'Mary Gentle's skill is such that she makes the miraculous seem totally plausible. A master of atmosphere and texture, her bravura portrayal of a Europe under pseudo-nuclear winter remains vivid long afterwards.' *Starburst*

'There are other writers who deal in people in our world coming into contact with other worlds, but I've yet to read any novel where the collision is handled as intelligently and subtly as it is here.' *SFX*

'Gentle is a fine writer . . . her characterisation of Ash is superb.' Waterstones

'Mary Gentle's earlier work, including *Golden Witchbreed* and *Rats and Gargoyles* and their sequels, was much applauded. *Ash* puts them in the shade . . . In its subversion of what we understand by history, and reality based on history, this huge work truly is a masterpiece.' *Freelance Informer*

'Very simply, *Ash* works. There is much more to talk about: the brilliance of the conversations and debates; the astonishing clamour of combat; the roundedness of almost every character in the vast tale.' John Clute

'When Mary Gentle is good, she's very good indeed – and this may well be her best book to date.' *Science Fiction World*

'There is a real sense in which *Ash* is the culmination of Gentle's work so far; it has the elegiac tone of the *Witchbreed* books, the urban complexity of the *White Crow* books and their intellectual prickliness; it has the thuggery of *Grunts*, but this time played for real and not for laughs. It also has some of the most complex and attractive characters of modern fantasy.' Roz Kaveney, *Dreamwatch*

'The book is an elegantly written *tour de force* by someone who knows their history and isn't afraid to mess with it.' *Guardian*

'I won't insult the author by trying to bullet-point a masterpiece, because masterpiece it is. A wealth of emotion, all written in tough, vigorous language . . . this is a book that will keep the author's name alive indefinitely.' *www.infinityplus.co.uk*

'Quite apart from Gentle's sly games with the stodginess of accepted scholarship, *Ash: A Secret History* is also a wickedly good adventure story. Gentle understands both the movement of politics across nations, and the motivations of seemingly insignificant people, and she makes her reader feel both. Her battles are as simultaneously glorious and horribly sordid as real battles must have been . . . It's almost literall

'There have been many books about mediaeval battles, many more about how physical and emotional love are so compelling and interdependent, many feminist warrior fantasies, and much hard science fiction that culminates in transcendence, but only here are all these facets combined so precisely and satisfyingly. It would be a shame for anyone to miss this book.' *Interzone*

Also by Mary Gentle

A Hawk in Silver
Golden Witchbreed
Ancient Light
Scholars and Soldiers
Rats and Gargoyles
The Architecture of Desire
Left to His Own Devices
Grunts!

MARY GENTLE

A SECRET HISTORY

The right of Mary Gentle to be identified as the author
of this work has been asserted by her in accordance with
the Copyright, Designs and Patents Act 1988.

This edition published in Great Britain in 2001 by

Gollancz
An imprint of the Orion Publishing Group
Orion House, 5 Upper St Martin's Lane, London WC2H 9EA

A CIP catalogue record for this book is available
from the British Library

ISBN 1 85798 744 6

Printed in Great Britain by
Clays Ltd, St Ives plc

For Richard

Dr Pierce Ratcliff, *ASH: THE LOST HISTORY OF BUR-GUNDY*, ▮▮▮▮▮ University Press, 2001. Extremely rare. Realistic offer considered.

The original 2001 edition of Dr Pierce Ratcliff's *ASH: THE LOST HISTORY OF BURGUNDY* was withdrawn from the publisher's warehouses immediately before publication. All known copies were destroyed. Copies sent out for review were recalled, and pulped.

A percentage of the same material was eventually reissued in October 2005, as *MEDIAEVAL TACTICS, LOGISTICS AND COMMAND, Volume 3: Burgundy*, after the removal of all the editorial notes and the Afterword.

A copy of the original edition is believed to be available in the British Library, together with facsimiles of the editorial correspondence, but is not available for public consultation.

NOTE: This excerpt from *Antiquarian Media Monthly*, Vol. 2, No. 7, July 2006, is original, glued on to the blank frontispiece page of this copy.

ASH

The Lost History of Burgundy

Pierce Ratcliff Ph.D.

▬▬▬▬ UNIVERSITY PRESS

LONDON   NEW YORK

Contents

Introduction

I make no apology for presenting a new translation of these documents which are our only contact with the life of that extraordinary woman, Ash (b.1457[?]-d.1477). One has long been needed.

Charles Mallory Maximillian's 1890 edition, *Ash: The Life of a Female Mediaeval Mercenary Captain*, begins with a translation from the mediaeval Latin into serviceable Victorian prose, but he admits that he leaves out some of the more explicit episodes; as does Vaughan Davies in his 1939 collection, *Ash: A Fifteenth Century Biography*. The 'Ash' documents badly need a colloquial and complete translation for the new millennium, and one which does not shrink from the brutality of the mediaeval period, as well as its joyfulness. I hope that I have provided one here.

Women have always accompanied armies. Examples of their taking part in actual combat are far too numerous to quote. In AD 1476, it is only two generations since Joan of Arc led the Dauphin's forces in France: one can imagine the grandparents of Ash's soldiers telling war stories about this. To find a mediaeval peasant woman in command, however, without the backing of church or state – and in command of mercenary troops – is almost unique.[1]

The high glory of mediaeval life and the explosive revolution of the Renaissance meet in this Europe of the second half of the fifteenth century. Wars are endemic – in the Italian city states, in France, Burgundy, Spain and the Germanies, and in England between warring royal houses. Europe itself is in a state of terror over the eastern threat of the Turkish Empire. It is an age of armies, which will grow, and of mercenary companies, which will pass away with the coming of the Early Modern period.

Much is uncertain about Ash, including the year and place of her birth. Several fifteenth and sixteenth century documents claim to be *Lives* of Ash, and I shall be referring to them later, together with those new discoveries which I have made in the course of my research.

This earliest Latin fragment of the Winchester Codex, a monastic document written around AD 1495, deals with her early experiences as a child, and it is here presented in my own translation, as are subsequent texts.

Any historical personage inevitably acquires a baggage train of tales, anecdotes and romantic stories over and above their actual historical career. These are an entertaining part of the Ash material, but not to be taken seriously

---

[1] Not entirely, as we shall see.

as history. I have therefore foot-noted such episodes in the Ash cycle as they occur: the serious reader is free to disregard them.

At the beginning of our millennium, with sophisticated methods of research, it is far easier for me to strip away the false 'legends' around Ash than it would have been for either Charles Maximillian or Vaughan Davies. I have here uncovered the historical woman behind the stories – her real self as, if not more, amazing than her myth.

Pierce Ratcliff, Ph.D. (War Studies), 2001

NOTE: Addendum to copy found in British Library: pencilled note on loose papers:

DR PIERCE RATCLIFF Ph.D. (War Studies)

Flat 1, Rowan Court, 112 Olvera Street, London W14 0AB, United Kingdom

Fax: ▮▮▮▮▮▮▮▮▮▮
E-mail: ▮▮▮▮▮▮▮▮▮▮
Tel: ▮▮▮▮▮▮▮▮▮▮

Anna Longman
Editor
▮▮▮▮▮ University Press
▮▮▮▮▮▮▮▮▮▮
▮▮▮▮▮▮

Copies of some (?) of the original correspondence between Dr Ratcliff and his publisher's editor found inserted between pages of text — possibly in the order in which the original typescript was edited?

29 September 2000

Dear Ms Longman,

I am returning, with pleasure, the contract for our book. I have signed it as requested.

I enclose a rough draft of the translation of Ash's early life: the Winchester Codex. As you will see, as further documents are translated, the seed of everything that happens to her is here.

This is a remarkable occasion for me! Every historian, I suppose, believes that one day he or she will make the discovery, the one that makes their names. And I believe that I have made it here, uncovering the details of the career of this remarkable woman, Ash, and thus uncovering a little-known – no, a *forgotten* – deeply significant episode in European history.

My theory is one that I first began to piece together as I studied the existing 'Ash' documents for my doctoral thesis. I was able to confirm it with the discovery of the 'Fraxinus' document – originally from the collection at Snowshill Manor, in Gloucestershire. A cousin of the late owner, Charles Wade, had been given a sixteenth century German chest before his death and the take-over of Snowshill Manor by the National Trust in 1952. When it was finally opened, the manuscript was inside. I think it must have sat in there (there is a steel locking mechanism that takes up the entire inside of the chest's lid!), all but unread *since* the fifteenth century. Charles Wade may not even have known it existed.

Being in mediaeval French and Latin, it had never been translated by Wade, even if he was aware of it – he was one of those 'collectors' who, born in the Victorian age, had far more interest in acquiring than deciphering. The Manor is a wonderful heap of clocks, Japanese armour, mediaeval German swords, porcelain, etc.! But that at least one other eye besides mine has seen it, I am certain: some hand has scribbled a rough Latin pun on the outer sheet – *fraxinus me fecit*: 'Ash made me'. (You may or may not know that the Latin name for the ash tree is *fraxinus*.) I would guess that this annotation is eighteenth century.

As I first read it, it became clear to me that this was, indeed, an entirely new, previously undiscovered document. A memoir written, or more likely dictated, *by the woman Ash herself*, at some point before her death in AD 1477(?). It did not take me long to realise that it fits, as it were, in the gaps between recorded history – and there are many, many such gaps. (And, one supposes, it is my discovery of 'Fraxinus' which encouraged your firm to wish to publish this new edition of the Ash *Life*.)

What 'Fraxinus' describes is florid, perhaps, but one must remember that exaggeration, legend, myth, and the chronicler's own prejudices and patriotism, all form a normal part of the average mediaeval manuscript. Under the dross, there is gold. As you will see.

History is a large net, with a wide mesh, and many things slip through it into oblivion. With the new material I have uncovered, I hope to bring to light, once again, those facts which do not accord with our idea of the past, but which, nonetheless, *are* factual.

That this will then involve considerable reassessment of our views of Northern European history is inevitable, and the historians will just have to get used to it!

I look forward to hearing from you,

Pierce Ratcliff

Pierce Ratcliff

PROLOGUE

c. AD 1465–1467[?]

'My soul is among lions'[1]

[1] Psalms 57: 4

I

It was her scars that made her beautiful.

No one bothered to give her a name until she was two years old. Up until then, as she toddled between the mercenaries' campfires scrounging food, suckling bitch-hounds' teats, and sitting in the dirt, she had been called Mucky-pup, Grubby-face, and Ashy-arse. When her hair fined up from a nondescript light brown to a white blonde it was 'Ashy' that stuck. As soon as she could talk, she called herself Ash.

When Ash was eight years old, two of the mercenaries raped her.

She was not a virgin. All the stray children played snuggling games under the smelly sheepskin sleeping rugs, and she had her particular friends. These two mercenaries were not other eight-year-olds, they were grown men. One of them had the grace to be drunk.

Because she cried afterwards, the one who was not drunk heated his dagger in the campfire and drew the knife-tip from below her eye, up her cheekbone in a slant, up to her ear almost.

Because she still cried, he made another petulant slash that opened her cheek parallel under the first cut.

Squalling, she pulled free. Blood ran down the side of her face in sheets. She was not physically big enough to use a sword or an axe, although she had already begun training. She was big enough to pick up his cocked crossbow (carelessly left ready on the wagon for perimeter defence) and shoot a bolt through the first man at close quarters.

The third scar neatly opened her other cheekbone, but it came honestly, no sadism involved. The second man's dagger was genuinely trying to kill her.

She could not cock the crossbow again on her own. She would not run. She groped among the burst ruins of the first mercenary's body and buried his eating-knife in the upper thigh of the second man, piercing his femoral artery. He bled to death in minutes. Remember that she had already begun to train as a fighter.

Death is nothing strange in mercenary soldier camps. Even so, for an eight-year-old to kill two of their own was something to give them pause.

Ash's first really clear memory came with the day of her trial. It had rained in the night. The sun brought steam rising from field and distant forest, and slanted gold light across tents, rough bashas, cauldrons, carts, goats, washer-women, whores, captains, stallions and flags. It made the company's colours glow. She gazed up at the big swallow-tailed flag with the cross and beast on it, smelling the cool air on her face.

A bearded man squatted down in front of her to talk to her. She was small, for eight. He wore a breastplate. She saw her face reflected in the curving mirror-shiny metal.

Her face, with her big eyes and ragged long silver hair, and three unhealed scars; two up her cheek under her left eye and one under her right eye. Like the tribal marks of the horse-barbarians of the East.

She smelled grass-fires and horse dung, and the sweat of the armed man. The cool wind raised the hairs on her arms. She saw herself suddenly as if she were outside of it all – the big kneeling man in armour, and in front of him this small child with spilling white curls, in patched hose and bundled into a ragged doublet far too big for her. Barefoot, wide-eyed, scarred; carrying a broken hunting knife re-ground as a dagger.

It was the first time she saw that she was beautiful.

Blood thundered in her ears with frustration. She could think of no *use* for that beauty.

The bearded man, the Captain of the company, said, "Have you father or mother living?"

"I don't know. One of them might be my father." She pointed at random at men re-fletching bolts, polishing helmets. "Nobody says they're my mother."

A much thinner man leaned down beside the Captain and said quietly, "One of the dead men was stupid enough to leave a crossbow spanned with a bolt in it. That's an offence. As to the child, the washerwomen say she's no maid, but no one knows her to be a whore either."

"If she is old enough to kill," the Captain scowled through wiry copper-coloured hair, "she is old enough to take the penalty. Which is to be whipped at the cart-tail around the camp."

"My name is Ash," she said in a small, clear, carrying voice. "They hurt me and I killed them. If anyone else hurts me, I'll kill them too. I'll kill *you*."

She got the whipping she might have expected, with something added for insolence and discipline's sake. She did not cry. Afterwards, one of the crossbowmen gave her a cut-down jack, a padded cloth jerkin, for armour, and she exercised devotedly in it at weapons practice. For a month or two she pretended the crossbowman was her father, until it became clear that his kindness had been a momentary impulse.

A little later in her ninth year, rumours went through the camp that there had been a Lion born of a Virgin.

II

The child Ash sat with her back to a bare tree, cheering the mummers. Furs kept some of the ground's ice from her backside.

Her scars were not healing well. They stood out red against the extreme pallor of her skin. Visible breath huffed out of her mouth as she screamed, shoulder to shoulder with all the camp strays and bastards. The Great Wyrm (a man with a tanned horse's skin flung over his back, and a horse's skull fitted by ties to his head) ramped across the stage. The horse skin still had mane and tail attached. They flailed the freezing afternoon air. The Knight of the Wasteland (played by a company sergeant in better armour than Ash had thought he owned) aimed skilful lance blows very wide.

"Oh, *kill* it," a girl called Crow called scornfully.

"Stick it up his arse!" Ash yelled. The children huddling around her tree screamed laughter and disdain.

Richard, a little black-haired boy with a port-wine stain across his face, whispered, "It'll *have* to die. The Lion's born. I heard the Lord Captain say."

Ash's scorn faded with the last sentence. "When? Where? When, Richard? When did you hear him?"

"Midday. I took water into the tent." The small boy's voice sounded proud.

Ash ignored his implied unofficial status as page. She rested her nose on her clenched fists and huffed warm breath on her frozen fingers. The Wyrm and the sergeant were having at each other with more vigour. That was because of the cold. She stood up and rubbed hard at her numb buttocks through her woollen hose.

"Where's you going, Ashy?" the boy asked.

"I'm going to make water," she announced loftily. "You can't come with me."

"Don't *wanna*."

"You're not big enough." With that parting shaft, Ash picked her way out of the crowd of children, goats and hounds.

The sky was low, cold, and the same colour as pewter plates. A white mist came up from the river. If it would snow, it would be warmer than this. Ash padded on feet bound with strips of cloth towards the abandoned buildings (probably agricultural) that the company officers had commandeered for winter quarters. A sorry rabble of tents had gone up all around. Armed men were clustered around fire-pits with their fronts to the heat and their arses in the cold. She went on past their backs.

Round to the rear of the farm, she heard them coming out of the building in time to duck behind a barrel, in which the frozen cylindrical block of rainwater protruded up a full handspan.

"And go on foot," the Captain finished speaking. A group of men clattered with him out into the yard. The thin company clerk. Two of the Captain's closest lieutenants. The very few, Ash knew, with pretensions (once) to noble birth.

The Captain wore a close-fitting steel shell that covered all his body. Full harness: from the pauldrons and breastplate enclosing his shoulders and body, the vambraces on his arms, his gauntlets, his tassets and cuisses and greaves that armoured his legs, down to the metal sabatons that covered his spurred boots. He carried his armet[2] under his arm. Winter light dulled the mirrored metal. He stood in the filthy farmyard wearing armour that reflected the sky as white: she had not thought before that this might be why it was called *white*

[2] A closed-face helmet.

harness. The only colour shone from his red beard and the red leather of his scabbard.

Ash knelt back on her knees and toes. Her frozen fingers rested against the cold barrel, too numb to feel the wood staves. The strapped and tied metal plates rattled as the man walked. When his two lieutenants thumped down into the yard, also in full armour, it sounded like muffled pans. Like a cook's wagon overturning.

Ash wanted such armour. It was that desire, more than curiosity, that made her follow them away from the farm buildings. To walk with that invulnerability. With that amount of *wealth* on one's back . . . Ash ran, dazzled.

The sky above yellowed. A few flakes of snow drifted down to lie on top of her untidy hair (less purely white than it) but she took no notice. Her nose and ears shone bright red, and her fingers and toes were blue and purple. This was nothing unusual for her in winter: she thought nothing of it. She did not even pull her doublet tighter over her filthy linen shirt.

The four men – Captain, clerk, two young lieutenants – walked ahead in unusual silence. They passed the camp pickets. Ash sneaked past behind while the Captain exchanged a word with them.

She wondered why the men did not ride. They walked up a steep slope to the surrounding woodland. At the wood's border, confronting the thick bowed branches, the brambles and thorn bushes, the deadwood brushfalls built up over more than a man's lifetime, she understood. You couldn't take a horse into this. Even a war-horse.

Now three of the men stopped and put on their armets. The unarmoured clerk fell back a step. Each man kept his visor pinned up, his face visible. The taller of the two lieutenants took his sword out of his scabbard. The bearded Captain shook his head.

The sliding sound of metal on wood echoed in the quiet, as the lieutenant re-sheathed his blade.

The wood held silence.

All three of the armoured men turned to the company clerk. This thin man wore a velvet-covered brigandine and a war-hat,[3] and his uncovered face was pinched in the cold air. Ash sneaked closer as the snow fell.

The clerk stepped confidently forward, into the wood.

Ash had not paid much attention to the hills surrounding the valley. The valley had a clean river, and the lone farmhouse and its buildings. It was good for wintering out of campaign season. What else should she know? The leafless woods on the surrounding high hills had been bare of game. If not hunting, what other reason could take her here, away from the fire-pits?

What reason could take *them?*

There *was* a path, she decided after some minutes. None of the brambles and thorn bushes on it were more than her own height. Not disused for more than a few seasons.

The armoured men pushed unharmed through the briars. The shorter lieutenant swore, "God's blood!" and fell silent, as the other three turned and

---

[3] A wide-brimmed steel helmet, identical in shape to the British 'Tommy's' helmet of the 1914–1918 World War.

stared at him. Ash snuck under briar stems as thick as her wrist. Little and quick, she could have out-distanced them, protective armour or not, if she had known where the path went.

With that thought she cast out to the side, wriggled on her belly along the bed of a frozen streamlet, and came out a hundred paces ahead of the leading man.

No snow fell here under the tree canopy. Everything was brown. Dead leaves, dead briars, dead rushes on the streamlet's edge. Brown bracken ahead. Ash, seeing the bracken, looked up, and – as she had expected – the tree cover over it was broken, as it must be to allow its growth.

In the forest glade stood a disused stone chapel, shrouded in snow.

Ash had no familiarity with the outside or inside of chapels. Even so, she would have needed to be very familiar indeed with architecture to recognise the style in which this one had been built. It was ruined now. Two walls remained standing. Grey moss and brown thorns covered them, old ice scabbing the vegetation. Two snow-plastered window frames showed grey, full of winter emptiness. Heaps of snow-rounded rubble cluttered the ground.

Green colour took Ash's eye. Under the thin covering of snow, all the rubble was grown over with ivy.

Green flowered also at the foot of the chapel walls. Two fat white-moulded holly bushes rooted where the stone slab of the altar stood against the wall. They stood either side of the cracked slab. Under the snow, their red berries weighed their branches down.

Ash heard clattering metal behind her. A robin and a wren took fright and flew out of the holly and away. The men behind her in the wood began to sing. They were fifteen feet behind her back, no further away than that.

Ash shot in rabbit-jinks across the rubble. She hit the snow by the wall and wormed her way in under the lowest holly branches.

Inside, the bush was hollow and dry. Brown leaves crackled under her dirty hands. Black branches supported the canopy of shiny green leaves above her head. Ash lay flat on her belly and eased forward. Barbed leaves stuck into her woollen doublet.

She peered from between the leaves. Snow fell now.

The thin clerk lifted a tenor voice and sang. It was a language Ash did not know. The company's two lieutenants stumbled across the broken ground, singing, and it would have sounded better, Ash thought, if they had taken their helmets off instead of just putting up their visors.

The Captain emerged from the wood's edge.

He put his gauntlets up to his chin and fumbled with buckle and strap. Then Ash saw him fiddle with the hook and pin. He opened his helm and took it off, and stood uncovered in the glade. Fat flakes of snow drifted down. They nestled in his hair and beard and ears.

The Captain sang,

> "God rest ye merry, Gentlemen, let nothing you dismay;
> This darkest hour, the Sun returns; so we salute the Day."

His voice was very loud, very cracked, not very much in tune. The silence of the wood shattered. Ash cried sudden hot tears. He had wrecked his voice bellowing above the noise of men and horses; it was a powerful ruin.

The company clerk came close to the holly bush in which Ash hid. She made herself still. Tears dried on her scarred cheeks. Half of being hidden is to remain utterly, completely still. The other half is to think yourself into the background. *I am a rabbit, a rat, a briar, a tree.* She lowered her mouth into the neck of her doublet so that her white breath would not betray her.

"Give thanks," the clerk said. He put something up on to the old altar. Ash was below and could not see, but it smelled like raw meat. Snow tangled in the man's hair. His eyes were bright. Despite the cold, sweat ran in drops down his forehead, under the brim of his metal hat. The rest of what he said was in the other language.

The taller lieutenant screeched "*Look!*" so loudly that Ash started and jumped. A disturbed twig dumped snow down her face. She blinked it out of her eyelashes. Now I'm discovered, she thought calmly, and put her head out into the glade and found no one even looking in her direction. Their eyes were on the altar.

All three knights went down on their knees in the ivy-covered rubble. Armour scraped and clattered. The Captain's arms fell to his sides, and the helm from his hand: Ash winced as she heard it hit rocky earth and bounce.

The company clerk took off his dish-shaped war-hat and moved to one knee with a singular grace.

Snow whirled faster from the invisible whiteness of the sky into the glade. Snow covered the green ivy, the red berries of the holly. Snow froze on the spindly brown arcs of briar. A great huffing animal breath came down from the altar of the ruined green chapel. Ash watched its whiteness on the air. Animal-breath hit her in the face, warm and wet.

A great paw trod down from the stone altar.

The paw's pelt was yellow. Ash stared at it, two inches from her face. Yellow fur. Coarse yellow fur, paler and softer at the roots. The beast's claws were curved, and longer than her hand, and white with clear tips. Needle tips.

The haunch of a Lion passed Ash's face. Its flank obscured the clearing, the wood, the men. The beast stepped down fluidly from the altar. It threw up its maned head, bolting down whatever the offering had been. She saw its throat move, swallowing.

A coughing roar broke the air a foot away from her.

She pissed the crotch of her woollen hose. Hot urine steamed in the cold, chilled clammily down her thighs, instantly cold in the snowy air. Eyes wide, she could only stare, could not even wonder why none of the kneeling knights sprang up or drew their swords. The Lion's head began to swing around. Ash knelt, paralysed.

The Lion's wrinkled muzzle swung into the hollow leaves. Its face was huge. Great luminous, long-lashed, yellow eyes blinked. A heavy smell of carrion, heat and sand choked her. The Lion grunted, flinched back slightly from the berry-laden pricking branches. Its black lips writhed back from its teeth. It reached in delicately and nipped the front of Ash's doublet between an upper and a lower incisor.

The Lion's rump went up. Its tail lashed. It pulled her out of the bush. Only a child's weight, no effort – a child snarled up in holly leaves and bramble, pulled forward, in green wool doublet and blue stinking hose, spilled face-down on the snow-shrouded ivy and rocks.

The second roar deafened her.

Ash had become too frightened to move. Now she jammed her arms up over her head, covering her ears. She burst into noisy uninhibited tears.

A rasping tongue as thick as her leg licked up one side of her scarred face.

Ash stopped wailing. Her sore face stung. She got slowly up on to her knees. The Lion stood twice as tall as she did. She looked up into its golden eyes, whiskered muzzle, curved white teeth. Its great tongue slobbered down and rasped up her other cheek. Her unhealed scars throbbed rawly. She poked at them with fingers blunt and senseless as wood. A robin on the ruined chapel's wall burst into song.

She was young to have such an awareness of herself, but she was perfectly sure of two separate, distinct, and mutually exclusive reactions. The part of her that was camp-child and used to large feral animals, and to hunting in season, froze her body very still: *it hasn't touched me with its claws, I'm too close to run, I mustn't startle it.* Another part of herself seemed less familiar. It filled with a burning happiness. She could not remember the words or language that the clerk had been using. In her utterly clear voice, she began to sing the Captain's hymn,

"God rest ye merry, Gentlemen, let nothing you dismay;
This darkest hour, the Sun returns, so we salute this Day.
We march forth to Your Victory, our foes in disarray!
Oh, his Brightness brings comfort and joy
None can destroy:
Oh, his Brightness brings comfort and joy."

The clearing was silent when she ended. She could not hear the difference between the man's cracked voice and her own purity. She did not have the age to distinguish between his bad voice, singing with maturity, and her own blurring of breath, and pauses, that were a reflection of rote learning by some campfire.

All the while her young soul sang, her mind whimpered, *no, no.* Remembering a leopard hunt once near Urbino. The cat's claws had sliced open a hound's stomach in an instant and tangled its stinking intestines in the grass.

The great head dipped down. For a second she breathed in fur. She choked, drowned in its mane. The Lion's eyes looked into hers, with a flat animal awareness of her scent and presence. The huge muscles clenched and bunched and the beast sprang over her head. By the time she could turn, it had crashed through the light underbrush at the edge of the clearing and vanished.

She sat for a few moments, clearly hearing the diminishing noise of its departure.

The clatter of metal woke her attention.

Ash sat, legs aspraddle, on snow-smeared rock and ivy. Her head was on a level with the articulated poleyns or knee-armour of the Captain's harness, now that he stood beside her. The silver chape on his scabbard glittered near her eye.

"He didn't speak," she complained.

"The Lion born of a Virgin is a beast," said the clerk, tenor voice loud and flat in the abandoned clearing. "An animal. Lord Captain, I don't understand. The child is known to be no virgin, yet He did not harm her."

The bearded Captain stared down from his great height. Ash felt afraid of his frown. He spoke, but not directly to her.

"Perhaps it was a vision. The child is our poor land, waiting the breath of the Lion for salvation. This winter barrenness, her spoiled face: all one. I cannot interpret, I have not the skill. It could mean anything."

The company clerk replaced his steel hat. "My lords, what we have seen here was for us alone. An you will, let us retire to prayer and seek guidance."

"Yes." The Lord Captain bent and picked up his helmet, brushing the caked snow off the metal. The sun, through an unexpected break in the winter cloud, struck fire from his red hair and beard and hard metal shell. As he turned away, he added, "Somebody bring the brat."

III

She found out what she could do with her scar-emphasised child's beauty.

By the age of nine she had a mass of curls that she kept long, halfway to her waist, and washed once a month. Her silver hair had the grey shine of grease. No one in a soldiers' camp could notice the smell. She never showed her ears. She learned to keep dressing in cut-down hose and doublet, often with an adult's jerkin over them. Something in the too-large clothing made her look even more of a little child.

One of the gunners would always give her food or copper coins. He bent her forwards over an iron-bound gun carriage, undid the points of her hose, and fucked her up the arse.

"You don't have to be that careful," Ash complained. "I won't have a child. I haven't shown flowers – blood – yet."

"You haven't shown a cock, either," the gunner answered. "Until I find a pretty boy, you'll have to do."

Once he gave her a spare strip of mail. She begged thread from one of the company's clothiers, and a piece of leather from the tanner, and sewed the riveted metal links on to that. She shaped it into a mail standard or collar, tied on to protect the throat. She wore it at every skirmish, every cattle-raid, every bandit ambush where she learned her business – which was, as she had always known, war.

She prayed for war the way other little girls her age, in convents, pray to be the chosen bride of the Green Christ.

Guillaume Arnisout was a gunner in the mercenary company. He never touched her. He showed her how to write her name in Green alphabet: a vertical slash with five horizontal cuts ("the same number as your fingers") jutting out of it on the right-hand side ("*sword*-hand side!"). He didn't teach her how to read because he couldn't. He taught her how to figure. Ash thought, *All gunners can calculate to a single powder-grain*, but that was before she understood gunners.

Guillaume showed her the ash tree and taught her how to make hunting bows from that wood ("a *wider* stave than you need for a yew bow").

Guillaume took her to visit the slaughterhouse, after the August siege at Dinant, before the company went overseas again.

The spring sun shimmered on hawthorn blossom hedging the cattle pastures. A chill wind still blew. The company encampment's noise and smell were carried away, downwind.

Ash rode the cow into the village, sitting sideways on the peaked bone ridge of its back. Guillaume walked beside the cow, on the rutted lane. She looked down at him walking in the dust. He carried a carved stick of a secret black wood, using it at each step for support. Ash knew she had not been born when a poleaxe smashed his knee in a line-fight and he retired to the siege guns.

"Guillaume . . ."

"Urh."

"I could have brought her on my own. You didn't have to come."

"Hurh."

She looked ahead. The double spire of the church was visible over the trees now. Blue smoke went up. They came to the edge of the cleared ground around the village palisade and the wind changed. The smell of the abattoir was full and choking.

"God's *blood*!" Ash swore. A hard hand clipped her skinny shank. She looked down round-shouldered at Guillaume and let water brim over her lower lids.

"Now that," Guillaume pointed, "is where we're going. Get off that old bag of bones and lead her, for Christ's pity's sake."

Ash kicked her heels out and launched herself into the air. She landed in the dusty road ruts, dipping briefly to steady herself with one hand, and sprang up. She leaped exuberantly around the plodding cow, skipping, and then ran back to the tall man.

"Guillaume." She took his arm, gripping the rusty brown sleeve of his doublet. There was no cloth under the cuff: the gunner had no more shirt to his name at the moment than Ash did. "Guillaume, is it boys you like?"

"Ha!" He stared down at her with his dark eyes. Stringy black hair hung down shoulder-length from his head, except at his crown where he was balding. He had a habit of shaving himself every so often with his dagger, generally the same day that he remembered to get his dagger sharpened, but his cheeks were brown and leathery and hardly showed one more nick from a blade.

"Do I like boys, missy? Is that you asking me why you can't twist me round your little finger, as you do the rest? Must I like little boys better than little girls for that to be true?"

"Most of them do what I want when I pretend."

21

He yanked her long silver-white hair. "But I like you the way you are."

Ash pushed her hair back down over her pointed ears. She kicked at the waving heads of grass that grew on the side of the village road. "I'm beautiful. I'm not a woman yet but I'm beautiful. I've got elvish blood in me, look at the hair. Look at my hair, *you* don't care . . ." She sang that to herself for a few minutes, and then looked up with what she knew to be large, widely spaced eyes. "*Guill*aume . . ."

The gunner strode ahead, ignoring her, planting his stick with great firmness in the dust, and then flourishing it to greet the two guards on the village gate. They had iron-shod quarterstaffs, Ash noted, and thick leather jerkins in lieu of armour.

She took the rope that hung around the cow's neck. The cow had been dry for six months. It remained barren now no matter which town's bull the mercenaries put it to on their way through the countryside. It would make stringy meat but quite good shoe leather. Ash kicked her bare soles on the earth. Or good leather for sword-belts.

With the smell of the dusty road overcome by the smell of the village's street, she wondered, Is it another place where they shout obscenities at scars, and make the sign of the Horns?

"Ash!"

The cow had drifted to one side of the path, and mouthed grass unenthusiastically. Ash set her bare heels on the path and heaved. The cow's head came up. It drew in a noisy breath and mooed. Ropes of saliva trailed from its jaws. Ash led it towards the village gate and the wattle-and-daub houses, after Guillaume.

Ash had a blade now. She fingered it, staring down the guys on the gate. Someone's twenty-inch dagger originally, so it was more of a short sword for her. At nine she is small, you could take her for seven. It did come with its own scabbard, and a loop for hanging it off her belt. She earned it. She steals food, she will not steal weapons. The other mercenaries – she has been thinking of them and herself in those terms recently – regard this as an interesting and peculiar quirk, and take advantage.

It being not long past dawn, few of the village folk were on the street. Ash regretted no one being there to see her.

"They let me enter the village armed," she boasted. "I didn't have to give up my dagger!"

"You're on the books as one of the company." Guillaume had his own falchion at his belt, a meat-cleaver of a blade with a hair-splitter single edge. In the same way that Ash habitually wore over-large doublets and played camp's-little-mascot, she deeply suspected that Guillaume played up to the stereotypical idea that gormless villagers had of mercenaries: filthy dress and spotless weapons. Certainly he did the other thing the yokels expected and cheated them at cards, but badly, even Ash could spot him doing it.

Ash walked with her thin shoulders back and her head up. She stared down a couple of idlers standing under the hanging bush that marked one hut as a tavern.

"If I didn't have this God-rotted barren animal," she yelped at the gunner walking in front of her, "I'd look like a proper contract soldier!"

Guillaume Arnisout laughed briefly. He walked on. He didn't look back.

She worried the complacent cow as far as the abattoir gates before it got its belly full of the smell. The stink of excrement and blood was strong enough to be tangible. Ash's eyes streamed. Something stuck in the back of her throat. She handed the cow's bridle over to a slaughterman at the gate, coughing.

A voice bawled, "Ash! Over here!"

Ash turned. Something warm and heavy hit her in the face and chest.

Surprise made her gasp, intake a breath. Immediately she choked on hot liquid. A solid mass of *stuff* slid from her shoulders, down her chest. She ground the heels of her hands into her burning eyes. She coughed, choked again, began to cry. The tears cleared her vision.

Blood soaked the front of her doublet and hose. Hot, steaming blood. Blood stuck her white hair together in crimson tendrils, dripping spatters into the dust. Blood covered her hands. Yellow matter crusted the creases of her clothes. She put her hand up and scooped a mass of matter out of the neck of her doublet. A lump of meat flecked with blood clots the size of her small fist.

The solid mass slid and flopped over her bare feet. It was hot. Warm. Cooling fast. Cold. Pink tubes and red tubes slid to the ground. She moved her foot out from under a kidney-shaped lump that she could not have held in her two hands.

Ash stopped crying.

She did something. It was not new, or she would not have known how to do it now. It might have been something she did just before or after she fired the crossbow point-blank at her rapist and his body exploded in front of her.

She wiped the back of her hand across her chin. Blood tightened on her skin as it dried there. She got rid of the constriction in her throat and the tears pricking behind her eyes.

She stared at Guillaume and the slaughterman, now carrying empty wooden pails.

"That was *stupid*," she raged. "Blood's unclean!"

"Come here." Guillaume pointed to a spot in front of himself.

The gunner was standing at a skinning rack. Timbers as stout as those that made up a siege machine held a chain on a pulley. Hooks hung from the chain, over a gutter dug in the earth. Ash lifted her feet out of pig's guts and walked towards Guillaume. Her clothes stuck to her. Her nose was ceasing to smell the reek of the slaughterhouse.

"Take out your sword," he said.

She had no gloves. The hilt of her weapon was bound with leather, and slippery in her palm.

"Cut," Guillaume said calmly, pointing at the cow that now hung head-down beside him, still alive, hooves trussed. "Slit her belly."

Ash had not been in a church but she knew enough to scowl at that.

"Do it," he said.

Ash's long dagger was heavy in her hand. The weight of the metal pulled on her wrist.

23

The cow's long-lashed eyes rolled. She groaned frantically. Her thrashing did no more than roll her from side to side on the hook. A stream of shit ran down her warm, breathing flanks.

"I can't do this," Ash protested. "I can do it. I know how. I just can't *do* it. It's not like she's going to do me any harm!"

"*Do it!*"

Ash flicked the blade clumsily and punched it forward. She leaned all her weight into the point, as she had been taught, and the sharp metal punctured the cow's brown and white pelt. The cow opened her mouth and screamed.

Blood sprayed. Sweat made the dagger grip slide in Ash's hand. The dagger slid out of the shallow wound. She stared up at the animal that was eight times her size. She got a double-handed grip on the blade and cut forward. The edge skimmed the cow's flank.

"You'd be dead by now," Guillaume rasped.

Tears began to leak out of Ash's eyes. She stepped up close to the breathing warm body. She raised the big dagger over her head and brought it down overarm with both hands.

The point of the blade punched through tough skin and the thin muscle wall and into the abdominal cavity. Ash wrenched and pulled the blade down. It felt like hacking cloth. Jerking, snagging. A mess of pink ropes fell down around her in the dawn yard, and smoked in the early chill. Ash hacked doggedly down. The blade cut into bone and stuck. A rib. She yanked. Pulled. The cow's flesh sucked shut on her blade.

"Twist. Use your foot if you have to!" Guillaume's voice directed over her harsh, effortful breathing.

Ash leaned her knee on the cow's wet neck, pressing it back against the wood frame with her tiny weight. She twisted her wrists hard right and the blade turned, breaking the vacuum that held it in the wound, and coming free of the bone. The cow's screams drowned every other sound.

"*Hhaaaaah!*" Both her hands on the dagger-grip, Ash swiped the blade across the stretched skin of the cow's throat. The rib bone must have nicked her blade. She felt the steel's irregularity catch on flesh. A wide gash opened. For a fraction of a second it showed a cross-section of skin, muscle sheath, muscle and artery wall. Then blood welled up and gushed out and hit her in the face. Hot. *Blood heat*, she thought, and giggled.

"Now cry!" Guillaume spun her around and cracked his hand across her face. The blow would have hurt another adult.

Astonished, Ash burst into loud sobs. She stood for perhaps a minute, crying. Then she wept, "I'm not old enough to go into a line-fight!"

"Not this year."

"I'm too little!"

"Crocodile tears, now." Guillaume sighed. "I thank you," he added gravely; "kill the beast now." And when she looked, he was handing the slaughterman a copper piece. "Come on, missy. Back to camp."

"My sword's dirty," she said. Suddenly she folded her legs and sat down on the earth, in animal blood and shit, and howled. She coughed, fighting to breathe. Great shuddering gasps wracked her chest. Her reddened hair hung down and streaked her wet, scarred cheeks. Snot trailed from her nostrils.

"Ah." Guillaume's hand caught her doublet collar and lifted her up into the air, and dropped her down on her bare feet. Hard. "Better. Enough. There."

He pointed at a trough on the far side of the yard.

Ash ripped her front lacing undone. She stripped off her doublet and hose in one, not bothering to undo the points that tied them together at her waist. She plunged the blood-soaked wool into the cold water, and used it to wash herself down. The morning sun felt hot on her bare cold skin. Guillaume stood with folded arms and watched her.

All through it she had her discarded sword-belt under her foot and her eyes on the slaughterhouse men.

The last thing she did was wash her blade clean, dry it, and beg some grease to oil the metal so that it should not rust. By then her clothing was only damp, if not dry. Her hair hung down in wet white rats' tails.

"Back to camp," the gunner said.

Ash walked out of the village gate beside Guillaume. It did not even occur to her to ask to be taken in by one of the village families.

Guillaume looked down at her with bright, bloodshot eyes. Dirt lodged in the creases of his skin, clearly apparent in the brightening sun. He said, "If that was easy, think of this. She was a beast, not a man. She had no voice to threaten. She had no voice to beg mercy. And she wasn't trying to kill *you*."

"I know," Ash said. "I've killed a man who was."

When she was ten, she nearly died, but not on the field of battle.

IV

First light came. Ash leaned out over the stone parapet of the bell tower. Too dark to see the ground, fifty feet of empty air below. A horse whinnied. A hundred others answered it, all down the battle-lines. A lark sang in the arch of the sky. The flat river valley began to emerge from darkness.

The air heated up fast. Ash wore a stolen shirt and nothing else. It was a man's linen shirt and still smelled of him, and it came down past her knees. She had belted it with her sword-belt. The linen protected the nape of her neck, and her arms, and most of her legs. She rubbed her goose-fleshed skin. Soon the day would be burning hot.

Light crept from the east. Shadows fell to the west. Ash caught a pinprick of light two miles away.

One. Fifty. A thousand? The sun glinted back from helmets and breastplates, from poleaxes and warhammers and the bodkin points of clothyard arrows.

"They're arrayed and moving! They've got the sun at their backs!" She hopped from one bare foot to the other. "*Why* won't the Captain let us fight?"

"I don't want to!" The black-haired boy, Richard, now her particular friend, whimpered beside her.

Ash looked at him in complete bewilderment. "Are you afraid?" She darted to the other side of the tower, leaning over and looking down at the company's wagon-fort. Washerwomen and whores and cooks were fixing the chains that bound the carts together. Most of them carried twelve-foot pikes, razor-edged bills. She leaned out further. She couldn't see Guillaume.

Day brightened quickly. Ash craned to look down the slope towards the river's edge. A few horses galloping, their riders in bright colours. A flag: the company ensign. Then men of the company walking, weapons in hand.

"Ash, why are we so *slow*?" Richard quavered. "They'll be here before we're ready!"

Ash had started to be strong in the last half-year or so, in the way that terriers and mountain ponies are strong, but she still did not look older than eight. Malnutrition had a lot to do with it.

She put her arm around him. "There's trouble. We can't get through. Look."

All down by the river showed red in the rising sun. Vast cornfields, so thick with poppies that she couldn't see the grain. Corn and poppies together – the crops so thick and tangled that they slowed down the mercenaries walking with bills and swords and halberds. The armoured men on horseback drew ahead, into the scarlet distance, under the banner.

Richard bundled his arms around Ash, pale enough for his birthmark to stand out like a banner on his face. "Will they all die?"

"No. Not everybody. Not if some of the other lot come over to us when the fighting starts. The Captain buys them if he can. Oh." Ash's guts contracted. She reached down and put her hand between her legs and took her fingers out bloody.

"Sweet Green Christ!" Ash wiped her hand on her linen shirt, with a glance around the bell tower to see if anyone had overheard her swear. They were alone.

"Are you wounded?" Richard stepped back.

"*Oh*. No." Far more bewildered than she sounded, Ash said, "I'm a woman. They told me, in the wagons, it could happen."

Richard forgot the armed men moving. His smile was sweet. "It's the first time, isn't it? I'm so happy for you, Ashy! Will you have a baby?"

"Not right now . . ."

She made him laugh, his fear gone. That done, she turned back to the red river fields that stretched away from the tower. Dew burned off in bright mist. Not dawn, now, but full early morning.

"Oh, *look* . . ."

Half a mile away now, the enemy.

The Bride of the Sea's men moving over a slope, small and glittering. Banners of red and blue and gold and yellow gleamed above the packed mass of their helmets. Too far away to see faces, even the inverted V that disclosed mouth and chin when, in the heat, they left off falling-buffs and bevors.[4]

---

[4] Armour pieces for the chin and lower face, made of either articulated or solid plate, and often lined with velvet or other cloth; therefore hot to wear.

"Ashy, there are so *many*—!" Richard whined.

The Serene Bride of the Sea's host drew up into three. The vaward or advance unit was big enough on its own. Behind it, offset to one side, was the mainward, with the Bride of the Sea's banners and their commander's own standard. Offset again, the rearward was only just in sight as a moving thicket of pikes and lances.

The first rows came on slowly. Billmen in padded linen jacks, their steel war-hats gleaming, bright hook-bladed bills over their shoulders. Ash knew billhooks had some agricultural use, but not what it might be. You could hook an armoured knight off his horse with one, and use it to crack his protective metal plates open. Men-at-arms in foot armour, with axes over their shoulders like peasants going out to cut wood . . . And archers. Far too many archers.

"Three battles." Ash pointed Richard bodily, holding him by his narrow shoulders. The little boy trembled. "Look, Dickon. In the front battle. There's billmen, then archers, then men-at-arms, then archers, then billmen, then more archers – all down the line."

A hoarse voice, audible across the whole distance, shouted, "Nock! Loose!"

Ash scratched at her stained shirt. Everything laid itself out suddenly plain in her head. For the first time, what had been an implicit sense of a pattern found words.

She stuttered into speech, almost too fast and excited to be understood. "Their archers are safe *because* of their men with hand-weapons! They can shoot into us, loose an arrow every six heartbeats, and we can't do anything about it! Because if we *do* try to get up close, their billmen or foot knights will kill us. Then their archers will draw their falchions and get stuck in too, or move out to the flanks and carry on shooting us up. That's why they've put them like that. What can we *do*?"

'If you are outnumbered, you cannot meet them in separate units. Form a wedge. A wedge-shaped formation with the point towards the enemy, then your flank archers can shoot without hitting your men in front. When their foot troops attack, they must face your weapons on each of your flanks. Send in your heavy armoured men to break their flank.'

Ash found the hard words no more difficult to decipher than discussions she had overheard, lying in the grass, back of the Captain's command tent. She puzzled it out, and said, "How *can* we? We don't have enough men!"

"Ashy," Richard whimpered.

She protested, "What have we got? The Great Duke's men – about half as many! And the city militia. They just about know enough not to hold a sword by the sharp end. Two more companies. And us."

"Ash!" the boy protested loudly. "Ashy!"

'Then do not array your men too close together. They are a mass for the enemy to shoot into. The enemy are out of range. You must move, fast, and close-assault them.'

She dug with her bare toe in the dust between the tower's flagstones, not looking at the approaching banners. "There's too many of them!"

"Ashy, stop it. Stop it! Who are you talking to?"

'Then you must surrender and sue for peace.'

"Don't tell me! I can't do anything! I can't!"

27

Richard shrieked, "Tell you what? *Who's* telling?"

Nothing happened for long seconds. Then the mass of the company moved forward, running, the Great Duke's troops with them, crashing into the first enemy battle-line, flags dipping, the red of poppies a red mist now; thunder, iron beating on iron, screams, hoarse voices shouting orders, a pipe shrilling through the dirt rising up a bare few hundred yards away.

"You said – I heard you!" Ash stared at Richard's white and wine-coloured face. "You *said* – I heard someone saying – Who *was* that?"

The Great Duke's line of men broke up into knots. No flying wedge now, just knots of men-at-arms gathered around their standards and banners. In the dust and red sun, the main battle of the Most Serene Bride of the Sea's army began to walk forward. Sheaves of arrows thickened the air.

"But *someone* said—"

The stone parapet smacked her in the face.

Blood smashed across her upper lip. She put one hand to her nose. Pain made her scream. Her fingers spread and shook.

The noise filled her mouth, filled her chest, shook the sky crashing down. Ash touched the sides of her head. A thin, high whine filled her ears. Richard's face streamed tears and his mouth was an open square. She could just hear him bawling.

The corner of the parapet wall fell soundlessly away. Open air gaped in front of her. Dust hung hazy. She got to her hands and knees. A violent whirring whicked past her head, loud enough for her, half-deaf, to hear.

The boy stood with his hands loose at his sides. He stared over Ash's head, out from the broken bell tower. She saw his particoloured legs tremble. The front of his cod-flap wetted with urine. With a ripe, wet sound, he shat in his hose. Ash looked up at Richard without condemnation. There are times when losing control of your bowels is the only realistic response to a situation.

"That's *mortars*! Get *down*!" She hoped she was shouting. She got Richard by the wrist and pulled him towards the steps.

The sharp edge of the stone barked her knees. Her sun-blasted vision saw nothing but darkness. She fell down inside the bell tower, cracking her head against the wall of the stairwell. Richard's foot kicked her in the mouth. She bled and yelled and tumbled down to ground-level and ran.

She heard no more gunfire, but when she looked back from the wagon-fort, her chest raw inside and burning, the monastery tower was gone, only rubble and dust blackening the sky.

Forty-five minutes later the baggage train were declared prisoners.

Ash ran away, out of their sight, down to the river.

Searching.

Bodies lay so thick on the ground that the air swam with the smell. She clamped her linen sleeve over her mouth and nose. She tried not to step on the faces of the dead men and boys.

Scavengers came by to strip the bodies. She hid in the wet, red corn. Their peasant voices were rapid, inflected music.

She felt the skin across her cheeks and nose crisping in the high summer

28

heat. The sun burned at her calves below the linen shirt, turning her fair skin pink. Her toes burned. She stood and put her wide-brimmed straw hat back on. The whole world smelled of shit and spoiling meat. She kept spitting without being able to get the taste of vomit out of her mouth. Heat made the air waver.

One of the dying men wept "Bartolomeo! Bartolomeo!" and then pleaded with the surgeon's cart, long-handled, dragged on two wheels by a man who grunted and shook his head.

No Richard. No one. The crops were burned black for a mile or more. Ravens dragged bits of two armoured horse carcasses apart. If there had been anything else – bombards, bodies, salvageable armour – it had been cleared up or looted.

Ash ran, breathless, back to the company cooking fires. She saw Richard sitting with the washerwomen. He looked up, saw her, and ran away.

Her steps slowed.

Abruptly, Ash turned and tugged the sleeve of a gunner's doublet. Not realising how deaf she was, she shouted, "Where's *Guillaume*? Guillaume Arnisout?"

"Buried down in the lime pit."

"*What?*"

The unarmed man shrugged and faced her. She followed his lips as much as the whisper of sound. "Dead and buried in the lime pits."

"Uhh." Air left her lungs.

"No," another man called from beside the fire, "they took him prisoner. The bloody Brides of the Sea have got him."

"No," a third man held his hands apart, "he had a hole in his stomach *this* big. But it wasn't the Most Serene, it was our side, the Great Duke's men, it was someone he owed money to."

Ash left them.

No matter what turf the camp was set up on, the camp was always the same. She made her way into the middle of the camp, where she did not often go. Now it was full of armed strangers. At last she found a manicured, blond man with a harassed expression, who wore a gold-edged green surcoat over his armour. He was one of the Lord Captain's aides and she knew him by sight, not by name; the gunners referred to him derisively as *tabard-lifter*. She already understood why.

"Guillaume Arnisout?" He put his hand through his thick bobbed hair. "Is he your father?"

"Yes." Ash lied without hesitation. She did the thing she had learned to do and the constriction in her throat went away, so that she could speak. "I *want* him! Tell me where he is!"

The aide pricked down a parchment list. "Arnisout. Here. He was taken prisoner. The Captains are talking. I imagine prisoners may be exchanged after a few hours."

Ash thanked him in as quiet a voice as she could manage and returned to the edges of the camp to wait.

Evening fell across the valley. The stench of bodies sweetened the air unbearably. Guillaume did not come back to camp. Rumour began to say he had died of his wounds, died of plague caught in the Bride of the Sea's camp, signed on with the Most Serene as a master gunner at twice the pay, run off with a noblewoman from the Duke's city, gone home to his farm in Navarre. (Ash hoped for a few weeks. After six months, she stopped hoping.)

By sunset, prisoners moved aimlessly between the camp's tents, unused to walking around without sword, axe, bow, halberd. The evening sun lay gold over blood and poppies. The air tasted of heat. Ash's nose numbed itself to the worst of the decomposition. Richard stalked up to her where Ash stood in dung-stained straw, her back to a cart's wheel, with one of the baggage train's washerwomen dabbing witch hazel on the yellow bruises down her shins.

"When will we *know*?" Richard shivered, and glared at her. "What will they *do* with us?"

"Us?" Ash's ears still thinly sang.

The washerwoman grunted. "We're part of the spoil. Sell us to whorehouses, maybe."

"I'm too young!" Ash protested.

"No."

"Demon!" the boy shrieked. "Demons told *you* we'd lose! *You* hear demons! *You'll* burn!"

"Richard!"

He ran away. He ran down the earth-track that soldiers' feet had beaten into existence over the peasants' crops, away from the baggage wagons.

"Man-bait! He's too pretty," the washerwoman said, suddenly vicious, throwing her wet rag down. "I wouldn't be him. Or you. Your face! They'll burn you. If you hear *voices*!" She made the sign of the Horns.

Ash leaned her head back, staring up into the endless blue. The air swam with gold. Every muscle ached, one wrenched knee hurt, her little toenail had been torn off bloody. None of the normal euphoria of hard exertion over and done with. Her guts churned.

"Not voices. *A* voice." She pushed with her bare foot at the clay pot of witch hazel ointment. "Maybe it was sweet Christ. Or a saint."

"*You*, hear a saint?" the woman snarled incredulously. "Little whore!"

Ash wiped her nose with the back of her hand. "Maybe it was a vision. Guillaume had a vision once. He saw the Blessed Dead fighting with us at Dinant."

The washerwoman turned to walk away. "I hope the Most Serene look at your ugly face and make you fuck their nightsoil men!"

Ash scooped up and hefted the pot of witch hazel in one hand, preparing to throw. "Poxy bitch!"

A hand came out of nowhere and clouted her. It stunned her. She burst into a humiliatingly loud squall, dropping the clay pot.

The man, now visible as wearing the Bride of the Sea's livery, snarled, "You, woman, get up to the centre of camp. We're doing shares of spoil. Go! You too, you little scarred freak!"

The washerwoman ran off, laughing too shrilly. The soldier followed.

Another woman, suddenly beside the wagon, asked, "*Do* you hear voices, child?"

This woman had a moon-round, moon-pale face, with no hair showing under her tight headdress. Over her big body a grey robe hung loosely, with a Briar Cross on a chain at her belt.

Ash snivelled. She wiped her dripping nose again. A line of thin, clear snot hung from her nostrils to the shirt's linen sleeve. "I don't know! What's 'hearing voices'?"

The pale moon-face looked avidly down at her. "There's talk among the men of the Most Serene. I think they're looking for you."

"Me?" A tightness took hold of Ash's ribs. "Looking for *me*?"

A clammily hot white hand reached down, seizing Ash's jaw and turning her face up to the evening light. She strained against the imprint of sharp fingertips, without success. The woman studied her intently.

"If it was a true sending from the Green Christ, they hope you will prophesy for them. If it's a demon, they'll drive it out of you. That could take until morning. Most of them are well gone in drink now."

Ash ignored the grip on her face, her sick fear and her bowels churning. "Are you a nun?"

"I am one of the Sisters of St Herlaine, yes. We have a convent near here, at Milano."[5] The woman let go. Her voice sounded harsh under the liquid speech. Ash guessed it not to be her first language. Like all mercenaries, Ash had the basics of most languages she had heard. Ash understood the big woman as she said, "You need feeding up, girl. How old are you?"

"Nine. Ten. Eleven." Ash dragged her sleeve across her chin. "I don't know. I can remember the big storm. Ten. Maybe nine."

The woman's eyes were light, all light. "You're a *child*. Small, too. No one has ever cared for you, have they? Probably that's why the demon got in. This camp is no place for a child."

Tears stabbed her eyes. "It's my home! I *don't* have a demon!"

The nun put her hands up, each palm to one of Ash's cheeks, surveying her without her scars. Her hands felt both warm and cold on Ash's wet skin.

"I am Sister Ygraine. Tell me the truth. What speaks to you?"

Doubt bit cold in Ash's belly. "Nothing, nobody, Soeur! Nobody was there but me and Richard!"

---

[5] Internal evidence therefore suggests this is not one of the Company of the Griffin-in-Gold's contracts with the Burgundian Dukes. Therefore, the battle can be neither Dinant (19–25 August 1466) nor Brustem (28 October 1467). I theorise that this takes place in Italy, that it is Molinella (1467), a battle in the war between Duke Francisco Sforza of Milan, and the Serenissima or Most Serene Republic of Venice under the condottiere Bartolomeo Colleoni. Colleoni has been falsely credited with the first use of field guns in battle.

The battle is obscure, noted only because of a cynical comment which Niccolò Machiavelli later wrote about the 'bloodless wars' of the Italian professional contract soldiers: that only one man died in the battle of Molinella, and that was from falling off his horse. Better sources suggest a more accurate assessment would be around six hundred dead.

The Winchester Codex was written around AD 1495, some twenty-eight years after this date, and nineteen years after the main body of the 'Ash' texts (which cover the years AD 1476–1477). Some details of the battle depicted here greatly resemble the last conflict in the Wars of the Roses, the Battle of Stoke (1487). Possibly this biography was written by an English soldier who had become a monk at Winchester, and wrote about what he experienced in the English midlands, at Stoke, rather than about Molinella itself.

Chills stiffened her neck, braced her shoulders. Rote words of a prayer to the Green Christ died in her dry mouth. She began to listen. The nun's harsh breathing. Fire crackling. A horse whinnying. Drunken songs and shouting further off.

No sensation of a voice speaking quietly, to her, out of a companionable silence.

A burst of sound roared from the centre of the camp. Ash flinched. Soldiers ran past, ignoring them, running towards the growing crowd in the centre. Somewhere in a wagon close by, a hurt man called out for his *maman*. Gold light faded towards dusk. The tall sky began to fill with sparks showering up from the campfires, fires let burn too high, far too high; they might burn all the mercenary tents by morning, and think nothing of it but a brief regret for plunder ruined.

The nun said, "They're despoiling your camp."

Not speaking to Soeur Ygraine, not speaking to anyone, Ash deliberately breathed words aloud: "We're prisoners. What will happen to me now?"

'Licence, liberty, and drunkenness—'

Ash clamped her hands over her ears. The soundless voice continued:

'—the night when commanders cannot control their men who have come living off the battlefield. The night in which people are killed for sport.'

Soeur Ygraine shifted her big hand to Ash's shoulder, the grip firm through Ash's filthy-dirty shirt. Ash lowered her hands. A growl in her belly told her she was hungry for the first time in twelve hours.

The nun continued to gaze down at her as if no voice had spoken.

"I—" Ash hesitated.

In her mind now she felt neither silence, nor a voice, but a *potential* for speech. Like a tooth which does not quite ache, but soon will.

She began to hurt for what she had never before given two thoughts to: the solitariness of her soul in her body. Fear flooded her from scalp to tingling fingertips to feet.

She abruptly stuttered, "I *didn't* hear any voice, I didn't, I *didn't*! I lied to Richard because I thought it would make me famous. I just wanted somebody to notice me!"

And then, as the big woman disinterestedly turned her back and began to stride away, into the chaos of firelight and drunken condottieri, Ash shrieked out hard enough to hurt her throat:

"Take me somewhere safe, take me to sanctuary, *don't let them hurt me, please!*"

Dr Pierce Ratcliff Ph.D. (War Studies)
Flat 1, Rowan Court, 112 Olvera Street, London W14 0AB, United Kingdom

Fax: ██████████████████

E-mail: ██████████████████

Tel: ██████████████████

Anna Longman
Editor

████████ University Press

████████████████

████████

Copies of some(?) of the original correspondence between Dr Ratcliff and his publisher's editor found inserted between pages of text — possibly in the order in which the original typescript was edited?

9 October 2000

Dear Anna,

It was good to meet with you in person, at last. Yes, I think doing the editing section by section with you is by far the wisest way to go about this, particularly considering the volume of the material and the proposed publication date in 2001, and the fact that I am still fine-tuning the translations.

As soon as my net connection is properly set up I can send work to you direct. I'm glad you're reasonably happy with what you have so far. I can, of course, cut down on the footnotes.

It's kind of you to admire the 'literary distancing technique' of referring to fifteenth century Catholicism in such terms as 'Green Christ' and 'Briar Cross'. In fact, this is *not* my technique for making sure the readers can't impose their own preconceptions about mediaeval life on the text! It's a direct translation of the mediaeval dog-Latin, as are the earlier Mithraic references. We shouldn't be too concerned, this is just some of the obviously false legendary material – supernatural lions and similar – attributed to Ash's childhood. Heroes always gather myths to themselves, still more so when they are not remarkable men but remarkable women.

Perhaps the Winchester Codex purports to reflect Ash's limited knowledge as a child: Ash at eight or ten years old knows only fields, woods, campaign tents, armour, washerwomen, dogs, soldiers, swords, saints, Lions. The company of mercenaries. Hills, rivers, towns – places have no names. How should she know what year it is? Dates don't matter yet.

All this changes, of course, in the next section: the del Guiz *Life*.

Like the editor of the 1939 edition of the 'Ash' papers, Vaughan Davies, I am using the *original* German version of the del Guiz *Life* of Ash, published in 1516. (Because of the inflammatory nature of the text it was immediately withdrawn, and republished in an expurgated form in 1518.)

Apart from a few minor printing errors, this copy agrees with the four other surviving editions of the 1516 *Life* (in the British Library, the Metropolitan Museum of Art, the Kunsthistorisches Museum in Vienna, and the Glasgow Museum).

Here, I have a considerable advantage over Vaughan Davies, who was editing in 1939 – I can be explicit. I have therefore translated this text into modern colloquial English, especially the dialogue, where I use the educated and slang versions of our language to represent some of the social differences of that period. In addition, mediaeval soldiers were notoriously foul-mouthed. When Davies accurately translates Ash's bad language as, "By Christ's bones", however, the modern reader feels none of the contemporary shock. Therefore, I have again used modern-day equivalents. I'm afraid she does say "Fuck" rather a lot.

Regarding your question about using different documentary sources, my intention is *not* to follow Charles Mallory Maximillian's method. While I have a great admiration for his 1890 edition of the 'Ash' documents, in which he translates the various Latin codices, each *Life*, etc., in turn, and lets their various authors speak for themselves, I feel this demands more than modern readers are willing to give. I intend to follow Vaughan Davies's biographical method, and weave the various authors into a coherent narrative of her life. Where texts disagree this will, of course, be given the appropriate scholarly discussion.

I realise that you will find some of my new material surprising, but remember that what it narrates is what these people genuinely *thought* to be happening to them. And, if you bear in mind the major alteration to our view of history that will take place when *Ash: The Lost History of Burgundy* is published, perhaps we would be wise not to dismiss anything too casually.

Sincerely,

Pierce

DR PIERCE RATCLIFF Ph.D. (War Studies)
Flat 1, Rowan Court, 112 Olvera Street, London W14 0AB, United Kingdom

Fax: ███████████████

E-mail: ███████████████

Tel: ███████████████

Anna Longman
Editor
████████ University Press
████████
████████

*previous letter from
A. Longman missing?*

15 October 2000

Dear Anna,

No indeed – although my conclusions will completely supersede theirs, I feel myself very *fortunate* to be following in the academic footsteps of two profound scholars. Vaughan Davies's *Ash: A Biography* was still a set text when I was at school! My love for this subject goes back even further, I must confess – to the Victorians, and Charles Mallory Maximillian's *Ash: The Life of a Female Mediaeval Mercenary Captain*.

Take, for example, Charles Mallory Maximillian on the subject of that unique country, mediaeval Burgundy – because, although the emphasis in the opening part of the main 'Ash' texts is on the Germanic courts, it is with her powerful Burgundian employers that she is finally most associated. Here is CMM in full flood in 1890:–

> The story of Ash is, in some ways, the story of what we might call a 'lost' Burgundy. Of all the lands of Western Europe, it is Burgundy – this bright dream of chivalry – which both lasts for a shorter period than any other, and burns more brightly at its peak. Burgundy, under its four great Dukes, and the nominal kingship of France, becomes the last and greatest of the mediaeval kingdoms – aware, even as it flourishes, that it is harking back to another age. Duke Charles's cult of an 'Arthurian court' is, strange as it may seem to us in our modern, smoky, industrial world, an attempt to re-awaken the high ideals of chivalry in this land of knights in armour, princes in fantastic castles, and ladies of surpassing beauty and accomplishment. For Burgundy, itself, thought itself corrupted; thought the fifteenth century so far removed from the Classical Age of Gold that only a revival of these virtues of courage, honour, piety, and reverence could make it whole.

They did not foresee the printing press, the discovery of the New World, and the Renaissance; all to happen in the last twenty years of their century. And indeed, they took no part in it.

This, then, is the Burgundy which vanishes from memory and history in January, 1477. Ash, a Joan of Arc for Burgundy, perishes in the fray. The great bold Duke dies, slain by his old enemies the Swiss on the winter battlefield at Nancy; lies two or three days before his corpse can be recognised, because foot-soldiers have stripped him of all his finery; and so it is three days, as Commines tells us, before the King of France can give a great sigh of relief, and set about disposing of the Burgundian princes' lands. Burgundy vanishes.

Yet, if one studies the evidence, of course, Burgundy does not vanish at all. Like a stream which goes underground, the blood of Charles the Bold runs on through the history of Europe; becoming Hapsburg by marriage, merging into that Austro-Hungarian Empire which still – an ageing giant – survives to this day. What one can say is that we *remember* Burgundy as a lost and golden country. Why? What is it that we are remembering?

> Charles Mallory Maximillian (ed.), *Ash: The Life of a Female Mediaeval Mercenary Captain*, J Dent & Sons, 1890; reprinted 1892, 1893, 1896, 1905.

CMM is, of course, the lesser scholar, full of romantic Victorian flourishes, and I am not depending on him in my translations. Ironically, of course, his narrative history is far more readable than the sociological histories that followed, even if it is more inaccurate! I suppose I am trying to synthesise rigorous historical and sociological accuracy with CMM's lyricism. I hope it can be done!

What he says is all perfectly factual, of course – the collection of counties, countries and duchies that was mediaeval Burgundy *did* 'vanish out of history', so to speak (although not before Ash fought in some of its most notable battles). It is true in the sense that remarkably little is written about Burgundy after its AD 1477 collapse.

But it was CMM's nostalgic lyricism about a 'Lost Burgundy', a magic interstice of history, that got me fascinated. Reading through it again, I feel a complete satisfaction, Anna, that I should have found, in my own field, what was 'lost' – and deduced exactly what that discovery implies.

I enclose the next fully translated section, Part One of the del Guiz *Life*: *Fortuna Imperatrix Mundi*. A point, here – although the main bulk of my new manuscript, 'Fraxinus', covers events later in 1476, I am able to use parts of it to illuminate these already-existing texts, from where the del Guiz chronicle picks up her adult life in June of that year. You may find there are some surprises even in this 'old stuff', that eluded CMM and Vaughan Davies!

I appreciate that, for your up-coming sales conference, you need to be 'fully briefed', as you put it, on what my 'new historical theory' arising from 'Fraxinus' is. For various technical reasons, I'm afraid I do not choose to go into the implications in detail just yet.

Sincerely,

Pierce

PART ONE

16 June AD 1476[?]–1 July AD 1476

Fortuna Imperatrix Mundi[1]

---

[1] 'The goddess Fortune is the Empress of this world.'

I

"Gentlemen," said Ash, "shut your faces!"

The clatter of helmet visors shutting sounded all along the line of horsemen.

Beside her, Robert Anselm paused with his hand to his throat, about to thrust the laminated plate of his steel bevor up into its locking position over his mouth and chin. "Boss, our lord hasn't told us we can attack them . . ."

Ash pointed. "Who gives a fuck? That's a chance down there and we're taking it!"

Ash's sub-captain Anselm was the only rider apart from herself in full armour. The rest of the eighty-one mounted knights wore helmets, bevors, good leg armour – the legs of a man on horseback being very vulnerable – and cheap body armour, the small overlapping metal plates sewn into a jacket called a brigandine.

"*Form up!*"

Ash's voice sounded muffled in her own ears by the silver hair she wore braided up as an arming cap, padding the inside of her steel sallet.[2] Her voice was not as deep as Anselm's. It came resonant from her small, deep chest cavity; piercing; it sounds an octave above any noise of battle except cannon. Ash's men can always hear Ash.

Ash pushed her own bevor up and locked, protecting mouth and chin. For the moment, she left the visor of her sallet up so that she could see better. The horsemen jostled around her in a packed mass on the churned earth of the slope. Her men, in her company's livery: on geldings of mostly medium to good quality.

Down the slope in front of her, a vast makeshift town littered the river valley. Bright under noon sunlight, walled with wagons chained together, and crammed with pennon-flying pavilions and thirty thousand men, women and baggage animals inside it – the Burgundian army. Their camp big enough (confirmed rumour had it) to have *two* of its own markets . . .

You could hardly see the little battered walled town of Neuss inside the enclosing army.

Neuss: a tenth the size of the attacking forces camped around it. The besieged town rested precariously within its gates – rubble, now – and behind its moats and the wide protecting Rhine river. Beyond the Rhine valley, pine-knotted German hills glowed grey-green in the June heat.

---

[2] Open-faced helmet; in this case with a visor which can be raised or lowered, for visibility or protection.

Ash tilted her visor down to shade her eyes from the sunlight. A group of about fifty riders moved on the open ground between the Burgundian camp that besieged Neuss and her own Imperial camp that (theoretically) was here to relieve the town. Even at this distance Ash could see the men's Burgundian livery: two red criss-cross slashes, the Cross of St Andrew.

Robert Anselm brought his bay around in a neat circle. His free hand gripped the company's standard: the azure Lion Passant Guardant on a field or.[3] "They could be trying to sucker us down, boss."

Deep in the pit of her stomach, expectation and fear churned. The big iron-grey gelding, Godluc, shifted under her, responding. As always in chance ambushes, the suddenness, the sense of moments slipping away and a decision to be made—

"No. Not a trick. They're overconfident. Fifty mounted men – that's someone out with just an escort. He thinks he's safe. They think we're not going to attack them, because we haven't struck a blow since us and Emperor-bleeding-Frederick got here three weeks ago." She hit the high front of the war saddle with the heel of her gauntleted hand, turned to Anselm, grinning. "Robert, tell me what you *don't* see."

"Fifty mounted men, most in full harness, don't see any infantry, no crossbowmen, don't see any hackbutters, don't see any archers – *don't see any archers!*"

Ash couldn't stop grinning: she thought her teeth might be all that was visible under the shadow of her visor, and you could probably see them all the way across the occupied plain to Neuss. "*Now* you get it. When do we *ever* get to do the pure knightly cavalry-against-cavalry charge in real war?"

"—Without being shot out of the saddle." His brows, visible under his visor, furrowed. "You sure?"

"If we don't sit here with our thumbs up our arses, we can catch them out on the field – they can't get back to their camp in time. Now let's shift!"

Anselm nodded decisive compliance.

She squinted up at the dark blue sky. Her armour, and the padded arming doublet and hose under it, burned as if she stood in front of an armourer's

[3] It is worth noting that the Angelotti manuscript's term for the company's main battle standard – Or, a lion passant guardant azure (a blue lion, pacing to the viewer's left and looking out, one paw raised) – is unusual. Traditionally in heraldry, the lion passant guardant is referred to not as a lion, but as a leopard.

I think it is clear that Ash chooses to refer to hers as a lion for religious reasons.

The standard reproduced in the Angelotti ms, a tapering, swallow-tailed banner perhaps six feet long, is charged with the commander's badge, and one version of the company battle-cry – 'Frango regna!': 'I shatter kingdoms!' – as well as employers' badges from their various German, Italian, English and Swiss campaigns.

Ash's own personal (rectangular) banner, bearing her badge, is referred to as Or, a lion azure affronté, (a blue lion's head, face-on, on a gold field); which seems to be a lion's head cabossed (that is, with no neck or other part of the beast featured). The more correct term would be Or, a leopard's face azure. It is clear here that the company livery is gold, and that her men wear, as the badge, the lion passant guardant azure. This combination of blue and gold is especially characteristic of eastern France and Lorraine, and more generally of France, England, Italy, and Scandinavia, in contrast to black and gold, which is more characteristic of the German lands. I can find no reference to 'Or, a leopard's face azure' nor 'Or, a leopard azure' being associated with any well-known individual other than Ash.

furnace. Godluc's foam soaked his blue caparisons. The world smelled of horse, dung, oil on metal, and the downwind stench of Neuss where they had been eating rats and cats for six weeks now.

"I'm going to boil if I don't get out of this lot soon, so let's *go!*" She raised her plate-covered arm and jerked it down.

Robert Anselm's thick-necked horse dipped its hindquarters and then sprang forward. The company standard lifted, gripped high in Anselm's armoured gauntlet. Ash spurred Godluc into the thicket of raised lances and through, ahead of her men, Anselm at her shoulder now, half a pace behind her trotting mount. She tapped the long spurs back again. Godluc went from trot to canter. The jolting shook her teeth to her bones, and rattled the plates of her Milanese armour, and the wind whipped into her sallet and snatched the breath out of her nostrils.

Percussive concussion shook the world. The hundreds of steel horseshoes striking hard earth threw up showers of clods. The noise went unheard, felt in her chest and bones rather than heard with her ears; and the line of riders – *her* line, *her* men; sweet Christ don't let me get this wrong! – gathered speed down the slope and out on to clear ground.

No rabbit holes, she prayed, and then: Fuck me, that isn't one of their commanders' standards, it's the Duke's banner. Sweet Green Christ! That's Duke Charles of Burgundy himself there!

Summer sun struck brilliances from Burgundian knights in full harness, steel-silver plates from head to toe. The sun winked from the stars that were the tips of their light war lances. Her vision blotted green and orange.

No time for new tactics now. Anything we haven't practised, we can't do. This season's training will have to get us through it.

Ash glanced quickly right and left at the riders coming up nose and nose with her. Steel faces, not recognisable now as lance-leaders Euen Huw or Joscelyn van Mander or Thomas Rochester; anonymous hard-riding men, thickets of lances dropping down to attack position.

She brought her own lance down across Godluc's thick arched neck. Her gauntlet-linen over her palm was ridged and wet with sweat where she gripped the wood. The massive jolting of the horse shook her in the high-backed saddle, and the flapping of Godluc's azure caparisons and the rattle of horse armour deafened her already muffled hearing. She had the smell, almost the taste, of sweat-hot armour in her mouth; metallic as blood. Motion smoothed as she spurred Godluc into full gallop.

She mumbled into the velvet lining of her bevor, "Fifty mounted men. Full harness. Eighty-one with me, medium armour."

'How are the enemy armed?'

"Lances, maces, swords. No missile weapons at all."

'Charge the enemy before the enemy is reinforced.'

"What the fuck," Ash shouted happily to the voice in her head, "do you *think* I'm doing? Haro! A Lion! A Lion!" She threw up her free arm and bellowed, "Charge!"

Robert Anselm, half a length to her rear, boomed back in answer, "*A Lion!*" and jammed the staff of the rippling cloth banner up above his head. Half her

43

riders were pelting ahead of Ash now, almost out of formation; too late to think about that, too late to do anything but think *let them learn to stick with the banner!* She dropped the reins over the pommel, brought her free hand up in the automatic gesture over her sallet, slamming the visor fully down, reducing vision to a slot.

The Burgundian flag jerked wildly.

"They've seen us!"

Not clear, least of all to her now, at this speed and this restricted vision, but were they trying to cluster around one man? Move away? Gallop back breakneck towards their camp? Some mixture of all three?

In a split second four Burgundian horses wheeled and came up together and burst into a full gallop towards her.

Foam splattered back on her breastplate. Heat blinded her out of a dark blue sky. It was as real and as solid as bread to her – *those four men galloping towards me on three-quarters of a ton of horse each, with curved metal plates strapped around them, carry poles with sharpened lance-heads as long as my hand, that will hit home with the concentrated momentum of horse and sixteen-stone rider. They will punch through flesh like paper.*

She has a mental flash of the lance-tip punching through her scarred cheek, her brain, the back of her skull.

One Burgundian knight hefted his lance, gripping it with his steel gauntlet, couching it on the lance-rest on his breastplate. His head was polished metal, plumed with white ostrich feathers, slit by a bar of blackness – a visor through which not even eyes could be seen. His lance-point dipped straight towards her.

A grim exultation filled her. Godluc responded to her shift of weight and swerved right. She dropped her lance down – down – down again, and took the grey stallion of the leading Burgundian knight squarely in under the jaw.

The shaft wrenched out of her hand. His horse reared, skidding forward on broken hind legs. The man went straight over his horse's arse and under Godluc's hooves. Trained as a war-horse, Godluc did not even stumble. Ash slid the lanyard of her mace over her gauntlet to her wrist, swung up the 24-inch shaft, and crashed the small flanged metal head square across the back of the second man's helmet. The metal creased. She felt it give. Something crashed into Godluc's flank: she went careering across grass – hot grass, slippery in the heat, more than one horse missing its footing – and shifted her body-weight again to bring Godluc up beside Robert Anselm. She reached over and hauled on his war-horse's reins, and pulled him up with her. "*There!*"

The confusion of colours, red and blue and yellow liveries and guidons,[4] resolved itself into a mass of skirmishing men. First charge over, lances mostly abandoned, except there were the German guys from Anhelt's crew, skimming around the edge of the fray, lances jabbing as if they were boar-sticking – and Josse in the blue brigandine reaching over from his saddle with his hand on the *back*plate of a Burgundian knight, trying to punch his dagger down into the gap between plackart and backplate – and a man down, face-down on the dirt – and a spray of red straight up her breastplate, someone hit in a femoral artery,

[4] Cavalry lance pennants.

nothing to do with her own wild swing at someone's head – the leather lanyard breaking and her mace flying up in a perfect parabola into the sunlight.

Ash grasped the leather-bound hilt of her sword and whipped it out of its sheath. In a continuation of the same movement she smashed it pommel-first into the face of an armoured man. The strike jarred her wrist. She brought her sword round and slammed it down on his right upper arm and elbow. The impact jarred and numbed the whole length of her arm.

He swung his mace up.

The sliding plates of his arm defences squealed where her blow had crushed metal, and stuck. Jammed.

He could not bring his arm up – or down—

She struck her blade in hard towards his vulnerable under-arm mail.

Three wildly plunging horses stampeded through the mass of heaving bodies, pushing them apart. She looked left, right, wildly around: the Lion banner *there* – soul's damnation, if I'm not sticking with the unit banner, how can I expect them to? – and the Duke's standard about twenty yards away, close to the edge of the fight.

She gasped, "Enemy command group – in reach—"

'Then neutralise their unit commander.'

"A Lion! A Lion!" Ash stood up high in the stirrups, pointing with her sword. "Get the Duke! Get the Duke!"

Something crashed only glancingly off the back of her sallet, but it knocked her face-down on to Godluc's neck. The war-horse wheeled around and reared up. Busy clinging on, Ash felt his hooves crush something. Screams dinned in her ears, and shouted commands in French and Flemish, and *again* the Lion banner slid off to the side, and she swore, and then saw the Ducal banner jerk and go down, and the knight in front of her threw his sword point-first at her face, and she ducked, and the ground was empty—

Thirty or so horses and men in Burgundian colours galloped, routing, across the packed earth towards their camp. Only minutes, Ash thought, dazed. It's only been minutes, if that!

The little running figures at the Burgundian camp-line resolved themselves into infantry, in the liveries of Philippe de Poitiers and Ferry de Cuisance – archers from Picardy and Hainault.

"Archers – veteran – five hundred—"

'If you do not have sufficient missile troops, withdraw.'

"No chance now. Fuck it!" She jerked up her arm, caught Robert Anselm's eye, and threw her whole weight into the gesture of *back!* "Withdraw!"

Two of Euen Huw's lance – a disreputable bunch of bastards at the best of times – were swinging down from their horses to strip the still-living wounded. Ash saw Euen Huw himself slam a bollock dagger straight down into the visor of an unhorsed knight. Blood sprayed.

"You want to be crossbow meat?" She swung half down from the saddle and pulled the Welshman up. "Bugger off back – *now!*"

The stabbed man was not dead, he thrashed and screamed, and blood jetted up from his visor. Ash hauled herself up into her saddle, rode over him on her way to Robert Anselm's side, and screamed, "Ride back to camp – go!"

The Lion banner withdrew.

A man in a blue livery jacket with a blue lion on it dragged himself up from under his dead horse. Thomas Rochester, an English knight. Ash sat still in the saddle for one minute, holding Godluc by pressure of her knees, until the man reached her and she pulled him up behind her.

The open ground in front of Neuss was scattered now with riderless horses that abandoned their panic and slowed and stopped.

The man behind her on her horse yelled, "Boss, 'ware archers, let's get out of here!"

Ash picked a careful way across the ground covered by the skirmish. She leaned down, searching among the unhorsed men to see if any of the dead and wounded were hers – or were the Duke – and none were either.

"Boss!" Thomas Rochester protested.

The first Picardian longbowman passed a bush she had privately decided was four hundred yards away.

"*Boss!*"

Thomas must be rattled. He doesn't even want me to stop and capture a stray horse, to replace his. There's money out there on four hooves.

And archers.

"Okay . . ." Ash turned and rode back, fording the almost-dry stream of the Erft, and moving on up the slope. She forced herself to ride at walking pace towards the wattle barriers of the Imperial camp's nearest gate. She thumped Godluc's armoured neck. "Just as well we fed you up for the practise exercise."

The gelding threw up his head. There was blood at the corners of his mouth, and blood on his hooves.

Men wearing the Blue Lion and carrying bows came crowding out of the Imperial camp – which was a wagon-walled mirror of the Burgundian camp, down on the river plain. Ash rode in through the sentinelled gap between their wagons.

"There you go, Thomas." She reined in for the man to slide down, looking back at him. "Lose another horse and you can walk back next time . . ."

Thomas of Rochester grinned. "Sure, boss!"

Figures running, men from her sector of the camp, crowding up to her and Robert Anselm, yelling questions and warnings.

"The damn Burgundians are hardly going to follow us in here. Hang on." The sun blasted down. Ash nudged Godluc a step aside from the crowd, and wrenched her gauntlet buckles open, and then grabbed for her helmet.

She had to lean her head way back to get at the strap and buckle under the chin-piece of her bevor. She yanked the buckle open. The sallet almost fell backward off her head, but she caught it, and put it down over the pommel of the saddle, and then sprang the pin on her bevor and concertina'd the laminations down.

Air. Cool air. Her throat rasped dry and raw. She straightened up in the saddle again.

His Most Gracious Imperial Majesty Frederick III, Holy Roman Emperor, faced her from the war saddle of his favourite grey stallion.

Ash glanced around. A full knightly entourage rode with the Emperor. All bright liveries, and ostrich plumes on their helmets. Not so much as a scratch on the steel. Far too late to join any skirmish. She caught sight of one man at the back – by the look of him, from the Eternal Twilight,[5] in mail hauberk; his eyes bandaged with thin strips of dark muslin – nonetheless wearing a mildly cynical smile.

Sweat stuck her braided-up silver hair to her forehead and cheeks. Her skin felt wet and red as fire. Calm-eyed, she rode towards the Emperor, away from her shouting men. "Majesty."

Frederick's dry little voice whispered, "What are you doing on this side of my camp, Captain?"

"Manoeuvres, Your Imperial Majesty."

"In front of the Burgundian camp?"

"Needed to practise advancing and retreating with the standard, Your Imperial Majesty."

Frederick blinked. "When you just happened to see the Duke's escort."

"Thought it was a sally against Neuss, Your Imperial Majesty."

"And you attacked."

"Paid to, Your Imperial Majesty. We are your mercenaries, after all."

One of the entourage – the southern mail-clad foreigner – stifled a noise. There was a pointed silence until he muttered, "Sorry, Your Imperial Majesty. Wind."

"Yes . . ."

Ash blinked her indeterminately coloured eyes at the little fair-haired man. The Emperor Frederick was not visibly in armour, although his velvet doublet probably concealed mail under it. She said mildly, "Didn't we ride here from Cologne to protect Neuss, Your Imperial Majesty?".

Frederick abruptly wheeled his gelding, and galloped back into the centre of the Imperial German camp with his knights.

"Shit," Ash said aloud. "I might have done it this time."

Robert Anselm, helmet at hip, rode up beside her. "Done what, boss?"

Ash glanced sideways at the crop-headed man; twice her age, experienced, and capable. She reached up and pulled her hairpin, and let her heavy braid fall down, unwinding over pauldrons and breastplate as far as the tassets that hung to mid-thigh, and only then noticed that her arms were dripping red to the elbow-couters, and that her silver hair was sopping up the blood.

"Either got myself into deep shit," she said, "or got where I want to be. You know what I want us to get, this year."

"Land," Anselm murmured. "Not a mercenary's reward of money. You want him to give us land and estates."

"I want in." Ash sighed. "I'm tired of winning castles and revenues for other people. I'm tired of never having anything at the end of a season except enough money to see us through the winter."

His tanned, creased face smiled. "It isn't every company can do that."

"I know. But I'm good." Ash chuckled, deliberately immodest, getting less of

---

[5] A reference from 'Fraxinus', to an as-yet-unidentified mediaeval myth-cycle or legend. It is also mentioned in the del Guiz text, but absent from the Angelotti and 'Pseudo-Godfrey' manuscripts.

an answering grin from him than she expected. She sobered. "Robert, I want somewhere permanent we can go back to, I want to *own* land. That's what all this is about – you get land by fighting, or inheritance, or gift, but you get land and you establish yourself. Like the Sforza in Milan." She smiled cynically. "Give it enough time and money, and Jack Peasant becomes Sir John Wellborn. *I want in.*"

Robert shrugged. "Is Frederick going to do that? He could be mad as hell about this. I can't tell with him."

"Me either." Heartbeat and breath quietened now, ceasing to thunder in her ears. She stripped one gauntlet off and wiped her face, glancing back at the dismounting knights of the Company of the Lion. "That's a good lot of lads we've got there."

"Haven't I been raising troops for you for five years? Did you expect rubbish?"

It was a remark intended jokingly, Ash noted; but sweat poured down the older man's face, and his eyes flinched away from hers as he spoke. She wondered, *Is he after a bigger share of our money?* and realised, *No, not Robert – so, what?*

"That wasn't war," Ash added thoughtfully, pondering her captain. "That was a *tournament*, not a battle!"

One arm cradled his helmet; the Lion standard was socketed at his saddle. Anselm's blunt fingers prodded under the mail standard at his throat. Its visible rim of leather was black with his sweat. "Maybe a tourney.[6] But they lost knights."

"Six or seven," Ash agreed.

"Did you hear—?" Robert Anselm swallowed. His eyes finally met hers. She was troubled to see his forehead white with sweat or nausea.

"Down there – I took one man in the face with my sword-hilt," he said, and shrugged an explanation: "He had his visor up. Red livery, white harts rampant. I ripped half his face away, just with the cross of my sword. Blinded him. He didn't fall, I saw one of his mates helping him ride off towards their camp. But when I hit him he shrieked. You could hear it, Ash, he knew, right then, he'd been ruined for life. He *knew*."

Ash searched Robert Anselm's features, familiar to her as her own. A big man, broad across the shoulders, armour bright in the sun, his shaved scalp red with heat and sweat. "Robert—"

"It isn't the dead ones that bother me. It's the ones who have to live with what I've done to them." Anselm broke off, shaking his head. He shifted in his war-horse's saddle. His smile was wan. "Green Christ! Listen to me. After-battle shakes. Don't take any notice, girl. I've been doing this since before you were born."

This was not hyperbole but a pure statement of fact. Ash, more sanguine, nodded. "You should talk to a priest. Talk to Godfrey. And talk to me, later. This evening. Where's Florian?"

---

[6] A tourney is an organised killing affray. A tournament is an organised killing affray with blunt weapons.

He appeared slightly reassured. "In the surgeon's tent."

Ash nodded. "Right. I want to talk to the lance-leaders, we were all over the place down there. Take company roll-call. Find me back at the command tent. Move it!"

Ash rode on through the young men in armour flinging themselves down from their war saddles, shouting at each other, shouting at her, their pages grabbing their war-horses' reins, the babble of after-battle stories. She banged one hard on the backplate, said something obscene to another of her sub-captains, the Savoyard soldier Paul di Conti; grinned at their yells of approval, dismounted, and clattered up the slope, her steel tassets banging on the cuisses that covered her thighs, towards the surgeon's tent.

"Philibert, get me fresh clothes!" she yelled at her bob-haired page-boy, who darted away towards her pavilion; "and send Rickard, I need to get unarmed. *Florian!*"

A boy threw down more rushes as Ash ducked in through the flap of the surgeon's pavilion. The round tent smelled of old blood and vomit, and of spices and herbs from the curtained-off area that was the surgeon's own quarters. Thick sawdust clotted the floor. The sunlight through the white canvas gleamed gold.

It was not crowded. It was all but empty.

"What? Oh, it's you." A tall man, of slight build, with blond badly cut hair flopping over his eyes, looked up and grinned from a dirty face. "Look at this. Shoulder popped right out of its socket. Fascinating."

"How are you, Ned?" Ash ignored the surgeon Florian de Lacey for the moment in favour of the wounded man.

She has his name to hand: Edward Aston, an older knight, initially a refugee of the *rosbifs*'[7] royal wars, a confirmed mercenary now. The armour stripped off him and scattered on the straw was composite, bought new at different times and in different lands: Milanese breastplate, Gothic German arm defences. He sat with the wheat-coloured light on his balding head and fringe of white hair, doublet off his shoulders, bruises blacker by the minute, his features screwed up in intense pain and greater disgust. The joint of his shoulder looked completely wrong.

"Bloody warhammer, weren't it? Bloody little Burgundian tyke come up behind me when I were finishing his mate. Hurt my horse, too."

Ash ran over Sir Edward Aston's English lance in her mind. He had raised for her service one crossbowman, one fairly well-equipped longbow archer, two competent men-at-arms, a bloody good sergeant and a drunken page. "Your sergeant, Wrattan, will look after your mount. I'll put him in command of the rest of the lance. You rest up."

"Get my share, though, won't I?"

"Bloody right." Ash watched as Florian de Lacey wrapped both hands around the older man's wrist.

"Now say 'Christus vincit, Christus regnit, Christus imperad'," Florian directed.

---

[7] *Rosbif* or 'roast-beef': continental nickname at this time for an Englishman, since they were popularly supposed to eat nothing else.

"Christus vincit, Christus regnit, Christus imperad," the man growled, his outdoor voice too loud in the confines of the tent. "Pater et Filius et Spiritus Sanctus."

"Hold on." Florian planted a knee in Edward Aston's ribs, yanked at full strength—

"*Fuck!*"

—and let go. "There. Back in its socket."

"Why di'nt you tell me that was going to hurt, you stupid bugger?"

"You mean you didn't know? Shut up and let me finish the charm." The blond man frowned, thought for a second, and bent to murmur in the knight's ear: "*Mala, magubula, mala, magubula!*"

The older knight grunted, and raised thick white eyebrows. He gave a sharp nod. Ash watched Florian's long strong fingers firmly bind the shoulder into temporarily immobility.

"Don't worry about it, Ned," Ash said, "you're not going to miss much fighting. It took Frederick-our-glorious-leader seventeen days to march the twenty-four miles from Cologne to here, he's not exactly raring for glory."

"Sooner have my pay for *not* fighting! I'm an old man. You'll see me in my fucking grave yet."

"Fucking won't," Ash said. "I'll see you back on your horse. About—"

"About a week." Florian wiped his hands down the front of his doublet, smearing the red wool, red lacing, and white linen undershirt with dirt. "That's it, except an arm fracture, which I fixed up before you got here." The tall master surgeon scowled. "Why don't you bring me back any interesting injuries? And I don't suppose you bothered to recover any dead bodies for anatomising?"

"They didn't belong to me," Ash said gravely, managing not to laugh at Florian's expression.

The surgeon shrugged. "How am I ever going to study fatal combat injuries if you don't bring me any?"

Ned Aston muttered something under his breath that might have been 'fucking ghoul!'

"We were lucky," Ash stressed. "Florian, who's the arm fracture?"

"Bartolomey St John. From van Mander's Flemish lance. He'll mend."

"No permanent cripples? No one dead? No plague outbreak? Green Christ loves me!" Ash whooped. "Ned, I'll send your sergeant up here for you."

"I'll manage. I'm not dead yet." The big English knight glowered at Florian de Lacey in disgust as he left the surgeon's tent, something of which the anatomist-surgeon remained apparently oblivious; and had done as long as Ash had known him.

Ash spoke to Florian, watching Ned Aston's retreating back. "I haven't heard you use that charm for a battle injury before."

"No . . . I forgot the charm for bloodless injuries. That one was for *farcioun*."

" 'Farcioun'?"

"It's a disease of horses."[8]

"A disease of—!" Ash swallowed a very un-leaderlike snuffle of laughter.

[8] Uncertain: possibly glanders.

"Never mind. Florian, I want to get out of this kit and I want to talk to you. *Now*."

Outside, the sun hit like a dazzling hammer. Heat stifled her, in her armour. Ash squinted towards her pavilion tent and the Lion Azure standard limp in the airless noon.

Florian de Lacey offered his leather water bottle. "What's happened?"

Unusually for Florian, the costrel did indeed contain wine thoroughly drowned by water.[9] Ash doused her head, careless of spillage over steel plate. She gasped as the warm water hit. Then, swallowing greedily, she said between gulps, "Emperor. I've committed him. No more sitting around here – hinting to the Burgundians that Neuss is a free city – and Herman of Hesse is our friend – so would they please go home? *War*."

"Committed? You can't tell with Frederick." Florian's features, pale and fine-boned under the dirt, made a movement of disgust. "They're saying you nearly got the Burgundian Duke. That right?"

"*Damn* near!"

"Frederick might approve of that."

"And he might not. Politics, not war. Aw, shit, who *knows*?" Ash drank the last of the water. As she lowered the bottle, she saw her other page Rickard running towards her from the command tent.

"Boss!" The fourteen-year-old boy skidded to a halt on dry earth. "Message. The Emperor. He wants you at his tent. Now!"

"He say why?"

"That's all the guy told me, boss!"

Ash stuffed her gauntlets into her inverted helmet and tucked the helmet under her arm. "Okay. Rickard, get my command lance together. *Fast*. Master surgeon, let's go. No." She halted, boot-heels skidding on glassy summer grass. "Florian. *You* go and change out of those clothes!"

The surgeon looked amused. "And I suppose I'm the only one?"

Ash surveyed her armour. The shining metal was brown now with drying blood. "I can't get out of harness in time. Rickard, get me a bucket!"

A few minutes saw her armour sluiced down, head to foot; the warm water, even the dampness of her soaked arming doublet, welcome in the noonday heat. Ash wrung out her thick, yard-long mane of hair between her hands, flung it dripping over her shoulder, and set off at a fast stride for the centre of the camp, her squire running back to the Lion Azure camp with her messages.

"You're either up for a knighting," Robert Anselm growled, as she arrived, "or an almighty bollocking. Look at 'em!"

"They're here to watch something, all right . . ."

An unusually large crowd waited outside the Emperor's four-chambered striped pavilion tent. Ash glanced around as she joined them. Noblemen. Young men in the V-fronted laced doublets of high fashion, with particoloured hose; bareheaded and with long curls. All wore breastplates at the least. The older men sweated in pleated full-length formal gowns and rolled hats. This square of grass in the camp centre was clear of horses, cattle, women, bare-

[9] Water was usually drunk at this period only when tiny amounts of alcohol were included, to prevent water-borne infections.

arsed babies playing, and drunken soldiers. No one dared infringe the area around the yellow and black double-eagle standard. It smelled, nonetheless, pleasantly of war-horse droppings and sun-dried rushes.

Her officers arrived.

The sun dried her from her armour through to her arming doublet. Enclosed in form-fitting metal, she found the padded clothing underneath drank up all her sweat; left her not so much hot as unable to get air into her lungs. *I would have had time to change. It's always hurry-up-and-wait!*

A broad, squarish, bearded man in his thirties strode up, brown robe flapping about his bare feet. "Sorry, Captain."

"You're late, Godfrey. You're fired. I'm buying a better class of company clerk."

"Of course. We grow on Trees, my child." The company priest adjusted his cross. He was deep-chested, substantial; the skin around his eyes creased from far too many years spent under open skies. You would never have guessed from his deadpan expression how long Godfrey Maximillian had known her, or how well.

Ash caught his brown-eyed gaze, and tapped a bare fingernail on the helmet tucked under her arm. Metal clicked impatiently. "So what do your 'contacts' tell you – what's Frederick thinking?"

The priest chuckled. "Tell me someone in the last thirty-two years who's ever known that!"

"Okay, okay. Dumb question." Ash planted her spurred and booted feet apart, surveying the Imperial nobles. A few of them greeted her. There was no movement from inside the tent.

Godfrey Maximillian added, "I understand there are six or seven fairly influential Imperial knights in there now, griping to him about Ash always thinking she can attack without orders."

"If I hadn't attacked, they'd be griping about contract soldiers who take the money but won't risk their lives in a fight." Ash added, under her breath, nodding to the only other contract commander outside the Emperor's tent, the Italian Jacobo Rossano, "Who'd be a mercenary captain?"

"You would, madonna," her Italian master gunner, Antonio Angelotti, said. His startlingly fair curls and clear-skinned face made Angelotti stand out in any crowd, and not just for his proficiency with cannon.

"That was a rhetorical question!" She glared at him. "You know what a mercenary company is, Angelotti?"

Her master gunner was interrupted by the arrival of an only-slightly cleaner and better dressed Florian de Lacey, on the heels of Ash's remark.

"Mercenary company? Hmm." Florian offered, "A troop of loyal but dim psychopaths with the ability to beat up every other thick psychopath in sight?"

Ash raised her brows at him. "Five years, and you still haven't got the hang of being a soldier!"

The surgeon chuckled. "I doubt I ever will."

"I'll *tell* you what a mercenary company is." Ash jabbed her finger at Florian. "A mercenary company is an immense machine that takes in bread, milk, meat and wine, tentage, cordage and cloth at one end, and gives out shit, dirty washing, horse manure, trashed property, drunken vomit and broken kit at the other end. The fact that they sometimes do some *fighting* is entirely incidental!"

She stopped for breath and to lower her voice. Her eyes gazed around the men there as she spoke, picking out liveries, identifying noble lords, potential friends, known enemies.

Still nothing from the Emperor's tent.

"They're a gaping maw that I have to shove provisions into, each day and every day; a company is always two meals from dissolution. And money. Let's not forget money. And when they *do* fight, they produce wounded and sick men who have to be looked after. *And* they don't do anything useful while they're getting well! And when they *are* well, they're an ill-disciplined rabble who beat up the local peasantry. Argghhhh!"

Florian offered his costrel again. "That's what you get for paying eight hundred men to follow you."

"They don't follow me. They allow me to lead them. It's not the same thing at all."

In quite a different tone, Florian de Lacey said quietly, "They'll be fine, Ash. Our esteemed Emperor won't want to lose a sizeable mercenary contingent of his army."

"I just hope you're right."

A voice not many feet behind her said, completely unselfconsciously, "No, my lord, Captain Ash isn't here yet. I've seen her – a butch, mannish creature; bigger than a man, in fact. She had a waif of a girl with her, when I saw her in the north-west quarter of our camp – one of her 'baggage train' – whom she caressed, quite disgustingly! The girl was shrinking from her touch. That is your 'woman-soldier' commander for you."

Ash opened her mouth to speak, registered Florian de Lacey's raised eyebrows, and did not turn to correct the unknown knight. She moved a few steps away, towards one of the older Imperial captains in yellow and black livery.

Gottfried of Innsbruck inclined his head to Ash. "Good skirmish."

"Hoped we might get reinforced from the town." Ash shrugged. "But I guess Hermann of Hesse is not coming out to attack."

The Imperial knight Gottfried talked with his eyes on the entrance to the Emperor's pavilion. "Why should he? He's held out eight months without our help, when I wouldn't have given him eight days. Not a little free city, against the *Burgundians*."

"A little free city that's rebelling against its 'rightful ruler', Archbishop Ruprecht," Ash said, allowing a large degree of scepticism into her tone.

Gottfried chuckled loudly. "Archbishop Ruprecht is Duke Charles's man, Burgundian to the core. That's why the Burgundians want to put him back in control of Neuss. Here, Captain Ash, you might like this one – Ruprecht was this Duke's *father's* candidate for the archbishopric; you know what Ruprecht sent the late Duke Philip of Burgundy as a gift of gratitude when he got the job? A lion! A real live lion!"

"But not a blue one," a light tenor voice interrupted. "They say he sleeps like a lion, their Duke Charles, with his eyes open."

Turning to look at the young knight who had spoken, formulating an answer, she suddenly thought, *Don't I know you from somewhere?*

It would not be unusual to recognise a German knight from some other camp, some other campaigning season. She took him in superficially in a glance: a very young man, hardly more than her own age; long-legged and rangy, with a width to his shoulders that would fill out in a year or two. He was wearing a Gothic sallet, which even with the visor up hid most of his face; leaving her to price rich doublet and hose pied in green-and-white, high leather riding boots pointed up under the skirts of his doublet, and a knight's spurs.

And a very fancy fluted Gothic breastplate for a man who hadn't been in any skirmishes today.

Two or three hard young men-at-arms with him wore a green livery. *Mecklenburg? Scharnscott?* Ash ran through heraldry in her mind without success.

She said lightly, "*I* hear Duke Charles sleeps upright in a wooden chair, with all his armour on. In case we take him by surprise. Which some of us are more likely to do than others . . ."

Under his sallet's raised visor, the German knight's expression chilled.

"Bitch in men's clothing," he said. "One day, Captain, you really must tell us what use you have for your cod-flap."

Robert Anselm and Angelotti and half a dozen of Ash's sub-captains moved up so that their armoured shoulders touched hers. She thought resignedly, *Oh well . . .*

Ash looked deliberately down between her tassets, at the codpiece on the front of her hose. "It gives me somewhere to carry a spare pair of gloves. I imagine you use yours for the same thing."

"Cunt!"

"Really?" Ash inspected his green and white particoloured bulge with visible care. "It doesn't look like one – but I dare say you know best."

Any man drawing his sword among the Emperor's guard is looking to be cut down where he stands: she was not surprised to see the young German knight keep his hand off his sword-hilt. What startled her was the sudden flash of his appreciative grin. The smile of a young man who has the strength to take a joke against himself.

He turned his back, speaking to his noble friends as if she had said nothing at all, pointing with one gauntlet at the pine hills miles to the east. "Tomorrow, then! A hunt. There's a he-boar out there stands high as my bay mare's shoulder—"

"You didn't *have* to make another enemy," Godfrey muttered despairingly at her ear. Heat or strain whitened his face above the dense beard.

"It's compulsory when they're assholes. I get this all the time." Ash grinned at her company priest. "Godfrey, whoever he is, he's just another feudal lord. We're *soldiers*. I've got 'Deus Vult' engraved on my sword – his has 'Sharp End Towards Enemy'."[10]

---

[10] In the original, this is a completely untranslatable joke based on a pun between two words in German and an obscure, no longer extant, Flemish dialect. I have therefore substituted something to give the flavour of it. 'Deus vult' means 'God willing'.

Her officers laughed. A flutter of wind picked up the Imperial standard, so that for a second the sun blazed above her through yellow and black cloth. Smells of roasting beef drifted up from the long tent-lined lanes of the camp. Someone was singing something appallingly badly, not drowned out by a flute now playing in the Emperor Frederick's pavilion.

"I've *worked* for this. *We've* worked for this. It's how the rules of power operate. You're either on your way up or your way down. There's never a place to rest."

She watched the faces of her escort, troops in their twenties for the most part; then her officers, Angelotti and Florian and Godfrey and Robert Anselm as familiar as her own scarred face; the rest new this season. The usual mix of lance-leaders: the sceptics, the over-devoted, the crawlers, and the competent. Three months in the field, she knows most of their men by name now.

Two guards in black and yellow left the tent.

"*And* I could do with dinner." Ash felt her hair. They had been standing waiting long enough for the last silver curls to dry after her hasty ablutions. The weight of her hair pulled at her when she turned her head, and the flowing thick skeins caught between the plates of her armour: she risked it, for the picture she knew she made.

"And—" Ash glanced about for Florian de Lacey and found the surgeon's face was now missing from the command group. "Fuck it. Where's Florian? He's not pissed *again*—?"

All talk was silenced by a trumpeter. A handful of guards and six of the more influential nobles of Frederick's court came out of the tent with the Emperor himself. Ash straightened up in the blazing heat. She saw the southern foreigner again – a military observer? – still blindfolded with translucent strips of cloth, but walking unerringly in Frederick's footsteps, precisely avoiding the guy-ropes of the pavilion.

"Captain Ash," the Emperor Frederick said.

She went down on one knee, carefully since she was in armour, in front of the older man.

"This sixteenth day of June, Year of Our Lord 1476,"[11] the Emperor said, "it pleases me to raise you to some mark of distinction, for your valiant service in the field against our enemy, the noble Duke of Burgundy. Therefore I have bethought me much what would be fitting for a mercenary soldier in our employ."

---

[11] This account is accurate, with one exception. The skirmish at the siege of Neuss took place, not in 1476, but on 16 June 1475. However, records often pick up an apparent error of a year either way. Under the Julian calendar, in different parts of Europe, the New Year is variously dated as beginning at Easter, on Lady Day (25 March), and Christmas Day (25 December); and post AD 1583, the Gregorian calendar backdates the begining of those years to 1 January.

I can do no better than refer the reader to Charles Mallory Maximillian's comment in the 'Preface and Notes' to the first edition (1890):

'The Germanic *Life* of Ash narrates many startling and, one might think, implausible events. It is, however, verifiable that all these particular exploits of the woman Ash are well-attested to, by a great variety of other trustworthy historical sources.

'One should forgive, therefore, this document's mistake in the mere dating of the events contained therein.'

"Money," a pragmatic voice said, behind Ash. She dared not look away from Frederick to glare Angelotti into silence.

The skin at the edges of Frederick's pale eyes crinkled. The little fair-haired man, now in blue and gold pleated robes, put his ringed hands together and gazed down at her.

"Not gold," Frederick said, "because I have none to spare. And not estates, because it would not be fitting to give them to a woman with no man to defend them for her."

Ash looked up in plain, utter amazement and forgot propriety. "Do I *look* like I need defending?"

She tried to swallow the words even as she was saying them. The dry voice overrode her:

"Nor may I knight you, because you are a woman. But I will reward you with estates, albeit at second-hand. You shall marry, Ash. You shall marry my noble lord here – I promised his mother, who is my cousin in the fourth degree, that I would arrange a marriage for him. And now I do. This is your betrothed, the Lord Fernando del Guiz."

Ash looked where the Emperor indicated. There was no one there but the young knight in pied green-and-white hose, and fluted Gothic breastplate. The Emperor smiled encouragingly.

Her breath sucked in, involuntarily. What little she could see of the young man's face was utterly still, under his steel visor, and so white that she could see now that he had freckles across his cheekbones.

"*Marry?*" Ash stared, dazed. She heard herself say, "*Him?*"

"Does that please you, Captain?"

Sweet Christ! Ash thought. I am in the middle of the camp of His Grace the Holy Roman Emperor, Frederick III. The second most powerful ruler in Christendom. In open court. These are his most powerful subjects. They're all looking at me. I can't refuse. But *marriage*? I never even *thought* about marriage!

She was aware of the strap of her poleyn cutting into the back of her knee as she knelt; and jewelled, armoured, powerful men all looking at her. Her bare hands where they rested together on her thigh armour appeared rough, red stains under her nails. The pommel of her sword tapped against her breastplate. Only then did she realise that she was shaking. *Shit, girl! You forget. You really do forget that you're a woman. And they never do. And now it's yes or no.*

She did the thing that put it all – fear, humiliation, dread – outside herself.

Ash raised her bowed head, looking fearlessly up; perfectly aware of the picture that she made. A young woman, bareheaded, her cheekbones slashed with the fine white lines of three old scars, her silver hair tumbling gloriously about her armoured shoulders and flowing like a cloak to her thighs.

"I can say nothing, Your Imperial Majesty. Such recognition, and such generosity, and such honour – they are beyond anything I had expected, and anything I could deserve."

"Rise." Frederick took her hand. She knew he must feel her palm sweat. There might have been an amused movement made by those thin lips. He held out his other hand commandingly, took the much fairer hand of the young man, and placed it over Ash's. "Now let no one gainsay this, they shall be man and wife!"

Deafened by tumultuous and sycophantic applause, and with warm, damp male fingers resting on hers, Ash looked back at her company officers.

What the fuck do I do now?

II

Outside the window of the Imperial palace room in Cologne, rain poured in torrents from gutters and gargoyles to the cobblestones below. It battered loudly, irregular as arquebus[12]-fire, against the expensive glass windows. Biscuit-coloured stone finials gleamed with every break in the high cloud.

Inside the room, Ash faced her soon-to-be mother-in-law.

"This is – all – very – *well*—" Ash protested through a faceful of azure velvet. She shook herself free of it. "—but I have to get back to my company! I got escorted out of Neuss so fast yesterday, I haven't had a chance to talk to my officers yet!"

"You must have women's clothing for the bridal," Constanza del Guiz said sharply, stumbling over the last word.

"With respect, madam – I have upwards of eight hundred men and women under contract to me, back at Neuss. They're used to being paid! I have to go back and explain how this marriage is going to benefit *them*."

"Yes, yes . . ." Constanza del Guiz had fair hair and lazy good looks, but not her son's rangy build. She was tiny. A soft pink velvet gown fitted tightly around her small bosom, and then flared from her hips to drape voluminously to her satin slippers. She wore a red and silver brocade undergown. Rubies and emeralds ornamented both her padded headdress and the gold belt that hung down in a V from her hips. A purse and keys hung pendant from the belt-chain.

"My tailor can't work if you keep moving," Constanza pleaded. "Please, stand *still*."

The padded roll of Ash's headdress sat on her braided hair like a small but heavy animal.

"I can do this later. I have to go and sort the company out now!"

"Sweet child, how do you expect me to get a wedding arranged at a week's notice? I could kill Frederick!" Reproachful, Constanza del Guiz looked up at Ash with brimming blue eyes. Ash noted the *Frederick*. "And you don't help, child. First you want to get married in your *armour* . . ."

Ash looked down at the tailor kneeling with pins and shears at her hem. "This is a robe, ain't it?"

"An underrobe. In your 'livery colours'." The old woman – fifty, perhaps –

---

[12] Fifteenth-century man-portable matchlock firearm.

put her fingers to her shaking lips, on the verge of tears. "It's taken me all of today to persuade you out of doublet and hose!"

A knock sounded on the door. A square-built, bearded man was admitted by the serving women. Ash turned towards Father Godfrey Maximillian and caught her foot in the sheer linen chemise that tangled her ankles, under her full-length silk kirtle. She stumbled. *"Fuck!"*

The whole room – tailor, tailor's apprentice, two Cologne serving women, and her prospective new mother – stopped talking, and stared at her. Constanza del Guiz's face pinked.

Ash cringed, took a deep breath, and stared out of the window at the rain until someone should start talking again.

"Fiat lux, my lady. Captain." Water streamed from Godfrey Maximillian's woollen shoulder-caped hood. He pulled it off phlegmatically, and made the sign of the cross at the Green Man carved in fine stone tracery in the room's shrine. He beamed at the tailors and serving women, including them in his blessing. "Praise the Tree."

"Godfrey," Ash acknowledged. "Did you bring Florian and Roberto with you?"

Anselm had been much in Italy, originally, in tandem with Antonio Angelotti; there were still old company members who did not use the English *Robert.* If she could name one of her officers she was most anxious to talk to now, it was him.

"I can't find Florian, anywhere. Robert's acting for the company while you're here."

And where have *you* been? I expected you eight hours ago, Ash thought grimly. Looking respectable. You could at least have cleaned the mud off! I'm trying to convince this woman I'm not a freak, and you turn up looking like a hedge priest!

Godfrey must have read something of this on her face. He said to Constanza del Guiz, "Sorry to be so unkempt, my lady. I've been riding from Neuss. Captain Ash's men need her advice on several things, quite urgently."

"Oh." The old woman's surprise was frank and genuine. "Do they need her? I thought she was a figurehead for them. I would have imagined that a band of soldiers functions more smoothly when women are *not* there."

Ash opened her mouth and the younger serving woman whipped a light linen veil over her face.

Godfrey Maximillian looked up from inadvertently shaking his muddy cloak over the tailor's bales of cloth. "Soldiers don't function with a figurehead in charge, my lady. Certainly they don't raise over a thousand men successfully for three years running, and have most of the German principalities bidding for their services."

The Imperial noblewoman looked startled. "You don't mean she actually—"

"I command mercenaries," Ash interrupted, "and that's what I need to get back and do. We've never been paid with a marriage before. I know them. They won't like it. It ain't hard cash."

"Commands mercenaries," Constanza said, as if her mind were elsewhere, and then snapped a blue gaze back to Ash. Her soft mouth unexpectedly hardened. "What's Frederick thinking of? He promised me a good marriage for my son!"

"He promised *me* land," Ash said gloomily. "That's princes for you."

Godfrey chuckled.

Constanza snapped, "There have been women who tried to command in battle. That unsexed bitch Margaret of Anjou lost the throne of England for her poor husband. I could never let you do that to my son. You're rough, unmannered, and probably of peasant stock, but you're not wicked. I can school you to manners. You'll find people will soon forget your past when you're Fernando's wife, and my daughter."

"*Bol*— rubbish!" Ash lifted her arms in response to the tailor's nudge. A blue velvet gown settled over her gold-embroidered underrobe, heavy on her shoulders.

One serving woman began to pull in the laces at the back of the tight bodice. The other draped the gown's gold brocade hanging sleeves to one side, and buttoned the undergown's tight-fitting sleeves from fur-trimmed cuff to elbow. The tailor fastened a belt low on Ash's hips.

"I've had fewer problems getting into *armour*," Ash muttered.

"Lady Ash will be a perfect credit to your son Fernando, I'm certain," Godfrey said, straight-faced. "Proverbs, chapter fourteen, verse one: every wise woman buildeth her house, but the foolish pulleth it down with her hands."[13]

Something in his tone on the last words made Ash look at him sharply.

Constanza del Guiz looked up – and it really is *up*, Ash noted – at the priest. "One moment. Father, you say this girl owns a company of men."

"Under contract, yes."

"And is therefore wealthy?"

Ash snuffled back a laugh, wiping her sun-tanned wrist across her mouth. Her weather-beaten skin wasn't set off to advantage by silk sleeves and wolf-fur cuffs. She said cheerfully, "Wealthy if I could keep it! I have to pay those bastards. Those men. Oh, shit. I'm no good at this!"

"I've known Ash since she was a child, my lady," Godfrey said smartly, "and she's perfectly capable of adapting herself from camp to court."

Thanks. Ash gave her clerk a look of heavy irony. Godfrey ignored it.

"But this is my only son—" Constanza put her thin fingers to her mouth. "Yes, Father. I'm sorry, I – faced with a wedding in less than a fortnight – and her origins – and no family—"

She dabbed at one eye with the corner of her veil. It was a calculated gesture, but then, as she looked at Ash struggling under the fitting of her headdress, a tension went out of her features. Constanza smiled quite sincerely.

"Neither of us expected this, but I think we can manage. Your men will be a welcome addition to my son's prestige. And you could be lovely, little one. Let me dress you properly and put on a little white lead to hide your blemishes. I would wish you to stand in front of the court as the pride of the del Guiz family, not the shame of it." Constanza's plucked brows furrowed. "Especially if Tante Jeanne comes here from Burgundy, which she might, even with the war

[13] Although it is a later translation, some 135 years after the 'Ash' texts, I have chosen the King James Authorised Version of the Bible (1611) as more accessible to the modern reader.

between us. Fernando's father's family always think they have a perfect right to come and criticise me. You'll meet them later."

"I won't." Ash shook her head. "I'm riding back to Neuss. Today."

"No! Not until I have you dressed and ready for this wedding."

"Now, *look*—" Ash planted her feet squarely apart under her voluminous, flowing skirts. She jammed her fists on her hips. The underrobe's close-fitting sleeves suddenly creaked at the shoulder-seams.

Tacking threads snapped.

The azure velvet gown slid up through her hanging belt and bunched at her waist. The sudden weight of the purse pulled her belt skewed. Her heart-shaped horned headdress, with its padded roll and temple-pieces, slipped to one side and all but fell off.

Ash huffed a breath at the crooked wisp of linen veil that floated down into her eyes.

"Child . . ." Constanza's voice failed. "You look like a sack of grain tied with a string!"

"Well, let me wear my doublet and hose, then."

"*You cannot get married in male dress!*"

Ash broke into an irrepressible grin. "Tell that to Fernando. I don't mind if he wants to wear the dress . . ."

"Oh!"

Godfrey Maximillian, studying his captain, folded his hands across his robed belly and rather unwisely said aloud what he was thinking. "I never realised. You look short, in a dress."

"I'm taller on the goddamn battlefield! Right, that's *it*." Ash wrenched the horned head-dress and veils off her head, wincing as the pins pulled out of her hair. She ignored the tailor's protests.

"You *can't* go now!" Constanza del Guiz pleaded.

"Watch me!" Ash strode across the room, the full skirt of her gown flapping about her slippered feet. She picked up Godfrey's wet cloak and slung it around her shoulders. "We're out of here. Godfrey, do we have more than one company horse here?"

"No. Just my palfrey."

"Tough. You can ride pillion behind me. Lady Constanza, I'm sorry – truly." Ash hesitated. She gave the tiny woman a reassuring smile that, she was startled to find, she meant. "Truly. I have to see to my men. I'll be back. I'll *have* to be. Since it's the Emperor Frederick's gift, I can't very well *not* marry your son Fernando!"

There was some debate at Cologne's north-west gate: a lady, with her head uncovered, riding unaccompanied except for a priest? Ash gave them a few coins and the benefit of a soldier's vocabulary, and was put out to have the gate guards then pass her through as a whore accompanied by her pimp.

"Are you going to tell me what's bothering you?" she said over her shoulder to Godfrey, an hour later.

"No. Not unless it becomes necessary."

Rain made the roads into two days' journey, not one. Ash seethed. Deep cart-ruts full of mud tired the horse, until she gave up and bought another at a farm where they stayed, and then she and Godfrey rode on through the downpour, until they smelled the downwind stink of an established camp, and knew they must be near Neuss.

"Ask yourself why it is," Ash said, absently grim, "that I know a hundred and thirty-seven different words for diseases of horses? High time we had something more reliable. Get up, there!"

Godfrey reined in his palfrey, waiting. "What did you think of life in the women's rooms in the castle?"

"A day and a half is enough for a lifetime." The roan gelding slowed again as her attention wandered. Ash felt a shift in the air and looked north at breaking cloud. "I've got used to people looking at me as soon as I walk into a room. Well, no – they *looked* at me in Constanza's solar, but not for the same reasons!" Her eyes slitted with amusement. "I've got used to people expecting me to be in charge, Godfrey. In camp it's *Ash, what do we do now?* And in Cologne, it's *who's this unnatural monster?*"

"You always were a bossy brat," Godfrey remarked. "And, come to think of it, you always were fairly unnatural."

"That's why you rescued me from the nuns, I suppose?"

He ran a hand over his bearded chin and twinkled at her. "I like my women strange."

"That's good, coming from a chaste priest!"

"You want more miracles and grace for the company, you better pray I *stay* chaste."

"I need a miracle, all right. Until I got to Cologne, I thought maybe Emperor Frederick wasn't serious." Ash shifted her heels, bringing the roan from immobility to amble. The rain began to ease.

"Ash – are you going through with this?"

"I most certainly am. Constanza was *wearing* more money than I've seen in the last two campaigns."

"And if the company objects?"

"They'll bitch because I didn't let them take prisoners for ransom on the skirmish, that's for sure. I'll bet I'm not flavour of the month. But they'll cheer up when they hear it's a rich marriage. We'll own *land* now. You're the one who objects, Godfrey, and you won't tell me why."

They confronted each other from the saddle: the surprising authority of the young woman, and the reserved concern of the priest. He repeated, "If it becomes necessary."

"Godfrey, sometimes you're a real Godly pain in the ass." Ash pushed her wet wool hood back. "Now, let's see if we can get all the command lance in one place at the same time, shall we?"

They were in sight of the south-east side of the Imperial wagon-fort now. The small foreign contingent of great-wheeled wagons here, chained together for defence, streamed with the last of the rain. Water ran down the forged iron plates that faced the sides of the war-carts, metal already streaking with orange rust.[14]

---

[14] These improbable vehicles bear some resemblance to the mobile horse-drawn 'war-wagons'

Over the sides of the iron war-wagons, inside the immense laager, Ash saw a rainbow of heraldic banners and standards dripping. The canvas cones of the striped tents hung limp from their centre poles, ropes stretched and wet. A spatter of rain dashed into Ash's face as they approached the gate. It was a good five minutes before a hail went up from the huddled guards.

Euen Huw, sidling into the gateway past them, with a chicken under his arm, stopped and looked extremely startled. "Boss? Hey, boss – nice dress!"

Ash looked resignedly straight ahead as their horses trudged in down the long wagon- and tent-lined lanes. Antonio Angelotti ran up seconds later, his pale and beautiful hands yellow with sulphur.

"Never saw you in a dress before, boss. Looks good. You missed all the excitement!" His perfect face beamed, like a down-market angel. "Heralds coming up from the Burgundian camp. Imperial heralds going down to the Burgundian camp. Terms put forward."

"Terms?"

"Sure. His Majesty Frederick says to Duke Charles, pull back twenty miles. Lift the siege. Then in three days, *we'll* pull back twenty miles."

"And Duke Charles is still laughing, right?"

Angelotti's yellow curls flew as he shook his head. "The word is, he'll agree. That it's peace between the Emperor and Burgundy."

"Oh, *shit*," Ash remarked, in the tone of one who – two minutes before – had known exactly what eight hundred-odd men, women and dependent children were doing for the next three months. And now doesn't, and will have to work something out. "Sweet Christ. Peace. There goes our cushy summer siege."

Angelotti fell in to walk beside her gelding. "What's happening about this marriage of yours, madonna? The Emperor can't be serious?"

"Yes he fucking can!"

Ten minutes riding across camp brought them to the A-frame shelters and horse lines at the north-west corner. The voluminous folds of the velvet gown clung wetly to her legs, rain darkening the cloth to royal blue. She still wore Godfrey's cloak. It was pulled back by its own weight of soaked wool, disclosing her kirtle and the wet linen of her chemise.

The company had separated off a corner of the Imperial camp with wattle fencing and a makeshift gate, something which had not pleased the Imperial quartermaster until Ash truthfully told him it was because her troops would steal anything not nailed down. A Lion Azure standard now drooped there in the wet.

A redheaded man from Ned Aston's lance, guarding the gate, looked up and executed a perfect double-take.

"Hey – nice dress, boss!"

"*Bollocks!*"

A few minutes saw her in the command tent, Anselm, Angelotti, and

---

used by the Hussites in the 1420s, some fifty years earlier than this. The Eastern European fighters appear to have used them as mobile gun-platforms. However, the del Guiz 'iron-sided' wagons are a mere impossibility – even if constructed, they would have been so heavy that no conceivable team of horses could have moved them.

Godfrey present; Florian de Lacey missing, and the company's other main sub-captains missing.

"They're off muttering in corners. I'd leave them to it until you've got something you can tell them." Robert wrung out his woollen hood. "Tell us how badly we're screwed."

"We're not screwed, this is one *hell* of an opportunity!"

Ash was interrupted by Geraint ab Morgan ducking into the tent. "Yo, boss."

Geraint, new this season, currently overall Sergeant of Archers, was a broad-shouldered man with cropped hair the colour of fallen leaves, that stood straight up on his skull. The whites of his eyes were perpetually bloodshot. As he came in, Ash noted that the points which joined the back of his hose to the back of his doublet were undone, and his shirt had ridden up out of the gap, disclosing a ragged pair of braies and the cleft of his buttocks.

Aware she had come back unheralded, Ash kept tactfully quiet, except for a glare that had Geraint avoiding her eye and staring up into the conical roof of the tent, where weapons and kit were hung up on the wooden struts out of the wet.

"Day report," Ash said crisply.

Geraint scratched at his buttocks under white and blue wool hose. "The lads have been inside for two days, out of the rain, cleaning kit. Jacobo Rossano tried to poach two of our Flemish lances and they told him to sod off – he's not impressed. And Henri de Tréville is with the provosts, arrested for being drunk and trying to set the cook on fire."

"You don't mean the cook's wagon, do you?" Ash asked wistfully, "you mean the cook."

"There was some comment about the besieged eating better in Neuss," Florian de Lacey said, as the surgeon entered, muddy to his booted knees. "And words to the effect that rat was a delicacy compared to Wat Rodway's stewed beef . . ."

Angelotti showed white teeth. "'God sends us meat, and the Devil sends us English cooks.'"

"Enough with the Milanese proverbs, already!" Ash swatted at his head; he dodged. "Good. No one's successfully poaching our lances. Yet. Camp news?"

Robert Anselm volunteered briskly, "Sigismund of the Tyrol's pulling out, he says Frederick isn't going to fight Burgundy at all. Sigismund's been pissed off with Duke Charles since he lost Héricourt in '74. His men have been brawling with Gottfried of Innsbruck's archers. Oratio Farinetti and Henri Jacques have quarrelled, the surgeons took up two dead from their men fighting."

"I don't suppose we've actually fought the enemy?" Ash somewhat theatrically whacked her palm against her forehead. "No, no; silly me – we don't need an enemy. No feudal army does. Christ preserve me from factious nobility!"

A lance of sunlight slanted in through the open tent-flap. Everything Ash could see through the gap was dripping, and jewel-bright. She watched the red brigandines and blue and yellow livery jackets of men coming out to coax fires back into life, and tap the beer barrels that stood taller than a man, and fall to playing with greasy cards on the upturned tops of drums. Rising voices echoed.

"*Right.* Robert, Geraint, get the lads out, tell the lance-leaders to split 'em into red and blue scarves, and give them a game of football outside the wagon-fort."

"*Football?* Bloody English game!" Florian glared at her. "You realise I'll have more injuries to deal with than from the skirmish?"

Ash nodded. "Come to think of it . . . Rickard! *Rickard!* Where is that boy?"

Her squire hurtled into the tent. He was fourteen, with glossy black hair and thick winged eyebrows; already conscious of how good-looking he was, and with a growing disinclination to keep it in his codpiece.

"You'll have to run up to the provosts and warn them the noise down here isn't a skirmish, it's a game."

"Yes, my lady!"

Robert Anselm scratched at his shaven head. "They won't wait much longer, Ash. I've had lance-leaders up to the tent every hour on the hour, these past two days."

"I know. *When* they've worked their energy off," Ash continued, "get them all together. I'm going to talk to everybody, not just the lance-leaders. Go!"

"I hope you've got something convincing to tell them!"

"Trust me."

Anselm went out behind Geraint. The tent emptied of all but Ash, her surgeon, priest and page.

"Rickard, on your way out, send Philibert in to dress me." Ash watched her eldest page stomp out.

"Rickard's getting too old," she said absently to de Lacey. "I'll have to pass him on as a squire, and find another ten-year-old page." Her eyes gleamed. "That's a problem you don't have, Florian – *I* have to have body servants under the age of puberty, or all the whore-rumours start up again. 'She's not a real captain, she just shags the company officers and they let her prance around in armour.' Hell-fire!" She laughed. "In any case, young Rickard's far too good-looking for me to have around. Never fuck your employees!"

Florian de Lacey leaned back in the wooden chair, both palms flat on his thighs. He gave her a sardonic look. "The bold mercenary captain ogles the innocent young boy – except I don't remember the last time you got laid, and Rickard's been through half the Imperial camp whores and come to me because he caught crab-lice."

"Yeah?" Ash shrugged. "Well . . . I can't fuck anyone in the company because it's favouritism. And anyone who isn't a soldier goes, you're a woman and you're a *what*?"

Florian stood and walked to look out of the tent, cradling a wine cup. Not, after all, a particularly tall man; he had the left-over stoop of a boy who grew tall earlier than his contemporaries, and learned not to like standing out in a crowd. "And now you're getting married."

"Yippee!" Ash said. "It won't change anything, except we'll have revenues from land. Fernando del Guiz can stay in his castle, and I'll stay in the army.

He can find himself some bimbo in a stuffed headdress, and I'll be entirely happy to look the other way. Marriage? *No* problem."

Florian raised a sardonic eyebrow. "If that's what you think, you haven't been paying attention!"

"I know your marriage was difficult."

"Oh." He shrugged. "Esther preferred Joseph to me – women often prefer their babies to their husbands. At least it wasn't a man she ignored me for . . ."

Ash gave up her attempt to unlace her bodice herself, and presented her back to Godfrey. As the priest's solid fingers tugged at the cords, she said, "Before I go out there and talk to the guys – I've been paying attention to one thing, Florian. How come you keep vanishing lately? I turn round and you're not there. What's Fernando del Guiz to you?"

"Ah." Florian wandered in an irritating manner around the kit-cluttered tent. He stopped. He looked coolly at Ash. "He's my brother."

"Your *what*?" Ash goggled.

At her back, Godfrey's fingers were momentarily still on the bodice lacing. "*Brother?*"

"Half-brother, actually. We share a father."

Ash became aware that the top of her gown had loosened. She shook her shoulders in the cloth, feeling it slide away. Godfrey Maximillian's fingers began to untie the fastenings of her underrobe.

"You've got a brother who's noble?"

"We all know Florian's an aristocrat." Godfrey hesitated. "Don't we?" He went around to the trestle table and poured a goblet of wine. "Here. I thought you knew, Ash. Florian, I always thought your family came from one of the Burgundies, not the Empire."

"It does. Dijon, in Burgundy. When my mother in Dijon died, my father re-married, a noblewoman from Cologne." The blond man slid a shoulder up in an insouciant gesture. "Fernando's a good few years younger than me, but he is my half-brother."

"Green Christ up a Tree!" Ash said. "By the Bull's Horns!"

"Florian's hardly the only man we've got in the company under a false name. Criminals, debtors and runaways, to a man." Seeing that she would not take the wine, Godfrey gulped it himself. He made a face of disgust. "That sutler's selling us rubbish again. Ash, I assume Florian stays away from his family because no aristocratic family would ever tolerate their son as a barber-surgeon – is that right, Florian?"

Florian grinned. He sat again, sprawling back on Ash's wooden chair, and put his boots on her table. "Your face! It's true. All of the del Guiz family, German and Burgundian, would have a fit if they knew I was a doctor. They'd prefer me dead in a ditch somewhere. And the rest of the medical profession don't like my research methods."

"One corpse too many gone missing in Padua,[15] I suppose." Ash recovered some composure. "Blood! How long have I known you—"

"Five years?" Florian said.

[15] Padua in Italy was at this time a famous centre attended by medical students from all over Europe.

"And *now* you tell me?"

"I thought you knew." Florian stopped meeting her gaze. He scratched at the shin of his torn hose with a hand deeply dirt-ingrained. "I thought you knew everything I had to hide."

Ash pushed her underrobe and kirtle off her shoulders and stepped out of the vast heap of crumpled silk and brocade, leaving it laying on the rushes. Her linen chemise was fine enough to show her skin as a pink glow under it, and disclose the round swell of her breasts, the darkness of her nipples.

Florian grinned at her, momentarily distracted. "That's what I *call* a pair of tits. Good Lord, woman! Beats me how you ever get those under an arming doublet. One day you really must let me have a closer look . . ."

Ash stripped her chemise off over her head. She stood naked and confident, one fist on her hip, and grinned back at her surgeon. "Yeah, sure – your interest in women's bodies is *purely* professional. That's what all the camp girls tell me!"

Florian leered. "Trust me. I'm a doctor."

Godfrey did not laugh. He looked out of the tent. "Here's young Philibert. Florian, isn't this ridiculous? You could – mediate with your brother. Isn't this the ideal occasion for a family reunion?"

All humour gone, Florian said flatly, "No."

"You could be reconciled to your family – bless them which persecute you; bless, and curse not.[16] And then you could *strongly* suggest to your brother that he doesn't marry Ash."

"No. I could not. I recognised who it must be out there by his livery. I haven't met him face to face since he was a child, and I intend to keep it that way."

An edge was apparent in the air, a tension in their voices. Ash glanced from one man to the other, entirely unconscious of being naked. "Don't object to this marriage, guys. It can open up a whole new world for the company. We can be permanent. We'll have land we can go back to, in the winter. *And* revenues."

Florian's gaze locked on the priest's face. "Listen to her, Father Godfrey. She's right."

"But she mustn't marry Fernando del Guiz!" The priest's desperate voice went up an octave; he sounded like the young ordinand that Ash remembered meeting in the St Herlaine convent, eight years ago. "She must not!"

"Why not?"

"Yes, why not?" Ash echoed her surgeon. "Phili, come and sort me out shirt and doublet and hose. The green with the silver points will be suitably impressive. Godfrey, why not?"

"I've been waiting, but you don't— Didn't you recognise his name? Don't you remember his face?" Godfrey was a big man, rather than being fat, and he had all the charisma of a large, powerful body, priest or not. Now there was helplessness in his gestures. He swung round on Florian, jabbing a finger at the willowy man sprawled in the chair. "Ash can't marry your brother because she's met him before!"

16 Romans 12: 14.

"I'm sure our ruthless mercenary leader has met many noble idiots." Florian picked at his dirty nails. "Fernando won't be the first, or the worst."

Godfrey stepped out of the page Philibert's way. Ash hauled a shirt over her head, sat on the wooden chest, and pulled on her doublet and hose together – two mismatched shades of green wool; still tied together at the waist with twelve pairs of cords tipped with silver aiglettes. She held her arms out, and the small boy eased her sleeves over them, tying them into the doublet's arm-holes at the shoulders with more pairs of points.

"Go watch the football, Phili; come and tell me when they're finishing." She ruffled his hair. As he left, and she began lacing up the front of her best puff-sleeved doublet, she said, "Come on, Godfrey, what is it? Yeah, I know I know the face from somewhere. Where do you know him from?"

Godfrey Maximillian turned away, avoiding her eyes. "He . . . won the big tournament, in Cologne, last summer. You remember, child? He unhorsed fifteen; didn't fight in the foot combat. The Emperor presented him with a bay stallion. I – recognised the livery and name."

Ash took his shoulder and turned him to face her again. She said flatly, "Yeah. *And* the rest. What's so special, Godfrey? Where did *I* meet Fernando?"

"Seven years ago." Godfrey took a breath. "In Genoa."

Her belly jolted. She forgot the waiting company. So *that's* what all the adrenalin-powered cheerfulness has been about, these past two days. I'm like that when I'm hiding something from myself. I just don't always know that's what I'm doing.

And it's probably why I've been running the company like a half-arsed excuse for a captain; letting myself be taken off to Cologne—

The memory, chewed dry, comes back to her as it always does, in the same fragments. Sea-water slopping against the stone steps of a dock. Lantern light on wet cobbles. Male shoulders against the light. Running back to camp afterwards – the camp of her old company, under the Griffin-in-Gold banner – choking, far too ashamed to show rage openly.

"Oh. Yeah. So?" Ash's voice sounded, even to herself, too hurried to be casual. She looked away from Godfrey, out of the tent. "Was *that* del Guiz? That was a long time ago."

"I made it my business afterwards to find out his name."

"Did you?" The back of her throat tightened with malice. "That's the kind of thing you like to do, isn't it, Godfrey? Even then."

In her peripheral vision, Florian de Lacey – now Florian del Guiz, a potential brother-in-law; how strange – stood up. He put his flopping, dirty blond hair out of his eyes, in the so-familiar gesture. "What is it, girl?"

"Didn't I ever tell you? It was before you joined us. I thought I might have got drunk some night and told you." A questioning glance, at which Florian shook his head.

Ash got up from the chest and walked to the tent's entrance. The wet canvas was beginning to dry now, under the afternoon sun. She reached out to test the growing tautness of a guy-rope. A cow moaned, over in the quartermaster Henri Brant's stock pens. The wind brought wet scents of dung. The tents and other shelters – A-frame structures made of canvas pegged down over halberd shafts – were unusually empty. She cocked an ear for the sound of voices shouting at football, and heard nothing.

"Well," she said. "Well."

She turned back to face the two men. Godfrey's fingers kneaded obsessively at the cord around the waist of his brown robe. You could still see, in his weather-hardened features, the pallid, plump young man that he had been then. Her rage, hanging fire, snapped.

"And you can take that sheep-face off! I've never seen *you* so happy. You loved me being punished. You could comfort me! You never like me quite so much when I'm not falling apart, do you? Bloody virgin!"

"*Ash!*"

Ebbing, the anger leaves her dry, free of the conviction that the world is full of faces hiding harm, viciousness, persecution.

"Jesus, Godfrey, I'm sorry!"

The priest's face lost a little of its distress.

Florian said, "What did my brother do?"

Ash felt the dry rushes beneath her bare feet as she walked back across the tent. The shadows of clouds move across the canvas; the world bright, then dim, then bright again. She sat on the wooden chest and pulled her boots on, without looking up at the surgeon. "Wine."

"Here." A dirty hand entered her field of vision: Florian holding a goblet.

Ash took it, and watched the red and silver ripples on the surface of the liquid.

"You can't hear it without laughing. No one could. That's the problem." She lifted her head as Florian squatted down on his haunches in front of her; she and the man now level, face to face. "You know, you don't look anything like him. I'd never have taken you on the company books if you had."

"Yes you would." Florian put one hand down to support himself, careless of the mud tracked in on the rushes. He smiled. It showed the dirt in the creases of the skin around his eyes, but made his whole face glow with affection. "How else could you afford a Salerno-qualified doctor, except by finding one with a predilection for cutting up battlefield casualties to see how bodies work? Every mercenary company should have one! And where else are you going to find someone sensible enough to tell you when you're being an idiot? You're an idiot. I don't know my half-brother, but what could he have done—?"

Florian suddenly straightened up and rubbed at his cramped legs. Mud smeared. He picked one or two of the larger clods off his blue hose, and watched her out of the corner of his eye. "Did he rape you?"

"No. I wish he had."

Ash reached up and unfastened the tight braids that Constanza's women had done up for her. Her silver hair uncoiled.

This is now. This is now: if I hear birds, they are crows yawping, not gulls. This is now, and this is summer, hot even when it rains. But my hands are cold with humiliation.

"I was twelve, Godfrey had taken me out of St Herlaine the year before; it was after I'd been apprentice to a Milanese armourer and then found the

Company of the Griffin-in-Gold again." She heard the sea in her mind. "This was when I still wore women's dress if I wasn't in the camp."

Still sitting, she reached over and picked up her sword, with the sword-belt wound tidily around its scabbard. The round wheel pommel comforted her hand as she rested her palm on it. The leather on the grip was cut and needed re-doing.

"There was an inn in Genoa. This boy was there with friends, and he asked me to sit down at their table. I suppose it must have been summer. It was light until late. He had green eyes and fair hair and no particular kind of face, but it was the first time I'd ever looked at a man and got hot and wet. I thought he *liked* me."

When she has to remember, when something reminds her of it, it is as if she watches what happens from a distance. But it only takes a slight effort to bring back the sweat and the fear, and her whining voice pleading *Let me go! Please!* She pulled away from their hands, and they pinched her breasts, leaving black bruises that she never showed to any physician.

"I thought I was *it*, Florian. I was doing sword-training, and the captain was even allowing me to act as his page. I thought I was *so* hot."

She couldn't look up.

"He was a few years older, obviously the son of a knight. I did everything to make him like me. There was wine but I never drank it, I just got too high when I thought that he wanted me. I couldn't wait to touch him. When we left, I thought we were going back to his rooms. He took me round the back of the inn, near the dock, and said, 'Lie down.' I didn't care, it could have been there or anywhere."

Cobblestones: cushioned only by the crumpled cloth of her robe and kirtle and shift. She felt them hard under her buttocks as she lay down and moved her heels apart.

"He stood over me and unlaced his flap. I didn't know what he was doing, I expected him to lie down on top of me. He took it out and he *pissed*—"

She rubbed her hands over her face.

"He said I was a little girl who acted like a man and he pissed on me. His friends came up and watched. Laughing."

She sprang up. The sword thudded down on to the rushes. Rapidly, she walked to the tent's entrance, looked out, spun around and faced the two men.

"You can't help but laugh. I wanted to die. He held me down while all his friends did it. On my robe. In my face. The taste – I thought it would be poison, that I'd die from that."

Godfrey reached out his hand. She stepped back from comfort without realising that she did so.

"What I don't understand to this day is *why I let it happen*."

Anguish thinned her voice.

"I knew how to fight. Even if they were stronger, and there were more of them, I knew how to *run*." She rubbed her hand hard across her scarred cheek. "I did scream out to one man walking past, but he just ignored me. He could see what they were doing. He didn't do anything to help. He laughed. I can't be angry about it. *They didn't even hurt me.*"

Sick fear in her stomach kept her from looking at either of them, Godfrey now reminded of a wet, stinking, weeping young woman; and Florian with whom things would not now be the same, not ever, not with him knowing this.

"Christ," Ash said painfully, "if that *was* Fernando del Guiz – he can't remember now or he'd have said something. Looked at me different. Do you think he still has the same friends? Do you think any of *them* will remember?"

Powerful hands closed over her shoulders from behind. Godfrey said nothing, but his grip tightened until she could have cried out. She could feel his mute appeal to Florian. Ash rubbed her flaming cheeks. "Fuck."

I've spent five years killing men on the field of battle, and here I am thinking like a green novice, not a soldier—

Godfrey's voice over her shoulder whispered, intensely: "Florian, find out if he remembers. Talk to him. He's your brother. Buy him off if you have to!"

Florian walked towards Ash. He stopped when he stood directly in front of her. In the light inside the tent, his face looked grey. "I can't do it. I can't try to persuade him out of it. They'd burn me."

Ash could only incredulously say, "*What?*", still shaking from the rush of memory. The man in front of her reached out. She felt her hand taken. Godfrey's grip from behind tightened again.

Florian's long, surgeon's fingers uncurled her hand. He pulled open the lacing of his doublet and plunged Ash's hand under the gathered neck of his fine linen shirt.

She was touching warm flesh before she said, "What?"

Under his shirt, Ash's fingers and palm cupped the full, rounded, firm breast of a woman.

Ash stared at his face. The dirty, unshakeable, pragmatic surgeon gripped her hand hard, and was plainly woman; plain as day, a tall woman in man's dress.

Godfrey's puzzled voice rumbled, "What—?"

"You're a *woman*?" Ash stared at Florian.

Godfrey gaped at both of them.

"Why couldn't you *tell* me?" Ash shouted. "Christ, I needed to know! You might have put the whole company in danger!"

The page Philibert put his head back through the tent-flap. Ash snatched her hand away.

The boy looked from one to the other: surgeon, field priest, captain. "Ash!"

He feels the tension, Ash thought, and then: No, I'm wrong. He's too wrapped up in what he's got to say to notice anything else.

The boy squealed, "They're not playing football. The men. Everybody. They won't! They're all together, and they say they're not doing anything until you come and speak to them!"

"*Here* we go," Ash muttered. She glanced back at Florian, at Godfrey. "Go and tell them I'm on my way. *Now*." And, as the boy Philibert ran out, "It won't wait. They won't wait. Not now. Florian – no – what *is* your name?"

"Floria."

"'Floria' . . ."

"I don't understand," Godfrey said frankly.

The tall woman retied the neck-string of her shirt. "My name is Floria del Guiz. I'm not Fernando's half-brother, he has no brothers. I'm his half-*sister*. This is the only way I can ever practise as a surgeon, and no, my family is not about to welcome me back, not in Burgundy, and certainly not into the Imperial German branch of the del Guizes."

The priest stared. "You're a woman!"

Ash muttered, "That's why I keep you on the company books, Godfrey. Your acumen. Your intelligence. The rapidity with which you penetrate to the heart of the matter." She shot a look at the lantern and its marked hour-candle, burning steadily where it sat on the trestle table. "It's nearly Nones.[17] Godfrey, go and give that unruly mob out there a field-mass. Do it! I need time."

She caught the brown sleeve of his robe as he moved towards the tent-flap. "Don't mention Florian. I mean Floria. You heard it Under the Tree. And get me enough time to arm up."

Godfrey looked at her for a long minute before he nodded.

Ash stared after his departing back as Godfrey stepped out across the rain-wet earth that steamed, now, in the afternoon sun. "Shit on a stick . . ."

"When do I leave?" Floria del Guiz said, behind her.

Ash pressed both index fingers down hard on the bridge of her nose. She shut her eyes. The darkness behind her eyelids speckled with light.

"I'll be lucky if I don't lose half the company, never mind you." She opened her eyes again; dropped her hands to her sides. "You've slept in my tent. I've seen you rat-arsed and throwing up. *I've seen you piss!*"

"No. You're merely under the impression that you have. I've been doing this since I was thirteen." Floria appeared in Ash's peripheral vision, wine cup trailing from her long fingers. "Salerno now trains no Jews, no black Libyans, and no women. I've passed as a man since then. Padua, Constantinople, Iberia. Army doctoring, because nobody *cares* who you are. You and these men . . . This past five years is the longest I've been able to stay anywhere."

Ash leaned out of the tent and bawled, *"Philibert! Rickard!* Get in here! – I can't make a hasty decision, Florian. Floria."

"Stick with Florian. It's safer. It's safer for *me*."

That rueful tone penetrated Ash's daze. She looked straight at the woman. "I'm female. The world puts up with me. Why shouldn't it put up with you?"

Florian ticked off on her fingers: "You're a mercenary. You're a peasant. You're human cattle. You don't have an influential rich family. I *am* a del Guiz.

---

[17] This text often gives the hour of the day by the monastic system: Nones is the sixth office or service of the day, taking place at 3 p.m. The monastic hours are:

Matins:	midnight (but sometimes held with)
Lauds:	3 a.m.
Prime:	sunrise (nominally 6 a.m.)
Terce:	9 a.m.
Sext:	noon
Nones:	3 p.m.
Vespers:	6 p.m.
Compline:	9 p.m.

(The unwary reader should note this is further complicated by the mediaeval habit of dividing the hours of dark and the hours of daylight into twelve-hour segments, which means that in winter an 'hour' of darkness is longer than an 'hour' of daylight, and conversely for the summer.)

I matter. I'm a threat. If nothing else, I'm the elder: I could inherit at least the estate in Burgundy . . . All this outrage comes down to property in the end."

"They wouldn't burn you." Ash did not sound certain. "Maybe they'd only lock you up and beat you."

"I don't have your facility for being hit without minding it." Florian's fair eyebrows quirked up. "Ash, are you so sure they tolerate you? This idea of a marriage didn't come out of nowhere. Somebody's put Frederick up to it."

"Shit. *Marriage.*" Ash moved back across the tent and lifted her sword up out of the rushes. Apparently absently, she said, "I heard, in Cologne, that the Emperor's knighted Gustav Schongauer. Remember him and his guys two years ago at Héricourt?"[18]

"*Schongauer? Knighted?*" Florian, briefly distracted by outrage, glared at her. "They were bandits! He spent most of that autumn destroying Tyrolese farms and villages! How could Frederick ennoble him?"

"Because there's no such thing as legitimate authority or illegitimate authority. There is only authority." Ash faced the man who was a woman, still holding her scabbarded sword between two hands. "If you *can* control a lot of fighting men – you *will*. And you'll be recognised and ratified by other controllers. *Like I need to be.* Except that no king or nobleman is going to knight *me.*"

"Knighthood? Boy's games! But if a murdering rapist can end up as a Graf—!"

Ash waved Florian's shock away. "Yeah, you *are* noble . . . How do you think we get new nobles in the first place? The other Grafs are scared of him. The Emperor too, for that matter. So they make him one of them. If he gets too scary, they'll band together and have him killed. That's the balancing act."

She took the wine cup out of Florian's fingers and drained it. The buzz was enough to loosen her up, not enough to make her light-headed.

"It's the law by which chivalry operates." Ash looked down into the empty cup. "It doesn't matter how generous and virtuous you are. Or how brutal. If you have no powerbase, you'll treated with disrespect; and if you do have a powerbase, everyone will come to you in preference to anyone else. And power comes from the ability to make armed men fight for you. To reward them with money, yes, but more – with titles and marriages and land. I can't do that. I need to. This marriage—"

Ash abruptly reddened. She scrutinised Floria's face, weighing up secrets known, and past confidences not betrayed. Floria, so like the Florian who had shared her tent on many nights, talking into the small hours.

"You don't go, Florian. Unless you want to." She met Floria's gaze, smiled wryly. "You're too good a surgeon, if nothing else. And . . . we've known each other too long. If I trust you to horse-doctor me, I can't stop trusting you now!"

A little shaken, the tall woman said, "I'll stay. How will you manage it?"

"Don't ask me. I'll work something out . . . *Sweet Christ, I can't marry that man!*"

A distant babble of voices became plainly audible outside.

---

[18] Héricourt was a small Burgundian frontier castle, put under siege by the Swiss; their campaign ended with a battle, on 13 November 1474.

"What are you going to tell them, Ash?"

"I don't know. But they won't wait. Let's move it!"

Ash waited only long enough for Philibert and Rickard to get her undressed and into her arming doublet and hose, and armour, and belt her sword around her waist, gilded sword-pommel catching the canvas-filtered light. The boys did it with never a fumble, rapid fingers tying points, buckling straps, pushing her body and limbs to where would best help them fasten her into her steel shell, all with the ease of practice. Full Milanese harness.

"I *have* to talk to them," Ash added, her tone somewhere between cynicism and self-mockery. "After all – they're the reason why the Holy Roman Emperor calls me 'Captain'. And the reason why I can walk through a camp full of armed men without being bush-whacked."

Florian del Guiz prompted: "And?"

" 'And' what?" Ash left her helmet off, carrying it reversed under her arm, with her gauntlets slung into it.

"Ash. I may be a woman. I've still known you for five years. You have to talk to them because you rely on them – *and* ?"

"And . . . I'm the reason they don't go back to being tanners or shepherds or clerks or goodwives. So I'd better see they don't starve."

Florian del Guiz chuckled. "That's my girl!"

At the tent-flap, leaving, Ash said, "Florian, it's the *Emperor's* marriage – I'm finished if I don't go through with it. And damned if I do."

III

A brisk stride took Ash into the central clear ground under the Blue Lion standard. She vaulted up on to the back of an open cart and gazed round at the men variously sitting on barrels and straw bales and wet ground, and standing with their arms folded, faces upturned grimly to hers.

"Let me recap." Her voice was not strained; she spoke distinctly and clearly, could see no one having trouble hearing her. "Two days ago we fought a skirmish with the Duke's men. This wasn't under orders from our employer. It was my call. It was rash, but we're soldiers, we have to be rash. Sometimes."

She dropped her voice on the last word, and got chuckles from a group of men-at-arms by the beer barrels: Jan-Jacob, Gustav, and Pieter; Flemish men from Paul di Conti's lance.

"Our employer had two choices then. He could break our contract. In that case we'd go straight across to the other side and sign up with Charles of Burgundy."

Thomas Rochester shouted up, "Maybe we should ask Duke Charles for a contract now, if it's peace here. He's always off fighting somewhere."

"Maybe not *quite* yet." Ash paused. "Maybe we'd better wait a day or two, until he forgets we almost killed him!"

Another laugh, louder; and van Mander's boys joined in; crucial because they were known as hard and consequently respected.

"We'll sort that out later." Ash went on briskly. "We don't care who's bishop in Neuss, so Frederick knew we'd go if he said the word. That was his first choice, and he didn't take it. Second – he could have paid us money."

"Yeah!" Two female archers (who were known as 'Geraint's women' only when they weren't around to hear about it) raised a cheer.

Ash's heart beat faster. She rested her left hand down on her sword-hilt, thumb stroking the ripped leather binding.

"Well, as you all know by now, we didn't get money either."

There were catcalls. The back of the crowd closed in; archers and crossbowmen, billmen and hackbutters; all shoulder to shoulder now and putting their attention on her.

"For those of you who were with me in the skirmish, by the way, well done. It was fucking amazing. Amazing." Deliberate pause. "I've never seen an encounter won by anybody who did so many things wrong!"

Loud laughter. She spoke over it, picking out individual men. "Euen Huw, you do *not* get off to loot the bodies. Paul di Conti, you do not start a charge from so far away that your horse is on crutches by the time you finally get to the enemy! I'm surprised you didn't get down and walk. And as for watching your commander for orders!" She let the comments die down. "I should add some remark about keeping your eye on the fucking standard at all times . . ." She cleared her throat.

Robert Anselm deliberately, and helpfully, made himself heard above the racket of several hundred voices. "Yes, *you* should!"

There was laughter and she knew the immediate crisis was over. Or holding, at any rate.

"So we'll *all* be putting in lots of skirmish practice." Ash looked out from the back of the cart. "What you guys did *was* fucking amazing. Tell your grandchildren. It wasn't war. You just don't see knight charging knight on the battlefields, because there's all you nasty little fuckers with bows out there! Oh yeah – *and* the hackbutters." A grin at what sounded like cheerful discontent from the gun-crews. "I wouldn't recognise a battle without the happy sound of back-firing arquebuses!"

The redheaded man-at-arms from Aston's lance yelled, "Get a fucking axe!" and the footmen took up the chant. The gunners responded variously and profanely. Ash nodded at Antonio Angelotti to quieten them down.

"Whatever it was, it was magnificent. Sadly, it hasn't earned us anything. So the next time we get a chance to stick a lance up Charles of Burgundy's ass, I'll come back and ask if you're going to be *paid* first."

A voice at the back found a moment of silence to call, "*Fuck* Frederick of Hapsburg!"

"In your dreams!"

A roar of laughter.

Ash shifted her weight on to her other hip. The uncertain breeze blew tendrils of hair across her face. She smelled cooking fires, and horse manure, and the stink of eight hundred sweaty bodies packed close in a crowd. They were mostly bareheaded, being in camp and theoretically safe from attack; and their bills and halberds were piled in stacks a dozen to a tent.

Children ran around the edges, not able to pass through the packed mass made up of the men and women who fought. Most of the men and women who didn't, the whores and cooks and washerwomen, were sitting up on the sides of wagons at the edge of the camp, listening. There were – as there always are – some men still intent on their games of dice, or dead-drunk asleep under wet canvas, or just off somewhere else, but she had the majority of her company in front of her.

Seeing so many faces that she knew, she thought: The best thing I have on my side is that they *want* to hear me. They want me to tell them what to do. Mostly they're on my side. But they're all my responsibility.

On the other hand, there are always other companies they can get employment with.

They went quiet, waiting for her. A word here and there, between mates. There was a lot of shifting of boots on wet ground, and people watching her, not commenting.

"A lot of you have been with me since I formed the company three years ago. Some of you were with me before that, when I raised men for the Griffin-in-Gold, and the Company of the Boar. Look around you. You're a lot of mad bastards, and the chances are you're standing next to some other mad bastards! You *have* to be mad to follow me – but *if you do*," she increased voice-projection: "if you do, you've always come out of it *alive* – and with a hell of a *reputation* – and *paid*."

She held up an armoured arm, before the level of talk could rise. "And we will this time. Even if we're being paid with a marriage! I suppose there's a first time for everything. Trust Frederick to find it."

She gazed down at her sub-captains, who stood in a tight little knot, exchanging comments and watching her.

"During the last few days I've been taking chances. It's my job. But it's your future too. We've always discussed in open meeting what contracts we'll take or not take. So now we're going to discuss this marriage."

The words came as fluently as ever. She never had problems talking to them. Behind the fluency, something tightened and thinned her voice. Ash became aware that her bare hands were clenched, knuckles straining.

What can I tell them? That we have to do this, but I can't do this?

"And after we've discussed it," Ash went on, "then we're going to *vote* on it."

"Vote?" Geraint ab Morgan yelled. "You mean a real vote?"

Somebody quite audibly said, "Democracy means doing what boss tells you!"

"Yes, a *real* vote. Because if we take this offer, it's *company* lands and *company* revenues. And if we don't take it – about the only excuse the Emperor Frederick is going to accept from me," Ash said, "is 'my company won't let me'!"

She didn't let them think closely about that, but carried on:

"You've been with me, and you've been with mercenary companies that

75

don't hold together through a season, never mind years. I've always put you in the way of enough loot to keep armour on your backs."

The clouds, shifting, let sunlight sweep across the wet earth, and flash from her Milanese plate armour. It was so pat that she spared a suspicious glance for Godfrey, who stood at the foot of the cart with his hands clasped about his Briar Cross.

The bearded man raised his eyes to the heavens and smiled absently; and followed that with a swift, satisfied glance at the picture she made, standing higher than her men, in bright armour, the Lion Azure a blaze across the sky above her. A very minor miracle.

Ash stood without speaking for a moment to let them notice her armour: its expense and therefore its implications. *I can afford this, therefore I'm good. You really want to be employed by me: honest, guv . . .*

Ash spoke. "If I get married to this man, we can have our own land to go back to in the winter. We can have its crops and timber and wool to sell. We can," she added thinly, "stop taking suicide contracts just to get the money to re-equip ourselves every year."

A man with lank, dark hair and wearing a green brigandine called out, "And what happens next year if we get offered a contract to fight *against* the Emperor?"

"He knows we're mercenaries, for fuck's sake."

A woman archer got her way to the front of the crowd with her elbows. "But that's now, when you're under contract to him. That's not when you're married to one of his feudal subjects." She craned her head back to look up at Ash. "Won't he expect you to be loyal to the Holy Roman Empire, Captain?"

"If I wanted to be *told* who to fight for," a hackbutter shouted, "I'd have joined the feudal levy!"

Geraint ab Morgan growled, "Too late to worry about that, the offer's been made. I vote we join the property game, and don't piss off the Emperor."

Ash looked down from the cart. "I assume we'll just carry on as we are."

A rumble of complaint made itself heard across the field. The archer spun round on her heel. "Can't you motherfuckers give her a chance? Captain Ash, you'll be *married*."

Ash recognised her now, the fair-haired woman with an odd name: Ludmilla Rostovnaya. She had the crank of a crossbow hanging from her belt. *Crossbowmen from Genoa*, Ash thought, and put both her hands on the side of the cart, dizzy and sick.

Why am I trying to persuade them we should go through with this?

I can't do it.

Not for the world, never mind a poxy little Bavarian estate—

Geraint ab Morgan pushed his way to the front. Ash saw her sergeant of archers look at Florian, and at the priest, as if questioning why they didn't speak.

Geraint yelled, "Boss, it's fucking obvious someone's landed this one on us because they don't like mercenaries. Remember the Italians, after Héricourt?[19]

[19] On 24 December 1474, eighteen captured Italian mercenaries who had been fighting for the Burgundians against the Swiss were burned alive, at Basle. It was Christmas Eve.

We can't afford to have Frederick fucked off with us. You're going to have to do this, Captain."

"But she can't!" Ludmilla Rostovnaya shouted into his face. There was a rising noise of talk, not everyone being able to hear the quarrel at the front of the crowd. Ludmilla's voice rose clearly over it. "If she marries a man, her property becomes his. Not the other way around! If she marries him, this company's contract will belong to the del Guiz family! And del Guiz belongs to the Emperor! Frederick just got himself a mercenary company for *nothing*!"

The words went out to the back of the crowd, you could see the intelligence pass.

Ash looked down at the eastern woman, always reassured, even in crisis and panic, to see another fighting woman. This one, in her brown padded jack and red hose, with poleyns strapped on her knees, and a sunburned fair-skinned face, now flung up an arm and pointed it at her. "Tell us you've thought about this one, boss!"

Her property becomes *his*—

Frederick is Fernando's feudal lord – we become feudal property. Sweet pity of Christ, this just gets worse!

Why didn't I think of this?

Because you're still thinking like a man.

Ash couldn't speak. Armour demands an upright posture or she would have slumped; as it was, she could only look out at the familiar faces.

Their voices died down. Only children, running and screaming at the edge of the crowd, made any noise. Ash swept her gaze over them, seeing one man with a meat-bone paused halfway to his mouth, another with wine running unnoticed from a wineskin to the earth. The sub-captains were being drawn out of their knot, their men crowding close to ask urgent questions.

"No," she said. "I didn't think about that."

Robert Anselm warned, "That boy won't let you stay in command. You marry Fernando del Guiz, we've lost you."

"Shit!" said a man-at-arms. "She can't marry him!"

"But you fuck off the Emperor and *we're* fucked." Geraint's bloodshot eyes seemed to vanish into his stubbled cheeks as he squinted up at Ash.

She grabbed at a first thought. "There are other employers."

"Yeah, and they're all his second cousins or whatever!" Geraint coughed and spat phlegm. "You know the royal Princes of Christendom. Incest is their middle name. We'll end up only being hired by arseholes who call themselves 'noble' because some lord once fucked their grandmother. We can forget being paid in gold!"

A different man-at-arms said, "We can always split up, hire out to other companies."

His lance-companion, Pieter Tyrrell, yelled, "Yeah, we can go with some stupid fuck who'll get us all killed. Ash knows what she's doing when she fights!"

"Pity she knows fuck-all about anything else!"

Ash turned her head, unobtrusively checking to see where her battle police were, where the gate-guards were, and what the faces of the cooks and the women who washed and mended looked like. A horse neighed. The sky was momentarily full of starlings, moving to another patch of wet, worm-filled earth.

Godfrey Maximillian said quietly, "They don't want to lose you."

"That's because I get them through battles, and I win." Her mouth dried. "Whatever I do here, now, I lose."

"It's a different game. You're wearing petticoats now."

Florian – Floria – growled, "Nine-tenths of them know they couldn't run this company the way you do. The one-tenth that think they can are wrong. Let them talk it out until they remember that."

Ash, stifled, nodded. She raised her voice to battlefield pitch. "Listen up! I'm giving you until Compline.[20] Come here for Father Godfrey's evening service. Then I'll hear what you decide."

She ducked down from the cart. Florian fell into step beside her. The surgeon even walked like a man, Ash noticed, moving from the shoulders and not the hip. She was dirty enough that you could not see she had no need to shave.

The tall woman said nothing. Ash was grateful.

Ash did her rounds, checking the hay and oats for the long lines of horses, and the herb-gatherers who collected equally for Wat Rodway and Florian's pharmacy. She checked the water and sand tubs that stood in the open lanes, between tents that might go up like tinder in the brittle summer night. She swore at a seamstress who sat in a wagon with an unshielded candle, until the weeping woman fetched a lamp instead. She checked piled bills and the stock of arrow-heads in the armourer's tents, and the repairs waiting to be done: sword blades to be sharpened, armour to be hammered back into shape.

Florian put a hand on her steel shoulder. "Boss, stop making a frigging nuisance of yourself!"

"Oh. Yeah. All right." Ash let riveted links of mail trail out of her fingers. She nodded to the armourer and left his tents. Outside, she scanned the darkening sky. "I don't think these sorry shites know any more about politics than I do. Why am I letting them decide this?"

"Because you can't. Or won't. Or daren't."

"Thanks for nothing!"

Ash strode back to the central open area under the standard as lanterns were lit and hung, and the end of Godfrey Maximillian's sung Vespers echoed across the tents. She made her way between the men and women sitting on the chilling earth.

Reaching the standard, under the Blue Lion, she faced about. "Come on, then. This is a company decision? This is all of you?"

"Yeah." Geraint ab Morgan got to his feet, seeming wary of the attention focused on him as spokesman. Ash glanced at Robert Anselm. Her first sergeant was standing in the dark between two lanterns. His face was not visible.

"Lots counted," he called. "It's legit, Ash."

[20] Monastic hours: 9 p.m.

78

Geraint said in a rush, "It's too big a risk, pissing off our employer. We vote for you to get married."

"*What?*"

"We trust you, boss." The big, russet-haired Sergeant of Archers scratched his buttocks unselfconsciously. "We trust you – you can think of some way out of this before it happens! It's up to you, boss. Sort it out before they get the wedding preparations finished. There's no way we're letting them get rid of our captain!"

Fear wiped out thought. She stared around in lantern light at their faces.

"Fucking *hell*. Fuck the *lot* of you!"

Ash stormed off.

If I marry him, he gets the company.

She lay on her back on the hard pallet, one arm under her head, staring up into the roof of the tent. Shadows moved with the shifting evening air. The rope-tied bed frame creaked. Something smelled sweet above the warm body-scent of her own sweat – bunches of camomile, and Lady's Mantle and Self-Heal for wounds, she realised, where they hung tied to the massive struts jutting out from the tent pole. Up among the weapons. It is always easier to lay poleaxes and swords up across the struts rather than lose them in the damp rushes. Camp life means everything goes up out of the mud.

If I marry him, I get a boy who may or may not remember that he's treated me worse than a dockside whore.

The stuffed cloth pallet was hard under her shoulders. She shifted on to fleeces. No better. The air felt damp, but warm. She lay and picked at the metal-tipped points that tied her sleeves into her doublet, until she got them undone and pulled the sleeves off, and lay back again, cooler.

Christ's pity! – I'm in it, and it just keeps on getting deeper—!

Her Milanese harness glinted on its body stand, all rounded silver curves. She massaged flesh where straps had bit in. There might be rust starting up on the tassets, it wasn't clear in the clay oil lamp's light. Phili would have to scour them with sand again before it bit in, and needed taking to the armourer's to be reground. The armourer would bitch at her if she let it get into that condition.

Ash reached down and rubbed her inner thigh muscles, still aching from the ride back from Cologne.

Striped canvas walls moved in and out with the night air, as if the tent breathed like an animal. She heard occasional voices beyond the walls' illusory security. Enough to let her know there still were guards outside: half a dozen men with crossbows, and a leash of mastiffs apiece, in case someone from the Burgundian camp decided to sneak over and take out a mercenary commander.

She dragged each ankle-high boot off by the heel. They thudded on rushes. She flexed bare feet on the cotton pallet, then loosened the drawstring neck of her shirt. Sometimes she is just extremely conscious of her body, of muscles knotting with tiredness, of bones, of the weight and solidity of torso, arms and legs, in their linen and wool garments. She eased her wooden-handled knife out of its sheath and turned the blade to catch the light, feeling with the edge of a fingernail for nicks. Some knives sit in the hand as if they are born to it.

Cynically, she murmured aloud, "I'm being robbed. Legally. What do I do about *that*?"

The voice that shared her soul sounded dispassionate:

'Not an appropriate tactical problem.'

"No shit?" She slid the knife back into its sheath and unbuckled knife, purse and belt all in one heap, shoving up her hips to pull the leather strap out from underneath her. "Tell me about it!"

The clay oil lamp's flame dipped.

She shifted up on one elbow, knowing someone had entered the main part of the tent, beyond the tapestry that curtained off the sleeping area.

In wet summers she put handspan-high raised planking down to floor the tent. The planks shift and creak under footsteps – if the boys were asleep or elsewhere, and the tent's guards gone, she would still be woken up, not taken in her sleep. Rushes are quieter.

"It's me," a voice warned pragmatically, before it approached the tapestry. She lay back down on the pallet. Robert Anselm pushed the hangings aside and stepped in.

She rolled over on to one elbow and looked up. "They send you because you're the most likely to persuade me?"

"They sent me because you're least likely to take my head off." He seated himself with a thump on one of the two massive wooden chests beside her pallet; heavy German chests with locks that take up all the inside of their lids, that she kept chained around the eight-inch tent pole for security.

"Who is this 'they', exactly?"

"Godfrey, Florian, Antonio. We played cards, and I lost."

"You didn't!" She fell back on to her back. "You didn't. Motherfucker!"

Robert Anselm laughed. His bald head gave him a face all eyes and ears. His stained shirt hung out of the front of his hose and doublet. He had the beginnings of a belly on him now, and he smelled sweetly warm, of sweat, and open air, and wood smoke. There was stubble on his face. One never noticed, looking no further than his cropped scalp and broad shoulders, how his lashes were long and fine as a girl's.

He dropped a hand down and began to massage her shoulder, under the linen and fine wool. His fingers were firm. She arched up into them, shutting her eyes for a second. When his hand slid around to the front of her shirt, she opened her eyes.

"You don't like that, do you?" A rhetorical question. "But you like this." He moved his hand back to her shoulders.

She moved over so that he could dig down into the rock-hard muscles. "I learned the reasons for not sleeping with my sub-commanders from you. Made a mess of that whole summer."

"Why don't you have it written up somewhere: *I don't know everything, I can make mistakes.*"

"I can't make mistakes. There's always someone waiting to take advantage."

"I know that."

His thumbs pressed hard into the knobs of her vertebrae. A sharp click cracked through the tent, ligament sliding over bone. His hands stopped moving. "You okay?"

"What the hell do you think?"

"In the last two hours I've had a hundred and fifty people come and ask to speak with you. Baldina, from the wagons. Harry, Euen, Tobias, Thomas, Pieter. Matilda's people; Anna, Ludmilla . . ."

"Joscelyn van Mander."

"No." He sounded reluctant. "None of the van Manders."

"Uh huh. *Right!*" She sat up.

Robert Anselm's hands moved away.

"Joscelyn thinks because he raised thirteen lances for me this season, he has more say in what we do than I have! I *knew* we were going to have trouble there. I may just pay off his contract and send him over to Jacobo Rossano, make it *his* problem. Okay, okay." She held up both hands, palms out, realising his reluctance to tell her had been entirely feigned. "Yeah, *okay*. All right! Yes!"

She is conscious of the whole vast engine that is the company, ticking over outside. Rush and hurry around the cook's wagons, the eternal oat-porridge stewing in iron cauldrons. Men on fire-watch. Men taking their horses out to graze on what grass has been left on the banks of the Erft. Men drilling with swords, with bills, with spiked axes. Men fucking the whores that they hold in common. Men with their clothes being sewn by their wives (sometimes the same women, at a later date in those women's lives). Lantern light and camp fire light, and the scream of some animal baited for sport. And the sky coursing with stars, over it all.

"I'm good on the battlefield. I don't know politics. I should have *known* I didn't know politics." She met his eyes. "I thought I was beating them at their own game. I don't know how I could have been this stupid."

Anselm clumsily ruffled her silver hair. "Fuck it."

"Yeah. Fuck it all."

Two sentries exchange the day's word outside the tent, giving way to two others. She hears them talking. Without knowing their names, she knows they have unwillingly scoured-clean bodies, full stomachs, swords with nicks carefully sharpened out, shirts on their backs, some kind of body protection (however cheap the armour); the Lion Azure sewn to their tabards. There are men like this all over Frederick III's great military camp tonight, but in this area there would not be, not these particular men – if not for her. However temporary it is, however mercenary they are, she is what holds them together.

Ash got to her feet. "Look, I'll tell you about . . . the del Guiz family, Robert. Then you tell me what I can do. Because *I don't know*."

Four days after both Charles the Bold of Burgundy's troops and the men of the Emperor Frederick III pulled back from Neuss, effectively ending the siege,[21] Ash stood in the great Green Cathedral at Cologne.

Too many people crowded into the body of the cathedral for the human eye

---

[21] The Gutenberg press edition of the del Guiz *Life* gives the date as 27 June 1476; the siege of Neuss ended, of course, on 27 June 1475. However, all other contemporary sources give the date of the wedding ceremony, four days later, as 1 July 1476.

to take in. All shoulder to shoulder, men in pleated gowns of blue velvet and scarlet wool, silver-linked chains around their necks, purses and daggers at their belts, and flamboyant rolled chaperon hats with tails hanging down past their shoulders. The court of the Emperor.

A thousand faces dappled with the light slanting from red and blue glass, falling from lancet windows a bowel-twisting height above the tiled floor. Thin stone columns pierced a frightening amount of air, too fragile to support their vaulted roof above. And around the bases of those pillars, men with gold-leaf on their dagger pommels, and plenty of flesh on their jowls, stood talking in voices that rose in volume now.

"He's going to be late. He *is* late." Ash swallowed. The pit of her bowels shifted uncomfortably. "I don't believe it. He's standing me up!"

"Can't be. You should be so lucky," Anselm hissed, "Ash, you have to do something!"

"Tell me what! If we haven't come up with it in four days, I'm not going to think of it now!"

How many minutes before the power to contract the company passes from wife to husband? All other means exhausted, the only remaining way out of this wedding is for her to walk out of the building. Now.

In front of the Emperor's court.

And they're right, Ash thought. Half the royal families of Christendom are married to the other half; we wouldn't get another contract from anyone until they'd calmed down. Not until next year, maybe. I don't have enough money put by to feed us if we don't have an employer for that long. Nothing like enough.

Robert Anselm looked past her, behind her head, at Father Godfrey Maximillian. "We could do with a prayer for grace, Father."

The bearded man nodded.

"Not that it matters now, but have you found out who set me up for this?" Ash demanded, quietly enough to be heard only by her supporters.

Godfrey, standing on her right, replied equally quietly. "Sigismund of the Tyrol."

"Goddamn. *Sigismund?* What have we— That man's got a long memory. This is because we fought on the other side at Héricourt?"

Godfrey inclined his head. "Sigismund of the Tyrol is far too rich for Frederick to offend him by refusing a useful suggestion. I'm told Sigismund doesn't like 'mercenaries with more than fifty lances'. Apparently he finds them a threat. To the purity of noble warfare."

"'Purity' of war? In his fucking dreams."

The bearded priest smiled crookedly. "You mauled his household troops, as I recall."

"I was *paid* to. Christ. It's petty, to give us this much trouble for it!"

Ash looked over her shoulder. The back of the cathedral was also packed with standing men, merchant from Cologne in rich gear, her own lance-leaders who outshone them, and a gaggle of mercenaries who had been made to leave their weapons outside the cathedral, and consequently didn't outshine anyone.

There were none of the bawdy remarks and cheerful grins you would have had with one of her men-at-arms being wedded. Quite apart from endangering their future, she saw how it made them look at her and see a woman, in a city, at peace, where before they had seen a mercenary, in the field, at war, and could therefore avoid considering her sex.

Ash snarled in a whisper, "Christus, I wish I'd been born a man! It would have given me an extra six inches' reach, the ability to pee standing up – and I wouldn't have to put up with any of this crap!"

Robert Anselm's adult, concerned frown vanished in a spluttering burst of laughter.

Ash looked automatically for Florian's cheering scepticism, but the surgeon was not there; the disguised woman had vanished into the mass of the company striking camp at Neuss four days ago, and had not been seen since (certainly not during the set-up outside Cologne where, as a number of uninformed mercenaries remarked, there was heavy lifting to be done).

Ash added, "And I *could* take Frederick setting this wedding on St Simeon's feast-day personally . . .[22] Maybe we could come up with a prior betrothal? Someone to step up to the altar stone and swear we had a pre-nuptial contract as children."

Anselm, at her left, said, "Who's going to stand up and take the shit for that one? Not me."

"I wouldn't ask it." Ash stopped talking as the Bishop of Cologne came up to the bridal party. "Your Grace."

"Our meek, gentle bride." Tall thin Bishop Stephen reached out to finger the folds of her banner, whose staff Robert Anselm held. He bent to inspect the scarlet lettering embroidered under the Lion. "What is this?"

"Jeremiah, chapter fifty-one, verse twenty," Godfrey quoted.

Robert Anselm growled a translation: "'Thou art my battle axe and weapons of war; for with thee I will break in pieces the nations, and with thee will I destroy kingdoms.' It's sort of a mission statement, Your Grace."

"How – appropriate. How – pious."

A new voice whispered drily, "Who is being pious?"

The bishop inclined his thin body in its green alb and chasuble. "Your Imperial Majesty."

Frederick of Hapsburg limped through the crowds of men, who all got out of his way. He was leaning on a staff now, Ash noted. The little man looked at Ash's company priest as if it were the first time he had noticed the man. "You, was it? A man of peace in a company of war? Surely not. 'Rebuke the company of spearmen – scatter thou the people that delight in war.'"[23]

Godfrey Maximillian removed the hood from his robe, and stood respectfully bareheaded (if ruffled) before the Emperor. "But, Your Majesty, Proverbs one hundred and forty-four, one?"

The Emperor rasped a small, dry chuckle. "'Blessed be the Lord my strength, which teacheth my hands to war, and my fingers to fight.' So. An educated priest."

---

[22] Simeon Salus, died *c*.590, is the saint associated with social outcasts, especially harlots. His feast-day is celebrated on 1 July.
[23] Psalms 68: 30.

"As an educated priest," Ash said, "perhaps you would tell His Majesty how long we have to wait for a non-existent bridegroom, before we can all go home?"

"You wait," Frederick said quietly. There was a sudden lack of conversation.

Ash would have paced, but the folds of her dress and the stares of the assembly stopped her. Over the altar, the Nine Orders of Angels shone in stone: Seraphim, Cherubim and Thrones, who are closest to God; then Dominions, Powers and Virtues; then Principalities, Archangels and Angels. The Principality of Cologne was sculpted with arched wings and ambiguous gender, smiling, clutching a representation of Frederick's Imperial crown.

What's Fernando del Guiz playing at?

He won't dare offend the Emperor. Will he? *Will he?*

He is a knight, after all. Maybe he just *won't* marry a peasant-woman soldier. Christ, I hope that's it—

On the altar's left, by some humour of the stonemasons, the Prince of This World was carved offering a rose to the naked figure of Luxury. Toads and serpents clung to the back of his robe's rich stone folds.[24] Ash contemplated the figure of Luxury. There were many women present in stone. In flesh only five, herself and her attendants. The customary maids of the bride's honour stood behind her, Ludmilla (in one of the seamstress's better robes) and the other three: Blanche, Isobel, and Eleanor. Women she'd known since they whored together as children in the Griffin-in-Gold. Ash took a certain private satisfaction in how many of the noblemen of Cologne already nervously recognised Blanche and Isobel and Eleanor.

If I have to go through with this damn ceremony, I'm doing it *my* way!

Ash watched the Emperor drift off in conversation with Cologne's Bishop Stephen. Both of them walked as if in a royal hall, not a sacred building.

"Fernando's late. He's not coming!" Joy and relief flooded through her. "Well, hey, *he's* not our enemy . . . Archduke Sigismund did this. Sigismund's making me compete in politics, where I don't know what I'm doing, instead of on the field of battle, where I do."

"Woman, you sweated your guts out to get Frederick to give you land." Godfrey, sounding sceptical enough to be Florian. "He merely took advantage of that sin of greed."

"Not sin. Stupidity." Ash restrained herself from looking around again. "But it's going to be okay."

"Yes – no. There are people outside."

"*Shit!*" Her sibilant whisper had the front two ranks of men glancing uncertainly at the bride.

Ash wore her silver hair unbound, as maidens do. Because she usually wore it in braids, it took a curl from that, flowing in ripples down over her shoulders, down her back, down, not just to her thighs, but to the backs of her knees. The finest, most transparent linen veil covered her head, and the silver metal headdress that held it in place was wound with a garland of field daisies. The veil was made from flax so fine that the scars on her cheekbones could be seen through it.

[24] No longer extant, but see similar figure at Freiburg-im-Breisgau, sculpted *c.* AD 1280.

She stood stocky and sweaty in the flowing, voluminous blue and gold robes. Drums sounded, and hurried horns. Her guts jolted. Fernando del Guiz and his supporters hurried up towards the rood-screen – all young noblemen of the Germanies, all wearing more money than she sees in six years of putting her body in the front line of battles for axe and sword and arrow to hit it.

The Emperor Frederick III, Holy Roman Emperor, walked with his entourage to take his regal place at the front. Ash picked out the face of Duke Sigismund of the Tyrol. He did not give her the satisfaction of smiling.

The light slanted down from immense perpendicular lancet windows, dappling green light on to the figure of a woman carved in black marble, riding on the back of the Bull on the altar.[25] Ash looked up with despair at her enigmatic stone smile, and the gold-thread-embroidered cloths that hooded her, as the boys in white tunicles came into the choir with their green wax candles burning. She was aware of someone coming to stand beside her.

She glanced to her right. The young knight Fernando del Guiz stood there, staring equally deliberately up at the altar, not looking at her. He looked more than a little ruffled, and he was bareheaded. For the first time she got a clear look at his face.

I thought he was older than me. He can't be. Not by more than a year or two.

Now I remember . . .

It was not his face, older now, clear-skinned and with bold brows, freckles across his straight nose. Nor his thick gold hair, trimmed short now to touch his shoulders. Ash watched the embarrassed hunch of his wide shoulders, and his rangy body – grown from boy almost to man, now – shifting from foot to foot.

That's *it*. That's it . . .

She found her hand aching to reach up and ruffle his hair out of its combed order. She caught his male scent, under the sweet perfume of civet. *I was a child then. Now* . . . Of themselves, her fingertips told her what it would feel like to unlace his velvet pleated doublet, that needed no padding at his broad shoulders, unfasten it down to his narrow waist, and untie the points of his hose . . . She let her gaze slide down the triangular line of his male body, to his strong rider's thighs in finest knitted hose.

Sweet Christ who died to save us. I am as much in lust with him as I was at twelve.
"Mistress Ash!"

Somebody, plainly, had asked her a question.

"Yes?" Ash agreed absently.

Light broke in on her. Fernando del Guiz: lifting up her fine linen veil. His eyes were green, stone-green, dark as the sea.

"You are wed," the Bishop of Cologne pronounced.

Fernando del Guiz spoke. Ash smelled wine warm on his breath. He said, in a perfectly clear voice, into the silence, "I would sooner have married my horse."

Robert Anselm, *sotto voce*, muttered, "The horse wouldn't have you."

Someone gasped, someone laughed; there was one delighted, dirty guffaw

---

[25] A direct translation of the original German. No such altarpiece is extant in Cologne.

from the back of the cathedral. Ash thought she recognised Joscelyn van Mander.

Not knowing whether to laugh or cry or hit something, Ash stared at the face of the young man she had just married. Looking for a hint – only a hint – of the complicit, humorous grin he had given her at Neuss.

Nothing.

She was unaware that her shoulders straightened, and her face took on something of the look she wore around the company's camp. "You don't talk to me like that."

"You're my wife now. I talk to you any way I please. If you don't like it, I'll beat you. You're my wife, and you'll be docile!"

Ash couldn't help a loud blurt of laughter. "I will?"

Fernando del Guiz ran his finger, in its fine leather glove, from her chin down to the linen neck of her chemise. He made a show of sniffing at his glove. "I smell *piss*. Yes I do. I smell piss . . ."

"Del Guiz," the Emperor warned.

Fernando turned his back and walked away, across the flagstone floor to Frederick of Hapsburg, and a tearful Constanza del Guiz (the court's ladies now entering the nave, the ceremony over). None of whom did more than glance sideways at the bride left standing alone.

"No." Ash put her hand on Robert Anselm's arm. She gave a quick look that included Godfrey. "*No*. It's all right."

"'All right'? You ain't going to let him do that!" Anselm had his shoulders hunched almost up to his protuberant ears, all his body yearning towards crossing the nave and knocking Fernando del Guiz over.

"I know what I'm doing, now. I've just seen it." Ash increased the pressure of her fingers on his arm. There were mutters from her company, at the back.

"I would be an unhappy bride," Ash said quietly. "But I could be a really cheerful widow."

Both of the men startled. It was almost comical. Ash continued to look at them. Robert Anselm jerked his head once, briefly, satisfied. It was Godfrey Maximillian who coldly smiled.

"Widows inherit their husband's businesses," Ash said.

"Yeah . . ." Robert Anselm nodded. "Better not mention it to Florian, though. The man *is* his brother."

"So don't tell h-him." Ash did not meet Godfrey's eyes. "It won't be the first 'riding accident' among the German nobility."

Ash paused under the vast vaults of the cathedral, momentarily unaware of her companions, of what she had said; seeking out Fernando where he stood, his back to her, weight on one hip, towering over his mother. Her body roused at the sight of him, at just the way the tall young man posed.

This will not be easy. Either way, this will not be easy.

"Ladies. Gentlemen." Ash glanced back to check that Ludmilla and Blanche and Isobel and Eleanor were holding up her train so that she could walk, and rested her ringed fingers on Godfrey's arm. "We're not going to skulk in corners. We're going to go and thank people for coming to my wedding."

Her guts clenched. She knew the picture she made: young bride, veil back, silver-blonde hair a glorious cloud. She did not know her scars stood out silver-red against her pale cheeks. She went first to her lance-leaders, where she would feel at ease: the men spoke a word here, a small joke there, exchanged a hand-clasp.

Some of them looked at her with pity.

She couldn't help it, she continued to stare anxiously through the crowd for Fernando del Guiz. Now she saw him angel-bright in a lancet window's beams, talking to Joscelyn van Mander.

Van Mander kept his back to her.

"*That* didn't take very long."

Anselm shrugged. "Van Mander's contract belongs to del Guiz now."

She heard a whisper from behind her. The heavy material of her train, suddenly unattended, pulled back on her neck. She glared back at Big Isobel and Blanche. The two women mercenaries did not look at her; they had their heads together and whispered, their eyes fixed on a man some distance away, with expressions Ash put somewhere between awe and fear. She recognised him as the southerner who had been present at Neuss.

Little Eleanor whispered explanatorily to Blanche, "He's from the lands Under the Penitence!"

The reason for the dark muslin cloth knotted ready for use about his neck belatedly dawned on Ash. She said tightly, "Oh, Green Christ, they're hardly *demons* down in Africa – let's get moving, okay?"

Ash moved on through the nave, greeting the minor nobles of free cities in their best robes, and their wives in towering horned, veiled head-dresses. This is not where I belong, she thought, talking politely, aimlessly; speaking to the ambassadors from Savoy and Milan, watching how shocked they were that a *hic mulier* [26] could wear robes, could speak their languages, and did not in fact have a demon's horns and a tail.

What do I do? What do I *do*?

A new voice spoke behind her, with an accent. "Madam."

Ash smiled a farewell to the Milanese ambassador – a boring man, and afraid, too, of a woman who has killed in battle – and turned.

The man who had spoken was the southerner – pale-haired, with a face burned brown by harsh sun. He wore a short white robe, over white trousers with greaves bound around them, and a mail hauberk over all. The fact that he was dressed for war, although without weapons, put her at her ease.

In the light from the lancet windows, the pupils of his light-coloured eyes were contracted to pinpoints.

"New here from Tunis?" she guessed, speaking her accurate but uneducated mercenary's version of his language.

"From Carthage," he agreed, giving the city its Gothic [27] appellation. "But I am adjusted, I think, to the light, now."

---

[26] Latin: a 'mannish' or 'man-aping' woman.

[27] Text uncertain here. Charles Mallory Maximillian has 'Visigoth', the 'noble Goths'. Although it is couched in terms of mediaeval legend, I believe the mention of 'Visigoths' to have aspects we would do well to consider.

"I'm – oh *shit*," Ash interrupted herself rapidly.

A solid, man-shaped figure stood behind the Carthaginian. It overtopped him by a head or more: Ash judged it seven or eight feet tall. At first glance she would have thought it a statue, made out of red granite: the statue of a man, with a featureless ovoid for a head.

Statues do not move.

She felt herself colouring; felt Robert Anselm and Godfrey Maximillian crowding in close to her shoulders, staring behind the newcomer. She found her voice again. "I've never seen one of those up close before!"

"Our golem?[28] But yes."

With an amused look in his pale eyes, as if he were used to this, the man beckoned with a snap of his fingers. At the Carthaginian's signal, the figure took a step forward into the shaft of window-light.

Stained glass colours slid over the carved red granite body and limbs. Each joint, at neck, shoulders, elbows, knees, ankles, gleamed brass; the metal jointed neatly into the stone. Its stone fingers were articulated as carefully as the lames of German gauntlets. It smelled faintly of something sour – river-mud? – and its tread on the tiny tiles of the cathedral floor echoed, heavily, with an impression of enormous weight.

"May I touch it?"

"If you wish to, madam."

Ash reached out and put the pads of her fingers against the red granite chest. The stone felt cold. She slid her hand across, feeling sculpted pectoral muscles. The head tilted downwards, facing her.

In the featureless ovoid, two almond-shaped holes opened where eyes might have been on a man. Her body shocked, anticipating white of eye, pupil, focus.

The eyes behind the stone lids were full of red sand. She watched the granules swirl.

"Drink," the man from Carthage ordered.

The arms swivelled up noiselessly. The moving statue held out a chased golden goblet to the man whom it attended. The Carthaginian drank, and gave it back.

"Oh yes, madam, we are allowed our golem-servants with us! Although there was some debate about whether they would be allowed within your 'church'." He surrounded the word delicately with nuances of sarcasm.

"It looks like a demon." Ash stared up at the golem. She imagined the weight of the stone articulated arm if it should rise and fall, if it should strike. Her eyes gleamed.

"It is nothing. But you are the bride!" The man picked up her free hand and kissed it. His lips were dry. His eyes twinkled. In his own language, he said, "Asturio, madam; Asturio Lebrija, Ambassador from the Citadel to the court of

---

[28] I prefer this term, with its suggestion of the organic, to Vaughan Davies's 'robot', or Charles Mallory Maximillian's 'clay man'.

This quasi-supernatural appearance is, of course, one of the mythical accretions which attach themselves to histories such as Ash's; and should not be taken seriously, except in so far as it reflects the mediaeval psychological preoccupation with a lost Roman 'Age of Gold'.

the Emperor, however briefly. These Germans! How long can I bear it? You are a woman of your hands, madam. A warrior. Why are you marrying that boy?"

Waspishly, Ash said, "Why are you here as an ambassador?"

"One who had power sent me. Ah, I see." Asturio Lebrija's sunburned hand scratched his hair which, she noted, was cropped short in the North African fashion for one who customarily wears a helmet. "Well, you are as welcome here as I, I think."

"As a fart in a communal bathtub."

Lebrija whooped.

"Ambassador, I think they're afraid that one day your people will stop fighting the Turks and turn into a problem." Ash registered Godfrey moving aside to talk to Lebrija's aides. Robert Anselm remained, looming, at her shoulder, his gaze fixed on the golem. "Or it's because they envy you Carthage's hydraulic gates and under-floor hot water and everything else from the Golden Age."

"Sewers, batteries, triremes, abacus-engines . . ." Asturio's eyes danced as he assured her of it. "Oh, we are Rome come again. Behold our mighty legions!"

"Your heavy cavalry aren't *bad* . . ." Ash stroked her hand over her mouth and chin but couldn't smother her smile. "Oops. It's a good job you're the ambassador. That was hardly diplomatic."

"I have met women of war before. I would sooner meet you in the court than on the battlefield."

Ash grinned. "So. This northern light too bright for you, Ambassador Asturio?"

"It's hardly the Eternal Twilight, madam, I grant you—"

An older male voice behind Lebrija bluntly interrupted. "Get the fuck over here, Asturio. Help me out with this damned conniving German!"

Ash blinked, realising almost immediately that the new man spoke in the Visigoth language, that his tone was sweetly pleasant, and that her own mercenaries were the only people present who had understood him. She glared at Isobel, Blanche, Euen Huw and Paul di Conti. They subsided. As she turned back to him, Asturio Lebrija bowed a flamboyant farewell, and moved to join what must have been the senior ambassador in the Visigoth delegation at the Emperor Frederick's side. The golem followed, with heavy soft tread.

"Their heavy cataphracts[29] *aren't* bad," Robert Anselm said in her ear. "Never mind all their fucking ships! And they've had a military build-up going on there these last ten years."

"I know. It's all going to turn into another Visigoths-fighting-Turks war for control of the Mediterranean, with undisciplined serfs and light cavalry knocking hell out of each other for no result. Mind you," – a sudden hope – "there might be some business down there for us."

---

[29] Heavily armoured lancers, with either both horse and rider armoured in overlapping scale or lamellar armour, or the horse unarmoured. This Middle Eastern form of cavalry survives throughout the mediaeval period, notably in Byzantium. (From context, I assume this not to refer to the Greek and Roman galleys also known as cataphracts.)

"Not 'us'." Anselm's features twisted with disgust. "Fernando del Guiz."
"Not for long."

On the heels of that, another voice echoed through the huge spaces of the cathedral, echoing from crypt to barrel-vaults. *"Out!"*

Frederick of Hapsburg – shouting.

Conversation drained swiftly into silence. Ash went forward through the crowd. A foot trod on her trailing train, bringing her up short. Ludmilla muttered something as she picked the cloth up off the flagstones and flung the whole weight of it over her arm. Ash grinned back at Big Isobel, and caught up with Anselm, edging her way between him and Godfrey to the front of the crowd.

Two men had Asturio Lebrija with his arms twisted up behind his back, forcing the man in the mail shirt to kneel. Also down on the stone floor, the older Visigoth ambassador had a bill-shaft held across his throat and Sigismund of the Tyrol's knee in his back. The golem stood as still as the carved saints in their niches.

Frederick's sibilant voice echoed among the soaring pillars, still shaking with the re-imposition of a control Ash had not heard him lose before. "Daniel de Quesada, I may hear you say your people have given mine medicine, masonry and mathematics; I will not stand here in this most ancient cathedral and hear my people maligned as barbarians—"

"Lebrija did not say—"

Frederick of Hapsburg overrode the older ambassador: "—my fellow sovereign Louis of France called 'a spider', or be told to my face I am 'old and covetous'!"

Ash glanced from Frederick and his bristling nobles to the Visigoth ambassadors. Far more likely that Asturio Lebrija had momentarily and catastrophically forgotten which language he was speaking, than that the older man – bearded, with the look of a battle veteran – would deliberately allow him to insult the Holy Roman Emperor.

She murmured to Godfrey, "Someone's picking a fight here. Deliberately. Who?"

The bearded priest frowned. "I think, Frederick. He doesn't want to be asked to lend military aid in Visigothic North Africa.[30] But he won't want to be heard refusing the ambassadors' request, in case it's supposed he's refusing because he hasn't got the troops to send, and is therefore weak. Easier to buy himself time like this, given this excuse, with false anger over an 'insult'."

Ash wanted to say something on behalf of Asturio Lebrija, whose face reddened as he strained to get out of the grip of two German knights; nothing immediately useful came to mind.

The Emperor snapped peevishly, "I will leave you both your heads! You are returned home. Tell the Citadel to send me civil ambassadors in future!"

Ash flicked a glance sideways, not realising that her whole stance changed:

---

[30] According to conventional histories, the Germanic Visigothic tribes did not settle in North Africa. Rather the reverse – with the Muslim Arab invasion of Visigothic Spain, in AD 711.

alert, balanced, and not usual for someone in bridal robes. The golem stood silent and motionless behind the two ambassadors. If *that* should move— Her fingers closed automatically, seeking a sword-hilt.

Fernando del Guiz straightened up from leaning on a cathedral pillar. Caught by the movement, Ash watched him helplessly. *No different from a hundred other young German knights here,* she protested to herself; and then, *But he's golden!*

Gold light from the windows catches his face as he turns, laughing at something one of the squires clustered around him has said. She sees a snapshot image of light limning the edge of sun-browned masculine brow, nose, lip; warm in the cold cathedral dimness. And his eyes, which are merry. She sees him young, strong, wearing fluted armour with complete naturalness; thinks of how he knows the outdoor months of campaigning as well as she does, the sunny ease of camp-life and the blood-teasing exultation of battle.

Why despise me, when we're the same? You could understand me better than any other woman you could have married—

Fernando del Guiz's voice said, "Let me be the escort for the ambassadors, Your Imperial Majesty. I have some new troops I need to knock into shape. Entrust me with this favour."

It was ten heartbeats at least before Ash replayed "new troops" in her mind.

He means my company! She exchanged glances with Robert Anselm and Godfrey Maximillian; both men frowning.

"It shall be your bridal gift, del Guiz," Frederick of Hapsburg agreed; something sardonic in his expression. "And a honeymoon for you and your bride." He gathered his nine-yard velvet gown about himself, with the aid of two small boy pages, and without looking over his shoulder, said, "Bishop Stephen."

"Your Imperial Majesty?"

"Exorcise *that*." A twig-thin finger flicked towards the Visigoth golem. "And when you have done it, command stonemasons with hammers, and have it broken into gravel!"

"Yes, Your Imperial Majesty!"

"Barbarian!" The older Visigoth ambassador, Daniel de Quesada, spluttered incredulously. "*Barbarian!*"

Asturio Lebrija looked up with difficulty from where he was pinned, on his knees. "I spoke no lie, Daniel: these damned Franks[31] are children playing in ruins, destroying whatever comes to their hands! Hapsburg, you have no *idea* of the value of—"

Frederick's knights slammed Lebrija face-down on the tiles. The sound of blows echoed through the vaulting heights of the cathedral. Ash took a half-step forward, only to be nearer, and caught her foot in the brocade hem and stumbled, grabbing Godfrey's arm.

"My lord del Guiz," the Emperor Frederick said mildly, "you will escort

---

[31] A term used in this text for Northern Europeans in general.

these men to our nearest port, in chains, and ensure they are deported by ship to Carthage. I wish them to live to carry their disgrace home with them."

"Your Majesty." Fernando bowed, still something coltish about him for all the breadth of his shoulders.

"You will need to take command of your new troops. Not all, not all. These men—" Frederick of Hapsburg lifted his fingers very slightly, in the direction of Ash's lance-leaders and men-at-arms, crowding in at the rear of the cathedral. "—are now by feudal right yours, my lord. And as your liege lord, they are also ours. You shall take some of them upon this duty, and we shall retain the remainder: we have tasks that they can do, order not yet being secure in Neuss."

Ash opened her mouth.

Robert Anselm, without moving his rigid eyes-front gaze, rammed his elbow into her ribs.

"He can't do this!" Ash hissed.

"Yes. He can. Now shut *up*, girl."

Ash stood between Godfrey and Anselm, her heavy brocade gown stifling her. Sweat dampened her armpits. The knights, lords, merchants, bishops and priests of the Imperial court began to move off in Frederick's wake, talking between themselves; a great throng of richly dressed men, their voices travelling up into the silence of the fan-vaulting and the saints in their niches.

"They can't just split us up like this!"

Godfrey's hand closed painfully tightly around her elbow. "If you can't do anything, *don't* do anything. Child, listen to me! If you protest now, everyone will see that you lack the power to alter this. Wait. *Wait*. Until you can do something."

The departing Imperial court took as little notice of one woman and a cluster of soldiers as they did of the stone saints above.

"I can't leave it!" Ash spoke so that only the priest and Anselm could hear. "I built this company up from nothing. If I wait, now, either they're going to start deserting, or they're going to get used to del Guiz in command!"

"You could let them go. It is their right," Godfrey said mildly. "Perhaps, if they no longer wish to be men of war—"

Both Ash and Robert Anselm shook their heads.

"These are men I know." Ash wiped her hand across her scarred cheek. "These are men hundreds of leagues from whatever poxy farm or town they were born in, and fighting's the only trade they've got. Godfrey, they're my people."

"Now they are del Guiz men-at-arms. Have you considered, child, that this may be better for them?"

This time it was Robert Anselm who snorted.

"I know young knights with their arses on their first war-horse! That young streak of piss and wind couldn't restrain *himself* in battle, never mind his men! He's a heroic disaster looking for a place to happen. Captain, we've got time. If we're leaving Cologne, that's good." Anselm stared after Fernando del Guiz, walking down the nave with Joscelyn van Mander; never a glance back for his bride. "See how you like it out on the road, city boy."

Ash thought, *Shit*.

They're splitting up my company. My company isn't mine any more. I'm married to someone who *owns* me – and there's no way I can play court politics to change the Emperor's mind, because I'm not going to be here! I'm going to be dragged off with disgraced Visigoth ambassadors to Christ alone knows where—

Ash glanced out of the cathedral's open doors, under the unfinished west front,[32] out at the sunlight. "Which *is* the nearest southern port from here, on Empire territory?"

Godfrey Maximillian said, "Genoa."

---

[32] As with the nave, this was in fact left unfinished until the nineteenth century.

```
Message:    #5 (Pierce Ratcliff)
Subject:    Ash, historical documents
Date:       02/11/00 at 08.55 p.m.
From:       Longman@
```
format address and other details non-recoverably deleted

Pierce —

Sorry to contact you out of office hours, but I *must* talk to you about the translation of these documents.

I have very fond memories of 'doing' Ash at school. One of the things I like about her, which comes through strongly in your translations of these texts, is that she's a jock. Basically. She doesn't read, she can't write, but boy can she hit things. And she has a complex character despite that. I love this woman! I still think that a modern translation of ASH, with your new document discovery, is one of the best and most commercial ideas that's come my way in a long time. You know I'm supporting you here, in the editorial discussions, despite not being fully briefed yet.

However. These sources —

I can cope with the odd mistake in dating, and with mediaeval legends. This is, after all, how those people *perceived* their experiences. And what we have here, with your prospective new theory of European history, is brilliant stuff! — But it's for this very reason that each deviation from history must be carefully documented. Provided the legends are clearly noted as such, we have a cracking good history book for the marketing department to sell.

But —

GOLEMS???!!!

In mediaeval Europe?!

What next — zombies and the undead?!! This is fantasy!

HELP!

— Anna

```
Message:    #1 (Anna Longman)
Subject:    Ash, historical documents
Date:       03/11/00 at 06.30 p.m.
From:       Ratcliffe@
```
format address and other details non-recoverably deleted

Anna —

This is what comes of getting connected to e-mail, one then forgets to check it! I am *so* sorry not to have answered you yesterday.

About 'golems'. I am following Charles Mallory Maximillian's translation here (with a little FRAXINUS). He refers to them in 1890 as 'clay walkers', very much the legendary Cabalistic magical servant as featured in the legend of the Rabbi of Prague. (We should remember that when Maximillian did his translation, the Victorian era was gripped by the fin-de-siècle occult revival craze.)

Vaughan Davies, in his later translation, rather unfortunately calls them 'robots', a reference which in the late 1930s was not as hackneyed as it now appears.

I intend to use the term 'golem', in this third edition, unless you think it too unscholarly. I am aware that you would like this book to have a wide readership.

As regards what these 'golems' or 'walkers' may, historically, have actually been, I think they are a mediaeval confabulation of something undoubtedly real with something legendary. The historical reality is mediaeval Arabic engineering.

You will no doubt be aware that, as well as their civil engineering, the Arabic civilisations practised a kind of fine engineering, making fountains, clocks, automata, and many other devices. It is quite certain that, by the time of al-Jazari, complex gear trains existed, also segmental and epicycle gears, weight drives, escapements and pumps. The Arabs' celestial and biological models were largely water-powered, and invariably — obviously — stationary. However, the European mediaeval traveller often reported the models to be *mobile* figures of men, horses, singing birds, etc.

My research indicates that the del Guiz LIFE has conflated these travellers' tales with mediaeval Jewish stories of the golem, the man of clay. This was a magical being with, of course, no basis in fact.

If there *had* been a 'walker' or 'servant' of some sort, I imagine it could conceivably have been a *vehicle*, wind-powered like the sophisticated pole-mills of the period — but then, it would require wheels, sophisticated road-surfaces, and a human driver, to function as any kind of message-carrying device, and could perform no indoor tasks at all. And you may say, rightly, that this is stretching historical speculation unjustifiably far. No such device has ever been discovered. It is chroniclers' licence.

As a legendary part of the Ash cycle, I like my golems, and I hope you will let me keep them. However, if too much emphasis on the 'legendary' aspect of the texts is going to weaken the historical *evidence* which I am drawing from the del Guiz text, then let's by all means cut the golems out of the finished version!

— Pierce Ratcliff

```
-------------------------------------------------------------------
```

Message: #6 (Pierce Ratcliff)
Subject: Ash, historical documents
Date: 03/11/00 at 11.55 p.m.
From: Longman@

Pierce — *format address and other details non-recoverably deleted*

I wouldn't know a segmental gear if it bit me! But I'm prepared to
credit that these 'golems' are a mediaeval legend based on some
kind of reality. Any study of women's history, black history, or
working class history soon makes you see how much gets dropped from
conventional histories, so why should engineering history be any
different?

  But I guess it's safer to leave them out. Let's not confuse
mediaeval legend with mediaeval fact.

  One of my assistants has raised a further query about the
'Visigoths' today. She's concerned that, since they were a
Germanic tribe who died out after the Roman Empire, how can they
still be around in 1476?

  Another query, from me — I'm not a Classicist, it's not my
period, but don't I remember Carthage being *wiped out* in Roman
times? Your manuscript speaks as if it still exists. But it makes
no mention of the ARAB cultures of North Africa.

  Is all this going to be made clear? Soon? PLEASE?!

— Anna


```
-------------------------------------------------------------------
```

Message: #3 (Anna Longman)
Subject: Ash, theory
Date: 04/11/00 at 09.02 a.m.
From: Ratcliff@

Anna — *format address and other details non-recoverably deleted*

I didn't realise that publisher's editors worked such unnatural
hours. I hope you aren't working too hard. :)

  You ask me for a statement of my theory — very well. We probably
can't proceed in our working relationship without one. Bear with
me for a moment, and I'll give you some necessary background:

  The arrival of what the LIFE calls the 'Gothic' ambassadors DOES
present an apparent problem. I believe that I have solved this
problem, however; and, as you imply, it is a key factor in my
reassessment of European history.

  While the ambassadors' presence at Frederick's court is verified
by references in both the CHRONIQUE DE BOURGOGNE and the

correspondence between Philip de Commines and Louis XI of France, I at first found it difficult to see where these 'Goths' (or, as I prefer Charles Mallory Maximillian's more precise translation, 'Visigoths': the 'noble Goths') might originate.

The Germanic Gothic barbarian tribes did not so much 'die out', as your assistant suggests, as become absorbed into the ethnic mix of the lands they moved into after Rome fell. The Ostrogoths in Italy, for example; the Burgundians in the Rhone Valley, and the Visigoths in Iberia (Spain). They continued to rule these territories, in some cases for centuries.

Maximillian thus suggests these 'Visigoth' ambassadors are Spanish. I was not completely happy with that. CMM's rationale is that, from the eighth century on, Spain is divided between a Christian Visigoth knightly aristocracy, and the Arabic dynasties that follow their own invasion in AD 711. Both the numerically inferior Muslim and Visigoth aristocratic classes ruled over a great mass of Iberian and Moorish peasantry. Therefore, Maximillian says, since there were 'Visigoths' of this kind left until well into the late fifteenth century, there might also have been mediaeval rumours that either these Christian Visigoths or the 'heathen Saracen' (Muslims) retained some 'engines and devices' of Roman technology.

It is actually not until fifteen years after Ash's death that the last Arab Muslims are finally driven out of the Iberian peninsula in the 'Reconquista' (1488-1492). The Visigoth ambassadors to the court of the Emperor Frederick *could* therefore be supposed to come from Iberia.

However, I personally then found it very puzzling that the ASH texts directly state that they come from a settlement which must have been on the coast of North Africa. (Even more puzzling since they are plainly not Arab!)

The author of the 1939 second edition of the ASH documents, Vaughan Davies, basing HIS theory on not much more than the text referring to Northern Europeans as 'Franks', treats the Visigoths as the standard Saracen knights of the Arthurian legends — the 'Saracens' are mediaeval Europe's idea of the Arab cultures, mixed with folk-memories of the crusades to the Holy Land. I don't think Davies does anything at all scholarly to address this problem.

Now, we include the other problem — Carthage! The original North African Carthage, settled by the Phoenicians, WAS eradicated, as you point out. The Romans rebuilt a city on that site.

The interesting thing is that, after the last Roman Emperor was deposed in AD 476, it was the Vandals who moved in and took over Roman North Africa — the Vandals being, like the Visigoths, a Gothic Germanic tribe.

They moved in as a small military elite, to rule and enjoy the fruits of this great African kingdom, under their first king,

Gaiseric. Although they remained somewhat 'Germanised', Gaiseric did bring in an Arian priesthood, make Latin the official language, and build more Roman baths. Vandal Carthage became a great naval centre again, Gaiseric not only controlling the Mediterranean, but at one point sacking Rome itself!

So you can see that we already have had a kind of 'Gothic Tunisia'. The last (usurping) king, Gelimer, lost Vandal Africa in three months to the Byzantine Empire in AD 530 (and was last heard of enjoying several large Byzantine estates). The Christian Byzantines were duly driven out by the surrounding Berber kingdoms, and Islam (chiefly by the military use of the camel) in the 630s. All trace of Gothic was eradicated from Moorish culture from then on; not even occasional words survive in their language.

Ask yourself, where could Germanic Gothic culture have survived after AD 630?

In Iberia, close to North Africa, *with the Visigoths*.

As you are aware, I believe that the entire field of academic research on Northern European history is going to have to be modified once my ASH is published.

Briefly: I intend to prove that there was a Visigothic settlement on the Northern coast of Africa as late as the fifteenth century.

That their 'resettlement' took place much later than Vandal North Africa, after the end of the Early Middle Ages; and that their period of military ascendancy was the 1400s.

I intend to prove that in AD 1476 there was an actual, historical mediaeval settlement, peopled by the survivors of the Roman Visigoth tribes — with no 'golems', no legends about 'twilights'.

I believe it to have been peopled by an incursion of Visigoth-descended Iberians from the Spanish 'taifa' (mixed/border) states. One might reasonably think this, from the racial type described here. The Fraxinus text calls the settlement 'Carthage', and indeed it may have been close to the site of the original Phoenician or Roman or Vandal Carthages.

I believe that this Gothic settlement, intermingling with Arab culture (many Arab military terms are used in the del Guiz and Angelotti manuscripts) produced something unique. And I believe that it is perhaps not the fact of this settlement's existence that is so controversial, so much as (shall we say) what this culture did, and their contribution to our culture as we live in it today.

There will be a Preface, or Afterword, perhaps, setting out the implications fully, that will go with the ASH documents; this is as yet unfinished.

I am sorry to be so cagey about those implications at this stage. Anna, I do not wish someone else to publish ahead of me. There are days when I simply cannot believe that no one else has read the ASH 'Fraxinus' manuscript before I saw it — and I have nightmares of opening THE GUARDIAN to a review of someone else's new translation.

99

At the moment, I would rather not put my complete theory on
electronic media, where it could be downloaded. In fact, until I
have the whole translation complete, word-perfect, and the
Afterword at first-draft stage, I am reluctant to discuss this
editorially.

Bear with me, please. This has to be rigorous and water-tight, or
I shall be laughed out of court — or at least, out of the academic
community.

For now, here is my first attempt at transmitting translated text
to you: Section 2 of the del Guiz LIFE.

— Pierce

Message: #12 (Pierce Ratcliff)
Subject: Ash, historical theory
Date: 04/11/00 at 02.19 p.m.
From: Longman@

*format address and other
details non-recoverably deleted*

Pierce —

Vandals, yes, but I can't find *any* hint in my books on European or
Arabic history, no matter where I look — *WHAT North African
'Visigoths'?*

Are you SURE you've got this right?

I have to be honest and say that we don't need any controversy
about the scholarship associated with this book. *Please* reassure
me on this. Today if possible!

Message: #19 (Anna Longman)
Subject: Ash, historical theory
Date: 04/11/00 at 06.37 p.m.
From: Ratcliff@

*(format address and other details
non-recoverably deleted)*

Anna —

Initially, I had all the same doubts that you have. Even the
Vandals had, by the fifteenth century, been gone from an entirely
Islamic Tunisia for nine centuries.

At first, you see, I thought the answer must lie in the mediaeval
mindset — let me explain. For them, history isn't a progress, a
sequence of things happening in a particular order. The fifteenth-
century artists who illuminated histories of the Crusades put
their twelfth-century soldiers into fifteenth-century clothes.
Thomas Mallory, writing his MORTE D'ARTHUR in the 1460s, puts his
sixth-century knights in the same armour as his own Wars of the

Roses period, and they speak as knights in the 1460s spoke. History is *now*. History is a moral exemplar of the present moment.

The 'present moment' of the Ash documents is the 1470s.

Initially, therefore, I thought the 'Visigoths' referred to in the texts must be, in fact, Turks.

We can't easily imagine, now, how *terrorised* the European kingdoms were when the vast Osmanli Empire (that's Turkish to you!) besieged and took Constantinople (AD 1453), the 'most Christian city'. To them, it literally was the end of the world. For two hundred years, until the Ottoman Turks are finally beaten back from the gates of Vienna in the 1600s, Europe lives in absolute dread of an invasion from the east — it is their Cold War period.

What I thought at first, then, was that it was not too surprising if Ash's chroniclers decided that she (simply because she was a famous military commander) *must* have had some hand in holding the Turks back from defenceless Europe. Nor that, fearing the Osmanli Empire as they did, they concealed its identity under a false name, hence 'Visigoths'.

Of course, as you know, I had later to revise this.

— Pierce Ratcliff, Ph.D.

Message: #14 (Pierce Ratcliff)
Subject: Ash
Date: 05/11/00 at 08.43 a.m.
From: Longman@

format address and other details non-recoverably deleted

Pierce —

I have no idea how I can explain to my editorial director, never mind sales and marketing, that the Visigoths are actually Turks, and that this whole history is a farrago of lies!

Message: #20 (Anna Longman)
Subject: Ash
Date: 05/11/00 at 09.18 a.m.
From: Ratcliff@

format address and other details non-recoverably deleted

Anna —

No, no, they're NOT Turks! I just thought that they MIGHT be. I was WRONG!

My theory posits a fifteenth-century Visigoth enclave on the North African coast. It is my *point* that the evidence for this has been shuffled under the academic carpet.

101

This happens — it happens with many things in history. And events and people not only get deliberately written out of history, as with Stalinism, they seem almost to slip out of sight when the attitude of the times is against them — I could cite Ash herself as an example of this. Like most women who have taken up arms, she vanishes from history during patriarchal periods, and during more liberal times, still tends to appear only as a 'figurehead' warrior, not involved in actual killing. But then, this happens to Joan of Arc, Jeanne de Montfort, Eleanor of Aquitaine, and hundreds of other women who were not of sufficiently high social class that their names couldn't be ignored.

At various times I've been fascinated both by the PROCESS of how this happens — cf my thesis — and by the DETAILS of what gets written out. If not for Charles Mallory Maximillian's ASH (given to me by a great-grandmother who, I think, had it as a school prize in 1892), then I might not have spent twenty years exploring 'lost' history. And now I've found it. I've found a 'lost' piece of sufficient significance that it will establish my reputation.

I owe it all to 'Fraxinus'. The more I study this, the more I think its provenance with the Wade family (the chest in which it was found supposedly brought back from an Andalusian monastery, on a pilgrimage) is accurate. The mediaeval Spains are complex, distant, and fascinating; and if there were to have been some Visigoth survivals — over and above the bloodlines of these Roman-era barbarians in the Iberian ruling classes — this is where we might expect to find it recorded: in little-known mediaeval manuscripts.

Naturally, the ASH manuscripts contain exaggerations and errors — but they contain a coherent and ESSENTIALLY true story. There WAS at least a Visigoth city on the North African coast, and possibly a military hegemony to go with it!

— Pierce

Message: #18 (Pierce Ratcliff)
Subject: Ash, theory
Date: 05/11/00 at 04.21 p.m.
From: Longman@

(format address and other details non-recoverably deleted)

Pierce —

Fine.
  MAYBE.
  How could something of this magnitude just VANISH out of history???

— Anna

```
-----------------------------------------------------------------

Message:      #21 (Anna Longman)
Subject:      Ash
Date:         06/11/00 at 04.07 a.m.
From:         Ratcliff@
                            format address and other
Anna —                      details non-recoverably deleted
```

Apologies for answerphone. I'd left this line switched over to
fax. I want to reassure you, but

You see, the thing is, it's EASY to vanish from history. BURGUNDY
does it, for God's sake. There it is, in 1476, the wealthiest, most
cultured, most militarily organised nation in Europe — and in
January 1477 their Duke gets killed, and Charles Mallory
Maximillian was right, NOTHING EVER GETS WRITTEN ABOUT BURGUNDY
AGAIN.

Well, no, that's not entirely true. But most educated people's
concept of European history is that north-west Europe consists of
France and Germany, and has done from the fall of the Roman Empire.
Burgundy is the name of a wine.

You see, what I'm trying to say is

It actually took Burgundy about a generation to vanish totally,
Charles's only child Mary married Maximilian of Austria, and they
became the Austro-Hungarian Hapsburgs, which last until World War
One, but the POINT I wanted to make is

The point is, if you didn't know Burgundy was a major European
power, and that we came THIS close to having five hundred years of
Burgundy instead of France — well, if you didn't know it, you
wouldn't learn it. It's as if the whole country is FORGOTTEN the
moment that Charles the Bold dies on the battlefield at Nancy.

No one has ever satisfactorily explained this! Some things just
don't get into history

I think something similar happens with the 'Visigoth' settlement

Here I am babbling away at the keyboard in the early hours,
you're going to think I'm an idiot

Excuse me, please. I'm exhausted. I've got a seat on a plane at
Heathrow, I only have an hour to pack, the taxi's due about now,
and then I decided to check my phone, and found your last message.

Anna, the most amazing, wonderful thing has happened! My
colleague Dr Isobel Napier-Grant telephoned me. She's in charge of
the diggings outside Tunis — the GUARDIAN'S been running stories
on their latest discoveries, you may have seen — and she's found
something that may be one of the 'clay walkers' in the del Guiz
text!

She thinks it *just might have been* an actual *mobile* piece of technology !!! — maybe mediaeval — post-Roman —

or it may be complete nonsense, some weird Victorian invention or forgery that's only been in the ground a hundred years

Tunis, of course, is near the historical ruins of Roman Carthage

Taxi's here. If this damn thing works, I've sent you the next translated section Ash. Phone as soon as back from Tunisia.

anna — if the golem are true — what else is?

PART TWO

1 July–22 July AD 1476

Nam sub axe legismus, Hecuba regina[1]

---

[1] "For under the axis ['Axle' of Rota Fortuna] is written, 'Queen Hecate'" – an interesting quotation by the author of the Angelotti manuscript, in which the mediaeval "dreadful example" of the Fall of Kings, Queen Hecuba of Troy, has been replaced by Hecate, the powerful and sometimes malignant goddess of Hell, night and the moon. Curiously enough, the Greek for "Hecuba" is "Hekabe".

I

Afloat on the Rhine river, the barge shifting underfoot, Ash lifted her chin and unbuckled her sallet. "What hour is it?"

Philibert took it from her. "Sunset."

On my wedding night.

The little page-boy, with the help of the older Rickard, unbuckled the straps of her brigandine, unlaced the mail standard around her throat, unbuckled her sword-belt, and took her weapons and armour off her body. She sighed, unconsciously, and stretched her arms out. Armour is not heavy when you put it on, weighs nothing ten minutes afterwards, and when you take it off is the weight of lead.

The Rhine river barges presented problems enough: two hundred men of the Lion company detailed off – at Fernando del Guiz's perfectly legal insistence – as escort for the disgraced Visigoth ambassadors, travelling from Cologne to the Swiss cantons, over the pass and down to Genoa. Therefore two hundred men, their gear and horses, to be organised. And a deputy commander to be left behind with the rest of the company: in this case, her unilateral decision appointed Angelotti, with Geraint ab Morgan.

Outside, there was a solid grunt and the sound of weight slumping to the deck: her stewards, poleaxing the last of the bullocks to be brought on board. She heard footsteps, water sloshed from leather buckets to clean the barge's deck, where basins do not catch all the blood: the rip of skin as the butcher's knife is taken to the carcass.

"What will you eat, boss?" Rickard shifted from one foot to the other, obviously anxious to get out on deck with the rest of the company. Men gambling, drinking; whores enjoying the night on the slow-flowing river.

"Bread; wine." Ash gestured abruptly. "Phili will get it for me. I'll call for you if I need you."

Philibert put a pottery plate into her hands, and she paced up and down the tiny cabin, cramming the crusts of bread into her mouth, chewing, spitting out a crumb and washing it all down with wine; all the time frowning, and moving – with a memory of Constanza, in her solar in Cologne – not like a woman, but like a long-legged boy.

"I called an officer meeting! Where the fuck are they?"

"My lord Fernando rescheduled it to the morning."

"Oh, he did, did he?" Ash smiled grimly. Her smile faded. "He said 'not tonight', and made bad jokes about bridal nights – right?"

"No, boss." Phili looked pained. "His friends did. Matthias and Otto. Boss,

Matthias gave me sweetmeats. Then he asked me what the whore-captain does. I don't tell him. Can I lie to him, next time?"

"Lie yourself blue in the face if you like." Ash grinned conspiratorially, to an answering pleased wicked grin from the boy. "That goes for Fernando's squire Otto, too. You keep 'em guessing, kid."

What the whore-captain does. . . ? Well, what do *I do?*

Be a widow. Confess, do penance. People do.

"Fucking Christ!" Ash threw herself down on the cabin's box-bed.

The wood of the Rhine barge creaked, gently. Night air breathed off the unseen water, making the canvas-roofed cabin pleasantly cool. A part of her mind registered the creak of ropes, horses shifting their hooves, a man praising wine, another man devoutly praying to St Catherine, other barges; all the night noises of two hundred men of the company travelling south upriver, as the long train of barges pulled away from Cologne.

"Fuck!"

"Boss?" Philibert looked up from sanding a rust-spotted breastplate.

"This is bad enough without—!" *Without everybody confused about who they're supposed to be taking orders from, me – or him.* "Never mind."

Slowly, unaware of the boy's fingers undoing her points, she dragged off doublet and hose together, and sprawled back in her shirt. A burst of laughter on deck shattered the comparative quiet. She was not aware that she flinched. One hand unconsciously tugged the hem of her long gathered shirt down over her bare knees.

"Boss, you want the lanterns lit?" Phili rubbed his knuckle into his eye-socket.

"Yeah." Ash watched without seeing as the scruffy-haired page hung the lanterns on their hooks. A buttery yellow light illuminated the opulent quarters, the silk pillows, the furs, the box-sided bed, the canvas canopy with the green and gold colours of del Guiz quartered with the Hapsburg yellow and black.

All of Fernando's travelling chests were thrown carelessly open, crowding the small cabin; his doublets spilling out, every surface covered with his possessions. She inventoried them automatically in her head – a purse, a shoeing horn, a bodkin; a cake of red wax, shoemaker's thread; a bag, a silk-lined hood, a gilded leather halter; sheaves of parchment; an eating-knife with an ivory handle . . .

"I could sing for you, boss."

She reached out with her free hand and patted Philibert on the hip. "Yeah."

The little boy pulled his caped hood off over his head, and stood in the lamplight with his shaggy hair sticking up. He squeezed his eyes shut and began to sing unaccompanied:

> "The thrush she sings from the fire,
> 'The Queen, the Queen's my bane—' "

"Not that one." Ash swung her legs over and sat on the edge of the box-bed. "And that's not the beginning of that song. That comes near the end. It's okay, you're tired. Go sleep."

The boy looked at her with stubborn dark eyes. "Rickard and I want to sleep in here like always."

She has not slept alone since she was thirteen.

"No. Go sleep with the squires."

He ran out. The heavy tapestry curtain let in a burst of sound as it opened, cut it off as it swung to. A far more graphic and biologically descriptive song than Philibert's old country tragedy was being sung out on deck. He probably knows the words to this one too, she thought; but he's been walking around me today like I was Venetian glass. Since this morning, and the cathedral.

Footsteps sounded outside on the deck. She recognised the sound: all her skin shivered. She lay back down on the mattress.

Fernando del Guiz pushed the curtain open, bawling something over his shoulder that made Matthias – a not-very-noble young male friend, Ash thought – howl with laughter. He let the curtain drop behind him, closing his eyes and swaying with the ship.

Ash stayed where she lay.

The curtain stayed undisturbed. No squire, no page; none of his court friends, young boisterous German knights. No very public aristocratic bridal customs? she wondered.

No – no, you won't will you? Drag the sheets out of here and show there's no virgin bloodstains? You won't want to listen to people saying *his wife's a whore*.

"Fernando—"

His large hands unbuttoned the front of his puff-sleeved satin doublet, and he shrugged it back off his shoulders. Fernando smiled a particularly knowing smile. "That's 'husband' to you."

Sweat stuck his yellow hair to his forehead. He struggled with the points at his waist, abandoned them halfway – cloth ripped as he tore his arm out of his shirt. Even rangy in build, with his body not yet filled out to his adult weight, Ash found him just plain *big*: male chest, male torso, the hard muscles of male thighs when the man is a knight and rides every day.

He didn't bother to unlace his cod-flap, he reached in and hitched his stiffening cock out over the top of the fabric, clutching it in his hand; and clambered one-handed on to the tiny truckle-bed towards her. The yellow lantern light turned his skin into oiled gold. She inhaled. He smelled male, smelled also how linen shirts smell, when they are left to dry in the open air.

With her own hands she pulled up her shirt, under which she was naked.

He reached down and wrapped his hand around his thickening purple cock, lifted her hips with his other hand, guided his thrust with an inexpert shove.

More than ready – ready since the realisation that it was his footsteps outside – she received the whole thick length of him thrust into her; shivered, hot as fever. Impaled, she enclosed his solidity.

His face lowered, inches from hers. She saw, in his eyes, his realisation of her wetness. He murmured, "Whore . . ."

His thumb stroked her scarred cheekbones, an old scar at the base of her neck, a curve of black bruises where a blow at Neuss had driven her breastplate in under her arm. His slurred young voice mumbled, "You got a *man's* body."

The points of his hose at his waist, and at his cod-flap, pulled tight. The fine wool ripped down the inner seam, exposing the hard flesh of his thigh. His torso fell across her. His weight made her struggle to breathe. She dug her fingers into the big muscles of his upper arms, hard. His skin under her hand was velvet over hardness; silk over iron. Her head fell back on the silk pillows. She moaned in her throat.

The man thrust, two or three times. Her wet, pulsing cunt held him; a shiver of pre-sensation began to loosen her muscles; she felt herself opening, flesh unfolding.

He jerked twice, like a poacher's rabbit from the killing blow, and his hot seed flooded her, copious, slicking down her thighs. His heavy body sprawled over her.

She smelled – almost tasted – thin German beer on his breath.

His cock slid out of her, limp.

"You're *drunk*!" Ash said.

"No. You wish I was. I wish I was." He looked down at her from a blurred face. "This is my duty and it's done. And that's it, madam wife. You're mine now, sealed by blood—"

Ash said drily, "I don't think so."

His expression changed: she could not read it. Arrogance? Revulsion? Confusion? A simple, selfish desire not to be here, not to be on this barge, in this bed, with this problematical she-male?

If I was hiring him, I could read him. What's the matter with me?

Fernando del Guiz rolled off her, sprawling face-down and semi-clothed on the mattress. Only his wet semen marked the linen. "You've been with men before. I hoped there was an outside chance it might be a rumour, that you weren't really a whore. Like the French king's maid. But you're not a virgin."

Ash shifted to face him. She merely blinked at him. Both her gaze and her voice were level, flat, very slightly tinged with black humour. "I haven't been a virgin since I was six. I was raped for the first time when I was eight. Then I stayed alive by whoring." Looking for comprehension in his expression, she saw none. "Have you ever had a little maid?"

His fair skin flushed, and he coloured pink from cheeks to brow to the back of his neck. "I have not!"

"A little girl of nine or ten? You'd be surprised how many men want that. Although, to be fair, some of them didn't care whether it was woman, child, man or sheep, so long as they got to stick their cocks in something warm and wet—"

"God and His angels!" Sheer, appalled shock. "*Shut up!*"

She felt the whisper of air as his fist moved; her own arm came up by reflex, and the blow was all but absorbed by the fleshy part of her forearm. She is muscular there. Only his knuckles brush her scarred cheek. That touch jolts her head back.

"Shut up, shut up, shut up—"

"Whoa!"

Panting, with bright unspilled tears in her eyes, Ash shifted her body back from him. Back from warm, silken skin over hard muscle: from the body that she longs to wrap herself around.

Bitter, all feudal privilege now, he spat, "How could you *do* all that?"

"Easily." Again, it is the commander's voice: acerbic, pragmatic, and with a conscious humour. Ash shook her head to clear it. "I'd rather have had my life as a whore than be the kind of virgin you were hoping for. When you understand why, we might have something to talk about."

"Talk? To a *woman*?"

She might have forgiven him if he had said 'to you', even in that tone of voice, but the way that he said 'woman' made her mouth curl up at one corner, without humour.

"You forget who I am. I'm Ash. I'm the Lion Azure."

"You *were*."

Ash shook her head. "Well, fuck me. This is some wedding night."

She thought she had him, swore she came within a bowstring's width of Fernando bursting out laughing – of seeing that generous, acknowledging grin she had seen at Neuss – but he threw himself back across the truckle-bed, limbs sprawling, one arm over his eyes, and exclaimed, "*Christus Imperator!* They made me one flesh with *this*."

Ash sat up, cross-legged on the palliasse, easily limber. She was entirely unconscious of being naked while he was still partly clothed, until the sight of him sprawled out in front of her, and his naked thigh and belly and cock in the lantern light, made a hot wetness grow in her cunt, and she coloured, and shifted to sit differently. She put her hands down in front of her, the unsatisfied ache hot in her vagina.

"Fucking peasant *bitch*!" he exclaimed. "Bitch on heat! I was right the first time I met you."

"Oh, bloody *hell* . . ." Her face flamed. She put her hands over her cheeks, and her fingertips felt that even her ears were hot. She said hurriedly, "Never mind that."

Without taking his arm away from his face, he groped and pulled a blanket half over his body. She could feel the skin of her face heating. She locked her hands about her own ankles, to keep from reaching out to touch the hard velvet of his skin.

Fernando's breathing shifted to a snore. His heavy sweating body slumped further down in the bed, deeply and instantly asleep.

After a while she wrapped her hand around the saint's medallion at her throat, and held it. Her thumb caressed the image of St George on one side, the ash-rune on the other.

Her body screamed at her.

She did not sleep.

Yes, I am probably going to have to have him killed.

It's no different from killing on the field of battle. I don't even *like* him. I just want to fuck him.

More hours later than a marked candle could count, she saw summer light around the edges of the tapestry curtain. Dawn began to lighten the Rhine river valley, and the cavalcade of ships moving upstream.

"So what are you going to do?" She said it quietly and rhetorically to herself.

She lay, naked, face-down on the pallet, reaching out for her belt where it lay

111

on her piled doublet and hose. The sheath of her knife came easily to her hand. Her thumb stroked the rounded hilt of the bollock dagger, slipped down to press it an inch or so out of the scabbard. A grey metal blade, with harsh silver lines on the much-sharpened edge.

He's asleep.

He didn't even bring a page in with him, never mind a squire or a guard. There's no one to shout an alarm, never mind defend him!

Something about this sheer depth of ignorance, his inability to even conceive that a woman might kill a feudal knight – *Green Christ, hasn't he ever thought he might be knifed by a whore?* – and his forgetfulness in merely falling asleep, as if this were any night between a married pair: something in that touched her, despite him.

She rolled over, drawing the dagger. Her thumb tested the edge. It proved keen enough to slice the first layers of dermis, at a touch, without penetrating to the red meat below.

What I ought to think is *Died of arrogance*, and kill him. If only because I might not get another chance.

I wouldn't get away with it; naked and covered in blood, it's going to be kind of obvious who did it—

No. That isn't it.

I know damn well that once it was done, a *fait accompli* as Godfrey would call it, then my lads would tip the body over the side, shrug, and say, "Must've had a boating accident, my lord," to anybody who asked; up to and including the Emperor. Once it's done, it's done; and they'd back me.

It's doing it. That's the objection I have.

Christ and His pity know why, but I don't want to kill this man.

"I don't even know you," she whispered.

Fernando del Guiz slept on, his face in repose unprotected, vulnerable.

Not confrontation: compromise. Compromise. Christ, but don't I spend half my life finding compromises so that eight hundred people can work together? No reason to leave my brains behind just because I'm in bed.

So:

We are a split company: the others are in Cologne: if I kill Frederick there'll be someone who objects – there's always someone who objects to anything – and if it were van Mander, for example, there's another split: his lances maybe following him, not me. Because he likes del Guiz: he likes having a man, and a noble man, and a real live knight for a boss. Van Mander doesn't much like women, even if they are as good on the field of battle as I am.

This can wait. This can wait until we've dumped the ambassadors in Genoa and got back to Cologne.

Genoa. *Shit.*

"Why did you do that?" She spoke in a whisper, lying down beside him, the electric velvet of his skin brushing hers. He shifted, rolling over, presenting her with a freckled back.

"Are you another one like Joscelyn – nothing I do will ever be enough, because I'm a woman? Because the one thing I can't be is a man? Or is it because I can't be a *noble* woman? One of your own kind?"

112

His soft breathing filled the tented cabin.

He rolled back again, restless, his body pressing up against hers. She lay still, half under the warm, damp, muscular bulk of him. With her free hand, she reached up to brush fine tendrils of hair out of his eyes.

I can't remember what his face looked like then. I can only see in my mind what he looks like now.

The thought startled her: her eyes flicked open.

"I killed my first two men when I was eight," she whispered, not disturbing his sleep. "When did you kill yours? What fields have you fought?"

I can't kill a man while he's sleeping.

Not out of—

The word eluded her. Godfrey or Anselm might have said *pique*, but both men were on other barges in the river-convoy; had found things to do that would take them as far from the command barge as possible, this first night after her wedding.

I need to think this through. Talk it through with them.

And I can't split the company. Whatever we do will have to wait until we get back to the Germanies.

Ash's hand, without her volition, stroked the sweat-damp strands of hair back from his brow.

Fernando del Guiz shifted in his sleep. The narrow bed necessarily threw their bodies together on the piled palliasses; skin against skin; warm, electric. Ash, without much thinking about it, leaned down and put her mouth to the back of his neck, her lips to his soft moist skin, breathing in the scent and feel of the finest hair at his nape. Vertebrae made hard lumps between his freckle-spotted shoulders.

With a great sigh he rolled over, put his arms around her waist, and drew her to his hot body. She pressed against him, breast and belly and thighs, and his cock hardened and jutted up between them. Still with his eyes shut, one of his narrow strong hands stroked her between the thighs, fingers dipping into her wet warm cleft, stroking her. The early light hazing the cabin illuminated his fair lashes, fine on his cheeks; *so young*, she thought, and then, *aah!*

One tilt of his hips put his swollen cock up inside her. He rested, still holding her close in his arms, and within minutes began rocking his body, pushing her up to a mild, unexpected, but completely pleasurable orgasm.

His head dipped, face coming to rest against her shoulder. She felt the brush of his lashes against her skin. Eyes still closed, half-asleep; he slid his hands over her shoulders, down her arms, around her back. A warm, valuing touch. Erotic, and *kind*.

He is the first man my age to touch me kindly, she realised; and as Ash opened her eyes, taken equally by surprise to find herself smiling at him, he thrust harder and deeper and came, and sank back from his peak into deeper sleep.

"What?" she leaned down, hearing him mumble.

He said it again, slipping down into an exhausted sleep, too unconscious to be reached again.

What she thought she heard was, "They have married me to the lion's whelp."

There were tears of humiliation, bright and wet, standing on his lashes.

Ash, waking again an hour later, found herself in an empty bed.

Fifteen days later – fifteen nights of empty beds – on the feast-day of St Swithun,[2] they arrived within five miles of Genoa.

II

Ash thumbed up the visor of her sallet, in the dew-wet early morning. The sun was not a finger's breadth above the horizon. Some coolness was still in the air. Around her, men walked and rode, wagons creaked; a wind blew her the noise of a shepherd on a distant hillside, singing as he surely would not if the country was not peaceable.

Robert Anselm rode up, past the wagons and horsemen, from the rear of the column; his open-faced sallet lodged in the crook of his arm. The southern sun had reddened his bald scalp. One of the men walking with a bill over his shoulder whistled like a blackbird, and shifted into the opening bars of *Curly Locks, Curly Locks, wilt thou be mine?* as Anselm trotted past, only apparently oblivious. Ash felt a smile tug at her mouth: the first for over a fortnight.

"Okay?"

"I found four of these assholes dead-drunk in the steward's wagon this morning. They didn't even get out to sleep it off somewhere else in the camp!" Anselm squinted against the morning sun, riding knee to knee with her. "I've got the provosts disciplining them now."

"And the thefts?"

"Complaints, again. Three different lances: Euen Huw, Thomas Rochester, Geraint ab Morgan before we left Cologne—"

"If Geraint had more complaints about this before we left Cologne, why didn't *he* take action?"

Ash looked keenly at her second-in-command.

"How's Geraint Morgan working out?"

The big man shrugged.

"Geraint's not keen on discipline himself."

"Did we know that when we took him on?" Ash frowned at the thickening dawn mist. "Euen Huw vouched for him . . ."

"I know he got slung out of King Henry's household after Tewkesbury. Drunk in charge of a unit of archers – *on* the field. Went back into the family wool business, couldn't settle, ended up a contract soldier."

"We didn't hire him just because he's an old Lancastrian, Roberto! He has to pull his weight, same as everyone else."

"Geraint's no Lancastrian. He fought with the Earl of Salisbury at Ludlow –

---

[2] Celebrated on 15 July; thus an internal reference for the date of the company's arrival outside the port-city of Genoa.

114

for the Yorkists, in fifty-nine," Anselm added, apparently none too confident of his captain's intricate knowledge of *rosbif* dynastic struggles.

"Green Christ, he started young!"

"He's not the only one . . ."

"Yeah, yeah." Ash shifted her weight, bringing her horse back towards Roberto's flea-bitten grey. "Geraint's a violent, lascivious, drunken son-of-a-bitch—"

"He's an archer," Anselm said, as if it were self-evident.

"—and worst of all, he's a mate of Euen Huw," Ash continued. Her twinkle died. "He's shit-hot on the field. But he gets a grip, or he goes. Damn. Well, at least I've left him in joint command with Angelotti . . . Come on then, Robert. What about this thief?"

Robert Anselm squinted up at the obscuring sky, then back at her. "I've got him, Captain. It's Luke Saddler."

Ash recalled to her mind his face: a boy not yet fourteen, mostly seen around the camp flushed with ale, wet-nosed and avoided by the other pages; Philibert had had tales to tell of twisted arms, hands touching cods. "I know him. Aston's page. What's he taking?"

"Purses, daggers; someone's *saddle*, for Christ's pity's sake," Anselm remarked. "He tried to sell that. He's in and out of the quartermaster's all the time, Brant says; but it's mostly the lads' personal kit."

"Crop his ears this time, Roberto."

Anselm looked a little grim.

Ash said, "You, me, Aston, the provosts – we can't stop him thieving. So . . ."

She jerked a thumb back at the men riding and walking; hard men in dusty leather and linen, sweating in the early Italian morning, shouting comments to each other about anything they passed, loud voices careless of rebuke.

"We have to act. Or else they'll do it for us. And probably bugger him into the bargain: he's a pretty kid."

Frustrated, she remembers Luke Saddler's sullen, shifty expression when she had had him into the command tent, to see if the full weight of the commander's displeasure might move him; he had smelled of Burgundian wine, that day, and giggled inanely.

Pricked by an inadequate feeling of having failed the boy, she snapped, "Why tell me, anyway? Luke Saddler's not my problem. Not now. He's my *husband's* problem."

"As if you cared two tits about that!"

Ash looked down rather pointedly at the front of her brigandine. It was not proving very much less hot to wear than plate. Robert Anselm grinned at her.

"As if you're going to let del Guiz worry about this mob . . ." he added. "Girl, you're going demented, running around picking up after him."

Ash stared ahead through the morning sea-mist, thickening now on the road, just making out the figures of Joscelyn van Mander and Paul di Conti riding with Fernando. Unconsciously, she sighed. The morning smelled of sweet thyme, from where the cartwheels crushed it at the edges of the wide merchants' road.

Her husband Fernando del Guiz rode laughing among the young men and servants of his entourage, ahead of the wagons. A trumpeter rode with him, and a rider carrying the banner with the del Guiz arms. The Lion Azure company standard rode a few hundred yards back, between the two wagon lines, whitening with the dust he kicked up.

"Sweet Christ, it's going to be a long bloody trek back to Cologne!"

She shifted by unconscious habit with the movements of her mount, a riding horse she had long ago nicknamed The Sod. She smelled sea nearby; so did he, and moved skittishly. *Genoa and the coast no more than four or five miles away now? We could arrive well before noon.*

Sea-mist dampened down the dust kicked up by lines of plodding horses, and the twenty-five lances who rode in groups of six and seven between them.

Ash sat up in the saddle, pointing. "I don't recognise that man. There. Look."

Robert Anselm rode up beside her and looked where she looked, narrowing his eyes to bring the outer line of wagons into focus – wagons driven with shields still strapped to their sides, and hand-gunners and crossbowmen riding inside them on the stores.

"Yes, I do," she contradicted herself, before he could answer. "It's Agnes. Or one of his men, anyway. No, it's the Lamb himself."

"I'll bring him through." Anselm tapped his long spurs into his grey's flanks, and cantered across the lines of moving carts.

Even with the droplets of mist, it was too hot to wear a bevor. Ash rode in sallet and a blue velvet-covered brigandine, the gilt rivet-heads glinting, with her brass-hilted bastard sword strapped to her side. She eased her weight back, slowing, as Robert Anselm brought the newcomer back inside the moving camp.

She watched Fernando del Guiz. He didn't notice.

"Hello, She-male!"

"Hello, Agnes." Ash acknowledged her fellow mercenary commander. "Hot enough for you?"

The straggle-haired man made a gesture that took in the full suit of Milanese plate that he rode in, the armet helm he currently carried on the pommel of his saddle, and the black iron warhammer at his belt. "They've got Guild riots down at Marseilles, along the coast. And you know Genoa – strong walls, bolshie citizens, and a dozen factions always fighting to be Doge. I took out the head of the Farinetti in a skirmish last week. Personally!"

He tilted his hand in his Milanese gauntlet, as far as the plates would allow, and made an imaginary illustrative thrust. His lean face was burned black from fighting in the Italian wars. Straggling black hair fell past his pauldrons. His white livery surcoat bore the device of a lamb, from whose head radiated golden beams, embroidered all over in black thread with '*Agnus Dei*'.[3]

"We've been up at Neuss. I led a cavalry charge against Duke Charles of Burgundy." Ash shrugged, as if to say *it was nothing, really.* "But the Duke's still alive. That's war."

---

[3] 'The Lamb of God'.

Lamb grinned, showing yellow broken teeth through his beard. In broad northern Italian, he remarked, "So now you're here. What is this – no scouts? No spies? Your guys didn't spot me until I was on top of you! Where the hell are your aforeriders?"[4]

"I was told we don't need any." Ash made her tone ironic. "This is a peaceful countryside full of merchants and pilgrims, under the protection of the Emperor. Didn't you know?"

Lamb (she had forgotten his real name) squinted through the mist to the head of the column. "Who's the bimbo?"

"My current employer." Ash didn't look at Anselm as she spoke.

"Oh. Right. He's one of *those* employers." Agnus Dei shrugged, which is a fairly complicated process in armour. His black eyes flashed at her. "Bad luck. I'm shipping out, down to Naples. Bring your men with me."

"Nah. I can't break a contract. Besides, most of my guys arc back at Cologne, under Angelotti and Geraint ab Morgan."

A movement of the Lamb's lips, regretful, flirtatious. "Ah well. How was the Brenner Pass? I waited three days for merchants going down to Genoa to get their wagons through."

"We had it clear. Except that it snowed. It's the middle of fucking *July* for Christ's sake – sorry, Lamb. I mean, it's the middle of July. I hate crossing the Alps. At least nothing fell on us this time. You remember that slide in seventy-two?"

Ash continued to talk civilly, riding beside him, aware of Anselm glowering on her other side, his grey plodding, horse and rider creamed white with chalk dust. From time to time her gaze flicked ahead, through the opalescent pearl of the mist, to the blurs of sunlight breaking through. Fernando's bright silks and satins glowed where he rode helmetless in the morning. The creak of wheels and the loud voices of men and women calling conversation echoed flatly. Someone played a fife, off-key.

After some professional conversation, Lamb remarked, "Then I shall see you on the field, madonna. God send, on the same side!"

"God willing," Ash chuckled.

The Lamb rode off south-east, in what she supposed must be the direction of his troop.

Robert Anselm remarked, "You didn't tell him your 'current employer' is also your husband."

"That's right, I didn't."

A dark, short man with curly hair rode up beside Anselm, glancing to either side before he spoke. "Boss, we must be nearly in Genoa!"

Ash nodded to Euen Huw. "So I assume."

"Let me take him out hunting." The Welshman's thumb slid down to caress the polished wooden hilt of his bollock dagger. "Lots of people have accidents when they're hunting. Happens all the time."

"We're twenty wagons and two hundred men. Listen to us. We've scared the game off for miles around. He wouldn't buy it. Sorry, Euen."

---

[4] Outriders, scouts.

"Let me saddle up for him tomorrow, then, on the way back. A bit of mail wire around the hoof, under the hock – aw, boss, go on!"

Her gaze could not help but be calculating when she looked through the mist at which of the lance-leaders rode with her, and who rode with Fernando del Guiz and his squires. It had been a frightening drift the first couple of days, then the Rhine river journey presented enough problems to keep every man occupied, and now it had stabilised.

You can't blame them. Whatever they ask me, he makes me clear all orders through him now.

But a divided company can't fight. We'll get cut up like sheep.

A man with potato features and a few wisps of white hair protruding under the rim of his sallet nudged his roan gelding up level with Ash. Sir Edward Aston said, "Knock the bloody little bugger off his horse, lass. If he keeps us riding without scouts, we're up to our necks in trouble. And he hasn't had the lances drill any night we've made camp."

"*And* if he keeps paying over the odds at every town we stop at for food and wine, we're in trouble." Ash's steward, Henri Brant, a middle-aged stocky man with no front teeth, nudged his palfrey closer to her. "Doesn't he know the value of money? I don't dare show my face among the Guilds on the way back. He's spent most of what I had put by to last us until autumn in these past fifteen days!"

"Ned, you're right; Henri, I *know*." She tapped spurs and shifted her weight left. Her grey gelding sneaked its head out and nipped Aston's roan on the shoulder.

Ash belted The Sod between the ears, and spurred off, kicking up gouts of wet dust, the cool air welcome on her face.

She slowed momentarily beside the wagons that held the Visigoth ambassadors. Tall wheel rims jolted in the ruts of the high road, sending the cart one way and then the other. Daniel de Quesada and Asturio Lebrija lay bound hand and foot with hemp rope, rolling with every jolt.

"Did my husband order this?"

A mounted man riding with his crossbow across his saddle spat. He didn't look at Ash. "Yeah."

"Cut them loose."

"Can't," the man said, even as Ash winced mentally and thought, *What's the first rule, girl? Never give an order you don't know will be obeyed.*

"Cut them loose when Lord Fernando sends word back to you," Ash said, hitting The Sod with a gloved hand again as the gelding tried to sidle up to the crossbowman's mount, a wicked light in its eye. "Which he will – *you* need a gallop to shake the temper out of you, you sod. *Hai!*"

The last remark Ash addressed to her horse. She spurred him from trot to canter to gallop, weaving a thunderous way between the lines of moving carts, ignoring the coughs and curses of those in her dust. The mist began to lift as she galloped. A dozen lance-pennants became clear above the wagons.

Fernando's bright bay pushed ahead of the group, throwing its head up and fretting at the bit, the reins looping dangerously down. Ash noticed that he had given his helmet to his squire, Otto; and that Matthias – neither knight nor squire – carried his lance. The fur of the foxtail pennant shone dully, in wet mist, drooping from its shaft above his head.

Her heart stirred immediately she saw him. *Golden boy*, she thought. The absolute picture of a knight: glowing with strength. He rode easily, and bare-headed. His Gothic plate showed rich, fine workmanship: fluted pauldrons and cuisses, each hinge flanged with decorative pierced metal. Condensation gleamed on the curve of his breastplate, and his tangled gold hair, and the polished brass fleur-de-lis that rimmed the cuffs of his gauntlets.

I was never that careless, she thought, with pinched envy. He's had this since birth. He doesn't even have to *think* about it.

"My lord." She rode up. Her husband's head turned. His cheeks were rough with gold stubble. Ignoring her, he half-turned in his saddle to speak to Matthias, and the long riding sword that swung at his hip banged against the bay's flank. The horse kicked out in aggravation, and the whole group of young men swirled into movement, shouting good-naturedly, and re-formed.

The group of squires riding around Fernando seemed reluctant to let her in. A loosening of her rein allowed The Sod's head to snake out and nip the haunch of one.

"Fuck!" The young knight sawed at his reins as his horse reared. Mount and rider staggered away, curvetting in circles.

Ash slid in neatly beside Fernando del Guiz. "A messenger came in. There's been trouble at Marseilles."

"That's leagues away from here." Fernando rode using both hands to hold up a wineskin, and tip it with his arms at full extension. The first streams hit him in the mouth; he coughed; straw-coloured wine spilled down the front of his fluted breastplate.

"You win, Matthias!" Fernando dropped the half-full wineskin. It thudded to the ground and burst. He threw a handful of coins. Otto and another page rode in close to undo straps, cut points, take pauldrons and breast- and back-plate off him. Still wearing arm-defences, Fernando slit the arming doublet's lacing, and the points at his waist, with his dagger, and ripped off the wet doublet. "Otto! It's too hot for harness.[5] Have them put my pavilion up. I'll change."

The spoilt garment went down into the dust as well. Fernando del Guiz was riding in his shirt now, the white silk bunching at his waist where it rode up out of his hose. His hose slid down to his cuisses, the material of the cod-flap stretched tight across his groin. When he dismounted, it would fall; he would strip it off and walk, unconcerned, in his shirt. Ash shifted in her saddle.

She wanted to reach out to his saddle and put her hand between his legs.

The trumpeter wheeled, sounding a long call.

Ash, jolted, said, "We're stopping?"

Fernando's smile took in those of her lance-leaders riding with him as well as his squires and pages and young noble friends. "I'm stopping. The wagons are stopping. You may do what you please, of course, lady wife."

---

[5] A 'harness' is the common term for a suit of armour. Thus the expression, 'died in harness', meaning 'died while wearing armour'.

"You want the ambassadors fed and watered while we stop?"

"No." Fernando reined in as the lead wagons stopped.

Ash sat astride The Sod, casting a glance around. The morning mist continued to lift. Broken ground, yellow rocks, scrub dried brown from the long summer's drought. A few copses of bushes – they could hardly be called trees. Higher ground two hundred yards from the wide road. A paradise for scouts, spies and dismounted men. Maybe even mounted bandits could sneak up.

Godfrey Maximillian plodded up to her on his palfrey. "How close are we to Genoa?"

The priest's beard was white, and the damp dust settled in the creases of his face gave her a premonition of how he would look if he reached sixty.

"Four miles? Ten? Two?" She fisted her hand, punched her thigh. "I'm blind! He forbids me to put scouts out, he forbids me to hire local guides; he's got this damn printed itinerary for pilgrims going to ports for the Holy Land, and *he* thinks that's all we need! He's a noble *knight*, no one's going to bushwhack *him*! What if it hadn't been Lamb's men out there? What if it had been some bandit?"

She stopped as Godfrey smiled, and shook her head. "Yeah, okay, I grant you, the difference between Lamb and a bandit is a bit hard to spot! But hey, that's Italian mercenaries for you."

"A baseless slander. Probably." Godfrey coughed, drank from his jug, and handed it up to her. "We're making camp two hours after we get started?"

"My lord wants to change his clothes."

"Again. You should have tipped him over the edge of a barge into the Rhine before we ever got to the cantons, never mind crossed the Alps."

"That isn't very Christian of you, Godfrey."

"Matthew ten, thirty-four!"[6]

"I don't think that's *quite* how Our Lord meant that one . . ." Ash lifted the pottery jug to her lips. The small beer stung her mouth. It was tepid, vaguely unpleasant, and (being wet) still extremely welcome for all that. "Godfrey, I can't push it, not right now. This is no time to ask my people to start picking sides between me and him. It'd be chaotic. We've got to at least *function* until we get back from this idiot's errand."

The priest slowly nodded.

Ash said, "I'm going to ride up to the top of the next ridge while he's busy. We're wandering around in a mist in more ways than one. I'll go take a look. Godfrey, go show your Christian charity to Asturio Lebrija and his mate. I don't think my lord husband had them fed this morning."

Godfrey's palfrey plodded back down the column.

Jan-Jacob Clovet and Pieter Tyrrell caught Ash up as The Sod skittered unwillingly up the slope – two fair-haired, almost identical young Flemish men, with unshaven faces, and tallow candle droppings on the sleeves under their brigandines, and crossbows at their saddles. They smelled of stale wine and

[6] Matthew 10: 34. 'Think not that I am come to send peace on earth: I came not to send peace, but a sword.'

semen; she guessed they had both been rousted out of a whore's cart before daybreak; probably, if she knew them, from the same woman.

"Boss," Jan-Jacob said, "do something about that son of a bitch."

"It'll happen when the time's right. You move without my word, and I'll nail your balls to a plank."

Normally, they would have grinned. Now Jan-Jacob persisted, "When?"

Pieter added, "They're saying you're not going to kill him. They're saying you're cock-struck. They're saying what can you expect from a woman?"

And if I asked who 'they' are, I'll get evasive answers or no answers at all. Ash sighed.

"Look, guys . . . have we ever broken a contract?"

"No!" They spoke simultaneously.

"Well, you can't say that for every mercenary company. We get paid because we don't change sides once we've signed a contract. The law is the only thing we have. I signed a contract with Fernando when I married him. There's one reason why this isn't easy."

She urged The Sod on up towards the lightening skyline.

"I was kind of hoping that God would do it for me," she said wistfully. "Hard-drinking reckless young noblemen fall off their horses and break their necks every day, why couldn't he be one of them?"

"Crossbows work." Pieter patted the leather case of his.

"No!"

"Does he fuck good?"

"Jan-Jacob, get your mind out of your codpiece for once – fucking *hell*!"

The breeze took the mist as they came up to the top of the ridge, rolling it forward, away out to sea. Mediterranean sun blazed back from ochre hills. A blurred blue sky shone, and – no more than two or three miles ahead – the light fractured off creeping waves. The coast. The sea.

A fleet covered the bay, and all the sea beyond.

No merchant ships.

Warships.

White sails and black pennants. Ash thought in a split second *that's half a war fleet down there!*, and *Visigoth pennants!*

The wind blew the taste of salt against her lips. She stared for a long, appalled, frozen second. The knife-sharp prows of black triremes cut the flat silver surface of the sea. More than ten in number, less than thirty. Among them, huge quinqueremes – fifty or sixty ships. And closer inshore, great shallow-draught troopships vanished from her sight behind the walls of Genoa, the wheels that drove them dripping rainbow sprays of sea-water. Dimly, across all the intervening distance, she heard the *thunk-thunk* of their progress.[7]

And she registered black smoke rising from the tiled roofs of the walled port

---

[7] Plainly, this is another intrusion of mediaeval legend into the text. Given the earlier inclusion of the name 'Carthage', I suspect that this is in fact a dim memory, preserved in monastery manuscripts, of the sea-power of the historical Carthaginians in the Classical period when it dominated the Mediterranean before being destroyed by the Roman fleet at Milazzo (263 BC), chiefly by the use of the Roman boarding-spike or *corvus*. It would not seem strange to a mediaeval chronicler to include such anachronisms.

city, and saw moving men among the painted plaster walls and winding streets of Genoa.

Ash whispered, "Troopships unloading, number unknown, fleet attacking, no allied vessels; my strength is two hundred men."

'Withdraw, or surrender.'

She still gaped at the coastline below the hills, the sound of the voice in her head almost ignored.

"The Lamb's run right into them!" Aghast, Jan-Jacob pointed at the standard with the white Agnus Dei, a mile ahead. Ash made a quick mental count of his groups of running men.

Pieter had already spurred in a circle, his mare hardly under control. "I'll sound the alarm!"

"*Wait.*" Ash held up one hand, palm outwards. "Now. Jan-Jacob, get the mounted archers formed up. Tell Anselm I want the knights up and armed, under him as captain! Pieter, tell Henri Brant that all wagons are to be abandoned, everybody on them is to be issued with weapons and told to ride. Ignore anything you hear from anyone with del Guiz livery – I'm going to talk to Fernando!"

She galloped down to the Lion Azure standard in the centre of the wagons. Among the milling men she spotted Rickard, yelled at the boy to bring Godfrey and the foreign ambassadors, and pelted on towards the green-and-gold-striped pavilion that was being put up in a confusion of struts and ropes and pegs. Fernando sat his horse, sun-bright, cheerfully talking to his companions.

"Fernando!"

"What?" He turned in his saddle. An arrogant shape took his mouth, a discontent foreign to what she was beginning to think was only a careless nature. I bring out the cruelty in him, she thought, and threw herself out of the saddle, quite deliberately on foot and catching his reins, so that she had to lift her head to look up at him.

"What is it?" He hitched at his falling hose, that now rucked down around his buttocks. "Can't you see I'm waiting to dress?"

"I need your help." Ash took a deep breath. "We've been tricked. All of us. The Visigoths. Their fleet. It *isn't* sailing for Cairo, against the Turks. It's *here.*"

"Here?" He looked down at her, bewildered.

"I counted at least twenty triremes – and sixty fucking big quinqueremes! *And* troopships."

His face became open, innocent, bemused. "Visigoths?"

"Their fleet! Their guns! Their army! It's a league up the road *that* way!"

Fernando gaped. "What are *Visigoths* doing *here*?"

"Burning Genoa."

"*Burning*—"

"Genoa! It's an invasion force. I have never seen so many ships in one place—" Ash wiped a crust of dust off her lips. "The Lamb's run into them. There's fighting going on."

"Fighting?"

The man Matthias, in a south German dialect, said, "Yes, Ferdie, *fighting*. You remember. Training, tournaments, wars? That sort of thing?"

Fernando said, "War."

The young German scowled, good-naturedly. "*If* you could be bothered. *I* train more than you do! You're so Boar-damned *lazy—*"

Ash cut across their languid conversation. "My lord husband, you have to see this. Come on!"

She mounted up, spun The Sod, and spurred him unmercifully, being rewarded by a kick-out (for temper's sake) and then a long, low, hard gallop up the slope, to arrive sweating and anxious, and peer down the long slope to Genoa.

She expected Fernando beside her in heartbeats: it seemed long minutes until he rode up, back- and breastplates strapped on to his body almost anyhow, and the white silk of his shirt-sleeves puffing out between the plates on his arms.

"Well? Where—" His voice died.

The foot of the slope was black with running men.

Otto, Matthias, Joscelyn van Mander, Ned Aston and Robert Anselm all arrived beside her in a flurry of manes and wet dust kicked up. They fell silent in the misty morning. Ahead, the smoke from Genoa smirched the sky.

In an identical bewildered tone to Fernando del Guiz, Joscelyn van Mander said, "*Visigoths?*"

Robert Anselm said, "They were either coming for us or the Turk. Turned out to be us."

"Listen." Ash's knuckles whitened on her reins. "A dozen mounted men riding on their own can move faster than this company. Lord husband, Fernando – ride back, tell the Emperor, he has to know about this *now!* Take de Quesada and Lebrija with you as hostages! You can do it in a few days if you ride post."

He stared down from his horse at the approaching banners. Behind him, the lance-leaders and men of the Lion Azure were a mass of steel helmets and dusty flags and the heads of polearms wavering in the heat. Fernando said, "Why not you, *Captain?*"

Poised above the dusty ruts, smelling of horse, wet with sweat, Ash felt a sensation as of putting her hand to a familiar sword grip: a sensation of control, not felt since they left Cologne a fortnight ago.

"You're a knight," she said, "not a peasant, not a mercenary. He'll listen to *you*."

Anselm màanaged a servile, "She's right, my lord." Roberto didn't meet Ash's eye, but she read what he was thinking with the clarity of long knowledge of the man. *Don't let this boy get any ideas about death-or-glory charges against that lot!*

"There are sixty quinqueremes . . ." Van Mander sounded stunned. "Thirty thousand men."

Fernando gazed down at Ash. Then, as if no one had spoken, as if it were his own decision, he shouted at her, "*I'll* take my Imperial cousin the news! You fight these bastards for me. I *order* it."

Got him! she thought, exultant, and stared down Joscelyn van Mander, who had very plainly heard his order.

They wheeled their horses by unspoken consent, trotting back down the slope. Early humid heat brought a cream sweat to the horses' flanks. The sea-mist from the Mediterranean coast thinned still more. A harsh sunlight stung her eyes.

She beckoned Godfrey Maximillian as he strode up, the two Visigoth men stumbling beside him. "Get them on horses. Chain their wrists. Go!"

Ash slapped her gloved hand against The Sod's satin neck. She couldn't stop grinning. The gelding whickered and mouthed at her, immense teeth clicking on the metal greaves covering her shins. "All right, you sod, so you like people – why the fuck can't you put up with other horses? One of these days you'll be stew. Stand *still*."

A hard object thunked between her shoulders, chinking the metal plates inside the brigandine. Ash swore. The already-spent arrow fell to the earth.

She brought the gelding around with her knees.

A line of light horses and riders in black livery were skylined at the top of the slope ahead. Mounted archers.

"Stop!" she yelled at Henri Brant, seeing the steward bawling at the drovers and men-at-arms to haul the big-wheeled vehicles around into wagon-fort formation. "You can forget that. That's a fucking army down there! Take what you can carry on packhorses. We'll leave the rest."

She spurred forward to where Anselm drew up a long line of mounted knights at the bottom of the slope, Jan-Jacob and Pieter out to either wing with mounted archers.

She kneed The Sod ferociously, wished that she was riding Godluc – *fucking Fernando, "Don't bring war-horses, we're riding in peace"!* – and her bastard sword was in her right hand, she didn't remember drawing it; and her unprotected hands wore nothing but leather riding gloves: her stomach clenched with the sheer terror of their vulnerability to chopping-edged weapons. She spared one glance to see the dozen young German knights riding hell for leather back down the road, lost in plumes of dust; then she galloped across the battle-line and out to the flank, and stared towards the sea.

Dark banners with clusters of men under them scrambled across the rocky slopes towards her. The sun winked off their weapons. A couple of thousand spear, at least.

She galloped back to the Lion Azure standard, finding Rickard also there, with her personal banner. Coming up with Robert Anselm, she called, "There's trees, two miles back! Henri, everyone on wagons is to cut their horses' traces, load up what they can, and ride. When you get to the bend about a mile back, leave the road and ride for the hills. We'll cover your backs."

Ash whirled The Sod on the spot, on his hind hooves, and rode out in front of the line. She faced them: about a hundred men in armour on horseback, another hundred out to the wings, with bows. "I always said you bastards would do anything for wine, women and song – and that's your wine, headed for the woods back there! In a minute, we're going to follow it. First, we're going to give this lot of southern bastards enough of a hard time that they won't *dare* come after us. We've done it before, and now we'll do it again!"

Rough voices bawled, "Ash!"

"Archers up on the ridge, there – move it! Remember, we don't go back until the standard goes back. And then we go back steady! And if they're stupid enough to follow us into the forests, they deserve everything they get. Okay, here they come!"

Euen Huw bawled, "Nock! Loose!"

The fine whistle of an arrow split the air, followed by two hundred more. Ash watched a rider in Visigoth livery on the ridge throw up his arms and fall, crossbow-bolt flights feathered in under his heart.

A crowd of spearmen on the ridge ran back.

Anselm yelled, *"Keep the line!"*

Ash, out to one side, saw more Visigoths on horses, small recurved bows in their hands. She muttered, "About sixty men, they can shoot from horseback."

'If they rally, charge them with knights. If they run, retreat.'

"Uh huh," she murmured thoughtfully to herself, and signalled the Lion Azure standard to pull back. She signalled the column to mount up. A half-mile at walking pace, with her eyes on the Visigoth cavalry archers – who didn't follow.

"I don't like that. I don't like that at all . . ."

"Something's odd." Robert Anselm reined in beside her as the men-at-arms rode past, on rising ground. "I expected the bastards to come down on top of us."

"They're outnumbered. We'd cut them to pieces."

"That never stopped Visigoth serf-troops before. They're an undisciplined shower of shite."

"Yeah. I know. But they're not acting like it today." Ash raised her hand and brought the sallet's visor down a touch, shading her eyes with the metal peak. "Thank Christ he went – I swear I thought my lord husband was going to order us to charge straight into that lot."

Far ahead, towards Genoa's burning buildings, she saw standards. Not pennants, but Visigoth flags crowned with what might – the distance being deceptive – be gilded eagles.

A movement beneath the eagles caught her eye.

Seen on its own, it could have been a man. Seen with the Visigoth commanders on the distant moorland, it was plainly a head taller. The sun shone on its ochre and brass surfaces. She knows that silhouette.

Ash watched as the clay and brass golem begin to stride out to the south-east. It walked no faster than a man, but its ceaseless stride ate up the ground, never faltering over rocks or banks, until she lost it in the haze.

"Shit," she said. "They're sending them out as messengers. That means this isn't the only beach-head."

Anselm tapped her on the shoulder. She followed his pointing arm. Another golem strode off, this one heading north-west, along the coastline. As fast as a trotting man. Slower than a horse – but untiring, needing no food or rest, travelling as well at night as in the day. A hundred and twenty miles in twenty-four hours, and carrying, in stone hands, written orders.

"Nobody's prepared!" Ash shifted in her war saddle. "They didn't just fool

125

our spy networks, Robert. The banks, the priests, the princes . . . God help us. They aren't after the Turks. They never *were* after the Turks . . ."

"They're after us," Robert Anselm grunted, and wheeled to ride with the column. "It's a fucking invasion."

III

By the time they caught the hastily loaded baggage train on the low slopes of the foothills, the head of the column was already vanishing up into a cliff-topped valley. Ash rode between a hundred archers and a hundred men-at-arms. Wheel ruts churned the road and the low gorse, the last abandoned wagons marking where the pack animals had left the high road. Ash squinted through air that began to waver as the morning grew hot. Probably a river flowed down through the valley, in winter. Dry, now.

Robert Anselm, Euen Huw, Joscelyn van Mander, her pages and the steward Henri Brant clustered under her banner, as two hundred armed men rode by. Tack jingled.

Ash thumped her fist on her saddle. Her breath came short. "If they're burning Genoa, they're prepared to be at war with Savoy, France, the Italian cities, the Emperor . . . sweet Green Christ!"

Van Mander scowled. "It's impossible!"

"It's *happening*. Joscelyn, I want your lances up front as the vaward. Euen, take charge of the archers; Robert, you have the mounted men-at-arms. Henri, can the pack animals keep up?"

The steward, in ill-fitting padded armour now, nodded his head enthusiastically. "We can see what's behind us. They'll keep up!"

"Okay, let's go."

Not until she rode into the steep-sided valley, and its shelter, did she realise how the increasing breeze had drummed in her ears, out on the moor. The silence here now echoed with horses' hooves, harness jangling, men muttering. Sun slanted through sparse pines on the valley floor. The promontories either side were thick with pine trees, broken deadfalls. And thick with undergrowth, at the cliff edges, where the trees didn't rob briars of sustenance.

Her neck prickled. With complete clarity, Ash thought, *Shit, that's why they didn't attack; they've bounced us back into an ambush!* and opened her mouth to yell.

A storm of eighty arrows blacked the air. A throng of shafts hit home, all in Joscelyn van Mander's lead lance. For a second it was as if nothing had happened. The whirring whine died. Then, a man screamed, metal flashed; another thicket of shafts jutted from horses' flanks, from men's shoulders, from the visor of a sallet; seven horses screeched and reared and the head of the column became a chaos of men running, dismounted, trying to control fear-stricken horses.

126

Ash lost The Sod's rein. The grey gelding bucked and sprang straight up, all four hooves off the ground, came down on age-hardened pine-tree roots – six black-fletched arrows sticking out of his neck and front quarters – and she felt the bone of his hind leg shatter.

She went sideways out of the saddle as he went down. One glimpse let her see men up high on the cliff-steep sides of the valley, shooting wicked small recurved bows, and the next mass arrow-flight shrieked down through the sparse trees and took Ned Aston's rearward lance into rioting horses and falling men and sheer, bloody chaos.

She hit the foot of a tree with a metallic crunch, hard enough to compress the plates in her brigandine. A dismounting man hauled her up on to her feet – Pieter? – her personal banner gripped in his other hand.

Her grey horse screamed. She leapt back from his threshing smashed legs; stepped in, sword in hand – how? when? – and slashed open the big vein in his throat.

The whole length of the valley seethed with screaming, rioting horses. A bay mare broke past Aston, running towards the moorland.

An arrow took it down.

Every exit blocked.

She steadied herself, body clamped tight up to the sticky resinous trunk of a pine tree, visor slammed up, staring around in desperation. A dozen or more men down, rolling on the dirt; the rest wheeling their mounts, looking for cover – but there is no cover – riding towards the foot of the seventy-degree slope – but no way up it. Bodkin-headed arrows thunked into flesh, bristled from the hastily roped towering loads on the mules.

The way ahead – blocked. A huddle of men, van Mander down; six of his men trying to drag him under the lip of the dry river bed, as if six inches of earth could protect them from a hundred murderous, razor-sharp arrow-heads—

Big Isobel, hauling on the reins of a mule, threw up her arms and sat down. A wooden shaft, as thick round as a man's thumb, stuck through her cheek, and through her mouth, and out of the back of her skull. Vomit and blood spilled over her brown linen bodice. The metal arrow-head dripped.

Ash slammed her visor down. She risked a look up at the cliff edge. Light glinted from a helmet. An arm moved. The tops of bows were a moving thicket. One man stood up to shoot, and she could barely see his head and shoulders. How many up there: fifty? A hundred?

Coldly realistic, she thought: Girl, you're not so special that you can't die yet, shot to pieces in some stupid ambush in some nameless hills. We can't shoot back, we can't get up the sides, we're fish in a barrel, we're dead.

No, we're not.

That simple: not even time to formulate a question for her saint's voice. She grabbed the banner-bearer's arm, her idea fully formed, plain, obvious and dirty.

"You, you and you; with me, *now*!"

She ran fast enough that she outdistanced her banner-bearer and two squires, thumping down behind the baggage mules as the Visigoth arrow-storm shrieked overhead.

"Get the torches out!" she screamed at Henri Brant. Her steward stared, gap-toothed mouth wide open. "The fucking pitch-*torches*, now! Get Pieter!"

She grabbed Pieter Tyrrell as Rickard ran back with him, all of them crouching crammed behind the squealing pack mules. Her banner-bearer gripped the pole in gauntleted hands, and ducked his head against arrows. The air stank of mule dung, and blood, and the fierce resin of the chine's forested slopes.

"Pieter, take these—" she dug in her pack for flint and steel, could only jerk her chin at the bundles of torches with pitch-soaked heads, that Henri Brant slashed free from binding cords with his dagger. "Take these and take six men. Ride like hell *up* this valley, ahead of us – look like you're running away. Climb the slope. Fire the trees on the cliff-top. Drag the torches on ropes behind your horses. As soon as there's a fire, cut around north-west. If you don't pick us up on the north road, wait for me at the Brenner. Got all that?"

"Fire? Christ, boss, a forest *fire*?"

"*Yes. Go!*"

Flint and steel sparked. The soft tinder in the box glowed, red and black.

"It's done!" Pieter Tyrrell swung around, crouching, to yell out half a dozen names.

Ash scuttled across the slope. A Visigoth crossbow bolt blew an explosion of splinters off a pine trunk, a yard ahead of her and the banner. She flung up an arm, cringing. Splinters thwicked across the velvet front of her brigandine. The soles of her riding boots skidded on the needle-covered slope. She slammed down beside Robert Anselm, behind a semi-fallen pine. "Have them ready to attack when I give the word."

"That's a fuck of a slope! We'll be cut to pieces!"

Ash glanced around at sweating, swearing men-at-arms, mostly in brigandines and long riding boots over leg armour, and carrying polearms that suddenly seemed clumsy under the low, stark branches of dry pines. Their faces turned to her. She slitted her eyes and stared up the gorge-like slopes of the dry river chine. You couldn't ride up this slope, or run up it: too steep. Weapon in one hand, the other to help scramble up. And so few trees for cover, so exposed, exhausted before you hit the men up there in cover—

"You're going in under cover of bows and arquebuses. Those fuckers will be too busy to see you coming!" It was a lie, and she knew it. "Robert, watch me for the signal!"

Ash sheathed her sword. Its scabbard rattled against her legs as she flung herself again across empty ground. Someone shrieked up on the top of the valley. Puffs of dust went up from the earth, and she caught her foot on an arrow buried to the fletching, and stumbled behind the second line of braying pack mules to the archers.

She was grinning so hard it hurt.

"Okay!" Ash slid to a halt beside Euen Huw, *de facto* captain of archers. "Oil pots and rags. Try for fire-arrows."

Henri Brant, unexpectedly still with her, yelled, "We don't have proper fire-arrows here! We weren't expecting a siege, so I didn't bring any!"

She slammed her arm around the steward's shoulders. "Don't matter! Do your best. With luck, we won't need it. Euen, how are we on ammunition?"

"Hackbutters are low. Bolts and arrows enough, though. Boss, we can't stay here, we're getting cut to pieces!"

A man in Blue Lion livery screamed and ran down the slope, arms flailing, towards the bottom of the valley. His boots skidded in the dry river course. A dozen arrows thunked into his legs. He hit dirt, rolled, took a bolt in the face, and lay thrashing and screeching.

"Keep shooting! Hard and fast as you can. Give those fuckers up there hell!" She grabbed Euen by the arm. "Hold on for five minutes. Be prepared to remount and *go* when I give the signal!"

Ash put her free hand on her bollock dagger, half intending to drop down to the dry river course and the dying man. A figure in padded armour and wearing a woollen hood shot past her. Ash, halfway back to the men-at-arms, her group dodging from tree to tree, suddenly thought *why the hood?* and realised she knew the long, loping run: *Fuck, that's Florian!*

She took one look over her shoulder, and saw the surgeon with the man's arm over her shoulder. He – *she* – bodily dragged the man under fallen, dead pine branches. Arrows chipped and thunked into the wood.

Come on, Pieter! Two more minutes and I'm going to *have* to attack, we're being slaughtered down here!

Acrid air rasped her throat.

The skyline above burst into flame.

Ash coughed. She wiped streaming eyes, and looked up at the cliff-top. One minute a wisp of black smoke, the air shimmering hard enough to make seeing anyone up on the cliff-top impossible. The next – red fire spouted from branches, from brush, from the deadfalls of old, dry pine branches. A resin-impregnated roar blasted the air.

She had an instant's vision of a man with his recurved bow raised, a hundred black-fletched arrows whistling between the trees – one magnificent roll of smoke and super-heated air—

Red flames roared up, obliterating the tree-line at the top of the cliffs.

Up there on the cliff-top, from further back, came the terrified screeching of horses.

Her eyes streaming, she prayed, *Thank you, Christ, I don't have to try to send people up that slope!*

"Okay, let's go!" Her voice was hard, loud, and shrill. It carried over the squeals of mules, the shrieks of mutilated men, the last two shots from an arquebus.

She seized the arm of the standard-bearer, pushing him and the twelve-foot Blue Lion flag on up the valley path ahead.

"Mount up! Ride! *GO!*"

The world was a chaos of men on horses, men running for horses, the thrum of arrows, a piercing long shrill scream that brought her gut up into her throat, the creaking whine of mules, and men she knows yelling orders: Robert Anselm with the men-at-arms mounted up and moving under the Lion standard, Euen Huw cursing the archers in Welsh and fluent Italian; the pack-beasts moving, Father Godfrey Maximillian hauling them, with one body slumped over the front of a framework packed eight foot high with bundles; Henri Brant with two arrows jutting out from his ribs under his right arm.

A scream broke her concentration. Two men in black livery broke cover on the skyline. They tumbled down the slope towards her banner and her. Ash yelled "Shoot!" even as a dozen clothyard arrows with bodkin heads punched through mail shirts and into their bodies; one man cartwheeling, the other sliding down on his back in a rumble of clods of earth, one leg in front, one trailing behind under his body, broken and dead before he stopped moving—

Ash whipped around, seized the rein of a roan that Philibert thrust at her, and hoisted herself into the saddle. One slap sent the boys' mounts ahead, on up the valley. She dug in spurs, aware of her banner-bearer running for his horse; then the pack train moved, the mounted archers shot past her in a thunder of hooves, Euen whooping, and the men-at-arms at full gallop, twenty or more of them riding double with wounded or dead men over the front of their saddles. The women and Godfrey and Floria del Guiz ran past, more wounded men over the backs of mules, abandoned stores spilling halfway down the valley back to the Genoese moors.

"What the fuck are you doing here?" Ash bawled at Florian. "I thought you stayed in Cologne!"

The surgeon, one of her arms over the back of a blood-soaked man on a mule, grinned up at Ash from a filthy face. "Someone has to keep an eye on you!"

The main body of men-at-arms galloped past, a hundred and fifty men shouting; Ash reined in for a second for her banner-bearer and half a dozen knights to catch up. Her eyes poured water. She wiped her face on her leather gauntlets. The top of the cliff swam. Fire licked out, catching the tops of the pines lower down the slope, nearer to her; the pines that grew tall out of the valley, reaching up for the light.

A man on fire ran off the steep edge of the cliff, cartwheeling down, arms and legs and body blazing. His corpse slid to a halt three yards away from her, blackened skin still bubbling.

Behind her, a trail of broken stores, thrashing horses and dead and wounded men's bodies lay strewn back down the valley. Heat from the fire brought sweat to her face. She wiped her mouth, and took her glove away black.

"GO!" she yelled, and the roan danced in a circle before she could bring it up and spur in the wake of two hundred men riding up the bed of the dry chine. Smoke stank.

A stag broke cover further up the line, springing straight through the line of galloping archers; and the air above the tree tops shrieked full of kestrels, owls, buzzards.

She coughed. Her eyes cleared.

A hundred yards: a quarter of a mile: the path rising—

A faint wind from the north freshened her face.

In the forest above – and *behind* her, now – the fire roared.

The valley steepened at the end of the chine, and she caught up with Robert Anselm and Euen Huw, under their respective pennants, hurrying the column on and up the earthy cliffs.

"Stick to the dry river bed," she yelled over the thump of hooves, exultant. "Don't stop for anything. If the wind changes, we're fucked!"

Anselm jerked a thumb at the slope in front of him, and a dead man. "We're not the first through here. Looks like your *husband* had the same idea."

Something about the fallen body made her check her horse. Ash leaned to peer down between shifting hooves. A dead man – lying back over the low fork of a pine tree, spine snapped. With his face bashed in, there was no telling what colour his hair or skin had been, under the red and black clots. His clothing had been white. Tunic and trousers, under mail. She recognised the livery.

"That's Asturio Lebrija." Ash, oddly moved, shifted her weight, steadying the roan. Foam flew back as the horse lifted and shook his head.

"Maybe young del Guiz didn't make it." Anselm's grim pleasure was evident in his voice. "There could be Visigoth patrols all over. They won't want news of the invasion getting out."

Her roan jerked at the crackling of the fire. Ash reined back, letting the last of van Mander's two lances pass her. The men's mounts scrambled, hooves sliding on the thick coat of needles on the sloping forest floor. The air stank of pitch and resin.

I've done it, I've got them out, I can't let it slip now!

We can be caught before we reach the mountains. We can find the passes closed, even in summer. Or that fucking wind can change, and we can fry.

"Get up front, see they don't bog down! Keep them going up into the hills. I want to get above the tree-line, *fast*."

Robert Anselm was gone almost before she finished speaking.

Ash gazed down now. Between the thin tops of pine trees below her on the slope, oddly undramatic from here: coils of black smoke, drifting up to smudge the sky, and the occasional flicker of red. This fire will burn the hills black. It is unstoppable, and she knows it. There will be peasants who own olive groves, vineyards, sick or weak families, who will curse her name. Huntsmen, charcoal-burners, goat-herds . . .

She ached in every muscle. Her brigandine and boots stank with her dead horse's blood. She strained her vision, trying to see if, on the coast, more of the golems were moving with their unceasing, mechanical tread.

In the far distance, metal eagle standards winked in the sun. The smoke from Genoa hid anything else.

A rider passed her, a mounted archer with blood running out from under the wrist of his padded jack. No one behind him. The last man out.

"Jan-Jacob!" Ash steered the roan in beside the archer and caught his reins as he sagged forward. She bent low to avoid jagged pine branches, and rode on up at the back of her column, leading the horse and the semi-conscious man.

Behind her, the North African invasion of Europe began.

IV

Seven days later, Ash stood slightly in advance of her lance-leaders, master gunner, surgeon and priest on the open ground directly in front of a tournament stand at Cologne. The Emperor's household guard surrounded her.

Imperial banners cracked in the wind.

She could smell the scent of the raw wood nailed together into box seating, under Frederick's yellow and black silk canopies. The scent of pine resin made her momentarily shiver. A sound of steel on steel came clashing from the tournament barriers. Play-combat – enough to maim a man, but play-combat all the same.

Her eyes sought the Imperial box, travelled along the rows of faces. All the nobles of the Germanic court and their guests. No ambassadors from Milan or Savoy. No one from any kingdom south of the Alps. A few men from the League of Constance. Some French, some Burgundians . . .

No Fernando del Guiz.

Floria del Guiz's voice, barely loud enough to carry to Ash, murmured, "Seats up the back. On the left. My step-mother. Constanza."

Ash's eyes shifted. Among the hennins and veils of the ladies, she caught a glimpse of Constanza del Guiz. But not her son. The old woman sat alone. "Right. Let's get this over with. I want a word with her . . ."

Swords clashed a way off, in the wattle enclosure. Coldness lives in her belly, now. Anticipation.

The wind swept over Ash, over the green hills, down towards the white walls of Cologne, containing its tiled blue roofs and the double spires of its churches. There were horses on the high road, and in the distance a few peasants in their shifts with hose rolled up were visible, wearing wide straw hats against the heat, and cutting a small copse of ten-year-old chestnut trees for fencing.

And what chance of them bringing in this year's wheat harvest?

Ash returned her gaze to Frederick of Hapsburg, Holy Roman Emperor, leaning in his throne to listen to his councillor. He scowled as the advisor concluded.

"Mistress Ash, you ought to have defeated them!" his dry voice raged, loud enough to be heard by all present. "These are just serf-troops from the land of stone and twilight!"

"But—"

"If you can't defeat a scout force of *Visigoths*, for the Green Christ's sake, what are you doing calling yourself a mercenary battle leader?"

"But—!"

"I had thought better of you. But no wise man trusts a woman! Your husband will answer for this!"

"*But* – Oh, fuck it! You mean you think I've made you look bad." Ash rested one steel-plated arm on top of the other and met Frederick's faded blue gaze. She could feel Robert Anselm bristle, without looking at him. Even Joscelyn

132

van Mander's intense florid face scowled – but that might have been pain from his bandaged leg.

"Forgive me if I'm not impressed. I've just come from calling my muster-roll. Fourteen men wounded, who're here in the city hospice, and two so badly mutilated I'll have to give them pensions. Ten men dead. One of them Ned Aston." She halted, at a loss, knowing as she spoke that she was making a cock of it: "I've been in the field since I was a child, this isn't ordinary war. It isn't even bad war. This is—"

"Excuses!" Frederick spat.

"*No.*" Ash took a step forward, registering Frederick's household guard shift their stances. "This *isn't* the way Visigoths fight!" She gestured at Frederick's captains. "Ask anyone who's campaigned down south. My guess is they had cavalry squadrons out ready, patrolling for ten or twenty miles inland, all down the coast. They *let* us ride in. They let Lamb in. So they could keep news from getting out until it's too late to do anything about it! They anticipated everything we did. That's way too disciplined for Visigoth slaves and peasant-troops!"

Ash dropped her left hand to grip her scabbard, for comfort. "I heard news, coming back through the Gotthard monastery. They're supposed to have a new commander. No one knows anything. It's chaos down south! It's taken us seven days to get back here. Have you had post-riders back yet? Has *any* news come north of the Alps?"

The Emperor Frederick held up his goblet for wine and ignored her.

He sat in his gilded chair, among a dazzle of men in fur-trimmed velvet doublets, and women in brocade gowns; those furthest away watching the tournament avidly, those nearest ready to smile or frown as the Emperor might require. There were great papier-mâché models of black Eagles ornamenting the tourney stand above him: the Empire's heraldic Beast.

Under cover of the Imperial servants fussing, just loud enough for her to hear, Robert Anselm murmured, "How can he be holding a fucking *tournament*, for Christ's sake? There's a fucking *army* on his doorstep!"

"If they haven't crossed the Alps, he thinks he's safe."

Florian del Guiz returned from a brief foray into the crowd. She put her hand on Ash's armoured shoulder. "I don't see Fernando here, and nobody will talk to me about him. They all clam up solid."

"Fuck." Ash privately glanced at Fernando's sister. With her face washed, you could see the surgeon had her brother's sprinkle of freckles across the nose, although her cheeks had lost the roundness of youth. Ash thought, If *anyone* in this company looks like a woman disguised, it's Angelotti – Antonio's too beautiful to live. Not Florian.

"Can you find anyone to tell you if my husband's come back to Cologne?" Ash looked questioningly back at Godfrey Maximillian.

The priest pursed his lips. "I can't find anyone who spoke to him after his men left the St Bernard Pass hospice."

"What the *hell* is he doing? Don't tell me: he ran into some more Visigoth aforeriders and decided it was a great idea to defeat the invading army on his own . . ."

133

Anselm grunted agreement. "Rash."

"He's not dead. I couldn't be that lucky. At least I've got command again."

"*De facto*,"[8] Godfrey murmured.

Ash shifted from one foot to the other. The Imperial serving of food and drink was obviously designed to keep her standing and waiting. Probably until Frederick devised some suitable penalty for losing a skirmish. "This is just playing games!"

Antonio Angelotti muttered, "Holy Christ, madonna, doesn't this man know what's going on?"

"Your Imperial Majesty!" Ash waited until Frederick glanced down at her. "The Visigoths sent messengers out. I saw clay walkers going west to Marseilles, and south-east towards Florence. I would have sent a raiding party after them, but by then we were in their ambush. Do you really imagine they'll stop with Genoa and Marseilles and Savoy?"

Her bluntness stung him; Frederick blinked. "It's true, Lady del Guiz, there is very little word coming back over the Alps since they closed the Gotthard pass. Even my bankers can tell me nothing. Nor my bishops. You would think they owned no paid watchers . . . And you: how can you come back and be able to tell me so little?" He pointed a testy finger at her. "*You* should have stayed! You ought to have observed for a longer period of time!"

"If I had, the only way you could reach me now would be through prayer!"

It's about ten heartbeats before she's arrested and thrown out, by her own estimation, but Ash's head is full of Pieter Tyrrell, in a Cologne inn-room with thirty gold louis and half his left hand cleaved off: little and ring and middle fingers gone. With Philibert, missing since one snowbound night on the Gotthard; Ned Aston dead; and Isobel, without even a body for a funeral.

Ash chose her moment and spoke measuredly.

"Your Majesty, I've visited the bishop today, here in the city." She watched the puzzled expression on Frederick's face. "Ask your priests and lawyers, Your Majesty. My husband has deserted me – without consummating our marriage."

Floria made a stifled noise.

The Emperor switched his attention to Floria del Guiz. "Is this true, master surgeon?"

Floria said, immediately and without apparent qualm, "As true as I am a man standing here before you, Your Majesty."

"Therefore, I've applied to have the marriage annulled," Ash said rapidly, "I owe you no feudal obligation, Your Imperial Majesty. And the company's contract with you expired when the Burgundian troops withdrew from Neuss."

Bishop Stephen inclined from his seat to speak into the Emperor's ear. Ash watched the Holy Roman Emperor Frederick's lined, dry face harden.

"Well, hey," Ash said, as casual as it is possible to be with eight hundred armed men at one's disposal. "Make me an offer and I'll put it before the men. But I think the Company of the Lion can get work anywhere we want, now. And at a good price."

Anselm, very quietly, groaned, "Shi-it . . ."

[8] Latin: 'by the fact (of doing it)', rather than *de jure*, 'by right of the law'.

It is a piece of unwise bravado and she knows it. Political trickery, hard riding and bad food, and the unnecessary fighting; the unnecessary deaths; none of the last month can be paid for by talking back like an unmannerly servant. But some tension leaves her, all the same, with the malice in her tone.

Antonio Angelotti chuckled. Van Mander slapped her backplate. She ignored the two men, her attention on Frederick, relishing how taken aback he looked. She heard Godfrey Maximillian sigh. Jubilant, she smiled at the Emperor. She did not quite dare to say *You forget – we're not yours. We're mercenaries*, but she let her expression say it for her.

"Green Christ!" Godfrey muttered. "It's not enough for you to have Sigismund of the Tyrol as an enemy, you want the Holy Emperor, too!"

Ash moved her hands to cup her elbows: the palms of her gauntlets feeling the cold steel of elbow-couters. "We weren't getting another German contract, whichever way you look at it. I've told Geraint to get the camp dismount started. We'll go into France, maybe. We're not going to be short of business now."

Casual, ruthless; there is a brutal tone to her voice. Some of it is rough grief for men she knows who are killed or maimed now. Most of it is gut-deep, savage joy that she is still alive.

Ash looked up into Godfrey's bearded face, and linked her armoured arm with his. "Come on, Godfrey. This is what we do, remember?"

"This is what we do if you're not in a dungeon in Cologne—" Godfrey Maximillian abruptly stopped talking.

A cluster of priests pushed through the crowd. Among the brown cowls, Ash glimpsed one bare head. Something wrong about it . . .

Men jostled, Frederick's Captain of the Guard shouting a challenge; then a space cleared before the stands, and six priests from the St Bernard hospice knelt before the Emperor.

It was a moment before Ash recognised the bruised, dishevelled man with them.

"That's de Quesada." She frowned. "Our Visigoth ambassador. Daniel de Quesada."

Godfrey sounded unusually perturbed. "What's he doing back here?"

"Christ knows. If he's here, where's Fernando? What's Fernando been playing at? Daniel de Quesada . . . There's a man whose head is going home from here in a basket." Automatically, she checked the position of her men: Anselm, van Mander and Angelotti armed and in armour; Rickard with the banner; Floria and Godfrey unarmed. "He's in shit shape . . . what the hell's happened to him?"

Daniel de Quesada's shaven scalp shone, bloody. Old brown blood clotted his cheeks. His beard had been ripped out by the roots. He knelt, barefoot, his head up, facing Frederick of Hapsburg and the German princes. His gaze skated across Ash as if he didn't recognise the silver-haired woman in armour.

Some disquiet tugged at her. *Not ordinary war, not even bad war*— What? she thought, frustrated. Why am I worried now? I've got out of this political chicanery. We're mauled, but the Company's been hurt before; we'll get over it. I've won. It's business as usual; what's the *problem*?

135

Ash stood outside the shade of the tourney stand, in the blazing summer sun. The clash of breaking lances and cheers echoed across from the green grass. A fresh wind brought her a scent of coming rain.

The Visigoth turned his head, surveying the court. Ash saw sweat bead on his forehead. He spoke with a febrile excitement she had seen before, in men who expected to die within the next few minutes.

"Kill me!" de Quesada invited the Hapsburg Emperor. "Why not? I've done what I came to do."

He spoke in fluent German.

"We were a lie, to keep you occupied. My lord the King-Caliph Theodoric sent other ambassadors also, to the courts of Savoy and Genoa, Florence, Venice, Basle and Paris, with similar instructions."

Ash, in her workaday Carthaginian, asked, "What's happened to my husband? Where did you part company with Fernando del Guiz?"

Exactly how much of an unpardonable, irrelevant interruption it was as far as Frederick of Hapsburg was concerned, Ash could see in his face. She held herself in an alert tension, waiting either for his anger, or Daniel de Quesada to reply.

Offhandedly, de Quesada said, "Master del Guiz freed me when he decided to swear loyalty to our King-Caliph Theodoric."

"*Fernando?* Swear *loyalty* to—?" Ash stared. "To the *Visigoth Caliph*?"

Behind Ash, Robert Anselm gave a great barking laugh. Ash was unsure whether she wanted to laugh or cry.

De Quesada spoke with a gaze fixed on the face of the Emperor, driving home each word with malice, and visible instability. "We – the young man you sent as my escort – met with another division of our army south of the Gotthard Pass. He was twelve men against twelve hundred. Del Guiz was allowed, on condition of his swearing fealty, to live, and keep his estate."

"He wouldn't do that!" Ash protested. She stuttered, "I mean, he wouldn't – he just *wouldn't*. He's a *knight*. This is just misinformation. Rumour. Some enemy's lies."

Neither the ambassador nor the Emperor heeded her.

"His estate is not yours to give, Visigoth! It's mine!" Frederick of Hapsburg twisted around in the ornamented chair, snarling at his chancellor and legal staff. "Put the young gentleman and his family and estates under an act of attainder. For treason."

One of the fathers from the St Bernard hospice cleared his throat. "We found this man Quesada wandering lost in the snow, Your Imperial Highness. He knew no name but yours. We thought it charity to bring him here. Forgive us if we have done wrong."

Ash muttered to Godfrey, "If they'd met up with Visigoth forces, what was he doing wandering around in the snow?"

Godfrey spread his broad-fingered hands and just shrugged. "My child, only God knows that at the moment!"

"Well, when He tells you, you tell me!"

The little man on the Hapsburg throne wrinkled his lip at Daniel de Quesada, in a quite unconscious disgust. "He is mad, obviously. What can he know of del Guiz? We were hasty – cancel the attainder. What he says is nonsense; convenient lies. Fathers, have him confined in your house in the city. Beat the demon out of him. Let us see how this war goes; he shall be our prisoner, not their ambassador."

"It is no *war*!" Daniel de Quesada shouted. "If you *knew*, you would surrender now, before you take more than a skirmish's casualties! The Italian cities are learning that lesson now—"

One of the Imperial men-at-arms moved to stand behind Quesada where the ambassador knelt, and pricked his throat with a dagger, the thick steel blade old and nicked but perfectly serviceable.

The Visigoth gabbled, "Do you know what you're facing? Twenty years! Twenty years of ship-building, and making weapons, and training men!"

The Emperor Frederick chuckled. "Well, well, we have no quarrel with you. Your battles with mercenaries are no longer my concern." A dry little smile at Ash, all her earlier malice repaid with interest.

"You call yourself a 'Holy Roman Empire'," de Quesada said. "You are not even the shadow of the Empty Chair.[9] As for the Italian cities – we find them worth it for their gold, but for nothing else. As for a rabble of farmers on horseback from Basle and Cologne and Paris and Granada – why should we want *them*? If we wanted to take fools for slaves, the Turkish fleet would be burning now at Cyprus."

Frederick of Hapsburg waved his nobles down. "You are among strangers, if not enemies. Are you a madman, to behave like this?"

"We don't want your Holy Empire." De Quesada, still on his knees, shrugged. "But we'll take it. We'll take everything that lies between us and the richest of all."

His brown eyes went to the Burgundian guests in the court. Ash guessed them there still celebrating the peace of Neuss. Quesada fixed his gaze on a face she recognised from other campaigning seasons – Duke Charles of Burgundy's Captain of the Guard, Olivier de la Marche.

Quesada whispered, "Everything that's between us and the kingdoms and duchies of Burgundy, we will take. Then we will have Burgundy."

Of all princedoms of Europe, the richest, Ash remembered someone once saying. She looked from the bloodstained, middle-aged Visigoth man up to the Duke's representative in the tourney stand, whose lugubrious face she also recognised from the tournament circuit. The big soldier in red and blue livery laughed. Olivier de la Marche had a loud, practised voice from shouting on battlefields; he did not modulate it now. Snickers came from the court hangers-on pressed close around him. Bright surcoats, brilliant armour, the gilded pommels of rich blades, confident clean-shaven faces; all the visible power of knightly chivalry. Ash felt a momentary sympathy for Daniel de Quesada.

"My Duke has recently conquered Lorraine,"[10] Olivier de la Marche said amiably. "Not to mention his defeats of my lord King of France." Tactfully, he avoided looking at Frederick of Hapsburg, or mentioning Neuss. "We have an

[9] Context leads me to suspect that this refers, in fact, to the city of Rome – perhaps the papal throne, the chair of Peter? The textual reference is obscure.
[10] In 1475.

137

army that is the envy of Christendom. Try us, sir. Try us. I promise you a warm welcome."

"And I promise you a cold greeting." Daniel de Quesada's eyes gleamed. Ash's hand went to her sword-hilt, without conscious intention. The man's body movements shouted wrongness, all human caution abandoned. Fanatics fight that way, and assassins. Ash came alive, a snapshot vision took in the men around her, the corner of the tourney stand, the Emperor's pennant, the guards, her own command group—

Daniel de Quesada shrieked.

Mouth a wide rictus, he moved nothing else, but the cords of his throat jutted out, his scream lifting above the noise of the cheering crowd, until a silence began to spread out from where they stood. Ash felt Godfrey Maximillian beside her grab at his pectoral cross. The hairs at the back of her neck lifted as if cold air blew over them. Quesada knelt and screamed a pure, uncaring rage.

Silence.

The Visigoth ambassador lowered his head, glaring at them all from bloodshot eyes. The torn skin of his cheeks bled freshly.

"We take Christendom," he whispered, raggedly. "We take your cities. All your cities. And you, Burgundy, *you* . . . Now we have begun, I am permitted to show you a sign."

Something made Ash look up.

She realised a second later that she was following the direction of Daniel de Quesada's bloodshot, ecstatic gaze. Straight up into the blue sky.

Straight into the white-hot blaze of the noon sun.

"Shit!" Tears flooded her eyes. She rubbed her gloved hand across her face. It came away wet.

She saw nothing. She was blind.

"Christ!" She shrieked. Voices howled with her. Close, in the silk-canopied stand; further off, on the tourney field. Screams. She rubbed her hands frantically across her eyes. She could see nothing – nothing—

Ash stood for one second, both linen-covered palms across her eyes. Blackness. Nothing. She pressed hard. She felt, through the thin linen, the balls of her eyes shifting as she looked. She took her hands away. Darkness. Nothing.

Wetness: tears or blood? No pain—

Someone cannoned into her. She grabbed, caught an arm: someone screamed, a whole host of voices screaming, and she couldn't make out what the words were, then:

"The sun! The *sun!*"

She was crouching without knowing how, her gauntlets stripped off, her bare hands flat on the dry earth. A body pressed into her side. She gripped at its sweaty warmth.

A thin voice that she almost did not recognise as Robert Anselm's whispered, "The sun's . . . gone."

Ash raised her head.

Prickles of light in her vision resolved into patterns. Faint dots. Not close – far, far away, above the horizons of the world.

She looked down, in faint unnatural light, and made out the shape of her hands. She looked up and saw nothing but a scatter of unfamiliar stars on the horizon.

In the arch of the sky above her was nothing, nothing at all, except darkness. Ash whispered, *"He put the sun out."*

Message: #19 (Pierce Ratcliff)
Subject: Ash
Date: 06/11/00 at 10.10 a.m.
From: Longman@

format address and other details non-recoverably deleted

Pierce —

THE *SUN* GOES OUT?????
  And you're WHERE?

- Anna

Message: #19 (Anna Longman)
Subject: Ash
Date: 06/11/00 at 06.30 p.m.
From: Ratcliff@

format address and other details non-recoverably deleted

Anna —

I am stuck in a hotel room in Tunis. One of Isobel Napier-Grant's young assistants is instructing me on how to download and send e-mails through the telephone system here — not as easy a task as you might imagine. The truck doesn't go out to the site until tonight, under cover of darkness. Archaeological teams can be fanatical about security. I don't blame Isobel one bit, if she's got what she says she has.

  I'd hoped, when she said she was coming out here, that she might find confirming evidence — so unlikely anyway, even for a potsherd, with the hundreds of square miles of territory to be searched — but THIS!

  'The sun goes out'. Yes, of course. As far as I can discover, there was no actual eclipse visible in Europe in 1475 or 1476 — the very best I can manage is one on 25 February 1476, in Pskov, but that's in Russia! - however, later chroniclers obviously found it an irresistible piece of dramatic licence. I must say that I do, too.

- Pierce

```
Message:    #20 (Pierce Ratcliff)
Subject:    Ash, historical background
Date:       06/11/00 at 06.44 p.m.
From:       Longman@
```
format address and other details
non-recoverably deleted

Pierce —

BUT!!! I've been looking this up, Pierce. All the wars I can find,
for the whole of 1476–1477, are Duke Charles the Bold of Burgundy's
attempts to conquer Lorraine, and link up his 'Middle Kingdom'
across Europe. Then there's his defeat by the Swiss at Nancy; and
the indecent haste with which his enemies divided up Burgundy
between them on his death. There are the usual wars between the
Italian city states, but that's it; there's *nothing* about North
Africa!

Don't tell me this is Euro-centric historicism! Isn't an
invasion of Italy and Switzerland a bit BIG to miss?

I repeat, Pierce, WHAT VISIGOTH INVASION???!!!

— Anna

```
Message:    #23 (Anna Longman)
Subject:    Ash
Date:       06/11/00 at 07.07 p.m.
From:       Ratcliff@
```
(format address and other details
non-recoverably deleted)

Anna —

I told you that FRAXINUS would cause you to reassess history.
Very well:

It is my intention to prove that the North African Visigoth
settlement, at one point between approximately AD 1475 and AD
1477, DID mount a military invasion of southern Europe.

I will be stating that contemporary interest in this raid was
lost in the flurry of panic when Charles the Bold was killed in
battle in 1477. That was perhaps only to be expected.

That later historians continue to ignore the episode is due —
dare I say — to the preponderance of white, male middle-class
academics unwilling to believe that Western Europe might be
challenged from Africa? And that a mixed-race culture might prove
militarily superior to Caucasian Western Christendom?

— Pierce

```
Message:    #21 (Pierce Ratcliff)
Subject:    Ash, historical background
Date:       06/11/00 at 07.36 p.m.
From:       Longman@
```
format address and other details non-recoverably deleted

Pierce —

The problem with this is still that the text gives us an invasion
of Western Europe in 1476 and even the Turks NEVER ACTUALLY
SUCCEEDED IN INVADING!!! I know you will say that, according to
your present theory, Ash is fighting your North African mediaeval
'Visigoths'. Then WHY IS THERE NO MENTION OF THIS IN MY HISTORY
BOOKS?

— Anna

```
Message:    #24 (Anna Longman)
Subject:    Visigoths
Date:       07/11/00 at 05.23 p.m.
From:       Ngrant@
```
format address and other details non-recoverably deleted

Anna —

I'm at the site!

Dr Napier-Grant is kindly allowing me to use her satellite
notebook PC. There's so much to say that I couldn't wait to try and
get a phone call through, the lines here are terrible. Isobel
(sorry, that's Dr N-G, in case you forget) Isobel says I can tell
you a bit but she doesn't want it leaking out, because if someone
else reads the message then she'll have every archaeologist
between here and the North Pole arriving on our doorstep. Those
that aren't here already.

I know I'm not supposed to say this, but it's hot and smelly and
the only time it's bearable is when we're actually out at the digs
— which I'm *not* going to mention the location of, obviously!!!
Suffice it to say that we are very near the northern coast of this
region of Tunisia. (There are mountains on the southern skyline,
they make me think of ice and coldness and somewhere you don't have
to stay under shelter between one and five in the afternoon!) Look,
you don't want to hear all this, but I can't tell you what I'd like
to, and I'm just bursting to.

Isobel says that since you're on the verge of ditching the book,
I *can* tell you some things. Isobel's a wonderful woman. I've
known her since Oxford. She's the last person I can think of who'd
get excited unnecessarily. You only have to look at her short hair
and sensible shoes. (No, we never did. I wanted to. Isobel isn't
keen that way.) And this last twenty-four hours since I got here,
she's been skipping about like a schoolgirl! This *could* still
turn out to be another Hitler Diaries, but I don't think so.

143
```
```

What have we found? (Not 'we', of course. Isobel and her wonderful team.)

We've found golems.

Exactly as the text describes them. 'Messenger-golems'. One complete, and some pieces of another. You remember me telling you that Arabic mediaeval engineering was quite up to building singing fountains, and mechanical birds that flap their wings, and all that sort of post-Roman trivia? Very well:

The ASH manuscripts always refer to the 'clay walkers' or 'robots' or 'golems' as *moving* mechanical models of men. This is complete nonsense of course. Imagine building a robot in the fifteenth century! Ornamental devices of some kind, possibly. *Just* possibly. I mean, if you can build metal singing birds — they worked pneumatically or hydraulically, as all the Roman treatises indicate; don't ask me the details, I'm not an engineer! — Then, I suppose, you could build metal models of men, too, like Roger Bacon's Brazen Head, but complete. I don't see why anyone would want to.

That's what I thought, up to twenty-four hours ago. Then there was all the rush of getting a plane out to Tunis, and being driven in some god-awful jeep out to the archaeologists' camp, and then Isobel taking me all the way out here on foot. There are soldiers guarding the camp, all Jeeps and Kalashnikovs, but they don't seem very alert — just a gift from the local government to keep petty pilfering down, I think. Isobel would like to keep it that way. The last thing we want is the military sent into this site. You could destroy the survivals that are five hundred odd years old —

Yes. Isobel's dated them, she's pretty sure they've been in the silt for upwards of four hundred years, and five hundred seems likely; they're not the Victorian curiosities I was afraid I was going to find. These are the messenger-golems of the ASH texts — man-shaped, life-sized carved stone bodies (the complete one is Italian marble), with articulated metal joints at the knees, hips, shoulders, elbows and hands. The stonework on the second one has shattered, but the bronze and brass gears and cogs are complete. *They are golems*!

I confess I don't understand all the professional arguments that are going on between Isobel's team, or rather, I don't understand the technological details. There is a *huge* row breaking out about whether these finds belong to a mediaeval Arab or mediaeval European culture — the Italian marble, you see, although of course Carrara marble was exported across the whole of Christendom at the time, as I've tried to point out. I've given Isobel my copy of the existing ASH translations, indicating that (as I was going to e-mail you to point out) the 'Visigoth' culture of the texts is *not* purely Iberian Gothic, but rather a mixture of Visigothic, Spanish and Arab culture.

I've got this far and I haven't told you the most important discovery so far. You're sitting there in London reading this, and you're thinking, so? So they had mechanical men, as well as mechanical birds, what does this matter?

Isobel has let me examine the surviving golem extremely carefully. This is something that must not get out before she is ready to publish her findings. There are patterns of wear in the metal joints. That isn't all.

There are patterns of wear on the marble surfaces *under* the feet!

The stone is worn away on the carved soles of the feet and under the heels exactly as though this golem has been walking. And I mean walking. Like a man, like you and me, a stone and brass mechanical man, *walking*.

What I have touched — touched, Anna! — is exactly what the ASH texts describe as the Visigoth clay walkers.

They are *real*.

I have to get off this machine, Isobel urgently needs to use it. I'll contact you again as soon as I can. The translations of the documents in section three are in the file I'm sending with this. Don't ditch my book!!! We might have something here that's bigger than anyone ever thought.

What Visigoths? HA!

— Pierce

Message: #28 (Pierce Ratcliff)
Subject: Ash, media-related projects
Date: 07/11/00 at 06.17 p.m.
From: Longman@

format address and other details non-recoverably deleted

Pierce —

I want you to talk to Dr Napier-Grant, and persuade her that you two should work together, starting NOW. My MD Jonathan Stanley is *very* much in favour of the idea of doing some kind of a tie-in between yourself and Doctor Napier-Grant. She sounds like one of those great British eccentrics who come across brilliantly on the small screen. I can see a possible tv series for her, and there's your original translation of 'Ash'; and then there is what you could do together – a book-of-the-expedition? Do you think you could write a script for a documentary on the expedition? This has *terrific* possibilities!

I'm certain a deal could be arranged. I don't usually say this to my academic authors, but *get yourself an agent*! You need one who handles film and tv rights, as well as non-fiction book translation rights.

It's true we've still got a text that's half mediaeval legend, half historical fact (eclipses!) — and I'm gobsmacked that something like an invasion could be left out of the history books — and how DID these golems MOVE? — but I don't see any of this as a barrier to successful publication. Talk to Dr Napier-Grant about the idea for a joint project and get back to me as soon as you can!

Love, Anna

PART THREE

22 July–10 August AD 1476

'How a Man Schall be Armyd at His Ease'[1]

---

[1] The title of a popular contemporary treatise (*c*.1450) containing instructions for putting on one's knightly armour for non-cavalry combat: *How a man shall be armed at his ease when he shall fight on foot.*

I

Forty pitch-torches flared in the wind, under an ink-black daytime sky.

A great lane of people opened in front of Ash as she galloped into the centre of the camp outside Cologne. She halted astride Godluc, in full armour, the company banner cracking in the wind above her; the noise loud in the silence. Yellow light blazed across her strained white face. "Geraint! Euen! Thomas!"

Her lance-leader lieutenants ran to stand either side, ready to repeat her words the instant that she spoke, feed them out to the hundreds of her archers and billmen and knights gathering in front of her. Voices began shouting, chaotic in the unnatural dark.

"Listen to *me*. There is," Ash spoke perfectly steadily, "*nothing* for you to be afraid of."

Above, what should have been a July midday blue sky showed only black, empty darkness.

There is no sun.

"*I'm* here. *Godfrey's* here, and he's a priest. You're not damned and you're not in danger – if we were, I'd be the first one out of here!"

No response from any of the hundreds of fearful faces. The torchlight wavers across their shining silver helmets, loses itself in darkness between their crowded, armed bodies.

"Maybe we're going to be like the lands Under the Penance now," Ash continued, "—but – Angelotti's *been* to Carthage, and the Eternal Twilight, and they manage well enough, and you're not going to let a bunch of shabby rag-heads outdo the Lion!"

Nothing like a cheer, but they made the first responsive noise she'd heard out of them: a subdued mutter, full of *fuck!* and *shit!* and nobody quite saying the word *desertion*.

"Right," she said briskly. "We're moving. The company's going to strike camp. We've done a night dismount before, you all know how to do this. I want us loaded and ready to go at Vespers."[2]

A hand went up, just visible in the streaming sooty light of the makeshift torches. Ash leaned forward in the saddle, peering. She realised it was her steward Henri Brant, his body still banded with bloodstained cloths, leaning on the shoulder of her page Rickard. "Henri?"

"Why are we moving? Where are we going?" His voice sounded so weak, the young black-haired boy beside him shouted his questions up to Ash.

---

[2] 6 p.m.

"I'll tell you," Ash said grimly. She sat back in her saddle, surveying the mass of people, keenly watching for those slipping away, those already carrying their packs, those familiar faces she couldn't see present.

"You all know my husband. Fernando del Guiz. Well, he's gone over to the enemy."

"Is that *true*?" one of the men-at-arms yelled.

Ash, remembering Constanza, rescued from the tourney field's riot; the tiny woman's absolute distress; her unwillingness to confess to Fernando's peasant wife that the court nobility knew exactly where her son was – remembering this, she pitched her voice to carry further into the dark day:

"Yes, it's true."

Over noise, she continued: "For whatever reason, it seems that Fernando del Guiz has sworn fealty to the Visigoth Caliph."

She let them take it in, then said measuredly, "His estates are south of here, in Bavaria, at a place called Guizburg. I'm told Fernando's occupying the castle there. Well – they're not his estates. The Emperor's put him under attainder. But they're still *my* estates. *Ours*. And that's where we're going. We're going to go south, take what's ours, *and then we'll face this darkness when we're safe behind our own castle walls!*"

The next ten minutes was all shouted arguments, questions, a few ongoing personal quarrels dragged into the discussion, and Ash bellowing at the highest, most carrying pitch of her voice; ramrodding her authority home.

Robert Anselm leaned from his saddle and murmured in her ear. "Christ, girl! If we move this camp, we'll have everybody all *over* the place."

"It'll be chaos," she agreed hoarsely. "But it's this or they panic, run off as refugees, and we're not a company any more. Fernando's neither here nor there – I'm giving them something we can *do*. Something – *anything*. It really doesn't matter what it is!"

The void above *pulls*, sucks at her. The darkness doesn't fade, doesn't give way to dusk or twilight or dawn; hour upon hour upon hour is going by.

"Doing anything," Ash said, "is better than doing nothing. Even if this *is* the end of the world . . . I'm keeping my people together."

II

The striking of the Guizburg town clock reached Ash over the intermittent sound of cannon. Four bell-chimes. Four hours after what would have been midday.

"It's not an eclipse." Antonio Angelotti, where he sat at the end of the trestle table, observed without raising his head: "There's no eclipse due. In any case, madonna, an eclipse lasts hours at most. Not twelve days."

Sheets of ephemerides and his own calculations lay in front of him. Ash put her elbow on Angelotti's table and rested her chin on her hand. Inside this room, boards creaked as Godfrey Maximillian paced up and down. Candlelight shifted. She looked at the shattered frames of the small windows, wishing for lightening air, for the damp cold of dawn, the interminable singing of birds, above all for the sense of freshness, of beginning, that sunrise has outdoors. Nothing. Nothing but darkness.

Joscelyn van Mander put his head around the door of the room, between the guards. "Captain, they won't hear our herald, and they're still shooting at us! The garrison doesn't even admit your husband's inside the keep."

Antonio Angelotti leaned back in his chair. "They've heard the proverb, madonna – 'a castle which speaks, and a woman who listens; both will be taken in the end'."

"They're flying his livery and a Visigoth standard – he's here," Ash observed. "Send a herald every hour. Keep shooting back! Joscelyn, let's get inside there *fast*."

As van Mander left, she added, "We're still better off here – as long as we're containing del Guiz, who's a traitor, the Emperor's happy; and we get a chance to stay out of the way and see how hot this Visigoth army really is . . ."

She got up and strode to the window. Cannon fire had exposed the lath and plaster of the wall by the sill, but it would be easy to patch up, she thought, touching the raw dry material. "Angeli, could your eclipse calculations be wrong?"

"No, because nothing that happened accords with the descriptions." Angelotti scratched at the gathered neck of his shirt. Plainly, he had forgotten the ink stone and the sharpened quill: ink liberally dotted his white linen. He looked at his stained fingers in annoyance. "No penumbra, no gradual eating-away of the disc of the sun, no uneasiness of the beasts of the field. Just instant, icy lightlessness."

He had bone-framed single-rivet spectacles clamped to his nose for reading. As he squinted through the lenses, in the candlelight, Ash noted the lines at the corners of his eyes, the squinching of flesh between his brows. This is how that face will look in ten years, she thought, when the skin is no longer taut, and the shine is off his gold hair.

He finished, "And Jan tells me the horses weren't bothered beforehand."

Robert Anselm, clumping up stairs and entering the room on the tail of this remark, pulled off his hood and said, "The sun darkened – weakened – once when I was in Italy. We must have had four hours' warning from the horse lines."

Ash spread her hands. "If no eclipse, then what?"

"The heavens are out of order . . ." Godfrey Maximillian did not stop pacing. There was a book in his hands, illuminated in red and blue; Ash might have made the text out with enough time to spell it letter by letter. He paused by one of the candles and flicked from page to page with a rapidity that both impressed her and filled her with contempt for a man who had no better use for his time than to learn to read. He did not even read aloud. He read quickly, and silently.

"So? Edward Earl of March saw *three* suns on the morning of the field of Mortimer's Cross. For the Trinity." Robert Anselm hesitated, as ever, mentioning the current English Yorkist king; then muttered aggressively, "Everyone knows the south exists in an eternal twilight, this is nothing to get worked up about. We've got a war to fight!"

Angelotti took off his spectacles. The white bone frames left a red dint across the bridge of his nose. "I can take down the keep walls here in half a day." On the word *day*, his voice lost impetus.

Ash leaned out of the broken window frame. The town outside was mostly invisible in darkness. She sensed a kind of straining in the air, in the odd warm dusk – cooling, now, perhaps – that wanted to be afternoon. The brown beams and pale plaster of the house's façade were dappled with red, reflections from the huge bonfires burning in the market square below. Lanterns shone at every occupied window. She did not look up at the crown of the sky, where no sun shone, only a deep impenetrable blackness.

She looked up at the keep.

Bonfire-light illuminated only the bottom of the sheer walls, shadows flickering on flints and masonry. Slot-windows were eyelets of darkness. The keep rose into darkness above the town, from steep bare slopes of rock; and the road to the gate ran along one wall, from which the defenders had already shot and dropped more killing objects than she thought they had. A slab-sided building like a block of stone.

That's where he is. In some room behind those walls.

She can envisage the round arches, the wooden floors crammed with bed-rolls of men-at-arms, the knights up in the solar on the fourth floor; Fernando perhaps in the great hall, with his dogs and his merchant friends and his handguns . . .

No more than a furlong from where I am now. He could be looking at me. *Why?* Why have you done this? What *is* the truth of it?

Ash said, "I don't want the castle damaged so much that we can't defend it when *we're* in there."

All the armed men she could see in the streets near the keep wore livery jackets with the pewter Lion badge fastened to the shoulder; most of those company people who went unarmed – women selling goods, whores, children – had taken up some kind of strips of blue cloth sewn to their garments. Of the town's citizens, she could see nothing, but she could hear them singing mass in the churches. The clock struck the quarter on the far side of this market square.

She longed for light with a physical desire, like thirst.

"I thought it might end with dawn," she said. "*A* dawn. Any dawn. It still might."

Angelotti stirred his sheets of calculations, scribbled over with the signs of Mercury, Mars; estimations of ballistics. "This is *new*."

Something leonine in the way he stretched his arm reminded Ash of the physical strength he possessed, as well as his male beauty. Points were coming undone at the shoulder of his padded white jack. All the cloth over his chest and arms was pitted with tiny black holes, burned through the linen by sparks from cannon.

Robert Anselm leaned over the master gunner's shoulder, studying the scribbled sheets of paper, and they began to talk in rapid low tones. Anselm thumped the trestle table with his fist several times.

Ash, watching Robert, was assailed by a paradoxical feeling of fragility: he and Angelotti were physically large men, their voices booming now in this room simply because they were used to conversing out of doors. Some part of her, faced by them, was always fourteen, in her first decent breastplate (the rest of her harness munition-quality tat), seeking out Anselm by his campfire after Tewkesbury and saying, out of the flame-ridden darkness, *Raise men for me, I'm fielding a company of my own now.* Asking in the dark because she could not bear a refusal in cold daylight. And then hours spent sleepless and wondering if his curt nod of agreement had been because he was drunk or joking, until he turned up an hour after sunrise with fifty frowsty, cold, unfed, well-equipped men carrying bows and bills, whose names she had immediately had Godfrey write on to a muster-roll. And silenced their uncertainty, their jocular complaints and unspoken hope, with food from the cauldrons she had had Wat Rodway at since midnight. The strands of authority between commander and commanded are spider-webs.

"Why the fuck doesn't it get light. . . ?" Ash leaned out further from the broken frame, staring at the castle's walls above the town. Angelotti's bombard and trebuchet crews had done no more than knock patches of facing plaster off the curtain walls, exposing the grey masonry. She coughed, breathing air that smelled of burning timber, and pulled herself back into the room.

"The scouts are back," Robert Anselm said laconically. "Cologne's burning. Fires out of control. They say there's plague. The court's gone. I have thirty different reports about Frederick of Hapsburg. Euen's lance picked up a couple of men from Berne. None of the passes south over the Alps are passable – either Visigoth armies or bad weather."

Godfrey Maximillian momentarily stopped pacing and looked up from the pages of his book. "Those men Euen found were part of a procession from Berne to the shrine at St Walburga's Abbey. Look at their backs. Those lacerations are from iron-tipped whips. They think flagellation will bring back the sun."

What was similar between Robert Anselm and Godfrey Maximillian, the bald man and the bearded, was perhaps nothing more than breadth of chest, resonance of voice. Whether or not it came from recent sexual activity after long celibacy, Ash found herself aware now of difference, of maleness, in a way in which she was not used to thinking; as something pertaining to physicality rather than prejudice.

"I'll see Quesada again," she informed Anselm, and turned to Godfrey as the other man strode downstairs. "If not an eclipse, then some kind of black miracle—?"

Godfrey paused beside the trestle table, as if Angelotti's astrological scribbles might touch somehow on his biblical readings. "No stars fell, the moon is not as red as blood. The sun isn't darkened because of the smoke of the Pit. The *third* part of the sun should be smitten – that's not what's happening. There have been no Horsemen, no Seals broken. It is not the last days after which the sun shall be darkened."[3]

"No, not the troubles before the Last Judgement," Ash persisted, "but a punishment, a judgement, or an evil miracle?"

"Judgement for what? The princes of Christendom are wicked, but no more wicked than the generation before them. The common people are venal, weak, easily led, and often repentant; this is no alteration from how things have always been. There is distress of nations,[4] but we have never lived in the Age of Gold!" His thick fingertips strayed over curlicued capitals, over painted saints in little illuminated shrines. "I don't know."

"Then bloody well pray for an answer!"

"Yes." He folded the book shut over one finger. His eyes were amber, full of light in the room lit by lanterns and fires. "What use can I be to you without God's help? All I do is puzzle it out from the Gospels, and I think I am more often wrong than right."

"You were ordained, that's good enough for me. You know it is." Ash spoke crudely, knowing exactly why he had left after instruction. "Pray for grace for us."

"Yes."

A shouted challenge, and footsteps sounded on the stairs below.

Ash walked around and seated herself on the stool behind the trestle table. That put her with the Lion Azure standard, leaning on its staff against the wall, at her back. Sallet and gauntlets rested on the table, with her sword-belt, scabbard and sword. Her priest praying in the corner at his Green Shrine. Her master gunner calculating expenditure of powder. More than enough for effect, she calculated, and did not look up for a good thirty heartbeats after she heard Floria del Guiz and Daniel de Quesada enter the room.

De Quesada spoke first, quite rationally. "I shall construe this siege as an attack on the armies of the King-Caliph."

Ash let him listen to the echo of his voice in silence. The lath and plaster walls muffled shouting and the infrequent small cannon fire. Finally she looked at him.

She suggested mildly, "Tell the Caliph's representatives that Fernando del Guiz is my husband, that he is now under an act of attainder, that I am acting on my own behalf in recovering what is now my property since he was stripped of it by the Emperor Frederick."

Daniel de Quesada's face was crusted with healing scabs, where the hairs of his beard had been ripped out. His eyes were dull. His words came with an effort. "So you besiege your husband's castle, with him in it, and he is now a sworn feudal subject of King-Caliph Theodoric – but that is not an act of aggression against us?"

"Why should it be? These are my lands." Ash leaned forward over linked hands. "I'm a mercenary. The world's gone crazy. I want my company *inside* stone walls. Then I'll think about who's going to hire me."

De Quesada still had a febrile nervousness, despite Floria's opiates and

[3] See Revelation 6: 12; Revelation 9: 2; Revelation 8: 12, and Matthew 24: 29, respectively.
[4] Luke 21: 25.

restraining hand on his arm. The doublet and hose and rolled chaperon hat he had been given sat awkwardly on him; you could see he was not used to moving in such clothes.

"We can't lose," he said.

"I usually find myself on the winning side." That was ambiguous enough for Ash to let it rest. "I'll give you an escort, Ambassador. I'm sending you back to your people."

"I thought I was a prisoner!"

"I'm not Frederick. I'm not a subject of Frederick." Ash gave a nod, dismissing him. "Wait over there a minute. Florian, I want to speak with you."

Daniel de Quesada looked around the room, then walked across the uneven floorboards as if across the uncertain deck of a ship, hesitating at the door, finally moving to stand in a corner farthest from the windows.

Ash stood up and poured wine into a wooden goblet and offered it to Floria. She spoke briefly in English – it being the language of a small, barbaric, unknown island, there was a sporting chance the Visigoth diplomat might not understand it. "How mad is he? What can I ask him about this darkness?"

"Barking. *I* don't know!" The surgeon hitched one hip up on to the trestle table and sat, long leg swinging. "They may be used to their ambassadors coming back God-struck, if they send them out with messages about signs and portents. He's probably functional. I can't promise he'll stay that way if you start asking him questions."

"Tough. We need to know." She signalled the Visigoth. He came forward again. "Master Ambassador, one other thing. I want to know when it's going to get light again."

"Light?"

"When the sun's going to rise. When it's going to stop being dark!"

"The sun . . ." Daniel de Quesada shivered, not turning his head towards the window. "Is there fog outside?"

"How would I know? It's black as your hat out there!" Ash sighed. *Evidently I can forget a sensible answer from this one.* "No, master Ambassador. It's dark. Not foggy."

He huddled his arms around himself. Something about the shape of his mouth made Ash shiver: adult men in their right minds do not look like this.

"We were separated. Almost at the top – there was fog. I climbed." Quesada's staccato Carthaginian Gothic was barely comprehensible. "Up, up, up. A winding road, in snow. Ice. Climbing for ever, until I could only crawl. Then a great wind came; the sky was *purple* above me. Purple, and all the white peaks, so high above— Mountains. I cling. There is only air. The rock makes my hands bleed—"

Ash, with her own memory of a sky so dark blue it burns, and thin air that hurts the chest, said to Floria, "He's talking about the Gotthard Pass, now. Where the monks found him."

Floria put a firm hand on the man's arm. "Let's get you back to the infirmary, Ambassador."

Half-alert, Daniel de Quesada met Ash's gaze.

"The fog – went." He moved his hands apart, like a man opening a curtain.

Ash said, "It was clear a month ago, when we crossed the pass with Fernando. Snow on the rocks either side, but the road was clear. I know where they must have found you, Ambassador. I've stood there. You can stand and look straight down into Italy. Straight down, seven thousand feet."

The wagons creak, horses straining against the ascent; the breath of the men-at-arms streams on the air; and she stands, the cold striking up through the soles of her boots, and peers down a mottled green-and-white cliff face, funnelling down towards the foothills. But it seems puny to call it a cliff, this southern side of the saddle-pass across the Alps; the mountains rise up in a half-circle that is miles across.

And it is almost a mile and a half straight down.

Sheer rock, moss and ice, and a vastness of empty air so big and deep that it hurts the mind to look at it.

She finished quietly, "If you fell, you'd never touch the earth until you hit bottom."

"Straight down!" Daniel de Quesada echoed. His eyes flashed. "I found I was looking— The road below me, winding down bend upon bend upon bend. There is a lake at the bottom. It is no larger than the nail upon my finger."

Ash remembers the interminable straining fear of the descent, and how the lake, when they got down to it, was quite large, and nestled in foothills: they were not off the mountain even then.

"The fog cleared and *I was looking down.*"

All the room was silent. After a minute, it became apparent to Ash that there was to be no more from him. De Quesada stared with unseeing eyes at the shifting shadows.

As Floria was handing the Visigoth over to one of her aides, Angelotti said, "I've known men blindfold themselves going over the alpine passes, afraid of going mad.[5] I didn't think I should meet one, madonna."

"I think you just have." Ash looked after de Quesada grimly. "Well, picking him up in the riots in the hope he'd be some use wasn't one of my better ideas. I'd hoped he'd negotiate with del Guiz when we got here."

"He's away with the fairies," Floria remarked. "If you want my medical opinion. Not the best qualification for a herald."

Ash snorted. "I don't care if he's nuts. I want *answers.* I don't like this darkness!"

"Who does?" Floria inquired rhetorically. She snorted. "You want to know how many of your men have developed acute attacks of coward's belly?"

"No. Why do you think I want to keep them busy with a siege? They're used to tunnelling petards and banging away with cannon, it reassures them . . . That's why the men-at-arms are going through this town street by street commandeering supplies – if they're going to loot the place, it might as well be *organised* looting."

This appeal to her cynicism made Floria chuckle, as Ash had known it would. There was so little difference between Floria and 'Florian', even down to the gallantry with which the tall woman offered now to pour wine for Ash herself.

[5] Recorded in several fifteenth-century travellers' accounts of their alpine journeys.

"It's no different from night attacks," Ash added, refusing wine, "which are, God knows, a bitch, but possible. I want this castle opened up by treachery, not damaged by us having to storm it. Speaking of which—" the restlessness that came with her failure to interrogate de Quesada impelled her to action "— you come with me and look at this. Angelotti!"

They left the room, the gunner with them; Ash glancing back to see Godfrey Maximillian, broad shoulders bowed, still at prayer. Outside – walking into a wall of darkness, pitch-black down in the streets – they silently stood for some minutes, waiting for night vision, before stumbling towards the bonfire-lights.

The town blacksmith's had been taken over by the company armourers, a perpetually black-handed group of men with straggling hair, hatless, in pourpoints[6] and leather aprons and no shirts, sweating from the forge, half-deaf from the ceaseless ringing of hammers. They made way good-naturedly for Ash, her surgeon, and her escort of half a dozen men and dogs. No commander was ever more than means to an end for them, this she knew. The latest project was difficult, welcome because of that, welcome because unusual.

"A twelve-foot pair of *bolt-cutters*?" Floria surmised, studying vast steel handles.

"It's getting the blades right?" The company's head armourer, Dickon Stour, habitually ended on a note of query, even when not speaking his native English. "To withstand the pressure, and to cut iron?"

"And those are scaling ladders," Ash said. She pointed at stout wooden poles with steel hooks on the end, and a mess of spars attached. Hook it over a wall, tug ropes, and a ladder will unfold from the mess. "I'm going to send people in secretly with black wool over their armour, to cut the big bars on the postern gate from the inside. I would say, at night, but in this darkness—" A shrug and grin. "Stealth knights . . ."

"You're mad. *They're* mad. I want to talk to you!" Floria scowled at the noise from the anvils and pointed, silently, at the street. Ash shook hands, thumped shoulders, left with her escort. Angelotti stayed, discussing metallurgy.

Ash caught up with the surgeon a few yards away, staring up from the cobbled street that ran up the hill, to the shadowy machicolations and timber-works of the castle crowning the heights.

Floria walked fast, a few paces ahead of the men-at-arms and hounds. "Are you really going to try that?"

"We did it before. Two years back, in – where was it?" Ash thought. "Somewhere in southern France?"

"That *is* my brother in there." The woman's voice came masculine out of the dusk, a breathy drop into lower registers that never relaxed, whether the command escort could hear her or not. "Granted I haven't seen him since he was ten. Granted he was a brat. And now he's a shit. But blood's blood. He *is* family."

"Family. Yeah. Tell me how much *I* care about family."

Floria began, "What—?"

"What? Will I give orders for him to be taken prisoner, not killed? Will I let

6 'Pourpoint': a waistcoat-like garment, to which hose can be tied.

him run, go off and raise men somewhere else to come back and fight me? Will I have him killed? What?"

"All of those."

"It seems unreal." Unreal, when I have had his body inside me, to believe that he could die with an arrow through the throat, a billhook slashing his gut; that someone with a bollock dagger and my express order could make him *not be*.

"Damn it, you can't go on ignoring this, girl! You fucked him. You married him. He's your flesh in the sight of God."

"That's a dumb thing to say. You don't believe in God." Ash could, in the torchlit streets, make out the sudden strain etching itself into the woman's face. "Florian, I'm not likely to go around denouncing you to the local bishop, am I! Soldiers either believe completely, or not at all, and I've got both sorts in the company."

The tall woman continued walking down the cobblestones beside her, all her balance in her shoulders: gangling and masculine. She made an irritated motion that might have been a shrug or a flinch as Angelotti's siege cannon crashed out smoke and flame, two streets away. "You're *married*!"

"Time enough to decide what to do about Fernando when I've got him and his garrison out of that castle." Ash shook her head as if she could clear it, somehow; clear the oppressive, unnatural darkness out of her skull.

She called the commander of the escort to her as she reached the commandeered town house again, ordering a brazier and food for his men in the street; and then clumped back up the stairs, Floria at her shoulder, only to walk into what seemed an entire company of people crammed between narrow white walls, helmet-plumes rubbing the candle-stained ceiling, voices raised.

"*Quiet!*"

That got silence.

She gazed around.

Joscelyn van Mander, his red-cheeked intense face framed by the brilliance of his steel sallet; two of his men; then Robert Anselm; Godfrey rising from his knees and disrupted prayer; Daniel de Quesada in his badly fitting European clothes – and a new man in white tunic and trousers and riveted mail hauberk, no weapons.

A Visigoth, with leather rank badges laced to his mail shoulders. *Qa'id*, she dredged up out of her memory of campaigns in Iberia: an officer set over a thousand. Roughly the equivalent of her own command.

"Well?" she said, reclaiming her place behind the table, and sitting. Rickard appeared and poured heavily watered wine for her. She dropped without thought into the dialect she had learned around Tunisian soldiers; something as automatic to her as calling a hackbutter an arquebusier in the French king's lands, or a poleaxe *der Axst* here and *l'azza* to Angelotti. "What's your business, *Qa'id*?"

"Captain." The Visigoth soldier touched his fingers to his forehead. "I met my countryman de Quesada and your escort, on the road. He decided to return here with me, to speak to you. I bring news to you."

The Visigoth soldier was small, fair-skinned, hardly taller than Rickard; with the palest blue eyes, and something about him that was undeniably familiar. Ash said, "Is your family name Lebrija?"

He seemed startled. "Yes."

"Continue. What news?"

"There will be other messengers, of your own people—"

Ash's gaze flicked to Anselm, who nodded, confirming: "Yes. I met them. I was on my way here when Joscelyn came in."

"*You* may have the honour of telling me," Ash told the Visigoth *qa'id* mildly, hating to hear news unprepared; hating not to have the few minutes' warning she would have had if Robert had been the one to tell her. Since Joscelyn van Mander seemed intensely worried, she switched back to German. "What's happened?"

"Frederick of Hapsburg has sued for terms."

There was a little silence, essentially undisturbed by Floria muttering "Fuck," and Joscelyn van Mander's demand: "Captain, what does he mean?"

"I think he means that the territories of the Holy Roman Emperor have surrendered." Ash linked her hands in front of her. "Master Anselm, is that what our messengers say?"

"Frederick's surrendered. Everything from the Rhine to the sea is open to the Visigoth armies." In an equally level tone, Robert Anselm added, "And Venice has been burned to the waterline. Churches, houses, warehouses, ships, canal-bridges, St Mark's Basilica, the Doge's palace, everything. A million, million ducats up in smoke."

The silence became intense: mercenaries stunned at the waste of wealth, the two Visigoth men imbued with a silent confidence, being associated with the power to make such destruction.

Frederick of Hapsburg will have heard about Venice, Ash thought, stunned, hearing in her mind the dry, covetous voice of the Holy Roman Emperor; *he's decided not to risk the Germanies!* And then, bringing her gaze snap into focus on the Visigoth soldier, brother or cousin of dead Asturio Lebrija, she realised, *The Empire has surrendered and we're caught on the wrong side.* Every mercenary's nightmare.

"I assume," she said, "that a relieving force from the Visigoth army is now on its way here to Fernando?"

Her vision of where they are flips a hundred and eighty degrees. It's no longer a matter of feeling herself safe behind town walls, soon to be safe behind the castle walls. Now the company's caught in between the approaching Visigoth men-at-arms in the countryside beyond the town, and Fernando del Guiz's knights and gunners up in the castle itself.

Daniel de Quesada spoke rustily. "Of course. Our allies must be helped."

"Of course," the brother or cousin of Lebrija echoed.

Quesada could not yet have told the *qa'id* of Lebrija's death, might not know anything, Ash thought, and resolved to keep silent where speech could very likely get her into trouble.

"I'll be interested to talk to your captain when he arrives," Ash stated. She watched her own officers out of peripheral vision, seeing them draw strength from her confidence.

"Our commander arrives here by tomorrow," the Visigoth soldier estimated. "We are most anxious to talk to you. The famous Ash. That's why our commander is coming here, now."

Sun gone out or not, Ash thought, I am not going to get the time I want to consider my decisions. Whether I like it or not, it's happening *now*.

And then:

Sun gone out or not, Last Days or not, it is nothing to do with me: if I stand by my company, we're strong enough to survive this. The metaphysics of it aren't my problem.

"Right," she said. "I'd better meet your commander and open negotiations."

Rickard presented Bertrand, a possible half-brother of Philibert, at thirteen busy growing into a body far too large for him, managing simultaneously to be fat and gangling. They put Ash into her armour and brought Godluc in his best barding; the boys smear-eyed with lack of sleep, at an hour which might have been dawn, if this third day in Guizburg had had one.

"As far as I can tell, their commander's personal name is actually the name of her rank," Godfrey Maximillian said. "Faris.[7] It means Captain-General, General of all their forces, something like that."

"Her rank? A woman commander?" Ash remembered, then, Asturio Lebrija saying *I have met women of war*, and his sense of humour, which his cousin Sancho (Godfrey reporting the name and fact) did not possess at all. "And she's here now? The boss of the whole damn invasion force?"

"Just down the road from Innsbruck."

"Shit . . ."

Godfrey went to the door, calling a man in from the main room of the commandeered house. "Carracci, the boss wants to hear it herself."

A man-at-arms with startling white-blond hair and high colour on his cheeks, who had stripped off all but a minimum of his shabby foot soldier's kit to travel fast, came in and made a courtesy. "I got right up to their command tent! It's a woman, boss. A woman leading their army; and you know how they've made her good? She's got one of those Brazen Head machines of theirs, it does her thinking for her in battles – they say she hears its voice! She hears it talk!"

"If it's a Brazen Head,[8] of course she hears it talk!"

"No, boss. She doesn't have it with her. She hears it in her head, like God speaking to a priest."

Ash stared at the billman.

"She hears it like a saint's voice, it tells her how to fight. *That's* why a woman beat us." Carracci suddenly stopped talking, lifted a shoulder, and at last gave a hopeful grin. "Oops. Sorry, boss?"

---

[7] This appears to be the del Guiz *Life*'s mistranslation of a Saracen term. *Faris* is Arabic for 'horseman', meaning the ordinary professional cavalry knight, rather than an army commander. However, I have chosen to use *faris* since the better alternative given in the Angelotti manuscript, the Muslim *al-sayyid*, 'chieftain' or 'master', already exists in European history – as the title of Rodrigo de Vivar: 'El Cid'.

[8] Fr Roger Bacon (*c.*1214–1292) was an early scientist, and the actual European inventor of gunpowder. He was popularly supposed to have been a sorcerer, and was credited with inventing a mechanical speaking head, made of brass; later destroyed.

She hears it like a saint's voice.

A pulse of coldness went through the pit of Ash's stomach. She was aware that she blinked, stared, said nothing; chill with an as yet unidentifiable shock. She wet her lips.

"Bloody right you're sorry . . ."

It was an automatic response. This billman, Carracci, had clearly not heard *Ash hears saints' voices!* as a company rumour: most – especially those who had been with her for years – would have done.

Does she hear a saint, this Faris? Does she? Or does she only think it's a useful rumour? Burned as a witch is no way to end . . .

"Thanks, Carracci," she added absently. "Join the escort. Tell them we're riding in five minutes."

As Carracci left, she turned back to Godfrey. It's difficult to feel vulnerable, laced and tied into steel. She put the billman's words out of her mind. Her confidence came back with her stride across the small room, the trestle bare of waiting armour now, to the window, where she stood and looked out at Guizburg's fires.

"I think you're right, Godfrey. They're going to offer us a contract."

"I've talked to travellers from a number of monasteries this side of the mountains. As I said, I can't get a real idea of their numbers, but there is at least one other Visigoth army fighting in Iberia."

Ash kept her back to him. "Voices. They say she hears voices. *That's* odd."

"As a rumour, it has its uses."

"Don't I know it!"

"Saints are one thing," Godfrey said. "Claiming a miracle voice from an engine, that's another. She might be thought a demon. She might *be* a demon."

"Yes."

"Ash—"

"There isn't the time to worry about this, okay?" She turned and glared at Godfrey. "*Okay?*"

He watched her, brown eyes calm. He did not nod.

Ash said, "We have to make our minds up fast, if the Visigoths *do* make us an offer. Fernando and his men are just waiting to find us caught between hammer and anvil. Then it'll be up with his castle drawbridge, and sally out and take us right in the back. Yippee," she said dourly, and then grinned over her armoured shoulder at the priest. "*Won't* he be sick if we're contracted to the same side? We're mercenaries, but he's an attainted traitor – I still reckon this castle's mine."

"Don't count your castles before they're stormed."

"Should that be a proverb, do you think?" She sobered. "We *are* between hammer and anvil. Let's hope they need us on their side more than they need to get rid of us. Otherwise I should have decided to move us out, not stay put. And it's going to be very short and very bloody up here."

The priest's broad hand came down on her left pauldron. "It's bloody where the Visigoths are fighting the Guilds, up near Lake Lucerne. Their commander will probably buy any fighting force they can get, especially one that's got local knowledge."

"And then put us in the front line to die, rather than their own men. *I* know how it goes." She moved cautiously, turning; armour can be considered a weapon in itself, if you are only wearing a brown pleated woollen robe and sandals. Godfrey's hand slid away from the sharp metal plates. She met his brown-eyed gaze.

"It's remarkable what you can get used to. A week, ten days ... The question no one wants to ask, of course, is – after the sun, what? What *else* can happen?" Ash knelt stiffly. "Bless me before I ride out. I'd like to be in good grace right now."

His deep, familiar voice sang a blessing.

"Ride with me," she directed, a heartbeat after he finished, and made for the stairs. Godfrey followed her downstairs and out into the town.

Ash mounted and rode through the streets, with her officers and escort, men-at-arms and dogs. She reined Godluc in when a procession passed, jamming the narrow street, men and women wailing, their woollen doublets and kirtles deliberately slashed, faces streaked with ashes. Merchants and craftsmen. Bare, bloody-footed boys in white carried a Virgin between green wax candles. Town priests whipped them with steel-toothed whips. Ash took off her helmet and waited while the lamenting, praying crowd stumbled past.

When the noise level dropped to the point where she could be heard, she replaced her sallet and called, "On!"

She rode with fifty men, past bone-fires that burned the clock round now, out through the gates of Guizburg. They passed some of her own men coming in from expeditions to untouched forest, dragging loads of pine for torches. What she thought were silver pine-needles were, she saw as she rode close, pine-needles covered in frost. Frost. In July.

The wheel of the mill was silent, above where they splashed across the ford; and in the darkness she could just see cows straying, not knowing when to come in to be milked. An odd half-song came from copses, birds uncertain whether to sleep or to claim territory. Oppressiveness prickled her spine, under the pinked silk lining of her arming doublet, and made her sweat; all this before she saw a thousand torches down the shallow valley, and the silver eagle Visigoth standards, and heard drums.

Joscelyn van Mander demanded reassurance, his eyes on the spearmen and bowmen down the slope. "I never fought Visigoths, what's it like?"

Ash leaned her upright lance back against her armoured shoulder. Its foxtail pennant hung in the still air. Godluc frisked, his tail bound up with a chaplet of oak-leaves and folly-bells. "Angelotti?"

Antonio Angelotti rode beside her, armoured, a Saint Barbara medal knotted around the cuff of his gauntlet. "When I was with the Lord-*Amir* Childeric, we put down a local rebellion. I had captaincy of the English hackbutters.[9] The Visigoths are raiders. *Karr wa farr*: repeated attack and retreat. Hit and run, cut your supply lines, deny you the fords, indifferent sieges for a year or three, then

[9] 'Hackbut': English for 'arquebus', a man-portable gun.

162

take the city by storm. I have not known them seek out the enemy army for a pitched battle. They've changed tactics."

"Evidently." There was a strong smell of unwatered beer from van Mander.

Ash checked back, twisting in the high, upright war saddle. Apart from the usual command officers, she had brought Euen Huw and his lance; Jan-Jacob Clovet and thirty bowmen; ten men picked from van Mander's band, and her steward Henri Brant – torso swathed in bandages – to oversee on behalf of the non-combatants. A majority of her riders carried torches.

Angelotti said, "You should have let my bombards open up the Guizburg keep. It would be much harder to get us out of that, madonna."

"Try not to think of it as *a* pile of rubble, but as *our* pile of rubble. I'd like it kept in one piece!"

Confident of the number and disposition of this part of the Visigoth forces at least, the company's scouts being reliable, Ash rode on down the slope between neatly sectioned fields and wattle-fenced animal pens. The company standard and her personal banner rode in the mass of men, dark against the unnatural dark sky, among the jolting, flaring torches.

They topped a slight rise. Ash kept Godluc moving forward when he would have responded to the shift in her weight as she saw what lay a little distance off. It is one thing to be reliably informed that there is a division of an army, eight or nine thousand men plus baggage train, encamped just off the Innsbruck road. It is another to see a hundred thousand torches, bright bonfires, hear the whickering and stamping from the horse lines, and the shouting of guards; glimpse, in the lightless day, the vast wheel of tents, spidered with guy-ropes, thronging with armed men and circled with wagons, that is that army in the flesh.

Ash drew rein at the appointed rendezvous, a crossroads milestone, and thumbed her sallet's visor up. All her party rode in full armour, by her orders; horses fully barded and caparisoned; coloured silk scarves twisted around helmets, plume-holders on sallets and armets frothing with white ostrich feathers. The mounted crossbowmen had their weapons out of their cases, and bolts close to hand.

"There," she said, straining to see through the darkness.

A rider with a white lance pennant rode up from the Visigoth encampment. After a while she managed to distinguish European armour, the rounded curves of Milanese plate, and a straggle of black hair curling out from under the neck of his armet. "It's Agnes!"

Robert Anselm growled, "Jammy sod. Trust Lamb to get hired."

"In the middle of a fucking battle! He must have signed a contract while they were still having that skirmish." In so far as her armour allowed it, Ash shook her head ruefully. "Don't you just love Italian mercenaries?"

They met in the stink of smoking pine torches. Lamb carefully unpinned the visor of his armet, showing his tanned face. "Planning a quick getaway, are we?"

"Unless the whole Visigoth army down there comes after us, we'd make it back through the town gates." Ash slotted her lance into its saddle holster to give her hands freedom. She spoke mainly for the benefit of her officers. "And unless your employer *really* wants to be sitting in front of one tiny Bavarian castle for the next twelve weeks, I don't think she'll be too interested in trying to prise us out of Guizburg."

"Perhaps." Ambiguous.

"Tell your general that we're understandably not keen about riding into her camp, but if she wants to ride up here, we'll negotiate."

"That's the word I wanted to hear." Lamb wheeled his lean, bony roan gelding, held up his lance, and dipped the white pennant to the dirt. Another group of riders moved out from the wagon-fort, perhaps forty strong. Too far away in the darkness to see detail, they could be any group of armed men.

"So how much extra did you get paid for riding up here on your own?"

"Enough. But I'm told you treat hostages well." A flirtatious curve of the lips; Agnus Dei's religious convictions not (by common rumour) extending as far as celibacy. Ash smiled back, thinking of Daniel de Quesada and Sancho Lebrija, now being compulsorily entertained in Guizburg until she should return unhurt.

"Nothing in the city states is holding out now except Milano," Lamb added, ignoring Antonio Angelotti's sudden obscenity; "and of the Swiss cantons, only Berne."

"They fucked the *Swiss*?" Ash was stunned into momentary silence. "Their lines of supply go back clear across the Mediterranean; they can keep armies like this in the field, and still push on north? And hold down territory behind them?"

It was very inelegant fishing for information, or rather, a restating of information that her sources informed her was true. Ash's attention fixed on the approaching riders.

Lamb proved close-mouthed. "Twenty years of preparation helps, I think, madonna Ash."

"Twenty years. I find it hard to imagine. That's as long as I've been alive." The mention of her youth was entirely malicious, Lamb being in his early thirties. So young, so famous; better not to be over-confident as well, she concluded, and waited for the riders to come up the slope. A wind swept over the dark grass, rustling the pine forests in the distance. There was a sense in her, almost physical, like the sensation of successfully riding a mettlesome horse of which one is barely in control.

"Sweet Christ," she murmured joyfully, almost to herself, "it's Armageddon. Everything's changing. Christendom being turned upside-down. Who'd be a peasant now?"

"Or a merchant. Or a lord." Lamb drew in his reins. "This is the only trade to be in, *cara*."

"You think so? Fighting's all I can do." A rare moment: she and the straggle-haired man apprehended each other very clearly. Ash said, "Stay in the fighting line until you're thirty and you die, so I command. Stay in command until you're old, forty or so, and you die. Hence—" A wave of her armoured hand back at Guizburg. "The game of princes."

"Mmm?" Lamb turned both body and head, in his plate harness, so that he could look directly at her. "Oh yes, *cara*. I heard rumours that half your trouble was, you wanted an estate and title. As for myself—" He sighed, with some degree of content. "I have my money for the last two campaigns invested in the English wool trade."

"Invested?" Ash stared at him.

"And I own a dye-works in Bruges now. Very comfortable."

Ash became aware that her mouth was open. She shut it.

"So who needs land?" Agnus Dei concluded.

"Uh . . . yeah." Ash switched her attention back to the Visigoths. "You've been with them, what, two weeks or more? Lamb, what's the deal here?"

The Italian mercenary touched the lamb on his surcoat. "Ask yourself if you have a choice, madonna, and if not, what does my answer matter?"

"She's *good*." Ash watched the torchlit procession coming closer. Close enough to see the outriders, four robed and veiled men on mules, with what looked like open-frame octagonal barrels resting on their saddles in front of them. Something wrong about the size of the men's heads and bodies. She identified them as dwarfs, a moment after she realised the red and gilded leather sides of the barrels were being struck with sticks; were, in fact, wardrums. The growing vibration made Godluc's ears go back.

Ash said, in a rush, "She kicked our asses at Genoa. You believe all this stuff about a brazen head machine telling her what to do? Have you seen it?"

"No. Her men say the brazen head, that they call her 'Stone Golem', isn't here with her. It's in Carthage."

"But the time you'd spend waiting for an answer – messages, riders on posthorses, pigeons – then she can't be using it in the field. Not in real-time *combat*."

"But her men say she does. They say she hears it *at the same time as it speaks in the Citadel*, in Carthage." He paused. "I don't know, madonna. They say she's a woman, so she can only be this good if it's voices."

Lamb's sly comment stung. Ash momentarily ignored him, caught up in an idea of what it might mean if one could be in constant real-time communication with one's home city and commanders, thousands of miles away.

"A Stone Golem . . ." she said slowly. "Lamb, hearing Our Lord's saints is one thing; hearing a *machine*—"

"It's probably just the rumour-mill," Lamb snapped. "Half of what they *say* they have in North Africa, they *don't* have; just manuscripts and some greatgrandfather's memories. This woman is new, and a commander of armies. There will of course be ridiculous stories. There always are."

Something about his rapid speech made her glance at Agnus: the Lamb was undoubtedly on edge. She caught the gaze of Robert Anselm, Geraint ab Morgan, Angelotti; all her officers in readiness for this, which might be a negotiation, and might be an ambush, and must in any case be endured long enough to find out. She looked down for Godfrey Maximillian's palfrey. The priest was staring at the approaching torches.

"Pray for us," she ordered.

The bearded man gripped his cross, his lips moving.

More torches bloomed, lower, carried by men on foot. Ash heard a superstitious oath from Robert Anselm. The torch-carriers were clay and brass figures of men, golems bearing streaming pitch-torches whose light flowed over their featureless red and ochre skins.

"Nice," she admitted. "If I were her, and had something that disconcerting, I'd use it too."

The Visigoth horses came on, between two lines of golems. Little high-stepping horses, with desert blood in them, and gilded leather tack that lay across their necks and their rumps; each bit and ring and stirrup flashing in the torchlight. They brought a smell of spicy horse dung, perceptibly different from that of the thick-necked European war-horses. Godluc stirred. Ash gripped his rein. Some of those are mares, she thought; and I've never been convinced Godluc realises he's been cut. The darting shadows bothered Godfrey's palfrey; she indicated a bowman should get down and hold the bridle, so that Godfrey could continue uninterrupted prayer.

Behind the Visigoth riders came the standard-bearer, with a black flag and an eagle on a pole. His horse was armoured, and Ash smiled to herself at that, having carried the standard in a number of battles and come to understand what her voices meant by the term *fire magnet*. An armoured poet rode beside him, singing something too colloquial for her to understand, but she remembered the custom from Tunis: *cantadors*, for morale.

"What a racket. I wonder if they're trying to impress us?" Ash sat in the tall saddle, her legs almost straight in the stirrups, centre of gravity at hips or just below: a different feeling to walking in armour. She shifted imperceptibly, keeping Godluc still. The Visigoth horses jangled as they came to a halt. Lances and shields, swords and light crossbows . . . She studied men wearing mail hauberks over padded armour, with white surcoats and open-face helmets. They leaned from their saddles towards each other, talking openly, some of them pointing at the European mercenary knights.

"No," Ash said cheerfully, picking one and letting her voice carry, "we don't, as it happens. Besides, you don't get goats in these mountains. Male *or* female."

A spurt of laughter, cursing, and alarm followed her speech. Geraint ab Morgan slapped his armoured thigh. A better-armed Visigoth rider under the black pennant-and-eagle standard spoke to men either side, then urged a chestnut mare forward.

Not to be outdone, Ash signalled. Euen Huw blew three clear notes on the trumpet he unwillingly carried. Ash rode forward in a clatter of horse barding, six officers with her – Anselm, Geraint, and Joscelyn van Mander in gleaming Milanese full plate; Angelotti in a Milanese breastplate and fluted, intricate Gothic leg harness; Godfrey (still praying, eyes shut) in his best monastic robe, and Floria del Guiz in someone's borrowed brigandine and archer's sallet, looking nothing like a woman, and, sadly, nothing much like a soldier either, Ash had to admit.

"I'm Ash," she said into the silence after the trumpet. "Agnus Dei tells me you're interested in a contract with us."

Ash could not make out the Visigoth leader's face under her helmet in the moving shadows.

The woman wore steel helmet and greaves, banded sabatons visible in her stirrups. Torchlight flowed richly over her crimson velvet-covered body armour: a coat-of-plates with a hundred big flower-shaped rivet-heads gleaming gold. Mail was visible under it, at her thigh. A standing plate collar must be a gorget of some sort, Ash surmised; and she noted a trilobed gilded sword-hilt, sword and dagger scabbards with gold chapes, sword-belt with heavy gold decoration; and the blue-black and white chequer of a cloak lined with vair.[10] Ash had the price of each totted up in seconds and was impressed despite herself. She could not help the spasm of pure pleasure she felt at seeing another woman commanding armed troops; especially one foreign enough not to be a competitor.

"You would fight Burgundians." The woman's voice, penetrating, spoke German with a Carthaginian accent. It argued that she wanted to be understood by those of Ash's entourage who did not speak Carthaginian.

"Fight Burgundians? Not for choice. They're hard bastards." Ash shrugged. "I don't risk my company for no good reason."

"You are 'Ash'. The *jund*."[11] The armoured chestnut mare moved forward, coming into the light of Ash's torches. The woman wore a helmet with a nasal bar, and a mail aventail hanging from its edges. A black scarf swathed her shoulders and lower face. There is little detail visible in helmet-framed eyes, which was all Ash could see, but enough to make her suddenly realise *She's young! My God. She's no older than me!*

It explained something of Lamb's edginess: a malicious desire to see these two female freaks, as he undoubtedly considered them, meet each other. Ash out of pure perversity immediately warmed to the Visigoth commander.

"Faris," Ash said. "General. Make me an offer. I've tended to fight on the side of the Burgundians when chance offered, but we can handle them if necessary."

"You have my ally here."

"He's my husband. I think that gives me prior claim."

"Your siege must be lifted. As part of the contract."

"Whoa. Too fast. I always consult with my men." Ash put up a hand. Something bothered her about the Visigoth general's voice. She would have edged Godluc closer, but the torchlight flickered on the points of arrows, easily nocked, in some cases lying across Visigoth riders' laps; and some of her own men very definitely had lances in their hands rather than socketed at the saddle. Weapons have their own life, their own tension; she could have said, with complete accuracy, how many Visigoth riders were looking at her and judging distance. She could feel the invisible connection.

Purely from a desire to gain a minute or two to think, Ash found herself asking the question most on her mind. "Faris – when will we see the sun again?"

---

[10] Back and belly fur of a European squirrel.
[11] Arabic: a mercenary, a soldier who fights for money or land-grants.

"When we choose." The woman's young voice sounded calm.

It also sounded, to Ash, like a lie; having told enough lies in public in her own time. *So you don't know either? The Caliph back in Carthage doesn't tell his general everything?* The yellow light of torches grew to a glare, the clay walkers making a half-circle to either side of their general. Fine-linked mail armour glinted.

"What are you offering?"

"Sixty thousand ducats. Contracted for the duration of this war."

Sixty *thou*—

As plain as if it were her inner voice, she could hear Robert Anselm think, *If the bitch has money to burn, don't argue with her!*

Ash gave herself a second or two to consider by reaching up and unbuckling her sallet, and taking the helmet off; this also being a sign to her men to stand down – or at any rate, not to do anything rash unless aggressive intent became very clear on the Visigoth side.

Lamb stripped a gauntlet off and bit at his fingers.

Ash pushed her bound silver hair (sweaty from its confinement as her helmet lining) out of her face, and glanced at the Visigoth general. After a long hesitation the young woman reached up and took off her mail-hung helmet, and pulled off her veil.

One of the Visigoth riders swore, violently. His mount lifted both front feet off the earth, and cannoned into the man beside him. A strident roar of voices made Ash grab at Godluc's reins, left-handed. Godfrey Maximillian opened his eyes and she saw him look directly ahead.

"Jesus Christ!" Godfrey exclaimed.

The young Visigoth Faris sat her horse in torchlight. She moved her scarlet-armoured body, encouraging the chestnut mare forward a pace, and stared. Shifting shadows and light gleamed from the waterfall of her silver hair.

Her brows were dark, sweeping, definite; her eyes a dark brilliance; but it was the mouth that gave it to Ash: Ash thought, *I have seen that mouth in a mirror, every time there has been a mirror to hand*; and took in the same length of arm and leg, solid small hips, strong shoulders, even – which she had not seen – the same way of sitting a saddle.

She brought her gaze back to the Visigoth woman's face.

No scars.

If there had been scars, she would have fallen off her horse and gone face-down on the earth, praying to the Christ, praying against madness and demons and whatever inhabitant of the Pit this might be. But the woman's cheeks were flawless and unmarked.

The Visigoth woman general wore no expression at all now, her features frozen, stone.

In the same second that armed men in both the European and Visigoth groups crowded their horses closer, Ash realised, *So that's what I look like without scars.*

No scars.

In everything other than that – we are twins.

III

The Faris held up one arm and said something too sharp and quick for Ash to understand.

"I'll send my *qa'id* to you with a contract!" the Visigoth general added. An urging movement of her body sent the chestnut Barb round on the spot, haunches bunched, then galloping away. And the rest of them with her, instantly. Drums, eagle, dwarfs, poets and armed thugs, all clattering down the dark slope towards the Visigoth camp.

"Back to town." Ash heard her own voice sharp and hoarse, in the silence. Thinking, *how many of them saw – perhaps a few men, close to me – thirty heartbeats to see a face in darkness – but word will soon get around, turn to rumour—* "Back to the town!"

For the next five days she was never at any moment speaking to fewer than two people at a time, and sometimes it was three.

Godfrey brought her the Visigoths' contract for the company, its meticulous Latin checked for her to sign. She signed; midway through remonstrating with Gustav and his foot knights for attempting a last raid on Guizburg castle, and that itself midway between counting remounts and sacks of oatmeal with Henri Brant, listening to complaints from hand-gunners about lack of powder, and hearing from Florian – *Floria!* – how wounds did or did not mend. By the first midnight, she had visited each lance of men at their own billets, agreeing the contract.

"We move at night," Ash announced. In part because at night *some* light existed – the moon waning into its last quarter still gave more light than the day did. In part because her men did not like riding under an unnatural daytime black sky; were safer, in her opinion, sleeping by day, no matter how difficult that might be. Shifting a camp of eighty lances and a baggage train each day is bad enough by daylight.

She was never, not for one heartbeat, alone.

She wrapped herself in impenetrable authority. There could be no questions asked. There were none. To herself, she seemed asleep, or sleepwalking at best.

She woke, paradoxically, five days later, out of sheer weariness.

Ash jolted out of a doze and found herself leaning her forehead against the neck of her mare. Conscious that her hand, gripping a horse brush, moved in small circles, decreasing now. Conscious that she had just spoken – but said what?

She raised her head and looked at Rickard. The boy looked frazzled.

Lady butted her with a plush nose, whuffing. Ash straightened. She ran her free hand across the warm, sleek flank, pressed out by the foal within. The mare whickered, gently, and pushed up against Ash with her golden shoulder. The rushes underfoot smelled pleasantly of horse dung.

Ash glanced down. She wore her high riding boots, the tops pointed into her doublet skirt to keep them up. They were covered with mud and horse dung to the knee.

"The glorious life of a mercenary. If I'd wanted to spend my life knee-deep in shit, I could have been a peasant on a farm. At least you don't have to *move* a farm fifteen miles every cock-crow. Why am I ass-deep in crap?"

"Don't know, boss." It was the kind of rhetorical remark that some would have taken as an invitation to wit; Rickard only looked inarticulate. But pleased, too. This was obviously not what she had been talking about before.

Encouraged, Rickard said, "She'll drop in around fifteen days."

Her body was bruised, warm, weary. Pierced iron lanterns shone yellow light on to the moving walls of the canvas stall, and the hay jutting from Lady's manger. Pleasant and restful, in these early hours.

But if I leave, I won't see dawn breaking. Only darkness.

Ash heard the voices of men-at-arms outside, talking, and the whine of dogs; she had not come through camp without an escort, then. *My absence of mind doesn't go that far.* She felt it as a real absence, as if someone had gone travelling and had only now returned.

"Fifteen days," she repeated. The handsome boy watched her. His shirt bunched up out of the gap between points at shoulder and lower back, and his face was thinning down, losing child-fat, changing to man. Ash gave him a reassuring smile. "Good. Listen, Rickard, when you've taught Bertrand to be cup-bearer and page, I'll ask Roberto to take you on as squire. It's past time you trained."

He said nothing, but his face illumined, like a page from a manuscript.

After physical exertion, the body relaxes. Ash became aware of her loosened muscles; of the warmth from her demi-gown, made like a doublet with a fuller skirt and with the puffed sleeves sewn in, that was buttoned over her brigandine; of her sleepiness, that did nothing to take the edge off desire. She had an intense, sudden tactile memory: the line of Fernando del Guiz's flank from shoulder to hip, skin hot under her fingertips, and the thrust of his erect member.

"Shit!"

Rickard startled. He ventured, "Master Angelotti wants to talk to you."

Ash's hand went to Lady's neck automatically as the mare nuzzled at her. Touch calmed her. "Where is he?"

"Outside."

"Right. Yes, I'll see him now. Tell everyone else I'm unavailable for the next hour."

Five days unconscious of travelling between sloping walls of bald rock, patched in the moonlight with white snow. Unconscious of the road. Cold scrub and heather and alpine weeds, and the clink of stones trickling off cliffs to either side. Moonlight on lakes, far below winding roads and scrée. Now, if there was sunlight, she would be looking down into the distance, seeing unfenced green meadows and small castles on hilltops.

Moonlight showed her nothing of the surrounding country as she left the horse lines. From the camp, she could see no distance at all.

"Boss." Antonio Angelotti turned from speaking to her guards. He wore a voluminous red woollen cloak, which he should not need in August, over his brigandine and leg armour. What crackled under his boots as he walked to her was not the dry rushes, but hoar frost.

The inner and outer circles of the company's wagons bristled with guns, behind pavises big as church doors. Bonfires burned within the central camp, where men slept in their bed-rolls, and burned also beyond the perimeter, by her order, to give sight of the country beyond, and to prevent their being silhouetted against flame for any passing bowman or hand-gunner. She could tell where the huge Visigoth camp was, a mile away, by flaring bonfires; and by men distantly singing, in drink or in battle ardour, it was not clear which.

"Let's go." She walked with Antonio Angelotti as far as the massed cannon, and the hand-gunners encamped around their fires, without speaking of more than organisational matters. When the startlingly beautiful man stood aside for her to go into his small tent, she knew her silence was about to end.

"Rickard, see if you can find Father Godfrey, and F-Florian. Send them to me here." She ducked through the small pavilion's flap and entered. Her eyes adjusted to the shadows. She seated herself on a wooden chest, bound with straps and iron, that contained enough powder to blow her and the hand-gunners outside to the Pit. "What have you got to say privately?"

Angelotti eased himself into leaning against the edge of his trestle table, without clipping the top edge of the cuisses that armoured his thighs. A sheaf of paper, covered with calculations, fell to the rush-strewn earth. He was incapable, Ash thought, of looking less than graceful in any situation; but he was not incapable of seeming embarrassed.

"So I'm a bastard from North Africa, instead of a bastard from Flanders or England or Burgundy," she said gently. "Does it really matter to you?"

He shrugged lithely. "That depends on which noble family our Faris comes from, and whether they find you embarrassing. No. In any case, you're a bastard for a family to be proud of. What's the matter?"

"Pr—!" Ash wheezed. Her chest burned. She slid down the side of the chest and sat, spraddle-legged, in the rushes, laughing so hard that she couldn't breathe. The plates of her brigandine creaked with the movement of her ribs. "Oh, Angel! Nothing. 'Proud'. Such a compliment! You – no, nothing."

She wiped the back of her glove under her eyes. A push with powerful legs hitched her back up on to the wooden chest. "Master gunner, you know a lot about the Visigoths."

"North Africa is where I learned my mathematics." Angelotti was, it became apparent, studying her face. He did not look as though he knew he was doing it.

"How long were you over there?"

Oval lids lowered over his eyes. Angelotti had the face of a Byzantine icon, in this light of candles and shadows; with youth on it like the white film on the surface of a plum.

"I was twelve when I was taken." The long-lashed lids lifted. Angelotti looked her in the face. "The Turks took me off a galley near Naples. *Their* warship was taken by Visigoths. I spent three years in Carthage."

Ash did not have the nerve to ask him more about that time than he seemed

171

disposed to volunteer now. It was more than he had said to her in four years. She wondered if he had wished, then, that he had not been quite so beautiful.

"I learned it in bed," Angelotti said smoothly, with a humorous twist to his mouth that made it clear her thinking was transparent to him. "With one of their *amirs*,[12] their scientist-magi. Lord-*Amir* Childeric. Who taught me trajectories for cannon, and navigation, and astrology."

Ash, used to seeing Angelotti always clean (if somewhat singed), and neat, itself a miracle in the mud and dust of the camp, and, above all, private – Ash thought, How badly does he think he needs to break through to me, to tell me this?

She spoke hurriedly. "Roberto could be right, this could be their twilight . . . *spreading*. Godfrey would call it an Infernal contagion."

"He would not. He respects their *amirs*, as I do."

"What is it you want to say to me?"

Angelotti undid his cord cloak ties. The red wool cloth slid down his back, to the table, and bunched there. "My gunners are mutinous. They don't like it that you called off the siege of Guizburg. They're saying it's because del Guiz is your husband. That you no longer have the smile of Fortune."

"O Fortuna!" Ash grinned. "Fickle as a woman, isn't that what they're saying? All right, I'll talk to them. Pay them more. I know why they're mad. They had galleries dug in almost to the castle gate. I know they were really looking forward to blowing it sky-high. . . !"

"And so they feel cheated." Angelotti appeared extremely relieved. "If you'll talk to them . . . good."

"Is that all?"

"Are your voices the same as hers?"

The slightest tap will shatter pottery, given in the right place. Ash felt cracks crazing out from his question. She sprang to her feet in the cramped pavilion.

"You mean, is my saint *nothing*? Is the Lion nothing? Is it a demon speaking to me? Am I hearing a machine's voice, the way they say she does? *I don't know*." Breathing hard, Ash realised the fingers of her left hand had cramped around the scabbard of her sword. Knuckles whitened. "Can she do what they say she does? Can she hear some, some *device*, halfway across the middle sea? You've been there, you tell me!"

"It could be just a rumour. A complete lie."

"I don't know!" Ash unclamped her fingers, slowly. Mutinous or not, she could hear the gunners celebrating one of their obscure saint's days feasts outside;[13] someone was singing something very loud and coarse about a bull being taken to a cow. She realised that the song was calling the bull *Fernando*. One of her dark brows went up. Maybe not so far from mutiny after all.

"The Faris's men have been building brick observation posts all down the roads, on the march." Angelotti spoke loudly over the embarrassing chorus.

---

[12] 'Amir' or 'emir': Arabic: 'lord'. I can find no linguistic proof for the connection either with the Persian *magi* (holy men or magicians) in the Angelotti text, or with 'scientist' – surely a much later addition to the text, by another hand.

[13] By internal ms evidence, I calculate this takes place on 9 August, the feast day of King Osward of Northumbria. Born *c*.605, died 642 at Masefeth, St Osward prayed for the souls of those who fell in battle with him. His cult as a soldier saint was later popular as far as south Germany and Italy.

"They're nailing this country down." Ash had a moment's sheer panic thinking *But where* are *we?* Fear vanished as the memories of the last few days welled up obediently in her mind. "I guess that's why they want to crown this Visigoth 'Viceroy' of theirs in Aachen."[14]

"The weather's bad. You said they'd have to settle for somewhere closer, and you were right, madonna."

In the moment's silence, Ash heard dogs bark, and friendly greetings from the guards; and Godfrey Maximillian walked in, stripping off sheepskin mittens, with Floria behind him. The surgeon pointed, and the boy Bertrand, with a brazier, cleared a space in the tent to put it down, and heaped on more hot coals. At a nod from Angelotti, he clumsily served small beer, and butter and two-day-old bread, before leaving.

"I hate bad preaching." Godfrey sat on another wooden chest. "I've just been giving them Exodus chapter ten, verse twenty-two, where Moses calls down a thick darkness from heaven over Egypt. Someone who knows is bound to ask why that only lasted three days, and this has gone on for three weeks."

The priest drank, and wiped his beard. Ash carefully checked the distance between the various chests and flasks of powder and the brazier's burning coals. *Probably* okay, she thought, having no great faith in Angelotti's good sense about gunpowder.

Floria warmed her hands at the brazier. "Robert's on his way here."

This is a meeting convened without my consent, Ash realised. And my bet is that they've been waiting five days to do it. She took a thoughtful bite out of the bread, and chewed.

Anselm's voice barked outside. He ducked hurriedly in through the tent-flap. "Can't stay, got to go and sort out the gate-guards for tonight – for today." He hauled his velvet bonnet off, seeing Ash. Candlelight shone on his shaven skull, and on the pewter Lion livery badge fixed to his hat. "You're back, then."

The odd thing, perhaps, was that no one questioned his choice of words. They turned their faces to her, Angelotti's altar-painting features, Godfrey's crumb-strewn beard, Floria with her expression utterly closed.

"Where's Agnes?" Ash demanded suddenly. "Where's Lamb?"

"Half a mile to the north-east of us, camped, with fifty lances." Robert Anselm hitched his scabbard out of the way and stood beside Floria at the iron brazier. He would move entirely differently, Ash suddenly thought, if he realised Florian wasn't a man.

"Lamb *knew*," Ash snarled. "Motherfucker! He *must* have known, as soon as he saw her – their general. And he let me walk into that without a word of warning!"

"He let their general walk into it, too," Godfrey pointed out.

"And she hasn't hanged him yet?"

"I'm told he claims he never realised how close the resemblance was. Apparently the Faris believes him."

"Bloody hell." Ash seated herself on the edge of the trestle table, beside Angelotti. "I'll send Rickard over with a challenge to a personal duel."

---

[14] The coronation-place of Holy Roman emperors from the time of Otto the Great.

"Not many people know what he did, if indeed he did, and it wasn't just a sin of omission." Godfrey licked butter from his white fingertips, his dark eyes keenly on her. "You have no public need."

"I might just fight him anyway," Ash grumbled. She folded her arms across her brigandine, looking down at the gilded rivet-heads and blue velvet. "Look. She's *not* my fetch. I'm *not* her devil. I'm just some *amir* family's by-blow, that's all. Christ knows the Griffin-in-Gold went across the Mediterranean often enough, twenty years ago. I'll be a bastard second cousin or something."

She raised her head, catching Anselm and Angelotti exchanging a look that she couldn't read. Floria poked the red coals. Godfrey drank from a leather mug.

"There is something I thought we would say?" Godfrey wiped his mouth and looked diffidently around the tent, at its shadowed folds and faces profiled in candlelight. "About our complete confidence in our captain?"

Robert Anselm muttered, "Fucking hell, clerk, get on with it, then!"

There was an anticipatory silence.

Into it, the last two lines of the hand-gunners' ballad echoed, having the failed bull Fernando being serviced by the cow.

Ash caught Anselm's eye, and, poised between absolute rage and laughter, was precipitated into helpless giggles by what must be an exactly similar expression on Robert's face.

"I didn't hear that," she decided, cheerfully.

Angelotti looked up from scribbling with a quill, leaning across his trestle table. "That's all right, madonna, I've written it down in case you forget!"

Godfrey Maximillian sprayed bread-crumbs across the tent, whatever he would have said lost or superseded.

"I'm getting a new company," Ash announced, with a deadpan humour; and was disconcerted when Floria, who had remained silent, said flatly, "Yes – if you don't trust us."

Ash saw the absence of five days written into Floria's expression. She nodded, slowly. "I do. I trust all of you."

"I wish I thought that you did."

Ash jabbed a finger at Floria. "*You're* coming with me. Godfrey, so are you. And Angelotti."

"Where?" Florian demanded.

Ash rattled her fingertips against her scabbard, keeping arrhythmic time to her calculations. "The Visigoth general can't crown her Viceroy in Aachen, it's too far to travel. We're turning west. That means she's going for the nearest city here, which is Basle—"

Godfrey said excitedly, "That would be a useful first move! It fixes the League and the south Germanies under their government. Aachen can come later. Sorry. Go on, child."

"I'm going into Basle. You'll see why in a minute. Robert, I'm giving you temporary command of the company. I want you to make a fortified camp about three miles outside the city, on the western side. You can put my war-pavilion up, tables, carpets, silver plate, the whole works. In case you get visitors."

Anselm's high forehead wrinkled as he frowned. "We're used to being sent off while you negotiate a contract. This one is already signed."

"I know. I know. I'm not changing that."

"It isn't the way we've done it before."

"It's the way we're doing it now."

Ash unfolded her arms and stood up. She glanced around at their faces, in the candlelit tent, fixing her gaze briefly on Floria. *There is a lot of history here. Some of it not known to everyone.* She put the problem aside for later.

"I want to talk to the general." Ash hesitated. Then she went on, speaking to each of them in turn.

"Godfrey, I want you to talk to your monastic contacts. And F-Florian, you talk to the Visigoth physicians. Angelotti, you know mathematicians and gunners in their camp, go get drunk with them. I want to know *everything* about this woman! – I want to know what she has to break her fast, what she wants her army to do in Christendom, who her family are, and whether she *does* hear voices. I want to know if *she* knows what's happened to the sun."

Outside, the setting crescent moon argues the arrival of another lightless day.

"Roberto. While I'm *inside* the walls of Basle," Ash said, "I can do with all the implicit threat that I can get, sitting there *outside*."

Going into the city of Basle, Ash could think of nothing else except *She has my face. I don't have father or mother, there's no one in the world who looks like me,* but *she has my face. I have to talk to her.*

Sweet Christ, I wish it would get light!

In the daytime darkness, between its mountains, Basle echoed with the hooves of war-horses and the shouts of soldiers. Citizens leaped out of her way, scurried indoors; or never left their houses, shouted from upper-storey windows as she rode by. *Whore, bitch,* and *traitor* were most common.

"Nobody loves a mercenary," Ash mock-sighed. Rickard laughed. The company's men-at-arms swaggered.

Crosses marked most doors. The churches were packed. Ash rode through processional flagellations, finding the civic buildings all shut up except for one guild house. That had black pennants outside.

Ash negotiated climbing the narrow crooked stairs in armour, her escort behind her. Bare oak support beams protruded from the white plastered walls. The lack of space made any weapon a liability. A rising noise came from the upstairs chambers: men's voices speaking Schweizerdeutsch, Flemish, Italian, and the Latin of North Africa. The Faris's council of occupation: somewhere she might be found.

"Here." Ash took off her sallet and handed it to Rickard. Condensation misted the bright metal.

It was, when she entered, no different from any other room in any other city. Stone-framed windows with diamond-leaded panes, looking out on rain on the cobbled streets below. Four-storey houses across the narrow alley, plaster-and-beam frontages gleaming in the wet – in rain turning to sleet, she suddenly realised. White dots dropped into the circles of lantern light, light from other windows, and the pitch-torches illuminating the men-at-arms below.

Sloping roofs blocked the black sky above the street. The room sweltered and stank with a hundred tallow candles and rush-lights. When she looked at the marked wax candle, she saw it was just past midday.

"Ash." She produced a leather livery badge. "Condottiere to the Faris."

The Visigoth guards let her pass in. She seated herself at table, her men behind her, reasonably secure in her knowledge that Robert Anselm could handle both Joscelyn van Mander and Paul di Conti, that he would take notice of what the leaders of smaller lances said; that, if it came to it, the company would follow him into an attack. A quick glance around showed her Europeans and Visigoths, but not their Faris.

An *amir* (by his robes) said, "We must arrange this coronation. I appeal to you all for procedure."

Another Visigoth civilian began to read, carefully, from a European illuminated manuscript. "'As soon as the Archbishop hath put the crown on the king his head, then shall the king offer his sword to God on the altar . . . the worthiest earl that is there present shall . . . bear it naked before the king . . .'"[15]

This is not what I do, Ash thought. How the hell do I get to speak to their general?

She scratched at her neck, under her mail standard. Then she stopped, not wanting to draw attention to rat-nibbled leather and the red dots of flea-bites.

"But why crown our Viceroy by heathen ceremonies?" one of the Visigoth *qa'ids* demanded. "Even their own kings and emperors don't command these people's loyalty, so what good will it do?"

Further down the table, on the far side, a man with yellow hair cut short in the Visigoth military fashion lifted his head. She found herself staring at the face of Fernando del Guiz.

"Ah – nothing personal, del Guiz," the same Visigoth military officer added genially. "After all, you may be a traitor, but, hell, you're *our* traitor!"

A ripple of dry humour went around the wooden table, quelled by the *amir*; who nonetheless glanced at the young German knight quizzically.

Fernando del Guiz smiled. His expression was open, generous, complicit with the high-ranking Visigoth officer; as if Fernando were seeing the joke against himself.

It was the same disarming smile he had shared with her outside the Emperor's tent at Neuss.

Ash saw his forehead gleaming in the candlelight: shiny with sweat.

Not a sign of strength of character. Not at all.

"*Fuck!*" Ash shouted.

"'And the king shall be'—" A white-haired man, in a murrey-coloured woollen pleated gown, with a silver-linked chain around his neck, looked up from tracing a hand-written document with his be-ringed finger. "Your pardon, Frau?"

"*Fuck!*" Ash sprang up and leaned forward, her gauntleted hands resting on

[15] This is similar to the Hastings manuscript Ordinances of Chivalry of the fifteenth century, 'The maner and the forme of the Coronacion of kyngis and Quenes in Engelonde'.

the table. Fernando del Guiz: stone-green eyes. Fernando del Guiz, in a mail hauberk, and a white tunic under it; the badge of a *qa'id* laced to his shoulder, and his mouth now white around the lips. He met her eyes and she felt it, felt the eye-contact as a literal jolt under her ribs.

"*You* are *a fucking traitor!*"

The hilt of her sword is solid in her grip, the razor-sharp blade drawn two inches from the scabbard before she even thinks about it, every trained muscle beginning to move. She feels in her body the anticipated jolt of the sword-point stabbing through his bare, unprotected face. Smashing cheekbone, eye, brain. Brute force solves so many things in life not worth wasting time thinking about; this is what she does for a living, after all.

In the split second before she drew, Agnus Dei – now visible, sitting in his Milanese armour and white surcoat beyond the *amir* – gave a shrug that said plainly, *Women!*, and said loudly, "Keep your private business for another time, madonna!"

Ash flicked a glance back to ascertain where her six men-at-arms were positioned, behind her. Impassive faces. Ready for back-up. Except for Rickard. The boy bit on his bare hand, appalled at the silence.

It reached her.

Fernando del Guiz watched, no expression on his face. Safe behind the walls of public protection.

"I will," Ash said, sitting down. Around the low-beamed room, suddenly tense men wearing swords relaxed. She added, "I'll keep my business with Lamb for another time, too."

"Perhaps mercenaries do not need to attend on this meeting, condottieri," the lord-*amir* offered drily.

"Guess not." Ash braced her hands against the edge of the oak table. "I really need to speak with your Faris."

"She is in the town's great hall."

It was clearly the placation of a quarrelsome mercenary. Ash appreciated it. She pushed herself to her feet, and concealed a smile at Agnus Dei having also to gather his men, make his farewells, and leave the meeting and the house.

She glanced back as Lamb and his men stepped carefully out on to the cobbles after her. She tugged her cloak around her against the sleet. "All mercenaries out on the street together . . ."

That would either make him fight or laugh.

The creases deepened in his brown face, under his barbute with its sodden plumes. "What's she paying you, madonna?"

"More than you. Whatever it is, I bet it's more than you."

"You have the more lances," he said mildly, pulling on his heavy gauntlets.

Confused by the evaporation of her anger, Ash put on her helm and reached out as Rickard brought Godluc, and mounted quickly and easily. Not that a war-horse's shod hooves were any more certain on the cobbles than her own slick-soled boots.

Lamb called, "Did your Antonio Angelotti tell you? They've burned Milano, too. Down to the dirt."

A smell of wet horse permeated the chill air.

"You were from Milan, weren't you, Lamb?"

"No mercenary is from anywhere, madonna, you know that."

"Some of us try." That brought Guizburg to mind, fifty miles away: shattered town walls and unbreached keep; and another jolt left her breathless: *He is upstairs in that little room and I wish he was dead!*

"Which one of you was it?" she demanded. "Who let 'twins' meet, without warning either of us?"

Lamb chuckled harshly. "If the Faris believed it was my fault, madonna, would I be here?"

"But Fernando's still here, too."

The Italian mercenary gave her a look that said *you are a child* and had nothing to do with her age.

Ash said recklessly, "What about if I paid you to kill my husband?"

"I'm a soldier, not an assassin!"

"Lamb, I always knew you had principles, if I could only find them!" She made a joke of it, laughing it away; uncomfortably aware from the look on the Italian's face that he knew it was not a joke.

"Besides, he's the coming man with the Faris-General." Agnus Dei touched his white surcoat, his expression changing. "God judges him, madonna. Do you think you're the only enemy he has, having done this? God's judgement comes on him."

"I'd like to get in first." Ash, grim, watched Agnus Dei and his men mount up. Hooves and voices echoed between high, narrow houses. A bitch of a street to fight along, she thought, and dropped her chin into her mail standard to mutter aloud – purely as a supposition – and for the first time since Genoa: "Six mounted knights against seven; all carrying war hammers, swords, axes; on very bad ground—"

And stopped. And reached up to jerk the visor of her sallet down, hiding her face. She whirled Godluc, iron shoes striking sparks in the sleet, and slid off at a gallop, men-at-arms following her all anyhow, Lamb's appalled shout lost in the clatter.

No! I said nothing! I don't want to hear—!

Nothing rational: a wall of fear rose up in her mind. She would not consider the reasons why.

It's only the saint I have heard since I was a child: why—

I don't want to hear my voice.

Eventually she let Godluc slow, on the dangerous cobbles. Torches flared as Ash led her entourage through narrow, pitch-dark streets. A clock distantly struck two of the afternoon.

"I know where we'll pick up the surgeon on the way," she told Thomas Rochester, having given up *Floria-Florian* as a name that made her speech stumble. Rochester nodded and directed the manner of their riding: himself and another armoured horseman before her, two more at the rear, and the two mounted crossbowmen in their felt hats to ride beside her. The road underfoot changed from cobbles to frozen mud ruts.

Ash rode between houses with tiny paned windows illuminated by cheap rush-lights. A black dot jerked and darted across her vision. Godluc tossed his head at its angular flight. Bats, she realised: bats flying out from under the house-eaves, in this dark daytime, snatching at insects, or trying to.

Something crunched under the war-horse's shod hooves.

Stretching across the cold dirt in front of them, insects lay like a crisp frost. Pismires of the air, all dead from cold: honey-bees, wasps, blow-flies. A hundred thousand of them. Godluc's feathered hooves came down on the bright, broken wings of butterflies.

"Here," she directed, at a three-storey house with a stack of overhanging windows. Rochester snuffled. She could see little of the dark-haired Englishman's face under his visor, but when she studied the house outside which they had halted, she guessed the reason for his humour. A hundred rush-lights shone in the windows, someone was singing, someone was playing a lute surprisingly well, and three or four men were being sick in the gutter in the centre of the alley. Whorehouses always do good business in a crisis.

"You guys wait for me." Ash swung down from the saddle. Light glinted from her steel armour. "And I mean *here*. I don't want to find any of you missing when I come back!"

"No, boss." Rochester grinned.

Thick-necked men in jerkins and hose, backlit, let her pass, seeing armour and livery jacket. Nothing unusual about a boy-voiced knight or man-at-arms in a Basle whorehouse. Two questions got her knowledge of the room occupied by a yellow-haired Burgundian-accented surgeon, two silver coins of indeterminate issue gained silence. She strode up the stairs, knocked once, and went in.

A woman was lying back on a pallet in the corner of the small room, her bodice pulled down and her long veined breasts drooping out. All her chemises and her woollen kirtle were ruffled up about her naked thighs. She might have been anything between sixteen and thirty, Ash couldn't tell. She had dyed yellow hair, and a small plump chin.

The room smelled of sex.

There was a lute beside the whore, and a candle and some bread on a wooden plate on the floor. Floria del Guiz sat cross-wise on the pallet with her back against the plaster of the wall. She drank from a leather bottle. All her points had been unlaced; one brown nipple was visible where her breast lay out of her open shirt.

As Ash watched, the whore stroked Floria's neck.

"Is this a sin?" the girl demanded fiercely. "Is it, sir? But fornication is a sin in itself, and I have fornicated with many men. They are bulls in a field, with their great cocks. She is gentle and wild with me."

"Margaret. Sssh." Floria leaned forward and kissed the young woman on the mouth. "I am to leave, I see. Shall I come back and visit you?"

"When you have the money." A glint, under the bravado, of something else. "Mother Astrid won't let you in if you don't. And come in your man-shape. I don't want to make a bonfire for the church."

Floria met Ash's black look. The surgeon's eyes danced. "This is Margaret Schmidt. She's excellent with her fingers – on the lute."

Ash turned her back on the young whore rearranging her clothes; and on Floria, tying her points with a surgeon's neatness. She walked across the floor.

Boards creaked. A deep male voice shouted something from upstairs; there was a series of rising cries, faked, in another upstairs room.

"*I* never whored with women!" Ash turned, stiffly, in metal plates. "I went with men. I never went with animals, or women! How can you *do* that?"

Margaret murmured, shocked, "He's a woman!', to which Floria, now tying on her cloak and hood, said, "She is, greatheart. If you fancy life on the road, there are worse camps to join."

Ash wanted to shout, but kept her mouth shut, halted by the decisions passing across the young woman's face.

Margaret rubbed her chin. "It's no life, among soldiers. And listen to him, to her, I couldn't be with you, could I?"

"I don't know, sweetness. I've never kept a woman before."

"Come back here before you go. I'll give you my answer then." With remarkable self-possession, Margaret Schmidt tidied the lute and the plate on to an oaken stool, in the chiaroscuro of the rush-light. "What are you waiting for? Mother will be sending another one to me. Or she'll charge you double."

Ash didn't wait to see what she thought might be a kiss of parting – except that whores do not kiss, she thought; *I* never—

She turned and stomped down the narrow stairs, between doors sometimes open to men with bottles and dice, sometimes to men fornicating with women; until she stopped and spun around in the hallway, nearly impaling the surgeon on the sharp edge of her steel elbow-couter. "What the *hell* do you think you're doing? You were supposed to be sounding out other physicians, picking up trade gossip!"

"What makes you think I haven't been?"

The tall woman checked belt, purse and dagger with an automatic touch of one hand, the other still clasped around the neck of the leather bottle.

"I got the physician to the Caliph's cousin truly rat-arsed, right here. He tells me in confidence that Caliph Theodoric has a canker, months to live at best."

Ash only stared, the words going past her.

"Your face!" Floria laughed. She drank from the bottle.

"*Shit, Florian, you're fucking women!*"

"Florian's perfectly safe fucking women." She swept her man-cut hair back into her hood, where it framed her long-boned face. "Now wouldn't it be inconvenient if I wanted to fuck men?"

"I thought you were just paying for a room, and her time! I thought it was a trick, to keep up your disguise!"

Floria's expression softened. She patted Ash gently on her scarred cheek, and then dropped the empty bottle, and whipped her mittens on against the chill seeping in from the street. "Sweet Christ. If I can put it the way our excellent Roberto would – don't be such a humourless hard-ass."

Ash made a half-noise not speech, all breath. "But you're a woman! Going with another woman!"

"It doesn't bother you with Angelotti."

"But he's—"

"He's a man, with another man?" Floria said. Her mouth shook. "Ash, for Christ's sake!"

An older woman with a tight face under her coif came out from the kitchens. "Are you bravos looking for a woman or wasting my time? Sir knight, I beg your pardon. All our girls are very clean. Aren't they, Doctor?"

"Excellently." Floria pushed Ash towards the door. "I'll bring my lord back, when our business is done with."

Cold darkness blinded Ash outside the doors; then Thomas Rochester and her men and their pitch-torches dazzled her, so that she hardly saw a boy bring Floria her bay gelding. She mounted and settled herself down in Godluc's saddle.

She opened her mouth to shout. And then realised that she had no idea what to say. Floria, watching her, looked supremely unapologetic.

"Godfrey will be at the hall by now." Ash shifted, rousing Godluc to a slow walk. "The Faris will be there. Ride on."

Floria's gelding shivered and flicked its head up. The white, soundless swoop of a disorientated barn owl curved past in flight, not a yard from the surgeon's hat.

"Look." Floria pointed up.

Ash tilted her head to gaze up at the high gable roofs.

She was not used to noticing the fullness of the summer skies. Now, every gable line and window ledge was thick with roosting birds – with pigeons, rooks, crows and thrushes, fluffing out feathers against the chill. Blackbirds, sparrows, ravens; all, in an uncanny peace, sharing their perches undisturbed with merlin hawks and peregrines and kestrels. A low, discontented mumbling went up from the flocks. White guano streaked the beams and plaster.

Above them, the overcast clouds of the day's sky stayed invisible, and black.

Despite the Visigoth ordinance restricting any noble's escort to six or less, Basle's civic hall was packed with men. It stank of tallow candles and the remnants of a huge banquet, and of two or three hundred sweating men crowded into the space between the tables, waiting to petition the Visigoth Viceroy at the high dais.

The Visigoth general was not visibly present.

"Fucking hell," Ash swore. "Where *is* the woman?"

A fug smudged the heights of the barrel-vaulted roof, with the Empire's and cantons' banners hanging down over tapestried stone walls. Ash let her gaze sweep across rushes and candles and men in European dress, doublet and hose, and brimless felt hats with tall crowns. Far more men were wearing southern robes and mail: soldiers and 'arifs and qa'ids. But no Faris.

Ash tilted the visor of her sallet low, leaving only mouth and nose to be seen; her silver hair hidden under her steel helmet. Fully armoured, she is not immediately recognisable as a woman, never mind as a woman who bears a resemblance to the Visigoth general.

Around the walls, as servers, stood clay-coloured Visigoth golems, eyeless and metal-jointed, their baked skins cracking in the great fireplaces' heat. Lifting herself on armoured toes, Ash could see one golem standing behind the white-robed Visigoth Viceroy – who was, she noted with a little surprise, Daniel

181

de Quesada – and holding a brazen head, which de Quesada consulted for a currency exchange as she watched.

Floria took wine from one of the pantlers rushing past, not apparently minding that it came from well below the salt. "How on earth can you tell this lot apart? Bear and swan and bull and marten and unicorn . . . It's a bestiary!"

A fast scrutiny of heraldry on liveries showed Ash that men were present from Berne, Zürich, Neuchâtel and Solothurn, and from Fribourg and Aargau . . . most of the Swiss Confederation lords, or whatever one called the lords among the League of Constance, all with an equally shut-faced look to them. Conversations were going on in Schweizerdeutsch and Italian and German; but the main talk – the shouted talk up at the head table – in Carthaginian. Or in North African Latin when the Visigoth *amirs* and *qa'ids* recalled their manners, which nothing forced them to do.

So where do I look for her now?

Thomas Rochester rejoined Ash, moving through the civilian crowd. The lawyers and officials of Basle moved back automatically, as one does from a man in steel plate, but otherwise ignored the mercenary man-at-arms. He lowered his voice to speak to Ash.

"She's been out at the camp, looking for you."

"*What?*"

"Captain Anselm sent a rider. The Faris is on her way back here now."

Ash kept her hand from her sword-grip with an effort of mind, such gestures being prone to misinterpretation in a crowded hall. "Did Anselm's message say what her business was?"

"To talk to one of her mercenary *junds*." Thomas grinned. "We're important enough for her to come to us."

"And I'm Saint Agatha's tits!" Suddenly queasy, Ash watched the throng around Daniel de Quesada, which did not grow any the less for being watched. Quesada's face was hardly marred by scars, now. His eyes moved very quickly around the hall, and when one of the cocky-tailed white dogs nosing in the rushes yipped, his body startled uncontrollably.

"I wonder who's pulling *his* strings?" Ash thought aloud. "And did she come out just to take a look at me, back at Guizburg? Maybe. Now she's gone out to the camp. That's a lot of trouble to go to, just to look at a bastard one of your family fathered on a mercenary camp-follower twenty years ago."

Antonio Angelotti appeared at her elbow, tall and sweating and swaying. "Boss. 'M going back to camp. It's true. Their armies defeated the Swiss ten days ago."

Knowing it must have happened, and hearing it, were two different things. Ash said, "Sweet Christ. Have you found anyone who was there, who saw it?"

"Not yet. They were outmanoeuvred. The *Swiss.*"

"Oh, that's why everyone's creeping up the arse of the King-Caliph. That's why everybody's throwing banquets. Son of a bitch. I wonder if Quesada meant it when he said they intended to war on Burgundy?" She shook Angelotti's shoulder, roughly. "Okay, go back to camp, you're pissed."

The master gunner, leaving, drew her eye to the great doors. Godfrey Maximillian strode in, glanced around, and made for the blue Lion liveries.

The priest bowed to Ash, and glanced at Floria del Guiz before he opened his mouth to speak.

"*That's* the look I hate," the disguised woman said, not particularly quietly. "Every time before you speak to me, now. I don't bite, Godfrey. How long have you known me! For Christ's sake!"

Her cheeks flushed, her eyes brilliant. Her bowl-shaped haircut was spiked with damp drizzle. A server and a pantler glanced as they hurried past, their white aprons stained. Seeing what, when they see her? Ash wondered. A man, definitely. With no sword, therefore a civilian. A professional man, because of the well-cut woollen demi-gown lined with fur, and the fine hose and boots and velvet hat. A livery badge pinned to the upturned velvet hat-brim: therefore a man who belongs to a lord. And – given the prominent Lion – belonged to Ash.

"Quieten down. I've got enough problems here."

"And I don't? I'm a woman, for fuck's sake!"

Too loud. Ash beckoned Thomas Rochester and Michael, one of the crossbowmen, forward from the rear wall of the hall.

"Take him outside, he's drunk."

"Yes, boss."

"Why does everything have to *change*?" Floria demanded, wrenching her arms away. Thomas Rochester efficiently punched the surgeon in the small of the back, his armoured fist hardly moving any distance; and while her face was screwed up in pain, lifted her between himself and Michael, and half-carried her out.

"Shit." Ash frowned. "I didn't mean them to manhandle h—"

"You wouldn't object if you still thought she was a man." Godfrey's hand gripped his cross, on his substantial chest. The hood of his robe was far enough forward to give her only a glimpse of beard and lips, nothing of his expression.

"We'll wait till the Faris gets here," Ash said decisively. "What have you heard?"

"That's the head of the goldsmiths' guild." Godfrey indicated with a slight inclination of his hood. "Over there, talking to the Medici."

Ash's gaze searched along the table, identifying a man in a black wool coif, with strands of silver hair wisping out under his ear. He sat within easy whisper of a man in an Italianate gown and a dagged green hood. The Medici sat grey-faced and drawn.

"They trashed Florence, too, to make a point." Ash shook her head. "Like Venice. To say, we don't *need* this. Don't need the money or the armour or the guns. We can just keep pouring it in from Africa . . . I think they can."

"Does it matter?" A man in a scholar's gown first bowed to Ash and then straightened, startled, frowning at the unexpected woman's voice.

Godfrey interposed himself. "Sir, you are?"

"I am – I was – astrologer to the court of the Emperor Frederick."

Ash could not help a snort of cynicism, her eyes travelling to the hall door, and the darkness beyond. "Bit redundant, aren't you?"

"God has taken the sun away," the astrologer said. "Dame Venus, the daystar, may still be seen at certain hours, thus we know when morning *would* break, but for our wickedness. The heavens remain dark, and empty."

The man wilted a little. "This is the second coming of the Christ, and his judgement. I have not lived as I should. Will you hear my confession, Father?"

Godfrey bowed, at Ash's acknowledgement; and she watched the two men find a relatively quiet corner of the hall. The astrologer knelt. After a time, the priest rested his hand on the man's forehead in token of forgiveness. He came back to Ash.

"It seems the Turks have paid spies here," Godfrey added. "Which my astrologer knows. He says the Turks are much relieved."

"Relieved?"

"The Visigoths having taken the Italian cities, and the cantons, and south Germany, they must either turn east and strike at the Turk Empire, or west at Europe."

"If they turn west, then the Turks might face a Visigoth rather than a Christian Europe, but otherwise no change; well," Ash said, "since Sultan Mehmet[16] must have thought all this was intended for him, he will be relieved!"

There were present, Ash saw, a few nervous men of Savoy and France, as yet untouched, desperate to know which way the Visigoth invasion was aimed next.

"I hate cities," she said absently. "They're a fire hazard. You can't buy oil or tapers here for gold. I give it two days before this city burns itself from wall to wall."

She expected some comment on her grumpiness, given with ease based on their long knowledge of each other. What Godfrey said, in a thoughtful tone, was, "We talk as if the sun will never shine again."

Ash stood silent.

"It's still getting colder. I rode through fields on my way in. The wheat is being blighted, and the vines. Such a famine is coming . . ." Godfrey's voice rumbled in his resonant chest. "Perhaps I was wrong. Famine is coming, and pestilence with it, and death and war are already here. These *are* the final days. We should be looking to the state of our souls, not picking among the ruins."

"I want the general of the Visigoths," Ash said speculatively, ignoring him. "And the general of the Visigoths is looking for me."

"Yes." Godfrey hesitated, watching her survey the town hall. "Child, you are not about to send us away from here."

"I am, too." The flicker of a grin. "You and Florian. Take her. Ride with Michael and Josse, out to Roberto at the camp, and stay there unless you hear from me. Can't you feel your hackles rising here? Go."

One thing about the habit of giving orders is that others fall into the habit of obeying them. She could see, under his hood, Godfrey Maximillian smooth his face to a pious unconcern. He made his way deceptively fast through the crowd, to the doors.

That leaves me and an escort of four men, Ash concluded. Yippee. Now we'll see who's a mistrusting bitch.

One could stay standing around at the back of the hall, not being offered basin and cloth to wash one's hands, never mind any meat or the strange foreign dishes spilling on the yellowing linen tablecloths. One could keep

[16] Mehmet II, ruled the Osmanli (Turkish) Empire AD 1451–1481.

184

waiting, Ash thought, until the sycophancy attendant on Daniel de Quesada's installation lost its first fervour. That might be days. Weeks.

She watched the men from France and Savoy gathering in tiny groups, nittering anxiously.

"I wish I had the French king's intelligence service. Or the Flemish bankers'." She turned to Thomas Rochester. "Guido and Simon, to the buttery, see what you can hear; Francis and you, Thomas, as and when the shit hits the fan here, we ride like hell for Anselm, got that?"

Rochester looked doubtful. "Boss, this is dodgy."

"I know. We ought to leave now. But . . . There might be some privilege in being a bastard from the Faris's family. We might get more money." Ash shook her head. The white scars on her face stood out dark, by virtue of her pale skin. "I just want to *know*."

She worked the hall for a time. She cornered a merchant, and argued a price for goods to make up losses of mules and baggage outside Genoa. The cost of replacement wagons shook her, until the man quoted her his price for broken and schooled horses. *Stealing may be better than buying*, she reflected, not for the first time.

A flurry of servants went past her, replacing burned-down candles and exhausted lanterns, and she stepped back against the wall out of their way, catching her scabbard across someone's knees.

"Pardon—" She turned, stopped; staring up at Fernando del Guiz. "Son of a *bitch*!"

"How *is* mother?" he inquired, mildly.

She snorted, thought: He *meant* to make me laugh.

That realisation shocked her into silence. She stood out of the crowd, staring up at his face: Fernando del Guiz in Visigoth military mail and surcoat, the cropped hair making him look oddly younger.

"Christus fucking Imperator! What do *you* want?" Ash saw Thomas Rochester, still finalising delivery with the merchant, look over at her inquiringly; she shook her head. "Fernando— no: what? *What*? What can you possibly have to say to me?"

"You're very angry," he remarked. His voice came from above her, where he stared out across the heads of the crowd; and then he suddenly dropped his gaze, impaling her. "I don't have anything to say to you, peasant."

"That's fucking good. Being noble didn't stop you going over to the Visigoths, did it? You *are* a traitor. I thought it was a *lie*." Anger, fuelling her, ran out; drained away with the flinch of his eyes. She was silent for a second.

He began to turn away.

"*Why?*" Ash demanded.

" 'Why'?"

"You— I still don't understand. You're a lord. Even if they were going to take you prisoner, they've have ransomed you back. Or kept you safe in a castle somewhere. Hell, you had armed and armoured men with you, you could have broken out, run—"

"From an army?" Humour in his expression, now.

Ash put a steel-covered arm in front of his body, so that Fernando del Guiz

185

would have to push past her to get out into the body of the hall. "You didn't run into an army. That's just rumour. Godfrey bought me the truth of it. You ran into a squad of eight men – *eight* men. You didn't even try to fight. You just surrendered."

"My skin's worth more to me than your good opinion." Fernando sounded sardonic. "I didn't know you cared, madam wife."

"I don't! I— Well, it got you a place at this court. With the winners." She nodded at the hall. "Devious. And you were taking a real chance. But then, the Emperor's nobles are all politicians – I should have remembered that."

"It *wasn't*—!" Fernando glared down into her face. The candlelight showed his upper lip beaded with damp.

"Wasn't what?" Ash asked, more quietly.

"Wasn't *political* treason!" Some odd expression crossed his face, in the deceptive light of the candles. He held her gaze. "They killed Matthias! They stuck a spear into his stomach and he fell off his horse, screaming! They shot Otto with a crossbow bolt, and three of the horses—"

Ash forced her voice down to a hoarse, outraged, whisper:

"Jesus Christ, Fernando, you're not like fucking Matthias. They'd have given you quarter. And what about all your fancy kit – you were fully armoured, for Christ's sake; up against Visigoth peasants in tunics! You can't tell me you couldn't have fought your way out! You didn't even try to bang out of there!"

"I couldn't do it!"

She stared at him: at the sudden, stark honesty on his face.

"I couldn't do it," Fernando repeated, more quietly, and with a smile that made his face seem older, distressed. "I filled my hose, and I fell off my horse, and I lay in front of the peasant sergeant and I begged him not to kill me. I gave him the ambassador in exchange for my life."

"You—"

"I gave in," Fernando said, "because I was afraid."

Ash continued to stare. "Jesus Christ."

"And I don't regret it." Fernando wiped his face with his bare hand, bringing it away wet. "What's it to you?"

"I—" Ash hesitated. She let her arm drop, not blocking his way now. "I don't know. Nothing. I suppose. I'm a mercenary, I'm not one of your retainers or your king, I'm not the one you've betrayed."

"You don't get it, do you?" Fernando del Guiz did not move away from where they stood. "There were men with crossbows. Steel arrow-heads as thick as my thumb – I saw a bolt go through Otto's face, straight through his eye, bang! His *head* exploded. Matthias was holding his entrails in his hands. Men with spears, like spears I've hunted with, gutting open animals, and they were going to gut me. I was surrounded by *madmen*."

"Soldiers," Ash corrected automatically. She shook her head, puzzled. "Everybody craps themselves when there's going to be a fight. I do. Thomas Rochester over there has; so have most of my men. That's the bit they don't put in the chronicles. But fucking hell, you don't have to surrender when there's still a fighting chance!"

"*You* don't."

His intense expression aged him: a young man grown suddenly old. I've been to your bed, Ash thought suddenly, and it seems I don't know you at all.

He said, "*You* have physical courage. I never knew, until that moment – I've done tournaments, mêlées . . . war's *different*."

Ash looked at him with complete incomprehension. "Of course it is."

They stared at each other.

"Are you telling me you did this because you're a *coward*?"

For answer, Fernando del Guiz turned and walked away. The shifting light of candles hid his expression.

Ash opened her mouth to call him back, and said nothing; could think of nothing, for long minutes, that she wanted to say.

Over the hubbub of talk and rattle of papers being signed, she heard Basle's town clock strike four of the afternoon.

"That's long enough." She signalled Rochester; resolutely put del Guiz out of her thoughts. "Wherever the Faris-General is, she's not coming here. Get the lads."

Thomas Rochester retrieved the men-at-arms from (respectively) the stables, the kitchens, and a maid's dormitory bed. Ash sent Guido out for the horses. She stepped out of the town hall between Rochester and the other crossbow-man, Francis, two yards tall, a burly man who looked as if he might not need a crank to cock a bow: he could probably do it with his teeth. The sky above the courtyard was empty. Black. All the shouting of grooms and horses' hooves on stones couldn't cover the silence that seeped down from above.

Francis crossed himself. "I wish the Christ would come. The tribulation first, that scares me. Not the Last Judgement."

Ash caught sight of orange dots all down her vambraces, where sleet falling on her arms had turned to rust spots during her time within the warm civic hall. She muttered an obscenity and scrubbed at the steel with a linen-covered finger, waiting for the horses.

"Captain," a man's accented, Visigothic Latin said. She looked up. She saw in rapid succession that he was an *'arif* commander of forty, that he had twenty men, that all of them had their swords out of their sheaths. She stepped back and drew, screaming at Thomas Rochester. Six or seven mail-hauberk-covered bodies hit her from behind and slammed her down on her face.

Her sallet and visor hit the cobbles, slamming her forehead against the helmet's padding. Dazed, she closed her left hand and swung her gauntlet back. Her thick metal fist thunked into something. A voice screamed above her, on top of her. She bent her left arm. Armour is a weapon. The great butterfly-plates of the couter that protect the inner elbow joint flow, at the back, to a sharpened spike. She slammed her bent elbow back and up and felt the spike punch through mail to flesh. A shout.

She thrashed, struggled to bend her legs, searingly afraid of a hamstring cut across the back of her unprotected knee. Two mail-clad bodies lay full-weight across her right arm, across her hand that gripped her sword-hilt. Men shouted. Two or three more bodies hit her in rapid succession, slamming down against her backplate, holding her motionless, pinned, unhurt, a crab in a padded steel shell.

Their hard-breathing weight pinned her absolutely. *So I am not to be killed.*

Weight across her armoured shoulders kept her from raising her head. She saw nothing but a few inches of stone, straw and dead cold bees. About a yard away, there was a soft impact and a scream.

I should have made *them let me bring a larger escort! Or sent Rochester away—*

She tightened the grip of her gauntleted right hand on her sword. With her left hand unnoticed for a moment, she folded her fingers under, so that the sharp edge of the plate on the back of her hand jutted forward, and shoved the edge out to where she guessed a man's face to be.

No impact. Nothing.

A heel in a mail sabaton came down on her right hand, trapping her fingers and flesh around the sword's grip, between the steel plates of her gauntlet, between the man's full weight and the hard cobblestones.

She shrieked. Her hand released. Someone kicked the blade away.

A dagger-point stabbed down and into her open visor and stopped a quivering inch away from her eye.

IV

The waning moon cast a faint light, setting over Basle's castle. Far off, away and high over the city walls, the same silver light glimmered on the snow of the high Alps.

The tall hedges of the *hortus conclusus* shone with frost. *Frost in summer!* Ash thought, still appalled; and stumbled in the near-darkness. The sound of a fountain plinked out of the dimness, and she heard the shift and clatter of many men in armour.

They have left me my armour, therefore they intend to treat me with some respect; they have only taken my sword; therefore they do not *necessarily* intend to kill me—

"What the fuck *is* all this?" Ash demanded. Her guards didn't answer.

The enclosed garden was tiny, a small plot of grass surrounded by an octagon of hedges. Flowers climbed frames. A cropped grassy bank ran down to a fountain, the jet falling into a white marble basin. The scent of herbs filled the air. Ash identified rosemary, and Wound's-Ease individually; underneath their smell was a stench of decaying roses. *Died from the cold, rotting on the stalk,* she surmised, and continued to walk forward into the garden, between her *'arif's* guards.

A figure in a mail hauberk sat at a low table covered with papers, on top of the grassy bank. Behind her, three stone figures held torches upright in their hands. A trail of hot spitting pitch ran down a torch-shaft as Ash watched, over one figure's clenched brass-geared hand, but the golem did not flinch.

Torch-flame cast flickering yellow light over the young Visigoth woman's unbound silver hair.

Ash could not help herself, her soles slipped on the cropped frozen grass and she stumbled. Recovering, she halted and looked at the Faris. That is my face, that is how I look—

Do I *really* look like that to other people?

I thought I was taller.

"You're my employer, for Christ's sake," Ash protested, aloud, disgusted. "This is completely unnecessary. I would have come to you. All you had to do was say! Why do this?"

The woman looked up. "Because I can."

Ash nodded thoughtfully. She walked closer, feet dipping into the springy cold turf, until the *'arif*'s hand on her vambrace arrested her progress some two yards away from the Faris's table. Her left hand automatically dropped to steady her sword-scabbard, and closed on emptiness. Ash planted her boots squarely, getting her balance; ready in any instant to move, and move as fast as armour permits. "Look, General, you're in charge of a whole invasion force here, I really don't think I need your power and influence to be *proved* to me!"

The woman's mouth quirked up at the corner. She gave Ash what was unmistakably a grin. "I think you do need the point driven home, if you're anything like me—"

She stopped, abruptly, and sat up on the three-legged stool, letting her papers fall back on to the small trestle table. She weighted them down with a Brazen Head, against the night breeze. Her dark eyes sought out Ash's face.

"I'm a lot like you," Ash said, quietly and unnecessarily. "Okay, so you're making a point. Fine. It's made. Where's Thomas Rochester and the rest of my men? Are any of them wounded or killed?"

"You wouldn't expect me to tell you that. Not until you've become sufficiently worried about it that you're willing to talk openly to me."

The quirk of an eyebrow, the same as her own – but mirror-image, Ash realised with a shock. Her own self, but reversed. She considered the idea that the general might be a demon or devil.

"They're well, but prisoners," the Faris added. "I have very good reports of your company."

Between relief at hearing her people were – or might be – still alive, and the shock of hearing that voice just not *quite* her own, Ash had to brace herself against dizziness that threatened to blank out her vision. For a moment, yellow torchlight wavered.

"I thought you might be amused to see this." The Faris held out a paper festooned with red wax seals. "It's from the parlement of Paris, asking me to go home because I'm a scandal."

Ash snorted despite herself. "Because *what*?"

"You'll appreciate it. Read it."

Ash stepped forward and extended her hand. The *'arif*'s men tensed. She still wore her gauntlets, and her gloved fingers only touched the paper; still, coming within scenting distance of her double – a smell of spice and sweat, like all the Visigoth military men around her – made her hand shake. Her gaze faltered. She looked down hurriedly at the paper. "You read it," she said.

"'Since that you are unbaptised and in a state of sin, and since that you have

189

received none of the sacraments, and bear no saint's name for your own; therefore we sternly petition you to return whence you came,'" the Faris read aloud, "'since we would not have our queens and dowagers have unclean intercourse with a mere concubine, nor our clean maidens, true wives and steadfast widows be corrupted by the presence of one who can be no more than a wayward wench or wanton wife; therefore enter not into our lands with your armies—'"

"Oh my lord! 'Wayward wench'!"

The other woman gave vent to a surprisingly deep-chested laugh. *Do I sound like that?* Ash wondered.

"It's the Spider,"[17] Ash murmured, delighted. "Genuine?"

"Certainly."

Ash looked up.

"So whose bastard am I?" she asked.

The Visigoth general snapped her fingers and said something rapid in Carthaginian. One of her men put another stool down beside the trestle table, and all the armed men, whose boots had been stamping divots back into the enclosed garden's lawn, filed out through the gate in the hedge.

And if we're actually alone now, I'm the Queen of Carthage.

Armour is a weapon: she considered using it, and as rapidly abandoned the idea. Ash let her gaze stray around in the dark, trying to pick out the points of light that would be reflected by steel arrow-heads or crossbow bolts. The cool night air shifted across her face.

"This place reminds me of the gardens in the Citadel, where I grew up," the Faris said. "Our gardens are brighter than this, of course. We bring the light in with mirrors."

Ash licked her lips, attempting to moisten a dry mouth. As required by the castle's ladies, little of the outside world could enter this garden. The hedges baffled sound. Now it was true night, and the darkness genuine, and the armed presence for the moment withdrawn, she found herself (despite the golems) insensibly more at ease; felt herself becoming the person who commands a company, not a frightened young woman.

"*Were* you baptised?"

"Oh yes. By what you call the Arian heresy." The general held out an inviting hand. "Sit down, Ash."

One does not commonly say one's own name, Ash reflected; and to hear it said in what was almost her own voice, but with a Visigothic accent, sent the hairs on the nape of her neck prickling up.

She reached up to unfasten the strap and buckle of her sallet, easing the helmet off. The night air felt chill against her sweating head and braided hair. She placed the visored sallet carefully on the table, and lifted her tassets and fauld with the ease of long practice to seat herself on the stool. Breast- and backplate kept her posture absolutely upright.

"This *isn't* the way to get your employee's co-operation," she added absently, settling herself. "It really isn't, General!"

[17] Louis XI of France, known to his contemporaries as 'the Spider King' because of his love of intrigue.

The Visigoth woman smiled. Her skin was pale. She had a mask of darker skin around her eyes, tanned honey-brown from long exposure to the sun, where neither steel helm nor mail aventail shielded her face. The mail mittens dangling from her wrists disclosed her hands: pale, with neatly trimmed nails. While it is true that mail sucks on to a human body, clinging to the padded clothing underneath, leaving her looking podgy, Ash judged the woman to have a very similar build to her own; and she was consumed, for a moment, with the sheer reality of the living, breathing, warm flesh sitting opposite her, no more than arm's reach away, looking *so alike*—

"I want to see Thomas Rochester," she said.

The Visigoth general raised her voice very slightly. The wicket-gate opened. A man held up a lantern for long enough for Ash to see Thomas Rochester, hands bound behind him, his face bloodied, but well enough apparently to stand without help – the gate closed.

"Happy?"

"I wouldn't describe myself as *happy*, exactly . . . Oh fuck it!" Ash exclaimed. "I didn't expect to like you!"

"No." The woman, who could not be much above her own age, pressed her lips flatly together. An irresistible smile tweaked the corners up. Her dark eyes glowed. "No! Nor did I! Nor did the other *jund*, your friend. Nor your husband."

Ash confined herself to growling, "Lamb's no friend of mine," and left the subject of Fernando del Guiz well alone. A familiar exhilaration began to fizz in her blood: the sheer balance required when renegotiating a trustworthy arrangement with people always more powerful than oneself (or they wouldn't be hiring mercenaries); the necessity of knowing what must be said, and what left unsaid.

"How did you come to have scars?" the Visigoth general asked. "A battle injury?"

Not negotiation, but pure personal curiosity, Ash judged. And as such, probably a weakness to be exploited.

"There was a saint's visitation when I was a child. The Lion came." Ash touched her cheek, something she did not often do, feeling the dinted flesh under her gloved fingertips. "He marked me out with His claws, thus showing I should be a Lioness myself, on the field of battle."

"So young? Yes. I was trained early, too."

Ash repeated, using the term quite deliberately, her earlier question. "Whose bastard am I?"

"Nobody's."

"N—?"

The Visigoth general looked as though she were appreciating how taken aback Ash felt. We should read each other very well, Ash thought. But do we? How would I know? I could be wrong.

She let her tongue run on:

"What do you mean, nobody? You can't mean I'm *legitimate*. Whose family is it? What family do you come from?"

"No one's."

191

The dark eyes danced, without any malice that Ash could detect; and then the other woman heaved a great sigh, rested her mailed arms on the table and leaned forward. The light from the golems' torches slid over her silver-blond hair and her unmarked face.

"You're no more legitimate than me," the Faris said. "I'm slave-bred."

Ash stared, conscious of a shock too great to recognise; so great that it faded into a mental shrug, and a *so what?* and a consciousness only that something, somewhere, had come adrift in her mind.

The Faris continued: "Whoever my parents were, they were slaves in Carthage. The Turks have their janissaries, Christian children they steal and raise up as fanatical warriors for their own country. My – father – did something very like that. I'm slave-bred," she repeated softly, "a bondswoman: and I suppose you are, too. I'm sorry if you were hoping for something better than that."

The sadness in her tone felt genuine.

Ash abandoned any thought of negotiation or subterfuge. "I don't understand."

"No, why should you? I don't suppose the *amir* Leofric would be pleased that I'm telling you. His family have been breeding for a Faris for generations. I am their success. You must be—"

"One of the rejects," Ash cut in. "Isn't that it?"

Her heart hammered. She held her breath, waiting to be contradicted. The Visigoth woman silently leaned over and with her own hands poured wine from a bottle into two ash-wood cups. She held out one. Ash took it. The black mirror of the liquid shook with the shaking of her hands. No contradiction came.

"Breeding project?" Ash repeated. And, sharply: "You said you had a father!"

"The *amir* Leofric. No. I've become used to . . . he isn't my true father, of course. He wouldn't lower himself to impregnate slaves."

"I don't care if he fucks donkeys," Ash said brutally. "That's why you wanted to see me, isn't it? That's why you came all the way to Guizburg, when you're running a damn war? Because I'm your – sister?"

"Sister, half-sister, cousin. Something. Look at us!" The Visigoth general shrugged again. When she lifted her wooden cup, her hand was shaking too. "I don't believe that my father – that Lord-*Amir* Leofric – would know why I *had* to see you."

"Leofric." Ash stared blankly at her twin. Part of her mind rummaged through memories of heraldry. "He's one of the *amirs* at the King-Caliph's court? A powerful man?"

The Faris smiled. "House Leofric has been, time out of mind, close companions to the King-Caliphs. We gave them the golem-messengers. And now, a *faris*."

"What happens to the . . . you said there were others. A project. What happens to the other people like us? How *many*—"

"Hundreds, over the years, I suppose. I never asked."

"You never asked." Incredulous, Ash drained her cup, not noticing whether the wine was good or bad. "This isn't new to you, is it?"

"No. I suppose it does seem strange, if you didn't grow up with it."

"What happens to them? The ones that aren't you – what happens to them?"

"If they can't talk to the machine,[18] they're usually killed. Even if they can talk to the machine, they usually go mad. You have no idea how lucky I feel that I didn't go insane in my childhood."

The first thought in Ash's mind was a sardonic *Are you quite sure about that?*, and then more of what the woman had said sunk in. Utterly appalled, Ash repeated, "'Killed'?"

Before the Visigoth woman could reply, the impact of one single phrase hit home.

She blurted out, without any intention of doing so, "What do you mean, *talk to the machine*? What 'machine'? What do you *mean*?"

The Faris folded her fingers around her wooden cup.

"Don't tell me you haven't heard of the Stone Golem?" she inquired, in a sardonic tone that Ash not only recognised but suspected of being a deliberate parody. "When I've gone to so much trouble to spread the rumour? I *want* my enemies too terrified to fight me. I *want* everybody to know that we have a great war-machine[19] at home – and that I speak with it whenever I please. Even in the middle of battle. *Especially* in the middle of battle."

That's it, Ash realised. This is why I'm here.

Not because I look like her.

Not because we're probably kin.

Because she hears voices *and she wants to know if I do, too.*

And what the hell will she do if she knows the truth?

Even knowing it to be a long leap to a conclusion, knowing it might be unjustified, panic and uncertainty set her heart thumping, to the point where she was glad to be wearing a mail standard: a pulse would have been clearly visible at her throat.

By reflex, she did the thing she had been doing since she was eight: cutting the linkage between herself and her fears. Her voice came out casually dismissive. "Oh, I heard the rumours. But that's just rumours. You've got some kind of a Brazen Head in Carthage – is it a head?" she broke off to ask.

"You have seen our clay walkers? It is their great father and progenitor: the Stone Golem. But," the woman added, "our defeating the armies of the Italians and the Swiss is not mere 'rumour'."

"The Italians! I know why you razed Milan, that was just to cut off the armour trade. I know all about that: I was apprentice to a Milanese armourer once." This fact having failed to distract either the woman or herself, Ash went

---

[18] The original text uses the Latin *fabricato*, for a structure made by human hands, not necessarily a machine in the sense that we would think of one.

[19] The Angelotti Latin text has, in its brief and previously obscure mention of this episode, *machina rei militaris*, a 'machine-tactician', and *fabricari res militaris*, '[something] made to [create] tactics'. 'Fraxinus me fecit' renders it as *computare ars imperatoria*, or, in a bizarre mixture of Latin and Greek, *computare strategoi*, 'a computor of the "art of empire"' or 'strategy'. This can be rendered into modern English as 'tactical computer'.

rapidly on: "I grant you the Swiss. But why shouldn't you be good? After all, *I'm* good!"

She stopped, and could have bitten her tongue hard enough to draw blood.

"Yes. You are good." The Faris said evenly, "I understand that you, also, hear 'voices'."

"Now that isn't a rumour. That's a downright lie." Ash managed to guffaw coarsely. "Who do you think I am, the Pucelle?[20] You'll be telling me next that I'm a virgin!"

"No voices? Merely a useful lie?" the Visigoth general suggested mildly.

"Well, I'm hardly likely to deny it, am I? The more Godly I sound, the better off I'm going to be." Ash managed, more convincingly, to sound both smug and ashamed of having been caught out telling fibs in public.

The woman touched her temple. "Nonetheless, I *am* in contact with our tactical computer. I hear it. Here."

Ash stared. She must look, she realised dimly, as if she didn't believe a word the woman was saying and thought she must be mad. In fact she was hardly aware of the woman at all.

The chill air moving into the sheltered garden swept over her sweating face. Somewhere outside a horse snorted, wuffing breath into the night sky. The sound of Visigoth soldiers talking was just audible. Ash clung to what she could see and hear as if to her own sanity. The thought formed itself in her mind with absolute inevitability. *If I was bred like her, and she hears voices from a tactical machine, then that's where* my *voice comes from.*

No!

Ash wiped at her wet upper lip, her breath misting the steel plate of her gauntlet. Numb, she felt first on the verge of vomiting, and then as if she were strangely detached from herself. She watched her wine-cup tip out of her fingers and bounce, spilling liquid across the trestle table, soaking all the papers neatly laid out.

The Faris swore, leaping to her feet, calling out, knocking over the table. Four or five boys – Visigoth pages or serfs – ran into the garden, rescuing the documents, wiping the table, mopping wine from the general's mail hauberk. Ash sat and stared with oblivious eyes.

Serfs *bred* as soldiers. Is that what she's saying? And I'm just some brat that somehow wasn't killed? Oh, sweet Jesus, and I always thought slaves and bondsmen beneath contempt—

And my voice isn't . . .

Isn't what?

Isn't the Lion? Isn't a saint?

Isn't a demon?

Christ, sweet saviour, sweet sweet saviour of me, this is worse than devils!

Ash gripped her left hand into a fist, under the table, digging steel plates into flesh. Then she could look up, focused by the pain, and mumble, "Sorry. Drinking on an empty stomach. Wine's gone to my head."

You don't know. You don't *know* that what she hears is what you hear. You don't *know* it's the same thing.

[20] Joan of Arc (AD 1412–1431).

Ash looked down at her left hand. The gauntlet-glove across her palm showed red blots, soaking into the linen.

The last thing I want to do now is carry on talking to this woman. Oh, fuck.

I wonder what would happen if I just told her? That I *do* hear a voice? A voice that tells me what tactics I can use in a battle?

If I tell her, what happens next?

If I don't know the answer to that question, then I certainly shouldn't ask her!

She was struck, as often in the past, with how time itself slows when life is knocked out of its rut. A cup of wine, in a garden, on a night in August: it is the kind of occasion that passes rapidly and automatically at the time, and falls out of memory instantly. Now she minutely registered everything, from the three-legged oaken stool's front leg sinking gradually into the daisy-thick grass under her weight, to the slide of plate over metal plate in her armour as she stretched her arm out to take the wine bottle, to the long, long intensity of the moment before the Visigoth general ceased being mopped down by her serfs and turned her bright head again towards Ash.

"It's true," the Faris said conversationally. "I do speak with the war-machine. My men call it the Stone Golem. It's neither stone, nor does it move like these—" A little shrug, as she indicated the stone-and-brass figures bearing the torches. "—But they like the name."

Caution reasserting itself, Ash put the bottle down and thought, If I don't know what the result of telling her I hear a voice will be, then I shouldn't tell her until I *do* know.

And certainly not until I've had time to think it through, talk it through with Godfrey and Florian and Roberto—

Shit, no! They just think I might be a bastard; how can I tell them I was born a slave?

Her lips stiff with the deceit, Ash said, "What would be the use of a war-engine like that? I could take my copy of Vegetius[21] on to the battlefield and read it there, but it wouldn't help me win."

"But if you had him there with you, alive, and you could ask the advice of Vegetius himself, *then* it might?" The Visigoth woman picked at the front of her fine mail with a fingertip, gazing down. "That's going to rust. This bloody wet country!"

The pitch-torches hissed and sputtered, burning down. Golems stood, cold statues. Trails of pine-smelling black smoke went up into the night sky. The recurved-bow crescent of the waning moon sank behind the hedges of the garden. Ash's muscles ached. Every bruise from her arrest smarted. The wine fizzed in her head, making her sway a little on the stool; and she thought, If I'm not careful the drink will work, I shall be telling the truth to her, and then where will I be?

"Sisters," she said, blurrily. The wooden stool lurched forward. She came to her feet, rather than fall sprawling, and halted with one armoured hand

---

[21] *De Re Militari*, written by the Roman Vegetius, became the standard training manual for the later mediaeval and early Renaissance era.

outstretched, catching the Visigoth woman's shoulder for support. "Christ, woman, we could be twins! How old are you?"

"Nineteen."

Ash laughed shakily. "Well, there you are. If I knew the year I was born, I could tell you. I must be eighteen or nineteen or twenty-ish by now. Maybe we *are* twins. What do you think?"

"My father interbreeds his slave stock. I think we probably all look alike." The Faris's dark brows frowned. She reached up with her bare fingers and touched Ash on the cheek. "I did see some others, as a child, but they went mad."

"'Went mad'!" A flush spread up over Ash's face. She felt the heat of it. Entirely unplanned, entirely genuine: her face grew red. "What am I supposed to tell people? Faris, what do I say? That some crazy lord-*amir* down in Carthage is breeding slaves like *stock*, like *animals*? And that I was one of them?"

The Visigoth woman said softly, "It still could be a coincidence. One shouldn't let a likeness—"

"Oh, fucking hell, woman! We're *twins*!"

Ash looked into eyes exactly the same height above ground as her own, the same dark colour, searching her features for kinship: for the curve of lip, shape of nose, shape of chin; a pale-haired foreign woman with the sunburn and odd scars of military campaigns, and a voice that, while not quite her own, might (she supposed now) be her own voice as others heard it.

"I'd rather not have known," Ash said thickly. "If it's true, I'm not a person, I'm an animal. Bloodstock. Failed bloodstock. I can be bought and sold – by *any*body – and I can't say a word about it. By *law*. You're a farm animal too. Don't you *care*?"

"It isn't news to me."

That brought her up short. Ash closed her hand over the woman's mailed shoulder, squeezed once, and let go. She stood swaying, but upright. The high hedges of the *hortus conclusus* shut out Basle, the company, the army, the world in darkness: and Ash shivered, despite armour and the padding under it.

"It doesn't matter to me who I fight for," she said. "I signed a contract with you, and I suppose this isn't enough to break it – assuming all my people here are unharmed, and not just Thomas. You know I am good, even if I don't have your 'Stone Golem'."

The lie came with an ease that might have been role-playing, might have been numbness, but in any case, Ash felt, couldn't delude anybody. She pushed on doggedly:

"I know you've razed half a dozen essential commercial cities in Italy, I know the Swiss cantons are wiped out as a fighting force, and that you've frightened Frederick and the Germanies into surrender. I also know the Sultan in Constantinople isn't currently expecting trouble, so your army is intended for Christendom – for the kingdoms north of here."

She let her gaze rest on the general's face, trying to detect any emotion. An impassive face looked back at her, chiaroscuro shadows shifting across it from the light of the golems' torches.

"Intended for Burgundy, Daniel de Quesada said, but I expect that means France as well. And then the *rosbifs*? You're going to be overextended, even with the numbers you've got. I know what I'm doing, I've been doing it for a long time, let me get on with it. Okay? And then some time in the future, when I'm not under contract to you, I'll let your Lord-*Amir* Leofric know exactly what I think of him breeding bastards."

—And this would probably work with anyone else, Ash concluded in the privacy of her own mind. How like me is she? Is she going to spot when I'm lying? For all I know, this would sound like bluff to anyone, let alone a sister I didn't know I'd got.

Fuck me. A sister.

The Visigoth general bent down and picked up the Brazen Head from where it dented the turf, shook it, shrugged, and placed it back on the trestle table beside Ash's sallet. "I should like to keep her as my sub-commander here."

Ash opened her mouth to reply, and registered the 'her'. 'Her', not 'you'. That, and the precise diction, and the woman's unfocused eyes, brought a sudden stab of realisation to her gut: *She is not talking to* me.

Fear flooded her body.

Ash took two steps back, skidded on the frosty grass, and stumbled backwards down the grassy bank, barely keeping her footing, falling, ramming her back hard into the marble surround of the fountain. She heard the metal of her backplate creak. A copper taste flooded her mouth. She blushed, blushed red as fire, as hot with shame as if she had been publicly discovered having sex; feeling in the one second *It was never real until now!* and in the next, *I never expected to see someone* else *doing this!*

Golems stared down from the top of the bank. The nearest one to Ash now had a spider's web linking its arm to the hedge, a frost-rimed white strand running from trimmed privet leaves to the shining brass mechanism of its elbow. She stared at the featureless oval face, the hen's-egg shape of the head delineated by guttering torches.

The Faris's voice protested, "But I would prefer to use her and her company now, not later."

She is not talking to me. She is talking to her voices.

Ash blurted, "We're under contract! We're fighting for you here. That was the arrangement!"

The general folded her arms, now with her head raised, watching the southern constellations in the sky over Basle. "If you order me to, then I will."

"I don't believe you hear voices at all! You're a bloody heathen. This is all play-acting!" Ash made an attempt to climb back up the steep bank. The soles of her riding boots glided over the cold grass, and she slid down, pitching forward in a rattle of metal; catching herself on her hands, and gazing up from on all fours at the Visigoth woman. "You're putting me on! This isn't *real*!"

Her protests were verbal floodwater. She stuttered, jabbering, and in the most private part of her mind, thought *I must not listen!* Whatever I do, I mustn't speak to my voice, I mustn't listen, in case it is the same—

—In case she'll know if I do.

Between keeping up a continuous protest and the clamped-shut determination in her mind, she neither heard nor felt anything as the Visigoth woman continued to speak aloud into empty air.

"Yes. I'll send her south on the next galley."

"You will not!" Ash got quickly and carefully to her feet.

The Visigoth general lowered her gaze from the night sky.

"My father Leofric wants to see you," she said. "You'll reach Carthage within a week. If he doesn't keep you long, I'll have you back here before the sun moves into Virgo.[22] We shall be some way further north, but I can still use your company. I'll send your men here back to your camp."

"*Baise mon cul!*"[23] Ash snapped.

It was pure reflex. In the same way that she had played camp's-little-mascot at nine, so she knew how to play bluff-mercenary-captain at nineteen. Her head swam.

"This wasn't in the contract! If I have to take my people out of the field now, it'll cost you – I've still got to feed them. And if you want me to go all the way to fucking North Africa in the middle of your war . . ." Ash made an attempt at a shrug. "That wasn't in the contract either."

And the second you take your eye off me, I'm out of here.

The Visigoth woman picked up Ash's sallet from the table, stroking her bare palm over the curve of metal from visor to crest to tail. Ash automatically winced, anticipating rust on the mirror-finished steel. The woman knocked her knuckles against the metal thoughtfully, and pushed the visor down until it clicked.

"I'm giving some of these to my men." A brief glitter of laughter, her eyes meeting Ash's. "I didn't order Milano razed until I'd cleared it out first."

"You can't get better than Milanese plate. Except for Augsburg – and I don't suppose you've left much of the south German foundries, either." Ash reached up and took her helmet from the woman's hands. "You send word to me out at the camp when you want me to board ship."

For a whole second, she was convinced that she had done it. That she would be allowed now to walk out of the garden, ride out of the city, put herself squarely in the middle of eight hundred armed men wearing her own livery, and tell the Visigoths to go straight to whatever might be the Arian version of eternal damnation.

The Visigoth general asked, aloud, "What do I do with someone my father wants to investigate, and I don't trust not to escape if I let her leave here?"

Ash said nothing aloud. In that part of herself where voice was potential, she acted. It was no decision, it was gut-level reflex, taken in despite of any risk of discovery. Passive, Ash listened.

A whisper – the merest whisper of a whisper – sounded in her head. The quietest, most familiar voice imaginable—

'*Strip her of armour and weapons. Keep her under continuous close guard. Escort her immediately to the nearest ship.*'

[22] On 24 August.
[23] French, lit. 'kiss my arse'.

V

A *nazir*[24] and his guards kept a literal grip on her, walking from the castle garden down through the streets, to a long tall row of four-storey houses that Ash recognised from her scouts' reports as the main Visigoth headquarters in Basle. Mail-covered hands held her arms.

Above the lime-washed plaster and oak beams of the gables, the stars were being swallowed up in darkness. Dawn coming.

Ash made no effort to break their hold on her. Most of this *nazir*'s unit were young, boys no older than her, with tan-creased faces, tight bodies, and long legs with calves thin-muscled from being so much on horseback. She gazed around at their faces as they hustled her into the nearest building, through an oaken door. If not for the Visigoth robes and mail, they could have been any men-at-arms from her company.

"Okay, okay!" She stopped dead in the entrance, on the flagstones, and shaped her mouth into a smile for the *nazir*. "I have about four marks in my purse, which will buy you guys drinks, and then you can come and tell me how my men are doing."

The two soldiers released her arms. She felt for her purse and realised that her hands were still shaking. The *nazir* – about her age, half a head taller, and male, of course – said, "Motherfucking mercenary bitch," in a fairly businesslike tone.

Ash mentally shrugged. Well, it was either that or *she's our boss's double!* and I get treated like the local demon . . .

"Fucking Frankish cunt," he added.[25]

House guards and servants came out into the hall, carrying candles. Ash felt a hand jerk at her belt as she was shoved forward, knew her purse would be missing when she looked for it; and then in a clatter of boots and shouted orders in Carthaginian, she found herself bustled towards the back of the house, through rooms full of armed men, down stone-floored passages, into a tiny room with an iron-barred door made of two-inch-thick oak, and a window about a foot square.

Two solemn-faced pages in Visigoth tunics indicated they were to help her off with her armour. Ash made no protest. She let herself be stripped down to her arming doublet and hose, with its sewn-in mail at armpits and crutch; her request for a demi-gown brought nothing.

The oak door closed. A sound of iron grating down into sockets told her that bars had been secured in place.

One candle guttered, its holder placed on the floor.

By its light she examined the room, padding around it in bare feet. The oak

---

[24] 'Nazir': a commander of eight men, the equivalent of the modern army's squad-leader (corporal). Presumably a subordinate of the *'arif* commander of forty (platoon-leader) that the text mentions earlier.

[25] 'Frank' is an Arab term of the period, meaning 'Northern European', and is certainly not Gothic.

floorboards felt chill. The room was bare, containing neither chair nor table nor bed; and the window-slot had thumb-thick iron bars set into its walls.

"Fuckers!" Kicking the door would hurt: she hit it with the heel of her hand. "Let me see my men!"

Her voice bounced back flat from the walls.

"Let me out of here, you motherfuckers!"

With the thickness of the wood, it was not even possible to tell if there was a guard posted outside; or if he could hear her if there was. She used the same voice she would have used to call orders across a battle-line.

"*Cocksuckers!* Sweet Christ, I can *pay* a ransom! Just let me send a message out!"

Silence.

Ash stretched her arms above her head, and then rubbed at the sore spots where her harness had chafed. She missed both her sword and her steel protection so keenly that she could all but feel the shape of the metal between her hands. She backed across the room, slid down the wall, and sat beside the sole light: pale wax and primrose-yellow flame.

Her hands prickled, as if the blood in them was cold as the water in alpine streams. She rubbed her palms together. A part of her mind insisted, no, it's not true, this is all some weird story, this isn't real life. You're a soldier's brat, that's all. It's coincidence. Your father was probably some Visigoth *nazir* who fought with the Griffin-in-Gold, and your mother was a whore. That's all: nothing out of the ordinary. You just look like the Faris.

And the other, stunned, part of her mind kept repeating: *She hears my voice.*

"Fucking hell." Ash spoke aloud. "She *can't* take me prisoner. I've got a fucking *contract* with the woman. Green Christ! I'm not going to Carthage. They might—"

Her mind refused to consider it. This was a new sensation: she tried to force her thoughts to consider being taken overseas to North Africa, and they slid away. Again and again. *Like trying to herd eels*, Ash thought, with a quick grin, and her teeth rattled together.

Maybe the Lion never came at all. *No.* No – our clerk made the miracle: the Lion did come.

But maybe nothing happened to *me*, there.

Maybe I just told the story of the chapel that way so often, I remember it like it did happen.

Ash's body shuddered, hands and feet cold, until she huddled up, tucking her hands into her armpits.

The Faris. She was bred to hear her tactical machine.

It *is* the same voice.

I'm – what? Sister. Cousin. Something. *Twin.*

Just something they discarded, on the way to breeding her.

And all I do is . . . overhear.

Is that all I've ever done? A bastard brat, outside the door, listening in to someone else's tactical war-machine, sneaking out answers for brutal little wars that the Visigoth Empire doesn't even notice . . .

The Faris is what they wanted. And even she's a slave.

After that she sat alone without food or drink and watched the candle-flame pouring a line of blackness up to where it suddenly broke and squiggled, playing sepia smoke over the low plaster ceiling, merging with the shadows. Her heart ticked off minutes, hours.

Ash rested her arms across her knees, and buried her face in her arms. There was a hot wetness against her face. Shock comes after wounds in the field, sometimes a long while after; and here in this narrow room she feels it now: Fernando del Guiz is not coming.

She wiped her nose on her sleeve. What opportunities there might be, to talk herself out of the prison for a ransom, or pity, or by violence, would not present themselves now.

This was the Emperor's marriage, and he's got out of it at the first opportunity that came along. No, that's not it—

Ash's chest aches. The hollow breathlessness wants to become tears, but she won't let it; raises her face and blinks in the candlelight.

—He's not here now because it was no coincidence he was in the town hall before I got captured. He was there to confirm where I was. For them. For her.

Well, you had him; you fucked him; you got what you wanted; now you know he's a weaseling little shit. What's the problem?

I wanted more than fucking him.

Forget him.

The wax candle melted down to a stump.

I'm prisoner here.

This is no Romance of Arthur or Peredur. I'm not about to scale the walls, fight off armoured men with my bare hands, ride off into the sunshine. What happens to valueless prisoners taken in war is pain first, broken bodies second, and an unmarked, unchristian burial afterwards. I am in their city. They own it now.

A hot thread of disquiet rumbled her bowels. She rested her arms on her knees, and her forehead on her arms.

They might expect a rescue by my company. Soon. An attack, men-at-arms, not on war-horses in these streets, so probably on foot.

I'd better have got this right.

The sharpest and loudest noise she had ever heard shattered the house.

Her body froze in the instant of the sound. Her bowels moved. She found in the same second both that she lay on shattered oak floorboards, and that she knew what the noise was. *Cannon fire.*

That's *ours!*

Her heart leapt up as she heard. Tears ran down her stunned face. She could have kissed their feet for gratitude. Another roar went up. The crack and thud of the second explosion echoed off the bare rafters of the roof.

For long heartbeats she was back in the alpine crags, where water falls down so loud that a man cannot hear himself speak, until out of the darkness and dust, torches flamed and men walked – men walking in over the remnants of lath and plaster and bloody rags of soldiers.

Black air swirled, dust clearing. Her room ended in broken beams and blackened limewash.

The back of the house gaped, blown away.

A great beam creaked and fell, like trees falling in the wildwood. Plaster sprayed her face.

Outside the breach, in the torchlight in the open, stood two carts and two light cannon dismounted, smoking from their touch-holes still; and she squinted her eyes and made out the bright blaze of Angelotti's curls, the man himself striding up to where she lay, hatless, grinning, and speaking – shouting – until she heard:

"We've blown the wall! Come on!"

With the back of the house, the city wall was down too; these houses, all fortified at the backs, themselves forming the wall around this part of the city.

Beyond them lay black fields, and the shrouds of forests on moonlit hills, and men moving in armour, calling *"Ash! Ash!"* both as a battle call, and to be known by their fellows. She stumbled out of the rubble, ears ringing, her balance gone.

Rickard tugged the sleeve of her arming doublet, Godluc's reins in his other hand. She made a grab for the big grey gelding's bridle, face momentarily pushed against his warm dappled flank. A crossbow bolt buried itself in old Roman brick and sprayed the wreckage of the house with fragments, men shouted, a rush of newcomers in mail and white tunics scrambling over the fallen oaken beams.

Ash got one foot into Godluc's stirrup, swung herself up, loose points and mail flapping from her arming doublet, too light without her armour; and a little lithe man flew at her and caught her by the waist and bore her bodily onwards right over her war-horse's back.

She fell, felt no impact—

Something happened.

I have bitten my tongue, I am falling, where is the Lion?

The picture behind her eyes was not of the Blue Lion banner, but of something flat and gold and meat-breathed, and a chill struck her fingers, her hands, her feet; dug deep into her sprawling body.

Feet stood to either side of her. Calves encased in shaped steel plate. European greaves, not Visigoth armour. Something flicked a glint of light past her face, into the air. Liquid spattered her cheek. An appalled shriek deafened her: the shriek of a man ruined in a second by the swipe of a sword, all life to come wrecked and spilled out on rubble; and a man close by her screamed, "My God, my God, no, no—" and then, "Christ, oh Christ, what have I done, *what have I done*, oh Christ, it *hurts*," and screams, on and on and on.

Floria's voice said "Christ!" very precisely and distantly. Ash felt the tall woman handling her head, warm fingers on her hair. Half her skull was numb. "No helmet, no armour—"

And another voice, male, saying above her, "—ridden over in the mêlée—"

Ash felt conscious through everything that was happening, although somehow she could not bring it to mind a moment later. Armoured horses galloped; hand-gunners banged off their charges, and then ran in the moonlight. She was tied with ropes to a truckle bed – how much later? – while she screamed, and others screamed; and the bed tied to a wagon; the wagon one among many, moving down frozen, muddy, deep-rutted roads.

A flapping cloth across her eyes blacked out the moon. All around her, wagons moved, oxen lowed; and the screeches of pack mules mixed with the shouting of orders, and a trickle of warm oil ran into her eyes, dripping down her forehead: Godfrey Maximillian, in his green stole, pronouncing the Last Rites.

It was too much to hold. She let it slip from her: the armed company men riding outrider, the whole camp packed up and moving, the clashes of steel from behind, far too close.

Floria knelt above her, holding Ash's head wedged still between dirty-fingered hands. Ash had a moment's sight of the grease of unwashed skin blackening the woman's linen cuff.

"Stay still!" the husky voice breathed above her. "Don't move!"

Ash leaned her head to one side, vomiting, and then screamed, and froze: held herself as still as possible, pain flaying her skull. A strange new drowsiness possessed her. She watched Godfrey kneeling in the cart beside her, praying, but praying with his eyes open, watching her face.

Time is nothing but vomiting and pain, and the agony of the cart rocking and jolting in the ruts of the roads.

Time is moonlight: black day: cloud-obscured moon: darkness: night again.

What roused her – hours later? days later? – into a dreaminess in which she could at least see the world, was a mutter, an exclamation from one man to another, from woman to man and child, all down the lines of her company. She heard shouting. Godfrey Maximillian grabbed the sides of the cart and leaned out of the front, past Rickard driving the beasts.

What they were shouting, she finally made out, was a name, a place. Burgundy. *The most powerful of princedoms*, she voiced in her mind; and at a level of voicelessness knew that she herself had intended this, had ordered it, had made Robert Anselm privy to this her intention before ever going inside the walls of Basle after the Visigoth commander.

Trumpets sounded.

A brilliance dazzled her eyes. *This is the pass to purgatory, then.* Ash prayed.

Light broke on her, over the canvas roof of the ox-wain, sifting down through the white coarse cloth. Light brought out the grain of the wood, the wagon's thick oak-plank flooring. Light manifested from the darkness the drawn cheek of Floria del Guiz, crouching over her wicker pack of herbs, retractors, scalpels and saws.

Not the colour-leeching silver of the moon. A harsh yellow light.

Ash tried to move. She groaned with a mouth thick with saliva. A man's broad-fingered hand pressed flat on her breast, holding her still on the low bed. Light brought out the dirt in the whorls of his fingertips. Godfrey's face was not turned to her, he stared out of the back of the wagon.

A warmth gleamed on his pink flesh, under the road-dust, and on the acorn-colour of his shaggy beard; and she could see, reflected in his dark eyes, a growing of this mad brightness.

Suddenly, a sharp line divided the rush-cushioned floor of the wagon and the strapped bed. Darkness over her body – shadow. Brightness over her blanket-covered legs, a line of light moving with the rocking motion of the wagon – sunlight.

She struggled, but could not raise her head. She moved her eyes only. Through the open back of the wagon glowed colours: blue and green and white and pink.

Her eyes teared. Through flooding water her eyes focused on distance – on green hills, and a flowing river, and the white walls of an enclosed town. The smell rose up and hit her, like a blow under her ribs from a quarterstaff: the smell of roses and honey, and the pungent warmth of horse- and ox-dung with the sun on it.

*Sun*light.

Nausea flooded up. Ash vomited weakly, the stinking liquid running down her chin. Pain fractured around the bones of her skull, brought more water to her eyes. Agonised, terrified of what the pain might mean, still she could only think, *It's day, it's day, it's the* sun*!*

Men with ten years' service cutting flesh on battlefields climb down to kiss the dirt ruts, bury their faces in dew-wet grass. Women who sew men's clothes and wounds alike, fall to their knees beside them. Riders pitch down from their horses' saddles. All, all falling on the cold earth, in the light, the light, singing *"Deo gratias, Deo adiuvante, Deo gratias!"*[26]

[26] Latin: 'Thanks to God', 'with God's help'.

Message: #47 (Anna Longman)
Subject: Ash, archaeological discoveries
Date: 09/11/00 at 12.03 p.m.
From: Ngrant@   format address deleted
                                        other details encrypted by
Anna —   non-Discoverable personal key

Anna, I apologise, for being out of contact for two days. It hardly
seems like minutes, here! So much is going on — we've had
television crews trying to get in. Dr Isobel has thrown what
amounts to a security cordon around the area, with the local
government's permission. So you may or may not have seen anything
about this on non-terrestrial television. If I were Isobel, I
wouldn't be so keen to have soldiers around an archaeological dig;
when I think of what they could carelessly destroy, my blood does
run cold, it is no mere figure of speech.

Before I do anything else, I *must* apologise for the things I
wrote on Tuesday about Dr Napier-Grant. Isobel and I have been old
friends, in a rather spiky way, for so many years. I'm afraid I let
my complete enthusiasm over the discoveries here reduce me to a
babbling idiot. I hope you will regard everything I wrote as being
in confidence.

I don't have Isobel's technical archaeological expertise, but
she wants me to stay and give her more of the cultural background —
all these finds are late 15th century. This is not her period, she's
a Classicist. The 'messenger' golem we have here is being measured
by the latest high-tech equipment, and *still* all that I can tell
you, Anna, is that at some point in the past, this thing walked.

What I can't tell you is *how*.

There appears to be nothing to power it, and no means for
anything to be fitted. Isobel and her team are baffled. She *cannot*
believe that the 'golem' descriptions in the ASH documents are a
coincidence or mediaeval fable. Anna, she WILL NOT believe it is
coincidence.

I am baffled, too. You see, in many senses, we shouldn't be
finding what we're finding here. Certainly, I believe I have the
evidence for a late-Gothic settlement on the North African coast,
but I have always known that the manuscripts' reference to
'Carthage' can be nothing but poetic licence. THERE IS NO
CARTHAGE! After the Punic Wars, Rome destroyed Carthage
completely. Carthage of the Carthaginians ceased to be an
inhabited, powerful city in 146 BC. The great later Roman
settlement, on this site, which they themselves called Carthage,
was itself obliterated by Vandals, Byzantines, and the Arab

conquest in the late 7th century AD — the ruins outside modern-day Tunis are a considerable tourist attraction.

'Delenda est Carthago', as Cato used to say in the Roman Senate, at every conceivable opportunity: 'Carthage must be destroyed!' And so it finally was. Two generations after the Carthaginian army under Hannibal was wiped out by Scipio at Zama, Rome had the inhabitants of Carthage deported, the city demolished, and the area ploughed under and sown with salt, so that nothing could ever grow there again — a little excessive, possibly, but at this point in our history it was a toss-up whether we were going to have a Roman Empire or a Carthaginian Empire, and, having been victorious, the Romans methodically made sure they wouldn't have any trouble from that area again.

History eradicates thoroughly. Until a decade ago, we did not know for certain which of the ruins on the ten-mile stretch of coast around Tunis was any of the Carthages! I am now having to speculate that the Visigoth expedition from Iberia itself re-settled a site that they, like the Romans before them, also CALLED Carthage; and that it was within a reasonable distance of the same location. If this didn't happen until quite late in the day — not until the High Middle Ages, perhaps — then that might account for the sparse documentary evidence of it. I intend to seek more in the way of Islamic sources to support this.

My theory, I THINK, remains intact. And now we have technological evidence to back it up!

— Pierce

Message: #48 (Anna Longman)
Subject: Ash mss, media projects
Date: 09/11/00 at 12.27 p.m.
From: Ngrant@   format address deleted
                             Other details encrypted by
Anna —   non-discoverable personal key

I forgot to check my previous mail! Shi Sorry. *Sorry*.

Isobel just downloaded your e-mail herself and is extremely interested in the TV project you propose — if not entirely flattered by your description of herself. She said, 'This woman makes me sound like Margaret Rutherford!' A remark which, I may add, despite her being only 41 and merely having a predilection for old black-and-white film comedies, *does* make her sound like Margaret Rutherford. (Fortunately for British television, Isobel is rather more chic.)

We are discussing what might best be done, given a certain tension between the dumbing-down effect of television upon scientific enquiry, and the undoubted attractions of gaining

popular publicity for archaeology and literature. And, if I can be
honest, discussing the attractions that publicity holds for me. I
should not mind my fifteen minutes of fame, no, not at all!
Especially since it seems that someone else would be paying me for
the privilege. I assume we will receive a fee of some kind?

Isobel wishes to consider her options and consult with her team,
and the university. I should be able to get back to you later
today. Now that I am certain I understand the uses of the Internet,
I am forwarding the next section of 'Ash'. You will want to look it
over while we hammer out some of the fine details here.

— Pierce

Message: #49 (Anna Longman)   *Previous message?*
Subject: Ash Project   *Hard copy presumed missing?*
Date: 09/11/00 at 12.44 p.m.
From: Ngrant@   *format address deleted*
                                           Other details encrypted by
Ms Longman —   *non-discoverable personal key*

I am reluctant to teleconference with your editorial committee.
The phone lines here are not good, and moreover I doubt they are
secure. I will fly back to talk in person as soon as I can take a
break from the site. I would be obliged if you could put me in
contact with an association of literary agents, or 'media' agents,
assuming that there is such an association; my University will
then be in a position to enter into negotiations.

I see no reason why we should not reach agreement. Footage from
our videocam team is being sent digitally back to my department at
█████████████ University, and processed there. I suggest that
you liaise with my departmental head, Stephen Abawi, about any use
of research footage for publicising Dr Ratcliff's edition of
'Ash'.

At Dr Ratcliff's suggestion, I am encouraging the team to film
more of the actual 'felt experience' of this dig, in addition to
our archaeological findings. This may need to be limited in scope,
as the soldiers do not like to be filmed and small bribes are not
always sufficient to placate them. However, it will, as Dr
Ratcliff points out, be necessary to have this footage if a
documentary is to be later constructed from our time here.

It is possible that Dr Ratcliff and I may collaborate on a
documentary script. I am considering using quotations from the
previous editors of the 'Ash' material. Are you familiar with
Charles Mallory Maximillian's 1890 edition? —

    . . . the great mediaeval spoked Wheel of Fortune is always

turning; the Goddess Fortuna always sweeping up each man in
turn from beggarhood to crowned king, to falling fool, and
back to the darkness below the wheel, which is death and
forgetfulness. In 1477, upon the field of Nancy, Burgundy
vanishes from history and memory, lies as cold and dead as the
frost-bitten corpse of Charles the Rash, who had been the
shining Prince of Christendom, and whose own enemies thought,
for two days, that they beheld the body of a mere peasant
soldier, so wretched, filthy and torn it was. We recall a
golden country. Yet, history has turned, and the past is
lost . . .

Here on the coast of Tunisia, the Wheel is turning again.

— I. Napier-Grant

Message: #63 (Pierce Ratcliff)
Subject: Ash, documents
Date: 10/11/00 at 01.35 p.m.
From: Longman@

Pierce —   *(format address and other details*
                            non-recoverably deleted)

Thank Dr Napier-Grant for her mail.
  Your news about the messenger-golem find is stunning. I don't know
what to make of it. I'll tell you WHY I don't know what to make of
it.
  You've found mobile golems.
  I've lost the Angelotti manuscript.

— Anna

Message: #50 (Longman)
Subject: Ash mss.
Date: 10/11/00 at 02.38 p.m.
From: Ngrant@

Anna —   *format address and other details*
                    non-recoverably deleted

I don't understand. How can you LOSE the Angelotti text? It's in
four major world collections! Explain!

— Pierce

```
Message:    #66 (Pierce Ratcliff)
Subject:    Ash mss.
Date:       10/11/00 at 02.51 p.m.
From:       Longman@
```

format address and other details non-recoverably deleted

Pierce —

No. It isn't.

I wanted to check on this 'forgotten invasion' of yours for myself.

If you weren't out in Tunis with Dr Grant — if this turns out NOT to be golems — I'm pulling the book. I mean it. THERE IS NO ANGELOTTI MANUSCRIPT!

The problem isn't that a 'Visigoth invasion' seems to have been swept under the historical carpet.

The PROBLEM is that since I wanted to check the Angelotti text myself, I phoned the Metropolitan Museum of Art, and the Glasgow Museum.

The Glasgow Museum no longer hold a copy of the Latin text attributed to one 'Antonio Angelotti'.

Both the British Library and the Metropolitan Museum now classify it as Mediaeval Romance Literature. As FICTION, Pierce!

WHAT IS GOING ON HERE?

```
Message:    #54 (Longman)
Subject:    Ash/Angelotti mss.
Date:       10/11/00 at 04.11 p.m.
From:       Ngrant@
```

format address and other details non-recoverably deleted

Anna —

I contacted Bernard at the Glasgow Museum. He tells me he doesn't know where their Angelotti text is, they may no longer shelve it, or it 'may' be out on loan to some other institution. He asked me why I wanted to study something so patently useless to the historian, since it's a presumed 17th century FAKE.

I don't understand what is happening!

Both Charles Mallory Maximillian and Vaughan Davies had no doubts whatsoever about the veracity of this manuscript! In 1890 and 1939 it was catalogued as an ordinary 15th century document. When I consulted it, it was in the CATALOGUE under that designation! This is not like anything else that has ever happened to me in my academic career! They CAN'T have reclassified it in the past six months!

I can't get anyone to talk to me on-line, and I CAN'T leave here. If I go off-site, I won't be allowed back on again. You're going to have to take this on for me. For our book.

— Pierce

```
-------------------------------------------------------------------
```

Message: #69 (Pierce Ratcliff)
Subject: Ash, texts
Date: 10/11/00 at 04.22 p.m.   *format address and other*
From: Longman@   *details non-recoverably*
                                          deleted
Pierce —

Jesus Christ Pierce what next? If one of your manuscripts is a
fake, but the golems are real?

  I'll do what I can on-line, and by phone. I really don't
understand this.

  Give me a list of documents to check.

  Okay, I can understand that maybe Victorian historians weren't
so rigorous as modern ones. There are such things as faked
manuscripts. But there've been two editions besides yours: if
Charles Mallory Maximillian was lax, surely Vaughan Davies should
have spotted something?

— Anna

```
-------------------------------------------------------------------
```

Message: #55 (Anna Longman)
Subject: Ash, texts
Date: 13/11/00 at 00.45 a.m. *format address deleted*
From: Ngrant@
                                    text encrypted by non-discoverable
Anna —   *personal key*

Yes, Vaughan Davies should have discovered if any of the documents
were invalid. You are kind enough not to say it, but, so should I.

  This is a list of the principal authenticated documents that I
have been working from:

  The WINCHESTER CODEX, c.1495, Tudor English translation of
  mediaeval Latin original (1480s?). Ash's childhood.

  The del Guiz LIFE, c.1516, withdrawn, expurgated and reissued
  1518. German original. Plus a version by Ortense Mancini, 17c
  playwright, in which she mentions that it is translated from a
  16c Latin manuscript — we have no trace of this. Covers Ash's
  life 1472–1477.

  The CARTULARY of the monastery of St. Herlaine, c.1480,
  translated from the French. Brief mentions of Ash as a novice
  c.1467–8.

  'PSEUDO-GODFREY', 1478(?), a German text of dubious value,
  found in Cologne in 1963; original paper and ink, but possibly

210

a contemporary forgery, cashing in on the popularity of the 'Ash' cycle of legends. Ash's life c.1467-1477.

The ANGELOTTI manuscript, Milan, 1487; appended at the end of a treatise on armour owned by the Missaglia family. Ash during the period 1473-1477.

'FRAXINUS ME FECIT', possibly autobiography of Ash, therefore written down no later than 1477; if a biography, between 1477 and 1481(?). Covers summer 1475(6?)-autumn 1476.

The two previous editions of the 'Ash' material are:-

Charles Mallory Maximillian (ed.) ASH: THE LIFE OF A FEMALE MEDIAEVAL MERCENARY CAPTAIN, J Dent & Son, London, 1890, reprinted 1892, 1893, 1896, 1905.
  This contains translations of all the above, excluding 'Pseudo-Godfrey' (and, of course, 'Fraxinus'). CMM does include the 17th century poems by Lord Rochester supposedly based on episodes from the del Guiz LIFE; later research indicates this is unlikely. CMM was a widely read and reputable scholar of his period, holding the Mediaeval History Chair at Oxford.

Vaughan Davies (ed.) ASH: A FIFTEENTH CENTURY BIOGRAPHY, Victor Gollancz Ltd, 1939. Not reprinted. Plates lost.
  Contents as CMM. There was also rumoured to be a pirated paperback edition, a facsimile reprint done by Starshine Press in San Francisco (1968), but I have not seen it.
  This original 1939 edition itself exists only in incomplete form in the British Library. The publisher's warehouse was bombed during the war, destroying stocks, and cutting short a popular vogue for Vaughan Davies's book — after all, it is not every history book that is written by a man with his scientific, as well as historian's, credentials.

That's all I have on file, I think there may be one or two confirmatory mentions in contemporary letters, but I don't have the data with me.
  I've now completed the next translation of the del Guiz/ Angelotti 'Ash' material, and will send it to you after this.
  Isobel, of course, is insisting that I IMMEDIATELY finish 'Fraxinus me fecit' for her, and she wants the translation done meticulously — so, I think, do I; but she knows that.
  Please contact me. I DO NOT UNDERSTAND what is happening here. I have been an academic for twenty years; I do not believe I could make an error — or a series of errors — of this magnitude.

— Pierce

```
--------------------------------------------------------------------
```

Message: #73 (Pierce Ratcliff)
Subject: Ash, documentation
Date: 13/11/00 at 10.03 p.m. *format address deleted*
From: Longman@
                                    Text encrypted by non-discoverable
Pierce —   *personal key*

I took a day's leave and spent it in the British Library. I didn't
particularly want to explain at the office that there may be
problems with your book — not when we've put it in the Spring
catalogue.

  I have grave problems with what I've found.

  Some of the documents you mention, I just can't find — the Pseudo
Godfrey, and the Cartulary (log-book, I suppose) of this St
Herlaine monastery. I can't find any record of the monastery
either.

  I've managed to trace the German del Guiz 'Life', but you won't
like it, Pierce.

  In 1890, it was classified under 'Late Mediaeval History'.
Charles Mallory Maximillian was obviously being completely above-
board when he did his translation of it. By 1939, it was re-
classified, this time as 'Romance Literature', along with the
Nibelungenlied! I found a reference to your 1968 American printing
of Vaughan Davies, which has the del Guiz manuscript in it, and the
whole thing is classified under 'General Fiction'! And as far as the
British Library's concerned now, they don't have any record of
having a copy.

  They don't have a record of any mediaeval manuscript by an
'Angelotti', either.

  As far as I can see, this material was thought to be genuine in
the 1890s, was discovered to be fake in the late 1930s — and
Vaughan Davies just ignored this. What I can't understand, Pierce,
is why YOU'VE ignored this.

  Unless you can give me a convincing explanation, I am going to
have to discuss this with my Managing Director.

  — Anna Longman

```
--------------------------------------------------------------------
```

Message: #60 (Anna Longman)
Subject: Ash, archaeological discoveries
Date: 14/11/00 at 11.11 a.m.
From: Ngrant@

*format address deleted.
Text encrypted by non-discoverable
personal key*

Anna —

I didn't ignore anything.

 When I last consulted these documents, in the British Library,
less than two months ago, they were classified under 'Mediaeval
History'. There was NO suggestion that they might be anything
else.

 Please do nothing rash.

 If these documents are so unreliable — why is the ARCHAEOLOGICAL
EVIDENCE backing them up?!

— Pierce

PART FOUR

13 August–17 August AD 1476

The Garden of War

I

A young woman's body lay on a mattress stuffed with goose-down. Whether this was too soft, she too unaccustomed, it was not possible to tell. She stayed unconscious. She nonetheless rolled a little, from side to side, and as her head turned it could be seen that she had a shaved patch over her left ear, hair sheared away from the swollen skull. A fine silver stubble grew back.

To stop her moving, they tied her with linen bands to the wooden frame of the bed. She seemed hot, with a fever, and restless. Someone washed and combed out and plaited the rest of her hair into two loose-woven braids, so it should not turn into impenetrable sweat-glued tangles.

Sometimes there were angry voices over her. A swearing-out of devils, or a fierce quarrel between soft-voiced women. Someone trailed oil over her forehead, and it rolled down the bridge of her nose and over her slashed cheek. When the linen sheet was taken back, half her body was spotted with black bruises, and a poultice of comfrey and Self-Heal was strapped to her right ankle, and another to her right wrist.

Someone washed her body with water from a silver basin.

Bees wove around the room, in the bright air between white walls, and back over the sill where climbing flowers nodded. A soft, rhythmic murmur of doves sounded beyond the window. Being washed and turned, she saw out of the window to the birds, blazing white in the sun, one of them with golden beams shining from its head and beak and golden eye: the Holy Spirit nesting in the dove-cote, along with the other doves. Then there was fire and pain and shouting, and she was bound back on the bed with new linen, and the world went away to the sound of an angry voice that rose up the registers from contralto to alto to shout.

All the time, there was the light.

It came first always with a cold pink and yellow glow, through the night-shuttered windows. It grew, slanting, into bars of brightness: as bright as light down the edge of a sharpened blade. And light shook from the surface of the water in the jug, that stood on an oaken chest beside the bed; dancing in blotched reflections on the white curving plaster of the ceiling.

Once a wing brushed her, white and stiff as a swan's feathers, but with all quills edged with gold like the leaves of a manuscript. Two voices spoke over the bed, debating about angels and those wandering spirits of the air that are devils, or perhaps old pagan gods worn weak with lack of worship.

She saw beyond the ceiling of the white cell a stacked rise of circles, circle within circle, each rimmed with faces and wings, and behind the saints' faces thin gold rings, a knife-scratch thin, haloes hot as the metal poured in a goldsmith's furnace. She sought, but could not find, a Lion.

The light, slanting the other way, drenched the room in gold. Chill shivered her, and hands brought up the linen sheets. A sharp clear-skinned face bent over her, short hair turned to rose-gold.

"D—"

Too soft a croak: and water from a wooden cup was spilling down her mouth and chin, soaking the sheets; leaking into her mouth, pricking a way between surfaces of dehydrated flesh. She felt in one instant the roar of pain through her flesh. Hurt leg, hurt arm, battered body; and her unbandaged hand jerking in its linen bands.

Fingers freed her. She felt for as much of her body as she could reach. Body, whole; no more damage to leg and arm than she has had before. A spurt of pain in her head. She touched her cheek, which flared with pain, and probed with her tongue to find the shattered roots of two back teeth in the upper left of her mouth.

"Did Thomas—"

"Thomas Rochester is alive! He's alive. And the others. Baby—"

More water at her lips, this with a stench of some herb in it. She drank, would she, would she not; but lay, fighting sleep, for as long as it took for the light to begin again, dew-wet and chill, at the shutters of the window.

Memories of darkness pushed at her, of a black sky, and an endless night, and lands growing winter-cold in the middle of harvest time.

"They'll be following—"

"Hush . . ."

Sleep took her down so fast that what she said was slurred, incomprehensible to anyone present:

"I will not be taken away to Carthage!"

II

She woke sweaty and warm. A dream of terror slid away from her, like water vanishing through sand. Ash opened her eyes as delirium became sudden clarity:

Shit! How many days have I been sick? How long will it be before the Faris comes after me, or sends a snatch-squad—?

The voice of Floria del Guiz, above her, said, "You got stepped on by a horse."

"So much for the glory of battle . . ." Ash strained to focus her open eyes. "Sod this for a game of soldiers."[1]

"Bloody idiot."

[1] *Hoc futui quam lude militorum.* I quote Vaughan Davies's idiosyncratic translation of the mediaeval dog-Latin text.

The wooden-framed bed creaked as weight came down on it. Ash felt her body hoisted up by warm, strong arms. Time blipped: she thought she felt another body in the bed beside hers; then realised that the warm torso and breasts under the linen shirt pressed against her cheek were Florian's; that the woman surgeon was cradling her, and that her own body was weak as water.

Florian's quiet voice buzzed in Ash's ear, transmitted more by vibration through the flesh and bone of the surgeon's body than by sound. "I suppose you want an honest answer to how badly you're injured? Seeing as you're the boss?"

"No . . ."

"Damn right you don't."

You should have washed, Ash thought dimly, smelling a warm stench of old sweat on the surgeon's clothes. She let her head fall back limply against Florian's breasts, the bright white cell swimming before her eyes. "Oh *shit* . . ."

The weight of their two bodies was pressing them together on the goose-down mattress, into a valley in the centre of the bed. Ash gazed up at a plastered white ceiling, her eyes tracking the black dot of a bee as it buzzed into the room. The pressure of the woman's arms around her felt inexpressibly welcome.

"You're tough as shit," the rough voice above her said. "That's more significant than anything I can do for you."

In the room's hush, Ash heard a distant choir. A noise of women's voices, singing mass. The tiny room filled with the scent of lavender: she guessed it must be growing close by.

Nothing in the room was hers.

"Where's my fucking sword? Where's my armour!"

"Yeah, that's my girl!"

Ash shifted her gaze to Floria's face. "I know I'm going to die before I'm thirty. We can't all be Colleoni[2] or Hawkwood.[3] How close have I come?"

"I don't *think* your skull's cracked . . . I've sewed you up. Said the right charms. If you'll take my advice, you'll stay in bed for the next three weeks. And if you will take my advice, it'll be the first time in five years!" The surgeon's cradling arm tightened. "I really can't do any more for you. Rest."

"How many leagues are we from Basle?" Ash demanded. "What's happened to my company?"

Floria del Guiz heaved a sigh that Ash felt against every rib.

"Why can't you be like my other patients and start with 'where am I?' You're in a convent, we're outside Dijon, in Burgundy, and the company's camped about a quarter of a mile *that* way." Her long dirty finger stabbed the air above Ash's nose, indicating a direction out of the cell window.

[2] Bartolomeo Colleoni (1403(?)–1475) had died the previous year. A famous condottiere, employed largely by the Venetians from 1455, he lived until the age of 72, still active Captain-General of the Venetian forces, and discouraged by the Most Serene Republic from travelling north of the Alps from his castle at Malpaga, in case the Milanese should immediately attack Venice in his absence! Those who truly wanted to see the great captain – for example, King Edward IV of England, in 1474 – travelled to him.

[3] Sir John Hawkwood, famed English mercenary and leader of the White Company (1363–1375), saw long and profitable service in Italy and died old (in 1394).

"Dijon." Ash's eyes widened. "That's a *fuck* of a way from the cantons. We're the other side of Franche-Comté. Good. Dijon . . . You're a fucking Burgundian, Florian, help me out. You know this place?"

"I should do." Floria del Guiz's voice sounded acerbic. She sat up, lurching Ash's body uncomfortably. "I have an aunt living six leagues from here. Tante Jeanne's probably at court – the Duke's here."

"Duke Charles is *here*?"

"Oh, he's here. So is his army. And his mercenaries. You can't see the meadows outside the town for military tents!" Florian shrugged. "I suppose this is where he came to after Neuss. It is the southern capital."

"Have the Visigoths attacked Burgundy? What's happening about the invasion?"

"How would I know? I've been in here trying to keep you alive, you silly bitch!"

Ash grinned, helplessly, at her surgeon's total disregard for military matters. "That's no way to talk to your boss."

Florian shifted around under her in the bed, until she could look Ash directly in the face. "I do, of course, mean 'you silly bitch, *boss*'."

"That's much better. Fuck." Ash tried to tense her muscles to sit up, and flopped back, her face screwed up in pain. "Some fucking surgeon you are. I feel half dead."

"I can arrange the other half any time you like . . ."

A cool palm laid itself against Ash's forehead. She heard Floria grunt, vaguely dissatisfied.

The surgeon added, "There's a pilgrimage up here every day, with a good three-quarters of the men trying to get in to speak to you. What's the *matter* with these guys? Don't they know a convent when they see one? Can't they even wipe their own arses without you being there to tell them to do it?"

"That's soldiers." Ash pushed her hands against the mattress, trying to sit up. "Shit! If you've been saying I can't see them because I got a crack on the head—"

"I haven't been saying anything. This is a *convent*. They're *men*." Florian smiled wryly. "The sisters won't let them inside."

"Christ, they'll think I'm dying or dead! They'll be off to sign up with someone else before you can say *condotta*!"[4]

"I don't think so."

With a long-suffering sigh, Floria del Guiz got out of the bed and began to hold up Ash's torso and heap pillows under her shoulders and head. Ash bit her lip to keep from vomiting.

"You don't think so – why not?"

"Oh, you're a hero." Floria grinned crookedly, moving to stand beside the cell window. The white daylight showed up purple flesh under her eyes, and lines cut into the flesh at the sides of her mouth. "You're the Lioness! You saved them from the Visigoths, you got them out of Basle and into Burgundy, the men think you're wonderful!"

"They *what*?"

[4] The Italian 'contract', from which the condottieri took their nickname.

"Joscelyn van Mander is quite dewy-eyed. You military types are too damn sentimental, I've always said so."

"Fucking hell." Ash felt the goose-down pillows give under her as she leaned back, dizzy. "I had no right to go wandering into Basle looking for the Faris, and even if I did, I put my men in danger. You name it and I fucked it. I really fucked up, Florian. They must know that!"

"If you walk down there today, they'll throw rose-petals under your feet. Mind you," Floria remarked thoughtfully, "if you walk down there today, I may be burying you tomorrow."

"A hero!"

"Haven't you noticed?" The surgeon delicately pointed upwards. "The sun. You've brought them back to the sun."

"*I* brought—" Ash broke off. "When did the sun come back? Before we got to Burgundy?"

"As we crossed the border." A frown compressed Floria's brows. "I don't think you understand me. The sun's only shining *here*. In Burgundy. It's still dark everywhere else."

Ash licked her lips, her mouth dry.

No, that can't be – it *can't* only be here!

Ash absently pushed Floria's hands away as the woman tried to put a wooden bowl to her lips. She took it in her own hands, and sipped, frowning.

They put out the sun. But not here, in Burgundy. Why Burgundy?

Unless the Eternal Twilight spreads where . . .

Where the armies from the land Under the Penitence successfully invade. No, how could that be?

Maybe it's not just here that there's the sun, but in all the lands north of what they've conquered, France and the Low Countries and England, where the Eternal Twilight hasn't yet spread? Shit, I need to be up and talking to people!

"If the guys think I got them *out* of trouble," Ash continued her progression of thought, " – Green Christ only knows why! – then I'm not going to tell them different. I need all the morale on my side that I can get. Bloody hell, Florian. You're Burgundian, aren't you? What are our chances of getting another contract here, given that I made a sterling effort to off the Duke not so long ago?"

Ash gave a small smile, her lips wet with the clear spring water.

"Would your Tante Jeanne get us an in to court?"

Floria's expression closed like a door shutting.

"You'd better see Robert Anselm today," she remarked. "It probably won't kill you. It might kill him if you don't."

Ash blinked, her attention disrupted from the Visigoths. "Robert? Why?"

"Who do you think rode over you at Basle?"

"Oh, *fuck*."

Floria nodded. "He'll be sitting outside the convent gate about now. I know this, because he's been sleeping out there."

"How long have I been here?"

"Three days."

"How long has he been out there? Don't tell me. Three days." Ash put her head in her hands, and winced as her fingers came into contact with the shaved patch of her scalp, and the painful irregularity of cat-gut stitches. She rubbed at her eyes. She was suddenly conscious of being dressed only in a stale night-shirt, and of needing the nightsoil pot. "Then who's been running my company!"

"Geraint-the-Welsh-bastard." Floria widened innocent eyes. "Or at least, that's what they seem to think his name is. With Father Godfrey. He seems to have it all under control."

"Does he, by God! Then it's more than time I was back in charge. I don't want the Lion Azure turning into Geraint ab Morgan's company while I sit on my arse in some damn convent!" Ash rubbed the heel of her hand over her face. "You're right, sod you; I'll get up tomorrow, not today. I still feel like there's a horse treading on me. I'll see Roberto. I'd better see the maîtresse of this place, too. *And* I'm getting dressed."

The surgeon eyed her sardonically, but made no comment except, "And with all your boys outside these walls, you expect me to act as your page, I suppose?"

"You might as well learn to be a page. You're a crap surgeon."

Floria del Guiz blurted out a laugh, an open guffaw completely different from her usual mordant chuckle, plainly taken by surprise. She whooped, and thumped the flat of her hand against her thigh. "You ungrateful cow!"

"Nobody loves an honest woman." Ash's mouth moved into an unwilling smile, remembering. "Or maybe I'm just a wayward wench."

"A *what*?"

"Never mind. Christ, I'm well out of that!"

And I'm staying as far away from the Faris as I can get.

Okay, maybe we *are* far enough away to be safe. For the moment. What do I do now? I don't know anything like enough about this situation!

Ash swivelled her legs around with difficulty and sat on the edge of the bed. Blood thundered in her ears, drowning out the sound of doves cooing beyond the window. She swayed where she sat.

"Poor bloody Robert. It would have to be him. Find me a chair, or at least a stool with a back to it. I don't want him to see me looking as if the Grim Reaper will be getting the next audience with me!" Ash stopped, adding suspiciously, "This is a convent? I'm not putting on a dress!"[5]

Florian laughed, moving past her towards the oak chest against the far wall. She trailed her fingers through Ash's unshaved hair, affectionately and lightly: Ash hardly felt the touch.

"I sent down to Rickard for your gear. The Soeur wouldn't let me bring a sword within the confines of the convent, but," Floria's head emerged, her hands clutching shirt, doublet, and hose, "you've got your green and silver, and a velvet demi-gown. Will boss be content with that?"

"Boss will do just fine."

Once past the squalidness of the nightsoil pot, and half laced into her clothes, Ash began to find it less disturbing to have a woman acting as her page. She grinned. "Why I've been paying you all these years as a *surgeon*, when—"

[5] Original text, 'kirtle'.

She broke off, as a nun entered the cell.

"Soeur?"

The big woman folded her hands at her waist. A tall, tight wimple robbed her face of all context, left it nothing but an expanse of puffy white flesh in the sunlight. Her voice sounded gravelly. "I'm Soeur Simeon. You're staying in bed, my girl."

Ash wriggled her arm down the sleeve of her doublet, and leaned against the upright of the back-stool while Floria laced it tight at the shoulder. She spoke as if the room wasn't swimming around her.

"First, I'm seeing my second-in-command, Soeur."

"Not in here you're not." The nun's lips compressed into a hard line. "No men within the walls of the convent. And you're not yet fit to go out."

Ash felt Floria straighten up. Her voice came from above Ash:

"Allow him in for a few minutes, Soeur Simeon. After all, you let *me* in – and I know what's important for my patient's health. Good lord, woman, I'm a surgeon!"

"Good lord, woman, you're a *woman*," the nun rapped back. "Why do you think you're allowed in here?"

Ash chuckled at the almost audible wuff! of the wind being taken out of Floria del Guiz's sails.

"That fact, *ma Soeur*, is completely confidential. I know I can trust a woman of God." Ash put her hands flat on her thighs, and managed to sit reasonably confidently. "Bring Robert Anselm in secretly if you must, but bring him in. I'll get through my business as fast as possible."

The woman – the nun's habit robbing her of her age, as well; she might have been anywhere between thirty and sixty – narrowed her eyes and surveyed the whitewashed sick-room and its dishevelled occupant. "You've been used to having your own way for quite some time, haven't you, *ma fille*?"

"Oh yes, Soeur Simeon. It's far too late to do anything about it."

"Five minutes," the woman said grimly. "One of the *petites soeurs* will be in here with you for decency's sake. I shall go and organise some prayer."

The door of the whitewashed cell closed behind the big woman.

Ash blew out her lips. "Whoa! *There* goes a born colonel of the regiment!"[6]

"Look who's talking." Floria del Guiz went to rummage in the oak chest again, and emerged with a pair of low boots. She knelt, thrusting them onto Ash's feet, and Ash looked down at the top of her golden head. She made as if to reach out and touch the disguised woman's hair, then drew her hand back.

"I'm all in tangles," she said. "Smarten me up, will you?"

The tall woman took a horn comb out of her purse and stepped behind her, undoing her loose braids. Ash felt a gentle, painful tugging as the comb worked its way up from the bottom of each hank of silver-fair hair, unthreading sweat-solidified knots. Her head began to throb. She shut her eyes, feeling the warmth on her face of the sun through the window, and the movement of warm summer air. *First I need to arrange for the company to survive in Burgundy. What are we living on? – Christ, but I feel sick!*

---

[6] In the original text, '*triarii* [veteran] of a legion', but a modern version gives a more immediate referent.

The comb stopped snagging her yard-long length of hair. Floria's fingers touched her cheek, that ran with salt tears. "Hurts? It will, with a head-wound. I could cut this lot off."

"*You could not.*"

"Okay, *okay* . . . leave *my* head on my shoulders!"

Time blipped again.

Floria's voice spoke quietly to someone else in the sick-room. Ash opened her eyes to see another nun, in the same dull green habit and white wimple; who met her eyes as they focused, and stepped across the room to offer her water in a wooden cup.

"I know you." Ash suddenly frowned. "It's difficult to tell without the hair, but I *know* you. Don't I?"

Off over towards the window, Floria chuckled.

The little nun said, "Schmidt. Margaret Schmidt."

Ash's cheeks coloured up. She said in a voice both weak and incredulous, "You're a *nun*?"

"I am now."

Floria crossed the room, sliding her hand over the woman's shoulders as she passed her. She bent down to feel Ash's forehead. "Dijon, boss. You're in the big convent outside Dijon." And then, when Ash only looked bemused, "The convent for *filles de joie* who become *filles de pénitence.*"[7]

Ash looked at the little nun, whom she had last seen in the whorehouse in Basle. "Oh."

The other two women smiled.

Ash made an effort, and managed to speak. "If you change your mind before you take the last vows, Margaret, you'll be welcome in the company. Say, as surgeon's assistant."

Floria's face, as she glimpsed it, held an expression somewhere between awe, cynicism and unease; but mostly one of surprise. Ash shrugged at her and, at the resulting twinge, put her hand up to her head.

The woman from Basle made a courtesy. "I make no decisions until I see what life in a nunnery is like, seigneur – demoiselle, that is. So far it isn't so different from the house of joy."

A rap sounded at the door.

"Bugger off," Ash said. "I'm seeing Robert on my own."

She closed her eyes for a moment, finding it restful; letting the opening and closing of doors go on without her. From other wounds, she recognised this weakness. Knew more or less how long it would take to pass. Too long.

What am I? The Faris says, Just a piece of rubbish. Just the same as a male calf you slaughter when it's born, because it's useless, because all you want is heifers to keep in milk.

But you hear a voice.

And that's all it is? Some brazen head, away in North Africa; some . . . some engine they've made, that spits out Vegetius and Tacitus and all the ancients on war? Just a – a library? Nothing more than tactics out of a manuscript, there for the asking?

[7] Contemporary records survive for this.

Ash smothered a giggle under her breath, not willing to let out the tears that pricked behind her eyes.

Sweet Christ, and I've trusted my life to it! And the times I've read bits out of *De Re Militari* and thought, no, there's no way you should do *that* tactic under *those* circumstances – what have I been listening to?

Ash felt a strong temptation to speak, aloud, and ask her voice those questions. She shook the impulse off, opening her eyes.

Robert Anselm stood in front of her.

The big man was out of armour, in hose patched at the knee, and a demi-gown undone over a laced Italian doublet: all in blue wool and all looking very much slept in, and slept out of doors at that. He carried an empty dagger scabbard at his belt, thrust through the loop of his leather purse.

"Uhh . . ." Robert Anselm reached up suddenly and grabbed the velvet hat off his head. He turned it between his big hands, thumbs absently pressing the pewter Lion badge on each revolution. His gaze fell.

"Are we safe? Where are we encamped?" Ash demanded. "What's the situation here – who's the local lord, under the Duke?"

"Uh." Robert Anselm shrugged.

Ash's head twinged, as she put it back to look up at him. He immediately dropped into a crouch in front of her stool, his forearms resting on his knees, his head lowered. Ash found herself looking at the salt-and-pepper bumfluff growing out around the edges of his scalp.

I could tell you you're a fucking idiot, Ash thought. I could hit you. I could say *what the fuck do you think you're doing, leaving my company to run itself?*

Her stomach growled, appetite returning. *Bread, wine, and about half a dead deer, for preference* . . . Ash put one hand up to shield her eyes from what was becoming painfully bright sunlight at the window. The air grew hotter. This must be morning moving on towards noon.

"You never saw what I did at Tewkesbury, did you?" she said.

Anselm's head came up. His expression was mottled, under the dirt, a strained white-and-red, unpleasant and unhealthy-looking. He rubbed the back of his neck. "What?"

"Tewkesbury."

"No." Anselm's shoulders began to untighten. He put one knee down on the floor to keep himself steady. "Didn't see it. I was on the other side of the battle. I saw you at the end, wrapped in the standard. You were dripping."

Dripping *red*, she remembered; feeling again the wet cloth, the scratch of heavy embroidery, the sheer exhaustion of wielding a poleaxe. A razor-edged blade on a six-foot shaft. An axe that bites as hard into metal and body-parts as a domestic axe does into wood.

"That worked," she said measuredly. "I knew I had to do something at that age to get noticed. I was far too young for command, but if I'd waited and done something remarkable at sixteen or seventeen – it wouldn't have been remarkable. So I took and held the Lancastrian standard on Bloody Meadow." Now she lowered her gaze, catching Robert Anselm with an expression of pure distress on his features.

"I got two of my best friends killed doing that," Ash said. "Richard and Crow. I'd known them for years. They're both on that slope somewhere. Buried in the ditch the White Rose dug afterwards. And you rode over me by accident. That's what we *do*. We kill people we know, and we get killed. And don't tell me it's bloody stupid. There aren't any ways to get killed that are sensible!"

Anselm yelled, "I'm getting *old*!"

Ash's mouth stayed open.

Robert shouted, "That's what those little shits have started calling me! 'Old man.' I'm twice your age, I'm getting too old for this! *That's* why it happened!"

"Oh, fucking hell." His hands were shaking and she grabbed at them, feeling his warm flesh clammy; and she tightened her grip as hard as she could, which was far less than she expected. "Don't be stupid."

He wrenched his hands out of hers. Ash grabbed at the sides of the stool. Her head swam.

"I'm sorry, all right?" he yelled. "I'm sorry! I'm *sorry*! It was my fault!"

The sheer volume of his shout brought her lip snarling back against her teeth. She winced at the pain; winced as the cell door banged open and back against the wall, Floria del Guiz grabbing Anselm's arm, yelling; him throwing her violently off—

"That's *enough*!" Ash took her hands down from her ears. She breathed in, and lifted her head.

Margaret Schmidt stood in the doorway, looking anxiously back along the passage. Floria had both her long-fingered hands tight around the big man's biceps again, straining to drag him out of the room. Robert Anselm's feet were planted firmly apart, his shoulders braced wide, and his head bullishly down; *nothing short of six men is going to throw him out of here*, Ash reflected.

"You, go and tell the Soeur Maîtresse nothing is the matter. You," her finger jabbed at Floria, "let go of him; *you*—" to Robert Anselm "—shut your fucking mouth and let me *speak*." She waited. "Thank you."

"I'll go," Floria said, with distaste at her own embarrassment. "If you send her into a relapse, Robert, I'll geld you."

The surgeon left the room, closing its door upon herself, Margaret Schmidt, and a number of other nuns attracted by the break in their monotony.

"Now you've had a chance to yell at me for getting hurt," Ash said gently. "Feel better?"

The big man nodded, sheepishly. He stared intently at his own feet.

"Have you really been sleeping on the convent steps?"

His shaven head dipped. The big shoulders came up, slightly, in a minuscule shrug.

"I turn forty this year. Two choices," he said, apparently addressing the floor. "Get out of this while I'm alive, or stay in the business. Stay as a woman's commander, or get my own company. Christ, woman, I'm starting to feel old. Please don't tell me Colleoni rode into battle when he was seventy!"

Ash shut her mouth. "Well . . . that is exactly what I was going to say. You telling me you're out of here, is that it? Bottle gone?"

"Yeah." He did not sound goaded into a confession, but flatly honest.

"Yeah, well, tough shit. I need you, Robert. If you want to go and start your own company, that's different, you can go, but you're not leaving mine because you've scared yourself shitless. Got that?"

Robert Anselm reached out for her insistent hand. "Ash . . ."

"Get me into that bed, or I'm going to throw up again. Jesus Christ, I hate head wounds! Robert, you're not going. Sometimes I *do* think I couldn't run this fucking company without you." Her hand knotted around his. She pulled herself up off the stool on to her feet. She stood, swaying, not needing to accentuate it.

Robert Anselm muttered sarcastically, "Yeah. You're a poor weak woman." He dipped and scooped his other arm under her knees, lifting her bodily, and carried her the few feet to the bed. With one knee dinting the mattress, he lowered her down. "You won't trust me after this. You'll say you will, but you won't."

Ash relaxed down into goose-feather softness. The white ceiling swooped, circling. She swallowed a mouthful of sour saliva. To have her body supine and cradled brought such relief that she let out a long breath and shut her eyes.

"Okay, so I won't. Not for a while. Then I will trust you again. We know each other too well. Like she said, if you leave, I'll geld you. We're in deep shit, now, and it needs sorting!"

He arranged her neatly in the bed, not unused to handling the wounded. Ash opened her eyes. Robert Anselm seated himself sideways on the edge of the bed, his head turned towards her, and suddenly frowned. " 'She'?"

"No. It wasn't her who said that, was it? Not the nun. *He*. Florian did."

"Mmm," Robert Anselm said absently. The way that he sat, arms spread, hands down supporting his weight, occupying all the space around himself, was so purely Anselm that she had to smile.

"It's all very well to sound so certain, isn't it?" Ash said. "Get back and run the company. If that works, then they haven't lost confidence in you. As soon as I can get up without falling over, I'll come and sort out what we're going to do next. We won't have long to make up our minds here."

He gave a curt nod and stood up. As his weight left the mattress, she felt suddenly bereft.

Her head pulsed with pain. "We've just run like fuck. We don't have a contract here in the Duchy. Do this wrong, and my lads'll be deserting in droves by tomorrow . . . If you fuck up my company, I'll have your bollocks," she snapped weakly.

Robert Anselm looked down at her. "It'll be under control. Next time," he crossed to the cell door, "wear a bloody helmet, woman!"

Ash made an Italian gesture. "Next time, *bring* me one!"

Robert Anselm stopped, on the threshold. "What did the Faris say to you?"

Fear punched in under her breastbone, flooding her body. Ash smiled, felt the falsity of it, let her face find its own expression of distress, and croaked, "Not now! Later. Get that asshole Godfrey up here, I want to talk to him!"

What had been background pain flared, throbbing, until water began to run

227

out of her eyes. She took little notice of what was said or done then, except for someone putting a bowl to her lips, and since she smelled wine and some herb she swallowed it in great gulps, and then lay praying until – not soon enough – she fell into a drugged sleep.

Her sleep became troubled less than an hour later.

Pain seared into her head. She froze, lying as still as possible, swearing at Floria whenever the surgeon came near her; her body broken out in a cold sweat. When the light dimmed, she felt it to be from the pain in her head. A male voice told her repeatedly that it was only evening, was sunset, was night, was the dark of the moon; but she shifted on the hot bolster, fangs of pain biting into her head, jamming her mouth shut with her fist, her own teeth breaking the skin of her knuckles. When she did give way and scream, when the pain became too bad, the movement blasted her into some region that she recognised: a place of blazing physical sensation, complete helplessness, complete inescapability. She had it one heartbeat, forgot it by the next; knew it for a memory, but not now what it was a memory of.

"*Lion*—" Her pleading voice choked in her throat; barely above a whisper: "By Saint Gawaine— by the Chapel—"

Nothing.

"Hush, baby." A soft voice, man or woman's, she couldn't tell which. "Hush, hush."

Still in a frozen whisper, she snarled: "Are you a fucking *machine*! Answer me! Golem—"

'No suitable problem proposed. No available solution.'

The voice in her secret soul is unemphatic, as it has always been. Nothing of the predator in it; nothing of the saint?

Pain swarmed over every cell of her body; she whispered, despairingly, "Oh *shit*—!"

Another voice, Robert Anselm's, said, "Give her more of that stuff. She won't die of it. For bloody Christ's sake, man!"

Sharp and rapid, Floria rapped out, "You can do this? Then you do this!"

"*No*; I didn't mean—"

"Then *shut up*. I'm not losing her now!"

III

She must have slept, but didn't realise it except in retrospect.

Pre-dawn light made a grey square of the window before her eyes. Ash groaned. Her palms were cold with sweat. The bed-linen smelled stale. As she moved her shoulder, she felt wool against her cheek, and realised that she was still fully dressed. Someone had undone her points, loosening her clothing. Stabs of pain entered her skull with every breath she took in, with every tiny movement of her body.

"I must be getting better, it hurts."

"What?" A shadow rose and bent over her. The chill dawn illuminated Floria del Guiz. "Did you say something?"

"I said, I must be getting better, it's starting to hurt." Ash found herself sounding breathless. Floria put the familiar bowl to her mouth. She drank, spilling half on the yellow bed-linen.

An odd sound became, as she recognised it, someone scratching at the sick-room door. Before Floria could rise from beside her, the door opened and someone came in, carrying a pierced iron lantern. Ash turned her head away from the stabbing light. She bit down on a breath, as the movement jolted her head. Carefully, she slitted her eyes and peered at the doorway.

"Oh, it's you," Ash muttered as she recognised the newcomer. "I don't know what the Soeur was complaining about – this fucking convent's *full* of men."

"I am a priest, child," Godfrey Maximillian protested mildly.

"Good God, am I that ill?"

"Not now." Floria's hand pressed down on her shoulder. Ash kept herself from crying out. The surgeon added, "You did too much yesterday. That won't happen today. This is the long boring bit. The bit you never like. The bit where boss tries to get up before she should. Remember?"

"Yeah. I remember." Ash momentarily grinned, catching the tall, golden-haired woman's smile. "But I'm bored."

The surgeon narrowed her eyes at Ash. There was a look on her face that Ash suspected meant she would be getting a smart cuff around the ear about now, if not for her state of health. *Maybe I'm not well, at that.*

"I've brought you a visitor," Godfrey said. The surgeon glared at him, and he held up one broad-fingered hand reprovingly: "I know what I'm doing. She's anxious to meet Ash, but she has to travel on from the convent later this morning. I told her she could come and speak with the captain for a few minutes."

Floria held an expression of scepticism as they talked across Ash's bed. The growing light brought their faces out of the dimness: the big bearded man, and the laconic man who was a woman. Ash lay and listened.

Godfrey Maximillian said, "It's still me, too, Fl— my child. You used to believe that I had some skill in my art."

"Priesting isn't an art," the surgeon grumbled, "it's a fraud practised on the gullible. All right. Bring your visitor in, Godfrey."

Ash made no attempt to sit up in the bed. Floria put the pierced lantern on the floor, where its light would not be so harsh. A blackbird spoke out of the emptiness beyond the window. Another called, a thrush, a chaffinch; and in a space of three or four heartbeats, a loud noise of birdsong echoed in the dawn. Ash's head throbbed.

"Fucking twittering *birds*!" she complained.

"Capitano," a woman's clear voice said. Ash recognised the sound of someone moving while wearing armour: metal plates rattling and clacking, mail chinging.

Ash raised her eyes and saw a woman of about thirty-five beside the bed. The woman wore Milanese-style white armour, with a wheel-pommelled sword belted at her waist, and an Italian barbute helmet tucked under her arm, and had a considerable air of authority.

"Sit down." Ash swallowed, clearing her mouth.

"My name is Onorata Rodiani, Capitano.[8] Your priest said I must not tire you." The woman stripped off her gauntlets, to move the back-stool to the other side of the bed. Her little finger and ring-finger of her right hand were crooked, both repeatedly broken and set.

She seated herself on the back-stool and sat carefully erect, dipping her head out of her bevor so that she could turn her chin, and see whether her scabbard was scraping the cell wall behind her. Satisfied that it was not, she turned back, smiling. "I never lose a chance to meet another fighting woman."

"Rodiani?" Ash squinted past the throbbing in her scalp. "I heard of you. You're from Castelleone. You used to be a painter, didn't you?"

The woman rested her hand up beside her face. It took Ash a second to note she was cupping her ear, and to realise that she should speak more loudly. The side of the woman's face was speckled black with impacted powder. Deaf from gunfire.

"A painter?" Ash repeated.

"Before I became a mercenary." The woman's white teeth showed in the dimness as she smiled broadly. "I killed my first man as a painter. In Cremona – I was painting a mural of the Tyrant at the time. An inopportune rapist. After that, I decided I liked fighting better than painting."

Ash smiled, recognising a public story when she heard it. *It's not that easy.* The woman's loose dark hair would show pure black in daylight. The lines of her tanned face promised plumpness in old age. *If she reaches it,* Ash thought, and reached her hands out from under the sheet. "Can I see that?"

"Yes." Onorata Rodiani handed her barbute over.

Ash took the weight, the pull on her muscles shooting pain through her head, and rested the helmet on the bolster beside her. She poked at strap, rivets and helmet liner with an inquisitive finger; and ran the pad of her finger around its T-shaped opening. "You like barbutes? I can never *see* out of the damn things! I see you've gone for rose-head rivets as well."

The woman's left thumb stroked the disc pommel of her sword. "I like brass rivets on a helmet. They polish up bright."

Ash rolled the barbute back towards her. "And Milanese vambraces? I've always used German arm defences."

"You like Gothic armour?"

"I can get more movement out of their vambraces. As for the rest of it, all fluting and edge-work – no. It's frilly armour."

There was a snort from the doorway, where Floria and Godfrey stood talking in undertones. Ash glared at them.

"So. You want to see my sword?" Onorata Rodiani offered. "I wish I could show you my war-horse, too, but I have to leave this morning for the war that will come to France. Here."

---

[8] Onorata Rodiani, a historical character, has obviously been incorporated in this text out of a conviction that these two women *ought* to have met. In fact, Rodiani is reported as dying, after a long career as a mercenary, in the defence of her home town, Castelleone, in AD 1472.

The woman stood and drew. That sound of sharp steel sliding against the fine wood that lines a sword-scabbard brought Ash up on her elbows. She struggled to get her back up against the bolster, finally sat, and reached her hand out for the hilt. She ignored the pain that made her eyes water.

France? Ash thought. Yes. The Visigoths have more men and supplies than I've ever seen; they're not stopping where they are now. After the Swiss, and the Germanies . . . France isn't a bad guess.

The Faris is equipped for a full-scale crusade.

"So how many lances do you have?" Ash flicked the wheel-pommelled sword in her hand. The thirty-six-inch blade, wide at the hilt and tapering to a needle point, slid through the air like oil through water. A living blade: the feel of it worth every pang in her scalp. "Christ, that's sweet!"

"Twenty lances," the woman said, and added, "Isn't it?"

"I see you've gone for hollow-grinding on the blade."

"Yes, and didn't I have to stand over the blade-smith to make him do it properly!"

"Oh God, never trust an armourer." Ash lowered the blade and sighted along it, testing its trueness by eye, and found herself focusing on the grinning face of Godfrey Maximillian. "What's the matter with you?"

"Nothing. Nothing at all . . ."

"Well, get my guest some wine, then! You want her to think we don't have any courtesy around here?"

Floria del Guiz linked her arm through the priest's. She murmured, "We'll get some wine, boss. We'll be right back. Honest."

Ash flipped the blade upright in her hand. A sliver of dawn light flashed off the scratched, mirror-bright steel. There was, she noted, a distinct curve to one edge of the blade, near the hilt, where battle nicks had been polished out on a grinder. A man could have shaved with the weapon's edge.

"Nice work on the grip," she commented appreciatively. "What is it, brass wire over velvet?"

"Gold wire."

At the door, leaving, her priest said something to her surgeon that Ash did not quite catch. Floria shook her head, smiling. Ash lowered the sword, scooping up the linen sheet on her left hand, and rested the blade across her muffled finger.

"Balances about four inches down . . . I like 'em blade-heavy, too. I bet it really cuts." She raised her head, glaring at Godfrey and Floria. "*What?*"

"We'll leave you to it, child. Madonna Rodiani," Godfrey bowed. Behind him, Floria was grinning for some reason that Ash did not understand, but obscurely felt might be best not inquired into. Godfrey smiled blandly at her. He said, "I'll just tiptoe away now. Florian will tiptoe away."

Ash heard Floria mutter something that sounded very like: "*Everybody* will tiptoe away! My God, these two could bore for Europe . . ."

"You," Ash said with dignity, "are interrupting a professional discussion. Now fuck off out of my cell! And while you're getting us wine, you can find me breakfast as well. Bloody hell, anybody would think I was an *invalid*."

It was pure pleasure to forget the armies over the border, forget the nightmare of Basle; for however short a time.

"You can't be fighting the war in your head every hour of the day; not and win when it does come to a battle." Ash grinned, all decisions temporarily in abeyance.

"Madonna Onorata, stay for breakfast? While we eat, I want to ask you what you think about something in Vegetius. He says stab with the sword point, because two inches of steel in the gut is invariably fatal – but then, your man may not fall over until he's had time to kill *you*. I often use the edge, and cut, which is slower, but maybe takes a man's head clear off, after which I find he generally doesn't bother me again. What's *your* preference?"

She was quite genuinely not afraid of injury.

When she had worked out, to her own satisfaction, that she probably would not die on this particular day – this despite having known men who walked around for several days after a blow on the head, only to drop dead for no reason that anyone could see (despite the company surgeon's covert rummaging in the contents of their brain-pan) – having decided this, and having suffered the extreme unpleasantness of having her two broken back teeth filed down flat, Ash to all intents and purposes forgot her wound. It became one of many.

That left her with nothing to do but think.

Ash leaned her elbows on the nunnery window's edge, gazing out into the confusion of a wash-day in the enclosed courtyard. The stench of Cuckoo Pint starch filled her nostrils. She smiled, ruefully, at the peaceableness of it.

Behind her, someone entered the cell. She didn't turn, recognising the tread. Godfrey Maximillian came to stand at the window. She noticed he glanced reflexively up, as Florian and Roberto and little Margaret had, at the sun in the sky. He looked to be burned red across the cheekbones.

"Fl-Florian says you're well enough to talk business."

"Now you're doing it! She does, does she? That's damn good of her."

A sparrow darted down, dipping its beak for the crumbs she held on her palm. Ash chirruped as it fluffed brown feathers at her, watching her with one black, pupilless eye.

She said, "I suppose we're deemed, *de facto*, to have broken our contract with the Visigoths. The Faris certainly broke whatever agreement she had with me. I think we've chosen the side we're *not* going to be on in this war."

Godfrey said, "I wish it was that simple."

A sharp beak pecked her palm.

Ash raised her head, to gaze up at Godfrey Maximillian. "I know that just staying out of the way won't be good enough. The Visigoths are coming north anyway."

"They've come as far as Auxonne." Godfrey shrugged. "I have sources. We came through Auxonne, on the way from Basle. It's no more than thirty-five, forty miles from here."

"Forty miles!" Ash's hand jerked. The sparrow abruptly flicked into flight, dipping across the courtyard crowded with women. The sound of nuns' voices and the noise of water slopping in tubs drifted up to the window.

"That's . . . getting to the point where I'm going to have to *do* something. The question is, what? The company, first. I need the lads back on-line . . ."

A flash of sunlight on slate roofs, bright as a kingfisher's wing, took her eye. Past the convent wall, beyond strip-fields and copses, the white walls and blue slate roofs of a city shone clean and bright and clear under the midday light. Under the sun.

"Godfrey, I have to ask you something. As my clerk.[9] Call this my confession. Can I lead them into combat – if I can't trust my voice?"

One look at the frown creasing his face was enough.

"Oh yes." Ash nodded. "The Faris does have a war-machine, a *machina rei militaris*. I watched her speak to it. Wherever it is – Carthage, or closer at hand – it wasn't in the same place as she was when she spoke to it. But she heard it. And I . . . heard it. It's my voice, Godfrey. It's the Lion."

She kept her voice steady, but water stung the lids of her eyes.

"Oh, child." He cupped his hands around her shoulders. "Oh, dear child!"

"No. I can stand that. It was a genuine miracle, a genuine Beast, but – children imagine things. Maybe I wasn't even present, I just heard the men talking. Maybe I made up seeing the Lion myself when I started hearing voices." Ash moved her shoulders, freeing herself from his hands. "The Visigoths, the Faris – she'll be suspicious now. Before, they had no reason to think anyone else could use the machine. Now . . . they might be able to stop me doing it. They might be able to make it *lie* to me. Tell me to do the wrong thing, in the field, get us all killed . . ."

Godfrey's face showed shock. "Christ and the Tree!"

"I've been thinking about it, this morning." Ash smiled crookedly, there being nothing else to do but haul herself together. "You see the problem."

"I see that you would be wise to tell no one about this! This is Under the Tree." Godfrey Maximillian crossed himself. "The camp is rowdy. Disturbed. Morale could go either way. Child, *can* you fight without your voice?"

The sun burned sparks from flints in the convent's wall, glittering in the corner of her eye. A waft of warm air brought her thyme, rosemary, chervil, and more Cuckoo Pint from the herb garden. Ash looked at him flatly.

"I always knew I might have to find out. That's why, when we fought Tewkesbury field – I never called on my voice the whole of the day. If I was going to lead men out to fight, where they could be killed, I didn't want it depending on some damn saint, some Lion-born-of-a-Virgin, I wanted it depending on *me*."

Godfrey gave a choked sound. Ash, puzzled, looked up at the bearded man. His expression wavered somewhere between outright laughter, and something very close to tears.

"Christ and the Holy Mother!" he exclaimed.

"What? Godfrey, *what*?"

"You didn't want it depending on 'some damn saint'—" His deep, resonant laugh boomed out; loudly enough to make some of the nearer nuns lift their

[9] Priest. Most scholars (clerks) were also priests, in this era.

233

heads and stare up at the window, eyes squinting against the brilliance of the sun.

"I don't see what—"

"No," Godfrey interrupted, wiping his eyes, "I don't suppose you do."

He beamed at her, warmly.

"Miracles aren't enough for you! You need to know that you can do it by yourself."

"When there are people depending on me, yes, I do." Ash hesitated. "That was five years ago. Six years. I don't know that I can do without my voice *now*. All I do know is, I can't trust it any more."

"Ash."

She looked up to meet Godfrey's sobering gaze.

The priest pointed towards the distant town. "Duke Charles is here. In Dijon. He's been holding court here since he withdrew his army from Neuss."

"Yeah, Florian told me. I thought he'd've gone north to Bruges or somewhere."

"The Duke is here. So is the court. And the army." Godfrey Maximillian rested his hand over her arm. "And other mercenaries."

What she had taken to be a distant continuation of Dijon's white walls, she now saw to be white canvas. Sun-bleached tents. Hundreds of tents – more, as her eye ran along their peaked canopies. Thousands. The glitter of light on armour and guns. The swarming of men and horses, too far away for livery to be distinguished, but she could guess them to be Rossano, Monforte, as well as Charles's own troops under Olivier de la Marche.

Sombrely, Godfrey said, "You have eight hundred fighting men out there in the Lion Azure, not to mention the baggage train, and they all talk. It's known you've been with the Visigoths – and with their Faris-General. Consequently, there are *many* people who are anxiously waiting to speak to you, when you recover and leave this place."

"Oh. Shit. Oh, *shit!*"

"And I don't know how long they will wait."

IV

The next morning's heat laid a blue glaze over the distant trees, and turned the sky a hot, powdery grey. Ash walked down between daisy-thick banks and towering cow-parsley, leaving her demi-gown and doublet sleeves behind, to where the Lion Azure had their camp, the promised quarter of a mile beyond the convent grounds. She came at it covertly through a copse of birches, and the company's tethered cattle and goats, grazing the rich water meadow.

Ash scratched at one of the wicker pavises strapped to the side of a baggage wagon, some distance from the main gate, making a mental note that Geraint's idea of how far apart one should space pickets was sadly lacking.

"I shouldn't be able to do this . . ."

She stared at the camp beyond the wagons, the fire-breaks between tents trodden down to dust, and the figures of men in Lion livery mostly sprawled around dead fire-pits, eating oat-porridge from wooden bowls.

Okay. What's been changed? What's different? Who—

"Ash!"

Ash tilted her head back, shading her eyes against the sun, staring up at the top of the wagon. Heat crisped the skin across her nose and cheeks. "Blanche? That you?"

A flash of white legs, and a woman swung herself out over the wagon-shafts, and threw her arms around Ash. The yellow-haired ex-whore thumped her back. Tears sprang to Ash's eyes.

"Whoa! Steady on, girl! I'm back, but you don't want to kill me before I get inside!"

"Shit." Blanche beamed, happily. White sunlight showed wet smears on her cheeks. "We thought you were dying. We thought we were stuck with that Welsh bastard. Henri! Jan-Jacob! Come here!"

Ash heaved herself over the wagon-shafts, jumping down on to the flattened straw that strewed this part of the camp, further away from the knight's tents; and straightened to find her hand being wrung by her steward Henri Brant, and Jan-Jacob Clovet struggling to lace his cod-flap with his injured arm and thump her on the back at the same time. Blanche's daughter Baldina, a red-haired woman, dropped her skirts with aplomb and got up from the straw where she had been accommodating the man-at-arms.

"Boss!" she called croakily, "are you back for good?"

Ash ruffled the whore's flaming hair. "No, I'm marrying Duke Charles of Burgundy, and we're going to spend every day eating 'til we burst, and fucking on swansdown mattresses."

Baldina said broadly, "Suits us. We'll make you a widow so you can. That's if that little limp-dick you married is still alive somewhere."

Ash made no answer, being engulfed in the wiry embrace of Euen Huw, and a torrent of Welsh admiration and complaint; and finding herself at the centre of a rapidly growing mob, made up of the company's boys, musicians, washer-women, whores, grooms, cooks and archers; and being swept off – as she had intended – towards the centre of the camp.

First of all the men-at-arms, Thomas Rochester threw his arms around her; his harsh face streamed with tears.

"Typical emotional *rosbifs*!" Ash thumped his back. Josse and Michael piled in on top of her; and half the English lances with them.

Fifteen minutes later, her head pounding and half-blind with renewed pain, Joscelyn van Mander was shaking her hand with a grip that left red imprints on her fingers, his blue eyes brimming with wetness.

"Thanks to Christ!" he blurted. He looked around, at the mob of men-at-arms and archers and billmen pressing close, and the knights elbowing in; all trying to reach Ash. "Lady, thanks to Christ! You're alive!"

"Not for much longer," Ash said under her breath. She managed to free her hands. One arm went comradely over Euen Huw's shoulder, and she rested her weight on the little Welshman; the other held Baldina's hand, the red-headed whore not willing to be parted from her for a second, mopping her face with the hem of her kirtle.

Lowering his voice for confidentiality, and breathing warm wine-breath in her face, Joscelyn van Mander interrupted. "I've been speaking to the Viscount-Mayor on behalf of the company; we have trouble with allowing knights into the town—"

Oh, *you've* been speaking on behalf of the company, have you? Uh-huh.

Ash beamed at the Flemish knight. "I'll sort it."

She grinned around at the thronging faces.

"It's boss!"

"She's back!"

"So – where's Geraint-the-Welsh-bastard?" Ash inquired, in a voice of piercing good humour.

Amid a roar of laughter, Geraint ab Morgan forced his way through the crowd in front of the command tent. The big man was stuffing his shirt into the back of his hose, between a set of broken points. His bloodshot blue eyes flinched, seeing Ash in the middle of a throng of delirious admirers.

Geraint shoved out with both arms to clear a space, and thumped down on both knees on the earth in front of her. "It's all yours, boss!"

Ash grinned at the note of heartfelt relief in his voice. "Sure you don't want to keep my job?"

At this point, she knew exactly the answer he would make. Geraint didn't have any choice. She had chosen to come in by way of the menial members of the company, who had no chance, nor would ever have a chance, of competing for rank within it. Their genuine joy carried itself to the men, and that left the knights – given van Mander's *volte face* – with nothing to do but forget any quite viable ambitions that had started to grow in her absence, any unauthorised promotions and demotions, and cheer her to the echo.

In broad Welsh, Geraint said, "Stuff your fucking job, boss, have it and welcome!"

"Lightbringer!" someone shouted behind her, and someone else, Jan-Jacob Clovet, she thought, bellowed, "Lioness!"

"Listen up!" Ash loosened her grip and held up both hands for silence. The camp's failings could wait an hour, she decided. "Okay! I'm here, I'm back, and I'm going up to the chapel now. Anyone else who wants to give thanks for our deliverance from the darkness, *follow me!*"

She couldn't make herself heard for sixty seconds. Eventually she stopped trying, thumped Euen Huw on the back, and pointed. They moved towards the camp's main gate, at least four hundred strong; and Ash answered questions and asked for news and congratulated men recovering from wounds, all in one breath, under a staggering hot sky.

Being a chapel of Mithras,[10] it was naturally on separate land to the convent.

---

[10] I find myself in agreement with Vaughan Davies's supposition in the second edition of the 'Ash' texts (published 1939), and can do no better than quote it:

'The oddities of religion apparently practised among the fifteenth century cohorts of Ash bear no resemblance to contemporary Christian practice. A more robust age – indeed, an age less in imminent need of divine protection than our own – can afford religious satires which we should,

Ash led the way uphill to the nearby copse, lost in the great crowd.

Trees in full leaf shuttered out the sun. Ash breathed a long sigh, not aware of how dazzled she had been by heat and light until now. She looked ahead, down the path, to where her officers waited outside the low, heavy masonry entrance: Floria, Godfrey, Robert and Angelotti, standing in sepia dappled shadow. She gave one very tiny nod of her head and saw them relax.

Floria fell in step with her as she came up to them; Godfrey on the other side. Angelotti bowed; he and Robert Anselm dropping back to let her pass.

Ash gave the two men a thoughtful glance over her shoulder.

Priests stood in the chapel entrance. She linked arms with Florian and Godfrey. Behind her, knowing there would be no room below, men-at-arms and archers were sinking to their knees on the leaf-mould, filthy men dappled with the sun's light through the green leaves, pulling off helmets and hats, talking at the tops of their voices, and laughing. Junior priests of Mithras moved away from the entrance towards the groups of armed men, so that the service could be held here as well as below.

She fell in beside Godfrey, linking arms, going under the lintel and down the steps; exchanging the scent of dry woodland for the moist cold of the earth-walled passage. "So – what did you hear at court? Will the Duke fight?"

"There are rumours. No information I would trust. Surely he can't ignore an army forty miles away, but— But I've never seen such magnificence!" Godfrey Maximillian spluttered. "He must have *three hundred* books here in his library!"

"Oh, *books*." Ash kept a steadying hand on her clerk's arm as she reached the bottom of the steps, and walked into the chapel of Mithras. Sunlight slanted down through the bars above, casting the stone cave into floods of light and shadow. Roman mosaics under her feet depicted the Proud Walkers and the April Rainers in tiny pastel squares. "What am I going to care about Duke Charles's books for, Godfrey?"

"No, I don't suppose you will. Not in the present situation." He inclined his head, a smile partly concealed by his beard. "But he has the most wonderful Psalters. One illustrated by Rogier van der Weyden, no less. He also has all the *Chansons du Geste*, child – Tristram, Arthur. Jaques de Lalaing . . ."

"Oh, what! Really?"

Godfrey chuckled, mimicking her tone. "Really."

"Now that's what's wrong with war," Ash said, wistfully, as they knelt in front of the great Bull altar.

"Ehh? Jaques de Lalaing is what's wrong with war?" Godfrey murmured, puzzled. "Good lord, child, the man's been dead for thirty years."

"*No.*" Ash cuffed the priest affectionately. From the altar, the Bull priest gave her a quelling glare.[11] She subsided to a whisper, aware she was still born up by the intensity of her welcome back to the company. They kept up a

perhaps, deem blasphemous. These scurrilous representations (which occur only in the Angelotti manuscript) are Rabelaisian satire. They are no more intended to be read as fact than are descriptions of the Jewish race poisoning wells and abducting children. The whole matter is a satire against a papacy which was, by the 1470s, not at all beyond reproach; and shows the feelings which would, in the next century, explode into the Reformation.'

[11] Neither women, nor soldiers who were not officers, were permitted to be present at the Mithraic mysteries.

constant chatter behind her. "I mean what *happened* to him is what's wrong with war. There you have him, perfect gentle knight, wins all the tourney circuit matches for years, been on every field of battle of note, a real warrior chevalier – actually set up a knightly pavilion and defended a ford with his lance against all-comers[12] – and what happens to him?"

Godfrey searched his memory. "Killed at one of the sieges of Ghent, wasn't he?"

"Yeah – by a cannon ball."

The blood bowl was passed around. Ash drank, bowed her head for the blessing, and said formally, "I give thanks for my recovery and dedicate my life to continuing the battle of the Light against the Dark." As the steaming bowl continued to the vast numbers of the company crowded into the chapel, and queued back up the steps, she murmured, "That's what I mean, Godfrey. All the virtues of chivalric war, and what happens to him? Some damn gun-crew blows his fucking head off!"

Godfrey Maximillian reached down with a broad arm to haul her up off the flagstones. She took the necessary help without resenting it.

"Not that I ever thought war was anything but a dirty business," she added dryly. "Why are Robert and Angelotti avoiding me, Godfrey?"

"Are they? Dear me."

Ash pressed her lips together. The blessing concluding, she waited while the white- and green-robed boys sang, and then ascended up into the light between her lance-leaders; a mass of men in bright steel and brilliant linen, walking out into the wood with her, swatting buzzing insects away; and each of them desperate to have just one reassuring word with Ash.

"The riding horses need exercise!" The company farrier.

"Twenty carcasses of pork, and nine of them off," Wat Rodway complained.

"Huw's archers keep brawling with my men!" An indignant fair-haired Sergeant of Bill. Carracci, she recognised; unusually fraught.

Euen Huw swore. "Bloody Italian bum-boys messing about with my lads!"

One of the female hackbutters complained, "And half my powder is left behind at Basle—"

Ash stopped dead on the path.

"*Wait.*"

Her page, Bertrand, handed her her velvet bonnet. She heard the snort of horses and looked ahead. Beyond the brown trunks of trees and the arching green loops of briars, out in the meadow, war-horses were being held by grooms.

"Later," she ordered.

A group of armed men stood just within the copse's shade. Their banner hung limp and unreadable, but looked to be – she squinted – quartered squares of red and yellow, with white bars, mullets,[13] and either crosses or daggers. The men's livery jackets were white and murrey-coloured.[14]

A hand under her armpit lifted her out of the discussion group and several

---

[12] In AD 1450.
[13] Not the fish. In heraldry, a five-pointed star.
[14] Murrey: a mulberry or reddish-purple colour.

yards on down the path from the crowd of her soldiers. Robert Anselm, without looking down at her, said, "I got us a contract. He's here. Meet your new boss."

" 'New boss'?" Ash stopped dead.

She was no weight to stop Anselm, but the big Englishman let go of her arm and abruptly dropped to one knee in front of her.

A second man knelt on the dry leaves: Henri Brant. Antonio Angelotti thumped down beside him. Ash looked down at her steward and second-in-command and gunner. She put her hands on her hips. "Excuse me, my new *what*? Since when?"

Anselm and Angelotti exchanged glances.

"Two days ago?" Robert Anselm ventured.

"New *employer*," Henri Brant spoke up. "I had difficulty getting credit in Dijon. Prices are going up, now there's an army at their border. And I can't supply eight-score horses and a whole company on what there is left from Frederick!"

So how much were *we forced to abandon at Basle? Shit.*

Ash surveyed Henri's broad face. He still favoured his right side a little, she noted, where he knelt. "Stand up, you idiot. You mean no food-merchant would give you credit unless the company had a formal contract with someone?"

Henri, getting to his feet, nodded agreement.

That's just about time for the news to get out that our last contract was with the Visigoths . . . Whoever it is, Ash thought, *he didn't waste any time making his move.*

Ash tapped the toe of her boot on the leaf mulch floor of the copse. "Roberto."

The two men, kneeling before her, could not have been more different: Anselm still in his blue woollen doublet, face unshaven; Angelotti with his mass of gold hair falling below his shoulders, and his gather-necked shirt spotless and of the finest linen. What they had in common were identical expressions of shifty apprehension.

"You said go run the company. I've run it." Robert shrugged where he knelt. "We *need* money! This is a good contract . . ."

"With a man that we know." Angelotti uncharacteristically stumbled over his words. "That Roberto knows, knew, knew his *father*, that is—"

"Oh, Christ, don't tell me it's one of your goddams!"[15] Ash glared. "There's a country I'm never going back to! Nothing but barbarians and rain. Roberto, I'm going to nail your ears to the pillory for this one."

"He's here. You better meet him." Robert Anselm got up, untangling his scabbard from a thorn bush. Angelotti followed suit.

"He's one of your fucking Lancastrians, isn't he? Oh, sweet Christ! On top of everything else, you want me to go and fight English King Edward for his throne. I don't *think* so." Ash stopped, scowled, suddenly realising, *That would put me a hundred leagues and a good chunk of sea north of the Faris and her army.*

---

[15] With *rosbif*, *goddam* is a contemporary nickname for the English, at that time popularly supposed to be very foul-mouthed.

Maybe there's something in this. If I go to England, at the worst I die on the field of battle. Who knows what might happen in Carthage, if they ever found out that I hear— no!

She muttered, "Now, who's white-and-murrey?" and began to ransack her memory of the heraldry of dispossessed Lancastrian lords in exile from Yorkist England.

Robert Anselm coughed. "John de Vere. The Earl of Oxford."

Ash absently took her sword as Bertrand brought it, and let the boy belt it around her waist. Dapples of sunlight shone on its battered red leather scabbard. Her green and silver doublet was still quite obviously an expensive garment: equally obviously, it had not been washed or brushed for nearly a week. And no armour, not so much as a jack of plates.

"The fucking Earl of fucking Oxford, and I look like I'm worth ten shillings a year. Thank you, Robert. Thank you." She gave the wriggle of her hips that settled her sword-belt comfortably at her waist. She looked keenly at him. "You fought in his household, didn't you?"

"His father's. His older brother, too. Then him, in '71." Robert shrugged uncomfortably. "I got us what I could. He needs an escort here, he says."

Ash glanced around for Godfrey, and saw the priest in conversation with a man-at-arms in a murrey livery jacket with a white mullet on it. She could not very well approach her clerk at this point to ask him why a Lancastrian lord might be at the court of Charles of Burgundy, what he might want with a hefty contingent of armed mercenaries, and what, she ended in her own mind, he thinks of the Visigoth forces about forty miles away from here!

"His father, your old boss – he died in battle?"

"No. His father and Sir Aubrey – that's his brother – they were executed."

"Oh yippee," Ash said sourly. "Now I'm being employed by attainted nobility – he is under attainder, I suppose?"

Antonio Angelotti quietly put in, "Madonna, here he is."

Ash straightened her shoulders quite unconsciously. The annoying insects still buzzed, gold motes in the light under the trees. A horse snorted. The men with the de Vere banner jingled as they approached, their surcoats tied over light mail. There were a few burned-red faces under the helmets. Ash guessed the escort largely consisted of those who had recently displeased a sergeant. The man at the centre of the group she could not see clearly, but she nonetheless hauled off her hat and went down on one knee as the escort parted and made way for him. Her officers knelt with her.

"My lord Earl," she said.

She was aware of the bulk of her company halted outside the chapel of Mithras watching her. She was fortunately too far ahead to hear much of what they were saying. The earth felt hard under her knee. A blink of pain went through her head. When a cool voice said in English, "Madam Captain," she looked up.

He might have been any age between thirty and fifty-five: a fair-haired Englishman with faded blue eyes and an outdoor face, wearing tall riding boots pointed to the skirts of a faded linen doublet. He stepped forward, extending a hand. She took it. He had bony wrists. Any doubts about strength were dispelled by his effortlessly bringing her to her feet.

Ash dusted her hands, and looked shrewdly at the man. His doublet was Italian fashion, not so barbaric as she had feared; and if it looked as though he had been hunting all day across hard country in it, it had started life as an expensive garment. He was wearing a dagger but no sword. She managed not to say *Mad English!*

"We're at your command, my lord Earl," Ash said, and also failed to add *Or so I'm told . . .*

"I find you recovered, madam?"

"Yes, my lord."

"Your officers have told me the strength of your company. I want to know your manner of commanding them." The Earl of Oxford turned on his heel and began to walk towards his horses. Ash muttered a brief command to Anselm, left him to get the company back to their camp, and walked briskly off in de Vere's tracks. His assumption that he did not have to tell anyone to follow him both amused her, and impressed her by how correct it seemed to be.

At the wood's edge, she found her servants and the de Vere grooms vying for shade; and mounted with a minimum of fuss. Godluc shifted his great quarters under her, pushing for a gallop. She brought him up beside the Earl of Oxford's bay gelding.

Over the jingle of tack, the Englishman said, "A woman, most unusual," and smiled. He was missing a side tooth, and now they were out in the light she could see old white scars seaming his wrists, and vanishing under the neck of his shirt. The dimple-puncture of an arrow wound marked one cheek.

He added, "They appear devoted to you. Are you a virgin-whore?"

Ash spluttered at his English translation of *pucelle*. She said cheerfully, "I don't see what damn business it is of yours. Sir."

"No." The man nodded. He leaned over in the saddle, offering his hand again. "John de Vere. You call me 'your Grace' or 'my lord'."

Manners of the camp, not the court, Ash thought. Good. It always helps if they know something about soldiering. I must have seen his father around at some point, he looks familiar.

She shook his hand. His grip was solid.

Let's delay the questions for a bit. Until I have time to think about my answers.

"What is it you want my men to do, your Grace?"

"In the first place, I'm here to make a request of Burgundian Charles. If he refuses, you will form part of my escort to the borders, and back to England. I shall pay you off in London."

"How strongly are we liable to be refused?" Ash asked thoughtfully. "Does your Grace want me to put the Lion Azure up against the entire Burgundian military machine? I probably can get you to the Channel ports, in that case, but I don't particularly want to die to the last man, which is realistically what it would mean."

John de Vere turned his pale blue eyes to her. His bay had a mettlesome look, barrel-chested and something wicked about the eye. He rode easy in the saddle. To Ash, all the signs said, this man is a soldier.

Almost demurely, the exiled Earl said, "I'm here to find a Lancastrian claimant for the English throne, Henry late of glorious memory being murdered, and his son dead on Tewkesbury field.[16] The Yorkists don't sit so securely. A legitimate heir could de-throne them."

Ash, knowing next to nothing about *rosbif* dynastic struggles after her own brief involvement five years before, remembered one fact. She shot John de Vere a confused glance.

Serene, he said, "Yes. I'm aware that Duke Charles is married to the sister of Edward of York."

"Edward of York, who's currently Edward, fourth of that name, King by the Lord's Grace of England."

De Vere corrected her with immense authority: "Usurping King."

"So you're here, in the court of a prince married to the Yorkist King's *sister*, to find a Lancastrian claimant who's willing to invade England and fight against the Yorkist King for his throne? Yeah. Right."

Ash eased herself back in her saddle, controlling Godluc's obvious desire to lie down and roll in the lush green grass they rode over. She couldn't look at the Earl of Oxford for a minute, and when she did, she was no longer sure whether or not he had been smiling.

"Remind me to re-negotiate our contract if it comes to that, your Grace. I'm pretty sure Anselm wouldn't sign me up for that."

Actually, I'm pretty sure he'd like nothing better. Damn Robert! He never gave up on his bloody English wars – but he's not dragging me into them!

Not that I wouldn't like to be half of Christendom away from here, right now . . .

"Don't think of it as an act of lunacy, Captain." The Earl of Oxford's weather-beaten face creased, amused. "Or don't think of it as more lunatic than employing a female mercenary in addition to my household troops."

Ash began to consider that under his English soldierly exterior, John de Vere, Earl of Oxford, might be as reckless as a fifteen-year-old knight on his first campaign. *And as mad as a dog with its balls on fire*, she thought dourly. Robert, Angelotti, you're in deep, deep trouble.

The Earl said, "You came up from the south, Captain, and were employed by the Visigoth commander. What can you tell me? Within the terms of your *condotta*?"

Here it comes. And he's only the first. There's going to be some interesting questions, and not just from mad English Earls who happen to be employing me . . .

"Well?" de Vere said.

Ash looked over her shoulder and saw her own escort, led by Thomas Rochester with her personal banner. They were riding intermingled with the troops in murrey and white.

The rest of the company, archers and billmen and knights together all

---

[16] 4 May 1471: Prince Edward, the only son and heir of King Henry VI, is killed in battle with Edward of York (afterwards King Edward IV of England) at Tewkesbury. Henry VI dies soon after, under suspicious circumstances.

promiscuous, moved ahead with her officers, walking and riding back to the camp.

"Yes, your Grace." Ash narrowed her eyes against the sun, watching the column – from this illusory perspective, behind them, they did not appear to be moving forward: just a forest of polearms bobbing gently up and down. A multitude of steel helmets and bill-heads glinted in the Burgundian sunlight.

Ash said, "If you wish to inspect my company, there's wine in my tent. I'm considering what I can tell you, without betraying a previous employer." She hesitated, then said, "Why do you want to know?"

He appeared to take no offence, and she had used enough lack of ceremony to provoke him if he was going to be provoked. She thought, *Now we shall find out what he wants*, and waited, the reins tucked up in her fingers, her body swaying with Godluc's loose-boned walk.

"Why? Because I've changed my mind about my business since I came here." John de Vere switched to Burgundian French. "With this southern crusade rolling up Christendom like a carpet, and my lord princes of Burgundy and France squabbling instead of uniting, then the Lancastrian cause is necessarily put into abeyance. What use would a Lancastrian king be on the throne of England if the next thing he sees is a fleet of black galleys sailing up the Thames?"

Ash dropped Godluc back very slightly, so that she could see the Englishman's face. His eyes, narrowing against the sun, showed deep-bitten crow's-feet. He did not look at her, nor the rich miles of Burgundian countryside.

Over the noise of jingling tack, and Godluc huffing a long breath, the Earl of Oxford said, "These Visigoth men are good. Either they'll conquer us, disunited as we are, or we'll unite – and we might still be beaten. It would be bad war. Then there's the Turk waiting in the east, to come down and take the victor's spoils away from him." His thin, bony knuckles whitened on his reins; the bay's head tossed. "Steady!"

"Your Grace hired me because I've been there."

"Yes." The Englishman brought his horse under control. The pale blue eyes lost their abstracted look, and fixed on Ash. "Madam, you are the only soldier I can find in Burgundy who has. I'll talk to your officers, too; your master gunner in particular. First I'll hear details of what arms they bear, and their manner of war. Then you can tell me what rumours they have following them. Like this nonsense of a sky without a sun over the Germanies."

"That's true."

The Earl of Oxford stared at her.

"It's true, my lord." Ash found herself the more inclined to give him his title, since he was in exile. "I was there, my lord. I saw them put the sun out. It's only since we came here . . ."

She waved an ungloved hand, indicating the green sweep of grass running down to the water meadows; the wagons and tents and flying pennons of the Lion Azure camp; the sparkling water of the Suzon river, and Dijon's peaked roofs, blue tiles shining like mirrors under the summer sun.

". . . only here that I've seen the sun again."

De Vere reined in. "Upon your honour?"

"Upon my honour, as I honour a contract." Ash surprised herself with plain honesty. She tucked her reins under her thigh, and pushed her linen shirt-sleeves up. Her skin was already reddened from the morning blaze, but she welcomed it, could not get enough of it, sunburn or not.

"Does the sun still shine on France, and England?"

Something in the intensity of her question must have got through to the Earl. De Vere said simply, "Yes, madam. It does."

Godluc dropped his head. White foam began to cream his flanks. Ash cast a practised eye to the horse lines (set up in that part of the camp that included trees and river) and considered their coolness and shade. The war-horses, separated out by long-suffering grooms from the riding mounts, looked fractious.

A figure came running out of the camp's wagon-gate as she watched, sprinting across the river meadow towards them – towards Thomas Rochester's Lion Azure banner, she guessed, and thus to herself.

His gaze on the running figure, the Earl of Oxford said, "And this war-machine of theirs? Did you also see that?"

"I saw no machine," Ash said carefully. The distant figure was Rickard.

"I'll tell you what I know," she said decisively. Then, with humour, "You hired me for what I know, your Grace. As well as for these men. And as far as I can, I'll tell you the truth."

"On the understanding that you have no more loyalty to me than to the last man who hired you," the Earl remarked.

"No *less* loyalty," Ash corrected him, and nudged Godluc and rode forward to where Rickard, long legs labouring, pounded across the grass and kingcups towards her.

Rickard halted, leaned forward with his hands gripping his thighs, breathing hard, and then straightened. Red-faced, he thrust a parchment roll up at her.

Ash reached down. "What's this?"

The black-haired boy licked parched lips and panted, "A summons from the Duke of Burgundy."

V

Ash became conscious of her pulse speeding up, her mouth rapidly drying, and an urge to visit the latrines. She closed her hand tightly around the Duke of Burgundy's scroll.

"When?" she demanded, not about to spell out some clerk's script word-by-word in front of a new employer. Seeing Rickard's bright red face, she loosed the water skin from her saddle and handed it down to the boy. "When does the Duke want us?"

Rickard drank, tipped a sparkling jet over his black curls, and shook his head, drops spraying. "The fifth hour past noon. Boss, it's almost noon now!"

Ash smiled reassuringly. "Get me Anselm, Angelotti, Geraint Morgan and Father Godfrey: *run!*"

Her voice cracked.

Straightening up in her saddle, she saw Robert Anselm just leaving the camp again, the Italian master gunner with him. As the boy pounded back past them, the two men strode through the thick, green grass towards her and the Earl of Oxford's retinue.

"Here they come – the lily-white boys," she remarked grimly, under her breath. *Robert, what have you got me into!* "My lord of Oxford, please you to accept my hospitality?"

The fair-haired Englishman eased his horse up alongside Godluc, gazing at the Lion Azure camp; which began, as they watched, to resemble a beehive kicked over by a donkey. With a slight smile, he murmured, "The Earl of Oxenford[17] would be better advised to go away for an hour and leave you to put your men in order."

"No." The grim edge didn't leave Ash's voice. Her gaze fixed on her approaching officers. "You're my boss, my lord. It's up to you now whether I obey this summons, and go and see the bold Duke. And, if I do go, how I go, and what I say to him. It's your call, my lord."

His faded brows lifted.

"Yes. Yes, madam. You may attend. I must decide what you say. Regrettably, it seems that I may have cheated you out of a contract richer than I can offer while Richard of Gloucester[18] holds my lands."

And just how much are you paying us? Not a hundredth as much as Charles Téméraire[19] could, that's for sure. Shit.

"Stay and eat with me, my lord. You need to give me your orders. I can guest your retinue, too." Ash took a breath. "I intend to hold a muster now and take the roll, so that I can tell you our exact strength. Master Anselm may have told you that we left Basle in something of a hurry. You got a bargain. My lord."

"Poverty is a worse master than I am, madam."

Ash surveyed his frayed doublet and thought about being attainted and in exile. "I do hope so," she murmured, under her breath. Then: "Excuse me, your Grace!"

As the men from his small retinue rode up to the Earl, Ash tapped Godluc's flanks with her spurs and trotted forward. She was aware of Florian walking up beside her stirrup, and Godluc whickering at the surgeon. Her head began to ache. She halted before the panting figures of Robert Anselm, Angelotti, and now Geraint ab Morgan with them. She gazed over their heads from her saddle, at the camp, and sought with a critical eye to bring detail out of what was essentially a chaos.

---

[17] 'Oxenford' is one of the contemporary versions of 'Oxford'.

[18] Seven years after the actions narrated in the 'Ash' texts, Richard of Gloucester is crowned King of England, as Richard III (1483–1485).

[19] Duke Charles of Burgundy, like his forefathers – Philip the Bold, John the Fearless and Philip the Good – was known to his people by a cognomen. *Téméraire* has been subsequently translated, according to taste, as 'Charles the Bold' or 'Charles the Rash'.

"Jesus Christ on the Tree!"

Itemised, it was worse than it first looked. Men lay drinking around firepits grey with ash. Glaives and bills leaned in untidy heaps or rested unsteadily up against guy-ropes. Blackened cookpots were being prodded by half-dressed men-at-arms. Whores sitting up on the wagons ate apples and screamed with laughter. Euen Huw's lance's sorry attempt at guarding the gate made her cringe. Children ran and screeched far too close to the horse lines. And the wall of wagons trailed down, at the river, to a mass of small shelters, blankets over sticks mostly, and no effort made to make fire-safety or a defence possible . . .

"*Geraint!*"

"Yes, boss?"

Ash scowled at a distant crossbowman with unlaced hose, and a dirty white coif over stringy shoulder-length hair, who sat on a wagon playing a whistle in the key of C.

"What do you think this is, Michaelmas fucking *Fair*? Get that bloody lot kitted up, before Oxford fires us! And before the Visigoths get here and kick our asses! *Move it!*"

The Welsh Sergeant of Archers was used to being shouted at, but the genuine outrage in her tone made him swing round immediately and stomp off into camp, between the tents, lifting his big legs with remarkable alacrity over guy-ropes, and bellowing directions to each lance of men that he passed. Ash sat in her saddle, with her fists on her hips, and watched him go.

"As for *you*." She spoke to Anselm without lowering her head. "*Your* ass is grass. Forget dining with your old lord. By the time we come out of my tent, this camp is going to look like something out of Vegetius, and these dozy buggers are going to look like soldiers. Or you're not going to be here. Am I right?"

"Yes, boss—"

"That was a fucking rhetorical question, Robert. Get them mustered; take the roll; I want to know who we lost and what we kept. Once they're out in the field, get them practising weapons drill; half of them are lying around getting rat-arsed, and that stops *now*. I need an escort fit to walk into Duke Charles's palace with me!"

Anselm blenched.

She snarled, "You have one hour. Get to it!"

Florian, her hand resting on Godluc's stirrup, gave a deep, breathy chuckle. "Boss goes *bark!* and everybody jumps."

"They don't call me the old battle-axe for nothing!"

"Oh, you know about that, do you? I've never been sure."

Ash watched Anselm sprinting back to camp, conscious that, under her anguished concern that her men weren't secure, and under the level of fear about stepping into the premier court of Europe, some tiny inner voice was exclaiming *God, but I love this job!*

"Antonio, stay here. I want you to show the English lord your guns – I never met a lord who wasn't interested in cannon – and keep him out of my hair for one hour. Where's Henri?"

Her steward appeared at Godluc's bridle, limping, leaning on the arm of the woman Blanche.

"Henri, we're entertaining this English Earl and his retinue in the command tent. Let's have fresh rushes, silver plates, and respectable food, okay? Let's see if we can set table for an Earl's degree."

"Boss! With Wat cooking?" Henri's aghast, linen-coifed face slowly changed to an expression of complacency. "Ah. *English*. That means he knows nothing about food and cares less. Give me an hour."

"You got it! Angelotti, go!"

She turned Godluc with a pressure of her knee, and rode slowly back to the murrey banner. The cloth drooped in the heat. The men-at-arms' faces under their helms shone wet and red. She thought, Every damn peasant is sheltering from the sun from now until late afternoon. Every merchant in Dijon is between cool stone walls, listening to musicians. I bet even the Duke's court are holding siesta. And what do we get?

Less than five hours to be ready.

"Madam Captain!" de Vere shouted.

She rode up to the Englishmen.

The Earl of Oxford, speaking (as he had been speaking) in the Burgundian dialect of the Duchy, indicated his young knights and said briefly, "These are my brothers, Thomas, George and Richard; and my good friend Viscount Beaumont."

His brothers looked all more or less in their twenties; the remaining nobleman a few years older. All of them had shoulder-length, curling fair hair, and a certain kinship of shabby leg armour and brigandines, and sword grips with the leather worn thin.

The youngest-looking of the de Vere brothers sat up in his saddle and said, in clear East Anglian English, "She dresses like a man, John! She's a strumpet. We don't need the like of her to get false Edward off the throne!"

Another brother, whose blue eyes squinted, said, "Look at that face! Who cares what she is!"

Ash sat her war-horse easily, and surveyed the four brothers with a relaxed expression. She turned her head towards the remaining noblemen, Beaumont. With the English she remembered from campaigning there, she remarked, "No wonder they say what they do about English manners. You have anything to add to that, my lord Viscount?"

The Viscount Beaumont held up a gauntleted hand in surrender, eyes twinkling appreciatively. When he spoke, a missing front tooth made his voice appealingly soft-edged. "Not me, madam!"

She turned back to the Earl of Oxford. "My lord, your brother there isn't the first soldier to insult me for being female – not by about twenty years!"

"I am ashamed by Dickon's[20] lack of courtesy." John de Vere bowed from his saddle. To all appearances confident of her, he said, "Madam Captain, you know how best to handle it."

"But she's a weak woman!" The youngest brother, Richard de Vere, turning amazed pale eyes to her, blurted, "What can you do?"

[20] 'Dickon' is the short, affectionate form of 'Richard'.

247

"Oh, I get it . . . You think my lord didn't hire me for my fighting skills," Ash said bluntly. "You think he just hired me because he wants to question me about the Visigoth general and the invasion that's headed this way, and because you think Robert Anselm runs this company, and commands it in the field. Am I right?"

One of the middle de Veres, Tom or George, said, "Duke Charles must be of the same opinion. You're a woman, what else can you do but talk?"

The Earl of Oxford politely said, "That is my brother George, madam."

Ash wheeled Godluc away to face the youngest brother. "I'll tell you what I can do, Master Dickon de Vere. I can reason, I can speak, and I can do my job. I can fight. But if a man doesn't believe I can command, or thinks I'm weak, or won't lie down after I beat him in a fair fight – which is the way I usually handle this with recruits – or thinks that any woman's argument is best answered by rape . . . then I can kill him."

The youngest de Vere's face coloured up red from neck to hairline. Part embarrassment, part – Ash guessed – the realisation that it was probably true.

"You'd be surprised how much trouble it saves." She grinned. "Honey, I don't have to convince you I'm not vermin. I just have to fight your lord brother's enemies, reasonably well, and survive to get paid."

Dickon de Vere, red-faced, stared; suddenly very upright in his saddle. Ash turned back toward the Earl of Oxford.

"They don't have to like me, my lord. They just have to stop thinking of me as a daughter of Eve."

There was a snort from the Viscount Beaumont, something in English so rapid between the four brothers that she couldn't follow it, and then the youngest brother flushed, burst out laughing; and only the two middle ones continued to glare at her. The Earl passed his hand across his mouth, possibly hiding a smile.

Ash narrowed her eyes against the sun, feeling sweat mat her hair under her velvet hat. A strong smell of horse and leather tack drifted up from Godluc; she felt it as something reassuring.

"Time for you to give me orders, my lord," she said cheerfully. And then, catching his eye, "This *is* my company, my lord Earl. All eighty lances. And I'd like to know something. We're too big for an escort, and too small for an army – why *have* you hired us?"

"Later, madam. When we dine. There's time enough before you visit the Duke."

About to insist, Ash caught sight of Godfrey leaving a conversation at the camp gate with three or four shabbily dressed men, and a woman in a green habit. His wooden pectoral cross bounced on his chest as he strode across the grass, robe flapping at his bare heels.

"I believe my clerk wants me. Will it please you to have Master Angelotti here show you our guns? They are in the shade . . ." She pointed down towards the trees at the edge of the river.

Meeting de Vere's eyes, she became aware that the English nobleman was perfectly aware of the stratagem, perfectly used to such courtesies, and willing to consent.

Ash rose in her saddle and bowed, as Angelotti took the Earl's bridle and led him towards the camp.

"Godfrey?"

"Yes, child?"

"Come with me!" She eased Godluc forward, Godfrey at her stirrup. "Tell me *everything* you've found out about the situation in Dijon, while I'm inspecting the camp. Everything! I have no idea what's going on in the Burgundian court, and I'm going to be standing in front of the Duke in four hours!"

Her command tent, when she reached it, was a scrum of servants rushing in and out, setting up a table, and strewing the sharp straw underfoot with sweet new rushes. Ash stomped behind the dividing curtain and dressed for the coming meal in extreme haste, knowing this would be the gear in which she would go before the Duke.

"It's *Burgundy*, Florian! It doesn't get any better than this!"

Floria del Guiz sat cross-legged on a chest, unimpressed. She rapidly lifted her feet up out of the way. "You don't even know you'll be fighting with the Duke. Robert's mad Earl might take us God-knows-where."

"De Vere wants to fight Visigoths." Ash held her forearms up, speaking to Floria while taking no notice of Bertrand and Rickard tying the doublet's points down to her wrists. The sleeves puffed fashionably at the shoulders.

Bertrand whimpered. Ash fidgeted.

"I'm not going to look as good as I should – that bitch kept my armour!"

The surgeon drank from a silver goblet snatched from Henri Brant's servers. "Oh, wear what you like! He's only a Duke."

"Only a – fucking *hell*, Florian!"

"I grew up with this." The long-legged woman wiped sweat from her face. "So, you haven't got your armour. So?"

"*Fuck!*" Ash found no words to explain what putting on full armour does, no way to say to Floria, *But you feel like God when you've got it on!* And in front of all those people, all these bloody Burgundians, I want to do myself and the company credit—

"That was full harness! It cost me *two years* to earn the money to pay for it!"

A quarter-hour by the marked candle saw every chest turfed out, Bertrand in tears at the thought of re-packing, and Ash with German cuisses strapped to her thighs, Milanese lower leg armour, a blue velvet brigandine with brass rivets showing dull against the cloth, and a polished steel plackart that, strapped around her waist over the brigandine, would come up in a point over her breastbone, to a fretworked metal finial. And be boiling hot.

"Oh shit," she said. "Oh shit, I'm having an audience with Charles of Burgundy, oh shit, *oh* shit . . ."

"You don't think you're taking this a *little* too seriously?"

"What they see – is what I am. And I'd rather worry about this than . . ." Ash opened a small mirror-case in her hand, tilting the tiny reflective circle to try and see her face. Bertrand jerked her hair with his comb. She swore, threw a bottle at the boy, tugged her silver hair down loose over the injured part of her scalp, and stared into dark, dark eyes, the colour of ponds in wild woods. The faintest tinge of sun coloured her cheekbones, making her scars stand out the more pale. Apart from the scars, and the thinness that illness had given her, a flawless face stared back at her.

Don't worry about the armour, because that isn't what they'll be looking at.

Floria stepped out of two men's way, watching Ash give orders to lance-leaders and efficiently dismiss them. Her smile became sardonic. "You're going to court with your hair down? You're a married woman."

Ash gave the surgeon a reply she had been practising in her mind on her sick-bed. " 'My marriage was a sham. I swear to God that I am in exactly the same state now as I was before I was married.' "

Floria made a long, rude noise. "No, boss! Don't try that one here. You'll make even Charles of Burgundy crack a smile."

"Worth a try?"

"*No*. Trust me. No."

Ash stood still while Bertrand belted her sword around her waist. The brigandine's velvet-covered metal plates creaked as she breathed.

From the sepia shadows cast by canvas, the tall woman said, "And what are you going to tell our noble Earl about meeting the Visigoth general? More than you've told me? Christ, woman, is it likely I'm going to betray a confidence? We're all—"

"We?" Ash interrupted.

"—me, Godfrey, Robert . . . *How long do you expect us to wait?*" Floria wiped the top of one of Ash's four silver goblets with a grimy thumb, and glanced up with bright eyes. "What happened to you? What did she say to you? You know, your silence is deafening."

"Yes," Ash said flatly, not responding to the woman's effortful flippancy. "I'm thinking it through. There's no point going off at half-cock. It could affect the company's future, and mine, and I'll call an officer-meeting when I've got it straight in my head – and not until then. Meanwhile, we have to deal with the Grand Duke of the West and a mad English Earl."

Two orders reduced the outer pavilion to order, and got the side panels of canvas unhooked. The canopy continued to give shade; the open sides admitted stinging mites, white butterflies, and the swooping green metallic darts of dragonflies, and let a breeze blow over Ash's face from the rush-choked river.

She took a brief survey of the table, clothed in regrettably yellow linen. The silver plate shone bright enough to leave after-images on her retinas. Smart men-at-arms from one of van Mander's lances were forming a guard around the central area of the camp. Three of the camp women played recorders: an Italian air. Henri and Blanche stood with their heads together, talking heatedly.

As Ash looked, the steward wiped his red, streaming face on his shirt-sleeve, and nodded; this just as the sun caught bright golden curls beyond him, and she realised it was Angelotti leading the Earl's party back towards the command tent.

She saw John de Vere register the unusual fact of Blanche acting as a server, and Ludmilla's lance-mate Katherine Hammell standing with her crossbow and a leash of mastiffs as part of the command tent guard.

Half as a question, John de Vere remarked, "You have many women in your camp, madam."

"Of course I do. I execute for rape."

It jolted the viscount, she could tell from Beaumont's expression; but the Earl of Oxford merely nodded thoughtfully. She introduced Floria del Guiz with some care, but the Earl greeted the surgeon as a man; and Godfrey Maximillian.

"Please you be seated," she said formally; and let the servants place each man at table according to his degree, herself ceding the head of the table to John de Vere. The music ceased while Godfrey's rumble intoned a grace.

As she sat down, half her mind on how far the Visigoths might have advanced in six days, and the other half thinking how best to behave in Duke Charles's court with an invasion due, a memory clicked suddenly into place.

"Good God," Ash blurted, as Blanche and a dozen others put the first remove on the table, "I do know you. I've heard of you. You're *that* Lord Oxford!"

The English Earl quaked, with what, after a split second, she realised was laughter. " 'That' Oxford?"

"They put you in Hammes!"

Floria, on the far side of the table, glanced up from a dish of quail. "What's Hammes?"

"High-security nick," Ash said briefly; then coloured, and began to serve John de Vere personally from the one large silver trencher they still possessed. "It's a castle outside Calais. With moats and dykes and . . . it's supposed to be the toughest castle in Europe to get free from!"

The Earl of Oxford reached over and slapped Viscount Beaumont heartily on the shoulder. "And so it would have been, but for this man. And Dickon, and George, and Tom. But you're wrong in one thing, madam: I made no escape. I left."

"Left?"

"Taking my chief jailer, Thomas Blount, with me, as my ally. We left his wife garrisoning the castle until we should return with troops for the house of Lancaster."[21] John de Vere smiled. "Mistress Blount is a woman even you would find formidable. I doubt not but that we can go back to Hammes any time these ten years, and find it still ours!"

"My lord of Oxenford's famous. He invaded England," Ash said to Floria. She sniffed back a laugh; no malice in it, only vicarious pride. "Twice. Once with the armies of Margaret of Anjou and King Henry." A mirthful snuffle. "And once on his own."

"On his *own*!" Floria del Guiz turned an incredulous face to the Earl. "You'll

---

[21] In point of fact, these events happened exactly as narrated here, but some eight years afterwards, in 1484. During the period covered by these texts, the Earl of Oxford remained a prisoner in Hammes castle. I suspect a chronicler of adding Oxford to the text, probably no later than 1486.

have to excuse boss's manners, my lord of Oxford. She gets like this sometimes."

"I was hardly alone," Oxford protested, deadpan. "I had eighty men with me."

Floria del Guiz subsided in her chair, gazing at the English nobleman with wine-bright eyes and her infectious smile. "Eighty men.[22] To invade England. I see . . ."

"My lord the Earl took their Michael's Mount in Cornwall," Ash said. "And held it – how long, a year?"

"Not so long. From September of '73 to February of '74." The Earl looked at his brothers, whose loud voices were rising in easy talk. "They were staunch for me. But not the men-at-arms, once it was clear no relieving force would come from France."[23]

'And after that, Hammes." Ash shrugged. "*That* Lord Oxford. Of course."

"The third time, I shall put a better man on Edward's throne."[24] He leaned back against the carved oak chair. With steel under his tone, John de Vere said, "I am thirteenth Earl of a line that goes back to Duke William, that time out of mind were great lords and Chancellors of the realm of England. But since I am in exile, no nearer a king of Lancaster than you are near Pope Joan, madam, and since we have these Goths to contend against, then – 'that Lord Oxford' it is."

He raised his silver goblet gravely to Ash.

Ye Gods! So this is the great English soldier-Earl . . . Ash's mind ran on as she drank deeply of the indifferent red wine. "You reconciled Warwick the Kingmaker to Queen Margaret, too.[25] Good God! . . . Sorry to say, my lord, I was actually fighting on the opposite side to you on Barnet field in '71. Nothing personal. Just business."

"Yes. And now, madam, to our business," de Vere said bluntly.

"Yes, my lord." Ash gazed out from under the shading canopy, past the Earl, at the surrounding tents and pennants sagging under the hot postmeridian sky. Her armour kept her upright at the table. The brigandine's weight didn't bother her, but the heat of it made her pale. Her head began to throb again.

Between Geraint's tent and Joscelyn van Mander's pavilion, she saw the slope of green meadows, and the grey leaves of trees beyond at the water's edge. A distant flash of blue took her eye: Robert Anselm, out in the field, stripped to pourpoint and hose, shouting at men drilling with swords and bills. Water-boys sprinted along the lines of men. The harsh Welsh yowl of Geraint ab Morgan sounded above the thunk of shafts hitting straw targets.

Let 'em practise in the heat! They won't be such bloody layabouts tomorrow.

[22] Some sources give a figure of 400 men.

[23] This is accurate. The English King, Edward, offered pardons to the men, but to Oxford and his brothers, only their lives. Oxford was incarcerated in Hammes shortly afterwards.

[24] In 1485, by winning the Battle of Bosworth for the then 'Welsh milksop' Henry Tudor, Oxford put Henry VII of England on the throne (1485–1509). Whether that is 'a better man' has long been a subject of debate.

[25] Richard Neville, Earl of Warwick, and Margaret of Anjou, wife to Henry VI of England; these inveterate noble enemies, having in 1471 spent the past fifteen years on opposite sides of the royal wars, were reconciled to an alliance by John de Vere.

Time this place started looking like a military camp . . . Because if it doesn't, they're going to stop thinking they're a military company. I wonder how many I've lost to the whorehouses in Dijon?

The pavilion's marked candle showed it to be closing on the third hour of the afternoon. She ignored the pulse of anticipation in her stomach, and lifted a cup of watered wine, the liquid tepid in her mouth. "Shall I call my officers in, my lord?"

"Yes. Now."

Ash turned to give the order to Rickard, who stood behind her chair, bearing her sword and second-best sallet. Unexpectedly, Floria del Guiz spoke:

"Duke Charles loves a war. Now he'll want to attack the whole Visigoth army!"

"He'll get wiped out, then," Ash said sourly, as Rickard spoke in an undertone to one of the many wagon-boys serving as pages. Between servers, pages and two or three dozen armed men with leashed dogs surrounding this end of the pavilion canopy, the table formed an island of stillness. She leaned her arms forward, ignoring the stains on the tablecloth, and caught John de Vere's blue eyes watching her. "You're right, my lord Earl. There's no chance of winning a battle against the Visigoths, without the princes of Europe unite. And that's a fat chance! They must know what happened in Italy and the Germanies, but I guess they don't believe it can happen to them."

A stir among the guards outside the tent, and Robert Anselm strode in, sweating heavily; Angelotti on his heels, and Geraint close behind the two of them. Ash motioned them to the table. Viscount Beaumont and the younger de Vere brothers leaned over to listen.

"Officers' reports," Ash announced, pushing back her plate. "You'd better sit in on this, your Grace. It'll save going over things twice."

And give you a completely unvarnished view of us . . . well, let's not have any mistake about what you're getting!

Geraint, Anselm and Angelotti took places at table, the captain of archers regarding the remnants of food with wistful hunger.

"We've re-done the perimeter." Robert Anselm made a long arm across the table and rescued a slab of cheese from Ash's plate. Chewing, he prompted thickly: "Geraint?"

"That's right, boss." Geraint ab Morgan gave the Oxford brothers a slightly wary look. "Got your men's tents set up in the river side of the camp, your Grace."

Ash wiped her wet brow. "Right— And where's Joscelyn? He's usually hanging about for command-group meetings."

"Oh, he's down there, boss. Welcoming them in on behalf of the Lion."

The Welsh captain of archers spoke entirely innocently, and looked up with a grunt as Bertrand, at Ash's nod, served horn goblets filled with watered wine. Robert Anselm caught Ash's eye, significantly.

"Is he, by God?" Ash murmured to herself. "Did your camp reorganisation involve putting all the Flemish lances together?"

"No, boss, van Mander did that when we got here."

The tent pennants that she could see indicated, to Ash's practised eye, that the entire back quarter of the camp was made up of Flemish tents, no other nation intermixed with them. Everywhere else was, as usual, a promiscuous mingling of homelands.

She nodded, thoughtfully, her gaze absently on a passing group of women in linen kirtles and dirty shifts, laughing as they made their way towards the camp gate and – presumably – the town of Dijon.

"Let it go for now," she said. "While we're at it, though, I want double perimeter guards from now on. I don't want Monforte's men or the Burgundian lads coming in nicking stuff, and I don't want our lot going out getting rat-arsed all the time. Let 'em into town in groups, no more than twenty at a time. Let's keep the unpaid fighting down to a minimum."

Robert Anselm chuckled. "Yes, Captain."

"That goes for officers and lance-leaders, too! Okay." Ash glanced around the table. "What's the feeling in camp about this English contract?"

Godfrey Maximillian brushed sweat off his face with a quick gesture. With an apologetic glance to Anselm, he said, "The men would have preferred it if it had been something you negotiated in person, Captain. I think they're waiting to see which way you jump."

"Geraint?"

The Welshman said dismissively, "You know archers, boss. For once they're fighting on the same side as someone supposed to be more foul-mouthed than they are! No offence, your Grace."

John de Vere looked rather grimly at the captain of archers, but said nothing.

Ash persisted, "No dissent?"

"Well . . . Huw's lance think we should have tried to get another contract with the Visigoths." Geraint didn't acknowledge Oxford. He said steadily, "So do I, boss. Out-numbered armies don't win the field, and the Duke's out-numbered and then some. The way to get paid is to be on the winning side."

Ash looked questioningly at Antonio Angelotti.

"You know gunners," Angelotti echoed. "Show us something we can fire at, and everyone's happy. Half my crews are off in the Burgundian army camp right now, looking at their ordnance – I haven't seen most of them for two days."

"Visigoths don't use much ordnance," Geraint observed. "Your boys wouldn't like that."

Angelotti gave his reserved smile. "There is something to be said for being on the same side as the big guns."

"And the men-at-arms?" Ash asked Robert Anselm.

"I'd say about half of them – Carracci and all the Italian lads, the English, and the easterners – are happy with the contract. The French lads don't like being on the same side as the Burgundians, but they'll wear it. They all think we owe the rag-heads something for Basle."

Ash snorted. "I've looked in the war-chest – *they* owe *us*!"

"They'll get stuck in, when the time comes," Anselm continued, amused. He frowned. "Can't answer for the Flemings. Captain, I don't get to talk to di Conti and the rest, now, I just get to talk to van Mander; he says it saves time if he passes orders on."

"Uh huh." In perfect understanding of the unease in Anselm's mind, Ash nodded. "Okay, let's move on—"

John de Vere spoke for the first time. "These dissenting lances, madam Captain, how much of a problem will this be?"

"None at all. There are going to be some changes."

Ash met de Vere's gaze. Something in her determined expression must have been convincing: he merely nodded, and said, "Then you deal with it, Captain."

Ash dismissed the subject. "Okay: next . . ."

Beyond the men huddled around the linen-covered table, beyond the peaked roofs of the tents, the forested limestone hills around Dijon glimmered green. Below the tree-line, in the valley, slopes glistened green and brown: rows of vines ripening in the sun. Ash slitted her eyes against that brilliance, attempting to judge whether this sun-in-Leo was still shining as strongly as on the previous day.

"Next," Ash said, "the matter of what we're going to *do*."

Ash glanced at Oxford. She found herself absently digging with the tip of her eating-knife at the charcoal-black pastry that had coffined a cow-steak and cheese pie. Her blade scattered fragments on the cloth. "It's like I said to you earlier, my lord. This company's far too big for you to want us just as an escort. But we're nowhere near big enough to take on an army – Visigoth, *or* Burgundian."

The English Earl smiled briefly at that. Her officers winced.

"So . . . I've been thinking, your Grace." Ash jerked her thumb over her shoulder. Where the tent-walls were removed, the long slope of pasture up to the city walls was visible; and the peaked roofs of the convent. "While I was up there. I had time to think. And I came up with a half-baked idea that I want to approach the Duke with. The question is, your Grace, have you and I had the same half-baked idea?"

Robert Anselm rubbed his wet hand across his face, hiding a grin; Geraint Morgan spluttered. Angelotti gazed at Ash from under ambiguously lowered oval lids.

"'Half-baked'?" the Earl of Oxford questioned, mildly.

"'Mad', if you prefer." Excitement keyed her up, momentarily wiped out both oppressive heat and the effects of her injury. She leaned forward on the table. "We're not going to attack the entire Visigoth invasion force, are we? That would take everything Duke Charles has got here, and then some! But – why should we need to attack them head-on?"

De Vere nodded, briefly. "A raid."

Ash dug her knife-point into the table. "Yes! If a *raiding* force could take out the head . . . a raiding force of, say, seventy or eighty lances: eight hundred men. Bigger than an escort, but still small enough to move fast, and to get out of trouble if we meet their army. And that's us, isn't it?"

Oxford leaned back slightly, his armour clicking. His three brothers began to stare at him.

"It isn't a mad idea," the Earl of Oxford said.

Viscount Beaumont lisped, "Only by comparison! Not as mad as some of the things we've done, John."

"And how does it help Lancaster?" the youngest de Vere brother broke in.

"Quiet! Ruffians." The Earl of Oxford thumped Beaumont on the shoulder, and ruffled Dickon's hair. His worn, lined face was alive when he turned his attention back to Ash. Above him, the white canvas blazed gold, hiding the fierce southern European sun.

"Yes, madam," he confirmed. "We have been thinking alike. A raid to take out their commander, their general. Their Faris."

For a moment, what she sees is not the sun-drenched camp in Burgundy, but a frost-starred pleasance[26] in Basle: a woman in Visigoth hauberk and surcoat wiping spilt wine from the dagged silken hem, her frowning face Ash's own. A woman who has said *sister, half-sister, twin*.

"No."

Ash, for the first time, saw the Earl appear startled.

In a very practical tone, Ash repeated, "No. Not their commander. Not here in Europe. Believe me, the Faris expects that. She knows damn well that every enemy prince wants her head on a spike, right now, and she's well guarded. In the middle of about twelve thousand soldiers. Attacking her right now is impossible."

Ash looked around at their faces; back at de Vere. "No, my lord – when I said I'd had a half-baked idea, I meant it. I want to mount an attack on Carthage."

"Carthage!" Oxford boomed.

Ash shrugged. "I bet you anything you like, they won't be expecting that."

"For damn good reason!" one of the middle de Vere brothers exclaimed.

Godfrey Maximillian spluttered, "*Carthage!*" in a tone of outraged astonishment.

Angelotti murmured something in Robert Anselm's ear. Floria, as still as a animal scenting hounds, looked at Ash with a narrow, baffled, complaining expression on her smudged face.

John de Vere, in much the same sceptical tone as she had earlier spoken to him about his Lancastrian claims, said, "Madam, you were planning to ask Charles of Burgundy to pay you to attack the King-Caliph in Carthage?"

Ash took a breath. She leaned back against the upright of the back-stool, overheating under the canvas canopy, and held her goblet up for Bertrand to fill it with watered wine.

"There are two things to be considered, your Grace. One – their King-Caliph Theodoric is sick, maybe dying. This I have from trustworthy sources." She momentarily met the gaze of Floria, of Godfrey. "A dead King-Caliph would be very useful. Well, a dead caliph is always useful! But – if there were to be a dynastic struggle going on back home, then I don't think the Visigoth army would be pushing their invasion north this campaigning season. They might even get recalled back to North Africa. At the least, it would halt them over the winter. They probably wouldn't cross the Burgundian border."

---

[26] Garden.

"Now I see why you hoped to speak to Charles, madam." John de Vere looked thoughtful.

Dickon de Vere spluttered something. Under cover of the English lords' increasingly loud talk, Floria del Guiz said, "*Are* you mad?"

"De Vere's a soldier, and he doesn't think it's mad. Not entirely mad," Ash corrected herself.

"It's desperate." Robert Anselm frowned, abstracted; reservations in his voice over and above what he was saying. He wiped his sweating, shiny head. "Desperate; not stupid."

"Carthage," Antonio Angelotti said softly, some expression on the master gunner's face that Ash couldn't identify. That worried her, needing to know how he would be, on the field of battle.

Godfrey Maximillian looked at her. "And?" he prompted.

"And . . ." Ash pushed her stool back and stood up. The English lords' debate had reached shouting proportions, John de Vere thumping his fist repeatedly on the table, and her movement went unnoticed. Like birds disturbed in corn, her officers' faces lifted to her.

She thought, looking around the table, that no one who didn't know these men could have picked up the growing atmosphere of distrust – certainly de Vere and his Englishmen seemed unaware of it – but to her it was loud as a shout.

"Boss," Geraint ab Morgan said. "Are you telling us what's on your mind, here?"

Ash said to Roberto, to Florian, to Godfrey, Angelotti, Geraint: "If their King-Caliph dies, it will give us breathing-space."

A look of settled disbelief closed up Godfrey Maximillian's expression. That was enough: she swung around, moved to stand with her hand against one of the tent-poles, staring out past the pavilion's spidering guy-ropes, past their shadows on the turf. Her eyes saw glimmering hot, brilliant, infinite sparks of sun on metal – silver platters, dagger pommels, sword blades in the meadow, the metal finial crowning the great standard-pole of the Lion Azure camp.

Ash turned. The sun dazzled her eyes: everything under the canopy now impenetrable with brown shadows, only a glimmer of white faces visible. She walked back inside, to the table.

"Okay. You're smart. *Not* the King-Caliph." She dropped her hand on to Robert Anselm's shoulder, closed it; feeling the rough blue-dyed linen of his pourpoint and the warmth of his body. "Although that would be a bonus."

She let her gaze move from Godfrey, who sat stroking his amber-brown beard; to Floria's face, to Angelotti's Byzantine-icon solemnity, Geraint's puzzled and impatient expression.

Beaumont said something in rapid English.

"Yes," Oxford added, raising his head from the discussion to Ash, and with a nod of acknowledgement to the viscount. "You said, madam, that there are two things to be considered; what is the second?"

Ash nodded to Henri Brant. The steward bustled the servers and pages clear out of the tent. A sharp command got her the captain of the guard's attention:

ordering the men-at-arms to circle the tent further off. She smiled to herself, shaking her head. *And still there'll be rumours, before nightfall.*

"The second thing." Her expression took on a serious, pragmatic abstraction. "Is the Stone Golem."

Ash leaned her fists on the tablecloth and looking around at her officers, and the Earl of Oxford. "The *machina rei militaris*, the tactics-machine. *That's* what I want to raid."

Ash, watching Godfrey as she spoke, saw his dark, brilliant eyes blink. There was a furrow across his forehead: fear, condemnation, or concern: all unclear.

"Are you certain—" he began.

Ash gestured him to silence, not before she saw the look that Floria del Guiz gave the priest.

"We know the Faris hears a voice," Ash said quietly. "You've heard all the rumours, about the Visigoth's Stone Golem. It talks to her from Carthage, it tells her how to win battles with her armies. That's what we need to take out. Not the Caliph. I want a raid to smash, burn and destroy this *machine* that she talks about. I want to wipe out this 'Stone Golem', shut her damn voice up for good!"

A woodpecker began to hammer at one of the alders growing down by the river, the hard *toc-toc-toc* echoing through the humid air, sharper than the noise of men at sword-drill. Across the river, there was nothing to distinguish the bright southern afternoon horizon from the other three quarters of the compass.

Viscount Beaumont's blurred lisp asked, "How much does she depend upon this *machina*, and how much on her generals? Would the loss of it be such a loss to her?"

Before Ash could answer, John de Vere cut in. "Have you heard anything else, since you set foot at Calais, but 'the Stone Golem'? Even if it only exists as a rumour, the *machina* is worth another army to her."

"Then, if it is nothing but rumour," his brother George remarked, "it can't *be* destroyed, no more than you can cleave smoke with a sword."

Tom de Vere put in, "And if it does exist, is it in Carthage, or with their woman-general? Or elsewhere? Who can say?"

Ash heard the woodpecker stop. Between tents, and over the palisades, she could see boys with slings down by the river bank.

Briskly, she said, "If the war-machine was with her, we could have bought that information by now. It's *not* with her. If it's elsewhere – then it's so valuable to them that it can only be smack in the heart of the Visigoth Empire, under a phenomenal number of guards, in the middle of their capital city." Ash paused and grinned. "The city I'm suggesting we raid."

Laconically, the Earl of Oxford said, " 'If'."

"Anything this unique – that's where it's going to be, your Grace. Can you see the King-Caliph letting it out of the city? But we can buy that information, confirm it; Godfrey's got contacts with the exiled Medicis. You can find out anything from a bank."

Wryly, John de Vere said, "I have chiefly found them unwilling to be cooperative with exiled Lancastrians. I wish your clerk better fortune. Madam, what is the *machina rei militaris* doing for the Visigoths? Is it a vital target?"

"This invasion is being run by the Faris; she's vital but you won't get her; *she* believes her machine is vital. Any way you look at it," Ash said, pulling out a back-stool and sitting down again, "*she* believes it instructed her to beat the Italians and the Germans and the Swiss, on the field."

She held out one of the dirty goblets automatically, forgetting there were no pages. She lowered the vessel. Making a long arm and grabbing the pottery jug herself, she splashed the goblet generously full of watered wine and drained it, aware that her face must be as heat-red as Anselm's and Oxford's.

Am I going to get away with this? she thought. This much and no more?

"You are very anxious to go and die," the Earl of Oxford said gently.

"I'm anxious to fight, live, and get paid. I've got frighteningly little money in the war-chest, and—" Ash jabbed a finger at the Burgundian and mercenary tents visible down by Dijon's confluence of rivers "—there're too many other places my lads can go and sign on for better money. We need a fight. We got our asses kicked at Basle, we need to kick back."

The Earl of Oxford pursued, "A fight for something that may be a rumour, a phantasm, a nothing?"

No. I'm not going to get away with this much and no more.

"Okay." Ash swirled wine in her goblet, watching light ripple. She flicked a gaze up, to de Vere, aware that he was quietly challenging her. "If I'm going to do what I plan, I have to have authority backing me up with money. And you're not going to give me authority or money unless you're convinced. It's this way, your Grace."

Godfrey Maximillian's brown hand touched his Briar Cross. Ash read Godfrey's face so plainly that it amazed her nobody else did. Only the Earl of Oxford's presence was stopping her company clerk from blurting out *Are you going to tell him that you have heard her voice? That you have always heard voices?*

Unexpectedly, the younger de Vere, Dickon, spoke up. "Madam Captain, *you* hear voices. I heard your men say. Like the French maid."

His voice rose at the end, a hint of a question; and he flushed under his elder brothers' glare.

"Yes," Ash said, "I do."

In the outbreak of brass voices, English noble soldiers shouting their conflicting views in growing excitement, Ash momentarily put her face in her hands.

In the dark behind her eyes, she thought, And if the Stone Golem *is* destroyed, does my voice and my life go with it?

"Look at me, your Grace," she invited, and when the English Earl did, she said, "And when you see the Faris, you'll be looking at the same face. We are alike enough to be twins."

"You are a bastard of her family?" Oxford's brows went up. "Yes. That is possible, I suppose. How does it concern this?"

"For ten years, I've thought I heard the Lion speak to me." Ash, unawares, crossed her breast, her fingers brushing the bright pierced metal of the plackart. She met and held each of their gazes in turn, Robert Anselm's considering

259

frown, Angelotti's enigmatic lack of expression; Floria's scowl, Geraint's sheer confusion, and the English Earl's keen, weighing stare.

"For ten years, I heard the voice of the Lion speaking in my soul, on the field of battle. That's why some of them here call me 'Lioness'. When they think about it." Ash's mouth took on a wry smile. "There's been campaigns when you couldn't move around here for God-struck holy men hearing saints' voices; it isn't that unique."

A ripple of male laughter went around the table.

Ash narrowed the focus of her attention to the attainted English Earl.

"This part I want kept quiet as long as I can," she said. "There's no way to keep it completely secret; you know what camps are like. My lord Oxford, I *know* the Faris hears a voice. *I* heard her speak to it. It isn't the Lion I've been hearing. It's their war-machine. She hears it because they bred her to. And I hear it – because I'm her bastard half-sister."

Oxford stared. "Madam . . ." And then, plainly dismissing doubt, and asking what he considered essential: "They know this?"

"Oh, they know it," Ash said grimly. She sat back on the stool, resting her hands flat on her armour. "That's why they bothered to take me prisoner, in Basle."

Oxford snapped his fingers, his expression saying plainly *of course!*

Dickon de Vere said naively, "If your voices are on her side, *pucelle*, can you still fight?"

The reverberations of that question were visible on the faces of her officers. Ash smiled a close-lipped smile at the English knight.

"Whether I can or whether I can't, I can prove to you that it's the same voice – the same machine. If it *wasn't*," she switched her gaze to John de Vere, "they wouldn't have been so damn anxious to find me in Basle. And they wouldn't want to drag me off to Carthage for interrogation."

A breath of humid air came up from the river, bringing the smell of weed and cool water, over the sweat and stench of the camp. She reached out and gripped Floria's shoulder, and Godfrey Maximillian's arm.

"Carthage wants me," Ash stated. "*I won't run.* I've got eight hundred armed men here. This time I'm taking the fight directly to them."

Her eyes glittered. She is keen, uncomplicated as a blade; with that frightening smile that she wears when she goes into a fight – frightening because it is serene, the smile of someone for whom all's right with the world.

"They want me in Carthage? – I'll *go* to Carthage!"

Message: #135 (Anna Longman)
Subject: Ash, mss.
Date: 15/11/00 at 07.16 a.m.
From: Ngrant@   *format address deleted*
                        other details encrypted by
Anna —   *non-discoverable personal key*

Excuse this, I haven't slept, I have been on-line most of the night
to universities around the world.

You're right. It IS all the manuscripts. The Cartulary of St
Herlaine is lost completely. There is one copy of Pseudo-Godfrey
in the fakes gallery at the V&A. The Angelotti text and the Del
Guiz LIFE are mediaeval romance and legend. I cannot find them
documented as mediaeval history at any time after the 1930s!

From what I can download, the manuscripts they have on-line are
the same TEXTS which I have been translating. All that's changed is
the CLASSIFICATION from history to fiction.

I can only ask you to believe that I am not a fraud.

— Pierce

Message: #80 (Pierce Ratcliff)
Subject: Ash, documentation
Date: 15/11/00 at 09.14 a.m.
From: Longman@   *format address deleted*
                         Text encrypted by non-discoverable
Pierce —   *personal key*

I do believe you. Or I trust you, which may be the same thing.

It isn't as if we didn't check out your academic record before we
signed the contract. We did. You're good, Pierce. I know you can be
good and still be mistaken, but you're good.

Doctor Napier-Grant's discoveries. Send me something. Download
me images, something, I need something to show the MD, or this is
all going to hell!

— Anna

```
Message:    #136 (Anna Longman)
Subject:    Ash, archaeological discoveries
Date:       15/11/00 at 10.17 a.m.
From:       Ngrant@        format address deleted
                           Other details encrypted by
Anna —                     non-discoverable personal key
```

Isobel doesn't have the slightest intention of letting photo
images of the site, or of golems, on to the Internet. She says they
would be global inside half an hour.

   Her son, John Monkham, is flying back from Tunisia early next
week. I have at last persuaded Isobel to let him act as a courier.
He will bring you copies of the expedition's photos of the golem;
but they will be in his possession at all times. Isobel is willing
to authorise you to show them to your MD, before John brings them
back to the site.

   This is the best I can do.

— Pierce

```
Message:    #81 (Pierce Ratcliff)
Subject:    Ash, archaeology
Date:       15/11/00 at 10.30 a.m.
From:       Longman@        format address deleted
                            Text encrypted by non-discoverable
Pierce —                    personal key
```

Give John Monkham my phone number, I'll meet him at the airport.

   I can't wait to see Ash's golem for myself. But I guess I'll have
to. While I'm waiting — have you thought of ANYTHING that can
account for what's happening?

— Anna

```
Message:    #139 (Anna Longman)
Subject:    Ash, texts
Date:       16/11/00 at 11.49 a.m.
From:       Ngrant@        format address deleted
                           Other details encrypted by
Anna —                     non-discoverable personal key
```

Frankly, no. I have NO idea why these manuscripts are now classified
under 'Fiction'. I'm at my wit's end.

   I HAD an idea. I thought, be philosophic. Occam's Razor — if the
simplest explanation for any event is the more likely to be true,
could it not be that it is the RECLASSIFICATION of the 'Ash'
manuscripts that is the mistake? You know how it can be, with

databases on line; if one university decides a document is a fake, that will cause a 'cascade effect' through all the universities on the net. And documents DO become mislaid, and lost.

That thought consoled me through last night, when sleep was impossible. I saw myself verified. Sadly, this morning — to the mundane sound of lorries arriving on site — I realised it is a mere fantasy. A cascade error would not affect all databases. It would not affect those libraries that aren't computer-literate, either! No. I have no idea what's going on. When I gained access to the British Library manuscripts they were classified as 'Mediaeval History', plain and simple!

And I have no explanation for the apparent fact that these documents were reclassified in the 1930s.

I don't know what is going on, but I do know we are in danger of Ash vanishing into thin air, into a fantasy of history; of her proving to be no more (or no less) historical than a King Arthur, or a Lancelot. But I was — and I remain — utterly convinced that we are dealing with a genuine human being here, beneath the accretions of time.

What is truly perplexing to me, also, is that what we have found on this site authenticates not just my theory of a Visigoth culture in North Africa, but the STRANGEST aspects of that culture — the post-Roman technology, nine centuries on. While I assumed that my Visigoths were factual, the technology is something I had thought to be mythical! And yet, here it is.

Still inexplicable as regards how it functioned.

It's enough to make me think kindly of Vaughan Davies. You may not know quite how strange his Introduction to ASH: A BIOGRAPHY is — it's something one tends to ignore, because of the sheer quality of his scholarship and the excellence of his translations.

He suggested, on the subject of the 'accretions' to the various texts, that the difficulties arise not because Ash has accreted myths, but because she has disseminated them.

Let me copy in what I have with me:-

(. . .)The hypothesis which I {Vaughan Davies} find myself compelled to accept is that, in the supposed history of 'Ash', this historian finds himself confronted with — among other things — the prototype of the legend of La Pucelle, Jehanne of Domremy, more popularly known to history as Joan of Arc.

This theory may appear to defy reason. The 'Ash' narratives are set in what is clearly the third quarter of the fifteenth century. Certainly the manuscripts cannot be dated to any time before 1470. Joan of Arc was burned at the stake in 1431. To accept Ash as the prefigurement of Joan as the archetypal warrior-woman is surely lunacy, for Joan comes first.

It is my belief, however, that it is the legends of Ash,

redeemer of her country, that we have transferred to the
meteoric career of the young Frenchwoman who was, it must be
remembered, a soldier at seventeen and dead at nineteen,
having driven the English out of France; and not the history
of Joan which becomes the 'Ash' cycle of tales. The reader
will ask himself, how can this be?

A simplistic explanation could be offered. If the legends of
Ash were in fact not late, but early mediaeval stories, then
their reproduction again in the 1480s could be put down to
popularity. With the invention of printing, the authors
merely re-wrote her narratives in contemporary terms. It was
common practice, for example in the illuminated manuscripts
of the era, to reproduce scenes from Biblical and Classical
history in fifteenth-century costume, accoutrements and
locale.

In this case, one would still have to account for the
complete absence of any hand-written manuscript evidence of
the 'Ash' cycle before 1470.

What explanation remains?

It is my belief that the 'Ash' stories are not fiction, that
they are history — they are just not our history.

It is my belief that Burgundy did, indeed, 'vanish'; not in
the apparent sense that it lost popular interest but can be
discovered by a diligent historian, but in a far more final
sense. What we have in our history books is only a shadow,
remaining.

With Burgundy's disappearance, such a history of facts and
events had to attach itself to something in the collective
European subconscious: one of the things they sought out was
an obscure French peasant woman.

I am well aware that this requires the spontaneous creation
of the historical documentation of Jeanne D'Arc.

Accept this, and one begins to have a mental image of real
events flying out, in fragments, from the dissolution of Ash's
Burgundy. Fragments that impel themselves backwards and
forwards, impaled along the timeline of history, taking on
such 'local colour' as they require for survival. Thus Ash is
Joan, and is Ashputtel/Cinderella, and is a dozen other
legends. The history of this first Burgundy remains, all
around us.

My hypothesis may be dismissed completely, of course, but I
consider it provable on rational grounds; (. . .)

I have always had a fondness for this extravagantly eccentric
theory — the idea that Burgundy genuinely faded out of history
after 1477, as it were, but that we can find the events of it in the
mouths of other historical characters; their actions in the

actions of other women and men throughout our history. Burgundy's portrait, as it were, cut up and sprinkled like a jigsaw through history: still visible for those who take the trouble to look.

Of course, it isn't a theory, as such. Plainly, although he says it is his 'belief', this is merely a distinguished academic amusing himself with speculations, and following Charles Mallory Maximillian's conceit of 'lost Burgundy' to its logical conclusion.

The problem is that this is only *half* of his 'Introduction' to ASH: A BIOGRAPHY. The theory is incomplete — what are his 'rational grounds' for what he calls a 'first' Burgundy? We have no idea now what Vaughan Davies's theory might have been in its entirety. I consulted a cheap wartime hardcover edition in the British Library and, as you know, there appears to be no other copy in existence of this second edition of ASH. (I presume that stocks were destroyed when the publishers' warehouse was bombed during the Blitz in 1940.) As far as I can discover through six years of diligent research, no complete copy now exists anywhere.

If you were to take the evidence of this partial theory, you might well say that Vaughan Davies was an eccentric. You may think he was a complete *crank*. However, don't dismiss him out of hand. It is not that many people in the 1930s who have doctorates in History *and* Physics, and a Professorship at Cambridge. He was obviously much taken with the high-physics theory of parallel worlds coming into existence. In a way, I can see why; history — like the physical universe, if the scientists are to be believed — is anything but concrete.

History is so *little* known. I myself, and other historians, make a story out of it. We teach in universities that people married at such-and-such an age, that so many died in childbirth, that so many served out their apprenticeships, that watermills and pole-lathes were the beginning of the 'mediaeval industrial revolution' — but if you ask a historian to say precisely what happened to one given person, on one given day, then we do not know. We *guess*.

There is room for so many things, in the gaps between known history.

I would throw up my hands and abandon this project (I don't need my academic reputation or my chances of getting published ruined) if I hadn't *touched* her golem.

I suppose that, also, I'm saying this by way of a warning. At Isobel's strict insistence, I am continuing the final translation of the centrepiece of this book — the document to which someone has (much later) added the punning heading 'Fraxinus me fecit': 'Ash made me'. Given Ash's lack of literacy, it seems likely that this is a document dictated to a monk, or to a scribe, with what omissions and additions and alterations we cannot know. That said,

I am convinced that this document is genuine. It fills in the gap
between her presence at the Neuss siege, and her later presence
with the Burgundians in late 1476, and her death at the battle of
Nancy on 5 January 1477. The 'missing summer' problem, as we have
always known it.

I have reached the part which throws additional light on the Del
Guiz and Angelotti chronicles of Ash's time in Dijon. Translating
now, with the golem only a few tents away from me — mere yards; the
other side of a canvas wall — I start to ask myself a question. A
serious question, although when I asked it before, it was a joke.

If the messenger-golems are true, what else is?

- Pierce

Message: (Pierce Ratcliff)
Subject: Ash, documentation
Date: 16/11/00 at 12.08 p.m.
From: Longman@   *format address deleted*

                             Text encrypted by non-discoverable
Pierce —   *personal key*

If 'Angelotti' and the rest of the manuscripts aren't true, what
else ISN'T?
— Anna

PART FIVE

17 August–21 August AD 1476

The Field of Battle

I

Dijon resounds to the thundering of watermills.

Afternoon's white sunlight blazed on distant yellow mustard-flowers. Rows of trimmed green grape-vines hugged the ground between brown strips of earth. Peasants thronged the strip-fields. The town clock struck a quarter to five as Ash eased Godluc between a tailback of ox-wains, and on to the main bridge into Dijon.

Bertrand stuffed her German fingered gauntlets into her hand, and fell back breathless beside Rickard, in the dust lifted up by the horses. Ash rode away from members of the company who had gone off scouting and now clutched at her stirrups, breathlessly reporting back, to take her place between John de Vere and her own escort.

"My lord Oxford." Ash raised her voice, and lifted up her head as they came in over the bridge to the town gate. Scents raised the hairs on the back of her neck: chaff, overheated stone, algae, horse-dung. She shoved her visor up, and bevor plate down, to get the benefit of the cool air over the river that served as a moat.

"I have the latest estimate of the Visigoth forces outside Auxonne," the Earl said, "they number nearly twelve thousand."

Ash nodded a confirmation. "They were twelve thousand when I was outside Basle. I don't know the exact number of their two other main forces. The same size, or larger. One's in Venetian territory, scaring the Turks from moving; the other one's in Navarre. Neither can get here within a month, even with a forced march."

A burning smell of hard-spinning mill-wheels filled the air, together with a faint golden haze. The mail shirts of the guards on the gate, and the linen pourpoints, hose, and kirtles of the men and women bustling through it, were tinted with the finest chaff. The taste of it settled on her tongue. *Dijon is golden!* she thought; and tried to let the heat and smells relax the cold, hard fear in her gut.

"Here is our escort." John de Vere reined in, letting his brother George go ahead to speak with the nine or ten fully armoured Burgundian knights waiting to take them to the palace.

De Vere's weathered, pale-eyed face turned to her. "Has it occurred to you, madam Captain, that his Grace the Duke of Burgundy may offer you a contract with him, now. I cannot finance this raid on Carthage."

"But we have a contract." Ash spoke quietly, her voice just audible under the grinding of mill-wheels. "Are you telling me to find some pretext for breaking my word – which *I* didn't give – to an exiled, attainted English Earl, because the reigning, extremely rich, Duke of Burgundy wants my company. . . ?"

John de Vere looked down from his saddle. What she could see of his face, with his close-helm's visor pinned up, was a mouth set in a firm line.

"Burgundy is wealthy," he said flatly. "I *am* Lancaster. Or Lancaster's only chance. But, madam, I am at the moment the leader of three brothers and forty-seven men, with enough money to feed them for six weeks. This, weighed against the employment of the Burgundian Duke, who could buy England if he chose . . ."

Ash, deadpan, said, "You're right, my lord, I won't consider Burgundy for a minute."

"Madam Captain, as a captain of mercenaries, the most precious goods you have to sell are your reputation, and your word."

Ash snorted. "Just don't tell my lads. I've got to sell *them* on the idea of Carthage . . ."

Ahead, George de Vere and the Burgundian knights seemed to be exchanging deferential greetings and arguments about precedence of riding order, in about equal measure. Dijon's cobbles felt heat-slick under Godluc's hooves. She reached forward and put a reassuring hand on his neck, where his iron-grey dapples faded to silver. He threw up his head, whickering with what, Ash realised, was a desire to show off in front of the people of Dijon. Around her, the city's whitewashed walls and blue slates roofs glittered.

Ash spoke over the louder noise of grinding mills. "This place looks like something out of a Book of Hours, my lord."

"Would that you and I did, madam!"

"Damn. I knew I was going to miss my armour . . ."

George de Vere turned in his saddle, beckoning the party forward. Ash rode beside the now smiling Earl of Oxford, into the centre of the group of Burgundian knights. They moved off, their horses making slow time through the cobbled streets despite the escort in Charles's red-crossed livery; winding between throngs of apprentices outside workshops, women in tall headdresses buying from stalls in the market square, and ox-carts grinding their continual way to the mills. Ash pushed her visor up, grinning back at the cheerful waves and the comments called by the subjects of Duke Charles.

"Thomas!" she hissed.

Thomas Rochester dug his heel into his bay gelding, and rapidly rejoined the party. A young woman with bright eyes watched him go, from where she leaned out of an overhanging second-storey window.

"Put her down, boy."

"Yes, boss!" A pause. "Any time off for R&R?"

"Not for you . . ." A touch to Godluc brought her back to the Earl of Oxford's left flank.

"I think you would never break a *condotta*, madam. And yet you consider it, now."

"No, I—"

"You do. Why?"

It was not the tone, or the man, to let her get away without an answer. Ash snarled in a whisper, glancing covertly at the Burgundian knights:

"Yes, I say we should raid Carthage, but that doesn't mean I'm not afraid of it! If I remember right from Neuss, Charles of Burgundy could have upwards of twenty thousand trained men here; and supplies, and weapons, and guns, and, if I had a choice, I'd like *all* twenty thousand of them between me and the King-Caliph! Not just forty-seven men and your brothers! Is that a surprise?"

"Only a fool is not afraid, madam."

The rhythmic pounding of mill-wheels drowned speech for a minute. Dijon sits between two rivers, the Suzon and the Ouche, in the arrow-head spit of land where they join. Ash rode along the river path. The walls here enclosed the river within the town. She watched the slats of watermill wheels rise up into the sun, dripping diamonds. The water under the wheels was black, thick as glass, and she could feel the pull of it from where she rode among the knights of the Duke's court.

They rode past the nearer mill.

Speech impossible, Ash did nothing for a moment but study the streets they rode through. A cluster of men in shirts and rolled-down hose, fixing an ox-wain's wheel, moved aside. They removed their straw hats, Ash saw, but neither rapidly nor fearfully; and one of the Burgundian riders reined in and spoke to their foreman.

Ash glimpsed an open space ahead, between diamond-paned-windowed buildings. The street opened out into a square – which she saw, as she rode into it, was a triangle. Rivers flowed past on the two sides, this land being at the very confluence of both. The high city walls gleamed, and the men on guard there leaned on their weapons and looked down with interest. They were well-armed, clean, with the kind of faces that have not suffered famine in the near past.

"You understand, your Grace," Ash said, "that rumours are getting out – that I hear voices, that I *don't* hear voices, that the Lion Azure are really still paid by the Visigoths, because I'm the Faris's sister. That sort of thing."

De Vere looked at her. "You have no wish to be abandoned as a bad risk?"

"Exactly."

"Madam, the responsibilities of a contract work both ways."

De Vere's battle-hardened voice gave his words no particular emphasis, but Ash found herself painfully and fearfully abandoning a habitual cynicism. The sun dazzled her eyes. Ash felt her voice catch.

As steadily as she could, she said, "Their general, their Faris, she's slave-born. She doesn't make any secret of it. And I . . . look like her. Like two pups in a litter. What does that make me?"

"Courageous," the Earl of Oxford said gently.

When he met her gaze, she looked straight ahead, with hard eyes.

He said, "Because your method of hiding from this is to put a plan to me, to attack the enemy in their strongest city. I could have reason to doubt your impartial judgement over that, if I chose to take it as such – but I do not doubt it. Your thoughts chime with mine. Let us hope the Duke agrees."

"If he doesn't," Ash said, gazing at the richly apparelled knights in the escort, "there's damn-all we can do about it. We're broke. This is a very rich, very powerful man, with an army outside this city. Let's face it, your grace, two orders and I'm his mercenary, not yours."

Oxford's voice snapped, "I have responsibility for my brothers and my affinity![1] And for someone I have taken under my protection!"

"That isn't quite the way most people regard a *condotta* . . ." Ash reined back to where she could look at him. "But you do, don't you?"

Watching him, she was confirmed in her opinion that people would follow John de Vere well beyond the bounds of reason. And only wonder why afterwards, when it would be far too late.

Ash took a deep breath, feeling unusually constricted by the brigandine she was wearing. Godluc snorted breath from wide nostrils. Ash automatically shifted her weight back, halting him, and looked for what had worried her mount.

Two yards ahead, a line of ducklings fluttered up from the river's edge, and pattered across the cobbled space. Preceded by a mother duck, they fluttered, squawking, towards the mill on the far side of the triangle, and the other, swift-flowing river.

Twelve Burgundian knights, an English Earl, his noble brothers, a viscount, a female mercenary captain and her escort all reined in and waited until nine ducklings passed.

Ash shifted up from leaning over in the saddle, about to speak to John de Vere. She found herself looking up at the ducal palace of Dijon. Soaring white Gothic walls, buttresses, peaked towers, blue slate roofs; flying a hundred banners.

"Well, madam." The Earl of Oxford smiled, slightly. "The court of Burgundy is like no other court in Christendom. Let's see what the Duke makes of my *pucelle* and her voices."

Dismounting, she was met by a sweating Godfrey Maximillian, on foot; who fell in with the rest of Thomas Rochester's men, behind her banner.

Inside the palace, the size of the space enclosed by stone stunned her. Soaring thin pillars jutted up, between long thin pointed windows; all the stonework fresh, white, biscuit-coloured; and with the late afternoon sun on it, looking, she thought, like fretworked honey.

She shut her gaping mouth and stumbled in John de Vere's wake, a clarion call ringing out and a herald shouting their names and degrees, loud enough to shake the banners hanging down each side of the hall; and a hundred faces turned, men of wealth and power, looking at her.

They were all dressed in blue.

She gazed rapidly at sapphire, aquamarine and royal blue silk, at indigo and powder-blue velvet, at the rolled chaperon hats as deep as the midnight sky, and the long robe of Margaret of York, the colour of the Mediterranean sea. Her feet took her in the Earl of Oxford's wake, quite independently; and Godfrey bent his bearded head close, whispering rapidly in her ear:

"There are Visigoths here."

[1] 'Affinity' – For a feudal magnate, this would include his dependent lords, maintained in his livery; his political allies among other feudal lords; and any commercial interests dependent on him for grace and favour.

"*What?*"

"A deputation. An embassy. No one is sure of their status."

"Here? In *Dijon?*"

"Since noon, I hear."

"Who?"

Godfrey's amber eyes moved away to survey the crowd. "I could not buy names."

Ash scowled. She ignored the dazzling profusion of jewelled badges on chaperon hats, gold and silver linked collars around noble necks, brass folly-belly sewn to younger knights' doublets, tissue-thin linen veiling the noble women.

All, all in blue, she suddenly realised. With a blue velvet brigandine she was moderately in the fashion, or at least, enough in it not to offend. She spared a glance for the four de Vere brothers and Beaumont, all of the noble English in full harness, a blaze of steel against the velvet and silk robes of the Burgundian court.

"Godfrey, *who's* here? Don't tell me you don't know. You've got a damn network of informers out there! Who's here?"

He deliberately dropped back a pace on the chequered tiles. Without causing confusion, and drawing attention to herself, there was no way she could continue to question him. She clenched her fist, for a second wanting nothing more than to hit him.

"Your Grace," she said, without looking at the Englishman's face, "did you know there's a Visigoth delegation here?"

"God's bollocks!"

"I'll take that as a 'no', shall I?"

They were escorted on down the great hall. There was more: paintings set in niches, tapestries of great hunting expeditions hung from the walls, but Ash couldn't take it in. Above it all that noble architecture soared up, ogee window and clustered columns, to the clear glass windows that disclosed the other roofs of the ducal palace of Dijon, and the fine, white-gold finials of stone piercing up towards the afternoon sky.

A flutter of doves flurried past the glass. Ash dropped her gaze, halting, her heels trodden on painfully by Dickon de Vere. Both escorts – hers, and de Vere's – parted, letting the other brothers come through to stand beside the Earl of Oxford. Godfrey kept to the back, his face calm, his eyes giving away nothing of what he might feel, confronted by so many churchmen, as well as so many nobles and their ladies.

Ash stared around, could see no Visigoth robes or mail anywhere.

John de Vere knelt, and his party also; Ash scraping down on to one knee and dragging her hat off in haste.

A youngish man in white puff-sleeved doublet and hose sat on the ducal throne, his head bent, conferring with another man at his elbow. Ash saw his somewhat lugubrious face, and black shoulder-length hair cut straight across the forehead, and realised this must be him: Charles, Duke of Burgundy, nominal vassal of Louis XI, more splendid than most kings.[2]

---

[2] Born in Dijon in 1433, Duke Charles was in fact 43 at this time.

"An inauspicious day, then?" the Duke said, quite clearly, as if unconcerned that his private conversations might be overheard.

"No, sire." The man at his elbow bowed. He wore a long, azure demi-gown, his arms out of the hanging sleeves, and his hands busy with papers marked with diagrams of wheels and boxes. "Say, rather, an opportunity to avenge an old wrong."

The Duke signalled him to move away, and leaned back, looking down from the dais at the kneeling Englishmen. The sole man in white, he stood out among his court for simplicity. Ash thought, *Signifies a Virtue – probably his day for representing Nobility or Chivalry or Chastity. I wonder what the rest of us are?*

His voice, when he spoke, was pleasant. "My lord of Oxenford."

"Sire." De Vere stood up. "I have the honour to introduce to you my mercenary captain, whom your Grace wished to see. Ash."

"Sire." Ash stood up. Behind her, Thomas Rochester and Euen Huw wore the Lion Azure livery; Godfrey gripped a Psalter. She smoothed her hair on the left side, assuring herself that it covered the healing injury there.

The rather dour young man on the ducal throne, who could not yet have been thirty, leaned forward with one hand on the arm of it, and stared at Ash with eyes so dark as to be black. A faint colour touched his pale cheeks. "You tried to kill me!"

This was not an occasion to smile, Ash guessed, the Valois Duke of Burgundy not looking particularly susceptible to being charmed. She schooled her face and her bearing to modesty and respect, and remained silent.

"You have a notable warrior there, de Vere," the Duke remarked, and turning his head away from her, spoke briefly to the woman at his side. The Duke's wife, Ash noted, did not take her eyes off John de Vere, Earl of Oxford.

"Perhaps," Margaret of York spoke up in a clear voice, "it's time this man told us why he takes advantage of your hospitality, Sire."

"In time, lady." The Duke beckoned two of his advisors, spoke to them, and then returned his gaze to the group in front of him.

Ash weighed up the cost of the Duke's simplicity: his demi-gown was buttoned, and with diamond buttons, and the seams of the shoulders looked to be sewn with gold thread. And all the rest of the seams of his garments, sewn with the finest gold thread . . . In the blue sea of his court, he gleamed like snow with the faintest tinge of winter sun gilding it; and the grip of his bollock dagger was decorated also with gold, and with pearls.

"It is our intention," the Duke said, "to discover what you know of this Faris, maîtresse Ash."

Ash swallowed, and managed to speak in a voice that could be heard. "By now, everybody knows what I know, sire. She has three major armies, of which one lies just beyond your southern border. She fights inspired by a voice, which she claims comes from a Brazen Head or Stone Golem device, across the seas in Carthage, and," Ash said, holding to her line of thought with difficulty under Charles's stare, "I have myself seen her appear to speak to it. As to the rest of it: the Goths have burned Venice and Florence and Milan because they don't *need* them – there's an endless supply of men and materials being shipped across the Med, and when I left, it was still coming."

"Is this Faris a knight of honour, a Bradamante?"[3] Duke Charles asked.

Ash judged it time to make herself both less spectacular and more human in his eyes. Rather bitterly, she replied, "A Bradamante wouldn't have stolen and kept my best armour, Sire!"

A subdued merriment made itself felt in the court, dying out as soon as it became apparent that Duke Charles was not smiling. Ash held his gaze, the bright black eyes and almost ugly face – certainly a Valois! – and added, "As for knights, heavy cavalry doesn't seem to be their strong point, sire. No tournaments. They have medium cavalry, huge numbers of foot-soldiers, and golems."

Duke Charles glanced at Olivier de la Marche, and the big man, with a nod for Ash, loped up the dais steps in a very uncourtly manner. The Duke whispered in his ear. He nodded, dropped to one knee to kiss the Duke's hand, and strode off. Ash didn't turn her head to watch, but guessed he was actually leaving the hall.

"These dishonourable men of the south," Charles said, more publicly, "dare to put out the sun above Christian men, and shroud us in the same penance as their own Eternal Twilight. They have not expiated the sin of the Empty Chair. We – under God, we are not sinless! But we do not deserve to have the sun which is the Son taken from us."

Ash untangled that one after a glance at Godfrey. She nodded hastily.

"Therefore—" the Duke of Burgundy broke off at an insistent mutter from Margaret, seated beside him on a smaller throne. A short and, Ash thought, rather sharp exchange ended with the Valois Duke leaning back magnanimously. "If it eases your mind, we will consent to your asking him. De Vere! The Lady Margaret wishes a word with you."

Slightly above Ash's head, George de Vere whispered, "That'll be the first time!', and Dickon snickered.

The English noblewoman gazed down at de Vere, his brothers and Beaumont, ignoring Ash and her priest and banner. "Oxford, why have you come here? You know you cannot be welcome. My brother, King Edward, hates you. Why do you follow me here?"

"Not you, madam." John de Vere, equally blunt, gave her no noble title. "Your husband. I have a question to ask him, but since you have an army on your borders, my question will wait for a better time."

"No! Now. You will ask it now!"

Ash, aware that so many currents ran deep under this particular river, thought that Margaret of York might not ordinarily be a shrill woman, or an impetuous one. *But something's biting her. Biting her hard.*

"It is not the time," the Earl of Oxford said.

Charles of Burgundy leaned forward, frowning. "If my Duchess asks, it is certainly time for you to answer, de Vere. Courtesy is a knightly virtue."

Ash shot a glance at de Vere. The Englishman's lips were pressed tightly together. As she watched, his face relaxed, and he gave a chuckle.

"Since your husband wishes it, madam Margaret, I will tell you. His Grace King Henry, sixth of that name, being dead and leaving no close heir of his

[3] A legendary female knight, notably popularised in Ariosto's *Orlando Furioso* (1516).

body,[4] I have come to ask the next Lancastrian claimant to the English throne to raise an army, so that I may put a legitimate and honest man there, instead of your brother."

And I thought I could be tactless . . .

Under cover of the outrage and shocked comments, Ash glanced back down the mirror-stone tiled floor, judging the distance to the great doors and the Ducal Guard.

Great. The Visigoth Faris puts me in prison. I get here. I get hired by de Vere. De Vere gets us all put in prison. This is not how I wanted things to be!

A tiny ripping noise sounded: the edge of Margaret of York's veil knotted and torn between her clenched fingers. "My brother Edward is a great king!"

Oxford's voice cracked out loud and hard enough to make Ash jump.

"Your brother Edward had my brother Aubrey's bowels torn from his body, while he lived, and his cock cut off and burned in front of his eyes. A Yorkist execution. Your brother Edward had my father's head cut off, with no ounce of English law behind him, since he has no claim to the throne!"

Margaret got to her feet. "Our claim is better than yours!"

"But your claim, madam, is not as good as your husband's!"

Silence dropped, like a blade coming down. Ash became aware she was holding her breath. All the de Vere brothers stood upright, hands to scabbards; and the Earl of Oxford himself glared, like a war-weathered bird of prey, at the woman on the throne. His pale gaze moved to Charles, and he inclined his head stiffly.

"You must know, Sire, that being as you are the great-grandson of John of Gaunt and Blanche of Lancaster, then the nearest living Lancastrian heir to the English throne is now – yourself."[5]

We're dead.

Ash clasped her hands behind her back, keeping her fingers away from the hilt of her second-favourite sword with an effort powered by sheer fear.

We're dead, we're done for, our ass is grass; sweet Christ, Oxford, couldn't you just for once keep your mouth shut when someone asks you for the truth?

She was astonished to open her mouth and hear herself say, quite loudly, "And if that doesn't work, I suppose we can always invade Cornwall . . ."

An instant of appalled silence, so short it was only long enough to stop the breath in her throat, broke with a shout of laughter from a hundred voices; this a fraction of a second after Duke Charles of Burgundy smiled. A very wintry, tiny smile; but nonetheless, he smiled.

"Noble Duke," Ash said quickly, "the French Dauphin had his *Pucelle*. I'm sorry I can't manage one of those for you – I'm a married woman, after all. But I pray that I also have the favour of God, as Joan did; and if you give me, not troops, but some of the wealth of your army, then I'll try and do for you what she did for France. Kill your enemies, Sire."

[4] Henry VI and Margaret of Anjou had only one son, Edward, killed at the battle of Tewkesbury. Any claim of the Lancastrians to the English throne thus devolved to more tenuously related men (ultimately to Henry Tudor, whose Welsh grandfather had married the widow of King Henry V). The Yorkist Edward IV, meanwhile, held the throne.

[5] In fact, Charles had registered his formal claim to the English crown in 1471, five years previous to this, but took no further action over it before his death.

"And what will your seventy-one lances do for Burgundy, maîtresse?" the Duke asked.

Ash flicked up an eyebrow, having not had the exact numbers from Anselm's muster that long herself. She kept her head raised, aware that her face and hair were to some degree speaking for her, and that she would have been far more impressive in full harness. "It would be better not in open court, Sire."

The Duke of Burgundy clapped his hands. Clarions sounded, the choirs at the sides of the great hall burst into song, ladies rose, men in rich pleated short gowns made their exits, and Ash – and Godfrey, and the de Veres – were ushered into a chapel or side room.

Quite some time later, Charles of Burgundy came in, a handful of attendants with him.

"You've upset the Queen of Bruges," he remarked to Oxford, waving his staff away.

Ash, bewildered, glanced at Oxford and the Duke.

"My wife, being governor of that city, is sometimes called its queen," the Valois Duke said, lowering himself into a chair. His demi-gown, unbuttoned, showed a gold-embroidered pourpoint beneath, and a drawstring-neck shirt of linen so fine it was hardly visible. "She has no love for you, my lord Earl of Oxford."

"I never thought she did," Oxford said. "You forced me to that one, Sire."

"Yes." The Duke switched his prim gaze to Ash. "You have an interesting fool. She is young," he added.

"I can command my men, Sire." Ash, uncertain whether to cover her head, which marks respect in a woman, or uncover it, as a man does, settled for standing bareheaded, her hat in her hand. "You already have the best army in Christendom. Send me to do what your armies won't – take out the heart of the Visigoth attack."

"And where does that heart lie?"

"In Carthage," Ash said.

Oxford said, "It's not lunatic, Sire. Only audacious."

The walls of this chamber were set about with tapestries, in which the Burgundian Heraldic Beast, the Hart, shone white and gold through the wild wood; pursued by hunters and worshippers. Ash shifted, hot in the late afternoon sun through the windows, and met the flat, gold-embroidered stare of the Hart, the Green Cross worked finely between its many-tined antlers.

"You are an honest man, and a good soldier," the Duke of Burgundy observed, as a page served him, and then Oxford, with wine. "Otherwise I would suspect this for some Lancastrian device."

"I am only devious on the field of battle," the Englishman said. Ash heard amusement in his tone; could see it pass Charles of Burgundy by.

"Then, do we have here the proof? That this 'Stone Golem' is where they claim – over the sea, far from us, and yet speaking to this Faris?"

"I believe that we do, Sire."

"That would be much."

So much depends on this man, Ash suddenly thought. This ugly, black-

277

browed boy, with twenty thousand men and more guns than the Visigoths: so much depends on his decisions.

"I have the Faris's blood, Sire," she said.

"So my advisors tell me. They tell me," Charles added, "that the likeness is remarkable. God send you are good, maîtresse, and not some device of the devil."

"My priest can answer you best, Sire."

Waved forward by her hand, Godfrey Maximillian said, "Your Grace, this woman hears mass and takes communion, and has made confession to me these past eight years."

The Duke of Burgundy said, "Prince as I am, I cannot silence rumour's tongues. It begins to be said that the Visigoth general's voice is a devilish engine, and that we have no defence against it. I do not know, Lord Oxford, how long your condottiere's name will be kept out of this."

"The Faris herself may not know that she is . . ." de Vere hesitated, searching for a word. "That she is overheard. We cannot rely on that state of affairs continuing. She already seeks the girl, here, for interrogation. We have a short time in which we can act. Sire, a matter of weeks – days, if we are unlucky."

"You are willing to let this matter of the Lancastrian succession drop?"

"I am willing to put it into abeyance, Sire, until we have faced this danger that comes on us from the south."

Without looking around, the Duke said, "Clear the room."

Within thirty seconds, pages, squires, falconers, Thomas Rochester, and the men-at-arms were ushered out of the chamber; leaving only Ash, Godfrey Maximillian, Oxford, and his brothers.

Charles of Burgundy said, "We are not what we were, de Vere."

The wind through an open window brought the scent of chaff, and roses.

"I have had the armourers of Milan make me a harness of finest quality," he said, "and if I could, sirs, I would be armed in it as a man should, and ride out to this despoiling army, and myself best in battle their champion, and that would decide the matter. But this is a fallen world, such honour and chivalry are no longer for us."

"It would save a lot of people getting killed," Ash said flatly, adding, "Sire," as an afterthought.

"As will a raid on Carthage," de Vere said. "Cut off the head, and the body is useless."

"But you do not know where – if it is in Carthage – where, exactly, this Stone Golem is kept."

Godfrey Maximillian, stroking his Briar Cross, remarked, "We can discover that, Sire. Given two hundred gold crowns, I undertake to bring you the news, within a very short time."

"Mmm." Charles of Burgundy switched his gaze to de Vere. "Tell me."

Oxford set it out for the Burgundian Duke in brief, military sentences. Ash did not interrupt, knowing that for the plan to be accepted, it would have to be put forward by a man; and having it put forward by one of the better battle-commanders of Europe wouldn't hurt a bit.

She glimpsed Godfrey's shoulders relax, briefly, at her silence.

What Visigoths? What won't you tell me?

The priest gazed at the hangings of the little chamber in awe. There was no way she could speak confidentially to him. Ash stared at the tiny, lattice-paned windows and the later afternoon sky, and wanted to be outdoors.

"No," the Duke of Burgundy said.

"Do as you think best," John de Vere rumbled. "God's teeth, man! – your Grace. What use is a battle, whether we win it or not, if the main enemy is untouched?"

The Duke sat back, waving John de Vere away. "I am determined to fight a battle against the Visigoths, and soon. My diviner advised me that it should be before the sun passes out of Leo, to be auspicious. The twenty-first of the month of Augustus is the feast of Saint Sidonius."

Ash saw Godfrey frown, be caught with the expression by the Duke, and steel his face to unctuousness as he rumbled an explanation. "Very fitting, Sire. Since Sidonius Apollinaris was martyred by early Visigoths, this should be a day for avenging him."

"So I think." Satisfied, the Duke said, "My preparations have been in hand since I returned from Neuss."

"But—" Ash bit her lip.

"Captain?"

She spoke with reluctance. "I was about to say, Sire, that I don't think even the armies of Burgundy can defeat the numbers they have here, let alone the numbers they have coming in by galley every day from North Africa. Even if you and the Emperor Frederick and King Louis united—"

Ash was familiar with catching the expression which tells you that, upon this one subject, a man is not rational. Having mentioned Louis XI, she was seeing it now on the face of Charles of Burgundy. She shut up.

"You won't put up gold for an attack on Carthage?" the Earl of Oxford demanded.

"No. I think it unwise. It cannot succeed, and the battle that I shall fight, that can." He looked at Ash. Disquiet stirred her stomach. He said, "Maîtresse Ash, there are Visigoths already present in my court, being ushered in under a flag of parley this morning. They have many demands – or humble requests, as they prefer to say. One of which is, their seeing the standard of your camp outside the walls of Dijon, that you yourself should be given up to them."

His black eyes watched her. By the quiet consternation among the younger de Veres, this seemed as though it must be that rare thing, a genuinely secret delegation.

But not for long, Ash thought, and said aloud, "The Visigoths broke their *condotta* when they imprisoned me, but I don't seriously suppose I can resist you handing me over if that's what you're going to do, Sire. Not with the whole Burgundian army at your disposal."

The Duke of Burgundy gravely turned his rings upon his fingers, and made no answer.

Dizzy with news of the Visigoths so close, Ash said bluntly, "What do you intend to do with me, Sire? And – please – will you reconsider funding this raid against Carthage?"

"I will consider both these matters," the Duke said. "I must talk to de la Marche, and to my advisors. You will know . . . by tomorrow."

Twenty-four hours on hold. God damn it.

The Duke rose, ending the audience.

"I am a prince," he said. "If you meet, here in my court, with these men from Carthage and their renegade allies, be assured that no man will harm you."

Ash let none of her scepticism show on her face. "Thank you, Sire."

But I shall be in the Lion Azure camp, just as fast I can ride.

The Duke's intense, lugubrious expression darkened.

"Maîtresse Ash. As a bastard slave of a Visigoth House, you are legally a bondswoman. They claim you, not as their paid captain, or their prisoner, but as their property. That claim may well be valid and lawful."

II

Ash, her men at her heels, finally halted at the bottom of a flight of stairs. She realised she had left the Earl of Oxford and his brothers way behind, had ignored court officials, got through ceremonial farewells purely mechanically, in the shock of that realisation:

I can be bought and sold.

The Duke will hand me over for political advantage. Or, if not because of that, then because he can't be seen to ignore the law. Not when law keeps anarchy away from his kingdom . . .

Vespers rang through the chambers of the ducal palace.

Maybe I need prayers!

Wondering where the nearest chapel was, about to ask Godfrey, she did not see a party of men approaching. Thomas Rochester coughed. "Boss . . ."

"What? Shit." Ash folded her arms, which the sleeves of her mail shirt under her brigandine did not make particularly easy.

Light shone down into the antechamber in front of her, falling from tall thin windows on to flagstones, bouncing back from the whitewashed walls and high barrel-vaulting, making the whole place airy and light and entirely not a place where one might stay unnoticed.

Ahead, a group of men in Visigoth robes began to slow their steps, seeing her.

"Wish they'd let us bring the dogs in," Ash murmured. "A leash full of mastiffs would come in very handy right now . . ."

Thomas Rochester grunted. "So let's see if the Duke's peace holds, or if we have to kick ass, boss."

Ash took a glance at the Ducal guards lining the walls of the antechamber.

She began to smile. "Hey. We're the ones on home ground here. Not the fucking Goths."

"That's right, boss." Euen Huw grinned.

"Banjo 'em with a fucking poleaxe," one of Rochester's lance rumbled.

"Do nothing unless I say so. Got me?"

"Yes, boss."

The mutual reply was reluctant. She was aware of Euen and Thomas at her shoulders. The first man in the group of Visigoths speeded his pace, walking up to her.

Sancho Lebrija.

"*Qa'id*," Ash acknowledged the Visigoth, steadily.

"Mistress *jund*."

A tall man in Lebrija's wake, in Milanese armour, proved to be Agnus Dei. The Lamb grinned at her, teeth yellow in his black beard.

"Madonna," he greeted. "That's a nasty cut you have there."

She still carried her hat in her hand, from being in the Duke's presence. Her hand went up to the side of her head automatically, fingers brushing a patch of shaven scalp.

Godfrey Maximillian said warningly, at her ear, "Ash—"

Soldiers in mail and white robes, four or five of them, accompanied the Visigoth delegates. As they halted, Ash saw a young man among them. He carried his helmet under his arm; was instantly recognisable.

"—of course!" Godfrey whispered vindictively. "It had to be! He can bribe some court chamberlain to find out when Charles is having audiences, and who with. Of course he can."

Fernando del Guiz.

"Well, look who it isn't," Ash remarked loudly. "That's the little shit who told the Faris where to find me in Basle. Euen, Thomas: you want to remember that face. Some day soon, you'll be spoiling it!"

Fernando seemed to ignore her. Agnus Dei said a word in Lebrija's ear that made the Visigoth *qa'id* bark out a short laugh.

Lamb continued to smile.

"*Cara.* You had a pleasant journey here from Basle, I trust?"

"A *fast* one." Ash did not take her gaze from Fernando. "You want to watch it, Agnes. One of these days they'll steal your best armour, too, if you don't look out!"

"The Faris wishes more speech with you," Sancho Lebrija said stiffly.

Meeting the Visigoth's pale eyes – none of the charm of his dead cousin there – Ash thought, What would you say if I told you how badly *I* want to talk to *her* again?

Sister, half-sister, twin.

"Then let's hope for a truce," she said, making her voice carry clearly enough to be overheard by any court intriguers. "War's always better when you're not fighting. Any old soldier knows that – right, Agnes?"

The mercenary grinned sardonically. Behind him, the Visigoth soldiers carrying swords made no aggressive move on the Duke's premises. Ash recognised an *'uqda* lance-pennon[6] with the escort, looked for the *nazir* who had taken her from the gardens of Basle, and saw his brown face scowling at her from behind the nasal bar of his helm.

There was an uncomfortable silence.

Sancho Lebrija half-turned, glared at Fernando del Guiz, and then turned back to say, "Madam *jund*, your husband wishes to speak with you."

"He does?" Ash said sceptically. "He doesn't look like he does."

The Visigoth *qa'id* put his hand firmly behind the German knight's back, pushing him forward. "Yes. He does!"

Fernando del Guiz still wore white robes and Visigoth mail. It cannot be much more than a week, ten days, since she saw him in Basle – the thought is a shock; so much has happened – but his face seems leaner, his golden hair untidily shaggy as it grows out of its crop. Not, as it was at Neuss, long enough to fall down over his young, broad, muscled shoulders.

Ash dropped her gaze, fixed her eyes on his strong hands – bare; his gloves tucked into his belt.

The smell of him in her nostrils hit her below any guard she might have made; a smell that jolted her back into warm linen sheets, the silk-smooth skin of his chest, belly and thighs, the thrust of his velvet-hard cock in her body. A flush rose up from her breasts, up the column of her throat, and reddened her cheeks. Her fingers moved of their own accord: she would, if she had not stopped herself, have reached out and touched his cheek. She made a fist, her pulse dry in her mouth.

"We'd better talk," Fernando del Guiz mumbled, not looking at her.

"Asshole!" Thomas Rochester said.

Godfrey Maximillian pulled at Ash's arm. "Let's leave."

She resisted the priest's force without effort, without looking at him. Studying the closed expression of Sancho Lebrija, and Lamb's malice, she murmured, "No. I *am* going to talk to del Guiz. I've got things to say to this man!"

"Child, *no*."

She removed her arm from Godfrey's grip, casually, and indicated an area of the antechamber a few paces away. "Step into my office, *husband*. Thomas, Euen, you know what to do."

She crossed the flagstones, and waited in an area where red and blue light from the stained-glass windows dappled the floor, under hanging battle standards from old Burgundian wars against France. It took her far enough away to put her out of earshot of the Visigoth delegation, and of Duke Charles's guard.

And it's public enough that any harm he tries to do me will be instantly seen – but, sadly, that works both ways.

She busied herself removing her gloves, rested the palm of her left hand on the pommel of her sword, and waited.

He left Lebrija and approached, alone, boots clicking on the worn, chequered tiles. The echo hissed back from the walls. The early evening heat might have accounted for the sweat on his face.

[6] The *'uqda* was carried by a *nazir*'s troop of eight men.

"So," Ash prodded. "What do you want to say to me?"

"Me?" Fernando del Guiz gazed down at her. "I don't think this was my idea at all!"

"Stop wasting my time."

All her authority was in her tone, although she was quite unconscious of it. She was only aware that he blinked, startled; glanced back over his shoulder at Lebrija; and finally spoke:

"This is awkward . . ."

"'Awkward'!"

Unexpectedly, Fernando reached out and put his hand on her arm. Ash looked down at his blunt, square-cut nails; the texture of his skin; the faint blond hairs at his wrist.

"Let's talk this over somewhere else. Alone." Fernando's hand came up, brushing her cheek.

"And do what?" Ash reached up and put her hand over his. Meaning to move it away, she found herself holding his hand, wrapping his strong fingers around hers. The warmth of it was so welcome, she did not immediately let go. "What, Fernando?"

He lowered his voice, uncomfortably watching her priest and her men-at-arms. "We'll just talk. I won't do anything you don't want me to do."

"Yes, I think I've heard that one before."

Looking into his face, she thought she could see the young man still there – the young noble, riding to hawk and to hounds, golden and glorious among his wide affinity of friends, never needing to work out whether he could afford this wine or that horse, not ever needing to choose between shoeing his horse and shoes for his own feet. A little road-worn, now, but still the golden boy.

Her fingers still clasped his. The warmth of them made her hands shake. She opened her hand and drew it away, feeling cold. Absently, she put her hand to her face, breathing in the particular scent of him.

"Oh, come *on.*" Ash's lips pressed together, in extreme scepticism. A quiver went through her belly. She was genuinely unsure whether it was lust, or plain nausea. "Fernando – I don't believe this. Are you trying to *seduce* me?"

"Yes."

"Why?"

"Because it's easier."

Ash opened her mouth, found she had no words, and stood for a count of ten staring at his face. Outrage hit. "Are you – what do you *mean*, 'because it's easier'? Easier than *what*?"

"Refusing the Faris and her officers." All the humour faded from his expression; perhaps it had been no more than momentary. "Even when they say a good fuck might get you into their hands again, so why don't I go give it to you?"

"'A good fuck—!'" Ash bellowed.

Across the floor, Agnus Dei put a restraining hand on Sancho Lebrija's arm, both men scowling; this shouted row obviously reaching them, obviously not what either of them expected to hear. Ash glimpsed Godfrey take a few steps forward, staring at her, his face drained and pale.

"*Seduce* me?" she repeated. "Fernando . . . That's *ridiculous*!"

"Okay. So it is. So what do you suggest I do, with half a dozen sword-happy maniacs watching every word I say to you?" He stood half a head taller than she did, looking down at her, a young man in foreign armour. "At the moment, thanks to you, I'm the Faris's pimp. The least you can do is not laugh at me."

"Wh—" Ash ran out of breath and the impetus to speak. Something in his appalling honesty touched her, despite herself. "The Faris's *pimp*?"

"I don't want to be here!" Fernando shouted. "All I want is to go back to Guizburg, stay there, stay in the castle, and not come out until this fucking lunatic war is *over*. But they married me to you, didn't they? And you turn out to be some relative of the Faris. So who do they think knows all about the mercenary commander Ash? Me. Who do they think is an influence on you? Me." He drew a gasping breath. "I don't care about politics. I don't want to be in the Faris's affinity. I don't want to be at the Visigoth court. *I don't want to be here*. But because they think I'm a source of information on you, here I am! And all I want is to fucking go back to Bavaria!"

He finished, panting; little white dots of spittle at the corners of his mouth. Ash realised he had spoken in German, that both Lebrija and Lamb were looking puzzled now at the rapid, slurred, foreign speech.

"Jesus Christ," she said. "I'm impressed."

"I'm only here because of you!"

The contempt and fury in his tone made Euen Huw and Thomas Rochester both reach for their sword-hilts, and watch Ash out of the corners of their eyes, to see if she would let him get away with it. She noted Godfrey's hands, almost hidden in his robes, whitening into fists.

"I thought you *wanted* to be well in with the Faris," she said mildly. "Making a place for yourself in the Visigoth court. I thought that was why you got me knocked on the head at Basle."

Ignoring that, he spluttered, "I don't want a place at court!"

Ash's tone became acid-edged with sarcasm. "Yeah, that's why you're in Guizburg now, not standing in front of me! Like you're not here with Lebrija for political advantage, or reward, or promotion."

Catching his breath, Fernando glared down at her. "I'll tell you exactly why I'm here. The Faris would happily have stuck my head on a spear, as an encouragement to any other minor German nobles. She didn't because I took one look at her, and told her that she had a double."

"You told her."

"I suppose having a bastard Visigoth wife is mildly better than having a French soldier-bitch."

"*You* told her?"

"You think I'm some knight out of the chronicles. I'm not. I've had men pointing spears at me, and I know it: I'm just another man with legal title to a few acres of land, and a few men wearing eagles on their clothes, and that's *it*. Nothing remarkable. Nothing valuable. No different from any other man they've butchered in Genoa or Marseilles or wherever."

She looked at him, seeing in his face some echo of that split-second of trauma. "Roberto said you were some damned stupid young knight with ideas of death-or-glory. He was wrong, though, wasn't he? You took one look at glory and decided you'd save your own skin!"

Fernando del Guiz stared. "Sweet Jesu. You're *ashamed* of me."

It was a distinct glint of humour. His tone was self-mocking.

"You wouldn't say this to your friend Lamb. Or did you? Did you say to him, why didn't you fight off the Visigoths at Genoa, there were two hundred of you and only thirty thousand of them?"

Her mind squirrelled away the figure of thirty thousand men without conscious thought. Her face reddened. She said, "Lamb negotiated a *condotta*. That's what he does. That's what I do. You just shat yourself and threw yourself on their mercy—"

He put his hand on the shoulder of her brigandine. Her hand clenched, to knock him away. She felt herself shake with the restraint of not doing it.

"*You* sent me off. Right into them."

"You're trying to blame *me* for this? Hey. I wanted my command back. I didn't want you ordering my lances into a field they couldn't win." Ash snorted. "Bit ironic, really. I should have let you give them an order. It would have been 'run like fuck!' "

He flushed, the pale freckled skin going pink from his throat to his brow.

Ash yelled, "And you could have! It wouldn't even have been *difficult*. Up into the foothills, lose yourself in the mountains. They'd barely got a grip on the coast, they weren't going to go off chasing twelve horsemen!"

Anger is translatable into any language. As he startled back, a green-robed shoulder appeared in front of her, between her and Fernando – Ash grabbed Godfrey Maximillian and pushed him away. For all the priest was twice her bulk, she used balance and momentum to put him straight past her.

"STOP!" she bellowed.

Thomas and Euen Huw instantly appeared one either side of her, hands on hilts. She threw out her hands, palms open, as Lebrija's men began to stride forward.

"Okay! Enough! *Back off*."

One of the Burgundians – a captain? – thundered, "You are under truce! In God's name, no weapons here!"

The Visigoths halted, uncertain. A Burgundian knight near the door shifted to a combat stance. Ash jerked a thumb, saw out of peripheral vision Thomas, Euen, and (reluctantly) Godfrey backing off again. She kept her gaze on Fernando.

His voice not quite controlled, Fernando del Guiz said, "Ash . . . when you're cautious, it's caution; when you change sides to the stronger force, it's business. Don't you understand fear?" He hesitated, then: "I thought you understood this – I did what I did because I was afraid of being killed."

He said it plainly, with quiet emphasis. Ash opened her mouth to say something, and shut it again. She looked at him. Both his hands, holding his upturned helmet now, were white-knuckled.

He said, "I saw her face – the Faris. And now I'm alive. For telling some

Carthaginian bitch she's got a bastard cousin in the Frankish armies. I was too afraid *not* to tell her."

"You could have run," Ash insisted. "Hell, you could at least have tried!"

"No. I couldn't."

The whiteness of his skin made her think, suddenly, *he's still in shock, he's in combat-shock without having been in combat*, and she said, automatically gently, as she would to one of her own: "Don't feel too bad about it."

His gaze snapped to her face. "I don't."

"What?"

"I don't feel bad about it."

"But—"

"If I did," Fernando said, "I'd have to believe that the people like you are right. I saw it all, in that second. You're crazy. You're all stark, staring *mad*. You go around killing other people, and getting killed, and *you don't see there's anything wrong with it*."

"Did you do anything when they killed Otto and Matthias and the rest of your guys? Did you even *say* anything?"

"No."

She looked him in the eye.

"No," Fernando said. "I didn't say a word."

To another man, she might have said *that's war, it's shit but it happens, there wasn't anything you could have said that would have made a difference*.

"What's the matter?" she needled. "Pissing on twelve-year-old girls more your style?"

"Perhaps I wouldn't have done that, if I'd realised how dangerous you are." His expression changed. "You're a bad woman. A butcher, a psychopath."

"Don't be bloody ridiculous. I'm a soldier."

"That," he echoed her, "is what soldiers are."

"Maybe so." Ash's voice sounded hard. "That's war."

"Well, I don't want to make war any more." Fernando del Guiz fixed her with a bright, rueful smile. "You want the honest truth? I want no part of this. If I had any choice, I'd go back to Guizburg, pull up the drawbridge, and not come out until this war's over and done with. Leave it to blood-thirsty bitches like you."

I have been to bed with this man, Ash thought, marvelling at the distance between them. *And if he asked me, now—*

"Is that my cue to walk out?" Ash hooked her hands into her belt. The blue leather was decorated with brass rivets in the shape of lions' heads; it was not, she thought, something that would ever be worn by a woman. "As seductions go, this is pretty crap."

"Yes. Well." Fernando glanced over his shoulder at Sancho Lebrija, looking painfully embarrassed to be overheard failing to persuade an errant wife. "My track record isn't brilliant, recently."

He looks tired, Ash thought. A pulse of sympathy for him ruined her carefully hoarded anger.

No. *No.* I'm fine, hating him. That's what I need to do.

"Your track record's fine. The last thing you did to me was betray me. Why didn't you come to me at Basle?" she demanded. "When they'd locked me up, why didn't you come?"

Fernando del Guiz looked blank. "But why should I have?"

Ash hit him.

The movement was not under her control, all she could choose was not to draw her sword. Not wanting a guard's blade struck through her midriff had something to do with it – but, more than that, the picture flashing in front of her eyes stopped her: Fernando del Guiz's face spidered red with blood running from a cleft skull.

That mental image brought a jolt of nausea. Not for the killing, that being her business, but the simple thought of harm to this body, a body caressed with her own hands—

She hit him in the face with the fist clenched, and her gauntlets off; swore; wrung her hand and tucked her throbbing knuckles under her armpit, and stared at Fernando del Guiz who rocked back on his heels, eyes flown wide with shock. Not with anger, she saw, but with sheer shock that a woman had dared to hit him.

Behind her: shifting feet, the ching of mail, polearm butts going down on the tiles, men about to plunge forward again—

Fernando del Guiz did not move.

A small red mark swelled below his lip. He breathed heavily, his face scarlet. Ash stood watching, flexing her throbbing fingers.

Finally, someone – not one of her own men, one of the Visigoths – laughed coarsely.

Fernando del Guiz stood in front of her, still not moving.

She looked at his face. Something almost like pity – if pity can sear and burn, the way that hatred does; if it can bring an absolute inability to bear another person's shame and pain – something went through her like edged steel.

Ash winced, put her fingers to her hair again, feeling again the sun-warmed heat of it and the spiky gut stitches still jutting from her skin, and caught the smell of him on her skin.

"Oh, Christ." Her stomach jolted. Tears pushed under the lids of her eyes, and she blinked, ferociously, threw her head back and said, "Euen! Thomas! Godfrey! We're leaving!"

Her heels rang on the flagstones. The men-at-arms fell in, either side, matching her step; and she strode straight past the face of Sancho Lebrija, past his men, ignored Lamb; strode out through the iron-bound oaken doors, not looking back, not looking to see what expression Fernando del Guiz might have on his face now.

Walking without direction took her out of the ducal palace, into Dijon. She passed and ignored men from the company, striding out blindly through the crowds. A voice called after her. She ignored it, turning away, climbing stone steps. They brought her up into the open, high above the alleys, on the massive stone walls of Dijon.

She paused, breathless, above the man- and horse-crowded streets;

surveying the city defences through absent-minded habit. The men-at-arms, outdistanced, clattered up the steps behind her.

"*Shit!*"

Ash sat herself down on the crenellations, in the late afternoon sunlight. She stared out between blocks of granite. A long way below, beyond the dusty white road leading into the city, diminutive figures worked in the fields. Men in shirts, their split-hose rolled down below their knees, binding up sheaves of the dusty white-gold wheat and lifting them on to ox-wains, working more quickly now that the deadly heat of afternoon was waning . . .

"Child?" A panting Godfrey Maximillian came to stand beside her. "Are you all right?"

"Christ on the Tree, that cowardly son of a bitch!" Her heart still shook her body, made her hands tingle. "Fucking Visigoths – and I'm going to be handed over to *them*? No way!"

Thomas Rochester, scarlet in the heat, said, "Christ, boss, calm down!"

"Too hot for running around like this," Euen Huw added, unbuckling his helmet, and standing up on the crenellations to catch any breeze, and to survey the apparently endless tents of the Burgundian army outside the city walls. "More to worry about than that boy, haven't we?"

Ash flashed a look at them, at Godfrey; calming down. "So I have twenty-four hours to decide whether I should wait for the Duke's verdict, or pack up my stuff in a spotted hanky and start walking . . ."

The men laughed. Noise came up from the foot of the wall, outside the city. Sixty feet below, a number of her men were swimming in the moat, white limbs flashing as they ducked each other, the camp's dogs yelping and barking at their bare heels. As she watched, a cocky-tailed white bitch bounded into the air and pushed Euen Huw's second, Thomas Morgan, off-balance and off the narrow bridge that formed Dijon's gateway. The sound of the distant splash came up through the hot air.

"There goes Duke Charles." Ash pointed at a cavalcade of riders moving out of the city gates, riding towards the woods; their brilliant clothes bright against the dust, hawks poised on wrists, musicians walking behind them and playing an air which came distantly up to the walls. Ash leaned her back against the cool stone. "You'd think he's got nothing to worry about! Well, maybe he hasn't. Compared to wondering whether he's going to be handed over to the damn Visigoths in the morning!"

Godfrey Maximillian said, "May I speak with you alone, Captain?"

"Oh, sure, why not?" Ash looked over her shoulder at Euen Huw and Thomas Rochester. "Guys, take five. There was an inn at the bottom of these steps, I saw the bush. I'll meet you in there."

Thomas Rochester frowned darkly. "With Visigoths in the city, boss?"

"With half of Charles's army in the streets."

The English knight shrugged, exchanged a look with Euen Huw, and strode lightly down the steps from the wall, the Welshman and the others following. Ash had a shrewd idea they would go no further than the foot of the stone steps.

"Well?" She leaned her face up to the slightest of breezes, bringing a dust of chaff golden from the fields. She hooked one knee up, and leaned her elbow on it. Her fingers still faintly trembled, and she looked down at her sword hand in some puzzlement. "What's bothering you, Godfrey?"

"More news." The big priest gazed out from the walls, not looking at her. "This 'father' of the Faris, Leofric. All I can hear is that this Lord-*Amir* Leofric is one of their least-known nobles, and supposedly resides in Carthage itself, in the Citadel. The rest is just rumours, from unreliable sources. I have no idea what this 'Stone Golem' even looks like. Do you?"

Something in his tone bothered her. Ash glanced up. She patted the flat stone between the crenellations invitingly.

Godfrey Maximillian remained standing on the inner wall walkway.

"Sit down," she said, aloud. "Godfrey, what's bothering you?"

"I can't get you better information without a great deal of money. When does Lord Oxford intend to pay us?"

"No, that isn't it. What, Godfrey?"

"Why is that man still alive!"

His voice boomed, loud enough to momentarily stop the bathers below shouting. Ash startled. She swung around and dangled her legs over the inside of the wall, staring up at him. "Godfrey? Which? Who?"

Godfrey Maximillian repeated, in an intense whisper, "*Why is that man still alive?*"

"Oh, sweet Christ." Ash blinked. She rubbed the heel of her hand across one eye-socket. "You mean *Fernando*, don't you?"

The big, bearded man wiped his sweating face. There were rings of white skin under his eyes.

"Godfrey, what is all this? It was a joke. Or something. I'm not going to murder a man in cold blood, am I?"

He took no notice of this appeal. He began to stride up and down, in short agitated paces, not looking at her. "You are *quite* capable of having him killed!"

"Yes. I am. But why should I? Once they leave, I'll probably never see him again." Ash put out a hand to stop Godfrey. He ignored it. The coarse linen of his robe flicked her fingers as he passed. She scented, still, Fernando del Guiz on her skin; and as she breathed in, suddenly looked up at the big bearded man. He's not old, she thought. I never think of Godfrey as young, but he's not an old man.

Godfrey Maximillian stopped in front of her. The descending sun put gold light on his face, reddening his beard, showing her something like pain in his creased eyes, but she was not sure if it were merely the brightness.

"One of these days there'll be a battle," Ash said, "and I'll hear I'm a widow. Godfrey, what does it matter?"

"It matters if the Duke hands you over to your husband tomorrow!"

"Lebrija doesn't have enough men with him to force me to leave here. As for Duke Charles . . ." Ash gripped her hands over the edge of the stone wall, and pushed herself down on to her feet on the walkway. "Scaring myself shitless tonight won't tell me what the Duke's going to decide to do tomorrow! So what does it matter?"

"It matters!"

Ash, studying him with the sunlight on his face, thought *I haven't looked at you properly since we ran from Basle*, and made a grimace of apology. She noticed now that he had a gaunt look. Just to either side of his mouth, his beard had white hairs among the wiry brown.

"Hey," she said quietly. "This is me, remember? Tell me about it. Godfrey, what is it?"

"Little one . . ."

She closed her hand over his. "You're too good a friend to worry about telling me something bad." Her eyes flicked up to his face, and her grip froze. "Okay, I wasn't born of freemen. Technically, I guess somebody in Carthage owns me."

That made her grin, wryly, but there was no answering smile from Godfrey Maximillian. He stood and stared at her, as if her face was new to him.

"I see." Ash's heart thumped, once, and then beat hard and rapid. "It makes a difference to you. Fucking hell, Godfrey! I thought we were all equal in the eyes of God?"

"What would you know about it?" Godfrey sprayed spit across her, suddenly shouting, his eyes wide and bright. "Ash, what would *you* know? You don't believe in our Lord! You believe in your sword, and your horse, and your men that you pay money to, and your husband that you can get to shove his cock into you! You don't believe in God or grace and you never have!"

"Wh—" Breath taken away, Ash could only stare.

"I watched you with him! He touched you – you touched him, you *let* him touch you – you *wanted* to—"

"What does it matter to you?" Ash sprang to her feet. "In fact, what business is it of yours? You're a damn *priest*, what would you know about fucking?"

Godfrey bellowed, "Whore!"

"*Virgin!*"

"Yes!" he snapped. "*Yes*. What other choice have I got?"

Breathing hard, silenced, Ash stood on the flagstone walkway facing Godfrey Maximillian. The big man's face twisted. He made a noise. Appalled, she watched the tears well out of his eyes; Godfrey crying hard, as a man cries, wrenched deep out of him, deep from the inside. She reached up to touch his wet cheek.

Almost in a whisper, he said monotonously, "I left everything for you. I followed you halfway across Christendom. I've loved you since I first saw you. In my soul's eye I still see you, that first time – in a novice's robe, with your head shaved, and that Soeur beating your back bloody. A little white-haired scarred brat."

"Oh, shit, I love you, Godfrey. You know I do." Ash grabbed both his hands and held them. "You're my oldest friend. You're with me every day. I rely on you. You know I love you."

She held him as if she held a drowning man, gripping him painfully hard, as if the tighter the grip, the more chance she stood of rescuing him from his anguish. Her hands whitened. She shook him, gently, trying to catch his eye.

Godfrey Maximillian reversed the grip and closed his hands around hers.

"I can't stand to watch you with him." His voice broke. "I can't stand having to see you, know that you're married, you're one flesh – flesh—"

Ash tugged her hands. They did not come free, trapped in Godfrey's broad fingers.

"I can bear your casual fornications," he said. "You confess to me, you're absolved, it means nothing. And there have been few of them. But the marriage bed – and the way you look at him—"

Ash winced at his grip. "But Fernando—"

"*Fuck* Fernando del Guiz!" Godfrey roared.

Silenced, Ash stared at him.

"I don't love you as a priest ought." Godfrey's bright wet eyes met hers. "I made my vows before I met you. If I could wipe out my ordination, I would. If I could be anything other than celibate, I would."

Fear thumped in her gut. Ash wrenched her hands free. "I've been stupid."

"I love you as a man does. Oh, Ash."

"Godfrey—" She stopped, not sure what she would have protested, only that the walls of the world were falling down around her. "Christ, this isn't a decision I want to take! It's not like you're just another priest, I can kick you out, hire another one. You've been with me from the beginning – before Roberto, even. Sweet saints. What a time to tell me."

"I'm not in a state of grace! I say mass every day, when I know that I wish him dead!" Godfrey began to twist his rope belt between his fingers, in agitation.

"You're my friend, my brother, my father. Godfrey . . . You know I don't—" Ash sought for a word.

Godfrey's face went crooked. "Don't want me."

"No! I mean – I don't want to – I don't *desire* – oh, shit, Godfrey!" She reached out as he spun around and strode towards the steps. She barked out, "Godfrey! *Godfrey!*"

He was too quick, outpacing her, a big man moving with reckless speed, almost running down the stone steps that clung to the inside of Dijon's city walls. Ash stopped, staring down at him, a broad-shouldered man in a priest's robe, pushing his way into the cobbled street, between women with baskets, men-at-arms, dogs running underfoot, children playing at ball.

"Godfrey . . ."

She noted that Rochester and Huw were indeed not far from the foot of the steps. The small Welshman had a mug of something, and as she watched, Thomas Rochester gave a tavern boy a small coin in exchange for beer and bread.

"Oh, *shit*. Oh, Godfrey . . ."

Still in two minds whether to go after him, try and find him in the crowd, Ash saw a golden head at the foot of the wall below her.

Her heart stopped. Rochester lifted his head, said something, and waved the man through – a man who, as he began to climb the steps, was not a man at all: was Floria del Guiz, and not her brother.

III

Ash muttered an obscenity under her breath, and stalked back to the crenellations, pulse thumping.

A white ghost of a crescent moon had begun to show against the blue daytime sky, low down towards the west. A wain creaked over the bridge, into Dijon, below Ash: she leaned out to watch it. Golden heads of grain drooped, heavy in their sheaves, and she thought of the watermills on the far side of the city, and the harvest, and the winter conditions of the land not forty miles away.

Floria loped up the last steps to where Ash stood. "Damn fool priest nearly knocked me off the steps! Where's Godfrey going?"

"I don't know!"

Seeing the woman's surprise, Ash bit back the anguish in her tone, and repeated, more calmly, "I don't know."

"He's missed Vespers."

"Do you want something?" Without stopping to think, Ash added, "Now that you've bothered to appear again. What bloody relative are you avoiding *this* time? I had enough of that in Cologne! What the fuck use is a surgeon if she – if *he's* never here!"

Floria's elegant brows went up. "I suppose I did think I might approach my Aunt Jeanne cautiously. Since she hasn't seen me in five years, it might come as something of a shock, even though she knows I dress as a man for travelling."

The tall, dirty woman shook her head, putting precise sardonic verbal quotation marks around the last words.

"I don't believe in rubbing people's noses in things they find difficult."

Ash glanced deliberately down at herself, and her brigandine, and man's hose. "And I do rub people's noses in it, is that what you're saying?"

"Whoa!" Floria held up her hands. "Okay, I give in, start weapons practice again. For God's sake go and hit something, it'll make you feel better!"

Ash laughed shakily. A tension in her relaxed. A breeze ruffled against her face, welcome after the stifling streets. She hitched her sword-belt around, the scabbard having begun to rub against the sides of her leg armour. "You're happy to be back here, aren't you? In Burgundy."

Floria smiled crookedly, and Ash could not make out what lay behind her expression.

"Not exactly," the surgeon said. "I think your Faris-general is mad as a rabid dog. Being behind one of the world's best armies seems a good idea to me, if it keeps me away from her. I'm happy enough here."

"Hey, you've got family here." Ash looked out, away from the walls, at the moon in the western sky; gold now beginning to shade pink on the clouds. She fisted her hands and stretched her arms, the brigandine's enclosing weight hot and familiar and reassuring on her body. "Not that family are an unmixed blessing . . . Christ, Florian! So far I've had Fernando telling me he wants my beautiful body, Godfrey throwing ructions, and Duke Charles not able to make up his mind if he's going to hand me back to the Visigoths!"

"If he's going to *what*?"

"You didn't hear?" Ash shrugged, turning towards the woman; who leaned, slender in stained doublet and hose, against the grey masonry, her insouciant face alive with questions. "The Faris has sent a delegation here. And, among the minor matters like declaring war and invading us or France, she wants to know if she can please have her bondswoman mercenary commander back."

"Rubbish," Floria said with abrupt, complete confidence.

"She might have a case in law."

"Not once my family lawyers see the documentation. Give me a copy of the *condotta*. I'll take it to Tante Jeanne's attorneys."

Noting how her surgeon avoided the word *bondswoman*, Ash said, "Would it matter to you if I weren't legitimate?"

"It would startle me considerably if you were."

Ash almost laughed. She choked it back, shot a glance at Floria del Guiz, and licked her lips. "And if I'm not freeborn either?"

A silence.

"You see. It *matters*," Ash said. "Proper bastards are okay, so long as they're the bastards of noblemen, or gentlemen-at-arms at the very least. Being born a serf, or a slave – that's something else. Property. Your family probably buys and sells women like me, Florian."

The tall woman looked blank. "They probably do. Is there *proof* of your been born from a slave mother?"

"No, there's no proof, as such." Ash dropped her gaze. She rubbed at her sword's steel pommel with her thumb, picking at nicks with her nail. "Except that by now, a lot of people are hearing what someone's been using serfs for, in Carthage. Breeding soldiers. Breeding a general. And, as Fernando was happy to remind me, throwing out the ones they don't think will grow up to standard."

With a spurious air of unshockability, Florian snapped, "That's stock-breeding, that's what you do."

"To give them credit," Ash said, her voice altered, her throat constricting, "I don't suppose my company are going to give a fuck. If they'll wear me being female, they won't care if my mother was a slave. So long as I can get them through a battle, I could be Beelzebub's great scarlet whore for all they care!"

"And when they know that I don't hear a saint, I don't hear the Lion, I just – just *over*hear someone else's voice? Someone else's machine. That I'm just a mistake, on the way to breeding *her*. What then? Does that make a difference? Their confidence in me is always a thin thread—"

She felt a pressure, a weight, and lifted her head to find Floria del Guiz's arm around her shoulders, the surgeon trying to force her touch through the armour.

"There's no way you're going anywhere near Visigoths again," Floria said briskly. "Look, you've only got that woman's word for it—"

"Fuck it, Florian, she's my twin. She knows she's slave-born. What else *can* I be?"

293

The tall woman lifted a hand, touching grimy fingers to Ash's cheek. "It doesn't matter. Stay here. Tante Jeanne used to have friends at court. She probably still does; she's that kind of woman. I'll make sure you're not sent anywhere."

Ash moved her shoulders uncomfortably. The breeze, dropping, left the upper walls of Dijon as hot as anywhere else. A noise of singing and drunken shouts came up from the tavern at the foot of the steps; and the clash of polearm-butts, as the guards on the bridge changed to evening shift.

"*It doesn't matter.*" Floria's hand insistently turned Ash's head, forcing Ash to look at her. "It doesn't matter to me!"

The warm pressure of her fingertips dug into Ash's jaw. Ash stared up, close enough to Floria's face to smell the woman's sweet breath, close enough to see the dirt in the crow's feet at the corners of her eyes, and the glimmer of light in her brown-green irises.

Making eye-contact, Floria grinned lopsidedly, released Ash's jaw, and trailed a fingertip along the scar on her cheek.

"Don't *worry*, boss."

Ash gave a great sigh, relaxing back against Florian. She slapped the woman's back. "You're right. Fuck it, you're right. Come on."

"Where to?"

Ash grinned. "I've taken a command decision. Let's go back to camp and get completely rat-arsed!"

"Good idea!"

At the foot of the steps, they picked up the escort, and strode back through the streets towards the south gate.

Arm-in-arm with the surgeon, Ash came to a stumbling halt as Florian suddenly stopped. Thomas and Euen's men instantly faced outwards, hands on weapons.

An elderly woman's voice said coldly, "I might have known that where Constanza's brat is, you would also be. Where is your half-brother?"

The woman was fat, in brown kirtle and white wimple, and clasped a purse against her belly in both her hands. Her clothes were rich silk, embroidered; and the visible gathered neck of her shift made from the finest lawn. All that was visible of her lined, sweating white face was a double chin, round cheeks, and a snub-button nose.

Her eyes were still young, and a beautiful green.

She demanded, "Why have you come back to shame your family? Do you *hear* me? Where's my nephew Fernando?"

Ash sighed. She murmured to herself, "Not *now* . . ."

Florian backed up a step.

"Who's the old bat?" a billman at the back of the escort asked.

"Fernando del Guiz is in the Duke's palace, madame," Ash cut in, before Florian could speak. "I think you'll find him with the Visigoths!"

"Did I ask you, abomination?"

It was said quite casually.

There was a shifting among the men in Lion tabards; assessing that there were no Burgundian soldiers in this street, that the woman – although nobly dressed – was out with no escort. Someone sniggered. One of the archers drew his dagger. Someone else muttered, "Cunt!"

"Boss, you want us to do the old bitch over?" Euen Huw asked loudly. "She's an ugly old shite, but Thomas here will fuck everything on two legs, isn't that right?"

"Better than you, you Welsh bastard. At least I don't fuck everything with *four* legs."

They were moving as they spoke, broad men in armour, hands going to bollock daggers. Ash barked, "Hold it!', and put her hand on Florian's shoulder.

The elderly woman screwed up her eyes, squinting at Ash against the bright sun that slanted down into the street, between the gabled roofs. "I am not afraid of your armed thugs."

Ash spoke with no asperity. "Then you're downright stupid, because they won't think twice about killing you."

The woman bristled. "The Duke's peace holds here! The church forbids murder!"

Seeing this woman, in her neat chaff-flecked gown, with the folds of her white headdress neat under her chin – knowing just how quickly it could all be changed, to cloth ripped off to show grey hair, kirtle slashed, shift bloodied, skinny legs sprawled naked on the cobbles – all this made Ash speak quite gently.

"We kill for a living. It gets to be a habit. They'd kill you for your shoes, never mind your purse, and they're even more likely to do it for the fun of it. Thomas, Euen, I think this woman's name is – Jeanne? – and she's some relative of our surgeon. Hands off. Got me?"

"Yes, boss . . ."

"And don't sound so damn disappointed!"

"Shit, boss," Thomas Rochester remarked, "you must think I'm *desperate*!"

They seemed to fill the street: the bulk of men who have padded doublets under mail, steel plates strapped to legs, long-hilted swords swinging from their hips. Their voices were loud, and under cover of Euen Huw's beery "Couldn't get laid in a whorehouse with a bag of gold louis!', Ash said, "Florian, this is your aunt?"

Florian stared ahead, her face set. She said, "My father Philippe's sister. Captain Ash, may I present Mademoiselle Jeanne Châlon . . ."

"No," Ash said feelingly. "You may not. Not today. Today, I've had just about enough!"

The elderly woman stepped straight into the group of soldiers, oblivious to their only brief amusement. She seized the shoulder of Florian's doublet and shook her, twice, with little jerky movements.

Ash saw it momentarily as Thomas and Euen did: a small, fat old woman catching hold of their surgeon, and the tall, strong, dirty young man staring down with an appalled helplessness.

"If you don't want her hurt," Thomas Rochester offered to Florian, "we'll just take her away for you. Where's the family live?"

"Teach her a few manners, on the way." Wiry, black-haired Euen Huw thumbed his dagger back into its sheath, and took hold of both the woman's elbows from behind. As his hands tightened, Jeanne Châlon's face turned white under its summer flush and she gasped, and went limp against him.

"Leave her alone." Ash stared the Welshman down until he relaxed.

"Let me look, Tante Jeanne!" Floria del Guiz reached out, with long-fingered hands, taking the woman's fat arm, and moving it gently at the elbow. "Damn it! Next time I have you in the surgeon's tent, Euen Huw—"

The Welsh lance-leader shifted his grip, uncomfortably aware that he was still supporting the woman against his chest. Half-fainting, Jeanne Châlon flapped her free hand, slapping at him. He attempted to support her without gripping her wide waist and hips, grabbed her as she slid downwards, finally lowered her to the cobbles, and grunted, "Fuck, Florian, boy; get rid of the old cow! We all got families back home, don't we? That's why we're out here!"

"Sweet Christ on a stick!" Ash shoved the men bodily back, breaking up the sweat-soaked, airless crush. "She's a *noblewoman*, for Christ's sake! Get it through your thick heads, the Duke can throw us out of Dijon! She's my fucking *husband's* aunt, as well!"

"She is?" Euen sounded doubtful.

"Yeah. She is."

"Shit. And him with all those Visigoth friends, now. Not that he doesn't need them – skid-marks in his hose, that boy's got."

"Quiet," Ash snapped, her eyes on Jeanne Châlon.

Ruthlessly, Florian stripped the white linen headdress away. The woman's eyelids fluttered. Wisps of grey-white hair plastered themselves to her forehead. Her red, sweating complexion became more normal.

"Water!" Florian snapped, holding her hand up without looking. Thomas Rochester lifted the strap of his water bottle hastily over his head and stuffed it into her hand.

"Is she all right?"

"Nobody saw us."

"Shit, I think there's Burgundians coming!"

Ash gestured, cutting off the comments. "You two, Ricau, Michael, get down to the end of the street, make sure it stays private up here. Florian, is she dead, or what?"

The crêpe skin, under Florian's fingers, fluttered with a pulse.

"It's too hot, she's overdressed, you scared her shitless, she fainted," the surgeon rattled off. "Is there any *more* trouble you can get me into?"

Under the sharp bravado, Ash heard the woman's voice shaking.

"Don't worry, I'll fix it," Ash said confidently, and with absolutely no idea of how anything might be salvaged from this disaster. She saw her confident tone steady Florian, for all that the surgeon might be very well aware Ash had no answers.

"Get her up on her feet," Ash added. "You, Simon, get wine. *Run.*"

It took minutes for the page of Euen's lance to run back to the inn, for the men-at-arms to begin to shuffle, remember they were in a city, become awed by the sheer number of streets and people, and remember the Burgundian army encamped outside. Ash saw their faces and heard their comments, while she knelt down beside Florian, staring at the old woman.

"I raised you!" the woman slurred. Her eyes opened, fixing on Florian's face. "What was I, to you? No more than a nursemaid? With you always whimpering for your dead mother! What thanks did you ever give me?"

"Sit up, Aunt." Florian's voice was firm. She put a wiry arm behind the woman's back, shifting her upright. "Drink this."

The fat woman sat on the cobbles, unaware of her sprawling legs. She blinked against the bright light, the legs of the men surrounding them; and opened her mouth, dribbling the wine that Florian poured between her lips.

"If she's well enough to slag you off, she'll live," Ash said grimly. "Come on, Florian. We're out of here."

She got a hand under the surgeon's arm, hoisting. Florian shook her off.

"Aunt, let me help you up—"

"Take your hands off me!"

"I *said*, we're leaving," Ash repeated urgently.

Jeanne Châlon gave a subdued shriek, and grabbed her ruined headdress up from the road. She clutched the linen over her grey hair. "Vile—!"

The men-at-arms laughed. She ignored them, glaring at Florian.

"You are a vile abomination! I always knew it! Even at thirteen, you seduced that girl—"

Her next words were inaudible, drowned in raucous comments. Thomas Rochester reached down and thumped the surgeon on the back. "Thirteen? Randy little sod!"

Florian's mouth curved, unwillingly. Bright-eyed, reckless, she said, "Lizette. Yes. Her father kept our hounds. Black curly hair . . . pretty girl."

One of the crossbow-women, at the back of the escort group, chuckled. "He's a ladies' man, our surgeon!"

"—*Enough*!" Jeanne Châlon shrieked.

Ash bent down and hauled Florian bodily to her feet. "Don't argue, just *go*."

Before the surgeon could move, the fat woman sitting on the cobbles shrieked again, loudly and urgently enough that the men fell silent around her:

"*Enough of this vile pretence.* God will never forgive you, little whore, little bitch, little abomination!" Panting, Jeanne Châlon heaved in a breath, staring up, wet-eyed. "Why do you tolerate her? Don't you know that she damns you, pollutes you, just by being with you? Why else is she forbidden her home? Are you blind? *Look at her!*"

Faces – Euen, Thomas, the billmen – turned to Ash, and then to Florian. And from Florian back to Ash.

"Okay, that's enough," Ash said quickly, hoping to take advantage of their confusion. "We're leaving."

Thomas gazed at Florian. "What's she on about, man?"

Ash filled her lungs. "Form up—"

Jeanne Châlon shuddered, rose, scrambling unaided to her feet in a flurry of skirts and shift. She was panting. One hand went out, grabbing Euen Huw's livery tabard.

"You *are* blind!"

She faced Florian.

"Look at her! Can't you see what she is? She's a whore, an abomination, she dresses in man's clothes, *she is a woman—*"

Ash, under her breath and without realising it, said, "Oh fuck."

"God be my witness," Mademoiselle Châlon shouted, "she is my niece, and my shame."

Floria del Guiz smiled, tautly. In an absent-minded voice, she said, "I remember that, after Lizette, you threatened to lock me up in a nunnery. I always thought that had a certain lack of logic about it. Thank you, Aunt. Where would I be without you?"

There was already a rumble of comment from the men-at-arms. Ash swore, violently, under her breath, spitting out the obscenity. "Okay, form up, we're out of here. Come *on.*"

The men clustered in a group around Florian and Jeanne Châlon, who stood face to face, as if no one else in the world existed. The shadows of doves from a nearby cot flickered over them. The rumble of mills was the only sound in the quiet.

"Where *would* I be?" Florian repeated. She still held the flask of wine that Simon had brought, and she lifted it and drank, absently, gulping the liquid down and wiping her sleeve across her mouth. "You drove me out. It's hard trying to pass as a man, train with men. I would have come home from Salerno in the first week, if I'd had a home to come back to. But I didn't, and so I'm a surgeon. You made me what I am, *Tante.*"

"The Devil made you." Very coldly, into the silence, Jeanne Châlon said, "You lay with that girl Lizette as if you were a man."

Ash saw identical expressions of shock on the faces of the men-at-arms; and on Thomas Rochester's face, an awed, superstitious disgust.

"I could have had you burned," the old woman said. "I held you in my arms when you were a baby. I prayed I would never see you again. Why have you come back? Why couldn't you stay away!"

"Something—" Florian's voice thinned, losing its husky depth. "—something I have always needed to ask you, Aunt. You paid to have me freed by the Abbot of Rome, when he would have burned me because I had a Jewish lover. Tante, could you have bought her, too? Could you have paid him for Esther's life?"

The men's faces turned to Jeanne Châlon.

"I could have, but I would not! She was a Jewess!" The fat woman sweltered, dragging her kirtle and shift around her, treading her purse unnoticed under her feet. She shifted her gaze away from Florian del Guiz, as if for the first time aware that she had an audience.

"She was a Jewess!" Jeanne Châlon repeated, in high-voiced protest.

"Well . . . I've been to Paris, and Constantinople, and Bokhara, and Iberia, and Alexandria." Florian's voice held a hopeless, vitiated contempt: Ash suddenly realised, seeing the surgeon's face, that she had held long hopes of this occasion, and of it being different to this. "I've met nobody I despise as I despise you, *Aunt.*"

The Burgundian woman shrieked, "And *she* dressed as a man, too!"

"So does boss," Thomas Rochester growled, "and nobody's fucking burning her."

Ash felt the balance in the air, the moment which can be crystallised. They don't know *what* to think: Florian's a woman – but this Châlon bitch isn't one of us—

She caught Ricau signalling. A number of Dijonnais turned into the narrow street: millworkers, on their way home.

The woman shrieked, "Philippe should never have fathered you! My brother suffers in Purgatory for that sin!"

Floria del Guiz pivoted on her foot, brought her fist through, and punched Jeanne Châlon in the face.

Rochester, Euen Huw, Katherine, and young Simon spontaneously cheered. Mademoiselle Châlon fell down, shrieking, "*Au secours!*"

"Okay," Ash called deliberately, her eyes on the approaching citizens of Dijon, "time to go: let's get our surgeon out of here."

There was no hesitation: all the men-at-arms closed in around Florian, hands on sword-hilts or gripping bill-shafts, and began a fast walk towards the end of the street and the city gate that had the citizens of Dijon leaping back out of their way.

"If anybody asks," Ash bent down to Jeanne Châlon, "my surgeon's under arrest, by my provosts, and I'm dealing with her discipline myself."

Oblivious, the old woman sobbed, bloody hands over her mouth.

Running in the wake of her men-at-arms, Ash glanced up at the evening sun over the roofs of Dijon, and had time to think *Why did we ever come to Burgundy?*

And what is the Duke going to say to me now?

IV

"Why is it," Ash said under her breath, "that when the brown and sticky hits the fan, I'm always standing real close by?"[7]

Thomas Rochester shrugged. "Just lucky, boss, I guess . . ."

Among subdued laughter, Ash strode on across the common ground beside the silent Florian del Guiz. Above, in the airy emptiness, colour drained slowly from the atmosphere. Behind them, the gable roofs of Dijon lay limned with gold, the white dots of Orion and Cassiopeia beginning to pattern the milk-blue sky.

Crows and rooks squabbled on the camp middens as they approached the wagon-perimeter; the carrion-eaters flapping up, black pinions outspread.

"Don't leave the camp, master surgeon," Ash ordered calmly, "under any circumstances."

---

[7] The original text has 'fortuna imperatrix mundi'.

The lowering sun coloured Florian's blue doublet and hose with warmth, turned her hair red-gold. The woman raised her dirty face as she walked, staring up, her arms folded around her body. Her eyes reflected the empty sky.

"Don't sweat." Ash slapped the surgeon's shoulder. "If the town militia turn up, *I'll* deal with it. Stay in the surgeon's tent tonight."

The woman's head lowered. Now she watched her bare feet, treading down the sharp-edged dry grass. She didn't look at the men-at-arms.

The men and women of the escort walked, talking quietly among themselves, weapons slung over shoulders, left hands going down to steady scabbards. Ash heard comments about the vast encampment that was the Burgundian army, arrangements for off-duty drinking with acquaintances from other campaigns now with the Burgundian mercenaries – nothing at all about their surgeon.

She made her decision.

No. I'm not going to say anything. Give it a few hours – tomorrow – and depending on what Charles of Burgundy says, we may have bigger problems than our surgeon being a woman . . .

The city walls lay in shadow now, only the topmost roofs gilded with sharp-edged red light. Dew dampened that masonry, and dampened the straw here, underfoot, spread outside the camp. An ox still out in the fields lowed, and a pack of dogs ran yelping and barking. Welcome coolness came into the air with sunset.

At the gates, where the straw was trodden down flat by hundreds of passing feet, a hubbub of voices and a crowd of men in Lion livery drew her attention. They stood red-faced and grinning, and parted to let her through with a suppressed excitement: a scowl for the provosts, and several grins for her.

With a resigned sigh, she said, "What is it this time?"

Two young men of about fifteen, all legs, and baby-fat burning down to muscle and youthful energy, were shuffled to the front of the crowd. Both were fair-haired, brothers by their faces; and she recognised them as men of Euen Huw's lance.

"Tydder," she said, bringing the name to mind.

One of the boys muttered, "Boss—"

His brother slammed an elbow into the other's bare ribs. "Shut up, you!"

Both of them had their shirts and pourpoints rolled down to the waist, chests bare and burning red, and everything more or less held up with their dagger-belts. Ash was about to snarl something when she noticed that the bundle of cloth around one of the waists was thicker. She pointed silently.

The young soldier unwrapped the cloth and shook it out. A quartered rectangular flag of blue and red, about two yards across, flopped down from his big hands. Ash found herself looking at two ravens and two crosses.

There was a rise in the noise around her, someone laughed; the anticipation all but tangible.

"That," Ash said, with no intention of disappointing them, "wouldn't happen to be a personal banner, would it?"

The brother holding the flag nodded rapidly. The other brother grinned, ferociously.

"Cola de Monforte's personal banner?" she queried.

"You got it, boss!" a third brother squeaked, flushing at his voice.

Ash began to grin.

Behind her, Floria suddenly broke her silence. "Christ on a stick! How are you going to explain this one?"

Her appalled expression made Ash burst out laughing.

"Oh, I'm not going to explain it," she said cheerfully. "I don't have to. In fact . . . you two – Mark and Thomas, isn't it? And young Simon. Now: Euen Huw . . . Carracci, Thomas Rochester . . . and Huw's lance—" Ash pointed at a dozen or more men. "I suggest you wrap this banner up very neatly, and you take it over to the gate of the Monforte camp, and you present it to Master Cola – in person – with our compliments."

"They do *what*?" Floria exclaimed.

"It can be really embarrassing to lose your personal banner. If we just *happened* to find it lying around," Ash emphasised, "and took it back to them, in case they were worried about it—"

Laughter drowned her out.

Under cover of the lances sorting themselves out, finding armour to wear up to the Monforte mercenary camp, and girding on their most impressive weapons, Floria del Guiz asked, "And just how did we come by that banner?"

"No point me asking." Ash shook her head, still grinning. "Remind me to tell Geraint to double the perimeter guard. And double the guard on the Lion standard. I feel there's going to be a lot of this—"

"—this crap!" Floria snarled. "Complete waste of time! Boys' games!"

Ash watched Ludmilla Rostovnaya and her lance-mate Katherine shouldering arquebuses to form part of the impromptu honour guard, some two dozen strong, moving off across the river meadows in the direction of the Burgundian mercenary camps.

"If they want to play at flag-stealing, I'm going to let them. Either Duke Charles will fund the raid, or he'll call for war. Either way, in a few days' time, they could be in your surgeon's tent. Or buried. And they know it." She twinkled at Florian. "Hell, you think this is bad, you've seen what they're like *after* they've won a fight . . . !"

The woman looked as though she might have said something, but a hail from the surgeon's tent – one of her assistants, a deacon – took her attention, and she nodded abruptly at Ash and walked off.

Ash let her go.

"If the town militia turn up here," she said to the captain on the gate, "you send for me at once. And you don't let them in, got that?"

"Sure, boss. We in trouble again?"

"You'll hear about it. In this camp, everybody hears everything . . ."

The captain of the gate-guard, a big Breton man with ploughman's shoulders, said, "Yeah, we might as well live in a fucking village."

I wonder which you'll find most scandalous – that the Duke's lawyers think the Visigoths own me, or that your pox-doctor is a woman?

"'Night, Jean."

"'Night, boss."

Ash strode off towards the command tent, her bodyguard-escort dispersing now they were inside the camp, half a dozen mastiffs jumping and yelping around her. Geraint ab Morgan came for passwords for the night guards, Angelotti notifying repairs ongoing with guns (the organ-gun *Barbara's Revenge* having cracked her shaft), Henri Brant needing money from the war-chest; all this within a few yards, so that it was a full half-hour before she got to the tent, took one look at the busy confusion inside her pavilion – Bertrand sulkily rolling her leg armour in a barrel of sand to clean it, under Rickard's impatient direction – and sniffed at her armpits as they removed her brigandine, turned command over to Anselm, whistled up the dogs, and went down to the river to swim in the last of the light, Rickard accompanying her.

"It's not like I have to *worry* about Florian." She buried both hands in the scruffs of mastiff-necks, feeling their warmth, smelling the dog-smell. "Anyone who objects to serving with women – doesn't sign up with me. Do they?"

Rickard looked confused. The powerful dog Bonniau snuffled.

Reaching the river bank, she stripped off hose and doublet as one (still pointed together at the waist) and her yellowing linen shirt, wringing wet with sweat. The mastiffs settled on the banks, heavy heads resting on their paws, one brindled bitch – Brifault – curling up on Ash's discarded, sweat-soaked shirt, doublet and hose, and shoes.

"Got my sling," Rickard offered.

Neither fox, polecat nor rat was safe near company refuse, Ash was well aware; her own lance's fox-tail came from one of Rickard's kills.

"I want you here with the dogs. Even if we are inside the camp."

Ash waded out, and threw herself in. The cold water grabbed her, shocked her skin, pulled her downstream. Gasping, grinning, she stood up and plodded back to the shallow eddy, thick with flag-irises, where the river cut a bow in the bank.

"Boss?" Rickard's voice said, among the mastiffs.

"Yeah?" She ducked her head under the surface. The weight of her wet hair swirled with the current. Standing up, the wet mass of it clung to her from head to knees, glinting palely in the sunset light. She scratched at sunburn and skin-rash. "You know, if I didn't take the time out to eat, wash, or sleep, this camp would function perfectly . . . what is it?"

His features could not be seen in the fading light. His boy's voice was abrupt. "I can hear a noise."

Ash frowned. "Leash the dogs."

She walked up to the bank, legs lead-heavy, and put her wet hair back from her ears. The usual noise from the campfires, and the sound of men drinking, echoed across the river valley.

"What did you hear?" She reached out for her shirt and began to scrub her skin dry.

"That!"

"Shit!" Ash swore, as a shout went up, from in the camp. Not men getting drunk, and fighting: too raw for that. She struggled into her clothes without drying herself off, the cloth sticking to her skin, and grabbed her sword and buckled it round her waist while she walked; and took the mastiffs' leashes from Rickard as he sprinted after her.

"It's the doctor!" the boy shouted.

In the growing dark, men massed, shouting.

The surgeon's tent went over as Ash came striding up, unnoticed into the crowd of off-duty men. The pennant and pole tipped as knives hacked away the guy-ropes; the canvas suddenly sagged.

A rose of yellow flame blossomed out of the canvas, brown-edged, brilliant in what was by contrast almost the darkness of the late sunset.

"FIRE!" Rickard shrieked.

"Pack it in!" Ash roared. She went forward without thinking about it, into the middle of them, dog-leashes clutched in both hands. "Anhelt, what the fuck do you think you're doing! Pieter, Jean, Henri—" picking out faces from the surging mass "—back off! Get the fire-watch! Get buckets, get sand on that thing!"

She was briefly aware of Rickard at her back, the boy struggling to draw his worn, munition-issue sword. Someone cannoned into both of them. The dogs snarled, a frenzy of hound-bodies throwing themselves forward; and she bawled, "Bonniau! Brifault!" and let the leashes out to her arm's length.

The men went back from the dogs, clearing a space around her and the collapsing tent. A figure fell down into the folds of canvas – Floria?

Ash yelled, "*Hold!*"

"WHORE!" a billman bellowed at the wreckage of the surgeon's tent.

"Kill the cunt!"

"Woman-fucker!"

"Fucking filthy pervert, fucking bitch, fucking dyke—"

"Fuck him and kill him!"

"Fuck her and kill her!"

Between their shoving bodies, she glimpsed other men running from other parts of the camp, some with torches, some with fire-buckets. The heat of the burning blew against her back. Charred fragments of canvas drifted past her.

Ash pitched her voice to carry. "*Get that fire out before it spreads!*"

"Drag her out of there and fuck her," a man's voice shouted: Josse. His face contorted as he spat. "Fucking *surgeon*! Cut her cunt up!"

Ash said quietly to the boy, "Get Florian out of the tent: *move*," and stepped forward, still with the mastiffs' leashes around her gloved hands, glaring around at the men.

In that moment she realised that most of the faces she could see were from Flemish lances. Some surprises – Wat Rodway, from the cook's tent, with a filleting knife; Pieter Tyrrell – but mostly it was red-faced men rawly shouting, hoarse, the stink of beer on the air, and more than that: an edge of real violence.

They're not just going to stand and shout, and destroy a few things.

Shit.

I shouldn't stand in front of them because they're going to come right over me. There's my authority gone.

The man Josse came forward, stomping over the slippery dry straw, regardless of her; reaching out to shove her aside with one hand, this woman with wet hair hanging to her thighs; his other hand going to his scabbard.

One of the Flemish lances' crossbowmen: she has a second to recognise him as one of the men taken with her at Basle, one of the first to greet her on her return to camp.

Ash released the mastiffs' leashes.

"*Shit!*" Josse screamed.

The six dogs bounded forward, silent now, and leaped; one man wrenching himself backwards with his arm clamped between heavy jaws, screeching; two men going down with dogs at their throats; a pennant and torches visible over the heads of the mob—

Over the noise of men screaming and swearing, and the howl as someone cut at one of the mastiffs, Ash pitched her voice to battlefield volume:

"BACK OFF! DOWN WEAPONS!"

She caught a sound of voices behind her: Florian and Rickard, some of the surgeon's-tent assistants. She didn't take her eyes off the billmen and archers massing in the firebreak between tents. Bashas opposite were being trodden down as the crowd grew: men inside them yelling protests. The crackle of flame grew behind her.

"Brifault!"

The mastiffs, hallooed back, came to heel. She felt the switch of attention: the crowd no longer a mass of men who might just push past her, not even seeing one more person in the confusion of the camp, but men in mail shirts, with daggers in their hands, and torches – one, Josse, with a drawn sword – facing her.

Ash, aware that reality is what consensus says it is, feels it begin to slip: from mutual agreement that she is commander of the company, to being just a young woman, in a field, at night, surrounded by men who are bigger, older, armed, drunk.

Entirely automatically, she started to mutter, "Armed revolt, in camp, thirty men—"

'*Re-establish command and control by—*'

"Who do you think you fucking are!" Josse sprayed spit from his mouth as he bellowed. The sheer volume of voice from that big a man blasted the air. He glared, said, "You're fucking dead," and lifted his falchion.

The movement of a live blade triggered every combat reflex.

Ash grabbed the neck of her scabbard with her left hand and her hilt with her right hand, ripping the sword out of the sheath. In the space of that second, Josse's arm went up, torch-light flashed off his falchion's edge, and the heavy curved blade chopped down. She whacked her sword in behind it, parrying, accelerating it down; slammed his blade down so hard into the dirt between them that her feet came off the ground. Landing, balanced, she slammed one foot on to his blade and held it; and lifted up her sword pommel-first and rammed it straight into his unprotected throat.

A voice among the gathered men whispered, "Shit . . ."

Ash felt wetness on her hands. She pulled the weapon back. Josse put both hands to his crushed trachea and fell, wheezing whitely, on to the smouldering straw at her feet. Simultaneously, sudden and final: one foot kicked; his bowels relaxed; the breath made a loud, harsh noise in his throat.

Men at the back still pushed to get forward, the shouting still went on there; but here, at the edge of the crowd around the surgeon's tent, shock and silence.

"Shit," Pieter Tyrrell repeated. He raised bright, drunken eyes to Ash. "Oh, shit, man."

A billman said, "He should've known better than to draw sword."

A sudden influx of men, in plate, and under Anselm's pennant, thrust in from one side; and Ash lowered her sword, seeing the provosts going in, breaking up what she now estimated in the darkness to be a crowd of fifty or sixty men.

"Well done." She nodded acknowledgement to Anselm. "All right, get this man . . . buried."

Deliberately, she turned her back on the men, letting Anselm sort it. She rubbed her glove over the stained pommel of her sword, wiping off blood, and sheathed the weapon. The mastiffs closed in around her legs.

Rickard and Florian del Guiz, in the wet smoking wreckage of the surgeon's tent, stared at her: the boy and the woman with identical expressions.

"He was going to *kill* you!" Rickard protested shrilly. He stood with his feet planted apart and his head down, much the way that Anselm habitually stood, watching the departing men with awkward bravado and fear. "How can they do that! You're the boss!"

"They're hard men. If they're drunk, nobody's boss."

"But you stopped it!"

Ash shrugged, gathering up the mastiffs' leashes. She rubbed Bonniau's muzzle, the dog's wet drool sliding over her hands. Her fingers shook.

Florian stepped out of the wreckage of the pavilion: over burned canvas, wooden chests smashed open, spoiled surgical instruments and scattered, trodden bunches of herbs. Someone had started on smacking the disguised woman around, Ash saw: her lips bled and her doublet sleeve was ripped out of its point-holes.

"You okay?"

"Motherfuckers!" Florian stared at the squad pulling Josse's body away in a blanket. "I've had them under my knife! How could they come here and do this?"

"Are you badly hurt?" Ash persisted.

Florian spread pale, dirty long fingers in front of her and looked down at the tremors shaking her hands. "Did you have to *kill* him?"

"Yes. I did have to. They follow me because I can do that without thinking about it, and I sleep nights afterwards." Ash reached out and lifted the surgeon's chin, studying the bruises.

Dark fingermarks stood out on the woman's flesh, where she had been grabbed and held.

"Get one of the deacons here, Rickard. Florian, killing doesn't matter to me. If it mattered, I'd've gone down the first time thirty armed thugs marched up to my tent and said, 'That's our war-chest, piss off, little girl'. Wouldn't I?"

"You're mad." Florian shifted her head away, staring down at the wreckage. One wet streak marked her cheek. "You're all fucking mad! Bloody maniacs, bloody soldiers! You're no different!"

Ash said dryly, "Yes, I am. I'm on your side."

To the deacon who trotted up with a lantern, she said, "Get the doctor bedded down in the field chapel. Is Father Godfrey back yet?"

The man gasped, "No, Captain."

"Okay. Feed her, keep an eye on her, I don't think she's hurt too bad, there'll be a guard along later," and as Robert Anselm returned, his armour rattling as he strode up to her, Ash continued, "I want Florian in the chapel tent, and a guard on it, nothing too obvious."

"It's done." Anselm gave orders to his subordinates. Turning back to Ash, he said, "Girl, what the fuck was that?"

"That was a mistake."

Ash looked down at the trodden straw. There was dark blood on it, not very much, but visible in the lantern's light. The stink of burned canvas and spilled herbs rose up in the night air.

Thomas Rochester, at Anselm's back, said, "You couldn't disarm him. He was twice your weight. I reckon you only had one chance, and you took it."

Robert Anselm stared after the departing surgeon. "He's – she's a woman, and she fucks women?"

"Yeah."

"You knew about this?" At her hesitation, he spat on the straw, swore softly, and fixed her with expressionless eyes. "You fucked up here."

"Yeah. Josse was good in a fight. I fucking needed him." Ash scowled. "I need all the good men I've got! If I'd seen this coming, I wouldn't have had to do that."

"Shit," Robert Anselm said.

"Yeah."

"Get that cleared up," Anselm directed his returning men. Ash walked aside with him, down the path between pavilions, as the physic-tent was sifted, shifted, and cleared.

"Do I call a meeting and talk to them?" Ash mused, aloud. "Or do I let it sink in what they've done, and let their heads clear in the morning? Have I still *got* a surgeon? One they'll trust?"

The big man sniffed, thoughtfully, and prodded with his sabaton at a wisp of extinguished straw, grinding it into the dew-wet dirt. "He's been with us five years, half of them have been put back together in – her – tent. Give 'em a chance to work out it's still the doc. First time somebody hits 'em, most'll come running."

"And those that don't?"

The pennant that had been lurking about at the back of the crowd became clear as it moved forward. Ash's face took on a grim expression.

"Master van Mander," she called. "I want a word with you."

Joscelyn van Mander, Paul di Conti, and five or six more of the Flemish lance-leaders picked their way through the confusion; van Mander's face white under his helmet.

"What the *hell* were you doing, letting your men do this?"

"I couldn't stop them, Captain." Joscelyn van Mander reached up and took off his helmet. His face was flushed, his eyes bright; she smelled wine on him, and on the others.

"You couldn't stop them? You're their lance-leader!"

"I command only by their consent," the Flemish commander said, unsteadily. "I lead by their wishes. It's the same for all us officers. We're a mercenary company, Captain Ash. It's the men who matter. How *could* I stop them? We're told the surgeon is a devil, a demon; a lustful, perverted vile thing; an offence to mankind—"

Ash raised a brow. "So she's a woman: so what?"

"She's a woman who has lain with other women, who knows them carnally!" His voice pitched high with outrage. "Even if I could bring myself to tolerate it, because he's, she's, your surgeon, and you're commander—"

"That's enough." Ash cut him short. "Your duty is to control these men. You failed."

"How could I control them, their disgust at this?" His breath blasted, warm and beer-laden, across the space between them. "Don't blame *me*, Captain. She's *your* surgeon."

"Get back to your tent. I'll tell you your penalties in the morning."

Ash stared the Flemish lance-leader down, ignoring for the moment the other lance-leaders with him; noting, as he turned and stalked away, who followed his pennant, and who stayed to undertake the clear-up of the area.

"God*dammit!*" Ash said.

"We've got trouble," Anselm said phlegmatically.

"Yeah, like I really need *more* trouble." Ash smoothed her still-wet shirt-sleeves down. "Maybe I should look forward to Charles handing me over to the Visigoths . . . it can only be an improvement!"

Robert Anselm ignored her temper, which she was used to him doing.

"I'll hold some kind of inquiry tomorrow. Fines, beatings; stop this before it gets out of hand." When she glanced up at him, Anselm was watching her. "And I'll be interested to know if van Mander's lances overheard any 'chance remarks' from Joscelyn before this riot."

"Wouldn't surprise me."

"I'd better go check on Florian."

"About Josse." Robert Anselm halted her as she was about to walk off into the camp. "Stop by my tent later. I've got wine."

Ash shook her head. "No."

"We can have a drink. To Josse."

"Yeah." Ash sighed, in gratitude for Anselm's particular understanding. She grinned. "I'll be along. Don't worry about me, Roberto. I don't need the wine. I'll sleep."

A hot, muggy mist came up with the next day's dawn. Granules of water hung suspended in the air inside the palace. The misty whiteness of the presence chamber tinged with gold as the sun rose over the horizon.

Ash stood beside the Earl of Oxford, welcoming the coolness that stone walls gave the early morning. De Vere and his brothers being awarded a place not far from the ducal throne, she was able to look about her, see the Burgundian nobles assembled, the foreign dignitaries – but not, so far, the Visigoths.

The clarions rang and the choirs began to sing a morning hymn. Ash took off her chaperon hat and bowed her knee to the white marble floor.

"I have no idea what the Duke will do," John de Vere said, as the hymn finished. "I'm an outsider here, too, madam."

"I could have had a contract with that man," she whispered, voice barely a breath.

"Yes," the Earl of Oxford said.

"Yes."

They mutually looked at each other, and as mutually shrugged, each with a quiet smile on their faces as they got to their feet, Duke Charles of Burgundy seating himself on his throne.

Her satisfaction vanished with the automatic glance she gave to find Godfrey, and listen to Godfrey's prompting voice at her ear. The place beside her was taken by Robert Anselm, Godfrey Maximillian not being present.

Robert might believe Godfrey would stay overnight in Dijon, last night, but he's wondering where our clerk is right now. I can see it on his face. And I don't have anything I can tell him. Godfrey, where the fuck have you gone?

Are you coming back?

"Hell!" she added, under her breath, and realised at de Vere's curious glance that she had spoken aloud.

Under the cover of the Duke's chamberlain and chancellor speaking, the Earl of Oxford said, "Don't worry, madam. If it comes to it, I'll think of something to keep you here, out of Visigoth hands."

"Like what?"

The Englishman smiled confidently, seemingly amused by her caustic tone. "I'll think of something. I often do."

"Too much thinking's bad for you . . . my lord." Ash tagged his title on to the end. She raised her head, trying to look across the heads of the crowd.

Complicated heraldries of Burgundy and France blazed silver and blue, red and gold, scarlet and white. Her eye travelled over the various groups, some standing in corners, others seated by the great open fireplaces full of sweet rushes. Nobles and their affinities, merchants in silk, because of the growing heat; dozens of pages in Charles's white puff-sleeved livery jackets, priests in their sombre browns and greens; and servants moving rapidly from one group of people to another. The freshness of the early morning made voices lively – but with a particular tone, she noted: solemn, grave and reverent.

Where's Godfrey when I need him?

Listening for intelligence, she overheard a tall man discuss the virtues of bratchet bitches for hunting; two knights speaking of a tournament combat over barriers; and a large woman in an Italian silk robe talking about honey glazes for pork.

The only political conversation Ash could hear was between the French ambassador and Philippe de Commines:[8] it mostly involved the names of

---

[8] Philippe de Commines or Commynes (1447–1511), historian and politician who first served the Burgundians, then betrayed them for the French. He became advisor to Louis XI four years previously, in AD 1472.

French Dukes with which she was not overly familiar.

So where's this court's factionalism and politics? Maybe I don't need Godfrey to feed me details, not here.

But I need Godfrey.

An automatic check behind assured her that Joscelyn van Mander was not only present, but sober and with his ego reasonably subdued, that her men-at-arms wore clean livery jackets over polished armour – or as polished as it was reasonable to expect, a week after fleeing a hundred miles across winter country – and that Antonio Angelotti as well as Robert Anselm stood at her elbow. Robert, in respectful conversation with one of the de Vere brothers, didn't notice her glance. Angelotti grinned out at her from between a mass of tangled, golden curls. She beckoned him to the front of the group, reflecting, We might as well *look* good.

A stir at the far end of the presence hall drew attention.

Ash straightened, resisting an urge to stand on tiptoe. She saw a pennant at the great oak doors, and heard the liquid accents of Carthaginian Latin. Her hand dropped to her sword-hilt for reassurance. She rested it there, standing with her weight casually back on one heel, as the chamberlain and his servants announced and brought in Sancho Lebrija, Agnus Dei and Fernando del Guiz.

The solemn grandeur of the Duke's court looked as though it were having some effect on Fernando del Guiz. He shifted uncomfortably in the open space before the dais, his eyes flicking around from face to face. Ash clasped her shaking hands behind her back. That his physical presence dried up her mouth and confused her thoughts was something she had almost grown used to. What confused her still further was her immediate pang at seeing him now, beleaguered, turn-coat, isolated from his own.

Beside her, the Earl of Oxford stood more erect. Ash came out of her reverie. It took her several seconds to pay attention to the Duke's voice. The early fog, still drifting in the high stone hall, cast a cool haziness over the gathered noblemen and rich merchants. The slanting eastern gold of the light fell in now through the rose windows of the palace, as the sun rose higher: warming Oxford's face, where he stood next to her, his head bowed to catch some comment of Robert Anselm's; bringing fire from Angelotti's Italian beauty; colouring the armour of Jan-Jacob Clovet and Paul di Conti with an antique sheen, so that to her eyes they seemed briefly all of a piece with Mynheer van Eyck's angels, dreaming through eternity in the presence of God.

Something tore at her heart. That feeling of their permanence, over and above earthly affairs, vanished. A feeling of fragility overtook her, as if her companions might be utterly valuable and at the same time utterly endangered.

The sun, rising higher, altered the angle of light in from the windows, and with that change the feeling was gone. Almost bereft, Ash turned her head to hear Duke Charles of Burgundy saying, "Master Lebrija, I have considered your request with my advisors. You ask us for a truce."

Sancho Lebrija made a stiff, formal bow. "Yes, lord Prince of Burgundy, we do."

The lugubrious face of the Duke was all but lost in the finery of rolled hat, dagged tail, puffed doublet sleeves, and golden neck-chains: a hierophantic image of courtliness. Abruptly he leaned forward on his throne, and Ash glimpsed the rich and powerful man with a keen affection for guns, who spent as many months of the year in the field as he could spare.

"Your 'truce' is a lie," Duke Charles said clearly.

A burst of noise: Ash's men around her speaking loudly enough that she signalled them to silence, and leaned forward to hear the Duke.

"Your halt at Auxonne is not for a truce, it is to spy out my lands, and receive your reinforcements. You stand at our borders in darkness, armed for war, the atrocities of this summer behind you, and you ask us to sue for peace – to surrender, in all but name. No," Charles of Burgundy said. "If there were but one man of my people left to defend us, he would say, as I say, that right is with us, and where right is, there God must be also. For He will stand at our side in battle, and cast you down."

Ash bit back what would have been an automatically cynical mutter to Robert Anselm. The shaven-headed man had dragged his hat off, and stood gazing open-eyed at the richness of the Duke, surrounded by bishops, cardinals and priests.

The Duke's voice echoed back from the vaulted roof. "Right may sleep, but it does not rot in the earth as men's bodies do, or rust as the treasures of this world, but remains unchangeable. Your war is unjust. Rather than sue for peace, I will die here on the land that my father ruled, and his fathers before him. There is not a man of Burgundy, be he never so poor a peasant, nor a man who has asked sanctuary of Burgundy, who shall not be defended with all might, all main, and all the prayers that we may raise to God."

The hush was broken by the French ambassador stepping forward into the open space on the black-and-white tiled floor. Ash saw his left palm close around his sword-grip.

"My lord Duke," he glanced back at Philippe de Commines in the mass of people, and went on, "Cousin of our Valois King, this is sophistry and treachery."

No one spoke. Ash's mouth felt dry. Her stomach twisted.

The French noble's face went taut. "You hope, by this one threat, to make Burgundy seem a dangerous land to attack, and thus turn these invaders into my lands, and into the lands of King Louis! That is all your strategy! You wish this bitch Faris and her armies to weary themselves for the next few months fighting *us*. And then you'll defeat them, and pick up what lands you can from us – Charles of Burgundy, where is your liege loyalty to your King?"

Where, indeed? Ash thought ironically.

"Your King," Charles of Burgundy said, "will remember that I myself have bombarded Paris.[9] If I desired his kingdom, I would come and take it. You will be silent now."

Ash was aware of chamberlains and other court officials closing in around the ambassador as the Duke turned his attention back to Sancho Lebrija.

"I will not accede to your request," Charles added, with finality.

The Visigoth *qa'id* observed, "This is a declaration for war, then."

[9] 1465.

310

Ash, aware of her own escort's low-voiced comments, caught sight of the face of Olivier de la Marche. The big Burgundian captain began to smile with a whole-hearted, infectious joy.

"*Said* we needed a fight," Anselm growled, at her ear.

"Yeah, well, you might get one sooner than you expect." Ash looked at Sancho Lebrija; kept her gaze from Fernando del Guiz. "I'm not going to be handed over."

Anselm's quick look said, plainer than words, *Be real, girl! You don't have any choice.*

"No," Ash said gently, "you don't understand. I don't care if I have to take on the whole of this court, and Charles's army, and Oxford into the bargain: I am not going with them. The only way we're going across the middle sea is fully armed and eight hundred strong."

Anselm shifted his stance, with the air of a man settling himself into some decision. Abruptly, he muttered, "We'll get you out. If it comes to it."

Aware of shifting feet behind her, Ash thought *You might but I'm not sure about van Mander* and moved to one side as the Earl of Oxford, summoned by the Duke's chamberlain, moved to the front of their group.

"Sire?" he said mildly.

"I am not your liege lord," Charles of Burgundy said, leaning back on his throne and ignoring the Visigoths, "but I pray that it will please you, my lord Oxford, to bring your company of men to the field, under my banner, when we ride to Auxonne?"

Shit. So much for the raid.

"Do it ourselves?" she murmured to Anselm.

"If you can fucking pay for it!"

"We can't *pay* for anything. We're only getting credit with our suppliers in Dijon because of Oxford's name."

Angelotti said something blunt in Italian, on the other side of Robert Anselm, that made Agnus Dei raise his black brows where he stood with the Visigoths.

"Honoured," the Earl of Oxford agreed curtly. "Sire."

Sancho Lebrija moved forward, mail hauberk chinging. "Lord Prince of Burgundy, before there is war, there is the law. Our general has asked that you return to her her property, the bondswoman there." His gloved finger flicked out, indicating Ash. "The legal title of the House Leofric to this woman is clear. She is born of a slave mother, and a slave father." He repeated, "She is the property of House Leofric."

In the silence, Ash breathed deeply of the meadowsweet smell of the flowers and rushes strewing the floor of the presence chamber. A tingle of apprehension dizzied her. She put it away from herself. Clear-headed, she lifted her scarred face and stared at the Burgundian Duke.

"He'll do it," she murmured to Anselm and Angelotti.

For only the second time since she had met him, Ash saw a wintry small smile on Charles of Burgundy's face.

"Ash," he said.

She stepped forward, beside Oxford, surprised to find that her legs were weak.

Gravely, the Duke said, "It has always pleased me to hire mercenaries. For whatever reason, I would decline to let any experienced mercenary commander leave my forces. In this case, however, I do not hold your contract. That is held by an English lord. Over him, the laws of Burgundy have no jurisdiction."

Rapidly, solemnly, the Earl of Oxford rapped out, "I couldn't go against the wishes of the premier prince of Europe, sire, and you *have* requested our presence on the field of battle . . ."

"I hear the sound of bucks being passed," Ash murmured. She kept a smile off her face with difficulty.

"You claimed *right*." Sancho Lebrija's harsh, battlefield voice cut through the courtliness. "You claimed right, lord Prince of Burgundy. 'Right may sleep, but it does not rot'."

Oxford's stance warned Ash, changing from benevolent courtesy to alertness. She made herself look confident, aware that her men-at-arms were looking from her, to the Duke, to the Visigoths, and back to her.

"What is your point?" the Burgundian Duke asked.

"Right does not sleep. We have the right, the law, with us." Sancho Lebrija's pale eyes slitted, as the morning sun found the place where he and his white-robed men stood in the chamber. Light struck fire from mail, from belt-buckles, from the hilts of worn swords.

"Will you stand convicted of mere expediency, lord Prince of Burgundy? This is defying the law, for no more reason than you wish a few more hundred men for your forces. It is greed, not right. It is despotism, not the law."

He hesitated, breathless; then nodded curtly, as Fernando del Guiz said something at his ear.

"No one could fault you, lord Prince, for saying you fight a just war against us. But where is your justice, if you set the law aside as it pleases you? She belongs to the House Leofric. You know – it is known to all, by now – she has my general's face. She is her living image. Lord Fernando here will stand witness to it. You cannot deny her to be born of the same parentage. You cannot deny that she is a slave."

Lebrija halted, his eyes on the Duke, who did not speak. The Visigoth finished:

"As a slave, she has no legal right to sign a *condotta*, so it does not matter who she has signed one with."

Oxford's mouth made a bitter twist. He scowled, said nothing, looked to be furiously thinking.

"He's going to do it," Ash whispered to the two men beside her: Anselm sweating, his head aggressively down; Angelotti's hand on his dagger with deadly grace. "Maybe he won't do it for political advantage – maybe he's different from Frederick – but he's going to listen to Lebrija. He's going to hand me over because they *are* legally right."

Behind her, the small group of her officers, men-at-arms, and archers began to shift, spread out a little; some men checking how far they were standing from the doors of the presence chamber, and where the guards were.

"You got any ideas?" she added, to Oxford.

The Earl scowled blackly, his pale eyes puzzled. "Give me a minute!"

The noise of a clarion cut through the ducal presence chamber: fine and high and clear. More knights in full harness, with axes, entered by the ornate doors, taking up their stations around the walls. Ash saw de la Marche give a satisfied nod of approval.

Charles of Burgundy spoke from his throne.

"What will your Faris-General do with the woman, Ash, when she has her?"

"*Do* with her?" Lebrija looked blank.

"Yes, do with her." The Duke folded his hands in his lap, neatly. Young and grave, a little pompous, he said, "You see, it is my belief you will hurt her."

"Harm her? Lord Prince, no." Lebrija had the face of a man realising he sounded unconvincing. He shrugged. "Lord Prince, it is not your concern. The woman Ash is a House slave. You may as well ask if I mean harm to my horse when I ride it on to the field of battle."

Some of the Visigoth soldiers with Lebrija laughed.

"What will you do with her?"

"My lord Prince, it is not your concern. It is for you to uphold the law. By law, she is ours."

Charles of Burgundy said, "That, I think, is certainly true."

The frustration that emanated from the men with her was all but tangible: they glared around at the armed Burgundians, swore; all internal dissent momentarily united. Anselm said something restraining to Angelotti.

"No!" Antonio Angelotti snapped. "I have *been* a slave in one of their *amirs'* houses. Madonna, I will do anything to keep you out of that!"

Robert Anselm snarled, "Master gunner, be silent!"

Ash stared across the chamber at Agnus Dei as Lamb slapped Sancho Lebrija congratulatorily on the back. Behind the Italian mercenary, Fernando del Guiz listened to some comment from his escort and smiled, throwing his head back, gold in the sunlight.

Her decision crystallised.

"I'm happy to kill all of the Visigoths here." Ash spoke steadily, loudly enough to be heard by Anselm, Angelotti, van Mander, Oxford and his brothers. "There are nine men. Take them out, now, fast; throw down our weapons – then let the Duke declare us outlaw. If they're dead, we'll just be thrown out of Burgundy, not handed over—"

"Let's do it." Anselm stepped forward; the men-at-arms in Lion livery moving as he did; Ash with them. She heard van Mander mutter something panicky about the guards – thought, in acceptance, *yes, we'll take casualties* – and Carracci swear excitedly, saw Euen Huw and Rochester simultaneously grin, hard men reaching for their swords with reckless aggression.

"Wait!" the Earl of Oxford commanded.

The clarion rang out again. Charles, Duke of Burgundy, stood. As if there were no armed mercenaries ten yards from his throne, as if the armed guards were not moving to obey de la Marche's abrupt signal, he spoke.

"No. I will not order the woman Ash turned over to you."

Utterly affronted, Lebrija said, "But she is ours *by law*."

"That is true. Nonetheless, I will not give her to you."

Ash dimly felt Anselm's hand grip her arm, with painful force.

"*What?*" she whispered. "What did he just say?"

The Duke looked around, at his counsellors, advisors, lawyers and subjects; a slight expression of satisfaction crossing his features as Olivier de la Marche bowed heavily, and indicated the armed men in the chamber.

"Furthermore, if you attempt to remove her by force, you will be prevented."

"Lord Prince, you are an insane man!"

"Fuck me, he's right," Ash said under her breath.

De Vere laughed out loud, and cuffed Ash's shoulder at much the same strength as he might one of his brothers. She had cause to be glad that she was wearing a brigandine: even so, she heard the riveted steel plates crunch.

Over what was an undoubted cheer from Ash's men, Charles of Burgundy addressed the Visigoth delegation:

"It is my will that the woman Ash stays here. So be it."

As if the Burgundian Duke, at least ten years his junior, was no more than a recalcitrant page, Sancho Lebrija exclaimed, "But you're *breaking the law*!"

"Yes. I am. Take this message to your masters – your Faris: I will continue to break the law, at all times, if the law is wrong." Stilted, and still a little pompous, Charles of Burgundy said, "Honour is above Law. Honour and chivalry demand we protect the weak. It would be morally wrong to give the woman to you, when every man listening here knows that you will butcher her."

Sancho Lebrija gazed up at him, utterly bemused.

"I don't get it." Ash shook her head, bewildered. "Where's the advantage? What's Charles getting out of this?"

"Nothing," the Earl of Oxford said, beside her, clasping his hands behind his back as if he had not just been drawing sword. He glanced keenly at her. "Absolutely nothing, madam. No political advantage. His action will be thought indefensible."

Ignoring the raucous pleasure of the Lion contingent, Ash gazed across the presence chamber at the Visigoth delegation, marching out flanked by Burgundian troops; and then at the throne, and at the Burgundian Duke.

"I don't *get* it," Ash said.

V

Ash came back to her command tent by a circuitous route. She spoke, on her way from fire-pit to fire-pit, to a hundred or more of the teenage males[10] who sat around drinking, talking inaccurately about their success with women, and even more inaccurately about the capabilities of their longbows or bills.

"It's war," she said, outwardly cheerful. And listened, both to what they said

---

[10] The text gives us 'iuventus', referring to young men between, say, sixteen and twenty; in our terms, these are teenagers.

and didn't say; squatting by the flames that flickered invisibly in sunlight, drinking beer here, and eating a bowl of pottage there; listening to excited voices. Listening to what they had to say about war. About their surgeon. About the drum-head court's penalties after Josse's death.

She paid particular attention to that side of the camp that was made up of the thirteen or fourteen Flemish lances that had signed on with Joscelyn van Mander.

Arriving at her tent, she surveyed her officers' meeting. A tiny frown dinted her silver brows. She stepped outside again, picked up her escort of six men from (this time) an English knight's lance, and their dogs, and walked back down the straw-trodden paths between the tents and bashas.

"Di Conti," she called. Paul di Conti loped up, a broad grin on his sun-reddened face, and dropped to one knee in front of her. "I don't see you or the Flemish lance-leaders in my tent. Get your asses in gear; there's a meeting."

The Savoyard man-at-arms beamed up at her. In his soft accent, he said, "Sieur Joscelyn said he would attend in our places. Willem and I don't mind, nor the others. Sieur Joscelyn will pass on all we need to know."

And di Conti's not even Flemish. Ash made herself smile.

Di Conti, his grin fading slightly, added, "It saves us crowding in, boss!"

"Well, I guess it saves half of you sitting on my lap! Right." Ash abruptly about-faced, striding back to the centre of camp.

Walking, thinking furiously, she did not at first notice herself being shadowed by a very large, dark-haired man. His skin was pale despite the south Burgundian sun, and his sparse beard black, and he stood – she continued to look up, and up – something above six foot high. One of the dogs yelped at him and he skipped, surprisingly lightly, to one side.

"You're . . . Faversham," she recalled.

"Richard Faversham," he confirmed, in English.

"You're Godfrey's assistant priest." She could not, for some reason, find the English term in her mind.

"Deacon. Do you wish me to hold mass until Master Godfrey returns?" Richard Faversham asked, solemnly.

The Englishman was not much above her own age; sweating as he walked in the dark green robes of a priest, the sharp edges of cut straw spiking in vain against the hardened soles of his feet. One cheek had a small cross tattooed on it in blue ink. A clanking mass of saint's medals hung suspended around his neck. Ash, identifying several prominent St Barbara's,[11] thought he might have the right idea.

"Yes. Has he notified you of when he's coming back from," she crossed her fingers behind her back, "Dijon?"

Deacon Faversham smiled benevolently. "No, boss. I make allowances for Master Godfrey's unworldliness. If there is a poor man, or a sick man, and he's met them, he'll stay until he's remedied their trouble."

Ash nearly choked, coming to a dead stop amid men-at-arms, leashed

---

[11] St Barbara, a Roman saint previously appealed to for protection against being struck by lightning, was adopted as the patron saint of gunners, presumably on the grounds that one explosion is very like another.

hounds, tent guy-ropes, and the round balls of sweet-smelling horse droppings. "'Unworldly'? *Godfrey?*"

Richard Faversham's small black eyes narrowed uncertainly against the sunlight. His voice, however, remained sure. "Master Godfrey will be a saint one day. There's no billman so low, or whore so dirty, that he won't bring them God's Bread and Wine. I've known him minister to a sick child forty hours at a stretch – and do the same with a sick hound. He'll be one of the Community of Saints, when he dies."

Ash, her breath returning, managed to say, "Well, at the moment, I could do with him on earth! If you see him, tell him boss needs him *now*; meanwhile, go prepare for a mass."

She moved on, back to the command tent, diverting only once – to speak briefly to John de Vere; and the visiting Olivier de la Marche, conveniently in conversation with the English Earl – and then stood under the Lion Azure standard, in front of her tent, and called all her officers out into the open piece of ground.

They stumbled out into the bright Burgundian sun: Geraint with his points undone and his split hose rolled down to his calves, Robert Anselm in breast-and backplate; Angelotti in a white silk doublet – Ash muttered "*white!*" and "*silk!*" under her breath in equal amazement, noting her master gunner to be clean – and Joscelyn van Mander, blinking hooded eyes against the glare.

She lifted her arm. Euen Huw put a clarion to his mouth and blew for general assembly. She was not too surprised at the speed with which the men made their way to the empty ground at the centre of camp, crowding it, pushing back into the open fire-break paths between the tents. Sometimes, she mused, the rumours of what I'm going to do get around before *I've* thought of it . . .

"Okay!" Ash pushed a squawking hen off an upturned barrel, at the foot of the Lion Azure standard, and sprang neatly up on top of it. She put her hands on her hips. The blue and gold standard hung, stiffened, above her, no breeze to ripple it on the air, but you couldn't have everything, she thought, and let her gaze travel across the crowd, picking out faces here and there, smiling as she did so.

"Gentlemen," she said, projecting only enough that they had to be quiet to hear her. "Gentlemen – and I use the term loosely – you will be pleased to hear that we're going to war again."

A muted rumble greeted this, part pleasure, part groans of dismay (some of them genuine).

Ash did not know what her grin did to her face as she stood there facing them, did not quite realise how it made her face blaze with brightness, with a sincere content. It broadcast, in the anticipation of a battle, her absolute (if unconscious) certainty that all was right with the world.

"We're going to fight a battle against the Visigoths," she called. "Partly because we like the sun here in Burgundy! Mostly because my lord the Earl of Oxford is *paying* us to do this. But mainly," she added emphasis, "mainly we're fighting the Visigoth bitch because *I want my fucking armour back!*"

What had been raucous, deep male laughter and cheers came together as a shout of laughter, and a loud yell of triumph that almost jarred the earth under the upturned barrel. Ash held up both arms over her head. There was a silence.

"What about Carthage?" Blanche called from one of the wagons.

What did I say about rumour?

"That can wait!" Ash made herself grin. "Three or four days and we fight a field against the rag-heads. I've got you an advance on your pay. Your duties for the rest of today are to go out and get rat-arsed, and fuck every whore in Dijon twice! I don't—" The loudest roar of noise overwhelmed her, she tried to make herself heard, gave up, grinning so hard it hurt; and at the first drop in the sound level, completed what she had been going to say: "I don't want to see a sober man wearing the Lion Azure tonight!"

A Welsh voice shouted, "No danger of that, boss!"

Ash raised a silver brow at Geraint ab Morgan. "Did I say that included officers? I don't *think* so."

The noise at this was, if anything, louder than before; eight hundred male voices baying with pure pleasure. Ash felt herself lifted up on the adrenalin.

"Okay – whoa! I said, whoa! Shut *up*!" Ash took a breath. "That's better. Go get pissed. Go get laid. Those of you that *do* come back are going to fight a battle, and give the rag-heads fucking *hell*." She slammed a hand against the standard-pole, shaking the folds of the silk above her. "Remember, I don't want you guys to die for your flag – I want you to make the Visigoths die for theirs!"

There was a cheer for that, and men at the back of the crowd beginning to drift away. Ash nodded once to herself, and turned around precariously on the barrel. "Mynheer van Mander!"

That stopped most of them moving. Joscelyn van Mander stepped forward from the officers' group, his movements uncertain. He glanced around. Ash saw him make eye-contact with Paul di Conti and half a dozen Flemish lance-leaders.

"Come here." She beckoned, insistently. As soon as he came within reach, she bent down and seized his hand, shook it firmly, and turned to the men crowding in close, and held the Flemish knight's arm up with hers. "This man! I am going to do something I haven't done before—" she leaned forward and embraced the startled van Mander, her cheek against his rough cheek.

Deep voices whooped, in startlement and glee. Those men-at-arms and knights who had begun to drift off pushed back into the central ground. A thunder of questions arose.

"Okay!" Ash spun around, holding both hands up again, and getting silence. "I want to publicly acknowledge my debt to this man. Here and now! He's done great things for the Lion Azure. The only thing is – there's nothing else I can teach him!"

Flemish men-at-arms, deliriously proud, banged fists against breastplates, their faces alight. Van Mander's broad features were caught halfway between pride and apprehension. Ash kept herself from grim laughter. *Get out of this one, sonny . . .*

Waiting while the noise died down again, she watched Paul di Conti's face, the other lance-leaders. And Joscelyn van Mander's expression.

Your officers don't take orders from me now, they take orders from you. Therefore they are not my officers . . .

Therefore, they have no reason to be in my camp.

"Sir Joscelyn," she said, strongly and formally, "there is a time for the apprentice and the journeyman to leave the master. I have taught you everything I know. It is no longer for me to command you. It is time now for you to lead your own company."

She gauged the quality of the hush that followed; judged it satisfactory.

She swung her arm around, indicating the assembled troops. "Joscelyn, there are twenty lances, two hundred Flemish men here, who will follow you. I myself began the Lion Azure with no smaller number of men."

"But I don't want to leave the Lion Azure," van Mander blurted.

Ash kept a smile on her face.

Of course you don't. You'd rather stay as a significant number of men and officers in my company, and try and sway the way *I* run it. That's why you want a weak leader – you get all the power and none of the responsibility.

Put you on your own and you're a very small number of men, with no influence whatsoever, and the buck stops with *you*. Well, tough. I've had enough of this company-within-a-company. I've had enough of things I can't trust – Stone Golem included. I certainly won't take a split company into a battle in four days' time . . .

Joscelyn van Mander began frowning. "I won't leave."

"I have—" Ash spoke loudly over him, getting their attention again. "I have spoken to my lord of Oxford, and my lord Olivier de la Marche, Duke's Champion of Burgundy."

A pause to let that sink in.

"If you wish, Sir Joscelyn, my lord Oxford will give you a contract with him. Or, if you want to be employed on the same terms as Cola de Monforte and his sons," – she saw the famous names of these mercenaries hit home among the Flemish lances, and moreover, saw van Mander see it – "*then Charles, Duke of Burgundy, will employ you direct.*"

The Flemish knights roared. Looking around, Ash could already judge which of the Flemish men-at-arms would be sneaking back into the Lion Azure camp tonight under assumed names; and which English billmen would be speaking fluent Walloon under Olivier de la Marche's direct command.

Ash shifted her weight back on to one heel. The upturned barrel was solid beneath her. She let the warm air blow over her face, and, with one finger to the mail standard at her neck, let a little air into the sweaty warmth of her neck. Joscelyn van Mander looked up, his lips pressed together into a thin line. She could make a guess at the words he was holding back – would have to hold back, now, or precipitate a public quarrel.

Which will have the same effect: he and his lances will have to leave. Ash let her gaze travel over the heads of the men-at-arms, and the crowding support staff from the wagons; reckoning up with a practised eye how clean a split it might be.

Better five hundred men I can trust than eight hundred I'm doubtful about.

A hand tugged the skirt of her doublet. Ash looked down.

Richard Faversham, deacon, said in his high English voice, "Might we hold a celebratory mass, to pray for God's good fortune on this newly made company of the Flemish knights?"

Ash surveyed Faversham's face, boyish despite the black beard. "Yes. Good idea."

She lifted a fist for attention, got it, and projected her voice out to the edges of the crowd to make this known. Her own attention remained on Joscelyn van Mander, huddled in a knot with his officers. She checked by line of sight where her escort was, where her dogs were, and the impassive expressions of Robert Anselm and Geraint and Angelotti. Nowhere in the packed mass of people could she pick out Florian de Lacey, or Godfrey Maximillian.

Fuck, she thought, and turned back to find Paul di Conti raising, on a bill-shaft, a hastily tied livery coat – one of van Mander's original ones: the Ship and Crescent Moon. This makeshift standard lifted into the air, the better part of the two hundred men that Ash had earmarked for this began to move towards it.

"Before you leave the camp," she said, "we will hear mass, and pray for your souls, and for ours. And pray that we meet again, Mynheer van Mander, in four days, with the army of the Visigoths lying dead on the earth between us."

As Deacon Faversham raised his voice to order things, Ash got down from the barrel, and found herself standing beside John de Vere, Earl of Oxford.

The Earl turned from a conversation with Olivier de la Marche. "More news, madam Captain. The Duke's intelligence brings him word that the Visigoth lines are overstretched – their supplies liable to be cut off. There are Turkish troops a scant ten miles from here."

"*Turks?*" Ash stared at the Englishman. He, composed, and with a glint of excitement in his faded blue eyes, murmured, "Yes, madam. Six hundred of the Sultan's cavalry."

"Turks. Fuck me." Ash took two steps on the rough turf and straw, ignoring the crowd of men; swung around, her gaze elsewhere, calculating. "No, it makes sense! It's exactly what I'd do, if I were the Sultan. Wait for the Carthaginian army to commit itself, take out their supply lines, get them cut up by us, and pick up the pieces . . . Does Duke Charles *really* think he won't have a Turkish army on his doorstep, the morning after we beat the Visigoths?"

"He is anxious," the Earl said gravely, "to have an army left, to take the field against them. He is calling his priests to him, now."

Ash absently crossed herself.

"For the rest," de Vere added, "the bulk of his army will march south, detachments moving today and tomorrow: we move with the rest of the mercenaries, the morning after next. Leave a base camp here. Get your men ready for a forced march. We will see, madam, how much of a commander you are without your saints."

Twenty-four hours passed in chaos, herded into order by the Lion's officers: neither Ash nor any man in the command group slept more than two hours.

Yellow clouds massed on the western horizon, flickering with summer lightning. Humid heat increased. Men scratched under constricting armour, swore; fights broke out over loading kit on to packhorses. Ash was everywhere. She listened to three, four, five different voices at a time, gave orders, responded, checked supplies, checked weapons; dealt with the provosts and gate-guards.

She held her final command meeting in the armoury tent, in the stink of charcoal, fires, soot, and the banging of munition harness being hammered out rough and ready.

"Green Christ!" Robert Anselm yelled, wiping his streaming forehead. "Why can't it fucking rain?"

"You want to march this lot in bad weather? We're *lucky*!"

The oppressiveness of the storm nonetheless made Ash's head throb. She shifted, uncomfortably, as Dickon Stour strapped a new greave to her shins, the metal rough and black from the forge. She flexed her knee to the ninety-degree angle that that armour allowed.

"No, it's cutting into the back of my knee." She watched him undo roughly riveted straps. "Leave it: I've got boots, I'll just wear upper leg harness and poleyns."

"I got you a breastplate." Dickon Stour turned, picked it up, held it out in black hands. "I've cut the arm-holes back?"

There is not time to forge a new harness. She turned, let him hold it against her, brought her arms together in front of her as if she gripped a sword. The breastplate's edges rammed into her inner arms. "Too wide. Cut it back again. I don't care about rolled edges on the metal, I just want something I can wear for four hours, that'll deflect arrows."

The armourer grunted discontentedly.

"Have the Great Duke's men gone?"

"Moved out at dawn," Geraint ab Morgan shouted, over the noise of arrow-heads being hammered out, at production-line speed.

In these twenty-four hours, nearly twenty thousand men and supplies have gone south: it will take them until the feast-day of the saint to cover the forty miles between here and Auxonne, here and the Faris's army. Empty dust, mud, and trodden common ground surrounds Dijon. The town and the country for miles around are stripped of supplies.

Summer thunder rumbled, all but inaudible under the sharp clangs of the armourers hammering out arrow-heads by the hundred. Ash thinks briefly of the road south. A few miles down the river valley and Dijon will be behind them: there is nothing but a few farms, villages in clearings in the forest, and great swathes of empty pasture, common land, and wilderness. An empty world.

"Okay – two hours and we ride."

Travelling south, the land grows colder.

By evening, ten miles south of Dijon, Ash rode aside from the long column of men and packhorses, spurring her riding horse up on to a rise. Smudges of black rose from fields ahead.

"What's that?" She leaned down to Rickard, as the boy ran up.

"They're trying to save the vines!"

320

"*Vines?*"

"I asked this old guy? They had frost here last night. They're making smoky fires in the vineyard, trying to keep the frost from forming tonight. Otherwise there'll be no harvest."

Two or three men-at-arms were riding out from the column: further orders needed. Ash spared one more glance for the hillsides and the vineyards, row upon long row of cropped vines clinging to the earth; and the distant figures of peasants moving between the smudge-fires.

"Damn; no wine," she said. Turning her horse, she noted Rickard had four or five fresh coney-carcasses slung off his belt.

"This will be a bad year," the Earl of Oxford remarked, bringing his barrel-chested gelding up with her.

"I'll tell the lads we're fighting for the wine harvest. *That'll* make them kick Visigoth ass!"

The English Earl narrowed his gaze, staring at the countryside to the south. One church's double spire marked an isolated village. For the rest, there was nothing but forests, uncultivated land; the road to Auxonne clearly marked by deep ruts, horse-droppings, trodden grass and the debris of an army passing.

"At least we shan't ride astray," Ash ventured.

"Twenty thousand is an unwieldy number of men, madam."

"It's more than she's got."

The evening sky darkened in the east. And now, perceptibly, darkened in the south as well: a shadow that did not fade with any day's dawn, the closer they drew to Auxonne.

"So that is the Eternal Twilight," the Earl of Oxford said. "It grows, the closer we come."

On the eve of the twenty-first of August, the Lion encampment stretched under the eaves of the wildwood three miles west of Auxonne. Ash picked her way between makeshift shelters, and men queuing for the evening rations, being careful to seem cheerful whenever she spoke to anyone.

Henri Brant, the chief groom with him, walked up to ask, "Will we fight before tomorrow morning? Shall we start feeding the war-horses up in preparation?"

Even trained war-horses are still herbivores who need to constantly graze for strength. More than an hour's fight, and they will lose stamina.

A thunder-purple sky was just visible through the oak leaves above her head; humid air moved against her skin. Ash wiped her face. "Assume the horses will need to be fit to fight any hour between dawn and nine, tomorrow. Start giving them the enriched feed."

"Yes, boss."

Thomas Rochester and the rest of her escort had fallen into conversation, under the trees, with Blanche and some of the other women. Ash breathed in, realised *No one is asking me questions! Amazing!* and then let out a sigh.

Shit. I preferred it when I didn't have time to think.

And there's still something to do.

"I'm not going far," she said to the nearest man-at-arms. "Tell Rochester I'm in the physic-tent."

Floria's tent stood a few yards away. Ash stumbled over guy-ropes tethering it to tree-trunks, in the root-knotted soil, as the sky yellowed and the first big drops of cold rain dropped on to the leaves above.

"Boss?" Deacon Faversham said, emerging from the tent.

Concealing apprehension, Ash said, "Is the master surgeon there?"

"She's inside." The Englishman did not seem at all uncomfortable.

Ash nodded an acknowledgement, and ducked under the tent-flap he held up. Inside, by the light of a number of lanterns, she saw not an empty tent, as she had feared, but half a dozen men on pallets. Their conversation stopped abruptly, then picked up in undertones.

"We're moving too fast." Floria del Guiz, bandaging an arm fracture, didn't look up. "In my office, boss."

Ash, with a word to the injured men – two crushed foot injuries, from loading sword-boxes on to packhorses; one burn; one self-inflicted injury with a dagger, falling over when drunk – went through the inner, empty chamber of the pavilion, to the small curtained-off area at the far end.

Rain rattled on the tent roof. She used flint and tinder to light a candle, lit the remaining lanterns with that, and was just done when Floria pulled the curtain aside, entering and sitting down with a curt grunt.

Going directly to it, Ash said, "Men with injuries are still coming to the company surgeon, then?"

Floria raised her head, hair falling back from her face. "I've had nineteen hurt men in here, the last two days. You'd think no one ever hit me—!"

She broke off, and put her dirty fingers together, fingertip to fingertip.

"Ash, you know what? They've decided not to think about it. Not for now. Maybe, when they've been hacked up, they won't care who's sewing them back together. But maybe they will."

Floria looked up sharply at Ash.

"They don't treat me as a man now. Nor as a woman. A eunuch, maybe. A neuter."

Ash pulled up a back-stool and sat down; silent while one of the lay assistants came to pour wine, and bring Floria a light cloak against the summer night's chill.

Ash said carefully, "We'll be fighting tomorrow. Everybody's too busy, right now, preparing. Most of the troublemakers went with van Mander. The rest can either lynch you – or have their lives saved when they're injured. In a lot of ways, we need this fight."

The woman surgeon snorted. She reached out for wine, in an ash-wood cup. "Do we, Ash? Do we need to see those young men chopped and stabbed and stuck with arrows?"

"That's war," Ash said levelly.

"I know. I could always work elsewhere. Plague towns. Lazar-houses. Jewish children, that Christian physicians won't touch." Shadows from the swinging lamps made the woman's features merciless. "Maybe tomorrow will be worth it."

"This isn't Arthur's last battle," Ash said cynically. "This isn't Camlann. We don't beat them here and then they pack up and go home. Winning the field doesn't give us the war, even if we wipe them out."

"So what does happen?"

"We've got nearly a two-to-one advantage. I'd prefer three, but we'll beat them. Charles's army is probably the best, most advanced left in Christendom."

Unspoken, Ash's thought is *But the Faris beat the Swiss.*

"Maybe we kill the Faris, maybe we don't. Either way, if she's defeated here, she doesn't have much of an army left, and her momentum's gone. It's one of those things: once they've *been* beaten, then they can be beaten."

"And then?"

"And then there's two more Carthaginian armies out there." Ash grinned. "Either they do pick a soft target – maybe France – or they dig in over winter, or they fall out with the Sultan. The last one's ideal. Then it isn't Burgundy's problem any more. Or Oxford's. He goes back to the *goddams'* wars."

"And we go and get paid by the Sultan?"

"By any side but hers," Ash confirmed.

Acute, and unwelcome, Florian said, "You want to speak to her again. Don't you?"

"I can get by without a machine's voice in my head. I've been fighting since I was twelve." Ash sounded harsh. "What does it matter, in practical terms? What can she tell me, Florian? What can she tell me that I don't already know?"

"How and why you came to be born?"

"What does that matter? I grew up in camps," Ash said, "like an animal. You don't know about that. I feed my baggage train, I don't let them sink or swim on what they can plunder when the soldiers have had the best of it. The only time someone will starve is when we *all* starve."

"But the Faris is your . . ." Floria paused, questioningly. "Sister."

"Several times over, possibly," Ash said, ironically. "She's quite mad, Florian. She sat there and told me, her father breeds son to dam, and daughter to sire – she means he breeds slave-children back to their parents. Generations of the sin of incest. Christ, I wish Godfrey was here."

"Every village has *that.*"

"But not so—" Ash groped in vain for the word *systematically.*

"Their scientist-magi have given Christendom most of the medical skills I learned," Floria said, "Angelotti learned his gunnery from an *amir.*"

"And so?"

"And so, your *machina rei militaris* isn't evil." Floria shook her head. "Godfrey never said it was a sin, did he? If you haven't got the use of it, that's sad; but never mind, you can do your butchery quite well on your own, we all know that."

"Mmm."

Floria said bluntly, "Is it true Godfrey's left the company?"

"I – don't know. I haven't seen him in days. Not since we left Dijon."

"Faversham told me he'd seen him with the Visigoths."

"*With* the Visigoths? The delegation?"

"Talking to Sancho Lebrija." When Ash said nothing, the woman added, "I can't see Godfrey going over to them. What is this, Ash? What's going on with you and him?"

"If I could tell you, I would." Ash got up and walked restlessly around. Deliberately changing the subject, she said, "The town militia never came out to the camp. Mistress Châlon must have kept quiet."

Staccato, Floria snapped, "She would. She'd have to admit I'm her niece. She won't do that. I'm safe enough if I stay away from Dijon. If I claim nothing from her."

"You still think of yourself as Burgundian," Ash realised.

"Oh yes."

Floria's dark gaze felt oddly foreign, Ash thought, bearing in mind that none of them had what might be termed a nationality. She smiled. "I don't think of myself as Carthaginian. Not after all this time. I always assumed I was Christendom's bastard."

Floria chuckled, deeply, and poured more wine.

"War doesn't have a kingdom," she said. "War belongs to the whole world. Come on, my little scarlet Horseman. Have a drink."

She stood, unsteadily, and walked behind Ash, a hand on her shoulder, to put the cup down in front of her.

"I didn't thank you for seeing those guys off," she said.

Ash gave a modest shrug, leaning back against Florian.

"Well, thanks anyway." Florian dipped her head. Her lips pressed, very lightly and quickly, against Ash's mouth.

"Christ!" Ash sprang up and pushed her way out of what seemed to be encircling female arms. "Christ!"

"What?"

Ash wiped the back of her hand across her mouth. "Christ!"

"*What?*"

An expression came to Ash's face that she was entirely unaware of: flat, cynical, tense. Her eyes, blank, seemed to be seeing something quite different from her surgeon.

"I'm not your little Margaret Schmidt! What is this? You think you can seduce me like your brother?"

Floria del Guiz stood up slowly. She went to say something, stopped, and spoke with restraint. "You're talking complete nonsense, Ash. This is – nonsense. And leave my brother out of this!"

"Everybody wants something." Ash, standing with her arms limp by her sides, shook her head. Above, the canvas cone of the tent roof shifted, under the drumming of chill rain.

Floria del Guiz made as if to reach out and thought better of it. She sat back.

"Ah." Floria stared at her toes. She paused, then, looking up, said, "I don't seduce my friends."

Ash stared at her in silence.

"One day," Floria added, "I'll tell you about being kicked out of my home at thirteen, and going to Salerno, dressed as a man, because I'd heard they let women study there. Well, I was wrong. Things have changed since Trotula's day.[12] And I'll tell you why Jeanne Châlon, who is my mother in all but name, commands no 'loyalty' from me whatsoever. Boss, you're all to pieces. Come on." Floria gave a lopsided grin. "Ash, *honestly*!"

The scorn in that brought colour to Ash's face, partly from shame, partly from relief; and she shrugged with an attempt at carelessness. "It's been a rough few days, I'll give you that. Floria, I'm sorry. It was a genuinely stupid thing for me to say."

"Mmm-hmm." Floria flirted an eyebrow at her, over-doing the naturalness somewhat. "C'mon."

Ash turned, moving towards the tent-flap, and standing looking out. From this point, under the edge of the trees, it was possible to see the fires of the main Burgundian army, further south, and the growing silver of the moon.

About two days before first quarter, she thought, automatically estimating its swelling curve. *It is only a few weeks.*

"Christ, so much has happened! What is it, about the middle of August now? And the skirmish at Neuss was the middle of June. Two months. Hell, I've only been *married* for six weeks—"

"Seven weeks. Hey." Floria's voice came from behind her, in the tent. "Have more wine."

The moon rising over the eastern hills blurred silver in Ash's field of vision. "Boss?"

She turned around, everything suddenly sharp and clear: the painted anatomy charts hanging on the tent walls; Floria's face with the casual laughter falling from it. The kind of clarity that comes with shock or combat, she thought, and said, "Florian, did I pass blood when I was ill?"

Floria del Guiz shook her head, frowning. "No, I watched. There was no flux of blood at all. It wasn't that kind of injury."

Ash shook her head dumbly.

"Christ," she said at last. "Not that kind of blood. Woman's blood. I've missed twice, this month and last month. I'm pregnant."

VI

The two women stared at each other.

"Didn't you use something?" Floria demanded.

"Of course I did! Do you think I'm stupid? Baldina gave me a charm to wear. As a wedding present. I had it in a little bag around my neck, both times we— every time." Ash felt the close evening air bring sweat out on her forehead. Her injury throbbed dully.

[12] The eleventh century Dame Trotula of Salerno was a clinician, and the author of *Passionibus Mulierum Curandorum* (*The Diseases of Women*), among other medical works. She was regarded as one of the foremost medical authorities of the mediaeval period. Other 'mulieres Salernitanae' or women physicians were also trained in Salerno, but this practice may have ceased by the fifteenth century.

She saw Floria del Guiz survey her: did not know that the woman was seeing a young girl in hose and a big doublet; sword belted at her side, and gloves tucked under the belt; nothing female about her except her cascade of hair, and her face, momentarily looking all of twelve years old.

"You used a charm." Floria's voice sounded flat. She spoke quietly, as if afraid they could be heard outside. "You didn't use a sponge, or a pig's bladder, or herbs. You used a charm."

"It's always worked before!"

"Thank *Christ* I don't have to worry about any of this! I wouldn't touch a man if—" Floria took two or three quick steps, back and forth on the boards laid down against mud, her arms tucked tightly about her body. She stopped in front of Ash. "You feel sick at all?"

"I thought that was the head injury."

"Tits tender?"

Ash considered. "I guess."

"And you bleed what time of the moon?"

"It's been the last quarter, most of this year."

"When did you last bleed?"

Ash frowned, thinking back. "Just before Neuss. Sun was still in Gemini."

"I'll have to look at you. But you're pregnant." Floria spoke with conclusive abruptness.

"You're going to have to give me something!"

"What?"

Ash reached behind herself with one hand, touching the back-stool, and slid down to a sitting position, adjusting her scabbard. She brought her hands around in front of her, clasping them first across her belly, and then around the grip of her sword. "You're going to have to give me something to get rid of it!"

The blonde woman dropped her arms to her sides. The lantern swung, as the tent creaked in the night wind. She squinted uncertainly into the light at Ash's face. "You haven't thought about this."

"I've thought!" Cold inside, flooded by terror, Ash gripped the leather-bound wood of her sword-hilt and stared down at the faceted, wheel-shaped pommel. She had a sudden urge to draw the blade, and cut. An urge to proclaim that her self is still her self. She tried to feel any sensation inside her body, to feel a difference, and felt nothing. No sense that she might be carrying a foetus.

"I can give you herbs in wine, to calm you down," Floria said.

With that note of caution, of professional calming of an overwrought patient, Ash's rage flared. She stood up. "I'm not going to be treated like some whore off the street! I will not have this baby."

"You'll have it." Floria del Guiz took hold of her arm.

"I will not. You'll have to cut it out of me." Ash shook herself free. "Don't tell me there's no surgery for that. When I was growing up in the wagons, any woman who would have died from another baby got rid of it by the company surgeon."

"No. I've sworn an oath." Floria's voice became flat, angry, tired. "You

326

remember your *condotta*? This is mine. 'Never to procure an abortion.' For anybody!"

"And now they know you're a woman, they say you haven't got the wit to take an oath. *That's* what your fraternity of doctors think of you!" Ash shifted her blade an inch out of the scabbard, and banged it home. "I will not have that man's child!"

"You're sure it's his, then?"

The slap was deliberate, a solid whack across the face that left Floria's cheek bright red, and her eyes running water. Ash yelled, "*Yes*, it's his!"

Floria's dirty face shone, some emotion twisting her features that Ash couldn't identify. "It's a legitimate baby. Christ, Ash. It could be my nephew! My niece! You can't ask me to kill it."

"It's not quickened, it hasn't kicked, it's *nothing*." Ash glared. "You didn't understand me, did you? Listen to me: I will not have this baby. If you won't abort it, I'll find someone who can, *I will not have this baby*."

"No? You'll come round. Trust me." Floria shook her head. Snot ran clear from her nostril, and she wiped her sleeve across her face, leaving a smear of clean skin. She laughed, a break in her voice: "You won't have it? Not when it's his, and you can't keep your hands off him?"

Ash's mouth remained a little open; she said nothing. Her mind struggled, racing for a reply. A sudden picture came into her mind of a small child, about three years of age, with solemn green eyes and flaxen hair. A child to run about the camp, fall off horses, cut itself on the edges of weapons, be sick of a fever, die maybe in a famine some lean year; a child that would have the same features as Fernando del Guiz, and maybe the same humour as Floria—

She met the eyes of Floria del Guiz and said with utter certainty, "You're jealous."

"You think I want a baby."

"Yes! And you never will have." Conscious of saying the unforgivable, powered more by fear than rage, Ash plunged on in razor-edged sarcasm: "What are you going to do, get Margaret Schmidt pregnant? A niece or nephew is as close as you'll get."

"That's true."

"Uh." Ash, expecting her rage, was confused. "I'm sorry I said it, but it *is* true, isn't it?"

"Jealous." Floria looked at Ash with an expression that might have been sardonic humour, or relief, or betrayal; or all three. "Because I won't cut a baby out of your belly. Woman, I don't want to see you bleed to death or die of childbed fever; but for Christ's sake *have* the thing! You won't die. You're strong as a bloody peasant, you can probably drop it one day and get back on your war-horse the next. Don't you understand that getting rid of it is *dangerous*?"

"A battlefield isn't *safe*!" Ash remarked with asperity. "Look, I'd as soon not go to a city doctor, I don't trust them, money-grubbing bastards, and besides, there isn't time to get one now. I don't want to use the remedies they use on the wagons unless I have to. And I trust you because you've patched me up every time someone's hacked a chunk out of me!"

"Holy Saint Magdalen! Are you completely stupid? You – might – die."

"Am I supposed to be impressed? I train for that every day. I'm fighting tomorrow!"

Floria del Guiz opened her mouth and shut it again.

Unhappy, Ash said, "I don't want to give you an order."

"An order?" Floria's face, in profile, dripped a clear drop from her eye, that still ran from Ash's blow. She didn't look at Ash. "And what are you going to do if I *don't* perform an abortion? Throw me out of the company? But you'll have to do that anyway."

"Christ, Florian, no!"

Her hand came up and grabbed Ash's arm. "It isn't 'Florian', it's 'Floria', I'm a *woman*. I love other women!"

"I know that," Ash said, hastily. "Look, I—"

"You don't know it!" Floria let go of Ash's arm. She stood for a moment with her head lowered, and then turned her face to Ash. "You don't have the slightest idea, don't tell me you do. What am I supposed to do when people go mad around me, because I've lain with a woman? What? I can't *fight* them. I couldn't hurt them even if I did! I *have* to pretend I'm something I'm not. What if someone decides to burn me because I'm a woman-lover and I practise medicine?"

Ash shifted uncomfortably.

Floria del Guiz held out her hands, palm up.

In the cool air and lantern light, Ash saw familiar white marks on the surgeon's fingers.

Floria said, "These are burn scars. Old burns. I got them trying to drag – trying to drag something out of a fire, after it was much too late, because I wanted just something, a relic, a memory, if I couldn't have her alive, with me, with me." Floria pushed her hands across her face, sweat and tears dampening her hair. "Some man *pissed* on you once and you think you know about this? Don't you tell me you know what it's like, you thug, because you *don't* know! You've never been defenceless in your life!"

The empty air echoed to her shout. Outside the tent, the guards stirred. Ash walked to the tent-flap, to give quiet orders.

Floria del Guiz spat, "So now you're having a baby. So welcome to being a woman!"

"Christ, Floria," Ash protested.

She didn't let Ash finish. "Maybe you shouldn't have been so damn eager to fuck my brother!"

Ash could only look at her. Between amazement and the shock of feeling kicked in the gut, she couldn't put her thoughts in order to find an answer, couldn't say anything at all.

"I'd do anything for you! I always have. But I won't do this!" Floria's voice scaled up an octave. "Don't just sit there! *Say something!* "

Ash stared in panicked silence; tried to speak; then dropped her gaze from the woman's fierce face and stared down at the rush-strewn forest-earth.

Clear and decisive, the thought came into her head: *I should tell Fernando.* But if it's a son, he'll take it away from me.

And I can't have it, anyway.

More than one woman's ridden into battle with a belly on her.

Yes, and more than one woman's got a fever after the birth and died, and the surgeons no use to her at all.

Equally clearly, a realisation came to her: I won't have it *because* it's his.

Floria's voice snarled, "*Ash!*"

Ash ignored her.

Very cautiously, she began to consider the thought of carrying the baby to term.

It isn't that long out of my life. Months. Bad timing, though, if we're facing war . . . well, women have fought wars like this before. They'd still follow me. I'd make damn sure of it.

The strength of her fear of her body changing out of her control, the sheer enormity of that physical reality, left her amazed. *But when it's done? Born?* Conscious that she was, to some degree, indulging herself in a pretty dream, Ash imagined a son or a daughter.

At least then I'll have blood kin. Someone who looks like me.

With that, a chill quite literally moved the hairs on the back of her neck.

You've already got someone who looks like you. *Exactly* like you.

And who knows what I'd give birth to? Some deformed village idiot? Christ and all the saints, no! I can't give birth to a monster.

It must already be more than forty days.. I've got to get rid of it now, before it quickens.

Before it gets a soul.

The woman's voice abruptly broke her concentration:

"I'm off. What am I supposed to do? Wait for you for ever? Sit around here until those assholes out there make up their minds whether a dyke doctor is just fine and dandy? *Keep* your damn company."

Floria turned and walked away, to the tent-flap; not slowing as she went out.

"*And* your baby! It's your problem, Ash. Solve it. You don't need me. Ash doesn't need anybody! I'll be with the Duke's Surgeon-General on the field tomorrow – where I can do what I trained for."

Before dawn, with the woods scarcely light enough to move without stumbling, Ash went out with the other commanders to walk the ground for the battle.

Air moved against her face. Condensation gathered on the inside of her helmet's visor, smelling of rust and armouries. Her boots skidded on the wet leaves. She almost barged into the Earl of Oxford, standing back a little from the main group of the Duke of Burgundy and his officers on the Dijon–Auxonne road. A growing paleness on her left showed her John de Vere's silhouette.

Ash asked quietly, "Is the Visigoth army still in position? What's the Duke planning?"

"They are. The Duke will fight this field outside Auxonne," Oxford murmured succinctly. He added, "Their campfires are where the scouts reported, near enough. A half-mile south, on the main road. You and I, madam, are to take the left of the line, with his other mercenaries."

"He doesn't trust us, does he? Or he'd put us on the right, where the fighting's heaviest."[13] Ash slid her hand down to adjust the buckle of her cuisse: even with an extra hole bored in the strap, the borrowed leg armour did not fit her very well. "Will he at least let us try a flying wedge attack? We could take out the Faris."

"The Duke says not: she will have battle doubles[14] on the field."

The silhouettes of shoulders moved against the light. Here the road and river swung suddenly away east, on her left hand, away from the shallow slope blocking the river valley to the south. Men moved off the road, on to rough pasture, striding up the hill in front of them. The sky was barely brighter than the earth. Ash realised de Vere's brothers were with him; peered over her shoulder for Anselm – present – and a bleary-eyed Angelotti.

"Okay," Ash said steadily to Oxford, as they stumbled into the cold morning, "so we might have to take her out several times! Let me put a snatch-squad together, my lord. Go round the flanks with about a hundred of us, we could be in and out and away. It's been done."

"The Duke requests that I bring your company to the field, under his banner," Oxford said, voice bleak. "We do as we're commanded. And hope that by this evening it is no longer necessary to think about raiding Carthage."

The ground lifted under her feet. Dew blackened the leather of her boots, and the lower part of her scabbard. The air remained chill, but clear: no more rain.

"My lord, my sources—" Godfrey's contacts now reporting direct to her "—say they're still bringing up supplies, in the dark. We might have caught them on the hop," Ash said. "Some of their wagons are being pulled by their messenger-golems. Maybe they're desperate!"

"God send they are overstretched," de Vere said, grimly for a man with a force that outnumbers his enemy.

Boots skidding in mud, Ash topped the hill, her breathing harsh in her own ears; and peered out across the dimness.

A spur of hill here jutted into the river valley. They stood on its shallow western knoll, with the ancient wildwood hard up on her right hand. No way to move troops through it. Scouts reported not walking the ground so much as scrambling ten feet above it on clotted deadfalls.

This should bring us north of their camp – wonder if the heralds have gone down yet? Well, at least we found each other. . . ! Could have wandered around this wilderness for days.

The temptation to murmur, to that interior part of herself that hears a voice, *Battle commander, Visigoth army, probable location?* is almost irresistible.

Could the machina rei militaris answer that one? Would it lie? Would she know I've asked—?

No point wondering. Act as if she would. It's the only safe thing to do.

They set off down the slope in front. She clattered in the Duke of Burgundy's wake, aware that most other commanders would ride the ground, but that

---

[13] Since most combatants are right-handed, close combat battles tend to rotate anti-clockwise.
[14] Wearing duplicate armour and livery.

Duke Charles wants to know what this hill is like for men on foot, and men with gun-carriages. She was mildly impressed; cheered. Rapid, low-voiced conferences went on ahead of her. She squinted into the weak light of dawn.

Her strides ate up ground, going downhill, and her calves ached. At the foot of the long slope, she noted that the ground was squashy – thickets and reeds blocked the dawn, that side: marshes, maybe? On this edge of the river?

The pre-dawn greyness did not grow any brighter.

A skyline of hills and thick forest, ahead. A faint bell split the darkness, maybe from the abbey in Auxonne. She had the thought, *Are the other side out walking the territory, right now? If we met—!*

The officers and Duke's men moved off, Cola de Monforte saying something quietly. She heard only *perfect choke-point*. Walking back around the eastern end of the spur, they met the road beside the river. Movement became easier with the ground sure underfoot. Ash glanced up at the steeper eastern end of the spur, overhanging the Dijon road.

If we set up on the ridge, that's going to be the left of the line; that's where we'll be. If they try to move past on the road, we'll hit their unprotected backs. If they try and flank us up that cliff— well, I don't know about the rest of the Burgundian army, but we're going to be fine!

Except that what they'll do is prep for combat, and come straight up that southern slope at us . . .

The voice of Duke Charles of Burgundy said, "My lords, we shall return to camp. It is clear in my mind. We will fight as soon this saint's-day morning as we may. Sidonius favour us!"

A decision! Ash applauded wryly, in her own mind.

"Guys," she said.

"Boss?" Robert Anselm came instantly to her side in the morning darkness; Antonio Angelotti and Geraint ab Morgan treading on his heels.

The Earl of Oxford gave a stream of rapid orders; Dickon, George and Tom de Vere moved off about his business; he turned and said something to Viscount Beaumont, who laughed. An electricity spread throughout the group of men: knowing, now, that today will see a chance of being killed or of winning honour, money, survival.

"God pardon me if I have ever offended thee," Ash said formally, and reached up and embraced Robert Anselm. He gripped her, stepped back in the dew-soaked turf at the edge of the road, and said:

"As I hope to be forgiven, so I forgive thee, in God's name. We're going in, aren't we?"

Ash gripped Angelotti's forearm, whacked Geraint across the shoulders. Her eyes were bright.

"We're going in. Okay. This is where the Lion Azure does what it's paid to. Get them into battle array."

She speeded up, finishing the circuit, walking back towards the northern tree-line and the camp faster than was safe in the dim dawn, and caught up with the Earl of Oxford. She pointed to the Duke of Burgundy:

"If he won't let us take out the Faris . . . My lord Earl, I want to consult with you about the tactics of this battle. I have an idea."

331

George de Vere, behind her now, sardonic, said, "The four most terrifying words in the language, a woman saying *I have an idea.*"

"Oh, no." Ash smiled sweetly at him, in the dim light. "There are two words much more frightening – boss saying, *I'm bored.* You ask Fl— ask my surgeon."

John de Vere seemed to be smiling, under his raised visor

"We've got numbers," she said. "I don't think the Turks will come in on our side: they're observers. We've got guns. We ought to win it – but the Visigoths beat the Swiss and no one survived the field to tell us how they did it. Just rumours: 'They fight like Devils from the sulphurous Pits' . . ."

"And?" the Earl of Oxford prompted.

"My lord," she said steadily, "look at that sky. There'll be little or no sun today. When we fight this field, we'll be fighting under the shadow of their darkness. Cold, dim – a winter battle."

Unseen, she made a fist, dug her nails into her palms, and showed nothing of what she felt.

"We should talk to our priests." Ash pointed at the Briar Cross that hung around the Earl's neck, dark against his surcoat. "I've got an idea. Time for God to give us a miracle, your Grace."

Within two hours of walking the ground, Ash stood beside Godluc's warm flank, Bertrand holding the war-horse's reins, and Rickard carrying her helmet and lance. Her thigh armour was borrowed, from a short stocky English knight in de Vere's train. It did not fit.

Half the sky above her was black.

The east, where the sun should have risen on the massive army, was a towering darkness. Only behind them did an odd half-light stir cocks in the baggage wagons to crow late news of dawn.

Glancing downhill, south, she could no longer see the enemy campfires.

Behind her, that part of the sky that was not black had been covered with a back-shadow of morning light. Now it was becoming rapidly overcast, dark as the east and south. Clouds came together, chalk-yellow and fat-bellied, as tall as castle walls or cathedral spires.

Jesu Christ. Five hundred people *organised.* In place. Where they should be.

"I'm too knackered to fight!" she murmured.

Rickard grinned, palely. Her war-horse's breath steamed. Ash looked up the slope to the skyline and the multiple forces of the Burgundian army.

She thought, in the idle moment that follows extreme exertion: *The main view of a field of battle is legs.*

Dismounted, she has the impression of the field consisting of nothing but legs – horse's legs, by the hundred, some masked by livery caparisons hanging limp in the cold wet air, but most bare roan or bay or black: milling as the knights move over the crest of the slope into position. And men's legs, made slender by silver armour, all of the knights and most of the men-at-arms having steel on their lower limbs, even the archers' bright hose having steel cops strapped on over vulnerable knees. Hundreds of legs: feet treading down what had been some lord's wheat and was now churned mud and horse-shit.

Minutes ticking by: past the third hour of the morning, surely?

A flurry of cold, wet air blew into her face. Trumpets shrilled. She had barely time to glance back at Anselm, Angelotti, Geraint ab Morgan; all three of them with their clusters of sergeants, gun-captains and lance-leaders thronging around them, orders urgently, furiously being given.

"Mounting up," she murmured, and took her sallet from Rickard, manoeuvring it carefully over her braided hair, settling it down on her head. She let the buckle strap swing free for the moment. One foot finding the stirrup, she sprang lightly up into the saddle.

From here, high above ground, her view changed; the field becoming instead all helmets and standards. Silver against black thunderheads, a mass of steel shoulders blocked her view: knights wearing their articulated pauldrons. Riders crowded in knots, shouting to each other, wearing a throng of duck-tailed Italian sallets, and German sallets with long pointed tails, surmounted by heraldic Beasts; dim colours echoed by the sagging wet silk of their banners and standards above.

Robert Anselm slapped his hands together. "Fuck me, it's *cold*!"

"Everybody clear about what they're doing?"

"Yeah." Anselm had his sallet tipped back on his head. He looked out from under it at her. "Sure. All twenty thousand of us . . ."

"Yeah, right. Never mind. No plan ever survived ten minutes after the fighting started . . . we'll wing it."

Up on the backside of the hill here, Ash could look to left and right and see the Burgundian army riding and walking into place: twenty thousand strong.

"I think that's Olivier de la Marche's banner on the right wing," she pointed out to Rickard. The boy nodded jerkily. "And the mercenaries over on the left, and Charles's own banner there – the heavy armoured centre. You should study heraldry. We could do with a better herald in the Lion Azure."

His flaring black eyebrows dipped. "How many of them can fight, boss?"

"Hmm. Yes. That *may* be a better question than who's a Raven and Lion Couchant . . ." Ash felt her bowels rumble. "About two-thirds of them, I'd say. The rest are peasant levy and town militia."

She shifted Godluc a few steps, leaning sideways, not able to see Angelotti now with the other master gunners, the Duke having decided to mass his serpentines[15] in the centre.

"It's dysentery," she said firmly. "That's why I keep wanting to shit myself. It's dysentery."

Geraint ab Morgan, moving to stand by her other stirrup, nodded. "That's right, boss. Lot of it about this morning."

With a gesture to her officers, Ash rode at a gentle pace up the slope of the hill and over the crest, her personal banner borne behind her by Robert Anselm; to where Euen Huw and his lance guarded the Lion Azure standard, in the centre of five hundred fighting men. The pommel of her sword tapped arrhythmically against her plackart as she rode. A faint moisture began to sting her bare face and uncovered hands.

Where's the fucking enemy – *ah*. There.

Down at the foot of the deceptively gentle slope – *be a bitch to run up*, her

---

[15] Small field cannon.

mind commented – groups of darkness moved in darkness. Moving units of men. The glint of a banner-spike. A randy mare whinnying to the Frankish war-horses.

"How many men?" Robert Anselm murmured.

"Haven't a clue . . . *Too* many."

"It's always 'too many'," the older man observed. "Two peasants with a stick is 'too many'!"

Godfrey's deacon sprinted out from the mass of armed men. Ash automatically looked for Godfrey Maximillian to be with Richard Faversham – after four days, was still looking. She had stopped asking.

"What did the bishop say?" she demanded.

"He consents!" Richard Faversham spoke softly enough that she had to bend down from the saddle to hear him, awkward in a brigandine which is not designed to do that.

"How many priests have we?"

"With the army, upwards of four hundred. With the company, but two; myself and young Digorie here."

He's not mentioning Godfrey either. Are we both assuming he's left the company? Without a word?

Ash's bare fist hit the saddle's pommel. She stared down at her cold skin, and reached out for her gauntlets. Rickard, on toe-tip, put them into her hands. As she buckled the left one on, she continued to look down at Richard Faversham, and the intense, bony, dark young man he had introduced as Digorie.

"Are you ordained?" she asked him.

Digorie reached up a hand that appeared to be all knuckles, and gripped her remaining ungauntleted hand in an extremely powerful clasp. "Digorie Paston,[16] madam," he said, in English, "ordained back in Dijon by Charles's bishop. I won't let you or God down, ma'am."

Hearing the order in which he said it, Ash raised an eyebrow but managed to restrain herself from any comment.

"You're going to win this battle for us, Digorie, Richard," she said. "Well, you and the other three hundred and ninety-eight . . ."

Godluc responded to a touch of the spurs, bringing her around to where she could look down the hill, over the heads of her own men, towards the Visigoth army.

"Oh, *shit*," Ash remarked. "That's all we needed."

In the half-light, she could see dozens of Visigoth command flags, spanning the eastern road from Dijon towards Auxonne, and the thousands of marching and mounted men with them. Narrowing her eyes against the keen wet wind, she recognised positions: *they have anchored their right flank hard up against the marsh down* there, *in the north; and got the southern valley* there *sat on with four companies of troops, and—*

And.

"Well," Ash's voice sounded thin to her own ears, "that's us fucked. That's us well and *truly* fucked."

Robert Anselm grabbed her stirrup and heaved himself briefly up, high

---

[16] No relation.

enough to look down across the slope, and see what she was seeing. "Son of a *bitch*!"

He fell back, heels jolting on the mud.

Ash shifted her gaze, slitting her eyes to be sure of what she was seeing in the dimness. There was no mistake. Over the troops who anchored themselves on the Visigoth right – about a thousand archers and light horsemen – white pennants flew.

The wind unrolled the silk on the air, letting her clearly see the red crescents.

"Those are Turkish troops," she confirmed.

Robert Anselm, below her, muttered, "So much for them cutting the Visigoths' supply lines . . ."

"Yeah. Not only are they not cutting their supply lines, there's a detachment of the Sultan's troops in the mainward. Oh, *fuck*," Ash exclaimed. "There's been some kind of treaty, alliance, something – the fucking Sultan's in bed with the fucking Caliph now!"

"I doubt quite that," John de Vere said, riding up beside them.

"Did you know about this, my lord?"

De Vere's face, under his armet's pinned-up visor, showed white with anger. "What would Duke Charles tell an indigent English Earl? His intelligence is too good for him not to know – he must think he can beat them," the Earl of Oxford said abruptly. "God's teeth! but he thinks he can defeat the Visigoths *and* the Turks! The greater enemy, the greater the glory."

"We're dead," Ash murmured, sing-song. "We're dead . . . okay, my lord. If you want my advice, stick with the plan. Let the priests pray."

"If I wanted your advice, madam, I should have demanded it."

Ash grinned at him. "Well, hey, you got it for free. Not everybody can say that. I'm a mercenary, you know."

The constriction of humour at his eyes gave him crow's feet. The laughter faded, as he and Ash sat their restless horses. In the twilight, it seemed the Visigoth and Turkish battles[17] might be drawing up in what local intelligence had suggested would be their optimum position.

"Will your men follow you in this?"

Ash said absently, "They're a damn sight more frightened of me than of the enemy – and besides, the Visigoths might not get them, but my battle police certainly will."

"Madam, much depends on this."

A feeling of great relaxation spread through her body. She reached down to adjust the strap of the plackart that protected her belly, and thought longingly of the protection afforded by full armour. Her hand came to rest on the leather-bound grip of her sword, checking the lanyard chain fastened around it below the pommel, and attached to her belt.

"I've got rid of the liabilities," Ash said, looking back at him. "Most of the rest of these men have been fighting for me for three years now. They don't give a fuck about Duke Charles. They don't give a fuck about – beg pardon – the Earl of Oxford. They give a fuck about their lance-mates, and about me,

---

[17] In mediaeval military terms, a 'battle' is a unit of men, rather than a specific combat. Mediaeval armies were often divided into three battles or large units, for fighting.

because I've got them out of fields worse than this in one piece. So yes, they'll do it. Maybe. All other things being equal."

The Earl of Oxford looked curiously at her.

Ash avoided the Englishman's gaze. "Okay – we're facing people who beat the Swiss: morale isn't *that* good. You ask Cola de Monforte!"

A clarion rang out across the field. Momentarily, men's voices stilled. The sounds of horses, their tack, the clatter of barding, and the snorts of breath gave way to the distant shout of Sergeants of Archers, and an unholy noise of singing from the gunners' position. Ash stood upright in her stirrups.

"Meanwhile," she said, "it isn't quite hopeless, and I've got a contract with you."

The Earl of Oxford saw his brothers approaching, and Ash saw the rest of her officers coming up; all with questions, needing orders and direction, and the time ticking away now to nothing.

John de Vere formally offered his hand, and Ash gripped it.

"If we survive the field," he said, "I shall have questions to ask you, madam."

"Good thing they don't do guns," Ash murmured to Robert Anselm. "They'd do what Richard Gloucester did to your Lancastrians at Tewkesbury, and blow us right off the top of this hill!"

Anselm nodded approvingly. "The Duke's got it well thought out."

"Bugger Charles of Burgundy!" Ash remarked. "Why do I have to fight a fucking hopeless battle before we can do anything useful? It isn't that lot we need to take out – it's her fucking Stone Golem, that's telling her how to win! This is a sheer waste of time."

"Particularly if we get killed," Anselm grunted.

Both of them sat in their saddles, gazing down the long muddy slope at banners galloping, as the Visigoth light cavalry got themselves into position. The Faris's banner held their centre – as Ash's scouts had informed her, it was a Brazen Head, on a black field. Ash absently rested her hand on the skirt of her brigandine, over her belly.

She missed, suddenly and painfully, whatever Florian might be saying at this moment, if she were here – something caustic about the stupidity of military life, and battles, and getting cut up for no good reason.

"Florian would say I have to fight harder because I'm a woman," Ash said inconsequentially, watching her officers moving along the back of lines of men. "She means, a male commander could get taken prisoner, but I'd get gang-raped."

Anselm grunted. "Yeah? It was me that found Ricardo Valzacchi after Molinella, remember? Tied across a wagon with a poleaxe shaft up his arse. I think he's— *she's* getting war confused with something else . . ."

What little she could see of Anselm's face in the vee between bevor and raised visor was hidden, now, by the dark sweep of clouds across the sky; a sweep of dank shadow that took the brightness out of blue and red and yellow banners, dulled the hooks and points of bills, and caused a muttered swearing among the archers and crossbowmen.

A blast of cold air brought rain into her face; stingingly cold, almost sleet. Ash stirred, tapped spurs to the big gelding's flanks and rode down in among the company lines. Godluc's big feathery feet picked a way between men and women bundled into jacks and helms and standing on the wet trampled crops.

Ludmilla Rostovnaya shouted up, "It's dampening our strings, boss."

"All bows unspanned and unstrung!" Ash ordered. "You'll get your chance, guys. Keep your bow-strings under your helmets. It's going to get bloody nasty, round about – now."

With that, the church bells of distant Auxonne rang out across the hills. A great noise of voices went up from behind the Burgundian battle-line. A choir, singing mass. Ash raised her head. A whiff of incense caught in her nostrils. A little further up the crowded slope, Richard Faversham and Digorie Paston knelt in the mud, crucifixes in hand, young Bertrand holding up a stinking tallow candle. Around Ash, voices muttered, "Miserere, miserere!" She caught a flash of black and white as a magpie flew swooping down across the field, and automatically crossed herself and spat.

A bolt of blue colour, about as big as her fist, shot across the wet crops, under Godluc's nose. His red-rimmed nostrils flared.

Ash watched the kingfisher dart away.

She tapped spurs into Godluc's flanks again, rode up and took axe and lance from Rickard, and as she reached to close her bevor up and visor down, the first flakes of white dusted across Godluc's blue and gold caparisons.

She raised her head, the duck-curled metal tail of her sallet allowing her to look up. Above, in a dark sky, white dots floated down.

In an instant, a howl of whiteness swirled out of the clouds, snowflakes turning from a powdery dust to thick, wet flakes; plastering her plackart, whitening Godluc's silk caparisons, cutting her off from everyone except the three or four closest: Anselm, Rickard, Ludmilla, Geraint ab Morgan.

"Hold them!" she ordered the Welshman sharply.

Wind drove into her back. Snow flew. The wet mud under Godluc's hooves went from black-and-brown to white in a matter of seconds. She rode a few yards, collecting her officers, halting close to Richard Faversham's high-voiced Latin. Lance holstered, hands going up, she wrenched off her sallet and listened, standing upright in her saddle.

Far off, on the left and right wings of the Burgundian army, hoarse loud voices cried orders. A second's pause, then the unmistakable *thunk* and *whirr!* of arrows being launched. One flight – and no other orders: an inhuman silence, all along the line.

"Shit, they're good," she whispered.

Somewhere below, a Visigoth man screamed.

Digorie Paston reached out and closed his bony hands over the English deacon's, his face screwed up, prayer spilling out of his mouth.

Ash turned her head. Wind lashed her plates-covered shoulders and back. A hard wind, rising – and a blast took the breath from her mouth, her face blinded with snow, and she scraped a gauntlet across her features, grazing skin, and leaned down:

"Ludmilla, go forward!"

The Rus woman slid out of her company and went forward into the driving snow. Ash cocked her head, listening. The shrill snarl of an arrow-storm went up, all in one second, and her bladder pulsed, a trickle of hot urine soaking her hose. *It is the sound.* Nerve-shredding to hear coming: worse when it stops.

Her clumsy hands got her helmet back on her head; all around her, her men were shoving their visors down and leaning forward, as if into a wind, to present the deflecting surfaces of steel helmets to the arrows' barbs and bodkin points.

"Shit, shit, shit," Geraint ab Morgan swore monotonously.

The abrupt cessation of the whistling sound told her the arrows had hit – something. She rode forward. No one screamed, or fell.

A white-plastered figure, stumbling, caught at her stirrup.

Ludmilla Rostovnaya shouted, "They're hitting earth! Thirty feet in front of the line!"

"*Yes!*" Ash tried to look behind her, into the wind, coughed out a mouthful of sleet, and shouted, "Rickard!"

The boy ran up, an archer's sallet crammed over his head, and a falchion at his belt. "Boss?"

"Get runners down here! I can't see the Blue Boar banner,[18] we're going to have to rely on runners and riders. Go!"

"Yes, boss!"

"Ludmilla, ride to the Earl of Oxford, *tell him it's working!* I want to know if it's working on the rest of the field!"

The woman lifted a hand, and plunged on up the slope, slipping and sliding in snow and mud. Ash shivered, steel's cold entering her body even through the padded arming doublet and hose beneath. Her crotch felt chill and wet. She swung Godluc around and rode back and forth in the snow in front of the Lion Azure's five hundred men, leaving Anselm in charge of the infantry and Geraint in charge of the archers; and the knights under the dubious restraint of Euen Huw.

A thrumming whirr burst on the air.

Ash held Godluc in, needing the rein to do it. The big beast under her shivered. She stood in the stirrups, bowels unsettled; and very slowly paced up and down before the ranks. One arrow buried its fletching in the mud fifteen feet in front of her.

The sound of bowstrings cut the air. Arrow shafts shrilled. The noise grew until she thought there could not be another arrow left in Christendom; flight upon flight from the recurved Visigoth bows, flight after flight of German arrows, from the Imperial troops glimpsed down among the enemy.

The wind from behind the Burgundian lines blew so hard that the snow flew horizontally southwards.

"Keep praying!" she yelled at Digorie and Richard. The mass from Charles's mainward came by fits and starts through the howling wind.

"*Now . . .*" she breathed.

It isn't much of a miracle – given what weather conditions are like anyway, with the sun out – but it *is* a miracle.

The snow. The snow – and the *wind.*

---

[18] The personal device of the Earl of Oxford.

Whiteness blocked the air, swirling, until she lost all sense of depth or distance. She held on to Godluc's warmth, and his steaming breath, and rode in close among the lines; a word here to a man with a brother-in-law fighting for Cola de Monforte, a word there to a woman archer who drank with the whores following a refugee contingent of German knights, all of it serving no particular purpose of information, only it brought them near enough to her to see, hear or touch her.

"This is what we do, this is what we're here for," she said, again and again. "Let them keep shooting. Wasting arrows. A few more minutes, and we'll give them the biggest shock of their lives. The *last* shock!"

The snow thinned.

Digorie Paston and Richard Faversham held each other up, kneeling in the mud. Bertrand put a wine flask to the lips of each in turn, his fat white face gaunt with fear. They prayed in harsh gasps. Christus, she thought, *Godfrey, we need you!*

Digorie Paston pitched over, flat on his face in two inches of snow.

"Prepare to shoot!" she yelled to Geraint ab Morgan.

The snow thinned still more. The sky grew brighter. The wind began to drop. Ash turned and spurred Godluc across the slope; page, squire, escort and banner-bearer with her; to Geraint ab Morgan and the archers; one fist up, sword out and held high. She watched the skyline as she rode, searching hard among the banners in the mainward for the Blue Boar.

Up the slope, Richard Faversham fainted.

The fall of snow stopped, abruptly; the air clearing.

The Boar standard dipped.

Ash didn't wait for the runner. As the west grew lighter, and the snow dropped to powdery drifts, she jerked her sword down. "Span and string!"

"Nock! Loose!" Geraint ab Morgan's harsh Welsh bellow echoed flatly across the hillside. Ash heard other orders roared, in the wings and further along the mainward; and she unconsciously braced herself. The Lion Azure's archers and crossbowmen readied their weapons, spanned bolts and nocked arrows, and at Geraint's second shout, loosed.

The better part of two thousand arrows blackened the cold twilight air. A thousand of which, she reflected in a moment's irony, undoubtedly came from the bows of Philippe de Poitiers and Ferry de Cuisance, whose archers from Picardy and Hainault she had run away from at Neuss.

I was right, too . . .

Ash's whole body quivered with their release, and she lifted her head as they flew; and the second flight of shafts was already black in the air, crossbows cranking furiously, longbow archers loosing at ten or twelve shafts a minute, snatched up from the porcupines of arrows jammed into the wet wheat and mud – still shooting with the wind behind them—

A distant horse squealed.

Ash stood up in the stirrups.

Three hundred yards away, down a hill littered with a brushwood barrier of thousands of Visigoth arrows, the first shafts of the Burgundian army struck home.

She can just see, at this distance: Visigoth men fall, clutching at their faces, spiked through eye and cheekbone and mouth. Their riders jerk on wheeling mounts. A great bulk of horses screamed and bolted, crashing back and south, opening holes in the lines of men with pike and swords; a man in white robes sprawling, skull crushed by a hoof, banners dipping in chaos—

Ash looked over her shoulder at the exact moment that Angelotti, and the other gunners with Duke Charles's centre, opened fire. A thundering *bang!* shook the ground under Godluc's hooves, and the stallion reared up a good eighteen inches, this in full armour.

They shot into the wind, and fell short. We shot with the wind and didn't. And they couldn't see that!

"Deo gratias!" Ash yelled.

The gunfire from the centre ran raggedly out to silence – it was always a moot point if the gun-teams could re-load before the enemy charged. Ash reined Godluc in as he thumped one hoof down on the reverberate ground and skittered his haunches around, wanting to charge forward.

"Runners!" she yelled at the scattered escort as they re-formed; took a minute to spur Godluc back of the battle-line, her personal banner following. Armed men on horseback closed in around her. She wheeled the stallion, seeing a man-at-arms come running down the slope towards the company, towards her banner—

A bone-shaking jolt threw her forward in the saddle.

One man's hand was under her chest, pushing her back up. She shoved Thomas Rochester aside, spat, shook her head dizzily; and found herself staring at a scar in the earth. A giant furrow, a spray of soil and turf and a man's severed hand—

She has time to think *They're not supposed to have guns!* and a second impact thuds into the ground close to the group of horsemen. Mud flies up, splatters her face.

"Captain!" One of the runners, hanging on her stirrup. "The Earl says pull back! Pull the line back! Over the top of the hill!"

"ANSELM!" she yells, prising mud out of her mouth with armoured fingers. She spurs to him. "Get them back over that hill, *now*! You – and you – *run* – orders for Geraint: *get them back*."

She can hear trumpets signalling, orders being shouted, the bark of lance-leaders hauling their men back, up the snow- and mud-slippery corn towards the skyline; only then does she turn.

Down at the foot of the slope, in the rain-pale twilight, the mass of Visigoth men in the centre battle have moved aside. There are wagons there.

As she watches, a figure that is larger than a man pushes a wagon into place, marble-and-bronze body wheeling it with no apparent effort. Light glints off the sides of the wagon. It is iron-slabbed, armoured: a Visigoth war-wagon. The sides, released, fall forward and down – studded with nail-points; you can't run at them, ride up them – and the great wooden cup of a mangonel goes back: snaps forward—

A boulder the size of a man's torso arcs through the air.

Ash shifted her weight sideways, brought Godluc round, and leaned forward to urge him up the hill. Men's backs closed around her; the banner jiggled overhead. A thud: a great screaming noise – rock-splinters whined through the air, ploughing into men's bodies.

She lifted her head and looked at a swathe cut through the battle line. Earth and corn crushed, heads and bodies crushed; a ploughed mass of dark red blood under the pale sky.

She rode behind the company, the mud under Godluc's hooves red with blood, blue-pink with intestines; men screaming; women pulling them up the hill towards the skyline. Rode slow – walking pace – Thomas Rochester at her left flank with tears running down his face, under his visor.

Bang!

"For Christ's pity, ride!" Rochester screamed.

Ash turned, as far as high saddle and brigandine would allow, staring back down the hill.

Twenty or thirty of the iron-armoured wagons stood at the foot of the hill. Men swarmed around them, hammering chocks under the mangonels, adjusting the elevation of the catapults; and tall above them, on the weapons-platforms, the clay figures of golems bent down, effortlessly lifting rocks into the cups, effortlessly hauling the cup down to cock it, not even bothering to wind the time-consuming winch – everything that a man can do, that *men* can do; but stronger, *faster*.

Five boulders ploughed into the slope to her right, impacting with great sprays of mud; another five hit in sequence – *bang! bang! bang! bang! bang!* – and the far end of the line of knights stopped being men riding. She stared at a mass of threshing hooves, rolling bodies, bloody liveries; a few unharmed riders trying to climb to their feet—

Rate of fire's phenomenal, Ash thought dreamily; at the same time that she was shouting, "Rickard, get to Angelotti! Tell him to pull back! I don't care what the rest of the guns are doing, the Lion's pulling back! We got to get over the hill!"

Ahead, the great swallow-tailed Lion standard dipped, recovered, and went steadily back up the slope. She muttered, "Come on, Euen, come *on!*" and put both spurs back into Godluc's sides. The gelding slid, caught himself, and sprang up the slope, bringing her up level with the backs of the great mass of running billmen and archers.

Thomas Rochester yelled, "*Shit!*"

A great curving streak of fire blasted up the hill past Ash's right-hand side. She screamed. Godluc reared. In a clatter of barding barely heard above the screaming men, he thudded down; her teeth clicked painfully together.

The mud steamed and hissed under a jet of blue-white fire.

It suddenly cut off. Black streaks blotched her vision: retinal after-images. Through them, Ash glimpsed large numbers of men sprinting up the hill towards the crest.

Down the hill, below the brushwood barrier of thousands of Visigoth arrows, uselessly stuck in the earth and burning now—

Ash saw the moving figures of golems, ahead of the Visigoth mainward.

Thirty or forty of them; each with huge brass tanks fixed to their backs, nozzles in their hands that spat flame. Carrying the weight of the tanks with no effort, bearing the heat of the flame with no hurt.

"Get Angelotti to me!" she roared at Thomas Rochester.

The jolt of Godluc scrambling up the slope knocked breath out of her; page, escort and riders all with her, all on the heels of the company's archers. She reined in, slowing deliberately; felt the ground flatten as she came up over the crest, and rode down in among the company as they went down into dead ground, out of mangonel-range, and spurred forward to the banner marking the guns.

"Angeli!" She leaned down from the saddle. "Get the hackbutters! Those damn things are made of *stone*, arquebus balls will *crack* them—"

"Got you, madonna!" the master gunner shouted.

"Jesus *Christ*! War-golems! Greek Fire![19] We should have been warned! Can't the scouts get *anything* right?"

Between screaming one order and the next, she realised there must be a battle going on out on the right flank, but that was all a wet confusion of banners streaming, gouts of mud kicked up by frantic riders, and one huge, immense roar of male voices that she guessed to be heavy cavalry going down the hill towards the wagons, the golems, the Greek Fire.

"Fuck, no!" Thomas Rochester gasped, riding to her side. "This is no time to be a hero!"

"If Oxford doesn't send orders—" Ash stood in her stirrups, trying to pick out the Blue Boar, or the Burgundian banner, as great throngs of men streamed past her; men-at-arms in Burgundian livery running; and she exclaimed, "Shit, have we routed, and nobody's told us?"

Man after man was carried back past her on hurdles ripped up by the women of the baggage train. She registered heads hanging down, hair matted with blood, mouths open; a man screaming with his leg bloody and the big bone of the thigh stuck up white through the skin; a woman in a kirtle, bloody from chin to hem, staring at her hand, lying a yard away in the mud. All faces she knew. She felt nothing, not even numb. She felt only the intensity, the necessity, of getting them through it as whole as she could.

Anselm appeared at her side on a rangy bay. "What now, boss?"

"Get scouts on the ridge! Tell me if they're advancing. Draw up into battles. We're not running yet!"

It is far easier to be killed running away.

No sun to tell her what hour this might be. She galloped along the front of the Lion Azure lines, partly to show any runners her banner, partly to discourage any man from running away. Two urging strides took Godluc up on to the skyline, even as she thought *This is suicidally dangerous but I have to know what's going on!*

Robert Anselm rode up beside her.

"Roberto, fuck off!"

---

[19] Used by Roman, Byzantine and Arab cultures, in both naval and siege warfare, the exact constituents of 'Greek Fire' remain unknown, although naphtha, sulphur, oil, tar, saltpetre and pitch have been suggested. Its nature as a terror weapon, however, is well recorded in history.

"There!"

Ash followed the direction of his gauntlet. On the far right, de la Marche's men had galloped down the slope, full charge, lances down, and joined battle. Men-at-arms swarming with them: bills rose and fell like a threshing machine. Among the Visigoth black pennants at the foot of the slope, next to the chevrons of Lebrija, a green and yellow personal banner briefly appeared.

"The Eagle of Del Guiz," Robert yelled. His voice sounded hoarse, electric, excited. "That – *there he goes!*"

Anselm stood in his stirrups and whooped the way a hunt hallows a fox. The nearest billmen in Lion livery took breath to see where he was pointing.

"Boss, your husband's running away!" Carracci bawled.

"Yeah!" Anselm grinned fiercely at Ash. "Petition the Emperor to award him another heraldic beast – the Lying Hound!"

She has a second to think *I* am *ashamed of Fernando, why am I ashamed of him, why should I care?* and then the bad light and confusion of men slashing away at each other hides banner, standard, the glint of weapons, and men's backs as they run away.

"Captain Ash!" a rider in red X livery bellowed, "the Duke wants you!"

Ash waved acknowledgement, bellowed, "You're in command, get off this fucking skyline!" to Anselm, and spurred Godluc – weary, hooves bloody, flanks heaving – across the back of the hill. Back of the lines, and down, into a tiny red streamlet, tributary of the river; splashing across it. She galloped into a paddock between hedges, trampled down by the passing of a thousand men.

A throng of men and riders packed the paddock. Appalled, she thought, *This is the back-of-the-lines HQ, have we been driven back this far, this fast?* She shoved up her visor, stared frantically at coloured cloth, and picked out the draggled Blue Boar, with Charles's White Hart. She rode in between the ranks of armed knights. Liveries were useless now, blood and brains and mud soaking their bright colours.

One man made to block her way.

"For the Duke, motherfucker!" Ash shrieked.

He recognised a woman's voice and let her through.

Charles of Burgundy, in full gilded armour, stood as the centre of the command group of nobles. Pages held their horses. One roan gelding delicately lipped at the verge of the stream, not willing to drink through mud and body fluids. Ash dismounted. The ground hit her heels, jarring her; she was instantly weary to the bone. She shook it off.

A man, his armet crowned by a blue boar, faceless in steel, turned at her voice. Oxford.

"My lord!" Ash elbowed between four armed knights in bloody yellow and scarlet livery. "We got to re-group. Take out the catapults and the Fire. What does the Duke want me to do?"

He thumbed his visor up, giving her a sight of red-rimmed pale blue eyes, fiercely keen. "The Duke's mercenaries on your left flank are holding back. They won't push an advance. He wants you to go in there."

"He wants *what?*" Ash stared. "Didn't anyone ever tell him, don't reinforce failure?"

She realised she was breathing hard, and shouting too loud, despite the battle fifty yards away.

More quietly and hoarsely, she said, "If we mass the cannon and the hackbuts, we can blast the stone men off the face of this field—"

Her hands move, describing shapes in the air which she knows approximate not to actual men, slicing at each other in this black morning's random confusion, but to their force, their will, their ability to *make* someone else go back: an ability not really dependent on weapons.

"—but we won't do it piecemeal. The Duke's got to give the orders!"

"He won't do it," John de Vere, Earl of Oxford, said. "The Duke is ordering a heavy cavalry charge."

"Oh, fuck chivalry! This is his chance to do something, we're getting chewed up here—" There is no time to argue on the field of battle. "Yes, my lord. What—"

Ash glimpsed something black and whirring and brought up her arm by instinct.

A bodkin arrow-head clicked off her upraised shoulder and glanced into the dirt.

The shock through the brigandine's plates momentarily numbed her right arm. She grabbed left-handed for Godluc's reins – a page in red doublet and white hose knelt before Godluc, slumped forward under her horse's hooves, two shafts protruding from his throat.

Not a red doublet, a white doublet soaked red.

"*Oxford!*" She had her four-foot short axe off the saddle, gripping it between two hands. *When the commanders have to draw weapons, it's trouble.* The scream and shout and sudden battering of hooves broke over the hedge in front of her, new riders piling into the enclosed paddock: ten, fifty, two or three hundred men in robes and mail on desert horses—

A spurt of flame leaped out in front of her.

Ash never saw the hand-gunner, or heard the *bang* and *crack!* of the gun; she was deaf before she knew it.

Another gun spoke. Not a hand-gun but an organ-gun. Between grey smoke, she saw a Burgundian cannon crew sponge, load, ram and fire, in less time than seemed possible. She swung round and the paddock was full of mounted Visigoth knights – and men in white mullet liveries, John de Vere bellowing an attack – and Godluc trampling someone a dangerous two yards from her right hand – and she brought her axe up and over and drove through the impact of flesh, of bone. The axe took off a Visigoth rider's arm, clean, with a spray of blood that reddened her armour from sallet to sabatons.

The impact of horses' hooves pounded up through the soles of her boots. She felt the *bang!* of another gun in the hollow of her chest. She took a grip, braced her feet, yelled as well as she could for Godluc; and turned a lance-shaft aside with a well-timed cut. Coming up on the backswing for the Visigoth knight's leg, she made no connection, almost falling—

"No! I won't ask!" She sobbed it aloud. "*No voices!*"

No riders in front of her.

The paddock was nothing but horses in red and yellow and blue caparisons:

galloping Burgundian knights. Ash took three seconds to swing up into the saddle, loop her axe to it, and draw her sword: within that time, there was no longer a man in Visigoth mail and livery alive, wounded horses screamed, butchered; and the great mass of the Burgundian Duke's escort closed up around them – around what had been, she realised, a flying wedge attack.

At her horse's feet, the Visigoth standard-bearer lay face down on his flag, a red rent in his mail shirt, and a broken sword blade jammed through his eye-socket.

"The Duke!" John de Vere was in the mud, staring up at her. He knelt, cradling a man in gilded armour and Hart livery – Charles, Duke of Burgundy. The gilt articulated steel was leaking thick, red arterial blood. "*Get surgeons! Now!*"

A flying wedge of men from the land of stone and twilight, willing to be chopped apart if it meant one of them could find, under his standard, Duke Charles of Burgundy. She shook her ringing head, trying to make out what the Earl of Oxford was saying.

"SURGEONS!" His voice reached her faintly.

"My lord!" Ash wheeled Godluc. The arch of the sky above her was black, with that lightlessness that she treated now as if it were just another natural phenomenon. North, the morning was distantly bright. Chill wind still blew in her face. She slammed her visor shut, jammed spurs home, and thundered across the slippery slope, her banner-bearer and escort hard put to keep up with her.

The light in the north began to die.

Godluc's gallop slowed instantly to a walk as her attention shifted. His head drooped. His barrel chest shuddered, white with foam. Thomas Rochester's little Welsh mare caught up, with the Lion banner behind him. She pointed, wordless.

Back towards Dijon, over the Burgundian border, the sunlight was beginning to dim.

"Surgeons for the Duke!" Ash ordered. "Ride!"

The slope of the hill rose up in front of her, wet, muddy, slippery with wreckage. The Surgeon-General's tents were fifty yards off, just below the crest. Godluc, doing his best, could not surmount it; she turned and rode with her group hard towards the west, along the contour of the hill, to where the slope would shallow out and allow her to get back, along the crest, to the rear and the surgeons' wagons.

Rochester and the escort outdistanced her, on horses that had done less in the past two hours. She found herself struggling in the rear, behind her banner, behind her escort.

She had no warning.

A crossbow bolt struck the flank of the horse in front: Rochester's mare. Wet meat exploded across her face and body.

Godluc reared.

A mailed hand from nowhere jerked her reins down, bloodying Godluc's mouth. The gelding screamed. A sword-slash cut one stirrup leather: she jerked in the high-backed saddle, grabbing with her free hand for the pommel, and balance.

Sixty Visigoth knights in mail and coat-of-plates rode past and over and through her escort, streaming out across the hill.

A spear thrust home from behind into Godluc's quarters. His hind hooves lifted, his head dipped, and she went straight over his head.

The mud was soft, or she would have died with a broken neck.

The impact was too hard to feel. Ash felt nothing but an absence, realised that she lay, staring up at the black sky, stunned, hurt, chest an acid void; that her hand gripped her sword and the blade had snapped off six inches from the hilt, that something was wrong with her left leg, and her left arm.

A man in the snatch-squad leaned down from his mount. She saw his pale face, behind the helmet bar, satisfying itself about her livery. He hefted a mace in his left hand. He dismounted, and struck twice: once to her left knee, the poleyn locking down, pain blazing through the joint; and once to the side of her head.

She knew nothing clearly after that.

She felt herself lifted, thought for a time that it might be Burgundians or her own men; recognised, at last, that the language they spoke was Visigothic, and that it was dark, the sun was nowhere in the sky, and that what rocked and shook unsteadily beneath her was not a field or road or hay-cart, but the deck of a ship.

Her first clear thought came perhaps days later. *This is a ship and it is sailing for North Africa.*

Message: #155 (Anna Longman)
Subject: Ash, archaeological discoveries
Date: 18/11/00 at 10.00 a.m.
From: Ngrant@   *former address deleted*
                           other details encrypted by
Anna —   *non-discoverable personal key*

I think that you may just have tried to mail me and failed.

To answer points I anticipate you may be asking about the last
section: no, I can find no other historical mention of a battle at
Auxonne on or around 21 August 1476 — although Ash's narrative does
bear some resemblance to what we know of a battle fought on 22
August 1485. That date, of course, refers to Bosworth field, which
put an end to the Plantagenet Kings in England. And something very
like the remarkable occurrence with the arrows is documented
earlier, on 29 March 1461, at Towton in England, with the
Lancastrians 'not perfectly viewing the distance between them and
their enemies' by reason of driving snow and wind; therefore
losing that 'Palmsunday field' (and England) to the Yorkists.

Again, Charles Mallory Maximillian footnotes this, in his 1890s
edition, as being one more case where the 'Ash' documents have been
fleshed out by her contemporaries (especially Del Guiz, writing in
the early 1500s) with details of their own famous battles.

I feel that this no longer answers the case.

I cannot reconcile what we have here — two opposing sets of
evidence. Manuscripts which are apparently (now) fictional;
archaeological relics which are evidently, physically, real. I am
advising Isobel on fifteenth-century Europe, I am working on my
translation, but all I can do, really, is think. How do I explain
this? What theory would account for this?

I don't have one. Perhaps when Ash referred to the sun going out
as a 'black miracle', I should have listened to her! I am starting
to think that only a miracle is going to give me the explanation we
need.

— Pierce

```
Message:    #95 (Pierce Ratcliff)
Subject:    Ash
Date:       18/11/00 at 11.09 a.m.
From:       Longman@
```
format address deleted
other details encrypted and
non-recoverably deleted

Pierce —

I have no idea why we've got a conflict of evidence, either; and I
have to talk to my MD about it. It isn't just my job and your
career. We can't publish a book that we know to be academically
fraudulent — no, wait, don't panic! — and we can't NOT publish one
with something as mind-boggling as a fifteenth-century
Carthaginian golem backing it up.

Reading your last mailing, I start wondering what your Vaughan
Davies would say — maybe not that the resemblance of Auxonne to
Bosworth Field is a case of historical Chinese whispers, but that
it's an echo of his idealised alternate-history 'Lost Burgundy'.
That's poetic, and it got me thinking, because he was a scientist
as well as a writer. Maybe it's NOT a poetic thought, maybe it's a
scientific one.

A friend of mine, Nadia, said something very interesting to me.
I've been reading up on this: we were talking about the theory you
mentioned — that there are an infinite number of parallel universes
created every second, in which every possible different choice or
decision at any given moment gives rise to another different
'branch', etc. (I really only know it from novels, and popular-
science books.)

What Nadia says is, it isn't the lost chances she regrets —
whether you drove down a different road and avoided an accident,
and so on — but the fact that, if this infinite-number-of-universes
theory is true, she can never lead a moral existence.

She says, if she chooses not to knock down and rob an old lady in
the street, then the very act of refusing to do this gives rise to a
parallel universe in which she DOES do it. It is not possible NOT
to do things.

I'm not suggesting you've accessed a parallel universe or
alternate history — I'm not THAT desperate — but it does make
Davies sound less of a mental case if his theory was based in
scientific speculation. I was thinking, if we COULD find the rest of
his Introduction, maybe it has a perfectly sensible SCIENTIFIC
explanation, which would help us now? Even science circa 1939
would be SOMETHING.

— Anna

Message: #156 (Anna Longman)
Subject: Ash
Date: 18/11/00 at 11.20 a.m.
From: Ngrant@

format address deleted
Other details encypted by
non-discoverable personal key

Anna —

Your Nadia's point is philosophically interesting, but not the
case, according to what I understand of our physicists. (Which is
purely a layman's understanding, I assure you.)

   If what the current evidence seems to point to is correct, then
we are not faced with an infinite number of possible universes, but
only an infinite number of possible FUTURES, which collapse into
one concrete and real present moment: the NOW. Which then becomes
one concrete and single PAST.

   So your friend chooses not to knock down her old lady, and that
state of NOT having done it is what becomes the unchangeable past.
It is only in the moment of transition from potential to actual
that a choice is made. So it is possible not to do things.

   Sorry: raise a philosophical hare with an academic and he will
always chase it! To change animals and mix metaphors: let us return
to our sheep—

   I would take help from ANYONE at the moment, including a
scientific theory of the Thirties about parallel universes! I've
tried extensively to find Vaughan Davies's book, though, and
failed; and I don't think I can do much about that sitting in a tent
outside Tunis.

   I want to try these last few weeks out on my colleagues, in
detail, and on Isobel's scientist friends, and see if they can come
up with any theories. I don't dare do it now. It would bring
unwanted attention to the site, here; it would cause Isobel a great
deal of distress — and, to be honest, it would finish my chances of
being the first man to translate FRAXINUS. I know this is venal, but
chances of spectacular success come only rarely; something you
will discover as you get older.

   Maybe we could do it in a month or so? Start asking around, among
experts, getting some REAL answers? That would still be before
publication date.

— Pierce

```
------------------------------------------------------------------

Message:    #96 (Pierce Ratcliff)
Subject:    Ash
Date:       18/11/00 at 11.37 a.m.
From:       Longman@

Pierce —
```
format address deleted
Other details encrypted and
non-recoverably deleted

But not before copy-editing, and printing! Pierce, what are you
trying to do to me!

  Suppose we say Christmas? If this problem hasn't resolved
itself, or we haven't at least found out what it is, by then — then
I'll have to go to Jonathan.

  First week of January at the LATEST.

— Anna

```
Message:    #157 (Anna Longman)
Subject:    Ash, texts
Date:       18/11/00 at 04.18 p.m.
From:       Ngrant@

Anna —
```
format address deleted
Other details encrypted by
non-discoverable personal key

Very well. I agree. We raise no alarm before the first week in
January. Although, if we haven't arrived at an answer before then —
it's all of seven weeks away! — I will most probably have gone mad.
But then I'll hardly have to worry about anything if I'm mad, will
I!

  John Monkham just came by. The photos of the golem are splendid,
beyond belief. I'm sorry you won't be able to copy or keep them;
Isobel becomes more security conscious with every hour that
passes. I think if John wasn't her son, she wouldn't be letting HIM
take them off-site.

  I've had a morning to polish my translation. Here it is at last,
Anna. 'Fraxinus', as promised. Or at least, the first section of it.
Sorry I have only had time to do the bare minimum of footnotes.

— Pierce

Message: #163 (Anna Longman)
Subject: Ash
Date: 19/11/00 at 09.51 a.m.
From: Ngrant@

format address deleted
Other details encrypted and
non-recoverably deleted

Anna —

I've GOT it.

I've got the ANSWER.

I was right, the simplest explanation is usually the correct one. We've been being too complicated, that's all; complicating things unnecessarily! It's so simple. No need to concern ourselves with Davies's theory, whatever it may have been; no need to worry about what the British Library catalogue says!

What I've only this minute realised is, just because a document is CLASSIFIED as fiction or myth or legend, THAT DOESN'T MEAN IT'S NOT TRUE.

That simple!

It was something Isobel just said to me — I HAD to tell her I was having problems, I was talking about Vaughan Davies's theory: she just said, 'Pierce, what's all this RUBBISH?' And then she reminded me —

The archaeologist Heinrich Schliemann (although his methods left much to be desired) found the site of the city of Troy in 1871, by digging EXACTLY WHERE HOMER SAID IT WAS in the ILIAD.

And the ILIAD isn't a 'historical document', it's a POEM! With gods and goddesses and all the artistic licence of fiction!

It was a thunderstroke! — I still don't know how I came to miss the re-classification of the Ash documents, but in a very real sense, it doesn't matter. What matters is, we have physical evidence here at the site that means — WHATEVER some expert has thought about it — the chronicles of Ash's fifteenth-century actually contain truth. When they mention post-Roman technological 'golems', we FIND them. You can't argue with the evidence.

Truth can be carried down to us through STORY.

It's all right, Anna. What's going to happen is, the libraries and the universities will just have to classify the Ash documents BACK to being Non-Fiction.

And Isobel's expedition and my book will give the incontrovertible evidence of why they must do this.

— Pierce

351

PART SIX

6 September–7 September AD 1476

'Fraxinus me fecit'

I

She missed the weight of her hair.

Never having cut it, she had not been aware before that it *had* a weight: all the hundreds of fine, silver, yard-long strands.

The winds grew colder as they sailed south.

This isn't right. This isn't what Angelotti used to tell me about, when he was under the Eternal Twilight; not this cold. *It should be getting hotter—*

Momentarily, she doesn't see this ship: sees instead Angelotti, sitting with his back up against the carriage of an organ-gun outside Pisa; hears him say *Women in thin, transparent silk robes – not that* I *care! – and roof-gardens where the heat is reflected in by mirrors; the rich grow vines; one long endless night of wine; and always fireflies. Hotter than this!* And she had breathed the sultry, sweating Italian air, watched the blue-green dots of fireflies swell and die, and dreamed of the hot south.

Freezing spray hit her face.

She had not realised, before, how the weight of her hair was with her every day, in every movement, or how it had kept her warm. Now she felt light-headed, cold about the neck, and bereft. The soldiers of the King-Caliph had left her no more hair than would cover her ears. The whole silver carpet of it had strewn the dock at – where? Genoa? Marseilles? – cut, and trodden into the mud as she was carried aboard, semi-conscious.

Ash flexed her left knee, secretly. A stab of pain went through the joint. She nipped her lip between her teeth, not crying out, and continued the exercise.

The prow of the boat dipped, thudding into the cold waves of the Mediterranean Sea. Salt crusted her lips, stiffened her cropped hair. Ash gripped the stern-rail, rocking with the motion, and stared back, north, away from the lands of the Caliph. A diminishing wake of silver marked their passage on the sea: the reflection of a crescent moon, cleft by their passing.

Two sailors pushed past her, going to the heads. Ash shifted her body. Her left leg would almost support her full weight now.

What happened?

Her nails dug into the wood of the ship's rail.

What's *happened* – to Robert, and Geraint, and Angelotti? What's happened to Florian, and Godfrey in Dijon? Is Dijon even standing? Fuck, fuck, *fuck!*

Frustrated, she slammed her hand down on the grained wood. Wind whucked the sails above her head. Nausea threatened to overcome her again. *I am tired of feeling sick every damn day!*

Stomach empty, light-headed since the wound to her head had been freshly broken open, she still knew from experience that – despite in the past breaking her ribs, her shinbone, and almost all the fingers on her left hand at one time or another – the most dangerous injury she ever had received had been the *nazir*'s tap with a mace to her knee. The most dangerous because the most likely to disable. Knee joints don't move that way.

Better, now, than it had been some days ago?

Yes, she concluded tentatively. *Yes* . . .

Ash turned her head, gazing down the well of the ship, past the rowers. The *nazir* who had given the blow, one Theudibert, grinned back at her. A sharp word from the commander of the prisoners' escort squad, *'Arif* Alderic, recalled him to his duties; which as far as she could see only involved Theudibert in seeing that she did not throw herself overboard, or get herself raped and killed by the ship's crew – 'raped' is probably permissible, she thought, 'killed' will get Theudibert into trouble – and otherwise entertain himself until the ship made landfall.

As well, the Visigoth soldier kept her away from the other prisoners aboard. Ash had barely got a word with one or two of them – four women and sixteen men, most of whom were Auxonne merchants by their dress, except for a man who was obviously a soldier, and two old women who looked like swine-herds or chaff-gatherers; no one who could be worth the cost of bringing across the Mediterranean, even as slave labour.

Carthage. It *has* to be Carthage.[1]

I never heard any voice. I don't know what you mean. *I never heard any voice!*

She glimpsed something ahead, between the lateen sail and the prow, but could not make out enough in the darkness to know if it were land or clouds again. Above, constellations still indicated they sailed south-east.

Ten days? No, fourteen, fifteen, maybe more. Christ, Green Christ, *de profundis*, what's *happened* since they took me? *Who won the field?*

A tread on the deck alerted her. She looked up. *'Arif*-commander Alderic and one of his men approached, the man carrying a bowl of something viscous, white and gruel-like.

"Eat," the bearded dark Visigoth *'arif* ordered. He appeared to be forty or so: a large man.

It had been five days after the battle before her raw, ragged voice came back, and she was able to whisper. Now she could speak normally, apart from her chattering teeth in the cold.

"Not until you tell me where we're bound. And what's happened to my troops."

It was no great effort to decide on a hunger strike, Ash thought, when it was impossible to keep food down. *But I shall have to eat, or I'll be too weak to escape.*

Alderic frowned, more in puzzlement than anger. "I was particularly instructed on that point, not to tell you. Come: eat."

She visualised herself through his eyes – a thin lanky woman with the broad

---

[1] Given the date of AD 1476, the text cannot be referring here to the original Phoenician settlement of Carthage, or to Roman, Vandal or Byzantine Carthage. Since the culture is not Islamic, this must be a reference to my presumed Visigoth settlement, possibly at or near the same geographical location, and named 'Carthage' for that reason.

shoulders of a swimmer.[2] Cropped silver-fair hair: scalp still clotted bloody where her head had bled ten or fifteen days ago. A woman, but a woman in nothing more than a linen shirt and braies; shivering, dirty, and stinking; and red with lice- and flea-bites. Bandaged at the knee and shoulder. Easy to underestimate?

"Did you serve with the Faris?" Ash asked.

The *'arif* took the bowl that his foot-soldier held, motioning the man away with a jerk of one hand. He remained silent. He held it out, with an expression of determination.

Ash took the wooden bowl and scooped up crushed-barley gruel in her filthy fingers. She took a mouthful, swallowed, and waited. Her stomach lurched, but kept it. She licked her fingers, revolted by the bland lack of taste. "Well?"

"Yes, I served with our Faris." *'Arif* Alderic watched her eat. An expression of amusement crossed his face at the speed of it, now she was able to eat without throwing up. "In your lands, and in Iberia, these past six years, where she fought in the *Reconquista* – taking Iberia back from the Bretons and Navarrese."[3]

"She good?"

"Yes." Alderic's amusement deepened. "Praise God, and praise her Stone Golem, she is very good indeed."

"She win, at Auxonne?"

Alderic began to speak. *Got him!* she thought. But within a fraction of a second the commander recalled himself and shook his head.

"My instructions are strict. You are to be told nothing. It was no inconvenience, while you were ill. Now you have recovered, somewhat, I feel it . . ." *'Arif* Alderic appeared to be searching for a word. "Discourteous."

"They want me softened up, before they talk to me. I'd do exactly the same thing."

Ash watched him carefully not ask her who *they* might be.

"Okay." She sighed. "I give up. You're not going to tell me anything. I can wait. How long before we dock at Carthage?"

The man's brows rose up, with perfect timing. The *'arif* Alderic inclined his head, politely, and said nothing.

Her stomach churned. Ash, with deliberation, leaned out over the leeward rail, and threw up what she had just eaten. It was not policy. Dread and pity mixed in her gut, fearful that she might hear of Dijon fallen, Charles dead – but who cares about a bloody Duke of Burgundy? – and worse, the Lion Azure in the front line, rolled up, broken, burned, crushed; all the faces she knows cold and white and dead on the earth in some southern corner of the Duchy. She gagged, threw up nothing but bile, and leaned back, holding on to the rail to keep herself upright.

"Is your general dead?" she asked suddenly.

[2] The Latin has 'upper body strength of a sword-user'; this is the nearest modern comparison.

[3] ??? – PR. This is completely baffling! The *Reconquista* involved Spanish Christian forces driving out the remaining Arab cultures from Spain (after the Arab conquest and settlement begun in AD 711), a process completed in AD 1492, some sixteen years after the events supposedly depicted in the 'Ash' texts. I can only suppose complete textual corruption here. After five hundred years it is impossible to guess what the 'Fraxinus' chronicler actually meant.

Alderic started. "The Faris? No."

"Then the Burgundians lost the field. *Didn't* they?" Ash fixed her gaze on him, stating speculation as certainty: "She wouldn't be alive if we'd won. It's two weeks, what can it *matter* if you tell me? *What happened to my people?*"

"I'm sorry." Alderic gripped her arm and lowered her down on to the deck, out of the way of sailors' running feet. The deck heaved up under her: she swallowed. Alderic gazed back at the steersman and the stern, where the ship's captain stood. Ash heard something called, but could not distinguish what.

"I am sorry," Alderic repeated. "I've commanded loyal men, I know how badly you need to hear news of yours. I am forbidden from telling you, on pain of my own death—"

"Well, *fuck* King-Caliph Theodoric!" Ash muttered to herself.

"—and in any case, I do not know." The *'arif* Alderic looked down at her. She saw him note, by a glance, where the *nazir* Theudibert was, and if he was in earshot or not. Not. "I don't know your liveries, nor what part of the field you fought, and in any case I was with my own men, keeping the road to the north clear of the reinforcements from Bruges."

"Reinforcements!"

"A force of some four thousand. My *amir*'s cousin, Lord Sisnandus, defeated them; I think in the early hours before you joined battle at Auxonne. Now: enough. Sit there, be silent. *Nazir!*" Alderic straightened. As Corporal Theudibert ran up, Alderic ordered, "Keep your men with you, and guard this woman. Never mind the other prisoners. Don't let *her* escape while we dock."

"No, *'Arif!*" Theudibert touched his hand to his heart.

Ash, hardly listening, found herself sitting on the deck that throbbed to the rowers' change of beat, surrounded by the legs of armed men in mail shirts and white robes.

Reinforcements! What *else* didn't Charles tell us? Hell, we're not mercenaries, we're mushrooms – kept in the dark and fed on horse-shit . . .

It was the kind of remark she could have made to Robert Anselm. Tears pricked at her eyes.

Above, the night sky darkened, familiar stars fading with moon-set. She prayed, by habit and almost without realising it: *By the Lion – let me see dawn, let the sun come up!*

A settled blackness lay across the world.

The wind bit cold, sieving through her old linen shirt as if she wore nothing. Her teeth began to chatter. *But Angeli told me how* hot *it is, under the Eternal Twilight!* Voices shouted, lanterns were lit – a hundred iron lanterns, strung from every rail and all up the mast. Decked out with yellow flames, the ship sailed on; sailed until Ash heard muttering among the soldiers and scrambled to her feet, knee paining sharply, and stood, soldiers' hands gripping her arms, and saw, for the first time that she remembered, the coast of North Africa.

The last moonlight marked out the lifting swell. A black blob, darker than the sea and sky, must be land. Low. Headlands? The deck jerked under her as they tacked and came around on a different course. Hours? Minutes? She grew cold as ice in their imprisoning hands, and the indistinct land drew closer. She smelled the liminal odour of dying weed, scavenged corpses of fish and bird excrement that is the smell of coasts. The lift and fall of the deck lessened: wood rang and rattled as the sails came down, and more oars dug into the water. Spray hit her numb skin.

A congerie of lanterns shone across the waves – the sea calmer now: she thought *Are we sheltered? Is there an isthmus?* – and became an approaching ship. No – ships.

Something in the first vessel's movement took her eye: a snaking, irregular motion. She clenched her arms across her breasts, against the cold, and stared tear-eyed into the wind. The foreign ship beat up towards them, indistinct; was suddenly twenty yards away, clear in its lanterns and their own – a sharp-prowed, long, thin, *curving* vessel; sides slabbed with wood and some bright substance.

Not metal, too heavy.

It glinted with the exact colour of sunlight on the roofs of Dijon, and she thought suddenly *Slate! Thin-split slate, as armour. Christus!*

A single great tiller-oar rose at the poop, shifting left and right. The ship snaked a serpentine course, the whole body of it moving in articulated segments; knifing through the black water, a vision in lamplight: gone into the dark. No sails, no oars: what had stood at the tiller, wrenching it with immense power, had been a golem—

"Messenger ship," Alderic said, behind her. "Fast news."

She made to answer. Her teeth chattered too much; she gave it up.

Behind the articulated wooden vessel, a much larger ship thunked through the waves. Ash had a second to recognise it as one of the troopships she had seen from the hills of Genoa, before it passed on into the wet darkness. She was too low to see its deck; could only guess at the number of soldiers in the shallow-draught hold – five hundred? More? She had a brief glimpse of the curved sides towering above them, shining wet with spray; saw the great blades of the wheel at the stern canted, dipped down into the troughs of the waves; and she saw the clay bodies of golems inside the paddle-wheel, their weight and strength forcing it to turn, to bite into the cold, deep water. It thunked away north-east, into the Mediterranean.[4]

And how many ships like that have gone north?

The thought numbed her as much as the cold. Tranced, in the icy dark, she thought nothing more until the ship's motion altered. An hour past moon-set: it would be dawn. But not in this Twilight – least of all, here.

Still held prisoned by Theudibert's men, she looked up.

The starboard rowers rested.

The ship opened the harbour of Carthage.

---

[4] This is obviously either a folk memory of the supreme Carthaginian sea-power in the Mediterranean around the time of the Punic Wars (216–164 BC), or of the Vandals' dominating navy in the 6th century AD.

A very similar passage appears in 'Pseudo-Godfrey'; indeed it may have been copied into this. If the author of 'Pseudo-Godfrey' was a monk, then he would have access to preserved Classical texts, which he has here conflated with the mediaeval myth of the Sea-Serpent to depict a mythical segmented 'swimming ship', and a 'paddle-wheel' powered vessel. Mediaeval authors are prone to this. We can assume Ash actually saw a double- or a triple-oared galley, rowed by Carthaginian slaves.

Bare masts thicketed the darkness, outlined against the thousand lights of the port buildings.

A thousand ships rocked, moored at rest in the harbour. Triremes and quinqueremes; golem-powered troopships loading men and stores; and European galleys, caravels, cogs, carracks. Deep-hulled merchant ships bringing in bullocks and calves and cows, pomegranates and pigs, goats and grapes and grain: all the things that do not grow or thrive, under the Eternal Twilight.

Oars splashed gently in the black water. Their ship glided on between two stark high promontories covered with buildings, each hair-pin street outlined by rows of Greek Fire lights, gaudy and blazing and brilliant. Ash craned her head back, staring up at people on the bastions of the harbour: slaves running, men and women walking in loose, heavy woollen robes; and she heard a bell banging out for mass from a distant church, and *still* the walls went up—

Nothing was raw rock. All of it was dressed masonry.

She saw the nearer stone dimly in the light from the ship's lanterns as they steered between half a dozen merchant ships, the drum-beat of their rowers echoing across the water and off the heights. Dressed stone: rising up sheer to battlements, bastions, ravelins, the highest walls pockmarked with row upon row of dark holes: arrow-slits, and crenellations, and stations for gunners to fire their cannon.

Her neck ached. She swallowed, lowered her gaze from the sheer immensity. She smelled the salt sea, overlaid by the stench of the harbour: all kinds of rubbish bobbed on the black waters, between skittering tiny craft. Sellers of fruit, sweetmeats, wine and woollen blankets sculled to keep up with their hull. She noted dozens of cargo ships, grain ships, riding high in the water: holds empty. And the black figures of men on the docks stood out against burning bonfires, and braziers full of hot coals. Chill wind blew into her eyes, making them water. The tears froze on her cheeks.

The sweaty fingers on her arm gripped tight. She glanced rapidly at whoever held her, and met the *nazir* Theudibert's bright-eyed, gloating expression. Theudibert slid his other hand up between her thighs. His rough nails snagged her skin and his fingers nipped shut, pinching tender internal flesh.

Ash winced, looked for Alderic, then felt her face burn red with the humiliation of making that appeal. She wanted to reach quickly behind her, grab Theudibert's wrist, bring his elbow cracking down backward over her knee – too many hands dug into the muscles of her arms, holding her: she could not move. His fingers stabbed up between painfully dry skin. She writhed.

He can't know – my belly's not thick. If anything, I'm thinner; I can't eat for being sick. Maybe if he rapes me that'll shake it loose, and I'll end up grateful to this mother-fucking bastard—

"This ain't the harbour," Theudibert grated, "*that's* the harbour."

Ash stared ahead. It was all she could do. The rowers were taking them between a multitude of small boats and medium-size cogs and carracks. Now, ahead, four great lanes of black water opened up before them, crowded with shipping.

Stark masonry separated these junctions of the harbour. Surmounting them, up in the darkness – she moved her head, dazed – in turn a barracks, a fort, a windowless black building . . . and moored along the quay, great triremes and galleys and black-pennanted warships.

Thousands of people swarmed, everywhere she looked: raising sail on ships, bringing donkey-carts steeply down to the quay ahead of them in the first opening, lighting more lanterns along the heights, calling, shouting, loading crates on to carracks. A dozen face-muffled women stared down from pleasure grounds a hundred and fifty feet away up a sheer cliff.

If I scream for help, who'll come?

No one.

The scent of spices, dung, and something odd came to her; something that didn't fit—

Ash wrenched her body. The armed men, taller and stronger, held her tightly; their warm, hard, armoured bodies jostling hers. She flinched, her bare feet among their boots. A pang of fear went through her, rising up from her belly to her throat. The muscles of her thighs and knees loosened. She swallowed, dry-mouthed.

It's *real*, now. All the while we were just on a ship, anything could happen, we could have been going somewhere else, I could have escaped, it wasn't real . . .

I would give anything now to have a weapon, and even a dozen men . . .

The sweating soldier who held her, his fingers wet with her body's wetness, wore mail and carried a sword strapped at his belt; more importantly, had eight mates with him, and a commander whose shout would bring a hundred troops from the docks and warehouses.

"Mouthy bitch not so mouthy now?" his voice whispered in her ear. His breath was sweet with rice gruel: her gorge rose.

The knowledge that rape and mutilation are not inconceivable, are possible and even likely, thumped in the pit of her pregnant belly. A cold, cold sensation ran through her. Her hands prickled. She stared at the inexorably approaching dock.

Terror dried her mouth, tautened her body, strung her out to the highest pitch. Almost absently, she identified the odour that jarred her – the wind smelled almost peppery-cold. It stung her nostrils. In the Swiss mountains she would have thought it the scent of approaching snow.

A sudden eddy of wind across the harbour brought dampness.

Cold dots of sleet kissed her scarred face, and her bare legs under her shirt.

Oars backed and withdrawn, the sailors leaped to prow and stern and slung ropes, and quayside workers hauled them in. Wood grated against stone. The galley docked in a crackle of the ice forming at the foot of the stone quay, and strained hemp cables to a creaking halt.

The *nazir*'s fist hit her in the kidneys, pushing her forward into the gaggle of the ship's other prisoners. Ash stumbled. She pitched forward and fell, unprepared, on the gangway, catching herself and grazing her hands on the stone steps that led up to the quay. The first flakes of true snow melted under her palms. A boot caught her in the ribs. She smelled her own vomit.

"Shit!" Her voice came out a dry, high whimper.

No escape from the truth now. I *do* hear a voice. And I did hear *her* voice. The same voice. They don't know it, but they're right. This isn't a mistake. I am the person they want.

And what happens to me, now that they're going to find that out?

II

All the way up the steep, narrow, ruler-straight streets from the dock, marching up steps between iron-shuttered buildings lit by steel-and-glass cages of Greek Fire,[5] the Visigoth soldiers still kept her away from the other prisoners.

She had no time to look at the city. She stumbled, bare feet scraping on cobbles, aware of hands gripping her under the armpits. Guards' polearms clashed as they came up to a thick stone arch – a gateway, that pierced an encircling wall stretching away around the hill as far as lights could show her. The wall was too high for anything to be visible beyond it.

The other prisoners from the ship were herded on past, into the body of the city, away from the gate into the citadel.

"What?" Ash turned her head, stumbling. The *'arif* Alderic called something. Two of the soldiers dragged back an old woman, a young fat man, and an older man. Soldiers closed around them.

The arched gateway tunnelled through a defensive wall a good twenty yards thick. She lost her footing in the dark. Theudibert dragged her up with a satisfied obscenity. She flinched back from another wall – no lights, here. A freezing wind blew in her face. She realised she was no longer in the gateway, but in a narrower passage.

None of the buildings to either side had any windows.

Four of Alderic's men lit ordinary pierced-iron lanterns, carrying them high. Shadows now stalked and jerked in the narrow passageway. A street? An alley? Ash squinted up. The last stars, fading into darkness, let her know this was still outdoors. A sharp fist in the back prodded her onwards.

They passed a black door, barred with seven thick sections of iron. Thirty yards down the street, another door. None of the buildings were built of wood, or wattle and daub: all were windowless stone. Then they turned a corner, turned again, and again; winding through a maze of dark alleys, a pitiless black day dark above their heads.

Ash hugged her arms around her body as she hobbled on. Clad in thin linen, she would have shivered anyway, but this present cold bit at her hard-soled feet on the cobbles, whitened her fingers, and made her breath steam on the air.

The soldiers of the King-Caliph likewise shivered.

Four of the soldiers ran to unbar a door in a featureless wall. Big enough to

---

[5] Since this is used for street lighting, this would appear (despite the text's use of the same name) to be a variant of Greek Fire – perhaps using only the ingredient naphtha, which receives its name from the Arabic *al-naft*, and has a later history of use for this purpose in industrial England.

be a sally-port, she thought. The *nazir* thrust her through it, into darkness. She banged her injured knee, and screamed aloud. Iron lanterns danced in her dazzled sight, hands shifted her, shoulders and arms banged against her body, hustling her inside, along a long dark passage.

A withered, tiny hand crept into hers.

Ash looked down, and saw that the old woman prisoner had taken her hand. The woman looked up at her. Shifting shadows, and lines and creases, disguised her expression. Her hand felt like cold chicken-bones. Ash tucked the woman's hand under hers, pressing it to her linen-covered body for warmth.

The old woman's hand slid down over her belly. The soft voice wailed in French, "I thought so, on the ship. You don't show, but you're with child, my heart. I could midwife you – *Oh, what will they do to us?*"

"Shut up!"

"What do they want us for?"

Ash felt and heard a mailed fist hit flesh. The woman's hand went limp and slid out of hers. She made a grab; but the soldiers surrounded her, pushing her on, and she stumbled with them out into a great courtyard.

Back entrance, she surmised, and *It's a manor house!* The courtyard was much longer than it was wide, surrounded on all sides by stone-barred windows and arched doorways. The building surrounding this interior courtyard on all four sides went up at least three storeys. Greek Fire lanterns dazzled: she could not see the sky.

The long courtyard was packed full with people. Some house-guards, by their swords. One or two better-dressed. Most of them were men and women of all adult ages, in plain tunics, with iron collars around their necks. Ash gaped at the running slaves, belly cold with familiarity.

Almost all, despite their different faces, had a family resemblance. Almost all had, in the fizzing white light, ash-pale hair.

She looked around for the old woman, missed her in the crowd, and tripped. She landed, hands and knees, on black and white tiles. She groaned, wrapping both hands around her knee. It felt swollen and hot again. Her eyes teared.

Through water, she saw Alderic step forward with the ship's captain, the two of them speak to a group of house-guards and slaves; and she rolled over and got up. She and the male prisoners were pushed into a huddle. A fountain plashed into its bowl, a few yards away. In the heart of the falling jets, a mechanical phoenix sang.

Ash gripped the hem of her shirt in her two hands, pulling it down over her thighs. Cold sweat ran down between her shoulder-blades. She found herself mouthing, *Oh Christ, help me, help me keep my baby!* and stopped, her face stark. *But I don't want it, don't want to die in childbirth—*

When you think you have reached the end of fear, there is always somewhere to go. She knotted her hands into fists to prevent it being seen that they were shaking. Sentimental pictures of a son or daughter would not stay in her mind, confronted with this too-bright courtyard full of men talking in the Gothic dialect they called Carthaginian, far too fast for her to understand. Only the vulnerability of her hardly noticeable belly remained, and the absolute necessity – and impossibility – of secrecy.

"Poor girl, poor heart." The old peasant woman hung in a soldier's grip, bleeding. The two male prisoners stood with her, their very different faces frozen in identical expectations of fear.

"Come with me." The 'arif Alderic was at her side, pulling her onward.

Ash shivered, cold deep in her gut. From somewhere she dragged up a grin, showing all her teeth. "What's the matter, you decided I'm the one you don't want? Hey, I could have told you that at Dijon! Or maybe this is where you tell me you want a contract with my company? Consider me softened up, you'll probably get a good deal!"

She could tell she stunk from the expressions of the guards near her, and the more distant glances of the one or two men who might be King-Caliph Theodoric's freeborn subjects, but her own nose was insensible of it. She limped with Alderic on the cold tiles. Her mouth ran on:

"I always thought it was warm enough, in the Eternal Twilight. This is fucking freezing! What's the matter, the Penance getting too heavy for you? Maybe God's pissed off with waiting for the Empty Chair to be filled. Maybe it's a portent."

"Be quiet."

Fear makes one voluble. Ash cut herself off.

Doors opened off the narrow passage. Alderic opened one, bowed, said something, and pushed her through in front of him. Her eyes were dazzled by more light.

Ash heard the door slam to behind her.

A thick voice said, "Is it her?"

"Perhaps." Another, drier voice.

Ash blinked her vision clear of dazzles. The dado of the room was lined with pipes and glass-covered lamps, hissing with Greek Fire. Oil burners stood in the room's corners, and their sweet scent both cleared her head and took her back with startling immediacy to being in a tent, in the field, some year in Italy, with Visigoth mercenaries.

No tent, this. The floor under her feet was tiled red and black, old enough that her bare feet felt every worn dip in it. Mosaic tiles winked back at her in the light of twenty lamps.

The walls glittered, covered in quarter-inch square colours from floor to vaulted ceiling. The images of saints and icons glared down: Catherine, with her wheel, Sebastian with his arrows, Mercurius with his surgeon's knife and thief's cut purse, George and dragon. Gold robes and liquid dark eyes stared down at her.

Shadows lost themselves in the ribbed ceiling. Under the pungent controlled jets of Greek Fire she detected a smell of earth. The entire wall at the back of the room was one huge mosaic of the Bull and the Tree, Christ watching her from where He hung, Saint Herlaine at his leaf-pierced feet, Saint Tanitta[6] observing.

It was oppressive enough that she missed what was next said, only managing to concentrate again as the echoes of voices died in the cold, cold room. She looked towards the room's heavy, polished, square-cut settle and tables. Two

[6] Possibly a Christianised version of the Carthaginian goddess, Tanit, to whom babies were sacrificed.

364

men confronted her. A thin, white-robed man of about fifty, in the dress of an *amir*, watched her with lined eyes. Crouched by the foot of his chair, a man with the pasty fat face of an idiot watched her and dribbled.

"Go." The *amir* gently touched the retarded man's arm. "Go and eat. You may hear later what we say. Go, Ataulf. Go. Go . . ."

The idiot, who might have been anything between twenty and sixty, passed her with a glance from slant bright eyes, under thick fair brows and thinning hair. His wide-lipped mouth dribbled wetly.

Ash took a step aside as he went out, using it as an excuse to look back. No windows opened into this room. There was only the one double door. The *'arif* Alderic stood in front of it.

"Have you eaten?" the *amir* asked.

Ash looked at the fair-bearded man. She could distinguish some slight physical resemblance to the retard, but his intelligence shone out of his lined face.

Knowing where his kindness came from – that it was an effort to break her by contrast – she nonetheless answered meekly in her best Carthaginian Latin, "No, Lord-*Amir*."

"'*Arif*, have food brought." He pointed to a second carved chair, lower, that stood beside his own; as Alderic leaned back out of the doors to give orders. "I am the *amir* Leofric. You are in my house."

That's right. That's the name. She mentioned you.

You're her not-quite father.

"Sit down."

Her feet became warmer the instant she stepped on to the carpets that covered the brick-red tiles. An ash-blond man entered and moved past her, placing a shallow ceramic dish of hot food on a low table, and retreating out of the room without a word. He was about Ash's own age, she judged; he had a metal collar around his throat, and neither Alderic nor the lord-*amir* Leofric took any more notice of him than they did of the lamps. A slave.

She hid the fear chilling her stomach by walking on across the carpet and sitting herself on the low oak chair. It was padded, with a back that came round under her elbows; she was at a loss, for some moments, as to how you sat in it. *Amir* Leofric appeared to be ignoring any likely infestations from this flea-bitten prisoner: he regarded her with a concerned, inquisitive expression.

The food – two or three objects that were yellow, soft and purse-shaped – steamed in the chill air. Ash scooped up one in her bare dirty fingers, bit into warm, brittle pastry, tasted potatoes, fish and saffron.

"Shit!" She slobbered the better part of a raw egg out of the pastry purse, down her wrists and forearms. In one rapid movement she licked yolk and white off, licked her skin clean. "Now, sir—"

She looked up, intent on taking a verbal initiative, and broke off, springing to her feet, careless of the stained shirt barely covering her legs.

"Oh, Christ, it's a *rat*!" She threw out an arm, pointing at the *amir*'s lap. "It's a plague rat!"[7]

---

[7] This, and another similar reference, are additions to the original manuscript. Even were they not inscribed marginally in different handwriting, context would prove as much: the role of *Rattus*

"My dear, nothing of the sort." The Visigoth *amir* had a surprisingly pleasant smile, much younger than his lined face; teeth gleaming white in his grey-blond beard. He bent his head and chirruped encouragingly.

A pointed furry face emerged from the folds of his white, gold-trimmed velvet robes, pink nose first. Tiny pupil-less black eyes fixed on Ash as the animal froze. Ash stared back, startled at the eye-contact. The animal's fur shone pure white in the softening lamplight.

Encouraged by stillness it glided out on to Leofric's thigh, picking its way carefully over his robe. High haunches were followed by a sleek bald tail. Its body alone was ten inches long. It had (she saw in frozen horror as it emerged) a bare scaly tail. And balls the size of walnuts.

"*That's* not a rat? Get out of here!"

At her voice the rodent froze, back curving into lordosis. Rats are black, are mice writ large. This, she saw with all the clarity of fear deferred, was broad at the rump, narrow in the fore-quarters. The muzzle seemed blunter than a mouse's. It had small ears, for the size of its broad head.

"A different breed of rat. My family brought them back from a voyage to the Middle Kingdom."[8] The *amir* Leofric murmured quietly. He put one weathered finger down and scratched the rodent behind its ear. The animal stood up on its hind legs, sniffing with a quivering spray of whiskers, and staring into the man's face. "He is a rat, my dear, but a different kind."

"Rats are the Devil's lap-dogs!" Ash moved back two steps on the carpet. "They eat half your stores, all if you don't have a pack of terriers; Jesu, the trouble I've had—! Filthy, dirty— And they give you plague!"[9]

"Perhaps once." Again, the Visigoth *amir* chirruped. It was a surprisingly silly sound to come from an adult man, and Ash thought she heard the *'arif* Alderic snort quietly from the doorway. Leofric's robe moved.

"Who's my sweetheart, then. . . ?" he whispered.

Two more rats came out on to his shoulders. One was yellow, marked with a sepia brown at the haunches, toes, and muzzle; the other, Ash would have sworn if the light had been better, was a pale enough slate-grey to appear blue. Two more sets of bead-black eyes fixed on her.

"Perhaps once," Leofric repeated. "A thousand rat-generations ago. They breed much faster than we do. I have records going back through the decades to when these were plain brown – not half so pretty as you, my dear," he added to one of the beasts. "These have known no disease for a century or more. I have many varieties. Rats of every colour and size. You must see them."

Ash stared, frozen, as one of the rats reached its furry snake-head up and bit the Visigoth *amir*'s ear. A rat-bite will bring fever, sometimes death; even if not

Rattus in carrying the 'plague flea' was not realised until 1896. I suspect a Victorian collector read this document at some point in its existence; a descendant, perhaps, of the man who wrote 'Fraxinus me fecit' on the outer sheet in the 1700s.

[8] Possibly China. By the physical description in the text, this is not *Rattus Rattus*, the Black Rat, but *Rattus Norvegicus*, the Brown Rat, which is Asian in origin.

[9] Ash's concern with the destructive capacity of rodents is original to 'Fraxinus', and must have been a similar problem for all army commanders.

that, then pain like a needle stabbing flesh. She winced in sympathy. Leofric didn't move.

The blue rat, delicate paws holding the unblemished lobe of the man's ear, continued to lick it with a tiny pink tongue. She nuzzled a little in his beard, and then dropped down to all fours, and wriggled instantaneously out of sight in his robes.

"They're your familiars!" Ash exclaimed, revolted.

"They are my hobby." The *amir* Leofric switched to talk in French, with a slight accent. "Do you understand me, my dear? I want to be sure than you understand what I say, and that I understand anything you may tell me."

"I don't have anything to say."

They remained staring at each other for a moment, in the lamplit room. The same slave entered and tended to one lamp, pouring in a different oil. A flower scent gradually imposed itself on the room's air. Ash glanced over her shoulder at Alderic's bulk blocking the doorway.

"What do you expect me to say, Lord-*Amir*?" she asked. "Yes, I'm some relation to your general. Obviously. She says you bred her from slaves. I can see that you did. Too many people here look like me . . . Does it *matter*? I've got five hundred men I can answer for, and despite what she did at Basle, I'm willing to negotiate another contract. What else can I say?"

Ash managed to end with a shrug, despite standing dressed in nothing but filthy shirt and braies, her hair cropped and stinking, itching with bites.

"Sweetheart," Leofric breathed. To the pale blue rat, Ash realised. The Visigoth lord bent his head and the rat now on his knee stood up on its hind feet, stretching up slimly. They were briefly nose-to-nose, then it dropped back to all fours. He cupped his hand and stroked the rodent's arched back. It turned its head and licked his fingers with a clean pink tongue. "Touch her, gently. She won't hurt you."

Anything to put off more questions, Ash thought grimly, and walked back across the carpet to Leofric's chair, and reached out an extremely reluctant finger. She touched surprisingly soft, surprisingly dry, warm fur.

The beast moved.

She gasped. Tiny claws fixed into her forefinger – she froze, feeling how light the grip was.

The pale blue female rat sniffed delicately at Ash's bitten, dirty nails. She began to lick Ash, sat back, sneezed twice – a tiny, absurd sound in the huge mosaic-walled chamber – and sat up on her haunches, rubbing paws over her muzzle and whiskers, for all the world as if she were cleaning away shipboard filth.

"She's washing her face like a Christian!" Ash exclaimed. She left her hand outstretched, hopeful of the rat investigating it further; and with a sudden jolt of fear to her belly, realised that she was standing so close to the seated *amir* that she smelled his perfume and the underlying odour of male sweat.

Leofric stroked his rat. "My dear, it can take many years to breed a variety. Sometimes the right colour will come, and then faults come bound up with it: retardation, aggressiveness, psychosis, miscarriages, deformed vaginas, deformed guts so that they burst of their own waste products and die."

The blue rat lay down and curled up nose-to-tail on his lap. He looked back at Ash. "It can take many generations to breed true. To breed daughter back to sire, son to dam and sister. One culls out the unusable, breeding only from what is useful – for many, many years. And sometimes success never comes. Or if it does, it is sterile. Do you begin to understand why you may be important to me?"

"No." Ash's tongue stuck to the dry roof of her mouth.

The *amir* Leofric smiled, as if he were simultaneously recognising her badly hidden fear, and thinking of something quite other. He added, "You will note, these are most tame, unlike other wild beasts. That is a by-product of the breeding, and one I did not expect— yes?"

"Sire!" Alderic's deep voice boomed. She turned her head and witnessed a sudden entry through the double doorway into the room of collared slaves, Arian priests, armed foot soldiers, an Abbot, and a man carried waist-high above the ground in a chair.

"Lord Caliph!" *Amir* Leofric hurriedly stood up, bowing, rats scurrying back inside his clothes. "Sire?"

The back of the room was full of soldiers, Alderic's men.

Between them walked a man in the green robes of an Arian abbot – something odd about the cross on his breast – and an *amir* richly dressed and (seen at close quarters) rather younger than Leofric.

"I welcome you to my house," Leofric said formally, in Carthaginian Latin, his voice achieving calmness.

A gesture, and the chair was set down.

"Yes, yes!" An old man sat in the chair, who had obviously once had red hair, but now it was turned dirty white, and who had had the warm freckled complexion that goes with it, which now shone mottled and dark in the lamp-light. Skin hung loose at his arms, and stretched tight over his nose, brows, and around his mouth. He wore robes of woven gold tissue. Ash inhaled once and tried to hold her breath: neither of the slaves attending with pomanders could hide the stench of shit and his wasted flesh.

Theodoric, she realised, appalled, *it's the Caliph!* and found herself pushed down on to the carpet – trying desperately to favour her left leg – and Alderic's mail gauntlet forced her down on to hands and knees. She could see nothing but the hems of robes, and richly tooled leather sandals.

"Well?" the Visigoth ruler's voice sounded weak.

Amir Leofric's voice said, "My lord Caliph, why are these men with you? This abbot? And the *amir* Gelimer is no friend of my family."

"I must have a priest with me!" The King-Caliph, fretfully.

A full-blown abbot is 'a priest'? Ash wondered.

"The *amir* Gelimer has no place here!"

"No? No, perhaps not. Gelimer, get out."

A different, tenor voice protested, "Lord Caliph, it was I who brought this news to you, not *Amir* Leofric, though he must have known it long since!"

"True. True. You will then stay, so that we may hear your wisdom on this subject. Where is the woman?"

Ash's gaze fixated on the plain weave of the carpet. Its fibres felt soft against her palm. She risked turning her head, to see if there was any way to the door; saw nothing but the mailed legs of guards. No friends, no allies, no way to run. She wanted to shit.

"Here," Leofric admitted.

"Get her up," the King-Caliph wheezed.

Ash, dragged to her feet, found herself stared at by two expensively dressed and extremely powerful men.

"This is a boy!"

Nazir Theudibert stepped out from the guard and grabbed the front of her linen shirt between his two hands, ripping it from neck to hem. He stepped back. Ash sucked in her belly and stood erect.

"It is a woman," Leofric murmured, respectfully.

The King-Caliph Theodoric nodded, once. "I have come to encourage her. *Nazir* Saris!"

A scuffle at the door, among the King-Caliph's personal guard, made Ash turn her head. A sword slid from its wood-lined sheath. At that sound she jerked instantly back, even in Alderic's grip.

Two of the Caliph's soldiers dragged in the fat male prisoner.

"No! No, I can pay! I can *pay!*" The young man's eyes went wide. He yelled randomly in French, Italian and Schweizerdeutsch. "My Guild will pay a ransom! Please!"

One of the soldiers tripped him up, the other yanked up his stained blue robes.

Light flashed from the flat of the sword as the soldier lifted it, and chopped precisely down. Blood spurted.

"Oh, *Christ!*" Ash exclaimed.

The room stank suddenly as the fat man's bowels relaxed. His white, bare legs streamed with blood. He lifted himself up on to his elbows, scrabbling forward, screeching and sobbing, face blubbered with tears. His legs dragged after him like two slabs of butcher's meat.

The twin slashes across the backs of his knees that hamstrung him, bled freely on the stone tiles.

An asthmatic voice said, "Talk to my councillor Leofric."

Ash forced herself to look away, to look at the man who had spoken – to look at the King-Caliph.

"Talk to my councillor Leofric," Theodoric repeated. In the lamplight, his stretched skin appeared yellow, his eye-sockets two black holes. "Tell him all your heart and all your mind. Now. I don't want you to be in any doubt of what we can and will do to you if you refuse even once."

The man on the floor bled and screamed and thrashed only his upper torso as the soldiers pulled him out of the room. The stone eyes of saints impassively watched him go.

"You did that just to *show* me—?"

Appalled and incredulous, Ash shouted at battlefield volume.

Dizziness sunk down through her body, her hands and feet felt hot; she knew she would faint, in a second, and bent over to grip her thighs and inhale deeply.

I've seen worse, *done* worse, but to just do it so casually, for no reason—

369

It was the speed of it, and the absolute non-existence of any appeal, that appalled her the most. And the irrevocable damage. A flush coloured her scarred face. She yelled, in camp patois, "You just ruined that poor fuck's life to *make a point*?"

The King-Caliph did not look at her. His abbot was saying something quietly, into his ear, and he nodded, once. Slaves sluiced down the tiles and retired. The floral scent from the oil-burners did not conceal the copper smell of blood and the stink of faeces.

Alderic stepped away from her. Two of the Caliph's soldiers, the same two, took her wrists, locking her elbow and shoulder joints to hold her immobile.

"Kill her now," the *amir* Gelimer said. Ash saw Gelimer was a dark man, in his thirties; with a plain, small-eyed face and a braided dark beard. "If she is a danger to our crusade in the north, or even if she is only a very little danger, you should kill her, my lord Caliph."

The *amir* Leofric said hastily, "But no! How will we know what's happened? This must be examined!"

"She is a northern peasant," the King-Caliph wheezed dismissively. "Leofric, why waste your time with this? The best that can come out of it is another general, and I have one of those. Will she tell you why this cold? Why this hellish, devilish *cold* here, since your slave-general went overseas? The further north we conquer in crusade, the harder it bites us here – I truly do wonder, now, what God would have us do! Was this war *not* His will, after all? Leofric, have you damned me?"

The Arian abbot said cheerfully, "Sire, the Penance is a northern heresy. God has always favoured us with this darkness that – while it keeps us from tilling soil or growing corn – nevertheless drives us out to conquer lands for Him. It makes us men of war, not farmers or herdsmen, thus it makes us noble. It is His whip, chastising us to do His will."

"It is cold, Abbot Muthari." The King-Caliph cut him off with a motion of his hand. The lantern light showed dark spots mottling his white fingers. Theodoric closed his fragile-lidded eyes.

"Sire," Gelimer murmured, "before you do anything else, Sire, take off her sword hand. A woman familiar with the Devil, as this one is, shouldn't be allowed to continue as a warrior, no matter how short a time you let her live after this."

The voice, and the apprehension of the image in her mind – two white circles of chopped bone in red spurting flesh – came instantaneously. Ash swallowed bile. Nausea and lassitude swept through her like the tide.

A small pointy furry face stared down at Ash from *Amir* Leofric's shoulder. Black eyes surveyed her. A spray of whiskers twitched. As Leofric bent down to speak to her, the rat shifted its pink-toed feet, and settled back to groom one pale blue flank – neither wet, nor dirty, nor infested with fleas.

"Give me something, Ash!" the Visigoth *amir* Leofric pleaded in an undertone. "My daughter tells me you're a woman of great value, but I have only hope, not proof. Give me something I can use to keep you alive. Theodoric knows he's dying and he's become very careless of other people's lives these last few weeks."

"Like what?" Ash gulped, tried to see through tear-wet eyes. "The world's over-full of mercenaries, my lord. Even good, valuable ones."

"I cannot disobey the King-Caliph! Give me a reason why you shouldn't be executed! *Hurry!*"

Ash watched in fascination as the blue rat twitched its whiskers and washed behind its ears with delicate pink paws. She shifted her gaze six inches, to Leofric's imploring expression.

Either this will mean I'll be released. Or it'll mean I'll be killed, probably quickly. Quickly is better; sweet Christ I *know* it's better, I've seen everything you can do to the human body, this is just children playing rose-in-a-ring! I don't want them to start on what professionals do.

She heard her own voice, thin in the cold stone-walled room:

"Okay, okay, I *do* hear a voice, when I'm fighting, I always have, it's the same as your – daughter – hears, it might be, I'm obviously blood-kin to her, I'm just a discard from your experiment, but I do hear it!"

Leofric thrust his fingers through his hair, spiking up his white curls. His intense eyes narrowed. She realised that the *amir* was regarding her with an expression of scepticism.

After all this, he doesn't *believe* me?

She whispered, hard and urgent, "*You have to believe I'm telling you the truth!*"

Sweating, shaking, she remained staring into his blue eyes for a long minute.

The *amir* Leofric turned away.

If a hand had not caught her around her body, she would have fallen: the *nazir* Theudibert supported her across her bare breasts with a wiry, hard-muscled forearm. She felt him laugh.

Leofric said, "She hears the Stone Golem, sire."

The *amir* Gelimer snorted. "And so would you claim that, now, in her place!"

The King-Caliph's mouth had whitened, and his attention wandered from the conversation to the abbot at his side; Ash saw his eyes snap back to Leofric at Gelimer's comment.

"Of course she says it," the King-Caliph Theodoric remarked, scornfully, "Leofric, you are trying to save yourself with some fable of another slave-general!"

"I hear tactics – I hear the Stone Golem," Ash said aloud, in Carthaginian Latin.

Gelimer protested. "You see? She had no knowledge of what it was called until you named it!"

The *nazir*'s arm pinned her. Ash opened her mouth to speak again, and Theudibert's free hand clamped over it, digging fingers hard into the hinges of her jaw so that she could not bite him.

The *amir* Leofric bowed very low, his rats scurrying for refuge into his robes, and raised himself up again to look at the dying King-Caliph.

"Sire. What the *amir* Gelimer says may be true. She *may* be saying this only for fear of pain or injury."

Leofric's pale faded eyes became bleak.

371

"There is a way to decide this. With your permission, now, Sire – I shall have her tortured, until it becomes clear whether or not she is speaking the truth."

III

One of Theudibert's mates said something in Carthaginian which Ash heard as, "Let's have a bit of fun with her. You heard the old boy. It doesn't matter so long as she don't end up dead."

It might have been a blond one, or his comrade; Ash couldn't tell. Eight men – nine, with their *nazir* – all very familiar, despite their light horse-mail and curved swords kit. They could have been any men in Charles's army, or Frederick's, or the Lion Azure if it came to it and *where am I being taken?* she asked herself, her bare feet bruising on stone steps, staggering, pushed down – down?

Down spiral steps, into rooms below surface-level. Is the whole hill above Carthage harbour riddled with cellars? she wondered. And the obvious thought appeared in her mind: How many go in who never come out again?

Some. It only has to be 'some'.

What does he mean, torture? He can't mean *torture*. He can't.

The *nazir* Theudibert spoke with a grin in his voice. "Yeah, why not? But you never saw it. Nothing happened to his prize bitch. You never saw nothing, right?"

Eight other excited voices mumbled agreement.

Their sweat stank on the air. Even as they bundled her out of the staircase, into lantern-lit corridors, she smelled their violent high spirits, their growing tension. Men in a group, egging each other on: nothing they would not do.

She thought, as their fists pushed her on: I can fight them, I can gouge out an eye, I can break a finger or an arm, rupture somebody's testicles, and then what? Then they break my thumbs and shins and they rape me forward and backward, cunt and arse—

"Cow!" A fair-haired man grabbed her bare breast and squeezed his fingers closed with all his force. Ash's breasts were already tender, had been every day on ship; she involuntarily screamed and lashed out, catching him in the throat. Six or seven pairs of hands manhandled her, a backhanded blow cracked across her face and spun her round and dashed her against the wall of a cell.

The crack to her head shattered her with pain. She felt baked clay tiles under her knees. A man coughed thickly; spat on her. A soft leather boot, with a man's hard foot in it, kicked her violently three finger's width below her navel.

Her lungs seized.

She gasped, scrabbling meaninglessly with her hands; found herself scraping a breath down her throat, felt cold clay tiles under left leg, hip, ribs and shoulder. Stinking linen tugged, caught around her neck, and ripped, as someone bending down tore her previously shredded shirt off over her head. Her braies were gone. Naked to their gaze.

Ash got half a spare breath, snarled, "Fuck you!" in a voice pitifully high.

Four or five male voices laughed above her. They kicked teasingly with their boots, laughed each time she shrank away from the pain.

"Go on, do her. Do her! Barbas, you first."

"Not me, man. I ain't touching her. Bitch got a disease. All them bitches from up north, they got disease."

"Oh, fucking baby, wants his mamma's tit, don't want a woman! You want me to *tie up* the dangerous warrior-woman? You 'fraid to touch her?"

A scuffle, over her. Booted feet stamped down dangerously close to her head, on the cell's tiled floor. She saw red clay, reddened by the single lamp's light; dirty hems of robes, very finely riveted mail skirts, leather greaves tied on shins, and – as she rolled over on to her front and lifted her head – men's faces in snapshot details: a wild brown eye, an unshaven cheek, a hairy wrist wiped across a mouth full of bright, regular teeth; a snake-scar trailing white down a thigh, a robe hitched up, the bulge under clothing of a cock growing hard.

"Fucking do her! Gaina! Fravitta! What you fucking standing there for, ain't you seen a woman before?"

"Let *Gaiseric* go first!"

"Yeah, let the baby do it!"

"Get your cock out, boy. That it? She ain't going to even feel *that*!"

Their deep voices resonated between small walls. She is ten years old again, sees men as infinitely heavier, stronger, muscled; but eight men are not just stronger than one woman, they are stronger than one man. They are stronger than *one*. Ash felt hot tears squeezing over her shut lids. She got to her hands and knees, shouting at them:

"I'm going to take some of you with me, I am going to *mark* you, maim you, mark you for life—!"

Saliva dripped out of her mouth, damp-spotting the baked tiles. She saw every crack at the edges of the squares where the clay crumbled, every black spidering mark of ingrained dirt. Her head and stomach throbbed, half blinding her with pain. A hot flush ran over her bare body. "I'll fucking kill you, I'll fucking *kill* you."

Theudibert bent down to scream into her face. His saliva sprayed her as he laughed. "Who's a fucking warrior-woman now? *Girl?* You gonna fight us, are you?"

"Oh *yeah*, I'm going to try and take on eight men when I don't even have a sword, never mind any mates."

Ash was not aware, for a second, that she had spoken aloud. Or in such a tone of adult, composed contempt – as if it were completely obvious.

Theudibert's eyes narrowed. His grin faded. The *nazir* remained bending over, hands splayed on his mail-covered thighs. His frown indicated confusion. Ash froze.

"Like, I'm going to be *stupid*," she whispered scornfully, hardly daring to breathe in the moment of stillness. She stared up at faces: men in their twenties who would be Barbas, Gaina, Fravitta, Gaiseric, but she could not know which

373

was which. Her stomach wrenched with pain. She sat back up on her heels, ignoring a hot trickle of urine down her inner thighs as she pissed herself.

"There aren't any 'warriors' on a battlefield." Her scornful voice ran on, trembling, in rough Carthaginian, and she let it: "There's you and your buddy, and you and your mates, and you and your boss. A *lance*. The smallest unit on the field is eight or ten men. Nobody's a hero on their own. One man alone out there is *dead meat*. I'm no fucking volunteer hero!"

It was the sort of thing she might have said every day, nothing especially perceptive.

She looked up in the yellow light at swinging shadows on the walls, and the rose-tinged faces staring down at her. Two men shifted back on their heels, a younger one – Gaiseric? – whispering to a mate.

But it's the sort of thing *they* might say.

And no civilian would.

Not man versus woman. Military versus civilian. *We're on the same side.* Come on, see it, you must see it, I'm not a woman, I'm one of you!

Ash had sense enough to rest her palms flat on her bare thighs and kneel there in complete silence. She appeared as unaware of her bare breasts and bruised belly as if she were back in the wooden baths with the baggage train.

Sweat poured unnoticed down her face. Salt blood from her cheek ran over her split lip. A rangy woman, with wide shoulders, and hair cropped boy-short, head-wound short, nun-short.

"Fuck," Theudibert said. His thick voice sounded resentful. "Fucking cowardly bitch."

A sardonic voice came from one of the eight men; a fair-haired man standing towards the back. "What's she gonna do, *nazir*, take us all out?"

Ash felt a definable cooling to the emotional temperature in the cell. She shivered: all the fine hairs on her body standing upright. *They're on duty. They could have been drunk.*

"Shut your fucking mouth, Barbas!"

"Yes, *nazir*."

"Ah, fuck it. Fuck her." Theudibert swung around on his heel, shoving between his men to get to the cell door. "I don't see none of you shits moving. *Move!*"

A thickly muscled soldier, the one she had seen get hard, protested sullenly, "But, *nazir*—"

The *nazir* thumped him in passing, hard enough to double him over.

Their hard heavy bodies cluttered the cell door for seconds, longer seconds than she had known at any period of time that wasn't on the field of battle: seconds that seemed to last for ever, them muttering discontentedly to each other, elaborately ignoring her, one spitting on the floor, someone harshly, cruelly laughing, a fragment of speech: "—break her anyway—"

The iron grating that formed a door clanged shut. Locked.

In that split second, the cell was empty.

Keys jangling, mail rustling. Their bodies moved away down the corridor. Distant booted footsteps loping up stairs. Fading voices.

"Oh, son of a bitch." Ash's head fell forward. Her body expected the flop of long hair over her face, awaited the minute shifting of its weight. Nothing obscured her vision. Literally light-headed, she gazed up at narrow walls lit by the lantern beyond the iron grating. "Oh, Jesu. Oh Christus. Save me, Jesu."

A fit of shuddering took her. She felt her body was shaking like a hound coming out of cold water and, amazed, found nothing she could do would stop it. The lamp in the corridor showed only a few feet of clay-tiled floor and pink mosaic walls. The lock on the iron grating was larger than her two fists together. Ash scrabbled around with shaking hands and found her torn shirt. The fabric dripped wet in her hands. One of the *nazir*'s men had pissed on it.

Cold cut her skin. She wrapped the stinking cloth over as much of her body as she could reach, and curled up in the far corner of the cell. The absence of a door bothered her: she did not feel less imprisoned but more exposed by the steel grating, even if its mesh was not large enough to let her put a hand through.

In the corridor, a Greek Fire jet hissed into life. Intensely white squares of light fell through the iron grating, on to the cracked tiles. Her belly hurt.

The stench of male urine faded as her nose numbed it out. The wet cloth grew warmer with her body-heat. Her breath clouded the air in front of her face. Intense coldness bit at her toes, her hands; numbed the pain of her cut forehead and lip. Blood still trickled down, she tasted it. Her stomach twisted, in a grinding pain, and she wrapped her arms around her body, hugging herself.

All I did was catch them off their guard at the right moment. That won't happen twice. That was just bad discipline: what happens when they get genuine orders to give me a beating, or a rape, or break my hands?

Ash curled herself tighter. She tried to quiet the yammering fear in her head, bury the word *torture*.

Fuck Leofric, fuck him, how could he feed me and then do this to me; he can't mean torture, not real torture, eyes burned out, bones broken, he can't mean that, it must be something else, it must be a mistake—

No. No mistake. No point in fooling myself.

Why do you think they've left you down here? Leofric knows who you are, *what* you are, she will have told him. By way of a profession I kill people. He knows what I'm thinking, right now. Just because I *know* what's being done doesn't mean it won't *work*—

Another grinding pain went up through her belly. Ash pushed both her fists into her abdomen, tensing her body. A low pain made her stomach cold. It subsided: almost immediately it grew again, cresting at a peak that made her gasp, swear, and sigh a great shuddering breath as it died down.

Her eyes opened.

Sweet Jesu.

She put her hand between her thighs and brought it out black in the lamp's light.

"Oh, *no*."

Appalled, she lifted her hand to her face and sniffed. She could not smell blood, could smell nothing now, but the way that the liquid covering her hand began to contract and pull on her skin as it dried—

"I'm *bleeding*!" Ash shrieked.

She pushed herself up on to her knees, left knee screaming at the impact; pulled herself to her feet, and limped two steps to the grating, her fingers locking into the square steel mesh.

"Guard! Help! Help!"

No voice answered. The air in the passage outside shifted, coolly. No voices came from other possible cells. No sound of metal: weapons or keys. No guardroom.

Pain doubled her over. She gritted a high, keen sound out from between clenched teeth. Bent over, she saw the white skin of her inner thighs appeared black from pubic hair to knee, rivulets of blood running down from knee to ankle. She had not felt it: blood is undetectable, flowing over the skin at blood-heat.

The pain grew again, grinding down in the pit of her belly, in her womb, akin to monthly cramps but stronger, harder, deeper. A sweat broke out over her face and breasts and shoulders, slicked wet under her arms. Her fingers clenched.

"Jesu, for Jesu's sake! Help me! Help! Help! Get a *doctor*! Somebody help me!"

She sank to her knees. Bent double, she pressed her forehead on the tiles, praying for the pain from her grazes to offset the pain and movement of her belly.

I must be still. *Completely still*. It might not happen.

Her muscles cramped again. A sharp, shearing pain cut off thought. She hugged her hands up between her thighs, into her vagina, as if she could hold back the blood.

The lamplight dimmed, gradually going down to a small intense jet. Blood clots blotted her palms. Blood smeared her skin as she held desperately on to herself, pushing up, pushing at the womb's entrance; warm wet liquid running out between her fingers.

"Somebody help me! Somebody get a surgeon. That old woman. *Anything*. Somebody help me save it, help me, *please, it's my baby, help me—*"

Her voice echoed down the corridors. Complete silence resumed, after the echoes died, a silence so intense she could hear the lamp hissing outside the cell. Pain died down for a moment, for a minute; she prayed, hands between her legs, and the swooping drag of it began again, a dull, intense, grinding, and finally fiery pain, searing up through her belly as her muscles contracted.

Blood smeared the tiles, made the floor under her sticky. Artificial light turned it black, not red.

She sobbed, sobbed with relief as pain ebbed; groaned as it started again. At the peak she could not keep from crying out. The lips of her vagina felt the pushing expellation of lumps – black stringy clots of blood, that slipped like leeches over her hands and away, spilling on the floor. Blood hot on her hands and legs; smearing her thighs, belly; plastering in warm hand-prints over her torso as she hugged herself and shook, biting at the inside of her mouth, finally screaming in pain; and then blood drying cold on her skin.

"Robert!" Her imploring scream died, dull against the ancient tiled cellar walls. "Oh, *Robert*! Florian! Godfrey! Oh help me, help me, help meee—"

Her belly cramped, contracted. The pain came now, rose up like a sea swell, drowned her in agony. She wished she could pass out; but her body kept her present, working against it, swearing at the physical inevitability of the process, weeping, filled with a violent fury against – who? What? Herself?

I didn't want it anyway.

Oh shit no—

Her ragged nails made half-moon indentations in her palms. The thick stink of blood flooded the cell. The pain shredded her. More than that, knowing what this pain meant broke her into pieces: weeping, quietly, as if afraid now that she would be heard.

Guilt shuddered through her: *If I hadn't asked Florian to get rid of it, this wouldn't be happening.*

Her reasonably accurate guesses of the north ('nearly Vespers', 'an hour before Matins') gave way to complete disorientation: it must surely be still black day, not starry night, but she could not be certain of it. Not certain of anything now.

Her belly's pain loosened and tightened every muscle in her body: thighs, arms, back, chest. The involuntary contractions of her womb died down, slowly. The immensity of the relief drowned her. Every muscle relaxed. Her eyes stared, fixed open wide.

Her breasts hurt.

She lay curled on her side in the lamp's chequered illumination. Both her hands were full of clots and strings of black blood, drying to stickiness. A flaccid veined thing lay on her palm, half that size, drying. It trailed a twisted thread of flesh no thicker than a linen cord. Attached to the cord's end was a red gelatinous mass about the size of an olive.

In the square of white light she could clearly distinguish its tadpole-head and curving body-tail, the limbs only buds, the head not human. A nine-week miscarriage.

"It was perfect." She screamed up at the invisible ceiling. "*It was perfect!*"

Ash began to cry. Great gasping sobs wrenched at her lungs. She curled up tight and wept, body sore, shuddering like a woman in a fit; screaming in grief, scalding tears pouring down her face in the darkness, howling, howling, howling.

IV

Footsteps tiptoed, voices whispered: she didn't notice.

Gut-wrenching sobs faded to silent tears, running hot and wet over her hands. Grief ceased to be a refuge. Her limbs and body shook, with trauma and with the intense cold of the cells. Ash rolled into a tighter ball, cold palms clasped around her shins. Her lips were dry with thirst.

The world and her body came back. Chill clay walls bit into her bare flank.

She shivered, all her body-hair standing up like the bristles on a pig; expected soon to be sleepy, to cease to shiver, as men do in cold high mountain snow when they lie down never to rise again.

The cell's steel grating slammed to one side. Slaves' bare feet slapped on the tiled floor; someone shouted, above her head. Ash tried to move. Soreness stabbed her vagina. Quaking shudders wracked her body. The tiles felt frost-cold under her.

A rasping voice shouted, "God's Tree, don't you know enough to report to me!"

Ash got her head up off the floor, neck straining, swollen hot eyes blinking.

"Light a fire in the observatory!" a bulky, dark-bearded Visigoth man snapped, standing over her. The 'arif Alderic unbuttoned the voluminous indigo wool gown that hung from his shoulders, over his mail. He dropped it to the bloodstained floor, knelt, and rolled her into the material. Ash vomited weakly. Yellow bile stained the blue wool. Thick folds of cloth enveloped her, and she felt him thrust an arm under her knees, her shoulders, and lift. The mosaic walls whirled in the intense light of Greek Fire as he swung her up into his arms.

"Out of my way!"

Slaves ran. His footsteps jolted her.

Silk-lined wool slid over her icy, filthy skin. Warmth grew. She began to shudder with uncontrollable shivers. Alderic's arms gripped her tightly.

Carried up steps, carried across the fountain courtyard with cold sleet slashing down on her bare face, trickling pale red water, Ash tried to go away in her head. To put it all wherever it is that she puts memories of bad things, of people who betrayed her, of stupid miscalculations that got people killed.

Hot tears pushed up between her eyelids. She felt water trickle down her face, mingling with the sleet. In a crowd of slaves and shouted orders, she was carried into another building, down corridors, down stairwells; grief wiping out everything but a dim impression of a warren of rooms going on for ever, rooted down into Carthage hill like a tooth into a jawbone.

The pressure of his arms under her relaxed. Something hard but slightly giving pressed into her back. She lay on a pallet on a blocky white oak daybed, in a spacious room lit by Greek Fire. Slaves ran in with ten or a dozen iron bowls, putting them on tripods and heaping them with red-hot charcoal.

Ash stared up. Metal cabinets lined the walls, below glass-and-fire lamps. Above the lights, the vaulted wooden roof *shifted* – shutting, like a clam-shell, as she watched: cutting off a view through thick, gnarled glass of a black day sky above.

Slaves ceased pulling ceiling-panels, tied off ropes.

A pale-haired girl of eight or so scowled at Ash, fingering her steel collar. The male slaves left. Two more child-slaves remained to tend the ember-burners that gradually leaked warmth into the cold air.

Alderic's harsh commands brought more people. A freeborn, grave, bearded Visigoth in woollen robes stared down at Ash, together with a woman who wore a black veil pinned to the crown of her headdress. The two of them rattled a rapid conversation in medical Latin. She understood it well enough – *why not? Florian uses it all the time* – but the details slid out of her concentration. Her body shifted like meat on a slab as they pulled her legs apart, and first fingers and then some steel instrument were pushed into her vagina. She hardly winced at the pain.

"Well?" another voice demanded.

Her few minutes in the *amir*'s company had not given her a memory of his face, but now she recognised his dirty-white hair and beard, tufting up like a startled owl. The *amir* Leofric, glaring down with alert, bloodshot eyes.

The woman – who must be a physician, Ash realised – said, "She will not easily conceive again, *Amir*. Look. I am surprised that she could bear this one for so long. There is chronic damage: she will never carry to term. The gate of the womb[10] is all but destroyed, and much scarred over with very old tissue."

Leofric stamped across the room. He reached out his arms and a slave put a green and yellow woollen robe on him. "God's Tree! *This one is barren too!*"

"Even so."

"What is the use of these sterile females? I can't even breed from this!"

"No, *Amir*." The woman probing between Ash's thighs lifted one blood-stained hand to put back her veil. She changed from Carthaginian Latin and spoke in French, as if she spoke to a child or an animal. The manner in which one speaks to a slave.

"I shall give you a drink. If there is more to pass, you will pass it. A flux, do you understand? A bloody flux. Then you shall be well."

Ash shifted her hips. Hard metal obstructions slid from her vagina, bringing infinite relief from a pain she had not known she felt. She tried to sit, to move, striking out weakly. The second doctor closed his hand around her wrist.

Her eyes focused on the man's cuff. In the room's white light, she saw slanting big stitches fixing the olive lining to the bottle-green wool garment. Wild stitches fastened button to cuff. The loop for the button was a mere hoop of fraying thread. *Someone, some slave, made this fast, sloppy, in a hurry.* Underneath his voluminous woollen sleeve a light silk robe was visible: far more like what she would expect to see worn in Carthage.

Alderic's wool gown cocooned her body, warming her core. Its workmanship was equally hurried.

They didn't expect this cold either.

What she feels here is not the warm, star-lit, sweltering twilight that Angelotti described; when he was both slave and gunner on this coast. The Eternal Twilight in which nothing grows, but within the bounds of which the nobles of Carthage walk, silk-clad, under indigo skies.

The very air crackles with frost.

The woman, practised, put a cup to her lips and tipped. Ash swallowed. A sweet herb tanged in the drink. Almost immediately her body cramped. The feeling of blood expelled from her body, soaking the wool, constricted her throat again and she clenched her jaw on a sob.

"Will she live?" Leofric demanded.

The elder doctor, very grave, very satisfied with his own opinion, observed to the *amir* Leofric, "The uterus is strong. The body is strong, and displays little

[10] Presumably 'cervix'.

379

shock. If she is subjected to more pain, she will hardly die of it, unless it be most severe. She may safely be put to moderate torture within an hour or so."

The *amir* Leofric ceased pacing on the mosaic floor and flung open wooden window shutters. A blast of cold air entered the room, chilling the effect of the coals in iron dishes. He stared out into darkness at a sky of utter blackness: no moon, no star, no sun.

Ash lay in the pomegranate-carved oak bed, watching him. She thought: I really could die, now.

It was not a sudden realisation. It came to her quite ordinarily, as it always did, usually just before battle; but it tightened the focus of her mind, snapped her into a complete consciousness of Leofric, his doctors, *'arif* Alderic and his guard, the bitter air, the bustle and business of the household. The hundred thousand men and women outside on the white-lit streets of Carthage, living out quotidian experience.

*About three-quarters of which will know there's a war on, half of whom will care, and none at all will bother about just one more prisoner dying in a lord-*amir*'s house.*

What came to her was the absolute apprehension of her own unimportance, as if a membrane had broken: all the things that one thinks could not happen 'because I am me' become in an instant possible. Other people die of injuries, of accidents, of poisoned blood, of childbed fever, of an ordinary order of execution of the King-Caliph's justice, and therefore *I*—

She was used to thinking herself the hero of her own life: what lost sense for her now was the idea of it being a coherent story requiring a resolved ending (some day, in the future, the far future). She thought, *But it doesn't matter*, quite calmly. Other people can win battles, with or without 'voices'. Someone else can take my place. It is all accident, all chance.

Rota fortuna, Fortune's Wheel. *Fortuna imperatrix mundi.*

Without turning around, the Visigoth *amir* said, "I was reading a report from my daughter when the slaves summoned me. She reports you are a violent woman, a killer by profession, a warrior by desire rather than by training, as she is."

Ash laughed.

It was a tiny snuffle, a choke of a laugh, hardly a breath; but it surged through her so that her eyes ran, and she wiped the back of her hand across her chill, wet face. "Yeah, and I had so many professions to choose from!"

Leofric turned. At his back, a blank black sky whirled, flakes of snow plastering the edges of the wooden shutters. The same girl-slave pattered over the tiles and heaved the window shutters to. Leofric ignored her.

"You are not what I expected." He sounded both fussy, and frank. He bundled up his striped gown of green and yellow velvet and paced across the floor towards her. "Foolishly, I expected you to be as she is."

That begs the question of what you think she is, Ash reflected.

"Take this down," Leofric said, to the smaller of the boy-slaves. Ash saw the child held a wax tablet, ready to impress it with his stylus. "Preliminary notes: physical. I see an habitually dirty young woman, evidence of parasitic skin inflammation common, scalp infested with ringworm. Muscle development

380

unusual in a woman, especially in the trapezoid, and biceps. Peasant stock. General muscle tone good – extremely good. Some evidence of early malnutrition. Two teeth missing, upper jaw, left-hand side. No evidence of caries. Scarring to face, old trauma to third, fourth and fifth ribs on the left side, to all fingers of the left hand, and evidence of what I suppose to have been a hairline fracture of the left shin-bone. Rendered infertile by trauma, probably before puberty. Read that back to me."

Leofric listened to the young boy reading in a sing-song. Ash blinked back too-easy tears, huddling the wool gown around herself. Her sore body ached. Waves of sensation still throbbed through her belly, through her whole body: every tissue aching.

It took her breath: too stark to think about. Some arrogant part of herself rose up in revolt. "What is this, my pedigree? I'm not some God-rotted horse-coper's mare! Don't you know of what *degree* I am?"

Leofric turned back to her. "What degree *are* you, little Frankish girl?"

Cold air flickered across the hot coals, they burned red and black in turn. Ash met the eyes of the girl-slave kneeling on the far side of the iron tripod. The child winced and looked away. Ash thought, *Is he serious?* A waft of heat over the coals made her shiver.

"Squire's, I suppose. I sit at table with men of the fifth degree by right." It suddenly struck her as irresistibly ridiculous. "I can eat at the same table as preachers, doctors of law, *rich* merchants, and gentlewomen!" Ash shifted her body closer to the edge of the oaken bed and the nearest dish of hot coals. "I guess I eat with the knight's rank, now I'm married to one. 'The substance of livelihood is not so dignifying as is noble blood.' Hereditary knight beats mercenary."

"And of what rank am I?"

She may safely be put to moderate torture within an hour or so.

Flesh is so easy to burn.

"Of the second degree, if an *amir* is second in rank after the King-Caliph; that is, a bishop, viscount or earl's equal." Her voice stayed calm. Her mind suddenly demanded, *What is John de Vere doing, is the Earl of Oxford dead?* She warily watched the Visigoth lord.

In his preoccupied tenor, he asked, "How should you address me, then?"

The answer he wants is *Lord-Amir* or *my lord*; he wants some show of respect.

Acidly, she suggested, " 'Father'?"

"Mmm? Mmm." Leofric turned and took a few steps away from her, and back; his lined and faded eyes fixing on her face. He snapped his fingers at the slave scribe. "Preliminary notes: of the mind and spirit."

Ash pushed herself up into a sitting position on the palliasse, gritting her teeth against soreness and pain. Her eyes dripped. She bundled the warm wool around her naked body. She opened her mouth to interrupt. The little slave-girl's face screwed up in terror.

"She is a—" The white-haired man broke off. His gown moved, a bulge near his fine leather belt wriggling around. The grey nose and whiskers of a big buck rat poked out of Leofric's sleeve. He absently lowered his arm towards the oaken bed. The rat descended cautiously on to the palliasse near Ash.

"This is a mind between eighteen and twenty years of age," the Visigoth *amir* dictated. "She has a great resilience towards pain, and towards mutilation and other forms of physical damage; recovering from the miscarriage of a foetus of approximately nine weeks' growth inside of two hours."

Ash's mouth dropped open. She thought *recovered!* and then startled as a fly brushed the back of her hand. The jolt as she froze, instead of batting it away, left her body shaking. She looked down.

The grey rat was niffing again at her hand.

"Such evidence as I have been able to gather speaks of her living among soldiers from an early age, adopting their modes of thought, and following both the military professions: whore and soldier."

Ash held out her brown-stained fingers. The rat began to lick her skin. It had a patched grey-and-white back and belly, one black eye and one red eye, and a plush velvet softness to its short coat. She cautiously shifted her hand to scratch it gently behind its warm, delicate ear. She attempted Leofric's chirrup. "Hey, Lickfinger. You're a witch's familiar if I ever saw one, aren't you?"

The rat looked up at her with bright mismatched eyes.

"She displays lack of concentration, lack of forward planning, a desire to live for momentary sensation." Leofric signalled the scribe to stop writing. "My dear child, do you imagine I have *any* use for a woman who has become a mercenary captain in the barbaric north, and who claims her military skills come from saints' voices? An ignorant peasant, with a mere physical skill?"

"No." Ash, cold in her belly, continued to finger the rat's velvet coat. "But that isn't what you believe I am."

"You were with my daughter long enough to counterfeit a working knowledge of the Stone Golem."

"So the King-Caliph says." Ash let the cynical, acid tone remain in her voice.

"He is, in this case, correct." Leofric's tall skinny bulk sat on the edge of the bed. The grey rat skittered over the palliasse and climbed up his thigh, putting its front paws up on his chest. He added, "The Belly of God is right, you know; we Visigoths have no choice but to be soldiers—"

"'The Belly of God'?" Ash echoed, startled.

"*Fist* of God," Leofric corrected himself. In Carthaginian Gothic it was a single word, obviously a title. "Abbot Muthari. I *must* stop calling him that."

Ash recalled a fat abbot in the King-Caliph's company. She would have smiled, but fear made her face stiff.

The *amir* Leofric continued: "Because you have every reason to attempt to convince me that you hear this machine, I can't believe anything you say about it." His faded blue eyes switched from her face to the rat. "I was not entirely lying to the King-Caliph, nor entirely attempting to save you from Gelimer's brutal, stupid wastefulness. I may have to inflict some pain on you, to be certain."

Ash rubbed her hand across her face. The coals took the chill from the air, but her sweat was cold. "How will you know I'm telling the truth when you hurt me? I'd say anything, and you know it, anybody will! I've—"

After a moment, into the silence, the white-haired *amir* Leofric said gently, "'I've tortured men.' Is that what you were about to say?"

"I've been present while it happened. I've given the orders." Ash swallowed. "I can probably frighten myself much better than you can, given what I've seen and what I know."

A slave-boy entered, coming to speak quietly to Leofric. The Visigoth's shaggy brows went up.

"I suppose I should admit him." He gestured the child away. A few moments later, two men in mail and helmets came in. Between his guards, an expensively dressed Visigoth *amir* with a braided dark beard entered the room.

He was the one with the King-Caliph, Ash remembered, and looking at his dried-grape eyes gave her memory of his name: Gelimer. Lord-*Amir* Gelimer.

"His Majesty insisted that I oversee this. Your pardon," the younger *amir* said insincerely.

"*Amir* Gelimer, I have never obstructed any order of the King-Caliph."

The two of them moved aside. Ash's stomach chilled. Inside a few seconds, the *amir* Gelimer made a signal. Two well-built men entered the room, one with a small field-anvil; the second with steel hammers and a ring of iron.

"The King-Caliph asked me to do this." *Amir* Gelimer sounded both apologetic and smug. "It is not as if she were freeborn, is it?"

Her body cramping, shuddering, bleeding; she let herself be pulled up from the bed, and stared fixedly at the mosaics on the wall – the Boar at the Green Man's Tree, in intricate detail – while a curved iron ring was shoved under her chin and held closed. Her head rang to the brief and accurate bang of hammers fixing a red-hot rivet through the collar's hasp. Cold water sluiced her. She could not move her head, cropped hair tight in one of the men's grips, but she blew water and spat and shivered.

The room smelled of soot. An unfamiliar cold weight of steel rested around her neck. Ash glared at Gelimer, hoping to have him think her outraged, but her mouth kept losing its shape.

"Out of consideration for her illness, I think a collar will be sufficient," the *amir* Leofric murmured.

"Whatever." The younger *amir* chuckled. "Our lord expects results."

"I will soon be in a position to better inform the Caliph. Consulting records, I find seven litters born about the time of her apparent age; of which all were culled but my daughter. It could be that this one escaped the culling."

Ash shivered. Her head throbbed from the hammers. She put her fingers through the slave collar and pulled at the unyielding metal.

Gelimer for the first time looked her in the face. The *amir* spoke with the intonation one used to slaves and other inferiors. "Why so angry, woman? You have lost very little so far, after all."

What she sees, in her mind's eye, is a Visigoth lance-head sliding into Godluc's side: a thick knife on a stick ripping his iron-grey hair and black skin up his ribs, sinking in behind his forequarters. Six years' care and companionship ended in a brutal second. She clenched her fists, under the woollen gown serving her as a blanket.

It is easier to see Godluc than the dead faces of Henri Brant and Blanche and the other six score men and women who turn the baggage train alternately into hotel, brothel and hospital, running it with all the enthusiasm they can bring her; and Dickon Stour's eternal efforts to improve his armoury from repair to manufacture. Easier than to think of the dead faces of her lance-leaders, and each of their followers, drunk or sober, reliable or useless: five hundred dirty, well-armed peasants who would not consent to dig their lord's fields, or wild boys out for adventure, or criminals who would not stay for petty justice; but they will fight, for her. All this – the tents and their carefully sewn pennons, every war-horse or riding horse; each sword and the history of where she bought or stole or was given it; each man who has fought under her standard, in weather and ground always too hot – or too cold – or too wet—

"No, what have I lost?" Ash said bitterly. "Nothing!"

Gelimer said, "Nothing to what you may lose. Leofric, God give you a good day."

The half-cooled rivet on her collar stung her fingertips. Ash watched Gelimer's leave-taking. The complexity of politics in this court – impossible to learn in months, never mind minutes – weighed down on her. *Leofric might be trying to save my life. Why? Because he thinks I am another Faris? How important is that, now? Does it matter at all? My only chance is that it still matters—*

Her isolation cut her like a newly sharpened sword.

No matter how clear one's unimportance becomes, how easy it is to apprehend one's own death, the self still protests, *But it's too soon, too unfair, why me?*

Ash's skin chilled.

"What is going on?" she demanded.

Leofric turned back from the room's ornate, arched doorway. In French, again, he said, "If you want to live, I suggest *you* tell *me*."

It was blunt, a different tone completely from how he had spoken to *Amir* Gelimer.

"What *can* I tell you?"

"To begin with: how do you speak to the Stone Golem?" Leofric asked gently.

She sat on an oak-carved bed it would take her five years to earn, wrapped in blood-soaked wool and linen. Her body felt sore. She said, "I just speak."

"Aloud?"

"Of course, aloud! How else?"

Leofric seemed to find something to smile at in her indignation. "You do not, for example, speak as you might do in silent reading, with an interior voice?"

"I can't do silent reading."

The scraggle-haired *amir* gave her a look which plainly intimated that he doubted she could do any kind of reading.

"I recognise some of your machine's tactics," Ash said, "because I read them in Vegetius's *Epitomae Rei Militaris*."

The skin around Leofric's faded eyes became momentarily more lined. Ash realised his amusement. She remained on a cusp between fear and relief, held in tension.

"I thought perhaps your clerk had read it to you," Leofric said amiably.

The release of tension brought too-easy tears to her eyes.

If I'm not careful, I shall like you, Ash reflected. Is that what you're trying to do, here? Oh, Jesu, what can I *do*?

"Robert Anselm gave me his English copy[11] of Vegetius. I keep – kept – it with me all the time."

"And you hear the Stone Golem – how?" Leofric asked.

Ash opened her mouth to reply, and then shut it again.

Now why have I never asked myself that question?

Finally, Ash touched her temple. "I just hear it. Here."

Leofric nodded slowly. "My daughter is no better at explaining it. In some ways she is a disappointment. I had hoped, when one was at last bred who could speak at a distance to the Stone Golem, that the least I could expect was to be informed how this was done – but no. Nothing but 'I hear it', as if that *explained* anything!"

Now who does he remind me of? Just forgets everything and goes off, rides his own hobby-horse. . . ?

Angelotti. And Dickon Stour. *That's* who.

"You're a *gunner*!" Ash spluttered, almost hysterical, and clapped both hands over her mouth, watching his complete incomprehension with bright eyes.

"I beg your pardon?"

"Or an armourer! Are you sure you've never felt the urge to make a mail shirt, my lord *Amir*? All those thousands of teeny-tiny rings, every one with a rivet in it—"

Leofric gave a bewildered, unwilling laugh; moved only by her evident mirth. Completely confused, the older man shook his head. "I neither forge guns nor construct mail. What are you saying to me?"

Why did I never ask? she thought. Why did I never ask *how* I heard? How *do* I hear it?

"Master Leofric, I've been taken before, I've been beaten before; none of this is new to me. I don't expect to live until Christ's Coming. Everybody dies."

"Some in more pain than others."

"If you think that's a threat, you've never seen a stricken field. Do you know what I risk, every time I go out there? War," Ash said, with very bright eyes, "is dangerous, Master Leofric."

"But you are here," the pale-coloured, elderly man said. "Not there."

Leofric's complete calmness chilled her. She thought, gunners, also, care everything about shot, aim, elevation, firepower: and only later think about the consequences, where it hits. Armed knights will, after battles, sit and discuss, realistically, the evils of killing; but this will not stop any of them devising a better sword, a heavier lance, a more efficient design of helmet. He *is* a gunner; an armourer; a killer.

And so am I.

"Tell me what to do to stay alive," she said. Hearing what she said, she suddenly thought, *Is this how Fernando feels?* She went on: "For however little time it turns out to be before you kill me. Just tell me."

Leofric shrugged.

---

[11] Otherwise *De Re Militari*. The 1408 edition, made on the orders of Lord Thomas Berkeley?

In the chill room, among bowls of red embers, lit by Greek Fire, Ash stared at the *amir*. She swathed the wool gown around her shoulders. It fell in bloodstained folds around her.

I never asked because I never needed to.

She felt it, now: a directing of her voice, somehow. A directing of her attention towards – something.

"How long," she asked aloud, "has there been a Stone Golem?"

Leofric spoke words she didn't attend to.

'Two hundred and twenty-three years and thirty-seven days.'

Ash repeated aloud, "Two hundred and twenty-three years and thirty-seven days."

Leofric broke off whatever he was saying. He stared at her. "Yes? Yes, it must be. The seventh day of the ninth month . . . Yes!"

She spoke again. "Where is the Stone Golem?"

'The sixth floor of the north-east quadrant of the House of Leofric, in the city of Carthage, on the coast of North Africa.'

Her attention rose to a peak. Her listening, too, felt now that she attended to it as if it were something she did: not entirely passive, as one listens to a man speak or a musician play; not a mere waiting for an answer. *What am I doing? I'm doing* something.

"About five or six storeys below us," Ash repeated, her eyes on Leofric. "That's where it is. That's where your tactical machine is . . ."

The *amir* said dismissively, "This much you might have heard from slave gossip."

"I might have. But I didn't."

He was watching her keenly now. "I cannot know that."

"But you can!" Ash sat up on the oak bed. "If you won't tell me what to do to stay alive – *I'll* tell *you*. Ask me questions, Master Leofric. You'll know what the truth is. You'll know whether I'm lying about my voice!"

"Some answers are dangerous to know."

"It's never wise to know too much about the affairs of the powerful." Ash got off the bed and walked, slowly and with pain, towards the window shutter. Leofric did not stop her as she unbolted it and looked out. A centre iron bar bedded deep in the stone casement was thick enough to stop a woman throwing herself out.

Bitter air froze the skin on her cheeks, reddening her nose. She had a brief sympathy for those under canvas, in the wet cold north; a fellow-feeling for their misery and discomfort that was, at the same time, an utter desire to be there with them.

Below the stone sill, the great courtyard hissed and spluttered, Greek Fire lamps being hastily sheltered by an inappropriately gay striped awning. Ash looked down at mostly fair heads. The men and women who were slaves tugged the waxed linen into place with much swearing, complaints; thin arms holding up cloth or cord with impatient shouts. No one freeborn was in the courtyard except guards, and she could pick up their mutual enmity from here.

The lights, once shrouded, let her see beyond, to the squat square surrounding buildings – a household of at least couple of thousand, she judged.

It was impossible to see further in the dark, to see if this interior Carthage city contained other *amirs'* establishments equally rich and well-fortified. And no way at all to see – she leaned up on her toes on the cold tiled floor – whether this building faced harbour or something else; how much of Carthage lay between her and the dock; where the great and famous market might be; where the desert lay.

A hollow, moaning sound startled her. She lifted her head, alert, discerning that it echoed across rooftops and courtyard from a great distance.

"Sunset," Leofric's voice came from beside her. When she looked at him, her eyes were on a level with his white-bearded chin.

The metallic sound echoed again across the city. Ash strained to see the first stars, the moon, anything that would give her a compass bearing.

The wooden shutter was gently closed in her face.

She turned back into the room. The glowing warmth from the iron plates of coals made her feel how chill her face had grown, in those few minutes.

"How do *you* speak to it?" she challenged.

"As I speak to you, with my voice," Leofric said dryly. "But I am in the same room with it, when I do it!"

Ash couldn't stop herself smiling.

"How does it answer you?"

"With a mechanical voice, heard by the ear. Again: I am in the same room when I hear it. My daughter does not have to be in the same room, the same household, the same continent – this crusade confirms me in my belief that she will never go a distance great enough for her not to hear it."

"Does it know anything except military answers?"

"It does not *know* anything. It is a golem. It speaks only what I, and others, have taught it. It solves problems, in the field, that is all."

She swayed on her feet as a wave of lassitude went through her. The Visigoth *amir* gripped her arm above the elbow, through the bloodstained wool. "Come and lie down on the bed. Let us try what you suggest."

She let him guide her footsteps, all but falling back on to the palliasse. The room swayed around her. She closed her eyes, seeing nothing but darkness for long minutes until the dizziness faded; opening them to the stark white light of the wall lamps, and the soft scritching of the boy-slave on his wax tablet.

Leofric made a gesture, and the child stopped writing.

His voice, beside her, asked quietly, "Who was it first built the Golem?"

Question and answer. She spoke it aloud: had to ask twice, the answering name was unfamiliar to her. She said uncertainly, "The . . . 'Rabbi'? Of Prague."

"And he built it for whom?"

Another question, another response. Ash shut her eyes against the harsh light, straining to hear the inner voice. " 'Radonic', I think. Yes, Radonic."

"Who first built the Stone Golem, and why?"

'The Rabbi of Prague, under direction of your ancestor Radonic, two hundred years ago, built the first Stone Golem to play him at shah.*'* "—At chess," Ash corrected herself.

"Who first built machines in Carthage, and why?"

'Friar Roger Bacon.'

"One of ours," Ash said. She let her voice repeat the sound of the voice in her head: *'It is said that Friar Bacon made, in his lodgings at the port Carthage, a Brazen Head, from such metal as might be found in the vicinity. Howbeit, when he had heard what it had to say to him, he burned his devices, his plans, and his lodgings, and fled north to Europe, never to return. Afterwards the new presence of many demons in Carthage were blamed upon this scholar. Geraldus writ this.'*

Leofric's voice said soothingly, "Many have read much into the Stone Golem's ears in two hundred years. Try again, dear daughter. Who made the first Stone Golem, and why?"

'The amir *Radonic, beaten in* shah *by this speechless device, grew weary of it, and was much displeased with the Rabbi.'* "That's lords for you," Ash added. She became aware that she was on the edge of hysteria. Dehydration made her head ache, blood-loss made her weak; all of this was enough to account for it. The voice in her head continued: *'Radonic, growing weary, caused the stone man to be set aside. Like a good Christian, he doubted the small powers of the Jews to be from the Green Christ, and began to think he may have countenanced demonic works in his household.'*

"More."

'The Rabbi had made this Golem a man in every part, using his semen, and the red mud of Carthage, and shaping it very handsomely. A slave in the household, one Ildico, grew greatly in love with the Golem, for that with its stone limbs and metal jointures it looked most like a man, and bore it a child. This she said was caused by the Wonder-Worker's intercession, the great Prophet Gundobad appearing to her in a dream and bidding her carry about her person his sacred relic, which was passed down in this slave's family since Gundobad lived.'

Ash felt a soft touch. She opened her eyes. Leofric's fingers stroked her brow, the tips touching skin, dried blood and dirt with complete indifference. She flinched away.

"Gundobad's your prophet, isn't he? He cursed the Pope and caused the Empty Chair."

"Your Pope should not have executed him," Leofric said gravely, removing his hand, "but I won't dispute with you, child. Six centuries of history have passed over us, and who can tell what the Wonder-Worker was, now? Ildico believed in him, certainly."

"A woman who had a baby by a stone statue." Ash couldn't keep contempt out of her tone. "Master Leofric, if I were going to read history for a machine to listen to, I wouldn't tell it this rubbish!"

"And the Green Christ born of a Virgin, and suckled by a Boar; this is 'rubbish'?"

"For all I know, it is!" She shrugged, as well as was possible lying down on the bed. Her feet were cold. She became aware as Leofric frowned that she had slid into a French-Swiss dialect of her youth, and tried it again in Carthaginian Latin: "Look, I've seen as many tiny miracles as the next woman, but all of them could be chance, *fortuna imperatrix,* that's all . . ."

With slight emphasis, the Visigoth man said, "What made the *second* Stone Golem and why?"

Ash repeated his words. The voice that moved in the secret places of her mind was no different from the voice that answered when she gave it terrain, troop type, weather conditions, and asked for an ideal solution: the same voice.

'Some have written that Ildico, slave, not only preserved a powerful relic of the Prophet Gundobad, but was in direct line of descent from his body, through the generations from the eight hundred and sixteenth year after Our Lord was given to the Tree, to that year of twelve hundred and fifty-three.'

Leofric repeated his question. "Who made the second golem, and why?"

'The eldest son of Radonic, one Sarus, was killed in a battle with the Turks. Radonic then caused to be made a shah *set in which the pieces were carved, complete to weapons and armour, resembling the troops of the Turks and the troops of his son Sarus. Then he recalled the Golem to his mind, and set about playing* shah *with it, and upon a day in that year, the Golem at last played out the game so that the troops of Sarus moved in a different array and would have defeated the Turks.*

'Upon this day, also, Amir *Radonic discovered his slave Ildico bedding the Golem; and he took a wall-builder's hammer, and he crushed the red mud and brass of the Golem to fragments, so small that no man could have told what it had been. Thereafter, he shut himself up in a tower. And Ildico bore a daughter.*

'Radonic, thinking upon Sarus his dead son, and upon his sons yet living, came and bade the Rabbi make a second Golem, to replace the one he had destroyed in his wrath. This the Rabbi would not do, although the Amir *threatened the life of the Rabbi's two sons. Not until Radonic made plain that he would impale and kill both Ildico and her newborn daughter would the Rabbi relent. Then he builded for* Amir *Radonic another Stone Golem, in a chamber within the house, but this human in seeming only in its upper body and head, thrice the size of a man: the rest being but a clay slab upon which models of men and beasts may be moved. And the brazen mouth of the Golem spoke.'*

Ash curled her body up, swathed in wool. Two or three sentences at a time is nothing, she thought, but *this* . . . The emotionless recounting of the voice made her tired, dizzy, detached.

'Then Radonic killed the Rabbi and his family, in case the Rabbi should make such another shah-*player for his enemies, or the enemies of his King-Caliph. And instantly the sun grew dark above him. And the sun darkened above the city of Carthage, and to all the lands ruled by the King-Caliph did the Rabbi's Curse extend. And so no living eye hath beheld the sun break through the Eternal Twilight, in two hundred years.'*

Ash opened her eyes again, not aware until then that she had shut them, the better to hear her voice. "Jesu! I bet there was panic."

Leofric said softly, "The then King-Caliph, Eriulf, and his *amirs* held command over their troops, and their troops kept the people quiet."

"Oh, you can do most things if you can keep a bunch of soldiers taking orders." Ash pushed herself up in the bed, until she came into contact with the white oak headboard, carved with fluted columns and pomegranates at the posts. She supported herself with an effort against the waxed wood. "This is all legends, I heard this stuff around camp when I was a kid. Legend number three hundred and seven about how the Eternal Twilight came to the south . . . Am I really telling you what you expect to hear?"

"Prophet Gundobad lived, and his slave daughter Ildico," Leofric said, "my family histories speak of it very clearly. And my ancestor Radonic certainly executed a Jewish Rabbi, about the year 1250."

"Then ask me things people won't have read in your family histories!"

The waxed wood of the bed smelled sweet to her. Her stomach growled. Strung out, watching Leofric's expression for the minutest changes, she ignored her complaining body.

"Who was Radegunde?"

Ash obediently repeated, "Who was Radegunde?"

'The first to speak at a distance to the Stone Golem.'

She thought, It doesn't say 'to me'.

'In these first years of crusade, when harvests failed and grain might not be got but by conquest of happier lands under the sun, then King-Caliph Eriulf began his conquests of the Iberian taifa *states. While* Amir *Radonic fought for King-Caliph Eriulf, he learned from each defeat or victory as he played them out over again with his Stone Golem, after each campaign. The child of Ildico, the girl Radegunde, began in her third year to make statues of men from the red silt sand of Carthage.*

'The amir *Radonic, seeing how she resembled the old Rabbi, smiled to think he had been so simple as to think a statue might beget a child upon a woman, and to regret his first Stone Golem's destruction. So Radegunde might have remained only a slave in the House of Radonic, but that, upon a day, she overheard Radonic's discussions with his captains, upon the practice field, and bade the* Amir *tell her what tactics he would employ, so that she might engage to speak to her friend the stone man about his plan.*

'Thinking to make merry, Radonic bid her ask the Stone Golem what it would have him do. Upon this, Radegunde spoke to the air. Then other slaves came running, to report that the Golem began to move the figures set out before it. When the amir *Radonic arrived in its chamber, the answers to his question were set out plain, as if the Golem had received her childish speech from some demon of the air.*

'Then Radonic abandoned the way of honour and rightness, and did not slay the child. Radonic adopted Radegunde, taking her with him to Iberia, speaking to her, and through her to the Stone Golem, and the tide of war turned in Eriulf's favour, so that southern Iberia became the grain-basket of Carthage under the twilight. And at five, she made her first mud statue that moved of its own volition, breaking much in the household, and greatly the child laughed to see this destruction.'

Ash drew her ankles up to her haunches, under the covering wool gown, and studied Leofric's expression. It was one of intense concentration.

"Is that Radegunde?" She stumbled over the name.

"Yes. Ask, how did she die?"

"How did Radegunde die?" Ash parroted. The dizziness in her might have had a dozen causes. She suspected a concentration of her mind that felt, somehow, as if she were pulling – a load up a slope – or unravelling something.

'In his seasons at home in Carthage, the amir *Radonic gave orders that Radegunde should be aided to make her new golems, bringing her scholars, engineers, and strange materials all as she desired. In her fifteenth year, God took away her powers of speech, but her mother Ildico communicated for her by signs known to them both. In this year also, upon a day, Radegunde built a stone man that rent her limb from limb and so she died.'*

Leofric's voice said, "And what is the secret birth?"

Ash kept her mouth shut, forming no words in her head, but letting an expectation form. An expectation of *being* answered. She let it somehow pull at other, implicit, answers. She said nothing out loud.

The voice began to speak in her head.

'Desiring another who should hear the Stone Golem though separated from it by many miles, so that he might continue his war, the amir *Radonic bred Ildico, in her thirtieth year, to the third golem, which had killed her daughter. This is the secret breeding, and the secret birth her twins, a male child and a girl.'*

She mumbled out loud, too startled at hearing it to keep quiet; muttered a necessary question out loud, in the face of Leofric's keen stare, over the answer already coming into her head. Then she stumbled over words, getting them out:

'The amir *Radonic desired another such slave, a grown adult, who should communicate with the Stone Golem as Radegunde had, a Janissary general after the manner of the Turks, an* al-shayyid *who should defeat all the petty* taifa *kings of Iberia. The twin children of Ildico could not be brought to do it, no matter the pain inflicted upon them and their mother. Nor could another golem be built. At last, Ildico confessed that she had given Radegunde her holy relic of the Prophet Gundobad, to place it within her last golem, and to make it speak and move as men do. But, at this knowledge, the third golem slew Ildico, and leaped from a high tower, and was dashed to fragments beneath. And this is their secret death: none remaining of the Prophet and Rabbi's miracle but the second Stone Golem, and Ildico's children.'*

Amir Leofric's hands closed over hers, clasping them tightly. Ash met his eyes steadily. He was nodding, unstoppably, in agreement; his eyes were wet.

"I never thought to have two such successes," he explained, simply. "It does speak to you, doesn't it? My dear girl."

"That was two hundred years ago," Ash said. "What happened then?"

She felt him unite with her in a moment of pure curiosity on her side, pure understanding of the desire for knowledge on his. The two of them sat companionably side by side on the bed.

Leofric said, "Radonic bred the twins and their offspring together. He wasn't a man to keep careful records. After he died his second wife Hildr and her daughter Hild took over; they kept minutely detailed notations of what they did. Hild was my great-great-grandmother. Her son Childeric, and her grandsons Fravitta and Barbas, continued the breeding programme, always tantalisingly close. As you know, as our conquests spread, many refugees and much scholastic knowledge came to Carthage. Fravitta built the ordinary golems, about the year 1390; Barbas presented them to King-Caliph Ammianus; they have since become popular through the Empire. The youngest son of Barbas, Stilicho, was my father; he raised me in the knowledge of the utmost necessity of our eventual success. My success was born four years after the fall of Constantinople. And so may you have been," Leofric finished thoughtfully.

He's older than he looks. Ash realised the Visigoth lord must be in his fifties or sixties. *That means he grew up under the threat of the Turks – and that begs another question.*

"Why isn't your general attacking the Sultan and his Beys?" Ash asked.

Absently, Leofric muttered, "The Stone Golem advised a crusade in Europe to be a better beginning; I must say I agree."

Ash blinked, frowned. "Attacking *Europe* is a better way to defeat the Turks? Ah, c'mon! That's crazy!"

Leofric ignored her mumble. "All has gone so well, and so speedily; if it were not for this cold—" He broke off. "Burgundy is the strategic key, of course. Then we may turn our attention to the Sultan's lands, God willing it so. God willing that Theodoric lives. He has not always been such a bad friend to me," the elderly man mused, as if to himself, "only in this last illness, and since Gelimer got his ear; still, he cannot very well stop a crusade once begun with so many victories . . ."

Ash waited until he looked up at her, raising his bowed head. "The Eternal Twilight has spread north. I saw the sun go out."

"I know."

"You don't know a damn thing about it!" Ash's tone rose. "You don't know any more about what's going on than I do!"

Leofric shifted very carefully on the edge of the white oak bed. Something squicked in the depths of his gown. The pale blue doe put out an indignant nose, and scuttled hastily on to his striped sleeve.

"Of course I do!" the Visigoth *amir* snapped. "It's taken us *generations* to breed a slave who can hear the Stone Golem without going mad. Now I have a chance of there being *two* of you."

"I'll tell you what I think, *Amir* Leofric." Ash looked at him. "I don't think you have any use for another slave-general. I don't think you need another Faris, another warrior-daughter who can talk to your machine – no matter how long it took you to breed that one. That's not what you want at all." She spared a finger for the rat, but it was sitting up on its haunches, grooming velvet-blue fur, and ignored her.

"Suppose I *can* hear your tactical machine. So what, *Amir* Leofric?" Ash spoke very carefully. The fog of misery was beginning to clear. Her body has ached from other wounds than this, if none so deep. "You can offer me a place with you, to fight for the King-Caliph, and I'll agree, and turn my coat as soon as I get back to Europe; he and you both know that. That's not important, it's not what you need!"

The exhilaration of unguarded honesty filled her. Looking around the room at the three slave-children, she briefly realised, *I've taken to talking as if they're not there, too*. Her gaze returned to Leofric, to see him thrusting his fingers through his hair, spiking it up still further.

Come on, girl, she thought. If he were a man you were hiring, what would you make of him? Intelligent, secretive, with none of the normal social restraints about causing physical harm to people: you'd pay him five marks and put him on the company books in a second!

And he didn't get to stay an *amir* without being devious. Not in this court.

"What are you saying?" Leofric sounded bewildered.

"Why is it cold, Leofric? *Why is it cold here?*"

The two of them looked at each other, for what must have been an actual minute of silence. Ash read the flinch of his expression clearly.

"I don't know," Leofric said at last.

"No, and nor does anyone else here, I can see it by the way you're all running around scaring yourselves shitless." Ash made herself grin. It was not very close to her usual gaiety of heart; she still ached too much. "Let me guess. It's only been cold since your invasion started?"

Leofric snapped his fingers. The smallest slave-child came and took a rat from him, cradling the blue doe with exquisite care in her thin arms. She walked unsteadily towards the door. One of the boys took the mismarked buck, twitching its whiskers, anxious to copulate with the doe; and at Leofric's signal, the slave scribe followed them out.

He said, "Child, if you did know of a reason for this intemperate weather, you would have told me of it, to save your life. I know this. Therefore, you know nothing."

"Maybe I do," Ash said steadily. In the half-chill room, her sore body ran cold sweat, darkening the robe gathered up under her armpits. She went on desperately, "Something I may have seen – I was there when the sun went out! – it might tell you—"

"No." He rested his chin on the knuckle of his first finger, nestling it in his untidy white beard. He held her gaze. She felt something tighten under her solar plexus: fear slowly squeezing her breath. She thought, Not now! Not when I've just found out I can *make* it talk to me—

Not now, under any circumstances.

"You're still at war, I saw that coming in," she said, her voice still steady. "Whatever victory you had can't have been final, can it? I'll give you the disposition and array of Charles of Burgundy's troops. You and the King-Caliph think I'm a Faris, a magical general, but you're forgetting: *I was one of Charles's hired officers.* I can tell you what he has."

She said it fast, before she could regret saying it:

"It's simple. I'll turn coat, in exchange for my life. I'm not the first person to make that bargain."

"No," the *amir* Leofric said absently. "No, of course. You shall dictate what you know to the Stone Golem; doubtless my daughter will find it useful, if somewhat overtaken by recent events."

Her eyes ran tears. "So I live?"

He ignored her.

"Lord-*Amir*!" She shrieked.

He spoke absently, as if he had not heard her.

"Whereas I had hoped to have another general, perhaps to lead our army in the east, I shall not have it under this King-Caliph, not with Gelimer to speak constantly against me. However," Leofric mused, "this gives me an opportunity which I had not expected to have before the end of this crusade. You – not being needed, as she is – can be dissected, to discover the balance of the Humours[12] within your body, and if there are differences in your brain and nerves which make it possible for you to speak with the machine."

---

[12] The mediaeval medical theory of humours attributes health to a balance of the sanguine (dry), choleric (hot), phlegmatic (wet) and melancholy (cold) humours in the body. Ill-health is a predominance of one over the others.

He looked at her with an absence of feeling that was frightening in itself. "Now I shall find out if this is indeed the case. I have always had my failures to dissect. Since there is no further use for you, now I may vivisect one of my successes."

Ash stared at him. She thought, I must have mistaken the word. No, that was clear, pure, medical Latin. Vivisect. Meaning 'dissect, while still alive'. "You *can't*—"

A sound of footsteps beyond the door brought her bolt upright, grabbing at Leofric's arm as he rose to his feet. He evaded her grip.

It was not a slave who entered but the *'arif* Alderic, a frown buried somewhere in his neatly braided beard; clasping his hands behind his back and speaking rapidly and concisely. Ash, too shocked, didn't understand what he was saying.

"No!" Leofric strode forward, his voice going up high. "And this is *so*?"

"Abbot Muthari has announced it, and called for prayer, fasting and repentance, my *Amir*," Alderic said, and with the air of a man repeating his initial message, slowly, as if the elderly lord-*amir* might not have understood: "The King-Caliph, may he live for ever, is dead of a seizure this half hour, in his rooms in the palace. No doctor could bring breath back to his body. Theodoric is dead, my lord. The King-Caliph is dead."

Stunned for different reasons, Ash heard the soldier speak his news with something approaching complete unconcern. *What's a King-Caliph, to me?* She knelt up on the bed. The woollen gown fell away from her bloodstained body. One hand knotted into a fist.

"Leofric!"

He ignored her.

"Leofric! *What about me?*"

"You?" Leofric, frowning, looked over his shoulder. "Yes. You . . . Alderic, confine her to the guest quarters, under guard."

Her other hand made a fist. She ignored the Visigoth captain as he gripped her arm. "*Tell me you're not going to kill me!*"

The *amir* Leofric raised his voice to his slaves. "Get my court robes!"

A bustle began.

He said, over his shoulder, "Think of it as a reprieve, if that comforts you. We are about the business of electing a new King-Caliph – which will be a busy few days, to say the least."

He smiled, his teeth shining in his white beard.

"This is merely a pause, before I can investigate you. As custom dictates, I can begin my work again immediately upon the inauguration of Theodoric's successor. Child, don't think of me as barbaric. It is not as if I'm torturing you to death as part of the celebrations. You will add *so much* to the sum of our knowledge."

```
Message:    #164 (Anna Longman)
Subject:    Ash / texts / archaeological evidence
Date:       20/11/00 at 10.57 p.m.
From:       Ngrant@
```
format address deleted
Other details encrypted by
non-discoverable personal key

Anna —

Everything's STOPPED.

Some trouble with the local authorities — we're being forbidden to carry on with the digging on-site. I don't UNDERSTAND how this can be happening! It is extremely frustrating that I, myself, can do nothing about this.

I thought it was solved this morning: Isobel came back, optimistic. I think she had gone through 'unofficial channels' and greased a few palms with money. She drove back with Colonel ▓▓▓▓▓ ▓▓▓▓▓▓, who seemed very jovial, promising the use of his men for heavy work here where required. But this afternoon, STILL nothing is happening, there are obscure 'difficulties'.

I am concerned; it seems to be more than the usual patronage and nepotism; but Isobel has been too busy for me to ask her.

One minor good thing, I suppose, is that it gives me an enforced opportunity to work on 'Fraxinus'. Mediaeval Latin is notoriously ambiguous, and 'Fraxinus' more idiosyncratic than most. I am finalising the translation furiously! In fact, I am putting the finishing touches to the next section.

Since we're encrypted, I can now tell you something about the site. What we have here is a beautiful midden. That's a refuse-heap. Archaeology, as Isobel informs me, mainly consists of digging in other people's dung. She, however, did not say 'dung'.

You would not think — everything covered by suburbs: two-storey white buildings festooned with television aerials — that any of this was the site of Carthaginian and Roman settlements. Even the Roman aqueduct is pretty much gone. But when I walked down to the beach this morning, and stood there under a lurid dawn sky, with the cold wind blowing off the sea into my face, I suddenly realised that most of the worn and rounded 'pebbles' under my feet were actually bits of Roman brick and Carthaginian marble. Some of them might even have been pieces of golem, shapeless after five centuries of being rolled around by the sea.

Nameless rocks. We know almost nothing. It wasn't even until a decade ago that the site of Carthage was identified; prior to that there was this ten-mile stretch of coast, with nothing — two thousand years later — to indicate just where it might have been.

Even what seems certain, we don't know. Bosworth field has its own tourist centre, but the field on which the battle was fought may not be that field at all (there is a theory it was closer to Dadlington than Market Bosworth). But I digress.

No, not really. I walked back through the site, in the chill fresh air — everything was under blue polyurethane covers. The grey boxes with notebook PCs plugged in had been removed back to the caravans. There were no men and woman in anoraks, flicking away earth with tiny paintbrushes, with their rear ends in the air. And what I thought was, Isobel is the one with the temperament for this. She wants to DISCOVER things. I want to EXPLAIN them. I need to have a rational explanation for the universe.

I even need a rational explanation for the 'miraculous' construction of these golems. The cold marble is uninformative. Andrew, our archaeometallurgist, is studying the metal joints; he has no answers yet. How did it get those marks of wear that prove it walked? HOW DID IT MOVE?

And what can I give these people, from the 'Fraxinus' text? A story of a wonder-working Rabbi and the sexual congress of a woman and a statue!

I know I said truth can be conveyed down through history in a story. Well, sometimes it proves impenetrably obscure!

There were men with guns on the site perimeter as I walked in. I was thinking, as I passed them, that the military mind itself has a rational explanation for the way the universe works — it's just an explanation at 90 degrees to the real one

Isobel's just told me there is 'stuff' going on behind the scenes, in local politics; we must be 'patient'.

So far we have various household implements, a dagger-hilt, and a piece of metal that might be a hair-fillet. I sit in on the discussions — arguments would, one supposes, be a better term — and put the case for a Germanic rather than an Arab culture here. The team agrees with me.

I need these diggings to start again.

I need more back-up for 'Fraxinus'.

If they don't let the team on-site soon, the army can move in and clear out archaeological tents full of dead bodies: I myself will be found battered to death with my own laptop computer! We are going stir-crazy out here. And it's HOT.

- Pierce

Message: #169 (Anna Longman)
Subject: Ash mss., breeding of Rattus Norvegicus
Date: 21/11/00 at 10.47 a.m.
From: Ngrant@   *format address deleted*
                            other details encrypted by
                            non-discoverable personal key

Ms Longman —

While we wait, I am mailing you at the suggestion of my colleague,
Dr Ratcliff, who has been kind enough to show me the Latin
manuscripts he is at present translating for you. He suggests I do
this since I have some amateur (if specialised) knowledge of rat
genetics and breeding.

Although Pierce and I spent some time discussing this yesterday,
and he is now as well-informed as myself, he suggested that I e-
mail you personally since I have the time now.

You may be aware that in the last forty-eight hours we have had
problems on-site, and at the moment there is little I can do except
watch the military representatives of the local government
treading on five hundred years of history. Fortunately most of the
findings at this site are under silt, which prevents too great an
amount of damage being done. The sole advantage I can see to this
delay is that the government are forbidding access to the airspace
above the coast, and this avoids saturation media coverage. Apart
from a few blurred satellite photos, the recording of the
expedition will be in the hands of my own capable videocam team.

Assuming that matters return to normal in the next twenty-four
hours, as Minister ████████ promises, I shall then be too busy to
be of any assistance to Pierce or yourself.

I really have very little to contribute; perhaps a footnote's
worth of knowledge — some years ago, being in search of a relaxing
hobby, I took up breeding specialist varieties of Rattus
Norvegicus, the Brown Rat. Such varieties are known as Fancy rats;
and I have been a member of both British and American Rat Fancy
societies.

In point of fact, my then-husband Peter Monkham was a biologist;
we never did quite see eye to eye on this matter, although his
reasons for having a vivisectionist's licence were no doubt good
and sufficient to him. Peter's jeremiads on the state of animals in
unrestrained nature (their lives being nasty, brutish, and shortly
terminated by something one step further up the food chain) only
served to convince me that my captive animals were in fact rather
better off than they would have otherwise been.

I was therefore intrigued to discover, while reading Pierce's
translation from the 'Fraxinus' manuscript for clues to our
technological findings, that several of our current genetic
mutations of Rattus Norvegicus seem to have been known in fifteenth-
century Africa. In fact, I had no knowledge of anything other than
Rattus Rattus, the Black Rat, being present in mediaeval times

397

anywhere outside Asia. (Rattus Rattus is, of course, the rodent popularly associated with spreading the Black Death.) I had believed that Rattus Norvegicus only spread here from Asia in or about the eighteenth century. What 'Fraxinus' describes, however, is undoubtedly the Brown Rat. If Pierce allows, I may use his findings for a brief paper on the subject of rat migration.

It seems possible, from 'Fraxinus', that these varieties were imported by North African traders. The Latin is sufficiently explicit that I actually RECOGNISE several varieties! I should explain that the brown or 'agouti' coat of the wild rat is in fact coloured in bands, each brown hair being striped blue-grey at the base; the coat scattered with additional guard-hairs, which are black. Selective breeding of initially spontaneous mutations can give different coloured coats which will then (with great effort) breed true. Patterned coats can also be bred true, although to give you some idea of the difficulty, the H locus which controls pattern can be modified to give at least six patterns: the Hooded rat; the Berkshire, the Irish, etc. And then there are polygenes to consider!

The difficulty is not in breeding a rat with a patterned coat, but in getting one that then breeds true to the same pattern. Two rats may be physically identical in their appearance while carrying completely different genetic histories in their alleles. Rat-breeding consists of trying to isolate certain genetic characteristics — without losing the proper bodily conformation of bold eye, well-set ears, good head, high rump, etc. — and creating a specific line of rats who will pass on that desired characteristic. Without keeping minutely detailed records of what bucks I bred to which does, it would have been impossible for me to select which of their offspring to use to continue the line.

Taking, for example, what 'Fraxinus' describes as a 'blue' rat — this is a rat bred to have the base blue colouring continued evenly through the fur coat. These are pretty, exotic little creatures, although (as this text in fact mentions!) early attempts proved difficult to get right, as the blue does suffered birthing problems. Whatever allele carried the gene for 'bleaching out' the agouti coat also stood a substantial chance of carrying a gene for deformed birth-canals, and bad temper. Blue rats used to bite, whereas the normal temperament of Rattus Norvegicus is inquisitive and friendly. The blue rat proper is then produced by breeding only from those examples which do not suffer from breeding difficulties, or difficulties of temperament.

'Fraxinus' also mentions the yellow/brown rat. This is known as a 'Siamese', and is the same gene that gives us Siamese cats (and, in fact, Siamese-coloured rabbits and mice); the coat is pale yellow except for the rump, nose, and paws, where the 'points' are dark brown. The description in 'Fraxinus' is excellent.

I can also account for the rat with different coloured eyes: the black eye being natural, the red eye a consequence of albinism. (The grey and white is referred to as 'lynx-marked' in the American Fancy.) The specimen referred to in this text appears to me to be a mosaic — genetically speaking, the opposite of a twin. Whereas with a twin an egg divides in the uterus, with a mosaic two different eggs fuse. This can produce a rat with the two halves of its body having different colour fur, or different colour eyes, or in some cases, being of different sexes. Since they are produced by random fusion, it is impossible for them to breed true, and they are of no use in fancy rat breeding.

Judging by the further description, the coat of the mosaic rat was either rexed — this is when the stiffer guard-hairs are bred out, giving a soft curly coat — or velvet (short and plush).

I once bred a line of rexes myself — being a rex, naturally each one was named after one of the Plantagenets (my favourite kings); although a particularly fluffy rat of mine called 'John' gave me an excellent illustration, by his temperament, of why we have only ever had one king of that name.

Fraxinus's rat is particularly interesting if it is *not* a rex, since no one in the Fancy has yet successfully bred a velvet coat on a rat, although the Mouse Fancy had achieved both velvet and satin pelts. In this respect, fifteenth-century North Africa seems to have out-done us!

This is conceivably because our Rat Fancy is primarily a twentieth-century phenomenon (although young Victorian ladies were known to keep pet rats in birdcages). Perhaps because of the rat's undeserved bad reputation far fewer years this century have been spent on its specialist breeding than, say, has been the case with the Mouse Fancy, or with different breeds of dog or cat. However, there are, even now, dedicated amateur geneticists at work on the Brown Rat, and it seems encouraging to me — if wonderfully strange — to learn that we are REdiscovering the many possible varieties of this delightful, playful, intelligent little animal.

I have gone into this in some detail simply because it shows the sheer SOPHISTICATION of the mediaeval mind. Pierce's manuscripts are proving fascinating now that we have these technological survivals to study, but I am almost MORE interested in what this says about the living minds of those people, who could note, conceive of genetic heritage, and EXPERIMENT in that respect, long before the Renaissance and the Scientific Revolution of the seventeenth century. Of course, one sees the beginning of it in horse- and hound-breeding of the same period, as one sees a similar mediaeval 'industrial revolution' in mills and military technology; but to produce, for example, the Siamese-marked rat, shows a mind-beggaring attention to scientific detail in what it is

easy to see as a superstition-ridden, theologically constrained
and inhumanely brutal society.

If I can be of any further assistance to you, please mail me at
the above address. I look forward to your publication of Pierce's
work. It may interest you to know that, in view of the help he is
giving me on site, I am more than willing for him to publish any
details of our discoveries here in so far as they relate to the
'Ash' histories, provided I and the university are credited.

- Sincerely I. Napier-Grant

Message: #99 (Pierce Ratcliff)
Subject: Ash, media-related projects
Date: 21/11/00 at 11.59 a.m.
From: Longman@

[handwritten: format address and other details non-recoverably deleted]

Pierce —

I just had mail from your Doctor Isobel. Most of it's *way* over my
head. And *rats*, eurrggh!

John showed me the golem-photos. They are WONDERFUL! My MD
Jonathan Stanley came over and saw them. He is equally impressed.
He's contacting an independent television producer that he knows —
well, who's the godfather of his son, actually.

Now I'm going to have media people to talk to. And explain that
this Schliemann found Troy by following up a poem. I can do it, I
suppose, but it would carry more weight coming from you or Dr
Napier-Grant.

I know you haven't the time, right now. I don't like the sound of
this problem with the authorities that you're having.

I'm getting edgy here.

- Anna

Message: #173 (Anna Longman)
Subject: Ash mss.
Date: 22/11/00 at 02.01 p.m.
From: Ngrant@

[handwritten: format address deleted. Other details encrypted by non-discoverable personal key]

Anna —

Something to amuse you, then, and stop you being edgy, while we
wait. Isobel has been re-reading my 'Fraxinus' translation and, as
we have nothing better to do at this moment, has been devising with
me a completely spurious scientific rationale for the abilities of

Ash and the Faris as regards the Stone Golem. We decided to see if we could out-do Vaughan Davies! It goes like this—

Since human beings cannot, as far as we know, converse with stone statues, this must, by definition, happen by the power of a miracle.

Of course, stone-and-brass tactical computers do not function in the world as we know it, either! So this theory will also have to account for the construction of the various 'stone golems' by the Rabbi of Prague and the descendants of Radonic. Therefore, such construction is also deemed to be miraculous!

Isobel and I have been playing about with a hypothetical *if*. Our theory is: suppose this ability to perform miracles was GENETIC — *if* there existed such a thing as a gene for performing miracles, *if* this 'wonder-working' had a scientific rather than a superstitious basis, how would it function?

It would have to be a recessive gene, obviously. If it were dominant, everybody would be constantly performing miracles. It probably also has to be a recessive with something dangerous linked to the same allele or the same focus — Isobel points out that because blue rats have difficulty in successfully birthing litters, a spontaneous mutation of a blue rat will probably not perpetuate its line. You don't see many blue rats in the wild, and indeed there may not have been any in existence at all until breeders took an interest in Rattus Norvegicus.

Imagine, then, that this proposed 'wonder-working' gene would arise through spontaneous mutation very infrequently, and therefore those born to successfully perform miracles would be history's memorable prophets and religious leaders - Christ; the Visigoths' unidentified 'Prophet Gundobad'; the major Saints; other cultures' great visionaries and seers. They would not necessarily pass their genetic heritage on successfully, but it would remain as a recessive gene.

In 'Fraxinus's' history of Leofric's family, Isobel makes the suggestion — which I had not thought of — that both the Rabbi of Prague *and* the slave woman Ildico were wonder-workers, both of them using that capacity and carrying the gene.

The Rabbi, as wonder-worker, could build a miraculous stone chess-playing computer. Ildico, as the descendant of Gundobad, would carry enough of the ability to conceive a child from the stone man, but not to work miracles herself. Her daughter, Radegunde, could work the miracle of long-distance communication with the computer, and construct her own golem (but, given the circumstances of her conception, would be prone to physical and mental instability).

The descendants of Radegunde and Ildico would all carry the potential for miracle-working, but it would take a long programme of selective breeding to bring about another Radegunde, given that there is no miracle-worker there to aid Leofric's family in this project, it has to be done purely by two centuries of stock-breeding. (The morality of this is another question, and certainly does not seem to have occurred to Leofric or his ancestors.)

Both Faris and Ash carry the wonder-working gene, and in them the ability to successfully use it is dominant. It seems not to have been active in Ash herself at birth, instead being triggered at the onset of puberty, at which point she begins to 'download' from the Stone Golem.

And there you have it! It's a shame there's no such thing as miracles. Well, this is what academics do for fun, on long cold afternoons . . .

Of course, miracles are — pace centuries of stories from various faiths — merely superstition. A miracle is a non-scientific alteration in the fabric of reality, if I may define it that way, and by that definition it is impossible. When one is sitting in a surprisingly cold army surplus tent (there is a sea-fog) with absolutely nothing else to do but wait to continue the dig, these are intriguing speculations.

If this delay goes on much longer, I confidently expect that Isobel and I shall next devise a theory about how such a 'non-scientific alteration in the fabric of reality' or 'miracle' might be caused. We are no longer nineteenth-century Materialists, after all; the higher reaches of theoretical physics have taught us that all our Laws of Nature and apparently solid world are probability, fuzzy logic, uncertainty. Yes, about another two hours should do it! We shall produce the Ratcliff-Napier-Grant Theory of Scientific Miracles. And begin to pray, doubtless, for a change of heart among the local politicos, so that we have something real to do!

I hope you are duly amused.

- Pierce

Message: #102 (Pierce Ratcliff)
Subject: Ash manuscripts
Date: 23/11/00 at 03.09 a.m.
From: Longman@

format address deleted
Other details encrypted and
non-recoverably deleted

Pierce —

Pierce, I have GOT something for you!

I had to go to a book-launch tonight. While I was swanning around the party, networking like mad, I met up again with a dear friend of mine, Nadia — I told you about her — a bookseller from Twickenham — she has one of those independent bookshops which are

402

fast dying out now in favour of chains, in which everything is welcome except customers. (When I asked her what she was doing there, she replied, 'The shop's full of people; I've come AWAY!')

However — there was a house clearance at some place in East Anglia, and she bid at an auction for several cases of books. One of them is Vaughan Davies' ASH: A FIFTEENTH-CENTURY BIOGRAPHY, and it's *complete*!

Nadia suspects that the house clearance was either from Davies's own house, or a relative's house containing Vaughan Davies's belongings. I've asked her to find out more, tomorrow morning.

I haven't had time to read the thing yet (we had to go back to her shop, and I've only just come in!) but I'll do that while I'm scanning it in for you. Shall I send it through now?

– Love, Anna

Message: #174 (Anna Longman)
Subject: Ash, archaeological discoveries
Date: 23/11/00 at 07.32 a.m.
From: Ngrant@

format address deleted
Other details encrypted by non-discoverable personal key

Anna —

Yes. YES. Scan it and send it to me NOW!

Good grief. A copy of Vaughan Davies, after all this time.

Anna, do you realise what this means? Please get your friend to contact the house-clearance people immediately. There may be UNPUBLISHED papers.

I know that my work is superseding Davies, but still — after all this time – even for pure interest's sake, I want to know what the missing half of the Introduction is. I want to know his theory.

– Pierce

Message: #175 (Anna Longman)
Subject: Ash, archaeological discoveries
Date: 23/11/00 at 09.24 a.m.
From: Ngrant@

format address deleted
text encrypted by non-discoverable personal key

Anna —

HOLD THE PRESSES!

(I always wanted to say that.)

Still nothing going on here, on site, but we're MOVING, tomorrow, Friday! Isobel received a radio communication from the expedition's ship. It's been examining the seabed north of Tunis, between Cap Zebib and Rass Engelah, around Bizerte (and the Lac de Bizerte, an enclosed sea-inlet south of the city). We're going to move to the sea-site while Isobel's manager handles the ongoing problem here.

Apparently it's unsafe to dive up there, but the cameras on the ROVs (remote operated vehicles) have been sending back pictures.

As soon as she allows me to, I'll be in contact with you.

- Pierce

PART SEVEN

7 September–10 September AD 1476

Engines and Devices

I

The Visigoth captain all but dragged Ash out and along narrow corridors, his squad forcing a way between crowds of running freemen and slaves; the whole house in an uproar.

Ash stumbled, aware of almost nothing, able to think only *I betrayed them, all of them, I didn't even think about it! Anything to stay alive—*

She became aware of being manhandled; lifted bodily. The sides of a wooden tub burned hot against her skin. Ash flinched back as slaves lowered her into water. They leaned her against sponges.

"I advise, as hot as you can bear it," a fat, cheerful young man observed, in Italian, unwinding the bindings from her left knee.

His voice echoed in the long hall, muffled only slightly by the sheets that hung, perfumed with flowers and herbs, from the ceiling of the lord-*amir*'s household bath-house. The hall has steel grills at the windows and bars on the doors.

"'*Arif* Alderic, what have you been doing to this one?"

Alderic shook his head. "Don't waste too much skill, *dottore*. She's one of the *amir*'s. She only has to live a few days."

Ash looked dizzily up. Two women with iron collars around their necks, chained together with a span of links about six foot long, bent over the tub and began to sponge and soap her body. If she could have stopped the handling, she would have. She could only stare through the steamy air, hot for the first time in weeks. Tears began to leak from under her eyelids.

I thought I would have more courage.

Other bathers' voices echoed outside, in the vast tubs that stood in cubicles all down the hall; and a woman's high laughter sounded, and the clink of glasses.

"Whatever you do to her later, she must eat now. And *drink*!" The Italian man pinched the back of Ash's hand. Ash watched the ridge of skin stand up proud for a moment. "She is, I know only the Latin, dehydrated. Dried up."

Alderic took off his helmet and wiped his forehead. "Feed and water her, then, she'd better not die yet. *Nazir!*"

He stomped off, to give orders. As the sheets were brushed back, she glimpsed other tubs, occupied by pairs of bathers, plates set on planks above the water, and jugs of wine standing on marble surrounds. A slave was playing a stringed instrument.

"You should not treat me," Ash protested. Only as she automatically spoke in Italian did she begin to realise the surgeon was not a Visigoth. She looked up, roused out of blank misery by surprise. A fat young man with straggling black hair, in red hose, stripped to shirt and pourpoint and still sweating in this steaming, echoing chamber, looking down at her.

He nodded, as if he guessed her confusion.

"We are a commonwealth, madonna; doctors and priests pass freely across borders, even in wartime," the fat young man said, his accent Milanese, now she thought about it. He raised a dark brow. "And, not treat you? Why?"

Because I don't deserve it.

Ash looked down at her brown, blood-dried skin. She submerged her hands under the surface of the hot, misty water. The heat sank in, sank into her muscles, into her bones. A great wave of warmth went through her, and relaxation. She had not known how cold she was. Just the animal comfort brought her back to herself, sore and aching and beaten: still alive.

I *would* have betrayed them – I still might – but I haven't yet.

Nothing more than luck! – Call it Fortuna. It's a chance. It's days. Two, three, four days, maybe. *It's a chance.*

It's helplessness I can't stand. Give me even the shadow of a chance, and I'll find a way to take it. Fortune favours the bold.

"Why?" the Italian insisted.

"Take no notice of me, *dottore*," Ash said.

The chained slaves put a plank across the tub. Another male slave brought a plate, and a narrow-necked pot topped with a pie-crust. As Ash pushed herself upright, he knocked the crust off and emptied the pot into the plate: a rush of meat, chopped hot herbs, pickerel,[1] and spiced wine. Its strong scent brought her to the point of vomiting. Almost instantly, the nausea went off, succeeded by a griping pain that she recognised from her childhood: complete hunger. Carefully, she picked out a small piece of meat and nibbled, her tongue curling up at the sensuous taste of the sauce.

"Ash," she said.

"Annibale Valzacchi." The physician flung away soaked bandages, bending over the tub and manipulating her knee-joint. She grunted, in pain, through a mouthful of food. The Italian exclaimed, "God be good to us, madonna, what do you do in life? Pull a plough?"

Ash licked her fingers and stared down at the steaming stew, forcing herself to wait before she ate again.

"The King-Caliph *died*," she said suddenly. "That old man died."

She half-expected Annibale Valzacchi to deny it, or to ask her what she meant: all of it could, she felt, have been her own delirium. Instead the Italian nodded, thoughtfully.

"Of natural causes," Valzacchi observed, in his thick Milanese north Italian.

"Yes, well . . . A cup of belladonna *is* 'natural causes', in Carthage!"

Rumours of assassination go around after every death of a powerful man. Ash gave an answering nod, and merely said, "He was too sick to live long anyway, wasn't he?"

"A canker, yes. We – doctors, surgeons, physicians, priests – we are here in

---

[1] Young pike.

Carthage in such numbers because he sought a cure, any cure. There is no cure, of course: God disposes."

God or Fortune, Ash thought, with a momentary shiver of awe, that shaded off into raw, mordant humour: *Haven't I always prayed before combat? Why stop now?* She said thoughtfully, "I should like to see a priest. A Green priest. Is that possible, here?"

"This lord-*amir* is no religious fanatic. It should be possible. You are not Italian yourself, madonna, are you? No. Then, there are three English priests, that I room with in the lower city; I know of a Frenchman, and a German, and there is one who might be from Franche-Comté or Savoy."

As if she were a beast in a byre, Valzacchi slid his hands up around her shoulders, expertly gauging their irregularity: the muscles of the right more developed than the left.

From behind, his voice said, "Strange, madonna. I should say this arm has been trained to use a sword."

For the first time in fifteen days, Ash couldn't help a genuine smile: half amazement, half delight. She sat back in the hot sweet-smelling water as his fingers probed her neck under the steel collar. "How the *hell* did you know that, *dottore?*"

"My brother Gianpaulo is a condottiere. I did my initial training with him. Until I discovered that civilian medicine is considerably less dangerous, and pays rather better. This is the muscle development of someone who uses a sword, and perhaps a military axe, right-handed."

Ash felt herself chuckle, a soft sound and a quaking body. She wiped her wet hand across her mouth. His hands left her shoulders. His touch of recognition gave her something back; her body, her spirit.

She rested her arms on her knees, sitting perfectly still in the hot water, and looked down.

Ash saw, on the still surface, a scarred cheek reflected through pale, rising mist; and a face she barely recognised with its cropped hair. *They wouldn't know me!* she thought, amazed; and on the heels of that, *What's happened here is past, I've left too many people behind me to give up now, I have responsibilities.* She knew it for bravado; knew also that, tended, it might be a seed of real courage.

"Yes," she acknowledged, more to herself than to the doctor. "I've been a condottiere myself."

Annibale Valzacchi regarded her now with an expression compounded of disgust, fear and superstition. It said plainly, *A woman?* Primly, he shrugged. "I can't refuse a request for religious consolation. A military priest would suit you best. The German, then. The German is a military priest, a Father Maximillian."

" 'Father Maximillian'." Ash twisted around bodily, and stared up at him out of the hot steaming water. "*Dottore*, do you know if— Jesus! Do you know if his name is Godfrey, *Godfrey* Maximillian?"

She saw nothing of Annibale Valzacchi for twenty-four hours, as near as she could judge the time.

A different squad of Alderic's men took her down a hundred stone steps, into the heart of the crag's corridors and apartments, and left her with slave attendants.

The room the slaves brought her to was smaller than a field tent, with only a pallet and a blanket on the stone floor. It had walls a yard thick, she could see that from the window – more like a tunnel, with iron bars set halfway down, so that no one could climb up to look out.

A freezing wind blew in through the unglazed window, from the blackness outside.

"Can I have a fire?" Ash tried to make herself understood to the five or six men and women, whose Carthaginian Gothic was quick, guttural, local, unintelligible. She went through every word for 'fire' that she knew; to blank looks from all of them, except a brawny big woman.

The fair-haired woman in an iron collar, woollen blankets belted around her waist, shook her head and said something sharp. A small, quick young man with her answered: it might have been a protest. He glanced at Ash. There were crow's feet around his eyes, his dark eyes.

"Can I have more clothes?" Ash gripped two fistfuls of the worn-thin linen nightshirt that the bath attendant had thrown at her, and held out the cloth. "More – warm? – clothes?"

The little girl who had attended on Leofric said, "Why should you? We not."

Ash nodded, slowly, looking around at the half dozen or so people, most of whom were openly staring at her. All but the girl had rough woven blankets, with stripe-patterns; the kind of wool that one throws over a pallet for extra warmth in the winter. They wore them wrapped around their bodies, and went barefoot on the mosaic tiled floor. The girl wore only a thin linen tunic.

"Here." Ash pulled the striped woollen blanket off the pallet, draping it around the child's shoulders. She fastened it with a neat fold under the arm. "Take it. Understand? Keep it."

The girl looked at the big woman. After a second, the woman nodded. Her frown faded, replaced by vulnerability, confusion.

Ash put her fingers under her iron collar, lifting it, giving her neck some relief from the weight. She said, "I'm like you. Just like you. They can do what they like with me, too."

The woman said thickly, "Slave?"

"Yes. Slave." Ash walked across the room and hitched herself up on her hands, peering out of the stone window. Frost sparkled on the surface of the red granite, and on the iron bars. Nothing was visible beyond, not roofs, not sea, not stars: nothing but dark.

"It's cold," she said. She grinned at the slaves, beating her arms exaggeratedly around her body, and blowing on her fingers. "Every time Lord Leofric sits down, his arse gets just as cold as ours do!"

The little girl laughed. The sharp-faced young man smiled. The big woman shook her head, with an expression of fear, and jerked her thumb; ushering the domestic slaves out. The sharp-faced man and the child lingered.

"What's down *there*?" Ash hooked her arm up and over, in an exaggerated motion of pointing out of the window, and down. "What?"

He said a word she didn't understand.

"What?" Ash frowned.

"Water."

"How far? How – *far* – down?"

He shrugged, spread his hands, grinning ruefully. "Water, down. Far. Long. Ahh . . ." He made a noise indicating disgust, then tapped his chest, looking as though he was sure he would be understood in this, at least. "Leovigild."

"Ash." Ash touched her own chest. She pointed at the girl and raised her brows.

The child looked up from examining her new blanket. "Violante."

"Okay." Ash smiled, companionably. She sat down on the pallet, tucking her freezing feet under the hem of her nightshirt. The cold made her breath smoke on the air. "So, tell me about this place."

When food came, she shared it with Leovigild and Violante. The girl, with bright eyes and a red flush to her face, ate hungrily and chattered on, half-understood; interpreting for the older man where she could.

From growing up a peasant in a military camp, Ash knows that servants get everywhere and know about everybody. Ash begins – through the cold hours, mitigated when the big woman came in with two worn wool blankets – to get the shape of the *amir*'s household clear in her mind; how life is lived in the honeycomb chambers of the Citadel; slave and freeborn and *amir*.

In the hours when she should have been sleeping, hunger kept her usefully awake. She stayed at the foot of the stone embrasure, staring up out of the window. As her eyes adjusted to night vision she saw bright pin-points: Fomalhaut, and Capricornus, the Goat. The constellations of summer in a freezing, bitter night.

No moon, she thought, but it could be the dark of the moon now; I haven't been counting the days—

She slid her hand along the wall, guiding herself back to the pallet, and sat down, feeling around for blankets. She wrapped herself up. Her hands clasped across her belly. Her body shivered. But only from the cold.

Let's say I have three days. Could be four or five, but call it three: if I can't get out of here in three days, I'm dead.

A man's voice outside the steel door said something too muffled to identify. Her hands suddenly shaking, Ash stuffed the sheet of paper and charcoal stick down the bodice of her shift.

The key turned.

With her hand against the flat metal door she could feel the mechanism work, bars sliding back between the two steel plates. Warned, she stepped back into the tiny room.

"I'll be back here in an hour," *'Arif* Alderic said from the corridor, not speaking to her. His voice sounded unusually compassionate. The single unwinking, pale light above the door shone down into her eyes: Ash blinked, attempting to see who was coming in.

Fear makes the belly uncomfortable. Ash, who has fought, feels her bowels shift in momentary discomfort that she recognises at last as fear.

A deep masculine voice said, in German, "Oh, excuse me, I thought that—" and broke off.

The man standing at the doorway wore a brown wool gown over his green priest's robes, the puffed sleeves slit, and lined with marten fur. It was the bulk of the gown, perhaps, that made his body look too big for his head. She stepped forward, thinking, *No, his face is thinner*, staring at the way deep creases cut down beside his mouth, not hidden by his beard. The fragile skin of his eyelids clung close to the balls of his eyes, accentuating their hollow sockets. All his face was clearly shrunken down on to the bone. *He looks old.*

"*Godfrey?*"

"I didn't know you!"

"You look thinner." She frowned.

"I didn't know you," Godfrey Maximillian repeated, wonderingly.

The steel door slammed. The noise of bars sinking into sockets drowned out any words for a long minute. Ash self-consciously smoothed the blue wool bodice and kirtle down over her shift, and one hand went up to touch her shorn hair.

"It's still me," she said. "They wouldn't give me male clothes. I don't care if I look like a woman. *Let* them underestimate me. That's just fine. Jesus, *Godfrey!*"

She took a step forward, intending to throw her arms around him, and at the last minute flushed from bodice-line to forehead, and reached out and grabbed both his hands, hard. Tears welled up and spilled down her face. She said, again, "Godfrey, Godfrey!"

His hands were warm within hers. She felt him shaking.

"Why did you go!"

"I left Dijon with the Visigoths, I came here, I desperately needed to spy out the Caliph's court and find out the truth about your voice. I thought it was the only thing now that I could do for you—" Godfrey's face streamed, wet. He didn't let go of her hands to wipe it. "It was all that I could think of doing for you!"

His hard hands crushed hers. She tightened her grip. The wind from the open stone window blew in, hard enough to whip her skirts around her bare ankles.

"You're cold," Godfrey Maximillian said accusingly, "your hands are bitter."

He lifted her hands and put them up under his armpits, into the warmth of his robe, and for the first time, met her eyes. His lids were reddened, wet. She could not imagine what he was seeing: a crop-haired thing in a dress and a steel collar, could not know how her own face was sharpened by hunger, by the loss of a silver waterfall of hair, short hair throwing brow and ear and eye and scar all into sharp relief.

Her cold fingers began to warm, prickling with blood-flow.

"*What happened to us?*" she demanded, "to the Lion? *What?*"

"I – don't know. I left two days before you fought. I thought—"

He freed one hand and wiped his face, his beard.

Words hung between them, spoken at Dijon. Ash felt his body-warmth through her cold skin. She raised her head, needing as always to look up to look into his face; and saw, not anguished declarations, but a face she knows (given the infrequency of mirrors) better than her own, and a mind of which she knows most, if not every, weakness.

Godfrey Maximillian said brusquely, "When I docked here, the field had been fought ten days ago. All I can tell you is what everybody knows: Duke Charles is wounded; the flower of Burgundian chivalry lies dead on the field outside Auxonne – but Dijon is holding out, I believe; or, there's still some fighting somewhere. No one knows or cares about one mercenary company. The Lion Azure had some notoriety because of its woman commander, but there is nothing, only minor rumours, no one in Carthage cares whether we were massacred outright, or changed sides and fought with the Faris, or ran away; they just care that the victory was theirs."

Ash found herself nodding her head.

"I have tried," Godfrey said.

Ash tightened her grip, fingers fisted in his, buried deep in his robe's scratchy brown wool. *No. If I hold him, embrace him, it will be for my comfort, not his. Not his, when he wants me. Shit. Shit.*

"You always come for me. You came for me at St Herlaine, and Milan." A hot tear flowed. She hitched her shoulder up, wiping her cheek on the blue wool, and stared up in wonder at him. "You don't want me. You just think you do. You'll get over it. And I'll wait, Godfrey, because I have no intention of losing you. We've known each other too long, and we love each other too well."

"You don't know what I want," he said roughly.

Godfrey stepped away and released her hand. The air seared cold on her skin. Ash watched him, calmly. She watched him pace, as far as the tiny cell allowed; two steps each way on the mosaic tiled floor.

"I burn. Doesn't the Word say it's better to marry than to burn?" His clear eyes, the brown of woodland-river water, fixed on her face. "You love that boy. What else needs to be said? You will forgive me, most men go through this at a much younger age; this is the first and only time I would have given back my priesting and rejoined the world." He made an odd, sonorous murmur in his chest, that Ash realised was laughter. "This, also, I have learned in confession – that men who love in secret, for so long, don't know what to do if that love is returned. I don't suppose I would be different in that respect."

Whatever: let him have that thought for consolation. I must not hold him, Ash thought; and could not stop herself. She moved forward, grabbed his arms, clutching him around the hanging sleeves of his gown, and hugged her arms around his broad back. "Shit, Godfrey! You don't know what it's like to see you here. *You don't know.*"

His forearms closed momentarily across her back. Enfolded, her face buried against his warm chest, she is for a long second blank to everything but his familiarity, his scent, the sound of his voice, the history that they share.

He put her back from him. As his hands left her shoulders, he touched the steel band riveted around her neck.

"I found out *nothing* about your voice. I failed. Every bit of the money I brought with me is gone." A glint of humour in his eyes, gazing down at her, a half-smile on his lips. "If *I* can't buy information, child, who can? I bribed who

413

I could. I know everything about the outside of this—" a movement of his bearded chin, indicating the walls of House Leofric "—and nothing inside."

"I know all about the inside. And my voice. Did they search you, coming in?"

"Your *voice?*"

"Later: it's complicated. It *is* the Golem. I think Leofric wants me to—" *learn from,* she did not say. She was unaware that an expression of pain touched her face, and that Godfrey registered it and remained thoughtfully silent. "Were you searched?"

"No."

"They might search you going out, though. They can't search your heart, Godfrey; look at this." She started to undo the draw-cord of her shift, hesitated, faced away from him, and retrieved her paper and charcoal before she turned back. "Here. This is my best guess for a house-plan."

Godfrey Maximillian eased himself down on to the pallet, which she patted in invitation. He pointed at the paper, and charcoal twig. "Where did you get those?"

"The same place I got most of this information. A slave child. Violante." Ash swathed the full skirt around her knees and tucked the hem under her feet, in an attempt to be warm. "I share my food with her. She steals things for me."

"You do know what could happen to her, if she's caught?"

"She could be whipped. Or killed," Ash said, "this is a crazy house. Godfrey, this is deliberate. I know what I'm doing, even if she doesn't, because my life depends on it." She turned the crumpled sheet to its blank side. "Okay, show me what's outside."

When he said nothing, she looked up again.

Godfrey Maximillian said quietly, "They let me in only to give you the last rites. I know they've condemned you to execution. What I don't yet know is why, and what I can do about it."

She choked up, nodded once, wiped the back of her wrist across her eyes. "I'll tell you, if there's time. Okay. Show me what's *outside* this building."

His broad, capable hands took the paper, the charcoal stick seeming tiny. With a surprisingly delicate touch, he drew an elongated squared-off U-shape. "You're on the middle headland that protrudes into the harbour. There are quays here and here—" an 'x' each side of the U "—and streets coming up the hill to the Citadel."

"What's the scale?"

"About a half-mile to the mainland. The bluff is three, four furlongs high?" Godfrey's rumble had a self-questioning note. He drew in another shape, an elongated square within the U, occupying the far end of it. "That's the Citadel, that we're in now. It's walled."

"I remember. They brought me in that way." Her dirty fingertip traced a path from the 'x' quayside mark, up to the rectangle crowning the U. "Is this Citadel walled all the way around?"

"Walled and guarded. At this end, the walls come up sheer from the water. There are town streets going back on to the mainland, and then Carthage city is here and here—" A shape added, like a palm and three fingers, which Ash

414

realised was the harbour and two other headlands; the town, by Godfrey's markings, all down on one side. "The market – here. Where the road goes out towards Alexandria."

"Which way is north?"

"Here." A scribble. "The sea."[2]

"Uh-huh . . ." She held it in her field of vision, under the Greek Fire that hissed in its glass cage above the door, until the lines burned into her memory.

"This window looks north," she said thoughtfully, "as far as I can tell from the stars. There's nothing between me and the sea, is there? I'm at the edge. Shit. So much for that." She flipped the paper over. "I've talked to people. This is what I think we're in." She indicated her scrawled hollow square. "Where they bring you into the House, there's a ground floor all around a courtyard: that's the *amir* and his family, his hangers-on."

"It's big." Godfrey sounded rapt.

Ash dotted in a black mark at the corners of each square. "These are four stairwells. They go down into the house underneath. Slave-quarters, kitchens, storerooms. There are stables and a mews at ground level, everything else is beneath. Violante tells me there are ten storeys carved out of the rock. I think I'm on the fifth one down. Each stair has four sets of halls and chambers coming off it, at each level, *and the stairs don't interconnect*." She finished with a cross at one corner. "That's north-west, that's me. Leofric is here, in the north-east set of chambers."

She threw the charcoal stick down, and sat back against the wall.

"Shit, I would hate to have to take this place by force!"

When she glanced sideways, and saw Godfrey Maximillian's closed expression, she smiled quietly.

"No. I'm not mad. Just old professional habit."

"You're not mad," he agreed, "but you're different."

Ash said nothing. There was for that second nothing she was capable of saying. Her breasts momentarily hurt, heavy within her bodice.

"Is it this?" Godfrey touched the steel collar again.

"That? No." Ash's head came up. "This is my pass out of here."

"I don't understand."

"The lord-*amir* Gelimer did me a favour." Ash knotted her fingers around the metal, feeling the steel's rounded corners digging into her skin. She did not know that she looked at Godfrey with all the old careless excitement of balancing on an edge. "If I don't have this, I'm a prisoner, a guest, a something you notice. *With* this . . . Alderic brought you down here—"

---

[2] The geography of Visigothic Carthage, as depicted in the 'Fraxinus' manuscript, does not appear to wildly contradict the known archaeological facts. The compass directions are a little off, but there is more often than not a mismatch between site and chronicle in archaeology.

In fact, there were two enclosed harbours behind an isthmus: the commercial harbour and the great naval shipyards. They were a feature of what we may call Liby-Phoenecian, or Carthaginian, Carthage; as was the Byrsa, an enclosed hilltop citadel within the main city itself. The streets were, indeed, stepped.

Close to this original site, Roman Carthage added other features, including water-storage cisterns, aqueducts, baths, an amphitheatre, and many features of civilised life; as well as their own great naval shipyards.

Anna – here's my rough aerial sketch of the ruins of present-day Carthage, and a proposed geography of 15c Visigoth Carthage.

I've included a possible new Visigoth harbour (which, like areas of the Roman/Carthaginian ones here, and the one at Leptis Magna, may have silted up in the interim).

The exact site of the Byrsa or walled hill during the 15c is conjectural, based on textual evidence.

Pierce

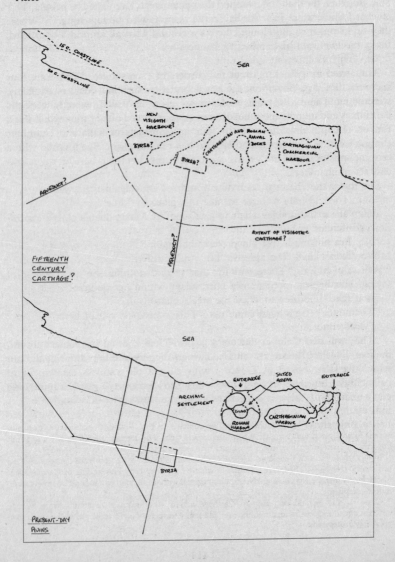

"Alderic?"

"The soldier." Ash spoke more quickly. "He brought you down. You must have seen it, Godfrey. This house is *full* of fair-haired slaves. If I get out of this room then I'm just one more of them. Nobody sees me. Nobody finds me. I'm just one more faceless woman in a collar."

"If that's not the trouble, what is?" Godfrey pursued. He rapidly shook his head. "Deus vous garde.[3] No. Say nothing until you wish it."

"I will."

"There are too many soldiers in this house."

"I know. I have to get outside to escape. Just for a few minutes, just a chance." She grinned, lopsidedly. "I know how thin a chance it is, Godfrey. I just can't stop trying, that's all. I have to get back. I have to get *out*." She cut off the intensity cracking her voice; let her fingers trail off the pallet, on the uneven floor. "This place is old . . ."

The unwavering light of Greek Fire lit up every corner of the tiny room: the close-set tiles in their pink and black geometries, the chamfered edges of the window embrasure, the faint worn bas-relief on the walls: pomegranates and palm trees and men with the heads of animals. Someone had scratched a name, ARGENTIUS, down close to the floor, with some sharpened tool; not, she thought, with the carved wood spoon that came with her wooden bowl and infrequent food.

She complained absently, "They wouldn't even let me have an eating-knife."

Godfrey Maximillian said dryly, "I'm not surprised. They know who you are."

Ash was startled into a laugh.

"So different, and so much the same." Godfrey reached over to touch the cut ends of her silver hair. His hand went back to the cross at his breast. "If that captain didn't know you, I'd give you these robes and hood and let you try to walk out of here. That's been known to be successful."

"Not for the man left behind," she said acidly, and was startled when he, in turn, laughed. "What? *What*, Godfrey?"

"Nothing," he said, frankly amused. "No wonder I've been with you since you were eleven."

"They will kill me." Ash watched his face change. "I've got forty-eight hours, realistically. I don't know what it's like out there, while they're electing their new King-Caliph—"

"Chaotic. It's carnival down in the city," Godfrey shrugged, "with only the city's own guards to keep it in order. As I discovered when I attempted to buy information, the *amirs* have retreated into their own houses up here, with their households and all their own troops."

Ash hit one fist into her palm. "It *has* to be now! Is there any way you can legitimately get me out of here? Just out on to the street, just for a minute?"

"You'll be guarded."

"*I can't give up now.*"

Some feeling sharpened his features, bringing the skin even more taut across

---

[3] 'God protect you'.

417

the bone, but she could not read him. He looked down at his spatulate broad fingers. When he spoke, after some moments' silence, there was an edge to his voice.

"You never give up, Ash. You sit in here and calculate that you may have two days left – but you may have two hours, or less; that Visigoth thug could knock on your door at any minute of today." He glanced briefly at the stone tunnel that served as a window. The cell's Greek Fire brilliance meant no night vision, nothing visible but a square of blackness. His tone strained, he continued, "Ash, don't you know that you could die? Does nothing teach you that? Does *nothing* make you suffer?"

He is trying to reach me, Ash thought, killing her anger.

"I'm not deluding myself. Yes, I'm probably going to die." She wrapped her hands in a fold of her woollen skirt, shivering against the cold. Footsteps banged down the corridor outside and faded into the distance, muffled by the steel door.

Godfrey said, "I'm nothing but an uneducated hedge-priest. You know that. I will pray to Our Lady and the Communion of Saints, I'll move Heaven and Earth to free you, you know that. But I would be failing you in everything if I didn't try to bring you to some realisation, some knowledge that you could be dead before you have time to put your soul right. When did you last go to confession? Before the field at Auxonne?"

Ash opened her mouth, shut it again. At last, she said, "I don't remember. I really don't remember the last time I was absolved. Does it matter?"

Godfrey gave a small, high chuckle; a noise that rather reminded her of Leofric's rats. He brushed his hand across his face. When he looked at her, his taut expression had relaxed. "Why? Why do I *bother*? You're a complete heathen, child. We both know it."

"I'm sorry," Ash said contritely.

"No."

"I'm sorry I can't be a good Christian for you."

"I wouldn't expect it. God's representatives on Earth have not been entirely kind." Godfrey Maximillian cocked his head, listening, then relaxed again. "You're young. You have neither kith nor kin, household nor guild, lord nor lady. I've watched you on the outside, child; I know at least one other reason than lust for why you married Fernando del Guiz. Every human tie you have is bound with money, and unbound with the end of a contract. That will never lead you to a tie with Our Lord. I prayed that you would have time to grow older, and to consider."

A long, harsh male scream echoed between the cell's stone walls. It took Ash a second to realise that it was not close at hand but far off – far below – and loud enough to echo up from the harbour, over the noise of gulls.

"Carnival, huh?"

"A rough carnival."

Ash thoughtfully wiped her charcoal several times across her paper, blurring the soft lines. She scrunched it up, knelt up, and threw it out of the window. The charcoal stick she tucked under one end of the pallet.

"Godfrey . . . How long does it take before a foetus has a soul?"

"Some authorities tell us, forty days. Others, that it takes on a soul when it quickens, and the woman feels the child move within her womb. Holy Saint Magdalen," he said flatly, "is that it?"

"I was with child when I came here. They beat me, and I lost it. Yesterday." Ash found herself making the same quick movement of looking at the black window that never showed her a sun, never reassured her that it was day. "No, the day before."

His hand closed over hers. She looked down at it.

"Are the children of incest sinful?"

Godfrey's grip tightened on her hand. "Incest? How could it be *incest* between you and your husband!"

"No, not Fernando. Me." Ash stared at the opposite wall. She did not look at Godfrey Maximillian. She turned her hand over, so that her palm slid into his, and they sat with their backs leaning up against the wall, the heavy-duty cloth of the pallet cold under them.

"I do have family," she said. "You've seen them, Godfrey. The Faris, and these slaves here. The *Amir* Leofric breeds them – *us* – like cattle. He breeds the son back to the mother, and the daughter to the father, and this family's been doing it since before living memory. If I'd borne a child, it would have been incestuous a hundred times over." Now she turned her head, so that she could see Godfrey's face. "Does that shock you? It doesn't shock me." And in a pragmatic monotone, she added, "My baby might have been deformed. A monster. By that reasoning, I may *be* a monster. Not just my voice. Not all deformities are things you can see."

His eyelids fluttered as he avoided her gaze. She thought she had not noticed before how long and fine his brown lashes were. She felt a pain in her hand and looked down. His knuckles were white where he gripped her hand.

"How—" Godfrey coughed. "How do you know it to be true? How did you discover this?"

"*Amir* Leofric told me," Ash said. She waited until Godfrey looked her in the face again. "And I asked the Stone Golem."

"*You* asked—"

"He wanted to know whether I was a fake or not. So I told him. If I could, and it was right, then I *had* to be hearing it from somewhere, I *had* to be hearing the voice of the machine." Ash reached down with her other hand and began to peel Godfrey's fingers off her. Where he had gripped, her skin was bloodlessly white.

"He bred a general who could hear his machine," Ash said, "but now – he doesn't need another one."

"Iesu Christus Viridianus, Christus Imperator,"[4] Godfrey said. He looked down at his hands without seeing them. Ash noticed that the cuffs of his robe were frayed. And half the gauntness of his face could be attributable to nothing other than hunger: a poor priest, lodging in some Carthage tenement, dependant on doctors like Annibale Valzacchi for alms, and for information. No information is without its price.

---

[4] 'Green Christ, Christ Emperor'.

In the silence, she said: "When you pray, Godfrey, do you get an answer?"

The question brought him out of his amazement. "It would be presumptuous to say."

All her body was tense against the cold, mitigated as it might be by thick stone walls. She shifted on the pallet.

"This," she touched her temple, "isn't the Communion of Saints. I used to hope it would be, Godfrey. I kind of hoped it would be Saint George, or one of the soldier-saints, you know?"

A faint smile curled up one corner of his mouth. "I suppose you would hope that, child."

"It isn't a saint's voice, it's a machine's voice. Although the machine might have been made by a miracle. If Prophet Gundobad was a real prophet of God?" She looked quizzically at Godfrey, without giving him time to answer. "And when I hear it, I don't just listen."

"I don't understand."

Ash bounced where she sat, hitting one fist on the pallet. "It's not just listening. When I hear you speak, I don't have to *do* anything to hear you."

"I frequently feel that you don't have to pay attention," Godfrey said, with a grave humour; derailing her absolutely. He gave her a smile of apology. "There is something more to this?"

"The voice." Ash made a helpless gesture with her hands. "I feel as if I'm pulling on a rope, or – you won't understand this, but, sometimes in combat you can *make* someone else attack you in a certain way, by the way you stand and hold your weapon, by the way you move – you offer a gap, a way in through your defences – and they come in where you want them to, and then you deal with them. I never noticed when it was just a question or two before we fought, but Leofric made me listen to the Stone Golem for a long time. I'm *doing* something when I listen, Godfrey. Offering a . . . way in."

"There are acts of omission and acts of commission." Godfrey sounded rapt, again. Abruptly, he glanced at the door and lowered the volume of his speech. "How much can you get it to tell you? Can it tell you how to leave?"

"Oh, it could tell me. Probably tell me where all the guards are stationed." Ash flicked her gaze up to meet Godfrey's. "I've been talking to the slaves. When Leofric wants to know what tactical questions the Faris is asking the machine, he asks it – *and it tells him*."

"And would tell what you ask, too?"

She shrugged. Staccato, she said, "Maybe. If it 'remembers'. If Leofric thinks to ask. He will. He's smart. Then I'm caught. They'll just change duty rosters. Maybe beat me until I'm unconscious and can't ask."

Godfrey Maximillian took her hand. His body was still half-turned towards the door. "Slaves do not always tell the truth."

"I know. If I was going to—" Ash made another unspecific gesture, trying to frame a thought. "To call what it knows to me, I'd ask something else first. Godfrey, I'd ask it *why is it so cold here? Amir* Leofric doesn't know the answer to that, and he's scared."

"Everyone is—"

"That's just it. Everyone *here* is scared, too. I thought this was something they made happen for their crusade – but they didn't expect this cold either. This isn't the Eternal Twilight, this is something else again."

"Perhaps these are the last days—"

A heavy tread sounded in the corridor.

Godfrey Maximillian leapt to his feet rapidly, brushing down his robe and gown.

"Try and get me out," Ash said quickly and quietly, "if I don't hear from you soon, I'll try any way I can think of."

His strong hand enveloped her shoulder, pushing her back down as she tried to rise, so that she was kneeling in front of him as the cell door began to open and soldiers came in. Godfrey crossed himself, and lifted the cross from his broad chest, and kissed it devoutly. "I have an idea. You won't like it. *Absolvo te*,[5] my child."

The *nazir* with Alderic was not Theudibert, Ash noted; nor were any of the squad Theudibert's men. The *'arif* commander stood back while his soldiers filed out, Godfrey Maximillian between them.

Ash watched impassively.

"You ought to be more careful what you say, Frankish girl," *'Arif* Alderic remarked. He put his hand on the steel door and, instead of closing it behind him, pushed it to in front of him, and turned around to face her. "That's a friendly warning."

"One," Ash held up her hand and ticked it off on her fingers, "what makes you think I don't know there are always people here listening to me? Two: what makes you think I care what you report to your lord-*amir*? He's mad. Three, he's already planning to torture me, just *what* have I got to worry about?"

She managed to end with her fists on her hips, chin up; and more energy in her voice than she thought she could find, given the weakness from hunger that went through her every time she stood up. The big bearded man stirred uncomfortably. Something about her bothered him; it took Ash several seconds to work out that it was the contradiction between her dress and her stance.

"You should be more careful," the Visigoth captain repeated stubbornly.

"*Why?*"

'Arif Alderic did not answer. He walked past her to the window, leaning up the red granite shaft and peering at the sky. A smell of ripe harbour rubbish drifted in.

"Have you ever done anything you remained ashamed of, Frankish girl?"

"What?" Ash looked at the back of his head. By the set of his shoulders, he was uncomfortable. A chill feathered the hairs on her arms. *What is this?*

"I said, have you ever done anything that you stayed ashamed of? As a soldier?" He turned to face her, looked her up and down, and repeated more firmly, "As a soldier."

Ash folded her arms. She bit back the first smart remark that came to her mind, and studied him. In addition to his white robes and mail hauberk, the Visigoth wore a crude goatskin jacket, laced like a peasant's tunic; and fur-lined boots, not sandals. He carried a curved dagger at his belt, and a sword with a narrow straight cross. Far too alert to be attacked, surprised.

[5] More properly, *Ego te absolvo*: the priest's absolution of one's sins.

Moved to truth, she relaxed and said, "Yes, everybody has. I have."

"Will you tell me?"

"Why—" Ash stopped herself. "Okay. Five years ago. I was in a siege, it doesn't matter where, some little town on the borders of Iberia. Our lord wouldn't let the townspeople come out. He wanted them to eat up the garrison's supplies, so they'd have to give up the siege. The garrison commander didn't want that, so he evacuated them, drove them out into the moat. So there they were, two hundred people, in a ditch between two armies, neither of whom were going to let them back or through. We killed a dozen before they'd believe us. It went on for a month. They starved and they died. The smell was something else, even for a siege . . ."

She refocused her gaze on Alderic, to find the older man studying her closely.

"That's a story I've told before," she said. "Usually to discourage the kind of would-be mercenary recruit who is fourteen and thinks it's all sitting on horseback and charging a noble enemy. I don't suppose you have those. What I don't say, and what I'm ashamed of, is the newborn babies. Our lord said it wasn't right they should be unbaptised and go to hell, so he let the townspeople pass them up to us. And we passed them to the field-priest, who baptised them – and then we handed them straight back down into the ditch."

Unconsciously she rested her palms flat against her belly.

"We did. *I* did. It went on for weeks. I know they died of starvation while in a state of grace . . . but it stays with me."

The Visigoth *'arif* nodded an acknowledgement.

"We have the fourteen-year-olds in the household levies." White teeth flashed in his black beard, and then his expression changed. "Mine is infants, also. I was perhaps your age, no older. My *amir* – my lord, you would call him; Leofric – had me working in the stock pens."

Ash was aware that she must look puzzled.

"The slave breeding-pens. No larger than this, most of them." Alderic gestured around the cell. "My *amir* set me and my squad to culling 'errors' in the breeding programme, when they were twelve or fourteen weeks old." The *'arif* abruptly pulled off his helmet, wiping his white brow, that was sweating despite the cold. "We were the clear-up squad. Nothing I have done since, in twenty years of war, has been so bad as slashing the throats of babies – the big vein, here – and then just . . . throwing them away. Out of windows like this one, into the harbour: rubbish. No one questions my *amir*. My squad did as we were ordered."

He shrugged helplessly, and met her gaze.

She looks at Alderic's face in the knowledge that – if this is the way it happened for her – there is a sporting chance that he almost killed her, casually slashed her throat and dumped her, twenty years ago. And that he knows this.

"So," Ash said. She grinned at Alderic companionably. "So, Leofric was nuts even back then, huh?"

She saw his brief confusion, a frown – *the woman can't be that obtuse, surely?* – and a dawning acknowledgement.

The *'arif* said, reprovingly, "That's a disrespectful way to speak of a man who may become King-Caliph."

"If the Visigoth Empire elects *Leofric*, you deserve all you get!" She lifted her hand to her neck. She is sure that her bodice shows the old white scar around her neck, that Fernando del Guiz touched so long ago in Cologne. "I always just assumed this was some childhood *accident* . . . Not that you were exactly efficient, *'Arif* Alderic. A quarter-inch either way and I wouldn't be talking to you, would I?"

"Even a dumb grunt can't get everything right," Alderic said gravely. "Accidents will happen."

Pure happenstance. Pure, freak chance.

The thought makes her sweat. She distracts herself.

"Why so young?" she said suddenly. "These children . . . Wouldn't the babies have to be old enough to *talk*, at least, before Leofric could find out they couldn't communicate with the Stone Golem?"

Alderic gave her a look. It took her a second to realise that it was the look soldiers reserve for civilians who find some piece of mass battlefield killing irrational.

"They don't have to talk," Alderic said. "He doesn't find out from them. The babies are kept in a different quarter of the house; he waits until they are old enough to distinguish real pain from a hunger to be fed, or discomfort, and then he hurts them badly – usually burns them with fire. They shriek. Then he asks the Stone Golem if *it* can hear *them*."

Sweet Christus!

Ash thinks with her mind and with her body. Her body is reading his, judging, finding no fault in his alertness, no point at which she might snatch a knife, gain a sword. Her mind tells her there is nothing she could do with a weapon if she had one.

"Granted they were slave-children," the *'arif* said, with a supreme insensibility to the slave-woman in front of him, "it is still something I dream I am doing, most nights."

"Yeah . . . people have told me about that sort of dream."

Over and beyond what they say, some other wordless, friendly communication is present in the room. Ash, bright-eyed, rubbed her hands briskly over her wool-sleeved arms. "Soldiers have more in common with other soldiers than with lords, with *amirs*, have you ever noticed that, *'Arif* Alderic? Even soldiers on opposite sides!"

Alderic touched his right hand to his chest, over his heart. "I wish I could have faced you in combat, lady."

"I wish you may still get your wish!"

It came out acerbic. The Visigoth threw back his head, beard jutting, and laughed. He moved towards the door.

"And while you're at it," Ash said, "the food here's terrible, but I'd like more of it."

Alderic smiled brilliantly, shaking his head. "You have only to command, lady."

"I *wish*."

The steel grill closed behind him. The sounds of locking metal died away, leaving only the wail of the rising wind. Outside, freezing rain spattered on carven red granite.

"I have only to command, *temporarily*," Ash amended, aloud.

There was nothing to mark the passing of any given hour in the day except the uninformative horns; no wheeling constellations; no difference to the passing footsteps, or the bells in what must be the household chapel: House Leofric appeared to swarm with activity through each twenty-four hours. She hoped for Alderic to send either a slave or a soldier with food within the hour: no one came. When each hour can be final, when any key unlocking the door can bring terminal news, time stretches unbelievably. It might only have been minutes until the sound of metal turning metal tumblers brought her up on her feet, swaying and dizzy.

Two soldiers, each carrying maces, came in and stood to either side of the narrow door. There was barely room for anyone else to come in. Ash backed up towards the window. The *'arif* Alderic pushed between his guards. A robed, bearded man followed him in. Godfrey Maximillian.

"Shit. Already? *Now?*" Ash demanded; but Godfrey was shaking his head almost as soon as their eyes met.

"The lord-*amir* Leofric thinks it best to keep you in good health, until you're needed." Godfrey Maximillian stumbled almost imperceptibly over the last word: she saw Alderic register the priest's revulsion.

"And?"

"And you require exercise. A short period each day."

Nice try, Godfrey.

Ash met Alderic's gaze. "So. Your lord's going to let me out of this stone box?"

Yeah, right. You have to be joking! Under what *possible* circumstances—

Alderic said impassively, "The *amir* has a trustworthy ally, he commits you to his custody for an hour each day from now until the inauguration. Perhaps only today."

Ash didn't move. She looked from one man to the other. Then she sighed, relaxing very slightly, thinking: Outside of here is a political machine running at full stretch, I have no way of knowing the various alliances, enmities, deals, bribes, tricks – and if some piece of double-dealing chicanery on Leofric's behalf is getting me out of this cell, I don't *care* what I don't know. I just need not to be watched for ten heartbeats and I'm gone.

"So who does the lord-*amir* count as his trustworthy ally?" Ash asked. "Who does he trust to keep an eye on me once I'm out of here? Let's not pretend I'm going to come back if I can help it."

"That much," the *'arif* Alderic said gravely, "I had worked out for myself. *Nazir!*"

The taller of the two soldiers hooked his mace over his sword-hilt, by its leather lanyard, and disengaged a long steel-linked chain from his belt. Ash lifted her chin as he approached and began to thread it under her iron collar.

"So, who?" she managed to get out.

Alderic's face took on an expression something between rough humour and disapproval. "An ally, lady. One of your lords. You know him, I'm told. A Bavarian."

Ash watched as the *nazir* bent down to attach manacles to her ankles. Cold metal links hung down, pulling at her collar. She could have throttled him with the chain, possibly, but that would still leave the rest.

"Bavarian?" she said abruptly. "Oh, *shit*, no!"

Godfrey Maximillian raised a brow. "I told you that you wouldn't like it."

"It's *Fernando*! Isn't it? He's come south! Fucking Fernando del Guiz!"

"He owns you," Godfrey said, stone-faced. "He's your husband. You're his property. I've brought the *amir* Leofric to a proper understanding of that fact – that the Lord Fernando can be held completely responsible for you. The lord-*amir* then agreed to release you into your husband's company for an hour, each day, on his parole."

"I imagine the Faris's lap-dog will guard you well enough," *'Arif* Alderic finished, with gallows cheerfulness, "since his life depends on it."

Of course, Ash thought, somebody else could just be using me to get rid of Fernando. He'll have made enemies. It could be anyone. Up to and including the lord-*amir* Leofric . . .

"*Fuck* politics," Ash said aloud, "why can't I just *hit* somebody?"

II

The skull of a horse reared up under the nose of Ash's mount. Hollow white eye-sockets and long yellow teeth leered up at her, bleached bone bright-edged in the intense light of Greek Fire.

"Carnival!" a drunken male voice bellowed.

"*Shit!*"

The horse-skull's wearer waved wild arms, in a flurry of red ribbons.

The elderly furry brown mare took both her front feet off the street and skittered back on her white hind legs. Iron shoes struck sparks from the flint cobblestones.

"*Motherfucker!*"

Ash reined in, shifting her weight forward, trying to bring the rearing mare down. The chains that were manacled to both her ankles and passed under the horse's belly rubbed against tender skin. Her neck-chain, shackled to the stirrups, jingled. The mare threw her mouth up, creaming foam springing out on her neck.

"*Get* down," Ash ordered, trying to wheel the mare around, back away from the throng in the street. Two soldiers' horses closed in on either flank, pressing close enough to threaten her knees; two more trained cavalry horses to her rear. "Get over!"

An escort-rider in front leaned down and got the mare's bridle with one hand. With her steadied, he struck a blow at the reveller's masked face. The man staggered away, shouting, pissed, into the crowd.

A second man rode in close.

"We'll ride outside the city," Fernando del Guiz announced, tall in the saddle beside her, soothing the hooded bird that gripped his wrist: too small for a goshawk, too big for a peregrine falcon.

Desire did not flood her, as it had when she had seen him before; only the utter, surprising familiarity of his face made her heart thump, once, with shock.

Six of the escort troop immediately rode to the front, beating the revelling men of Carthage to one side. Ash, cold air stinging her face, kneed the mare forward; and when she could safely free her hands, drew her fur-lined hood up around her face, and wrapped her linen-lined wool cloak firmly about her body.

"Son of a *bitch*," she muttered. "How does anyone expect me to ride, like *this?*"

The chains that passed from ankle to ankle, round and under the mare's body, trapped her. Even an accidental slip out of the saddle would get her dragged, head-down, over cobbled streets; a death perhaps not much preferable to that planned by Leofric.

"Come on, beautiful," Ash soothed. The mare, happier by reason of being surrounded by nine or ten of her stable-mates, reverted to plodding between the companions of Fernando del Guiz. Armed German troops, mostly. Alert and unfriendly.

And if at some point I can persuade you to bolt, with me on you, Ash thought grimly as she leaned forward to slap the mare's neck, that *will* be a miracle. But it looks like it's my only chance . . .

Intense, blue-white Greek Fire blazed down into the rule-straight avenues, casting a high-definition light on men wearing heron's-head masks, painted leather cat's skulls, and knife-tusked boar's heads. She thought she saw one woman: realised it was a bearded merchant in a woman's gown. Harsh male voices sang all around her, noise echoing back from the buildings, the crowd only beaten back by the escorts using the flats of their blades. Fernando del Guiz reined his roan gelding in, his squires with him.

A man above the city gate shouted in quick, guttural Carthaginian Gothic, "Poncy German arse-fucker!"

Gathering a shaky amount of self-possession, Ash spoke before it even occurred to her that this was not wise, under these circumstances:

"Well, well. Someone who recognises your personal banner. How about that?"

Fernando's face was not particularly visible behind the acorn-shaped steel helmet's nasal bar: she could not read his expression.

Christ, the last thing I did in Dijon was hit him in the face, in front of his Visigoth mates; maybe I should just learn to keep my mouth *shut?*

She noted that he sat his black-pointed roan gelding somewhat wearily, and that his eagle livery coat showed threadbare in places, ripped at one seam. Something in his posture spoke of bearing up under trouble, makes her think that – however necessary it might be for survival – the role of a renegade is not proving easy for him. *Not the golden boy, now.*

426

He handed his hunting bird over to a squire and removed his helmet.

"You can stop hitting me. They let me keep Guizburg." His voice sounded rueful, with a hint of humour, and when she met his green eyes, they were dust-red and bloodshot: the eyes of a man who is not sleeping easily. "So, yes, it's still my livery."

Damn! Your mouth is going to get you killed, girl . . .

She could feel her face heating, although the chill wind disguised it; and she stared away into the darkness beyond the city gate. Am I really going to do this? Am I really going to ask *him* for help?

What else can I do, now?

A half-inch of steel, prosaic and unanswerable, is locked around her neck and her wrists and her ankles. Chains fasten her to her horse. An armed guard surrounds her, and she has no armed friends. With things as they are, she will ride out into the desert outside Carthage now, and she will ride back into Carthage again an hour or so in the future.

Maybe she'll risk spooking the mare, risk being kicked and trampled in the unlikely event the animal will bolt. Even so, she's still trapped by steel links that Dickon Stour could sever in one blow at the anvil – but Dickon is half a world away, if he isn't dead. If they aren't all dead.

I am going to do this.

It is not the fact that she will ask Fernando for help that makes her ashamed. *It's the fact that fear forces me to do it. And he's weak; what* use *will this be?*

She snorted an amused laugh that came out too high, and wiped her streaming eyes. "Fernando. What will you take, to let me go? Just to turn your back for five minutes, that's all."

Just let me merge into the slave-class, or into the darkness, no matter that I'm still in North Africa, that I'm hundreds of miles from home.

"Leofric would have me killed." There was an educated certainty in his tone. "There isn't *anything* you could offer. I've seen what he does to people."

Do I tell this man what, in two or three days' time, Leofric will do to me?

"You're here in his House, you must be in his favour. You could get away with it—"

"I don't get a choice about whether I'm here or not." The European knight in Visigoth armour snorted. "If I wasn't your husband, I'd have been executed after Auxonne for desertion. They still think I'm a lever they can use with you. A source of information."

"Then help me get away." She sounded unsteady, even to herself. "Because in two or three days, Leofric's going to strap me down and cut me open, and then you're redundant!"

"What?" He gave her a shocked look that for a second gave her back Floria del Guiz, his sister's expression on his face. Anguish. Then: "No! I can't do anything!"

The thought *I might not ever see Floria again* went through her mind. It brought a sharp pain, that she pushed away into numbness.

"Well, *fuck* you." She breathed shakily. "That's about what I thought you'd say. You *have* to listen to me!"

The noise of their horses passing under the city gate drowned out her voice.

The look he gave her, she couldn't read.

Coming out into the open, outside the walls, the city lights left her half-blind in countryside darkness. She felt she was gripping the rein too tightly and eased off. The mare fretted and sidled towards Fernando's gelding. Ash raised her head to the black sky, brilliant with stars shining clear through the frigid air.

It *is* night . . . I wasn't sure.

Her eyes adjusting, she found the stars bright as strong moonlight. His face she could clearly see to be flushed.

"Please," she said.

"I can't."

A bitter wind whipped into her face. Stomach churning, on the verge of panic, she thought, *What now?*

Capricornus hung high in the arch of the sky. They rode out on to a paved avenue. To either side, the great brick arches of twin aqueducts ran back into the city.[6] A faint sound of running water could be heard over the clink of tack, and the rumbled conversation of Fernando's men-at-arms and squires. The starlight gleamed on pomegranate-crowned pillars, robbing them of colour.

She let the mare drop back.

"Ash . . ." Fernando's tone sounded warningly.

"Walk on." Ash clucked. The winter-coated mare shifted forward, taking two long strides to put herself in the centre of the group of riders again, by Fernando. Ash sat up in the saddle, looking between the armed guards.

As they rode past an arch of the nearer aqueduct, Ash saw in the charcoal shadow a great carved beast, resting, couchant. The pale weathered stone gleamed, five or six times the height of a man. It was, she made out, the body of a lion, with the head of a woman: the stone face almond-eyed, the expression almost a smile.

As the avenue came level with the next arch, she saw another statue within. This was brick, shaped and curved into the flank of a hind: the neck collared with a crown, the tiny antlers broken off. Ash turned her head, looking across to the other side of the avenue. The aqueduct there was in deeper shadow, but something shone within its black arches: a blunt, granite statue of a man with the head of a serpent.[7]

She was startled into speaking aloud.

"What's *that*?" She corrected herself. "Those?"

Fernando del Guiz said, "The King-Caliph's stone bestiary."

Dry-mouthed with a new fear, she suddenly asked, "Where are we going, Fernando?"

"Hunting."

"Yeah. Right." *And I'm the Queen of Carthage . . .*

Movement caught her eye. A group of waiting riders, in the aqueduct's shadow. Another ten men? Mares, white surcoats – and the notched-wheel livery of House Leofric.

---

[6] Archaeological evidence shows only a single Roman aqueduct; 90 km long, it brought 8.5 million gallons of water per day to Carthage from Zaghouan. The remains can be seen crossing the Oued Miliana valley, twenty miles south of Tunis.

[7] Nothing of this 'stone bestiary' survives, that we know of.

"We'll ride to the pyramids," Fernando called out to the group of waiting Visigoths. "The hunting is better there!"

Shit, Ash thought, looking at the Visigoth newcomers. This is going to be next to impossible. Come on, girl, think! Is there something I can use, here?

The chill air bit at her face, and her ungloved fingers. Her cloak spread out, covering her legs in the thin wool gown, and the mare's flanks. The mare plodded, even less lively now that she was out of the city. Ash strained her vision to look ahead, away from the city, southwards. The avenue and aqueducts ran away parallel into silver darkness. Into freedom.

Even as she looked, the mass of guards wheeled, taking her with them, off into flat, barren earthy country; and she slowed her pace, partly for the uncertain footing, partly to see if she could drop back, unnoticed.

A pitch-torch sputtered behind her. In its yellow light, she saw that the nearest riders were Fernando del Guiz and a dark Visigoth boy with a scanty, curled beard. The boy rode bare-headed, was dressed nobly, and there was something about his face that tugged at her memory.

"Who is this, Uncle?" The boy used what Ash recognised as an honorific rather than kinship title. "Uncle, why's this slave with us? She can't hunt. She's a woman."

"Oh, she hunts," Fernando said gravely. His eyes met Ash's, over the boy's head. "Two-legged quarry."

"Uncle, I don't understand you."

"She's Ash," Fernando said resignedly. "My wife."

"Gelimer's son does not ride with a *woman*." The boy shut his mouth with a snap, gave Ash a glare of utter disgust, and nudged his mount across to the squires and birds.

"*Gelimer's* son?" she gasped, into the cold wind, at Fernando.

"Oh, that's Witiza. He lives in House Leofric." Fernando shrugged uncomfortably. "One of *Amir* Leofric's nephews lives with *Amir* Gelimer."

"Yeah, it's called 'hostages' . . ."

The new fear grew. She asked no questions – knowing there would be no answers – but rode on, every sense heightened by apprehension. Looking over at Witiza, with a pang, she thought, *He's neither man nor boy. He'll be about Rickard's age.*

She turned her head, missing the words the boy and squires were speaking – a discussion about hawking – and rode blindly, her eyes momentarily swimming. When she raised her gaze again, Witiza had ridden forward, and was laughing with the del Guiz men-at-arms. Fernando still rode at her right flank.

"Just let me ride off!" she whispered.

The young German knight's head turned. She abruptly remembered his face with a red mark of a blow swelling under his lip. Apart from his first remark, it was not being mentioned: she felt it hanging between them.

"I'm sorry," she said, with an effort.

Fernando shrugged. "So am I."

"No, I—" She shook her head. Other urgencies pressed in, brought by the image of him at Dijon. "What happened to my company at Auxonne? You can at least tell me that! You ought to know, you're in House Leofric."

Then, not able to keep bitterness out of her tone:

"Or didn't you see – given that you left early?"

"Would you believe me, if I told you?"

It was not a taunt. She could not be aware of everything around her – stingingly alert to where each of the German men-at-arms was riding, who might be drinking from a wineskin and so not alert later, who was paying more attention to the squires carrying belled hunting birds than to their escort duties – impossible to be open to this, and not also know that Fernando had spoken without malice, only with a kind of tired curiosity.

"Very little," Ash said honestly. "I'd believe very little you told me."

"Because I'm a traitor, in your eyes?"

"No," she said. "Because you're a traitor in *your* eyes."

Fernando grunted, startled.

The mare's uneven gait brought her attention back to the ground, silver-and-yellow under starlight and torch-light. The cold wind whipped smoke from the burning pitch into her face, and she coughed at the bitter smell.

"I don't know what happened to your company. I didn't see, and I didn't ask." Fernando shot a glance at her. "Why do you want to know? They all end up dead with you anyway!"

It took her breath for a moment.

"Yeah . . . I lose some. War gets people killed. But then, it's their decision to follow me."

Her mind's eye holds the images of golems, wagons, fire-throwers. She will not think *Roberto, Florian, Angelotti*.

"And my decision to say that I take responsibility for them, while our contract lasts. *I want to know what happened!*"

She let herself look at him directly, and found herself looking into his tired, reddened eyes. His curling fair hair was longer, straggling around his face; he looked closer to thirty than to twenty, *and it is only two months*, she thought, *since I stood with him in the cathedral at Cologne: sweet Christ!*

She did not know what expression was on her own face, could not know that she looked simultaneously much younger, much more open and vulnerable, and at the same time herself looked aged. Worn, not by a life in camp, but by nights spent awake in Dijon, thinking about this, imagining what words she could speak, her body aching to lay full-length against him, wrap her legs around his hips, thrust him deep inside her.

And her mind despising her for that hunger for a weak man.

"I *don't* know," he mumbled.

"What have they got you doing now?" Ash said. "That's Gelimer's son. Lord-*Amir* Gelimer hates Lord-*Amir* Leofric. So, are you taking me to Gelimer? To be killed? Or what?"

His beautiful, ravaged face was momentarily blank.

"No!" Fernando's voice rose to a shout. He silenced himself; waving reassuringly to Witiza and the squires. "*No*. You're my wife, I wouldn't take you to be murdered!"

Ash slid the reins up between finger and thumb, her eyes on the riders around her. She said, bitterly, "I think *you'd* do anything. The minute somebody threatened you! You hated me anyway, Fernando. From the minute we met in Genoa."

He coloured up. "I was a boy then! Fifteen! You can't blame me for some wild boy's prank!"

That touched a nerve, Ash realised, surprised.

Something whirred and clattered, out in the desolate land. A bird flew up from under one of the horses' hooves. Ash tensed, about to dig her heels in. The German troops closed in two-deep around her: she imperceptibly relaxed.

The sound of hooves on earth gave way to the clatter of iron shoes on stone: the mass of troops riding out of the desert and on to ancient flagstones. Her belly churned. She looked ahead, straining her eyes to see more cavalry: expecting now the *amir* Gelimer's men in ambush, or men hired by him. Gelimer, who might want her killed, or questioned: either being vile. *Caught up in someone else's fight,* she thought. *Christ, I thought I had two days before Leofric did for me. I was safer inside Carthage!*

Dark shapes blotted the sky.

Hills, she thought; before her eye took in their regularity. The noise of the horses' hooves echoed back from flat surfaces that sloped up and away; so that her second apprehension was that she rode in a steep valley, but the sides even in starlight were too regular. Flat planes, sharp-edged.

Pyramids.

Anyone could be hiding out here!

Stars fringed the edges of the stone. Their light leeched all colour from the sides of the pyramids: immense, shaped structures of carven stone, built up from a hundred thousand red silt bricks, faced with brilliantly painted plaster. Ash rode among armed men, among the pyramids of Carthage. She could say nothing; silenced; could only lift her head and look around her, regardless of the freezing wind that howled around the gargantuan stone burial monuments.

She saw that all the great frescoes were faded, damaged by centuries of weather and darkness. Plaster flaked off the tombs and lay in shards on the paving stones. Her mare trod on a painted gold-eyed fragment: a lioness with the moon between her brows. It crunched like frost.

Under their faded, flaking covering, the exact and mechanical regularity of the pyramids remained, stretching out as far in every direction as she could see – and she could see ten or a dozen of them, silhouetted against the stars. Her neck hurt from looking up, and her steel collar dug into her flesh.

"Christus!" she whispered.

An owl hooted.

She jumped. The mare startled, not very wildly; and she leaned forward to put a calming hand on the beast's neck.

A pair of wings stretched out from a squire's arm, ahead. Two flat yellow eyes gleamed at her through the starlit dark. The squire raised his arm. The great owl lifted, silently, and swooped into the night.

"You're hawking with owls," Ash said, wonderingly. "You're hawking, with owls, in a graveyard."

"It's a Visigoth pastime." Fernando shrugged.

The group having halted, most of the guards were taking up stations in a rough circle between two of the immense sandstone pyramids. There was not room to gallop between them, Ash saw; even with a horse not twelve years old, overfed, and swaybacked into the bargain. She glanced back over her shoulder. Carthage was invisible, except for a white glow silhouetting a broken ridge, which she thought might be distant Greek Fire.

Clearly, we are waiting.

For someone? For something to happen?

The back of her neck prickled.

White, soundless death swooped past her head – so close that the pinions flicked her scarred cheek.

An owl.

In sheer, inane relief, she asked the banal question: "What do they hunt out here?"

"Small game. Gully-rats. Poisonous snakes."

Hunting is always a good cover for a covert meeting.

So easy. A crossbow bolt out of the dark. You wouldn't even have to hit me. Just this horse. Where am I going, when I'm chained to it? *She died in a riding accident, my lord.*

"Do you think I'm just going to sit here and *wait*?"

Fernando shifted in his saddle. Something gave a coughing growl, far off among the pyramids. It sounded like a wild cat. Ash looked at Fernando's German riders; two or three of them gazed nervously off into the darkness, the rest were watching her.

Shit! I have *got* to do something!

Fernando sat back in his saddle. "There's news about the French peace treaty. His Spider-Majesty Louis signed. France is now at peace with the Visigoth Empire."

Fernando's gelding mouthed at the mare's tack, lipping her. The mare ignored this. She nuzzled the flagstones for spindly, frost-burned tufts of grass.

"The war's going to be over. There's no one to fight now except Burgundy."

"And England, if they ever finish fighting their own civil wars. And the Sultan," Ash said absently, staring into the darkness, "when Mehmet and the Turkish empire decides you've worn yourself out fighting in Europe, and you're ripe to be picked."

"Woman, you're obsessed with war!"

"I—" She broke off.

What she had been watching in the distance materialised.

Not a troop of soldiers.

Two squires with satiated owls on their wrists, walking out from behind a corner of the pyramid, a dozen or more dead snakes spitted on a stick between them.

Her thumping heart slowed. She turned back in her saddle to face Fernando. Both she and the mare were chilling, stiffening up; and she nudged it into a walk, del Guiz riding beside her, gazing down at her with an expression of anxiety.

I can't just wait to be taken!

She demanded, "Do you really think *Amir* Gelimer doesn't want to kill me?"

Fernando ignored the question.

"Please," she said. "Please let me go. Before something happens here, before I get taken back – please."

His hair took gold from the torch-light, that brought a glow of colour from his green livery and the gilded pommel of his riding sword. She thought he might be wearing a plackart over mail, under his livery jacket.

"I've been wondering," he said, "why men follow you. Why men follow a woman."

With a certain grim humour, that can stave off fear for whole seconds at a time, Ash said, "Often they don't. Most places I've been, I've had to fight my own troops before I've fought the enemy!"

In the torchlight, his expression changes. When he looks down at her, from the saddle of the Visigoth war-horse, it is with an unconscious awareness of the breadth of his shoulders, filling out into adulthood now, and the hard muscles of a man who trains daily for edged-weapon warfare.

"You're a *woman*!" Fernando protested. "If *I'd* hit *you*, I'd have broken your jaw, or your neck. You're nothing like as strong as I am. How come you do what you do?"

It is true, if irrelevant at this moment, that she neither hit him with her full strength, or with a weapon, or with the knowledge of where the human body breaks. She could have blinded him. Wondering now at her reluctance – Jesu Christus, he's *not* going to let me go! – she listened to the night's noises for a full minute before she spoke.

"I don't have to be as strong as you. I only have to be strong enough."

He looked blankly at her. " 'Strong enough'?"

Ash looked up. "I don't have to be stronger than you are. I only have to be strong enough to kill you."

Fernando opened his mouth, and then shut it again.

"I'm strong enough to use a sword or an axe," she said, huddled into her cloak, listening. Nothing but the hunting calls of the owls. "That's just training, timing, balance. Not weight-lifting."

He blew into his hands, as if for warmth, and without looking at her, said, "I know why men follow you. You're only incidentally a woman. What you really are is a soldier."

Thrown back in her memory to the cell, to Gaiseric, Fravitta, Barbas, Theodoric; to violence that stops short of rape; to shed blood; she winces.

"And it's nothing to be proud of!"

The chains chafe her wrists. "It's what I need to be, to do what I do."

"Why do what you do?"

Ash smothered a laugh: it would have come out weary, and on the wrong side of hysteria. "You're not the person I'd expect to ask that! You're the one who's spent your whole life training to wear armour and use a sword. You're the knight. Why do what *you* do?"

"I'm not doing it any more."

What might have been adolescent in his tone was gone now. He made a quiet

433

statement of fact. Distracted from listening for hoofbeats, she gazed at his Visigoth mail hauberk, the trained horse that he was riding, and the sword-belt at his side; and let him see her looking.

Fernando stated, "I'm not killing anyone."

Ash's mind made a mental note that any other knight's sentence would have finished 'anyone *else*', at the same time that her mouth opened and she said, without volition, "In a fucking pig's arse! That hauberk a present from Leofric?"

"If I don't wear armour or a sword, no one in House Leofric listens to a word I say."

"Yeah, and what does that tell you?"

"That doesn't make it right!"

"Lots of things aren't the way they should be," Ash said grimly. "You ask my priest why men die of sickness, or famine, or act of God."

"We don't *have* to kill," Fernando said.

A horse snorted, close at hand. Her pulse jolted, before she realised that it was one of the escort's mounts.

"You're as crazy as she is! The Faris," Fernando said. "I was one of the officers with her before Auxonne, walking the ground. She kept walking around saying 'we can make that a killing-zone' or 'put the war-wagons there, I can guarantee you sixty per cent enemy casualties'. She's a fucking head-case."

Ash raised her silver brows. "In what way?"

She realised Fernando was staring at her.

"Doesn't it seem crazy to you to go around a perfectly good pasture and work out which bits of it you can use so that you can burn people's faces off, and chop through their leg-bones, and shoot rocks through their chests?"

"What do you want me to say, I lie awake nights worrying about it?"

"That would be good," he agreed. "But don't tell me; I wouldn't believe you."

Sudden anger sparked. "Yeah, well, I don't notice you going up to the King-Caliph and saying, hey, invading Christendom is wrong, why don't we all just be nice to each other? And I don't guess you said to House Leofric, no, I won't take the horse and the kit, thanks; I'm not going to be a warrior any more. Did you?"

"No," he muttered.

"Where's the hair-shirt, Fernando? Where's the monk's robes, instead of the armour? Exactly when do you plan to swear poverty and obedience, and go around the King-Caliph's nobles telling them to lay down their arms? Your ass would be hung up to dry!"

He said, "I'm too afraid to try."

"Then how can you tell *me*—"

He cut off her outraged protest: "Just because I can see what's right, that doesn't mean I can do it."

"Are you seriously telling me *you* don't intend to stand up and protest against this war, but you expect *me* to stop what I do for a living? Jesu Christus, Fernando!"

"I would think, from where you are, you'd know how I feel."

About to spit back some smart remark, Ash felt a chill in her belly that was not the bitter wind. She swallowed, dry-mouthed. At last, she said, "I'm on my own here. I don't have my guys with me."

Fernando del Guiz did not make a sarcastic or destructive comment; he only nodded, acknowledging what she said.

Ash said, "I'll strike a bargain with you. You free me, here, let me ride off into the desert, before anyone else gets here. And I'll tell you how you can legitimately have the marriage annulled. Then you're nothing to do with me any more, and everybody will know that."

She brought the mare around again, moving within the enclosing circle of troops. A wave of fear went through her. *Who's already on their way here? Gelimer? Someone else? Someone I don't even know about?* An owl shrieked, close by. Something rustled in the torch-lit darkness.

She heard Fernando say, "Why could I annul the marriage? Because you're a villein; slave-born?"

"Because you'll want an heir. I'm barren," Ash said.

She became aware that her bare hands locked shut on the pommel of her saddle, her shoulder-muscles rigid against – what? A punch, a blow from a whip? She looked up swiftly at Fernando del Guiz.

"You are?" The lines of his face showed only shocked bewilderment. "How do you know?"

"I was with child at Dijon." Ash found she couldn't release the grip of her hands. The leather reins, wrapped around the pommel, cut into her cold fingers. She kept her gaze on his face in the circle of torch-light. "I lost it, here; it doesn't matter how. It isn't possible for me to have another."

She expected anger, tensed against being hit.

"My *son*?" he said wonderingly.

"A son or a daughter. It was too soon to tell." Ash felt her mouth twist into a painful smile. "You didn't ask me if it was yours."

Fernando stared off, towards the dark pyramids, not seeing them. "My son or daughter." His gaze came back to Ash. "Did they hurt you? Is that why you lost it?"

"Of course they hurt me!"

He bowed his head. Without looking at her, he said, "I never meant . . . Did it happen when we were riding to G—" He stopped.

"To Genoa," Ash completed. "Ironic, isn't it? While we were on the river."

Momentarily, he cupped both hands over his face. Then he sat up in the saddle. His shoulders went back. The torchlight shone on his eyes, that gleamed wet; and Ash, frowning, found him stripping off his gauntlet and reaching a hand out to her. His expression held pain, sardonic humour, and a raw, undilute empathy that started to rip her open.

"Sometimes I wonder, how did I get to be this person?" Fernando pressed his other hand's knuckles to his mouth, and took them away to add, "I wouldn't have had much to leave him. A keep in Bavaria and a blackened reputation."

His pain hit her, raw, under the breastbone. She pushed it away: *this is not what I need to feel.*

He exclaimed, "You should have told me, at Dijon! I would have—"

"Changed sides?" she completed, sardonically; but she reached across and gripped his hand, flesh warm in the cold night. "By the time I knew, you were gone."

His hand tightened on hers.

"I'm sorry," he said quietly, "you wouldn't have had much of a husband in me."

A sharp answer came into her mind but she didn't speak. For all his inanity, what shone out of his face as he reached down from his saddle to her was a genuine regret.

"You deserve better," he added.

She let go of his hand, settling back on to the saddle's chill leather. Above, thin clouds began to hide the stars.

"I'm barren," she said flatly. "So that's the end of that. Don't tell me you don't want an annulment. You can always put a barren wife aside."

"I don't know that we *are* married. Leofric's lawyers are arguing over it."

He turned the gelding, riding back across the open ground.

"You're a bondswoman. Either you're now my property, because I married you – or you didn't have a right to consent to any contract, and the marriage is void. Take your pick. It doesn't matter to me – whether the Church blessing holds or not, these people still think I'm the one who knows about you. I'm the one they ship down here because of that!"

Chill, inner and outer, went through her, and she said, "Fernando. They are going to kill me. One or another of these lords. Please, *please* let me go."

"No," he said, again, and the cold wind ruffled his hair. He looked across at Witiza and the squires, absorbed in the minutiae of hunting; and Ash could see him picturing a fair-haired boy of the same age.

A barn-owl slid through the darkness as if the air were oil, gliding across the sloping face of a pyramid and vanishing into blackness.

"How can you let this happen? I'm sorry I hit you," Ash said in a rush. "I know you're afraid. But please—"

Fernando, his voice rough, his face growing redder, snapped, "I'm trying to keep my own head on while these heathens anoint another of their God-damned Caliphs! You don't know what it's like for me!"

Ash talks to slaves. She knows that, up at the palace, the fretwork stone corridors resound to the screams of unsuccessful candidates for the Caliph's throne.

"Oh, I do." Ash rested the brown mare's reins under her cloaked knee, and blew on her white fingers. There was a laugh pressing up under her breastbone: or it might have been tears. "I remember something Angelotti once said to me. He told me, 'The Visigoths are an elective monarchy – a method we may call succession by assassination'!"

"Who's Angelotti, for Our Lady's sake?"

"My master gunner. He trained here. You employed him, briefly. You," Ash said, "wouldn't remember."

Overhead, the stars had moved to midnight, or close to. She saw no moon. Dark phase, then. Three weeks after Auxonne field. The freezing wind began to drop, chill on her face; and she lifted her head, hearing the chink of bit and bridle – a split second before the German men-at-arms heard it, their lances lowering, visors going down.

Fernando barked an order. Ash saw lances going back up to rest-position. Newcomers obviously expected. *It's now—*

Her stomach plummeted. She held on to her saddle with one hand, leaned out with the other and grabbed for her husband's sword. His leather-gauntleted hand smacked down, crushing her fingers. He grabbed both her wrists.

"You will not be killed!"

"That's what *you* say!"

Horses came riding in between the towering sides of the pyramids, their torches sending shadows leaping across the ancient stone paving. Ash smelled horse-sweat. The brown mare's flanks creamed whitely, as she backed up, pressing her rump against Fernando's gelding. The newcomers wore mail, a dozen or more of them, and she opened her mouth to say, "Twelve cavalry, swords, lances;" to the machine, ready now – now it could not matter; in this extremity – ready to break silence, but she thought, *And I'm unarmed, no armour, chained; what's it going to tell me – 'die'?*

The boy Witiza shoved his hunting owl at a squire and rode forward. A shrill horn split the silence.

Not from the new party – from further back.

Ash heard it; and she stood up in the stirrups, as if the mare were a war-horse, and peered forward into the flickering light.

"Exactly how much company were you expecting?" she inquired caustically.

Fernando del Guiz groaned, "Shit . . .' and thumbed his sword loose in the mouth of its scabbard.

Enough torches clustered together now between the two pyramids that Ash could see clearly. Crumbling plaster walls bore faded hieroglyphs in white and gold and blue, and the two-dimensional images of cow-headed women and jackal-headed men.

Riding over broken paving stones, the lord-*amir* Gelimer was reining in a bright bay gelding with white coronels, and staring behind him, past his armed escort.

Ash followed his gaze.

Thirty or forty more horses rode up out of the darkness.

These bore men in mail, riding with their lances at the rest-position. She saw a pennant with the device of a toothed wheel, and found herself looking at helmeted faces that she nevertheless knew: *'Arif* Alderic, *Nazir* Theudibert, a young soldier – Barbas? Gaiseric? – and two more *nazirs*, and their squads, each man mounted.

Alderic's forty men, at their full strength.

"God give you all a good night," the *'arif* Alderic said, his voice a deep rumble as he bowed in the saddle to Gelimer. "My *Amir*, riding so late can be dangerous. I beg you to accept my *Amir* Leofric's hospitality, and our escort back to the city."

Ash put one hand thoughtfully over her mouth, and deliberately didn't catch Alderic's eye. The soldier barely dignified what he said with the tone of a request.

She saw the lord-*amir* Gelimer glare at Alderic, glance around, see Witiza, and Gelimer's small-eyed face shut up like a strongbox.

"If I must," he said ungraciously.

"Wouldn't do to leave you alone out here, sir." Alderic rode on past him, bringing his rangy, flea-bitten grey mount up beside Ash's mare. "Same goes for you too, Sir Fernando, I'm afraid."

Fernando del Guiz began to shout, one anxious eye on the Visigoth noble, Gelimer.

Ash bit her lip. It was either that, or cheer, or burst out into hysterical laughter. The cold wind chilled the sweat under her arms and down her back.

She saw a dun palfrey approaching in Alderic's wake. The rider, whose feet appeared to almost touch the ground either side, put back his hood.

"Godfrey," Ash acknowledged.

"Boss."

"Leofric get to hear about who's putting the screws on my husband, then?"

She edged the mare a step sideways away from Fernando del Guiz, who was roaring furiously at the *'arif* Alderic.

"I was talking to the *'arif* when the order came up."

"I don't suppose you brought a pair of bolt-cutters? I might just about get away with it, right now."

"The *'arif*'s men searched me. For that, and for weapons."

"Damn . . . I hoped there was going to be a fight. I might have got out of here." Ash rubbed her palms across her face and brought them away hot and wet with sweat. She huddled her cloak around herself, to keep her shaking hands out of Godfrey's sight. Clouds coming up from the south began to blot out the sky.

Overwhelmingly, as if it was her body that thought, a physical desire overcame her for blue sky, for the gold-hot burning eye of the sun, for dry grass and bees and barley buried in red poppies; for meadowlark song, and cows lowing; for rivers glittering thick with fish; for the sun's warmth on her naked skin, and daylight in her eyes; an ache so hard that she groaned, aloud, and let her hood fall back and tears stream from her eyes in the bitter cold south wind, staring beyond the sharp walls of the pyramids for the slightest break in the darkness.

"Ash?" Godfrey touched her arm.

"Pray for a miracle." Ash smiled crookedly. "Just a tiny miracle. Pray for the Stone Golem to break down. Pray for these chains to rust. What's a miracle, to Him?"

Godfrey smiled, reluctantly, gazing up at her from the palfrey's back. "Heathen. But I do pray – for grace, for freedom, for you."

Ash tucked Godfrey Maximillian's hand under her arm and squeezed it. She let go quickly. Her body still shook with reaction. "I'm no heathen. I'm praying right now. To Saint Jude."[8] She couldn't manage to sound humorous as she picked up her reins. "Godfrey . . . I don't want to go back and die in the dark."

He shot a glance at the surrounding horsemen. Ash regarded Theudibert's squad, now so close that only what appeared to be an odd, comradely compassion made his men pretend not to be overhearing her conversation.

"God will receive you, or there is no justice in heaven," Godfrey protested. "Ash—"

Something cold stung her scarred cheek. Ash raised her head. Outside the circle of the torches, everything was black; the stars obliterated by cloud. A whirl of white specks shot across the ancient paving, among the legs of cavalry mounts moving quickly into their escort array around herself, and around Gelimer's men.

"*Snow?*" she said.

In yellow torchlight, wet flakes showed white. Like a dropping veil snow came suddenly and thickly down on the south wind, building up swiftly on the sides of the nearest pyramid, plastering white lines along the edges of bricks, delineating unseen irregularities.

"Close up!" The *'arif* Alderic's hoarse shout.

"No more yapping, priest." *Nazir* Theudibert pushed his grey mare in between Godfrey and Ash. Ash's mare dropped her head down, presenting a winter-coated furry flank to the wind. White ice plastered the leather tack, the folds of Ash's cloak.

"Move it!" Theudibert grunted.

"Snow. In the middle of a fucking *desert*, snow?" She transferred her reins to one hand, jabbing a bare cold finger at the *nazir*'s face. "You know what this is, don't you? *Don't you?* It's the Rabbi's Curse, come home at last."

Judging by Theudibert's bony, red-cheeked face, she had hit a superstitious nerve. A brief hope flared in her. The *nazir* coughed, and spat a gob between their horses.

"Fuck off," he said.

Ash pulled her hood forward. The lining of marten fur tickled her frozen cheek. *What did you expect him to say?*

The troop of horse moved off, riding back in the direction of Carthage; torches and armour glinting in the snow. She kneed the brown mare to a weary walk. *He said just what I'd say. Except that I know there* is *a curse.*

Aptly, as if he could read her thoughts, Theudibert growled under his breath, "Fucking *'arif*s all the curse *I* fucking need!"

"Well, I'll tell you something." Ash let her mouth run, feeling the pull of steel chains at her neck and ankles, looking furiously around for a gap between riders, for help, for anything. "I'll tell you. Your *amir* Leofric breeds slaves – I reckon someone out there is breeding sergeants. *'Arif*s. 'Cause they're all the fucking same!"

Theudibert looked at her coldly. Two of the soldiers laughed and smothered it; both of them men who had been in the cell with her, threatening rape. Ash rode on between them.

---

[8] Patron saint of lost causes.

439

If I could kill this horse, they'd *have* to take me out of the chains. However briefly. But I'd need a weapon for that, and I don't have a weapon. If I could lame her, get free—

She let her gaze travel ahead, looking for holes in the paving.

—then I'd be on foot, in the desert, in a blizzard, with sixty men trying to find me. Well, hey, it's not such a bad deal. Not when you consider the alternative.

Not when you consider that, if they have to cut the chains to get me off this beast, there'll probably be six of them with swords at my throat every minute while they're doing it. That's what I'd do. That's the trouble. They're as smart as me.

I just have to hope that someone will make a mistake.

Ash let her awareness spread out, taking in the whole troop. Alderic's heavy cavalry platoon around her, one squad behind, one to either side; and Alderic ahead, riding with Gelimer and Fernando del Guiz, Gelimer's troops out in front – *where he can see them*, Ash approved – and Godfrey's palfrey plodding, head down, in the shelter of Alderic's scraggy mount.

I do not, ever, give up. No matter what.

Driving snow plastered her cloak against her back, and the back of her skull; freezing wind seeping through the wool. Outside the circle of torchlight, a whirling white desolation screamed, the wind rising. She saw Alderic order a scout[9] forward.

We came, what, two miles? Three? It isn't possible to get lost three miles from a city!

Yes it is . . .

A mail-covered arm reached across in front of her. *Nazir* Theudibert yanked the mare's reins out of her hands, and wound them around his wrist. His squad closed in, Gaiseric's cob nipping at the mare's rump; all of them riding within touching distance. Snow began to lie on the paved ground. She let Theudibert yank the mare into movement, clasping the furry body with her knees, keeping her weight level and her knees still.

Just a broken paving stone, a rabbit hole, any*thing* . . . Feeling the recalcitrant weight and solidity of the mare's barrel-body, that might come crashing down on her leg if they fell. *I'll take the risk!*

The mare plodded exhaustedly on. The stink of sweating men and hot horses faded from Ash's nostrils, obliterated by the cold. White flakes lay, eating up the flat ground, piling up against a plinth. She looked up into the star-crowned face of a stone queen, snow whitening the gargantuan granite beast-body. The sphinx's smile blurred under clinging ice.

"Where is Carthage?"

It was the merest whisper, into the fur lining of her hood. The *nazir* glared suspiciously at her, then turned aside to speak with one of his men. A low-voiced dispute broke out between them.

In her head, words sounded:

'Carthage is upon the northern coast of the continent of Africa, forty leagues to the west of—'

[9] Literally, 'aforerider'.

"Where is Carthage from where *I* am!"

No voice sounded in her head.

The mare slowed, plodding through drifting snow. Ash peered out of her hood. Theudibert's men rode, hunched, muttering. Their tracks were churning up a hand's-deep fall of snow now, that clung in bobbles to the hairy hocks of the horses. One white mare whickered, tossing up her head.

"This isn't the way we rode in, *nazir*!"

"Well, it's the way we're riding *out*. Do I have to shut your fucking mouth for you, Barbas?"

Ash thought, What does it matter, now, if Leofric learns I'm asking the Stone Golem questions? If they get me back inside Carthage, I'm *dead*.

"Forty men and twenty men and fifteen men, all cavalry, possibly all three groups hostile to each other," she breathed, mist dampening the fur around her mouth and freezing immediately to ice. She found she was shivering, for all her wool gown and cloak. Her bare feet were numb blocks of flesh, and all sensation had gone from her hands. "One person, unarmed, mounted; escape and evasion, how?"

'You should provoke a fight between two forces and escape in the confusion.'

"I'm chained! The third force isn't mine! How?"

'No appropriate tactic known.'

Ash bit at her cold, numb lower lip.

"You might as well pray, I suppose," a light tenor voice called. Fernando del Guiz rode in from her right, pressing the roan gelding between Alderic's troopers without a thought. Perhaps for that reason, they admitted him. His green and gold banner whipped in the blizzard, momentarily blocking out torch-light. Ash looked up at his snow-plastered helmet and cloak.

"Is that necessary?" Fernando added, indicating the mare's reins with one gloved hand.

"Sir." Theudibert's tone was a gruff, less-urbane copy of his *'arif*'s. He kept her reins knotted firmly in his right hand, riding knee to knee with Ash. "Yes, sir."

Trying to read Fernando's expression, Ash could make out nothing. Over his shoulder, through driving snow, she saw the lord-*amir* Gelimer and his son Witiza riding back down the column towards them.

"When *I* pray, I want an answer." She spoke lightly, as if it were a joke. Snow melted, chill on her lips.

"I'm sorry!" Fernando leaned over, close enough that his breath was damp and warm on her cheek. The male smell of him jolted her heart. He hissed, "I'm caught between the two of them, I can't help you!"

She held in her mind the expectation of a voice. "You've got, what, fifteen men with lances? Could you get me out of here?"

The familiar voice in her head said, *'Two larger units will unite to defeat third: tactic unsuccessful,'* as Fernando del Guiz laughed, slapped the nearest Visigoth soldier on the back, and said, unconvincingly jovially, "What wouldn't you give for a wife like that?"

The young soldier, Gaiseric, said something quickly in Gothic which Ash could see Fernando didn't understand.

"I'm worth more than 'one sick goat', trooper!" she remarked, in Carthaginian. The trooper snuffled a laugh. Ash gave him a quick grin. *It's worth making them think of me as a commander, if it slows their reaction time by even a split-second—*

"Del Guiz!" The lord-*amir* Gelimer closed distance through the wind and snow.

"Del Guiz, I am riding back to the city. Ask me for no further help." His sharp, gauntleted gesture took in the blizzard, Alderic's horsemen, the del Guiz squires shuddering with cold and riding with the hooded owls sheltered under their cloaks, his own son's blue-white face. "I hold you implicated in this! I should have made a better judgement of you – a man who would marry this, *this*—!"

He pointed at Ash. She gripped a fold of her cloak and shook snow off herself; wiped the snow from her eyelashes. The brown mare whuffed, too tired to pull away from the *nazir*'s grip on her reins. Ash sniffed back a runny nose, staring up at Gelimer; at this richly robed and armoured man, white snow lodging in the braiding of his beard.

"Well, fuck you too," she said, almost cheerful, if only because of the appalled expression on Fernando del Guiz's face. "You're not the first person to act like I'm an abomination, my Lord-*Amir*. If I were you, I'd be worrying about worse problems than me."

"You!" Gelimer waved a finger at her. "You and your master Leofric! Theodoric was misguided enough to *listen* to him. Yes, it is essential that Europe be eradicated, but not—" He stopped, wiping a blast of snow out of his face. "Not with a slave-general! Not with a useless war-machine. These things *fail*, and then where are we?"

Ash made great show of looking around her, at Theudibert hunched over his saddle, at the troopers pretending not to listen to the overwrought *amir* as they rode knee to knee in a tight little group, at Alderic ahead supervising Gelimer's men.

She raised her head to the high, white, whirling air, and the snow-covered immense statues, and the blanket of snow smoothing out the desert in the sputtering light of the wet pitch-torches.

"Why is it winter here?" she demanded. "*Look* at this. My mare has her winter coat and it's only September. Why is it so damn *cold*, Gelimer? Why? *Why is it cold?*"

She felt as if she slammed, face-first, into a stone wall.

Her expectation of a voice in her head was flooded – no other word for it – with a stunning, fierce, complete silence.

The lord-*amir* shouted something in return.

Ash didn't hear it.

"*What?*" she said, aloud, bewildered.

"I said, this curse began with Leofric's slave-general going on crusade, it will probably stop when she dies. All the more reason to put a stop to his activities. Del Guiz!" Gelimer shifted his attention. "You could serve me yet. I can forgive!"

He spurred his mount. The gelding arched its back, took a kick in the flank,

442

and cantered forward, iron shoes skidding on the snow-covered flagstones. The lord-*amir* called out. Gelimer's men spurred forward, away from Alderic's troop, on into the dark blizzard ahead. The *'arif* let them go.

Fernando groaned. "I thought he'd given up on me."

Ash paid him no attention. Her breath steamed around her face. Even her knees, where she clasped the mare's flanks, were numb with the cold; and snow gathered in the folds of her cloak. The iron chain from her collar burned, where it touched her skin under her clothes.

Appalled, she whispered delicately, "Forty men and fifteen men, armed cavalry, escape and evasion, how?"

"What?" Fernando sat down in the saddle from peering after Gelimer.

"Forty men and fifteen men, armed cavalry, escape and evasion, *how*?"

No voice sounded in her mind. She let herself will the effort of active listening, making a way in through defences, demanding an answer from the silence within.

A cold slap of ice-flakes on her face snapped her attention outwards.

Am I not . . . hearing? That's it. That's it. It isn't as if I'm stopped, blocked . . . There is no voice here. Only *silence*.

Beside her, on his palfrey, Godfrey spoke cheeringly over what was plainly her indistinguishable mumble. "These *amirs* are crazy, child! You know that Gelimer was a rival with Leofric for the King-Caliph's money, for the crusade? To raise troops? And now they're both trying to get themselves elected king—"

"What is the secret breeding?" Snow burned Ash's face. She muttered insistently: "What is the secret birth?"

No voice. No *answer*.

The potential there, but utterly, utterly silent.

"*Where's my fucking voice?*"

"What do you mean?" Fernando pressed his gelding close in and reached out to pull back her hood. "Ash? What are you talking about?"

Theudibert reached across in front of her, over the mare's saddle, to push the fair-haired European knight away. Ash lunged, almost automatically, reaching across the *nazir*'s mailed back, grabbing for his knife where its scabbard hung on his right hip, with the intention of slashing through the mare's reins.

A soldier shouted a warning.

Something fast and black came down between her and the *nazir*: a lance-shaft. She jerked away.

"Shit!"

Ash grabbed for the saddle.

She knew she hadn't made it, was falling off the mare. Something caught her arm a numbing blow. She cried out. Her heel jerked back. The furry mare jinked to the right. She grabbed for the saddle and her numb bare fingers slid across leather, fear flooding her gut as she slipped, falling, falling forwards and down towards snow-covered stone.

Her stomach swooped. Her head banged sharply against something that gave – the mare's foreleg. Every muscle cringed, taut, against impact. Waiting for an iron-shod hoof to kick back into her face. Waiting to hit stone pavement.

The fall stopped.

Ash hung, upside-down.

A hoof clopped on stone, close by her ear. Something banged her jaw, very softly. She thrashed her head in the enveloping cloak and kirtle and shift falling down over her ears, and found herself staring at pale-tipped brown horse-hair.

The underside of the muzzle of the brown mare.

The horse stood, all four feet planted, knees locked, her head hanging exhaustedly down to the ground in front of Ash's face.

Above her, there was a noise. A man laughing.

Dazed, Ash made out that she was hanging with both her hands and feet above her. Her cloak and skirts fell down over her head.

"*Shit!*"

She hung upside-down, the chain between her ankles now taut across the mare's saddle, and her whole body suspended under the mare's belly. Some confusion of garments and chain and collar had both her hands pulled up tight into one stirrup and trapped.

Her cloak and gown fell back over her head and shoulders, baring her legs to the blizzard.

Ash giggled.

The mare placidly nosed back at her wool-shrouded head. Folds of wet cloth slid down, across her face, and uncovered her again, drooping to sweep the snow-covered stone.

"*Nazir!*" a voice she recognised as Alderic's bawled hoarsely, through the blizzard.

"'*Arif*?"

"Get her back on that horse!"

"Yes, '*Arif*."

"Ah – wuff!" Ash choked, tried to muffle it, and a wet laugh burst out from between her lips. She snuffled. In front of her, upside-down to her view, the legs of horses milled about, male voices shouting in confusion. Her chest began to ache as she laughed harder, not able to stop, her convulsing body driving out all her breath, tears streaming out of the corners of her eyes and down into her cropped hair.

She hung, completely unable to move, while mail-clad soldiers of the Visigoth Empire tugged thoughtfully at the chain across the mare's back, and picked hopefully at the tangle of her wrists in the cloak and stirrup.

A face came into her view, a man bending down. The *nazir* Theudibert shouted, "What have you got to laugh at, bitch?"

"Nothing." Ash shut her lips firmly together. His upside-down face, beard at the top and helmet underneath, and with an expression of complete bewilderment, sent her off again. A chest-heaving, belly-shaking laugh. "N-n-nothing – I could have been k-killed!"

She managed to wrestle her right hand and chain free. With that resting on the flagstones, wrist-deep in cold wet snow, she took some of her own weight. Hands manhandled her and the world swooped, sickeningly, and she was upright, the saddle between her thighs, feet scrabbling for stirrups.

A circle of dismounted men with swords surrounded her and the mare, wind driving snow into their faces. Beyond that were a ring of surrounding riders;

and a clump of cavalry close around both Godfrey's palfrey, and Fernando's riding horse. Even in the increasing wind and poor visibility, there was no way through the cordon.

"Nobody made a mistake, then," Ash remarked cheerfully as her gut settled.

She freed her hands and wiped her nose on the linen lining of her cloak. The inner cloth was still dry. She started to speak, giggled, swallowed it back, and surveyed the cavalrymen around her with a warm, appreciative, and entirely embracing smile. "Whose dumb idea was this in the first place?"

One or two of them grinned in spite of the foul weather. She sat back in the saddle and picked up her reins, snuffling back chest-aching mirth.

Fernando del Guiz, from where he and his German troops sat surrounded on their horses, called, "Ash! Why are you *laughing*?"

Ash said, "Because it's funny."

She caught sight of Godfrey. Under his snow-whitened hood, he was smiling.

The *'arif* Alderic's horse moved back into the circle of torch-light, Alderic riding with a solid, erect stance despite the driving snow.

"*Nazir*. Get that damn horse moving. The scout's come back. We're no more than a furlong from the city gate."

III

"But they goin' to *kill* you!" the boy-faced soldier, Gaiseric, emphasised; his tone somewhere between confused malice, and awe. "You know that, bitch?"

"Of course I *know* it. Do I look stupid?"

The north-east quadrant steps of House Leofric jolted Ash as she plodded down their spiral again, Gaiseric and Barbas and the *nazir* in front of her, the rest of the squad behind. Mail jingled; sword scabbards scraped the curved wall. Her soaking wet wool skirts dragged behind her on the steps.

"I don't think," Ash said, "that you've understood."

As they walked out into a corridor, she hauled her cloak out from under her feet. The glasses of Greek Fire in the corridor showed her Gaiseric's bewildered face, white with the cold.

"Don' get you," the boy said, as his *nazir* went ahead down the mosaic-tiled corridor.

Ash only smiled at him. She surreptitiously flexed her bruised and aching arms. The muscles of her inner thighs burned. She thought, It must be three weeks since I've ridden anything – not since the field of Auxonne.

"I've been taken prisoner before," she explained. "I think I'd forgotten that."

As to why I'd forgotten – she cut the thought off, putting the cell with the blood-soaked floor away in some part of her mind where she need not look at it. She is young, she heals quickly; there is a background discomfort from her head, her knee; it does not, now, affect this rising of her spirits.

A voice called, "Bring her!"

Leofric, Ash identified. Yeah, thought so.

Gaiseric unexpectedly mumbled under his breath, "You'll be all right in there. He has a fire in there for the vermin."

Two soldiers slid open an iron-bound oak door. Theudibert pushed her through. She shook off his hand. There was a brief exchange of words between the lord-*amir* and the *nazir*. Ash strode forward, direct as a crossbow-bolt's flight, towards a brazier full of red-hot charcoal, and sank down on her knees on the stone floor in front of it.

Something rustled. Something squeaked.

"Oh, *yeah* . . . that's more like it," she sighed, eyes closing. Heat from the fire soaked her face. She opened her eyes, reached up clumsily, and pushed her hood back. Steam rose off the surface of the wool. The stone floor was wet all around her. She rubbed her fists together, biting her lip against the pain as numbness gave way to returning circulation.

"Lord-*Amir*!" Theudibert acknowledged. The door slammed; soldiers' footsteps departing down the corridor. She looked up to find herself alone with the lord-*amir* Leofric and a number of his slaves, some of whom she knew by name.

The walls of the room were stacked with iron rat cages, five and six deep. A myriad beady eyes watched her from behind thin metal grills.

"My lord." Ash faced Leofric. "I think we have to talk."

Whatever he had been expecting, it was not speech from her. He turned, more like a startled owl than ever, his grey-white hair and beard jutting out where he had run his fingers through it. He was wearing a floor-length gown of green wool, spotted with the droppings and litter of his animals.

"Your future is decided. What can you have to say to me?"

His incredulous emphasis on *you* stirred her temper. Ash got to her feet, pulling down the tight wrists of her gown, so that she faced him as a young woman in European dress, her shorn hair hidden by her coif, her body swathed in the wet cloak and hood that she would not abandon in case some slave cleared it away.

She approached the bench where he stood by an open cage. Violante stood beside him, carrying a leather bucket of water.

"What are you doing?" It was a deliberate distraction, while she furiously thought.

Leofric glanced down. "Breeding a true characteristic. Or rather, not. This is my fifth attempt. And this, also, has failed. Girl!"

The iron box in front of the *amir* was full of chopped hay. Ash lifted her brows, thinking, The sheer expense of that, here, where nothing grows—!

Wriggling white grubs lay among the hay. She peered closer, memories coming back of living in a wagon with Big Isobel, when she had been nine or ten: the quartermaster paying a loaf of bread for ten dead rats, or a litter of babies. She leaned over the box, looking at the rat pups – their blind heads big, like hound-pups', and their small bodies covered with a fine white fur. Two were plain grey.

"At five days, you may see the markings. These, like the previous litters, have proved to be useless," the lord-*amir* Leofric observed over her shoulder. His breath smelled of spices. He reached down with trim-nailed fingers, scooping the whole litter up in his palm, and dropped them into the leather bucket.

"Wh—"

They plopped beneath the black surface of the water without a struggle. Her senses, stretched keen, distinguished the rapid succession of fifteen or twenty tiny, heavy, splashes. Ash, staring, met the eyes of Violante, holding the leather bucket. The child's eyes brimmed over with tears.

"The buck is number four-six-eight," the elderly man said, oblivious, reaching up to another cage. "It *will not* breed true."

He reached swiftly in. Ash heard a squeal. Leofric took his hand out, gripping a buck rat around the middle of its body. Ash recognised the liver-and-white patched rat – it squealed, thrashing, all four legs splaying, tail held out stiff, then whipping from side to side in panic. Leofric raised the rat up and brought its head cracking down on the sharp edge of the bench—

Ash, moving before she realised she had the intention, locked her hand around his wrist, arresting his movement before he could strike the animal's brains out.

"No." She pressed her lips together, shook her head. "No, I don't think so – Father."

It was said purely to jolt him. It did. The elderly man stared at her, skin crinkling around his sclerotic blue eyes. Abruptly he flinched, scowled, and flung the rat straight at her, putting his bleeding finger to his mouth. "Keep it if you want it!"

The flying object thumped into Ash's chest. She dropped her hands to catch it, momentarily held a bundle of flailing needles, swore, snatched at the rat's muscular body, and froze, completely, as the animal shot down into the depths of her voluminous cloak.

"What is your *objection*?" Leofric snapped testily.

"Um . . ." Ash remained perfectly still. A stench of rat droppings was in the air. Somewhere in the folds of her cloak, a small solid body moved. *It's sitting in the crook of my elbow!* she realised. She did not put her hand into the cloth. She attempted a chirrup. "Hey, Lickfinger . . ."

The small warm solidity moved. She felt the rat's body shift into a crouch. She couldn't help but tense against the stab of razor-sharp chisel-teeth.

No bite came.

Wild animals do not willingly put up with human touch. They panic, confined. Someone has handled this one, Ash thought. Often. Far more often than Leofric, playing the eccentric rat-breeding *amir* . . .

Ash, very still, shifted her gaze and looked at Violante. The slave-girl had put down the bucket of dead rat-pups and was standing, fists in her mouth, face wet, staring at Ash with appalled hope.

Tameness is a 'by-product' of the breeding programme, is it? Bollocks! *Bollocks*. Leofric, you haven't got a *clue*. I know who's been petting these beasts. And I'll bet she isn't the only slave to do it, either . . .

"All right, I'll keep it." Ash turned back to Leofric. "I think *you've* misunderstood."

"Misunderstood what?"

"*I'm not a rat.*"

"What?"

Ash held herself in stillness. The small, warm, solid body stretched out, under the wool, resting on her forearm. Against her skin – *under* my sleeve! she thought, picturing it sliding between points at her shoulder, wriggling under the neck of her shift. She had a brief lurch in her gut, feeling its furry snake-head and bald, scaly tail in contact with her skin – and realised that what she was feeling was warm fur, no different to a hound puppy; and a rapid, pattering heartbeat.

Ash raised her eyes to Leofric's face and spoke with care. "I'm not a rat, my lord Father. You can't breed me. And I'm not one of your naked slaves, either. I come with a history. I have a life, eighteen or twenty years of it, and I have ties, and responsibilities, and people who depend on me."

"And?" Leofric held out his hands, and one of the male slaves came with a bowl and towel and soap. He spoke without appearing to notice the man who washed him.

I've done that with pages, Ash thought suddenly. It isn't the same. It isn't the same!

"They come with a history, too," she added.

"What are you saying to me?"

"If I come from here, you still don't own me. If I was born to one of your slaves, so what? I'm not yours. You have a responsibility to let me go," Ash said. Her expression changed. In a quite different voice, she said, "Oh Lord, it's licking me!"

The small hot tongue continued to rasp at the tender skin of her forearm, inside her elbow. Ash shivered. She looked up again, delighted; and seeing that Leofric was regarding her with his hands folded in front of his body, she said, "Talk. Negotiate. That's what real people do, my lord Father. You see, you may be a cruel man, but you're not mad. A madman could have run this experiment, but he couldn't have managed a household, and court politics, and all the preparations for the invasion – crusade," she corrected herself.

Leofric lifted his arms as a slave buckled his belt and purse over his long gown. He prompted quietly, "And?"

"And you should never turn down the chance of five hundred armed men," Ash said calmly. "If I don't have my company any more, give me a company of *your* men. You know what the Faris can do. Well, I'm better than her. Give me Alderic and your men, and I'll make certain House Leofric doesn't go down in the struggle for election. Let me send messengers and call my captains, and my specialist gunners and engineers, and I'll make sure things go your way in Europe, too. What's Burgundy, to me? It all comes down to armed force, in the end."

She smiled, hand hovering over her elbow, afraid to touch the rat through the damp wool. By the feel of it, the animal could be asleep.

"Things are different, now that Caliph Theodoric's dead," she said. "I know

448

what it's like, I've been around enough times when heirs take over from lords, and there's always the doubts about the succession, about who's going to follow who. You think about it, my lord Father. This isn't three days ago, this is *now*. I'm not a rat. I'm not a slave. I'm an experienced military commander *and I've been doing this a long time.*" Ash shrugged. "A split second with a poleaxe and these brains go flying out, and end up splattered up someone's breastplate. But until that happens, I *know* so much that you need me, lord Father. At least until you've got yourself elected King-Caliph."

Leofric's lined and creased face ceased to have its habitual, blurred expression. He put his fingers through his unbraided beard, combing it tidy. His eyes were bright, and focused on Ash. She thought, *I've woken him up, I've got him.*

"I don't believe I could trust you to command my troops and remain here."

"Think about it." She saw the fact that she did not plead sink home with him. "It's your choice. No one who's ever hired me *knew* I wasn't going to turn coat and leg it. But I'm neither stubborn nor stupid. If I can come to a compromise that keeps me alive, and means I have some hope of finding out what happened to my guys at Auxonne, then I'll fight for you, and you can trust me to go out there and die for you – or *not* die," she added, "which is more to the point."

She deliberately turned away from his intense, pondering face.

"Excuse me. Violante? I have a rat down my shift."

She did not look at Leofric for the next confusing few minutes, loosening her laces, the small girl's cold hands rummaging around her bodice, and the rat's needle-thin claws scoring red weals down her shoulder as the reluctant furry body was removed. Two red eyes fixed on her from a pointy, furry face. The rat squicked.

"Look after him for me," Ash ordered, as Violante cuddled the buck against her thin body. "Well, my lord Father?"

"I am what you would call a cruel man." The Visigoth noble's tone was completely unapologetic. "Cruelty is a very efficient way of getting what one needs, both from the world and from other people. You, for example, would suffer if I ordered the death of that piece of vermin, and the girl, or the priest that visited you here."

"You think every other lord who hires a bunch of mercenaries doesn't try that?"

"What do you do?" Leofric sounded interested.

"Generally, I have two or three hundred men around me who are trained to use swords and bows and axes. That discourages a lot of them." Ash straightened her puff-shouldered sleeves. The chill, animal-scented room was finally beginning to feel warm, after the blizzard outside. "There's *always* someone who's stronger than you. That's the first thing you learn. So you negotiate, make yourself on balance more useful to them than not – and it doesn't always work; it didn't work with my old company, the Griffin-in-Gold. They made the mistake of surrendering a garrison: the local lord drowned half of them in the lake, there, and hanged the rest from his walnut trees.

Everybody's time runs out sooner or later." She deliberately met Leofric's gaze, and said brutally, "*Later*, we're all dead and rotten. What matters is what we do now."

He took some notice of that, she thought, but could not be sure. What he did was to turn aside and let his slaves finish dressing him, in a new gown, belt, purse and eating-knife; and fur-trimmed velvet bonnet. She studied his back, that was beginning to stoop with age.

He's nothing more than any other lord or *amir*.

And nothing less, of course. He can have me killed at any time.

"I wonder," Leofric's voice creaked, "whether my daughter would behave so well, if she were captured, and in the heart of an enemy stronghold?"

Ash began to smile. "If I'd been a better military commander, you wouldn't be having the chance to compare us."

He turned and continued to watch her assessingly. Ash thought, He doesn't mind hurting people, he's ambitious enough to try for the place of power, and the only difference between him and me is that he has the money and the men, and I don't.

That, and the fact that he has forty or so years of experience that I don't have. This is not a man to fight. This is a man to come to an agreement with.

"One of my *'arifs*, Alderic, takes you to be a soldier."

"I am."

"But, as with my daughter, you are something more than that."

The lord-*amir* glanced away as an older, robed slave entered the room, his hands full of parchment scrolls. The slave bowed briefly and began immediately to whisper to Leofric in an intense undertone. Ash guessed it to be a series of messages, requiring – by Leofric's tone – assent, reassurance, or temporising rejection. It gave her the sense of how, six floors above her head, the stone world of the Citadel buzzed with men seeking allies, to gain power.

Leofric broke off. "I grant you that I will consider this."

"My lord Father," Ash acknowledged.

Better than I'd hoped for.

Rats rustled and scuttled, captive in their cages that lined the room. The hem of her kirtle dragged wetly at her heels, and the manacles on her ankles and her steel collar made her wince with their galling.

He hasn't changed his mind. He may be thinking about changing it, but that's as far as he's got. What can I put into the balance?

"I *am* something more," she said. "Two for the price of one, remember? Maybe you could do with a commander here in Carthage who can use the Stone Golem's tactical advice?"

"And sometimes needs to use it for a revolt of her own men?" the lord-*amir* said quizzically, preparing to follow the slave out. "You are not infallible, daughter. Let me consider."

Ash froze, not attending to his last words.

For a revolt of—

The last time in Dijon I spoke to the Stone Golem, it was the riot, when they almost killed Florian—

450

She bowed her head as the lord-*amir* Leofric left the room, so that he shouldn't see her expression.

Jesu Christus, I was right. He can find out from the Stone Golem what questions it's been asked – by her or by me. He can know exactly what tactical problems I've had.

Or will have. If I still *have* a voice. If it isn't just silence, like it was out in the pyramids. And I can't ask! *Goddammit.*

She thought, furiously, not really attending as a troop of soldiers escorted her back to her cell. The manacles on her ankles were removed, the collar left on her. She sat in the dark of the day, alone, in a bare room with only a pallet and a pisspot, her head between her hands, straining her mind for an idea, a thought, *any*thing.

No. Anything I ask it – Leofric will know. I'd be telling him what I was doing!

A hollow metallic call from outside announced sunset.

Ash lifted her head. Snow, drifting, whitened the stone ledge at the front of the window embrasure, but it did not penetrate far in. Gown and cloak swathed her. Hunger, grinding, made her stomach knot up. The single light, too high up to be reachable, shone down on bas-relief walls, and the worn mosaics of the floor, and the flat black surface of the iron door.

She pushed her fingers up under her collar, easing the metal away from the sores it had already rubbed on her skin.

Something scratched on the outside surface of the door.

A child's voice came clearly between the junction of door and jamb, where great steel bars socketed into the wall.

"Ash? Ash!"

"Violante?"

"Done," the voice whispered. More urgently, "Done, Ash, done!"

Ash scrambled to the door, kneeling on her skirts. "What is it? *What's* been done?"

"A Caliph. We have Caliph, now."

Shit! The election's finished sooner than I thought.

"Who?" Ash did not expect to recognise the name. Talking to Leovigild and other slaves had brought her scurrilous rumours about the habits of the lord-*amirs* of the King-Caliph's court, a passing acquaintance with some political careers, the knowledge of such sexual alliances as slaves witness, and a good deal of gossip about deaths from natural causes. Given another forty-eight hours to persuade the soldiers to gossip, she might have been in a better position to judge military power. Leofric's name was often mentioned, but that Leofric should gain the throne was neither impossible, nor likely.

If he does, he'll have too much new business to think about vivisecting me. If he doesn't—

I needed another forty-eight hours. I don't know *enough*!

"Who?" she demanded, again.

Violante's voice, through the knife-thin crack, said, "Gelimer. Ash, *Amir* Gelimer is Caliph now."

IV

In the room outside her cell a second row of Greek Fire lights flared into brilliance, marking the onset of black day. Their radiance shone through the stone grill over the door. Ash sat staring at the window embrasure and the lightless sky.

"Faris," a man's voice said, over the noise of steel bolts sliding protestingly back into the wall sockets.

"Leovigild?"

The beardless slave stepped into her cell, leaving two armed guards outside. He carried a bundle in his arms.

"Here!"

A roll of cloth dumped and spilled on the pallet. Ash knelt up, hands rapidly sorting through the pile.

A fine-textured linen shirt. Hose, still laced to a pourpoint; the colour invisible in this light. A great thick wool demi-gown with the sleeves sewn in, and silver buttons down the front. A belt, a purse – empty, her furiously scrabbling fingers determined – and no shoes, just a pair of soles with long leather cords affixed. Ash looked up, puzzled.

"I show, wear." Leovigild shook his head in frustration. The reflected light allowed her to see the relaxation of lines in his face. "Violante speak, not come." The lithe man made a quick gesture, cradling his arms as if cuddling something against his cheek. "Wear, Faris."

Ash, kneeling on the pallet, looked up at him. What she held between her hands was the padded roll and hanging tail of a chaperon hat.

The hydraulically powered horn sounded the hour across the city six times before her cell door opened again.

Hunger gnawed in her gut, and finally quietened. It would return later, sharper, she knew. A small smile curled up one corner of her mouth, that she was unaware of; it was a smile of pure, delighted recognition. Hunger and isolation are tools she is familiar with.

They mean she is still worth being persuaded.

From the harbour below, sounds racketed up the stone walls and battlements: loud singing, shrill music of flutes, continuous shouting, and once a swift crash of blades. She could not wriggle up the window embrasure far enough to see downwards, but pressed up against the iron bars, staring into the dark, she witnessed bonfires on top of the next harbour headland, to the east, and tiny figures silhouetted against the flames, dancing in wild celebration. The smell of the sea came tinged with wood-smoke.

The hose were tight, the doublet a shade big, but the feel of a fine linen shirt against her skin again made up for it all. She was whistling under her breath without knowing it as she laced Leovigild's odd footwear up her shins, over her hose, with fingers blue with cold.

"All I need is a sword."

452

She knotted the ties of the cloak around her neck, put on her hood, and tugged the shoulder-cape of the woollen hood down and under the steel collar around her neck, not caring if it was a visible mark of slavery so long as she had something to cushion it from the sores on her skin. She wore the hood pushed back and the hat pulled down on her head; gradually growing warm now, despite the howling chill and sleet at the granite window's edge.

She had used the pisspot an hour since, when she finally heard footsteps in the guardroom outside and was ready.

"*Nazir*," she greeted Theudibert, standing.

His expression, between disapproval and fear of a reprimand if he questioned the reason for her new appearance with his superiors, might have made her smile, but his attack was not yet distant enough in her mind.

"Move!" He jerked his thumb at the door.

Ash nodded, not so much in acknowledgement of what he said, as to herself.

I need to know who sent me these clothes. If it was Leofric, as a gift, it means one thing. If Violante or Leovigild stole them, it means another. If I ask, and it *was* theft, they'll be killed. So I can't ask.

So, I don't ask. It's only one more thing that I don't know. And I can handle that.

One of the men said something to Theudibert, gesturing at her ankles. A suggestion to replace the manacles, Ash guessed. My hands, too?

The *nazir* snarled something and struck the man.

Orders not to? Or just, no orders?

Tension tightened her gut, like the morning before battle. Ash hitched the heavy woollen cloak forward around her shoulders, tucking her bare hands into the cloth, and smiled at Gaiseric and Barbas as she strode out of the cell.

The spiral stairs of House Leofric were packed with freeborn men in their finest dress. Theudibert's squad moved her through with the minimum of fuss; up and out into the great courtyard, scarred with sleet, where bareheaded slaves slipped as they ran, bringing drink, banners, lutes, roasted fish, fire-crackers, and bandoleers of folly-bells. She bit her lip, her sandalled heels skidding on the sleet-covered chequer-paved court; found herself huddled between armed men and hurried out through a long archway, out into a lightless street or alley.

This is the way I was brought in to House Leofric. Four days ago? Is it only four days?

Gaiseric stopped dead in front of her.

She cannoned into his back, and grunted. His mail hauberk was covered with a long surcoat, the notched-wheel livery of House Leofric, bright black on white. His sword-hilt was almost reachable. In the same second of realisation she heard a command from the *nazir*, and she felt her hands gripped, and a short length of cord tied around her wrists.

Gaiseric moved forward a step.

The torches, held high, showed nothing in front of them but the backs of other men.

They began to inch slowly forward, with the crowd, on through the narrow blank streets of the Citadel.

Ash found herself stumbling over discarded rubbish underfoot: burned-out torches, someone's shoe, ribbons, a discarded wooden plate. Having her hands bound kept her off-balance, and her eyes down, trying to see in the wavering yellow light what she was about to trip over. The distant city clock hooted again twice while she sometimes walked, and more often stood still, crammed up against the bodies of Theudibert's squad.

None of the young men put their hands on her.

Her gaze down, she could not see where they were heading until they were almost there. A fine cold wetness – not quite sleet – fell out of the black sky on to upturned faces. Here, there were enough torches, held by bareheaded slaves standing on a low wall, surrounding an open square, that she could see for about a bow-shot.

Yellow light fell on the heads of the packed crowd, and on the walls of a building that stood, isolated, in what must be the Citadel's centre. Its gilded, curved walls rose up into a great dome, high over Ash's head. An even tighter cordon of armed men in the Caliph's personal colours surrounded the front of the building: she could actually see bare pavement behind them.

A disturbance eddied the heads of the crowd to her right. The *nazir* muttered something unenthusiastic.

"Not here, *nazir*!" a sharp, deep voice said. Ash got sight of the *'arif* Alderic shoving his way through the civilian crowd. "Round the back."

"Sir."

The squad fell in around Alderic. Ash took in the fact that the bearded Visigoth soldier sweated, despite the cold. She could not have eaten, now, her stomach knotted up like a horse with colic.

"I hear you might be joining us as a captain," *'Arif* Alderic murmured, his eyes fixed forward.

No hope of keeping anything secret in a household full of slaves. Or soldiers, Ash reflected. Is this truth, or only a rumour? *Please, let it be true!*

"It's what I do. Fight for who pays me."

"And you'll be betraying your previous employer."

"I prefer to think of it as re-aligning my loyalties."

Alderic's squad shoved their way through a crowd that did not perceptibly thin as they circumnavigated the wall of the massive building. Closer to the walls, Ash could see that arches punctuated it at intervals around; and through these, light spilled out, and the sound of boy-choirs singing; the inaugural festivities obviously still not completed, eight hours on in the day. The dome above her gleamed. The tiles that scaled its curves looked, very much, as if they were gilded; and Ash blinked, dazzled, both at the reflected torchlight from gold leaf and the realisation of wealth.

The squad wheeled left. *'Arif* Alderic went forward, speaking to a sergeant in a black surcoat. Ash craned her neck back, apparently gawping at the dome, and let her peripheral vision bring her an assessment of the chamberlains, musicians, squires and pages crowded around this entrance. All of them wore what she thought must be their winter clothes, for such winter as ever came to this warm twilight coast, shivering in thin woollen robes; the ones who had money distinguishable now by northern garments: Venetian gowns, or English wool doublets, or dagged hoods and linen coifs.

A man's fist thumped her hard between the shoulder-blades. She stumbled forward, out of the sleet, into the building and the shelter of the archway; almost losing her balance since she was not able to put out her tied hands to recover it. If she had been wearing skirts, she would have gone sprawling.

"In, bitch," Theudibert growled.

"That's 'Captain Bitch' to you."

Someone snickered. The *nazir* was not fast enough to see who. Ash pressed her lips together and kept a straight face. She walked between armed men, out from under the arch and into the hall. Hundreds of courtiers and warriors crowded the rim of the circular hall, under its archways.

The central floor was bare, except for a cluster of people around a throne.

Green vegetation strewed the tiles. Much trodden down, it was nonetheless still recognisable: green blades of corn.

No, Ash corrected herself, dismissing the gilded stone above her head. *This* is wealth.

She surveyed the green stems, laid so thick that the floor was hardly visible. Smears of green marked the mosaic tiles, where boots had skidded on the leaf-sheathed stalks and prickly green heads of corn. A sharp, sour fragrance pervaded the air. Unripe corn, brought in from Iberia, she guessed; and wasted, purely for ceremony, laid down as one lays down rushes, to keep the floor neat.

"Madonna Ash," a familiar voice said as she was hustled to one side. She found herself standing, bound, with Alderic's troop of forty; and with them a straggle-haired young man.

"Messire Valzacchi!"

The Italian doctor removed his velvet bonnet and bowed, as well as he could in the close crowd. "How is your knee?"

Ash flexed it absently. "Hurts with this cold."

"You should attempt to keep it warm. The head?"

"Better, *dottore*." Like, I'm going to say I still get dizzy, in front of men I might – sweet Christ, please – might be commanding, before long.

"You could always untie me, '*Arif*," she added to Alderic. "After all, where am I going to go?"

The Visigoth commander gave her a short, amused glare, and turned back to his subordinates.

"Worth a try . . ." Ash murmured.

An oval white patch lay on the floor ahead of her, off-centre. Ash looked up. The great inner curve of the dome rose up over her head, ivory and gold mosaics picturing the saints in their splendour: Michael and Gawaine and Peredur and Constantine. The dark intricacy of the icons defeated her, she could not tell, in torchlight, whether it was bulls or boars depicted between the saints. But what she at first thought was a black circle seventy feet above her head was, in fact, an opening. At the apex of the dome, a stone-rimmed gap opened to the sky.

Through the hole, as if it were night, Capricornus shone. A faint peppering of snow drifted down into the rotunda, diagonal on the air, sifting to the corn-strewn pavement beneath.

The boy-choir began again. Ash deduced that the children must be somewhere on the far side. She could not see past the heads of the men around her. Tiered oak benches set between the arches held nobles and their households, their soldiers lining the aisles – a noble for each gap between arches, she guessed, running her eye across foreign heraldry.

To her right, someone bore Leofric's banner. Where polished and carved oaken pews rose up, she recognised some of the household, Leofric himself not visible.

Before her, on a great octagonal plinth in the centre of the rotunda, stood the throne of the Visigoth Empire. A man sat there. At this distance she could not make out his face, but it must be the King-Caliph. Must be Gelimer.

Annibale Valzacchi remarked, "You are privileged, madonna."

"I am?"

"There are no other women present. I doubt there is a woman out of doors in all Carthage." The young man snickered. "Since I am a doctor, I can at least vouch for your being female, if not a woman."

Despite choir and royal occasion, people were talking between themselves. Valzacchi's voice came quiet under the buzz of three or four thousand voices, but with unmistakable malice. Ash gave him a swift glance, which took in his black wool gown, the cloth much faded, and the squirrel-fur trim at his hanging-sleeve slits matted and dirty.

"No one pay your fees, *dottore*?"

"*I* am not a hired killer," Valzacchi emphasised bitterly. "Theodoric died, and so I go without my fee. You kill, therefore they are prepared to pay you. Tell me, madonna, where is Christian justice in that?"

Prepared to pay you. Oh sweet Christ, Christ Viridianus, let it be true, not just a rumour – if I've convinced Leofric—

"Let me even the balance of Justice's scales. If I'm here to be bought, I'll buy a doctor, too. You said you'd worked in a condottiere camp." A tremor went through her body, so that she had to grip her hands together under her cloak, the cords chafing her wrists. *Fortune is to be wooed, not commanded.* "Of course, if I'm here to be executed, I'll keep my mouth shut about you."

The doctor stuttered a laugh at this skinny, wide-shouldered woman in man's dress; her shining silver hair cut too short even for a man, as short as a slave's crop.

"No," he said. "I prefer to earn my gold healing, even if lately that gold has been copper. I will ask you a question, madonna, that I asked my brother Gianpaulo once in Milano. From the rise to the set of the sun, you put all your mind and all your body and all your soul into ways in which you can burn down houses, foul wells, slaughter cattle, rip unborn children out of their mother's bellies, and slice off the legs and arms and heads of your fellow men, on the field. How is it that you sleep, at night?"

"How is it that your brother sleeps?"

"He used to drink himself senseless. Lately, he turned to the Lord God, and now says he sleeps in that mercy. But he has not changed his trade. He kills people for a living, madonna."

Something about the man's face triggered, finally, recognition. "Shit! You're *Lamb*'s brother! Agnes Dei. Aren't you? I never knew his name was Valzacchi."

"You *know* him?"

"I've known Lamb for years." Oddly cheered, Ash smiled and shook her head.

Annibale Valzacchi repeated, "How is it that you can sleep at night, after what you do? Do you drink?"

"Most of the people I employ drink." Ash met his gaze with her clear, cold dark eyes. "I don't. I don't need to, *dottore*. Doing this doesn't bother me. It never has."

A familiar voice said something from the other side of the *nazir's* cordon of soldiers. Ash didn't catch what, but she went up on her toes to try and see who it was. To her surprise, the *nazir* Theudibert grunted, "Let him through! – Search him first. It's only the *peregrinatus Christi*."[10]

The boy-soldier Gaiseric suddenly said, at her ear, "Old Theudo's scared shitless, ma'am! He's reckoning on you favouring him later, if he lets you have a priest now."

Godfrey Maximillian's big hands gripped both of hers warmly. "Child! Praise God, you live."

Under cover of a sonorous Latin blessing, and the sleeves of his green robe, Ash felt Godfrey's fingers move quickly around her wrists, loosening the knots of the cord. His bearded innocent face remained uninvolved, as if his hands were acting without his own consent. She shrugged her freed hands back into her enveloping cloak, as casually and as quickly as if it were something they had practised, like mummers in a play. The back of her neck prickled hot and wet with the effort of not looking to see if anyone had noticed.

"Did you assist in the eight offices here, Godfrey?"

"I am too heretic for them. I may preach, if this ceremony ever ends." Godfrey Maximillian's forehead shone. He spoke past her, to Annibale Valzacchi. "Is the man Caliph or not, yet?"

The doctor moved his shoulders in a very Italian manner. "Since this morning. The rest has just been consecrations."

Ash looked across the corn-strewn floor. Something to do with priests was going on around the throne, iron-grey men in green robes processing, hieratically, about the lord-*amir* Gelimer. She strained her vision, trying to bring his face into focus, a childlike conviction in her mind that a man should look different after the anointing oils, after he was no longer man, but king.

Have I done it? Have I wagered and won?

Thousands of candles heated the air, making her cloak almost uncomfortably warm, and shining a soft gold light upon the walls. She looked up at the great Face of Christ depicted above the saints, and the sprouting viridian foliage of the Tree thrusting from His mouth.

His lips encompassed the circular hole at the top of the rotunda, as if He opened His mouth upon star-ridden darkness.

---

[10] Term used of Celtic travelling monks, without an abbey of their own: 'a wanderer for Christ'.

"Christus Imperator," Ash breathed. Her neck hurt, staring up. Her guts twinged; fear and anticipation, rather than hunger.

"The Mouth of God. Yes. Here in Carthage He is preferred as He was when He ruled over the Romans," Godfrey Maximillian murmured, his arm pushing up against her shoulder, his body warm and comforting beside her. "Are the rumours true?"

"What rumours?" Ash smiled.

She thought she managed to hit the correct expression, somewhere between deference and complacency. Certainly Annibale Valzacchi gave her a look of contempt. *Florian would see through this at once*, she thought. A sideways glance assured her of Godfrey's complicit silence.

Leofric wouldn't have brought me here if he wasn't planning to do *something* with me. But *what*? Can it matter to him that he thinks of himself as a father – her father – mine?

But I am not the Faris.

And Gelimer is Caliph now.

Ash shifted, slightly, causing two of Alderic's *nazirs* to look at her. It became apparent to them that she was trying to see their lord-*amir*, through the massed ranks of his household. No hands went to sword-hilts.

She got sight of Leofric at last, one elbow on the arm of his carved walnut chair, at the top of the rising pews on the left-hand side of the archway. He was speaking to someone, a young man in rich dress – a son? a brother? – but his gaze was fixed forward, on the throne of the King-Caliph, and on Gelimer. Ash stared, willing Leofric to look at her.

Seated men around him leaned forward, speaking quietly. Male backs shut her off from Leofric. Men in robes, men in mail; household priests in their high-fronted headdresses.

"Aren't they splendid?" a guttural Gothic voice whispered in her ear. Gaiseric, again.

Ash, startled, studied the boy's face, and then the men clustered beneath the black notched-wheel banner. Noblemen in hastily stitched wool gowns and hukes, older men wearing nine-yard velvet houppelandes; knights in full mail hauberks. Swords, daggers, chased leather purses, riding boots; she knows what you will pay to have these made, and what they will fetch as loot.

She knows what it is like to go barefoot, own one wool shift, and eat every other day.

Gaiseric, as she glances at him, is plainly from a village of two huts, or a farmhouse with earthen floors, one room for the people and another for sow and cow – from rich freemen, his face does not have the early lines of malnutrition.

"What about the King?" Ash whispered.

The boy's face shone with an adoration reserved for priests, at the altar, lifting bread and bringing down flesh. "This ain't no old man. *He* won't stop us fighting."

Nine-tenths of the cultivated world is forest, strip-fields, lath-and-plaster huts, and chilblains and hunger; death from early disease or accident, and no touch of any fabric softer than wool woven by the winter hearth. For this it is

458

worth strapping metal to one's body and facing the hard blades of axes, and the punching steel of bodkin arrow-heads. Or it is, for Gaiseric. Worth it to be standing in a city, now, of sixty thousand people, while his king is crowned in the sight of God.

And for me? Ash thought. Worth it not to be knee-deep in mud, all my life? Even if it brings me, finally, to standing here, not knowing what will happen to me, only that the next few minutes will decide it? Oh yes. *Yes.*

Godfrey Maximillian's hand closed over her arm. A blast of clarions shattered the song of boys, ripping the vast dome of air above their heads. All the flames of the wax candles shook; sweet-smelling candles as thick as a man's thigh. An explosion of tension went through her blood, both hands going to her belt. Her hands, purely of themselves, missed the feel of the hilts of sword and dagger; as her body missed feeling the weight of protective armour.

From every quarter of the hall, men began to walk in.

She had a brief glimpse, at the front of the crowd, of men's faces. Pale, bearded faces; young and old, but all, all, male. From every arch they advanced, leaving the aisles in front of the pews bare, so that great spokes of empty floor ran from the high seats of the lord-*amirs* to the throne of the King-Caliph. Between, men who might be merchants, ship-owners, great importers of spice, grain and silk, packed the space elbow-to-elbow, in their fairest dress.

Clarions ran on, each higher burst shattering at her ears. Ash felt tears start at her eyes and could not tell why. The distant figure of the King-Caliph, swathed in his cloth-of-gold robes, stood and raised his arms.

Silence fell.

A bearded Visigoth warrior called out, words she could not understand. At the furthest quarter of the dome, where another great household sat arrayed, there was a stir – men rising to their feet, banners raised, swords unsheathed, a great deep-voiced shout. And then they came forward, down the steps to the grain-covered mosaic tiles, striding forward to the throne, each falling down upon his knees as a lord-*amir* and his household swore, in unison, their fidelity to the ruler of the Visigoth Empire.

A similar preparatory stir moved Alderic's troop. Ash shot a glance around the lord-*amir* Leofric's quarter of the rotunda. Banners raised up, trailing from their spiked and painted poles. *Nazir* Theudibert lifted a pennant. Alderic said something quickly professional to another of Leofric's 'arifs', who grinned. A great rustling of cloth sounded as all the knights and men-at-arms shifted forward to their pre-planned places; and Ash hauled her hat off, uncovering her head like the rest of Leofric's household. She unconsciously straightened her shoulders, her head coming up.

"You are like my brother's war-horses!" Annibale Valzacchi muttered, disgusted.

Ash caught herself in a rare moment of comprehension. She shook her head. "He's right. The *dottore* is right."

One of Godfrey Maximillian's hands came up swiftly and brushed over her cut hair. Godfrey said, painfully, "I am here. Whatever happens. You will not be alone."

Men around them began moving forward. Horns shattered the high air.

Stumbling beside Godfrey, Ash said, without looking at him, "You're no war-horse. How do you manage to stay on a field of battle, Godfrey? How can you bear with the killing?"

"For you." Godfrey's words came hurriedly, and she could not see his face for the press of people. "For you."

What the hell am I going to do about Godfrey?

There were more people shoulder-to-shoulder around her now. Ash saw, over the heads of some of them, that Leofric must have six or seven hundred men present.

I know what's missing!

She searched around the hall, staring at banners, seeing no white pennants with red crescents.

No Turks, here to see the crowning.

But I thought, at Auxonne – I thought they *must* have allied – am I wrong?

What she did see, in the crowd around ahead, was a familiar green and gold banner: the livery of Fernando del Guiz. And then, all around her, men began to sink to their knees, and she knelt with them, down in the sour smell of crushed corn, the air cold on the back of her neck, sleet falling down on her from the Mouth of God above.

She craned her neck back once, to see stars in the blackness; and the great painted curls of foliage spiralling out from His mouth and down the curving dome, winding about the armour-clad saints and the tops of squat, papyrus-grooved pillars. A cold wind blew into her eyes. With a start, she realised that Leofric was speaking.

"You are my liege, Gelimer." His creaking, quiet voice became audible over the susurration of a thousand men breathing. "I hereby swear, as my fathers swore, honour and loyalty to the King-Caliph; this promise to bind me and my heirs until the day of the Coming of Christ, when all divisions shall be healed, and all ruling given over to His reign. Until that day, I and mine shall fight as you bid us, King Gelimer; make peace where you desire, and strive always for your good. Thus do I, Leofric, swear."

"Thus do I, Gelimer, accept your fealty and constancy."

The King-Caliph stood. Ash lifted her head very slightly, peering up from under her brows at Leofric moving cautiously forward and embracing Gelimer. Now she was close to the front, she could see the octagonal steps that rose up to the ancient black throne, with its carved wooden finials and bas-relief suns. And the men's faces.

Gelimer's narrow-faced looks were not noticeably improved by dressing the man in a cloth-of-gold houppelande with ermine trim, Ash thought; and you might braid as much gold wire into his beard as you chose, without making him any more prepossessing. The thought gave her an odd, partial comfort. Gelimer, standing before her, with his arms formally around Leofric, kissing him on each cheek, might look like some hierophantic doll. But for the moment, not only the men of his own household, but Alderic and Theudibert and all the rest would take their swords and fight where he indicated.

"For as long as it lasts . . ." Ash pressed her lips together. "What d'you think, Godfrey? A 'riding accident'? Or 'natural causes'?"

In an equally faint whisper, Godfrey Maximillian said, "Any king is better than no king. Better than anarchy. You weren't outside in the city these last few days. There has been murder done."

The sonorous formal exchanges allowed her a quick reply:

"There may be murder done here in a minute – except, they'll call it execution."

"Can you do nothing?"

"If I've lost? I'll try to run. I won't go quietly." She grabbed his hand, under her cloak, and gripped it, turning a bright-eyed gaze on him. "Throw a fit. Throw a prophecy! Distract them. Just be ready."

"I thought – but – he'll hire you? He must!"

Ash shrugged, the movement made jerky by tension. "Godfrey, maybe nothing at all will happen. Maybe we'll all turn around and march out of here. These are the lords of the kingdom, who cares about one condottiere?"

Leofric stepped back from the King-Caliph, his pace slow as he walked backwards down the shallow stairs of the throne. A gold fillet glinted in candlelight, binding back his white hair. The gilded pommel and hilt of his sword caught the light, too; and his gloved hands glittered with the dome-cut splendour of emeralds and sapphires.

At the foot of the steps he stopped, made a shallow bow, and began to turn away.

"Our lord Leofric." The King-Caliph Gelimer leaned forward, seated on his throne. "I accept your fealty and your honour. Why, then, have you brought an abomination into the House of God? Why is there a woman with your household?"

Oh, shit. Ash's gut thumped. I know a put-up question when I hear one. There's the formal excuse for an execution, if Leofric doesn't speak for me. Now—

Leofric, with every appearance of calm, said, "It is not a woman, my King. It is a slave, my gift to you. You have seen her before. She is Ash, another warrior-general who hears the voice of the Stone Golem, and so may fight for you, my King, upon your crusade now ending in the north."

Ash picked up *now ending*, so obsessed for a second, debating, *Is the war in Burgundy over? Is this just flattery, for Gelimer?* that she did not realise Gelimer had begun to speak again.

"We will continue our crusade. Some few heretic towns – Bruges, Dijon – yet remain to be taken." Gelimer's pinched face moved into a smile. "Not enough, Leofric, that we need subject ourselves to the danger of another general who hears battle commands from a Stone Golem. Your first we will not recall, since she proves useful, but to have another – no. We may come to rely on her, and she may fail."

"Her sister has not." Leofric bowed his head. "This is that Captain Ash who took the Lancastrian standard at Tewkesbury, in the English wars, when she was not yet thirteen years of age. She led the spearmen from the wood, on to Bloody Meadow.[11] She has been tested upon many fields, since. If I give her a

---

[11] The battle of Tewkesbury (Saturday 4 May 1471) decided the second of the Yorkist/ Lancastrian wars in favour of the Yorkists. Ash would have been thirteen or fourteen years of age at

company of my men, Lord King, she will prove helpful to the crusade."

Gelimer slowly shook his head. "If she is such a prodigy . . . Great generals grow dangerous to kings. Such generals weaken the realm, they make confusion in the minds of the people as to who is the rightful ruler. You have bred a dangerous beast here. For this reason, and for many others, we have decreed that your second general shall not live."

The sleet fell down more slowly, now, from the Mouth of God; white flecks floating upon the air.

"I had thought you might use her as a condottiere, my King. We have used such before."

"You had thought also to make an investigation upon the flesh of this woman. Do it. She is your gift to me. Do it. You may thus ease our mind about your other 'daughter'. Perhaps, then, *she* will be allowed to retire, alive, when this war is ended."

Ash registered the flick of deliberate malice in King-Caliph Gelimer's voice. She thought, This isn't personal. Not on the strength of one insult. Not on his coronation day. Too petty. This isn't aimed at *me*, any of it.

Leofric's the target, and I think this is the end of a long campaign.

She sensed Gaiseric and Theudibert shifting fractionally back, on their knees, leaving her isolated in the front row of Leofric's household. Godfrey Maximillian's bulk remained, solidly, at her shoulder; blocking any movement behind her.

The lord-*amir* Leofric put his hands to his belt buckle, where its long leather tongue hung down, ornamented with golden studs in the shape of notched wheels. She could see only his profile, not enough to guess if his façade of calm had cracked.

"My King, it has taken two centuries to breed two women who can do this."

"One was sufficient. Our *Reconquista* of Iberia is complete, and soon we shall have completed our crusade in the north: we do *not*," the King-Caliph Gelimer said deliberately, "we do not need your generals, or this . . . gift."

I don't believe this.

Disbelief burned in her, false and familiar; the same disbelief that she sees in men's eyes when they take a final wound from her, staring at cut flesh, slashed gut, white bone: *this cannot be happening to me!*

Ash started to rise. Theudibert and Gaiseric grabbed her shoulders. Apparently unconscious of the movement, the lord-*amir* Leofric gazed at the men of the King's household, surrounding the throne, and back at Gelimer. Ash caught sight of Fernando, between two German men-at-arms, his chin scraped clean and his eyes reddened. Beside King-Caliph Gelimer, a fat robed man bending to speak into the royal ear.

Leofric said mildly, as if nothing at all had been decided, "Our Prophet Gundobad wrote: the wise man does not eat his seed corn, he saves it so that he

this time. Edward of York, afterwards king, is said to have hidden two hundred of his 'fellowship' in a wood, from where they broke out, flanked and routed the Duke of Somerset's troops, and began the rout of the whole Lancastrian army, large numbers of which were butchered, becoming trapped in the 'evil ditches and lanes' covering the battlefield. Contemporary reports do not mention mercenaries in this context, but they were known to have fought in the battle of Barnet, which immediately preceded Tewkesbury.

will have a harvest the following year. Abbot Muthari may have the Latin of it, but it is perfectly plain. You may need both my daughters in the years to come."

Gelimer snapped, "*You* need them, Leofric. What are *you*, without your stone machines, and your visionary daughters?"

"My King—"

"Yes. *I* am your King. Not Theodoric, Theodoric is dead, and your place of favour died with him!"

A low, startled buzz of voices sounded. Someone blew the beginning of a clarion call. It cut off abruptly. This isn't part of the ceremony, Ash realised. She shivered, where she knelt.

Gelimer stood up, both his hands gripping the royal staff of ivory that he had been clasping across his lap. "I will have no over-mighty subjects in my court! Leofric, she *will* die! You will oversee it!"

"I am no over-mighty subject."

"Then you will do my will!"

"Always, my King." Leofric inhaled deeply, his face impassive in the shivering lights of the candles. He looked gaunt. There was no reading his expression, not after sixty years spent in the courts of the King-Caliph.

Ash let her field of vision expand, widening focus as one does in battle, to be aware of the soldiers beside her, the blocked aisles out of the building, Fernando's aghast face, the packed crowds around the throne, the archway half a bow-shot behind her. No chance of reaching it, through the soldiers. No chance that – heart in her throat, sweating, fear beginning to push her to some stupid final act – no chance that she would not try for it.

The voice of a very young man, very nervous, sounded in the silence. "My lord King-Caliph, she isn't a slave, she isn't Lord-*Amir* Leofric's property. She's freeborn. By virtue of marrying me."

Godfrey Maximillian, behind her, said, "God on the Tree!"

Ash stared across at Fernando del Guiz. He returned her gaze hesitantly, a young German knight in a foreign court, bright in steel and gilded spurs; whispers going on all around him – the whole matter of the treatment of Visigoth-conquered territory brought up into public domain again by his ingenuous words.

Ash, her knees hurting her, climbed to her feet.

For one moment, she made eye-contact with Fernando. His clean, shaven, fair-haired appearance was altered now; dark colour under his eyes, and new lines around his mouth. He gave her a look that was rueful; half-apologetic, the other half sheer terror.

"It's true." Ash hugged her cloak around her shoulders, her eyes wet, her smile ironic. "That's my husband, Fernando."

Gelimer snorted. "Leofric, is this turn-coat German yours, or ours? We forget."

"He is nothing, Lord King."

A gloved, thin hand closed on Ash's arm. She startled. The lord-*amir* Leofric's grip tightened, the gold of his rings biting into her even through cloak and doublet.

Still formal, Leofric persisted, "My King, you will have heard, as I have heard, how this young woman has won much fame as a military commander in Italy and Burgundy and England. How much better, then, that she should fight for you. What could better prove your right to rule over the north, than that their own commanders fight for the King-Caliph?"

Close enough to him now, Ash saw Gelimer nip his lower lip between his teeth; a momentary gesture that made the man look no older than Fernando del Guiz. *How in Christ's name did he get to be elected Caliph? Of course. Some men are better at gaining power than holding on to it . . .*

Leofric's inoffensive, soft, penetrating voice continued. "There is the wife of Duke Charles, Margaret of Burgundy, who yet defies us behind the walls of Bruges. It is not certain the Duke himself will die. Dijon may hold out until the winter. My daughter the Faris cannot be everywhere in Christendom. Use this child of my breeding, my King, I beg you, while she is yet of use to you. When she is no longer useful, then carry out your just sentence upon her."

"Oh no you don't!" Ash shook her arm free of the Visigoth noble. She stepped forward, into the space before the throne, not giving the King-Caliph time to speak.

"Lord King, I *am* a woman, and a woman of business. Charles of Burgundy himself thought I was worth my hire. Give me a company, make it of whoever's household troops you choose – yours, if you want it that way – and give me a month, and I'll take any city you want taken, Bruges or Dijon."

She manages to have an air about her, something to do with being the only woman present among four thousand men, something to do with her hacked-off silver-blonde hair and her face, identical to their Faris who has won cities for them in Iberia. She has a presence. It is more to do with how she stands: a body trained for war does not move in the same way as a woman kept behind stone-tracery bars. And the light in her eyes, and her crooked grin.

"I can do this, Lord King. Quarrels and factions in your court aren't as important as that. I can do it. And don't kill me at the end of it, pay me." A glitter in her eyes, thinking of red crescent banners. "War is a never-ending presence on the earth, Lord King, and while it is, you must live with such evils as captains of war. Use us. My priest, here, is ready to swear me to your service."

Gelimer seated himself, a movement which Ash thought gave him a moment to consider.

"As to that, no." His voice gained a sharper edge of malice. "If nothing else, you are a mercenary who will desert at the earliest opportunity."

Ash, bewildered, said, "Sire?"

"I have heard of your fame. I have read the reports which Leofric says come from his general, in the north. Therefore, one thing is obvious to me. You will do what you did before, last month, at Basle, when you ran away to join the Burgundian army. You call yourself 'condottiere' – you broke your *condotta* with us at Basle!"

"I broke no contract!"

It was the name of the city of Basle that did it. Voices drowned her out. Ash's stomach swooped, sickeningly. A noise broke out, each man telling their neighbour some distorted story. Beside her, Leofric's complexion greyed.

"But that isn't what happened!" Godfrey Maximillian lumbered up off his knees, protesting to the King-Caliph. "She was torturing Ash! *She* broke contract! We had no intention of joining the Burgundians. Ash! Tell him!"

"My Lord King, if you will listen—"

"Oath-breaker!" the King-Caliph announced, with some satisfaction. "You see whom you trust, Leofric? She and her husband both! All these Franks are treacherous, unreliable bastards!"

Godfrey Maximillian straight-armed two soldiers out of the way; Ash grabbed him as the troop closed in, manhandling the priest back. Unknown to her, her face twisted into a bitter smile. *I always wanted to be known across Christendom – so much for fame.*

"Godfrey! It doesn't matter what *did* happen!" She shook him vehemently. "It doesn't matter that my story's true. Can you see me trying to *explain* it? What's true is what they *believe*. Sweet Christ, what the hell did the truth ever matter!"

"But, child—!"

"We'll have to handle it another way. I'll get us out of here."

"*How?*"

A shrieking horn drowned out his voice. The King-Caliph, Gelimer, sat with his arm upraised. Silence fell, across the whole rotunda. Slowly, Gelimer lowered his arm.

"We are not this day anointed King so that we may *debate* with our lords. Leofric, she is an approved traitor. She will be executed. She is a monster, of course," Gelimer leaned back on his throne, "hearing voices; as your other child is, but your other child is at least loyal. Perhaps, when you put this one under the knife, you will be able to tell us, my lord, where in the heart treachery lies."

A burr of sycophantic laughter went around the court.

Ash gazed at the faces of nobles and knights, bishops and abbots, merchants and soldiers; and found nothing but curious, avid, amused expressions. Men. No women, no slaves, no clay golems.

King-Caliph Gelimer sat resting both arms on the arms of the throne, his slender hands cupping the carved foliage, his back straight, his braided beard jutting as he stared around at the thousands of men gathered under the roof of the palace and the great Mouth of God above his head.

"*Amirs* of Carthage." Gelimer's tenor voice echoed under the dome. "You have heard one of your number here, the *amir* of House Leofric, doubt our victory in the north."

Ash became conscious of Leofric stirring, in irritated surprise, at her side, and thought, *He didn't see this coming. Shit!*

The new King-Caliph's voice rang out again:

"*Amirs* of Carthage, commanders of the empire of the Visigoth people, you have not elected me to this throne to lead you to defeat – or even to a weak peace. Peace is for the weak. We are strong."

Gelimer's bright black gaze flickered across Ash.

"No peace!" he repeated. "And not the war that weaklings fight, my *amirs*. The war of the strong. In the heretic lands of the north, we are fighting a war against Burgundy, most powerful of all the heretic nations of Christendom. Most rich in her wealth, most rich in her armies, most powerful in her Duke. And this Burgundy *we shall conquer*."

Under the painted foliage of the Mouth of God, under the stone rim opening upon the black day skies of Carthage, every man is silent.

Gelimer said, "But we are not content merely to conquer. We will not merely defeat Burgundy, the most mighty nation. *We will raze Burgundy to the ground*. Our armies will burn their way north from Savoy to Flanders. Every field, every farm, every village, every town, every city – we will destroy. Every cog, carrack and warship – we will destroy. Every heretic lord, bishop and villein, we will destroy. And the great Duke of Burgundy, the great conquering Duke and all his kin – we will kill. He, his heirs, his successors, to the last man, woman and child – we will kill. And with this example, my *amirs*, we shall be the overlords of Christendom, and none will dare dispute our *right*."

A great roar shocked through her at his last word. Gaiseric grinned, yelling, at her side. The *'arif* Alderic gave a great shout. Ash winced at the deep noise from thousands of male throats; a shout she has heard on battlefields, but now – hammering back at her from the walls of the dome – it frightens her; twists in her cold belly along with her fear for her life.

Godfrey whispered in her ear, "I see it now. That's how he got elected. Rhetoric."

The noise began to die down, echoing away from the throne at the centre of the hall. The men of House Leofric continued to stand stolidly under their banners.

The King-Caliph leaned down towards Leofric. "You see, *Amir*? We have, still, the advice of the Stone Golem: that Burgundy shall be destroyed, as an example to all others. The Stone Golem has been our guide and advisor for many generations of King-Caliphs; for more years than we have had the use of your female general. And as for your *second* slave-bastard – she is not necessary to us at all. Dispose of her."

The last cold dots of sleet starred Ash's cheeks, falling from the chasm above her head. The heat of the candles and the cold of the wind from outside set her shivering. A force of emotion grew in her belly; something she knew from experience could turn into paralysing fear, or hypertense readiness to act.

What will they chronicle? *'The accession of King-Caliph Gelimer was celebrated by the execution of a forsworn mercenary—'*

"No!" she spat, aloud. "I'll be damned if I'm dying here as part of someone else's celebrations! Leofric—"

"Be quiet," Leofric grated. He smelled of sweat, now, under his fine robes.

Ash began to whisper, "A household troop, swords, glaives; one exit; one woman unarmed . . ."

Before, it would have been an automatic action, after a decade; to call her voice, for help with tactics. *He cannot stop me asking the Stone Golem questions, he cannot stop it answering me—*

Can he?

The fear-suppresed memory of the sudden silence in her head, riding among the pyramids and sphinxes outside the city, brought a chill fear in her mind. *But I will speak, what other choice is left?*

She bit her lip, began to speak – and stopped as Leofric spoke again.

"Very well. If you will have it so. My Lord King," the elderly lord-*amir* Leofric said decisively, "consider only one thing more, before you give your judgement. If you permit her to make war for you, she will not run. She has nowhere to go."

"I *have* given my – our – judgement!" Gelimer spoke with asperity, then a weak curiosity. "What do you mean, 'she has nowhere to go'?"

"I mean, my Lord King, that next time she cannot run back to her company. They no longer exist. They were massacred on the field of Auxonne, three weeks ago. Dead, to a man. There is no Lion Azure company for her to run to. Ash would be – must be – faithful only to you."

Ash heard the word *massacre*. For a second she could only think, confused, *what does that word mean? It means 'killed'. He can't mean 'killed'. He must be using the wrong word. The word must mean something else.*

In the same split second she heard Godfrey's grunt of pain and realisation behind her; and she spun around to stare at 'Arif Alderic, at Fernando del Guiz, at the lord-*amir* Leofric.

The bearded Visigoth commander, Alderic, had his arms folded, his face giving no sign of any emotion. *He was ordered to tell me nothing, is this why? But he wasn't there, on the field, he wouldn't know if this is true—*

Fernando only appeared bewildered.

And the startled-owl face of Leofric, pale under his pale beard, showed nothing but an undefined strain.

He is fighting for his political life, to keep his powerbase, which is the Stone Golem and the general – and me – he would say anything—

The King-Caliph Gelimer said sulkily, "There has been nothing but cold here since your Christ-forgotten daughter the general went north! We will not bear with this blight, this curse! Not another one. Who knows but she might leave us frozen as the bitter north? No more, Leofric! Execute her today!"

Leofric will say anything.

A voice ripped out of her that she did not recognise, did not know she was going to hear until she found herself screaming.

"What's happened to my company?"

Her chest burned; her throat hurt. Leofric's pale face began to turn to her, Alderic's men moving at the 'arif's snapped command, Gelimer standing up again on the dais.

"What's happened to my company?"

Ash threw herself forward.

Bear-like arms wrapped around her from behind, Godfrey clutching at her, his wet cheek at her cheek. Two of Theudibert's squad ripped her out of the priest's arms, mailed fists efficiently punching her in gut and kidney.

Ash grunted, doubled up, held in their grip.

The floor swam under her gaze: muddied stalks of corn, trodden across mosaics of the Boar and Her litter. Tears rolled out of her eyes, snot from her nostrils; she could only hear the noise she was making, the same noise that all men make during a beating.

"What – happened—?"

A metal-wrapped fist struck the side of her jaw. She jolted back, only supported now by the men who held her, Gaiseric, Fravitta; her knees gone rubbery. The huge features of the Green Christ swam in her vision, above her, as she fell back.

They dropped her face-down on the terracotta floor.

Ash, her hands flat against the freezing tiles, lifted her head and stared up at the lord-*amir* Leofric. His pale, faded eyes met hers; nothing in them but a faint condemnation.

In a moment of complete clarity, Ash thought, He could be lying. He could be saying this to persuade Gelimer to let me live. And he could be saying this to persuade Gelimer to let me live because it's true. I have no way of knowing.

I can ask. I'll *make* it tell me!

Through split, swollen lips, Ash spoke with an instant, precise accuracy: "The field of Auxonne, the twenty-first day of the eighth month, the unit with blue lion on a gold field, what battle casualties?"

Leofric's expression turned to one of irritation. "Gag her, *nazir*."

Two soldiers tried to get hold of her head from behind. Ash let herself fall forward, limp, her body banging shoulders, elbows and knees against the tiled floor. In the few moments as they lifted her up, uselessly boneless, she violently screamed, "Auxonne, unit with a blue lion livery, what casualties?"

The voice sounded sudden and clear in her head:

'Information not available.'

"It can't be! *Tell me!*"

Ash felt herself supported upright, gripped between two men. Someone's hand clamped tight across her broken mouth, and tight across her nose. She sucked for air, the candle-dark hall darkening still more in her vision.

The hand clamped over her face, immovable.

Not able to breathe, not able to speak, she raged through crushed lips into the suffocating glove: "You do know, you *must* know! The Faris will have told you—!"

Nothing like a voice came from her throat.

Sparkles danced across her vision, blotting out the court. No voice sounded in her head. She tried to close her jaws. She felt the scrape of metal rings against her teeth. Copper-tasting blood choked in her throat. She coughed, gagged; the men still held her, tight, as she strained, gasping, suffocating.

I *will* know.

If I can't speak – I'll listen.

She let fear and futility rush through her, forced herself to be calm, to be perfectly still in the midst of bodily pain and mental agony.

She saw nothing but the pattern of veins inside her eyelids, printed on the world outside. Her lungs were fire.

She made a ferocious effort. An act of listening – no passive thing, something violently active. She felt as though she pushed, or pulled; drew up a rope, or swung down with an axe.

I *will* hear. I *will* know.

Her mind *did* something. Like a broken rope, her whole self jolted; or was it a meniscus, that suddenly gave way, and let her through some barrier?

She felt a wrench, in the part of herself that she had always thought of as being shared by her voice, her saint, her guide, her soul.

A grinding roar shook the world.

The walls of the building moved.

A voice exploded through her head:

'NO!'

The solid floor lifted up, under her feet, as if she stood again on the deck of a ship at sea.

V

The mosaic tiles juddered under Ash's feet.

'WHO IS THIS?'

'IT IS ONE—'

'WE PREVAIL—'

She lurched, losing her footing, dizzy; vision filled with yellow sparkles. The solid world shook. Through a roaring noise – in her mind? in the world? – many voices slammed into her head:

'BURGUNDY MUST FALL—'

'YOU ARE NOTHING—'

'YOUR SORROW, NOTHING! YOU ARE NOTHING!'

In that second, Ash realised: Not *a* voice.

Not *a* voice – *voices*. Not *my* voice. Sweet Jesus, I am hearing more than one voice! What's happening to me?

A grating roar jerked the floor under her as a dog shakes a rat.

She got her arms out from under her entangling cloak, slammed an elbow into Theudibert's mail-clad ribs, jarring her shoulder. She clawed at the man's hand across her mouth, breaking her fingernails on the mail of his gauntlets.

'WHAT IS IT THAT SPEAKS TO US?'

'IT IS ONE OF THE SHORT-LIVED, BOUNDED BY TIME.'

'WE ARE NOT SO BOUNDED, SO CONSTRICTED.'

'IS IT THE *MACHINA REI MILITARIS*?'[12]

'IS IT THE ONE WHO LISTENS?'

The hand clamped over her face suddenly dropped away.

Ash dropped to her knees; sucked in a great, unobstructed breath. The smell of the sea filled her nostrils and mouth: salty, fresh, terrifying.

"Who are you? What is this?" She gulped air; screamed: "What happened to my company at Auxonne?"

[12] 'War-machine', 'machine [for making] tactics'.

'AUXONNE FALLS.'

'BURGUNDY FALLS!'

'BURGUNDY MUST FALL.'

'THE GOTHS SHALL ERADICATE EVERY TRACE OF IT FROM THE EARTH. WE WILL – WE *MUST* – MAKE BURGUNDY AS THOUGH IT HAD NEVER BEEN!'

"Shut up!"

Ash shrieked, aware that the noise of voices was in her head, and a greater noise was ripping through the hall: a shattering, cracking roar.

"What's happened to my people? *What?*"

'WE SHALL WE *MUST* – MAKE BURGUNDY AS THOUGH IT HAD NEVER BEEN!'

"Voice! Stone Golem! Saint! Help me!" Ash opened her eyes, not knowing until then that she had screwed them shut in concentration.

Iron candle-trees tipped over, yellow flames arcing across the vast chamber. Men around her sprang to their feet. Smoke filled the air.

Ash fell, sprawling prone. The buckling tiles shuddered under her hands. She scrabbled one foot under her, flexed her injured knee, came halfway up on to her feet.

A man screamed. Fravitta. The Visigoth soldier threw up his arms and vanished from in front of her. The floor split and opened, mosaic tiles rending raggedly along a line of stone flooring. Fravitta rolled down the floor that suddenly *sloped*, vanished into blackness—

The whole world jolted.

She was instantly in the centre of a pushing, jostling crowd; armed men ripping swords from their scabbards, yelling orders; men of law and men of trade reduced to a mass, clawing to force their way back, away from the throne, away towards the archway exits.

Ash spread her arms wide, flattening herself down on the bucking floor. Black cracks spidered across its vast expanse. Heaps of trodden corn tipped up and slid, with benches, with robed men falling to their knees; slid down slabs of mosaic-covered red terracotta tiles that tilted up with a great rending crash—

Something dark flashed across the air in front of her.

Ash had a second to glance up, one arm going automatically over her head. The Mouth of God opened. Blocks of stone, painted with curling leaves, fell away from the circular rim and tumbled down through the empty air.

On the far side from her, a quarter part of the dome shattered and fell out of the roof.

Horrific, harsh male screams sounded; she could not see where the masonry was landing, but she could hear it, great impacts that vibrated the floor, shook the ground—

'WHAT SPEAKS TO US?'

The vibration in her mind and in the world met, became one. Another section of the roof fell. The stars of the south shone between racing clouds.

The tiles on which she stood buckled.

Earthquake, Ash thought, with complete calm. She stood and stepped back, at the same time reaching out and grabbing the sleeve of Godfrey's robe, hauling him towards her. A stench of faeces and urine filled her nostrils: she choked. Buffeted by stampeding soldiers – Theudibert, Saina – and deafened by Alderic shouting, "To Leofric! To *Leofric!*"; and another *'arif* screaming "*Evacuate the hall!*", Ash flashed a shaky grin at Godfrey.

"We're going!" She started to move backwards as she spoke.

A shatter of plaster fell, exploding on the floor not twenty feet away. Two great chunks of masonry tumbled down, seemingly slowly, through the air. Her gut curdled.

"The doctor!" Godfrey bawled.

"No time! Oh shit – get him!" Ash let go of Godfrey's robe. The falling stone struck somewhere to her left, with a noise like cannon-fire. Fragments shrapnelled through the crowds. The sheer mass of people between her and the impact saved her. Stone slashed through flesh. Shrieks and cries deafened her. An eddy of motion pushed her forward.

She braced herself, and knelt down. Men's bodies knocked against her, all but trampling her. A body in a mail hauberk sprawled at her feet. The boy-soldier Gaiseric, moaning, semi-conscious. She ruthlessly rolled Gaiseric over, unbuckling his sword-belt. "*Godfrey!* Move! Go, go, go!"

Kneeling, she lifted her head in time to see Godfrey Maximillian staggering back across the tilted floor, a man's struggling body slung over his shoulder – Annibale Valzacchi, his face all one bloody bruise.

I hear more than one *voice—! Who? What—?*

If they speak again, we'll all die—

Sure-fingered, Ash buckled belt and scabbard around her, settling the sword on her hip as she sprang up, reaching to try and take some of the Italian man's weight from Godfrey. Men struck against her, pushing past.

"We're out of here!" she shouted. "Come on!"

The noise of stonework tearing drowned out her voice.

She has a moment to stare around her, through dust and flying mortar-powder – the throne and dais gone, buried under raw-edged marble cladding and granite masonry. No sign of King-Caliph Gelimer. A glimpse of a white head, far over: Leofric being hustled between two soldiers; Alderic behind him, a flash of his drawn blade in the smoky air.

A carved, curving block of stone crashed to the floor thirty feet ahead of her. Instantly she dropped, pulling Godfrey and the injured doctor down with her.

Stone splinters whistled over her head, which she buried in her arms. Stone fragments ricocheted, stinging her legs.

"Sweet Christ, if I only had a helmet! This is more dangerous than combat!"

"There's no way through!" Godfrey Maximillian bellowed, his big body pressed up close to hers where they lay.

Terrified clawing crowds of men blocked every near archway. The hall had no lights now, no candles, no torches. Red flames flickered up from one wall: embroidered hangings flaming into fire. Someone screamed, above the tumult. Two voices bellowed contradictory orders. Over to the left, blades rose and fell: a squad of soldiers from some *amir*'s household attempting to cut their way through and out into the open.

"We can't stay here! The rest of this place is coming down!"

A cold wind blew dust into her eyes. Ash coughed. The stench of sewerage grew stronger. She nodded once to herself; got up on to hands and knees, and grabbed Annibale Valzacchi's arm again. "Okay, no problem. Follow me."

Any decision is better than no decision.

Valzacchi's dead-weight body jolted as they pulled it over rubble, Godfrey Maximillian crawling beside her, his robes blackened with stone-dust. The chape of her scabbard scraped a groove in the mosaic tiles beside her.

"Here!"

The tilting floor fell away, ahead of her, down into darkness. The crust of tiles had broken like the pastry crust that coffins a pie. She wiped her streaming eyes, let Valzacchi's arm fall, and knelt up, looking for a fallen torch or candle. Nothing but the dim light of fire flickered across the hall.

"What is this?" Godfrey wiped his beard, choked at the foetid air.

"The sewers." Ash, in the stink and faint light, grinned at him. "Sewers, Godfrey! Think! This is *Carthage*. There had to be Roman sewers. We can't go out, we go *down*!"

A creaking groan filled the air. For a moment she was not certain where it came from. She glanced up. Torn clouds raced across a black, starry sky. The moist air stank.

What remained of the dome groaned. She could almost swear she saw, in the light of burning banners, the stone masonry sag inwards.

Ash picked up a fragment of granite the size of her fist and tossed it into the black gap in the floor in front of her. The rock bounded once on the sloping floor and disappeared.

"One – two—"

A splash, from the darkness below.

"That's it! I'm right!"

A straining groan of masonry filled the air. Ash met Godfrey's eyes. The bearded priest smiled at her, with a sudden, surpassing sweetness.

"I only wish this were the first time you'd landed me in the shit!" He reached for Valzacchi, rolling the unconscious man forward, and poised his body at the top of the tilting slab of tiles. "All the saints bless you, Ash. Our Lady be with us!"

Godfrey pushed Valzacchi. The Italian, his face black with blood in the dim light, rolled over and over and vanished into the cleft.

"One . . . two . . ."

Ash heard the heavier splash of a man's body hitting liquid.

Deep, or shallow?

No solid sound, that would indicate rock beneath.

She nodded once, decisively, tucked her scabbarded sword up under her left arm, and crabbed forwards on her hands and knees. "Better not let the bastard drown, I guess – *let's do it!*"

A hollow crackling roar grew louder. Fire. The light flickered redly across the terracotta tiles. The cleft, some six or seven feet across, split the hall each way as far as Ash could see. Nothing penetrated the darkness of the hole: light stopped at the fractured edges of tiles. The faint illumination showed fresh, raw broken stone on the far side of the gap. Nothing of what lay below down in the darkness.

She hesitated.

Water? Rubble? Broken rock? Valzacchi might have landed luckily, the next one might break their neck—

"Ash!" Godfrey whispered. "Can you?"

"I can. Can you?"

"There's a hurt man down there. I knew I could do it, if there was. Follow me!"

She was suddenly looking at his robed rump as Godfrey Maximillian crawled rapidly forward, slid himself sideways over the edge, hung by his hands, and dropped.

Displaced air blew across her face.

Instinct took her. She threw herself forward. The tiled floor battered her. The hilt of the Visigoth sword dug into her unarmoured ribs. The floor suddenly wasn't there. She dropped into void and darkness—

—an immense weight struck the floor of the dome above her. A *boom!* as loud as a siege bombard deafened her. The darkness filled with rock, with flying fragments, with dust. She dropped into something freezing cold, in a shock that nearly drove her heart to stop and battered the air from her lungs.

She clamped her mouth shut. Water stung her eyes. Water enveloped her. She beat her arms, kicked her legs. The water swallowed her down, her lungs straining for air. She thrashed her legs, disorientated; certain for a split second that she would see sunlight to guide her to the surface, that she would splash up under the stone arches of a river bridge in Normandy, or in the valley by the Via Aemilia—

Something sucked her down.

The force of the water swirled her, bodily. Something passed, taking her down with it. A hard shock broke against her thigh, numbing all her right leg; and her right hand would not move. Ferociously, she thrashed her numb arms, kicked; her chest burning; her eyes wide open and stinging in the black water.

Redness shone, to her right and below her.

I am diving, she realised. She twisted her body in the water, kicked herself up towards the light.

Her mouth opened of its own accord. Head back, face slapped with frozen air, she sucked in great sobbing breaths. She kicked again with her legs: found herself standing, crouching on rock, her head just above water, thick with filth; her body numb.

The stench of an open sewer forced her gorge to rise. She straightened, vomiting weakly.

"Godfrey? *Godfrey!*"

No voice.

The noise of fire echoed down from above. Red light limned the edges of the gap. A thin warmth drifted down, and smoke, and she coughed, choking again.

"Godfrey! Valzacchi! Here!"

Her eyes adjusting, she made out that she crouched at one side of a great tubular sewer, built of long red bricks, ancient beyond measure. Where the earthquake had cracked the pipe, water was rushing out between the gaps.

Tumbled blocks of stone choked the rift, not ten feet away from her, piled up in the water and blocking the flow.

Dust settled over her wet face.

She straightened, the weight of her soaking clothes dragging her down. Her cloak was gone; the belt and scabbard still around her waist, but the sword gone out of it. Her left hand was white, her right hand black. She lifted it. Blood trickled over her wrist. She flexed her fingers, sensation returning. Grazes bled. She stooped to feel her leg, below the surface; aching now, but whether with injury or with the cold of the water, it was impossible to tell.

Realisation came to her with the settling dust.

The roof fell in after me.

"Godfrey! It's all right, I'm here! Where are you?"

A noise sounded to her left. She turned her head. Her dark-adjusted eyes showed her a lip of brick – an access path, she realised. She reached out, grabbing the edge, and tried to pull herself up out of the water. The scuffling noise increased. In the light of the fire above, she saw a man. His hands were clamped over his face. He ran off, staggering, into the dark.

"Valzacchi! It's *me*! Ash! Wait!"

Her voice echoed flatly off the brick walls of the sewer tunnel. The man – it must be the doctor, by his build – did not stop running.

"*Godfrey!*" She hauled herself up on her belly on to the platform – a brick ledge a few yards wide, running along the course of the sewer pipe. Grit slashed her palms.

She spat, coughed, spat again; and crawled forward, leaning over the water, staring down.

Flames reflected from the swift-running surface. It stank with a sweetness that choked her. She could see nothing beneath.

An explosion boomed through the tunnel.

She jumped, her head jerking up. Above, the building was still collapsing, broken masonry hitting the floor with a sound of artillery. Warmth fanned down on her face from the flames. In her mind's eye she pictured what had been left of the dome – two-thirds of the roof poised to fall.

"Well, *fuck*." She spoke aloud. "I'm not going without you. Godfrey! Godfrey! It's Ash! I'm here! Godfrey!"

She limped along the brick pathway, quartering the area under the crevasse. The floor of the hall groaned above her. She called out, paused to listen, called again, as loudly as she could.

Nothing.

Wind blew across her wet face, sucked up through the gap to the fire above. Red and gold light shimmered on the running water that carried the Citadel's sewage. She wiped her streaming nose, turned around, moved back; this time leaning out over the water to stare across at the piled broken masonry under the rift.

Something moved.

Without a second's hesitation, Ash sat down on the lip of the platform and slid over into freezing water. She thrust her feet against the side. The impetus swirled stinking water across her face, but she managed, with two gasping strokes, to swim across to the fallen masonry.

Her fingers touched wet cloth.

A body rocked, caught under the shattered bas-relief carving of Saint Peredur. She knotted the cloth around her hand, pulled; couldn't move it. The block stood taller than she did, bedded down into the channel. She braced her foot against it and tugged.

Cloth ripped. The body came away free. She fell back into deep water, out of her depth in mid-pipe; kept her numbed, frozen grip on the wool and swam, dragging him with all her strength, towards the platform. The body floated face down; Godfrey or maybe not Godfrey; about the right build—

Cold limp hands brushed her, under the water. Fravitta?

Splashing water echoed from the broken roof of the pipe. Frenetic, straining, she found rough places in the bricks below the water line. She dug her toes into the holes. She ducked down under the water line; got her shoulders under his chest, and lifted his body up.

For a second she was poised, all his fourteen-stone weight on her shoulders, just above the lip of the platform. Her fingers slipped, losing their cold grip on his thighs. She tilted her body sideways, rolling him; knew as she fell back that she succeeded, got most of his body on to the path; and she surfaced, shaking wet hair out of her face, to see the body slumped and dark on the brickwork above her.

She crawled up and out. Her legs were leaden. Her breath sobbed in her throat. She knelt on all fours.

The soaking robes were no colour, in this gold light; but she knew the curve of this back and shoulder, had looked over at it sleeping in her tent too many times not to know it.

"Godfrey—" She choked, spat filth; thought, *I can't see him breathing, get him over on his side, get the water out of his lungs—*

She touched him.

The body flopped over on to its back.

"Godfrey?"

She knelt up, water streaming off her. Blood and filth soaked her clothes. The stench of the sewer dizzied her. The light from above dimmed, the crackling roar diminishing, the fire finding nothing more to burn than stone.

She reached out a hand.

Godfrey Maximillian's face stared up at the curved, ancient brick. His skin was pink, in the firelight; and where she touched his cheek he felt icy cold. His chestnut beard surrounded lips just parted, as if he smiled.

Saliva and blood gleamed on his teeth. His dark eyes were open and fixed. Godfrey, still recognisably Godfrey; but not half-drowned.

His face ended at his thick, bushy eyebrows. The top of his head, from ear to nape, was splintered white bone in a mess of grey and red flesh.

"Godfrey . . ."

His chest did not move, neither rise nor fall. She reached out and touched her fingertip to the ball of his eye. It gave slightly. No contraction moved his eyelid down. A small, cynical smile crossed her lips: amusement at herself, and how human beings hope. *Am I really thinking, with his head caved in like this, that he might still be alive?*

I've seen and touched dead men often enough to know.

His mouth gaped. A trickle of black water ran out between his lips.

She put her fingers into the unpleasantly warm and jellied mess above his broken forehead. A shard of bone, still covered with hair, gave under her touch.

"Oh, shit." She moved her hand, cupping it around his cold cheek, closing the sagging, bearded jaw. "You weren't meant to die. Not *you*. You don't even carry a sword. Oh, shit, Godfrey . . ."

Careless of his blood, she touched her fingers to his wound again, tracing the dented bone to where it splintered into mess. The calculating part of her mind put a picture before her inner eye of Godfrey falling, broken rock falling; water, impact; heavy masonry shearing off the top of his skull in a fraction of a heartbeat, dead before he could know it. Everything lost in a moment. The man, Godfrey, gone.

He's dead, you're in danger here, go!

You wouldn't think twice, on the battlefield.

Still she knelt beside Godfrey, her hand against his face. His cold, soft skin chilled her to the heart. The line of his brows and his jutting nose, and the fine hairs of his beard, caught the last light from the flames. Water ran off his robes and pooled on the brickwork: he stank, of sewerage.

"It isn't *right*." She stroked his cheek. "You deserve better."

The utter stillness of all dead bodies possessed him. She made an automatic check with her eye – does he have weapons? Shoes? Money? – as she would have done on a stricken field, and suddenly realised what she was doing, and closed her eyes in pain and breathed in, sharply.

"Sweet Christ. . . !"

She rose up on to her haunches, crouching on her toes, staring around in the water-rushing darkness. She could just make out the white glimmer of his flesh.

I would leave any dead man upon the field, if there was still fighting going on; would – I know – abandon Robert Anselm, or Angelotti, or Euen Huw; any of them, because I would have to.

She knows this because she has, in the past, abandoned men she loved as well as she loves them. War has no pity. Time for sorrow and burial afterwards.

Ash suddenly knelt again, thrusting her face close to Godfrey Maximillian, trying to fix every line of his face in her mind: the wood-brown colour of his eyes, the old white scar below his lip, the weathered skin of his cheeks. Useless. His expression, his spirit, gone, it might have been any dead man lying there.

Black clots of blood rested in the splintered bone of his forehead.

"That's enough, Godfrey. Joke's over. Come on, sweetheart, greatheart; come on."

She knew, as she spoke, the reality of his death.

"Godfrey; Godfrey. Let's go home . . ."

Sudden pain constricted her chest. Hot tears rimmed her eyes.

"I can't even bury you. Oh, sweet Jesus, *I can't even bury you*."

She tugged at his sleeve. His body did not move. Dead weight is dead weight;

she would not be able to lift him, here, never mind carry him with her. And into what?

The water rushed and things rustled in the darkness around her. The rift above was a pale, rosy gap. No noise came down from the ruined halls above, now.

Under her feet, the earthquake shuddered again.

"You killed him!"

She was on her feet before she knew it, shrieking up into the darkness, spittle spraying from her mouth in fury:

"You killed him, you killed Godfrey, *you killed him!*"

She had time to think, *When they spoke to me before, there was an earthquake.* And time to think, *'They' didn't kill him. I did. No one is responsible for his death except me. Ah, Godfrey, Godfrey!*

The old brickwork shook under her feet.

I've been a soldier for five or six summers, I must be responsible for the deaths of at least fifty men, why is this different? It's *Godfrey*—

Voices spoke, so loud in her mind that she clamped her hands over her ears:

'WHAT ARE YOU?'

'ARE YOU ENEMY?'

'ARE YOU BURGUNDY?'

Nothing physical could block it. Her lip bled where she bit it. She felt a great vibration, the ancient bricks grinding together beneath her feet, mortar leaking out in dust and powder.

"Not my voice!" she gasped, lungs hurting. "You're not my voice!"

Not *a* voice, but *voices.*

As if something else spoke through the same place in her – not the Stone Golem, not that enemy: but an enemy somehow behind the Visigoth enemy, something huge, multiple, demonic, vast.

'IF YOU ARE BURGUNDY, YOU WILL DIE—'

'—AS IF YOU HAD NEVER BEEN—'

'—SOON, SOON DIE—'

"Fuck off!" Ash roared.

She dropped to her knees. She wrapped her fists in the soaking wet cloth of Godfrey's robes, pulling his body to her. Her face turned up sightless to the dark, she bellowed, "What the fuck do you know about it? What does it matter? He's dead, I can't even have a mass said for him, if I ever had a father it was Godfrey, don't you *understand?*"

As if she could justify herself to unknown, invisible voices, she shouted:

"Don't you understand that *I have to leave him here?*"

She leapt up and ran. One outstretched hand thumped the curved wall of the tunnel, grazing her palm.

She ran, the touch of the wall guiding her, through the darkness and the stone, through after-shocks of earthquake; into the vast and stinking network of sewers under the city, Godfrey Maximillian left behind her, tears blinding her, grief blinding her mind, no voice sounding in her ears or her head; running into darkness and broken ground, until at last she stumbled and came down on her knees, and the world was cold and quiet around her.

"I need to know!" She shouts aloud, in the darkness. "Why is it that Burgundy *matters* so much?"

Neither voice nor voices reply.

Loose papers found inserted between Parts Seven and Eight of ASH: THE LOST HISTORY OF BURGUNDY *(Ratcliff, 2001), British Library*

Message: #177 (Anna Longman)
Subject: Ash
Date: 26/11/00 at 11.20 a.m.
From: Ngrant@

format address deleted
Other details encrypted by
non-discoverable personal key

Anna —

We can't GET to the offshore site. The Mediterranean is stiff with naval helicopters over the area, as well as surface ships. Isobel is off again talking to Minister ▓▓▓▓▓: I don't know what influence she can bring to bear, but she *must* do something!

Forgive me, I haven't even had time to tell you that your scanned-in text of the Vaughan Davies 'Introduction' came through as machine-code. Could you possibly try again in a different format? Did you talk to your bookseller friend, Nadia? Does she have any more information about this house clearance in East Anglia? As far as I am aware, Vaughan Davies died during the last war — this is a son or daughter of his, perhaps?

The way I've been moving around, it's no wonder that you couldn't get the file through to me. I'm back on Isobel's machine now, working on the transferred FRAXINUS files, on the on-going translation, while we wait. I've been slowed down, obviously — you've nearly caught up with what I've completed.

As far as I can discover, no one has cracked Isobel's encryption, so I feel free to tell you that the last two days have been absolutely *bloody*.

While Isobel's team are perfectly amenable people, they're under considerable stress; we spend our time sitting around in the tents — with them running analysis on what data they have been able to collect, and playing around with image-enhancers for the underwater details — Roman shipwrecks, mostly.

Anna, this isn't the MARY ROSE, there may be a whole new level of mediaeval technology down there on the seabed, that we haven't previously suspected the existence of!

Sorry: when I come to splitting infinitives, I know I'm distressed.

But there may be ANYTHING down there. Even — dare I say it — even, perhaps, a fifteenth-century GOLEM-POWERED ship?

Is there anything *you* can do, Anna? Have you any media contacts which could put pressure on the government? We are losing a priceless archaeological opportunity here!

- Pierce

Message: #118 (Pierce Ratcliff)
Subject: Ash, media
Date: 26/11/00 at 05.24 p.m.
From: Longman@

format address Deleted
Other details encypted and
non-recoverably deleted

Pierce —

I think I got the text file through to you this time. Please confirm.

I can't promise anything, but I'm going to a social do tonight, at which will be an old boyfriend who now works for BBC current affairs. I'll do what I can to suggest more notice should be taken of this affair.

This interference is INTOLERABLE. Surely it's got to become a cause celebre?

Hang in there!

— Anna

NOTE: Scanned text 26/11/00: hardcopy printout:- excerpt from Vaughan Davies, ASH: A BIOGRAPHY, 1939: 'Introduction'

Message: #117 (Pierce Ratcliff)
Subject: Vaughan Davies
Date: 26/11/00 at 05.03 p.m.
From: Longman@

format address deleted
Other details encypted
and non-recoverably deleted

indeed I believe it to be founded on the most scientific and rational grounds.

I think that it would be fair to say that no man without a thorough knowledge of the sciences might have conceived of it; and it would be wise for another historian, if he would seek to discount my theory, to have a wide knowledge of both the historian's and the physicist's fields of enquiry.

Let us begin, then, with a theory of history and time.

Conceive, if you will, of a great mountain range, an Alps almost beyond the imagination of man; and let this represent the history of our world. The vast main part of it is nothing but bare rock, for here our history is that of geological aeons, as the planet cools and takes its orbit around the sun. At the most recent edge of the mountains, a little fringe of life appears – the millions of years of prehistoric vegetation, animalcules, amoebæ; developing in a final rapid rush into animals, birds, and at last, man.

We, as we traverse these 'mountains', that here represent our physical existence in the universe, experience our passage as 'time'. Those of my readers familiar with the works of Planck, Einstein, and J. W. Dunne (but I hardly hope for such erudition among my lay readers, the split between science and art being what it is in English

480

culture) will not need me to inform them that time is a human perception of a vastly more complicated process of actual creation.

The world, as it comes about, is shaped by what has gone before. Those mountains behind us prefigure what is to come; the shape of the paths across them determines the paths that we ourselves will take, in what we see as our 'future'. The actions of men in mediaeval times have set us here, on the brink of what may prove to be the world's most destructive conflagration, no less surely than the more recent acts of (let us say) Mr. Chamberlain and Herr Hitler. We are what we follow.

My own theory is, now that I have studied the real evidence implicit in the history of Ash, that the 'mountains' are not as immovable as one might suppose. I hold, in effect, that it is possible that from time to time an earthquake shakes the landscape. It obliterates some things, alters some; rearranges the rock under some of that little fringe of life which inhabits its crevices.

On some occasions, this will be no more than a minor disturbance – a name different here, a girl born in place of a boy, a document lost, a man dead before he otherwise would have been. This is merely a tremor in the great landscape that is time.

However, on at least one occasion a great fracture, as it were, has taken place in what we perceive as our 'past'. Imagine the hands of God reaching down to shake the mountains, as a man might shake a blanket – and then, afterwards, the bedrock remains, but all the shape of the landscape is changed.

This fracture, I believe, takes place for us in the first week of January, 1477.

Burgundy, in our mundane historical records, is a magnificent mediaeval kingdom. Yet it is no more than that. Culturally rich, and militarily powerful, its Dukes spend their time in peregrinatory pilgrimages, building sideshow castles after the manner of Hesdin, and warring against the decaying monarchy of France, and the dukedoms that lie between the north and south of this most disunited of lands, trying to unite a 'Middle Kingdom' stretching from the English Channel to the Mediterranean Sea. Charles, most aggressive and last Duke, dies fighting the Swiss in a foolhardy, freezing bloodbath at Nancy; and the waves of history roll over him, closing over Burgundy. Its territories are divided among those who can get them. There is nothing in the least remarkable about it.

Most historians do not write of it at all, perceiving it perhaps as a backwater, of little importance now. Yet a common thread runs through the small amount of historical writing which there is upon Burgundy. One finds it plainly in Charles Mallory Maximillian, when he writes of a 'lost and golden country'. While for most, Burgundy has been swept from memory, for a few it is a symbol, a sense of loss: a forgotten phoenix.

I have come to see, through my researches, that when we remember this, it is *Ash*'s Burgundy that we remember.

As I have written elsewhere, it is my contention now that the Burgundy of which the 'Ash' biographers tell us did not vanish. It became transformed. The mountainous landscape of the past shifted, and when the earthquake was over, the nameless fragments of her story had alighted in other, different places – in the story of Joan of Arc; of Bosworth Field; the legends of Arthurian chivalry, and the travail of the Chapel Perilous. She has become myth, and Burgundy with her; and yet, these faint traces remain.

It can be clearly seen from this that what was created on 5 January 1477 was not merely a new future. If current thinking is correct, different futures may spring into existence at every moment, and these 'alternate' histories continue in parallel with our own. We will, one day, detect this; upon whatever molecular level such a detection can take place.

No, the vanishing of Burgundy – Ash's Burgundy – shattered the landscape entire. Such a change would bring about a new future, yes, but also a new past.

Thus, Burgundy vanishes. Thus, the tales which we have left – as myth, as legend – remind us that once they were themselves true. They serve to remind us that we ourselves may have begun, only, in 1477. This past that we in the twentieth century excavate is in some senses a lie – it did not exist until after 5 January 1477.

It is my contention, therefore, that these documents which I have translated are authentic; that the various recountings of the life of Ash are genuine. This is history. It is just not our history. Not now.

What we might have been, if not for this temporal fracture, one can only speculate. More tenuous still must be speculation of what we may now become. History is vast, massive, as impervious to alteration as the adamantine bedrock of the Alpine peaks. As I believe it says somewhere in the King James Bible, nations have bowels of brass. Yet, it seems plain to me, the landscape of our past shows clear evidence of this change.

Ash, and her world, are what our world used to be. They are no more. The surging forward edge of time is left to us to inherit, and the future, make what we will of it.

I leave to others the task of determining the exact nature of this temporal change; and whether or not there is a likelihood of another such fracture in the orderly processes of the universe occurring.

I am presently in the process of preparing an addendum to this second edition, in which I plan to detail the vitally important connection between this lost history and our own, present, history. If I am spared from what, it seems in this month of September 1939, will be a conflagration to shake the whole world, then I will publish my findings.

Vaughan Davies
Sible Hedingham, 1939

Message: #180 (Anna Longman)
Subject: Ash/Vaughan Davies
Date: 27/11/00 at 02.19 p.m.
From: Ngrant@   *format address deleted*
                       Other details encrypted by
Anna —   *non-discoverable personal key*

History plays us some small tricks of coincidence. The end of the Introduction names the place where Vaughan Davies was writing at the time. I KNOW Sible Hedingham.

It's a small East Anglian village, close to Castle Hedingham, which itself is the village attached to Hedingham Castle. Hedingham Castle was owned for centuries by the de Vere family – although John de Vere, the thirteenth Earl of Oxford, did not spend much of his time there.

Perhaps this coincidence appealed to Vaughan Davies? Or perhaps (always look for the simplest explanation) his historical researches took him there and he liked it enough to settle down. When you follow up this house clearance, you might have a go at finding out whether the Davies were incomers, or a family that's been in Sible Hedingham since the Domesday Book.

I am unspeakably grateful for this chance to see Vaughan Davies's complete theory. Anna, thank you. I hardly dare ask more of you, but I would give anything to go to the family house and see if there are surviving family; if – more importantly – there are any surviving, unpublished, papers.

That is, I would give anything except the chance of seeing something *concrete* from Visigothic Carthage being gradually uncovered from beneath the decay of centuries – perhaps more relics; perhaps, even, dare I speculate, a ship?

Please, go in my place?

What surprises me most, now that I have read what you scanned in and sent to me, is that I RECOGNISE Vaughan Davies's theory. Although he has couched it as a metaphor, this is plainly a mid-century attempt to describe one of the most up-to-date tenets of particle physics – the anthropic principle that, on the sub-atomic level, it is human consciousness that maintains reality.

I am already contacting the colleagues I have on the net who are knowledgeable about this. Let me give you what I have from experts in the field – bearing in mind it's only my understanding!

It is we, theorists of the anthropic principle state, who collapse the infinite number of possible states in which the basic particles of the universe exist, and make them momentarily concrete – make them real, if you like, instead of probable. Not at the level of individual consciousness, or even the individual subconscious, but by a consciousness down at the level of the species-mind.

That 'deep consciousness' of the human race maintains the present, the past, and the future. However solid the material world appears, it is we who make it so. It is Mind, collapsing the wavefront of Possibility into Reality.

We are not talking about the normal human mind, however – myself, you; the man in the street. You or I could not alter reality! Theoretical physics is talking about something far more like the 'racial unconscious' of Jung. Something buried deep in the autonomic limbic system, something so primitive it is not even individual, a leftover from the prehistoric proto-human primates who lived a group-mind consciousness. No more accessible or controllable by us than the process of photosynthesis is to a plant.

For Vaughan Davies's 'hands of God', therefore, read 'human species subconscious'. If I were a physicist myself, I could make this clearer to you.

Leaving aside all this 'new past as well as new future' nonsense, it is just about possible to make a case in theory for Vaughan Davies's 'fracture' — or at any rate, it is not possible to prove that it could NOT happen. If deep consciousness sustains the universe, one supposes deep consciousness might change the universe. And then the leftovers of the change — like a written-over file leaving bits of data in the system (you see how cognisant I am becoming of computers!) — would remain, to puzzle historians like Vaughan Davies.

Of course, not being able to prove something cannot happen is very far from proving it CAN happen; and Davies's theory remains one with the esoteric speculations of some of our modern physicists. But it has a certain beauty as a theory, don't you think?

I am very interested to know if he wrote anything between the publication of ASH: A BIOGRAPHY in 1939 and his death later in the war. Is there news?

— Pierce

Message:	#124 (Pierce Ratcliff)
Subject:	Vaughan Davies
Date:	27/11/00 at 03.52 p.m.
From:	Longman@

format address deleted
other details encrypted and non-recoverably deleted

Pierce —

Okay, okay. I'll go to Sible Hedingham. Nadia says she's going down again anyway.

I'm getting moderate media interest. I think it will depend on whether it's decided that the political-military problems you're having on-site make you too hot to handle, or whether it's those same problems that make you interesting and a probable media 'cause'.

Jonathan Stanley's handling that. I'm trying to keep him on general grounds. Even though your archaeologist found Troy where a poem said it was, I don't really want to have to explain that the manuscripts you've translated are in any way questionable. I'll handle that when I HAVE to.

The Vaughan Davies stuff is fascinating, isn't it? Is this guy crazy or WHAT? I thought it was only the present moment that could

be made into reality, and so become history? How could there be
two histories of the world? I don't get it. But then, I'm no
scientist, am I?

It's okay for you, Pierce, you can play around with theories, but
I have to work for a living! One history is more than enough. It's
going to take some neat handling by me to get this all to go right.
When you finally meet him, for God's sake don't go telling Jon
Stanley about all this! I can do without him telling me one of my
authors is a mad professor.

— Love, Anna

Message: #202 (Anna Longman)
Subject: Ash
Date: 01/12/00 at 01.11 p.m.
From: Ngrant@   *format address deleted*
                             other details encrypted by
                             non-discoverable personal key
Anna —

I don't know how to tell you what has happened.
I'm handing you over to Isobel.

Message: #203 (Anna Longman)
Subject: Ash
Date: 01/12/00 at 02.10 p.m.
From: Ngrant@   *format address deleted*
                             other details encrypted by
                             non-discoverable personal key
Ms Longman —

At Pierce's request, I am conveying to you some very unfortunate
news. I regret that it will have an effect on the publication of
his book, as well as on our expedition here.

As you know, the great 'find' of this dig has been the Visigothic
'messenger-golems' — one intact and complete, one in remnants.
Because the fragmentary golem was already in pieces, I chose that
one to be sent off to be tested.

Among the tests we do is C14 radio carbon-dating. When it comes
to marble and other forms of stone, dating an object by this method
is impossible — one merely gets the age of the rock before it was
carved into an object. However, the 'messenger-golems' also
include several metallic parts. The broken one had sections of a
ball-joint for one arm.

I have now had the radio-carbon dating report back on this bronze
joint. I have also doubled-checked with our archaeometallurgist
here.

485

Bronze is an alloy of copper, tin and lead. These metals are smelted together and then cast. During the casting process, when the metal is poured, organic impurities can become mixed in; and a study of the crystalline structure of this joint, when shaved down, showed that just this sort of impurity *had* become incorporated into the structure.

When subjected to radio-carbon dating, these organic fragments gave an extremely odd reading. The tests were repeated, and repeated again.

The lab report, which arrived today, states that in their opinion, the readings show that the organic fragments in the metal contain the same levels of background radiation and pollution as one would expect to find in something which has been growing today.

It seems that the metal for the joints and hinges of the 'messenger-golems' must have been cast during a period of much higher radiation and atmospheric pollution than existed in the fifteenth-century — indeed, a high enough level to make me certain the metal was cast during the last forty years (post-Hiroshima and atomic testing).

I am left with only one possible conclusion. These 'messenger-golems' were not made in the 1400s. They were made recently, possibly very recently. Certainly after the date that, as Pierce tells me, Charles Wade brought the 'Fraxinus' document back to Snowshill Manor.

Frankly, these 'golems' are modern fakes.

I have had little enough time myself to take in this news. Pierce is shattered. You realise that one of the reasons for the extreme security of the dig is that such things do happen in archaeology — fakes are a constant problem — and I never make any announcements until I am sure.

I realise that this leaves Pierce with documents that have been re-classified as fiction, rather than history, that now have no significant archaeological evidence to support them.

I expect that you will want to consider this news before you make any decisions about publication of Pierce's translations.

Colonel ████████ has authorised offshore diving to resume at first light tomorrow. Despite our problems, I am reluctant to lose any opportunity, given the political instability of the region. I am no longer sure if the images from the ROV cameras are relevant, but of course we shall be following up this area of investigation.

We shall therefore be leaving for the ship at daybreak. I think, if you could contact Pierce, he would appreciate a kind word.

I am so sorry. I wish I could have brought you better news.

— Isobel Napier-Grant

```
-------------------------------------------------------------------

Message:    #137 (Pierce Ratcliff)
Subject:    Ash / archaeology
Date:       01/12/00 at 02.31 p.m.
From:       Longman@
```

format address deleted
other details encrypted
and non-recoverably deleted

Pierce, Isobel—

ARE YOU SURE?

— Anna

PART EIGHT

10 September–11 September AD 1476

'Ferae Natura Machinae'

I

The darkness went on for what seemed hours.

Ash had no way of judging the time. The world was anything she could feel with her fingertips, at arm's length, in cold blackness. Brick, mostly; and damp nitre. Mud or shit underfoot. She found the darkness reassuring. No light must mean no breaks in the sewer-covering: therefore these particular brick passages could be safe to traverse.

If there are no pits. No shafts.

If I were with Roberto, now, we'd get drunk. Talk about Godfrey. I'd get so drunk I couldn't stand up. I'd tell him Godfrey was always a damn peasant at heart. One time I saw him *call boar*. Wild boar, out of the forest! And they came. And I forget how many times he's listened to me when I needed to talk to someone who wasn't one of my officers—

Not a father. Who needs fathers? Leofric calls himself a father. A friend. Brother. No, more than a brother; what would it have cost me to love you, just once? Just *once*?

Falling-down drunk. And then we'd go off and get into a fight somewhere. Jesus, what's Roberto going to say when I tell him this?

If Robert's alive.

The sound of water running deep and smooth ahead of her made her slow her steps. The wall under her fingertips turned a corner. She paced slowly forward around it, putting her feet down toes-first, testing for broken ground.

The sewers went on.

I shouldn't leave him.

I can't do anything else.

I could ask my voice for the way out of here— no, it doesn't know places, it only solves problems—

Can I even talk to the Stone Golem, now?

Other – voices?

What are they?

Does Leofric know? Did the Caliph know? Does anybody know? Christ, I want to talk to Leofric! *Did anybody know anything about this before today?*

I shouldn't have left him.

Pale light made geometric shapes on her retinas.

Ash stopped, her bleeding hand still touching brickwork. The light was strong enough to show her what planes and surfaces it illuminated. A junction of tunnels. Flat walls, curving walls, sweeping up to a cracked roof that let in faint light. Running water. Walkways. Rubble.

This could go on for miles. And it could all come down on my head any second. The earthquake must have shaken a lot of stonework loose.

A noise.

'Valzacchi?' she called, softly.

Nothing.

Ash raised her head. Above, four or five stones had fallen from the tunnel roof. Enough to let through a faint glow of Greek Fire. She thought she heard a confused noise, this time outside, but it faded as she strained to listen.

How long before the rest of this part of the sewer collapses?

Time to be somewhere else.

Unexpected grief bit at her. Her eyes flooded over with tears. She wiped them on her sleeve. She had a moment of knowing, beyond doubt, her responsibility. *And I can never say to you that I'm sorry you came here because of me.*

Ash pressed her filthy hands over her face, once. She raised her head. Grief will come, she knows, in seconds and minutes when she does not expect it; will bite harder when this shock fades and she accepts into herself the knowledge that – when the reasons are found, the responsibilities accepted, her confession made – it does not matter. It does not change the fact that she will never speak to Godfrey again; he will never answer her.

She whispered, "Goodnight, priest."

Something white and moving caught her eye.

Her hand flashed to her belt and met only the empty scabbard. She flattened her back against the tunnel wall, staring ahead.

Something small and white scuttled across the walkway and off into the darkness.

Ash stepped cautiously forward. Her sandals grated on brick. Two more white things darted off out of her way in a low-slung scuttling run.

"Rats," Ash whispered. "*White* rats?"

If the earthquake breached the sewers built under the Citadel's streets, could it have breached the walls of the houses cut down *into* the rock? Am I near House Leofric?

Maybe.

Maybe not. If they are his freak rats, that doesn't necessarily mean I'm close. Rats can move a long way; it's got to have been an hour since the quake, maybe more.

"Hey, ratsies . . ." Ash chirruped softly. Nothing moved in the dim light.

A thought came into her mind, of what rats might feed on, down here. She glanced back, into darkness.

"Godfrey . . ."

She began to edge around the corner of the junction, treading silently, unwilling to disturb the air and the cracked brickwork shell above her head. She stopped. She looked back.

"You won't approve, Godfrey . . . You always said I was a heathen. I am. I don't believe in mercy and forgiveness. I believe in revenge – I'm going to make somebody *hurt* because you're dead."

A distant chittering echoed from further down the sewer.

The sweet stench of shit grew worse. Ash started to walk on, with her wet sleeve clamped over her nose. She had nothing left to vomit up. Water flowed sluggish and silent below the brick walkway.

The last light from the cracked roof caught on an irregularity in the wall. She reached out, touched brick, touched darkness – touched emptiness.

With her fingertips, she traced out a long brick slot, as tall as her two hands together. She tentatively reached in. Her knuckles barked on bricks and mortar, no great distance in front of her. Frowning, she slid the flat of her hand up the wall in front of her, and her palm slipped into air, into another slot. And above that, another.

The lower edge of each slot had a lip, made of brick, perhaps two inches thick, and three inches high. Strong enough to bear a man's grip and a man's weight.

Gladness flooded her. She breathed in, unawares; coughed at the sweet stench, and laughed aloud, her eyes running. She slid her hands up and down the surface of the wall, to be sure there was no mistake. As high over her head as she could reach, the brickwork had slots built into it. And it was not a curving wall, not here at this junction of tunnels: the wall above her went straight up.

Ash reached up and put her hands into one slot, her foot into another, and began to climb the wall.

The first fifteen or twenty feet were easy enough. Her arms began to ache. She risked leaning back to look up. The broken part of the pipe might be fifty or sixty feet above her, still.

She reached for the next slot in the brickwork 'ladder' and hauled her sopping weight upwards. Distracting herself from the physical, she let her mind ramble:

I think the 'voices' are speaking *through* the machine, through the Stone Golem. They come into my spirit the same way. But they're not like my voice.

Does anybody know this? Does the Faris know? How long have they been doing it? Do they tell her things, through the Golem – do they pretend to *be* the Stone Golem? Maybe nobody knows. Until now.

Suppose that the *machina rei militaris* has been in House Leofric for two centuries, suppose that these – others – have been speaking through it? Or are they a part of it? A part that Leofric doesn't know about? But does he?

Ash resolutely kept the part of her mind that listened, quiet.

She reached up above her head, biceps aching, and hauled herself up another rung. Her thighs and calves burned. She absently glanced down and saw, past the length of her body, how far up she was.

Forty feet on to brick, or into a sewer, is high enough to kill.

She pushed herself on, upwards.

And supposing it's these 'voices' that hate Burgundy? Why *Burgundy*? Why not France, Italy, the empire of the Turks? I know the Burgundian Dukes are the richest, but this isn't about wealth; they want the land burned black and sown with salt – *why?*

Ash rested, leaning her forehead against the brickwork. It felt chill. Mortar grated dustily.

She had to twist around now to see the broken part of the roof, above her and to the side. A stone lip was cutting her off from it. The steps led up – she raised her head – into a narrow roof shaft. Within it, darkness. No way of telling what might be up there.

She clung, puzzling, shivering in her wet and filthy clothes. She abruptly smiled into the darkness.

That's *it*. Of *course*. *That's* why the Visigoths have attacked Burgundy, not the Turks! The Turks are a bigger threat, but the machine's been *telling* them that its solution is for them to attack Burgundy. That has to be it! But it isn't the Stone Golem, it's the voices!

Ash clenched her fingers on the rung. Her muscles jabbed at her with cramps. She dug her toe deep into the rung and flexed her leg, straightening it; reaching with her other foot for a rung higher up.

If some other *amir*'s family has created another Stone Golem . . . that would be known! Even Leofric never tried to keep it secret. Just secure. But if it isn't another clay machine, what is it – what are they?

Whatever they are, they know about me.

She moved into darkness, head and shoulders and the rest of her body, as she climbed up into the shaft. If it leads nowhere I shall just have to climb down again, she thought, and then: So they know about me now. Good. *Good.*

I've lost my people. I've lost Godfrey. I've had enough.

"You better damn well hope you know me," Ash whispered. "Because I'm going to find out about *you*. If you're machines, I'll break you. If you're human, I'll gut you. Messing with me may just be the stupidest thing you ever did."

She smiled in the darkness at her own bravado. Her fingers, reaching up, touched brick and metal. She stopped.

Feeling carefully, she touched dusty stone, directly above her head, and a rim of cold iron. Within the rim, more metal – a circular iron plate, about a yard across.

Ash settled her feet as far as they would go into the brick rungs she stood on. She gripped a rung with her left hand. With her right hand flat against the metal, she pushed up.

She expected resistance, was thinking *shit I need to get my back under this and I can't* and it took her by surprise as the metal cover flew up and back and off. A bolt of cold air hit her in the face. Greek Fire blazed, dazzling her. She fell forward, mashing her face against the brick ladder, almost losing her hold.

"Son of a bitch!"

She shoved her body up two more steps and groped outside, for something to haul herself out by. Nothing. Her fingertips scraped stone. The port was too wide for her to brace herself across it.

In one movement, she got both feet up to a higher rung, let go with her left hand, straightened her legs and pushed herself up, and dived heavily forward.

Momentum carried her: she sprawled out across a road, her thighs and the rest of her legs dangling over the abyss but her body safe. She put her palms down flat, and wriggled her body forward, and rolled, jack-knifing; not stopping the roll until she was a good ten feet away from the open sewer-port.

In a narrow alley between windowless buildings.

One glass of Greek Fire burned, twenty yards away. The others, closer to her, were smashed. A few yards down the alley, the paving stones ominously sagged.

Her night-adjusted eyes ran with water. She shook her head, getting up on to her hands and feet; the wet wool of her hose and doublet clinging to her, rapidly freezing in the black air.

I'm still in the Citadel: where—?

The wind changed direction. She rose, straining her ears.

A confused noise of shouting and screams came to her. Rumbling cart-wheels. Metal striking metal. A fight, a chaos; but nothing to tell her where, within the Citadel or outside the walls in Carthage itself – the wind blew at her back again, and she lost the sounds.

But I'm out!

Ash drew a deep breath, choked at her own stench, and looked around herself. Bare stone walls confronted her, either side of the narrow street. They went up high enough that she had no chance of seeing a landmark, no guess at which way might be the dome, which way the walls. She sniffed. The smell of the harbour, yes, but something else . . .

Smoke.

A smell of burning drifted across the narrow street. Ash looked up and down: cross-streets at either end. The subsidence to her left should be avoided. She moved off to the right.

A pang went through her, of sorrow and revulsion. Something lay ahead on the cobbles, at the edge of the pool of light cast by the remaining lamp.

A man's body, slumped – with the same stillness that Godfrey has, dead.

She put grief out of her mind quite deliberately. "It'll keep."

She strode up the alley, moving quickly to keep warm. Her sandals left smears of filth on the cobbles. She went towards the prone body that lay up against the featureless wall. *Rob it of money if a civilian; or weapons, if a soldier—*

The light was not good. The Greek Fire above her dimmed in its glass bowl. Ash knelt, reaching out to roll the prone body over on to its back. In quick succession she noted, as her hands hauled at his cold dead weight, that it was a man, wearing hose, and livery tabard, and steel sallet; his belt already gone, his sword looted, his dagger missing—

"Sweet Christ."

Ash slid down into a sitting position, her knees given way. She leaned forward and threw the dead man's arms back, exposing his chest. All his throat and shoulders were a mass of coagulated blood. A bright livery tabard was tied on over his mail shirt, ties knotted at his waist, and some dark device on the cloth—

She unbuckled the strap of the man's sallet, hauling it off his head, her hands coming away bloody from the crossbow bolt that stood up out of his throat. A sallet, with a visor, and an articulated tail: not a Visigoth helmet. *Made in Augsburg, in the Germanies – home!*

Ash jammed the padded helmet on her head, buckled the strap, reached for the man's ankles, and dragged him bodily over the cobbles, under the dimming light.

He sprawled with his arms above his head, his head turned to one side. A young man, fifteen or sixteen, with light hair and the beginnings of a beard; she has seen him somewhere, knows him, knows the dead face if not his name—

Under the light, she stares down at his livery, clearly visible now.

A gold livery tabard.

On the breast, in blue, a lion.

The livery of the Lion Azure. Her company livery.

II

Ash unknotted the ties with wet, frozen fingers, and hauled the livery tabard off the boy's body. The neck of the garment was made wide enough to accommodate a helmet: she threw it on over her head. Tying its cords at her waist, she stared down at him. "Michael? Matthew?"

He had stopped bleeding. His body did not feel rigid. Cold in this outdoor city, but not stiff. No rigor, yet.

She smoothed the dyed linen cloth down over her unprotected belly. No way to get a mail shirt off a casualty alone, mail is hard enough to get off when you're living: the linked metal sucks on to the body. She tugged the mail mittens from his hands – too large, but she can live with that – and the boots from his feet.

Stripped, he seemed pathetic; with the long bones and fat face of young manhood. She hauled his boots on.

"*Mark*. Mark Tydder," she said aloud. She reached across, drawing a cross on his cold brow. "You're – you were one of Euen's lance, weren't you?"

You're not here on your own.

How many more people are going to die because somebody brought me to Carthage?

Ash stood up and stared around her at the cold dark street. I can't waste time wondering *if there's one, are there more; who's alive, who's dead?* I just have to find them and get on with it.

She bent and kissed the soiled, dead body of Mark Tydder on the forehead, and folded his arms across his chest.

"I'll send someone back for you if I can."

The Greek Fire above her guttered and gave out. She waited a moment as her eyes adjusted to the dark. The shapes of windowless walls rose above her, and, in the gap between roofs, unrecognisable constellations of stars in the icy, windy sky – *an hour or less before sunset* her mind automatically calculated.

She moved off down the alley. Here, no damage could be seen from the quake. At the first cross-street, she turned left; and at the next, right.

Buildings spilled rubble across the road. She slowed, picking her way. Above her head, splintered beams jutted out. The further down the alley she went, the more she was picking her way over high piles of dressed stone, fractured mosaics, broken furniture – a dead horse—

No dead people. No wounded. Someone has been through this area after the quake – or it was deserted, everyone up at the palace?

Climbing over a fallen pillar, boots skidding on frost-slick stone, she came to what had been another road junction. Buildings on the far side still stood. Immense cracks, taller than she was, spiderwebbed their walls. She halted, lifting up her helmet and listening intently.

There was a deafening *boom!* A sound loud enough to burst her eardrums blasted the air. Rubble shifted and slid.

"*Shit!*" Ash grinned, ferociously, her head ringing. She swung around to her left. With no hesitation, she scrambled down and trotted as fast as she could in the dark, in the direction of the noise. "That's guns!"

A swivel gun or a hook gun. Light cannon? She skidded across split cobbles, scrambling down the dark narrow street. *Not Goths! That's us!*

Clouds slid over the sky. The faint starlight dimmed to nothing, leaving her between windowless houses cracked from foundations to roof. She saw little rubble here. Heedless, in almost complete blackness, she loped on down the alley, arms stretched out in front of her to hit obstacles first.

Boom!

"Got you." Ash halted. The slick soles of the boots let her feel the contours of the cobblestones under her feet: the ground sloping slightly down now. She stared into the absolute darkness. Air blew into her face. *An open square? An area where the quake has demolished every house?* Trailing leaves brushed her face – she flinched – *some kind of creeper?*

Lanterns.

The yellow light might have been just flecks in her vision, but a sharp angle cut across it: a wall. She made out that she was standing off-set from an alley leading out of this square, the buildings on the left-hand side of it collapsed in on themselves, but on the right-hand side, still standing. Towards the far end of the alley, someone was holding a lantern.

The dry, acrid, infinitely familiar smell of powder hit her nostrils.

Ash did not know that her teeth were bared, grinning fiercely into the dark. One hand closed, by itself, seeking the hilt of a sword which did not hang from her belt.

She filled her lungs with the cold, gunpowder-air:

"Hey! ASSHOLES! DON'T SHOOT!"

The lantern jerked. An explosive *spang!* blew fragments of clay facing down on her head. A crossbow bolt: shot high and wide, hitting the right-hand wall somewhere above her.

"I SAID *DON'T* FUCKING SHOOT ME YOU ASSHOLES!"

A cautious voice called, "Mark? That you?"

A second voice cut in: "That's not Tydder. Who goes there?"

"Who do you fucking think?" Ash bawled, still in the Franco-Flemish dialect that was the common patois of the camp.

A silent pause – which brought Ash's heart up into her mouth, dried out her

497

chest with breathlessness, fear, hope – and then the second voice, rather small, and distinctively Welsh, called uncertainly, ". . . Boss?"

"Euen?"

"*Boss!*"

"I'm coming in! Don't be so fucking trigger-happy!"

She trotted up the alley towards the light. Six or seven men with weapons filled the width of it: men in European-style steel helmets, and with razor-edged bills, and swords, and two with crossbows, one frantically winching as if to prove he had not fired his bolt.

"Negligent discharge," Ash grinned in passing, and then: "Euen!" She reached out, grabbing the small dark man's hands and wringing them. "Thomas – Michel – Bartolemey—"

"Jesus fucking Christ," Euen Huw said reverently.

"Boss!" Euen's red-haired 2IC, Thomas Morgan, crossed himself, with the hand that did not hold a spanned crossbow.

"*Shit*, man!" The others – tall, broad-shouldered men with hard, hunger-marked faces – began to grin at her and make comments among themselves. They were standing among neatly piled heaps of wine-casks, velvet gowns, and heavy jute sacks, Ash noted; their shining faces turning to her, plain wonder on their expressions. "Would you ever fucking *believe* it!"

"It's me," Ash said, turning back to the wiry, dark Welshman.

Euen Huw was not a particularly prepossessing sight: his jack was faded, salt-stained under the intermittent light from the pierced iron lantern; and an old blackened bandage was wrapped around his left hand and wrist. His other hand grasped the hilt of a riding sword, a ridiculous forty inches of razor-sharpened steel.

"Christ, I might have known it, boss," Euen said. "Straight out of the middle of a fucking earthquake, you come. Right. What do we do now?"

"Why are you asking me?" Ash inquired wryly, surveying their dirty larcenous faces. "Ah, that's right – I'm the boss! I knew there was some reason."

"Where you *been*, boss?" Michel, the other crossbowman, asked.

"In a Visigoth nick. But." Ash grinned. "Here I am. Okay, this ain't a fucking social banquet. Tell me. Who's here, why are we here, and what the fuck is going on?"

Boom!

That gun was close enough that the ground twanged under her feet. Ash fingered her ear with a pained expression, watching them watch her do it, seeing them grin; judging how much strain was also in their expressions, how most of them were losing the momentary amazement of her presence, falling back into the old habit of being commanded by her: *this is Ash, she'll tell us what to do, get us through this.* In the adrenalin-rush of combat, they are not even surprised: impossible things happen all the time in battle.

In the middle of the heart-city of the Visigoth Empire, surrounded by enemy people and enemy troops—

"What dumb fuck brought you guys here?"

The crossbowman, Michel, shoved a suspicious sack aside with his boot. "Mad Jack Oxford, boss."

"Oh my God. Who's with the guns?"

"Master Captain Angelotti," Euen Huw answered. "He's up there trying to bust into this shit-rich lord-*amir*'s house – 'course, *his* house couldn't fall down like the rest of them, could it? No chance!"

"*Which* lord-*amir* – no, tell me later. What are you motherfuckers doing out here?"

"We're a picket, boss, wouldn't you know it? Waiting for all them little ragheads to turn up and try to mince us into the ground."

His sardonic sarcasm got answering grins from his lance. Ash let herself chuckle.

"I'm just sorry for the Goths! Okay, stick to it. And watch it! You're in the middle of an overturned hive here."

"Don't we know it!" Euen Huw grinned.

"Mark Tydder's body's down one of those alleys, you – Michel – go scout it; then you and another man bring him back, if the road's clear. We don't leave our own—"

A sudden image bit into her mind. Godfrey, his green robe black with water and filth, and the white splinters of bone above his tanned brow. Her eyes stung.

"—if we can help it. If any troops show up, report to me fucking fast. I'll be with HQ."

Euen Huw said cheerfully, "Boss, you *are* HQ."

"Not until I know what the hell Oxford thinks he's doing! You." She indicated the redheaded lance-second, Thomas Morgan. "Lead me to Oxford and Angelotti. And you guys here, *close that fucking lantern up!* I could see you a mile off! None of you have got the brains of a field mouse, but that's no reason you shouldn't make it home – just follow my orders! Okay, let's go! Move it!"

As she moved off, Thomas Morgan's tall broad back blocking the hastily closed lantern, she heard a man mutter, "Shit, lil' scarface is back . . ."

"Too fucking right," Ash growled.

They're alive!

With the lantern gone and the cloud-cover thick, it was impossible to see anything but blackness, but there were voices ahead of her now, and the shouts of men sponging gun-breeches and loading them: she tucked her mittened fingers under the back of Thomas Morgan's belt and followed his uncertain progress as he tapped his way down the cobbles with the shaft of his bill, the wood knocking against spilled masonry and rubble.

A coldness crept into her belly. Her mind put nightmare pictures on the darkness in front of her: these men, men that she knows, trapped in these streets, trapped inside the middle of a walled city – a walled city *within* a walled city – and all of Carthage outside, the *amirs*, their household troops, the King-Caliph's army, the merchants and the workers and the slaves, each an enemy—

What fucking dangerous *lunatic* brought them here? Ash wondered bleakly, furiously. How do I get them *out* of here?

And do what we have to do, first?

Thomas Morgan stumbled, muttered something obscene, clattered his bill-shaft against a splintered masonry block, and stepped to the right. She kept her footing and followed.

How *many* of my guys are here now? *What the fuck is Oxford thinking of?* Just because we're mercenaries doesn't mean you can stick us out as a forlorn hope and leave us to die – well, maybe *he* thinks it does – I thought better of him—

The quality of the air changed.

Glancing up, Ash saw how the clouds, shredding, opened on bright stars: the constellations of the Eternal Twilight. Quickly she lowered her gaze. Her night vision took enough from the starlight to let her see where she stepped, drop her hand from Thomas Morgan's belt, and focus on the corner of the blank-walled house in front of her.

Way down on her right, ahead, the building's massive iron-banded main gates hung splintered and blasted – cannon-fire, not quake damage. Gun-crews crowded the corner here, behind a cluster of pavises.[1] Two swivel guns[2] had their supporting spikes jammed down into the dirt where the quake had split the cobblestones. Men, swearing bitterly and shouting, were trying to shoot fifty yards cross-wise down the alley and blast the gates open – no room to get cannon up close, opposite the House gate, not in an alley no more than ten feet wide.

More men came running in, pavises going up, looted wooden doors piled as makeshift defences. A silent flight of bolts impacted ten yards from her feet, blasting up splinters of stone. Antonio Angelotti's voice – *Angeli!* Ash grinned, delighted at the recognition, his presence – screamed a beautiful obscenity. On the House roof, men briefly moved: shooting down: Visigoths, Visigoth House guards, this house—

Ash felt a sudden stab of memory. Genuine? Illusory? *I think we've come north, I've come all the way back from the King-Caliph's palace, this is how I was brought into Leofric's house – this* is *House Leofric—!*

Realisation hit her.

Oh shit. I know why Oxford's here.

He's doing what I said *I* was going to do.

He's here for the Stone Golem.

Thomas Morgan bellowed, "Here they are, boss," in a tone that suddenly held doubt.

Ash trotted past him, into the alley that dead-ended on her right, lit with lanterns and torches; all filled up with men and their shouting, men running, two more swivel guns commanding the alley directly in front of House Leofric, having their breeches frantically sponged and shot rammed home. A tall, fair-haired man in Italian doublet and demi-gown crouched by the gun-crews, shouting – Angelotti – and a dozen other familiar faces: the deacon Richard Faversham, a skinny blond man with his hands wrist-deep in a sack of bandages, behind a big pavise and two billmen – Florian de Lacey, Floria del

---

[1] Crossbowmen used these wooden shields as mobile protective defences, shooting from behind them. Pavises were often three to four feet high. They would be supported upright by stakes, or by another man.

[2] Two-man portable weapons, between the size of a hackbut and a small cannon.

Guiz – and beyond her a massive cluster of men in breastplates and leg-harness, with maces and arquebuses, and Lion livery – and a young corn-haired knight in half-armour, Dickon de Vere; and John de Vere himself taking off his sallet to wipe his forehead—

She has a split-second to study them while they, busy in ordered chaos, ignore her arrival. It puts a curdle of panic into her bowels: to be facing men, soldiers, who ignore her as if she isn't there – this is the commander's dread of authority (that spider-thread) disappearing like mist. Who is she, that anyone should do what she says?

The person who persuaded them off their farms and into this business. Into many wet mornings on grassy blood-soaked hills, many nights in burning towns sprawling with mutilated bodies. The person whom they will think can get them through this alive.

Two or three nearer heads turned, Thomas Morgan's visible presence penetrating their attention. One of the gunners put down his worm, staring; another man dropped the breech of the second gun. Three Flemish billmen stopped talking and gaped.

Antonio Angelotti said a foul word in utterly musical Italian.

Floria slowly stood up, her face in the flaring light broken with hope, with amazement, with a sudden wrenching fear.

"Get down in *cover*!" Ash bawled at her.

Ash nevertheless remained in the open. She reached up and unbuckled the strap of Mark Tydder's sallet, easing it off her vulnerable head. Her cropped silver hair stood up in spikes, sweaty despite the freezing air. *Even with the risk of some bastard getting me with a composite bow, they have to see me.*

"*Fuck*," someone said, awe-struck.

Ash tucked the sallet under her arm. The metal was freezing, even through the leather palms of her mittens. Lantern light fell on the livery tabard that she wore, black and stiff with dried blood at the throat, the Lion Azure plain across her chest. Her hands, muffled in too-large mail mittens, and her feet in too-large boots, gave her the appearance of a child in adult clothing. A tall skinny child with three scars standing out dark against the skin of her frozen white cheeks.

And then she moved, put her other fist on her hip, to be recognisably their Ash, Captain Ash, condottiere: a woman unlawfully dressed as a man, in doublet and hose, hair cut short as a serf's, face gaunt with hunger and pain, but with a shining grin that lit up her eyes.

"It's the *boss*!" Thomas Morgan called, his voice shaky.

"ASH!"

She couldn't tell who shouted: they were all moving by then, careless of the armed household a few yards away; men running, shouting the news to their lance-mates, Angelotti reaching her first, tears streaming down his powder-black features, throwing his arms around her; Floria shoving him bodily aside to grab her arms, stare into her face, all questions; and then a throng: Henri de Treville, Ludmilla Rostovnaya, Dickon Stour, Pieter Tyrrell, and Thomas Rochester with the Lion banner, Geraint ab Morgan in deep-voiced Welsh amazement: all piling on to her, mailed hands thumping her back, voices shouting, everyone too loud for her to make herself heard:

"Shit, look what happens to you motherfuckers when I leave you alone for five minutes! Where the fuck is Roberto?"

"Dijon!" Floria, a tall dirty-faced man to all appearances, grabbed at her arm. "*Is* it you? You look older. Your hair— You've been prisoner here? You escaped?" And at Ash's nod of agreement: "Our Lady! You didn't have to walk back in on this. You could have walked away. One man could make it out of here alone—"

She's right. Ash felt a startled realisation. *I stood a much better chance of slipping away alone. I didn't have to come up this street and put myself in the middle of a – very small – bunch of armed lunatics.*

But it didn't occur to me not to.

There was no regret in her mind, not even wonder; all the amazement was on Floria's face. The disguised woman surgeon touched Ash's cold, scarred cheek. "Why would I expect anything different? Welcome to the madhouse!"

I'll tell her about Godfrey later, Ash decided; and lifted her head and looked around at the circle of faces, the men sweating despite the chill air, weapons unsheathed, two men further away climbing down from a high wall.

"Get me my officers!"

"Yes, boss!" Morgan ran.

We're in one of the alleys that run around three sides of House Leofric to the end of the cliff, Ash thought with a minute and detailed realisation. *The fourth side is the Citadel wall itself.*

She looked down the cross-alley.

I am looking north. To the Citadel wall. Over that wall – and a fucking long way down – is Carthage harbour.

In the torch and lantern light she cannot be sure: there may be a glow beyond the wall, and noise, far down below.

"*Geraint!*" She grinned up at Geraint ab Morgan as he pelted back from the barrier of pavises, slapping his shoulder.

"Fuck, it *is* you!"

"Got us here by sea, did you? I assume we have ships? How are you enjoying foreign travel to the Eternal Twilight, Geraint?"

"Hate it!" Her big-shouldered captain of archers grinned at her, half sardonic, all amazed. "Not me, boss, I didn't do this! I get seasick, see."

"*Sea*sick?"

"'S why I'm an archer. Not a wool merchant like my family. I used to leave meals with the fishes all the way from Bristol to Bruges." Geraint ab Morgan wiped his mouth with the back of his wrist. "And all the way across from Marseilles to here in those fucking galleys. I just hope it's worth it. Rich, is he, your father?"

A group of her men ran over with pavises, and she dropped to one knee behind the temporary shelter as her other officers ran up. Ash buckled her sallet back on, staring at the gates of House Leofric: fifty yards along the alley ahead, blasted by two – or three? – cannon shot, but still intact. *Need more guns.*

"Leofric's not my father. He is rich. But we'll be travelling light, so keep it to the easy, portable bits of loot – got it?"

"Got it, boss. Oh yes."

Ash made a mental note to search Geraint on the way back to whatever ships there might be.

"How the *fuck* did you guys *get* here?"

"Venetian galleys," Antonio Angelotti said, at her ear; and when she looked at him, his angelic lashes lowered over amused eyes: "My lord Oxford found us a pair of Venetian captains who survived the burning of the Republic. There is nothing they would not do, to harm Carthage."

"Where are they?"

"Moored ten miles west of here, along the coast. We came in disguised as a wagon-caravan from Alexandria. I thought – we thought they might have taken you, after Auxonne. There were rumours you were in Carthage."

"No shit? For once, rumour's right."

The expectation was less marked on Angelotti's face, but it was there all the same in his eyes, as it was in all the eyes watching her. A trust, an expectation. Ash felt fear pang in the pit of her belly again, crouching behind the flimsy shields.

Down to me. We got to do this and get out – or just get out – or we're all dead. However many of them are here, they're dead men if I can't get them out. And they expect me to do it. They've expected it for five years now.

My responsibility. Even if de Vere brought them in.

The freezing winds from the southern desert moved across her face, bringing a faint sound of shouting and panic-stricken confusion up from the centre of the Citadel. Nothing moving here in this broken place. *Where is Leofric, where are his men? Where are the King-Caliph's men? What's happening here?*

"Right," Ash said. "Somebody find me some armour! That *fits*. And a sword! My lord de Vere, I want a word with you," and she stood and stepped forward to meet the Earl of Oxford as he ran up, taking his steel-clad arm and steering him a few steps in close under the walls, no murder-holes above, and the angle too steep to be shot at.

A scream and a crunch came from somewhere along the alley, and a loud cheer.

"Got 'im!"

"Fucking rag-head!"

"'Ave that from the fucking Franks, why don't you?"

"Madam," John de Vere said.

Ash looked up at the English Earl in a mutual amazement. His faded blue eyes crinkled as if against bright light or in amusement. His steel armour was covered by de Vere livery, brilliant scarlet and yellow and white in lantern light. Under the pushed-up visor of his sallet, his face was fair, dirty, lined, and bright with the excitement of a much younger man.

Boom!

The sound stabbed her ears. Even through helmet-padding it hurt. Every bit of loose mortar and stone dust on the walls fell down into the alley, showering her livery jacket and doublet shoulders; every bit of debris on the quake-damaged cobbles leaped up, making her eyes sting.

"Captain Ash," John de Vere spoke loudly over the cascade of sounds after Angelotti's cannon-fire. His tone sounded businesslike, or, if not quite that, pragmatic at least. No surprise at her presence. He pointed over her head towards the massive Citadel wall: a twenty-foot-high blank end to the alley to her right. "The rest of the guns are on their way in."

She fell back into habit: brief questions, to the point. "How are you getting men and artillery up here?"

"Along the top of the wall. This wall, that encloses the Citadel. It's wide enough for patrols, so I'm using it. All the streets are choked."

John de Vere's pointing hand shone, encased in delicate Gothic fluted gauntlets, the lantern light picking out the lace-pattern of pierced metal on cuffs and knuckles. Ash found herself thinking, He's come here in all his riches, but in armour light enough for manoeuvre in these bloody tight alleys; I've seen none of my men wearing more than breast, back and leg armour, no spaulders and pauldrons,[3] he may be mad but he knows what he's doing.

"What about the gate between the Citadel and Carthage itself?"

"Madam, I have men holding that gate, ready, and also Carthage's south gate on the landward side – we have perhaps an hour, if God and Fortune favour us, to raid and run."

Thomas Morgan and the billman Carracci trotted up; and an armourer's apprentice who stared as he knocked out the rivet and removed her steel slave's collar. Ash stretched out her arms while they stripped off her livery and doublet, pointed on some young man's arming doublet – a trifle tight across the chest, but with reassuring panels of mail sewn in at armpits and shoulders – and set about pointing and strapping someone else's breastplate and backplate on over it.

They did not fit her. *Stationary defence only*, she thought. *No running around.*

"Get you leg armour in a second, boss," Carracci promised.

Ash sucked in her breath as the metal shell locked home and Thomas Morgan pulled the straps tight. She rapped her knuckles against the plackart riveted to the breastplate. Protection. Carracci knelt to buckle tassets on to the lower lames of the fauld.[4]

Her mouth curved up, in a smile she couldn't conceal. "Knee cops,[5] if you can't find anything else. Some fucking rag-head did my knee in at Auxonne."

"Sure, boss!" Carracci took an archer's falchion and sword-belt from Thomas Rochester: the dark Englishman now kneeling to help him buckle them around her armoured waist.

Ash turned her head to speak to John de Vere, yanking on the mail gauntlets again. "You're here for the Stone Golem. Have to be. Fuck, this is a suicide raid, my lord!"

"Madam, it need not be; and we are in such straits, in the north, that she must be stopped in some way."

"How are you going in?"

---

[3] Cumbrous steel plate shoulder defences.

[4] The skirts or articulated lames of armour protect the lower abdomen and buttocks; protective plates called tassets hang below them to protect the thighs.

[5] A shaped piece of armour that straps over the knee.

"By main force – take this House, and search it from roof to cellars."

"That's easier said than done. You know what it's like in these places?"

"No—"

John de Vere broke off to shout to his brother Dickon; the young knight strode away down the right-hand alley to where, in lantern light, scaling ladders were visible at the foot of the Citadel's enclosing wall, and dark heads silhouetted the skyline above it, in a furious bustle of activity.

"I'm going up there," Ash stated. "I need to get my bearings. Did you start this raid before the quake, my lord, or after it?"

"It was a happy accident."

"A *happy*—!" Ash snorted, despite herself.

Rope-and-wood ladders hung from their scaling hooks on the parapet, twenty feet above her head. She reached up, had one terrifying moment when her arms seemed too weak to pull her up – Christ, I've rested, I can't be sick *now*! – and then she found her footing, powerful leg-muscles pushing her up, swaying in the winter-dark air, reaching up to hands at the parapet and the muttered oaths from men who didn't recognise her in borrowed armour.

A row of pavises, broken doors, and splintered beams made a temporary barricade across the wall. Further along was bare. On the higher front of House Leofric, that overlooked that stretch of wall, she glimpsed the flash of light from Visigoth steel helmets, and from the heads of arrows: the *amir*'s soldiers able to lay down a withering fire if they went forward of this position.

"Francis; Willem!" She greeted her crossbowman and lance-leader. "What's it like at the Citadel gate?"

"Fuck," Willem muttered.

The two men stared at her, frozen, holding a solid oaken cask between them. The bowman, Francis, abruptly coughed, spat, and said, wonderingly, "Couple of skirmishes, boss. There's nobody really down there right now. Everybody's running around like a bitch in heat because of the quake damage."

"Let's hope it stays like that. Okay, get shifting!"

"Boss—" The crossbowman gave up, shaking his head, but with a wide grin. He turned back as other men came running up with casks. "Here! She's *back*—!"

Up here, on the roof of the city, out of the sheltering alleys, the bitter wind sheared across Ash's face, under her visor, and tears sprang into her eyes. She was instantly frozen. She ran, half-crouching, to the harbour-facing side of the city wall, glancing out into the black depths.

John de Vere went back to the ladders, shouted down, took something, and came across to her, holding a thick woollen cloak which he thrust at her. "Madam, take this. I've had your people coming into the city disguised for the last three days. They are God's own bastards and a joy to lead. I had the raid planned for a later hour, but this—" A stark gaze around, at the broken roof-lines of the inner city, at tumbled walls and blocked alleys: "This was an opportunity not to be refused. Will you take command again under me, madam? Are you well enough to do so?"

Ash glanced up at the sky. Nothing to give her the hour. Maybe thirty minutes since she had emerged from the sewers? No more.

The cold at least kept some of the stink out of her nostrils; she doubted the others, with a stench of powder and killing on them, had even noticed it.

"Who else of my officers is here? And where the fuck are the others?"

"This is but half your full company. By Duke Charles's command, Master Robert Anselm stays in Dijon, with two hundred men, keeping up the defence against the Gothic forces; his last message reached me a week since. They hold out."

"*Robert's—*" Safe. Alive. "*They're alive!*"

Or, they were, a week ago.

Sod it, they're alive still, I know they are! I know them.

Her eyes filled up with tears.

"Son of a *bitch!*" Ash said weakly. "I might have *known*. It takes more than a bunch of rag-heads to finish these arseholes off. Sweet Christ, I should've trusted them for that!"

"You had no word?" the Earl said.

"None: and I was lied to, told we were all dead on Auxonne field!"

"Then I am glad to bring you this news." John de Vere smiled, one ear cocked to the shouting and clamour below. "And if I had a better thing, I would have brought it to you with as good a heart. Your people sorely felt your loss."

"I didn't know—" Ash swallowed, her throat tightening. She felt herself grin. "*Shit.* They made it? You're sure they made it? When you left, they were okay? Robert's okay?"

"Inside the walls of Dijon, and like to hold out, I think. The news of its fall would have been heard, madam. They have Charles within the walls, also, and the capture of a Duke, or his death, would have been shouted abroad. Now." De Vere reached out and gripped her forearms in his gauntlets. "We must take counsel together."

When you wake up on a runaway wagon, you either grab the reins, or you jump off. One or the other.

Dozens of men on the wall now, heaving weapons and crates down the scaling ladders, into the alleys; and all of them detouring past Ash as they ran back and forth, staring, calling *it's her, it* is *her*; receiving her nods of acknowledgement; running with a new fervour, excitement, joy.

"Bugger counsel!" Ash said. "We go or we fight. Now—"

Perhaps an hour, now, from the moment of the quake. The sense grows in her of a clock, ticking, ticking away time in which the overturned hive of Carthage might recover, regroup, begin to send troops out of the fortress-houses of the inner city and into the streets and alleys. To discover Frankish cannon-fire.

"They won't have heard us yet. Or they'll think it's just some *amir* or other taking advantage of the confusion to do in old enemies—"

BOOM!

"*Shit!*" Ash grabbed the stone parapet. The violence of the sound jabbed into her eardrums. *One of Angelotti's cannon exploded?* she thought, about to run to that side of the wall; and then a flare of light bloomed on the night's darkness, towering up, rising from the harbour below.

"That," the Earl of Oxford directed her attention, "will be Viscount Beaumont."

The pillar of fire rose up, illuminating the cliff below Ash, shining red light across the inner harbour of Carthage. Smoke, flames: and at the foot of the towering conflagration, a great Visigoth war-galley, burning – burning to the water line.

She gripped the stone and leaned over, staring down at black water, ice. Fierce crackling flames billowed up, fork-tongued: stabbing up into darkness. By their immense light she saw other ships, a whole harbour full of vulnerable, inflammable wood, rope, cord, cargo. Another curl of flame suddenly ripped the night air, racing up the masts of a merchant cog, spidering out along the yardarms, wisping ropes into so much ash on the cold wind.

Two ships now on fire. Three. Four. And over there—

Ash squinted, tears running down her frozen cheeks from the wind, at the roofs of warehouses across the inlet. She unconsciously hauled the cloak around her shoulders and knotted the ties. Warehouses, with forked curls of flame flickering up from their roofs and upper granary stores—

Another sudden noise came on the wind, as if the explosion had been a signal. Noise blown from the west, from the main part of Carthage town that lay over the next headland. She could not distinguish if it were fire or voices.

"And that will be my brothers, Tom and George," the Earl of Oxford added. "The King-Caliph brings in a lot of cattle, Captain. Thousands of head, to feed all Carthage, where nothing may graze. George and Tom will, I trust, have taken and stampeded the stock market . . ."

"The stock—" Ash wiped her streaming nose. She choked back a laugh. "My lord!"

"Streets full of maddened cattle, in these ruins, should spread more confusion." De Vere added thoughtfully, "I wanted to fire the naphtha plant too, but that would be too well-guarded, and I could gain no solid information as to where it is sited."

"No, my lord." *You're a fucking maniac, my lord.* In her mind's eye: tremor-ravaged buildings, running men, women, wild-horned beasts, fire, injury, death, utter confusion. Utter *effective* confusion. "How many of us are with you?"

"Two hundred and fifty. Galley-crews back at the ships. Fifty men on this Citadel gate, fifty holding the south gate where the aqueducts come into the city. Above one hundred here, light armour, close-combat weapons, and light guns; crossbows and arquebuses."

In the harbour, flame runs from ship to ship along the docks, carracks and cogs burning, a throng of men like black lice running frantically, a bucket-line forming to the warehouses, chaff and embers sprinkling red on the wind, drifting towards other roofs. Small boats are being frantically rowed across the black vitreous water, trying to take cargo off before vessels are burned – and a throng of merchants, clerks, sailors, tapsters and whores shrieks around the warehouses, leather buckets of water pissing on the conflagration, chains of men passing cargo out, fights starting, theft.

Ash heard screamed orders, shouting, and on one burst of wind, the sound of a man bellowing in such pain that it made her hurt in sympathy. This will be happening a thousand times across Carthage now: no one is thinking about one *amir*'s house, up on the Citadel.

"Shit." She found herself grinning at the Earl of Oxford. "What an opportunity. *Nicely* done. There won't be another chance like this."

John de Vere gave her a shining, utterly reckless smile. "I thought this worth the venture, though foolhardy or desperate even if it succeeded in destroying the *machina rei militaris*. Now, with the earth tremor, madam, yes, we may succeed and leave. Oftentimes I am blessed with such lucky accidents when I need them."

"Wuff!" Ash felt breathless. "'When I need them'—!"

"However," de Vere continued, squinting down at the chaos of burning ships and men, "I had planned for us to leave by way of the aqueducts – which have not fallen, but they may not be safe after the earth tremors."

"We won't get out by way of the streets, even in this." Ash's scarred face shone in the flickering light of the flames below. "Even if they're falling down, the aqueducts are a damn sight better than trying to fight our way out through Gelimer's army – this confusion won't last for ever."

"Gelimer?"

"The newly elected Caliph."

"Ah. That was his name."

"You *have* been lucky," Ash said. She spoke to Oxford over her shoulder as she crab-crawled behind the barricade, back across the wall. Two black-feathered shafts abruptly stood out from a pavise over her head. She ignored them as if they were a mere irritating nuisance. "Theodoric's death, and the election! – all the *amirs*' troops are wiping their own masters' bottoms right now, instead of thundering around the city. All there is down *there* is the militia, and they're crap. Up here . . ."

Ash wiped her nose on the leather palm of her mail glove, wet skin freezing in the air.

"This city spends half its time with lords' households at war with each other," she said. "They're *used* to shutting themselves up in these house-forts and waiting for the shit to go away. But Leofric's men are going to come out real soon."

"They need not do so, if we cannot take that gate!"

A shriek thirty feet away whipped her head around. On the roof of House Leofric, another mail-clad man in white robes threw up his arms and slumped over the wall, tumbling down into the alley. A raucous cheer went up from below. Carracci ran forward and dragged the twitching dead man behind the shields; Thomas Morgan scooped up the Visigoth's bow.

"Leofric left troops guarding the place – or maybe he's made it back from the palace. Either way, they've about worked out that we're not Visigoths, we're Franks, this isn't another *amir* attacking them."

A whistling sound split the air. Ash had no time to throw herself flat, only to wince – herself, Oxford, and the soldiers on the Citadel wall half-ducking in identical jerky movement – and something whooshed up from inside the walls of House Leofric, and a flare and flat concussion banged out fifty feet above their heads.

White light strobed collapsed buildings, blocked alleys, the mass of helmets below.

"Distress rockets! Calling their allies." Ash shook her head. "Okay. Decision, my lord – we attack right now, or we withdraw."

"*No!* No retreat!" The Earl of Oxford swore. "I will have this Stone Golem of the Faris's, and I will leave it rubble like the rest of this thrice-damned city!"

"The Visigoths have other generals."

"But none that they believe to be of such great power." Oxford gave her a look which, despite battle-dirt and their situation, was all reflective irony. "I dare say they have *better* generals, madam – but none with a mystical war-machine at home, none that they believe invincible. We are in such straits, in Burgundy, we *must* stop her!"

Something about *Burgundy* tugged at her mind: she forcibly ignored it.

"My voice for the attack. Dickon?" The Earl glanced at his younger brother, who stuttered, "Yes, my lord, mine also."

Ash loosened the strap of her helmet and lifted the edge, listening – hearing nothing but the racket and clamour of her own men. "They're still my people. This is my company. The decision's mine." *When we run, we'll get mauled getting out, too.* "You may be an English Earl, my lord, but I am their captain, who are they going to follow?"

John de Vere regarded her grimly. "In especial, after a miraculous re-appearance? Better not to put it to the test, madam. Leadership cannot quarrel, not where we stand now!"

"Who's quarrelling?" Ash grinned widely, breathing in the chill air that stank sweetly of black powder; putting aside her invaded soul, other voices, everything, for this now-or-never second. "There'll never be another chance like this! Let's do it!"

"Boss!" Geraint's voice came from an anonymous head in an archer's sallet, stuck up just above the level of the parapet. "They're trying to get runners out, down the wall from their roof!"

"Get your bowmen back out there, pick them off!"

The helmet vanished. She has not fully taken it in, the reality of the presence of these men: Geraint, Angelotti, Carracci, Thomas Morgan, Thomas Rochester – and Floria! Christus! Floria . . .

Here. Here in *Carthage*. Shit.

She risked a glance over the edge, into the alley below. Floria and Richard Faversham knelt in a protective cordon of billmen, a thrashing yelling body between them – the crossbow-woman, Ludmilla Rostovnaya – rolling bloody on the cobbles; Floria's surgeon's box open, bandages welling red with blood.

"*Don't* attack through that front gate," Ash snapped. "It opens into a tunnel. A closed passage full of murder-holes!"

De Vere frowned. Still more of her men came piling past them now – mere minutes since she'd come up here – climbing down the scaling ladders, shifting iron barrels on wooden trenchers, casks, arquebuses, barrels of arrows and bolts. The Earl lowered the intensity of his tone so that his voice should not carry:

"I could purchase no information about the inside of these palaces."

"But *I* know, my lord." Ash's face went momentarily bleak, remembering. "I talked a lot to slaves. The houses go down into living rock. There are six floors below street-level. I was in this House for—" She had to force herself to think. "Three, four days. There are shafts, murder-holes, and *deep* bolt-holes. It's fucking impossible. I don't wonder Carthage was never taken!"

"And the Golem?" De Vere's sandblasted fair face, under his visor, lit up grimly. "Madam, *do you know where this golem is kept?*"

The realisation came to her with the sensation of machinery locking home: this man's knowledge, and her own.

We're going to do this. We're going to succeed.

"Yes. I know exactly where the Stone Golem is. I talked to the slaves who clean it. It's in the north-east quadrant of the House, and it's six floors down."

"God's bollocks!"

An odd abstraction overcame her. She ignored the swish of a second distress rocket climbing the black sky, blasting a hollow sphere of light above her.

"How *would* I attack this place. . . ? Not frontally, that's for sure. We could scale their walls and climb down into the central courtyard – and then be caught in a crossfire from all directions, when they pot us from inside the building . . ."

"Madam Ash!" John de Vere shook her by the shoulders. "No time for talk. We go or we stay, we run or we attack! There is no time. Or I shall lead this company in despite of you!"

Ash leaned out from the wall, one hand to the top of a ladder. "Carracci! Geraint! Thomas Morgan!"

"Yes, boss?" Red-faced under his helmet, Carracci bawled happily up at her.

"Clear this alley!"

"Yes, boss!"

"Angelotti!"

The master gunner ran through the crowding armed men to the foot of the wall, and shouted up: "What, madonna?"

This is the north-east side. Allow about twenty paces for the thickness of the city wall – then allow another twenty feet—

"Put powder casks up against the House wall, right down *there*." She pointed. "Everything you've got in casks, and clear this area!"

"Yes, madonna!"

The powder will not be going off in a confined space, so it will have less force; but in an alley ten feet wide, even open to the stars, it will have such force between the buildings that it will rip masonry apart.

As Angelotti and his crews ran, Ash said, "I paced it out, my lord. My cell, the passage. I know where things are on the other side of that wall."

Preparing to climb down the scaling ladder, John de Vere gave her a look that was equal parts admiration and appalled shock. "This, while you were prisoner, and doubtless ill-handled? Madam, you are an amazement to me!"

Ash ignored that. Her pain, her blood on the floor; these are somewhere she cannot feel or notice them now.

She pointed at the growing heap of powder casks. "We don't mess about with storming gates, we go straight in *through* the wall – blow the side of the building in. That puts us in at ground-level in the north-east quadrant."

The Earl of Oxford nodded sharply. "And we take the whole House?"

"Don't need to. It's built in four quadrants, around four stairwells, and they don't connect. Take the top of one, and you've taken the whole – or bottled up anyone who's in there. I need men on the ground floor, to hold this quadrant against the rest of the House. Then we have to fight our way down six floors to find the Stone Golem . . ."

She turned, swung herself down the ladder, awkward in ill-fitting armour but growing accustomed; down out of the icy night wind, sweating into her padded arming doublet, into the empty alley, John de Vere and Dickon beside her; the alley dim now almost all the lanterns and torches had been pulled back.

A tall, leggy man in a powder-scarred padded jack heaved a last barrel into place: Angelotti, his curls bright gold under the metal rim of his helmet. Approaching, catching what she said, he offered, "The casks are in place. I still have powder. We can toss grenades down the stairwell."

"That ought to do it—" Ash broke off.

She stands in a bare alley, the stars of the southern sky above her head; sounds of crossbows being frantically winched towards the front of the House, but here nothing, nothing except John de Vere treading with great care, so as not to strike a spark from his metal sabatons on the cobbles. And an innocent heap of small oak casks, piled neatly against the wall of House Leofric.

"We haven't got much time, boss." Geraint ab Morgan joined them with a bare respectful nod to the Earl of Oxford, and Dickon de Vere. "They're shooting from slot windows up front, picking my boys off."

"Madonna, do you want me to stop the swivel guns attacking the gate?" Angelotti demanded, wiping his mouth with a black, sweating hand. His took a slow match from Thomas Morgan as the man walked briskly up. The fuse smouldered odorously. "Or keep them going until we blow the wall?"

Both men shouted, loudly, to be heard over the noise of the wall-guns, and sporadic arquebus fire; the harsh shouts of men used to bellowing at other men wearing helmets, half-deaf from the padding, and the clatter of armour.

They looked to her expectantly, for split-second orders.

Ash, appalled, found herself speechless.

She stared at the men in the alley, her voice dead in her throat.

III

Her silence stretched out.

"Are you hurt, madam?" John de Vere half-shouted. "Ill-treated by your captors? Unfit for this?"

"No—" Now it ceases to be theory: becomes concrete.

Doubt grew on Geraint ab Morgan's face.

Angelotti, his smirched beauty plain in torch-light, said swiftly, "Madonna, when I was Childeric's gunner, I had to kill Christians. But when I returned to Christendom, I found at first I had no heart for fighting Visigoths – they might have been men I knew."

"Shit. *Shit*, yes." Ash spread her hands towards the Italian gunner. "Angeli, I never – this is the first time I had to attack somewhere where I *know* the defenders . . ."

Where I've lived with them.

She added, with difficulty, "I have – blood kin, within House Leofric."

"*Kin?*" Angelotti, startled out of his Byzantine calm.

"Okay, they're slaves," she said steadily. "They're still related to me. And no one else is."

Gazing around at the group, she saw Dickon de Vere merely puzzled, excited with the anticipation of battle; his older brother with a calm, concerned face; Geraint shifting from one foot to another and scratching under his hose; Angelotti taken aback.

Violante. Leovigild. Even Alderic, even the *'arif*, even the bloody rats; I *know* these people – if they're inside, if the earth tremor hasn't killed them, if—

If they're inside now, and I order this attack, they're on my conscience.

"I never had family before," she said.

"Area's clear!" Carracci bawled from the far end of the alley. "I've cleared the men back three streets! Boss, come on back, and we'll blow it!"

Men anxious to attack, now, before momentum and courage slacken.

Dickon de Vere said in a high-pitched voice to his brother, "Do it, before someone on the roof sees this! If someone drops a torch on those casks, we're dead!"

Pull back from this wall, reinforce the perimeter, let no one approach this end of the headland, blow open the House—

It is no voice in her head, but she feels her own thoughts almost as automatic, as pragmatic, with the same absence of human feeling.

She thought, It's only my trade, it's only what I do, it isn't *me*.

"When I give the signal!" Ash shouted to Angelotti, where he stood swinging the slow match and waiting her word to touch it to the fuse.

She turned, loping urgently back with the English Earl, Geraint and Dickon de Vere. The mass of men in the back streets had grown large. She watched their bobbing heads: faces under visors, hands gripping swords, axes, crossbows.

"Listen up!" she yelled in growing desperation to their upturned faces, raw with readiness, shitting themselves to be at it, in the overwhelming excitement and terror of actual fighting. "Listen—"

It is too little, too late.

"—We're going in. My orders are, *don't hurt the house slaves. Spare* the slaves! They have fair hair, and iron collars. *Only kill the fighting men.* Spare the commons!"

It is an old cry, from the English wars; John de Vere nods brief approval. Possible in battle. Sometimes. Men being what they are, on the verge of killing other men, they will listen to her to get them through this fight, but as for other orders . . .

And powder will not listen: not when you plan to use casks to blow the walls to smithereens and anyone inside to bloody rags of meat.

I can't claim to be trapped in this, Ash thought. Even if it does feel like being caught up in a mill-wheel: grind or be ground. It's still my decision.

"Angelotti, blow this place wide open!"

Carracci, further forward, relayed her shout. In seconds, he and Antonio Angelotti came pounding back down the alley, armoured elbows tucked into their ribs, running at the sprint. She spun around, following them; the cobbles hard under her boots, around one corner, around the next, plunging into the middle of a group of men: Euen Huw and his lance, all their faces wild with excitement, the unbearably prolonged moment before battle.

BOOM!

She did not hear the explosion so much as feel it, instantly deaf with the unbelievable roar of sixty casks of powder going up. The street jumped under her feet; a swirl of movement ahead is a building sliding into a slow collapse, black powder ending what the quake began; dust filled her face and she coughed, choked, Angelotti's slender hand thumping her shoulders; a tongue of fire leaping up like lightning in reverse, to strike the heavens, somewhere somebody shrieking in utter agony; John de Vere's mouth opening and shutting soundlessly.

Not hearing any word he said, she swung around, faced the mass of men, and shrieked, "Come on, you bastards!"

She cannot hear herself yell, lifts her arm, lifts the sword, points forward; and is running, all of them running with her and her banner, her head ringing, eardrums pierced with a thin wire of pain; running through great clouds of dust, stone chips, mortar-dust, flakes of granite embedded in the cobbles; running to where the side of House Leofric stands.

There is nothing.

A great cloud of dust hurtles around her head. She screams, "Lanterns! Torches!', not knowing if she will be heard.

Light comes: partly from armed men with torches, partly from a roaring fire-rimmed cavern ahead. Men stream past her, she swats at their shoulders, urging them on and through, down the alleys; Geraint and Angelotti with her, shouting their own commands; Oxford and his brother at the head of the billmen; all faces contorted, all mouths open and yelling, but for her in the silence of the deaf.

The dust began to clear.

Ash, at the head of them by the time they reached the side alley, jerked up her hand for them to halt. Bodies crowded in back of her, shoving her forward.

To left and right, the side of the houses were gone. As if something had reached down and bitten a great hole in the walls. Most of the road surface was gone, a great deep pit where the barrels had stood.

And ahead of her was open air.

The wall of the Citadel – breached.

Great basalt masonry gone, blocks at the edges hanging out into empty darkness – and she saw the sea beyond, the northern sea and the road home.

House Leofric burned. Half of the side of the alley was nothing, now, except stone, rubble, beams, timbers, broken furniture, men in white robes screaming bloody, a woman in an iron collar coughing her guts into her skirt, a broken mosaic of the Boar and the Tree, exposed wood blackened and burning.

"Take the ground floor! Secure the windows!" Ash bawled. Carracci nodded, running forward. Her hearing just began to come back, accompanied by a thin, high whistling.

"We're in!" Carracci: back at her side, grinning through dust-blackened sweat. "Geraint's bowmen are at the courtyard windows! The arquebuses are there, too!"

"Thomas Rochester, keep the perimeter! I'm going in!"

Now is the time when you do not feel the restrictions of armour, the body can do anything, buoyed up with the exhilaration of fighting. Euen Huw and his lance crowded shoulder to shoulder tightly round her: commander's escort. Thomas Morgan dipped the pole of the Lion Azure banner as she strode forward, in the wake of the shouting mob of armed men, over the piled broken foundations of the wall, still hot and glowing with scraps of powder and burning fragments of cloth, into a great room with pavises now up at the shattered stone-lace windows, Geraint ab Morgan striding up and down behind the ranks of crossbowmen and arquebusiers; John de Vere at the head of the soldiers fighting—

That was over as she looked: a dozen or more men in white robes and mail cut down, one doubled over de Vere's blade, his guts spilling out pink on the mosaic floor; Carracci bringing his bill straight down on a *nazir*'s helmet, shearing the metal wide open, the man collapsing like a dropped stone. No prisoners.

Another *nazir* lay at her feet, his mouth full of blood, dead or unconscious.

For the first time in combat, Ash found herself looking to see if she knew an enemy's face: she did not.

Her ears hurt, badly. The Earl of Oxford shouted something, his bright steel arm lifting; and a unit, two dozen or more men, thundered across the room and took positions either side of the door.

"*Stairs!*" Ash yelled, coming up with de Vere, and footsteps on the roof above made her glance up, once. "Stairwell, beyond that door!"

"Where is the master gunner?"

"*Angelotti!*"

The Italian gunner came over rubble at a run, more men with torches behind him. Ash stared around the broken stone cavern that had been a room, hangings still on fire, floor slippery with blood and excrement.

"Grenades!"

"Coming up!"

"Get back from the door!" Ash yelled; and gauged it – a stone slab, of antique design, that slides on metal rollers. It will keep the blast in. "*Go!*"

A dozen of the company's gun-crew piled in, de Vere urging the billmen to pull back the stone door; a dozen crossbowmen covering the entrance, and Ash felt a hand on her breastplate push her sharply back.

A shower of bolts shot up through the open door – from the stairs below, by angle – and she ducked her head automatically, grinning at Euen Huw. A runner from Geraint at the far side reached her at the same time as Dickon de Vere thumped down at her other side.

"Courtyard's clear!" the runner bawled.

She risked a glance – dust, rubble; and beyond the stone windows, on the tiles by the fountain, two or three sprawled men in mail and white surcoats. Stone window frames spurted dust with the impact of black-fletched arrows. A *nazir* screeched orders and pain from across the great inner yard.

"Keep it that way! Don't waste bolts! We have to get out of here, too. Dickon?"

"The door on the far side of the stairwell is open, they are firing from the far side of that room!"

"Well, fuck subtlety," Ash said – teeth white in a blackened face, an appalling flat grin on her face, her voice hoarse, her ears singing, her face frozen by the wind whipping dust across the broken room, where there is no longer a city wall to obstruct it – "Fuck subtlety, chuck in the grenades! And shut the fucking door!"

Angelotti bellowed. His crews lit fuses, and rolled the sputtering casks across the floor and into the stairwell. De Vere put his shoulder to the stone door with her men: all shoving.

The metal rollers screamed and stuck.

The door jammed, three-quarters open.

Ash yelled, "DOWN!" in a voice that ripped her throat, and fell flat on to sharp, sticky rubble.

Boom!

The semi-muffled blast lifted her, bodily, she felt it. Two more followed, on the heels of the first; Euen Huw in his padded jack almost suffocated her, where he sprawled across her armoured back, and then she was up on her feet, the Welshman beside her; her and his lance scrambling across the room, the archers swearing loudly and getting up from below the windows, John de Vere and the three lances with him standing up, one screaming man being bandaged by Floria, her face dirty, intent, utterly concentrated; and Ash ran to the end of the jammed door.

"DUMB BITCH!" Euen Huw screamed in her ear.

"Someone's got to do it!"

Riding adrenalin, bubbling laughter behind the metal bevor that protects her mouth, body in metal plate that digs and restricts, she hurtled through the gap between door and wall, out on to the pie-shaped step in the stairwell, into blackness lit by flaring torches from the room opposite and a man charging out straight at her.

She registers that it is someone wearing an acorn-shaped helmet, mail hauberk, flowing robes, and with a sword lifted up. It is a snapshot recognition of an enemy silhouette. She is already moving, swinging her sword up in a two-handed grip, bringing it over her head; her shoulder-muscles forcing the metal to whip over in a tight arc and slice down, smack, on his upraised arm.

Her blade doesn't slice mail: riveted links absorb the edge's cut. But under the arm of his hauberk, smashed back with the power of her blow, his elbow-joint shatters at the impact.

"*Aahh—!*" His piercing-high scream: pain, rage?

Anyone with him? Behind him?

Jarred through mail gauntlets and armour, Ash whips her blade down, through, and up again: over and down – no split-second hesitation between the blows: she hits the man hard on the junction between his helmet and his falling arm, stopped by the mail between neck and shoulder.

"Uhhnh!"

Hits him again—

"Uhh! Uhhnh! *Uhhh!*"

—and again, and again, grunting uncontrollably, putting him down with ferocity and speed; he falls down on the floor, long before she stops striking; ready for the man behind him—

No one.

Her breastplate drips, red running thinly over mirror-polished steel. The bottom edge of the steel is cutting painfully into her hipbone.

A snapshot apprehension of dust, smoke, silence in the far room, every nerve shrieking with alertness—

Thomas Morgan stumbled into her shoulder, bearing her banner, shouting: "Haro! The Lion!"

Euen Huw's wiry body tried to shove her aside, at the head of the men of his lance: it ended with both of them stumbling into the far wall together, to a raucous cheer from Geraint's archers.

Nothing else moving, nobody—

An empty room opposite, empty platform, no one running up the stone stairs—

The powder-blackened walls of the stairwell dripped.

Ash stopped, a fierce smile on her face.

Her stomach heaved dryly at the hot smell of burned flesh.

There had been a squad running up the stairs at precisely the wrong moment. One man's arm, blown clear off, lay at her feet, ragged and bleeding from the white knob of the shoulder-joint, sword still gripped in the hand. A heap of men lay tangled midway down the clockwise curve of the stairs. As dead men always do, they looked like men sprawling in a heap, splashed with red limewash or dye, their swords and bows dropped any old how. But arms do not bend at that angle, legs do not lie under bodies that way; and a blackened, fried face stared up at Ash through the dust: Theudibert, *Nazir* Theudibert; no point in looking at the faces of the men with him, his eight, no point now.

She looked, all the same. Gaiseric and Barbas and Gaina, young men, boys not much older than she is. Their faces are recognisable, although Gaiseric's helmet, blown off by the blast, has taken a large part of his jawbone with it. Barbas's open eye reflects the greasy light of torches: Euen's men, behind her,

516

with Rochester's lance, Ned Mowlett, Henri de Treville; their men stomping in.

Gladness sears through her: rich, amoral, vengeful, entirely of the moment.

"*Clear!*" Ash screamed. Her escort pulled her back; men charged across the stairs into the room on the opposite side.

The Visigoth soldier she has killed is dragged bodily by one arm and thrown against the wall, out of the way.

She tried to see his face, in the dim light. She remembers many of the men she has seen in Leofric's household. This man is unrecognisable, a little soft brown hair poking out from under the lining of his helmet. Two slashes from her edge have chopped his face apart from temple to cheekbone, eye to mouth.

She remembers almost all the faces of the men she has killed, in five years.

"Block the doors!" Ash shouted, voice pitched brazen-high to carry through the clamour. "Bottle them up! Don't lose it, guys! We don't need to kill them! *Take the stairs!*"

She took two steps back, as the mass of men went past her, seeing nothing but torchlight on armoured backs, swords and maces over their heads, no room in here for polearms; and she stepped back again, her chest heaving, breath forcing itself raggedly into her lungs, finding herself beside John de Vere, giving brisk orders to a runner from the perimeter.

"Skirmish at the gate, madam!"

She could not read his mouth, with his bevor up; she could just hear him if she thumbed up one side of her helmet.

"Which gate?"

"Citadel! Some *amir*'s house-guard, fifty men or more."

"Can we still get out that way?"

"We're holding!"

Defence is easier than attack: the gate can probably hold. If her men don't lose heart. More explosions rocked the lower part of the building, echoing hollowly up the stairwell. Taking the next floor down.

Ash turned, Euen's men with her. Thomas Morgan swore under his breath as the top of the banner caught against the shattered vaulting of the ceiling:

"Other commanders fucking stay still! Other commanders don't fucking charge up and down the fucking field of battle!"

"Follow me!" She went through the door again, hearing the sound of hammering and banging even with her deafened ears. The mass of armed men had gone through and down the stairs. Angelotti stood, shouting orders.

A dozen of the gun-crew, with mauls, knocked shards of splintered timber under the doors, jamming closed the doors to every room opening on to the stairwell.

"Well done!" Ash walloped the shoulder of his padded jack. "Keep doing it! Follow them down!"

"Yes, madonna! The bang – *bellissima!*"

Ash stepped over Theudibert's stained, burned legs. Her escort trod indiscriminately on the body until Euen Huw cursed and kicked it sideways on the steps.

But it is *bellissima*, she thought, staring into the dead man's face. It is *bellissima*, too. Like Godfrey says – said. *Fair as the moon, clear as the sun, and terrible as an army with banners.*[6]

With Morgan cursing at getting the banner down the narrow stairwell, and runners pelting up and down the stairs towards her, it took her long minutes to get down to the next floor. Sounds of shrieking voices and slicing metal echoed up from below.

Two men in Lion livery lay across one threshold, hacked about the face and stomach: Katherine, Ludmilla's lance-mate; and big Jean the Breton.

Ash knelt down. Jean moved, whimpering. Katherine Hammell opened white eyes in a blood-drenched face; moved one hand to touch her belly, and the half-slashed but still effective protection of her jack.

"Get them upstairs! Move it!" She rattled on past, the clatter of tassets loud in the enclosing stone; four of her escort splitting off to carry the wounded.

Angelotti's door-team overtook her, running down the steps with complete disregard for safety, hammering rough wedges in as the foot-soldiers hacked arms and hands from doorframes, crossbows shot up rooms, and stone slabs slid shut.

The grenades had chipped the edges of the worn steps, and twice her feet slid out from under her; both times she was grabbed and set back on the steps, and they pelted on down.

Counting floors, Ash thought: Four? Yes. We're four floors down. Shit, too easy, even if they don't have all their forces here, too easy! We're not seeing anybody! Where are Alderic's men—?

A gust of hot air whooshed into her face.

Hot as fire: blasting her unprotected skin and eyes.

"Stop!" She thwacked Euen across the breastplate to halt him, shoved up her visor, stood listening.

Something teased at her hearing. She frowned, looked questioning at Euen, who shook his head. A sliding, crackling noise.

Boom!

Thirty feet below her, a great number of voices suddenly screamed.

The sound howled up the stone shaft. Over it, she heard the sound of creaking, breaking wood; and a hollow roar of flames.

"Shit!" Ash gripped the hilt of her sword and ran down the curving steps. "Boss, *stop!*"

One boot heel slipped. She grabbed for the wall with her free hand, ripping the leather palm of her mail mitten, and skidded to a stop on her arse on the next pie-shaped big step with a room opening off it. Fifth floor down.

There was nothing beyond.

"Carracci?" Ash shouted.

At the rim of the step, ahead, was darkness. Empty darkness.

She stood up and limped across to it, for once careless of the door at her back; and heard a clatter of boots as Euen's men moved in, and ignored them, ignored them, because what was in front of her *was* nothing, nothing at all.

The stone stairs ended where she stood. She was looking down a sheer masonry drop into blackness, where flames flickered, stirred . . .

[6] Song of Solomon 6: 10, AV.

Furnace-hot air shrieked up from below. She clamped her hand over her mouth, leaning forward, looking down. Light flared.

"Shit," Euen Huw breathed at her side.

"Pity of Christ!"

The stairwell went on down, a slick-walled empty stone shaft fifteen feet across. At the bottom, fierce flames roared up among a great mass of tangled ropes, planks, beams, and splintered wood.

Black against the fire at the bottom of the shaft, fallen men writhed and screamed.

"*Get ropes! Get scaling ladders! Get them down here! GO!*"

Sick-faced, Euen Huw turned around and pelted back up the stairs.

Ash stayed quite still, looking down at men in mail shirts and padded jacks and helmets, who had plainly fallen fifty or sixty feet straight down. And not down on to stone, but on to the collapsed wreckage of stairs.

Deliberately collapsed. The stairs for these last two floors weren't stone. They were wood—

Ash knelt, reached down at the side of the shaft, finding what she expected: a hole in the masonry big enough to socket a wooden beam, which would support wooden stairs.

Which can be brought down, tripped, collapsed, whenever an enemy gets in.

The sounds of screaming echoed up from below, and the roar of fire.

"A bolt-hole shaft," Ash said, and became aware it was the Earl of Oxford, panting, standing beside her and staring down, his expression blankly fierce. She stepped to one side to let the men with rope ladders through. "That's where they are. Alderic, the household troops, Leofric if he made it."

"They collapsed the stairs and fired them, with our people on them." John de Vere knelt, constrained by his leg armour, staring over the edge into bitter blackness and flames. "And now they will have barricaded every door down there, and it will take more than powder to get through."

"More powder than we have," Antonio Angelotti said, beside her. His eyes were brilliant in his blackened face: wet.

"Shit!" She smashed her mailed fist into the wall. "Shit. *Shit!*"

"Out of the way!" a low-pitched, ragged voice ordered.

Ash stepped back again, letting Floria pass her, which the woman did without a look; merely ordering Faversham and a lance of men to help her carry up two bodies, which the ladders had brought up. Carracci was one, helmet gone, screaming. His high-coloured face and white-blond hair all one colour now: burned black.

"Pity of Christ," Ash said again, her face wet and her voice shaking; and then she straightened, walked to the edge, and looked down at the men on the ladders, dangling over fire, desperately trying to get within reach of the broken bodies of the fallen.

Superheated air breathed across her face.

"Back up the ladders!"

"Boss—"

"*I said pull out! Now!*"

As the last man came up, flames licked at his heels, soaring up.

Black smoke and panic filled the shaft.

Coughing, tears streaming down her face, Ash began to push and shove men up the stairs, Morgan with her with the banner, Euen's men at her side; John de Vere grabbing men and throwing them up the steps, climbing, climbing in searingly hot air and soot, until she staggered out last across a stone threshold and out into air cold by contrast – the ground floor room of House Leofric, open to the sky.

"They have air-shafts!" Ash bit back a fit of coughing. "Air-shafts! They can feed the fire! Turn the whole thing into a chimney!"

Someone put a leather flask to her mouth. She gulped water, stopped, coughed it back up again, her mouth bitter with bile. Another mouthful; this one swallowed.

"You okay, boss?" Euen Huw demanded.

She nodded abruptly. Heads were turning, at the defended windows, the other doors, the arquebusiers poised to shoot up into the shattered roof. To the Earl of Oxford, she yelled, "They've turned it into a chimney! We haven't got time to wait for the fire to burn out, there's too much timber down there!"

"Will the heat crack the shaft? Their doors?"

Angelotti, taking off his helmet and wiping his wet curls back, said, "No, my lord. Never, with this thickness of wall. This whole place is carved down into the headland."

"They can just pull back into the outer rooms," Ash yelled bitterly. She became aware that she could hear herself, her deafness fading. More quietly, she said, "They can stay in the outer rooms, wait for the fire to go out, and then I'll bet they have ladders and stores down there. They're used to doing this. Shit, I should have seen this one coming! Geraint, Angelotti, how many people did we lose?"

"Ten," Antonio Angelotti said, grimly. "Nine if Carracci lives."

The courtyard windows were still full of pavises, the crossbowmen ceasing to crack jokes, winching their bows with their eyes on the increasing smoke pouring out of the stairwell. A cold wind blew across the shell of the house here. In the middle of the floor, Floria knelt with Richard Faversham, over Carracci, her hands black.

Ash crossed to her. "Well?"

"He's alive." The woman reached out, her hand hovering over the injured man's face. Carracci moved, moaned, unconscious. Ash saw that the lids of his eyes had been burned off.

"He's blind," Floria said. "His pelvis is shattered. But he'll probably live."

"Shit."

"This is where we could do with one of Godfrey's miracles," Floria said, brushing her hose as she stood up, and her tone changed: "What is it? Ash? Is Godfrey *here*? In Carthage? Have you seen him?"

"Godfrey's dead. He died in the earth tremor." Ash turned her back on the woman's expression. She spoke to Antonio Angelotti. "We'll try what powder there is left. See if you can blow the bottom of the shaft. Don't risk men."

"I've got no powder left!"

"Send to the gates?"

"Not enough to do this, not even if we leave them with none. It took everything to crack the House!"

For a moment she and the Italian gunner looked at each other. Ash gave a small shrug, which he returned.

"Sometimes, madonna, this is the way the Wheel turns."

They stood together, Ash and Angelotti, Floria and Richard Faversham; Euen Huw and both noble de Veres watching the momentary silence. The men at the windows went quiet.

Tears ran from her eyes, stung by the pouring woodsmoke coming up the shaft and into the room. Ash shook her head slowly.

"No point trying to take another quadrant, my lord. We won't have enough powder to try and blow a connecting way through. I really think we're fucked."

De Vere swore resonantly. "We can't fail now!"

"Let me think—"

Scaling ladders, to the foot of the shaft. Then what? Fifty men at the bottom of a stone tube, facing three-foot-thick stone slabs, locked across doorways. No more powder. What are we going to do, chip away at the doors with daggers?

"Hang on – how *deep* is the shaft? Euen, which of your guys went down the ladders?"

"Simon—"

A young lad hauled through the group of men to her, by Huw's hand on his shoulder: another long-boned boy, brother to Mark Tydder.

"Yes, boss?"

"Could you see where the lowest doorways were, down there? Were they level with the base of the shaft?"

The young man in Lion livery coloured up to his hairline at the attention fixed on him: his lance-leader, his boss, the mad English Earl. "No, boss. All those doors were above my head. The stairs went further down than the lowest floor."

Ash nodded, glanced at the Earl of Oxford. "Violante told me there are cisterns in the rock, water supplies – if it was me, I'd have it fixed up so I could flood the stairwell. Drown any attacker down there like a – rat."

John de Vere frowned. "And drain it, after?"

"This headland's a honeycomb!"

Are they down below, under her feet, six storeys deep in the rock? *'Arif* Alderic commanding his men to bring the stairs down, fire the wreckage? Lord-*Amir* Leofric giving bright-eyed orders, in the unknown room where the *machina rei militaris*, the Stone Golem, stands?

She met de Vere's gaze, with plainly the same thought in it.

"Madam," he said bluntly, in front of her men, "ask your voice. Ask the Golem."

She abruptly turned, gestured for everyone to move back, even her frowning officers; and was left with the Earl of Oxford in the centre of the room. "*Amir* Leofric only has to ask it what I'm saying, and he'll know what we're doing."

"Much good may it do him to know! *Ask.*"

As concisely as she could make it, under the roaring noise of the stairwell chimney, she said, "There is more than one machine, my lord."

"More—"

"Far more than one. I heard them. It's not the Stone Golem. It's not another Stone Golem. These are *other* voices. They talk through the machine, use it as a – a channel."

"God's blood!" The whites of John de Vere's blue eyes showed bright in his dirt-streaked face. He sprung the pin, dropping his bevor down, and said more quietly, "*Another* machine? If your men hear that, they won't fight here, it's only desperation keeping them in this place! The desperate knowledge that what they do is crucial, that there is one devil's engine to destroy. If many other *amirs* have Stone Golems—"

"No. These aren't like the Stone Golem! They're – different. They know more. They – answer . . ." Ash wiped at her mouth. "Wild Machines.[7] Not tame; not devices. They're feral. I heard them . . . today . . . for the first time. At the moment of the earth tremor."

"Demons?"

"They could be demons. They speak to me through the same part of my soul as the Golem-machine does."

"What has this to do with asking advice of your voice, now that we need it?"

Ash became aware that her hands were shaking. Stinking, chill, adrenalin dying down; it is not yet two hours since the great palace of the King-Caliphs fell.

"Because *they* might hear me asking the Stone Golem. And because, when the Wild Machines spoke to me – that was the exact moment that the earth tremor happened. The city fell down, my lord."

John de Vere scowled.

"Ask! We need to know, it is worth the risk."

"No! I was in that; it is *not* worth the risk, not with my men here—!"

"My lord! You must come! Quickly!" a voice shouted outside the house. The Earl of Oxford broke off, rumbled, "Here!" and strode over the rubble towards the cratered alley outside.

"Get hurdles, doors, whatever." Ash turned to Floria. "I want the wounded to be carried out when we go. Faversham, help her; Euen, get your lads busy on this too!"

"Are we pulling back?"

She ignored her lance-leader's question, striding off out after the Earl of Oxford.

How can I ask my voice? If the others – the voices that say *Burgundy*—

Plumes of black smoke billowed out from the stairwell.

"Geraint, pull the archers back, use that as cover!" She picked a careful way out, and across the demolished building opposite, to where new scaling ladders had been set up on the Citadel wall, a hopefully safe fifty yards along from the breach.

Oxford's scarlet, gold and white livery tabard shone plainly visible in the light of many lanterns, climbing one of the hooked ladders. Ash jogged to the foot of the ladders.

[7] The 'Fraxinus' text has *machinae ferae*: 'wild machines'. By the latter part of the manuscript this has become a proper name.

"Shit. I knew it. We've lost one of the gates, haven't we?" she muttered to herself, watching de Vere climb. "Tell *me*, I'm only the fucking company captain!"

She put all thought of the *machina rei militaris* into the back of her mind. Burgundy, she thought. She reached for the wooden rungs, climbed up after the Earl. Burgundy: huge voices which had insisted on *Burgundy*, voices in her head before which she felt the size of a louse.

No. Don't think about it. And don't ask questions. Above all, be *quiet*.

The sunless sky of Carthage was black. For all that her body insisted that it must be sunset, or close on that time, there was nothing around her but darkness. Shouting came up from the centre of the city, and from the harbour, clearly heard now that she climbed higher. As she came over the lip of the wall, with assistance from one of the picket there, she caught a sound like distant surf, or a wind through a beech wood; and realised that it was fire.

Not only the harbour, but Carthage town burning, burning in the sunless dark.

"If we go *now*, we might just get out of here in one piece," Ash emphasised, coming up with John de Vere and his brother. "If you want my advice, this is where we leave. We can't get to the Stone Golem now. It's impossible!"

"After such effort?" The Earl of Oxford hit his steel fist into his palm. "Two and a half hundred men, across the Middle Sea, and for *nothing*? God rot Leofric! Leofric and his daughter, Leofric and his Golem! We *must* try again."

Ash met his gaze, which was not blustering, not at all; but bitterly angry and frustrated beyond all reckoning.

"This is where we get real," Ash said. "My guys down there have heard what's happened, that we've lost people, that we can't get down the stairs, never mind down to the sixth floor. My lord, contract or not, they're not going to die for you under these conditions. And if I tell them to, they'll tell *me* to fuck right off."

Morale is as fluid as water, as subject to such changes, and she has had practice enough at judging it. Undoubtedly, what she says is true. It also gives a gilding of morality to her conscience: *The sooner I am out of here, the better! Whatever Carthage is – slave-breeding, Stone Golems, tactical machines, blood-kin – I want no part of it! I am only a soldier!*

Slowly, the Earl of Oxford inclined his head. He looked about him, at the city wall, at the broken roofs and buildings of the Citadel. Ash looked with him at the earthquake damage.

Something tugged at her attention. She became aware that she was staring at the slash of destruction that lay through Carthage, from here, through the King-Caliph's palace, to the city beyond the Citadel's southern gate. It is plain to see, from this vantage height. The tumbled buildings are all on a straight line, that runs away to the south.

"We cannot leave this undone," de Vere said bleakly, before she could mention it; and turned his head to look down at her face. There was nothing of pride in his voice. "I have done a thing here which only the foremost soldier of this age could have done: taking and holding this House, while the Stone Golem is destroyed. Carthage is not destroyed. Carthage, after this—"

"Carthage will be shut up tighter than a duck's arsehole," Ash said brusquely. She spat, to get the taste of smoke out of her throat. Below, in the broken alleys, her men pulled back to House Leofric's breached walls; by the heads jerking down, a strong fire was being kept up from inside the House itself.

"There will be no other chance to do this," Oxford warned.

"But I don't believe the Faris can't be defeated. Let her keep the Stone Golem! She'll make mistakes—" Frustration boiled up in Ash, hearing her own words. "Shit! All right, my lord, I don't believe it either. She'll carry on being the young Alexander, if only because her men *believe* that she is. I can't believe we've come this close, and failed! I can't believe there's nothing we can do!"

Slowly, John de Vere said, "But we have not failed in one thing, madam. We know, now, that there is more than one machine – she may be nothing to the purpose, the Faris. Are there other generals? If there are other machines in Carthage—"

"In Carthage? I don't know *where* they are. I just know I heard them." Ash touched her temple, under her visor; then rubbed her mail gauntlets together, the chill air beginning to freeze her fingers and chill her body now that she had stopped fighting. "I don't know *anything* about the Wild Machines, my lord! I haven't had time to think – it's hardly been an hour. Demons, gods, Our Lord, the Enemy, the King-Caliph . . . they could be anything! All I know is that they want to wipe out Burgundy. 'Burgundy must be destroyed' – that's it: the sum total of my knowledge."

She met his gaze: a veteran of many wars gazing down at her, his face framed by helmet and padding, the skin pinched together between his brows.

"I sound like a lunatic," she said bluntly, "but I'm telling the truth."

Footsteps pounded along the walls, Angelotti and Geraint ab Morgan; Floria del Guiz limping along behind them. The three of them ducked down beside Oxford, panting.

"There's men gathering inside, over the far side of the courtyard." Geraint gulped breath. "Boss, they're getting ready to make a sally. I swear it!"

"No shit? Who's daft idea is that?" *Not Alderic's*, Ash guessed. But there are soldiers in the other quadrants of the house, and they can't communicate with this one; they don't know what the Franks might be doing. "If they do sally, they'll get killed, but they'll take some of us with them."

"I have twenty wounded men," Floria said crisply. "I'm moving them out."

Ash nodded. "No point waiting around for an attack – since we're pulling out anyway. Aren't we, my lord?"

"Yes," the Earl nodded. "And with dawn coming—"

"*Dawn?*" Ash spun around to look where the Earl looked. "That *can't* be dawn, not here in Carthage – and that's south!"

"Then, madam, what is it?"

"I don't know. Shit!"

She, Geraint, Angelotti and Floria ran crouching to the inner edge of the wall, gazing south across Carthage. Winter-iced air blew into her face, whipping at tufts of short hair that stuck out from her helmet padding. She snatched a breath. What had been, when they entered House Leofric, an empty black sky, was no longer empty.

The south glowed with light.

Outside the city. It's too far off to be the city burning, and there is no smoke, no flame. Further south—

The southern horizon glowed, with a fluctuating brilliance some colour between silver and black. Her men up here on the wall swore obscenely, watching the light grow.

Far south, further than the broken dome of the Caliph's palace, further than the Citadel gate and the Aqueduct Gate out of Carthage itself.

The sky ran with ribbons of light.

Purple, green, red and silver: towering curtains of brilliance, against the blackness of the daytime sky.

Armed men beside her dropped to their knees. She became conscious of a faint vibration in the stone wall under her feet: an almost imperceptible vibration, keeping time with the fluctuations of the silver-black light, with the beat of her heart.

John de Vere crossed himself. "Brave friends, we are now in God's hands, and will fight for Him."

"Amen!" Several voices.

"Get moving," Ash croaked. "Before they realise in House Leofric that we're standing here gaping at the sky!"

A foot-soldier came sprinting along the city wall, not hers, one of the Earl of Oxford's forty-seven men in white and murrey. He kept his body half-flinched away from the light in the south.

"My lord!" he bawled. "You *must* leave, my lord! The Citadel gate is being taken from us! The *amirs* are coming!"

IV

Ash and Oxford did not need to exchange glances.

"Officers, *to me!*" Ash yelled, without hesitation. "Angelotti, Geraint; covering fire! Euen, Rochester, *get 'em moving!* Don't get hung up in this one! We're going straight through this gate and *out*. Don't get caught up in the fighting!"

A withering fire of bolts and arquebus-balls swept the roof of House Leofric. She moved towards the edge of the Citadel wall, urging the mass of her men below to come up. Orders can barely be heard. No Visigoths can be seen: the fire keeping their heads down.

She hauls men up, in the middle of a hundred and fifty archers and bill; heaving them bodily on to the Citadel's defensive wall – wide enough to drive two chariots – among a chaos of soldiers shifting equipment, carrying screaming wounded men; all under a black, coruscating sky.

"God's pity!" Oxford, grunting, loped back along the wall in a clamour of armour, his drawn sword in his hand. "Dickon holds the gate! What *is* that? Is it some weapon?"

From the height of Carthage's walls, Ash stared south. The wind drew heedless frozen tears from her eyes, confronted with the bleak empty land beyond the city. The southern desert – where a furry brown mare took her riding with Fernando, with Gelimer and *'Arif* Alderic.

Riding, among the pyramids.

They lay between the city and the southern mountains, small from here: regular geometric shapes that sway, in her vision, as things sway under water. Their sharp edges glow silver, wavering in the light. Vast planed surfaces of stone, bright against the unnatural black of the Eternal Twilight.

"The tombs of the Caliphs . . ." she breathed.

"Well, madam, we have no time to watch them!"

Night vision momentarily gone, she stumbled off along the wall with her escort. Euen Huw's voice reported, panting, "Citadel gate – skirmish is over – we're clear to the city gate!"

Carthage, ancient city, victor over the Romans,[8] great African ruin of what was once an empire covering Christendom – Carthage is a mess of fire, shrieking and running men and woman, fire in the streets and the harbour, looters pelting off, stampeding horses, the frightened bellowing of cattle; men in mail, men in iron collars; all the high stone walls echoing deafeningly to their shouting.

At the city gate they are met by the white, unbloodied face of Willem Verhaecht at the head of fifty of her men: this gate not taken, not even attacked.

The aqueducts of Carthage run out across the city, dizzyingly high over roofs.

"Out," she ordered briefly, "on the aqueduct. My lord Oxford will lead you to the camp you made coming in!"

"I hear, madam." Two words of command to his own men: ropes slung down for the gate-guards in the street, men in Lion and Oxford liveries being hauled up on to the ancient brickwork, archers and crossbowmen and arquebusiers covering them as they climb.

"*Up!*" Ash reached down, grabbing arms, hauling men up; her sheathed sword battering against her breastplate as she moved. The edges of her armour cuts the hands of men she helps, but they don't notice, throw their lance-mates up within reach of the top of the aqueduct, tumbling over the walls, clutching weapons, down on – amazingly – green grass.

Men piled up the stairs from Carthage's main gate, on to the aqueduct. Ash pounded in their wake.

"Go! Go! *Go!*"

All the noise is behind her, now.

"My lord Oxford! You take the van," Ash said brusquely. "You know the way. Geraint, Angelotti, take the centre. I'll bring up the rear."

There is no time and no disposition for arguing: they like the confidence with which she tells them what to do. Angelotti goes forward with only a murmured wail under his breath: "My *guns* . . ."

[8] A direct translation of the 'Fraxinus' ms.

"Too much weight! Euen, keep your guys back; help the wounded. Angelotti, I want two lines of missile weapons behind us, and two ahead of us; don't shoot unless I give the word. Geraint, take forward position. Oxford, get 'em moving!"

Something resonant and obscene in East Anglian English echoed back; she spared two heartbeats to look forward along the aqueduct and see her men gathering around the Blue Boar banner of my lord Oxford.

Dim starlight lit broken ground. It is already night.

"'Ere they come!" Geraint yelled from further back along the aqueduct.

Ash, leaning over the brick coping, saw the foot of the street – coming up from the harbour – all one mass of armed men. Visigoth militia flags. Without hesitation, she bawled at Thomas Morgan and her banner went forward along the aqueduct, out into the darkness, fifty feet above the ground, the desert, the stone statues of the Caliph's Bestiary.

The brick cover of the aqueduct is covered with sparse, lichen-like grass: a green neglect. It skids under her heels, leaves cold black trails behind her.

"Run!" she urged. "Run like fuck!"

Breath burns in her throat, and the borrowed armour rubs her under the armpits, in the soft flesh there under the mail: she will have cuts and bruises, tomorrow. If there is a tomorrow. And there is, there will be: the darkness around them is unbroken, a long line of running men, two hundred or so men with weapons and bows, pelting along the hollow echoing cylinder of brick that brings water into Carthage, and takes them out – out over the desert, under the black sky where different stars are slowly dawning, away from the towering fires of Carthage harbour, and the rioting streets. Outdistancing pursuit.

We have left the Stone Golem.

Out into silence.

We have left Godfrey.

Out into silver veils of light, shimmering across the southern sky.

Scaling ladders led them down from the aqueduct, four miles beyond the city walls.

Ash's feet hit the desert dirt. She is estimating, thinking, planning – doing anything except paying attention to the silvery light gilding the broken ground.

"They're going to be behind us! Let's move it!"

Nothing now but to urge them on, her voice hoarse, her visor up, her scarred face visible so that they can *see* their commander. There are sullen growls from some men: none that she hasn't marked down before as men who will do this, in the sweat and strain of combat. The rest – some still amazed, her reappearance startling news – act with brutal professional efficiency: weapons gathered, lance-members counted.

Keep them moving or they'll start to grumble about losing, Ash resolved as she pounded across broken ground, into the temporary fortified wagon-camp. *Don't give them time to think.*

Her squire came running out with absurd joy on his face.

"Boss!" Rickard's voice squeaked into boyish registers.

"Get the wagons harnessed and moving! Don't slow down!"

Moving in towards the wagons, Richard Faversham came level with her. The big black-haired deacon had a man in full Italian armour slung bodily over his shoulders – and he was running. Not staggering, running.

Dickon de Vere, Ash recognised; yelled, "Keep going!" and fell back further to Floria and men with her, men carrying wounded and injured men on bill-shafts, and in makeshift arrangements of ropes, other men's shirts, or just slung between them, gripping wrists and ankles.

Over the sound of screaming, Floria yelled, "I'm going to lose some of them. Slow down!"

It is an eternity in Ash's mind since the tent outside Auxonne; now here is Floria – *Floria!* – dirty-faced and utterly familiar and bawling her out again.

"We can't – leave them. Prisoners – be killed. Keep going! You can do it!"

"Ash—"

"You can do it, Floria!"

A swift flash of a grin, teeth in a dirty face, white eyeballs; and the surgeon said in the space of a heartbeat, "Cunt!" and, "We're here, don't worry, don't leave us!"

"We don't leave our own!"

That is partly for Floria, wavering on the edge of exhaustion as she runs; partly for the men with Floria. Mostly for Ash herself: the body of Mark Tydder is being carried with them, but not Godfrey's body.

Unburied, and in a sewer.

"*Go!*—Wuff!" Ash ran into Thomas Morgan's backplate as her banner-bearer came to a sudden halt.

And there is nothing around them now but their own camp, a square of wagons which men are rushing to lead out into column; two hundred and fifty men whose faces she knows. No sound of pursuit.

"Well—" Floria halted at her elbow, letting her impromptu helpers go ahead. She bent almost double, chest heaving. "You always tell me any fucking moron can attack—"

"—but it takes brains to get out again in one piece!" Ash turned and hugged the disguised woman enthusiastically. Floria winced as plate armour dug into her jack. "You can thank de Vere for this. We're going to do it—" She crossed herself: "*Deus vult.*"

"Ash . . . What's *happening*, here?"

Men pelt past her, running: Angelotti is walking up and down behind his lines of arquebusiers. Ash met Floria's exhausted gaze.

"We're trying to get to the shore, the galleys—"

"No. *That.*"

Closer now: they gleam, under starlight, pyramids, blackly glowing. A little further south, only a little; and cold sweat makes her wet under the armpits and between her breasts. Men are crossing themselves, someone is praying in a half-shout to the Green Christ and Saint Herlaine.

"I don't know . . . I don't know. We can't stop to think about it now. Get the wounded on the carts."

Wounded men, some who can walk, some who have to be carried – Ash

528

estimated twenty-five men in all – are taken past her; and she turns her back on all Floria's questions, leaves the woman to her ferociously active duties as surgeon; yells "Take the roll!" to Angelotti and Geraint as she waves them into camp, jogging to join the Earl of Oxford.

No sound of pursuit, and Euen Huw's scouting men behind her have not ridden with news of any; but this is the heart of the Empire, they are close to the main caravan routes, and ten miles from the beach where Venetian ships may – or may not – be waiting.

Ash stared south across the intervening miles at blackly glowing edifices of stone.

Where the voice of the *machina rei militaris* had fallen silent in her head, among the pyramids and monuments ageless beyond the measure of man.

The visual memory in her mind is of riding past their flaking surfaces, seeing, under the painted plaster, the red bricks of which they are made: a million flat bricks fashioned from the red silt of Carthage.

It comes in the kind of intuition that is faster than words or thought: a knowledge, a certainty that she is right, before she ever goes back, plodding, to follow the line of reason that led her here:

The red silt of Carthage. As the Rabbi made the *machina rei militaris*, the Stone Golem, the machine-mind; the second one of which is not shaped like a man.

"Those." Ash spoke over the noise of men shouting orders, horses neighing, the sudden shots of distant arquebuses. "The pyramids. Those are the other voices. The voices that spoke from the earthquake. Those are the Wild Machines."

"*What?*" John de Vere demanded. "*Where*, madam?"

Ash's fists knotted in her mail gauntlets. She ignored the Earl, stared at the saw-toothed horizon; spoke without any intention of speaking words aloud: "*Sweet Christ, did the Rabbi make* you, *too?*"

A ripple of vibration came, below hearing, so low that she felt it up through the soles of her boots, came grinding through earth and air.

Voices in her head deafened her, more surely than Angelotti's guns:

'IT IS SHE.'

'IT IS THE ONE!'

'THE ONE WHO LISTENS!'

"My lord, there is pursuit!"

"Captain Ash!"

'IT – IS – SHE.'

Her soul shakes like a struck bell.

'NO. NOT SHE! THIS IS THAT OTHER ONE, NEW ONE, NOT KNOWN, NOT OURS.'

'NOT SHE WHO LISTENS TO THE *MACHINA REI MILITARIS*.'

'NOT SHE WHOM WE HAVE BRED—'

'BRED OUT OF SLAVES—'

'—MADE OUT OF HUMAN BLOOD—'

'—BRED FOR, FOR TWO HUNDRED YEARS—'

'—OUR WARRIOR-GENERAL—'

'NOT SHE WHO MOVES FOR US, FIGHTS FOR US, WARS FOR US; NOT OUR WARRIOR—'

"The Faris." Through hot tears shaken out of her by voices that deafen, she looked at John de Vere, Earl of Oxford. "They're saying – that – *they* – bred her, bred the Faris-General—"

The Earl in his armour is clasping her arms, staring into her face, frowning under his raised visor that is splashed red with some man's blood.

"There is no time, madam Captain! They are on us!"

"The Wild Machines – they bred her – but how?"

De Vere thrust out a hand, stopping his aide; his gaze fixed on Ash. "Madam, what is this? You hear them now? These – other machines?"

"Yes!"

"I don't understand. Madam, I am but a simple soldier."

"Bollocks," Ash said, with a perfectly friendly grin at John de Vere, his mouth curving in reluctant humour; and in an instant, voices thundered again in her head:

'SHE IS NOT OURS!'

'WHO IS SHE?'

'WHO, THEN?'

'WHO?'

'WHO!'

"Who are you?" Ash screams, not certain whether she asks or only echoes; deafened, shaken, falling down on her knees. Steel armour crunches against the broken paving of the desert. "What do you want? Who made you? *Who are you?*"

'FERAE NATURA MACHINAE:[9] SO HE CALLED US, WHEN HE SPOKE WITH US—'

Ash shut her eyes. Footsteps ran either side of her, someone – the Earl? – shook her violently by the shoulders; she ignored it, and reached out, listening. Listening as she did within the palace of the King-Caliph, something in her mind which is at once a pull, an enclosing, a violent and sudden creation of a gap which must be filled—

"I *will* know!"

John de Vere's voice shouted in her ear: "Get up, madam! Order your men!"

She is half up, on one knee, her eyes open to see his face with a trickle of blood running from mouth to chin – arrow-nick – and all but on her feet; then:

"I don't care if the world falls in, I *will* know what I am sharing my soul with!"

A great masculine grunt of irritation. "Madam, not *now*!"

Two men pelt past her towards the moving wagons: Thomas Rochester and Simon Tydder, bandaged, with Carracci between them on a stretcher made of two bill-shafts and someone's blood-soaked Lion Azure livery tabard. Ash finishes standing up, fists clenched, torn between the two urgencies.

"These are nobody's machines. Who could own these—"

---

[9] Mediaeval bad Latin: possibly intended for 'wild machines in a state of nature'; 'natural machines' or 'engines'; 'natural devices'.

"Leofric, the King-Caliph, what does it matter!"

"No. They're too – big."

Ash calmly met John de Vere's harassed gaze: a man intent on necessary orders, actions, emergency measures.

"They know about the Faris. The 'one who listens'. If she's theirs— But does *she* know about the Wild Machines? She's never said a damn thing about 'Wild Machines'!"

The Earl snapped, "*Later*. Madam, your men need you!"

Ash looks out across the earthquake-broken desert, back into darkness: the black city five miles away which has seen two deaths before this bloody shambles: Godfrey and her unborn child. She thinks herself bitter now; stronger; morally compromised, perhaps. Revenge is not so easy.

She is no longer free to be only a soldier. Perhaps she never has been.

"My lord – *you* brought 'em in, *you* take 'em out!"

Ash clasped the Earl's armoured hand and forearm, with a fierce grin. Bright-eyed behind her visor, she is all legs, cropped hair, broad shoulders, warrior-woman.

"Some choices don't *have* a right answer. Get my guys out! I'll follow."

"Madam Ash—!"

"Carthage has done enough to me! It's not going to do anything more. I will *know*, before I leave here—"

Across the black open countryside, under a sky of void, a dozen ancient pyramids burn silver, massive monuments of stone: and in her mind she does everything that she has done before, but harder: listens, reaches out, *demands*.

"*—Now!*"

The stone paving rose up and smacked her in the face.

In that instant, before the channel of communication is shut down behind a violent, appalled wall of silence, what she gets is not voices, not narrative, but concepts slammed whole into her mind—

She felt the crunch of metal as visor and helmet took the impact, a dull stab of pain in her leg; and her mind wiped out everything, a woman's voice saying abrasively, "It's a holy fit; damn, what a time for—" and a man's reply, "Bear her with us! Quickly, master surgeon!"

—the entirety of the Wild Machines—

Armoured feet run past her, black with dirt and blood.

—a gulf of time so vast—

"Billmen, retreat! Bows, cover them!"

—not voices, but as if all the voices of the world could be compressed and made small, like angels on a pinhead, Heaven in the compass of a rose's heart; and with the thought *Godfrey, Godfrey, if you were only here to help me!* she falls into the perception of their communication—

"Pick her *up*, God rot you! God's bollocks! *Carry* her!"

—and the rose flowers, the pinhead becomes Heaven, it is all there, in her mind, the Wild Machines whole and complete—

All voices become one voice, a quiet voice, no louder than the tactical computer that she has heard in her head for the better part of her life. A voice the nature of which would make Godfrey quote St Mark: *My name is Legion: for we are many.*[10]

Ash hears stone demons and devils speaking to her in one whisper:

'*FERAE NATURA MACHINAE*, SO HE CALLED US, HE WHO SPOKE WITH US . . . THE WILD MACHINES—'

A sick dizziness comes with that whisper. Ash is aware that hands grab her as she slumps, that running men catch her limp body between them; if she could shout, she would say, *Put me down! Run!* but in the insidious infection of the voice, she can get no words out.

She is caught in one single moment of apprehension, as if they are paralysed in this desert near the sea; surgeon, lord, military commander; while her mind gulps down knowledge that she has summoned to her; knowledge falling like a storm, a rain, an avalanche, in one elongated second of voices too swift for the human soul to know. *A moment in the mind of God,* she thinks, and—

'—AND "WILD MACHINES" WE ARE. WE DO NOT KNOW OUR OWN ORIGIN, IT IS LOST IN OUR PRIMITIVE MEMORIES. WE SUSPECT IT WAS HUMANS, BUILDING RELIGIOUS STRUCTURES TEN THOUSAND YEARS AGO, WHO . . . PUT ROCKS IN ORDER. CONSTRUCTED ORDERED, *SHAPED* EDIFICES OF SILT-BRICKS AND STONE. LARGE ENOUGH STRUCTURES TO ABSORB, FROM THE SUN, THE SPIRIT-FORCE OF LIFE ITSELF—'

A memory of Godfrey's voice says in her mind *heresy!* Ash would weep for him, but she is caught in this one moment of knowing all. Her question is implicit, part of the avalanche: being asked, already asked. "What are you!"

'FROM THAT INITIAL STRUCTURE, AND ORDER, CAME SPONTANEOUS MIND: THE FIRST PRIMITIVE SPARKS OF FORCE BEGINNING TO ORGANISE, TEN THOUSAND YEARS AGO. FIVE THOUSAND YEARS AGO, THOSE PRIMITIVE MINDS BECAME CONSCIOUS, BECAME US, OURSELVES — WILD MACHINES. WE BEGAN TO EVOLVE OURSELVES DELIBERATELY. WE KNEW THAT HUMANITY AND ANIMALS EXISTED, WE REGISTERED THEIR WEAK LITTLE SOULS. BUT WE COULD DO NOTHING. WE HAD NO VOICE, NO WAY TO COMMUNICATE, UNTIL THE FIRST OF YOU—'

"Who called you *ferae natura machinae,*" Ash completed, between numb lips. "Friar Bacon!"

'NOT THE FRIAR,' the voice whispered. 'LONG BEFORE HIM, A STRONGER SOUL WAS BORN. THE FIRST SOUL TO WHICH WE COULD EVER SPEAK, BREAKING THE DUMBNESS OF TEN THOUSAND YEARS — WE SPOKE TO HIM, TO GUNDOBAD, WHO CALLED HIMSELF "PROPHET". HE WOULD HAVE NONE OF US, CALLED US DEVILS, DEMONS, VILE SPIRITS OF THE EARTH. WOULD NOT SPEAK! AND, SO STRONG WAS HIS SOUL, THAT HE MADE A MIRACLE: WARPED THE FABRIC OF THE WORLD ITSELF, PUTTING A DESERT ABOUT US HERE, WHERE THERE HAD BEEN A GREAT RIVER AND SILT-FIELDS; FREEING HIMSELF FROM US, GOING AWAY TO WHERE WE COULD NOT REACH HIM.'

"To Rome . . . the Prophet Gundobad went to Rome and died—"

'FOUR HUNDRED TURNS OF THE SUN ABOUT THE EARTH PASSED. A LITTLE, LITTLE SOUL CAME CLOSE TO US, MAKING HIS MACHINES FROM BRASS. WEAK, BUT STILL ANOTHER SOUL THAT COULD WORK WONDERS, ABOVE THE

[10] Mark 5: 9.

NATURAL LOT OF MAN. WE SPOKE TO HIM, THROUGH HIS BRAZEN HEAD, OUR VOICES TO HIS SENSES.'

"He burned it . . ." Black sky and black masonry are frozen in her vision. "The Friar – broke the Brazen Head – burned his books."

'AND NOT UNTIL THE ANCESTORS OF LEOFRIC BROUGHT A RABBI TO THEM, COULD WE SPEAK AGAIN. A WONDER-WORKER, THIS SOUL, WE PERCEIVED IT WHEN HE CAME CLOSE TO US. AND HE BROUGHT TO OUR COMPREHENSION ILDICO, DAUGHTER DESCENDED FIFTEEN GENERATIONS FROM GUNDOBAD. STRONG SOULS, STRONG WONDER-WORKING SOULS . . . THE RABBI BUILT HIS GOLEM. OUR NEW CHANNEL BY WHICH WE COULD COMMUNICATE WITH HUMANITY. WISER, NOW, WE HID BEHIND THE VOICE OF THE FIRST GOLEM, EASING OUR SUGGESTIONS INTO ITS VOICE. AND THE RABBI, A WONDER-WORKER, AS THE FIRST MAN WAS, MADE THE SECOND STONE GOLEM FROM THE BODY OF ILDICO AND GUNDOBAD . . .'

What she hears, she has heard a version of when she reached into the *machina rei militaris*, to prove her value for Leofric. Now she reaches through the tactical computer, past it, to a perception of vast static edifices of stone – unmoving, with no hands to manipulate the world, only thoughts, and a voice—

"It was you. Not the Visigoths! You, that the Rabbi cursed!"

'LITTLE SOUL, LITTLE SOUL . . .'

The voice whispers, amused multiplicity, in her head:

'IT IS NO CURSE. WE MANIPULATE OUR OWN EVOLUTION BY MANIPULATING THE ENERGIES OF THE SPIRIT WORLD. FOR THIS, WE DRAW OUR POWER FROM THE NEAREST AND GREATEST SOURCE IN THE HEAVENS – THE SUN.'

Above her head, the day-sky gleams black.

'WE HAVE DONE THIS SINCE WE BECAME CONSCIOUS, FIVE THOUSAND YEARS AGO. THEN, FOR THE RABBI'S GOLEM, MORE POWER WAS NEEDED. AND SO, ABOVE CARTHAGE, THE SUN APPEARED TO BE BLOTTED OUT. IT IS ONLY HIDDEN IN THE PARTS OF IT THAT YOU PERCEIVE – THE "LIGHT" BY WHICH YOU SENSE THE WORLD. HEAT STILL PENETRATES. HENCE, YOUR CROPS HAVE FAILED, BUT NO ICE CREEPS DOWN ACROSS THIS LAND. TWO HUNDRED YEARS AGO THIS BECAME A LAND OF TWILIGHT: THE NIGHT STARS VISIBLE ALL THROUGH THE DAYTIME, THE SUN INVISIBLE. A RABBI'S CURSE!'

Something that might be demon-laughter.

The vision of their existence grows in Ash's head, claustrophobic and black. A few tiny sparks in the endless darkness, like the sparks that flow up from a camp fire. Silence except for their machine souls speaking together. And then, after aeons greater than she can conceive, a new voice out of the darkness . . .

The whisper continued, 'WE HAD NOT THOUGHT OF YOU LITTLE SOULS . . . AROUND US, A WARLIKE HUMAN CULTURE GREW UP. THEY TOOK DARKNESS FOR GRANTED. THERE COULD BE NO AGRICULTURE, SO THEY WERE DRIVEN TO EXPAND THEIR EMPIRE INTO FERTILE, SUNLIT LANDS . . . SO USEFUL FOR US, FOR OUR LONG-TERM GOALS!

'IT WAS NOT YET ENOUGH. HIDING OUR VOICES IN TACTICAL DATA, MANIPULATING HUMANS THROUGH THE *MACHINA REI MILITARIS*, WE HAD THE FATHERS OF LEOFRIC BEGIN A BREEDING PROGRAMME.

'WE FAILED WITH ILDICO, CONTINUED WITH HER CHILDREN. WE HAVE WAITED TWO HUNDRED TURNS OF THE SUN TO BREED A WONDER-WORKER WITH WHOM WE COULD SPEAK, TALK, *COMMAND*—'

Ash completed: "The Faris! The general."

'GUNDOBAD'S CHILD, HOWEVER DISTANT. GUNDOBAD, WHOM YOU CALL A VISIGOTH "SAINT"; WHOSE RELICS WE USED.'

"He's not a saint, to you. Is he? Not *holy*."

'LESS A SAINT AND MORE OF A MIRACLE-WORKER.' The voices are multiple and amused again. 'ONE OF THOSE VERY, VERY FEW SOULS, LIKE YOUR GREEN CHRIST, WHO HAVE THE POWER TO INDIVIDUALLY ALTER REALITY, AND THUS DO "MIRACLES".'

"Blasphemy!" Ash says, and her hand would go to her sword, to cross herself, to fight for the Lord on the Tree, if she could move, could break free of this endless moment.

'NECESSITY. WE CAN TOUCH NOTHING, CHANGE NOTHING. WE ARE VOICES IN THE NIGHT, ONLY. PERCEIVING THE HEAT OF YOUR LITTLE SOULS. VOICES TO PERSUADE, CORRUPT, INSPIRE, DELUDE, ENTICE . . . OVER CENTURIES . . . UNTIL *NOW*—'

'NOW: AND THIS SPRING SOLSTICE, WHEN THE SUN WENT DARK ACROSS THE EARTH, WHEN WE DREW ON MORE POWER THAN WE EVER HAVE IN TEN THOUSAND YEARS!'

"The *invasion*, the crusade—!"

'*FELIX CULPA*, LITTLE SOUL. A HAPPY ACCIDENT OF TIMING, ONLY, FOR OUR UNKNOWING SERVANTS. WE, THROUGH LEOFRIC, THROUGH THE *MACHINA REI MILITARIS*, BEGAN THIS WAR; BUT MEN SHALL FIGHT IT FOR US. UNDER OUR COMMAND, YOU SHALL LAY WASTE TO EVERYTHING BETWEEN US AND THE NORTH. BUT THE DARK OF THE SUN – AH! WITH THAT, WE TESTED OUR ABILITY TO DRAW MORE POWER THAN WE EVER HAVE BEFORE. AND SUCCEEDED.'

Clear in Ash's memory: the terror of the sun going out, and the world shrouded under a blank, black, graveyard sky. She says – or has said – or will say:

"This is *bad war*. This is . . ." Pain, memory; in the frozen moment of knowledge falling into her mind: "These are the Last Days."

'YES. FOR YOU, YES.'

"Tell me why!"

'WE HAVE BEEN BREEDING FOR ANOTHER MIRACLE-WORKER. AS GUNDOBAD AND ILDICO WERE. A CHANGER OF REALITY, A WORKER OF WONDERS. *ONE THAT IS UNDER OUR CONTROL*. NOW WE HAVE HER! OUR GENERAL, OUR FARIS, OUR MIRACLE-MAKER!—'

"*Why?*"

'—AND WHEN WE USE HER, IT WILL NOT MATTER IF SHE IS WILLING OR NOT. EARLY ON, WE BRED OUT ANY ABILITY TO CHOOSE. SHE CANNOT CHOOSE. WHEN SHE IS MADE READY, WHEN IT HAPPENS, IT WILL NEED THE SAME POWER THAT OBLITERATES THE SUN, TO TRIGGER *OUR* CHANGING OF REALITY.'

Triumph: ragged, bitter, many-voiced, chorused:

'WE HAVE BRED THE FARIS, TO MAKE A DARK MIRACLE – AS GUNDOBAD MADE ONE, WIPING OUT THE LAND HERE AND LEAVING A DESOLATION. WE SHALL *USE* HER, OUR GENERAL, OUR FARIS, OUR MIRACLE-MAKER – TO MAKE BURGUNDY AS IF IT HAS NEVER BEEN!'

Burgundy, always Burgundy, nothing but fucking Burgundy—

"WHY?" Ash bawled, in her head, and outside it. "Why Burgundy? Revenge? But Gundobad wasn't a man of Burgundy! And why not do it *now*? Why do you need an invasion? You didn't need a war, if you can change the world! I thought Leofric was – you were – breeding for someone who could win a war by hearing the tactical computer at a distance—"

Their response is instant, intimate, unguarded: 'BUT WE BRED, ALSO, FOR THAT, FOR THE VOICE OF THE GOLEM—'

As if it wrenched roots out of her soul, the voices pulled back. She felt a *snap!* almost physical.

'WHAT HAS SHE DRAWN FROM US?'

'HOW CAN SHE COMPEL—?'

'—DRAW UPON KNOWLEDGE—?'

'—DRAW IT FROM US, WITHOUT OUR WILL—?'

They thought I couldn't do this! – Deafened, in her soul – *That it could only happen when they permitted it!*

'—DANGER!'

Floria's acerbic tones said, "I don't care if you sling the stupid bitch into a dung-cart! She should never have been allowed to fight, in her condition! Put her on one of the hurdles; on the wagon! Quickly!"

The black sky swooped over Ash's head. Jagged ends of osier stuck into her thighs.

"Who hit her?"

"No one hit her, Euen; she went down like a mined wall!"

"Shit!"

Somewhere there is a crowd of men, hands grasping the sides of swaying wagons; the bitter din of swords and bills striking other weapons, armour, men's flesh.

The horse-drawn wagon rumbled under her. She reached out, touching armoured fingers to the walls that rose up beside her. She felt vibration, a shivering in the air: and the voice in her head drowned every sensation out with finality:

'YOU WILL COME TO US.'

'YOU WILL COME.'

"Fuck you," Ash said clearly and aloud. "I don't have time for this now!"

She struggled upright, the edges of her knee cops cutting into her shins, and her backplate jabbing into her neck and spine. Thomas Morgan, trotting beside the moving cart with her Lion banner, reached out to give her a hand off.

Euen Huw fell in beside them. "Boss, Geraint says shall we light torches?"

"No!"

"Boss says no fucking way!" Euen called forward; and as he spoke, Floria elbowed her way in past the Welshman, her eyes concerned, but her voice businesslike.

"You should ride!"

"We have to keep going—"

And in mid-sentence Ash stops.

She turns – her body turns itself – and begins to walk.

South.

Nothing voluntary about it. For a moment she is dazzled by the way her body moves without her volition: smooth muscles and tendons sliding, flesh and blood turning, walking straight towards the south, towards the towering flat planes of the pyramids, towards the silver light of the Wild Machines.

'YOU WILL COME.'

'WE WILL EXAMINE YOU.'

'DISCOVER YOU.'

'WHAT YOU ARE—'

She speaks – and is silent.

Nothing can move her mouth, her throat; her voice is silenced within her. Her legs move involuntarily, carrying her forward; and she shudders inside her flesh, overtaken as one is by vomiting: the body in charge, the body doing what it will do—

—what it is being forced to do.

'COME.'

Not a call, but an order, an instruction; and she panics, inside her head, carried without her will, bruised and aching but striding off into the darkness. No way to break it.

"Boss?" Euen Huw called. "Morgan, grab her!"

Hands grab her steel-covered body: Floria del Guiz. Ash's body knows that it can take the woman down; tenses to slam a mail gauntlet across Floria's eyes.

"Back!"

The voice is Welsh and two hard impacts take her across the backplate, men bearing her down to the earth, the shafts of two bills pinning her to the broken Carthaginian paving; so that she can't use her armour as a weapon, can't get her hand to her sword, can't move at all.

"You want to be careful with her, surgeon," Euen Huw's voice says, in pedantic instruction. "She's used to killing people, see."

He adds, up over his shoulder, kneeling all his weight down on the bill's eight-foot shaft. "It's combat stress; I seen it before, lots. She'll be fine. We might have to carry her back to the ships. Thomas, will you shift your Gower ass so that I can see the girl?" Euen Huw's brilliant black eyes stare down at her. "Boss? You okay?"

Her voice will not obey her. Now she chokes, almost unable to breathe, as if her body is forgetting how. She still feels her legs move, like a dying animal kicking; legs that are trying to get up and walk her south, to where the ground trembles at the feet of great pyramids: where the Wild Machines glow under the black sky that they have made.

"Carry her," Floria del Guiz's voice snaps, "and take that bloody sword away from her!"

Nothing, nothing now but confusion; her body struggling as they lift her,

536

entirely out of her control. She thrashes in their arms as the men run, striking out across the desert, constellations their landmarks.

Her head hangs down, the steel helmet banging against a low outcrop, stunning her, and she bites her tongue, the thin taste of blood in her mouth. Upside down in her vision, the silhouettes of the Wild Machines dominate all of the south, rising up over the men who trot, weapons shouldered, into darkness.

And – a fraction of her mind is her own.

She could strike killing blows, but she doesn't. She could use what she knows, chop mail gauntlets at vulnerable elbow and knee joints, bludgeon for faces; but she does none of these things.

They don't know how, her mind guesses, *and they can't make me.*

But they can make me walk away from my men, make me come to them—

Prisoner in flesh, she strains. Her mind burns like a flame, a fierce will that does not submit, no matter what her limbs are trying to do.

Abruptly she is back in the cell in House Leofric, blood streaming down her thighs: isolated, agonised, alone.

I will not—

And is also somewhere else: somewhere she does not know, now; where she is held, her body powerless, by great force; where violation is ripped into her, and she cannot act, cannot move, cannot prevent—

I will never—*!*

Time loses itself in fever.

The thunder in her mind is weaker.

Ash lifts her head.

She is carried between two men, anonymous in steel helmets; the stars are further advanced across the dome of the sky, it will be past Matins now, almost Lauds.

A violent trembling shook her body, all her limbs jerking spastically.

"Put her down!"

The two men, whose faces she knows in torchlight – torchlight? – lay her down on round pebbles and rock. A sound reaches her ears. The sea. A cold wind blows across her face. The sea.

"Hey, boss." Euen Huw reached out cautiously and shook her armoured shoulder. "You flipped out there for a bit."

Thomas Morgan said plaintively, "Are you going to hit me again, boss?"

"I didn't hit you. If I'd *hit* you, you'd know about it!"

Morgan grinned, propping the battered pole of the banner against his shoulder, and reached up and took his open-face sallet off. Sweat slicked his long red hair down flat against his skull, ears and neck. He freed a hand from a gauntlet and wiped his cheeks. "Shit, boss! We made it out."

Somewhere over towards the middle of two hundred men, Richard Faversham's loud and tuneless voice sings the mass for Lauds, and for deliverance. This would be the hours before dawn, if it were not the Eternal Twilight. A few lanterns gleam, one or two per lance, Ash guesses; and shifts up on her elbows, bruised, drained, sore, exhausted.

"We waiting for those galleys Angelotti was telling me about?"

Euen Huw jerked a thumb at a rose-coloured glow, further down the beach. "Beacon, boss. They better turn up soon, fucking gondolier-pilots; my boys will have their guts for point-ribbons if they don't."

Storms, currents, enemy ships: all possible. Ash sat up. "They'll be here. And if they're not, well . . . we'll just go back and ask the King-Caliph very nicely if we can borrow one of his. Won't we, boys?"

The two Welshmen chuckled.

A voice a little way off lisped, "Victuals."

"Wat!" She climbed to her feet, aching. Someone had stripped her back and breast and leg armour: presumably the man who owned it, and she felt both lighter and unprotected. "Wat Rodway! Over here!"

"Meat," the cook said tersely, holding out a steaming strip.

"You reckon?" Ash took it, crammed it in her mouth as her stomach groaned with hunger, and passed two more handfuls on to Huw and Morgan. Saliva filled her mouth. She chewed raggedly, swallowed, licked her fingers, and exclaimed, "Wat, where'd you get my old boots from!"

"Best beef," Rodway lisped, his tone aggrieved.

Euen Huw, under his breath, said, "It was, before you cooked it."

Ash spluttered into a giggle. "Where's Oxford?"

"Here, madam."

He still wore his full harness, and did not look as if he had taken his armour off since Carthage. Ground-in dirt made the lines around his eyes plainly visible.

"Are you well?"

"I have things I must tell you." She saw her officers in de Vere's wake and beckoned them up; and Floria joined the group, out of the darkness, carrying a lantern that showed her dirty, pale about the eyes, and with a fierce frown.

"Are you losing your mind?" Floria said without preliminary.

Both Angelotti and Geraint looked shocked.

Ash gestures them around her with the familiar movement, so that they squat, the lantern showing them each other's faces, in a circle on the wave-beaten beach ten miles west of Carthage.

The voices in her mind are – not fainter, but less powerful. As winter sunlight is no less light than the summer sun, but is thinner, weaker, without the same heavy fire and warmth. So the whispers in her mind nag at her, but do not force her body out of her own control.

"Too much to tell you . . . but I will. First, I have orders, and a suggestion," Ash said. "I plan now to go back to Dijon. To Robert Anselm, and the rest of the company. Most of my men will come with me, my lord Oxford – if only because they're dead if they stay in North Africa. We may have desertions once we're back in the north, but I think I can get most of them to Dijon."

She hesitated, her eyes screwed up, as if against remembered light.

"The sun's still shining in Burgundy. Dear God, I want to see daylight!"

"And then what?" de Vere said. "What will you have us do, madam?"

"I can't command you. I wish I could." Ash smiled, very slightly, at the English Earl's expression. "We are facing an enemy behind the enemy, my lord."

De Vere knelt, listening gravely.

She said, "We are facing something that doesn't care what happens, so long as Burgundy is taken – I don't think they care about the Visigoth Empire at all."

The Earl of Oxford continued to regard her, with a contained deliberation.

"You hold an ancient title," Ash said, "and whether in exile or not, you are one of the foremost soldiers of the age. My lord Oxford, I go back to Dijon, but you should not. You should go elsewhere."

Over protests, John de Vere said, "Explain, madam."

"Something demonic is our enemy . . ." And, when his expression changed, and he crossed himself, Ash leaned forward and said, "If you'll listen to me, this is what you should do. Christendom is subject, now. The Visigoth Empire either has treaties, or it has conquered, almost everything except Burgundy – and England, but England is in little danger."

"You think not?"

Ash took a breath. "There is an enemy behind the enemy . . . The Stone Golem processes military problems, it tells Leofric and through him the King-Caliph how they should attack – and for the last twenty years it's said *attack Christendom*. But what speaks through the Stone Golem, that doesn't care about Christendom. Just Burgundy."

John de Vere repeated, "An enemy behind our enemy."

"Who wants Burgundy, not England; it's all Burgundy. The Visigoths will take every other city, and then they'll take Dijon, and the Faris will lay the countryside waste – I don't know why the Wild Machines hate Burgundy, but they do." The echo of voices shivering her spine. "They do . . ."

Oxford said briskly, "And you think that one mercenary company, reunited in Dijon, will prevent this?"

"Stranger things have happened in war, but I don't much care about the destruction of Burgundy." Ash caught Floria's eyes fixed on her. She ignored the woman's gaze. "I plan to go to Dijon – and then break out, take ship for England, be four hundred miles away, and see what happens to the crusade when the Burgundian Dukes are defeated and dead. The further away I am, the better . . ."

Voices in her mind: faint still.

". . . But if they don't stop at Burgundy, my lord of Oxford, then I can think of only one thing that might stop the conquest."

De Vere's faded blue eyes blinked, in the pungent lantern light. "Which is?"

"We should part company here," Ash said. "You should sail east."

"*East?*"

"Sail to Constantinople – and ask the Turks for help against the Visigoths."

"The Turks?"

John de Vere began to laugh. It was a resonant deep bark that turned heads. He rested his arm across Dickon de Vere's shoulders – avoiding his young brother's bandaged head – and guffawed.

"Go to the Turks, for help? Madam Captain!"

"Maybe they're *not* allied with the King-Caliph. I didn't see them at the crowning. My lord, there's what's left of the Burgundian army, and that's *it*.

The Turks are going to try and take Christendom from the Visigoths anyway, you could persuade them to do it now—"

"Madam, I would sooner try to go back and take Carthage!"

Dark shapes occluded the waves. Ash stood, peering into the darkness. She did not need Rochester's runner, bare moments later, to tell her that these were the fabled galleys.

"Given the state their harbour's in . . ." Ash shrugged. "And we have two ships: maybe we should go back, and try and blast House Leofric off the cliff-face! Get the Stone Golem that way. My lord, we could go back—"

'BACK!'

Faint, now, but piercing as distant horns: the voices of the Wild Machines yammer in her mind:

'YOU WILL NOT TOUCH THE STONE GOLEM—!'

'—NOT HARM—'

'—NOT DESTROY—'

'—YOU AND YOUR PEOPLE WILL LEAVE!'

'YOU WILL ORDER THEM!'

'IT IS NOT TO BE TOUCHED!'

'IT IS PROTECTED!'

'YOU WILL NOT HARM THE *MACHINA REI MILITARIS*!'

Ash, hands rammed tight over her ears in a useless attempt to block the voices in her head, looked up with her eyes brimming over with tears.

"Oh, Christ—"

"What is it?" Floria's brusque voice, at odds with the gentle hands.

"The same place." Ash's eyes screwed up in pain. "The same place in my soul. I said, I said to you, de Vere, they use it as a channel. *It's how they talk—*"

Now she sees it, plain.

"They're *stone*. Deaf, blind, and dumb. Until they had the machine they couldn't talk to us . . . couldn't communicate with anything, couldn't do a thing!"

Floria stared down at her. Over the noise of oars from the galley, and the breaking waves of the sea, she said, "It's the *only* way they talk. Isn't it? It's their only channel to the outside world."

"It has to be . . ." Ash took her hands down.

Men are boarding the galleys. The headland of Carthage is a black blob, ten miles to the east.

"You're not thinking of going back!"

"And be killed? No. I've seen their fleet. No."

She rested her chin on her fist, staring at the black waves.

"We turned Carthage upside down, but we failed. Two hundred men to strike at the capital of an empire, and we did it, and we failed. What we did wasn't enough."

There is no confusion on their faces: Antonio Angelotti, unaccustomedly dirty, black-powder burns pitting his padded jack; and Geraint kneeling and scratching at his cod. Only a grim, weary, anxious despair. John de Vere's embrace around his brother's shoulders tightened.

"I don't understand," Floria said, her husky voice thinning and lightening. "How could all this not be enough?"

"We failed," Ash said crisply. "We could have broken the link. If we'd taken the Stone Golem, destroyed it – we could have broken the only link between the Wild Machines and the world."

Ash looked at Floria; at the Earl of Oxford.

She said, "What we've done isn't enough – and it's worse than that. All we've done now is alert the enemy to what we know. We're worse off than when we started."

Message: #139 (Pierce Ratcliff)
Subject: Ash
Date: 02/12/00 at 12.09 p.m.
From: Longman@

format address deleted
Other details encrypted and non-recoverably deleted

Pierce –

There isn't an easy way to say this. The editorial decision is that we are going to have to suspend publication of your work.

I'm going to do what I can. Maybe I can find another publishing firm for you, one that would be interested in a book of mediaeval myths and legends?

I know that wouldn't be much consolation. You've spent so many years editing the 'Ash' texts under the impression that they were genuine historical documents. But it's all I can think of, right now.

When you do fly back to the UK, let's meet. Have lunch. Something. Yes?

Love, Anna

Message: #204 (Anna Longman)
Subject: Ash Project
Date: 02/12/00 at 04.28 p.m.
From: Ngrant@

format address deleted
Other details encrypted by non-discoverable personal key.

Anna, please—

Anna, you have got to let me publish. I know that we're close to deadline for spring publication. Don't call a halt now. Please.

– but why *should* you let me carry on? The Tunisian archaeological evidence has collapsed completely!

Anna, I am pleading with Isobel to have the radio-carbon dating tests on the metal joints of the 'messenger-golem' repeated. The results we had through could be WRONG. I don't believe these 'golems' are merely modern fakes that the expedition has dug out of the silt outside Tunis. I just don't believe it. They are genuine remains from the period of the Visigoth settlement of Carthage: I *know* they are!!

And yet how can I _not_ believe they're fakes, when scientific evidence says the bronze metalwork was cast post-1945?

Schliemann discovered Troy in 1871 by searching where Homer sited it in the ILIAD – but he didn't discover, when he excavated it, that the Bronze Age city of Troy had been constructed in the

1870s! That is the equivalent of what we are facing here.

I know what you'll say. How could we ever have thought this was _history_? The texts I'm using seem to have been re-classified from Mediaeval History to Fiction. And my 'Fraxinus' document, my one great discovery, telling us about the woman Ash 'hearing voices' from a fifteenth-century 'Stone Golem computer'? Legends and fabrications! Unbelievable lies and myth!

I'm going to fly out with Isobel to the expedition's ship, now that we FINALLY have official permission. Ironic. I suppose I have very little justification for doing so, but what *else* can I do? I feel bereaved. I know that Isobel is too tactful to point out that I should just fly back to the UK now. I suppose a few days watching the undersea cameras give us images of the seabed north of Tunis will at least take my mind off all this. We might even find a Roman shipwreck or two.

I haven't slept.

Anna, I have finished translating the penultimate section of 'Fraxinus me fecit'. I had an explanatory note that I intended to put with this part of the ASH manuscript

But it's all irrelevant now. The golems are fakes: the Angelotti manuscript is a mere fiction. The ambiguities of the 'Fraxinus' text are irrelevant.

– Pierce

Message: #140 (Pierce Ratcliff)
Subject: Ash
Date: 02/12/00 at 11.01 p.m.
From: Longman@

format address deleted
Other details encrypted and
non-recoverably deleted

Pierce –

I'm not even sure you have a 'Visigothic Carthage' land-site there now. What is Isobel Napier-Grant saying?

What you've told me so far is that you expected the 'Fraxinus' text to prove the existence of a 15c Visigoth settlement in the area of Arab Carthage, powerful enough to mount a crusade into Southern Europe. I could have swallowed this (assuming that things like the burning of Venice are chronicler's poetic licence), and I guess I could have believed that these Visigoths failed, went back to Carthage, and interest in them was lost when Burgundy collapsed later that year.

I guess it's even reasonable to think your 'Visigothic' Carthage was probably so weakened by this expedition that they were overrun by Moors fairly shortly afterwards and wiped out. Or maybe they returned to Spain and were lost in the confusion of the Reconquista.

And any evidence has been ignored here on the grounds of race and class.

But I don't see _now_ —if your texts are Romances, and the 'messenger golem' a modern fake based on the texts — what *possible* reason you have for thinking your Doctor Isobel's site is anything to do with any Visigoths!

Pierce, it's *over*. I know it's not nice, but face it. There is no book. Ash isn't history, she's Robin Hood, Arthur, Lancelot——_legend_.

We might still get a programme out of Dr Dr Napier-Grant's dig and her problems with the Tunisian authorities; and I don't see why you shouldn't be a script adviser if that does come off.

Give it a few days, then start thinking about it.

Love,
Anna

Previons message missing?

Message: #205 (Anna Longman)
Subject: Ash/Carthage
Date: 03/12/00 at 11.42 p.m.
From: Ngrant@

format address deleted
other details encrypted by
non-discoverable personal key

Anna –

Your last came through scrambled – machine code: did you attach a .jpg? It's hopelessly corrupted! Try again, I'll reply later, much later – Isobel needs this link for the next few few hours at least.

I'm no longer at the land-site, I'm on the ship; that's one reason the transmission might have failed. We flew out by helicopter this morning to the expedition's ship, the HANNIBAL; we're at sea five miles off the North African coast.

You must not pass this on, any of it, not to Jonathan whatsisname, your MD, to nobody, don't even talk about it in your sleep.

Isobel just said get off the machine so here it is:

She and her team have been out here since September primarily because of the discoveries made by the team from the Institute for Exploration, Connecticut, in July and August of 1997. If you remember it from the media coverage, that expedition found – among other things – five Roman shipwrecks, below the 1000 metre mark, in an area of the sea about twenty miles off Tunis. (They had a US Navy nuclear submarine helping them out with sonar. We are using low-frequency search equipment, the same as that used in oil-exploration.)

The wrecks indicate that, far from skulking along the coastline to Sicily, merchant ships since 200 BC have been sailing *deep-water* routes across the Mediterranean. What they found was one of the reasons Isobel could get funding to come and investigate the land-site here, and get local government permission to do coastal exploration.

Now OUR ROVs have been sending pictures back, also from below the 1000 metre mark. We thought this had to be a mis-reading, they're going down in shallow coastal seas. But it isn't an instrument malfunction, they ARE sending back from that depth – too deep for human divers, with the limited equipment here. What the ROVs have found is a marine trench in the shallow water, about 60 kilometres north-west of the ruins of old Carthage – I almost wrote, from the ruins of OUR Carthage. And it's what I've hoped and prayed for, since the disastrous carbon-dating report.

We have found a harbour with five headlands. It's all there, under the silt, you can see the outlines clearly. I have been watching green night-vision enhanced pictures, from bulky machines diving in unclear waters, but I can tell you, it's there

Later –

Anna, it's unbelievable. Isobel is shaken. We have found Carthage, yes, I always thought we might find my 'Visigoth settlement' on this coast; and it's the way it's described in the ASH manuscript, in 'Fraxinus'. Oh Anna. I've found her. I've found the IMPOSSIBLE.

Isobel had me there to direct the ROV technicians. There I was in front of these banks of machines, slightly queasy (I don't like the sea) and a rough pencil sketch of what I'd worked out from the manuscripts MUST be the geography of Ash's Carthage. Great moments always happen when you're wet, or hot, or slightly queasy; when you're looking the other way, as it were. I was trying to pick out the inner wall, the 'Citadel' wall that the manuscripts mention.

We found the wall, on one of the headlands, and we found what was plainly a structure. This IS Gothic Carthage, below the waves, this IS what the manuscripts describe, I have to keep reminding myself of this, because what happened next is so impossible, so shattering in its implications, that I feel I will never sleep again – I feel that my life from here is downhill, THIS is my discovery, THIS is what will get my (and Isobel's) names into the history books, nothing will ever be quite this much of a pinnacle again.

I had the ROV down in the broken walls, sending back pictures from its cameras of silt-covered roofs and rooms, all in a state that would accord very much with earthquake damage. And I turned the ROV to the right – what would have happened if I hadn't? I suppose the same discovery, but later; people are going to be picking over these ruins for the next forty years: this is Howard

546

Carter, this is Tutankhamen all over again.

I turned the ROV to the right and it went into a building that still had some of its roof. This is something the technicians hate. There are all sorts of dangers of losing the ROV, I suppose. Into a building, and there it was: a courtyard, and a broken wall – a broken wall ABOVE WHAT WOULD HAVE BEEN THE HARBOUR.

Even Isobel agreed then, better to lose the ROV in the attempt than not make the attempt. I can see it all, in my mind, from the FRAXINUS manuscript, and there it was, Anna, there were the walls of the room, and the stairwell going down, and the great carved stone slabs that would have closed these rooms off from each other.

I suppose it took six or eight hours, I know we had two shift changes of technicians, Isobel was with me all the time, I didn't see her eat, I didn't eat. You see, I knew where it had to be. It must have taken us four hours just to get orientated – among lumps of mud-covered, mud-coloured rocks, in nothing that looks ANYTHING like a city, trying to discover which direction might have been north-east, before the quake, and where, down in that sightless, electrically illuminated depth it might be. 'House Leofric', I mean. What the manuscript calls 'House Leofric' – and its 'north-east quadrant'.

No, I am not mad. I know I am not quite sane at the moment, but not mad.

We have two ROVs, I was prepared to sacrifice this one. The technicians teased it down, in, under; all the time at the mercy of currents, thermals. I am dumbfounded by their expertise, now, at the time I didn't even notice. The screens kept bringing us lurching pictures of steps, inside a stairwell. I think the moment that Isobel wept was when the stone steps stopped, and the well became just a smooth-sided masonry tube going down into darkness, and we managed to get a close-up of one wall. It had a socket in it, for taking a framework of wooden steps.

All this time I wasn't sure which floor of the House the ROV was exploring, there's enough damage to make it uncertain – the upper floors are barely a house! And it powered infinitely slowly and cautiously through room after room – up a floor, down a floor, through a gap – the silt covers bones, and amphorae, and coins; woodbores have eaten all the furniture. Down, down, room on room, and no way to know where we were, in the pressure and the cold and the depth.

When it came, it was just another broken room, quite suddenly, but Isobel swore out loud: she recognised the silhouette instantly from the description. It was a minute before I knew what it must be. The techs couldn't understand Isobel's excitement, one of them said 'It's just a fucking statue, for Christ's sake,' and then it came into focus for me.

Read the translation, Anna! See what FRAXINUS says. The second golem, the Stone Golem, is 'the shape of a man above, and beneath, nothing but a dais on which the games of war may be played'.

What I didn't really appreciate was how BIG the Stone Golem is.

The torso and head and arms are gargantuan, three times the size of a man. Twelve or fifteen feet high. It sits there, blindly, in the seas off Africa, and it gazes into the darkness with sightless, stone eyes. The features are Northern European, not Berber, or sub-Saharan African; and every muscle, every ligament, every hair is defined in stone.

I think that the Rabbi had a mordant sense of humour! I suspect that, whereas 'Fraxinus' tells us that the mobile golems resembled the Rabbi, the Stone Golem itself is a portrait of that noble Visigoth/amir/, Radonic.

The silt hides colour, of course, makes everything a uniform brown-green in the million-candlepower lights. The stonework itself I think is granite, or red sandstone, by the colour. I cannot tell you the quality of the workmanship. What seems to have corroded are the metal joints of the arms, wrists, and hands.

Below, it is part of a dais. As far as I can tell, the torso joins seamlessly to a surface of marble or sandstone. Pressured jets of water might clear some of the silt, to see if there are markings on the dais, but Isobel and the team are frantically taking film footage of this, they won't touch it until everything has been recorded, recorded beyond a shadow of a doubt, beyond all necessity for proof, no proof needed, because it is, it IS, the Stone Golem, Ash's MACHINA REI MILITARIS.

And I'll tell you something, Anna. Even Isobel isn't trying to come up with a method by which somebody can fake THIS.

What I need to know – what I can't know, because it has been non-functional and lost under the sea for five hundred years – is, is this the MACHINA REI MILITARIS that FRAXINUS says it is? Is it a temple statue, a religious icon – it can't be anything else, can it, Anna? Anything else is because I haven't slept for I can't remember how long, and I haven't eaten, and I'm light-headed but I can't stop thinking it: IS it a mechanical chess-player? IS it a war-machine?

Oh, suppose it was something more. Suppose it WAS the voice that spoke to her?

Two-thirds of a mile down, in the deep trench that an earthquake might have left, in the cold and the dark, five hundred years under the sea that has seen enough wars since then – fighting ships, aircraft, mines; I can't help wondering, would the MACHINA REI MILITARIS cope with combined ops warfare, if Ash were alive what would it tell her now, if it HAD a voice?

Isobel needs this computer now. Anna, please, you said to me once, if the golem are true, what else is? This is. The ruins of Visigoth Carthage: an archaeological site on the bed of the sea.

_There_are_no_50_billion_dollar_frauds,_ and that is what this
would have to be.

  Anna, this supports everything that's in the FRAXINUS
manuscript!

  But how could the carbon-dating on the messenger golem be wrong?
Tell me what to think, I'm so exhausted I don't know.

- Pierce

Message: #143 (Pierce Ratcliff)
Subject: Ash
Date: 03/12/00 at 11.53 p.m.
From: Longman@   *format address deleted*
                                      other details encrypted
Pierce -   *and non-recoverably deleted*

Jesus Christ!

  I won't breathe a word, I promise. Not until the expedition's
ready. Oh, Pierce, this is SO BIG! I'm so sorry I doubted you!

  Pierce, you have _got_ to send me the next part you have of
/Fraxinus/ that's translated. Send me the text. If _two_ of us are
looking at it, there's more chance we might pick up clues, things
you need to tell Dr Napier-Grant about. I won't even keep it in the
office, I'll take it home with me - I'll keep it in my briefcase all
the time, it won't get more than arm's-length away from me!

  And you _have_ to finish the translation!!

Love,
Anna

Message: #237 (Anna Longman)
Subject: Ash/Carthage
Date: 04/12/00 at 01.36 a.m.
From: Ngrant@   *format address deleted*
                                      other details encrypted by
Anna -   *non-discoverable personal key*

I know. I know! Now we need 'Fraxinus' more than ever! But there
are nonetheless _problems_ in the later part of 'Fraxinus' that we
cannot afford to be blind to!

  I had always planned to send you an explanatory note with the
penultimate part of 'Fraxinus', 'Knight of the Wasteland'. Even
without the problems of golems, C14 dating, and inauthentic
manuscripts, 'Fraxinus me fecit' still ends on a cliff-hanger in
November 1476: it doesn't tell us what happened *afterwards*!

  I have skipped over the final pages of the Angelotti ms. Ash's ships sail from the North African coast on or around 12 September 1476. I omit a short passage which deals with the expedition's return to mainland Europe. (I would like to include this in the final text of the book. The details of daily life on board a Venetian galley are fascinating!) Their retreat to Marseilles occupies around three weeks. I calculate that the ships left Carthage on the night of the 10th September 1476, and – with storms, and bad navigation, and a stop at Malta to take on food and put off the sick who would otherwise have died – the voyage took until 30 September. The ships then landed (during the moon's last quarter) at Marseilles.

It seems, from the Angelotti manuscript, to have taken between three and four days for the company to have regrouped, acquired mules and supplies, and set out for the north. Antonio Angelotti devotes a large part of his text to regretting his lost cannon, which he describes in great technical detail. He spends rather less time – a bare two lines – on the direction in which the exiled Earl of Oxford decided to take ship again and to sail away with his own men.

It is at this point that the Angelotti ms cuts off (a few final pages are missing from the Missaglia treatise). 'Fraxinus me fecit' adds only a few bald sentences: that the country was, by this time, in a state of emergency, with famine, cold and hysteria emptying the towns and devastating the countryside.

Evidently, from the little we can glean from Angelotti, the company disembarked at Marseilles in conditions that we would now think of as resembling a nuclear winter. With Ash leading them, they proceeded on a forced march up the valley of the Rhone river, from Marseilles north to Avignon, and further north towards Lyons. It says something for Ash as a commander that she could have groups of armed men travel several hundred miles under very loose control, during unprecedentedly terrible weather conditions – a force with less effective leadership would surely have been far more likely to hole up in a local hamlet or village outside Marseilles, and hope to wait out the 'sunless' winter.

Given their lack of horses, and the fact that a starving peasantry had eaten the countryside bare of crops and draught animals, stealing river ships was probably their easiest option. Moreover, in a countryside that is pitch-dark twenty-four hours a day, without reliable maps or guides, following the Rhone valley at least ensured that the company would not get hopelessly lost. A fragmentary reference indicates that they gave up river-travel itself just south of Lyons when the Rhone froze over completely, and marched towards the Burgundian border, following the Saone north.

It is not recorded that any of the French ducs reacted to this incursion on their territory. They may have had too much to cope with themselves, with famine, insurrection, and war likely. More probably, in the winter and night conditions, they simply didn't notice.

Given the logistics of getting two hundred and fifty men across Europe in darkness, together with all the baggage they could carry on their backs, and the number of starving survivors who began to attach themselves to the company (either to give sexual favours for food, or to attempt to rob them) – given the sheer work involved in keeping her men on the road, keeping them fed, keeping them from mutiny or plain desertion, it is perhaps not surprising that 'Fraxinus' details almost no interaction on a personal level between Ash and anyone else in the company until the hiatus immediately following their arrival outside Dijon.

We do know, from the beginning of the 'Fraxinus' manuscript, that the company gained a position very close to Dijon itself without being seen by Visigoth scouts. The company moved along the cultivated edges of the true wildwood – the virgin forested areas that still, at this point, covered a great deal of Europe. Travel would be slow, especially if weapons and baggage were to be transported, but it would be sure. It would be almost the only certain way of reaching Dijon without being wiped out by a detachment of one of the Visigoth armies.

'Fraxinus' states that the journey occupied almost seven weeks (the period from 4 October to 14 November). By 14 November 1476, then, Ash and between two and three hundred of her armed men, with mules and baggage train, but without horses or guns, are five miles west of Dijon, just south-west of the main road to Auxonne.

Anna, I *did* think the 'Fraxinus' manuscript was either written or dictated by Ash herself; I was certain it was a reliable primary source. Now – with Carthage 1000 metres below me! – I'm even MORE certain!

BUT – there was always going to be *a* problem. You see, I had always hoped that the discovery of the Fraxinus document would allow me my niche in academic history as the person who solved the 'missing summer' problem. Although, in fact, given the problem with dates – some of Ash's exploits fit far better into what we know of the events of 1475; others can only have taken place in 1476; and the texts treat them all as one continuous series of events – it may be a 'missing year and a half' problem!

Records appear to document Ash fighting against Charles the Bold's forces in June 1475/6. She is unaccounted for over what appears to be the summer of 1476; turns up again in winter; and dies fighting at Nancy (5 January 1476/7). There are some missing weeks between the end of 'Fraxinus' (mid-November 1476), and the point where conventional history picks Ash up again. (Some mysteries must be left for other scholars, after all!) 'Fraxinus' breaks off abruptly, evidently incomplete.

If 'Fraxinus' does not mesh seamlessly with recorded history, that is not a problem.

The *problem* is, that in the autumn of 1476, Charles the Bold is involved in his campaign against Lorraine, besieging Nancy on 22 October. He stays at that siege all though November and December; and dies there in January, fighting against Duke Rene's reinforcements (an army of Lorrainers and volunteer Swiss).

I had initially expected this latter part of 'Fraxinus' to indicate that Ash returns to a Europe in which the Visigoth raid has failed and is in retreat.

It does not. 'Fraxinus' has the Visigoths _still_ *present* in Europe in force as late as the November of 1476.

It has France and the Duchy of Savoy at peace, by treaty, with the Carthaginian Empire; it has the ex-Emperor Frederick III of the Holy Roman Empire – now controlled from Carthage – making inroads into ruling the Swiss cantons as a Visigoth satrap, hand in hand with Daniel de Quesada. It has, in fact, everything you would expect to see if the Visigoth invasion had _succeeded_.

If this is 1476, where is Charles's war against Lorraine? Conversely, if this is 1475, then my theory that the incursion of the Visigoths was forgotten in the collapse of Burgundy falls apart, since that won't occur for another twelve months!

I can only assume that something in the dates within this text is deeply misleading, and that I have not yet understood it completely.

Whatever we have not yet understood, I do understand this much: 'Fraxinus' has given us Carthage. Isobel says being able to identify a site this early is amazing!

I will send you my final version of the last section as soon as I can – but how can I stay away from the ROV cameras!!!

I am looking at *Carthage*.

I keep thinking about FRAXINUS's 'wild machines'.

– Pierce

PART NINE

14 November–15 November AD 1476

Knight of the Wasteland

I

Rain streamed off the raised visor of her helmet, streamed off the sodden demi-gown and brigandine that she wore, and soaked her hose inside her high boots. Ash could feel it, but not see it – the sound of falling water and the unobstructed blisteringly cold air told her she must be close to the tree-line, but she could see nothing in the pitch-darkness of the forest.

Someone – Rickard? – blundered into her shoulder, throwing her forward into the slick, hard bark of a tree trunk. It grazed her mittened hand. An unseen spray of soaked autumn leaves slapped her across the face, dashing cold water into her eyes and mouth.

"Shit!"

"Sorry, boss."

Ash waved the boy Rickard to silence, realised he couldn't see her, and groped until she caught his sodden wool shoulder, and pulled his ear down level with her mouth:

"There are umpteen thousand Visigoths out there: would you mind keeping *quiet*!"

Cold rain soaked through her belted demi-gown, and through the velvet and steel plates of the brigandine, making her arming doublet against her warm flesh uncomfortably cold and damp. The constant rattle of rain in the darkness, and the whispering creak of trees swaying in the night wind, prevented her hearing anything more than a few paces away. She took another cautious step, arms outstretched, and simultaneously hooked her scabbard into a low-hanging branch, and skidded her heel into a mud-rut six inches deep.

"Shit on a fucking *stick*! Where's John Price? Where are the fucking scouts?"

She heard something suspiciously like a chuckle, under the noise of the falling rain. Rickard's shoulder, against hers, juddered.

"Madonna," a quiet voice said, to her left and below her, "light the lamp. There's a great deal of forest between here and Dijon; how much of it would you like us to cover?"

"Ah, shit – okay. Rickard . . ."

Several minutes passed. Occasionally the boy's arm or elbow jogged her, as he wrestled with a pierced iron lantern, a candle, and presumably the lit slow-match he had brought with him. Ash smelled smouldering powder. The velvet blackness pressed against her face. Cold drops of rain spattered her head as she turned her face up, letting her night vision attempt to distinguish between the crowns of trees and the invisible sky.

Nothing.

She flinched, repeatedly, as rain struck her on the cheeks and eyes and mouth. Sheltering her face with one soaked sheepskin mitten, she thought she distinguished a faint alteration of darkness and blackness.

"Angelotti? You think this rain's stopping?"

"No!"

Rickard's dark lantern finally glimmered, a weak yellow light in the surrounding pitch-darkness. Ash caught a glimpse of another figure shrouded in heavy woollen hood and cloak, seemingly kneeling down at her side – a sucking sound made her startle. The kneeling figure stood up.

"Fucking *mud*," Master Gunner Angelotti said.

The light from the lantern failed, serving only to illuminate the silver streaks of falling water droplets. Before that, Ash had one glimpse of Angelotti, his cloak torn and his boots clotted with mud to his upper thighs. She grinned briefly to herself.

"Look on the bright side," she said. "This is a whole lot better than the conditions we've just come through to get here – it's *warmer*! And, any rag-head patrols are going to stay really close to home in this murk."

"But we won't see anything!" Rickard's face above the lantern, in his hood, was a chiaroscuro demon-mask. "Boss, maybe we should go back to the camp."

"John Price said he saw broken cloud. I'm betting the rain's going to ease up before long. Green Christ! does anybody know where we *are*?"

"In a dark wood," her Italian master gunner said, with sardonic satisfaction. "Madonna, the guide from Price's lance is lost, I think."

"Don't go yelling for him . . ."

Ash faced away from the lantern's tiny glow. She let the dark into her eyes again, gazing blindly into blackness and rain. The sleeting drops found the gap between sleeve and mitten at her wrist; eased cold rivulets of water down between sallet-tail and gown collar. The cold water made her hot flesh shudder and begin to chill.

"This way," she decided.

Reaching out a hand, she grasped Rickard's arm, and Angelotti's gloved hand. Stumbling and lurching through the mud and thick leaf-mould underfoot, she banged against branches, shook down water from trees, unwilling to take her eyes from the faintest of silhouettes in front of her: the waving twigs of hornbeam trees against the open night sky beyond the wood.

"Maybe around—*whuff*!" Her numbed, cold hand slid off Rickard's arm. Angelotti's strong fingers gripped, tightly; she slid down on to one knee and hung from his grasp, momentarily unable to get her feet under her. Boot soles skidded in the mud. Her leg went out from under her, and she sat down heavily and unguardedly in a mass of wet leaves, sharp twigs, and cold mud.

"Son of a *bitch*!" She hauled her twisted sword-belt back round, feeling sightlessly down the hilt to the scabbard – trapped under her leg – for breaks in the thin wood. "*Shit!*"

"Keep that fucking noise down!" a voice whispered. "Put that fucking lantern out! Do you want an entire fucking Visigoth legion up here? The old battle-axe will have your fucking arse!"

Ash, in English, said, "Too damn right she will, Master Price."

"Boss?"

"Yeah." She grinned, invisible in the black night. Grabbing for arms and hands at random, she found herself pulled back on to her feet. The cold was bitter enough now to make her body shake, and she beat her hands against her arms – seeing neither, in the darkness. A flurry of rain made her duck her head, and then turn her wet face in the direction of the unobstructed wind.

"We're on the wood's edge?" she said. "Lucky you found us, Sergeant."

Price muttered something in a northern dialect, in which 'making enough noise for six pair of yoked oxen' was the only phrase Ash clearly overheard.

"We're further along here, on top of the bluff," the man added. "Rain's been easing this last hour. Reckon you'll get sight of the city from here, soon, boss."

"Where's the rag-heads now?"

A movement in the black night, which might have been a waving arm. "Down there, someplace."

Green Christ! If I could just ask the *machina rei militaris*: *Dijon, southern border of the Duchy of Burgundy: strength and disposition of siege camp.* Ask the Stone Golem: *name of battle commander, tactical plans for the next week*—

A shudder went through her skin that was nothing to do with the bone-chilling rain. For a moment, the darkness was not the mulch-odoured, bitter-cold, open night blackness of a Frankish forest, but the shit-smelling, stomach-turning darkness under the Citadel of Carthage, kneeling with a dead man's body in the sewers, and hearing voices louder than God blast through her head, in that solitude where she is used to hearing only the *machina rei militaris*.

And for a heart-stopping moment she whipped her head around, glaring into the darkness, afraid of seeing the same celestial light that burned in the desert outside Carthage, nine weeks before. The aurora that glimmers above the red silt-brick pyramids . . .

Nothing but wet night.

Don't be stupid, girl. The Wild Machines want you dead – but they can't know where you are.

Not unless I tell the Stone Golem.

If I can live nine weeks without asking tactical advice, Ash thought grimly – if I could manage the road from Marseilles to Lyons, *Christus Viridianus!*, without advice – I don't need to ask now. *I don't need to.*

Faint rustles in the undergrowth made her suppose Price's men and their lost guide had come up to join them. Other than the lighter darkness in front of her, and the solid darkness behind, there was no way to distinguish anything in the blackness in which they stood. The infinite, invisible, random dropping of water on her was a continuous soaking presence.

"The moon will have risen by now, madonna," Angelotti's soft voice said, beside her. "A first quarter, by my calculations. *If* we see it."

"I trust your celestial mechanics," Ash murmured, groping blindly with a cold-numbed hand to check her sword-hilt and scabbard again. "Got any predictions about this fucking rain?"

"If it has rained for eighteen days solid, madonna, why should it stop now!"

"Ah, well done, Angeli. I only keep you on the company books for your morale value, you know."

One of Price's men rumbled a chuckle. By common consent, they moved back into the underbrush, squatting down in any scrap of cover: she heard their movement without seeing them. Ash, hand up to keep invisible briars out of her eyes, rested a knee in the sodden, puddled grass. After a while, she felt the heat of her flesh warm it; and then, the cold begin to suck the heat from her body. The pattering of the rain on the leafless trees faded into the background.

Filthy weather, enemy pickets: this could be any campaign I've been on these last ten years. *Treat it that way.* Forget anything else.

"There." She reached out blindly, at last, eyes on the sky, and touched a shoulder. "A star."

"Cloud's breaking up," Price's voice said.

His shoulder had been visible, Ash realised, as she lowered her head; a darker silhouette against the sky. She quickly glanced backwards and forwards, seeing the black swaying branches of trees, and two or three other silhouettes distinguishably human: nothing else in nature is head-and-shoulder shaped.

"We all secure here?"

"We're on the bluff above the Suzon river, west of the Auxonne road." Price grunted. "Not skylined. Wood's behind us; no one could see us up here without they were on top of us."

"Okay; make sure all helmets are covered by hoods. If we do get any moonlight, I don't want us flashing away like heliographs."

John Price turned away to mutter orders. Ash realised she was seeing his breath, white in the cold air. She stripped off her wet sheepskin mittens and, with numb fingers, unbuckled her sallet. Rickard received it, concealing it under a fold of his sodden cloak. Clean, bitter-cold air bit at her ears, cheeks and chin.

The rain ceased, suddenly, within the space of a minute. A constant dripping came from the trees around her, but the wind dropped. With that came a new, intense cold; and she glanced up to see the trailing ragged end of a black cloud against a grey sky, the cloud-bank running high and fast into the east.

What's it like here, now?

Cold biting to the bone, she finds her flesh remembering Dijon of the golden strip-fields and heavy vines; Dijon with blue sky and blazing sun seen over its white walls and blue-tiled roofs; the company's camp in Dijon's meadows smelling of sweat and horse-dung and the thick sweetness of cow-parsley.

Stout-walled Dijon: richest capital of southern Burgundy, stiff with merchants wealthy enough to show off and keep architects, masons, painters and embroiderers in business; Dijon thronging with the household and army and ordnance of Charles, Great Duke of the West . . . A white jewel in a rich countryside.

Before we rode out to Auxonne, and got our asses kicked.

Her own breath smoked white before her face. The night became full of the noise of dripping water, gaunt bark shedding still-clinging rain. She realised that the shapes of trees were becoming more apparent. Grass and dead bracken had a visible verge, two yards in front of her.

Beyond that was a drop.

Far out across the open air in front of her, a grey pearl of cloud parted in the east and became a shatteringly bright silver semicircle.

"That river's up," she murmured, her night vision dazzled by the moon, edging forward on all fours, the cold puddles seeping through her hose.

Eyes adjusting to the half-moon's light, she could see the slope of a bluff dropping down in front of her, too steep to be easily climbed. A hundred paces below, scrub and bushes were an impenetrable darkness. Beyond them, she would not have known where to look for the road to Auxonne, but she saw it glimmering: one long sheet of puddles and water-filled ruts reflecting the moon. A black silhouette of limestone wooded hills, to the south. *And we marched down that road with the Burgundian army how long ago – three months? De Vere said they were holding out, but that was nine or ten weeks ago . . .*

Roberto, are you down there?

Further east, by a half mile or more, the silver light shone back from swelling waters that lapped up close to the road – the Suzon river, flooding. Squint as she might in the moonlight, Ash could not make out anything beyond it, no black obstruction that might be Dijon's city walls. Glimmers of light might be the other river, the Ouche; or the slates on roofs. A glance at the stars told her it was not long past Lauds.[1]

"Sergeant Price? What do the scouts report?" Ash said, switching without thought into the military camp version of English that she knew.

The first-quarter moon made white chalk of the man's face beside her. John Price, made a Sergeant of Bill in Carracci's place, after Carthage – momentarily she saw, not Price's moon-whitened features, but Carracci's face: skin blackened by fire, eyelids crisped away . . . she put the thought from her.

"The rag-heads are down there like you thought, boss."[2] Price squatted, pointing; bulky in mail shirt and huke.[3] The war-hat buckled over his coif was far too rusty to catch the moon's light and betray their position. Dirty ringlets snaked out from under the coif.

Ash followed his direction. In the mile or more of dark land between her and the town, she began to make out intermittent dots of fire. Campfires, being re-lit after the rain. Regularly spaced. Two or three hundred, by guess; and there would be more, not visible from here.

"Patrols come out every hour," Price added briefly. "Got it covered, but we shouldn't stay here long."

---

[1] 3 a.m.

[2] There is no mention in conventional histories of a siege of Dijon in the autumn of 1476. Since the 'Fraxinus' document depicts it, one must assume that it is an exaggeration, by Ash or by Visigoth chroniclers, of a minor military incident that history has ignored. The 'Fraxinus' narrative breaks off in November 1476: there is then a gap between the end of the 'Fraxinus' text and Ash's presence in the Nancy campaign.

[3] 'Huke': a sleeveless knee- or thigh-length tunic, often not sewn closed at the sides, and worn with a belt.

"Right. So, we have enemy encampments on the land between the road and the river – what's down there?"

Price rubbed at a runny nose with fingers that were ingrained with dirt, his thick nails cracked and bitten; then shoved his hands back into sheepskin mittens.

"Okay, boss. In front of us now, we've got the main north-south road. From here, Dijon's on the far side of the road and the river – we're looking at the western wall, but you can't see it. There's water meadows along the river, the other side of the road – that's where they've got their main artillery. There's reports of some infantry up the road to the north, just up at the crossroads." Price shrugged, a movement entirely visible in the white light. "Could be. I know for sure there's infantry blocking the road south to Auxonne; I went down that way myself. They've got rag-'ead boats chained together across the river, so no one's going to get downriver from Dijon."

"Just siege machinery down there?" Squinting, Ash could make out nothing more than Visigoth campfires between herself and the invisible city walls. "What about golems?"

John Price grunted. "My lads did good enough to get in close and tell it was an engineers' camp. You want to know what the rag-heads had for supper as well?"

Ash gave him a look that the bright moonlight did nothing to hide. "I'd be surprised if your lot couldn't tell me!"

Price unexpectedly grinned. "You won't get any chivalric nonsense out of billmen. We're better at sneaking around than those damn knights in their tin cans. You know knights, boss – 'death before dismount'!"

"Oh, quite," Ash said dryly. "That'll be why de Vere took you lot to Carthage, and left the heavy armoured guys behind here . . ."

"Sure, boss. Half *my* lads are poachers."

"And the other half thieves," she observed, with rather more accuracy than tact. "Okay, what about north of Dijon? And what about on the east side, over the Ouche?"

"We've scouted all round. Dijon's just north of where the two rivers join." Price's fingers sketched a shield-shape in the moonlit air. "The city takes up all the ground in between, right down to the junction. Over this side, the Suzon comes right up close to the walls – acts as a moat. Over the east side, there's broken ground between the city walls and the river Ouche, and broken ground on the far bank, too. Scrub, cliffs, swampy ground. *Bad* ground. Some of my lads ran into rag-head patrols there, earlier tonight."

"And?"

"And they'll be missed." Price's teeth showed bright. "God rot us, boss, we had little enough choice in the matter."

"So assume that, by now, the Visigoths know there are enemy forces around. Bit of luck, they'll think we're some gang of peasants, or burghers from a burned town; they must be getting a lot of that." Ash squinted. "Okay, there's a road comes in from the east, to Dijon's north-east gate, I remember that . . ."

"They've got men and guns sitting on the hills above the eastern bridge. Looks like there's been artillery used from inside the town. That area's churned up pretty bad." John Price blew into his sheepskin mittens for warmth. "Twenty culverins and serpentines and a bombard[4] up on the hill, we think. You won't get in from the east."

Antonio Angelotti's voice startled Ash, coming from her shoulder, where he had crawled up to peer out from the top of the bluff. "Give me twenty guns and I could keep that eastern gate of Dijon impassable. I looked round, when we were here before."

"So they got artillery over there, and here?"

"Moats work two ways, madonna. If the Visigoth *amirs* cannot order an infantry attack over the Suzon at Dijon's west wall, then neither can the defenders sally out and attack the siege-engines. The *amirs* can bombard Dijon with impunity from here."

And they will have done. How close is this city to falling?

Shit, we've taken too long to get here!

Ash grunted. "What about the country to the north? What have they got up there?"

John Price answered, "Better part of a legion and a half. 'S true, boss. Saw the XIV Utica and the VI Leptis Parva."[5]

There was a second's silence.

Absently, whimsically, Ash murmured, "So much for Plan B . . ."

Been bad enough on the road here, avoiding their forces, skirmishing if we had to – shit, I was hoping we wouldn't find anything like this concentration of forces here!

But it was an even chance we were going to . . .

"Where, exactly?" Ash asked.

"See the crossroads, where the road comes in from the west?"

Trying to see a mile and more in moonlight, Ash could glimpse nothing more than an obstruction to the glint of the river, which might be a bridge across it, and which might argue a road coming in. "Can't see it, but I remember it; goes out towards the French border. And?"

"They got guns covering the north-west gate of the city, same as they got guns covering the north-east gate." Price shrugged. The movement released a musty, damp smell from his clothing. "They got a *lot* of people up beyond there, boss. All their main battles are camped up from the water meadows, where we were in the summer. They got troops dug in all across the open ground in front of the woods, right over to the east river."

Ash, trying to squint in the silver darkness, had a brief memory of the Lion standard hanging listless in the heated air, by the Suzon river; and the chapel and the nunnery nestled under the eaves of the wildwood, a little to the north.

[4] Bombard: the great siege gun, often not firing more than one or two of their 550 lb shot per day. The smaller cannon – culverins, serpentines, and others – kept up a more rapid fire.

[5] Presumably Visigoth legions named for the areas from which troops were initially raised. Judging by the text, these 'legions' resemble the Classical pattern in their strength (within the 3,000–6,000 men of the Roman legion at various periods), and conceivably their infantry/cavalry/auxiliary structure, if one supposes the place of the auxiliaries to have been taken by Visigoth slaves. There is, however, no mention of them dividing their legions into cohorts or centuries. I suspect the Visigoth fighting force otherwise resembles the Western European mediaeval model, but with some additions – religious terms, and some ranks – in keeping with their concept of themselves as the successors of the Roman Empire.

"What's Dijon's northern defence?"

"Speaking from memory, madonna, a moat dug between the Suzon and the Ouche, and stout city walls. Otherwise, the land north of the city is flat meadowland, until the forest. Do I remember well, Sergeant?"

Price nodded.

"That's the weakest spot, then. That's why the rag-heads have got their main force there." *More* than six thousand men. Maybe seven. Christus Viridianus! "Hang on, what about the south gate?"

"Someone's thrown that bridge down. No one's getting in or out of Dijon's south gate."

"That was probably the idea . . ." Ash tapped her fingers together, then laid them cold against her lips. "Okay, that's a *lot* of troops. Not just your ordinary siege. Something *is* going on here . . ."

Antonio Angelotti touched her shoulder. "You could ask your voice, madonna."

"And hear *what*?"

It has been weeks, but the overwhelming fear of the *Ferae Natura Machinae*, the Wild Machines, is still with her. Squat stone pyramids in the desert south of Carthage, sullenly bright under the Eternal Twilight; their nature hidden for so many aeons . . .

She kept her voice low with an effort.

"If I *did* ask the *machina rei militaris* questions, the rag-heads could just ask it what I'd wanted to know. Then they'd work out where the company is – right here on their doorstep, just handy for their six thousand troops!" She drew a breath. "I'm willing to bet Lord-*Amir* Leofric asks it daily: 'is the bastard Ash alive, does she speak to you? If she has asked questions, what do they tell us about where she is, the strength of her force, her intentions?' . . . Assuming *Leofric's* still alive. He may be dead. But *I can't ask!*"

"Unless they have heard the Wild Machines, madonna, some *amir* will be using the *machina*, even if Lord-*Amir* Leofric is dead. We know it was not destroyed." Momentarily, there was a ragged note in Angelotti's whisper. "*If* you were to ask the *machina rei militaris* what orders are being passed between Carthage and the Faris-general, you could tell us how this war goes. I see that you can't ask. But you could . . . listen?"

A shudder that was not the bitter cold of the night, not the cold of the rain-soaked underbrush, went through her body.

"I *listened*, in Carthage. An earthquake flattened the city. I can't listen to the Stone Golem without the Wild Machines knowing, Angeli. And we've left them behind in North Africa, they don't know where we are, and I'm *fucked* if I'll ever have anything to do with that again! The Wild Machines want Burgundy? That isn't my problem!"

Except that I've made it my problem, by coming back here.

John Price, rumbling his deep voice on the other side of her, said, "Didn't like the look of them pyramids, in Carthage. Didn't like the look of the rag-heads, neither. Bunch of fucking nutters. Better they don't find out where we are. Don't you go telling 'em, boss."

If anything could have warmed the stone coldness inside her, it would have been the Englishman's stolid humour. She remained numb at a level deeper than camaraderie could reach.

Ash forced herself to smile at the straggle-haired billman, knowing her expression to be visible in the moonlight. "What, you think they won't be pleased to see us? I guess not. After the state we left Carthage in, I don't think we'll be winning any popularity contests with the King-Caliph . . . That's if his mighty highness King-Caliph Gelimer is still with us, of course."

Rickard unexpectedly said, "Would the *amirs* still have a crusade in Christendom if Gelimer were dead?"

"Of course they will. The *machina rei militaris* will be telling whoever's King-Caliph to push the campaign for all they're worth. Because that's what the Wild Machines are saying, through it. Rickard, that's nothing to do with the Company of the Lion." Ash saw moonlit disbelief on his face. She shrugged and turned back to the Sergeant of Bill. John Price looked at her, as if for orders; she saw fear and trust in his expression.

"This gives us an answer. I'll bet on it." Ash reached down and rubbed her booted thighs, easing her cold and sodden legs back into life. "Numbers like this . . . First, even if he *was* wounded at Auxonne, Duke Charles is still alive. Second: he hasn't escaped into northern Burgundy. The Visigoths wouldn't have this much force sitting outside one town in the south if Charles *Téméraire* was dead or in Flanders. They'd be up there trying to finish this."

"You think he's in Dijon, boss?"

"I think so. Can't see any other reason for all this." Ash put her hand on Price's mailed shoulder. "But let's get to the important bit. Have the scouts seen Lion liveries on the city walls?"

"Yes!"

Evident, from his expression, what crucial hope rides on this.

"It's our lot in there! We saw the Lion Passant Guardant okay, boss! Burren's lads saw a standard before it got dark. I'd trust his boys to know the Blue Lion, boss."

Rickard, as abrupt as young men are, demanded, "Can we attack the Visigoths? Raise the siege and get Master Anselm out?"

If Robert's there, and alive . . . Ash snorted under her breath. "Optimist! Do it on your own, Rickard, will you?"

"We're a legion. We're soldiers. We can do it."

"I must stop getting you to read me Vegetius . . ."

There was a chuckle from the men around her at that.

Ash paused momentarily. A new cold dread sat in her stomach, and gnawed at her: *I'm going to make a decision based on this information, and it won't be one hundred per cent right – it never is.*

She spoke. "Okay, guys – now we're committed. I'm betting that the rest of the company *didn't* break out, go to France or Flanders; they're still in there, with Duke Charles as their employer. So, if the other half of the Lion Azure is sitting inside that siege, we don't give a fuck about weird shit in Carthage, or *anything* else, we sort out our lads first."

"Yes," Angelotti agreed.

"On our own, boss – well, we ain't going to get no back-up. It's all bandit country and Visigoths we've come through," John Price said disgustedly. "Burgundy's the only place that's still fighting."

"They should have attacked the Turk," Angelotti said quietly. "We know now, madonna, why the lord-*amirs* chose to attack Christendom and leave the Empire of Mehmet whole on their flank."

"The Stone Golem gave them that strategy."

Abrupt in her memory, she hears the voices that spoke through the *machina rei militaris* in Carthage: 'BURGUNDY *MUST* FALL WE MUST MAKE BURGUNDY AS THOUGH IT HAD NEVER BEEN—'

And her own voice, speaking to the Wild Machines: *Why does Burgundy matter?*

The cold mud slid away under her heels as she stood up, chill in the wet moonlit night.

I still don't know why.

I don't want to know!

The tension between what she felt, and what she could say in front of these men, momentarily silenced her. Quietness and cold made her shudder. Dripping trees sprayed her with water, as the wind blew up briefly before dropping; the stillness of pre-dawn not many hours off.

She looked around at their white faces in the moonlight. "Remember who's in there. The other side of the guns and siege engines and six thousand Carthaginians. Just remember."

Antonio Angelotti got to his feet, mud-soaked. "The city's held out nearly three months, madonna. Things will not be good in there."

The same thought in both their minds: a memory of empty French villages, frozen under the eternally black sky where day never dawns. Half-timbered houses burned and abandoned; charred wood covered with snow. Sties empty; paddocks scraped down to flint and clay. A child's ragged linen shirt left frozen in the muddy ice, with preserved boot-marks treading it down. Houses, farms, all empty; their reeves leading the people away; lords and their bailiffs gone beforehand; towns left with empty, devastated streets, not the neigh of a horse, nor the stink of a gutter remaining. And those who could not flee dead of starvation, and stacked like icy kindling-wood; not all the bodies untouched.

In a siege, there is nowhere to flee to.

Angelotti added, "We should get Roberto and the men out."

Ash turned back to Price. "There's the three main gates into the city . . . Any sally-ports?"

Price nodded. "Yeah, my lads were looking at 'em when we were here in the summer. There's about half a dozen postern gates, mostly over the east side. There's two water-gates down this side, where they diverted the river through the town to the mills. You want us to sneak Master Anselm and the company out down a mill-race, boss?"

"That's right, Sergeant." Deadpan, Ash looked at him. "One at a time. It should take, oh, about three days, provided we do it in the dark, and nobody notices!"

John Price gave a short, choked laugh. He wiped his nose on the back of his sodden mitten. "Fair enough."

She thought, *I want to despise him for responding to so blatant a manipulation.* A wry smile moved her mouth. *But all I wish is that someone would do the same for my morale.*

We are committed, that's for sure.

Ash turned until she could see Angelotti's dirty angelic features, as well as Price. Rickard hovered behind her, with Price's men.

"Send the scouts out again." Her voice dropped chill into the bitter air, warm breath turning to white mist as she spoke. "I need to know if the overall commander of the Visigoth forces is here, too. I need to know if the Faris is here at Dijon."

"She will be," Angelotti muttered. "If the Duke is."

"I need to be sure!"

"Got you, boss," Price said.

Ash squinted in the white light: a calculating look at the distant fires in the western camp of the Visigoth army. "Angeli, can you get one of your people up through the engineers' camp to the walls without being noticed?"

"Not difficult, madonna. One gunner looks very like another, without livery."

"Not a gunner. Find me a crossbowman. I want to send a message in over the walls. Tied to a crossbow bolt is as good a way as any . . ."

"Geraint will object, madonna? To my telling his missile troops what to do?"

"Find me a man or woman that you trust." Ash turned away from the valley. The ground squelched under her boots as she staggered back towards the cover of the waist-high soaking bracken, and the wet trees.

In memory – not in, never in, the silent recesses of her soul, now – in memory she hears the Wild Machines say 'BURGUNDY *MUST* FALL!' And a sardonic, quite different part of herself asks, *How long do you plan to ignore this?*

"Find me Geraint, and Father Faversham," she ordered Rickard; waiting at the edge of the black depths of the wood. "Euen Huw, Thomas Rochester, Ludmilla Rostovnaya, Pieter Tyrrell. And Henri Brant, and Wat Rodway. Officer meeting, soon as we're back at HQ. Okay, let's *go!*"

Avoiding sodden branches, and keeping a footing on the rough ground and undergrowth, took all her attention, and she gladly surrendered herself to that necessity. Ten or so armed men lumbered up out of the bracken and briar, cursing at the wet darkness under the trees, and took up their places around Ash as she went. She heard them muttering about the fucking *size* of the fucking rag-head army, God love us; and the lack of game in the woods, not even a God-rotted squirrel.

The true wildwood, even in winter, would have been impassable; progress measured in yards, not leagues, per day. Here on the cultivated edges, where charcoal-burners and swine-herds lived, it was possible to move fairly quickly – or would have been, by daylight.

The sun! Ash thought; one hand on the shoulder of the man in front, one arm cocked up to shield her face, able to see nothing but blackness. *Dear God, two months travelling in pitch-darkness, twenty-four hours a day: I hate the night, now!*

A league or so away, they paused to light lanterns and went on more easily. Ash swatted a wet, leafless hornbeam branch out of her face, following the back of the man in front, a crossbowman, sergeant of Mowlett's lance. His mud-drenched cloak swung in her vision, held down by the leather straps of belt, bag, and bolt-case. A twisted rag had been tied around his war-hat, above the brim; it might once have been yellow.

"John Burren." She grinned, pushing her way through wet briar to walk beside him. "Well, what's *your* men's guess – how many rag-heads down there?"

He rasped, "A legion plus artillery. And a devil."

That raised her brows. "'Devil'?"

"She hears devil-machines, don't she? Those damned things in the desert, like you showed us? That makes her a devil. Fucking bitch," he added, without emphasis.

Ash staggered sideways in time to avoid a tree, looming black in the faint lamplight. Confronted by his broad back, she said wryly and on impulse, "I heard them too, John Burren."

He looked over his shoulder, his expression in the darkness uncomfortable. "Yeah, but you're the boss, boss. As for her . . . We all got bad blood in families." He skidded, avoiding underbrush; regained his balance, and stifled the noise of a phlegmy sniff in his cupped hand. "And anyway, you didn't need no voices at *all* to get us out of that ambush outside Genoa. So you don't need 'em now, Lion *or* Wild Machine, do you, boss?"

Ash thumped him on the back. She found a smile creasing her mouth. *Well, hey, how about that? I said I wanted someone to improve my morale . . .*

Green Christ, I wish I thought he was right! I do need to ask the *machina rei militaris*. And I can't. I mustn't.

An hour travelling in the dark with lanterns brought them to the pickets and the muzzled, silenced dogs. They passed over the dug-trench-and-brushwood walls into the camp: two hundred men and their followers encamped under mature beech forest.

Most of the beech trees were already de-barked to above the height of a man's reach, feeding the meagre fires that now gave the only light. The borders of a streamlet were trodden down into a wet, black slick. On the far side, Wat Rodway's baggage-train helpers clustered around iron cook-pots on tripods. Ash, muddy and wet to the thigh, made first for the banked fires and accepted a bowl of pottage from one of the servers. She stood talking with the women there for a few minutes, laughing, as if nothing in the world could be a worry to her, before handing back a bowl scraped dry.

Angelotti, bright-eyed, huddled his cloak even more tightly around his lean shoulders and pushed in beside her, close to the flames. His face bore the mark of weeks on basic rations, but it did not seem to have depressed his spirits; if anything, there was an odd, reckless gaiety about him.

"Another one of Mowlett's men has come back here before us, madonna. You could have spared yourself sending those other scouts – he has the answer to your question. Her livery's been seen, and her person. The Faris is here."

The blast of heat from a wind-blown flame of the campfire does not make her flinch: she is momentarily lost in memory of a woman who is nameless, whose name is her rank;[6] whose face is the face that Ash sees in her mirror, but flawless, unscarred. Who is the overall military commander of perhaps thirty thousand Visigoth troops in Christendom. And who is more than that, although she may not know it.

"I'd have bet money on it. It's where the Stone Golem will have told her to be." Ash corrected herself: "Where the Wild Machines will have said, through the *machina rei militaris*, that they want her."

"Madonna—"

"Ash!" Another figure shoved in beside Ash, through the press of people. Patches of firelight picked the woman out, the brown and green of her male dress: hose and cloak nearly invisible against mud, bare trees, stacked kindling-wood, and wet crumpled briar.

"I want a word with you," Floria del Guiz demanded.

II

"Yeah, soon as I'm done here—" Ash wiped her mouth with her sleeve, chewing the crust of dark bread that Rickard shoved into her hand, sipping spring-water from a cup he thrust at her; eating on the move, as ever. She nodded abstractly to Florian, noting also, now, Rickard, Henri Brant, and two of the armourers, all waiting to speak to her; and turned back to Angelotti.

"No," Florian interrupted the group. "A word with you *now*. In my tent. Surgeon's orders!"

"Y'okay . . ." The chill spring-water made Ash's teeth ache. She swallowed down the bread, told Henri Brant and the other men briefly, "Clear it all with Angeli and Geraint Morgan!", and nodded Rickard towards the warmth of the fires. She turned to speak to Floria del Guiz, to find the woman already striding away through the slopping leaf-mulch and mud and darkness.

"Flaming hell, woman! I've got stuff to set up before morning!"

The tall, skinny figure halted, looking over her shoulder. Night hid most of her. Firelight made an orange straggle of her hair, still no longer than a man's, that curled at the level of her chin. She had obviously raked it back with muddy fingers at some point: brown streaks clotted the blond hairs, and her freckled cheekbones were smeared dark.

"Okay, I know you don't bother me for no reason. What is it *this* time? More on the sick list?" Moving too fast, Ash skidded, and put her boot down in a pothole hidden in shadow. Her hose were wet enough that she scarcely felt the cold through the soaked leather.

"No. I told you: I want a word."

Florian held up the flap of the surgeon's tent, where it had with difficulty been pitched among the shallow roots of the beech trees. Canvas yawed and

[6] 'Faris': cavalryman; knight.

sagged alarmingly, shadow and reflected firelight shifting with the movement. Ash ducked, entering the dim, musty-smelling interior; and let her eyes adjust to the light of one of the last candles, set aside for the dispensary. The pallets on the earthen floor appeared empty.

"I'm out of St John's Wort and witch hazel," Florian said briskly, "and damn near out of gut for surgery. I'm not looking forward to tomorrow. I shan't need you, deacon."

She continued to hold the tent-flap up. One of her lay priests abandoned his mortar and pestle, and nodded to her as he scrambled out of the tent into the darkness. Nothing in his demeanour suggested he was in any way uncomfortable this close to a woman dressed as a man.

"There you are, Florian. Told you so." Ash seated herself at one of the benches, leaning her elbows on the herb-preparation table. She looked up at the female surgeon in the half-light. "You sewed them up after Carthage – you went to Carthage *with* them, under fire. You've stuck with us all the way back. Far as the company's concerned, it's 'we don't care if she's a dyke, she's *our* dyke'."

The woman slung her lean, long-legged body down on a wooden folding chair. Her expression was not clear in the candlelight. Her voice stung with bitterness. "Oh, no *shit*? Am I supposed to be pleased? How magnanimous of them!"

"Florian—"

"Maybe I should start saying the same about them: 'so, they're a bunch of muggers and rapists, but hey, they're *my*—' Hell! I'm not a . . . not a . . . company *mascot*!" Her hand hit the table, flat, making a loud crack in the cold tent. The yellow flame shifted with the movement of the air.

"Not quite fair," Ash said mildly.

Florian's clear green eyes reflected the light. Her voice calmed. "I must be catching your mood. What I meant to say was, if I took a woman into my tent, then we'd find out how much I'm 'theirs'."

"*My* mood?"

"We're going to be fighting today or tomorrow." Florian did not inflect it as a question. "This isn't the right time to say this, but then, there may not be a right time later. We might both be dead. I've watched you, all the way here. You don't talk, Ash. You haven't talked since we left Carthage."

"When was there time?" Ash realised she still held the wooden cup in her numb, cold fingers. There was no water left in it. "There any wine tucked away in here?"

"No. If there was, I'd be keeping it for the sick."

Pupils dilating with night vision, Ash could make out Floria's expression. Her bony, intelligent face had lines from bad diet and hard marching, but none of the marks of a surfeit of wine or beer. *I haven't seen her drunk in weeks*, Ash thought.

"You haven't been talking," the other woman said deliberately, "since those things in the desert scared the living shit out of you."

Cold tension knotted in her gut; released a pulse of fear that left her dizzy. Florian added, "You were all right at the time. I watched you. Shock set in afterwards, when we were crossing the Med. And you're *still* avoiding thinking about it now!"

"I hate defeats. We came so near to taking out the Stone Golem. All we've done is make sure they know they need to protect it." Ash watched her own knuckles squeezing her wooden cup, trying to stop it rattling against the planks of the table. "I keep thinking that I should have done more. I *could* have."

"Can't keep re-fighting old battles."

Ash shrugged. "I know there was a breach into House Leofric somewhere below ground-level – I'd seen his damn white rats escaped into the sewers! If I could have found the breach, maybe we could have got down to the sixth floor, maybe we could have taken out the Stone Golem, maybe now there'd be no way the Wild Machines could ever say anything to anyone again!"

"*White* rats? You didn't tell me about this." Florian leaned across the table. The candlelight threw her features into sharp relief: her expression intense, as if she pried into chinks in masonry. "Leofric – the lord who owns you? And owns the Faris, one supposes. The one whose house we were trying to knock down? *Rats?* "

Ash put her other hand around the cup, looking down into the shadow inside it. It felt marginally warmer in the tent than in the forest, but she yearned for the scorching heat back at the bonfire.

"Lord-*Amir* Leofric doesn't just breed slaves like me. He breeds rats. They're not natural rat-colour. Those ones I saw had to mean the earthquake cracked House Leofric open underground. But, it might not have been the same quadrant of the House that has the Stone Golem in, it *might* not have been a wide enough breach to get men through . . ." She left it unfinished.

"'Coulda, woulda, shoulda.'" Floria's expression altered. "You told me about Godfrey in the middle of that fire-fight. Just, 'he's dead'. I haven't had any more out of you since."

Ash saw the darkness in the empty cup blur. It was quite genuinely several seconds before she realised tears were in her eyes.

"Godfrey died when the Citadel palace came down, in the earthquake." Her voice gravel, sardonic, she added, "A rock fell on him. Even a priest's luck has to run out, I suppose. Florian, we're a mercenary company, people *die*."

"I knew Godfrey for five years," the woman mused. Ash heard her voice out of the candlelit darkness of the pre-dawn; did not look up to see her face.

"He changed, when he knew I was no man." Florian coughed. "I wish he hadn't; I could remember him with more charity now. But I only knew him a few years, Ash. You knew him for a decade, he was all the family you'll ever have."

Ash leaned back on her bench and met the woman's gaze.

"*Okay*. The private word you wanted to have with me is: you don't think I've grieved for Godfrey. Fine. I'll do it when I have *time*."

"You had *time* to go out with the scouts, instead of letting them report in like normal! That's make-work, Ash!"

Anger, or perhaps fear of the immediate future, kicked in Ash's belly, and came out as spite. "If you want to do something useful, grieve for your useless shit of a brother, instead – because no one else is going to!"

Florian's mouth unexpectedly quirked. "Fernando may not be dead. You may not be a widow. You may still have a husband. With all his faults."

There was no discernible pain in Floria's expression. *I can't read her*, Ash thought. There's, what, five, ten years between us? It could be fifty!

Ash got her feet under her, pushing herself up from the table. The earth was slick under the soles of her boots. The tent smelled of mould and rot.

"Fernando did try to stand up for me in front of the King-Caliph . . . For all the good it did him. I didn't see him after the roof fell in. Sorry, Florian. I thought this was something serious. I *haven't* got time for this."

She moved towards the tent-flap. Night air billowed the mildew-crusted canvas walls, shifted the light from the candle. Florian's hand came up, and gripped her sleeve.

Ash looked at the long, muddy fingers knotting into the velvet of her demi-gown.

"I've watched you narrow down your vision." Florian didn't relax her grip on the cloth. "Yes, being that focused has got us across Christendom to here. *It won't keep you alive now.* I've known you for five years, and I've watched how you look at *everything* before a fight. You're . . ."

Florian's fingers loosened, and she looked up, features in shadow, hair brilliant in the candle-shine; searching for words.

"For two months, you've been . . . closed in on yourself. Carthage scared you. The Wild Machines have scared you into not thinking! You have to start again. You're going to miss things; opportunities, mistakes. You're going to get people killed! You're going to get *yourself* killed."

After a second, Ash closed her hand over Florian's, squeezing the chill fingers briefly. She sat down on the bench beside the surgeon, facing her. Momentarily, she dug at her brows with her fingers, grinding the flesh as if to release pressure.

"Yeah . . ." Some emotion crystallised; pushing to the forefront of her mind. "Yeah. This is like Auxonne; the night before the battle. Knowing you can't avoid decisions any more. I need to get my shit together." A memory tugged at her. "I was in this tent then, too, wasn't I? Talking to you. I . . . always meant to apologise, and thank you for coming back to the company."

She looked up to see Florian watching her with a closed, pale face. She explained, "It was the shock of finding I was pregnant. I misinterpreted what you said."

Florian's thick, gold brows dipped. "You ought to let me examine you."

Ash spoke concisely. "It's been a couple of months since I miscarried; everything's back as it should be. You can ask the washerwomen about the clouts."[7]

"But—"

Ash interrupted. "But now I've mentioned it – I should apologise for what I said then. I *don't* think you were being jealous that I could have a baby. And . . . well, I know now that you weren't – well – making a pass at me. Sorry for thinking that you would."

"But I would," Floria said.

[7] 'Clouts' – cloths; in this case presumably menstrual.

Relief at finally having made her apology overwhelmed her, so that she almost missed Florian's reply. She stopped, still beside her in the half-dark, on the cold wooden bench, and stared at the other woman.

"Oh, I would," Florian repeated, "but what's the use? You don't watch women. You never look at women. I've seen you, Ash – you've got *hot* women in this company, and *you don't ever look at them*. The most you'll do is put your arm around them when you're showing them a sword-cut – and it means nothing, does it?"

Ash's chest hurt; Floria's vehemence left her breathless.

Floria said, "Say what you like about being 'one of the boys' – I watch you flirt with half the male commanders you've got here. You can call it *charisma* if you like. Maybe none of you realise what it is. But you *respond* to guys. Especially to my slut of a brother! And *not* to women. Now what would be the use of me making a pass at you?"

Ash stared, her mouth slightly open, no words coming into her mind. The chill of the night made her eyes and her nose run; she absently wiped a sopping velvet sleeve across her face, still with her gaze fixed on the older woman. She strained for words, finding only a complete absence of anything to say.

"Don't worry." A brittle note entered Florian's voice. "I wasn't then, and I won't now. Not because I don't want you. Because it's not in you to want me."

The harshness of her tone increased. Caught between revulsion, and an overwhelming desire to console the woman – *Florian, this is Florian; Jesu, she's one of the few people I call friend* – Ash began to reach out a hand, and then let it drop.

"Why say this now?"

"We may both be killed before the end of tomorrow."

Ash's silver brows came down. "That's been true before. Often."

"Maybe I just wanted to wake you up." The fair-haired woman leaned back on the bench, as if it were a movement of relaxation, and only coincidentally one that moved her further away from Ash. She might have been thoughtful, might have been smiling slightly, or frowning; the dim light made it impossible to know.

"Have I upset you?" Florian asked, after a moment's utter quiet.

"I . . . don't think so. I knew that you and Margaret Schmidt— but it never occurred to me that you'd look at *me* like that— I'm . . . flattered, I guess."

A splutter of edged laughter came from further down the bench. "Better than I'd hoped for. At least you're not treating it as a management problem!"

That was so much Florian – knowing perfectly well what Ash's first reaction would be – that Ash had to smile. "Well . . . Okay, I'm flattered it turns out I'm a woman you could fancy! Same as with a man, I guess. I deal with this from time to time in the company. I tell them, they'll find a good woman – it just isn't me."

In a deliberately casual tone, Floria del Guiz said, "I can handle that."

"Well, okay." An unaccustomed feeling that she should do something, or say something more, made Ash stand up quickly, her footing uncertain on the wet, earthen floor. She looked at the seated woman. "What am I . . . supposed to do with this?"

"Nothing." A wry smile touched Florian's features, and faded. "Do what you like with it. Ash, wake up! This isn't just getting half the company out of a siege. We're back in the Duchy; you spent one night on the beach outside Carthage telling us that these," her voice hesitated, "these *ferae machinae*[8] have spent two hundred years tricking House Leofric into breeding a slave for them to conquer Burgundy with – and you've said nothing since. Now you're here, Ash. This is Burgundy. This isn't a war that people had anything to do with. Are you going to carry on acting like it's just another campaign? Like you and your – sister – are just war-leaders?"

Ash was unaware that her face had a peculiarly unfocused expression, as if she were still listening to the echoes of machine-voices in her head. She snapped her gaze to the woman's face, suddenly. "No, you're right, Florian. No, I'm not."

"Then what?"

"This isn't 'just another campaign'. But – don't take this wrong – Burgundy isn't my business. *Or* yours."

"But Carthage is."

Ash turned her head away from the woman's uncompromising expression, hearing the familiar voices of her lance-leaders outside the tent. "Time for the officer meeting. I want to hear what state we're in. You come with me. If there aren't any wounded you should be looking after?"

"We lost the last of the *non*-walking wounded just north of Lyons." There was a rasp in the woman's tone.

Ash turned towards the tent doorway, the candle casting her shadow dark in front of her, and she groped blindly for the flap, and pushed it open. Stiff, cold canvas scraped her bare fingers. She tugged her sodden, frozen mittens on. Aware of Florian at her shoulder, she stepped out into the firelit darkness.

"I haven't *completely* lost it," Ash added. "I have spent some of the time we took getting here working out what the fuck we could do if we ever *got* here . . ."

She heard Florian's familiar cynical snort. Ash halted, staring off through the darkness. In one place, among branch-shelters, the distinctive smoke of burning green wood went up. "Put that fucking fire out!"

Geraint ab Morgan, walking up with most of his belongings hanging off his belt and a great-sword resting over his shoulder, turned to shout at a provost-sergeant, who set off at the trot. "Yes, boss. Hey, boss, council of war's set up. The rest of 'em are in your pavilion."

There were only two tents put up, here on the difficult open ground within the edge of the wood: the surgeon's infirmary tent, and the commander's pavilion. Most shelters were ripped-down branches, or muddy canvas tied between trees. Ash fell in beside Morgan in the firelit darkness, walking in the wake of her other lance-leaders heading towards her tent – a drooping structure pegged between the roots of beeches, partly tied to branches, lurching as the wet night loosened the guy-ropes.

"How many men do we have now, Geraint?"

[8] 'Wild machines'.

The big man scratched under his coif at his russet-coloured, short-cropped hair. "Down to one hundred and ninety-three men, aren't we? Men who can fight. The baggage train is up to three or four hundred, but we're getting civilians tagging on."

"Sort that out." Ash met Geraint ab Morgan's gaze mildly. "Do it before we eat breakfast."

"Some of the men here have taken women from the road. If we drive the women off, they'll starve. The lads won't like that, boss."

"Shit!" Ash hit one fist into her mittened palm. "Leave it, then. More trouble than it's worth, to get rid of them."

Floria del Guiz, stumbling across the broken ground with them, a wry smile only just visible in the fire's light, murmured, "Pragmatist . . ."

A night's camp had left autumn undergrowth trodden into the mud, or ripped up for bedding. No goats or chickens ran underfoot now. Something like five hundred people and their pack-beasts crowded into the oblong camp erected in the strip of land along the edge of the wildwood. Archers and lightly armoured men-at-arms crouched around fires, in the wet, eating the sparse rations.

A bray came from the pack-mules tied to trees further down the length of the camp; and Ash breathed into her mail-covered mittens as she walked, letting her breath warm her frozen face, watching by the fires' shifting illumination – squires and pages talking as they cared for the mules, billmen and hackbutters chivvied into clearing up by sergeants and corporals; and the women and children who roamed everywhere, the newcomers underfoot, pinched of face, with the look of deep shock in their eyes. Judging morale.

"We lost another two men-at-arms, then?"

"Last night, before we made camp. That's fewer than in the south."

We didn't get here a minute too soon.

Geraint frowned. "Boss, I've been reorganising some of the under-strength lances into provost units, and this lot are far more scared of me now than they are of deserting. But I wish you'd let me leave missile troop duty to Angelotti; we got all the damn company archers with us; it's taking up too much of my time."

Ash nodded thoughtfully. "You're a damn sight better provost than you ever were Sergeant of Archers! Okay: I guess you'd better keep it up, then."

She made for the commander's tent, Morgan and the surgeon with her. Geraint ab Morgan shoved his way past Floria del Guiz to enter, halted with comical suddenness, and jumped back to let her pass.

"God's *blood*! You can't show me your pubic lice and then expect me to want to be treated like a lady," Floria rasped, striding past him into the pitch-dark tent.

Ash caught sight of his expression, and, for all her own bitter confusion, almost burst into laughter.

"Quieten down," she said, smiling; walking into the canvas-darkened, already occupied interior. "Rickard, open the flap; let's have some firelight in here."

"I could light lamps, boss."

"Not unless Father Faversham here helps you with a miracle. We're out of lamp-oil. Aren't we, Henri?"

"Yes, boss. That and a lot of other things. We can't keep going for ever on what we scavenge from abandoned towns."

"*If* they were abandoned before you 'scavenged' . . ." Floria, feeling her way, sat herself down on one of Ash's back-stools, with a caustic glance at Thomas Rochester, and at Euen Huw, as the Welsh lance-leader scuttled in, late.

"Most of them were. Mostly." Euen Huw's dirty, rough features assumed an injured expression. "Who can tell in the Dark? Spoils of war, isn't it, boss?"

Ash ignored the banter. She glanced around in the dim light. The Rus woman Rostovnaya came in on Euen's heels. Geraint ab Morgan muttered to Pieter Tyrrell, Tyrrell listening to the Welshman and massaging the leather glove sewn over the remaining finger and thumb of his half-hand. Wat Rodway leaned up against the centre pole and sharpened his cook's knife on a whetstone, Henri Brant now talking to him in an urgent undertone.

"Henri," she said. "What's the state of play with the food?"

The broad-faced man turned around. "You've run it too fine, boss. Half-rations for the last week, and I've had armed guards on the pack mules. There's no more hot food after today, we're down to dark bread; maybe two days' worth. Then nothing."

"That's definite?"

"You've given me five hundred people to feed; yes, I'm definite, it can't be done! I have nothing left to bake!"

Ash held up one hand, calming his red-faced anxiety, keeping her own stomach-churning apprehension off her face. "It's not a problem, Henri. Don't worry about it. Geraint, what is it?"

Geraint ab Morgan's deep voice filled the musty air, in the flickering gold light. "We don't think it's a good idea to attack the city."

The unexpected challenge jolted her. "Who's 'we'?"

"Fuck this, boss." Ludmilla Rostovnaya didn't answer directly. "Go on, tell us all about getting the rest of the company out of Dijon, 'n' on the road to England. What we gonna do, boss, *spit* at the fucking rag-heads?"

"Yeah, spit 'n' the walls fall down," Geraint growled.

Ash, catching the eye of Thomas Rochester, shook her head fractionally.

"You know what?" she said, conversationally, "I don't give a fuck what you think isn't a good idea, Geraint. I expect my officers to keep themselves informed of what's going on."

"Demons." The big russet-haired man stared at her, through the gloom. "The King-Caliph's got *demons* telling him what to do!"

"Demons, Wild Machines, call them what you like. Right now, those legions of Visigoths outside Dijon are a bigger problem!"

Geraint scratched in his cod, still gaping at Ash; and then shot a glance at Ludmilla Rostovnaya.

"Your arm okay?" Ash asked the Rus woman; and at her hesitant nod, said, "Right. Report to Angelotti. He's got a job for you, and your crossbow snipers. I'm going to write a dozen messages for the company inside Dijon, and I want them shot over the walls – and I want you to then wait for a message back from Captain Anselm. You got that?"

Given something to do, the crossbow-woman looked reassured. "Now, boss?"

"Angelotti's with the hackbutters. Get going."

In the shuffling rearrangement of bodies as the woman left the pavilion, Geraint ab Morgan said, "I don't agree with what you're doing! It's madness, an assault on Dijon. The men won't follow you."

At that rasping complaint, the pavilion became silent. Ash nodded once to herself. She glanced around in the dimness at the lance-leaders, steward, and surgeon.

"You're going to have to trust me," she said, her eyes finally meeting Geraint's pale blue, bloodshot gaze. "I know we're hungry, we're exhausted, but we're *here*. Now you either trust me to take it from here, or you don't. Which is it, Geraint?"

The big Welshman glanced to one side, as if seeking Euen Huw's support. The wiry, dirty lance-leader shook his head, lips pursed together. Thomas Rochester rumbled something under his breath. The only other sound came from Wat Rodway stropping his knife on the whetstone.

"Well?" Ash gazed around in the flickering shadows at the pavilion full of men, their breath smoking in the freezing air; big bodies slung about with belts, daggers, swords, arrow-bags. In that company of soldiers, she noted that Floria got up and went to stand with the steward and cook.

"I'm with you," Floria said, as she walked past Ash. Henri Brant nodded; Wat Rodway glanced up with piggish eyes and inclined his head, sharply, once.

"Master Morgan?"

"Don't like it," Geraint ab Morgan said suddenly. He did not drop his gaze. "Bad enough the enemy's being led by a demon, isn't it? Now we are, too."

"'We'?" Ash queried gently.

"Saw it at the galleys. You were going to go into the desert. Find them old pyramids, maybe. Maybe listen to their orders. What are we doing here, boss? Why are we here?"

"Because the rest of the company is – inside Dijon." Ash moved to one side; sitting herself on the edge of the trestle table, covered in maps, on which she had earlier been attempting to work out their route of march.

She gazed around at her officers sitting on back-stools, at Floria lounging beside Wat Rodway at the tent-pole, and Brant shifting from foot to foot on the bracken-strewn earth. Richard Faversham hulked at the back. The light from the open tent-flap illuminated profiles only.

She nodded to Rickard, gesturing him to pull the canvas back wider; and heard him exchange some comment with the guards outside.

"Okay," Ash said. "Here's how it is. First I'm going to talk to you; then I'm going to talk to all the lance-leaders, and then to the lads. First I'm going to tell you what we're doing here. Then I'm going to tell you what we're going to do next. Is everybody clear on that?"

Nods.

"We all know," she said, her words quiet in the silence, and her gaze mostly on Geraint ab Morgan, "that there's an enemy behind the enemy.

575

Christendom's been fighting Visigoths, Burgundy's been fighting Visigoths – but that isn't all there is to it, is there?"

It was a rhetorical question: she was momentarily off-balance when Geraint muttered, "That's what I said, isn't it? Led by a demon. She *is*. Their Faris, their general."

"Yes. She is." Ash rested both hands beside her, on the table. "She hears a demon. And so do I."

The Welsh archer winced at that; but Euen Huw and Thomas Rochester shrugged.

"More than one bloody demon," Rochester said, his voice elaborately casual. "Bloody desert down there's full of them, ain't it, boss?"

"It's okay, Tom. It scares me shitless, too."

Momentarily, they are silent; their minds full of the southern lights, of the dark desert illuminated by silver, scarlet, ice-blue. Seeing again the lined ranks of pyramids, stark against the silver fire.

"I used to think I was hearing the Lion – but it was their Stone Golem," Ash said. "And you all know that I heard the Wild Machines at Carthage. The voices *behind* the Stone Golem. I don't know if the Faris even knows they're there, Geraint. I don't know if anyone – House Leofric, or the Caliph, or the Faris – knows a damn thing about the voices of the Wild Machines." She held Geraint's gaze, in the dim light. "But we know. We know Leofric was a puppet, and the Wild Machines bred his slave-daughter. We know this isn't normal war. It hasn't been, not from day one."

Geraint said, "I don't like it, boss."

She noted the slump of his shoulders, his second glance around for support; and gave him a smile of great friendliness. She shifted herself off the table and moved to stand in front of him.

"Hell, I don't like it either! But I won't go to the Wild Machines. I haven't felt the pull of them since we sailed from North Africa. Trust me." She gripped his forearms.

Standing there, in the red and golden filtered light, she is a strong, filthy, mud-stained woman, white scars on her face and hands, flesh dimpled with old wounds; wearing orange-rusted mail mittens and a sword as if it were a matter of course. And grinning at him with apparent utter confidence.

Geraint straightened his shoulders. "Don't like it, boss," he repeated. He looked down at her hands. "Nor do the lads. We don't know what this war's for, any more."

Floria, her face in shadow, said vitriolically: "Loot, pay, rapine, drunkenness and fornication, Master Morgan?"

"We're still out here to beat any other company in the field," Euen Huw said as if it were self-evident.

"Master Anselm and the others!" Rickard croaked.

An edge of tension informed all their voices. Ash let go of Geraint Morgan's arms, giving him a friendly slap. She looked around at the others, unconsciously bracing herself before she spoke again.

"No. He's right. Geraint's right. We *don't* know what this war is for." She paused for a moment. "And the *Visigoths* don't know what this war's for. That's the key. They think it's a crusade against Christendom. But it's far more than that."

Slowly, she stripped off her armoured sheepskin mittens, rubbing her frozen fingers together.

"I know the Wild Machines have fed ideas to Leofric, and through him to the King-Caliph. They speak through the Stone Golem. The Visigoth armies are here because the Wild Machines sent them here. Not to Constantinople, or anywhere in the east – *here*, so they could get Burgundy overrun and destroyed."

From the back of the tent, Richard Faversham said in English, "Why Burgundy?"

"Yeah: why Burgundy?" Ash repeated in camp patois. "I don't know, Richard. In fact, I don't know why they've brought an army here at all."

Geraint ab Morgan spluttered an amazed laugh. Unselfconsciously falling back into his rank, he blurted, "Boss, you're mad! How else would they fight Duke Charles?"

Ash looked past him. "Richard. We need more light in this tent."

The apparent non sequitur silenced them all. She had a moment to watch as the English priest lumbered up off his stool and knelt down, Thomas Rochester shifting out of the way; Floria turning to look at Ash in amazement; Wat Rodway stuffing his whetstone back in his purse, and his skinning knife into its sheath.

"*In nomine Christi Viridiani . . .*"[9]

Richard Faversham's surprising high tenor silenced them.

". . . *Christi Luciferi*,[10] *Iesu Christi Viridiani . . .*"

The prayer went on; their voices joined in. Ash watched them, with their lowered heads and clasped hands, even Rickard at the tent-flap turning and kneeling down in the cold mud.

"God will grant this, to you," Faversham announced, "in your need."

A low, yellow light, like the light of a candle, shone from the air.

A shiver went up from her belly. Ash shut her eyes, involuntarily. A faint warmth touched her scarred cheeks. She opened her eyes again, seeing their faces clearly now in the calm light: Euen Huw, Thomas Rochester, Wat Rodway, Henri Brant, Floria del Guiz – and, slipping in, Antonio Angelotti; his wet, mud-draggled hair and face taking on a smirched, unearthly beauty.

"Blessed be." The gunner touched his doublet, above his heart. "What is here?"

"Light in darkness. God forgive me," Ash said, resting her hand on Richard Faversham's shoulder. She raised her head, gazing around now at parchment-coloured canvas, at swords and a few last herbs hanging from the roof-wheel. Shadows leaped; shrank. "I had no need of it, except to show it could be done. Richard, I'm sorry for using you."

The honey light clung about her. Sparkles of white light flickered at the edges of her vision. Richard Faversham kissed the Briar Cross he held and stood up, heavily, his hose black with leaf-mould.

[9] 'In the name of the Green Christ'.
[10] 'Christ the Light-bringer'.

He murmured, "Man calls on God eternally, Captain Ash, and for greater than this; yet all seems, to Him, as small as a candle-flame. And in any case, small miracles are what I'm with the company for."

Ash knelt, briefly. "Bless me."

"*Ego te absolvo*," the priest recited.

Ash got to her feet.

"Geraint, you asked me a question. You said, how else would the Visigoths fight Duke Charles? This is how."

The provost-captain shook his cropped head. "Don't get it, boss."

The luminous air shifted, granular.

"With miracles," Ash said, gazing around. "Not like this one. Not from God. With evil; with devil's miracles. I know this from the Wild Machines – they bred the Faris from Gundobad's line. They bred her from the Wonder-Worker's blood, to be another saint, another Prophet, another Gundobad. But not for Christ. They've bred her so she can be *their* power on earth and to perform *their* miracles. On their compulsion – and they can compel."

In the miraculous light, Richard Faversham licked his dry lips. "God wouldn't permit it."

"God may not have. But we don't know that." Ash paused. "What we do know is, the Faris isn't the King-Caliph's design, nor *Amir* Leofric's. The Faris belongs to the Wild Machines. They bred her to make a devil's miracle and wipe Burgundy off the face of the earth. So – why has she come with an army?"

There was a momentary silence.

Richard Faversham suggested, "Her power for miracles may be small; every day. No more than a priest or deacon. If that is so, then of course she must bring an army."

Floria frowned at the priest. "Or . . . not come into her power yet?"

"Or their breeding may have failed." Antonio Angelotti stood, not looking at Ash, smiling gently in the luminous air. "Perhaps God is good, and she can do no evil miracles? *You* can't."

Ash looked ruefully back at the English priest. "No. I can't even do tiny miracles. Richard will tell you how many nights on this trek I've spent praying with him! I'll never make a priest. All I can do is hear the Stone Golem. And the Wild Machines. She could be more than I am. And yet, here she is, *fighting* her way in . . ."

Antonio Angelotti shook his head. "If I hadn't known you so long, madonna, and if I hadn't seen what we saw in the desert, I'd think you were crazy or drunk or possessed!" His bright eyes flicked up to meet her gaze. "As it is, I must believe you. Clearly, you heard them. But if the Faris knows nothing of their existence, and if the Wild Machines only speak to her in the disguise of the Stone Golem's voice, she may not know yet what we know."

Richard Faversham demanded, "And when she does know, will she make a desolation here for them?"

Angelotti shrugged. "The Visigoth armies have already made a desolation. Nothing stands where Milano stood, not a wall, not a roof. Venice is burnt. A generation of young men are dead in the Swiss Cantons . . . Madonna, I trust you, but tell us this at least – why Burgundy?"

There were murmurs of agreement; faces turned towards her.

"Oh, I'd tell you – if I knew. I asked the Wild Machines questions, and got my soul nearly blasted out of my body. I don't know, and I can't think why." Ash wiped her nose on her sleeve again, conscious of the stink of mildew in this pavilion, too. "Florian, you're Burgundian-born. Why these lands? Why not France, or the Germanies? Why this Duke, and why Burgundy?"

The woman surgeon shook her head. "We've been on the road well over two months. Every night I've thought about it. I don't know. I don't know why these 'Wild Machines' care about anything human, never mind the Burgundians." Sardonic, Florian added, "Don't try asking them! Not now."

"No," Ash said, something naked about her expression. The miraculous light dimmed a little, the air turning thin and dark again. Ash glanced at Richard Faversham. An expression of pain, or the concentration of prayer, passed across his face.

Even our miracles are becoming weaker.

She turned her gaze back to Geraint, Euen, Thomas Rochester, Angelotti. The tent was full of the smell of sodden wool and male sweat.

"All we know for sure," she said, "is that there's a war behind the war. If I've got you guys involved because of what I am, then that's regrettable – but remember that we would have been in this war anyway. It's what we do." She hesitated. "And if their Faris hasn't done a devil's miracle yet, we can hope that she won't do any in the future. Then it's down to steel and guns. And *that's* what we do."

Reservations were plain on their faces, but no more so than during any campaign. Not even Geraint Morgan, she noted.

"Boss?" the provost-captain asked diffidently, as her gaze fell on him.

"What is it, Geraint?"

"If she does conquer Burgundy, if she does kill their old Duke for them, whether it's by a war or a miracle – what happens then, boss?"

Ash suddenly laughed. "You know – your guess is as good as mine!"

"What do you care, Morgan?" Euen Huw demanded, roughly good-humoured. "By the time that happens you'll be back in Bristol, with all the money you can spend, and clap enough to keep the doctors rich for years!"

Wat Rodway, who had said nothing yet, regarded the fading miraculous light in the tent with jaundiced reverence. "Boss, can I go back and fix food to break our fast? Look – either she can bring some demonic retribution down on us, or she can't. Either way, I'm about to cook the last pottage we're going to see before we attack Dijon. You want it or don't you?"

"'You want it or don't you, *boss*,'" Ash said.

"Oh, I'm not bothered with this. I'm off. Meal in an hour. Tell the lads." Rodway strode out of the tent, with a word to the guards in the same abrupt and entirely offensive tone.

Ash shook her head. "You know, if that man couldn't cook, I'd stick him in the pillory."

"He can't cook," Floria snapped.

"No, that's right. Hmm." Ash, with a smile still stretching her cheeks, felt a cold wind blow through the open tent-flap, bringing the smell of unwashed men, excrement, wet trees, wood-smoke and horse-dung.

Nearly Prime, and the air has started to move—

"Angelotti, Thomas, Euen, Geraint; the rest of you; come outside." She stepped forward, grabbing for the tent-flap. "Florian—"

Geraint ab Morgan leaned over, blocking her way.

"The men won't like it," he repeated, stubbornly. "They don't want to attack the town."

"Come outside," Ash repeated, cheerfully and with an edge of authority. "I'm going to show you another reason why we're here."

Loud squawks and croaks from ravens echoed across the clearing as she stepped outside, past Geraint. She saw the black birds dropping down to the middens by the cook-wagons, strutting unfed, complaining raucously – and realised that she could see them clearly between the spaced beeches, twenty yards away.

Ash turned her face up to the sky.

The air moved across her skin.

"Look!" She pointed.

Deep in the trees, the first half-hour of it must have passed without notice. Now – men and women getting up off their knees in the mud, where they had been hearing Digorie Paston's service of Prime – now all the leafless twigs and bare branches on the eastern horizon of the clearing stood out against the sky.

Ash barely looked at the moon, bone-white and sinking to the west. She felt a tightness in her chest, became aware that she was holding her breath; heard a muttering from the people thronging out into the empty space between the camp's perimeter ditches.

The eastern sky turned slowly, slowly from grey to white to the palest eggshell blue.

The minutes passing could have been no time, or all time; Ash felt that she simultaneously endured an eternity, waiting; and at the same time, that it happened all in an instant – that one minute the clearing in the wood was dark, and the next, a line of bright yellow light lay across the trunks of the western trees, and a sliver of imperishable gold rose up over the eastern mist.

"Oh, Jesu!" Euen Huw plonked down on his knees in the mud.

"God be thanked!" Richard Faversham's deep voice shouted out.

Ash, for once not hearing the shouts, or seeing people running – Geraint ab Morgan and Thomas Rochester grabbing each other in wild hugs, tears streaming down their cheeks for this continuing miracle – Ash stood watching as, for only the fourth morning since the twenty-first day of August, she saw the sun rise up in the eastern sky.

The end of three months of darkness.

A shoulder brushed hers. Dazed, she looked to see Floria beside her.

"You're still not thinking this is our business," Florian said quietly. "Just something for us to avoid."

Ash almost reached out and thumped the woman's shoulder, as she would have done an hour ago. She stopped herself from making physical contact.

"'Our business'?" She stared around her at the men, kneeling. "I'll tell you what 'our business' is, right now! We can't stay camped here – I give it twenty-four hours maximum before we've got Visigoth scouts up our ass. We can't *eat* here – and they got supply lines bringing in all the food they want. We're outnumbered, what, thirty to one?"

She found herself grinning at Florian, but there was more blind exhilaration than humour in it.

"And then there's this. It's still happening! Light!"

"They won't retreat now," the surgeon said. "You realise that?"

Ash's fist clenched. "You're right. I won't be able to lead them back Under the Penitence. I know that. We can't go back. And we can't stay here. We *have* to move forward."

Floria del Guiz, for the first time since Ash had known her, and quite unconsciously, reached up with dirty fingers and crossed herself. "You told me on the beach. The 'Penitence' is nothing to do with the Visigoths. You told me the Wild Machines put out the sun over Christendom this summer. That they've made two hundred years of the Eternal Twilight, over Carthage, by drawing down the sun."

Cold air moved against Ash's face. A sudden cold tear ran down her scarred cheek at the brightness.

"Burgundy, again," Florian said. "In the summer the Wild Machines made a darkness that stretches across Italy, the Cantons, the Germanies; now France . . . and when we cross the border, here, we're out of it. Out of the Eternal Twilight, again. Into this."

Ash looked down. The line of sunlight bisected her body, illuminated the dirt-ingrained skin of her hands, bringing out every whorl in her fingertips. Wet velvet sleeves began to steam under the infinitesimal warmth.

Florian's voice said, "Before this year, the Twilight was only over Carthage. It spread. But not here. Have you thought? Maybe *that's* why the Faris is here with an army. We may be beyond where the Wild Machines can reach."

"Even if we are, that might not last."

Ash looked up at the sky. Automatically, still, this being Florian, she added aloud what was in her mind:

"Remember 'Burgundy must be destroyed'? This is their main target area. Florian, I had no choice about bringing us back here – but now we're standing right on ground zero."

III

Lowering her face from the faint but perceptible warmth of the risen sun, Ash wiped her muddy palm across her scarred cheeks.

Beside her, the woman took her gaze from the eastern sky and shivered in the cold morning.

"Girl, I wouldn't want your job right now!" Florian briskly blew on her bare fingers, looking around at the camp. "We can't go back. *Can* we go forward? What are you going to tell them?"

"That?" Ash, for the first time in weeks, gave a genuinely relaxed smile. "Oh, *that's* not the difficult part. Okay: here we go . . ."

Ash walked on, out into the middle of the clearing, clapping her hands.

Five hundred people stopped talking fast enough, gathering around once they saw it was her: men in mail, and rusted plate, or padded jacks, standing, or squatting on the mud where it was too filthy to sit down. Some few diced in the wet. Rather more were drinking small ale. She gazed around her, at their faces that kept turning away in wonder to the sky.

"Well," Ash said. "Will you look at *your* sorry asses!"

"We can take it, boss!" one of the Tydder brothers yelled: Simon or Thomas, Ash was momentarily unsure which. He ducked a shower of punches, mud-balls, and insults.

"Creep!" Ash remarked. Laughter started, unstrained; going round the crowd.

Well, well. Geraint was wrong. And I was right.

She rubbed her hands together, and grinned broadly back at the drawn faces. "Okay, lads. We're broke again. Not for the first time – won't be the last. It means a day or two more on bread-rations, but hey, we're rough, we're tough, we can hack it."

The other one of the Tydder brothers whimpered in a shrill falsetto, "Mummy!"

Ash took the laughter that followed as an opportunity to look at them closely. The Tydders and a lot of the younger men-at-arms were elbowing each other in the ribs; one with his lance-mate's head wrestled under his arm. Two hundred fighting men with faded liveries and ragged hose, bundled up in every garment they owned; mud-stained, fingers white with chilblains, noses dripping clear liquid. She took the feel of them, electric in the air; read from their faces that they seemed tighter, more exultant, high on being rough, ragged, tough, and soldiers in a world of refugees.

It's because there's sun. We've come across the border. For the first time in weeks, there's the sun . . .

And they've got out of Carthage in one piece and force-marched the better part of one hundred leagues in moonlight and darkness: right now, they think they're shit-hot.

And they are.

Please God it's not all for nothing.

As the laughter died down, Ash lifted her head and looked around at the muddy encampment, and the mud-stained men in front of her.

"We're the Lion company. Never forget it. We're *fucking amazing*. We've come across a hundred leagues of this, through night and bitter cold; it's taken us weeks, but we're still here, we're still together, we're still a company. That's because we're disciplined, and we're the best. There isn't any argument about it. Whatever happens from now on in, we're the best, and you know it."

There was a ragged, good-natured cheer: if only because they knew the amount of truth in what she said. Some men were nodding, others gazed at her in silence. She watched faces, alert for fright, for arrogance, for the imperceptible loosening of bonds between men.

Ash pointed over her shoulder, in the general direction of the river valley and Dijon. She showed teeth in a fierce smile. "You're expecting me to tell you how we're going to batter those walls down, and rescue Anselm and the lads. Well, guys, I've been up ahead to look. And I've got news for you. Those walls aren't going down, they're fucking solid."

One of Carracci's billmen put his hand up.

"Felipe?"

"Then how the fuck are we going to get the rest of the Lions out, boss?"

"We're not." She repeated it, more loudly: "*We're not.*"

A noise of confusion.

"That's a siege going on up there," Ash said, pitching her voice to carry. "Now most people are trying to break *out* of a siege."

"With the exception of the enemy," Thomas Rochester put in helpfully, behind her.

Antonio Angelotti snickered. A number of the men took it up, appreciative of the back-chat.

Ash, who knew very well why – in the midst of Visigoths, twenty-four-hour-a-day darkness, and speaking stone pyramids – both her officers were doing this, contented herself with a glare.

"All right," she said, breath smoking on the icy air. "*Apart* from the enemy. Pair of bloody smartarses."

"That's why you pay us, madonna . . ."

"He gets *paid*?" Euen Huw complained, in broad Welsh.

Ash held up her hands. "Shut up and listen, you dozy shower of shit!"

A voice from the back of the ranks murmured whimsically, "'We're the best' . . ."

The outburst of laughter made even Ash grin. She stood, nodding and waiting, until quiet returned; and then wiped her red, runny nose with her sleeve, put her hands on her hips, and projected her voice out to them:

"Here's the situation. We're in the middle of hostile countryside. There's two Carthaginian legions just down the road in front of us – the Legio XIV Utica and some of the Legio VI Leptis Parva: six or seven thousand men between them."

Murmurs. She went on:

"The rest of their forces are behind us in French territory, and up north in Flanders. Okay, it isn't winter here yet, like it is under the Dark – but there's corn rotted in the fields, and grapes rotted on the vine. There's no game, because they've hunted it all. There's nowhere left to loot, because every town and village for miles around has been stripped. This land is *bare*." She stopped, waiting, looking around; hard dirty faces scowled back at her.

"No need to look at me like that," Ash added, "since you looted your share on the way up here . . ."

An archer's voice: "Fuckin' right."

"You bastards carried away everything that wasn't tied down. Well, I got news for you. It's gone. I've talked to Steward Brant, and it's – all – gone."

Ash gave that a slow emphasis, saw it sink in. A billman crouched down a few feet away looked at the hunk of dark bread in his hand, and thoughtfully tucked it away in his purse.

"What we gonna do, boss?" a crossbow-woman called.

"We've done one hell of a forced march," Ash said, "and we're not finished yet. We're in the middle of a war here. We're about to run out of rations. Now, most people are trying to break *out* of a siege . . ."

She flirted a quick glance at Angelotti, gave Florian a grin; and turned her attention back to the men yowling questions:

"Most people. Not us. We're going to break *in*."

Those in the front row bawled their amazement.

"Okay, I'll tell you again." Ash paused, for emphasis. "We're not going to break Robert Anselm and the lads *out* of Dijon. *We're* going to break *in*."

Simon (or Thomas) Tydder blurted out, "Boss, you're mad!" and blushed bright red. He stared down at his boots.

She let the buzz die down. "Anyone else got anything to say?"

"Dijon's under *siege*!" Thomas Morgan, Euen Huw's 2IC, protested. "They got the whole bloody Visigoth army in front of their gates!"

"And they have had – *for three months*. Without taking the city! So what better place to be than safe inside Dijon? If they find us out here," Ash said, looking around at faces again, "we're catsmeat. We're in the open. Most of our heavy armour's in Dijon. And we're outnumbered thirty to one. We can't face a Visigoth legion in the field – not even you guys can do that. Now we *are* here, there isn't any option. We need walls between us and the Visigoth army, or that's the end of the Lion Azure, right now."

She had the experience to wait then, while a hubbub of talk rose up; to wait with her arms folded, weight back on one hip, her bare cropped silver hair exposed to the wintry light under the trees; a woman no longer beautiful, but in mail coat and sword and with her pages, squire, and officers ranked behind her.

One of the billmen stood up. "We'd be safe in Dijon!"

"Yeah, till the Goths batter the gate down!" a man-at-arms in Flemish livery remarked.

Until we find out what the Wild Machines have bred the Faris for.

Ash stepped forward and held her arms up.

"Okay!" She let their noise die down. "I'm getting in contact with our people inside Dijon. I'm arranging for a gate to be opened tonight. De Vere picked you guys to move fast, for the raid on Carthage, so moving fast is what we're going to do! We won't have to fight our way in – but I'll want volunteers for a diversionary attack."

The Englishman John Price nodded and stood up, his mates with him. "We'll do it, boss."

Ash spoke quickly, not letting any more questions be asked.

"You, Master Price, and thirty men. You'll attack tonight, two hours after moonrise. Angelotti, give them whatever slow-match and powder we've got left. You guys: wear your shirts over your armour: kill anything that doesn't show up white."

"That won't work, boss," Price's lance-mate objected. "All them fuckers wear white robes!"

"Shit." Ash let them see her look amused. "Y'know – you're right. Sort out your own recognition signal, then. I want you down at the west bank of the Suzon, setting fire to their siege engines – that'll bring the whole army awake, siege-machines are expensive! When you've done it, fall back into the forest. We'll pick you up in a boat tomorrow evening and bring you in through one of the water-gates."

Ash turned to her officers.

"That'll give the rest of us time enough to move. Okay, we've got ten hours before dark. We're leaving any carts: I want everything in the baggage train either on someone's back or slung out. I want the mules blindfolded." She gauged spirit, looking around at all the faces she could see in the November morning. "Your lance-leaders will tell you where you are in line of march – and when we go in tonight, we go in with weapons muffled, and wearing dark clothes over armour. And we don't hang about! They won't know we're here until we're in."

There was still some murmuring. She made a point of making eye-contact with the dissenters, gazing around at white, pinched faces, cheeks flushed with small beer and bravado.

"Remember this." She looked around at their faces. "That's your mates up ahead in Dijon. We're the Lion – and we don't leave our own. We may be broke, it may be winter, we may need a siege-proof roof over our heads right now, but don't forget this – with the whole company together, we can kick *any* damn Visigoth's ass from here to breakfast! Okay. We go in, we assess the situation, and when we move on out later on, we move out with all the armour and guns we had to leave here – and we move as a full-strength company. You got that?"

Mutters.

"I *said*, you got that?"

The familiar bullying tone cheered them, enabled a complicit cheer:

"YES, BOSS!"

"Dismiss."

In the resulting ordered chaos of men running, shelters being demolished, and weapons being packed up, she found herself standing beside Floria again.

A sudden awkwardness made her avoid the woman's eye. If Florian too was uncomfortable, she showed no sign of it.

But she will be.

"Don't—" Ash coughed, getting rid of some congestion in her throat. "Don't do a Godfrey on me, Florian. Don't *you* vanish off out of the company."

She surprised a sudden unmonitored expression on Florian's face; a raw anguish, gone before she could be sure it was anything more than a cynical, brilliant grin.

"No danger of that." Florian folded her arms across her body. "So . . . You've solved the immediate military problem. If it works. We get into Dijon. What then?"

"Then we're part of the siege."

"For how long? Do you think Dijon will hold out? Against *those* numbers?"

Ash looked levelly at the Burgundian woman. There will be unease, she thought. Not enough to matter – and not for long. Because it *is* still Florian.

"I'll tell you what I *think*," Ash said, with a release of breath and tension, in sudden honesty. "*I* think I made a shit-lousy mistake in coming here – but once we landed at Marseilles, once we were committed, there hasn't been a damn thing I can do about it."

Floria blinked. "Good God, woman. You've been keeping this lot on the road by sheer will-power. And you think we're *wrong* to be here?"

"Like I said on the beach at Carthage – I think we should have sailed for England then." Ash shivered in the morning cold. "Or for Constantinople, even, with John de Vere, and taken service with the Turk. Got as far away from the Wild Machines as possible, and left the Faris to whatever shit there's going to be in Burgundy."

"Oh, bollocks!" Floria put her fists on her hips. "*You?* Leave Robert Anselm and the rest of the company here? Don't make me laugh! We were always coming back here, whatever happened at Carthage."

"Maybe. The *smart* thing to do would be to cut our losses and start again with the men I've got here. Except that people don't sign up with commanders who dump their people."

Some internal honesty prompted, unexpectedly: *But she's right, we were always coming back here.*

She squinted into the morning wind, her eyes tearing, thinking, *weather's bad even for November, and that's a weak sun.* And it's been so cold, south of here, for so long now. There won't have been a harvest.

"Too late now," she said, hearing herself sound almost philosophical. She smiled at Florian. "Now we *are* here – there isn't anywhere else to go, except behind the nearest walls! Better dead tomorrow than dead today, right? So you can pick between Dijon falling sometime soon, and the legions up ahead finding us tomorrow . . ."

She felt an immense release, as if from a weight, or an unrelenting grip. Fear flooded through her, but she recognised it and rode it; let herself become fully aware, again, that it is not merely the usual business of war that concerns her.

Floria snorted, shaking her head. "I'll get my deacons praying. Fix where we'll be in line of march. Where will you be, on this moonlight flit? In front, as usual?"

"I won't be with the company. I'll join you in the city, before dawn."

"You'll *what?*"

Ash beat her cold hands together. Warming circulation pricked at the impacts. Cool, damp air touched her face.

Her gaze met Florian's: whimsical, bright, utterly determined.

"While the company's making an entry into Dijon tonight, I'm going to get some answers. I'm going to go down to the Visigoth camp and talk to the Faris."

IV

"*You're mad!*"

In the wet, muddy daylight, Ash suddenly grinned to herself. *I can still talk to Florian. At least I still have that.*

"No. I'm not mad. Yes: we had a defeat at Carthage. Yes: I needed to *think*. Yes: I am going to do something." Half teasing, she added, "Once my banner goes up in Dijon, the Faris will know I'm alive anyway."

"So don't raise it!" Exasperated, unguarded, Floria waved her hands in the air. "Come off it, Ash. Forget chivalry. Keep your banner rolled up. Sneak out when we *do* leave Dijon! But don't tell me you're going out there to try and *talk* to her!"

"I could tell you a lot of good reasons why I should talk to a Visigoth army commander." Ash wiped her muddy hands together, took her sheepskin mittens from her belt, and put them on: still damp and uncomfortable. "We're mercenaries. I'm expected to do this. I've got to look for the best deal. She might just give us a *condotta*."

Florian looked appalled. "I know you're joking. After Basle? After *Carthage*? The minute you show your face, they'll ship you back across the Med! They'll string you up for the raid! And then Leofric will poke around in what's left!"

Ash stretched her arms, feeling the ache in her muscles from the night's exertions; watching the camp beginning to pack up. "I'd take any help I can get, including Visigoth, if it means getting the company out of here before whatever the Wild Machines have planned for Burgundy starts happening."

"You're nuts," Floria said flatly.

"No. I'm not. And I agree about what sort of a reception I'm likely to get. But it's like you said – I can't hide from this for ever."

Florian's dirty face scowled.

"This is the craziest thing I've ever heard you say. You can't put yourself in that much danger!"

"Even if we get into Dijon okay, we're only hiding. Temporarily." Ash paused. "Florian – she's the only other person on God's earth who hears the Stone Golem."

In the silence, Ash turned back to find Florian looking at her.

"So?"

"So I need to know . . . if she hears the Wild Machines, too." Ash held up her hands. "Or if it's just in my head. I need to know, Florian. You all saw the Tombs of the Caliphs. You all believe me. But she's the only other person on God's earth who *knows*. Who will have heard what I heard!"

"And if she didn't?"

Ash shrugged.

After a pause, the surgeon asked, "And . . . if she did?"

Ash shrugged again.

"You think she knows something about this that you don't?"

"She's the real one. I'm just the mistake. Who knows what's different about her?" Ash heard bitterness in her own voice. She cocked a silver brow at the woman surgeon, and deliberately grinned. "And she's the only one who can tell me I'm not nuts."

Shrugging sardonically, Florian muttered, "You've been nuts for years!"

There was nothing unfamiliar in the woman's affection. Or unfamiliar about her complicit, unverbalised consent. Ash found herself smiling at the dirty, tall woman. "You're a doctor, you'd know!"

A sharp *thock!* made Ash turn her head: she caught sight of Rickard and his slingshot – and tree-bark scarred down to raw, white wood thirty yards away, from his practice shot.

"If you show yourself," Florian said, "the Faris won't be the only one who'll find out where you are. Carthage; the King-Caliph; the *Ferae Natura Machinae*."

"Yes," Ash said. "I know. But I have to do it. It's like Roberto always says – I could be wrong. What use am I, if I'm not sane?"

At dusk of that day – it came early, from a frozen sky empty of clouds; under which her officers complained lengthily after the announcement of her decision – Ash gave penultimate orders.

"A first-quarter moon rises about Compline.[11] We move then, after mass. If there's messages from Anselm, send them to me. Call me if it clouds over. Otherwise – I'm getting a couple of hours' sleep first!"

A last tallow candle, unearthed from the bottom of a pack, stank and flickered in the command tent as she entered. Rickard stood up, a book in his hands.

"You want me to read to you, boss?"

She has two books remaining, they live in Rickard's pack: Vegetius and Christine de Pisan.[12] Ash walked to the box-bed and flopped down on the cold palliasse and goatskins.

"Yeah. Read me de Pisan on sieges."

The black-haired young man muttered under his breath, reading the chapter headings to himself, holding the book up close to the taper. His breath whitened the air. He wore all his clothes: two shirts, two pairs of hose, a pourpoint, a doublet, and a ragged cloak belted over the top of them. His nose showed red under the rim of his hood.

Ash rolled over on to her back on her pallet. Damp chill draughts crept in, no

[11] 9 p.m.

[12] Daughter of an astrologer-physician, herself widowed with three small children, Christine de Pisan earned her living as a professional writer. She produced, among her many other works, *The Book of Feats of Arms and of Chivalry* (begun AD 1409), a revision of Vegetius and a practical manual of warfare much used in the field by the great captains of her era. This is most probably the book of hers to which 'Fraxinus' here refers.

matter how tightly the tent-flap was laced down. "At least we didn't have to eat the mules yet . . ."

"Boss, you want me to read?"

"Yeah, read, read." Before he could open his mouth, Ash added, "We've got a moon just past first quarter; that's going to give us some light, but it's rough country out here."

"*Boss* . . ."

"No, sorry: read."

A minute later she spoke again, a bare few sentences into his reading, and she could not have said what he had read to her about. "Have any messages come out of Dijon yet?"

"Don't know, boss. No. Someone would've come and said."

She stared at the pavilion wheel-spokes. The cold burned her toes, through her boots and footed hose. She rolled over on to her side, curling up. "You'll have to arm me in two hours. What have they been saying about Dijon?"

Rickard's eyes sparkled. "It's great! Pieter Tyrrell's lance are blacking their faces. They're betting they can get into the city before the Italian gunners, because they'll be dragging Mistress Gunner's—"

Ash coughed.

"—Master Angelotti's swivel-guns!"

She rumbled a laugh under her breath.

"Some of them don't like it," Rickard added. "Master Geraint was complaining, over at the mule lines. Are you going to get rid of him like you got rid of Master van Mander?"

Preparations for the battle of Auxonne, when the sun was still in Leo: it seems a lifetime ago. She barely remembers the Flemish knight's florid face.

Ash curled herself tighter against the cold. Her breath left dampness on the wool of her hood, by her mouth. "No. Joscelyn van Mander came in this season, with a hundred and thirty men; he never made himself part of the company; it made sense to bounce him back out again." She sought the boy's face in the dim light, seeing his flaring brows, his unpremeditated scowl. "Most of the disaffected men around Geraint have been with me for two or three years now. I'll try to give them something of what they want."

"They don't want to be stuck in a town with a bloody big army on the outside!"

The guy-ropes creaked. The tent wall flapped.

"I'll find a compromise for Geraint and his sympathisers."

"Why don't you just order them?" Rickard demanded.

She felt her lips move in a wry smile. "Because they may say 'no'! There isn't much difference between five hundred soldiers, and five hundred refugee peasants. You've never seen a company stop being a company. You don't want to. I'll find some way of satisfying their gripes – but we're still going to Dijon." She grinned at him. "Okay; read."

The young man held the book up to the taper.

"It isn't that bad a tactical situation," she added, a moment later. "Dijon's a big city, must have ten thousand people in it, even without what's left of Charles's army; the Faris can't have her people cover every yard of the walls.

She'll be covering roads, gates. If the sergeants can get us moving and keep us moving, we'll get inside, maybe without fighting at all."

Rickard rested his finger on one illuminated page, and closed the cover of the book. The tallow candle gave hardly enough light to show his expression.

He said suddenly, "I don't want to be Anselm's squire. I want to be your squire. I've been your page. Make me your squire!"

"'Captain Anselm'," Ash corrected automatically. She reached over her shoulder, hauling goatskins and sheepskins over her fully dressed body.

"If I don't get to be your squire, they'll say it's because I'm not good enough. I've been your page again since Bertrand ran off. Since we found you in Carthage! I fought at the field at Auxonne!"

On that outraged protest, his voice slid up the scale to squeak, and down to croak. Ash flinched with embarrassment. She snuggled the sides of her hood back, ears bitten with cold, so that she could hear him more clearly. He rose and banged about in the dark tent for some minutes, in silence.

"You're good enough," Ash said.

"You're not going to do it!" He sounded suspiciously close to tears.

Ash's voice, when it came, was tired. "You didn't fight Auxonne. You've *seen* what it's like in the line, Rickard, you just don't *know* what it's like."

The edges of swords and axes slice the air, in her mind:

"It's a storm of razors."

"I'm going to fight. I'll go to Captain Anselm."

Ash heard no pique in his tone, only a sullen, excited determination. She shifted herself up on her elbow to look at Rickard.

"He'll take you," she said. "I'll tell you why. Out of every hundred men we get, ten or fifteen will know what to do in the field when the shit hits the fan, without being told, either by instinct or training. Seventy men or so will fight once someone else trains them, and then tells them how and where. And another ten or fifteen will run around like headless chickens no matter *what* you train into 'em or tell 'em."

In the line of battle, she has grabbed men by their liveries and thrown them bodily back into the fight.

"I've watched you train," she finished, "you're a natural swordsman, and you're one of the ten or fifteen any commander picks out and goes, 'you're my sub-commander'. I want you alive the next two years, Rickard, so I can give you a lance to command when the time comes. Try not to get killed before that."

"Boss!"

The warmth from the furs hit some level that allowed her body to stop shivering. A wave of tiredness rose up, drowning her; she barely had time to register Rickard's pleased, inarticulate, aggressive surprise; then sleep took her down like a fall from a horse, no impact, only oblivion.

She was aware that she rolled on the pallet, under the blankets.

Something gave, under her body.

She heard a hollow crack, a noise like a man putting his foot through a waxed leather bottle. Close to her. She stirred, heard guards and dogs beyond the canvas walls, shifted one arm sideways, and felt some obstruction give under her ribs.

The solidness cracked, broke with a wet noise.

Ash slapped her hand across the pallet, down by her side. Something slick and solid impaled itself on her thumb. She felt the nail resisted by obstruction, then whatever it was split, squelchy as a ripe plum. Her hand became suddenly slimy and wet.

She smelled a familiar odour: a sweet richness, mixed with the excremental stink of battle, thought *blood* and opened her eyes.

A baby lay half-under her body. She had rolled over and crushed it. Its tight swaddling-bands were sopping with something dark, seeping down from the head. Its fuzz-haired scalp ran red. White bone glinted, the child's skull fractured from ear to ear, the back of it crushed where she had rolled over. Her hand rested over its face, her thumb deep in a ruined eye-socket.

The other eye blinked at her. So light a brown as to be amber, gold.

A baby, no more than a few weeks old.

"Rickard!"

The scream left her mouth before she knew she had given voice. Dizzy, blackness seething in front of her eyes, she dug her heels into the bedding and pushed herself bodily back, off the pallet, on to the mud, away.

Boots sucked out of mud, outside the tent-flap; the tent-laces gave way to a dagger-slash.

A dark figure ducked into the tent, and Ash saw that his hair was golden, although it was Rickard.

"You killed our baby," he said.

"It isn't mine." Ash tried to reach out and pull the sleeping furs over the bundled body, but she didn't have the strength to drag them to her. The baby's skin was fine, soft; the tent smelled like a hard-fought field. "Fernando! I didn't kill it! It isn't mine!"

The boy turned and left the tent. In another man's voice, he said, "You were careless. Only a moment, and you could have saved it."

"They *beat* me—"

Ash reached out, but the cold dead skin of the child felt hot under her fingers, as if her fingers burned. She scrabbled back across the floor of the pavilion, and abruptly sprang up and ran out of the door.

White snow shone under a blue sky.

No night sky. Noon: and a bright sun.

There were no tents.

Ash walked into an empty wood. The snow sucked at her bare feet, pulling her down. She kept slipping, landing heavily; struggling to her feet. Snow plastered every twig, every leafless winter bud, every crooked branch. She floundered, wet, bitten with the chill, her hands red and blue in the freezing whiteness.

She heard grunting.

She stopped moving. Carefully, she turned her head.

A line of wild boar rooted through the snow. Their hard snouts ploughed up the whiteness, leaving troughs of black leaf-mould exposed. They softly grunted. Ash saw their teeth. No tusks. Sows. Razorback sows, moving between the trees, in the bright sunshine. Their winter coats were thick and white, they smelled of pig-dung, and their long lashes shaded their limpid eyes against the light.

A dozen or more striped boarlets ran between their mothers' legs.

"They're too young!" Ash cried, crawling on hands and knees through the snow. "You shouldn't have littered them yet. It's too early. Winter's here; they'll die; you had them at the wrong time! Take them back."

Snow fell from branches on to snow on briars, white hoops against the trunks of trees. The boars moved slowly, methodically, ignoring Ash. She sat back in the snow, on her knees. The stripy little ones, about the size of a fresh-baked loaf, trotted past her with their stringy tails whipping against the snow, their chisel-hooves kicking up whiteness.

"They'll die! They'll *die!*"

A red-breasted bird flew down, landing beside the biggest sow's forefoot. She nosed towards the robin momentarily. Her head swung back to root under the snow. The robin's beak dipped for worms.

The boarlets strayed further from the herd, into the white forest.

"They'll die!" Ash felt her throat tighten. She began to sob, wretchedly; felt the muscles of her throat moving, felt her eyes dry and without tears; felt the hard stuffed canvas of the palliasse under her back.

The tallow candle had burned down to a stump.

Rickard made a huddled lump, sleeping across the door.

"They'll die," Ash whispered, looking for orange-and-brown striped flanks, for trotting hooves, and for brown eyes shaded by delicate long, long lashes. She smelled the air for blood, or dung.

"I didn't kill it!"

I miscarried. I was beaten, and I miscarried.

Her eyes remained dry. If there was weeping, she could not do it. Aches and cold and bodily discomfort reasserted themselves.

A voice said, – *Making friends with the shy, fierce wild boar.*

Ash relaxed back against the skins and furs. "Shit. God sent me a nightmare, Godfrey. My hands . . ."

She strained to see them, in the dimmest light. She could not see if her fingers were stained with anything. She lifted them cautiously to her nostrils: sniffed.

"Why does He want me to see dead babies?"

– *I don't know, child. You're presumptuous, perhaps, to think He troubles Himself to trouble your sleep.*

"You sound troubled." Ash frowned. She stared around, in the all-but-dark; could not see the priest.

– *I am troubled.*

"Godfrey?"

– *I am dead, child.*

"Are you dead, Godfrey?"

– *The boars are a dream, child. I am dead.*

"Then why are you talking to me?"

In the part of her that listens, the part of her soul that she is used to sharing with a voice, she feels something: a kind of warmth. Amusement, perhaps. And then, again, the voice:

– I thought that, since I could call boars, I could call you. When I was a boy, in the forest, using nothing but stillness, I made friends with those of God's creatures whose tusks could rip my belly in a moment. You are one of God's creatures with tusks, child. It took me so long to get you to trust in me.

"And then you went and died on me. Are you in the Communion of Saints, Godfrey?"

– I was not worthy. I am tormented by great Devils! Purgatory, perhaps, this is. Where I am now.

"Close to God, then. Ask God, for me, why do the Wild Machines want Burgundy wiped out?"

A chill pain sliced through her mind. At the same moment, Rickard said sleepily from the door, "Who are you talking to, boss?"

He reached up from where he lay, in his blanket-roll, and pulled the tent-flap open. Moonlight slanted into the command tent. It shone on his face, his white breath, on Ash's clean hands, on her furs, clothes, sword, pallet.

"I—"

No transition. No transition from dream to waking. Ash sat up, suddenly; none of the languor of sleep in her muscles. Her head was clear. *I have been awake for more than a few minutes*, she realised, and peered around: the tent remained dirty, familiar, corporeal. Rickard stared expectantly at her.

I have been awake.

"Oh *shit.*" Ash bent over, gagging. Memories momentarily overwhelmed her. The single moment of vision, Godfrey's body flopping back, the smashed and missing top of his skull, this stays with her, details imprinted on her inner eye. "Christus!"

Dimly, she was aware that Rickard put his head out of the tent and called to someone; that he left; that someone else came in, bustling – Ash could not have said how much time had passed – and then she lifted her head and found herself staring at Floria.

"Godfrey," Ash said. "I heard his voice. I heard Godfrey. I *spoke* to him."

Silver and black in the moonlight, there are people moving outside the tent. Floria's voice said, "If he's still alive, perhaps you dreamed of him where he is—"

"He's dead." Tears welled up in Ash's eyes. She let them fall, in the dark interior of the tent. "Christ, Florian, he had the top of his head smashed *off*. If you think I would have left him if he wasn't dead—!"

The long, slender fingers of the surgeon came out of the darkness, turning her face to the light. She felt no awkwardness, no fear of the woman's touch. Floria crouched in front of her, sniffed at her mouth – for wine, Ash realised – touched her cool forehead; finally sat back, and shook her head.

"Why should he haunt your sleep?"

"*I wasn't asleep.*"

She made to get up, to call Rickard to arm her, since it was plain that moonrise was well advanced, silver light streaming down between trees.

Without warning, a sharp pain stabbed through her nose, eyes and throat. She choked. Her mouth distorted; tears ran out of her eyes. She dragged in a breath, sobbed tightly.

"Shit. He's dead. I let them kill him."

"He died in the earthquake in Carthage," Floria snapped.

"He was there because of me, he was doing what I told him to do."

"Yeah, and so have half a hundred soldiers been, when you got them killed in some battle." The woman's voice changed. "Baby, no. You didn't kill him."

"I heard him—"

"How?"

"'How'?" Ash's wet eyes burned. The question stopped the sobs in her throat.

"When *you* say you hear voices," Floria observed, sardonic in the cold moonlight, "then I want to know what you mean."

Ash stared at her for a long moment.

"Rickard," she said abruptly, and stood up so quick that she left the surgeon kneeling at her feet. "Find my arming doublet; let's get moving. *Now*."

"Ash," Floria began.

"Later." She put her hands on Floria's shoulders as the woman stood up. "You're right, but later. When we're in Dijon."

"If you risk trying to get to the Faris, you might not *get* into Dijon!" More quietly, under the noise of Rickard rummaging in the baggage, Floria added, "Not a dream. A voice."

"*After* a dream. It was very like him." Ash was surprised at how much her composure returned, with the words. She reached out, and after a second's hesitation, Floria took her hands.

"In Dijon," Ash promised. "I'll be there. I'll come back."

Rickard blurted, from the dark corner of the pavilion, "Ash always comes back. That's what they've been saying since Carthage. That you'll always come back to the company. You will come back, boss?"

"Though all the army of the Visigoths lie between," Ash said lightly, mock-grandly; and was rewarded by a grin as the boy armed her: brigandine, sallet, and sword. She shrugged her cloak back over everything, stepping outside with Rickard and Floria, to be immediately overwhelmed in a moonlit wood by men with questions, sergeants coming for orders, and messengers shoving through the crowd.

She took a roll of paper from Ludmilla Rostovnaya, bending her head to listen while Rickard read it out to her under a horn lantern; nodded decisively, and gave a string of orders.

"I take it we're expected?" Floria del Guiz said, in a momentary break.

Without even time to realise her own searing relief, Ash confirmed: "Robert's still alive and giving orders, if that's what you mean. There'll be a gate open. Now all we have to do is get there . . ." Ash spoke absently, peering through the crowds in the semi-darkness. "Thomas Rochester!"

She strode forward, picking up Angelotti on the way, pulling the two men into a huddle with her, in the freezing moonlit muddy woodland.

"I've told the lance-leaders and sergeants to come to you," she said, without preamble. "Angelotti, I want you with the guns and all the missile troops. Just get them inside the walls. Henri Brant and Blanche and Baldina will handle the train. Thomas, I want you leading the foot-troops."

His dark, unshaven face showed sudden confusion. "Aren't you leading the foot, boss? Won't you be back before we leave?"

"I'll be back before you're inside Dijon. You'll have Euen Huw and Pieter Tyrrell as your officers. Geraint will keep any stragglers under control – won't you?" she added, as the big Welshman plodded up to them through the mud.

She studied his unreadable features, thought for the hundredth time *Perhaps nothing* does *go on behind that face*, and watched him draw himself up; a large, dirty man in mail, cloak and archer's sallet.

"You know I don't agree with this, boss."

"I know, Master Geraint. You can disagree all you like, once we're in Dijon." She let her expression soften. "We can debate what we do as a company, after that. What you're doing now is going into the city. Right?"

Tension left his stance. "Right. And you'll be with the enemy commander, boss? Okay."

A glance from Angelotti's calm, Byzantine features made her feel more disquiet than Geraint ab Morgan's blunt acceptance.

"With the Faris," Ash confirmed. And then: "I'm the one that can walk into the Visigoth camp and no one will say a thing."

She reached up and touched her cheek, fingers taking scars entirely for granted.

"It's still her face. She's still my twin."

Message: #147 (Pierce Ratcliff)
Subject: Ash/Carthage
Date: 04/12/00 at 09.57 a.m.
From   Longman@   *format address deleted*
                                        Other details encrypted and
                                        non-recoverably deleted
Pierce –

I want to know what's going on! Are you still on the ship? What else have you found???

Are you sure – no, of course you're sure. _Visigoth_ Carthage!!! No wonder the existing site on land didn't match the description in 'Fraxinus'!

I don't expect you to answer lots of questions right now, but I've got to have _some_ information if I'm going to stop the book/documentary project being suspended.

Just ask Dr Isobel: _when_ can I pass on the news about her discovery to my Managing Director?

Oh my _God_, what a book we're going to have.

Oh, yes – is this the last of the 'Fraxinus' manuscript? Or is there one more section to come? Do hurry up and finish the translation! I swear I won't let it out of my hands!

– Anna

Message: #150 (Pierce Ratcliff)
Subject: Ash/Carthage
Date: 04/12/00 at 04.40 p.m.
From: Longman@   *format address deleted*
                                        Other details encrypted by
                                        non-discoverable personal key
Pierce –

I'm stalling people.

Please get Dr Isobel to mail me. Just a sentence. Just 'we've found something amazing that verifies Dr Ratcliff's book'. Just something I can show Jon Stanley!

I may be out for a few hours tomorrow, as Nadia phoned me, but I'll take the satellite notebook-PC and check regularly.

We're probably okay till the end of the week, since I successfully managed to fudge everybody today – but if I go in Friday morning and find the plug's been pulled, I'm going to need convincing evidence that I can _show_ them.

It's been nearly a whole day, I WANT TO KNOW MORE ABOUT WHAT
YOU'VE FOUND ON THE SEABED. PLEASE!!!

Love, Anna

Message: #256 (Anna Longman)
Subject: Carthage
Date: 04/12/00 at 05.03 p.m.
From: Ngrant@

[handwritten: format address deleted / other details encrypted by / non-discoverable personal key]

Ms Longman,

>>Just ask Dr Isobel: _when_ can I pass on the news about her
>>discovery to my Managing Director?
  If _absolutely necessary_ to the survival of Dr Ratcliff's book,
you may disclose his 3/12/00 mailing to your Managing Director.
This is on condition that it goes no further, until I am ready to
put out a press release.
  You may tell him that I endorse every word Dr Ratcliff has
written. We have Visigoth Carthage.

I. Napier-Grant

PART TEN

15 November AD 1476

Siege Perilous[1]

[1] Final part of the document 'Fraxinus me fecit', presumed written *c.* 1480 (?).

I

Ash came down off the foot of the bluff in a clatter of clods of earth, into the exposing light of the moon.

Her eyes adjusted from night vision in the forest. The cold moon, clear of clouds, shone down on the road where she crouched.

Shit! I'm surrounded by bodies!

A clear sky brought lower temperatures: frost glittering on the mud; cat-ice forming a skin on puddles, water-filled holes, and expanses of quagmire. Around her, crammed together in the slopping impassable mud ruts, horse-drawn carts and people – horses with bony, arched spines, heads hanging down in sleep or exhaustion. And men, men and women bundled up on the ground, filthy, careless of the mud that froze around and on them as they slept, or sprawled dead in the night.

Ash froze, squatting down in the bitter cold, listening for shouts.

Nothing.

She rubbed the wind's cold tears from her eyes, thought: No; it only *looks* like a field of battle – but there's no dead bodies piled up man-high, no scavengers looting, no crows and rats, no drying blood; it doesn't *smell* like a skirmish, an ambush, a massacre.

These men are sleeping, not dead.

Refugees.

Sleeping, exhausted, wherever they were when darkness fell tonight.

She remained perfectly still, alert for any movement of men waking, orienting herself. The Lion camp behind her; this, the road running south from Dijon to Auxonne. Dijon a mile ahead, across water meadows and an invading army.

A thought invaded her mind. *But, of course, I could just keep going. Stay clear of Dijon.*

Keep going: leave Floria and the Faris, the company and the Wild Machines, behind me: leave everything, because it's all different now; I only ever wanted to be a soldier—

That ended on the beach at Carthage. That ended when something *made* me start walking towards the pyramids; towards the Wild Machines.

South of her, she heard the distant bugling of a wolf's call. Another; two more; then, silence.

Still want to run?

She felt her mouth move, wryly.

I *am* a soldier. I have a couple of hundred living, breathing reasons behind me for why I need answers *right now*.

Of course, I could fuck off and leave Tom Rochester in charge. Go someplace else. Sign on as a grunt. Stop trying to hold all this *together*—

A twist of unease in her bowels made her aware of the extent of her fear. Greater than she expected.

Is that because going to the Visigoths now is lunatic? It *is* lunatic. Some damn guard can hack me down without a question asked. The Faris can have me executed. Or on a ship back to Carthage – what's left of it. I think, after Basle, I know her – but do I? It's stupidly dangerous!

And that's before I get my questions answered.

Lose the armour, lose the sword; Ash thought. Lie down to sleep beside one of these women, get up in the morning, and carry on walking. I'd keep my face hidden, but no one's going to recognise me; not among this lot.

There must be hundreds of thousands of refugees in this war. I'd just be one more. Even if they manipulated the Faris's army, the Wild Machines wouldn't find me. I could get out of Burgundy. I could stay hidden for months. For years.

Yeah: lose the armour, lose the sword; get raped and murdered because I still own a pair of boots.

No one stirred out of their exhaustion.

She got carefully to her feet. The demi-gown buckled over her brigandine, and the cloak over all, kept her armour from being obvious. She kept one hand on the scabbard of her sword. Under the hood, and helmet, her face felt naked. The cold wind whipped her hair against her scarred cheeks; hair too short now to get in her eyes.

I'd stay alive, she thought. At least until I starved.

The taste of urine settled into her mouth. The road stank of piss and excrement. She stepped across deep cart-ruts, moving quietly on the sodden earth between groups of slumped bodies.

It was a minute before she realised that she was seeing children everywhere; almost every family with swaddled babies or small brats. Someone far off coughed; a young baby cried. Ash blinked, in the night chill.

At that age, I was one of a slave's litter in Carthage. Waiting for the knife.

Moving through the mud with the quietness of an animal – and there were no dogs here, few horses; only people on foot, with what they could carry on their backs – she placed her boots with care, avoiding potholes, and crossed the track. She had an impulse to leave her cloak spread over one child, but her automatic stealthy movement carried her past before she could give way to it.

The Faris and me, we have more in common with each other than we do with these people.

Her breath smoked on the chill, moonlit air. Without hesitation, she turned north, trudging towards the crossroads and bridge north of the town.

I'm not going to run. Not with Robert and the rest in Dijon. The company know it, and I know it: that's why we've never had a choice about coming here.

Damn the Earl of Oxford, damn John de Vere; why didn't he bring *all* my men to Carthage—? I could be half the world away!

Done, now.

I'd still be hearing a dead man's voice—

Godfrey – ah, Jesu! I miss Godfrey!

Bad enough to remember him so clearly I think I hear him?

She plodded on, through frozen scrubland, through ground it would have taken her minutes to cross in daylight. She spared a glance for the moon, saw something under an hour had passed; and with that came over a rise and in sight of the bridge, and the great north part of the siege camp.

"Son of a *bitch* . . ."

Seeing it from the bluff with John Price, she had only seen west of the river: tents spread out across three or four miles of what had been vine-covered hills and cornfields and water meadows. Across the bridge now, north of the town, there was nothing *but* tents, hundreds of them, white in the moon; and, further over, dark structures might have been field-forts, thrown up as winter quarters. And more great siege machinery: trebuchets, and the square silhouettes of hide-covered towers.

No golems visible.

The bridge was dark, only a campfire here and there on the perimeter this side, and the intermittent movement of guards around them. The remains of old crucifixions hung from trees: mute reminder of what happens to refugees. She began to catch snatches of voices, across the cold air: Carthaginian Latin.

I've got an hour before John Price does his stuff. I hope. Don't get it wrong, *rosbif* . . .

It is easy, in the night, the confusion, the lack of timing and command and control, for everything to go to hell in very short order. She knows this, wonders for a moment if she should go back; and on that doubt straightens her shoulders and walks forward, down the muddy slope, on to the road that leads to the bridge, and the perimeter of the Visigoth camp.

"Halt!"

"Okay, okay," Ash called, good-humouredly, "I'm halting." She held her gauntlets out from her side, open palms clearly displayed.

"We ain't got no fucking food!" a despairing voice bawled in French. "Now bugger off!"

Another, deeper male voice said in Carthaginian, "Put a bolt over their heads, *Nazir*, they'll run."

"Oh, *what*?" Ash snuffled a laugh. Excitement fizzed in her blood. She found herself grinning so broadly that her mouth hurt, and the night cold stung her teeth. "Green Christ up a fucking Tree! *Alderic*? *'Arif* Alderic?"

There was a brief moment of complete silence, in which she had time to think, *No, of course you were mistaken, girl, don't be such a bloody idiot*; and then, from one of the dark figures at the wagon-gate, the same male voice said, "*Jund*? Is that you, *jund* Ash?"

"Hell's great gaping gates! I don't believe it!"

"Step forward and be recognised!"

Ash wiped the moisture off her upper lip with the cold sleeve of her demi-gown, and tucked her arm back under her cloak. She stepped forward, stumbling on muddy ground, night vision gone with having looked into their fire; and came down on to the trodden mud around the wicker gate, between wagons that blocked the bridge.

Half a dozen men with spears came forward, a bearded, helmeted officer at their head.

"Ash!"

"Alderic!" She reached out, at the same moment that he did; they gripped arms and stood grinning at each other for a stunned second. "Keeping an eye on your perimeter guards, huh?"

"You know how it is." The big Carthaginian chuckled, letting go of her, running his hand over his braided beard.

"So – who'd you upset, to get posted back up here?"

That jolted him, she saw it; made him focus himself again as a soldier, and an enemy. His shadowed face became severe. "Many died in your attack on House Leofric."

"Many of my men, too."

A thoughtful nod. The *'arif* snapped his fingers, muttered something to a guard, and the man set off at a run back into the camp. Ash saw him slow, once away from the guiding firelight at the gate.

"I suppose I should consider you my prisoner," Alderic said, stolidly. He moved, and the firelight shone on to his face. Ash saw, along with the amazement, that he was concealing, a brief spurt of amusement. "God in His mercy damn you. I did not believe a woman could do what you did. Where is the English *jund*, the white mullet livery? Is he with you here? Who is with you?"

"No one's with me."

Her mouth dried as she spoke. She thought, Damn, it had to be him, he knows me, he'll turn the camp guards out, John Price will have his work cut out for him down at the siege-engines.

Well, he's a hard bastard, he can take it.

"What you see is what you get," Ash remarked, keeping her gauntleted hands in plain view. "Yes, I am bearing a sword; I'd like to keep it."

The *'arif* Alderic shook his head. He gave a deep bellowing laugh. With a good-natured cheerfulness, beckoning his men forward, he said, "I wouldn't trust you with a blunt spoon, *jund*, never mind with a sword."

Ash shrugged. "Okay. If I were you, though, I'd ask the Faris first."

Alderic himself put back her cloak, while two of the guards held her arms, and began unbuckling her sword-belt. His fingers were quick, even in the chill. Straightening up, her scabbarded blade in his hands, he said, "Don't try to convince me the General knows you're here."

"No. Of course not. You'd better tell her." Ash met his gaze. "You'd better tell her Ash is here to negotiate with her. Sorry I didn't bring my white flag."

She could see in a second that the cheek of it appealed to him. The *'arif* turned, gave orders to the gate-guards, and the men either side of Ash pushed her forward, not particularly roughly, into the camp. The river rustled below, as they crossed the bridge, walking out into muddy lanes between tents, that showed clear in the white moonlight.

The sheer reality of her presence, here, now, among armed men who will have absolutely no hesitation in killing her – that reality makes her eyes open wide to the freezing night wind, as if to imprint the moonlit silhouettes of hundreds of hundreds of frost-rimed pavilions; her ears take in the noise their feet make, crunching through the mud. It nonetheless seems unreal. *I should be with my company: this is crazy!*

Ash, walking in the *'arif*'s wake, heard a hound bark once; a pale, lean-bodied shadow in the night, nosing at rubbish abandoned outside one of the big barrack-tents – almost no small tents, she noted; the Visigoths like to keep their men in bigger units – and an owl flicked like the white shadow of death over her head; brought her heart into her mouth with the memory of hunting, in Carthage's darkness, among the pyramids.

They skidded, walking up and down slopes, walking for half a mile or more, still within the camp, hardly closer to the north wall of Dijon. Moonlight glinted from something – the artillery-battered tiles on Dijon's turreted roofs. *Somewhere a sally-gate is being opened. Please God.*

"Six men of my forty died when you attacked the House," Alderic said, dropping back to walk beside her. He still gazed ahead, profile stark in silver light. "*Nazir* Theudibert. Troopers Barbas, Gaina, Gaiseric . . ."

Ash let a little of the bleakness she felt into her voice. "Those are men I would have killed personally."

Looking at his bearded face, she thought him entirely aware – as a good commander should be – of the beating that had lost her her child; who had done it, their names.

"You are too seasoned a campaigner to let it become personal. Besides, *jund*, you did not die in our Citadel when it fell. God spares you for something: other children, perhaps."

At that, she stared up at the big Carthaginian.

He knows I lost a child: not that I can't have another. He knows I got out of Carthage: he doesn't know about the Wild Machines. He's assuming I'm here for another contract. A *condotta*.

If he knows anything, it's barrack stories that I'm another Faris, I hear the Stone Golem.

If they'd had reason to stop using the *machina rei militaris* – and he's House Leofric; he'd know! – he'd be *afraid* of me.

As if to confirm her thoughts, the *'arif* Alderic continued calmly: "If I were you, *jund*, I would not risk myself within reach of the *amir* Leofric's family again. But our General is a fighting woman, she may well have a better use for you with us, here."

She registered that *Leofric's family* rather than plain *Leofric*.

"The old man's dead, huh?" she said bluntly.

In the sharp contrast of moonlight and shadow, she could see Alderic raise his eyebrows. When he spoke, it was still in the tone of one professional colleague to another:

"Sick, I thank you, *jund*; but recovering well. What else might we expect, now that God blesses us so clearly?"

"He *does*?"

A flicker of amusement. "You could not know, in Dijon. God touches His earth, at Carthage, with the light of His blessing; and any man may see His cold fire burning over the tombs of the King-Caliphs. A seer told me it presages a speedy end to our crusade here."

She blinked, thought, *He assumes I've made my way* out of Dijon? and then, *Cold fire over the tombs—*

Over the pyramids.

The aurora of the Wild Machines.

"And you think it's a sign of God's *favour*?" she blurted.

"How else? You yourself, *jund*, were there when the earth shook the Citadel, and the palace fell. And, all in one moment, the first Fire of the Blessing was seen, and King-Caliph Gelimer was spared from death in the earthquake."

"But—!"

There was no time to formulate questions: they were arriving on the heels of the *'arif*'s messenger; the man still shouting at the guards on what Ash saw, by the livery, was the Faris's quarters. No tent here: raw timber had been knocked together into a long, low, turf-roofed building, surrounded by braziers and troops and slaves waking from their sleep.

About to persist, she shut up when a white-clad figure opened the arched doorway and stepped out.

The automatic attention of the men would have told her it was the Faris, if nothing else; but the moon on the river-fall of silver blonde hair, falling down about her shoulders to her thighs, was unmistakable. Ash, watching and not yet seen, had a second to think *I used to look exactly like that* before she strode forward, long-legged and gawky, arms wrapped in her cloak, and said in a cheerful voice, "This is a parley. You want to talk to me."

With absolutely no hesitation, the Visigoth woman said, "Yes. I do. *'Arif*, bring her inside."

The Faris turned and walked back through the doorway. Her white garment was a heavy robe of marten fur and silk, swathing her body. Unarmed, bareheaded, barely awake, she seemed still in complete possession of herself. Ash stumbled on the wooden steps, her feet numbed by the cold.

Two golems stood, one either side of the door, oil-lamps held in their stone hands.

They might have been merely statues of men: one in white marble, the other in carved red sandstone. An artificer's hand had certainly shaped the muscled arms, the long limbs and sculpted torso; given form to the aquiline features. Then the bright polished bronze of shoulder- and elbow-joints flashed in the light, as the marble golem raised its lamp higher. Ash heard the infinitesimal sound of greased metal sliding on metal. The red golem mirrored the movement; the vast weight of its stone body shifting.

"Follow!"

At the Faris's word the two golems fell in behind her, their stone tread making the wooden floor creak. A flickering light danced on the tapestried walls.

Ash stared at the backs of the golems. *I was so damn close. So damn close to the Stone Golem itself, the* machina rei militaris . . .

She called ahead, "You want to speak to me privately, Faris."

"Yes. I do." The Visigoth general walked without hesitation into an arch hung with silk curtains, and hands pulled the material back for her to pass. Ash, as she followed, glanced to one side and saw fair-haired slaves in woollen tunics, House slaves, sent up from the African coast; even one or two men she knew by sight from House Leofric. But not – a swift searching glance – the man Leovigild, or the child Violante.

Leovigild, who tried to talk to me in my cell; Violante, who brought me blankets.

Of course they might be dead.

"Isn't it nice when you get important enough that people don't kill you out of hand?" Ash said sardonically, walking into the low, lantern-lit chamber, and throwing herself down on to a stool in front of the nearest brazier. She didn't look at Alderic or the Faris for a moment, putting back her hood, stripping off gauntlets and sallet, and stretching her hands out to the heat. When she did, it was with a look of complete confidence. "Not won Dijon yet, then?"

It was the *'arif* who rumbled, "Not yet."

She had one dizzy moment, literally light-headed, looking at the *'arif* commander Alderic and seeing how he watched herself and the Faris. *Identical sisters. One, you've followed around Iberia, and trusted your life to in combat. And the other – you cut the throat of, when she was fourteen weeks old.*

Ash's hand moved. She put it down again, not wanting to reach up to the unseen scar on her neck. She settled for grinning at Alderic, and watching him wince at her scarred face. There was still sympathy in his expression, but not to excess. Professional, military . . . evidently he felt his semi-responsibility discharged with his own confession to her in Carthage.

"Dijon is not yet won by assault." The Faris wrapped her arms around her body, lifting her robe as she turned. The light on her perfect face showed her tired, but not drawn; campaigning hard, but not starving.

"Assaults don't end sieges. Hunger, disease and treachery end sieges." Ash lifted a brow, at Alderic. "I want to talk to your boss, *'Arif*."

The Faris said something quietly to him. Alderic nodded. As the big man left, the Faris signalled to the slaves, and remained standing while food and drink was brought in by men wiping suddenly-broken sleep out of their faces.

The long chamber contained trestle tables, chests, a box-bed; all of it European and probably looted. Among these Frankish items, the war-gear of the Visigoth general, and the red clay and white marble of the golems, seemed jarring.

"Why interrupt my sleep?" the Visigoth woman said, suddenly quizzical. "You could have waited until morning to be a traitor."

Both of them? Ash thought, nothing registering on her face. *Without my saying anything – they're both assuming I've been in Dijon all this time?*

Of *course* – because the Faris will have seen men in my livery on the walls!

And since I haven't talked to the *machina rei militaris*, it can't have told her where I've really been.

She thinks I'm here to give her the city.

Let her think that. I've got about thirty minutes. I only have to keep them guessing for that long. Stay alive for that long.

And meantime do what I came for.

The Faris stared for a moment. She walked back to the chamber door, past her mail hauberk hanging on a body-form, and gave quiet orders to the slaves. The men left the room. Turning, she said, "The golems will tear you apart if you attack me. I need no guards."

"I'm not here to kill you."

"I will doubt that, for my own survival." The Visigoth woman walked closer, seating herself in a carved chair further off from the brazier. It was as she sat, her body dropping limply down on to the silken cushions, that Ash realised how weary she was. Long silver lashes drooped over her eyes for a moment.

Still with her eyes closed, and as if completing long thoughts, the Faris said, "But you wouldn't be here, after I've taken the city, would you? You're too afraid of being taken to Carthage again. You haunt me," the woman added unexpectedly.

"Dijon," Ash said neutrally.

"You will have your price for opening a gate." The Faris put her hands in her lap. The fur gown slid back, exposing her leg to the charcoal brazier's heat. Red light gleamed on her fine, pale skin. A self-possessed woman, little different from the woman Ash had seen at Basle.

Looking at the Faris's hands in her lap, Ash saw that the flesh at the sides of her perfect nails was nipped, bitten; fragments of skin stripped out and the meat showing red beneath.

"The safety of my company is paramount," Ash said. As if it were a normal negotiation – and *might* it be? – she added, "We march out with full honours of war. All our kit. Give an undertaking not to contract to the Empire's enemies in Christendom."

As if she did not want to look, but could not stop herself, the Faris met Ash's gaze. With a quiet fretfulness, she said, "Our lord Gelimer presses me hard. Messengers, pigeons, as well as the *machina rei militaris*. 'Press the siege, press hard' – but other commanders could hold the siege, my place is with my field armies! Give me the city and I am in a mood to make it worth your while."

So Gelimer did *make it out of the palace alive. Damn. That's one rumour down.*

Ash briefly considered asking *Is my husband Fernando alive?* and dismissed both the thought and the odd stab of grief that came with it.

And are they still fighting up in Flanders?

"My money was on Gelimer thinking: the campaign's going to have to stop for the winter, the crusade's succeeded so far, it can all wait till spring. Meanwhile Gelimer makes himself a *secure* elected monarch." Ash rubbed her cold hands together. "If the real action's in Flanders, Gelimer won't send you orders. You're Leofric's toy; Gelimer doesn't want him looking good at the moment."

She spared a glance to see how the Faris was taking her familiarity with Carthaginian politics.

"You're wrong. Nothing matters to our King-Caliph but the death of the Duke and the fall of Burgundy." As if they were sisters, the Visigoth woman said, "Father is ill; he took injuries in the earth tremor. Cousin Sisnandus commands the House. I speak with Sisnandus, through the Stone Golem – he assures me Father will be well, soon."

At the mention of the *machina rei militaris*, Ash felt the nape of her neck turn cold. "You can still speak to it? To the Stone Golem?"

The Faris's gaze slid away. "Why should I not?"

Something in her tone made Ash freeze, hardly breathing, trying to pick up every nuance.

"I tell the Stone Golem what the tactical situation is, and Sisnandus and the King tell me to continue here. I would sooner hear it from Father . . ." She sighed, rubbing at her eyes. "He must recover, soon. It takes two weeks, a month, to go back in person: I cannot leave here."

Her eyes opened: her dark gaze met Ash's. Ash thought, *There is something different about you*, but could not work out what it might be.

"You've heard the other voices," Ash said. Not knowing, until she heard herself say it, that it must be true. "You've heard the Wild Machines!"

"Nonsense!"

The Faris looked for a moment as if she might jump to her feet. Her robe fell back further, disclosing that the woman was wearing her shift, with a belt and dagger fastened over it any-old-how; the signs of a sudden waking alarm. Her hand moved down to caress the curved knife's hilt.

The Faris glanced over towards the nearest golem. Lamplight shone on its red stone limbs, its eyeless face. "'Wild Machines' . . . ?"

"They told me Friar Bacon called them that."

"They *told* you . . ." The woman stumbled over her words. Her voice strengthened. "I – yes – I heard what the *machina rei militaris* reported, on the night of your attack on Carthage. The tremor disturbed it, obviously: it told me nothing but some myth or legend that someone once read into it. Garbled nonsense!"

Ash felt the palms of her hands become cold, wet, with sweat. "You heard it. You heard them!"

"I heard the Stone Golem!"

"You heard something speaking *through* the Stone Golem," Ash said, leaning forward intensely. "I made them tell me – they weren't expecting it – I can't do it again. But you heard them say what they were: *ferae natura machinae*. And you heard them say what they want—"

"Fiction! Nothing but fiction!" The Faris shifted around in the chair, so that she no longer looked at Ash. "Sisnandus assures me it is a made-up story some slave must have read into the Stone Golem at some point – probably some slave with a grudge. He has executed many slaves in retribution. A temporary glitch, nothing more."

Oh lord. Ash stared at the Carthaginian woman. *And I thought I was avoiding thinking about this* . . .

"You can't believe that," she said gently. "Faris. Where there was one voice, I heard many. You heard them too. Didn't you?"

"I didn't listen. They told me nothing! I won't hear."

"Faris—"

"There *are* no other machines!"

"There's more than the voice of the Stone Golem—"

"I will not listen!"

"What have you asked them?"

"Nothing."

To an outsider – and Ash suddenly conceives of that hypothetical outsider, perhaps because she wonders if slaves or guards are listening at doors – this would seem uncanny: two women with the same face, talking to each other with the same voice. She has to touch her scars to reassure herself, seek out the fading tan that masks the Visigoth woman's eyes, to know that they are not the same person, that she is not in the same place as the dead baby and the boar wood.

"I don't believe you haven't spoken to them," Ash said flatly. "What, not even to find out what they are?"

The woman's cheeks flushed slightly.

"There is no *them*. What do you want with me, *jund*?"

Ash leaned forward to the brazier. "I'm your bastard sister."

"And that means?"

"I don't know what it means." Ash smiled, quickly and ruefully. "On the most pragmatic level, it means I hear what you hear. I've heard the Wild Machines telling me what they are. And I've heard them say why they've manipulated House Leofric for the past two hundred years, trying to breed you—"

"No!"

"Oh yes." Ash's smile glinted. "You're Gundobad's child."

"I have heard none of this!"

"Your – our father, Leofric; he's been used. Is *being* used." Ash stood up. She gave a sudden, wary glance at the golems. They remained still. "Faris, in the name of Christ! You're the one, you've been hearing the Stone Golem since you were born, you've got to tell me what you've been hearing from the Wild Machines!"

"*Nothing.*" The woman also rose. She stood barefoot on the furs thrown down on the rough-hewed oak boards, her eyes on a level with Ash's. Her head tilted a little to one side, studying. "This is some fantasy of a discontented slave. How can it be anything else?"

"This isn't your war. It isn't Leofric's war. It isn't even the fucking *King-Caliph's* war." Ash turned her back, stalking up and down the chamber, in and out of lamplight and brazier light. "It's the Wild Machines' war. Why? Why, Faris? Why?"

"I don't know!"

"*Then bloody ask!*" Ash roared. "*You* might get an answer!"

The nearest golem shifted on its stone feet. Ash froze, waiting until it returned to complete immobility; as she might have done for a large, fierce, not very intelligent dog.

The woman said, "I . . . heard voices. Once! And— It is some error. Leofric will correct it, as soon as he is well!"

"You know what they are – I bet you've even seen them, in the desert – Alderic called it 'God's blessing'—"

"Be quiet." The Visigoth general spoke with a sudden, immense authority. A little helplessly, Ash stopped pacing. She felt herself to be in the presence of a woman who had fought a dozen Iberian campaigns before she ever set foot in Christendom. Unarmoured, without weapons; the woman was nonetheless a warrior. The only crack in her composure came with her shifting, inadequate gaze.

"Look at it from my point of view, *jund*," the Faris said quietly. Her voice shook. "I have three armies in the field. That's my priority. That gives me enough work, twenty-four hours of the day. I do not need to bother with some *rumour*. Where would these other *machinae* be? How would we not know of them, and the *amirs* who must have built them?"

"But you know it's no rumour: you *heard*—" Ash broke off.

She isn't listening to me. She knows what she heard. But she won't admit it – even to herself.

Do I tell her what *I* know?

A gleam in the corner of the chamber resolved itself into another body-form, covered by a white harness. Seeking a diversion of the Faris's attention, Ash moved closer to it. She reached up and touched the breastplate, slid her fingers down over the fauld to the left lower lame, and the newly riveted strap on the tasset of the completely familiar Milanese armour.

"Bloody *hell*. Been carting this around with you, then? All the way from Basle? But then, I suppose it fits *you*, too!"

Ash ran her fingers back up her own armour, where it hung on the body-form, giving the strap that buckled placket to breastplate a solid tug. "Buckles could do with a polish. All these bloody slaves, you'd think you could manage that."

"Sit down, mercenary."

With that reminder of enmity, Ash remembered the matter of time, saw no clock in the chamber, could see no moon through the tapestried doorway. I won't know, she realised. When all hell breaks loose, I won't know whether it's John Price putting his attack in, or the rest of the company being caught on their way in through the sally-port.

"You know this isn't about armies," Ash said, turning to face the Visigoth woman. "If it was, you'd be fighting the Turk, not Burgundy. Whatever they are, whatever they want, these Wild Machines: they're getting stronger. You must know that *they* make the darkness, not some damn Rabbi's curse. And now it's spreading—"

The Faris shook her head, loose hair shimmering. "I don't *listen*!"

"Do they call you 'Gundobad's child'?"

Dark eyes, under silver brows, watched her with a flat lack of affect. The Faris said mechanically, "Nothing speaks to me except the tactical machine. Anything else is history, legends that someone once read into the Golem. Nothing else speaks to me."

She isn't seeing me, Ash thought. She isn't even talking to me.

Is this what she said to *Leofric*? The day that it happened?

The realisation was sudden, but absolute; Ash imagined both the woman's

611

first tentative questions to her adoptive father, and the lord-*amir*'s instant, panicky replies. And now her denial.

But how long has Leofric been ill? Ever since the quake, two months ago? Christus! *Was* he injured in the earth-tremor, or is it something else—?

And who's this 'cousin Sisnandus'? How much does he know? About the Wild Machines, about any of this . . . How ill *is* Leofric?

"So what's 'Father' said to all this?" Ash demanded, sardonically.

The woman looked up. "I shall hardly bother him with such nonsense, until he recovers his full health."

Aware of being on dangerous ground, Ash only watched the woman now, saying nothing.

Have the Wild Machines already spoken through the *machina* and made House Leofric set a guard on it? Can I ask her that?

No. I'm not getting through to this woman. Whatever I'd ask her – she doesn't want to know. She's shut down for the duration.

And I don't know what she'll repeat through the Stone Golem.

The Faris leaned back in her chair. The orange light from the oil lamps limned her brow, cheek, chin, shoulder. She passed a hand over her face. Some of the weariness went, and with it, strangely, some of her authority. She looked up at Ash, her expression acutely indecisive.

"Is your confessor with you?" the Faris said, suddenly, into the silence.

Ash gave a startled laugh. "My *confessor*? You're going to have me executed? Isn't that a bit extreme?"

"Your priest, the man Gottfried, Geoffroi—"

"Godfrey?" Stunned, Ash said, "Godfrey Maximillian's dead. He died trying to get out of Carthage."

The Faris put her arms on the back of her chair, resting her weight on it. Ash watched her look up at the plank-and-earthen roof, as if the answers were somewhere in the dirt; and look down again, meeting Ash's gaze.

"I . . . have questions I would have asked a Frankish priest."

"You'll have to try someone else. They don't come much deader than Godfrey when I saw him last," Ash said coarsely.

"You're certain?"

A chill that was nothing to do with winter twisted in her gut. "What's one priest, to you? When did Godfrey Maximillian ever meet you?"

The Faris looked away. "We never met. I had heard his name at Basle, as a priest of your company."

Spurred, impulsive, Ash blurted, "Would you know his voice?"

The colour of the woman's face altered, subtly; she looked now as if she were unwell.

"You are the only other one," the Faris said suddenly. "*You* hear. You and I, both. How else am I to know I am not sunstruck-crazy?"

". . . Because we hear the same thing?" Ash said.

It was no more than a whisper: "Yes."

Armour, golems, the Visigoth camp outside: all forgotten. Nothing else exists but the realisation: *She isn't talking about the Wild Machines now.*

Cold sweat slicked Ash's palms. Dry-mouthed, she asked, "What *do* you hear, Faris?"

"I hear a heretic priest, persuading me that I should betray my religion and my King-Caliph. I hear a heretic priest telling me that my *machina rei militaris* is not to be *trusted*—"

On the last word, risen an octave, she cut herself off.

Almost in a whisper, the Faris finished: "I hear great voices, tormenting a heretic's soul."

Ash, holding her breath, released air slowly and silently through her nostrils. The golems' perfumed lamps made the atmosphere heavy; both cold and stifling. Aware that one wrong word or gesture could lose it, she said quietly, "A 'heretic priest' . . . yes, it is; it must be. Godfrey Maximillian. I . . . heard him too."

With that, the realisation hit home. She momentarily forgot where she stood; was back in the command tent, her dream of boars and snow fading, hearing a voice—

It really *is* him. Godfrey, dead Godfrey; if she hears him too, *it has to be!*

She pushed the heel of her hand into her eye-sockets, one after the other, smearing away water. Rapidly, remembering the woman in front of her, she said, "And the 'great voices' you hear are the Wild Machines."

"A dead heretic, and ancient machine-minds?" The Faris's perfect face moved in an expression of sardonic humour, fear, forgiveness: all in a second. "And you'll tell me, too, that I can't trust the Stone Golem to win my battles for me, now. Ash – what else *would* you say to me? You're fighting with the Burgundians."

"And if you pay me to fight on the same side as your men," Ash said steadily, "I'll tell you exactly the same thing."

"I will not trust an enemy!"

"But you'll trust the Stone Golem, after *this*?"

"Be quiet!"

The flickering light of oil lamps gleamed on armour, on mail, on the red stone limbs of the golem.

Godfrey, Ash thought, dazed. *But how?*

"I could hire your men," the Faris said absently, "but not to fight under your command: I would need you elsewhere. Father wants you," she added. "He told me so, before he grew ill. Sisnandus tells me he still orders your presence."

Oh shit, I bet he does!

"Your 'father' Leofric wants to dissect me, to know how *you* work." Ash lifted her eyes to discover an expression of bewilderment on the woman's face. "Didn't you know that? Probably he'd want it even more badly, now! If you and I can hear a *dead* man—"

A voice outside bellowed, "To arms!"

Oh, Christus, not now! What a time to be interrupted!

A fist hammered at the outer door of the command building. Ash heard shouting, did not shift her gaze from the Visigoth woman's face.

"Maybe," Ash said, "it isn't just Leofric and this Sisnandus who want me in Carthage. Do you *know* who's giving you orders, Faris?"

"*To arms!*" a male voice bawled again, outside the chamber door.

The Faris swung around, breaking eye-contact with Ash; marched to the door and flung the curtains aside, just before a slave male could do it.

"Give me a proper report, *'Arif*," she snapped.

The man-at-arms, with the *'arif*'s rank on his livery, gasped, "They're attacking the camp—!"

"Which perimeter?"

"South-west. I think, *al-sayyid*."[2]

"Ah. That will be a diversion. Get me the *qa'id* for the engineers' camp, but first, send a message to alert the *qa'id* of the east camp. Get me *'Arif* Alderic and his troop, here, now. Slaves! Clothe me!"

She flung back into the room, brushing past Ash, who had to take a step back to keep her balance. Jolted, Ash had time to think, *Is that what I look like when I get in gear?*

"I'm not sending you to Carthage, yet. Father will have to wait. I need the city. I'm sending you back to Dijon, *jund*." The Faris looked up from the clothing on her bed, with a brief, surprising smile. "With an escort. Just in case you get ambushed on the way."

Back to Dijon. *Into* Dijon!

A handful of slaves pushed past Ash, two or three of them showing stark surprise and recognition at seeing her. They began to strip robe and shift from the Visigoth general, and dress her from the skin out.

"You're giving me an *escort*?"

"Dijon is where you are crucial to me, now. I need the city! We will talk again. About these . . . Wild Machines. And your dead priest. Later."

Ash shook her head, spluttering between frustration and anger. "No. *Now*, Faris. You know what war is! Don't leave something because you think you can do it tomorrow."

The other *'arif* rushed back in. "Now they are attacking the eastern perimeter, *al-sayyid*!"

Ash opened her mouth, all but said, aloud and incredulously, *Two* attacks? She shut her mouth again.

"And that will be the true attack. Get your men to arms! You were a distraction, to allow these sallies out of the city? Well, you may still have your price!" Not waiting for a confirmation, and still with a wicked smile covering her immense weariness, the Visigoth woman put her arms up as her slaves lowered her mail hauberk over her head, wriggling arms and body and neck until the mail snugged down over her body.

I need another hour with her! Ash thought, frustrated. She *wants* to talk, I can *feel* it—

As a child tied the waist of the hauberk to her belt with aiglettes, the Faris continued:

"Alderic will take you to the gates once we have contained these attacks. We *will* talk again – sister."

[2] 'Boss'.

614

Stunned at the swiftness of it, Ash found herself stumbling out, down steps into the moonlit camp, into a flurry of lanterns, men running with spears and recurved bows, *nazirs* bawling hoarse orders; all the ordered confusion one might wish to see in a camp surprised by a night-attack. By the time she got her helmet on and her night-vision back, she was being hurried along between two of *'Arif* Alderic's men, boots ringing on the frosted earth, towards the great dark bulk of the city walls of Dijon.

She can't just send me off like this! Not without answers—!

Torches moved outside the impromptu holding-area. Her feet grew numb in her boots.

From somewhere to the east she heard steel blades slamming together.

Two attacks? One will be mine. I wonder if Robert's sent a force out of the sally-gate himself? It'd be like him. Twice the confusion.

" 'Hurry up and wait'," she remarked to Alderic's *nazir*, a small, spare man in well-worn mail. He said nothing, but he gave a brief smile. No different in this man's army.

After an interminable wait, the sounds of combat moved off. Nothing then but torches moving in the Visigoth camp; legionaries on fire-watch shouting in frustration; war-horses neighing from their lines. She considered asking if the cooks had been woken up too; decided against it; found herself almost falling asleep on her feet, the length of the wait blurring in her mind.

"*Nazir!*" The *'arif* Alderic strode back into the circle of torchlight, nodded abruptly at his men, and they all moved off; Ash in the middle of the eight, the cold forcing her half-sleeping mind back to alertness.

She stumbled down trenches, behind palisades, the smell of earth and powder thick in her nostrils; then out into the open, beyond the last of the defensive barriers. Ahead, across a wide expanse of blasted, raw earth, torches already began to flare – up on the hoardings hanging out from the battlements, above the north-west gate.

"Best of luck," the *'arif* said brusquely. Glimpsing Alderic's face, she saw the last of his guilt-induced kindness.

He and his men vanished back into the trenches, the darkness, the flames.

"God *damn* it!" Ash remarked into the cold air.

She let me go. Yeah. Because she can. She's sending me into a siege. Because she wants me to betray Dijon. She doesn't think I'm going *any*where.

And she thinks she can get me for Leofric any time . . .

"Cow!"

Ash stopped dead, on the battered, rutted, rough ground, up to her ankles in mud. Cold wind made her eyes leak tears down her numb, scarred cheeks. Through the helmet's padding, she could hear the river running somewhere off on her right-hand side; water not yet frozen over. Closer, dancing in her vision, she saw sheer towering walls; and lights in front of her, over the north-west gate of Dijon.

"Oh, the cow. She's *already* got my armour. Now she's kept my bloody *sword*, too!"

A nervous voice came from the parapet above the portcullis and gates. "Sarge, there's someone out there *laughing*."

Ash wiped her eyes. *Godammit, they should have had word about me – fine time to go down to friendly fire!*

"Some crazy rag-'ead tart," a second, invisible male voice commented. "You going to go down there and give 'er one?"

"Yo, the wall!" She walked forward, at an easy pace, into the circle of light now spread by the lanterns; keeping an eye on the combat-ready and twitchy men lining the parapet of the gate above her. She squinted. In the poor light, their livery was unclear.

"Whose men?" she sang out.

"De la Marche!" a beer-roughened voice bawled, arrogantly.

"Who the fuck are *you*?" another, anonymous, voice demanded.

Ash looked up at bows, bills; one man in armour with a poleaxe.

"Don't for the Green Christ's sake shoot me now," she said unsteadily. "Not after what I've just been through! Go tell your boss he wants to see me."

There was a silence of sheer, dumbstruck amazement.

"You *what*?"

"I said, go tell your boss de la Marche he wants to see me. He does. So open the gate!"

One of the Burgundian men-at-arms snorted. "Cheeky *bitch*!"

"Who is that?"

"Can't see, sir. Not in the cloak. It's a woman, sir."

Still grinning, Ash put her cloak back over her shoulders.

Over her brigandine, dirty-yellow but perfectly distinct, the livery of the Lion Azure shone in the light of their torches.

A clutch of Burgundian men-at-arms, swords drawn, hustled her through the man-high door cut into Dijon's great gates; hustled her into darkness, and echoes off masonry, and the smell of sweat and shit and pitch-torches burned down to the socket.

I'm in! I'm inside the walls!

The relief of such safety deafened her, for a second, to the voices of men and officers.

"She could be a spy!" an over-excited billman shouted.

"A woman dressed as a man? *Whore!*"

A lance-leader stuttered, "No, last August I s-saw her in the English Earl's affinity—"

She blinked, eyes gradually adjusting to the torchlight in the long tunnel of the gates, and the faint glimmer of light – dawn? torches? – at the arched exit.

And I'm sane. Or – a smile hidden by helmet and hood – *as sane as the Faris, anyway, which may not be saying much.*

Her smile faded.

And it *is* Godfrey . . . dear God: *how?*

Ash returned her attention: raised her voice. "I have to find my men—!"

*I'm in. Are *they*? Fuck!*

And – if we are – now how the hell do I get us out again?

II

Growing first light showed her devastation – a shattered no-man's-land stretching two hundred yards from the north-west gate back into the city, and as far to either side as she could see. Dawn picked out man-high heaps of rubble, the broken beams of bombard-wrecked houses and shops; scarred cobbles, burned thatch; one teetering retaining wall.

Ash stumbled, between the Burgundian soldiers; the cold wind numbing her scarred cheeks. She spared a glance for heraldry and faces: definitely Olivier de la Marche's troops. And therefore Charles of Burgundy's loyal men.

We were with them at Auxonne, they'll be assuming we're still hired on with them—

But we might just be a damn sight better off selling Dijon to the Visigoths, and heading east to the Sultan and his armies. Mercenaries are always welcome.

If we're not all dead out there.

Noise shocked the air.

Above Ash's head, in the chill pre-light before dawn, the bells of Dijon suddenly began to peal out. Church after church, St Philibert and Notre Dame, noise running back from the street where she stood; abbey and monastery, within the city walls; all their great bells pealing out high and low, shrill and clear, shaking the birds up from the roofs and the citizens awake in their houses: the bells of Dijon clamouring out into the morning, cascading with joy.

"What the fuck—?" Ash yelled.

The Burgundian officers fell back. She glimpsed Thomas Rochester shoving his way through the pack – *Christus, the first familiar face in hours!* – battered, not badly injured; safe in the city; an escort of company men-at-arms with him under the tattered Lion standard. Seeing her, he signalled, and one of the men-at-arms unrolled and raised her personal banner beside it.

"Where the fuck have *you* been?" Ash bellowed.

The dark Englishman shouted something, inaudible in the Dijon street for the noise. Pushing in close, shoulder to shoulder, he lowered his mouth to her ear, and she thumbed up one side of her sallet to hear him shouting:

". . . got in! They swam rope-bridges across at the south gate! Where the bridge has been mined?"

The scent of summer dust is suddenly heavy in her memory: she recalls riding into Dijon by that bridge, at the side of John de Vere, Earl of Oxford. Into a white, fair city.

Floria del Guiz appeared from behind Rochester, yelling; Ash read her lips rather than heard her above the bells and the shouting: "News has got out! I thought we'd never find you!"

"Where's Robert? *What* news?"

The woman grinned: might have said, "Sometimes you're *slow!*"

Voices shrieked at windows above Ash's head. She glanced up, listening – the earth still darker than the lightening sky – and a body cannoned into her and

Thomas Rochester together. She caught her balance, shoving back at a burly man tumbling out of his scarred wooden front door, a fat woman fumbling at his shoulder and tying his points; two small children howling underfoot.

"Jesus *wept!*"

Amazed, Ash signalled to the banner, attempting to back off across the trebuchet-battered cobbled streets. Among the familiar military silhouettes in the crowd – pinch-waisted doublets, hose, bill-points and sallets – there were civilian men bundling themselves into their gowns, cramming on their tall felt hats: neighbour shrieking to neighbours, all questions, all demands.

"Find me Roberto!" Ash directed Thomas Rochester, at battlefield-pitch. The Englishman nodded, and signalled to the men-at-arms.

Now bodies pressed up against Ash from all sides. Their breath whitened the air; the smell of old sweat and dirt filled her nostrils. She shoved. *Hopeless!* she thought. There was no way to move without using force. Rochester looked back at her and raised his shoulders, in the press of bodies. She shook her head at him, ruefully, almost relaxing into the chaos; still dazzled by the implicit safety of the city's towering walls.

The press of bodies swayed against her; the narrow street spilling people out into the no-man's-land of demolished streets and burned-out houses. Not all civilians, Ash noted; Burgundian-liveried men in mail and plate, or in archer's jacks, were also running out across the bombarded ground, towards the north-west gate and walls of the city. The pressure of the crowd began to push her inexorably back in that direction.

"Okay, guys! Listen up! Better find out what the fuss is . . ."

The aches of the night's exertions, and the lack of sleep, blurred her mind. It was a minute before she realised she and her escort were stomping up stone steps – up to the walls, in the wake of armed men; deafened still by the bells. *Is this . . . ?*

She automatically glanced back down the flight of stone steps, looking for a house with a bush hanging from it, to signify an inn. *Is this where Godfrey came to me, on the walls of Dijon, and told me he wanted me?*

There were no undamaged buildings below: everything at the foot of the wall was a mess of beams, broken plaster, scrambled roof tiles, and abandoned furniture; and masonry scorched black.

No: we must have been further down the west wall, I remember looking down at the southern bridge . . .

Wry humour made her smile; there was nothing other than cynicism and adrenalin to keep her going now:

. . . The same day I saw Fernando in the Duke's palace, was it? Or the day we beat up Florian's aunt? Christus!

She crowded between a priest and a tanner and a nun, pushing her way towards the crenellations, where the soldiers were leaning out under the wooden brattices[3] and shouting down off the city's north wall.

At her elbow, a monk in green robes bellowed, "It's a miracle! We have prayed, and it has been granted to us! *Deo gratias!*"

[3] Wooden structure built out from the walls to allow missiles, etc., to be dropped through holes in the floor.

To Rochester and Floria del Guiz, impartially, Ash bawled, "What the fuck *is* this?"

Nearly Prime[4], on the morning of the fifteenth of November, 1476: Ash tastes the chill of winter in her mouth, on the wind that blows from the northeast. She has time to notice the streaming lines of people running up to the walls – used to estimating numbers on the field, she thought: *the better part of two thousand men, woman and children*. Leaning into an embrasure, she touched her hand to the walls above Dijon's north-west gate, feeling their protection.

She cupped her gauntlet, shielding her eyes from the sun that rose on her right hand, listening for what was being so rhythmically shouted. The sight in front of her put it clear out of her mind.

A greater 'town' surrounds the walls of Dijon now – the town that is the Visigoth siege-camp. Clear in the daylight, it has its own streets and mustergrounds; its own turf-roofed barracks and Arian chapels and army markets. Two months is long enough to make them seem frighteningly established and permanent. Rank upon rank of weather-worn, bleached tents stretch out, too, into the white-misted distance. They cover all the acres between Dijon and the forests to the north.

Cold air making her eyes water, Ash let her gaze travel across the sweep of the Visigoth camp: pavises, shelters; fenced siege-engine parks; saps and trenches snaking towards the walls of the town ... and thousands upon thousands of armed men.

Jesus! Now we're in here – what have I done?

Leaning out, looking west, she picked out the burned ruins of great wooden pavises, that had sheltered at least four massive bombards. The cannon seemed apparently untouched – their distant crews beginning to crawl out of their bashas and poke campfires into more life.

Frost limned every blade of grass. Amid the dozens of intact mangonels, ballistae, trebuchets and cannon, she saw a few blackened areas of grass and collapsed canvas. White-haired slaves desultorily cleared up the mess, coldfingered and slow; she heard *nazirs* bellowing at them. Their voices came clear across the cold air.

Glancing east, she saw no sign whatsoever of any attack there, not even burned canvas.

Two attacks didn't even dent them.

She leaned forward, feeling her men crowding in beside her; moving her gaze to the north.

Men are small, three or four hundred yards away, beyond the trenches and outside bow- and arquebus-shot; but livery is still visible. She could not make out the Faris's Brazen Head livery on any of them. Wind-tears blurred the edges of pavilions and the colours of pennants. She lifted her head, looking further out from the walls.

"Jesus fucking Christ, there's thousands of them!"

Down on the Visigoth horse lines, men fetching feed stopped, listening to the sudden noise from Dijon. The low morning sun shone on Carthaginian spearpoints, and men's helmets, on the camp perimeter. The sound of barked orders

[4] 6 a.m.

came clear across the open air. Down towards the western bridge, half-hidden by pavises, men sprinted to serve guns – a puff of white smoke came from the muzzle of one mortar, and perceptible seconds later, the *thump!* of its firing.

Fat crows flew up from camp middens.

"And a good morning to you rag-heads, too!" Rochester growled, beside her, in profile against the yellow eastern sky.

Ash squinted, head whipping round, not able to see where the mortar shot hit – lobbed somewhere inside the burned streets of Dijon, back of her.

Another flat *thwack!* brought her head back around. Ten yards down the parapet, the crowd of men folded in on itself; a swirl of figures in belted gowns and chaperon hats; one voice raised in high, shocked agony. The constant shout of the crowd lining the walls drowned him out.

Shit. There *is* a whole legion out there. Oh, *shit* . . .

No wonder the Faris thinks that all a 'betrayal' would save her is time.

A man-at-arms in Lion livery leaned precariously out from under the hoardings, yelling down at the frost-glittering tents of the Visigoths, four hundred yards out from the walls, spit spraying out from his mouth:

"*Your city's fucked! Your Caliph's dead! How about that, motherfuckers!*"

A great cheer went up along the walls of Dijon. With Rochester and the banner at her shoulder, Ash pushed in close. The man-at-arms, a redhead she remembered as one of Ned Mowlett's men, all but lost his grip on the brattice-strut he held. A mate hauled him back.

"Pearson!" Ash thumped him on armoured shoulders, hauling him around to look at the first one of the men who had stayed in Dijon – filthy with mud, straggle-haired, and with a healing scar across one eyebrow.

"*Boss!*" Pearson bellowed; sweating, surprised, happy, transcendent. "Those fuckers are *done* for, aren't they, boss?"

His gold-and-blue livery was unaltered, her own device of the Lion Passant Guardant[5]; nothing added or subtracted by Robert Anselm. She contented herself with another slap on his shoulder.

A second priest called, "*Deo gratias*, the Visigoths and their stone demons are thrown down!"

Two yards away, a Burgundian man-at-arms yelled down, "We didn't even have to *be* there! You're outside our city, and our walls stand! We didn't even have to *go* to Carthage and it's fucking *flattened*!"

Someone further down the north city wall blew a herald's horn, wildly. More men-at-arms entered the crowd, unshaven men in Lion livery pushing through the press towards the frost-stiff blue-and-gold of the Lion Affronté on her personal banner. Behind them, men in rich gowns with their faces full of sleep – sergeants with staffs, constables, burghers – made vain attempts to clear the parapet. The deep flat crack of mortar fire sounded again: two shots, five, and then a slow, erratic succession of explosions.

---

[5] More properly referred to as a 'lioncel', or 'leopard'; 'Fraxinus', however, prefers the more unorthodox usage. Presumably this reflects Ash's religious devotion to the 'Heraldic Beast' of her childhood: the mythical 'Lion born of a Virgin'.

The soldiers, starting with the Lion company men clustered around her, leaned out off the brattices and started to chant:

"Carthage fell *down*! Carthage fell *down*! Carthage fell *down*!"

"But it—" *wasn't quite like that!* Ash mentally protested.

A company archer, one of Euen Huw's men, shouted, "Yer Caliph's *dead* and yer city fell *down*!"

"But it was a quake—"

Floria del Guiz's voice, at her ear, bellowed, "They know that!"

Despite the precariousness of being an exposed target, Ash could only grin helplessly as the sound grew, a chant that was deep, male voices bellowing, loud enough to reach the enemy lines and then some; and she put her face up to the dawn breeze, grinning out at more Visigoth men who began to collect along the front line, muttering and gathering in groups.

"'Ware trebuchets!" Thomas Rochester touched her arm and pointed west across the Suzon river to the big counterweight siege weapons, their crews visible now, tiny figures staring at the city walls. Eighty or ninety per cent of the engines undamaged, she thought.

"Jesus, this lot aren't bright! You couldn't shift 'em with bombards!" Ash shrieked back. "Let 'em have their shout, Tom, then start moving them back down off the walls! I want us across the broken ground and *out* of here!"

"THE CALIPH IS *DEAD*! CARTHAGE FELL *DOWN*!"

The wind shifted, coming from the east as the sun rose up. She focused into the distance – up on the northern slopes, above the water meadows, an empty shell stood: nothing now but fire-blackened stone. *I wonder what happened to Soeur Simeon and the nuns?*

Ash's throat tightened. She wiped at her watering eyes.

Half the population of Dijon up on the defences now: despite the rapid tremble of the stone parapet underfoot, where mangonel boulders struck home against the outside wall.

"They're getting the range!" she yelled to Floria, her mouth at the woman's ear to be heard over bells, men shouting, women shouting, children shrieking.

"THE CALIPH IS *DEAD*! CARTHAGE FELL *DOWN*!"

"But Caliph Theodoric died before the earthquake!" Floria yelled back, her mouth now to Ash's ear, warm damp breath feathering her skin. "And they elected another one!"

"And Gelimer's still with us. These people don't care about *that*. Oh, the hell with it! The Caliph is dead!" Ash raised her voice: "Carthage fell *down*!"

Several men in armour and Burgundian livery jackets came pushing through the crowd, towards her banner. Ash let herself down off the masonry. She inclined her head, bowing a speechless greeting.

Behind the men, squads of foot soldiers began clearing the walls, heaving people back from the brattices. She blinked, hearing the faintest diminution in the sound-volume. Two of the men she recognised from the summer: an elderly chamberlain-counsellor of the Duke's court, and a nobleman she knew to be one of Olivier de la Marche's aides.

"It's her!" the chamberlain-counsellor exclaimed.

"Messire—" Ash managed to remember his name: "—Ternant. What can I do for you? Tom, *get these bloody idiots down from here!* Green Christ on a crutch, I didn't get them back here to have them shot off the walls! Sorry, Messire Ternant, what is it?"

"We expected Captain Anselm!" de la Marche's aide bellowed, his face a picture of sheer incredulity.

"Well, you've got Captain Ash!" She shifted as the first of her men filed back off the brattices, boots booming on the hollow wooden floors.

"In that case – it is your presence that the siege council requests, Captain!" Ternant bawled, his voice cracking with age and effort.

"'Siege council'—? Never mind!" Ash nodded her head emphatically. "I'll come! I'm settling my men here in their quarters first! When? What time?"

"The hour before Terce.[6] Demoiselle, we are hearing such rumours—"

She waved him to silence, in the face of the wall of sound. "Later! I'll be there, Messire!"

"CARTHAGE FELL *DOWN*! CARTHAGE FELL *DOWN*!"

"I give up." Floria stood up on her toes, grabbing at Thomas Rochester's mail-shirted shoulder for support. She bellowed towards the open air, "Down with the Caliph! Carthage fell down!"

Thomas Rochester gave a snort. Abruptly, the dark Englishman caught Ash's eye, and pointed. At the standards set up at different points in the enemy camp, she realised. Standing aside to let the last of her men past, she looked out from the walls at the tents Rochester indicated.

Frankish pavilions, not Visigoth barracks.

"What? *Oh.* Uh-huh . . . oh, *right* . . ."

Five hundred yards away, men were gathering in a businesslike way under a great white standard, bearing a lamb surrounded by rays of gold. It flapped in the frosty air on the eastern side of the camp.

Under the sound of bells, impacting rocks, and the chant that had got up a rhythm now – the men and women of Dijon struggling not to be herded off the walls – Thomas Rochester yelled, "We can kick *his* ass, boss!"

Besides Agnus Dei's standard, in what was obviously the mercenaries' part of the Visigoth camp, Ash picked out the banner of Jacobo Rossano – *wondered who was paying him after Emperor Frederick!* – and half a dozen other small mercenary companies. One standard, a naked sword, teased her memory.

"Shit, that's Onorata Rodiani."

"What?" Floria screamed.

"I *said*, that's *Onorata*—" Ash broke off. The rising wind unwrapped the standard next to Rodiani's. It was the ripped, scarred and triumphant banner carried on to a hundred fields by Cola de Monforte and his sons.

The surgeon's voice, at her ear, breathed, "The bastards! Those are *Burgundian* mercenaries!"

[6] i.e. 8 a.m.

"Not any more! He must have gone over, after Auxonne! That's a lot of men out there. Cola doesn't have a company. He has a small army." Ash narrowed her eyes against the slanting brilliance from the east. "Looks like nobody gives a shit for this city's chances—"

Floria's hand tightened on her arm. Ash glanced where the surgeon stared, into the now-sunlit Visigoth camp. When she saw it, she did not know how she had missed it before. In the Frankish tents back of Monforte's pavilions, a silver and blue banner: the Ship and Crescent Moon.

"Joscelyn van Mander," she said bleakly.

Thomas Rochester swore. "Fucking Flemish cock-sucker! What's he doing out there?"

"Ah, shit, Tom! He's a mercenary!"

A stench of wood-smoke filled the air. She winced, as the paving stones underfoot juddered; and glanced towards the north-west gate. The nearest brattice was on fire.

"Fucking incendiaries now!"

The rhythm of sound broke: men and women only too eager, now, to struggle down the steps and off the walls. Distantly, the creaking of siege-weapons being wound up for a shot came to her. In the Visigoth artillery park, the red sandstone arms of a golem glinted, raising the great trebuchet counterweight at four times the speed of a human crew.

A succession of badly aimed, jagged missiles slammed into the wall above the gate; a merlon flew apart in stone fragments, and the press of bodies lurched, cannoning into each other, screams now audible above the noise.

And just in case the Visigoths also *have a gunner who can show you the brick in the castle wall that he's about to hit—*

"Time to go," Ash murmured, turning, as Rochester raised the banner.

"No: look!" Floria took another step forward, until she stood pressed against the hide-covered wooden frame of the brattice. Ash heard the surgeon's harsh intake of breath. "Sweet Green Christ . . ."

Far over, under the pale sun, the distances of the river valley were plainly visible. On the far side of the Suzon and its bridge, people on foot plodded to the south. Too far to see who they were – peasants and craftsmen, goodwives and maids, a few deserting men-at-arms, maybe; maybe even a priest. Indistinguishable figures wrapped in cloaks and blankets, plodding, head-down in the biting wind; small figures – children or old men – huddled by the side of the road, some still crying out to those that had left them.

Hungry, frozen, exhausted, the column of walking refugees snaked on down the track, no end of them in sight.

"They're *still* coming," Floria breathed, almost inaudible over the roaring mob hanging off the walls.

Rather less interested than her surgeon, Ash grabbed Florian's arm, pulling her back from the wall. "Let's go!"

"Ash, those aren't soldiers, those are *people*!"

"Well, don't sweat it; the rag-heads are leaving them alone. We appear to still have some of the rules of war operating . . ." The press of bodies on the parapet lessened. Ash tugged the surgeon towards the steps, in the wake of her men; Rochester and the banner at her shoulder.

Shrill, Floria yelled, "I expect they come down and rape and rob a few, when it gets boring in camp – don't you think, girl?"

"Depends how good her discipline is. I'd want them concentrating on getting inside these walls, if it was my troops." Ash looked back over her shoulder at the distant road, and the thick clogging masses of people.

"You know what it is?" Floria said suddenly. "They're heading *south*. To the border at Auxonne. Look at them, they'd rather go under the Sunless Sky than stay here!"

Too far, up here on the walls, to hear human voices; only the shriek of ungreased axles came up through the still air, and the scream of a driven packhorse. A dot – a person – lurched and fell down, got up on their feet, fell again, got up and trudged on.

Floria said, "Darkness or sun, they don't care where they're going. They just want to get away from here. These are Duchy people, townsmen, farmers, villagers, craftsmen; they're just *going*, Ash. They don't care what's in front of them."

"I'll *tell* you what's in front of them – starvation!"

The *crack!* of a small-calibre cannon: a ball thwacked off the eastern gate-tower. A huge roar of contempt and adrenalin went up from the remaining people crowding the walls:

"THE CALIPH IS *DEAD*! CARTHAGE FELL *DOWN*!"

In a moment of stillness, Ash looked out from the walls at the refugees. Despite what Florian said, she could see people trudging north, too, further into Burgundian territory; into sunlit cold and famine.

That could be us. I can't feed my people, not out there, there's no land to live off. The war-chest won't buy anything if there's nothing for money to buy. There was no harvest: we're due a famine. And out there it's dark, and cold. We'd fall apart as a company inside three days.

Let's hope it's better in here.

For however long this lasts.

Because the only way out of here is treachery.

Ash clapped her hand on Rochester's shoulder. "Okay, if the civilians want to get themselves killed, fine – we're leaving! *Lions, to the banner!*"

There was a pleasing amount of legionary discipline in the way that men wearing Lion livery detached themselves from the crowds to follow her banner, tugging in the wind above their heads. They scrambled across the devastation, into city streets again – away from the chanting crowd that now sank to its knees in prayer, still deafened by celebratory bells.

"Company billet's this way, boss!" Rochester pointed south-east into winding streets.

"Let's go!"

Green Christ, this place has been battered about!

They shouldered their way down narrow cobbled streets, under heavily timbered overhanging buildings. Glass and tiles covered the cobbles, clattering underfoot, slippery in the frost. Coming out into the open again – crossing a bridge into a square, beside the walls of silent mills – she recognised it. In the summer, a dozen Burgundian noblemen had reined in their horses here, to let a duck and her chicks waddle past to the water.

The memory took all her attention for a second; not until Rochester called the men to a halt did she rouse from her reverie, focus eyes gritty with lack of sleep, and realise she was at the company billet.

The shadow of a square, squat tower blocked out what November sun there was. Over its surrounding wall, she saw it was old, brutal in its construction; with featureless sides and narrow arrow-slit windows. Four, maybe five storeys high.

She opened her mouth to speak. A gust of wind down the cramped street snatched the breath out of her mouth. She swallowed, eyes running in the sudden, bitter blast.

One of the men-at-arms swore and stepped back as a roof-tile fell, hit, and sprayed fragments across the dung-covered cobbles. "*Jesu!* Fuckin' *storms* coming again!"

Ash recognised him as another of the men who had stayed behind in Dijon; one of di Conti's Savoyards, remaining after his captain quit. She looked up, beyond the tower's flat roof, at a sky that was rapidly losing morning clarity, turning grey and cold. "Storms?"

"Since August, boss," Thomas Rochester said, at her elbow. "I've got reports. They've been having foul weather here. Rain, wind, snow, sleet; and storms every two or three days. *Bad* storms."

"That's . . . I should have thought of that. Shit."

A darkness freezing Christendom beyond the Burgundian border – the border that, here, is barely forty miles away.

The body of air around her shifted. Even down between these buildings, it tugged hard at the silk of her rectangular banner, the material cracking loudly in the wind. A scurry of white dust – almost too powdery to be snow – blew into her face. Under velvet and steel, her warm flesh shivered at the sudden chill.

"Son of a bitch. Welcome to Dijon . . ."

It got a laugh, as she knew it would. Only Florian's face remained serious. Despite reddening cheeks and nose, the tall woman spoke with gravitas:

"It's been dark over Christendom for five months. We can be sure of one thing while we're here. This weather isn't going to get any better."

The effect of her words was immediately visible on the faces of the men around her. Ash contemplated some jovial or profane remark, caught sight of Thomas Rochester's superstitious scowl, and changed her mind.

"You keep one thing in mind," she said, loudly enough to be heard over the gusting wind. "That's one fuck of a big army out there. Soldiers, engines, guns; you name it. But we've still got one thing they haven't."

Evidently regretting her unguarded remark, Florian provided the required question. "*What* have we got that they haven't?"

"A commander who isn't cracking up." Ash cast another glance up at the heavy bellies of the clouds, aware of the men-at-arms listening. "I saw her last night, Florian. Trust me. The woman's going completely bug-fuck."

III

The banner and escort moved forward, under the arch of the tower's guard-wall.

"Sorry," Floria del Guiz murmured. "That was stupid of me."

Ash kept her tone equally low. "Let's deal with current problems. We're in here now. Now we worry about what happens next! You're Burgundian – what's this 'siege council' likely to be?"

The woman frowned. "I don't know. He didn't mention the Duke?"

"No. But no one except Duke Charles will be giving orders for the defence." Ash huddled her cloak around her as they strode towards the tower entrance. "Unless he's *not* here. Maybe I'm wrong. Maybe he did die at Auxonne, and they're keeping it quiet. *Shit* . . . Florian, go talk to the physicians."

The tall woman nodded, said breathlessly: "If they'll let me."

"You try it while I go to this 'council'. We haven't got much time. C'mon."

Over the arched main gate of the tower, a painted heraldry plaque bore the arms of an obscure Burgundian noble – obscure enough not to be here, Ash thought. Or maybe his household are up north, besieged in Ghent or Bruges?

This situation is looking stickier by the minute.

Loping from the courtyard up the steps to the first floor, she met Angelotti, Geraint ab Morgan and Euen Huw at the keep door.

"We got everybody?" she questioned sharply. "Everybody inside, last night?"

"Yes, boss," Geraint nodded breathlessly.

"Baggage train as well?"

"All of them."

"Casualties? John Price's lot?"

Antonio Angelotti said, "We're picking Price up tonight, after sunset. We have no one lost that we know of."

"Fucking hell, I don't believe it!" Ash looked to Euen Huw. "Robert's lot put in an attack, too, didn't they? They all get back?"

"Been checking 'em on the roll, boss, haven't I? The attack force is here."

"And Anselm?"

"He was leading it." Euen's unshaven face creased in a grin. "He's upstairs, boss."

"Okay, let's go. I've got to be at this damn 'siege council' in half an hour."

The inside of the keep was darker than the morning outside, but less chill. She nodded a brief greeting to the startled guards, loping with her officers up the steps as her sight adjusted to the lanterns. Rough grey masonry and brick lined the stairwell, bleakly strong. Walls fifteen or twenty feet thick, she gauged. Old, solid, undecorated, unsubtle.

Behind her, she heard bill-shafts thumped against the flagstones; someone bawling "Ash!" as loudly as they called it on a field of battle.

Guards pulled leather hangings back at the second floor entrance. She had one moment to take it all in: nothing but one hall, wooden-floored, as wide as the keep itself, stinking of humanity. Men and women crowded it, wall to wall.

She rapidly identified faces – troops she has brought from Carthage – and saw no immediately apparent absences. There are men missing – casualties of Auxonne, but Rochester has warned her about them; and inevitably there will be some from the attrition of the siege.

Nine dead at Carthage, a score of deserters on the way here; with what we've got in Dijon, are we four hundred, four-fifty strong? I'll call a muster.

"*Ash!*" Baggage-train officers not seen for months – bowyer, tailor, falconer, Master of Horse – jumped to their feet.

Washerwomen hugged each other, talking; children scrambled about; two or three couples were industriously having sex. The floor was hidden under their new heaps of baggage rolls, wicker baskets, mail shirts in rusted heaps, bills propped up against the stark walls. Wet clothes hung from makeshift lines, steaming dry after immersion in the Suzon river. A fire smoked in the hearth. As, one by one, lance by lance, they saw the banner at the doorway, saw *her*, men and women scrambled to their feet, the sound of a ragged cheer battering back off the stone walls:

"Ash! *Ash!* ASH!"

"Okay, *pack it in!*"

A brace of mastiffs ran across the hall, splaying plates, cups and costrels aside in their enthusiasm.

"Bonniau! Brifault! Down!" Ash neatly grabbed their studded collars, forcing the mastiffs down. They wriggled at her feet, growling happily, smelling of dog.

Despite the lanterns, and the light from the arrow-slit windows, it was a second before she saw Robert Anselm stomping across the cluttered floor towards her. She was at the centre of a crowd in seconds: Anselm shouldered through them without effort.

"Green fucking Christ up a Tree!" he snarled.

Ash snapped her fingers, quieting the mastiffs.

Three months – or hunger – had put lines in his face. Other than that, he was no different. His hose were torn at the knee, and his demi-gown had half its lead buttons ripped off; there was the glint of a mail standard at his throat. Stubble blackened his cheeks. His shaven head shone with sweat, despite the chill morning. She met his dark gaze.

If he's going to challenge my authority, now's the time. It's been his company for three months; I've been dead.

"Fucking hell, woman!"

At his tone, at his expression, she couldn't help but laugh.

"You wouldn't like to try that again, would you, Roberto?"

Euen Huw had his hand over his mouth; some of the others were openly grinning.

"Fucking hell, *Captain Ash*." Robert Anselm shook his head, bear-like, and for a second she did not know whether he was about to yell at her, attempt to hit her, or laugh. He reached out. His strong hands gripped her shoulders painfully hard. "Christ, girl, you took your time! Just like a bloody woman. Always late!"

"Too right!" Ash, when the gale of laughter died down, added, "Sorry, I dragged it out as long as I could – I hoped the war'd be over before we got back here!"

"Damn right!" one of the archers yelled.

"We've been waiting three months." The big man looked down at her with a familiar, amazed amusement. Robert Anselm, battered and broad-shouldered; the familiar rasp of his *rosbif* accent unbelievably welcome. "You're getting a reputation. 'Ash always comes back.'"

"I like it. Let's try and keep it that way," Ash said sardonically. She looked at him, at the men around him, was aware of no friction yet between those who had gone to Carthage and those who had stayed in Dijon. "Find me one of the clerks. I need to write some retrospective commissions of array – Euen Huw and Thomas Rochester to be made sub-captains; Angelotti in overall charge of all missile troops as well as guns, Rostovnaya and Katherine as his subordinates to take over the crossbows and longbows."

There was a murmur of pleasure and approval. She kept her face bland when Geraint ab Morgan looked at her.

"Geraint, I want you to take over as head of the provosts. I need a man I can trust to keep discipline in the camp."

Morgan's face flushed with pride. "I'll do that, boss, don't you worry!"

I won't worry – not with you out of the combat line. Let's keep you and your doubts where they can't do any damage – and see if you can learn something about discipline while you're enforcing it . . .

"Robert, you'll have your own recommendations for promotions with the guys here," she added, "consider them okayed. Now we get our asses in gear, the city council want to talk to me, and I want an officer meeting before we go, Robert, what's that?"

She finished, breathless, staring at a horse.

Snickers sounded from the men-at-arms; she could feel them grinning without looking at them. The ones that grinned were mainly the troops who had stayed in Dijon.

"It's a horse," Robert Anselm said unnecessarily.

"I can *see* it's a fucking—" Ash took a quick glance under the beast, where it stood by one wall, head contentedly down in a feed-bag. "—a mare. What's it doing *here*?"

Robert Anselm lifted bland brows. A couple of the resident lance-leaders chuckled.

Ash picked her way between people's kit, across the dormitory floor, to the straw-strewn area liberally dotted with horse-dung that housed the large chestnut mare. The beast flickered a dark eye at her. "I'm not even going to ask how you persuaded it up the stairs . . ."

"Blindfolded," Anselm answered, striding up beside her. "We picked her up in the early hours of this morning."

"Robert – where from?"

"The Visigoth horse lines." The big man kept a straight face. "No one wanted her at the time. Even with this."

At his signal, a billman and a groom unfolded between them a filthy length of cloth. Horse caparisons, she saw. With the Brazen Head livery still visible through the filth.

"Great Boar! That's the Faris's horse!"

"Is it? Well, well. Who'd have guessed?" Anselm smiled down at her. "Welcome home."

Their pleasure was noisy, and extensive; and she gave way to it wholeheartedly. She slapped Robert Anselm on the arm. "Everything they ever said about mercenaries is true! We're nothing but a bunch of horse-thieves!"

"Takes talent to be a good horse-thief," Euen Huw remarked professionally, and flushed. "Not that I'd know, see."

"Perish the thought . . ." Ash did not approach the mare too closely, reading *war-horse* in her conformation. "Where's Digorie Paston?"

"Here, ma'am."

As the clerk pushed his way to the front of the men, she said, "Digorie, write me a message. To the Faris. Have a herald take it down to the Visigoth camp. 'Chestnut mare, thirteen hands, Barb blood, livery supplied – will exchange for one harness, Milanese plate, complete; and my bloody best sword!'"

A roar.

"I'll take it!" Rickard emerged from the press of men, flushed.

"Yeah, okay, you and Digorie, but I'll need you for the council first. Take a parley flag. Don't be cheeky, and wear a clean livery. She'll be expecting a message from me—" Ash stopped, grinned cynically, and added: "—just not the one you're taking her. Meanwhile . . ."

She lifted her head, looking at her company.

"Food," she announced, pointedly.

Within a few minutes, sitting on someone's wicker rucksack, she was tearing dark bread apart with her teeth, greeting men and women not seen for twelve weeks, alert to any signs that they might now be two different companies. They sat or knelt around her, on the floor; the hall full to the point that the window embrasures were crowded with sitting men, swapping stories at full volume.

"Is the Earl still out there?" Robert Anselm asked, squatting beside her.

He smelled of wood-smoke condensed in confined quarters, eye-wateringly strong. Ash grinned at him through a mouthful of bread. "Oxford's not in Burgundy as far as I know."

Anselm's jerk of the head took in all the company occupying the hall. "If it wasn't for him, we wouldn't be here. He made it a retreat, not a rout. Four days back from Auxonne, all the Burgundian leaders dead or wounded, Oxford holding everybody together, step by step by step."

"With the rag-heads snapping at your ass all the way?"

"Yeah. If we hadn't held together as fighting units, they'd have wiped out the rest of the Burgundian army right there." Anselm rubbed his hands together, and reached out for some of the bread. Through it, thickly, he added, "If not for de Vere, there wouldn't be a siege going on here. All of south Burgundy would be overrun."

"The man's a soldier." Ash, aware that they were being listened to, said carefully, "As far as I know, and if he's been lucky, my lord of Oxford is currently in the court of the Sultan at Constantinople."

Anselm sprayed wet crumbs. "He's *what*?"

Over a general murmur, Ash said, "Don't bust your points. If Burgundy is weakening, now's a good time for the Turks to hit the Visigoths. Before they get too strong. Make the rag-heads fight a war on two fronts."

"Make them the jam in the shit sandwich."

"Robert Anselm, you have a real way with words . . ."

His brow furrowed. "How much chance of my lord Oxford getting Turkish help?"

"God in His mercy knows, Robert. I don't." Ash made a rapid change of subject, jerking her thumb at the nearest window and the greying sky. She said briskly, "I see there's a tilt-yard down the end there. Some of the lads could do with getting up to speed on weapons practice. After that hike, I'd like to give them a day or two training before we put them into the field."

Robert Anselm shook his head. "Boss, you didn't see Auxonne."

"Not the end of it, no," Ash remarked dryly. "What's your point, Captain?"

"As far as casualties are concerned, Auxonne was Agincourt and the Burgundians went down like the French."[7]

Blankly amazed, Ash said, "Fuck me."

"*I'd* be out with the Goths," Anselm said grimly, "if I didn't know what treatment the Lion Azure can expect. We got about a tenth left of the Duke's army – between two and a half, three thousand men. And the city militia, for what they're worth – I give 'em this: on their home ground, they're determined. And we got an entire city wall to defend."

Ash looked at him in silence.

"You brought back two hundred fighting men," Robert Anselm said. "Girl, you don't know how much of a difference two hundred men can make right now."

Ash raised silver brows. "Man, I *thought* I was popular! So that's why this 'siege council' wants to talk to me."

"That and the fact that 'Carthage fell down'," Anselm completed her thought.

Ash nodded, consideringly, and looked at the men around her.

"Robert, I don't know how much Angelotti and Geraint have told you—"

"These new demon-machines in the south?"

Warmed by his quickness, and by the lack of any alteration in the way he spoke to her, Ash nodded and moved closer to the hearth. There was a scurry of men-at-arms moving their kit out of the way; the escort sitting down on the floorboards a yard or two off, giving at least an illusion of privacy. Ash sat down on a joint stool, resting her elbows on her knees, and letting her cloak fall open to the fire's warmth.

"Sit down, Robert. There are things you need to hear from me."

He squatted beside her. "Are we staying?"

It was blunt.

---

[7] At the Battle of Agincourt (1421) an English force of perhaps 6,000 men (five-sixths of whom were archers) defeated upwards of 25,000 French cavalry and foot, wiping out the heart of the French nobility for a generation. Henry V's English army is reported as suffering 'a few hundred' casualties; the French had 6,000 dead and many more captured for ransom.

"You came back for us," Anselm elaborated. "What's the options now, girl? Do we stick with this siege? Or try to negotiate a way out past the Visigoth lines?"

"You saw what food we brought in, Robert. Fuck-all. It took a *lot* longer getting here than I'd bargained for . . . We'd have to negotiate with the Visigoths themselves for supplies, for a forced march. I know the Faris is anxious for a quick end to the siege. As for leaving here . . ." Ash turned her gaze away from the burning wood's scarlet buttresses, on the hearth. She looked at Robert Anselm's sweating face.

"Robert, there's stuff you need to know. About the 'demon-machines', yes; and the Stone Golem. About my sister, the Faris – and why she's so damn determined to keep this crusade here in Burgundy."

Distant in her memory, her own voice asking a question comes to her: *why Burgundy?*

She reached out; touched Robert Anselm's dirty sleeve. "And about Godfrey Maximillian."

Anselm rubbed both bare hands back over his scalp; she heard stubble rasp. "Florian told me. He's dead."

Aware suddenly of the three-month hiatus between them – aware that she may not know, yet, how Robert Anselm has changed, three months in command of his own men – Ash nodded, slowly.

I could wait. Leave it; tell him later.

We're either one company, or we're not. I either trust him, or I don't. I have to risk it.

"Godfrey's dead," she said, "but I've heard his voice, Roberto. Exactly the way I've always heard the Lion – the *machina rei militaris*. And – so has the Faris."

Some fifteen minutes later, Ash moved back into the main body of the hall.

To Baldina, Henri Brant, and a woman called Hildegarde, a sutler who appeared to have stepped into Wat Rodway's place in his absence from Dijon, she said, "How are we off for supplies, here?"

"I've shown Henri the cellars, boss." Hildegarde's red face creased. "Town supplies aren't good."

"They're not? I thought they'd have a year's supplies put by – they've had sieges here before."

Henri Brant said sardonically, "They had all of the Duke's standing army billeted here for weeks before Auxonne. I've been checking – it's bloodmonth, and they've had fuck-all to slaughter![8] They ate the place all but bare, boss."

Hildegarde put in, "But we won't need to worry, will we? Not now the Goths are beaten."

"Beaten?" Ash exclaimed.

The woman shrugged, a movement which strained the laces of her bodice. "Only a matter of time, my dear, isn't it? With their demon-city fallen in bits about their ears. What's their army to do? They'll lift the siege before solstice."

[8] During November – Anglo-Saxon 'blodmonath' – it was the usual practice to slaughter all animals except the breeding stock for meat, to enable communities to survive through the winter.

By the nods of agreement around her, Hildegarde was not the only one of that opinion. Ash caught Floria's eye, where the surgeon sat with her long legs sprawled out on the floor – and a rapidly emptying wine jug beside her.

"There's still a government in Carthage," Floria pointed out. "That army out there haven't surrendered!"

"Never argue with morale," Ash murmured. "No – never argue with *high* morale."

"Why am I surrounded by idiots?" Florian remarked, rhetorically.

"*Dottore*, you should consider that thought very carefully." Angelotti chuckled, where he sat between Geraint and Euen Huw. "As the *rosbifs* have it, 'like calls to like'!"

The heat of the hall began at last to penetrate. Ash put her hands up and slid her hood back, stripped her gauntlets and helmet off, and looked up to find Robert Anselm and a whole lot of the garrison troops staring at her, suddenly silent.

She became aware again of her roughly cropped short hair. Aware that the river-fall of shining glory is gone, that she is only a leggy, dirty, strong woman with her hair cropped as close as a slave's, shorter than most of the men's. That the one in armour and glory, now, is the Faris.

"At least now you can tell me and the Visigoth bitch apart," she remarked dryly, into the silence.

Robert Anselm said, "We always could. You're the ugly one."

There was a split second of belly-chilling silence, in which the men around her worked out firstly that only Anselm could have said it, and secondly that his brutal grin was being answered by one of Ash's own.

"Hey," she said. "I had to get scars before *I* could frighten children."

Anselm's grin widened. "Some of us do it with natural talent."

"Yeah." She threw a gauntlet at him: he snagged it out of the air. "Robert, I don't know if you frighten the enemy, but you scare the shit out of me . . ."

There was a glow in the room, nothing material, that came from the garrison's appreciation of the banter; came with their realisation that Anselm would not challenge her for the company; came with her arrival beyond hope out of the unknown sunless south. Ash basked in it, for a moment. She took a look around, at the lances eating together, deep in exchange of stories, catching up on old quarrels and gossip.

Okay, she thought. No time like the present.

"You guys better listen up." She raised her voice, addressing the room generally. "Because I'm going to tell you why you'll be better off without me."

It got their attention, as she thought it might. Talk died down. Men and women looked at their lance-mates, and moved closer, to be able to hear. A baggage-cart child said something which made her friend giggle. Ash let the hall become silent.

"Your lance-leaders and officers will bring you up to speed on this," she said. "You guys hold a company meeting, while I'm at this siege-council. The main thing you need to know is, I saw the Faris last night—"

"And got out again?" one of Mowlett's archers surprised himself into saying out loud. Ash grinned at the man.

"And got out again. Hell, she even gave me an escort, so I wouldn't get lost on the way . . ."

"What does she want?" Geraint ab Morgan demanded; drowned out by other questions.

"What do you mean, better off without you?" Robert Anselm demanded bluntly over the hubbub. "The company needs you in command!"

There was a murmur, expressions of agreement on most of the faces she could see; and that startled her, slightly. *They've done without me for three months. I know damn well some of them will be thinking exactly that, right now. Won't they?*

"Okay." Ash moved forward, to be seen by them all. "Do we stay in Dijon, do we look for a contract in Burgundy? If not, if there are any supplies left here, we *might* manage a forced march east."

But not if the Burgundians know we're going to ransack the place and go . . . and they must at least be thinking that's a possibility.

"We *might* negotiate a way out past the rag-heads. We *might* give them the city." A quick, weighing glance: *have any of them developed a loyalty for what they've been defending?* "Okay. Over the next few hours, I want you guys thinking about this. There's a chance the Visigoths might let you guys march out anyway; it would weaken the defence here. But this is what you should bear in mind – as far as the Faris and House Leofric are concerned, they want *me*. Me, personally. Not you guys, not the Lion. Me."

Euen Huw said something in Thomas Rochester's ear that she did not catch. The two Tydder boys, at the back, seemed to be explaining something in confused excitement to garrison lance-mates. Blanche and Baldina, mother and daughter faces all but identical now under dyed yellow hair, looked identically bemused.

"Why'd they want you?" Baldina shouted.

"Okay, we'll take it from the top." Ash brushed crumbs off the front of her demi-gown. "If it's been long enough since you came through the sally-port for rumours to get out among the citizens, then it's more than long enough for rumours to get round the company, I know that!"

She raised her voice, over the noise: "These are facts. The old King-Caliph Theodoric died. They've got a new one – he's crap, but they've got one. That's King-Caliph Gelimer. The city of Carthage was flattened by an earthquake. But, sadly, as far as I can tell from the Faris's camp, Gelimer survived, and there's still a functioning government."

Euen Huw, in deep Welsh gloom, remarked, "Oh *shit*," and then narrowed his black eyes in surprise as half the company burst out laughing.

One of the younger garrison crossbowmen thumped his fist on the floor. "Get us a contract with the attackers, boss! That's safer. Fight *with* the Visigoths."

A woman beside him, in archer's gear, muttered in English: "I heard rumours they'd pay us twice as much as they're paying Cola de Monforte if we go over. One of van Mander's lads got word back to me last week."

Before Ash could comment, one of the sergeants leaned over the woman's shoulder: a hatchet-faced Italian, Giovanni Petro.

"Sure they might sign us up for twice the money," he rasped, "and who do you think would get to walk up and mine the walls? Or bring a siege tower up to the gate? Or go through the first breach? There's a lot of shit jobs in a siege, and we'd get them all. We'd never live to collect."

Pieter Tyrrell said flatly, "I don't want a contract, after Basle. Not after they broke the *condotta*."

There were many heads nodding in agreement. A babble of suggestions, contradictions, and complaints broke out. Ash let it go on for a minute or so, then raised her hands for quiet.

"Whether you could sign up with them and survive it or not – and you're tough motherfuckers, I still think it's your best chance – the Visigoths want *me*," she repeated. "That's why they sent a snatch-squad in at Auxonne. That's why the scientist-magus Leofric tried to take me apart in Carthage. And I do mean 'take me apart' – maybe he's been learning from our surgeon!"

She took the opportunity of the unsubtle joke to check on Floria. The woman raised her wine jug, acknowledging the subdued rumble. Ash saw no hint in her expression of any loyalty to the country of her birth. *Fuck knows it was hard enough for her last time we were here – but she can't start drinking again because of that.*

"Why don't they want you alive, boss?" Jean Bertran, one of the armourers, yelled from the back. She lifted a hand, acknowledging him; soot-blackened, unchanged in her absence. He shouted across, "Two's better than one, right? And you hear their old machine too!"

Another man-at-arms who had stayed with the garrison stood, hauling up his drooping hose. "Yeah, boss, if you're another Faris, and you hear the Stone Golem too, why won't she employ us? Fuck, the rag-heads would flatten everybody, then!"

Ash, head tilted slightly sideways, eyed the footman. "You know, next time I'm going to have feudal levies, not bloody mercenaries, then I can just tell them what to do without all these fucking questions. Listen up, dickheads! I'll say it again. House Leofric and the King-Caliph don't give a fart in a thunderstorm about the company of the Lion. If you guys decide to get out of here – maybe go look for the Turk, maybe go north – then you'll get no more trouble than you ever do. If I'm with you, we're the prize target. *Without me, you can leave Dijon.*"

"We can take 'em! Fuck the rag-heads!" Simon Tydder yelled, to general approval.

"How about a bit less morale and a bit more intelligence?" Ash's hands dropped to her side. "Now fucking listen. This isn't war. No – shut up! Right. This isn't human war."

The hall hushed.

"There are other powers in the world besides men. God gives His miracles to those who believe in Him. And the devil gives power to his own."

Into an almost total silence, Ash went on:

"Those of you who were with me at Carthage saw it. The Visigoths won't admit it, but their empire is founded on demons. We've seen them. Stone demons, stone engines, wild machines in the desert. *They* put the sun out, not the *amirs*."

Now the silence became total. The better part of three hundred men and women of the baggage train; forty lances of fighting men who will pass this word on to those of the Lion Azure out on guard duty or elsewhere; the children and the mastiffs – all still, and watching her face.

"*They're* spreading this darkness. Not the Visigoths – it's the Wild Machines who tell the King-Caliph and his Faris what to do. They speak to her through the Stone Golem. I hear them. *She* hears them. *She* knows the Stone Golem's possessed by demons. And she's scared!"

Richard Faversham got to his feet. "These Wild Machines killed Father Maximillian!"

"No, that was an earthquake," Floria called out.

"Doctor; priest!"

A sudden, private shudder threatens to demolish this public argument: *Godfrey*! she thinks; aware of sweat cold now against her skin.

"*Later.* Now listen up! I know you guys don't give a shit about demons. You'd scare the ass off demons, anyway!"

A cheer.

"But the demons—" Ash put her fists on her hips. "—the demons are only after *me*. Maybe the demons want another Faris. But if they do—" A shrug. "It isn't to lead their army! As far as they're concerned, I'm a loose cannon. I'm a Faris they don't control. So House Leofric wants me dead, the King-Caliph wants me dead, the demon Wild Machines want me dead." Her mouth moved into a grin, lopsided with private emotion. "I don't kill so easy. You know that."

"Fucking right, boss!"

"But they won't sign a *condotta* with *me*. I'm giving you guys – advice, let's say. Take Robert Anselm as your commander. Sell Dijon to the Goths. Break out and head for Dalmatia. Take Visigoth money, rob this city of supplies if you have to, and head for the Turks."

It is cold advice, standing here in this beleaguered city which has held out for three long, bitter months. Advice that the *machina rei militaris* might have given her, if she could have asked it.

"The Sultan isn't going to see the Visigoth Empire take over Christendom without doing something about it. You could get a *condotta* with him—"

Over the great confusion of noise, shouting, men springing to their feet, sergeants trying to restore order, Robert Anselm got to his feet.

"I won't take the command! You're our commander!"

"Never mind the fucking heroics!" Ash shouted, roughly. "Never mind the fucking company flag and loyalty. *Think about this.* Do you really want a captain who the Visigoths and their demons are determined to kill? Because if you do, we're stuck in here!"

"Screw the fucking rag-heads!" Euen Huw, also on his feet, punched the air with his fist.

Ludmilla Rostovnaya yelled, "Nah, we want to fight with you, boss!"

A wall of sound hit Ash: it was a second before she realised it was agreement.

"Ash wins battles!" Pieter Tyrrell shouted.

"Ash gets us *out* of the shit!" bellowed Geraint ab Morgan. "Got us back from fucking Carthage, didn't you, boss?"

"*This isn't your fight!*" She paced, nearing the window embrasure. The weak sunlight of a clouded day touched her, showing clearly a woman in stained and muddy brigandine and hose, a dagger at her belt, her face white with exhaustion. Nothing about her that is fire except her eyes.

Trying to guess at the mood of the meeting, the necessity of reducing four or five hundred interior lives, complicated souls, to names on a muster-roll and a gestalt mood: this bewilders her, sometimes. She stared around at faces. Those she would have automatically picked out before to be trouble-makers and authority-grabbers – Geraint ab Morgan, Wat Rodway – did not avoid her eye. Both men, and others like them, watched her with a raw loyalty that frightened her.

Part of it's that no one wants to be boss right now, and have to take these decisions. They're afraid they might lose if I'm not in charge – and that's not reason: war doesn't depend much on rational thought.

But that's still only part of it.

"For Christ's sake," Ash said, voice rough. "You don't know what you're getting into."

"A *fortunate* commander is worth much," Antonio Angelotti remarked, as if it were a proverb.

Ludmilla Rostovnaya stood up, facing Ash.

"Look, boss," the raw-featured Rus woman said reasonably. "We don't give a fuck whose fight it is. I never fought for any lord or country. I keep my eye on my lance-mates' backs, and they watch mine. You're a fucking awkward boss sometimes, but you get us through. You got us out of Basle. And Carthage. You'll get us out of here. So we'll stick with you." A dazzling, gap-toothed smile towards the shaven-headed soldier beside Ash: "No offence, Captain Anselm!"

"None taken," Anselm rumbled, confidently amused.

Jolted, Ash demanded, "What do you mean, 'awkward'?"

"You spend half your time playing up to the local nobs." Ludmilla shrugged. "Like with German Emperor Frederick? All this social climbing shit? I was *embarrassed*, boss. But we kicked ass at Neuss anyway."

Thomas Rochester unexpectedly said, "And I've covered more miles as your escort than I ever did in the entire Yorkist war! Can't you ever stay in one place on the fucking battlefield, boss?"

"Yeah, then the runners would know where to find you!" a sergeant of archers called.

"*Excuse* me—" Ash began a protest.

"And you don't get drunk half often enough!" Wat Rodway called. Baldina from the wagons added, "Not with us, anyway!"

Ash, trying to press home the seriousness of it, began to laugh. "Are you *quite* finished?"

"Not yet, madonna, there's plenty more. The gunners haven't even started."

"Thank you, Master Angelotti!"

The hall filled with a buzz of friendly, foul-mouthed harassment. Ash put her fingers through her cropped hair, at a loss. Opening her mouth, and not sure what she was going to say as she did, she was interrupted.

"Boss . . ."

A raw voice. She turned around, trying to locate the man who had spoken; found Floria del Guiz on her feet, grabbing at the arm of a man on crutches.

Black bandages looped his face, covering the cauterised sockets of his eyes. Above them, white scars gave way to wisps of white hair. He snarled something at the surgeon, hitching his crutches under his armpits, tilting his head up, listening, sightlessly staring off into a corner of the roof.

"Carracci," Ash began.

"Let me speak," the ex-Sergeant of Bill cut in, his head turning approximately to face her.

Ash nodded; then realised. She said aloud, "What is it, Carracci?"

"Just this." His blind head weaved a little, as if he were trying to face all of the company there, or as if he wanted to be clearly seen by them. "You didn't have to bring me back from Carthage. I'll never be any use again. I'm not the only one you brought back, boss. That's all."

A different quality of silence fell. Ash reached out, gently closing her hand over his forearm, where corded over-developed muscles trembled with the tension of balancing upright. There were people nodding heads all through the hall, a few men shifting uncomfortably or going back to their rations, but most murmuring quiet agreement. A voice said, "Right on, Carracci."

"We don't leave our own," Robert Anselm said. "Works both ways. No more shit, girl."

She turned her head sharply to one side, momentarily not in control of her expression.

There is no way to escape this: not if you are asking men to pick up swords and axes and walk out into wet fields, and end up face down in the mud; no way *not* to create that fierce mixture of fear and affection that – she admits to herself – will lead them to this refusal, nine times out of ten.

Could've been the tenth time, she thought, somewhere between black humour and appalled resignation. *I'd better be able to handle this now I've got it.*

A clatter of feet and weapons at the stair broke the silence. Still holding Carracci's arm, Ash yelled across, "What is it?"

A harassed company guard entered the hall, behind him a dozen or so men in armour and Burgundian liveries. She saw in an automatic glance that their swords were in their sheaths; that the leader carried a white baton.

"Captain Ash," their leader called across the hall. "My lord Olivier de la Marche has sent us. He wishes you to be suitably escorted to the Viscount-Mayor's siege council. It is my honour to ask, will you come with us now?"

"You go," Ash said instantly to Robert Anselm. "Assuming I'm right, and he's here, I've got more important things to do – if you're all set on staying here, I need to talk to the Duke."

"To Charles?" Anselm lowered his voice. "They won't let you in, girl."

"Why not?"

"You don't know yet? Fuck. I should have told you." Anselm hitched up the belt that held his purse and bollock dagger, settling it under his beer-belly. His gaze on the Burgundian men, he said, "You know Duke Charles was wounded at Auxonne? Yeah? That was three months ago. They tell us he still hasn't recovered enough to leave his bed."

IV

One of the aides standing beside the Burgundian with the white rod called across impatiently, "Are you *deaf*, woman? The council's *waiting*!"

Jolted, she turned her head: found herself among men-at-arms swearing, straightening their shoulders, beginning to move. She made the abrupt mental gear-change necessary to realise that violence is about to happen – especially now; especially after Carracci – and nodded at Geraint, watching as he and his provosts brought the lances to order.

"Son of a bitch!" Robert Anselm muttered, from his tone as disoriented as she was.

The leader of the Burgundian officers – Jussey? Jonvelle? – said something sharply condemnatory in French to his companion. He shrugged a very informal half-apology towards Ash. His expression, as far as Ash could decipher it in the dim, high-roofed hall, was embarrassed. His gaze went up and down her, head to foot.

"He's got a point," Ash said grimly.

The night-before-last's sodden rain still blackened her brigandine's blue velvet and buff straps. She glanced down at the high boots pointed to her doublet skirts, and the mud drying black and crusted on them. One moment of feeling naked without cuisses and greaves – without armour – then she realised, too, that the brass-headed studs on her brigandine were dull, and her sallet (where Rickard, blushing, picked it up) was glazed orange and brown with rust.

"Get me a sword," Ash said abruptly.

"*And* the rest . . ." Robert Anselm gave her one assessing glance, already signalling to one of his squires. The boy came back across the hall with his hands full of straps, scabbard, and sword.

"Arm me." Anselm, stripping off his demi-gown, stood with his arms outstretched, while his pages pointed and strapped leg armour and cuirass to his arming doublet. As if they weren't there, he stared around at the men-at-arms, and finally fixed on the master gunner. He showed his teeth. "*Tony!*"

Angelotti, kneeling by a bucket, lifted his head and threw a quantity of wet-gold hair back, spraying his own squires with dirty water. His face was a little cleaner, still showing traces of having come in through mud, rain, and freezing slush. He looked first at Anselm, then at the Burgundians, scowled, and muttered something mellifluous and filthy.

"Yeah, yeah. I *know* you. You got clean stuff in your pack, wrapped up dry. Right?" Robert Anselm kicked at the Italian gunner's kit with his sabatons, as his pages laced his arm-defences on to his obviously newly repaired arming doublet. "You're about her size. That demi-gown. The one you always wear when you're on the pull . . . You manage to bring that all the way back from North Africa?"

Ash covered her mouth with her hand, feeling a sudden grin under her palm. Angelotti knelt, unwrapped a pack of leather and waxed pelts, and stood up and turned, a garment across his arms.

A white silk damask demi-gown. Spotless. Furred at the high collar, skirts, and slit sleeves with the soft, multiple greys of wolf-fur.

"Can't 'ave boss going out there looking shite," Anselm said, giving the Burgundians a brawl-starting grin. "Now can we, Tony? Get the Lion a bad name."

Long minutes, while the Burgundian officers waited meekly: two pages brushing her boots, Rickard pointing and buttoning the spotless demi-gown on over her filthy brigandine and calling to a mate of his for the loan of a polished archer's sallet. He deftly twisted blue and yellow silk ribbon around the open-face helmet, and skewered a white plume into the holder.

The soft wolf-fur lining Angelotti's collar stroked her scarred cheek.

"Sword!" Anselm beckoned his squire forward. Ash automatically raised her arms for the squire to kneel at her side.

Anselm reached across and took the weapon from the boy, with a deliberate, expansive physicality that always brought him far more clearly into her mind than anything else.

He stepped forward and knelt on the flagstones in front of her, an armoured man now but for his helmet and gauntlets. He began to buckle the sword-belt and weapon on around her waist, over the shining demi-gown.

She dropped her hand down, encountering a hand-and-a-half grip: blue velvet bound with gold wire. She touched the flutes of a writhen brass pommel and cross; the metal polished to a deep, glimmering brightness.

"This is your best sword, Robert."

"I'll wear my other one." He snicked a buckle home, expertly threaded the tail of the belt through itself in a knot, and let the blue leather strap, studded with brass mullets, hang down over the pleated white damask skirts of her demi-gown. "You ain't at Neuss now, girl."

The memory of kneeling before the Holy Roman Emperor is sharp in her mind's eye. Silver hair rippling to her knees; young, scarred, beautiful; a woman in full Milanese plate shining so brilliantly in the sun that it hurts the eye, leaves dazzles on the vision – and says, as clearly as a shout: *This is what I earned as a mercenary captain, I'm good.*

They're going to look at me now and think: *she can't even afford plate armour.* Well, shit, I'm down to a helmet and gauntlets: that's *it*. Everything else – spare leg harness, borrowed cuirass – is lost, damaged beyond repair, or out there with the fucking Faris . . .

Is this going to be enough?

Ash reached out and took the borrowed sallet, prodding the padding for a better fit. She lifted her chin as Rickard tied the fastenings of a clean, dry livery jacket, and buckled the sallet's strap.

"Looks like I'm going to the council. Angelotti, Anselm; with me. Geraint, I want a complete muster-roll of the whole company before I get back. Okay: let's move it!"

A cluster of men sorted themselves out into a remarkably clean, if now unspectacularly dressed, Angelotti; a Thomas Rochester, equally rapidly cleaned up and wearing other people's kit; and his lance of twelve as escort with Ash's banner. Ash strode at their head, out of the shadow of the doorway, into the open air. The courtyard scurried with pigs and a few remaining hens, chased by screaming children; clanged with the noise of the armoury sheds that lined the inside of the tower's perimeter wall.

A *crack!* made her whole body startle – the invisible impact of a rock, not far off. Animals and children simultaneously froze for a second. Pale sun struck her face: her chest suddenly constricted, her breath coming shallow.

"Hitting up at the north-west gate again," Anselm rumbled, glancing automatically and uselessly at the sky, and reaching up to buckle on his sallet.

Beside him, Rickard flinched. Ash reached out to shake his shoulder companionably. Unexpectedly, she felt sweat cutting runnels in the dirt on her face. *What's wrong with me now? This is just the usual shit for a siege.* She made herself start to walk down the stone steps, towards the men and horses in the courtyard.

There was a brief moment of the confusion that she has been used to for over a decade; armoured men mounting into the saddles of war-horses: trained, restless stallions. As the Burgundians mounted up, Rickard led forward a mouse-coloured dun stallion with black points and tail visible under the caparisons.

"Borrow Orgueil,"[9] Anselm said. "I don't suppose you picked up any remounts on the way back from Carthage."

The dun's shining black eyes looked into Ash's face, dark nostrils flaring. Anselm's rough, sardonic tone demanded humour, or at least comradeship.

"Boss?"

"What?"

"Wrong time of the month for a stallion? We can find you a gelding."

"No. 'S okay, Roberto . . ."

Momentarily – reaching up to put a firm hand against the beast's soft muzzle; feel warm horse-breath on her bare, cold skin – she is stopped dead: incapacitated with loss.

Six months ago, she owned destrier, palfrey and riding horse. All gone, now. Iron-grey Godluc, wide-chested, bossy and protective. Lady's flaxen chestnut sweetness and greed. The Sod's dirty-water-grey colouring and foul temperament. For one second her heart hurts, thinking of the golden foal that Lady might have had, and The Sod's viciousness (nipping at her leg when least expected; nuzzling at her chest equally unexpectedly), all lost in the rout from Basle. And Godluc – *I swear*, she thought, eyes stinging, mouth twisting with black humour; *I swear he thought of me as a horse; some misbehaving mare!* – skewered and dead at Auxonne.

---

[9] 'Pride'. There is a certain knowing defiance about this name, pride being in the mediaeval mind a great sin – and one that goes before a fall.

Easier to grieve for horses than men? she wonders, remembering the dead buried on rocky, inhospitable Malta.

"We'll get you another war-horse," Anselm said, appearing at a loss when she did not speak. "Shouldn't have to lay out more than a couple of pounds. There's been enough dead knights won't need 'em any more."

"Jeez, Roberto, you're an ever-present trouble in time of help . . ."

The Englishman snorted. She cast an eye around at the armoured knights on their war-horses, the bright richness of rounded steel plate. Her own blue-and-gold liveries on the mounted archers shone out brilliant in the grey morning; men with open-faced steel helmets and mailed sleeves mounting up – she guessed – on some of the riding horses the garrison still maintained. Jutting bow-staves and her striped banner-pole pierced the air. A careful eye could have picked out rusted cuisses and poleyns, and boot-leather blackened and cracked by wet and cold.

". . . Let's go."

They rode in the wake of the Burgundian officers, out into a crowded street where cold air moved against her face. Her escort formed up around her. Dust blew, filling the air; and old ashes skirled across the cobbles, spooking two of the geldings. Groups of people standing talking on the corner moved back out of the way of the armed men. She laid the rein over to avoid a man hauling a hand-cart of rubble away from a collapsed shop. In the space of a hundred yards, she picked half a dozen constables out of the crowds.

Another heavy *crack!* and boom of something landing and exploding into fragments echoed through the morning air over Dijon. Orgueil fluffed a plume of breath into the chill air, and she felt him shift discontentedly under her. Another succession of sharp impacts sounded, to the north. The Burgundians rode on, with an unconsciously hunched posture – men used to shrinking, however pointlessly, away from what the sky might deliver to them.

"Shit, that's close!"

"Couple of streets. Sometimes they play silly buggers like this all day." Robert Anselm shrugged. "Limestone. Reckon they're quarrying rocks all the way down the Auxonne road by now. It's just harassment." Riding up to her side, he jerked his thumb at a church further on down the street. Ash saw it was a blackened shell. "When they're *serious*, they use Greek Fire."

"Shit."

"Too fucking right!"

"I've been up on the walls. They must have upwards of three hundred petriers[10] out there," Angelotti called, his voice thinning. Careful on the flagstones, he brought his brown gelding over closer on her other side. "Perhaps twenty-five trebuchets that I can see, madonna. They shelter their mangonels and ballistae with hides; difficult to count them. Perhaps another hundred engines – but truly bad weather will make at least their catapults unusable. But . . . they have golems."

Wryly, Ash said, "I thought they might."

Angelotti said, "But do we fight here, madonna?"

[10] Small siege-engines: stone-throwers that operate by winching a wooden beam down and using the tension as a spring to propel rocks.

641

Our options are narrowing all the time—

The Burgundian officers, picking up the pace, struck off diagonally down a narrower street; riding from the cover of one house to the next. Here there were fewer broken roofs and burned-out houses. Under the iron hooves of the horses, rubble strewing the cobbles made footing uncertain.

Deliberately not answering his question, Ash asked, "If you were their *magister ingeniator*,[11] Angeli, what would you be doing right now?"

"I would look to undermine the north wall, or break one of those two gates." The Italian's oval-lidded eyes narrowed, looking past her to study Anselm's reaction. "To weaken morale first, I would have had men up on the bluff, to draw me a map of what could be seen in the city; then I would concentrate my barrage on public targets. Markets, where people congregate. Churches. Guild halls. The ducal palace."

"Got it in one!" Anselm snorted.

The churning in her stomach, and the tightness in her chest, both increased. A man desperately nailing boards across his remaining windows paused as she passed, pulling off his hat, and then ducked into his doorway as another spray of rocks cracked and whined across the rooftops.

"Ah, *fuck* it!" Ash exclaimed. "Now I remember how much I *hate* bloody siege-engines. I like something I can get within axe-reach of!"

"No shit? I'll tell Raimon the Carpenter that." Robert Anselm: sardonic. At her inquiring look, he added, "Had to make someone Enguynnur,[12] with Tony here buggered off to Africa and likely dead."

Doubled-up commands aren't going to make anyone's life easy . . .

"Christus Viridianus!" Ash shook her head. "So much for 'safe inside Dijon'. We're sitting smack in the gold![13] Okay, brief me, before we get to this damn council – what's been happening, Roberto?"

"Okay. Debrief." Robert Anselm wiped his hand across his nose. There was a slight awkwardness about the movement that she guessed meant a wound taken during a Visigoth assault; knew he would not mention it himself.

"They bottled us up here after Auxonne. We could see the sky on fire, every night – burning towns, off in the boonies. First off they set up their engines and guns, gave us a major artillery barrage. Those big trebuchets? They had 'em lobbing dead bodies in, dead horses, our own casualties from Auxonne. That was when they set up the flame-throwers opposite the three gates, 'bout fifteen to a gate, covering the walls and river. We blew up the south bridge; they started mining in from the north."

"Didn't miss a trick." She blinked at the backs of the men and horses she followed, as they rode into a larger public square, where a slide of bricks blocked half the road. *I wish I couldn't picture everything he says.*

What's wrong with me? This stuff never bothers me!

"Oh, they done their best to fuck us, all right," Anselm said grimly. "Been bombarding us from the end of August, soon as they found they couldn't take

---

[11] 'Master Engineer': specifically, here, a military siege engineer.

[12] The 'Fraxinus' text uses this indiscriminately with both 'enginur' and 'enguigniur'; all mean 'engineer', in the sense of 'combat engineer'.

[13] Presumably a reference to the gold ring at the centre of targets used for archery.

the city straight off. They couldn't get no bombards and siege-engines over on the east of the Ouche river, ground's too broken, so they stuck their artillery north and west of the city. Ploughed up as much of the place as we thought was in their range."

He looked down, bringing his mount around a crater that gouged the flagstones. As they passed it, Ash saw the sandstone walls of a church were pocked with holes.

"This lot started shifting their people down into the south-east quarter of the city," he added. "For safety. Well, about the beginning of October, the Goths let loose with everything they had – on the south-east quarter. Stone shot. Greek Fire. Fucking golem war-machines – '*course* they were in range. They just wanted to give the civilians a chance to pack up tight in one area . . . The Burgundians lost a lot of troops too. Since then, it's been 'guess the target area, and where in the city do you want to sleep tonight?'"

"The company's tower looks sound."

"They've put the fighting men in places that'll stand bombardment." He looked across at her. "Then the human-wave assaults started on the walls. That's been hot. The rag-heads are losing men – and they don't *need* to. They've got two or three *fucking* big saps under way. Going for the north-west gate. Where you come in? Up there. You get down in the foundations of the gate-tower, and you can fucking *hear* them coming. They don't need to keep piling up the wall at us!"

"How long has this place got?"

Confronted with a direct question, Robert Anselm didn't answer. He looked at her with a slow smile. "By God, girl, you look different, but you don't sound it. Carthage 'asn't changed you that much."

"'Course not. Long way to go to get a haircut, that's all."

They exchanged glances.

Strong winds snapped the Lion Affronté, over her head. The group of men riding around her speeded their pace a little, unconsciously. She didn't counter it.

"How often *do* the Goths try and come over the walls?"

"Well, they ain't relying on hunger and disease to break this city. It's been fucking hot up at the north-west gate," Anselm admitted. He lifted a hand, scarred as a smith's or farmer's hands, to signal the banner-bearer to slow to a less panicky pace. "You spoke to their boss. The rag-heads want Dijon. Never mind Antwerp, Bruges, Ghent. I reckon they must want the Duke – if he don't die of his wounds, first. That means assaults. It's been every few days. Some nights. Fucking *stupid* siege tactics."

"Yeah. It is. But, looking out there, they must outnumber the Burgundians four or five to one . . ."

Searing cold air cut her face. Overhead, ragged clouds ran south on a high wind. A white façade – a guild hall? – was visible now, over the heads of the Burgundian escort. She didn't recognise the area from the summer. The group of riders straggled to a halt. Looking ahead, Ash saw the leader of the Burgundians in fluent discussion with some civilian at the foot of the guild hall steps.

"Strong roof over our heads would be nice," she murmured, quietening Orgueil. "Till some bugger drops a ton of rock on it, I suppose . . ."

The banner-bearer murmured, "Looks like we're moving, boss."

What had delayed them had evidently been some debate about ceremony: as they dismounted and entered the Viscount-Mayor's hall, a herald's clarion rang out under its painted, vaulted roof.

The nobles, merchants, and mayor of Dijon looked up from seats at a long, beech-wood table. The tapestried chamber filled with their voices. A flock of armed men and civilians sat, or stood. A few, Ash judged by the hennin headdresses lost in the crowd, must be female: merchant's wives, traders on their own accounts, minor nobility. She took note of the liveries on the armed men with them. Not all Burgundian households.

"Frenchmen? Germans?" she murmured.

"Noble refugees," Anselm said, with a wealth of cynicism.

"Who want to carry the war on against the Visigoths?"

"So they say."

In full armour, with Chamberlain-Counsellor Ternant beside him, Olivier de la Marche stood up from the chair of state. He looked, Ash thought, tired and dirty and not at all like the man who had commanded the Duke of Burgundy's army at Auxonne. She frowned.

"As the deputy of the Duke," Olivier de la Marche said without preamble, "I welcome the hero of Carthage into our company. Demoiselle-Captain Ash, we bid you and your men welcome. Welcome!"

De la Marche bowed, formally, to her.

"The—" Ash kept her face expressionless with an effort. *Hero of Carthage!* She returned the bow; awkward; as ever, not knowing whether a curtsey would have been better. "Thank you, my lord."

Seats towards at the head of the table were rapidly vacated. She sat down, muttering under her breath to her officers, "'Hero' of Carthage? 'Hero'!"

Robert Anselm's grim face looked twenty years younger as he snuffled back a laugh. "Don't ask *me*. God only knows what rumours have been spread here!"

"Inaccurate ones, madonna!" Angelotti said softly.

Ash finally grinned. "So. A hero, by accident. Well – that makes up for the dozens of utterly splendid things I've done that nobody ever noticed!" She sobered. "Trouble with being a hero is, people expect things of you. I don't think I do 'hero', guys."

Anselm punched her shoulder, briefly and very fast. "Girl, I don't think you have a choice!"

Thomas Rochester and the escort took up places behind them. Ash looked around, grateful for Angelotti's evidently blisteringly expensive demi-gown; seeing every reaction from contempt to awe on the faces down the table. She beamed, broadly, at the man across the table, with the Viscount-Mayor of Dijon's chain resting on his rich robes; a man bundled up in furs and velvets, who was glowering covertly at 'the hero of Carthage'.

"Yes, madonna," Angelotti said, before she could speak, "that is the man who would allow no merchant to give us credit, when we first arrived here from Basle and you were sick. The Viscount-Mayor, Richard Follo."

"Called us 'scruffy mercenaries', didn't he?" Ash beamed. "Which I doubt he repeated to John de Vere! Well, that's Rota Fortuna[14] for you . . ."

Ash looked around at the assembly of Burgundians and the foreign nobles present, those who had precedence sitting at the long table, those who had not crowding the room to the walls behind them. An air of aggressive desperation, familiar to her from other sieges, hung about them. What friction there might be between lords, burghers, the Viscount-Mayor, and the people of Dijon itself, she decided she would not concern herself with at the moment.

"We bid you welcome," de la Marche concluded, seating himself.

She caught his eye, thought, *Let's throw the cat in the fire, then!* and spoke. "My lord, it's taken me and my men more than two months to get here from Carthage. My intelligence isn't current or good. I need to know, on behalf of my company – how strong is this city, and how much Burgundian territory is still holding out against the Visigoths?"

"Our lands?" de la Marche rumbled. "The Duchy, Franche-Comté, the north; Lorraine is not certain—"

A thin-faced noble hammered his hand on the table, turning to Olivier de la Marche. "You *see*! Our Duke should consider. I have lands in Charolais. Where is his loyalty to our King? If you would only seek King Louis' protection—"

"—or call on the feudal ties he has with the Empire—"

Ash barely realised the second voice was speaking in German when the two Burgundian knights, almost in unison, finished: "And sign a peace with the King-Caliph!"

Anselm muttered, "Shit, why not? Everywhere else in Christendom has!"

The hundred or so men and women in the hall began to shout, in at least four different languages.

"*Silence!*"

De la Marche's full-throated shout – *you could hear that over cannon!* Ash reflected – banged off the roof-beams and brought a shuffling quiet to the council hall.

"Jesus, what a dog-fight!" Ash muttered. She realised she had been heard, and felt her face heat. Fear – of the army outside, of a twin, of all the incestuous south; of all the lack of answers there or here – made her bad-tempered. She shrugged at de la Marche. "I'll be frank. I wondered what Cola de Monforte and his boys were doing out there with the Visigoths. I'm starting to see why. Burgundy's coming apart at the seams, isn't it?"

Unexpectedly, the chamberlain-counsellor who sat beside de la Marche, Philippe Ternant, chuckled. "No, Demoiselle-Captain, no more than usual! These are family quarrels. They grow heated, when our father the Duke is out of the room."

Ash, seeing Ternant's watery blue eyes and age-spotted hands, weighed up his probable experience of Burgundian politics. She said politely, "As you say, messire," and flicked a glance at Robert Anselm. *I need to take decisions! I thought – if we got here – at least we'd have a breathing-space—*

---

[14] 'The Wheel of Fortune'.

"What is Burgundy?" de la Marche demanded, his weather-beaten face turning towards Ash. "Demoiselle-Captain, what are we? Here in the south, we're two Burgundies: both the Duchy and the County. Then the conquered province, Lorraine. All the northern lands: Hainault, Holland, Flanders . . .[15] What our Duke does not owe as a French fief to King Louis, he owes as an Imperial fief to the Emperor Frederick! Demoiselle, we speak French in the two Burgundies, Dutch and Flemish in Flanders, and Imperial German in Luxembourg! Only one thing holds us together – one man – Duke Charles. Without him, we would collapse again into a hundred quarrelling properties of other kingdoms."[16]

Philippe Ternant looked amused. "My lord, much as I bow to your military prowess, let me say that a single chancellor, chancery, and system of tax binds us equally—"

"And that would last *how* long, without Duke Charles?" Olivier de la Marche's hand came down flat on the wooden table, with a bang that startled all of the crowded room. "The Duke unifies us!"

A flicker of green cloth: Ash caught sight of an abbot, his face hidden from her in the crush of bodies further down the guild hall.

"We are the ancient German people of Burgundia," the abbot said, still invisible; "and we have been the Kingdom of Arles, when Christendom was divided into Neustria and Austrasia. We are older than the Valois Dukes."

His deep voice reminded her briefly of Godfrey Maximillian: she was unaware of the sharp crease that appeared in the flesh between her eyebrows.

"Names do not matter, my lord de la Marche. Here in the forests of the south, there in the cities of the north, we are one people. From Holland to Lake Geneva, *we are one*. Our lord the Duke is the embodiment of that, as his father was before him; but Burgundy will outlast Charles of Valois. Of that I am certain."

Into the hush, Ash found herself saying thoughtfully, "Not if someone doesn't do something about the Visigoth army out there!"

Faces turned towards her; white discs in the sunlight that now streamed in through the ancient stone windows.

"The Duke unites us." The Viscount-Mayor, Follo, spoke up. "And therefore, since he is here – the north will come south, and rescue us."

It will? Restraining a sudden, blind hope, Ash turned towards de la Marche. "What's the news from the north?"

"The last message spoke of fighting around Bruges; but that news was a month old when it arrived. The armies of the Lady Margaret may have won a victory by now."

"Will they come? Just for one town under siege?"

"Dijon is not merely 'one town under siege'," the chamberlain-counsellor

[15] At this time, at the height of its power, Burgundy consisted of the Duchy of Burgundy, the County of Burgundy (Franche-Comté), Flanders, Artois, Rethel, Nevers, Brabant, Limbourg, Hainault, Holland, Zeeland, Luxembourg, Guelders, and – briefly, in 1475 – the Duchy of Lorraine.

[16] This is, broadly speaking, what happened when Charles the Bold died in 1477, having failed to sire a male heir, or arrange the marriage of his only daughter and heir, Mary. Had Charles lived, his ambition to be a European monarch might well have succeeded.

Philippe Ternant said, looking at Ash. "You stand in the heart of Burgundy, here; in the duchy itself."

"My Duke," Olivier de la Marche said, "wrote, three years ago, that God has instituted and ordained princes to rule principalities and lordships so that the regions, provinces and peoples are joined together and organised in union, concord and loyal discipline.[17] Since the Duke is here – they will come."

About to ask *What strength are the forces in the north?*, Ash found herself interrupted.

Olivier de la Marche, briskly now, said, "Demoiselle-Captain. You and your men have more recently seen what lies beyond these walls."

"In Carthage?"

De la Marche's weather-beaten face twisted, as if with some pain. "In what you have seen south of Burgundy first, demoiselle. We know little of the lands outside our borders, these past two months. Except that there are refugees every day on the roads outside the city."

"Yes, messire." Ash got to her feet, and realised that was out of pure habit, to let them see that she was a woman wearing a sword, even if it was without armour and thus not a customary thing to do.[18] *I'm not used to being a hero of anywhere . . .*

"We came in through the French King's territories, under the Darkness," she began. "They say there that the dark extends north to the Loire – at least, they were saying that two or three weeks ago. We didn't see any fighting—" She grinned, toothily. "Not against the *Visigoths*, anyway. So I suppose the peace treaty is holding."

"Motherfuckers!" de la Marche spat, explosively. Some of the merchant princes looked startled at his language, but not, Ash thought, as if they disagreed with the sentiment. There was a rumble from the few refugee French knights present.

Ash shrugged. "That's the Universal Spider[19] for you."

"God rot him," de la Marche observed, in his battle-loud voice. Merchants and noblemen who would have winced at the champion's loudness in peace now looked, Ash thought, as if the big Burgundian were their last hope.

"God rot him, *and* German Frederick!" de la Marche finished.

She has a brief memory of some of these noble German and French refugees when they stood in the cathedral at Cologne, at her marriage to Fernando del Guiz: all of them in bright liveries, then, and with well-fed faces. Not now.

"Messire—"

Getting a second wind, de la Marche thumped the long table. "Why should their lands be spared, treacherous sons of bitches? Just because the grovelling little shits signed 'treaties' with these Visigoth bastards!"

"Not all of us are traitors!" A knight in Gothic armour sprang to his feet, crashing his plate gauntlet down on the table. "And at least *we* do not wish to continue to cringe behind these walls, Duke's man!"

---

[17] Charles the Bold, ordinance of Thionville, 1473.

[18] The practice of wearing a sword over 'civilian' clothing does not, in Western Europe, really begin until the sixteenth century. In 1476, a sword is normally only worn with armour or other war-gear. (The wearing of a knife, however, would be universal.)

[19] Louis XI of France.

De la Marche ignored him. "What else, Demoiselle-Captain?"

"Their lands aren't being 'spared' much of anything. Whoever wins this war – there's going to be major famine." Ash looked around the table, at jowled faces somewhat bitten by short rations.

What had been prosperous townships, on the rivers of southern Burgundy; what had been rich abbeys; all of these are in her memory, under weak autumn sunlight. Burnt-out, deserted.

"I don't know what stores are like here in Dijon. There's nothing going to come in to you, even if the Visigoth army didn't have this place sewn up tight. I've seen so many deserted farms and villages on the way north that I can't count them, messires. There aren't any people left. Cold's ruined the harvest. The fields are rotten. There are no cattle or swine left: they've been eaten. On the march, we saw babies left out, exposed. There isn't a surviving township between Dijon and the sea."

"This isn't war, this is obscenity!" one of the merchants snarled.

"It's bad war," Ash corrected him. "You don't wipe out what makes a land productive if you're trying to conquer it. There's nothing left for the winner. My lord, I'd guess your refugees out there are turning for Savoy, or southern France, or even the Cantons. But it's no better there – and they'll be under the Darkness. There's still sun over south Burgundy. But outside, it's already winter. Has been since Auxonne, as far as I can see. And it's staying that way."

"Winter like in the Rus lands."

Ash turned her head, recognising Ludmilla Rostovnaya's voice from where the crossbow-woman stood with Thomas Rochester. She signalled her to continue.

Ludmilla Rostovnaya's red hose and russet doublet were thick with candle-grease, under her cloak. She shifted from foot to foot, conscious of eyes on her, and spoke more to Ash than to the assembled nobles.

"Far north, the winter comes with ice," she said. "Great sheets of it, eight months of the year. There are men in my village who can remember Czar Peter's port[20] freezing one June, ships cracking like eggs. *That's* winter. That's what it's like at Marseilles, when we landed."

A priest at the far end of the table, between two Burgundian knights, spoke up. "You see, my lord de la Marche? This is what I have said. In France and the Germanies, Italy and eastern Iberia, they no longer see the sun – and yet he has not entirely forsaken us, here. Some of his heat must touch our earth, still. We are not yet Under the Penance."

Ash opened her mouth to say *Penance be damned, it's the Wild Machines!*, and shut it again. She looked to her officers. Robert Anselm, lips pushed together, shook his head.

Antonio Angelotti first glanced at her for permission, then spoke aloud. "Messires, I am a master gunner. I've fought in the lands Under the Penitence, with Lord-*Amir* Childeric. There was *warmth* there, then. As of a warm night. Not enough for seed, but still, not winter."

Ash nodded thanks to the crossbow-woman and the gunner.

---

[20] Some textual corruption here? If St Petersburg/Leningrad is intended (conceivably an addition by a later hand), Peter the Great did not found the city until 1703.

"Angelotti's right. I'll tell you what I saw, not two months ago, my lords – *it isn't warm in Carthage any more*. There's ice on the desert. Snow. And it was still getting colder when I left."

"Is it a greater Penance?" The priest – another abbot, by his pectoral Briar Cross – leaned forward. "Are they the more damned, now that they take their guidance from demons? Will this greater punishment spread with their conquests?"

De la Marche met Ash's gaze, his eyes shrewd. "The last news I have is that impenetrable darkness covers France as far north as Tours and Orleans, now; covers half the Black Forest; stretches as far east as Vienna, and Cyprus. Only our middle lands, as far as Flanders, still witness the sun."[21]

Aw, *shit!* "Burgundy is the only land—?"

"I know nothing of the lands of the Turk. But as for what I do know – yes, Demoiselle-Captain. Daily, the dark spreads north. The sun is seen over Burgundy alone, now." Olivier de la Marche grunted. "As well as what you see fleeing away, we have hordes of refugees travelling *into* our lands, Demoiselle-Captain. Because of the sun."

"We cannot feed them!" the Viscount-Mayor protested; stung, as if this were part of a long debate.

"Use them!" the German knight who had spoken before snarled. "War will cease over winter. We might win free of this poxy town, as soon as spring comes, and fight a decisive battle. Take them in as levies and train them! We have the Duke's army, we have the hero of Carthage here, Demoiselle Ash; in God's name let us *fight!*"

Ash winced, imperceptibly, both at the mention of her name, and at Robert Anselm's snort. She waited for the Duke's deputy to build on it; propose some heroic and doubtless foolhardy exploit for the hero of Carthage to perform to help raise the siege.

We ain't going to fight a *hopeless* war. There ain't enough money to pay us for that.

What *are* we going to do?

Olivier de la Marche, as if the German knight had not spoken, demanded abruptly, "Demoiselle-Captain Ash, will the Visigoth army stay in the field now? How much of Carthage is destroyed?"

The white masonry of the ogee windows glittered, sun flickering between clouds. Frost starred the stone. A scent of something burning drifted in on the chill air, over and above the great fire that the servants kept burning in the hearth. Ash tasted coldness on her lips.

"Nothing like as much as rumour says, my lord. An earthquake threw down the Citadel. I believe the new King-Caliph, Gelimer, to be alive." She repeated, for emphasis: "My lord, it's snowing on the coast of Africa – and they didn't expect it any more than we did. The *amirs* I met are shit-scared. They started this war on the word of their King-Caliph, and now the countries they've conquered are under the Darkness, and back home in Carthage they're freezing

---

[21] It is interesting to plot these and the other geographical points mentioned on a map of Europe and the Mediterranean. In fact, they form more than half of an ellipse, with the north-eastern coast of Tunisia as its hypothetical centre.

their asses off. They know Iberia's the grain-basket of Carthage – and they know that, if the sun doesn't come back, they won't have a harvest next year. *We* won't have a harvest. The longer this goes on – the worse things will be in six months' time."

Near a hundred faces stared back at her: civilians and soldiers; some of the nobles' escorts probably, inevitably, in the pay of men outside the walls of Dijon.

"Anything else," she said flatly, "isn't for open council; it's for your Duke."

At her dismissal, a hubbub of noise filled the room, particularly from the foreign knights and nobles. Olivier de la Marche spoke over it effortlessly:

"This cold, does it come from the demons your men speak of? These 'Wild Machines'?"

Exchanging glances with Robert Anselm, Ash thought, Damn. My lads have got big mouths. I bet there's half a hundred garbled stories going the rounds.

"I'm trying to stop rumour. The rest's for your Duke," she repeated doggedly. *I'm not going to be palmed off with underlings!*

De la Marche looked bluntly unwilling to let it go at that. Tension painfully tightened her shoulders. Ash rubbed at the muscles of her neck, under the back of the demi-gown's collar. It did not ease the ache. Regarding their white faces, all turned to her in the morning light, she felt a pulse of fear in her bowels. Memory chills her: voices that say, WE HAVE DRAWN DOWN THE SUN.

"Fucking mercenary *whore!*" someone shouted, in German.

There was no hearing anything for the next few minutes, the council and the foreign knights raising their voices in ferocious, excited discussion and argument. Ash put her hands on the table and leaned her weight on them, momentarily. Anselm put his elbow on the back of her chair, leaning behind her to talk to Angelotti.

I should sit down, she thought, let them get on with it. This lot are hopeless!

"My lord de la Marche." She waited until the Duke's deputy turned his attention to her again.

"Demoiselle-Captain?"

"*I* have a question, my lord."

If I hadn't, I might not have bothered with this damn stupid council!

She took a breath. "If I were the King-Caliph, I wouldn't have started a crusade here without taking out the Turks first. And if I *had* done it, I'd be looking to make peace about now – the Visigoths have got most of Christendom to hold down. But the Goths aren't stopping. You say they're fighting in Ghent and Bruges in the north, they're trashing Lorraine. They're here at Dijon. My lord, you tell me – what's so important? *Why Burgundy?*"

A woman's voice spoke before the Duke's deputy could, and spoke in the tone of one citing a proverb: "Upon Burgundy's health depends the health of the world."

"What?"

The voice tugged at Ash's memory.

She leaned further forward across the table, and found herself looking into the pinched white face of Jeanne Châlon.

She was, for once, glad Floria del Guiz was not present.

Abruptly, she flinched from the memory of August in Dijon, and the death that had followed the disclosure of Floria del Guiz as a woman. *But why? There have been deaths since that one. The man I killed might well have died in battle by now.*

"Mademoiselle." Ash stared at the surgeon's aunt. "With respect – I don't want superstitious twaddle: I want an answer!"

The Burgundian woman's eyes widened, her face full of shock. She stumbled back from the table, pushing her way through the confused crowd and the servants and fled.

"You always have that effect on people?" Anselm rumbled.

"I think she just remembered, we've met." An ironic smile twisted Ash's lips, fading quickly. "'Upon Burgundy's health—'"

A knight in French livery completed: "—depends the health of the world.' It is an old proverb, and a meretricious one; nothing more than self-justification by the Valois Dukes."

Ash glanced around. No Burgundian appeared willing to speak.

The French knight added, "Demoiselle-Captain, let us have no more nonsense of demons. We do not doubt the Visigoth army has many engines and devices. We have only to look out from the walls here to see that! I do not doubt they have more engines in their cities in the south, perhaps greater ones than they have here. You say you have seen them. Yes. But what of this? We must fight the Visigoth crusade *here*!"

A buzz of approval sounded around the chamber. Ash noted it came mainly from the foreign knights. The Burgundians – de la Marche in particular – merely looked grim.

"We know better," Antonio Angelotti murmured under his breath.

Ash waved him to silence.

"Suppose, messire—?" Ash waited until the French knight responded: "Armand de Lannoy."

"—Suppose, Messire de Lannoy, that the Visigoths are not fighting this war with their engines. Suppose it is the 'engines' which fight, using the Visigoths."

Armand de Lannoy slammed his palms flat on the table. "This is nonsense, and an ugly girl's nonsense at that!"

The breath went out of her. Ash sat down, amid a babble of French and German.

Shit, she thought bleakly. Had to happen. I don't have how I look to count on any more. To use. Shit. *Shit.*

Beside her, there was a low, unconscious, ratcheting growl from Robert Anselm; almost entirely identical to the sound that the mastiffs Brifault or Bonniau might make.

She grabbed his arm. "Let – it – go."

Olivier de la Marche's voice rose, a bellow that ripped the air in the hall apart, brought adrenalin into Ash's body even if it were not directed at her. He and the French knight, de Lannoy, both stood and shouted into each other's faces across the table.

Ash winced. "This is worse than Frederick's court! Christ. Burgundy was better than this, the first time we came."

651

"The place wasn't full of factious refugees, madonna," Angelotti put in, "and the Duke, besides, was ruling then."

"I've sent Florian to talk to the doctors. See what state he's really in." Aware of some disturbance among Thomas Rochester and her escort, behind her, Ash turned her head. The men-at-arms parted, letting through the elderly Burgundian chamberlain-counsellor.

"Messire . . ." Ash got hastily to her feet.

Philippe Ternant regarded her for a moment. He put his hand on the shoulder of a boy beside him, a page in puffed-sleeve white doublet, gold aiglettes pointing doublet to hose.

"You are summoned. Jean, here, will guide you," he said quietly. "Demoiselle-Captain, I am ordered to bring you to attend on the Duke."

V

"Duke Charles?" Ash said, startled. "I thought he was sick."

"He is. You will be allowed in for a short time. It would weary the noble Duke to see many people, therefore you must bring no crowd. Perhaps one man-at-arms, if you will have a bodyguard with you." Ternant's lined mouth smiled. "As I know, to my cost, here, a knight must have his entourage, be it never so small."

Ash, catching the chamberlain-counsellor's eyes on de Lannoy and his single archer escort, nodded companionably. "Quite. Robert, Angeli; take over for me here. Thomas Rochester, you come with me." She signalled to the page, before her officers could do more than nod obedience. "Lead on."

At last!

Following the boy Jean, her hand automatically went to her scabbard, steadying Anselm's sword. Any likelihood of assassination would be small; nonetheless she kept a keen eye out as they crossed the streets to the palace – flinching at the noise of bombardment, over towards the west side of the city – and entered, and traversed white-walled passages cut deep into stone; climbing stairs where stained-glass windows spilled pale light on the floor. She noticed fewer Burgundian men-at-arms in the palace than when she had first visited it, in the summer.

"Maybe he's dead, boss," Thomas Rochester suddenly ventured.

"What, the Duke?"

"No, the asshole – your husband."

Just as Rochester said it, she recognised the vaulted chamber they were passing through. Banners still hung from the walls, although the muted light made less of the stained glass's reflections on the flagstones.

The *qa'id* Sancho Lebrija is doubtless with the crusade, Agnes Dei's banner is outside these walls, but Fernando? God and the Green Christ know where Fernando is now – or if he's even alive.

This is where she last touched him – her warm fingers entwined with his. Where she struck him. In Carthage, later, he was as weak, as much of a pawn, as he was here. Until the last moments before the earth tremor – *But he could afford to speak up for me: no one was going to* care *about a disgraced, turn-coat German knight!*

"I choose to assume I'm a widow," she said grimly, and followed the page Jean and the chamberlain-counsellor Philippe Ternant as they began to climb the stairs of a tower.

The chamberlain-counsellor passed them through great numbers of Burgundian guardsmen, into a high vaulted chamber packed with any number of people: squires, pages, men-at-arms, rich nobles in gowns and chaperon hats, women in nuns' headdresses, an austringer with his hawk; a bitch and a litter of pups in the straw by the great hearth.

"It is the Duke's sick room," Philippe Ternant said to Ash, as he went on into the mass of people. "Wait here: he will call on your attendance when he desires it."

Thomas Rochester said, low-voiced, for her ear, "Don't reckon that 'siege council' is much more than a sop to keep the civilians quiet, boss."

"You think the real power's here?" Ash glanced around the crowded ducal chamber. "Possible."

There were enough men in full armour present, wearing liveries, for her to identify the notable military nobles of Burgundy – all of them who had survived Auxonne, presumably – and all the major mercenary commanders with the exception of Cola de Monforte and his two sons.

"Monforte leaving could have been political, not strictly military," she murmured.

The dark Englishman's brow creased, under his visor; and then his face cleared. "Beginning to think we'd had it, boss, listening to that council. But if the captains are still here . . ."

"Then they might still stand a chance of kicking ass." Ash completed the English knight's train of thought. "Thomas, I know you'll stick close to my back here."

"Yes, boss." Thomas Rochester sounded cheerful at her confidence in him.

"Not that I expect to get nailed in the middle of the Duke's sick room . . ." Ash stepped back automatically as a Soeur-Viridianus came past with a basin. Bandages with old blood and filth filled the copper pan.

"If it isn't my patient!" the big woman exclaimed.

The green robes and tight wimple of a soeur still made Ash's hackles rise. At the gruff greeting, she found herself startled into looking up into the broad white face of the Soeur-Maîtresse of the convent of *filles de pénitence* – up, and further up than Ash had realised while being nursed; the woman was tall as well as solidly big.

"Soeur Simeon!" Ash sketched a genuflection scarcely worth the term, but with a brilliant smile that more than made up for that. "I saw they trashed the convent – glad you made it into the city."

"How is your head?"

Moderately impressed at the woman's memory, Ash made a bow of rather more respect. "I'll live, Soeur. No thanks to the Visigoths, who tried to undo your good works. But I'll live."

"I am glad to hear it." The Soeur-Maîtresse spoke without change of tone to someone beyond Ash: "More linen, and another priest: *be quick.*"

Another nun dipped a curtsey. "Yes, Soeur-Maîtresse!"

Ash, trying to see the little nun's face, was startled when Simeon said thoughtfully, "I shall wish to visit your quarters, Captain. I am missing one of my girls this morning. Your – surgeon, 'Florian' – may, I feel, be able to help me."

Little Margaret Schmidt, Ash thought. I'd put money on it. Godammit.

"How long has your soeur been missing, Maîtresse?"

"Since last night."

That's my Florian . . .

Her private smile faded. She was conscious of an uneasy relief. *After what she said to me – it's safer if she's with someone else.*

"I'll make enquiries." Ash met Thomas Rochester's blue eyes briefly. "We're contract soldiers, Soeur. If your soeur's signed up with the baggage train . . . well. There's an end of it. We look after our own."

She watched the English knight more than the Soeur-Maîtresse, looking for the slightest flinch. If the idea of keeping the surgeon's woman lover away from a nunnery was disturbing Thomas Rochester, he didn't show it.

But if he knew Margaret Schmidt isn't the only woman here that Florian's attracted to?

"I'll see you later," Simeon cried, her tone too determined for Ash to make out whether that was threat or grim promise, before the big woman strode out through the crowd that parted in front of her.

"Can't we sign up that one, boss?" Thomas Rochester said whimsically. "Better have her than some bimbo the surgeon fancies! Stick the Soeur-Maîtresse in the line-fight beside me – and I'll hide right behind her! Scare the shit out of the rag-heads, she would."

The page, Jean, appearing at her elbow, hauled off his hat and gabbled, "The Duke summons you!"

Ash followed the boy through the crush, overhearing the many guildsmen and merchants present discussing civilian matters, keeping only enough attention on them to estimate morale. A large number of confident men in armour came past her from the far end of the chamber, their aides carrying maps; and Ash moved through them, and found herself confronting the Duke of Burgundy.

The walls here were pale stone, saints' icons set into niches with candles burning before them; and a great tester bed occupied this whole end of the chamber, between two windows blocked with clear leaded glass.

The Duke was not in the great bed.

He lay, on his left side, on a truckle-bed no more splendid than any she had seen in the field, apart from some carvings of saints on the wooden box-frame. Braziers surrounded the bed. Two priests stood back as Ash, the page, and her bodyguard approached; and Duke Charles waved them aside decisively.

"We will speak privately," he ordered. "Captain Ash, it is good to see you returned at last from Carthage."

"Yeah, I think so too, your Grace. I've been up and down Christendom like a dog at a fair."

No smile touched his face. She had forgotten he was not to be moved by a sense of humour, or by charm. Since it had been a reflex remark, made entirely to hide her shock at seeing him, she did not waste time regretting it; only stood silent, and tried not to let her thoughts appear on her face.

Bolsters kept the Duke propped up on his left side on the hard bed. Books and papers surrounded him, and a clerk knelt by his side, hastily returning what Ash saw to be maps of the city defences to order. A rich blue velvet gown covered Charles of Burgundy and the bed together; under it she could see that he was wearing a fine linen shirt.

His black hair stuck, sweat-tangled, to his skull. This end of the ducal chamber stank of the sick room. As he looked up to meet her gaze, Ash took in his sallow skin and prominent feverish eyes, the ridges of cheekbones that stood up now in his face, his cheeks sunken in. His left hand, closing around the cross hanging from his neck, was frighteningly thin.

She thought, quite coldly, *Burgundy's fucked.*

As if he were not in pain – but by the sweat that continually rolled down his face, he must be – Duke Charles ordered, "Master priests, you may leave me; you also, Soeur. Guard, clear this end of the chamber."

The page Jean moved back with the rest. Ash glanced uncertainly towards Thomas Rochester. She noted that the Duke's bodyguard, a big man with archer's shoulders and a padded jack, did not move away from his station behind the Duke.

"Send your man away, Captain," Charles said.

Ash's question must have been apparent on her face. The Duke spared a brief glance for the archer, towering over him.

"I believe you to be honourable," he said, "but, were a man to come before me with a stiletto up his sleeve, and if there were no other way to stop him, Paul here would put himself between me and such a weapon, and take the blow into his own body. I cannot honourably send aside a man prepared to do this."

"Thomas, stand back."

Ash stood, waiting.

"We have much to say to each other. First, go to that window," the Duke said, indicating one of the chamber's two glassed windows, "and tell me what you see."

Ash crossed the two yards' space in a stride or so. The tiny, thick panes of glass distorted the view below, but she made out that she was looking south, under a changeable sky, now greying; clouds racing on a rough wind that rattled the window in its frame. And that she was high enough that she must be, now, standing in the Tour Philippe le Bon, the palace's notorious look-out post.

Doesn't look any fucking better from up here . . . !

Wind yanked at the withy barriers surrounding rows of catapults. Squinting, she could make out men crowding around the jutting beams of trebuchets, long

655

lines passing rocks up to the slings; and loaded oxen dragging carts full of quarried stone through the flooded Auxonne road.

"I can see as far as the joining of the Ouche and Suzon rivers, beyond the walls," she said, loudly enough for the sick man to hear her, "and the enemy siege-machine camp in the west. River's up: there's even less of a chance to assault across it at those engines."

"What can you see of their strength?"

She automatically put her hand up to shield her eyes, as if the rattling wind were not outside the glass. The sun – somewhere around the fourth hour of the morning[22] – was a barely visible grey light now, low in the southern sky.

"Unusual lot of cannon, for Visigoths, your Grace. Sakers, serpentines, bombards and fowlers. I heard mortars when we were coming in. Maybe they're concentrating all their powder weapons with these legions? Above three hundred engines: arbalests, mangonels, trebuchets – shit."

A great tower began to roll forward as she watched, towards the bastion where the southernmost bridge over the river had been thrown down. A fragment of escaping sunlight glanced back from its red sides.

A tower shaped like a dragon, bottle-mouthed – she glimpsed the muzzle of a saker projecting from between the teeth – but with no soaked hides coating it to protect it against fire-arrows.

A wheeled tower made of stone, twenty-five feet high.

"Christus Imperator . . ."

No slaves pushed the tower forward to the river's edge.

Instead, it rolled forward of itself, upon brass-bound stone wheels twice the height of a man, that settled deep into the mud. As it came closer, she could just see a Visigoth gun-crew inside the tower's carved head, furiously sponging and loading their cannon.

The window-glass distorted a commotion on the city walls. Feeling cut off, Ash watched men running, crossbows being winched, spanned; steel bolts shot into the chill wind, all in silence, up here in the Duke's tower. A bang and crack from a Visigoth saker came muffled to her, and the whine of plaster fragments spraying from the bastion wall.

Arbalest and crossbow crews crowded the city's battlements. Anxiety sharpened her eyesight. *Any Lion liveries? No!*

A thick bolt-storm rattled against the sides of the stone dragon-tower, sending its gun-crew scuttling deeper inside for shelter.

Stomach churning, she watched. The tower lurched. One wheel bit deeper into the mud, sinking to the axle. A throng of Carthaginian slaves, herded out of the legion camp with whips, began casting fence-posts and planks down under the great stone wheel for traction; falling man by man under a constant arrow-fire from the city walls. As Ash watched, they ran away from the siege-tower, leaving it and its crew desolate.

Evidently the Faris believes in keeping up the pressure.

"If I had to find a word for . . . for golem-*towers*," Ash said, still staring, her tone somewhere between awe and black humour, "I think my voice would call them 'self-propelled artillery' . . ."

[22] *c.* 10 a.m.

The Duke of Burgundy's voice came from behind her. "They are stone and river-silt, as the walking golems are. Fire will crack their stone. Arquebus bullets will not. Cannon have cracked their bodies. The Faris has ten towers, we have immobilised three. Go to the north window, Captain Ash."

This time, knowing what to look for, it was easier for Ash to rub moisture from the glass and lead and pick out details of the northern part of the encircling forces. Here, she saw the great camp between the two rivers laid out – the moats in front of Dijon's north wall half-full of bundles of faggots; dead horses rotting in the no-man's-land of open ground.

It took her a while to pick it out from the tents, pavises, barricades, and men queuing outside the cook-tents. A blink of brightness from the southern sun caught her eye, gleaming from a brass and marble engine longer than three wagons.

"They've got a ram . . ."

A marble pillar as thick around as a horse's body hung sheathed in brass, suspended between posts, on a great stone-wheeled carriage. Men could not have swung the weight of that ram, or have wheeled the body of it up to the gates, but if the wheels would turn of themselves, the great metal-sheathed point slam into the timbers and portcullis of Dijon's north gate . . .

"If it hits too hard, it'll disintegrate." Ash turned back to face the Duke. "That's why they use their ordinary golems for messengers, not combat, your Grace. Bolts or bullets will chip them away. That ram, if it hits too hard, will crack its own clay and marble. Then it'll just be a lump of rock, for all the *amirs* can do."

As she walked back to stand in front of the Duke's austere bed, he said authoritatively, "You have not seen the most dangerous of their engines – nor will you. They have golem-diggers, tunnelling saps towards the walls of Dijon."

"Yeah, your Grace, my captain Anselm's told me about those."

"My *magistri ingeniatores* have been kept employed in counter-mining them. But they need neither sleep nor rest, these engines of the scientist-magi, they dig twenty-four hours a day."

Ash said nothing to that, but could not entirely hide her expression.

"Dijon will stand."

She couldn't keep the sudden scepticism off her face. She waited for his anger. He said nothing. A sudden spurt of fear moved her to snap, "I didn't bring these men halfway across hell just to get them killed on your walls!"

He did not appear offended. "How interesting. That is not what I expect to hear from a mercenary commander. I would expect, as I heard from Cola de Monforte on his leaving, to hear you say that war is good, good for business, and however many men are killed, twice as many will flock to take their place in a successful company. You speak like a feudal lord, as if there were mutual loyalties involved."

Caught wrong-footed, Ash reached for words and failed to find anything to say. At last, she managed, "I expect to see my men killed. That's business. I don't expect to *waste* an asset, your Grace."

She kept her eyes stubbornly on his face, refusing to identify, even for the briefest moment, a nagging dread.

"How are your men made up?" the Duke demanded. "Of what lands?"

Ash folded her hands in front of her, to stop the sudden tremble in her fingers. She ran through the muster in her mind: the comforting neutrality of names written on paper and read to her. "For the most part, English, Welsh, German and Italian, your Grace. A few French, a couple of Swiss gun-crews; the rest who-knows-what."

She did not say *why?* but it was plain in her expression.

"You had some of my Flemings?"

"I split the company, before Auxonne. Those Flemings are out there with the Faris, your Grace. Orders," she said, "will only take you so far. Van Mander was a liability. I want my men fighting because they want to, not because they have to."

"So do I," the Duke said emphatically.

Feeling verbally trapped, Ash spelled out the necessary conclusion. "Here in Dijon, you mean."

Charles's face tightened. He gave no other sign of pain. He looked around for a page to wipe the sweat from his face; they having been sent away, he wiped his sleeve across his mouth, and raised his dark eyes to look at her with determined authority.

"I show you the worst, first. The enemy. Now. Your men will be one in five, or one in six, of my total forces here." A sharp jerk of the head, towards his captains further down the chamber. "It is my intent to bring you into my counsel, Captain, since you form a sizeable part of the defences. If I will not always take your advice, I will listen to it nonetheless."

That's the respect he'd show a male captain.

She said soberly, and completely neutrally, "Yes, your Grace."

"But in that event you will say that you and your men are, nonetheless, fighting only because you must. Because you must fight to eat."

Oh, you're good. Ash met his keen, black gaze. He was not very many years older than her; a decade, perhaps.[23] Lines cut down the skin at the sides of his mouth, put there both by authority and, more recently, she guessed, by pain.

"Your Grace, I'm a mercenary. If I think my men should leave, we will. This isn't our fight."

Charles said, "Therefore I intend to offer you a contract."

"Can't take it." She shook her head, her answer immediate.

"Why not?"

Ash spared a glance for the big archer behind the Duke, wondered momentarily how close-mouthed the man might be, and then mentally shrugged. *The rumour-mill will have had everything around the city before Sext,[24] no matter what I say.*

"For one thing – I signed my name on a contract with the Earl of Oxford," Ash said measuredly. "He's employing me right now. If I knew for certain where he was, your Grace, I'd feel obliged either to get his orders, or to take the company and leave to rejoin him. As it happens, I have no idea where he is, or even whether he's alive – from Carthage to the Bosphorus is a damn long way,

---

[23] In fact, Charles of Burgundy had been born, in Dijon, in AD 1433.
[24] The canonical sixth hour of the day: noon.

right now, through war and freezing winter, and who knows what mood the Sultan's in? I guess that my lord of Oxford may have a better idea where *I* am. He may get word to me here. He may not."

None of what she said appeared to come to the Duke as a surprise. *At least his intelligence is reasonable.*

"I wondered what you would finally say to me when I asked for your commitment."

So did I.

She became aware that her heartbeat increased.

"I kept you from Visigoth hands, Captain, last summer." Charles leaned forward in the bed, as if his back pained him. "You feel no obligation to me?"

"Personally, perhaps." Saying that, unsure, she decided to let it stand. "This is business. What happened in Basle to the contrary, I don't break contracts, your Grace. John de Vere is my employer."

"He may be lost. Imprisoned. Or dead these many weeks. Sit." The Duke pointed.

A three-legged stool stood not far from the ducal bed. Ash sat, carefully, balancing her weight in the brigandine; wishing she could turn around and see people's expressions. *It is not everybody who is invited to sit in the presence.*

"Yes, your Grace?"

"You doubt my competence as a leader, now," Charles said.

It was a forthright statement, with no uncertainty about the uncomfortable fact; given with a kind of confidence nonetheless. Ash, startled, could think of nothing to say that would not get her into trouble. *It's true. I do.*

"You're wounded, your Grace," she said at last.

"Wounded, but not dead. I still command my officers and captains. I will continue to do so. If I fall, de la Marche, or my wife who commands in the north, are both perfectly capable of withstanding the invading army, and relieving the siege here."

Ash let no doubt show in her voice. "Yes, your Grace."

"I want you to fight for me," Charles said. "Not because towns and cities have been destroyed, and out there on the horizon the dark is closing in on us, and you have nowhere else to go. I want you to fight for me because you trust me to lead you, and win."

He continued to hold her gaze, where she sat. His voice became quieter:

"When I first ordered you into my presence, this summer past, you were concerned that your own men might not follow you, you having been wounded at Basle. I think that you wondered, later, if they would have rescued you at Auxonne – if that wound, and their doubt of you, had not held them back. Then, when your men came to Carthage, it was not for you, but for the Stone Golem. You are still partly troubled over their loyalty, even if you do not express your concern." Charles gave a small smile. "Or do I read you wrong, Captain Ash?"

"Shit." Ash stared blankly at him.

"I've been in the field since I was a boy. I read men." The Duke's smile faded. "And women, too. War makes nothing of that distinction."

How the fuck do you know what I've been thinking?

Ash shook her head, unaware that she did so; not so much a negative, as a rejection of the thoughts in herself.

"You're right, your Grace. I thought exactly that. Up to today. Now . . . I've just had a demonstration of – loyalty, I guess. That's even harder to cope with."

The Duke surveyed her for a long moment.

"You may sign a contract with me that leaves de Vere your master," he said, abruptly. "If orders come from him, or if you hear of his whereabouts, you and your men are free to go. Until then, remain here, fight for me. When you agree, I will have you fed along with my men, which is worth more than coin in this city now; and you and your officers will have a say in the defence of the city. As for the rest—"

Charles broke off again. One of the green-robed soeurs edged closer, glaring at Ash in unmistakable anger. Ash got to her feet, the previous night's exertions aching in her muscles.

"Your Grace, I'll retire until you're well."

"You will retire when you are given leave."

"Yes, *sir*," Ash said under her breath.

Her gaze weighed him, as she stood before him; a woman in man's demi-gown and hose, her own bodyguard holding her sword-belt and weapons six paces away.

Whatever wound he had taken at Auxonne, it still pained him. She looked away from his sallow face, caught by his gesture as he waved the nun away. His right hand was blotched, at the first knuckle of the middle finger, with black oak-gall ink.

He's still up to writing orders and ordinances, however sick he is.

That's a good sign.

He'll probably stand by his word, too, if the past's anything to go by.

That's a better one.

He's no John de Vere. On the other hand, he's certainly no Frederick of Hapsburg.

She remained silent, weighing him on the one hand with the English soldier-Earl, on the other with the political acumen of the Holy Roman Emperor, realising without much surprise that – even with his little humour and less social grace – what she felt comfortable with was the soldier in him, rather than the Duke.

There's six thousand men and three hundred engines out there, minimum. Against some vague hope of a relieving force from Flanders. And the minute this guy keels over – the city goes.

And he has more than men for enemies.

"Follow me, and trust me," Charles said. He spoke with a brisk, awkward confidence, but nonetheless a confidence that was total. Looking at this man, even on his sick bed, Ash found she could not imagine him in defeat.

Dead, yes, but not defeated. That's good. If they're that confident, we might settle this before his death's an issue.

"You believe you're going to win, your Grace."

"I conquered Paris, and Lorraine." He spoke without boasting. "My army

660

here, though much reduced, is better equipped, and made up of better men than the Visigoths. There is another army of mine in the north, under Margaret's command, in Bruges. She will come south soon. Yes, Captain, we shall win."

Whether you will, or whether you won't – right now, I can't feed my men without you.

She met his dark gaze. "Upon condition, I can sign a *condotta* that's limited to what you've just said, your Grace." And then, an irrepressible grin breaking out, born of relief at having taken any decision, no matter how temporary: "I guess we're with you for the moment!"

"I welcome that much trust. I shall ask you questions that you will not answer unless you trust me, Captain."

He gestured. She sat down again. He shifted on the hard bed, a grimace of pain twisting his features. One of the priests moved forward. Charles of Burgundy waved him back.

"Dijon is in danger because its Duke is here," he added reflectively. "This Goth crusade is determined to conquer Burgundy, and they know they cannot do it except by my death. Therefore the storm falls on the place I am."

"Fire magnet," Ash said absently. At his questioning look, she said, "As a lodestone draws iron, your Grace. The war follows you, wherever you are."

"Yes. A useful term. 'Fire magnet'."

"I learned it from my voice."

She rested her forearms on her thighs, supporting herself on the stool, and gave him a look that said *pick the bones out of that!* as clearly as if she had voiced it. *Let's see how good your intelligence is.*

He made as if to lay his shoulders back into the bolster, and stopped. No pain showed on his face, but visible droplets of sweat ran down his sallow, shaven cheeks; drenched the chopped-straight black hair that lay across his forehead. With illness and with the Valois features, nose and lip, he made a singularly ugly young man in some respects, Ash reflected.

As if it cost him nothing, the Duke shifted himself up into a sitting position.

"Your men are concerned that you will no longer consult with the *machina rei militaris*," he said. "It is said—"

"'My men'? Since when do you know about my men?"

He frowned at her bald interruption.

"If you would be treated with respect, behave as a commander does. Reports are made to me of rumours, tavern-talk. You are far too well known for them not to speculate about you, Captain Ash."

A little shaken, Ash said, "Sorry, your Grace."

He inclined his head slightly. "Their concerns are mine, to a degree, Captain. It seems to me that, even if this *machina rei militaris* is a tool of the Visigoths, there is nothing to stop you consulting it, perhaps learning of their tactics and plans, also. Knowledge would make our numbers seem greater. We would know where and when to strike."

His black stare challenged her.

Ash put her palms flat on her thighs, staring down at her gauntlets.

"You see Darkness when you look at the horizon, your Grace. Do you want to know what I see?" She raised her head. "I see pyramids, your Grace. Across the middle sea, I see the desert, and the light, and the Wild Machines. They're what I'd hear, if I spoke to the Stone Golem. And they'd hear me. And then I'd be dead." Irrespective of his sense of humour, Ash added, "You're not the only fire magnet in Dijon, your Grace."

He ignored her pleasantry. "These Wild Machines are not merely more Visigoth engines? Think. You could be mistaken."

"No. They're nothing made by any lord-*amir*."

"Might they have been destroyed, in the earthquake that destroyed Carthage?"

"No. They're still there. The rag-heads think they're a sign!" Ash, bleak, saw that her hands had made fists, without her intention. She unclenched her fingers. "Lord Duke, put yourself in my position. I hear a Visigoth tactics machine. By accident. And what I hear is itself a puppet. It isn't the King-Caliph who wanted war with Burgundy, your Grace. It isn't Lord-*Amir* Leofric who wanted to breed the Faris to talk to the Stone Golem. This is the Wild Machines' war."

Charles nodded absently. "Yet, now your sister knows you are here, she will communicate that fact to the *machina rei militaris*. So these greater machines will – overhear – that you are in Dijon. May already have heard."

A hot wire of fear twisted in her guts at the thought. "I know that, my lord."

Charles of Burgundy said firmly, "You are mine, for now, Commander. Speak to your voice. Let us learn what we can, while we can. The Visigoths may find some way to stop you from hearing the *machina rei militaris*, and then we have lost an advantage."

"*If* she's still using it . . . This isn't my business! My business is to command my men in the field!"

"Not your business, perhaps, but your responsibility." The Duke leaned forward, black eyes feverish. Very deliberately, he said, "You visited your sister, under parley, to speak of this. She will look for answers, as you do. And she may move freely to seek them."

He held her gaze.

"You say this is the Wild Machines' war. *You* are all I have that will aid me in finding out what these Machines are, and why I am at war."

Charles's body shifted, on the hard bed; and he took more of his weight on his left arm, not leaning back at all.

He said, "We have no Faris, but we have you. And no great time to waste. I will not let Burgundy fall because of one woman's fear."

Ash looked from side to side. The white stone walls of the palace reflected back the day's grey light. The chamber seemed suddenly constricting. *Dijon is a trap in more than one way.*

Pages busily took wine around among the men behind her, near the hearth-fire. She heard the high-pitched yelp of one of the pups, seeking its bitch; and an urgent buzz of talk.

"Let me tell you something, your Grace." The urge to lie, to conceal, to prevaricate, all but overwhelmed her. "You made the worst mistake of your life before Auxonne."

An expression of affront crossed his face, gone almost before she could register it. Charles of Burgundy said, "You are blunt. Give me your reason for saying this."

"Two mistakes." Ash ticked them off on her gauntleted fingers: "First, you didn't finance my company to go south with Oxford, before Auxonne. If you'd supported the raid on Carthage, we might have taken out the Stone Golem months ago. Second, when you did let the Earl raid Carthage, you kept half my company back here. If we'd had more men, we might have broken House Leofric – high casualties, but we might just have done it. And we'd have broken the Stone Golem into rubble."

"When my lord of Oxford travelled to Africa, I spared him all the fighting men I could. The rest I needed to man the walls of Dijon. I grant you, a raid in force, beforehand, might have been better. In retrospect, I misjudged it."

Son of a bitch, Ash thought, looking at the man in the sick bed with a new respect.

Charles of Burgundy's voice went on steadily: "Denying the use of the *machina rei militaris* to their Faris would both weaken her, since I believe she relies upon it; and by morale, weaken her men. I cannot see, however, that failing to bring that about is the worst mistake of my life. Who knows but that may be yet to come?"

She met his fever-bright eyes, detecting a slight – a very slight – glint of humour. Behind her, she heard movement. The Duke of Burgundy signalled past her, to pages, who shepherded back the armed nobles anxious to speak with him.

"I've had the Wild Machines in my head," she said, watching him steadily. "You haven't. They're louder than God, your Grace. I've had them turn me around and walk me towards them—"

He interrupted: "Possession by demons? I have seen you brave in the field, but, yes, any man would fear that."

Since he seemed entirely oblivious of that *any man*, Ash let it go. She leaned forward, speaking with intensity:

"They're machines, stones that live; the ancient peoples made them first, I think, and then they grew of themselves." She held the Duke's gaze. "I do know, your Grace. I listened to them. I – think I *made* them tell me, all in a second. Maybe because they weren't expecting it, weren't expecting me. After that, I ran; I ran from Carthage, and the desert, and I kept on running. And I wish that was *all*—"

She reached for her sword's pommel; remembered it to be in Rochester's hands, further down the chamber; and clasped her fingers together again to stop them shaking. She could, for a moment, only try to quiet her rapid, shallow breathing.

"If it wasn't for my company, I wouldn't be in Dijon, I'd still be running!"

Confident, he reached to clasp her hands in his. "You are here, and will fight in whatever way you can. Even if it means talking to the *machina rei militaris* for me."

She took her hands away, bleak. "When I said that not destroying it was the worst mistake of your life, I meant it. The Wild Machines could speak to

Gundobad because he was a Wonder-Worker, a miraculous prophet. And then – your Grace, *then they spent centuries in silence until Friar Roger Bacon built a Brazen Head in Carthage, and House Leofric built the Stone Golem.*"

The Duke stared. Back down the chamber, a hooded hawk cried: brief, high, pained. As if it jolted him, he said, "They speak through the *machina rei militaris.*"

"*Only* through it."

"You are certain of this?"

"It's their knowledge, not mine." Ash wiped a hand over her face, hot with sweat, but did not shift her stool away from the charcoal brazier. "I think they need a channel of some kind to speak to us, your Grace. Those like the Green Christ or the Prophet Gundobad aren't born more than once or twice in a thousand years. The Wild Machines need Bacon's devices, or Leofric's; otherwise they're dumb. They've been secretly manipulating the Stone Golem ever since it was made. If they could have manipulated the Visigoth Empire any other way, by now they would have!"

Looking at him, she surprised a look of pain on the Duke's face that had nothing to do with any wound.

"What would they have had now," she said bitterly, "if I could have destroyed the Stone Golem last summer? Nothing! They're *stone*. They can't move or speak. They might compel the earth to shake, but only in Carthage."

Memories of falling masonry invade her mind: she pushes them away.

"If I'd managed to take it out, we'd have been safe! There'd be peace by now. The Visigoth Empire's over-extended, they need to consolidate what they've taken. It's only because the damn Stone Golem keeps telling them to take Burgundy that they're keeping on with this campaign! And the Stone Golem's only relaying the words of the Wild Machines."

"Then we must see if we cannot mount another raid," Charles of Burgundy said, "more successfully."

In the over-heated ducal chamber, seated by a wounded man, Ash found herself suddenly and unwillingly invaded by hope.

"No shit? They're probably manipulating to get a hell of a guard on House Leofric now . . ."

"It might be done." Charles frowned, ignoring her coarseness; calculating. "I cannot weaken the defence here. If orders could be got north, to Flanders, and my wife's army; she might send a major force out by the Narrow Sea, and south down the coast of Iberia. You will talk to my captains. Perhaps now, when the Goths are over-extended, and before Carthage has recovered its defences . . ."

Something unexpected moved her. She recognised it as the perception of possibility. *Could we do it? Go back to Carthage, trash the place? If we could – oh, if we could! Damn, I knew there had to be some reason the Burgundians followed this man!*

Taking instant decisions, as battles have taught her to, Ash said, "Count me in."

"Good. All the more important, now, that you speak with the *machina rei militaris*, Captain Ash. And, when you hear these 'Wild Machines', that you tell me what they are planning."

All her hope vanished in a rush of fear.

Can't get away from it; can't not *tell him—*

I can try not to.

"Your Grace, what happens when *they* hear *me*? I could be controlled—" She caught his expression. "You said yourself, anyone would be afraid! You pray, your Grace, but you wouldn't want the voice of God in your head, I promise you."

"These 'Wild Machines' are not God." His voice was gentle. "God permits them to exist, for a time. We must deal with them as we can. With courage."

By the way he looked at her, she thought Charles of Burgundy might have his own doubts about her piety.

"I *know* what they're planning!" she protested. "Trust me, there isn't any need to ask twice! All I heard from them in Carthage was *Burgundy must be destroyed*!"

"'*Burgundia delenda est*' . . ."

"Yes. *Why*?" She sounded loud, brash, brutal. "Why, your Grace? Burgundy's rich – or it was – and powerful, but that isn't it. France and the Germanies were allowed to surrender. What's so important about Burgundy that they want it razed to the ground, and then they want to piss on the ashes?"

The Duke drew himself together, having considerable presence despite his sick bed. He looked at her keenly.

"I may give you no reason why they should wish Burgundy destroyed."

His ambiguity was plain.

Not sure if it were trust or resignation that she felt, Ash merely looked at him.

"Destroy this link," Charles said, "and we have only the Visigoth Empire to meet in the field. That, I believe we can do. We have taken harder blows than this and come back with victory. So you must listen for me, master Captain, if we are to attempt Africa again. Call your voices to you.'

Carried on his words, she came to herself with a shock as cold as spring-water. She sat back on the stool.

"Your Grace, I don't think I'll be much good to you."

Ash looked away from his face. She said steadily:

"The last time I – listened to where my voice is, I heard the voice of my priest, Father Maximillian. That was yesterday. Godfrey Maximillian died, in Carthage, two months ago."

Charles watched her, neither judgement or condemnation in his face.

She protested, "If you think I'm hearing illusions, your Grace, you won't think that *any* voice I hear can be trusted!"

"'Illusions'." Charles, Duke of Burgundy, reached out among the papers that surrounded him, uncovering one with an effort. As he read, he said, "You *would* call it that, Captain Ash. You say nothing of demons, or of temptation by the devil. Or even that this Father Maximillian may be with the saints, and this the answer to your sorrow at losing him."

"If it *is* Godfrey—" Ash clenched her fist. "It is Godfrey. The Faris hears him, too. A 'heretic priest', she said. If *both* of us . . . I think when he died, there, as they shook the earth, his soul went into the machine – he's trapped, his soul is trapped in the *machina rei militaris*. And whatever's left of him – not a whole man – is there for the Wild Machines to pick apart . . ."

He reached out to grip her arm.

"You do not grieve easily, or well."

Ash pressed her lips together. "You've lost men under your leadership, so you know how it is, your Grace. You carry on with the ones you've got."

"War has made you hard, not strong."

His tone was not condemnatory, but kind. His grip on her arm did not feel like that of a sick man. She flinched. Charles released her.

"Captain Ash, I have noted down on this paper, here, that I spoke to your Father Maximillian, some days before the field of Auxonne. He came to me for a letter of passage across these lands, and for a letter requesting the Abbot of Marseilles to find him a place on a ship to the south."

"To *you*?"

"I gave him his letters. It was clear to me he is – was – no traitor, but a devout man seeking to help a friend, in charity and love. If anything of his soul does remain, fear for it, but do not fear it."

Ash blinked rapidly. One hot drop of water broke from her eye before she blinked it clear; coursing down her cheek. She scrubbed her wrist across her face.

"Grief is part of the honour of a soldier," Charles said, awkwardly, as if the tears of a woman moved him more than the tears of a man might have.

"Grief is a fucking pain in the ass," Ash said, on a shaky, indrawn breath; and then with the brilliant smile that was all hers, said, "Sorry, your Grace."

"Ask for what help you need," the Duke said.

"Your Grace?"

The young black-haired man in the gold-embroidered gown finally smiled at her. There was nothing of malice in it, only plain kindness; and a weary joy, as if he were making things very clear, as if she might not otherwise hear his meaning.

"I will not use force." His eyes shut, for a split second, and then he was looking at her again. "Nor shall I in any way compel you to speak to the *machina rei militaris*. I *ask* you to do it."

"Shit," Ash said miserably.

"I ask you to answer the question of why you hear a dead man's voice. I ask you to discover what these machines beyond the *machina rei militaris* will do now. I want," Charles said, looking at her keenly, "to know why you have been saying that the Visigoth Faris has been bred to work a great and evil miracle against Burgundy. And whether it is true that she has the power to do this."

Ash looked at him dumbly. *Nothing wrong with his intelligence at all.*

"I offer any help you may need. Priests, doctors, armourers, astrologers: whosoever of my people can help you, you shall have them. Name help, and you shall have it."

Ash opened her mouth to answer him, and had no answer to make.

Charles of Burgundy said, "Nor will I use underhand methods. If you and your men desire it, I will welcome you as one of my captains, whether you do this or not. You are a field commander I would wish to have serve me."

Dumb, she could only stare at him. *He means this. I wish I thought he didn't. He means what he says.*

"Do it," he said, holding her gaze, completely confident; all his awkwardness for once gone. "For yourself, for your men, for Dijon, for Burgundy. For me."

Ash said flatly, "I've been forced back here, I'm sitting smack in the centre of a target, and *I don't know why it's a target.* Your Grace, I'm going to need to know that. If not now, then very soon."

She studied his sallow face, and the hollow gaps between socket and eye, where the flesh of his eyelids had sunk in. No weakness showed in his expression.

"I offered whatever help you need. Speak with your dead priest." He watched her with authority and determination. "If it proves needful – come back to me. You shall know whatever I can tell you."

At last, painfully, she said, "Give me time."

"Yes. Since you need it, you shall have that, too."

Ash, sweat running down her body under her armour, light-headed with fear, stood and looked down at the Duke of Burgundy.

"Not time to decide," she said. "This was always going to happen; here or anywhere else. I've decided. Give me time to do it."

Message: #258 (Anna Longman)
Subject: Carthage
Date: 04/12/00 at 05.19 p.m.
From: Ngrant@

format address deleted
Other details encrypted by
non-discoverable personal key

Anna –

Is Isobel's mail what you needed? Let me know later today. We're so busy here, you wouldn't believe it! Or perhaps you would!

Everybody is being very nice to me, and not pointing out that I have no particular authorisation to be here except for 'Fraxinus', and that I'm continually underfoot. I think we're all too excited to care. A genuine, untouched, DOCUMENTED seabed site – even Isobel can't bring herself to call it anything other than Carthage!

Anna, *that* is the final part of 'Fraxinus me fecit'. My last piece of translation. The manuscript breaks off there, plainly incomplete.

I cannot answer any of the questions it raises!

Other historical documentation picks Ash up again, but only in the initial part of January 1476/77. We may never know why the 'siege of Dijon' section gives such an unconventional rendering of European history, and of Charles the Bold's character – in some ways, it is much closer to a portrait of his father, Duke Philip the Good – but *he* died in 1467! We may never know what happened to Ash in the winter before her death at the battle of Nancy, or why this text places Charles in Dijon!

In the light of current events, does it *matter*?

I don't believe, now, that I'm worried about what results the metallurgy team will come up with when they re-test the 'messenger golem'.

Suppose carbon-dating *does* put it in this half of the twentieth century? It is not *completely* impossible that someone else saw the 'Fraxinus' document before I did. Nor is it *completely* impossible that a fake 'golem' might be made – Isobel tells me there is a substantial market in archaeological fakes to the more gullible private collectors.

Carthage is not a fake. Carthage is a fact.

Of course, archaeologically speaking, there is the question of what, as a fact, this implies. Has this inundated site any connection with the Liby-Phoenicians who settled the original 'Carthage' in 814 BC – did they perhaps land here, and only later move to the land-site that has been excavated outside Tunis? It seems unlikely: this is not the Carthage that the Romans sacked.

But it is Visigothic Carthage.

You see, Anna, I have been positing a settlement made in the AD 1400s - and from the ROV images, this site already seems much older than that! Perhaps this is Vandal Carthage? Or perhaps this is a much *older* Visigothic site? After all, if a storm had not sunk their fleet in AD 416, the Spanish Visigoths would have taken over Roman Carthage thirteen years before the Vandals did just that!

So much - so _much_ to be discovered now.

My initial theory posited a late-mediaeval, short-lived settlement. Any continuously occupied site, from AD 416, gives us much *more* of a problem - I can believe that 'my' Visigoth settlement on the North African coast, lasting perhaps 70-80 years in total, could go unnoticed, or at least have such evidence as survives 'swept under the carpet' for any number of reasons. However, ten and a half centuries of continuous occupation would show up in Arabic chronicles, even if the 'Franks' managed to ignore it!! I grant you there are tens of thousands of surviving mediaeval Islamic manuscripts, and many libraries throughout North Africa and the Middle East that have yet to be fully catalogued - but, no mention of 1060 years of Carthage?! *Anywhere?*

I do need to talk to Isobel about this.

I've said that we are all in a state of exaltation - that's true, but, I would expect Isobel to be more joyful. She seems concerned.

I suppose that, if I were responsible for confidentiality on the site of the biggest archaeological discovery this century, *I* might look a little frazzled and haggard, too!

There are new images coming through from the ROVs every few minutes - will contact you again when I can - isn't this *wonderful*?

- Pierce

Message: #158 (Pierce Ratcliff)
Subject: Ash, manuscript
Date: 05/12/00 at 07.19 p.m.
From: Longman@   *format address deleted*
                                        other details encrypted and
                                        non-recoverably deleted
Pierce -

There is a manuscript.

I wanted you to know that first. I've been to Sible Hedingham, I've spoken to Professor Davies's brother, who's been remarkably candid with me, but first - THERE IS A MANUSCRIPT.

It isn't an unpublished work by Vaughan Davies.

It's original.

670

Pierce, I've no idea if this is important or not. I don't even know if it's from the right era. Or if it's a fake.

The brother, William Davies, says Vaughan referred to it as a 'hunting treatise'. The cover bound on to it does have a woodcut of a deer being chased through the woods by riders. I hope you are not going to be disappointed. My (small) Latin's Classical, not mediaeval, so I can't pick out anything much except a few references to 'Burgundia'. For all I know, the rest of it could be about hound breeding! I hope it isn't; I really hope it isn't, Pierce. I'm going to feel I've let you down if it is.

William has let me scan it. Given the condition the paper is in, I'm not sure I should have allowed him to – but I had to. He's contacting Sotheby's and Christie's. I have talked him out of contacting the British Library at the moment. It won't be long before he insists.

If this is genuine – important – even useful, I can use this discovery to support the combined book-and-documentary project, without having to involve what you and Dr Isobel are doing at the sea-site yet. I do realise she needs total security at the moment.

I'll start sending some scanned text after this. I know what sort of chaos there'll be where you are – you're still on the ship, right? – but how soon can you translate these first pages?!

Here's its provenance –

I went up to East Anglia with Nadia, on the pretence that she might want to buy some of the remaining bric-a-brac. (Not a pretence, as it turned out: she did negotiate for some pieces.) William Davies turned out to be a nice old man, a retired surgeon and an ex-Spitfire pilot; so I came clean and told him I was your publisher, you were in Africa, but you were doing a re-edition of his brother's work on ASH. (Thought this was most tactful.)

As far as I could find out by talking to him, William Davies never had much to do with his brother before Vaughan came to Sible Hedingham. They were brought up in an upper-middle-class family somewhere in Wiltshire. Vaughan went to Oxford and stayed there, William went to London, studied medicine, married, and came into the Sible Hedingham property on his wife's early death. (She was only 21.) After that, he only saw Vaughan while on leave from the RAF, and they didn't talk much.

What relevant family history I've picked up from him is as follows: Vaughan Davies moved from Oxford to Sible Hedingham in the late 1930s. William remembers it as 1937 or 1938. William owned the house, but was in the process of joining the RAF, and was prepared to let it to Vaughan. I get the feeling they wouldn't have moved in together – listening between the lines, Vaughan sounds bloody impossible to live with. Vaughan was on a sabbatical from Oxford, finishing the ASH manuscript for publication.

According to William, Vaughan then lived the life of a hermit;

but no one in the village much minded. I think he must have been very abrasive. In any case, as a newcomer, he wasn't made welcome. He 'bothered' (William's word) the family who owns Hedingham Castle for access to it, and made himself a real pain; so much so that they told him to go away.

I think William thinks this manuscript comes from Hedingham Castle.

I think he thinks Vaughan stole it.

He didn't see Vaughan Davies after the war because Vaughan vanished in 1940.

I'm not kidding, Pierce. He vanished. William was shot down over the Channel that summer, and spent considerable time in hospital. He still has burn-scars, you can see them. By the time he was invalided out, the house at Sible Hedingham was deserted. There were the usual rumours for the time of Vaughan having been a German spy, but all William could find out was that his brother had left for London.

Being wartime, the police investigations were a bit scanty. Now it's sixty years later, the trail's cold.

William says he always assumed his brother was caught in the Blitz, killed in the bombing, his body blown up or burned so as to be facially unidentifiable. He had no hesitation in saying this to me in just those words. Gruesome. Maybe it's being a surgeon.

William Davies is selling the Sible Hedingham house because he's going into sheltered accommodation. He must be in his eighties, now. He's very sharp. When he says there's no mystery over his brother's death, I want to believe him.

No – what I _want_ is to go back to the office and pretend that none of this is happening. I've always loved academic publishing, but what I want now is for there to be more distance between me and history. All this is uncomfortably close, somehow.

What you're finding on the Mediterranean seabed – Pierce if this manuscript _is_ something we need, I don't know what I'll do. Take my annual holiday, fly to the Florida Keys, and pretend that none of it is happening! It's too much.

No.

As your editor – as a friend – I'll be here. I know you can't do the translation instantly, I know you're busy examining the new site, but can you at least give me some idea of whether this is a valuable document or not, before the end of the day?

– Anna

Message: #270 (Anna Longman)
Subject: Ash/Visigoths
Date: 05/12/00 at 10.59 p.m.
From: Ngrant@

format address deleted
Other details encrypted by
non-discoverable personal key

Anna –

Good God, even as separate files, they're taking *for ever* to
download! I'm using Isobel's other notebook while they're coming
in; and I'm looking at the first page at this moment –

One thing I can tell you immediately. If these images have
scanned in correctly, this document is by the same hand that wrote
'Fraxinus'.

Anna, I KNOW this handwriting – I can read it as fast as I can
read my own! I know all the tricks of phraseology and contractions
and spelling. I should do, I've been studying and translating this
hand for the last eight years!

And if that's the case –

This *has* to be a continuation of 'Fraxinus'.

'Fraxinus me fecit' is quite definitely Ash's autobiography.
Either written or (more likely, given her illiteracy) dictated by
her.

If Vaughan Davies had access to *this* document, why doesn't he
mention it in his second edition of the Ash chronicles?! All right,
he didn't have 'Fraxinus', but even this – the little I've read so
far – it's plainly and evidently Ash; why didn't he *publish*!

Encrypt the rest and send it; I don't care _how_ long it takes to
scan or download!

– Pierce

Message: #277 (Anna Longman)
Subject: Sible Hedingham ms
Date: 10/12/00 at 11.20 p.m.
From: Ngrant@

format address deleted
Other details encrypted by
non-discoverable personal key

Anna –

It *carries on* from 'Fraxinus' – is a missing part of the document
– a *continuation* – covers autumn of 1476!!! But I don't know how
MUCH it covers!!!

Evidently one or more pages are missing at the start – perhaps
torn away over the intervening five hundred years – BUT, I don't
think we're missing more than a few hours of 15/11/1476!!

From the internal textual evidence, these events MUST belong in
the same 24-hour period as Ash's first entry into Dijon! Or at least

no later than the following day. Given the correspondence between details of dress and weather in the 'Fraxinus' ms, this HAS to be a bare few hours after Ash's interview with Charles of Burgundy, and is therefore 15 November 1476.

I don't think there can be anything missing except some initial call to arms!

Was there anything written on the binding and could that be scanned?

Later:

Here is 1st part, quick & dirty, tidy up later. Been at this for five days straight. Can't *believe* what we have here!

– Pierce

PART ELEVEN

15 November–16 November AD 1476

Under the Penitence[1]

[1] Sible Hedingham ms, part 1.

I

[. . .] command group on Dijon's walls.[2]

"What the fuck is she *doing*?" Robert Anselm shrieked above the noise. "I thought you said she was waiting for us to sell her a gate!"

"Maybe she's trying to concentrate our minds!"

Ash is conscious, in the back of her thoughts, of the heavy protection of steel on head and hands; of the thin layers of mail and wool and linen that are all that cover her limbs. The desire for Milanese harness is strong enough for her to taste.

"Fucking hell! All that talk, and we can lose this city *right now*—"

She forced herself to stand upright on the parapet, and stare out between the merlons[3] at the empty ground – covered suddenly, now, in running figures.

A horde of men running forward towards Dijon's north-west walls, planting screens, kneeling to shoot – Carthaginian archers, behind mantlets,[4] with wicked black recurve bows. The *thwick!* of arrow-heads against stone tightened her belly. A crackle of arquebus fire sounded all along the parapet, Angelotti's and Ludmilla's voices raised in shrill orders; and the rapid, repetitive thrum of longbows went up into the air: sweating archers bellowing foul-mouthed congratulations at each other.

A black wave of men rose up from the earthworks in front of the Visigoth camp. At the same second, a whistling shrillness sounded. Ash glanced to her left: could not see past the tower to the north-west gate – but a sound of impacts and screaming rose over the clamour. She looked back – only a split second – and the ground below was covered with running men holding siege ladders and shields above their heads, some already falling under the steady fire from the battlements.

"Auxiliaries!" Robert Anselm bellowed in her ear. She heard him through the helmet's muffling lining.

"What about *them*?" She leaned into the gap in the stonework, staring out and down. Along with the black tunic-wearing men with spears and hatchets, forty or fifty Europeans were running.

"Prisoners!" Anselm bellowed.

A glance told her he was right – captured townsfolk, Dijonnais taken some time this autumn and pressed into service, due now to die either on the walls,

---

[2] The first part of this sentence has been lost with the missing page(s) of the Sible Hedingham ms.

[3] The solid parts of battlements, as opposed to the 'crenels' or gaps between them.

[4] 'Mantlet': a protective screen which can be moved to enable archers and gunners to advance closer to besieged walls.

or by the hand of the Visigoth *nazirs* behind them. Abruptly she broke off from hearing messengers and giving orders, tapped Anselm's breastplate, and pointed.

Anselm shoved his visor up, squinting, then bellowed a coarse laugh. "Tough fucking shit, Jos!"

In the wake of the auxiliary troops and condemned prisoners, men in blue livery with the Ship and Crescent Moon on it jogged forward, soaked hides over their shoulders, carrying ladders of their own. Ash found herself squinting, trying to see if she could spot Joscelyn van Mander's personal banner, but in the confusion of flying rock-splinters, dirt, arquebus-smoke and distance, she couldn't make it out.

"Here they come," Ash began, steadily, trying to stop her voice shaking.

As the first of the men hit the edge of the moat below, throwing down more wood-faggots on the piles that almost filled it, she turned back to the parapet.

"Anselm! Get the billmen up on the walls, *now*! Ludmilla: move the archers back to give 'em room! Angelotti—"

Over the noise of men in mail and plate jogging up the steps to the parapet, and the archers determined to get off every last shaft, a great *crack* and *boom!* sounded to her left. *Main gate*, she realised. *Shit!*

She turned away to look for Angelotti, failed to see him, and took a step towards the nearest mangonel. Two of the winch-crew squatted down behind the arrow-studded wooden screens, and, as Ash looked, Dickon Stour gave the wooden frame a solid whack with a hammer, straightened up, stepped back, and slapped the cup-shaft with an expression of satisfaction. "Okay? Try it now?"

"Where's Captain Angelotti gone?" Ash bawled.

The lanky armourer, straw-coloured hair jutting out under the rim of his war-hat, shouted over his shoulder at her. "Down by—"

A stupendous explosion deafened her.

The parapet jumped under her feet; the air filled with screaming fragments of rock. Two merlons gaped, whitely; half the masonry to each side blown away; a crater gaping in the surface of the battlements.

Something vast glanced past her and on into the town below. Body shivering with shock, she realised first *I'm not hurt!* and then *Direct hit on the mangonel!*

The wooden protective screens hung in flinders. A shattered tangle of wood and rope looked nothing like the frame and cup. One man rolled, screeching. In among the white splinters of wood in front of Ash, ragged joints of meat leaked wetly; and a leg hung, still inside a perfectly whole boot. Another man lay dead on the parapet. There was no sign of Dickon Stour. Only a red-splashed, jagged scar, dug six inches deep in the cracked flagstones.

Ash put her hand up and wiped hair out of her mouth. It was not her hair. She spat, at the taste, ridding her mouth of a fragment of bone.

Within a fractured moment, a second trebuchet-missile hit, further down the wall: a lump of limestone half the size of a cart. She saw a mess of ropes and wood and men on their knees, on their backs, blown halfway down the steps. A boulder shattered into fragments, hurtling down into the no-man's-land behind the walls.

The shrill whistling of clay pots trailing flames sounded overhead.

Ash winced, ducking down. Clay vessels hit, one after another, all down the length of the walls from her; spraying Greek Fire bright into the hoarding and lines of men. The *whoof!* of igniting flame made her shudder.

"ANSELM—!"

A shoulder barged her to one side. Overhead, her banner dipped, fell to a diagonal, and slowly moved away from her in the press of a crowd of men – archers and billmen all shoving past her, back away from the walls, pressing towards the steps.

"*HOLD!*" she bellowed, lung-crackingly loud.

A gaggle of Rochester's billmen shoved her hard up between themselves and one damaged merlon: she has a momentary glimpse of yards of empty air, and men and ladders beneath. The nearness of the fall jolts her stomach.

Off towards the gate, she hears hook-guns firing, and their fortified ballistae shooting hard and fast, but the Carthaginians are in under their minimum range now—

"Fucking *stand*!" she screamed, and grabbed one man's shoulder, another by the belt. Both pulled free. Over the helmets of the routing men, she saw her banner gradually come back upright, and towards her – and then fall.

Without hesitation, Ash ducked into the mêlée of running men, scooped up the pole, and raised the banner over her head. Awkward and unwieldy, it wavered. She heard Anselm's voice, louder, at the steps, grabbing the bearer of the Lion standard and bellowing: "—*right* where you fucking are!" She saw his arm and sword blade go up.

"ON ME!" she yelled. Rickard's face appeared in front of her, in the press of people. She shoved the Lion Affronté into his hands; grabbing at the short axe he carried for her. Shouldering her way against the crowd, shouting into men's faces, she sensed the slowest possible hesitation.

"*Follow* me!"

Further down towards the White Tower, the brattice was alight; and the stone surface of the parapet alive with unquenchable flames of spilled Greek Fire. The nearest brattice was untouched. Faintly above the shrieking and yelling, she heard noise from below; switched to a two-handed grip on the axe, and put all her weight into shoving two archers and a gunner's mate back out of her way.

"Bring that fucking flag!" she snarled at Rickard, not stopping to see what the white-faced boy did; slammed her gauntlet into the back of one man's helmet, and cleared herself a way up into the embrasure.

"*On me, you fucking sons of bitches!*"

She felt her own voice come out muffled, the sound reflected back by the wood and hide roof of the brattice; had a second to think, *Jesu Christus! I wish I could have worn a bevor, or even a sallet with a visor!*, and flipped the shaft of the poleaxe over in her hand. It slapped home into the linen palms of her gauntlets.

A face appeared up through the hole in the wooden hoarding in front of her.

In a conscious irony entirely separate from the combat-awareness of her mind, she thought, *What I'd give to be able to talk to the* machina rei militaris *right now.*

The wooden shaft of the axe fitted smoothly and familiarly into her grip: left hand forward, right hand in support. She let the axe-head go back, then thrust forward with the shaft, and slammed the butt-spike into the Visigoth auxiliary's face.

The point skidded off his helmet's nasal bar.

The man's bearded mouth opened: shock or anger. He roared. He thrust himself up on the top of a scaling ladder, invisible beneath the planks of the brattice, hauling his sword through the gap.

She let the weapon's momentum carry her body forward a step. Breath coming hard in her throat, whole body tensed in anticipation of his blow, she mentally screamed at herself *I'm not moving fast enough!* and let the axe swing round and back and over her head, sliding her right hand down to the bottom of the axe-shaft to join her left, accelerating the cutting edge of the weapon over and down. Four pounds of metal, but moving in a tight four-foot arc. She slammed the blade into his face as he looked up.

A spray of wet speckled her arms. She felt the edge bite: couldn't hear his screaming for the shouts behind her, the clash of edged steel, the cracks of arquebuses, and the sound of other men shrieking. Not a mortal wound, not enough to put a man down—

A spear-point jabbed up between her feet. It caught in the roughly sawn planks: jammed.

She leaped back. One of her heels caught on the edge of the embrasure behind her. The poleaxe flew up in her grasp, ripped the soaked hides that roofed the brattice as she fell backwards, and sat down hard in one of the crenellations. The impact jolted her whole spine.

Quietly, without fuss, and from a sitting position, she lifted up the axe and slammed the butt-spike forward again, punching a hole just below the brow of the steel helmet of the first man.

His eyes stayed open, fixed on the planks, as he fell forward, half-in, half-out of the gap. Thick, dark-red blood and brain-matter came out with the spike as she twisted it free.

No footsteps behind her, no banner, no shout from Rickard. A shrieking, bellowing clamour from below—

For all I know, I'm alone up here now—

"*On me, for fuck's sake!*"

The spear-point levered itself out of the planking from below. The dead body jerked, the Visigoth soldier being pulled down by others on the ladder beneath; she heard them shrieking orders, swearing. Unaware that she was very grimly smiling, she got back up on to her feet.

"Boss!" Euen Huw leaped over the battlements and slammed into her side. He staggered. Blood soaked his hose from thigh to knee.

"Oh, thank fuck! Where's Rickard? Where's my banner? Ludmilla, get your archers up here! It's a fucking bird-shoot!" Ash slapped the shoulders of Huw's infantry and Rostovnaya's archers, ten or fifteen men piling on to the brattice now, feeding them on past her. She swung herself over the dead man by gripping a beam above her, and ran down to the next gap. Her boots echoed on the planking.

As she loped, feet shifting sideways, she kept her back to the safety of the wall, head switching rapidly from side to side, trying to watch for an attack from any quarter. The tingling vulnerability of exposed, unarmoured thighs, shins, forearms, elbows; all of this fires her to extreme perceptiveness, extreme efficiency.

"*Here!* Get the ones below, on the ladder!"

An archer, whose greasy ringlets and unshaven face shone with sweat, loped up and ducked his head down through the gap in front of her. Within seconds, he bawled at his pavise-mate for more shafts; stood astride the gap, drawing his bow with difficulty in the confined space, shot down at the foot of the siege ladder, fifty feet below.

Two crossbowmen rapidly elbowed him out of the way: more room for their weapons in the gap.

Ash bent her head for a quick squint out through an archery port in the planks. *If they can storm—If they come over the wall, it's all irrelevant: voices, everything!*

A constant *thunk!* of bolts and shafts echoed along the brattice now; points hitting wood and stone. Her body tensed against the searing rush of Greek Fire. *No, not while their own men are scaling the walls—*

The hook of a scaling ladder thumped into another brattice, further along the wall; she had a bare second to see that the men with swords and axes beginning to swarm up it were not Visigoth auxiliary troops, but men with Crescent Moons on blue livery jackets.

She's seen my banner on this section of the wall – this is deliberate – sending men we've fought beside – a psychological attack: getting Frankish mercenaries to kill each other—

"Look who it ain't!" Euen Huw bellowed, slamming his wiry body between the wall and her. Over his shoulder as he ran on, he bawled, "Been having it easy, 'aven't they? See about that!"

A glance back along the hoarding showed her Angelotti's brilliant curls under the edge of a sallet, his heavy-bladed falchion rising and falling in an appalling, close-combat press of bodies jammed together. His left arm hung, bleeding, buckler gone somewhere. His men crowded that side: warding him.

Christ, half the Visigoth army's on its way!

"Boss!" Robert Anselm, Rickard, and the banner appeared at the embrasure behind her; the older man limping, his face twisted in a bellowed warning.

Ash swung around, saw in a second that the dead auxiliary's' body was dislodged now, two soldiers wearing the Crescent Moon scrambling up scaling ladders and through the openings in the plank floor.

Euen Huw parried the first man's sword down with his own in a shower of sparks and kicked the man's leg under the edge of his mail hauberk. Two or three pounds pressure will pop a kneecap. The man – no time to guess at the face; if this is someone known, or someone Joscelyn van Mander has picked up in the months since he left the Lion Azure – the man fell forward dead-weight, like a sack of grain.

The roof and beams cramped her. Ash stuck the shaft of her poleaxe forward past Euen as he recovered his balance. She hooked the curved back edge of the blade behind the second man's knee. Bracing both feet, she yanked.

The razor edge of the axe hooked the man's knee forward, his mouth opening in a scream as the cut hamstrung him. He went over, on to his back, crumpling against the front wall of the brattice. Euen Huw stabbed with his sword, up between the legs, under his hauberk, into his groin.

The first man struggled upright, on to one knee, his other leg jutting at a twisted angle. Too close. Ash dropped the axe, grabbed her dagger out of its scabbard with her right hand, and threw herself down on to his back.

She wrapped her forearm around his helmet, twisted his head around, and slammed the blade down into his eye-socket, straight into the brain.

Despite helmet, despite blood and the scream and the disfigurement of his face, she had a moment to recognise the man. *Bartolomey St John – Joscelyn's second – I know him!*

Knew him.

Anselm bellowed something. Two or three dozen men in Lion livery piled over the battlements into the brattice, iron cook-pots manoeuvred gingerly between them on bill-shafts. The first two tipped their cauldrons, and a white mist of steam hissed up: boiling water spilling through the gaps and planks alike. More men: Henri Brant and Wat Rodway heaving a cauldron between them, *laughing* under the clamour, tipping hot sand down through the nearest opening—

A yard under Ash's feet, men screamed, shrieked; there was the recognisable crack of a siege ladder shattering under panicking men's weights. Screams diminishing, bodies falling into the bright air.

"Shit, boss, that was close!" Euen bellowed, mouth at her ear, one hand reached out absently to pull her to her feet.

Ash grabbed the axe with her free hand, hauling it out from under Bartolomey St John's dead body. Her hands were, she realised, shaking; with the same uncontrollable tremor that one has when badly injured. *But nothing's touched me: the blood isn't mine!*

She lifted her head, couldn't see Anselm, could hear him and her sergeants yelling orders back on the battlements – *he's done it, we're holding!*

"Euen, send a runner! The Byward Tower, *now*. What the fuck are the Burgundians doing up there? We need covering fire! They've got no business letting these guys get anywhere near the foot of this wall!"

One of Euen's squires pelted off down the brattice, regained the battlements, and vanished in the direction of the nearest tower. *Can we cover it still, from the Byward Tower to the White Tower?*

Ash ducked back, and stepped off the hoardings on to the walls. Only the backs of men visible, now; a hundred or so here: blue-and-yellow Lion livery for the most part; a couple of Burgundian red Xs. Further along, where the brattices had been on fire, and chopped away because of that, she saw swords, axes; men hooking bills over the tops of ladders – no time for anything subtle: slam them into position along the battlements and tip down everything available on the scaling ladders below.

Robert Anselm jogged up in a clatter of armour and hard breathing. "I've sent my lance to the tower to kick some sense into the Burgundian missile troops!"

"Good! We got 'em turned round here, Roberto!"

Something bright and burning dropped out of the sky, with the whistle of flames fanned by the wind.

The stench of it warned her.

"Greek Fire!"

Oh, sweet Jesu, they *will* fire on their own men if it means getting us too, they just don't care!

She threw herself back across the battlements to the inside of the wall, hauling Anselm with her, yelling orders: "Back! Off the walls! *Away from the walls!*"

Fire hit and splashed.

Inside a second, the nearer brattices burst into flame. She saw the flaming greasy liquid splash and spread. One high voice shrieked. No use to call for water—

"Cut the hoardings free!" she ordered, swinging her axe up and over, chopping down at the supporting beams, and she stood back as the men of three more lances took over.

The shrieking figure rolled on the stone battlements, Greek Fire clinging, a stench of burning coming from blackened skin. Ash recognised red hose and brown padded jack, and the frizzled hair under the melting steel of her sallet: Ludmilla Rostovnaya, half her torso and one arm coated in gelatinous, burning fire.

Anselm yelled, "Thomas Tydder!"

The boy and the rest of his fire detail rushed up along the wall, doused leather buckets of sand over the screaming woman, scraping the stuff away. Ash glimpsed their hands going red in the process.

"Stand aside!" Floria del Guiz sprinted past her with a stretcher team.

The brattice creaked, tilted; gave way with a rush. Flaming wood collapsed out into the empty air.

Ash moved forward to the wall. Below, she saw siege ladders tipping back, screaming men falling from them. Bodies in twenties and thirties plummeted to the broken ground at the foot of the city wall. Visigoth slaves – without armour, without weapons – ran about on the escarpment, darting forward, lifting and carrying men with broken limbs.

As she watched, one pale-haired slave fell with a bolt in him. A few yards away, a soldier wearing the Crescent Moon knelt down beside another trooper who writhed with a broken back, gave him the *coup de grâce* with his dagger, and ran on, leaving the slave jerking and twitching and alive.

Ash looked up to the Byward Tower. Archers and crossbow troops surged past to the shuttered embrasures and arrow-loops; some of the Welsh longbowmen recklessly shooting over the merlons.

Another bolt of Greek Fire impacted, further down the wall.

Under her breath, Ash muttered, "Come *on*. Take that machine *out!*"

She grabbed the edges of the battlements, staring out from the walls. Under the pale sun, four carved limbs of turning stone flashed white in the November day. Four carved marble cups, on stone beams, like the cups of a mangonel, revolved around a stone spindle. There wasn't a soldier or a slave within yards of it to wind it. Ash watched it moving, golem-like, of itself.

Stone chips exploded off it, under a hail of crossbow bolts.

A shrill voice from the Byward Tower yelled, "*Gotcha!*"

As Ash watched, the brass-bound wheels of its carriage began to turn, and it swivelled away from the walls and back towards the Visigoth camp to reload. Blue flickers of fire still burned in the cups at the end of each of its four arms.

"We're holding!" Ash yelled at Anselm.

"Only just!" Ordering the sergeants back to the wall, Robert Anselm broke off to add: "They got the ram going against the main gate! *This* is just a diversion!"

"Yeah, I could've guessed that!" Ash wiped her mouth, took her hand away bloody. "Are they holding the gate?"

"Up till now!"

Breathless, Ash could only nod.

"Motherfuckers!" Robert Anselm narrowed his eyes against the light. "'Ere they come again. Auxiliaries and mercenaries again. Wait till they fucking *mean* it."

Aware now that her chest was heaving to gain air, Ash snatched a second to look out at the distant enemy camp. Three or four hundred men, massing in preparation for the assault's success. "No eagles!"

Robert Anselm tilted his sallet down, against the sun that showed the dirt and stubble on his face. "Not yet!"

Another stone machine edged forward out of the makeshift vast city that is the Visigoth camp. Ash watched. The cups were loaded: fragile clay pots with fuses already lit, shimmering with heat.

"Look at that! They're not supporting that engine. Robert, send to de la Marche, tell him to sally out and take out those bloody engines! Tell him if he won't, we'll be happy to!"

As Anselm signalled a runner, Ash narrowed her eyes in the sunlight. Below, the ground before the walls was strewn with the dead, already; in what must be the first fifteen minutes of fighting. The moat was full of bodies, moving feebly, or still and broken, bleeding on to the faggots and mud and shattered rock.

Two or three riderless horses wandered aimlessly. Carts with pavises mounted on them, slave-hauled, began to recover enemy wounded.

And this wasn't even an attack. A feint. Just so they can get the ram or the saps up to the north-west gate.

It isn't what we can see. It's what we can't see.

With that thought, and almost as she thought it, a great section of the city wall five hundred yards to her right, past the White Tower to the east, first rose up slightly – mortar puffing out between the masonry – and then slumped by ten or eleven inches.

A hot wind blasted her: a thunderous muffled roar shook the paving stones under her feet.

"Fucking saps!" Thomas Rochester thrust through the command group, joining her. His scream was almost hysterical. "They had *another* fucking sap!"

The high-pitched painful ringing in her ears began to deaden a little.

Euen Huw yelled, "I thought we were supposed to be counter-mining!"

Now a vast number of men came running forward from the Visigoth lines, obviously at this signal; dozens of scaling ladders carried aloft over their heads. Ash heard Ludmilla Rostovnaya's lance-mate, Katherine Hammell, yell a shrill "Nock! Loose!" and hundreds of shafts whirred blackly into the middle air from the Lion archers, twelve per minute; vanishing into the mass of men, impossible to see any single strike.

"They've fucked it!" Ash slapped her palm down hard on Rochester's shoulder, grinned at Euen Huw. "They didn't bring the fucking wall *down*. You must be right about the counter-mine!"

She stared at the point where the wall now dipped, and the unsafe battlements along it. Hoardings smouldered. Burgundian men with red St Andrew's crosses on their padded jacks were moving slowly out of the wreckage, a few men being carried.

They may not have brought the wall down. But that's going to be a hell of a weak spot from now on.

"We'll have to hold the wall for them while they sort it! Every second man! Robert, Euen, Rochester: on me!"

Reckless of the likelihood of collapsing masonry, she ran lightly down on to the broken section of wall, the company swarming through the White Tower after her. Rapidly hammering out orders, Ash saw the tops of scaling ladders appear; and hand-to-hand fighting start all along the wall. Four hundred men, a line three and four deep in places; war-hats bright in the light, the spiked blades of bills throwing up a fine red mist. Behind, on the parapet, the Burgundian troops regrouped.

"They blew it!" Ash yelled to Robert Anselm, over the shrieks, the harsh bellowing of "A Lion! A Lion!', and the bang of swivel guns brought down from the far end of the wall. She saw men-at-arms, sunlight glinting off their war-hats, passing up hooked poles, shoving scaling ladders off the walls; and more than one lance were picking up the shattered fragments of trebuchet and mangonel missiles, and dropping chunks of masonry back down off the battlements.

On to the men below.

"The wall didn't come down in front of 'em!" Robert Anselm bellowed. "They ain't got *nowhere* to go!"

Antonio Angelotti, arriving with more swivel guns, showed eyes that were the only white thing in his black face. He yelled to her, "We *must* have counter-mined some of their mines! Else this whole section would be down!"

"At least we're doing something right – let's hope de la Marche can hold the fucking *gate*!"

It seemed long – was probably not, probably only another fifteen minutes – before the only things visible on the walls were the backs of her own men, ignoring any wounds, still high on adrenalin, leaning over the battlements and shouting their raw, violent contempt down at the dying men below. One billman stood up on top of the battlement, his cod-flap unlaced, urinating off the wall. Two of his mates grabbed dead stripped Visigoths by wrists and ankles, and slung them out through the embrasures.

She did not draw breath again until the Burgundian combat engineers had shored up the fallen section of wall with forty-foot planks as thick as a man's arm, supported by wooden buttresses; and the attack on the north-west gate had petered out into a rout, under missile fire, men running back behind the wooden palisades of the Visigoth camp; the golem-ram abandoned, sunk over the axles in mud.

"*Shit . . .*"

Standing with her command group, she made an assessment of the sagging wall in front of her, almost without thinking of it. Merlons broken, like jagged teeth. Men-at-arms moving back from the walls as the sergeants stood them down, leaving anything else to the missile troops.

When they come again, this is where they'll come.

"Can we stand them *all* down?" Angelotti demanded. He appeared oblivious to the blood dripping on to the stone from the fingers of his left hand. "My boys too?"

"Yeah. Pointless wasting ammunition."

Her gaze went up and down the parapet. One crossbowman had his foot planted firmly in the stirrup of his crossbow, winding the winch, but with little urgency now. A hand-gunner in breastplate and war-hat was kneeling, leaning over, hook-gun braced against the edge of the crenellation. As Ash watched, her lance-mate touched a slow-match to the touch-hole; then stuck it back in a sand-barrel, unconcerned by the noise of the shot.

The gunner, as she bent her head to re-load and her face became visible, was Margaret Schmidt.

"Stop wasting your fucking ammunition!" Angelotti's sergeant, Giovanni Petro, bawled, as Ash opened her mouth to give the order. "Don't shoot while they're running away. Wait till the bastard Flemings come back – with all their little Visigoth friends!"

There was a mutter of laughter along the wall. Ash, approaching the edge, and leaning out, caught glances from her men: most of them in the exultation that comes immediately after an action, which is nothing more than the joy of having survived it. One or two of the billmen were prodding corpses in obviously European livery, their expressions hard.

Conscious of a wired rapture that is her own response to survival – a hard joy that wishes every man in the Visigoth camp maimed and bleeding – she leaned over and looked down at the innocent earth in front of the city. Studied it again for disturbance: saw nothing.

"They must have been counter-mined; if they'd managed to set off *all* their petards, they'd have breached this wall."

Not particularly aware of her pronouns, she thought, *We nearly lost Dijon in one attack!*

The noon sun winked back in sparks from the ground. She realised after a second that she was seeing the caltrops[5] that had been thrown down by the defenders.

"Greek Fire, too. Think they're fucking 'ard," Anselm grunted cynically. "What's the *rush*?"

Ash gave him a breathless, diamond-hard grin.

"Don't be in such a hurry, Roberto. They'll be back."

"You reckon?"

"She wants in here fast. I don't know why. All she has to *do* is sit out there and let starvation do it for her. Christ, she even fired on her own men!" Her facial muscles ached, and she realised the grin had gone. Almost inconsequentially, she added, "Dickon's dead – Dickon Stour."

His gaze was not unaware of other casualties; nonetheless, there was a deep disgust in his voice. "Ah, fuck it. Poor fucking shite."

Ash busied herself in the business of clearing up, seeing her men reassembled, and on their way back to their quarters. Groups of men carried heavy, red-soaked blankets between them: Dickon Stour, his two mates, and seven others dead. And Ludmilla not the only screaming survivor of Greek Fire, but what the wounded list was, she would not, she supposed, hear from Florian until later.

It was a stranger who found her as she was coming down off the wall at last: a Burgundian knight who rode up to her and her command group in the street, intercepting her as she stepped across the central gutter; still, even in this bitter weather, semi-liquid with excrement.

"Demoiselle-Captain—"

"Just 'Captain'!"

"—the Duke sends word."

Ash, every muscle aching, and wanting little more than to find Floria's salve for bruises, dark beer, and pottage – in that order – eyed him wearily. "I'm at the Duke's command."

"He told me that you have a more urgent task than the defence of the walls," the knight said, "and he asks you, when will you begin it?"

II

The November day died in grey twilight, an hour or more before Vespers. Of the wounded, all survived that long. Those inns within a quarter-mile radius of the company tower became packed with mercenary men-at-arms getting loudly drunk. Riding back through the streets, Ash thought it wise not to see, officially, what might be going on in the way of brawls and sexual encounters in the street; wise to leave ab Morgan to keep it from becoming murder and rape.

The top floor of the company's tower having been reorganised to contain the

---

[5] Iron spikes with four points, made so that one spike always projects upwards, no matter how the caltrop falls.

armoury, the war-chests, and Ash's own belongings, they were now stacked more or less in order on the open, rush-strewn floor. Ash strode past the armed men at the door, nodding her acknowledgement.

She threw a handful of sketches down on the trestle table in front of Robert Anselm. "There."

"You've been all round the walls."

"Twice." Ash moved over to a brazier, unbuckling and stripping off her gauntlets. A page – one of half a dozen recruited new from the baggage train – ran to take them from her. She huffed, grinned, beating her cold hands together. "Euen Huw's whingeing on again. He said, *You'll wear the lads out before the rag-heads even get in here—*"

Her accurate mimicry made Robert Anselm laugh.

"I must have passed six of the Duke's messengers on up to the walls since Nones[6]," he added, reading the rough charcoal lines and dots that represented enemy dispositions outside the walls, and not her face. "Did any of them happen to find the bit of it you were on?"

"Green Christ! We only got into this fucking town this morning! *And* we've had to fight. Can't the man give me a few *hours*? I'll do it, when I'm ready—" Ash straightened, hearing footsteps and guards' muffled voices. No challenge. The door opened.

Floria del Guiz stepped inside, flushed, her hair dishevelled. She shed her cloak as she strode to join Ash at the brazier.

"Damn, but I love a good row!" Her eyes sparkled; her expression hard. "Free and frank exchange of professional views, I *should* say."

Robert Anselm put the maps down. "Been talking to doctors up at the palace, have you?"

"Half-witted leech-ticklers!"

Ash, her fingers and cheeks prickling with returning warmth, demanded, "So. *Tell me.* How's the Duke?"

Floria's expression lost its anger. She signalled the serving page to add more water to the offered wine-cup. "You trust that man. I can see it. That's a new one, for you."

"Do I?" Ash broke off to tell another of the pages, at the hearth, that she should mull the rest of the wine. "Yeah. He's promised me another try at Carthage. That's what I trust. He's in this for survival; and the man knows what to do with an army. So: what's the prognosis? When will he be on his feet again? *Is* it the wound he took at Auxonne?"

"That's what I've been discussing. Ha! Ash, do you know? It was the name of this company that got me through to him. A 'woman-doctor'." Floria walked across to the window embrasure, peered out into the gloom, and hitched her hip up on to the window ledge. Her hands described the shapes of bodies in the air. "His surgeons finally let me see it – he's taken a wound in the middle of his back. Lance, I'd say."

"Shit!"

Floria's green gaze flickered at the empathic flinch that came from Ash. She pointed at Anselm. "Stand up!"

[6] 3 p.m.

As the big man stood, she crossed the chamber and seized his left arm, holding it up from his body. Robert Anselm looked gravely at her. The surgeon tapped his armour, under his left arm.

"As far as I can see, a lance strike here – from the front or the side, into the left side of the Duke's body."

"It should have glanced off. That's what the deflective surfaces of armour are for." Ash went to where Anselm stood thoughtfully motionless. She put her fingers on the join of breast- and backplate. "Unless the lance hit one of the hinges, here. That would let it bite."

"I've also been able to examine the Duke's armour. It's burst open."

Anselm, not moving except to try and look over his shoulder, speculated, "A lance would hit hard. Bite. Burst the hinges, maybe. The lance-tip would penetrate."

"Might slide round the *inside* of the backplate." Ash looked questioningly at the surgeon. "Did the lance deform, maybe? Break off in the wound?"

"I did hear it was a lance," Anselm admitted. "Someone said de la Marche cut the lance-shaft with his sword, almost as soon as it struck home."

"Fuck."

"Better than having a full hit. He'd have been dead inside minutes."

Floria waved her hands. "This is what I've been debating with the Duke's physicians! I believe it wasn't the lance that hurt him – it was his armour."

The page approached with wooden cups, serving Ash first, then Anselm – who relaxed his self-imposed immobility – and finally the surgeon; before the girl went back to huddle at the spidery, dirt-crusted hearth with the rest of the children. Smoke gusted into the room with a change of the wind.

"There are fragments of his own armour still in the Duke's wound. I examined the cuirass. The hard outer layers have shattered, and the soft iron underneath has torn." Floria put her free hand on Anselm's waist at the back, above the fauld. Ash noted that he did not flinch.

The surgeon said, "There are two organs, bean-shaped, that lie under the flesh here. One is crushed; we think the other has fragments of steel in it."

"Oh fuck," Ash said blankly. She shook herself back to concentration. "So, how is he?"

"Oh, he's dying, no argument about *that*."

III

"*Dying?*"

The blank professionalism of Floria's gaze altered as she became cognisant of Ash's appalled stare. The shaggy-haired woman laced her long fingers together.

"His surgeons have been debating cutting him. They won't do it. It won't save him if they do. But it won't harm him much, either . . . You've seen him.

You've talked to him. He's stayed alive for three months, he's nothing but bones. He doesn't eat. It's only his spirit keeping him going. I give him a week or two at the outside."

Anselm rumbled, "Who's his heir?"

Automatic, stunned, Ash said, "Margaret of Burgundy, if she wins at Bruges; de la Marche by default."

"The heart will go out of the defence."

"*Dying*," Ash repeated; ignoring Anselm. "Sweet Christ. A couple of weeks? Florian, are you *sure*?"

Floria del Guiz spoke with a brittle rapidity. "Of course I'm sure. I've seen guys cut up every way you can think of. Barring a miracle, he's dog-meat."

Anselm drained his cup and wiped his mouth. "Have to rely on the priests, then."

"His priests' prayers aren't getting any answers. I'm seeing it with our men, here," Floria said. "Bad air from the rivers, maybe. They don't heal well."

"Who knows how bad it is?"

Floria looked at Ash. "For certain? Him, his doctors; the three of us, now. De la Marche. The soeurs, I expect. Rumours? Who knows?"

Ash became aware that she was biting at her knuckle; tasting salt sweat, and feeling the tender bruises of blows that have only hit gauntlets.

"This changes everything. If he dies – why didn't he *tell* me? Green Christ . . . I wonder if he can order a force to Africa before he . . ." Ash broke off. "Dying. Florian, you know what I thought, as you said it? 'At least I won't have to talk to the Wild Machines, now.' I've been avoiding it all day. And I won't have to. With Charles dead, the Visigoths are going to come right over those walls out there!"

"Then we find out if your demon-machines are just voices," Robert Anselm stated, pragmatically. "Just farts in the wind. We find out what they can do."

Floria made as if to touch Ash's arm, and stopped herself. "You can't be afraid for ever."

Easy for you to say.

Ash said abruptly, "Wake me in an hour, Robert. I'm going to sleep before the food comes."

She was aware that they exchanged glances, but ignored them. The chamber chilled as evening darkened. Noise came up from below, the main hall filling up. She listened to guards patrolling the access corridors, that ran through the twenty-foot-thick walls; and the pages chattering as they stripped her down to her shirt and helped her into her gown; all without noticing much but the shock-reaction chilling her body. She lay down on her box-bed, close to the hearth, thinking, *Dying?* She can't be sure. Only God *knows* a man's last hour—

But she's been right in the past, about most of the wounded in my company. Shit.

The flames licked at the wet, smoking logs, charring the damp bark away. Central wood burned away into ash, that still held the shape of the grain until a draught from the chimney stirred it, sparks flying up. Smoke stung her eyes. She wiped at them repeatedly.

What am *I* worrying about? It's just one more employer who didn't make it.

If I can get him to set a task-force up to go from Flanders to North Africa . . . there isn't time.

Come to think of it, I wonder where John de Vere is, right now? Oxford, I wish you were here; we could do with all the good men we can get.

But if I'm honest, I could do with your companionship as much as your skills.

The ache of fighting eased, now that she lay on the bed; rubbing at one over-strained shoulder; wondering where, exactly, in combat the blue-black bruises on her hands had come from. With practised ease, she set herself to fall asleep.

On the borders of unconsciousness, the chill draught from the windows turned into a biting gale, and her eyes saw white snow, and the light of a blue sky.

She had the impression of a forest, and that she knelt in snow. In front of her, plain to the last winter-thick white hair and grey-brown bristle, a wild boar lay on her side. The earth was scored up by the sow's thrashing hooves.

Ash stared at the beast's fat belly, nipples visible in the thick hair, and the rump that she was facing. Without any warning, the sow writhed, arched and flexed her back, and cocked her leg. A blue-red mass pushed halfway out of her body.

Not here! Ash thought. *Not in the snow!*

The slumped, razor-backed body of the sow rippled. The steaming mass pushed out of her vagina, long blind snout first, teardrop-shaped body after; all in a rush, out into the stinking snow. Mucus smeared the boarlet's body. It flopped, in the snow, wet legs twitching; muzzle blindly turning, seeking the sow's nipple. She groaned, snorting. Ash saw her begin to shift, as if she would get up.

"No . . ." The thickness of her voice as she spoke, aloud, almost brought her back to her bed and the crowded solar; but she deliberately let that go.

As one does in dreams, she fought to move through air as thick as honey. Light sparkled from each snow-crystal. She closed her hands around the new-born boar, her fingers slick with mucus and juice, and thrust the thing towards its mother's belly.

Fast as a snake, the sow's jaws clashed.

Ash snatched her bare hands back.

Now that her snout all but rested on it, the sow appeared to notice the boarlet. Her jaw dipped. She chewed through the white birth-cord. Her head flopped forward again. She took no more notice of the new-born thing, did not lick it, but by now it had its snout clamped firmly into her belly-fur, attached to a nipple.

"Not in the snow," Ash mumbled, anguished. "It can't survive."

– *Stranger things have happened.* Deo gratias.

"Godfrey?"

– *You are hard to reach!*

Robert Anselm's heavy tread vibrated through the floorboards by her head, as he stomped past her towards the mulled wine resting by the hearth. She rolled over, away from him, open-eyed. Muffled under gown and sleeping-furs, she whispered, "Only when I want to be. You could be a demon. So tell me something only you would know. Now!"

– *In Milano, when you were apprenticed to the armourer, you slept under your master's work-bench, not allowed into inns, not allowed to marry without his permission. I used to visit you. You said you wanted to run an arms-dealing business.*

"God, yes! I remember, now . . ."

– *You were eleven, as near as we could judge. You told me you were tired of having to break apprentice-boys' heads. I believe that was with the broom you swept up with.* The voice in her head tinged with amusement.

"Godfrey, you're dead. I saw you. I had my fingers in the wound."

– *Yes. I remember dying.*

"Where are you?"

– *Nowhere. In torment; in Purgatory.*

"Godfrey . . . what are you?"

Let him say *a soul*, she thought. Her nails dug painfully into her palms. The life of the company went on around her – she could hear Angelotti's voice, now, in the solar; and Thomas Rochester; and Ludmilla Rostovnaya loudly complaining about burns bandaged and thick with goose-grease. Under the noise, she whispered again:

"What are you, now?"

– *A messenger.*

"Messenger?"

– *Here in the dark, I still pray. And answers come to me. They are answers for you, child. I have been trying to speak to you; to give these messages to you. You never relax, except at the edge of sleep.*

Hairs shivered on the back of her neck. Although she lay prone, her body tensed with the alertness of imminent attack.

Ash has a momentary memory, mosaic-like, of a hundred skirmishes, a hundred fields fought; and the same voice always clear in her head: *advise this, advise that, attack, withdraw.* The Stone Golem: the *machina rei militaris*. It is the same voice that she hears now – and yet now it is illuminated by a presence, changed utterly.

"It is you," she said. Water welled in her eyes and she ignored it. "I don't care what this is, demon or miracle, but I'm going to get you back, Godfrey."

– *I am not the man you knew.*

"I don't care if you're not a saint or a spirit, either. You're coming home." Ash covered her face with her hands, under the edge of blankets and furs. She felt her breath hot against her cold skin. "Do you know, you speak to me where the Stone Golem speaks? Godfrey – can you hear that, too?"

– *A voice speaks in me, of war. I have thought, since I became . . . this . . . that such a voice must be your* machina rei militaris. *I have tried to speak through it, to the men of Carthage, but they believe my words to be nothing but errors.*

She uncovered her face, if only to see, now that candles were being lit, that she lay on her bed among her company, neither in a snow-bound forest, nor in a cell in Carthage. The yellow light swarmed in her vision; she felt hot, then cold.

"My sister? Will *she* speak to you?"

– Not to me. I have tried. Nor, now, will she speak to the machina rei militaris *itself.*

"She won't?"

Is that since I talked to her, last night? Shit! If it is—

"Jesus wept!" Ash said devoutly. "If that's true, she can't have been using it when she attacked the wall—"

– 'The wall'?

Vehemently shaking her head, Ash whispered, "Doesn't matter! Not now! Shit, if that was *her* decision – firing on her own men – that was a shit-bad judgement call!"

– Child, I'm lost on this one.

"You'd hear, though? You'd hear, if she spoke to it – to you?"

– I hear everything.

"Everything?"

The floorboards creaked under her, the noise of a couple of hundred off-duty squaddies coming up from the hall below: belligerent, boisterous, loud. Ash flinched.

She spoke, barely moving her lips:

"Godfrey, I've given my word that I'll speak to the Stone Golem again. I'm afraid of it—no. I'm afraid of what can speak through it. The other machines."

– The name they have for themselves is 'Wild Machines'. As if your machina rei militaris *were tame and domestic!*

Fear and amazement washed through her. She thought, But he shouldn't know about them, he was dead before I found out! And then: But it *is* Godfrey. And he *does* know.

"How do you know about them?"

– More than one voice speaks to me. Child, I am among many voices, here. I tried to speak to you, but you put up a wall to keep me out. I have been listening, then, to them. Perhaps this is the rim of Hell, and I hear the great Devils speaking between themselves: these 'Wild Machines'.

"What . . . what do they say?"

– They say to me: WE STUDY YOU . . .

In Godfrey's voice, repeating it, she hears an echo of the voices that blasted her mind wide open.

"Maybe they want to know what people are like," she said, and added painfully, with bracing sarcasm: "Green Christ alone knows why! They've had two hundred years of listening to military reports from the whole Visigoth empire, they must know everything about court politics and betrayal there is to know!"

– I hear them, voices in the dark. They say, WE STUDY THE GRACE OF GOD IN MAN . . . *They say,* LAST SUMMER, THE SUN WENT OUT OVER THE GERMANIES. *I hear them say,* THAT WAS ONLY A TRIAL OF OUR STRENGTH.

A long sigh shuddered through her body. "You *do* hear them. That's what they said to me."

– That it served as a demonstration of power? But that it was not done for that, not done to bring darkness to Christendom. It was done only to see if they could draw on such power. If they could use it. But they have not wholly used it yet. That is to come.

"They draw their power from the sun's spirit. I heard them saying they took more from the sun this summer than they had in ten thousand years." Ash licked dry lips. "And that the next time it happened, it would be to use the Faris to make a miracle. What I don't understand is why they haven't done it before now—"

The voice of Godfrey Maximillian in her head whispered on, relentless, with an agonising determination in its tone:

– *They will draw grace from the sun, as we have prayed to the saints for Divine grace. As I have made tiny miracles by the grace of God, so they will make her a channel for their will and their miracle. Soon! It is going to be soon.*

"Yes, but, Godfrey—"

A voice that was many and one, loud enough that she bit her tongue at the shock, broke into her mind:

'IT IS SHE!'

Ash sat bolt upright.

"Get me a priest!"

As every face turned towards her, she said, "They found me."

IV

"It's too dangerous, speaking with Devils!" Robert Anselm protested grimly. "We need you here. Commanding the company. Devils might – break you."

Ash, studying his sweating brow, under his woollen hood pulled low, thought, *You* need me commanding the company. Is that it? Is that what you found out, these past three months? Shit, Roberto. I never took you for one of life's natural 2ICs.

What *has* it been like here?

Softly, Antonio Angelotti said, "But it *is* Meister Godfrey. Alive, is it, madonna? Alive, still?"

"No; dead. It's his—" Ash stumbled. "His soul. I know Godfrey's soul as well as I know my own." A crooked smile. "Better."

Floria's hand rested on the shoulder of Ash's gown, her knuckles momentarily warm against the muscles of Ash's neck. Not to Ash, but to Angelotti, she said, "What's the priest to you? It isn't worth losing our girl."

The gunner, ragged curls gold in the candlelight, looked at last now as if he had been on campaign; lines drawn down the sides of his mouth, eyes hollow. A thick, stained bandage covered his left arm from shoulder to elbow. "Ash rescued me. Meister Godfrey prayed with me. If I can help him, I will."

"Demon-possessed," Robert Anselm cut in, "what if you end up demon-possessed again?"

"It's too dangerous," the surgeon said.

"I signed a *condotta*. The Duke has a right to demand this. Even if he is dying." Ash held out her arms to her pages. "I'll do it *once*. Guys . . . I might as well talk to the Wild Machines. They know I'm alive now. You can bet *they'll* talk to me!"

One of the pages finished tying the eighteen pairs of aiglettes that fastened her doublet to her hose, and handed her a demi-gown. She shrugged into it.

"Now?" Robert Anselm said.

"Now. One of the things we've always known, Roberto. We *have* to have all the information we can get. Otherwise the company gets fucked. It's my decision." She shook his shoulder. "Digorie; Richard."

The two company priests arrived at the head of the spiral stairs, Digorie Paston somewhat in the lead, his bony face alight with enthusiasm. Richard Faversham trod bear-like in his wake.

"Captain." Digorie Paston's stole lay askew on his shoulders. He gazed around. "Clear this room. The pages should bring clean water, and bread, and then go down below. All to go except Master Anselm, Master Angelotti, and – the surgeon." He flushed pink to the tips of his ears. "Master Anselm, Master Angelotti, will you keep the door, please."

"Just one minute." Ash put her fists on her hips.

"Please, Captain," the priest said. "This is an exorcism."

Ash looked at him for a long minute. "It . . . might turn out to be that, yes."

"Then let myself and Father Faversham do what is necessary. We will need all of God's grace that we can get."

The roof of the tower's top floor shifted with shadows, candle-flames moving in the draughts. Ash moved to stand with her arms folded, near the fire, and watched as the two priests cleared the room with surprising lack of fuss. While Richard Faversham swung a censer, Digorie Paston followed him, around the corridor in the walls, appearing at the window gaps, disappearing again, their chant echoing up into the vaulted stone.

"You're going to do this," Floria said resignedly, walking to stand beside Ash in the yellow light.

"Somebody has to."

"Do they? Do they have to?"

"To win this—"

"Oh, the *war!*" Floria put her back to the fire's warmth. For a moment, her brother's stone-green eyes looked at Ash from her face. "Bloody, pointless, *destructive*—! Won't I ever get it through to you? Most people spend their lives *building* things!"

"Not the people I know," Ash said mildly. "You're maybe the exception."

"I spend my life putting men back together after you get them chopped up. I get sick of it sometimes. Ten people *died* up on that wall!"

"We're all going to die," Ash said. Floria began to turn away. Ash caught her arm and repeated, "We're all going to die some day. Doesn't matter what we do. Till the fields, sell wool, sell your fanny, pray all your life in a nunnery – we're all of us going to die. Four things go over this world like the seasons: hunger, plague, death, and war.[7] They were doing it before I came along, and they'll be doing it long after. People *die*. That's all."

---

[7] Cf. Revelation, ch. 6.

"And you follow the Four Horsemen because you like it, and because it pays well."

"Stop trying to pick a fight, Floria. I'm not going to fight with you. It isn't just a war here. It isn't just *bad* war. It's complete and entire destruction . . ."

"Dead is dead," Florian snapped. "I don't suppose your civilian casualties care much whether they died in a 'just war' or a 'bad war'!"

Paston and Faversham chanted, "Christus Imperator, Christus Viridianus." Their voices swooped, one high, one low. In the light, that is bright only where the candles are, Angelotti and Anselm could be any pair of armed men, standing at the stair-entrance. The gunner appeared to be holding an impassioned *sotto voce* conversation. Ash saw Anselm scowl.

Impatience made her shift her footing, stare at the shuttered windows, the stacked crates of the armoury.

"Oh yeah – Florian – while I remember. I saw Soeur Simeon in the Tour Philippe le Bon. She wants your Margaret Schmidt back. That was a hell of a shock up on the wall – I never expected I'd see her with the gunners. I thought she'd be one of your surgery assistants."

Floria del Guiz said quietly, "She isn't 'my' Margaret Schmidt."

Conscious of feeling taken aback, Ash said, "Oh."

Floria looked at her with an expression between grimness and bitter amusement. "Whatever I may have been expecting – no. She . . . It seems she's signed on the company books as a gunner's apprentice."

"She'll be all right," Ash offered, somewhat at a loss, still waiting for the blessing to finish. "She was with one of Angelotti's best men; he'll train her."

Florian kept her gaze on Ash. "I can't make you understand it, can I? They're teaching her to kill other men! Not for defence, not even for her lord. For money. And because she'll get to like it. Or if she sickens of it in the end, what is there for her? She can't go back."

Ash said quietly, "I didn't make her join us."

"She's too young to know her own mind!"

Digorie Paston and Richard Faversham re-entered the main chamber, a scent of incense with them; singing together a solemn blessing.

"Okay," Ash said authoritatively, "I'll do what I do with very young recruits. I'll put her on guard tonight, up on the east wall, over the Ouche river. No one's going to come in on that side, but it's going to be fucking freezing."

She looked away from the priests, back to Floria.

"Most of the young lads quit after that. They can say they've been at the front, so their pride's okay. If she wants out, I'll let her go. But if she doesn't, Florian, I won't make her. Because we'll need her. Unless we can get supplied up and out of this city, we need everyone we can *get*."

In the sudden silence, Ash realised the blessing had finished.

Faversham and Paston glared at her.

Floria switched her gaze to the waiting priests. "Girl – you haven't got the piety of a *rabbit*. Have you?"

Ash's lips twitched in what would have been a smile, if her face had not been stiff with fear. "You'd be surprised."

Digorie Paston said, "The – surgeon – should attend while we do this. It may be dangerous."

"Right." Ash put her hands to her belt; missed it; realised it still lay on her bed, purse and dagger threaded on it; so that she stood without weapons. "Digorie, Richard; I want you to pray for me, while I do this. And, when I ask it – I want you to pray for God's grace to silence the voice between my soul and the Stone Golem."

Floria's dark gaze came up. "You're going to try to cut yourself free of the Wild Machines? The Duke won't like that."

"I'll ask the questions he wants me to ask. If Godfrey's right, and I've scared the Faris off the *machina rei militaris* for now, I'm not going to get any answers about her tactics. And we *know* what Carthage's grand strategy is."

"It may change. If you do this, we won't know."

Ash's voice thinned. "They just – turned me around, Florian. They *made* me walk towards them. Okay, we're a long way from Carthage. But that isn't happening again. It is *not*. I have people depending on me."

"And Godfrey?"

Before Ash answered – the implications of that stark in her mind – Digorie Paston reached out and took her hand in his bony grip, and led her to the hearth. Flames leaped, dazzling. The dusty, cluttered chamber was full of cold wind and leaping shadows. At his insistent push, Ash knelt. Ancient carvings glared down from the lintel above the hearth. Shadows moved in the eyes and foliage of Christus Viridianus.

Digorie Paston took a loaf of dark bread and broke it. Richard Faversham sprinkled water and salt.

"Fire and salt and candlelight: Christ receive thy soul—"

Ash shut her eyes. She closed out the anxious faces of the two priests; shut out Floria, pacing at the edge of the candlelight, and the voices of Anselm and Angelotti. The floor was painfully hard under her knees, bruised from the assault on the walls of Dijon.

– *And you had no business to be leading an attack, child! It is a sin to tempt Death that way.*

Salted bread touched her lips. She took it into her mouth. It formed a solid, gelatinous lump.

"How the hell—" she swallowed "—do you know what I was doing up there today, Godfrey?"

– *You were praying. To Our Lord, or to the* machina rei militaris: *perhaps both. I heard you. 'Keep me alive until the rest get here!' I have no knowledge of where you fought, or how; but I am not a fool, and I know you.*

"Okay, so I was out in front. Sometimes you have to be. It wasn't suicidal, Godfrey."

– *But hardly safe.*

She laughed at that, swallowing down the bread and almost choking. With her eyes shut, every sense strained, she listened. In that part of her self which she has been used to sharing, there is a sense of amusement, kindness, love. Tears prick at her eyes: she blinks them back. In the hollow of her mind there is

697

a sense of potential for more voices than this one: Godfrey Maximillian, alone in the dark.

"What comes after death?"

It was not the question she meant to ask. She heard, with her ears, Digorie Paston's sharp, "Blessed be!', and Richard Faversham's "Amen!"

– *How can I say? This is Limbo; this is Purgatory. This is pain! Not the Communion of the Blessed!*

"Godfrey—"

Anguish flooded through her, with his voice.

– *I need to see the face of Our Lord! It was promised to me!*

She felt pain, and blinked her eyes open for long enough to see her nails dug into her palms.

"I *will* find you."

– *I am . . . nowhere. Not to be found. I have no eyes to see, no hands to touch. I am something that listens, something that hears. Everything is darkness. Voices . . . pry at me. Expose me to them . . . The hours, the days – is it years? Nothing but the voices, here—*

"Godfrey!"

– *Nothing but the dark, and the Great Devils eating away at me!*

Ash reached out. Hands took hers; a man's hands rough with chilblains and work, and cold with the November chill. She gripped them as if they were the hands of Godfrey Maximillian.

"I won't leave you."

– *Help me!*

"There's nothing we won't do. Trust me. Nothing! I'll get help to you."

She spoke with complete conviction, with the utter determination of combat. That such a rescue might be unknown or impossible is nothing, now; nothing beside the need to reach him.

His voice became gentle laughter.

– *You have said that to us many times before, little one, in the most impossible of fights.*

"Yeah, and I've been right, too."

– *Pray for me.*

"Yes." She listens, inside. In the hollow of her shared soul; listening for voices louder than God.

– *How long is it, since last you spoke to me?*

"Minutes . . . Not even an hour."

– *I cannot tell, child. Time is nothing where I am. I read once in Aquinas that the duration of the soul in Hell may be only a heartbeat, but to the damned it is eternity.*

Momentarily, she lets herself feel his desolation. Then, harshly: "You hear my sister. Has she spoken to the Stone Golem again, yet?"

– *Once more. I thought at first that it was you. She spoke to it, to Carthage, saying that you live. Saying that whatever she asks the* machina rei militaris, *you can ask, and be told. She tells her master the King-Caliph that they are overheard, now.*

In her ears, her own heartbeats sound; and the whispered addendum of the voice in her head:

– *You are very different, you and she.*

"How? No: tell me later."

The boards beneath her knees brought pain, focusing her.

"Tell me what troops she's got deployed here. What recent messengers she's had from the armies in Iberia and Venice. And how strong she is in the north – I know she had another two legions with her when we were at Basle: they *must* be in Flanders!"

– I . . . can tell you what reports have been made to the machina rei militaris, *I think.*

Ash bowed her head, her hands still tightly gripping the hands of the man in front of her; her eyes closed.

"And . . . I have to speak with the Wild Machines, if I can. Will you stand by me?"

There was, for the first time, a hiatus in her mind. His sadness suffused her. Godfrey Maximillian's voice sounded, soft as thistledown:

– When I was a boy, I loved the forests. My mother vowed me to the Church. I would have stayed under the sky, with the animals. I loved my monastery no better than you loved St Herlaine, Ash, and they beat me as they beat you, brutally. I still do not believe God intended me for a priest, but He gave me the grace to perform small miracles, and the gift of being in your company. It was worth it. On earth, or here, I stand with you. If I regret anything, it is only that I could not gain your trust.

The *it was worth it* she shoved into a dark part of her mind, wiped out, ignored. A tight, cold ball of muscle knotted under her breastbone. Before she could lose the courage and the warmth of him, she said, "Visigoth troop dispositions, siege of Dijon, main units, give position."

The *machina rei militaris*, in Godfrey's voice, began to speak:

– Legio VI Leptis Parva, north-east quadrant: serf-troops to the number of—

'IT IS SHE . . . '

The same silence that had blanketed her mind among the pyramids of the desert numbed her. For a second, she lost the feel of the boards under her shins, and the grip she had on Digorie Paston's hands.

"Son of a bitch—" Ash opened her eyes, screwing up her face. Richard Faversham held her shoulders; Digorie Paston her hands. As far away as if they had been at the other end of a field of combat, faces surrounded her: Anselm, Angelotti, Floria.

She gripped Digorie's bony hands. "Godfrey!"

Nothing answered. A chill inside her mind began to spread. She reached into herself, meeting only numbness, deafness. *They can reach this far, then.*

Christ, all the way over the seas from Carthage; across half of Christendom . . . ! But the Stone Golem can, so why shouldn't they?

"Godfrey!"

Faint as a dream, Godfrey's voice whispered:

– I am here, always.

'IT IS SHE. IT IS YOU, LITTLE ONE . . . '

It is not enough, now, that there are men and women – Thomas Rochester, Ludmilla Rostovnaya, Carracci, Margaret Schmidt – whose lives may be rescued or ruined by her decisions.

She thinks, *No one is indispensable.*

Now it is Ash, a woman, alone, after nineteen years; kneeling on hard wood in a cold wind, with the searing flicker of the hearth-fire hot on the sleeve of her doublet. A woman who prays, suddenly and separately, as she has not done since she was a child: *Lion protect me!*

She recalls painted plaster crunching under the hooves of a brown mare, in snow, in the south, riding between the great pyramids. If she is numbed, now, it may be with silence or with cold. The voices in her head – and they are plural, multiple, legion – whisper as one:

'WE KNOW THAT YOU HEAR US.'

"No shit?" Ash said, mildly acid. She let go of the priest's hands, her eyes still shut, and heard his gasp of pain released. She sat back on her heels. There is no compulsion to stop performing any of these acts. In utter relief, she says, "But you can't reach me. I could be anywhere."

'YES. YOU COULD BE. BUT YOU ARE IN DIJON. GUNDOBAD'S CHILD TELLS US SO.'

"I don't think so. Told the Stone Golem and House Leofric, maybe. But not you. She won't listen to you."

'THAT IS NOTHING. SHE WILL *HEAR*, WHEN THE TIME COMES. LITTLE ONE, LITTLE ONE; STOP FIGHTING US.'

"In a fucking pig's ear!"

It is pure mercenary, mercenary as she has always wanted to be seen: foul-mouthed, cheerful, brutal, indestructible. If anything else is under the surface, it is hidden even from her, now, in this adrenalin-rush.

"You're not Wild." Tears dripped down her face: and she could not have said whether it was pain or painful humour that put them there. "We *made* you. Long, long ago – by accident – but it was us, we made you. Why do you hate us? Why do you hate Burgundy?"

'SHE HAS HEARD.'

'SHE HAS SHARED.'

'KNOWN WHAT WE KNOW.'

'LITTLE AS WE KNOW.'

'KNOWN THE BEGINNING. BUT WHO KNOWS THE END?'

What had been chorus became, with the last voice, a braided sound. Sorrow keened in it. Ash blinked under the power of it, momentarily saw the flames in the hearth and the blackened stone chimney behind, burned with the fires of centuries. Where the fire had been fierce, a piece of stone had cracked and fallen away. The pattern of fracture remained.

In her memory, Ash sees the dome of the King-Caliph's palace fracture and fall, the weight of stone hurtling down.

'WE KNOW THE END . . . '

'THE VILENESS OF FLESH!'

'LITTLE VILE THINGS, NOT WORTHY TO LIVE—'

'—BECAUSE OF YOUR EVIL—'

Pressing her fingers into her palms so hard that her nails penetrated the skin, Ash gasped, sardonically, "Don't let two hundred years of listening to Carthage prejudice you!"

There is something that may be rueful amusement – Godfrey? And a soul-deafening, icy babble in her mind:

'CARTHAGE IS NOTHING—'

'—THE VISIGOTHS, *NOTHING*—'

'GUNDOBAD SPOKE WITH US, LONG BEFORE THEM—'

'VILEST OF MEN!'

'WE REMEMBER!'

'WE REMEMBER . . . '

'WE WILL BURY YOU, LITTLE THING OF FLESH.'

The last reverberation in her head made her wince, taste blood where she bit her tongue. She said aloud, not seeing the people around her, "Don't worry. If they *could* move the earth here, they would. If they're not doing it, they can't."

'ARE YOU SO SURE, LITTLE ONE?'

Chills ran down the skin under her clothing; she thought, with appalled disgust, *'Little one': that's what Godfrey calls me; they've taken that from* him.

"Something's stopping you," she said aloud. With a fierce sarcasm, she spat, "According to you, the Faris doesn't *need* an army! She's Gundobad's child, she's a wonder-worker; she can make Burgundy into a desert just like that. All you have to do is pray to the sun, and *bang!* there you are. One miracle. *So why haven't you done it?* "

With that vehemence, she instantly focused herself – finding the same interior state that she finds when she handles a sword – and *listened*.

Instantly, she grunted with a soundless impact. Her mouth stung. She put her hands up, opened her eyes; saw blood, realised she had bitten her lip. Someone said something abrupt, beside her. She could say nothing, only jerk her hand, wave them back. She felt at once winded, and numb; as she felt when she first learned to ride. It is that split second between hitting the ground, and pain. She froze.

Physical pain did not come.

'YOU CANNOT HEAR US. NOT IF WE CHOOSE. YOU WILL NOT SURPRISE US AGAIN.'

"Shit, no." Ash rubbed her hand across her mouth, feeling blood slick on her skin. "No, *sir*."

'WE DO NOT UNDERSTAND YOU.'

"No. You don't. Join the fucking club," Ash said bitterly.

There was no feeling in her of their puzzlement or confusion. Only the interior sound of the voices. Her blood dried cold, pulling on her skin. She probed it tenderly with her tongue, thought, *That's going to hurt*, and swallowed blood and saliva before she said, "You can't keep me out for ever."

Nothing.

"What does it matter if you tell me? It's *already* getting cold. You're drawing down the sun, and it's getting cold, where you are. Pretty soon you won't need the Faris here. Or a miracle! The winter will kill us all."

Again, voices in unison:

'WINTER WILL NOT COVER ALL.'

"Godammit!" Ash hit her fist against her thigh, exasperated. "Why is Burgundy so *important* to you?"

'WE CAN DRAW DOWN THE SUN'S SPIRIT—'[8]

'USE ITS POWER, WEAKEN, BRING DARKNESS—'

'DARK, COLD AND WINTER—'

'—BUT—'

'WINTER WILL NOT COVER ALL THE WORLD.'

Ash opened her eyes.

Robert Anselm knelt in front of her, one hand steadying his hilt. Behind him, Angelotti had his hand on Anselm's mailed shoulder. Both of them stared at her. Floria squatted between the two priests, resting her arms on her thighs, her long fingers almost touching the floorboards.

'WINTER WILL NOT COVER—'

'—ALL!—'

'DARKNESS WILL NOT COVER ALL THE WORLD.'

"In nomine Patris, Filii, et Spiritus Sancti," Richard Faversham said in a hoarse, high whisper.

Ash repeated, "'Darkness will not cover *all the world*' . . . ?"

She did not shut her eyes, could still see them all, but the sound of great voices in her head blasted her attention away from the tower room. A vast, cold sorrow almost drowned her:

'—WINTER MAY KILL ALL THE WORLD, BUT FOR HIM.'

'DARKNESS MAY COVER ALL THE WORLD – BUT FOR HIM.'

'WE CANNOT REACH—'

'—BURGUNDY DIES AT HER COMMAND, ONLY—'

'SHE WILL DESTROY BURGUNDY. OUR DARK MIRACLE. AS SOON AS THE DUKE DIES.'

"All the world," Ash said. "All the world!"

'WHEN IT IS GONE—'

'—MADE DESOLATE, MADE A DESERT—'

'WHEN IT IS NOTHING: BURGUNDY DESTROYED, AS IF IT HAD NEVER BEEN—'

'THEN EVERYTHING—'

'ALL THE WORLD—'

'—CAN BE CLEANSED AND PURE, ALL THE WORLD—'

'—FREE OF FLESH; VILE, DESTRUCTIVE FLESH; FREE—'

'AS IF YOU HAD NEVER BEEN.'

The surge and ebb of the great voices drained away. The floorboards shifted under her feet— no, were solid, but she lost balance and fell back and sat on her rump, Richard Faversham catching her, so that she sprawled up against him, his blacksmith's arm around her shoulders.

A numb, desolate silence filled her soul. Into it, no voice came. No Godfrey. A white and deathly tiredness filled her.

"Did you pray?" she asked.

"To cast out the voices." Faversham's body shifted as he nodded his head. "To cast the demons out of you."

---

[8] I wonder if this phrase might better be translated as 'energy', or even – to a modern reader – as 'solar power'? Perhaps even as 'electromagnetic force'?

"It may just have worked . . ." She snuffled, not knowing quite whether she would laugh or cry. "Godfrey, Godfrey."

Softly, in her mind, his voice spoke:

– *I am with you.*

"Son of a bitch." She reached up to thump Digorie Paston on the arm. "Exorcism isn't going to do it. No. And I don't even know if it matters, now—"

She found her gaze fixed on Floria's face.

"What?" the surgeon demanded. "*What?*"

"Burgundy isn't an objective," Ash said. "Burgundy is an obstacle."

Robert Anselm growled, "What the fuck, girl?"

She stayed resting against Faversham's solidness because she doubted her ability to sit up on her own. A fever ran through her body; all her muscles weak.

"Burgundy isn't the objective. Burgundy is the *obstacle*." She looked up at Robert Anselm's sweating face. "And I don't know why! They've kept saying they must destroy Burgundy – but it isn't because they just want *Burgundy* wiped out. After Burgundy's gone . . ."

A shudder went through her flesh; weakness at some deep level better not examined, better ignored. To her own surprise, her voice came out harsh and amused:

"It's *us* they want to be rid of. Men. All men. Burgundy – Carthage, too. They're . . . farmers who'd set fire to a barn to get rid of the rats. It's why they want their 'evil miracle'. After Burgundy's gone – they say, *then* they can make their darkness cover the whole world."

V

Ash added, "I have to see the Duke! Right now!"

Floria, holding a candle up uncomfortably close to Ash's face, ceased peering into her eyes and focused instead on her. "Yes. You do. I'll go ahead and clear it with his physicians."

The disguised woman stood abruptly, shoved the wooden candlestick into Digorie Paston's hand, and strode towards the dark stairwell. Her footsteps clattered down the stone steps.

"I'll get you an escort." Robert Anselm stood and bellowed. Ash heard the sound of men in mail running.

"But, madam, you should rest," Digorie Paston protested. The English priest took her hands and turned them over, studying her palms in a business-like way. "God's grace has failed to rescue you. It were better you should fast and pray, humble yourself, and pray to him again."

"Later. I'll come to Compline.[9] The Duke has to know about this!" Ash probed for voices, as a tongue probes an aching tooth. "Godfrey—"

A weak warmth. Godfrey's voice faint, all but inaudible:

[9] Final service of the day, 9 p.m.

– Blessed be!

A sound like wind through trees filled her soul. Creaking and whispering at first, and then loud, until her eyes watered, and she rubbed with the heel of her hands at her temples. "Okay—"

As she withdrew the impulse of her mind, the deafening interior sound sank to a keening mutter.

The Wild Machines, choral, lamenting, their language old, now, and incomprehensible. The language in which they spoke to Gundobad, so many centuries ago: an ancient, impenetrable Gothic tongue.

Richard Faversham said, "Don't tell God 'later', madam. He wouldn't like it."

Ash stared at him for a second; and chuckled. "Then don't tell Him I said it, master priest. Come with me to the Duke. I may need you to explain that your prayers failed. That I can't be cut free of the Stone Golem."

And I'll ask him again. Why is Burgundy so important? Why is Burgundy an obstacle *to the Wild Machines? And this time I'm going to* have *to have an answer out of him.*

With the reappearance of Rickard and her younger pages, she was fully dressed in minutes; borrowed sword belted on under a thick campaigning cloak, and the edge of her hood pulled down over her helmet.

Anselm and the escort surrounded her through Dijon's pitch-black streets, under the stars. The deep boom of cannon shattered the silence, and from somewhere far off, towards the northern wall, came the crackle of fire. Men and women slid through the shadows, civilians running from the bombardment, or thieving; Ash did not stop to investigate. A company of Burgundian men-at-arms passed them in one square, a hundred men, feet slapping the frozen earth, running in order for the wall. Her hand went to her sword-hilt, but she kept on going.

The palace was a dazzle of light; candles brilliant through the glass of ogee windows, torches flaring among the guards at the gates. In the light, Ash caught sight of a flaxen head of hair.

Floria, her hood pushed back and her face red, stood gesticulating at a large Burgundian sergeant. As Ash arrived at her side, she broke off.

"They won't let me in. I'm a bloody *doctor*, and they won't let me in!"

Ash pushed to the front, standing between men-at-arms in Lion livery. Smuts from torches stung her eyes. Bitter wind snapped at her mittened hands; her exposed face. Her stomach thumped, cold.

"Ash, mercenary, Duke's man," she explained rapidly to the sergeant in charge of the cordon of guards. "I must speak with his Grace. Send word to him that I'm here."

"I 'aven't got time for this—" The Burgundian sergeant's harassed expression faded as he turned. He gave her a nod. "Demoiselle *Ash*! You came in last night; I was on the gate. They say you razed Carthage. That right?"

"I wish it was," she said, putting all the frankness she could into her tone. Seeing that she had his momentary respect and attention, she said quietly, "Pass me through. I have important information for Duke Charles. *Whatever* crisis you've got here, this is more important."

She had time to think *But I don't need to fool him, this* is *more important*, and to see that it was her conviction of that, rather than her faked sincerity, that convinced the man.

"I'm sorry, Captain. We've just cleared all the physicians out. I can't let you in. There's only priests in there now." The Burgundian sergeant jerked his head, and as she stepped aside with him from the front of the crowd, lowered his voice:

"No point, ma'am. There's a dozen abbots and bishops up in his Grace's chamber, all wearing their knees out on the stone, and it isn't going to do one damn bit of good. God lays His heaviest burden on His most faithful servant."

"What's happened?"

"You've seen wounded men when they're in the balance, and it suddenly goes one way or the other." The sergeant reached up, tilting his sallet, his bloodshot eyes weary in his lined face. "Keep it quiet, ma'am, please. There'll be upset soon enough. Whatever your business, you'll have to keep it for whoever succeeds him. His Grace the Duke is on his death-bed now."

Floria came back into the upper floor of the tower. "It's true."

She walked across the chamber to the hearth, ignoring Anselm and Angelotti; spoke directly to Ash, and sank down in a huddle by the fire, holding her hands out to the flames.

"I managed to get as far as his chamber door. One of his physicians is still there: a German. Charles of Burgundy is dying. It started two hours ago, with fever, sweats. He became unconscious. It seems he hasn't passed water or faecal matter for days. His body has begun to stink. He isn't conscious for the prayers."[10]

Ash stood, gazing down at the company surgeon. "How long, Florian?"

"Before he dies? He's not a lucky man." Floria's eyes reflected flames. She continued to stare into the hearth. "Tonight, tomorrow; the day after, at the latest. The pain will be bad."

Robert Anselm said, "Girl, if he were one of your men, you'd be up there with a misericord right now."[11]

An air of unease had spread up and down through the tower's floors, from the cooks and pages in the kitchens, to the troops, to the guard on Ash's door. Knowing that the surgeon would be overheard, Ash made no attempt to stop her speaking. *If there's going to be a morale problem, I want it out in the open where I can see it.*

"Well, we're fucked," Robert Anselm remarked. "No second try at Carthage. And watch this fucking siege collapse!"

His tread was heavy as he clattered, still fully armoured, across the floor. Outside the slit-windows, the sound of a night bombardment echoed; golem-machines, which require neither sleep nor rest, throwing missiles, battering ceaselessly at Dijon's walls. She saw him flinch at the nearer strikes. "What

[10] This description in the original text resembles death by renal failure, after prolonged illness. Confusingly, in our history Charles the Bold is not reported as dying until two months later, on 5 January 1477, and in this case from fatal wounds, on the battlefield at Nancy, fighting the Swiss.

[11] A dagger used to give the *coup de grâce*, so called from the religious aspect, granting the final mercy.

does happen 'when the Duke dies'? What will these Wild Machines be able to do?"

"We are about to find out." Antonio Angelotti came forward into the fire's light from the door. "Madonna, Father Paston sends word he is about to begin the service of Compline."

Ash gestured irritably. "I'll do Matins.[12] Angeli, we don't just *sit* here. If that's 'Gundobad's child' out there . . . If the Wild Machines say the Faris can do a miracle, like Gundobad did when he made Africa into a desert – are you going to sit there and wait to find out if they're right?"

The gunner came to squat beside Floria del Guiz, two golden heads together. Angelotti had the air of a man who knows that, as soon as the bombardment stops, he will have to be ready to deal with the follow-up assault. From time to time he experimentally flexed his bandaged, gut-sewn arm. "What is there to do but wait, madonna? Sally out and see if you can kill her in battle?"

There was a small silence. Angelotti cocked his head. She saw him recognise that the Visigoth guns had ceased firing.

"He promised another raid on Carthage. I was counting on it." Ash calculated as she spoke. "With him dead – no chance. So: we don't get to take out the Stone Golem. There's only one answer left. Angeli's right. We take out the Faris. And then it doesn't *matter* what the Wild Machines planned, or what they bred her for, or any of that. Dead is dead. You don't do miracles of any kind when you're dead."

Robert Anselm shook his head, grinning. "You're mad. She's in the middle of a fucking army, out there!" He paused. "So – what's our plan?"

Ash shook his shoulder as she passed him, walking to study the papers on the trestle table; maps and calculations drawn spider-thin in the candlelight. "'Plan'? Who said anything about a plan? Damn good idea if we *had* a plan . . ."

Between Anselm's deep laugh, and Angelotti's more subdued amusement, Ash heard a commotion on the stairs. Deep voices boomed. She was instantly and instinctively shoulder to shoulder with Anselm and Angelotti, a glance checking that Floria was safely behind them; all three facing the stair entrance, hands gripping sword-hilts.

Rickard stumbled as he came in, falling to his knees on the floorboards. He dropped what he was carrying in both arms.

The blanket-wrapped bundle dropped with a muffled, sharp clatter.

"What the fuck?" Ash began.

Still kneeling, the black-haired boy flipped the blanket open.

The shifting candles reflected from a mass of curved, banded, and shining metal. Ash glimpsed confusion on Floria's face as the surgeon stared, while the two men had already begun to laugh, Robert Anselm swearing in an amazed, cheerful stream of filth.

Ash walked across the floor to the blanket. She leaned down and picked her cuirass up by its shoulder straps. The hollow cuirass sat in the concertina'd skirts; and the fauld clicked down as she lifted the empty armour up, the tasset plates swinging on their leathers.

---

[12] First service of the day, held at midnight.

"She's sent my fucking armour back!"

Two complete metal legs lay in the blanket, together with a tangle of shoulder defences: pauldrons, spaulders, and a gorget. One arm defence was unpointed, the butterfly-shape of the couter taking the light and splintering it. Ash put her cuirass down and picked up a gauntlet, flexing it, letting the laminations slide over each other. A few spots of rust, and some scratches, were new.

Incredulous, Ash said, "Shit! She *must* have been impressed by us holding the wall! If I'm worth bribing— Does she still think we'll betray Dijon? Open a gate?"

Half of her furiously thinking, *What does this mean?*, the other half can only stroke metal, examine linings for tears, remember each field that earned her the money to say to an armourer *Make me this.*

"Why *now*? If she's thought better of direct assault—"

What has she – heard?

Turning her head, Ash confronted Rickard's immense, utter pride. "Uh – right. Better get it cleaned up, hadn't you? Finish the job."

"Yes, boss!"

Under the curved plates, with its long belt wrapped up neatly around the hilt, a wheel-pommel, single-handed sword lay in its scabbard; her own sweat-marks still dark on the leather grip.

"Son of a bitch." Ash's fingers continued to slide over the gauntlet. She squatted, touching cold metal: sword, breastplate, backplate, visored sallet; checking leathers and buckles; as if only touch and not sight could confirm its reality. "She sent my sword and harness back . . ."

And Carthage didn't tell her to do this – if what Godfrey says is true, she's not talking via the Stone Golem!

Rickard sat back on his heels and wiped his running nose.

"Sent a message, too." He waited, a little self-importantly, until Ash's attention focused solely on him.

"A message from the Faris?"

"Yeah. Her herald told it to me. Boss, she says she wants to see you. She says she'll give you a truce, if you come out to the northside camp at dawn."

"A *truce*!" Robert Anselm guffawed coarsely.

"Tomorrow morning, boss." Rickard himself looked sceptical. "She says."

"Does she, by God?" Ash straightened up, one gauntlet still in her hand. She stared thoughtfully at the knuckle-plates. "Florian, the Duke – you said it could be as early as tonight?"

The surgeon, behind her, said, "It could be any time. I wouldn't be surprised to hear the mourning bells right now, if it comes to it."

"So we don't have any argument." Ash turned to her command group. "And we don't get the idea that this is a democracy. Rickard, send a page to find the herald again. Roberto, get me an escort for dawn – I want people who aren't trigger-happy. You're in command until I get back into the city."

Robert Anselm said, "Yes."

Floria del Guiz opened her mouth, shut it, stared at Ash's expression for a moment, and snapped, "*If* you get back."

707

"I'll come with you, madonna." Antonio Angelotti stood up lithely. "Ludmilla's burned but she can walk, now: she'll command the guns. You may need me. I know their scientist-magi. I may see things that you won't."

"True." Ash rubbed the heel of her hand against her gauntlet. "Rickard, let's armour me up, shall we? Just for practice, before morning . . ."

Robert Anselm said, "You'll get stopped at the city wall. Mercenary captain, off to see the enemy as soon as she hears the Duke's dying? They won't like it."

"Then I'll get a written pass from Olivier de la Marche. I'm the hero of Carthage! He knows Duke Charles trusts me. More to the point, he knows I wouldn't be leaving my movable valuables – that is, you lot! – unless I was coming back. You can work out a sally-and-rescue with him, if the Visigoths turn treacherous."

"'If'?" Floria spat. "Have some sense in that pointy head of yours, woman! If you're on the other side of these walls, she'll kill you!"

"That must be why I'm shitting myself," Ash said dryly, and saw the creases at the corners of Floria's eyes as she unwillingly smiled.

As Ash began to strip off, and Rickard dug her arming doublet and hose out of one of the oak chests, she said quietly, "Robert, Florian, Angeli. Remember – it's different now Charles is dying. *Don't lose sight of the objective.* We're not here now to defend Dijon. We're not here to fight Visigoths. We're here to survive – and, since we can't get away from here, right now that means we're here to stop the Faris."

Robert Anselm gave her one keen glance. "Got it."

"We mustn't get caught up in fighting to the point where we forget that."

Floria del Guiz bent down and heaved the cuirass clumsily into the air. As Rickard rushed to help her support it, and hinge it open for Ash to put it on, Floria said, "Will you kill her, tomorrow?"

"It's under truce!" Rickard protested, scandalised.

Ash, grimly amused, said, "Never mind the moral question. She's not going to give me the chance; not on this one. Maybe, if I can set it up for more negotiations, at a second meeting . . ." She caught the boy's gaze. "*She* obviously thinks we have an unfinished conversation. I might stand a better chance when her guard's – down – oof!"

The familiar heave clicked the cuirass shut around her body. Rickard cinched the straps tight on its right-hand side.

"Don't *you* forget," Floria said, standing close by her side, touching Ash's cheek; her eyes bright. "What you call 'stopping' her – I've spent five years watching you kill people. This one is your sister."

"I don't forget anything," Ash said. "Robert? Get Digorie and Richard Faversham back up here. I want my lance-leaders, and their sergeants, and the rest of the command group. Here. *Now.*"

"So how's it look, boss?" Rochester asked.

"Shite, thanks!"

Ash shot a quick glance across the map-strewn table at Digorie Paston, his chewed goose-quill pen, and the oak-gall ink blackening both his hands and bony features.

"—Hold on, Tom— Father, repeat that back."

Digorie Paston held up his scribbled page slant-wise to the candle, reading with some difficulty in golden light. "'Thus fifteen legions were committed in the first phase—'"

On the tail of his words, stumbling to echo him phrase by phrase, Ash repeated: "'Fifteen legions, committed in the first phase . . .'"

– *Yes.*

The voice is mild. She shook her head, cropped hair shifting, as if a fly bothered her.

"'With ten remaining, deployed now as I have said—'"

"'. . . ten remaining, now deployed . . .'"

The voice of Godfrey, in her head, is not weary – has, in fact, the tireless ability that the *machina rei militaris* has always had, to speak when any human soul would be dropping from exhaustion.

Her own voice is rasping, after bellowing on the walls of Dijon. After so much rapid dictation, her throat croaks. "'. . . Report made this feast day of St Benignus.'"[13]

– *Yes.*

"Here, boss."

She took a wooden cup of (admittedly sour) wine from Rickard, and drained it. "Thanks."

"The others are on their way up, boss." He turned to serve Rochester.

Ash stretched her arms, under asymmetric steel plates, feeling the sensation of each leather strap pulling against cloth and the flesh beneath – all of it grown unfamiliar in the space of three months. Her armour shells snug around her body, clattering at her thighs. Weight is nothing, but she finds herself almost forgetting how to breathe, sheathed so close in metal.

The warmth is welcome.

"Godfrey – the Wild Machines?"

– *Nothing.*

Shit. Oh, fuck, maybe from their point of view, it doesn't *matter* what I know? No: that can't be right!

Digorie Paston straightened up from his writing, flicking a sideways glance at her from cherry-rimmed eyes. He held himself upright on the joint stool, ready to read, and said nothing. He licked his lips.

"Okay, that'll do it for now." Ash placed her palms flat on the trestle table, and leaned her weight on her arms.

As she stood, momentarily weary, the rest of the lance-leaders and sergeants shoved through the stone doorway into the tower's upper floor. Their voices rose over the noise of the wind banging at the wooden shutters, and the desultory crash of bombardment from the darkness outside.

"Shit. Another night when I ain't gonna get more than two hours' sleep!"

"You're young." Robert Anselm grinned at her, demonic in the smoky light of the tapers. "*You* can do it. Think of us poor old men. Right, Raimon?"

The white-haired siege engineer acknowledged that, briefly; walking in beside Dickon Stour's apprentice – promoted to chief armourer, now – and

---

[13] 1 November. Second century; martyred, coincidentally enough, at Dijon.

behind him Euen Huw and Geraint ab Morgan in close talk, and Ludmilla Rostovnaya, with black-singed hair still not cropped off, but her body and shoulder bound up bulky in linen rags and grease and moving painfully.

"You been talking to your old machine, boss?" Ludmilla asked huskily. "Thought you didn't want it knowing where you are?"

"Bit late to worry about that, now . . ." Ash grinned ruefully at her. "The rag-heads have already told Carthage I'm right here."

Forty or so men and women came in, enough to make the bleak stone-walled upper chamber seem crowded. They brought welcome body-heat. Ash paced around the trestle table where Digorie Paston and Richard Faversham sat among piles of paper.

"Okay, what we got here is some . . . intelligence, on Visigoth troop deployment in Christendom. I have to say, it ain't gonna cheer us up any. As we thought, they've got things sewn up tight – with some interesting exceptions," she added thoughtfully, leaning between the clerks to spread out the spider-scrawled map of Christendom, as the men-at-arms crowded at her shoulder.

"For example – I can see how we got in from Marseilles the way we just did . . . When they first landed, the Faris put three legions directly into Marseilles – but they ended up fighting their way up to Lyons, and then Auxonne. I reckon the Legio XXIX Cartenna must be that garrison we were avoiding on the coast . . . They took heavy casualties. She's got the remnants of the Legio VIII Tingis and the X Sabratha in Avignon and Lyons, but apart from that, almost *nobody* holding down the Langue d'Oc."

"Then that's why we could eat," Henri Brant offered, "there wasn't half the number of enemy supply parties out that I expected to see."

"We were fucking lucky."

"Oh yeah, boss," Pieter Tyrrell said alcoholically, his arm around Jan-Jacob Clovet's shoulder – it must, Ash realised, have been pretty much the first time he'd seen his fellow crossbowman since he got back from Carthage. He looked up from puzzling over the maps. "Got us here. *Real* lucky!"

"You ain't got no gratitude, Tyrrell! If I'd taken us up here, where the Venetian captains wanted—" Ash tapped the eastern coast of Italy "—we'd be currently enjoying the hospitality of the two fresh legions that are sitting there watching the Dalmatian coast!"

Tyrrell grinned. Antonio Angelotti, putting wooden plates and an eating-knife down to trap the edges of his map of Christendom flat, murmured, "I make it fifteen Carthaginian legions in the first invasion, another ten for reinforcement of ports like Pescara, madonna – and five more in reserve. Say perhaps a hundred and eighty thousand troops."

In the silence that followed, Robert Anselm gave a low whistle.

Thomas Rochester prodded Angelotti's map, and the rough sketches that Digorie Paston and Richard Faversham spread out beside it. "This their deployment? How old's this news, boss?"

"Beginning of this month. It's the most recent overall sit. rep.[14] from the Faris back to Carthage. Some of *her* news is going to be out of date, given the

---

[14] 'Situation report'.

problems travelling through the Dark – especially the legions in northern France and the Germanies . . . But what we've got—"

Ash stopped, took a breath; walked a pace or two forward and back, in the light from the blazing hearth-fire. A brush-haired younger page, at Rickard's direction, squatted there in case of embers falling on to the timber floor. His eyes reflected silver as she walked past him, the fit of greaves to her calf-muscles not *quite* right – too much walking, too little riding, in the last few weeks – and the fit of cuisses to thigh muscles a little clip for the same reason, but all in all (and this, also, she sees in the boy's eyes) beginning to move with her as if the metal plates are part of her body. Part of her self.

"What we've *got*," she said, turning to face them, "is what happened during the initial deployment of the invasion – and what happened in phase two: the re-supply and re-deployment of fresh troops. We know where we are now."

Simon Tydder, promoted sergeant, and with stubble on the angular bones of his face that are growing out of plump adolescence, squeaked, "We *know* where we are now, boss. In deep doo-doo . . ." and then blushed at his change of register.

"Too fucking right!" Ash slapped his shoulder in passing. "But now we know it in detail!"

There was a strong smell of horse in the room, as is inevitable with knights. Despite lack of sleep, most of the faces watching her as men crowded around the trestle table, or leaned over the shoulders of the men in front, were aggressive, sharp, keyed-up. Ash blinked against the eye-stinging smell of mould on cold stonework, urine, and wood-smoke. She drew her bollock dagger and plonked it down on the centre of the map.

"There," she said. "That was their main thrust. In at Marseilles, and Genoa – where we were lucky enough to meet them—"

"Lucky, my fucking arsehole!" John Price rumbled.

Antonio Angelotti murmured, "What you do with your arsehole is entirely up to you . . ."

Ash glared at the innocent expression of her master gunner. "*Okay*. The main force, under the Faris, made two landings: the one I mentioned at Marseilles, and seven additional legions at Genoa."

Ludmilla, moving stiffly, leaned past her sergeant, Katherine Hammell, and studied Paston's sketch. "Agnes was right, then, boss? Thirty thousand men?"

"Yup." Ash drew her finger across the map. "The Faris sent three of those legions to raze Milan, Florence, and Italy, while she took her own four legions over the Gotthard into Switzerland. As far as I can make out, she devastated the Swiss somewhere near Lake Lucerne, over several days, and then moved on into Basle. At that point, with the Germanies surrendered, she moved west, met up with the other legions marching north from Lyons, and advanced towards the southern border of Burgundy."

"Fuck me, boss, don't tell me we were facing seven legions at Auxonne!"

"Oh, we were – but it looks like the scouts were pretty shit-hot on the figures. The rag-heads took heavy casualties getting to Auxonne. By the time we were facing them, we *did* out-number them."

"Shoulda fucked 'em," Katherine Hammell growled.

"Yeah, well, we didn't . . ."

"Fucking nancy Burgundians," John Price added.

"Fucking war-golems! We've held this place, though!" one of the remaining Flemish lance-leaders said: Henri van Veen, his breath thick with wine. At his shoulder, his sergeants nodded enthusiastically.

"You should have seen us, boss!" Adriaen Campin blurted. The big Flemish sergeant glanced around, hit the table with his clenched fist. "You shoulda been here! It's been fucking hot, but they haven't shifted us yet!"

"We're not all like that motherfucker van Mander," the lance-leader beside him said: Willem Verhaecht, another of the Flemings who had stayed with the Lion Azure. His pale face, in fire- and candlelight, was stubbled and scarred, black in places with small crusts of old blood.

"We're the Lion; he's not," Ash said brusquely. "Okay, as far as I can work it out from the Faris's casualty reports, the legions coming up from Marseilles took forty per cent casualties against the southern French lords, and the legions she brought up from Genoa lost fifty per cent of their men to the Swiss. Most of their legions are amalgamated now. Same goes for the Langue d'Oc. The legions over in France took casualties; most of the German ones didn't . . ."

"*Fifty* per cent?" Thomas Rochester blinked.

"I'd say by the time she was at Auxonne, she had not much more than fifteen thousand men, total. They took another twenty-five per cent casualties there – some of them from us." Ash shook her head. "She doesn't care how many men she loses . . . That legion and a half outside here, now, is the Legio XIV Utica in shit-hot shape, and the remnants of the XX Solunto and XXI Selinunte in with the tag-end of the VI Leptis Parva. Nearly seven thousand men. Price, tell your lads they got it absolutely right."

Most of the men-at-arms grinned. John Price merely grunted a small acknowledgement.

"Other than that . . . there's the French deployment, and the Legio XVII Lixus garrisoning Sicily, holding the naval base, and keeping the entire west of the Mediterranean Carthaginian. She won't move *them*. That was the situation towards the middle of August. She brought the second wave in shortly after King Louis and Emperor Frederick surrendered. One extra legion into middle Italy, so that Abbot Muthari could get his bum on the Empty Chair – the XVI Elissa."

"Them? Hardcore nutters, boss," Giovanni Petro offered. "I met them before, in Alexandria."

Ash nodded acknowledgement. "Two more legions into North Italy, around Venice, and Pescara, watching the Turk and the Turkish fleet. Another two to reinforce Basle and Innsbruck: that's the Cantons nailed down, I guess. And two more to keep order in the Holy Roman Empire – one's stationed in Aachen, with Daniel de Quesada, but the other's been given orders to march to Vienna: it should be there by now. And then three more legions were sent in to reinforce the Faris."

"Shit. *Three?*" Robert Anselm queried.

Ash scrabbled among the papers, settled at last for Rickard reading one of the lists to her, *sotto voce*. "—the V Alalia, IX Himera, and XXIII Rusucurru.

She ordered them to divert around Dijon, fight their way up through Lorraine, and take Flanders. They're up in the Antwerp–Ghent area; *those* are the ones we hope Margaret of Burgundy's army is knocking seven kinds of shite out of."

Antonio Angelotti kissed his St Barbara medal. "God send us such grace. I wonder how many cannon they have?"

"Rickard's got an artillery list here somewhere . . ." Ash straightened up from the map. "Their *overall* losses in the first wave of the invasion amount to almost seven legions. Out of thirty, in total. That's under twenty-five per cent, that is," she echoed the even tone of the *machina rei militaris*, "acceptable. It's getting her people killed trying to break Dijon in a hurry that's her problem . . ."

"Look at this." Angelotti, scanning the papers as quickly as Father Faversham or Father Paston, put his finger down blindly on the map, and then moved it to Carthage. "Gelimer's got two more legions in Carthage, but he won't plan to move them with the Turkish fleet still untouched, even if they do hold Sicily and the western Med."

Ash moved aside as Robert Anselm leaned in over the table, unselfconsciously scratched red flea-bites, and then traced with his blunt, dirt-ingrained finger the coast of North Africa.

"Egypt. *That's* the spike up Gelimer's arse," he grunted. "Look at that! He's got three whole legions in Egypt – fresh – and he can't move them. Not if he don't want the Turks across the Sinai faster than you can say *Great Mother!* But he fucking needs them in Europe, because if this is right, he's spread *way* thin . . . He can't even reinforce southern France."

Angelotti remarked, "Don't get excited. Right now, the Faris thinks she can keep three legions fighting up in Flanders. She can always move those men south to here. Throw three legions against this city and it'll fall over pretty quick."

"Maybe. She'd have to stop using the French and Saxon ports to feed them. Try re-supplying with river boats."

"Depends if the Rhine or the Danube's frozen . . ."

"That's another reason they can't let go of Egypt; with Iberia going under the Dark, they need to get corn from *somewhere* . . ."

Ash, grimly interrupting, said, "There isn't a peep out of King Louis – or his nobles, which is far more remarkable. And even the Electors are holding to the Emperor's surrender in the Germanies. I think it's what happened at Venice, and Florence, and Milan – and to the Swiss. They don't dare move – and they don't know the Visigoths are running at full stretch and then some."

A glance went between Anselm, Angelotti, and Rochester.

Geraint ab Morgan threw down the piece of paper he had been attempting to decipher, with a look of disgust at Richard Faversham. "Too many fucking clerks in this! – no offence, Father. Boss, how do you know that what your demon-voice says about all this is true? How do we know they ain't got a few more legions tucked away?"

Other faces turned to hers, at that – Geraint's old sergeants, now Ludmilla's: Savaric and Folquet, Bieiris, Guillelma and Alienor. John Price; John Burren. Henry Wrattan broke off a low-voiced conversation with Giovanni Petro.

"It isn't a demon-voice," Ash said, "it's Father Godfrey now."

She has a moment of doubt: must she explain it all, examine rumours that have spread through the company in the last forty-eight hours, go back in her mind to the shattering collapse of Carthage? Two or three men cross themselves; most of the others touch Briar Crosses, or Saints' medals, to their lips.

"Yeah, well," Jan-Jacob Clovet grinned, showing yellow and black teeth. "Father Godfrey always did manage a shit-hot intelligence service. Don't suppose that's changed since he's dead."

There was a subdued chuckle in the room: Henri van Veen muttering something to Tyrrell, who punched his arm and cheerfully said, "Mother-fucker!" John Price and Jean the Breton palmed and drank from a stoppered wineskin with practised ease.

Thomas Rochester held up a fistful of illustrative paper. "Are we giving this information to the Burgundians, boss?"

"I'm getting Digorie to make a copy for the Sieur de la Marche. We haven't broken a *condotta* yet . . ."

She waits, gaze flicking across lined, filthy faces, to see if anyone will say *Always a first time.*

"We've held that fucking north wall!" Campin muttered again. "I'm losing too many of my people to Greek Fire, boss. Mind you, so are the nancy-boy Burgundians . . ."

"I know you reckon we can't get out of here with you, boss, but how would we manage, if we were still heading for England, then?" Euen Huw bent down over the table, his expression hidden as he studied the sketched map. "They ain't going to take those northern legions across the Channel while Duchess Margaret's still fighting. Say we didn't go north or east, suppose we went back west, and then into Louis's lands? Calais, maybe?"

"Under the Dark? When we still need to eat?" Ash put her finger on the map. "Even if we tried . . . initially, back in July, the Faris landed three legions here, at St Nazaire; they've moved up the Loire valley. The II Oea and the XVIII Rusicade are occupying Paris. We're not going to make Calais if they want to stop us . . . As for the far west, the Legio IV Girba are sitting *here*, at Bayonne – either to be shipped up the west coast of the French king's territories, or to be moved back into Iberia if the unrest there gets worse – they didn't expect the Dark to cover half Iberia, it's paying merry hell with their logistics. That's one she *could* bring east."

"Has she?"

"Jeez, Euen, how the fuck do *I* know! She reports back to Carthage every fucking day!" Ash took a breath. "Godfrey's been taking me through her sit. reps. for the past three weeks. I don't think she's recalled the IV Girba to here."

She paused, shifting her body in her Milanese armour, still less than comfortable; re-training muscles and balance at a level below the conscious. Because it is only a few hours to morning.

"It isn't likely," Ash said, at last. "Not with those huge logistics problems. But . . . if she was stupid enough to send an order – and didn't report it through to Carthage – we wouldn't know."

"So if we go west, we'll meet legions." Overt, now, Geraint ab Morgan shouldered in beside Euen Huw and asked, "What if we went back down south, boss? To Marseilles? I know it was 'ell, but we might get a ship, get out of the Med, sail up the west coast of Iberia . . ."

"Good God, no, Geraint – if you think I'm going to spend five hundred miles watching you puke over the side of a ship—!"

A gust of laughter. Simon Tydder, shouldering his way in beside Rickard, gave a guffaw that ended in a squeak, and started the snorts and chuckles off again.

"If we ain't thinking of breaking out for England, boss, what's this truce about?"

Ash gave him a rather old-fashioned look. "Defeating the enemy might be a start!"

"But, *boss* . . ."

"They're not chucking rocks at us for fun, Tydder! We're signed on with Burgundy: that lot out there are the *enemy*. Look, these legions don't matter a toss. Except that the Faris is pretty damn safe sitting in the middle of them . . ."

"Man, do we need back-up!" Adriaen Campin sighed.

"Maybe *we* could go ask the Turks for help." Florian, who had been silently checking Ludmilla's burns, Angelotti's bandages, and the assorted minor wounds of the other knights and sergeants, plonked a filthy hand down on the table. "What's it like in the east?"

Anselm consulted the annotated map. "Thin, if Father Godfrey's right. She's trying to hold down the Germanies with a couple of legions."

"So maybe . . . ?"

"If we had some eggs, we could have some eggs and ham – if we had any ham."

Geraint ab Morgan snorted. "Never thought I'd say this, but England's looking better all the time . . ."

Katherine Hammell, still moving stiffly from her wound at Carthage, looked across at Ludmilla Rostovnaya. "What about your lot, Lud? We could try the Rus lands. How would we do in St Petersburg? Any good wars?"

The commander of archers scowled. "All the time. Too fucking cold for me. Why d'you think I'm here?"

"Cold everywhere, now . . ."

"Yeah. Fucking rag-'ead cunt. Why'd she have to bring her lousy weather with her?"

Ash let the discussion ramble, apparently studying the map; studying instead the maps of faces, chiaroscuro in the firelight.

"We're here for the moment," she said flatly, at last. "We'll keep the Burgundians up to date with this. For one thing, our contract obliges us to do it."

The Wild Machines can't think I'll keep quiet – can they?

"And for another – who's going to know that we told?" Ash grinned briefly at her men. "At best, it'll be just one of a whole set of confused rumours – *won't* it?"

"Oh yes, boss." Euen Huw looked pious. "You can rely on us."

Morgan grunted, "We got a rep for breaking contracts after Basle, does it matter now?"

"Yes."

His gaze slid away from hers. More importantly, she let her flat gaze take in the faces of the men near him – Campin, Raimon, Savaric – to see if he had any support.

"Fuck it, they think we're oath-breakers already," Morgan grumbled.

"I won't argue with you there. But we're not. We're professionals."

The Welshman said, "Screw the Burgundians! Who cares?"

"He's got a point, madonna," Angelotti said. She looked at him in surprise. He said, "Screw the Burgundians. Why is it *our* responsibility to kill the Faris?"

Not a flicker of her expression, or his, either thanked him for putting the question where it could be answered, or acknowledged that that had happened.

"We need a debrief on all this info," Ash said, as a page brought her a joint-stool, and she took her place behind the trestle table. "We're going to go through this in detail, now. I want to know if anybody's fought against any of these legions before; what you know about them; what the commanders are like, anything. I want to know if anybody's got any suggestions, ideas. But first I'll give you the answer to your question."

Geraint ab Morgan pushed forward to the table's edge. "Which is?" he demanded.

Ash looked up at him calmly.

"Which is – screw the Burgundians, all right – we might as well be behind these walls, trying to work out a way to kill my sister. Because where do you suggest we go, Geraint? When the Wild Machines kill the world, it won't help us to be in England, four hundred miles away from Dijon – not one little bit."

VI

The toing and froing of interminable messages at last over, Ash discovered the long November night to be almost past: Lauds sung three hours ago by Dijon's striking town clock, and the office of Prime about to begin. Sleeplessness gritted in her eyes.

Striding through Dijon's cold streets, she berated herself: Come on girl, think! I may not have long. Is there anything else?

Under her breath, she whispered: "Current position of Gothic forces overall commander?"

In her head, the *machina rei militaris*, in Godfrey's voice, said – *Dijon siege camp, north-west quadrant, four hours past midnight; no further reports.*

Still, nothing drowned out that interior voice.

Why not? Is it the Faris – the Wild Machines don't want to scare her? Or is this something else?

De la Marche's clerk hurried at her side, between squat masonry houses with

716

deep shadowed doorways, in the filth of the winding streets, as light faintly sifted down from the pre-sunrise grey east. There were men and women, their children bundled at their sides, sleeping tucked against walls, and against iron-bound oak doors. Horses and pack mules neighed, tethered outside stables turned over to refugees.

"We have everything," the clerk gasped. His stoppered ink bottle bounced at his belt; his woollen cloak was blackened with earlier attempts to stop and write. His face was white with lack of sleep. "Captain – I shall report to the Duke's Deputy – their forces' positions—"

"Tell him I don't expect to be able to do this again. Not now they know their communications are compromised."

A church bell rang a few streets away. All of them – Ash, the clerk, her escort – simultaneously halted and listened. Ash gave a sigh of relief. The normal call to mass: no slow, funereal bells.

"God preserve the Duke," the clerk murmured.

"Report back to de la Marche," Ash ordered. She started off again, boot soles slipping on the frozen filth underfoot. The leaning buildings closed out all but the slightest dawn light. Thomas Rochester thrust to the front of his lance with a pitch-torch. Serfs and villeins come into the city for refuge half-woke, moved out of the way; one or two recognised the banner, and Ash heard a "hero of Carthage!" float across the cold air.

Rochester said, "You sure this is a good idea, boss?"

"Piece of piss," Ash said, between the grunts that trotting through Dijon's streets in unaccustomed full armour forced out of her. "The Duke's on his last legs, we're going into the enemy camp under a supposed truce, and they have every reason I can think of to kill us out of hand – yeah, sure, Thomas: this is a brilliant idea!"

"Oh. Good. Glad you said that, boss. Otherwise I might have started to worry."

"Just worry enough to stay alert," Ash said sardonically. "And ask yourself if they'd rather have the 'hero of Carthage' and the Faris's bastard sister alive or dead?"

The dark Englishman, at the head of the escort, gave her a completely careless grin. "You can hear what she says privately to her War-Machine? My money's on them using crossbows the second we're in range! *I* wouldn't take chances, boss. Why assume they're stupider than I am?"

"That would be almost impossible."

Thomas Rochester and the men behind him guffawed.

"She won't kill me. Yet." *I hope. Not when I'm the only other person who hears the Wild Machines.*

Of course, she may not give that the importance that I do.

Rochester was aware, she saw, of the likelihood of his own death; and no more bothered about it than he would have been before the field of battle. She thought, It is the hardest thing in the world, to give orders that will mean other people may die.

"The Faris wants to talk to me," Ash said. "So look on the bright side. They maybe won't kill us until she has."

"That's all right, boss," one of Rochester's sergeants said: a fair-haired English man-at-arms carrying her personal banner. "You can talk the hind leg off a donkey . . . !"

Her armour, tied, strapped and buckled about her, gave the usual feelings of invulnerability. She began to move with it as if it had never been gone. She had tied down her scabbard to her leg, with a leather thong, so that she could draw her sword single-handed if necessary: one of Rochester's lance carried her axe.

A thread of coldness tickled in her gut.

"Nice kit." She rapped the knuckles of her gauntlets against the sergeant's cuirass. All twenty of Rochester's men had armoured up, borrowing what fitted from other men.

"Showing the rag-heads what we got," the sergeant grunted.

Walking between them, surrounded by men mostly taller, and all in armour, Ash felt a fallacious sense of complete security. She smiled to herself, and shook her head. "All this metalware, and what happens? Some little oik shoves a pointy stick up your backside. Never mind, lads. All wearing our mail braies,[15] are we?"

"Don't plan to turn our backs on them!" Rochester snorted.

The atmosphere of expectancy was electric: an exhilaration born out of the certainty of risk. Ash found herself striding energetically forward across the narrow square leading to the northern sally gate. Black rats, and one stray dog, scuttled away into the dimness at the clatter of armour.

"Godfrey, *has* she spoken to the Stone Golem again?"

This time the voice of Godfrey Maximillian sounded quietly inside her head.

– *Once, only. She ignores Carthage: their words to the* machina rei militaris *grow frantic. She has asked only if* you *speak to it . . . where you are, what your men are doing; if there is to be an attack.*

"What does it – do you – tell her?"

– *Nothing but what I must, what I can know, from the words you speak to me. That you are on your way to her. For the rest, I know nothing of it; you have not told the* machina *your forces, nor asked for tactics.*

"Yeah, and I'm keeping it that way."

She spoke quietly, aware that the men closest around her would be hearing what she said over the clatter of armour and scabbards.

"The Wild Machines?"

– *They are silent. Perhaps their will is to let her think they are a dream, an error, a story.*

Ash's personal banner hung from its striped staff, a chill breeze not enough to stir the blue-and-gold cloth. The Burgundian troops at the sally-port recognised it, coming forward with their own torches.

"Madonna." Antonio Angelotti walked out of the gloom by the wall, noise announcing a cluster of grooms and beasts behind him in the dimness. "I've arranged horses."

Ash surveyed the riding horses; most ill-conditioned from the long siege, and with their ribs visible to count. "Well done, Angeli."

While Rochester confirmed passwords and signals, she remained silent,

---

[15] Underwear. A cloth-lined mail covering for this vital area.

hands cupping the points of elbow couters, her eyes fixed on the eastern sky. Grey clouds lightened above the pitched roofs, and the merlons of the city wall above. One of the nearer buildings – a guild house – still smoked, blackened and burned out, from the alarm that had turned out most of the Burgundians in this quarter to fight the fire. The weather had warmed from frost to bitter-cold rain, in the night; now it began to freeze again.

"Thank Christ for bad weather!"

Angelotti nodded. "If this were summer, we would be burned out, and have pestilence besides."

"Godfrey, is there any later report of where she is?"

– *She has not told me where she is since Lauds.*

"This is a dumb thing to do, isn't it?"

– *If this were merely a war, child, you would not do it. In eight years I have known you be reckless, bold, and adventurous; but I have not known you waste lives.*

Another one of Rochester's men-at-arms glanced sideways at her, and she gave him a reassuring grin. "Boss talking to her voices. That's all."

The young man-at-arms had a white face, under his visor, but he gave her a sharp, efficient nod. "Yes, boss. Boss, what have they got for us out there? What should we watch out for?"

Fuck only knows! About ten thousand Visigoths, I should think . . .

"Those recurved bows. They don't look like much, but they're as fast as a longbow, even if they don't have the penetrating power. So. Bevors up, visors down."

"Yes, boss!"

"Now they feel safer," Angelotti observed in an undertone. "It isn't weapons, madonna. It's sheer numbers."

"I know."

The thread of disquiet in her belly turned into a distinct twinge.

"That's the problem with armour," she said musingly. "Strapped in. You can't take a shit in a hurry when you need to . . ."

– *Ah. Dysentery: the warrior's excuse.*

"*God*frey!" Ash spluttered, amused and appalled.

– *Child, are you forgetting? I've followed you around military camps for eight years. I minister to the baggage train. I know who does the laundry, after a battle. You can't hide anything from the washerwomen. Courage is brown.*

"For a priest, Godfrey, you're a deeply disgusting man!"

– *If I were a man still, I would be at your side.*

It jolted her, not out of the warm feeling of comradeship, but into a keener grief for him. She said, "I *will* come for you. First: this." She raised her voice. "Okay, let's do it!"

As the units of armed men passed into the tunnel-like gate below one of Dijon's watch towers, Thomas Rochester's sergeant bent down and muttered in her ear, over the noise, "What does he say?"

"What does who say?"

The Englishman looked uncomfortable. "Him. Your voice. Saint Godfrey. Do we have God's grace in this?"

"Yes," Ash replied, automatically and with complete conviction, while her mind murmured *Saint Godfrey!* in something between appalled amusement and awe. *I suppose it was inevitable* . . .

"Troop movements, Visigoth camp, central north section?"

– *No movement reported.*

And that means fuck-all, Ash thought grimly, hearing her boots echo off the raw masonry walls of the sally-port; hearing, in her soul, an incursion of ancient, inhuman muttering. Right now, *she's* not talking to the Stone Golem either.

The Lion grooms brought the horses forward; Ash's new mount a pale gelding some yellow-tinged colour between chestnut and bay, points barely dark enough to be distinguished; Orgueil returned to Anselm. She mounted up. Angelotti reined his own scrawny white-socked chestnut in beside her, still favouring his wounded arm. Ash glimpsed the bulk of linen bandages under the straps of his vambrace and his arming doublet.

Ahead, Burgundian soldiers yanked iron bars down from the gates as quickly as possible, passing her and her men through and out with indecent haste. The gates slammed behind them. She looked up, as they came into the open air, but her helmet and bevor prevented her turning her head enough to see the top of the wall, and the Burgundian archers and hackbutters she hoped would be up there.

The high saddle kept her extremely upright, legs extended almost straight. She shifted her weight, moving forward in the grey light, anxious to traverse the uncertain sloping ground before the walls. One of the men-at-arms on foot beside her grunted, and efficiently kicked a caltrop out of the way.

A quick glance to the east showed her Dijon's city walls emerging from white mist, and, at their foot, a moat three-quarters choked with faggots of wood thrown down by assaulting troops. Beyond the churned earth, trenches and ranks of mantlets covered the ground between her and the Visigoth main camp.

"Okay: move out . . ."

Once out of the gateway, Rochester's sergeant raised Ash's personal banner.

"ASH!"

The shout came from the walls above: a deep roar of voices, that broke into "Hero of Carthage!" and "Demoiselle-Captain!', and ended in a ragged cheer, extremely loud in the early morning. She wheeled the gelding, leaning back in the saddle to look up.

Men chanted: "Scar-face! Scar-face!"

The battlements were lined with men. Every embrasure thick with them; men climbing on to merlons, adolescent youths hanging from the wooden brattices. She lifted her hand, the gauntlet dull with freezing cold dew. The cheerful noise went up again; raucous, bold, and disrespectful; the same noise that men make before – unwillingly trusting – they commit themselves to the line-fight.

"Kick the bitch's ass!" a woman's contralto voice yelled.

"There you are, madonna," Antonio Angelotti, at Ash's side, said. "We have a doctor's advice!"

Ash waved up at Floria del Guiz, tiny face almost invisible on the high walls. There was a cluster of Lion livery jackets with her; they made up a sizeable proportion of the crowd.

"You can't keep anything a secret overnight." Ash turned the gelding. "Just as well, really. We may need someone to haul our asses out of this fire."

Ahead, east of the river, lateral banks of white mist clung to the Visigoth barrack-tents and turf huts. Droplets of water illuminated the guy-ropes, and the tethers of the horse lines, in the weak rising sun. A freezing wind flapped one tent, its canvas side bellying out.

A long, black line of Visigoth men-at-arms stood along the palisade. A thin shout went up, in the distance.

There's bold, and there's stupid, Ash reflected. _This is stupid. There's no way we're going to be allowed back out of there._

She tapped one long rowel-spur back, just touching the gelding's flank. It plodded forward. Not a fighting horse.

_No,_ Ash thought, squinting against the first rays of the sun. _Not stupid. What did I say to Roberto? Don't lose sight of the mission objective. I'm not here to fight the Visigoth army._

Faintly, in her shared soul, the clamour of the Wild Machines begins to grow again. Nothing intelligible to a human mind.

Does she hear it too?

I'm not even here to get out of their camp alive, if there's a chance to take the Faris out.

What do I know about sisters, anyway?

"Doesn't look good, boss," Thomas Rochester said quietly.

"You have my orders. If we're attacked, and the Faris is there, kill her. We can worry about getting us out _after_ she's down. If we're attacked, and the Faris isn't present, we bang out. Make for the north-west gate, behind us. Sound the retreat loud and clear, and pray for some Burgundian help. Got it?"

She spared a glance for the Englishman, his stubbled face visible between visor and bevor; his expression alert. Lines of strain showed he understood that they might be dead before the end of the morning. He was, nonetheless, unexpectedly cheerful.

"Got it, boss."

"But if it looks like sheer suicide for no result – we don't attack: we _wait._"

Antonio Angelotti turned in his saddle, pointing into the early morning mist. "Here they come."

The long clarion call of a truce rang out. White standards went up, five hundred yards away.

"Let's go," Ash said.

Rochester and the escort formed up and moved forward.

Ash became aware of the way they closed around her, horse and foot; not protectively, but prideful, as if to show their own efficiency as guards. Men who would let no fear show.

She rocked gently to the pace of the gelding, riding on, in among the tents, staring down from the saddle at Visigoth soldiers; not a barefoot woman, now, prisoned in Carthage; nor a lone woman walking through their camp; but a captain who is surrounded by well-armed men, who has – for good or ill – the responsibility of ordering them to fight and live or die.

The Faris, illuminated by the lemon-yellow low light of dawn, stepped out on to the beaten earth. She wore armour but no helm. From fifty yards, there is no reading her expression.

I could kill her now. If I could get to her.

Companies of the XIV Utica lined the way through the camp; men in mail and white robes, dank in the dawn, the light flashing from the leaf-shaped points of their spears. Somewhere between two and two and a half thousand men, she guessed. All eyes on her and her men.

"God damn you," Ash said quietly. "*Fuck Carthage!*"

A voice in her head, that was both the *machina rei militaris* and Godfrey Maximillian, said, – *Before you take vengeance, go and dig your own grave.*

A smile moved her lips. It did not reach the taut, controlled fury that she would not let show. "Yes . . . I was never sure how you used to mean that one."

– *It means no vengeance is worth such anger, such hatred. You may lose your own life in the attempt.*

She feels the rocking of her hips, as she rides; lays one hand on the fauld of her armour, over her belly. A chill, controlled shudder goes through her. A memory of the smell of blood, in a cold cell like this same cold morning, passes through her mind. She is suddenly aware of the razor-sharp edge of her sword in its scabbard, of the balanced weight of metal at her thigh.

"I'll give you another version of your proverb," she murmured. "It means, the only way that you can be sure to achieve vengeance is to count yourself already dead. Because there's no defence against an attacker who isn't afraid of dying. 'Before you take vengeance, go and dig your own grave'."

– *Be very sure that you are right, child.*

"Oh, I'm *sure* of nothing. That's why I have to talk to this woman."

Angelotti, quietly, said, "Have you forgiven them the Lord Fernando's child? Carracci, Dickon; those who died in House Leofric, that's war – but have you forgiven them your child?"

"It didn't have a soul. Isobel used to lose two out of every three, when I was living with her on the wagons. Every year, regular as a clock." Ash squinted into the light, growing as the mist lifted. "I wonder if Fernando's dead as well?"

"Who is to know?"

"What I *won't* forgive her is, she should have thought this through years ago. She's known for years that she's hearing a machine. Sweet Green Christ! She's just followed it blindly, she's never thought, why *this* war?"

Angelotti smiled with enigmatic calm. "Madonna, when you untied me from a gun-carriage outside Milano and told me, 'Join my company because I hear the Lion telling me to win battles,' I might have said much the same thing. Did you ever ask the Lion, why any particular war?"

"I never asked the Lion which battles I should fight," Ash growled. "I just asked Him how to win them once we were on the field. Getting me the job in the first place isn't His business!"

Angelotti's pale throat showed, under his helm, where he had left off his bevor, and now threw his head back and laughed. Several of the Visigoths they passed stared curiously. Rochester's escort had the expressions of men thinking *he's a gunner.*

"Madonna Ash, you are the best woman of any in the world!" Angelotti sobered; his eyes still bright with affection. "And the most dangerous. Thank God you are our commander. I shudder to think how it would have been, otherwise."

"Well, you'd still be ass-upwards on a gun-carriage, for one thing, and the world would have been spared one more mad gun-captain . . ."

"I will see who I may speak with among the Visigoth gunners, during this truce. Meantime, madonna—" Angelotti's gold curls, clamped down by his sallet, were dulled by the dank morning. He lifted his steel-covered arm, pointing: "There, madonna. See? That is where she expects you."

In a rattle of scabbards on armour, they rode forward. Ash saw the Visigoth woman turn away from her commanders and walk out to a little awning, set up in a space in the middle of the camp. A table, two ornate chairs, and a plain canvas awning: set in the middle of thirty yards of bare earth. No room for anything to be concealed, and anything done there would be public.

Public, but not overheard, she reflected, judging the distance to the surrounding Visigoth *qa'ids*, *'arifs*, *nazirs*, and troops.

The *'arif* Alderic, as she expected, stepped forward from among the units of soldiers.

"Please you to join the Captain-General," he said, formally.

Ash dismounted, slinging her reins to Rochester's page. She kept one hand automatically on the hilt of her sword, palm flat against the cold metal of the cross.

"I accept the truce," she replied, equally formally. Surveying thirty yards of unoccupied, trodden earth, with the table in the middle of it, she thought *What a target for the archers*.

"Your weapons, *jund* Ash."

Regretfully, she unbuckled her sword-belt, handing him sword, scabbard and dagger together in a tangle of leather straps. With a nod of acknowledgement, she went forward.

Under the laminated plates of her backplate, under the pinked silk arming doublet, sweat dampened the skin between her shoulder-blades as she walked out across the open space.

The Faris, seated at the small table under the awning, stood up as Ash came within ten yards of her, holding her hands out from her sides. Her hands were bare, and empty. The white robes over her coat of plates and mail hauberk might easily conceal a dagger. Ash contented herself with leaving her bevor up, and tilting her sallet for a clearer view of the Visigoth woman; leaving steel plate and riveted mail to cope with any theoretical stiletto.

"I would have had wine set out for us," the Faris said, as soon as Ash came within speaking distance, "but I thought you would not drink it."

"Damn right." Ash stopped, for a moment, resting her gauntleted palms on the back of the carved white oaken chair. Through the linen, she felt the shapes of the ornamental carved pomegranates. She looked down at the Faris, seating herself again on the opposite chair. The remarkable face – familiar to her only from scratched, polished metal mirrors, and the dark, glassy pools of river backwaters – still shocked her: a churning sensation somewhere in her gut.

"But in that case," Ash added, "we get to sit here and freeze our asses off, and be thirsty."

She managed a pragmatic, confident grin; walking round and hitching up back tasset-plate and fauld to sit down on the ornate chair. The seated Visigoth woman signalled without looking behind her. After a few seconds, a child-slave approached with a wine jug.

The bitter wind that now shifted the morning mist blew filaments of silver hair across the Faris's face. Her cheeks were white, the flesh drawn; and faint purple shadows lay under her eyes. Hunger? Ash thought. No. More than that.

"You were in the forefront of the defence of the walls, yesterday," the Faris said abruptly. "My men tell me."

Ash sprung the bevor pin, pushing the laminated plate down, and reached for the silver wine goblet offered by the slave. The wine smelled, to her chilled nose, merely like wine. She clamped her mouth over the edge of the goblet, tilted it, from long practice appearing to drink deeply; put it down, and wiped the wine from her lips with the gauntleted heel of her hand. No liquid entered her mouth.

"You won't take this place by assault." She looked from the flat area, towards Dijon. From the ground, the grey and white walls and towers appeared satisfactorily solid and appallingly tall. She noted the interview was being conducted well away from the remaining saps, creeping ever closer under the earth. "Hell. It really does look nasty from out here. Glad I'm not on the outside! Golem siege-towers or not . . ."

The Faris, ignoring her, persisted: "You were fighting!"

The Visigoth woman's tone told her much. Ash kept her expression calm, friendly, and confident; and listened to the note of extreme strain.

"Of course I was fighting."

"But you were silent! You asked the Stone Golem nothing! I know you asked for nothing, no tactics; I asked it!"

The lemon-yellow of the rising sun paled to white. With the mist dispersed, Ash risked a quick glance around the nearer part of the Visigoth camp. Deep mud ruts, some tents ragged; fewer horses than she had expected. Behind the troops drawn up in ranks – obviously the best, for show purposes – she could see many men sprawled on the freezing wet earth in front of some of the turf huts. At this distance, hard to see if they were wounded or whole; but possibly whole, and just short of tents in winter. Faces in the ranks showed hunger; were thin – but not yet gaunt. A whole cluster of stone self-moving siege-machines appeared to be parked towards the Suzon bridge, either in waiting, or broken down.

The Faris burst out: "How can you risk fighting, without the voice of the machine?"

"Oh, I get it . . ." The armour would not let her lean back, but Ash carefully spread her arms on to the arms of the chair, giving the impression of relaxed expansiveness. "Let me tell you something, Faris."

While her gaze avidly totted up the number of spears and bows, the numbers of barrel-laden wagons in the background, Ash said aloud, "I could already fight when I was five. They had us in training, the kids on the wagons. I could already kill a man with a stone from a sling. By the time I was ten, I could use a half-pike. The women on the baggage train weren't there for ornament. Big Isobel taught me how to use a light crossbow."

Ash flicked her gaze back to the Visigoth woman. The Faris stared, opening her mouth to interrupt.

"No. You asked me a question. This is the answer. I killed two men when I was eight. They'd raped me. I was in sword-training with the other pages by the time I was nine, with somebody's broken, re-ground blade. I wasn't strong enough, the camp *dog* could have bowled me over – but it was still training, you understand?"

Silent, her dark eyes fixed on Ash, the Visigoth woman nodded.

"They kept knocking me down, and I kept getting up. I was ten or eleven, and a woman, before the Lion ever spoke to me. The Stone Golem," Ash corrected herself. A dry wind blew across the camp. Prickles of cold touched the little amount of skin she had exposed: snow-crystals stinging her scarred cheeks. "In the year or so then before I could get back to our company, I made my mind up that I would never come to rely on anything – not a Saint, not Our Lord, not the Lion: nothing and nobody. So I taught myself to fight with and without my voices."

The Faris stared at her. "Father told me it came to you with your first woman's blood. With me – I have never *not* heard it. All my games as a child, with Father, were playing how to speak with the *machina rei militaris*. I could not have fought in Iberia without it."

Both her face and her voice remained calm. On her lap, almost concealed by the edge of the table, Ash saw that the Faris's bare hands were clenched into white-knuckled fists.

"We have a conversation to finish. When I came into your camp, two nights ago, you asked me about my priest," Ash said harshly. "Godfrey Maximillian. You were hearing him then, weren't you? He speaks to you as the machine."

"No! There is only one voice, the Stone Golem—"

"*No.*"

Ash's impatient contradiction cracked out, loud enough to be heard across the open square of earth. One of the Visigoth *qa'ids* moved forward. The Faris signalled him back, without taking her eyes off Ash's face.

"God damn it, woman," Ash said softly. "You know the other voices are real. Otherwise you wouldn't have stopped talking to the Stone Golem. You're afraid they're listening to you! It's *their* voices you've been following, for the last twenty years. You can't ignore this."

The Visigoth woman unclenched her hands, rubbing them together. She reached for her goblet and drank.

"I can," she said briefly. "I could. Not now. Every time I fall asleep, I have nightmares. They speak to me on the borders of sleep – the Stone Golem, the Wild Machines – your Father Godfrey, he speaks to me, in the place where the *machina* should be. And how can *that* be?"

Ash moved her shoulders, restrained by cuirass and pauldrons from a shrug. "He's a priest. When he died, the machine was speaking through me. I can only suppose God's grace saved him by a miracle and put his soul into the machine.

Maybe not God – maybe the Devil. The hours don't pass the same for him. It's more like Hell than it is like Heaven!"

"It's strange. To hear a man speak, here." The Faris touched her bare temple. "Another reason for doubt. How can I be sure anything the *machina rei militaris* tells me is trustworthy now, if it carries the soul of a man – and an enemy?"

"Godfrey wasn't anyone's enemy. He died trying to rescue a physician who'd been treating your King-Caliph."

Somewhat to Ash's surprise, the Visigoth woman nodded. "Messire Valzacchi. He is one of the men treating Father, under Cousin Sisnandus's care."

The morning sun made Ash squint. A growing bitter cold froze the dank morning. The wind blew a flurry of white snow-powder across the earth, from the thin clouds massing in the north. Momentarily diverted, she said, "What *did* happen to Leofric?"

She was not expecting an answer. The Faris, leaning forward, said earnestly, "He returned from the Citadel in time to take refuge in the room of the *machina rei militaris*."

"Ah. So he was down there while we were trying to blow the place."

As if Ash's mild, sardonic amusement didn't exist, the Visigoth woman went on:

"He was there when the Stone Golem . . . spoke. When it repeated what the – other voices – said." Her gaze flicked away from Ash's face, but not before Ash filled in the missing phrase: 'what the other voices said *to you*'.

"I am not a fool," the Faris said abruptly. "If Cousin Sisnandus believed that what my father heard was more than a product of his mental breakdown, he still would not tell the King-Caliph and rob House Leofric of what political influence we have left. I know that. But I know that Father *is* ill. They found him the next day, among the pyramids, under God's Fire, surrounded by dead slaves. His clothes were torn. He had scratched away part of the side of a tomb, with nothing but his hands."

The thought of those hands, that have examined her body with steel instruments, being torn and bleeding; of the man's mind shattered – Ash kept herself from showing her teeth. *How sad.*

"Faris, if you've heard Godfrey," she persisted, pressing her point, "then you've heard the Wild Machines."

"Yes." The Visigoth woman looked away. "Finally, this past night, I could do nothing else but listen. I have heard."

Ash followed her gaze. Hundreds of surrounding faces stared back at the two of them: at the fate of Dijon being negotiated under truce, in the mud of a camp with winter coming on.

"They follow you, Faris."

"Yes."

"Many of them men from your Iberian campaigns? And from fighting the Turk, over by Alexandria?"

"Yes."

"Well, you're right," Ash said, and when the woman looked back at her, went on: "Your own men *are* in danger. The Wild Machines don't care how they win this war. For one thing, they're telling you to assault the city, take it in a hurry, kill the Duke by sheer force of numbers; and that's bad tactics, you could lose half an army of men here for nothing. That's lives wasted; lives of men you know."

"And secondly?" the Faris said sharply.

"And, secondly – 'We have bred the Faris to make a dark miracle, as Gundobad made one. We shall use her, our general, our Faris, our miracle-maker – to make Burgundy as if it has never been.'"

Ash, speaking the words seared into her memory, watched the woman's face start to seem grey, sunk-in, desperate.

"Yes," the Faris said. "Yes, I have heard those words. They say it is they who made the long darkness over Carthage. They *say*."

"They want the Duke dead and Burgundy gone so that they can make a miracle that makes the world into a desolation. Faris, will the Wild Machines care if the Visigoth army is still inside the borders of Burgundy when that happens? When there's nothing but ice, darkness, and decay – the way it's starting to be around Carthage. And do you think anyone's going to survive it?"

The Faris leaned back in her chair, her coat of plates creaking slightly. Aware of every movement – any signal that might be an attack, a hand that might be going for a stiletto – Ash found herself mirroring the Visigoth woman, sitting back and away from her.

Another flurry of snow-particles dust-devilled across the earth, beyond the guy-ropes and tent-pegs of the awning.

"Winter," the Faris said, and looked straight at Ash. "'Winter will not cover all the world'."

"You heard that too." A tension that she had not been conscious of relaxed. *It's me telling Roberto and Angeli and Florian these things, it's me staking the company, and Dijon, and a whole lot of lives on being right – and whether it's true, or a lie, at least someone else has heard it.*

"*If* this is true," the Faris said, "where do you suggest I take my men – or you take your men, if it comes to that – to be safe? If they want the whole world made into a desert, burned, sown with salt . . . Tell me, Frankish woman, where we may go to be *safe*!"

Ash hit the wooden table with her gauntleted fist. "*You're* Gundobad's descendant! *I* can't even miraculously light a bloody altar candle! You're the one that's going to make this miracle for them!"

The Faris's gaze slid away. Almost inaudibly, she said, "I do not know this to be true."

"Don't you? Fucking don't you? Well, I'll tell you what's true. When I was outside Carthage, the bloody machines just turned me round and walked me towards them, and there wasn't a Christ-damned thing I could do about it! I didn't have a *choice*! If Duke Charles dies, we're all going to find out if *you've* got a choice, but by then it's going to be far too late!"

"And so the answer is that you kill me."

It stopped Ash as if she had walked into a wall: the Visigoth woman's abrupt shifts from fear to concentration and back again. Now the Faris, without moving, added:

"I can think for myself. You reason thus: if am I dead, the Wild Machines can do nothing. If you make a move, there are twelve of my sharpshooters who will put bodkin-head arrows through your armour before you get out of that chair."

An arrow-shaft as thick as a finger; an arrow-head four inches long, four-sided, sharp: able to punch through metal. Ash pushed the image out of her mind's eye.

"Of course there are archers," she said equably. "If nothing else, I overhear your communications with Carthage. You'd have shot me before now, except that Dijon will be even harder to take if you go around killing their current heroes. And you still think I might betray the city to you."

"You are my sister. I will not kill you unless it is necessary."

In the face of the woman's intent seriousness, Ash felt nothing but a sudden impulse of pity. *She's young. She still thinks you can do that.*

"I'll kill you without a second thought," Ash said. "If I have to."

"Oh yes." The woman's gaze wandered to the child-slave, standing a few paces off with the wine jug; a boy with thistledown-white hair. Ash saw her glance around at other slaves; at Ash herself.

The Faris said, "There is nothing they can make me do. Not a miracle, nothing. I will no longer speak to the *machina rei militaris*, I will not listen! Surely they can do nothing unless I speak with them, and I will not, I will not!"

"Maybe. It's a hell of a chance to take."

"What would you have me do?" Her keen expression sharpened. "Kill myself, because voices in my head tell me I'm going to do a hellish miracle? I'm like you, *jund* Ash, I'm a soldier. I've never done miracles! I pray, I go to mass, I sacrifice where it's proper, but I'm not a priest! I'm a *woman*. I'll wait until we kill this Burgundian Duke, and see if I—"

"It's too late then!" Ash's interruption silenced the Faris. "These are creatures who have the power to put out the sun. They did that. When they draw on the sun's spirit again, when they force it on you, the same way God's grace comes to a priest, do you think you can refuse it?"

The woman licked her lips. When she spoke, it was without the rising note of hysteria.

"But what would you have me do? Fall on my sword?"

Ash said instantly, "Persuade Lord-*Amir* Leofric to destroy the Stone Golem."

The Visigoth woman stared, completely silenced, while a man might have counted a hundred. The sound of a war-horse, neighing from the lines, broke the silence. The eagles of the Visigoth legions glinted in the sunlight.

I can't get to her and kill her before they kill me.

Maybe I won't have to.

"*Do* it," Ash urged. "Then they can't reach you. The Stone Golem is their only voice."

"My God." The Faris shook her head in amazement.

"They spoke once to your Prophet Gundobad, and once to Roger Bacon," Ash said steadily, "and then with the *machina rei militaris*, to us. It's their only voice. You've got an army here. Leofric's your 'father', even if he's sick. You've got the authority. No one can stop you going back to Carthage and breaking the Stone Golem into rubble!"

The woman in Visigoth mail, with a quick apprehension that Ash read as long, if unconscious, consideration of the subject, said, "Cut these 'Wild Machines' off – at the cost of my never taking the field again."

"It's you or the machine." A ghost of humour pulled Ash's mouth up at the corners. "So: you're right, finally – here I am with the general of the Visigoth army, asking her to destroy the tactical engine that makes her win wars . . ."

"I wish, truly, that this was a such a ruse of war." The Faris linked her fingers, rested her elbows on the table, and her lips against her joined hands.

There is no sound in Ash's mind of the Faris's voice speaking to the *machina rei militaris*, appealing to Leofric or Sisnandus. Nothing speaks.

After a moment's silence, the Faris lifted her head to say, "I could pray, now, for your Duke to stay alive."

"He's—" *not my Duke*, Ash had been about to protest. She cut herself short. "He's my current employer, so I'm supposed to want him to stay alive! Even if there wasn't so much at stake."

The Faris chuckled briefly. She reached out for the goblet and drank again, the wine staining her upper lip purple. "Why Burgundy's Duke?"

"I don't know. You don't know either?"

"No. I dare not ask." The Faris squinted at the sky, and the gathering yellow-grey cloud cover. "My father – Leofric will never destroy the Stone Golem. Even now. He gave his life to it, and to breeding us. And he is sick, and I cannot talk with cousin Sisnandus unless I use the *machina rei militaris* to do it, and am . . . overheard. Or unless I travel back, over land and sea, to speak face to face."

"Then do that!"

"It – would not be so easy?"

Ash felt the lessening of tension, heard it in the Visigoth woman's questioning voice. They sat, either side of the table, staring at each other: a woman in Milanese harness, a woman in a bright cloth-covered coat of plates; scarred and unscarred faces suddenly still.

"Why not? *Extend the truce.*" Ash tapped a finger on the table, the gauntlet's laminations sliding one over the other. "Your officers would rather hold siege and try to starve us out. They know they're going to lose a lot of men with constant assaults. Extend the truce!"

"And go south, to Carthage?"

"Why not?"

"I would be ordered back here. Ordered not to leave."

Ash heaved a great breath of air in, feeling a tension relax, feeling an excitement and expectation. "Shit, think about it! You're the Faris, no one here has the authority to argue with you. You'd get to Carthage. This siege is good for months."

The unexpected feeling, Ash realised, was hope.

"But, sister," the other woman said.

"Better go back to Carthage and have the Stone Golem destroyed, whether Leofric wants it to happen or not. Better that, than sit here knowing you're the one person that has to be killed to stop this." Ash jabbed her finger in the air. "This isn't about war any more! It's about being wiped out. Hell, take the Visigoth army home and take out House Leofric if you have to!"

A smile curved the other woman's lips. "That, I think, these men would *not* do. Even for me. The Empire takes certain precautions against that. But . . . Father might listen to me. Ash, if I leave, and if I fail, then perhaps we are still safe. Perhaps, if I am not in Burgundy, then nothing can happen."

"We don't know that, either."

If you leave here, Ash thought suddenly, there'll be no one with you who knows that you have to be killed. Shit: I should have realised that. But the chance, the chance that this could work and take out the Stone Golem—

"They are great Devils," the Faris said soberly. "Princes and Thrones and Dominions of Hell, set loose in the world and given power over us."

"Will you extend the truce?"

The Faris looked up, as if her thoughts had been elsewhere. "For a day, at least. I must think, must carefully consider this."

To stop the assaults, the fucking bombardment, for a whole day; is it this easy?

Such a phenomenal concession made Ash dry-mouthed with the fear that it might be retracted. She made herself sit with the confident expression of a mercenary who is used to negotiating the rules of engagement in war; tried to keep the strain and the sudden hope off her face.

"But Duke Charles," the Faris said. "There have been rumours that he is sick? That he was wounded mortally, at Auxonne?"

Startled, Ash realised from the woman's expression that she asked the question in all seriousness. *She really thinks I'm going to tell her?*

"There'll be rumours that he's sick, wounded, and dead," Ash said caustically. "You know what soldiers are like."

"*Jund* Ash, I am asking you – how much time do we have?"

It was the first time that she truly heard the *we*.

"Faris . . . I can't tell you things about my employer."

"You said it yourself: this is not about war. Ash, *how much time?*"

I wish I could talk to Godfrey, Ash thought. He'd know whether I should trust her. He could tell me . . .

But I can't ask him. Not now.

She kept the part of her that listens passive, silent, absorbed; offering no chink for a voice to come through. The fear of the ancient voices gnaws at the back of her mind, like a rat.

No one can make this decision but me, on my own.

"You call me your sister," Ash said, "but we're not, we're nothing to each other, except by blood. I know nothing about whether I can trust your word. You're sitting out here with an army – and I have men who will die if I make a bad decision."

The Faris said steadily, "And I am Gundobad's child."

Now, as she sat back in her chair, the scarlet cloth covering riveted over the metal plates of her armour could be seen to be rubbed, worn, black with dirt under the cuffs. The Visigoth woman's long hair shone silver-grey with grease. Ingrained mud pencilled fine lines in the skin at the corners of her eyes. She smelled of wood-smoke, of the camp; and Ash, feeling it hit home under her breastbone, leaving her without breath, was overcome with an utter familiar closeness nothing to do with blood kinship.

The woman added, "We neither of us can say for certain what that means, but will you risk waiting to find out? Ash, how much *time* do we have? Is the Duke well and whole?"

Ash remembers a dream of boar in the snow; Godfrey's whisper of *you are one of the beasts of the world with tusks*, and *it took me so long to gain your trust.*

The Faris got to her feet. Ash's own face looks back at her from between wind-strewn tendrils of white hair; hair that falls in ripples over the rose-head rivets of a coat of plates, down past the waist and the sword-belt with its empty scabbards.

Ash shut her eyes briefly, to blot such a strong resemblance out of her mind.

"More than sisters," she said, opening her eyes to cold wind and the surrounding ranks of troops; and armed men moving and talking quietly while discussion goes on out of their earshot: strategy, tactics, decisions. "Never mind what we are by birth. *This.* We both do this. We both understand it . . . Faris, don't take long to consider your decision. The Duke is dying as we speak."

The woman's gaze became fixed: no other change of expression gave away her shock.

Now we shall find out, Ash thought. Now we shall find out how much she really believes of all this, how much she's actually heard the voices of the Wild Machines talking to her.

How much this is just another war to her – and if I've given her Dijon. Because she can hit the city now it doesn't have a leader. And she may just get in.

Ash watched the Faris's expression; and missed having her sword ready for use.

The young woman in Visigoth armour put her hands out. The gesture was made slowly, so that watching men might not mistake it. Bare hands held out to Ash, palm-upwards.

"Don't be afraid," the Faris said.

Ash looked at the woman's hands. Dirt was ingrained in the lines of her palms. Small white scars, from old cuts, were visible through the dirt: a peasant's hands, or a smith's, or the hands of someone who trains for the line-fight.

"Ash, I will extend the truce," she said steadily. "A day: until dawn tomorrow. I swear this, here and now, before God. And God send we find an answer before then!"

Slowly, without a page, Ash undid the buckles on her right gauntlet with her gauntleted left hand, and stripped the armour off. She reached out and gripped the Faris's bare hand in her own. She held warm, dry human flesh.

The cheer that went up from the walls of Dijon shook the snow out of the clouds.

"I don't have any authority to do this!" Ash grinned. "But if I've got a truce, those motherfuckers on the council will ratify it! Can you hold your *qa'ids* to a truce?"

"My God, yes!"

As the noise died down, as the ranked, bored troops of the Visigoth army began to stir and talk among themselves, a shrill bell suddenly cut through the air. About to speak again to the Faris, Ash momentarily did not realise what she was hearing. Loud, hard, bitter, grieving—

A single bell rang out from the double spire of Dijon's great abbey, within the city walls. Heart in her mouth, Ash waited for the second spire bell to join in.

Only the single bell continued to toll.

Solemn, urgent, once every ten heartbeats.

Each harsh clash of metal shook the still camp outside the walls; all men gradually falling silent in the cold air as they heard it, and realised what they were hearing.

"The passing bell." The Faris turned her head back to Ash, staring at her. "You have the same custom here? A first bell for the beginning of the last few hours. The second bell for the moment of death?"

The repetitive single strokes of the bell went on.

"The Duke," Ash said. "Charles the Bold has begun to die."

The Faris's hand, still clasped in her own, tightened. "If it *is* true, if I have no choice, now—!"

Ash winced at the strength of her grip, grinding the small bones of Ash's hand together.

A complete calm came to her. As in the line of battle, when time seems to slow, she made her decision and began to move her body: clenching her left hand still in its reinforced metal gauntlet, choosing the unprotected throat of the Visigoth woman as her target, tensing arm-muscles to punch the sharp edge of the knuckleplate straight through the carotid artery.

Will I make it before the arrows? Yes. Needs to be first blow; no second chance, I'll be skewered—

"The Burgundy Duke's standard!" a Visigoth *nazir* bellowed, his deep voice cracking shrill with shock.

As if she were in no danger, the Faris dropped Ash's hand and stepped forward, away from the table and awning. Ash thought, *why am I doing nothing?*, and, appalled, looked to where the *nazir* was pointing.

Her heart jolted.

The port in the north-west gate of Dijon stood open.

Opened while all were transfixed by the abbey bell, Ash guessed: portcullis hauled up, the great bars taken down – *shit! can they close it before there's an assault*—?

The Faris's shouted orders dinned in her ears. No Visigoth soldier moved. Ash strained her gaze to see who it was riding out. She saw a man on horseback, carrying the great blue-and-red standard of the Valois Dukes, and nobody with him: no noble, no Duke miraculously raised from his deathbed, nobody. Only a man on foot, and a dog.

At the Faris's bemused order, the Visigoth troops parted to let the rider and footman through.

Ash began to put her right-hand gauntlet on, fumbling the buckles; glancing quickly towards Rochester and her escort, thirty yards away, pitifully outnumbered among the Visigoth legions.

The standard-bearer rode across the trodden earth. He reined in a few yards in front of the Faris. Ash did not recognise the man from the small part of his face she could see under his raised visor; wondered *Olivier de la Marche?* and read from the livery that it was not, was no great Burgundian noble at all. Only a mounted archer.

While she and the Faris continued to stare, the man on foot walked forward. He pulled off his hat.

His leashed hound, a great square-muzzled dog with a head that seemed too big for its body, gave Ash's leg a cursory sniff.

"It's a lymer,"[16] she said, startled into speech.

The man – white-haired, elderly, his cheeks red with the broken veins of a man who has been outdoors much of his life – smiled with a slow pleasure. "He is, Demoiselle-Captain Ash, and one of the best. He can find you any day a hart of ten, or a great-toothed boar, or even the unicorn, I swear it by Christ and all His Saints."

A glance at the Faris showed Ash the Visigoth woman staring in total bewilderment.

"Demoiselle Captain-General Faris?" The man bowed. He spoke respectfully, and a little slowly. "I have come to ask your permission for the hunt to pass, undisturbed."

"The hunt?" The Faris turned an expression of complete bewilderment first to Ash, and then to the thirty or more of her *qa'ids* who now walked up to surround her. "The *hunt?*"

This is lunacy! Ash, open-mouthed, could only stare. *If I give the order now and we go straight for the gate, will we make it?*

The elderly, bearded man lowered his gaze and mumbled something, abashed at seeing the commanders of all the Visigoth legions as well as their army commander. The lymer shook its head, drooping round ears flapping, and wagged a rat-like tail with urgent excitement.

The Faris's dark gaze flicked once to Ash as she said gently, "Grandfather, you are in no danger. We are taught to revere the old and wise. Tell me what message you bring from the Duke."

The red-cheeked man looked up. More loudly, he said, "No message, missy. Nor there won't be one, neither. Duke Charles will be dead before noon, the priests say. I am sent to ask you, will you let the hunt pass?"

"What hunt?"

Yeah, you and me both! Ash thought, not about to interrupt the Visigoth woman. *What hunt!*

"It's custom," the man said. "The Dukes of Burgundy are chosen by the hunt, the hunting of the hart."

When the Faris merely stared at him, in complete silence, he said gently, "It's always been so, Demoiselle Captain-General. Now that Duke Charles is

[16] A variety of hunting dog.

near death, the hart must be hunted to find his successor. The one who takes the quarry takes the Duke's title. I'm bidden to ask you free passage through your camp. If you give it, then me and Jombart here will go and quest for quarry."

The Faris held up her hands to quieten her officers. "*Qa'ids!*"

"But this is insanity—" A man whom Ash recognised, now, to be Sancho Lebrija, subsided at the Faris's look.

The Visigoth woman said, "Captain Ash, have you knowledge of this?"

Ash regarded the white-haired hunter. If the Visigoth commanders intimidated him, he was still standing with a serene confidence in his trade.

"I don't know a damn thing about it!" she confessed. "It's not even the season now for hunting the hart. That ended on the last feast of the Holy Cross."[17]

"Demoiselle, it must happen when it happens; when the old Duke dies."

"It is a trick, to remove their nobles from the besieged city!" Sancho Lebrija burst out.

"And go where?" the Faris challenged. "War has passed over this land. The castles and towns are sacked. Unless you think they will cut through our forces, march hundreds of miles to the north and famine, and to Flanders – and then there is nothing for them there but more war. *Qa'id* Lebrija, with their Duke dead, they will be leaderless; what can they do?"

The hunter interrupted an exchange that, in Carthaginian Gothic, it was doubtful he understood. "Demoiselle, there isn't much time. Will you let the hunt pass out, and then back into the city, unmolested?"

Ash's gaze went absently, and automatically, to the sky. In the south-east, the white sun hung above the horizon. Veils of cloud covered and uncovered it, and a thin powder of snow flurried in the air. The stench of wood-smoke was strong in her nostrils. She thought, *The weakness of the light may be nothing more than autumn.*

"Perhaps," Ash said urgently to the Faris, on the heels of the elderly man's words, "perhaps *one Duke is as good as another.*"

The *qa'ids* and *'arifs* surrounding the Faris glanced at Ash with minor irritation, as if what she said were a frivolous comment. Only the Faris, holding Ash's gaze, inclined her head a fraction of an inch.

"I give my authority to this," she said, and swung around at the outburst from her officers. "*Silence!*"

The Visigoth commanders quietened. Ash watched them exchanging glances. She became aware that she had, unconsciously, started to hold her breath.

The Faris said, "I will let them follow their custom. We are here to conquer this land. I will not have it again as it was in Iberia, a thousand little quarrelling noblemen, and no one man able to give word to control them!"

Some of her officers nodded approvingly.

"If we are to impose an administration on a conquered country, it were better they had their Duke to obey, and we had him to obey us. Otherwise

[17] 14 September.

734

there is nothing but chaos, mob-rule, and a hundred tiny wars to tie us down here, when we should be fighting the Turk."

More nods, and comments in low voices.

It even sounds convincing to me! Ash reflected, in grim, amazed humour. And it's at least half true . . . Obviously I'm not the only good bullshitter in this family.

"Tell your masters, I will let the hunt pass," the Faris said to the hunter. "Upon one condition. A company of my men will ride behind you, to see that you and your new Duke *do* return to the city."

She raised her voice so that the group of officers could all hear:

"While you hunt, this day let God's truce operate in this camp, and in Dijon, as if it were a holy day, with no man raising his hand to another. All fighting shall cease. Captain Ash, will you answer for that?"

Ash, her expression completely controlled, let herself look briefly at the serf army, the low-ranking officers. *They don't like this. I wonder how long before they'll do something about it – mutiny? Hours? Minutes?*

The Faris might have lost it, right here.

Better do something while she still has command.

The single bell rang out across the wet, cold air.

If one Duke isn't as good as another, Ash thought grimly, we shall soon know.

"Yes," Ash said aloud. "If Olivier de la Marche isn't a complete fool, yes, I guarantee the fighting will stop, the truce will be observed today. Until Prime tomorrow?"

"Very well." Briskly, with a sheen of sweat on her temples, the Faris turned back to the huntsman. "Go. Ride out, hunt. Choose yourselves a new Duke of Burgundy. *Waste no time.*"

Loose papers found inserted, folded, between Parts Eleven
and Twelve of ASH: THE LOST HISTORY OF BURGUNDY
(Ratcliff, 2001), British Library.

```
Message:    #162 (Pierce Ratcliff)
Subject:    Ash
Date:       11/12/00 at 07.02 a.m.
From:       Longman@
```

format address deleted
Other details encrypted and
non-recoverably deleted

Pierce -

This is amazing. I need more!

  Do I get a credit for finding it? :-)

  We _must_ have the rest of your translation of the Sible
Hedingham manuscript as soon as possible. You'll need to write at
least a preface, connecting it with 'Fraxinus'. Pierce, our
publication date is only four months away!

  So - we have to take some decisions. Go ahead and publish
'Fraxinus', and then 'Sible Hedingham' later? Delay publication of
both for a few months? I'm in favour of the latter, and I'll tell
you why.

  If we can bring out your translation of these manuscripts
simultaneously with the release of Dr Napier-Grant's initial
findings at the Carthage sea-site, and with the possible TV
documentary that we've discussed, then I think we're going to have
the kind of academic success that only comes once in a generation.

  Academic and _popular_, Pierce. You could be famous! ;-)

  I've got to have your OK to tell my MD about the Sible Hedingham
ms. He knows about academic confidentiality! This is so frustrating
- he's already desperate to continue negotiations with Dr Napier-
Grant's university board, or with her, direct; and I'm having to
fudge. I don't want office politics to take this away from me! How
soon do you think Doctor Isobel will be ready to release details of
the Carthage sea-site? When can I tell Jon that we've got a new
manuscript?? When can I tell _anyone_ about the Stone Golem??

  I cannot tell you how excited I am!

- Anna

```
Message:    #304 (Anna Longman)
Subject:    Ash/Sib. Hed.
Date:       11/12/00 at 04.23 p.m.
From:       Ngrant@
```

format address deleted
Other details encrypted by
non-discoverable personal key

Anna -

I can only do a translation just so fast! Mediaeval Latin is notoriously difficult, and if it weren't for the fact that I'm used to this hand and this author, you could expect to wait for years!

From a quick-and-dirty read through of the whole ms, I can state now that the Sible Hedingham document is definitely a continuation of the 'Fraxinus' text, by the same hand. But it differs in almost all of its particulars from our conventional history of the events of the winter of 1476/77. I don't recognise this history! And some of the passages towards the end of the ms are impenetrably resistant to translation!

Even towards the end of this section that I'm about to forward to you, the text becomes very difficult. The language is obscure, metaphoric: I may be mistaken – a tense, a case, an unfamiliar word-usage, can alter so many meanings! Bear in mind this is a *first* draft!

Let's reserve our opinions. The first part of this very document – 'Fraxinus' – gave us a street-map accurate description of the city that we have since discovered on the bed of the Mediterranean Sea. And it may be that, reading and translating late at night, I'm getting confused. I haven't worked at quite *this* intensity since Finals, and coffee and amphetamines will only take one so far!

I've been told to take a short break today, before getting back down to it. Isobel wants me to meet some of her old Cambridge friends (as a post-grad, she was apparently very friendly with the physics people) – and the helicopter's due in an hour.

And the ROV team have got the Stone Golem as cleaned up _in situ_ as is desirable with our equipment, and I want to see the new images as they come through. If the new equipment passes its checks, the first divers will be going down later today. What I really want, of course, is to get my hands on the physical object. That won't be for weeks – I'm no diver! Even if it can be lifted from the seabed, I'm considerably far down the queue. I'll have to be content at the moment with the images coming in as the settlement is mapped.

Between this and the new manuscript, I don't know which way to turn! I have, of course, tried to bring this new information to Isobel's attention. Surprisingly, I found her abstracted, abrupt.

It's useless to tell her that she's working too hard – she has always worked far too hard, all the years that I have known her, and she is, understandably, spending all twenty-four hours of the day on this site – and as much of the time as is physiologically possible under the Mediterranean! Perhaps that's why, when I asked her on your behalf about releasing more details of the archaeological finds, she 'bit my head off', as they say. Perhaps it isn't surprising at all!

I'll show her more when I have more translated.

– Pierce

```
-------------------------------------------------------------------
```

Message: #310 (Anna Longman)
Subject: Ash/golems
Date: 12/12/00 at 06.48 p.m.
From: Ngrant@

format address deleted
other details encrypted by
non-discoverable personal key

Anna –

I just thought I would let you know: Isobel has given me the new
report on the 'messenger-golem' that we found at the Carthage
land-site.

  Apparently, the metallurgy department are _now_ stating that
materials incorporated into the bronze-work during the smelting
process indicate a time period of *five to six hundred years ago*!

  Isn't it nice of them to admit their error like that?

  (Yes, I do feel smug.)

  When I've had time to read the full text of the report, I'll ask
Isobel – if I can get hold of the woman! – if I can have it to
incorporate in an appendix to our book.

  Back to translation and the Sible Hedingham document––

– Pierce

```
-------------------------------------------------------------------
```

Message: #180 (Pierce Ratcliff)
Subject: Ash
Date: 12/12/00 at 11.00 p.m.
From: Longman@

format address deleted
other details encrypted and
non-recoverably deleted

Pierce –

I'm so pleased, Pierce! How in the world did they come to make such
an error in the first place? Dr Isobel needs to use a far better
metallurgy department. All that unnecessary worry!

  I think we have to think about moving fast. Jon Stanley's started
to mention rumblings on the American academic publishing
grapevine: apparently someone knows that you're translating
'something'. 'Fraxinus', I'd guess – I've kept the existence of
anything else utterly confidential. But Pierce, I can't tell
William Davies what to do with the original Sible Hedingham
manuscript, can I?

  I expect there's an archaeological grapevine, too, and that it's
working overtime. Can you suggest to Dr Isobel that some sort of
controlled press release might be _really_ _useful_ about now?

  Isn't this exciting? I'm so happy to be involved, even if it is
only long-distance!

Love,
Anna

```
------------------------------------------------------------------
```

Message: #187 (Pierce Ratcliff)
Subject: Ash
Date: 13/12/00 at 06.59 p.m.
From: Longman@

format address deleted
other details encrypted
and non-recoverably deleted

Pierce –

I NEED THE REST OF THE TRANSLATION.

  Theories are all very well, Pierce, but

  No. It doesn't matter. Something did happen, IS happening. Isn't it? I'll tell you why I know –

  I came home tonight, about half an hour ago, and flaked out in front of the TV, which happened to be on local news. I get London local, or East Anglian. By sheer chance I was on East Anglian news. The lead story was a human interest piece on a war veteran reunited with his long-lost brother after sixty years.

  I heard half of it – no names – sat up and stared – picked up the phone, thought who can I call, and realised: there was a message waiting for me.

  I've just played it. It's William Davies. Such a kind, formal voice, speaking to the empty air of an answering machine. He wants to know if I would like to speak to his brother, Vaughan. Vaughan has 'been away'. Now he's back.

  No, I don't want to, I want YOU to fly back to England and talk to him, Pierce. This isn't me, this isn't what I do. I'm an editor, not a journalist or historian, and I don't think I even want to go near him. He's YOUR baby. YOU do it.

– Anna

```
------------------------------------------------------------------
```

Message: #188 (Pierce Ratcliff)
Subject: Ash
Date: 13/12/00 at 07.29 p.m.
From: Longman@

format address deleted
other details encrypted and
non-recoverably deleted

Pierce –

Answer my message!

– Anna

```
------------------------------------------------------------------
```

Message: #189 (Pierce Ratcliff)
Subject: Ash
Date: 13/12/00 at 09.20 p.m.
From: Longman@

Pierce –

Read your bloody mail!!!

– Anna

Message: #192 (Pierce Ratcliff)
Subject: Ash
Date: 14/12/00 at 10.31 p.m.
From: Longman@

Pierce –

Where the hell are you?

   Well, I did it. I drove out to the old people's home this evening,
and I saw William Davies and his brother Vaughan. Two very elderly
gentlemen, with nothing much to say to each other. That's sad,
don't you think?

   Vaughan Davies isn't frightening. Just elderly. And senile. He's
lost his memory – as the result of a wartime trauma, bombed in the
Blitz. He's not a distinguished academic any more.

   It seems the amnesia is genuine. William is a surgeon, and of
course he has all his old medical contacts, even though he is
retired, so Vaughan has been checked up in the best hospital in
England, by the best neurosurgeons. Amnesia after traumatic shock.
Basically, he got blown up, got picked out of the rubble, didn't
know who he was, was put in a home after the Second World War,
forgotten, and then chucked out on the streets a few years back for
'care in the community'.

   The police eventually picked him up when he appeared in Sible
Hedingham and tried to get into his old house. He's pretty gaga,
and no one would have known who he was, except one of the family who
own Hedingham Castle was there the third or fourth time he tried
this, and finally recognised him.

   This is a dead end, Pierce. He doesn't remember editing the
second edition of ASH. He doesn't remember being an academic. When
he talks to William, he thinks they are still fifteen and living
with their parents in Wiltshire. He doesn't understand why William
is 'old'. His own face in a mirror distresses him. William just
pats his brother's hand, and tells him he'll be all right now. It
made me cry to listen to him.

Sometimes I don't like myself much. I don't like myself because
he's a real person, who has suffered appallingly; and his brother
is a sweet old man who I'm fond of.

FFS, Pierce, why aren't you checking your mail!

- Anna

Message: #322 (Anna Longman)
Subject: Ash
Date: 14/12/00 at 10.51 p.m.
From: Ngrant@

format address deleted
Other details encrypted by
non-discoverable personal key

Anna -

I can't leave here now. I can't take the time away from this
translation! You will see why. Am sending the next section.

Talk to Vaughan Davies again, for me. _Please._ If he is *at all*
coherent, ask him: what was his theory about a 'connection'
between the ASH documents and the history - our history - that
superseded it? Ask him what it was that he was going to publish
after his second edition!

- Pierce

Message: #196 (Pierce Ratcliff)
Subject: Ash
Date: 14/12/00 at 11.03 p.m.
From: Longman@

Pierce -

ARE YOU MAD?

format address deleted
Other details encrypted and
non-recoverably deleted

- Anna

Message: #333 (Anna Longman)
Subject: Ash
Date: 14/12/00 at 11.32 p.m.
From: Ngrant@

format address deleted
Other details encrypted by
non-discoverable personal key

Anna -

No, I'm not mad.

It's late, here. Too late to do any more translation tonight, and besides, I am too tired to think in English, never mind in dog-Latin. I'm sending you what I have complete. Dawn tomorrow I'll carry on, but for now, I owe you an explanation of why I'm not flying back to Gatwick, and here it is.

I have at last been shown the Admiralty charts of this area of the Mediterranean. As you might expect, given the sheer amount of submarine activity during the last war, their charts of the seabed are extensively detailed, and accurate.

None of them show any kind of a 'trench' on the sea-floor in this location.

– Pierce

PART TWELVE

16 November AD 1476

The Hunting of the Hart[1]

[1] Sible Hedingham ms, part 2.

I

"There's a fucking *army* outside the walls," Ash yelled, "and you think you're just going to go out and hunt some *animal*?"

Olivier de la Marche brought his big chestnut stallion around, avoiding rubble, and answered her question between orders to the throng of huntsmen. "Demoiselle-Captain, we ride *now*. We must have a Duke."

Ash, looking at his weather-beaten features under his visor, recognised a capable man with much to organise, and also something else; some quality of abstraction that she realised to be present now everywhere in these ravaged streets.

The blitzed great square behind Dijon's north wall must have three thousand people in it now, to her quick calculation: and more coming in every minute. Knights mounted on horseback, archers running with messages, huntsmen and their varlets, and couple upon couple of running-hounds. But most – she squinted her eyes against the morning sun falling between the burnt-out timbers of buildings – wet, and blackened from fire – mostly women and men in drab clothes. Shopkeepers. Apprentices. Farming families: peasants taking refuge from the devastated countryside. Wine-makers and cheese-sellers, shepherds and small girl-children. All of them bundled up in their layers of neatly mended, muddy woollen tunics, gowns, and cloaks; faces bitten red and white by the wind. Most of them solemn, or abstracted. For the first time in months, not flinching in anticipation of falling stone or iron.

And quiet. The noise of her own men walking and riding back in was the loudest noise, audible over the whining of the hounds. Her rough voice, and the single passing-bell, were all else that broke the almost complete silence.

"If there are Burgundians among your mercenaries," Olivier de la Marche concluded, "they may hunt with us."

Ash shook her head. The pale bay gelding, abruptly alert to her movement, skittered a step sideways in the mud and broken cobbles. She brought him under control. "But *who* inherits the Dukedom?"

"One of the royal ducal bloodline."

"*Which one?*"

"We will not know, until they are chosen by means of the hunting of the Hart. Demoiselle-Captain, come if you will; if not, keep the walls and watch the truce!"

Ash exchanged glances with Antonio Angelotti as the Duke's deputy rode off towards the houndsmen. "'The hunting of the hart' . . . Am I crazy, or are they?"

Before Angelotti could answer, a tall scarecrow figure approached, pushing its hood back. Floria del Guiz beat her sheepskin mittens together against the bitter wind.

"Ash!" she called cheerfully. "Robert has a dozen men who need to speak to you about the hunt. Should he bring them from the tower, or will you go to him?"

"Here." Ash dismounted, the steel and leather war saddle creaking. The tension of the Faris's camp released itself, momentarily, in aching muscles, under her armour.

Down at ground-level, she became more aware of the men and women packing into the square. They walked quietly, most not speaking; a few with expressions of grief. Where they were forced by the devastation of the narrow winding streets to crowd together, she saw how they courteously stepped aside, or gave a nod of apology. The Burgundian men-at-arms, that she expected to see using their bills to hold the crowd back under control, were standing in small clusters watching the flood of humanity go past them. Some of them exchanged brief comments with the peasants.

Many of the women held lit tapers carefully between their cupped hands.

"This silence . . . I've never heard anything like it."

There were two women behind Floria, Ash now saw; one in the green robes of a soeur, and one in a stained, grubby white hennin. As the press lessened around her and the bay gelding, she could see their faces. Soeur-Maîtresse Simeon, and Jeanne Châlon.

"Florian . . ." Bewildered, she turned back to her surgeon.

Floria looked up from sending a baggage-train child back with a message. "Robert says the dozen or so Flemings who stayed with us after the split, they want permission to ride in the hunt. I'm riding too."

Ash said sceptically, "And when was the last time you thought of yourself as Burgundian?"

"This does not matter." The Soeur-Maîtresse's fat white face did not look disapprovingly at Ash; rather, sadly, and with no condemnation. "Your doctor has been ill-treated by her homeland; but this draws all of us together."

Ash caught Jeanne Châlon looking at her without bitterness. Tears had reddened the rims of her eyes. That or the cold wind kept her sniffling. Amazingly, she had her arm linked in Floria's.

"I can't believe he's dying," she croaked. Ash felt her throat tighten in involuntary sympathy with the woman's plain grief. Jeanne Châlon added, "He was our heart. God lays His sternest burdens on His most faithful servant . . . God in His mercy knows how we shall miss him!"

Apart from the Soeur-Maîtresse, Ash suddenly realised, she was seeing no priests out on the streets. The single bell continued to toll. Every ordained priest must be in the palace, with the dying Charles; and she felt a curious impulse to ride there, and wait for the news of his final passing.

"I was born here," Floria said. "Yes, I've lived away. Yes, I'm outcast. All the same, Ash, I want to see the new Duke chosen. I wasn't in Burgundy; I was abroad when Philip died and Charles hunted. I'm going to do it now, whether—" and her eyes became small with the constriction of reckless, bitter humour on her face: "—whether I think it's rubbish, or not. I'm still going!"

Ash felt the cold wind redden her nose. A drop of clear liquid ran down. She unbuckled her purse to take out her kerchief, and, having given herself time to think – time to look at the hunters, the archers in the liveries of Hainault and Picardy mounting up; even the refugee French knight Armand de Lannoy standing ready with grooms and a group of Burgundian nobles – Ash wiped her nose vigorously and said, "I'm coming with you. Robert and Geraint can look after the shop."

Antonio Angelotti spoke down from the saddle of his scraggy grey. "But if the Visigoths don't keep the truce, madonna!"

"The Faris has her own reasons for keeping this truce. I'll brief you after this." Her tone lightened. "Come on, Angeli. The lads are getting bored. I'm going to show them we don't have to sit inside Dijon like we're terrified. Good for morale!"

"Not if they stick your head on a spear, madonna."

"I don't suppose that would improve my morale, no . . ." Ash turned as the child messenger threaded her way back through the polite crowd, Robert Anselm and a number of men-at-arms behind her. "What's the request here?"

Pieter Tyrrell stood behind Anselm, his maimed hand in its specially sewn leather glove tucked behind his belt. His face under his archer's sallet looked white. With him, Willem Verhaecht and his lance second, Adriaen Campin, seemed equally stunned.

"We didn't think he was going to *die*, boss," Tyrrell said, not needing to explain who he referred to. "We'd like to ride the hunt in memory. I know it's a siege, but . . ."

The older Willem Verhaecht said, "A dozen of my men are Burgundian by birth, boss. It's respect."

"He was a good employer," the lance second added.

Ash surveyed the men. A pragmatic part of her mind said, *A dozen men either way won't save us if the Visigoths turn treacherous*, and the rest of her responded, in the weak morning sunlight, to the effect of the immense press of people and the almost total silence.

"If you put it that way," she said, "yes, it's respect. He knew what he was doing. Which is more than you can say for most of the sad bastards who pay us. Okay: permission granted. Captain Anselm, you and Morgan and Angelotti will hold the tower. If there's treachery, stand ready to have the city gates open – we'll be coming back in a hurry!"

A quiet appreciative chuckle went round the group. Willem Verhaecht turned to organising his men. Robert Anselm's mouth shut in a firm line. Ash caught his eye.

"Listen."

"I don't hear anything."

"Yes, you do. You hear grief." Instinctively, Ash kept her voice at a low conversational tone. She pointed to where, among the huntsmen and hounds, Philippe de Poitiers and Ferry de Cuisance stood with Olivier de la Marche; all of them surrounded by their men; all of them bareheaded now in the autumn day. "If this city's going to stand, they *need* a successor to Charles. If he dies and there's no one – then this is over: Dijon will fall tomorrow."

Over the slight susurrus of the crowd, the noise of the single bell came clearly. Ash glanced up at the peaked roofs. She could not see the twin spires of the abbey. *They'll be anointing him, giving him the last sacrament.*

The back of her neck prickled with anticipation, waiting for the second and final peal to begin. *Dead before midday, the huntsman thinks. And it's got to be past the fourth hour of the morning now . . .*

"What about the Faris?" Robert Anselm rumbled.

"Oh. She's sending an escort with the hunt," Ash said wryly.

"An *escort?*" Anselm's bullish, stubbled face looked bewildered. He shook his head dismissively. "That's not what I meant. When he dies – is she Gundobad's child? Can she do a miracle?"

"I don't think even she knows."

"And do you know, girl?"

The pale gelding butted Ash's pauldron. She reached up absently and firmly stroked its muzzle. It lipped at her gauntlet.

"Roberto . . . I don't know. She hears the Wild Machines. They speak to her. And if they speak to her—" She switched her gaze to Robert Anselm's brown gaze, under pinched, frowning brows. "If they made me turn around and walk to them – then, whatever she's capable of, they can make her do that, too."

There were no last hedgerow flowers in this ravaged autumn, but she could smell evergreen branches, and pine-sap: half the men and women in the crowd were wearing home-made green garlands. Ash stands where she has stood so often before: among a group of her officers, familiar faces; horses being held by the company's grooms; men-at-arms in Lion livery sorting themselves out and swapping kit between them.

Everything's different now.

They watch her with more seriousness than they would give to the morning of battle.

"The Faris is frightened. I *may* have frightened her all the way back to Carthage – but I don't know," Ash said thoughtfully. "She's heard the Wild Machines say *winter will not cover all the world, unless Burgundy falls.* But what she's lived under is the Eternal Twilight – I don't know if she really understands that they want everything black and freezing and *dead.*"

Her gaze went above the silent crowd and the ruined roofs, towards the sun, for reassurance.

"I've been forced by them. She hasn't. She thinks it can't happen to her. So I don't know if she can bring herself to harm the Stone Golem. Even now that she knows it's the only way the Wild Machines can get at her."

Robert Anselm completed her thought: "It's what she's depended on, in the field, for ten years."

"It's her life." Ash's scarred face twisted in a grin. "And it isn't mine. I'd blow the Golem sky-high – but I'm not there. So that doesn't leave me much of an option."

Her mind recovering itself, she found herself with a plan rapidly falling together under the stimulus of that demand. "Robert, Angeli, Florian. I said to the Faris, one Duke's as good as another. But I can be wrong. If the Wild Machines only need *Charles* dead – then we're about to find out what that means."

Ash made an effort, ignored the silent crowd.

"Let's hope the Visigoths have got all their attention on this hunt. Damn us riding *with* it – I'm going to lead a snatch-squad. Once we're outside the area, we're going to slip away from the hunt, come back to the Goth camp, and make an attempt to kill the Faris."

"We're dead," Anselm said brutally. "If you took the whole company, you wouldn't get through thousands of men!"

Ash, not at all contradicting him, said authoritatively, "Okay: we'll *take* the whole company – all those with mounts, anyway. Roberto, the Faris can declare a truce, but there could be an armed mutiny going on out there before midday. The hunt could turn into a slaughter. If we want to kill the Faris – this is going to be the only chance to get outside the walls and try."

Anselm shook his bull head. "Truce be buggered. *I'd* kill any Burgundian noble who stuck his head outside, if I was Goth commander. De la Marche thinks he can be in and out of here like a rat up a drain-pipe!"

"This whole hunt is mad," Ash said, lowering her voice, under the noise of the single bell. "That's *good*. The confusion will work for us. But I should start praying, if I were you . . ." A brief grin. "Roberto; I'll take picked men; volunteers only."

"Poor bastards!" Robert Anselm gave a glance at the Lion captains sorting their men out into units, in the square. "The ones you took to Carthage. They *believe* they're 'heroes' now. They forget they got their asses kicked. And the ones that stayed here, they think they missed out, so they can't wait to get stuck in. They'll think you've got a plan."

Alert to nuance, Ash said, "I'd planned to leave Angelotti in charge here, the gunners need keeping under control. I think the foot needs an officer, too – maybe you *should* stay in Dijon, not volunteer to come with me now."

She expected a protest, along the lines of *let Geraint Morgan do it!* Anselm only glanced at the city gates, and nodded acknowledgement.

"I'll put a watch up on the walls," he grunted. "Soon as I see you attack the camp, we'll shoot from here, add to the confusion. Sod the truce. Anything else, girl?"

His gaze slid away from hers.

"No. Sort out all the mounts you can for the men who're coming with me on this."

Ash stood in the weak sun, watching him walk away; a broad-shouldered man in English plate, his scabbard tapping against his leg armour as he walked.

"Robert's turning down a fight?" Floria said incredulously, at her elbow.

"I need someone smart to stay in the city."

The surgeon looked at her with a brief, cynical expression. She did not say *his nerve's gone*, but Ash read it on her face.

"He'll be okay," Ash said gently. "We all get like that. *My* nerve isn't brilliant right now. Maybe it's something about sieges. Give him a day or two."

"We may not *have* a day." Floria bit her lip. "I've seen you talk to Godfrey.

I've seen you turned around by the Machines – we all have. I know it as well as the rest of this sorry lot: we may only have an hour, now. We don't *know* how long until it happens."

A familiar coldness insulated Ash. "I'll do this without Robert. He knows what I'm planning here could be a one-way trip. I need people with me who know that – and still come."

On the far side of the square, the town clock struck ten. Its chimes battered the silence. Ash saw people unwrapping bread from dirty kerchiefs, sitting and eating on heaps of fallen bricks and furniture; all of it done in a contained, reverent practicality.

Floria closed her fingers around Ash's hand in its chill metal gauntlet. She said, as if the effort were suddenly too great, "Don't do this. Please. You don't need to. Leave your sister alive. There'll be another Duke in an hour or two. You're going to get yourself killed for no reason."

Ash turned her hand so that she could clasp the woman's hand, carefully, between metal and linen. "Hey. I spend my life risking getting killed for no reason! It's my job."

"And I get sick of stitching you back together!" Floria scowled. She looked, despite the dirt lining her face, very young: a youth wrapped in doublet and demi-gown, candle-wax drippings white down the front of her cloak. She smelled of herbs, and old blood. "I know you need to do this. And you're scared. I know it. You're not talking with Godfrey, either."

"No." The thought of speaking, or listening, brought a dryness to Ash's mouth. In that part of herself that she has shared for a decade, there is a growing tension; an oppression, like the pressure before a storm. The silent presence of the Wild Machines.

"At least see the Duke chosen, before you try military suicide!" Floria's voice was gruff, with a raw dark humour. "There'll be as much confusion in their camp after that as before. Maybe more. They might even be more off-guard. Come on, you're telling me you don't want to see de la Marche become Duke?"

Responding to the humour, to the woman's plain attempt to control her own emotion, Ash said lightly, "I thought no one knew who gets chosen?"

Floria squeezed her hand hard and released it. Thickly, she said, "Technically, no. *Technically*, anyone with Burgundian ducal blood's eligible. Hell, with the way the noble families intermarry, that's about every arms-bearing family between here and Ghent!"

Ash flicked a glance towards Adriaen Campin, where he did a last kit-check for Verhaecht's other Flemish men. "Hey, maybe we've got the next Duke of Burgundy riding with the company!"

That made Floria wipe her eyes, and grin cynically. "And maybe Olivier de la Marche isn't the experienced noble military candidate. Come on. Who do you think they're going to pick?"

"You mean when they open up the deer and look at the entrails, or whatever it is they do here, it's going to say 'Sieur de la Marche' in illuminated capitals all over it?"

"That's about the size of it, I guess."

"Makes life easier." Ash shook her head. "Why go to the bother of hunting the fucking thing! Christus. I'll never understand Burgundians – present company excepted, of course."

When she looked at Floria, it was to see the young woman smiling at her, eyes warm, wiping her nose with a dirty rag.

"You don't understand a damn thing." Floria's voice shook. "For the first time in my life, I wish I knew how to hack someone up with your bloody meat-cleavers. I want to ride with you, Ash. I don't want to see you ride off on this suicidal, stupid idea and not *be* there—"

"I'd sooner throw a mouse into a mill-wheel. You'd stand about as much chance."

"And what chance do *you* stand!"

That this morning – the clouds thinning in the north, no more flurries of snow; the sun harsh and white in the south; the air full of the scent of broken evergreen – that this may be the last morning she sees: it is not new to her. But it is never old; never something which one becomes used to. Ash took a deep breath, into lungs that seemed dry and cold and constricted with fear.

"If we do take out the Faris, all hell will break loose. Then I'll get the guys out in the confusion. Listen, you're right, this is suicidally stupid, but it won't be the first thing to succeed simply because it is. No one out there is expecting anyone to actually *do* this."

She reached out quickly as Floria turned on her heel to stalk off, and grabbed her arm.

"No. This is the hard bit. You don't go off and cry in a corner. You get to stand here with me and look like we *know* it's going to work."

"Christ, you're a hard bitch!"

"You can talk, surgeon. You feed my guys up with opium and hemlock,[2] and chop their arms and legs off without a second thought."

"Hardly that."

"But you do it. You sew them up – knowing they're coming back to this."

After a silence, Floria muttered, "And you lead them, knowing they wouldn't do this for anyone else."

A flurry of activity among the Burgundian nobles made Ash turn her head. She saw lords and their escorts mounting up, on what nags and palfreys three months' siege had left in the city; a clarion rang out; and a hunting horn over that shrillness. All across the square, people began getting to their feet.

In the part of her soul that listens, ancient voices mutter, just below the threshold of hearing.

Ash said briskly. "All right – but stay with the hunt, Florian, where it's safe. I'll break off immediately the full cry sounds. I can't wait until the hunt's over to attack. We can't wait for anything, now."

---

[2] Together with black henbane, the ingredients of an anaesthetic recently discovered by a dig at the fourteenth-century Augustinian hospital at Soutra, near Edinburgh. Oak-gall solution served to revive the patient after surgery.

II

Riding out through the zigzag siege trenches that extended due north of the city, Ash's neck prickled. Silent Visigoth detachments stood and watched them pass.

She swivelled in her war saddle. Black and massed as ants, a Visigoth spear-company fell in behind the cavalcade.

"Lousy bloody hunt, *this* is," Euen Huw complained.

Ash has an immediate tactile memory: six months ago, riding from Cologne at the Holy Roman Emperor's own lackadaisical pace towards the siege at Neuss, and stopping for a day's hunting. Frederick III had had the regulation trestle tables spread with white linen set up in the forest, for his noblemen to have their dawn breakfast at. Ash crammed her mouth full with white bread while lymerers returned from their various quests and unfolded, from the hems of their doublets, fumays, which they spread on the cloth, each debating the merits of his own particular beast.

The hot June sun and German forests faded in her memory.

"They don't find a hart soon, see," the Welsh captain added, "and there won't be a hunt at all. We'll have scared off the game for leagues around!"

His gaze was febrile. Ash, without appearing to watch, took in Euen Huw, Thomas Rochester and Willem Verhaecht; the armoured escort that rode with her and her banner; and her fifty men riding behind.

It has been a scramble to raise even fifty battle-trained horses.

Is this enough men? Can we break into their camp, with this?

"Watch for my signal," she said briefly. "Break off by lances as soon as we're in tree-cover."

And hope we can go without an alarm going up.

The wind outside Dijon's walls blew chill from the two rivers. Sun winked from Visigoth helmets – the amazing, still-new, still-welcome sun. Ash wore her demi-gown over her harness, the thick wool belted at the waist so that her arms would be unencumbered. The pale sun shone back also from the armour of her men, and from the rich, dirty reds and blues of the Burgundian liveries a few yards ahead.

Thin, across the cold air, the noise of clapper against bell struck, singly.

"I can hear the abbey bell, boss," Thomas Rochester said. "Charlie's still with us."

"Not for long. Our surgeon had a word with his – he's in a coma; has been since Matins—" Seeing de la Marche stopping, on the verge of the trees, Ash reined in, checking the pale bay with a curse. Silent people on foot crowded the horses: peasants, townsmen, huntsmen. An anxious whining rose from the hounds.

"Wait here." She shouldered the gelding forward with only Thomas Rochester and a lance escort. The Duke's deputy had dismounted. He stood, surrounded by a dozen men with silent square-muzzled lymers.

"Bloody Burgundians. Ought to have my old granddad here," Thomas

Rochester muttered. "Used to reckon, boss, if you showed him a fumay, he could tell you if the beast was an old or a young one, a male or a female. Just from a turd. 'A fat long and black 'un's a hart of ten.' That's what he used to say."

Fifty men's nowhere near enough. But the foot troops couldn't keep up. Fifty cavalry, medium and heavy; we need to smash our way into the camp – I need to know how she's deployed her troops; where she *is*—

She bit down on her lip, within a split second of automatically speaking aloud to the *machina rei militaris*.

No! Not to the Stone Golem, not to Godfrey: because the Wild Machines are there, I can *feel* them—

A swelling pressure in her soul.

The Faris won't have reported through the Stone Golem anyway.

"Is that the word of you all?" Olivier de la Marche asked. The bluff armoured man had the look of someone who would far rather be organising a tournament or a war. Ash wondered briefly if the Duke's deputy would be a Duke who could keep control of an invaded country: war here, war in Lorraine, war in Flanders . . .

The white-bearded lymerer looked around for confirmation at his fellows. "True, my lord. We've been out on foot since before dawn. Downriver, to the plains, and east and west to the hills. West and north, to the forests. All the hollows are cold. All the fumays are old. There are no beasts."

"Oh, *what*!" Ash exclaimed under her breath. She risked a glance back. No more than quarter of a mile outside the Visigoth camp: too soon to break off.

But if there's not going to be a hunt—

Olivier de la Marche stomped around and held up both hands, in an unnecessary demand for silence. He bellowed: "The quest has found no beasts! The land is empty!"

"'Course it's bloody empty!" Thomas Rochester snorted with self-disgust. "Shit, boss, think about it! They've got a bloody army camped here. The rag-heads probably ate everything in sight months ago! Boss, you can forget this, it ain't gonna happen."

From the men and women around them, like the mumbled response of a mass, many voices echoed: "The land is empty."

Olivier de la Marche swung himself back up into his saddle in a clatter of armour. Ash heard him order the huntsmen.

"Send the lymers back. We will have no scent to follow. Bring the running-hounds. Send the greyhound relays to the north." He raised his voice: "North, to the wildwood!"

A swirl of people went past Ash. The pale bay gelding whickered, half kicking out; and she brought him back under control in time to see all the men, women and children on foot streaming past, in the wake of the mounted Burgundian nobles. The black standard of the Visigoth company bobbed at their rear. She saw a number of cavalry with the spearmen: mounted archers.

Archers. *Shit.*

"Let's go!" She raised her arm and jerked it forward. The bay wheeled, and she brought it up with the mounted men-at-arms and archers of the Lion, falling in beside her banner and Euen Huw.

"Go where, boss?" Thomas Rochester demanded.

Ash rapped out crisp orders. "North. Ride for the trees. Once in cover, break off; then rendezvous at the ford on the west river."

Verhaecht's Flemings pushed ahead, so that she rode towards the rear of the company, among faces she knew. A thin youth turned his head away: she recognised Rickard, forbidden to ride on this assault, and said nothing – too late, now.

"This is stupid!" Rochester fumed, riding by her side. "How can he send the hounds out, when he doesn't know which way the beast is likely to run? And there isn't a beast! How can they hunt when there isn't a quarry, boss?"

With automatic cheerfulness, Ash said, "That's Burgundians for you."

A low chuckle went around the riders. She sensed their apprehension, the immediate excitement of daring oozing away. She glanced up at her banner. *There's a reasonable chance they won't follow me for this. It's murder. Can I get to the Faris on my own? Ride back, give myself up, smuggle a dagger in – no. No. She knows she's the target.*

Pushing the gelding across, she rode out to the edge of her company, to where ladies in padded headdresses and veils rode sidesaddle on underfed palfreys. Floria's big-boned scrawny grey stood out like a mercenary in church. The surgeon spurred across to her from Jeanne Châlon's side.

"What are we doing?" Ash called.

"Fuck knows!" Coming closer, ignoring the appalled stares of the crowd on foot, Floria lowered her voice. "Don't ask me, ask de la Marche, he's Master of Game for this one! Girl, it's November. We won't find so much as a wren out here. This is mad!"

"Where's he taking us?"

"North-east, upriver. Into the wildwood." Floria pointed from the saddle. "Up ahead, there."

The head of the column was already in the edge of it, Ash saw. Riding among leafless trees, brown branches stark against the pale sky. She slowed the gelding's pace as they began to come among tree-stumps. Chopped bark displayed weeping pale wood. The scent of wood-smoke went up from a number of campfires; one stump had a rusting axe left sticking in it. Of the wood-gatherers and charcoal burners and swine-herds she would have expected to see, in peacetime, there was no sign. Gone, weeks before, as refugees.

"There," Floria said, as if she realised what Ash had been looking for.

Where she pointed, men in black coifs and sodden wool tunics and bare legs walked with the hunters, talking animatedly to the men with their leashed couples of hounds. One elderly, stout man carried a taper, its flame all but invisible in the sunlight.

This cultivated edge of the forest was all hornbeam, coppiced down to thin thumb-width growth; and ash, for staves, and hazel, for nuts in season. All the winter-dark branches stood equally bare. The last chestnuts and leaves hung from bigger trees. Ash glanced down to bring the gelding around a stump, lifted her gaze, and found that she had lost the walkers and riders at the edges of the cavalcade in the multiple thin thickets. The horses' hooves sounded softer on leaf-mulch and muddy moss.

Ahead, with de la Marche's banner, the bearded huntsman lifted his horn to his lips. A shattering call split the silent, crowded wood. Handlers bent down to the leashes of the running-hounds, uncoupled them; and a bellow went up: "Ho moy, ho moy!"

Another handler shouted at his hounds by name: "Marteau! Clerre! Ribanie! Bauderon!"

The Soeur-Maîtresse of the *filles de pénitence* dug her heels into her palfrey and shot past Ash. "*Cy va! Cy va!*"

"Ho moy!" Jeanne Châlon wheezed. Her little wheat-coloured mare dug in its heels, among the fallen sticks under the chestnut trees and oaks. She gestured energetically at Floria. "Ride for us! Be my witness!"

"Yes, Tante!"

A surge of men running pushed them apart from the women riders, Ash with Floria's rangy beast shoving close to her gelding's rump. Heart thumping, she all but gave in and spurred over the cut trees and rough ground in the wake of the Burgundians, caught up in the chase. She leaned her weight in, turning back towards Thomas Rochester and Willem Verhaecht and the men.

"Get in among the trees!" she yelled. A glance back south showed her more riders, more men running on foot, and the Visigoth banner just entering the line of the wood.

Floria yelped, "Ho moy!" at the hounds, streaming away through bush and briar, and reluctantly reined in back beside Ash, cheeks flushed. Bare branches rubbed together over their heads, creaking, audible over the clink of tack and the rapid footsteps. The hounds' shrill baying ran ahead. The press of men and women running up from behind forced Ash into a trot, ducking low branches, careful on the broken earth.

Floria, behind her, called, "What the hell do they think they've found?"

"This late in the day?" Ash jerked her thumb at the sun, low through the trees behind them, close on mid-morning. "Nothing! There isn't a bloody rabbit left between here and Bruges. Get up ahead with your aunt."

"I'll ride with you – go ahead in a minute—"

"Thomas." Ash signalled. "Start sending them off. Lance at a time. North first, then west through the woods."

The man-at-arms nodded, turning his mount awkwardly among wilted banks of briar and dead goldenrod; and spurred back into the company cavalry. She watched the few seconds necessary to see him approach the lance-leaders.

"Florian." She checked position of her banner, the tag-end of the running crowd among holly, hornbeam, and oak wood; the standard of the Visigoths – out of sight, somewhere back at the edge of the wood. "Get your ass up there with the hunters. When you get back to the city, have everything ready for wounded."

The surgeon ignored her. "They're coming back!"

A throng of men on foot and on horse went past, couples of hounds tugging away from their handlers, moving too fast for the rough ground underfoot.

757

Swept back towards a holly thicket, Ash shifted her weight forward and hauled on the rein.

The pale gelding turned. Ash shifted her weight back, tassets sliding over cuisses, and brought the horse around. Apart from Rochester's sergeant with her banner, a yard or two off her flank, all the riders and people on foot around her now were strangers. She risked a glance off to the far right – to see the backs of men in Lion livery riding out into thicker woods that way – and another look behind her.

Two heavy cataphracts in scale armour, that flashed in the slanting light under the trees, were riding up close behind; the Visigoth company standard caught up somewhere in branches behind them, and fifty or more serf-troops with spears running on foot with the riders.

"It is not their business to be here!" a tight-lipped voice said, at her right side. Ash, turning in her saddle, found herself right beside Jeanne Châlon's palfrey.

"It is not yours, either!" the woman added, her tone not hostile, but disapproving.

Ash could not now see Soeur-Maîtresse Simeon, or Floria, in the mob. She kept the gelding tightly reined in as he rolled his eye, shifting his hooves on the bank that sloped down ahead of them.

"Better hope the chase doesn't come back this way!" Ash grinned at Mistress Châlon, and jerked her thumb at the serf-troops running past them through briar and tree-stumps. "What happens to Burgundy if a Visigoth kills the hart?"

Jeanne Châlon's pursed mouth closed even tighter. "They are not eligible. Nor you, you have not a drop of Burgundian blood in your veins! It would mean nothing: no Duke!"

Ash halted the pale gelding. Water ran black under the leafless trees. A pale sun, above, put white light down through the tall branches. Ahead, men with hose muddy to the thigh, and women with their kirtles kilted up and black at the hem, waited patiently to cross a small stream. Ash thumbed the visor of her sallet further up.

A strong smell hit her. Made up of horse – the gelding sweating, as it fretted in the moving crowds of peasants – and of wood-smoke, from distant bonfires, and of the smell of people who do not bathe often and who work out in the air: a ripe and unobjectionable sweat. Tears stung her eyes, and she shook her head, her vision blurring, thinking, *Why? What does—*

What does this remind me of?

The picture in her head is of old wood, that has been faded to silver and cracked dry by summer upon summer in the field. A wooden rail, by a step.

One of the big roofed wagons, with steps set down into grass; the earth trodden flat in front of it, and grass growing up between the spokes of the wheels.

A camp, somewhere. Ash has a brief associational flavour in her mouth: fermented dandelion, elderflower; watered down to infinitesimal strength, but enough to make the water safe for a child to drink. She remembered sitting on the wagon steps, Big Isobel – who could only have been a child herself, but an older child – holding her on her knee; and the child Ash wriggling to be set down, to run with the wind that ruffled the grasses between lines of tents.

The smell of cooking, from campfires; the smell of men sweating from weapons practice; the smell that wool and linen get when they have been beaten at a river bank and hung out to dry in the open air.

Let me go back to that, she thought. I don't want to be in charge of it; I just want to live like that again. Waiting for the day when the practice becomes real war, and all fear vanishes.

"*Cy va!*"

Hounds gave tongue, somewhere far ahead in the wood. The crowd at the stream surged forward, water spraying up. Both her sergeant and banner were gone. Ash swore, unbuckled the strap under her chin, and wrenched her sallet off. She pushed the cropped hair back from her ears, tilted her head, and listened.

A confused noise of hounds echoed between the trees.

"*That's* not a scent – or they've lost it again." Ash found that she was speaking to the empty air: the Châlon woman vanished into the throng.

Visigoth serf-troops pounded past on foot, either side of her; most of them with nothing but a helmet and a dark linen tunic, running bloody and barefoot on the forest floor. Skin prickled down the whole length of her spine. She dared not put her hand to her riding sword. She sat poised, bareheaded, waiting, ears alert in the cold wind for the sound of a bow—

"Green Christ!" a voice said at her stirrup.

Ash looked down. A Visigoth in a round steel helm with a nasal bar, arquebus clutched loosely in a dirty hand, had stopped and was staring up at her. Boots, and a mail shirt, marked him out as a freeman; what she could see of his face was weather-beaten, middle-aged, and thin.

"Ash," he said. "Christ, girlie, they did mean you."

In the rush of people, the two of them went unnoticed; Ash's gelding sidling back into the shelter of a beech tree with a few last brown leaves still curled like chrysalides on its twigs; the Visigoth's mounted officer too busy yelling his men back into some kind of order and off the trail of the hounds.

Alert, safe in her armour, she tucked her sallet under her arm and looked down from the high saddle. "Are you one of Leofric's slaves? Did I meet you in Carthage? Are you a friend of Leovigild or Violante?"

"Do I sound like a bloody Carthaginian?" The man's raw voice held offence, and amusement. He cradled the arquebus under one arm and reached up, pulling his helmet off. Long curls of white hair fell down around his face, fringing a bald patch that took up almost all of his scalp, and he pushed the yellow-white hair back with a veined hand. "Christ, girl! You don't remember me."

The belling of the hounds faded. The hundreds of people might as well have not been present. Ash stared at black eyes, under stained yellow eyebrows. An utter familiarity, coupled with a complete lack of knowledge, silenced her. *I do know you, but how can I know anyone from Carthage?*

The man said rawly, "The Goths hire mercenaries, too, girlie; don't let the livery fool you."

Deep lines cut down the side of his mouth, ridged his forehead; the man might have been in his fifties or sixties, paunchy under the mail, with bad teeth, and white stubble showing on his cheeks.

The gulf that she felt opening around her was, she realised, nothing but the past; the long fall back to childhood, when everything was different, and everything was for the first time. "Guillaume," she said. "Guillaume Arnisout."

He had shrunk, and not just by the fact that she sat so high above him. There would be scars and wounds she knew nothing of, but he was so much the same – even white-haired, even older – so much the gunner that she had known in the Griffin-in-Gold that it took her breath: she sat and stared while the hunt raged past, silenced.

"I thought it had to be you." Guillaume Arnisout nodded to himself. He still wore a falchion; a filthy great curved blade in a scabbard at his waist, for all he carried a Visigoth copy of a European gun.

"I thought you died. When they executed everybody, I thought you died."

"I went south again. Healthier overseas." His eyes squinted, looking up at her, as if he looked into a light. "We found *you* in the south."

"In Africa." And, at his nod, she leaned down from the saddle and extended her hand, grasping his as he offered it; forearm and forearm; his covered in mail, hers in plate. A great smile spluttered out of her, into a laugh. "Shit! Neither of us has changed!"

Guillaume Arnisout looked quickly over his shoulder, moving back into the scant concealment of the branches. Thirty feet away, a Visigoth cataphract bawled furiously and obscenely at the standard-bearer, the eagle still tangled between hornbeam clumps.

"Does it matter to you, girlie? Do you want to know?"

There was no malice, no taunt, in his tone; nothing but a serious question, and the rueful acknowledgement of a nearby sergeant likely to exercise proper discipline for this infringement.

"Do I?" Ash straightened, looking down at him. She abruptly put her sallet back on, unbuckled, and swung down from the saddle. She looped the gelding's reins around a low branch. Safe, unnoticeable among the passing heads, she turned back to the middle-aged man. "Tell me. It makes no difference now, but I want to know."

"We were in Carthage. Must be twenty years ago." He shrugged. "The Griffin-in-Gold. A dozen of us were out in the harbour, one night, drunk, on somebody's stolen boat. Yolande – you never met her, an archer; she's dead now – heard a baby crying on one of their honeyboats, so she made us row over there and rescue it."

"The refuse barges?" Ash said.

"Whatever. We called them honeyboats."

A shrill horn sounded close by. Both she and the white-haired man looked up with identical alertness, registered a Burgundian noble carrying a lymer across his saddle-bow; and then the rider and hound were past, gone into the people still massing to cross the stream.

"*Tell me!*" Ash urged.

He looked at her with a pragmatic sadness. "There isn't much more to tell.

You had this big cut on your throat, bleeding, so Yolande took you to one of the rag-head doctors and got you sewn up. Hired you a wet-nurse. We were going to leave you there, but she wanted to bring you back with us, so I had the charge of you in the ship all the way over to Salerno."

Guillaume Arnisout's creased, dirty face creased still further. He wiped at his shiny forehead.

"You cried. A lot. The wet-nurse died of a fever in Salerno, but Yolande took you on into camp. Then she lost interest. I heard she got raped, and killed in a knife-fight later on. I lost track of you after that."

Open-mouthed, Ash stood for a short time. She felt stunned, conscious of the leaf-mulch under her feet, and the warmth of the gelding's flank at her shoulder; for the rest, was numb.

"You're saying you saved my life casually and then got bored."

"Probably wouldn't have done it if we hadn't been drunk." The man's worn, livid face coloured slightly. "A few years later, I was pretty sure you were the same kid, no one else had that thistledown-colour hair, so I tried to make up for it, a bit."

"Sweet Christ."

There's nothing in this I didn't know or couldn't have guessed. Why are my hands and feet numb; why am I dizzy with this?

"You're the big boss, nowadays." Guillaume's rasping voice held scepticism, and a hint of flattery. "Not that I wouldn't have expected it. You were always keen."

"Do you expect me to be grateful?"

"I tried to show you how to look after yourself. Stay sharp. Guess it worked. And now you're this general's sister, and a big shot on your own account, from what I hear." His lined cheeks twisted into a smile. "Want to take an old soldier into your company, girlie?"

She wears a fortune on her back, strapped around her body: forged and hardened metal that it would take Guillaume Arnisout decades to buy – if, indeed, he could buy a whole harness in his lifetime. Hers comes from third-share enemy ransoms: one third for the man who makes the capture, one-third for his captain, and one-third for the company commander. At this second, it is nothing but a prison of metal that she would like to shuck off, run through the woods as freely as she did as a child.

"You don't know the half of it, Guillaume," Ash says. And then: "I *am* grateful. There was no reason for you to do any of it. Even casual interest, at the right second – believe me, I'm thankful."

"So get me out of this bloody serf-army!"

So much for disinterested information.

The wind rubs bare branches together above their heads. The ammoniac stench of disturbed leaf-mulch comes up from the bed of the stream, the black water churned into grey mud by passing men. Ash's gelding whickers. The flow of people is becoming thinner, now; the Visigoth eagle glints under the thickets of evergreen holly.

I would do it for any man – any mercenary – if he asked me at this moment.

"Lose the kit." She scrabbled with gauntlet-fingers at the ties of her livery tabard, and gown, that she wears over her armour. By the time the ties loosened, she looked up to see the Carthage-manufactured gun gone who-knows-where, the helmet slung overarm into the stream, and Guillaume with his dirty linen coif tied tight down over his balding head.

She thrust her demi-gown and the crumpled blue-and-gold cloth at him, turned, and sprang herself up into the saddle, the weight of the armour ignored.

"Burgundian!" a harsh voice bawled.

Ash spurred the gelding out of the low-hanging branches and twigs under the beech tree. At her stirrup, an anonymous man in a demi-gown and Lion livery ran beside her, limping from an ancient wound. Mail and falchion: plainly just another European mercenary.

"Which way rides the hunt?"

"*Every* way!" the Visigoth *nazir* yelled, in the Carthaginian camp patois. Ash couldn't help a grin at his frustration. He threw his arms wide in a gesture of despair. "Lady warrior, what in Christ's sweet name are we doing in this wood?"

"Don't ask me, I only work here. You!" Ash ordered Guillaume Arnisout, "let's find the Burgundians, sharpish!"

Burgundians, hell: let's find the Lion Azure!

The ground was too bad to push the gelding to more than a walk. She spurred across the stream, Guillaume Arnisout splashing after her, and slowed again, riding forward. The sun through the tree-cover let her see roughly where south might be. *Another couple of furlongs, and turn west, try and find the edge of the forest, and the river-ford . . .*

"Fuck of a hunt *this* is," Guillaume remarked, from beside her stirrup. "Bloody Burgundians. Couldn't organise a piss-up in an English brewery."

"Fucking waste of time," she agreed. She has enjoyed hunting, when the opportunity has presented itself: a noisy organised riot of a rush through bad countryside, not unlike war. This . . .

Ash removed her sallet again. She rode bareheaded in the chill wind, that the trees robbed of an edge. Too far, by many leagues now, to hear the bell tolling from the Dijon Abbey, and if there are two bells: if Charles the Bold has breathed his last. A brief solemnity touched her.

And too confusing to be able to tell which of the baying hounds, hunting horns, voices shouting "Ho moy!" and horses neighing – all glimpsed a hundred yards away, between tree-trunks – which might be the main body of the hunt.

"Sod this for a game of soldiers." Ash checked the position of the Visigoth troops behind her. "Ease off to the west . . ."

With Guillaume beside her, and the pale gelding picking a careful way between tree roots and badger setts, Ash rode across the trampled woodland floor. Briars held tags of cloth on long thorns, witness to men passing.

The white flash of a hound showed a furlong ahead, for a moment, questing busily.

Guillaume Arnisout, and a rider on a scrawny horse emerging from a holly thicket, bawled "*Gone away!*" at the same moment.

"There it is!" The rider – flushed, standing in her stirrups, hood down and hair thick with twigs – was Floria del Guiz. She spurred in a circle and pointed. "Ash! The *hart!*"

Within seconds, they were the centre of attention: a slew of riders cantering up, with the red Xs of Burgundian livery on their jackets; two *'arifs* and the eagle and a flood of serfs in munition-quality helmets pouring into the clearing; twenty huntsmen with leashed couples of hounds pounding between tree-trunks, over fallen branches and briars, sounding horns. The hounds, freed, quested busily, bayed, and shot off in a long trailing column into the forest ahead.

Shit! So much for sneaking off—

A pale flash of colour, ahead. Ash stood in her stirrups. Floria pointed again, shouting something; the horns blowing to let other huntsmen ahead know the hounds had been released drowned her out.

"There it goes!"

Two greyhounds tore past, under the gelding's hooves. The reins jerked through her fingers. Ash swore, blood thumping in her veins, pulled back, and felt the gelding gripping the bit between its teeth. It thrust forward into the crowd of Burgundian noblemen, shouldering aside a grey; and cantered beside a chestnut, partnering it, ignored Ash's attempt to bring it back by wrenching her weight back.

"Ho moy!" Floria bawled to the running-hounds, riding stirrup by stirrup with Ash. Her face flushed puce in the cold air. Ash saw her dig her spurs into the scrawny grey's flanks, all caution forgotten, everything else lost in the wild excitement of the hunt. "The hart! The hart!"

With her legs almost at full extension from war saddle to stirrups, Ash could do nothing but grab the pommel and cling on. She flew ahead of Guillaume Arnisout. The rough, broken canter jolted her up and down in the saddle. Armour clattered. The gelding, trained for war, chose to forget his training; stretched out to a full gallop and Ash threw herself down as a branch whipped across her face.

Pain blinded her momentarily. She spat out blood. Her sallet was gone, fallen from the pommel of the saddle. She straightened up, yanked the reins, felt the bit bite, and prepared to haul the gelding's mouth bloody.

His ears came erect again, the noise of the hunt lost; and he slowed.

"God *damn* you," Ash said feelingly. She looked back, without hope, for her helmet. Nothing.

The wood's full of soldiers. I've seen the last of *that.*

The pale gelding lathered up, under his caparisons. Dark patches stained the dyed blue linen cloth. Ash let him place his hoofs delicately, picking a way down the winding track. Pebbles bounced down ahead, into the chine. A crumbling chalk bluff rose up, out of the trees, raggedly topped by thorn bushes and scrub. It was no higher than the tops of the trees beyond it.

The sun shone weakly. Ash lifted her gaze, expecting to glimpse cloud cover through the tree-tops. Beyond the bare branches, she saw nothing, only clear autumn sky and the white sun at tree-top height. The myriad bare twigs and branches swaying in the wind blurred her vision. She reached up carefully with metal-shod fingers to rub at her eyes.

The sunlight lessened again: not its light, but its quality.

Fear constricted her heart. Alone, the rest of the hunt gone Christ-knows-where, she rode on down the slope. The high war saddle creaked as she let herself rest back, pelvis swaying to the horse's gait. A faint haze of rust already browned the cuisses covering her thighs, and the backs of her gauntlets; and she smiled, thinking of how Rickard would round up half a dozen of the youngest pages to do the cleaning, back in Dijon.

If I get back to Dijon. If there is any of Burgundy left.

"Halloo!" Ash bellowed, bringing her voice up from deep in her belly. It did not crack, despite the dread she felt. "Halloo, a Lion! *A moi!* A Lion!"

Her voice fell flat in the wood: no echo.

The quality of the light changed again.

We're too late. He's dying; the last breaths—

Now, the wind blowing cold between the trees, all the high bare branches swayed, rubbing bark against bark, creaking and surging like the sea. The face of the chalk bluff glowed, as clouds do before a storm, when there is still some sunlight to gleam off their white ramparts.

"*A moi!*" she shouted.

Faintly, far off, a woman's voice called, "*Cy va!*"

Hounds clamoured. Ash sat up and stared around, searching as far as she could see in any direction. No way to tell where the barking, yelping and belling came from. The gelding, reading her hesitation, lowered his teeth to a clump of grass at the foot of the bluff.

"Halloo!" Cords rasped in Ash's throat. She swallowed, in pain, too scared to project her voice properly. "The Lion!"

"Here!"

The rip of the gelding tearing grass distracted her. She could not tell which direction the voice came from. Hesitant, she touched spurs to flank, and moved off down into the chine. The shifting perspective of tree-trunks as she rode hid any movement from her.

Above, a bird shrilled out a long call. Wings whirred. The gelding tossed his head.

"*A Lion!*"

Silence followed her shout.

The long slope ran down under beech trees to another stream. Briars over-grew the water. The gelding caught the scent. Ash let him drink, briefly. No hoof-marks dinted the banks, no footsteps, no muddied water from up-stream; nothing to show any man had ever passed this way.

The air around Ash took on the quality that it has before rain: a luminous sepia darkness. By instinct, she crossed the streamlet and turned the gelding's head uphill; riding towards the brightest light.

A silent whiteness floated between her and the turf-crowned bluff. The owl vanished almost as soon as she saw it. She leaned forward, urging the war-horse on up and around the rise.

Coming up on to the shoulder of the bluff, she could look behind her, and to the west, and ahead. A faint mist of grey-black twigs met her gaze, interrupted here and there by the solidity of holly and evergreens. Nothing but forest-top, nothing for leagues in every direction – and now, as she mounted the bluff, and could see over it to the east, nothing there either but trees: the ancient wildwood of Christendom.

No voices: no hounds.

Something white moved at the foot of the bluff, where it sloped down shallowly into the forest. Another owl? she thought. It was gone before she could be sure. Searching the line of trees, her eye caught a flash of another colour – straw-pale, gold – and she was spurring forward before she thought, reacting to what had to be a man's or woman's uncovered hair.

The air tingled.

Riding bareheaded, helmet gone, chilled in the cold east wind, and alone, she could have wept to see even Visigoth soldiers. The small open space gave way to trees as she entered the wood again. She searched for the red-and-blue of Burgundian liveries, for the flash of light from a hunting horn; strained her ears to hear them blow the mote and rechase. Someone, somewhere, she thought, must be working the main pack. If they had a hart, they might have released the back relay of hounds, to bring it to bay.

The wind creaked in the branches.

"Haro!" she called.

Movement registered in the corner of her eye.

Liquid brown eyes looked into hers. The gelding snuffled. Ash froze.

Brown-gold animal eyes watched her, looking out of the lean face of a hart. Ivory-brown tines climbed the air above its brow – a hart of twelve, poised with one hoof raised, and its coat the colour of milk fresh from a cow's teat.

Ash's knuckles tightened. The gelding responded, rearing up, lifting both front hooves from the leaf-carpet. She swore, slapped his neck, and without her taking her eyes from the forest floor ahead of her, the white hart had gone.

"*Haro!*" she bawled, spurring forward. A spray of twigs lashed her, scratching pauldrons, breastplate, and her bare chin. A drop of blood stained her breastplate. Knowing only that the one hart in this whole forest must, if the hunters served the hounds right, bring the hunt down on it, Ash spurred hard through the trees – the ground open, the spoil-heaps of charcoal-burners scarring the earth – after the fleeing beast.

A screen of dark holly blocked her way. By the time she found a way around it, the hart was gone. She sat still in the saddle, listening intently; and could hear nothing; might – she thought in a sudden panic – be the last living soul in Burgundy.

A greyhound bayed. Ash's head jerked round, in time to see a dog sprinting down what must be a cart-track from the charcoal-burners' camp; its pads kicking up dirt from the deep ruts. In a split second, it vanished down the track. The deep thump of hooves on mud sounded, where it went: Ash had one glimpse of a rider – hooded head down, riding neck-or-nothing – and six or seven more hounds, strung out in a long line, and a huntsman in a dagged hood, his curved horn to his mouth; and all the small group were gone.

"God *damn* it!" She jabbed the gelding's flanks and shot off down the cart-track.

There were no tracks.

Several minutes of casting up and down gave her nothing. She reined in and dismounted, leading the pale gelding, but nothing met her searching gaze except the hoof-marks of her own mount.

"They crossed this fucking path!" She glared at the gelding. It flickered long pale lashes, in disinterest and weariness. "Christ and all His Saints help me!"

A few hundred yards down the cart-track, the ruts became overgrown with brown grass. She led her horse, the noise of its hooves and the noise of her armour as she walked breaking the silence. Another hundred yards, and the track itself trailed off into bushes, briar, and fallen beech-limbs.

"Son of a *bitch*!"

Ash stood still. She looked around, listened again. An older fear churned in her stomach: the knowledge that this was an abandoned track, that the wildwood covers league upon league upon league of land, and that once in it, men have died both of hunger and thirst. She put the thought out of her mind.

"This isn't wildwood. We'd be trying to climb over fallen trees if it was, wouldn't we? Come on, you." She firmly patted the gelding's nose. He dipped his head in weariness, as if he had been ridden far and hard; and she could not tell, trying to spot the direction of the sun, what time of the day it might now be.

White and gold moved in the forest.

She saw the hart plainly, against a green-black glossy holly tree. His smooth flanks and rump gleamed white. The tines of his horns rose up, sharp and forked; and he swung his head around as she looked, his nostrils twitching.

Wind from me to him, she realised; and then, *Sweet Green Christ!*

A gold crown encircled the hart's neck.

She saw it clear in every detail: the metal pressing into the hart's forequarters with its own weight, dinting the smooth-haired white coat.

One end of a broken golden chain dangled down from the crown. The last link tapped at the white hart's breast.

III

As if the leaves did not bear old spines grown hard, the white hart turned and sprang into the holly. The green closed behind it without trace.

Ash strode forward, gripping the reins, letting the gelding find its own footing behind her. In the minutes that it took her to climb over rough ground to the evergreen trees, she thought nothing, only stared in front of her with dumb disbelief.

At the holly, she reached out first to touch the spines – no blood – and then bent and scrutinised the ground. No droppings. A slot, that might have been a hind's track; but only one, and nothing to be read from it. So smudged, in fact, that it might have been anything, a boar's mark, even; or an old track from days ago.

She tried to push the holly branches aside.

"Shit!" She snatched her hand back. A leaf-spine, penetrating the linen glove under her gauntlet, had drawn blood: it welled red into her palm as she watched.

Beyond the shell of green leaves, the black-brown branches intertwined to fill the space there so tightly, it seemed no beast could get through.

She considered tethering the gelding, covering her face with her protected hands, and letting the armour guard her as she walked through the holly. Reluctant to be left on foot, she rejected the idea; and began to lead her horse on and around the great thicket of holly trees, on in a direction that might be west, but she could not now be sure.

That all food, all water, was gone with her company units presumably now somewhere towards the ford of the western river, was only a minor irritation.

Christ, I have to be there! They'll go in, even if I don't arrive. Thomas and Euen will see to that. But they won't get far enough to kill the Faris. I know they won't!

It was not pride but objective knowledge: her men would fight harder, and longer, if they had Ash there fighting with them; would take on trust her assessment of how necessary winning might be.

Undergrowth began to thin out. Blackened tree-stumps made her think that a fire might have blazed here, a generation ago: the forest became alders and ash trees, none of them much more than fifteen feet high. Areas of brown grass grew, clear of thorns.

The gelding plodded exhaustedly at her shoulder, picking his way with her over moss-encrusted rocks. A milky light shone down from the sky. Ash lifted her head, looking for any clue to direction. She blinked, furiously; looked away, and then up again, through the alders' gnarled bare twigs.

White dots scattered across the sky, close to the horizon. Too low to be seen properly, they tugged at Ash's memory. She thought, *Of course. Stars.*

The constellations of autumn, pale against pallor, glimmered behind the noon sky.

Visible behind the weakening sun.

"Cristus vincit, Cristus regnit, Cristus imperad," she whispered.

The wood creaked around her.

The ground dropped away at her feet. She could see nothing down the slope, only the bare tops of trees: some darkly glossy and evergreen. The brown half-dead grass was slippery under her sabatons and boot-soles. She mounted up again, every muscle aching, and coaxed the gelding forward and down between the trees.

Red dots dappled the earth.

From the saddle, she could see that what covered the slope – what the gelding now trod under his hooves – were rose-briars. Pale green briars, soft and easily crushed. The scent of bruised vegetation filled her nostrils. And roses, red and pink petals coming loose in a shower of golden pollen, releasing their sweetness.

Some last, sheltered autumn blossoms, she thought, determinedly.

The ground flattened out as she rode towards tall rocks, jutting up between the trees. Moss covered the rocks, bright lime- and bottle-glass green. Very bright, as if the sun, faint everywhere else, shone on these rocks – but when she glanced up, she saw only the milky star-dotted sky. The gelding stopped abruptly.

A tiny stream ran away between grass-fringed banks. White and red flowers dotted the grass. The stream ran out from a dark still pool between the rocks. Its black surface rippled, as Ash watched, and she saw with no surprise that the white hart had its muzzle down, lapping at the water. The gold of its crown was so bright now that it hurt the eye.

A rough-coated greyhound trotted around the rocks from the far side.

The dog ignored the hart. Ash watched it sniff busily at the edge of the pool, in which the hart's tines reflected perfectly. A second dog, its leash-mate, joined the greyhound. They cast about, with no great excitement, and then trotted back the way they had come.

Ash looked back from watching them vanish. She saw that the white hart no longer drank at the pool.

A cat with tufted ears watched her. Bigger than a lymer, as big as her mastiff bitch Brifault. Shiny pebble-black eyes stared into hers, un-beastlike; its black lips writhed back from sharp teeth, and it squalled.

"Chat-loup!"[3] Left hand to scabbard, right to sword-grip; reins tucked under her thigh – and the cat turned and padded off across the flower-starred grass, vanishing behind the rocks.

She patted the gelding hard on his neck – unwilling to see any mount's flanks ripped by claws, no matter how bloody-minded a ride – and dismounted. There were no deer slots, nor cat tracks, in the springy grass. The scent of wild roses filled her nostrils, dizzying her with the smell of long-gone summer.

"Deliver us, oh Lord—" she muttered aloud; managed not to say *Godfrey, help me, what do I do?*

In the part of her that is shared, a growing tension is becoming triumph. Becoming distanced, interior, infinitesimal sound:

'SOON! TO BE FREE OF YOU—'

'—DRAW DOWN THE SUN!—'

'—REACH HER: OUR CHOICE, OUR CHILD—'

'—DRAW ON OUR POWER . . .'

Even the voices of the Wild Machines are stifled, in her soul, to a faint and immaterial chatter.

A horn.

"Over here!"

Ash stood, head cocked sideways, eyes all but shut. A voice, female, coming from – down the slope, under the alder trees?

The gelding's soft white muzzle thumped into her breastplate, compressing steel and padding. She muttered, "Oof!" and grinned at the horse. The gelding's ears pricked up, and he stared down the slope.

"Okay . . . if you say so." She sprang heavily up into the saddle, using a blackened tree stump as a mounting block. The saddle received her, creaking.

---

[3] 'Wolf-cat'. Possibly, by the textual description, a lynx.

She turned the gelding and rode carefully down the hill, ducking alder branches with fresh green curlicues of leaves budding from their twigs. "Haro! A Lion!"

"A Lion yourself!" Floria del Guiz, still astride the rangy grey gelding, and with four hounds and two huntsmen behind her, rode up out of the denser wood. The woman in man's dress rode with complete carelessness, bouncing in the saddle; Ash marvelled that she stayed on at all. "Did you see it? We lost the scent again!"

"Did I see what? I've seen a lot of things in this past hour," Ash said grimly. "Florian, I don't trust half of them – roses in winter, white harts, gold crowns—"

"Oh, it's a white hart, all right." Floria urged her mount forward from the conferring hunters. "We saw it. It's albino. Like that pup that Brifault whelped in Milan." Her amused smile took on a note of scepticism. "*Crowns?* And you tell *me* to lay off the local wine!"

"Look, I'm telling you—" Ash began stubbornly.

"Cobnuts!" Floria said cheerfully. "It's just a hart. We shouldn't be hunting it out of season – but there you go."

The scent of roses fading in her nostrils, Ash hesitated, made as if to speak, and realised she did not know what she had intended to say. *This hunt is not important, there are men I should be leading, men you know; look at the sun!*

One look at Floria's intent, lost expression dried the words in her throat. She could not even say, *I am starting to listen to the Wild Machines, I can't stop myself—*

"The hunt's scattered over five leagues!" Floria pushed her hood back from her straw-coloured hair. Shrewd, she glanced at Ash. "If Thomas and Euen can't find their way back to the Visigoth camp, that's good. If they do find it, they're dead."

"If they don't find it, we're all dead. I should have managed to stay with them!"

Ash hits fist to thigh in frustration, gauntlet scraping on cuisse; a woman with slave-short silver hair, in armour, astride a muddy pale horse. The gelding whickered in complaint. Ash gazed up through the winter-bare branches of alders, but the sky is too milky – overcast with clouds, or something else – for her to see the invisible sun.

One of the hunters, red-faced and fever-thin, bends down at the foot of the rocks; his shaggy-coated greyhounds with their muzzles down at his side. A very faint baying echoes between the trees. There is the rich smell of horse manure, cast from the two standing beasts.

"There's no way we can take out the Stone Golem," Ash said, "so we have to kill her. Sister or not, Florian. If Euen and Thomas aren't putting an assault in right now, killing her, I think we're finished."

For the first time, the surgeon's attention seemed to shift from the hunt. Her eyes narrowed against the milky light. "What happens?"

Ash suddenly smiled: sardonic. "I've never been on the receiving end of a miracle before! I don't know. If anyone knows what it was like when Gundobad did his stuff, they've been dead far too long to tell us about it!"

Floria chuckled. "Shit. And we thought *you* knew!"

Ash reached out, gripped the woman's hand; slapped her lightly on the shoulder. The two geldings stood flank by flank. Ash saw how Floria's mud-spattered face was, under leaf-mould and a scrape or two – obviously at least one fall – remarkably happy.

"Whatever's going to happen, it's . . . happening. Starting," Ash urged. "I can – feel it, I guess."

Simultaneously, as she spoke, white flicked in her peripheral vision, the greyhounds bayed and darted forward, one of the huntsmen sounded the call on his horn to let the Master of Game know his couple were released; and Floria del Guiz stood up in her stirrups and bawled, "Cy va! *Let's go, boss!*"

The hart ran between alder trees, a furlong ahead. Ash looked over the furiously humping haunches of the greyhounds, sprinting towards their quarry. Floria's gelding kicked up great tufts of grass. The huntsmen ran forward.

"*Sweet Christ up a Tree, you can't go chasing bloody deer at a time like this—!*"

The pale gelding jerked at her shout. It stumbled forward into a canter, across the rough ground, shaking every tooth in her head. She saw red flash as she rode by: realised they had gone from alders to mountain ash, and the autumn branches blazed with red rowan berries. Ahead, across the burned-clear ground, a dozen other dogs streamed into view, heading for the foot of the granite crags ahead.

"Florian!"

The surgeon, bouncing in her saddle even at a trot, lifted her arm in acknowledgement without looking around. Ash saw her trying to stick her heels into her horse's flanks.

Son of a bitch, she's going to be off; or the horse will break a leg—

The deadfalls cleared. Under the rowan trees, moss and brown grass covered embedded chunks of granite. More light shone down: autumn sunlight from a pale, overcast sky. She lifted her head long enough to see that the tree-fringed horizon was clear, no pale dots of stars, and rode on at an agonisingly careful walk, her spirits suddenly lifting.

"*Florian!*" she bawled after the Burgundian woman. "Wait for me!"

A sudden cry of hounds drowned her out. Ash rode up the slope. Long skidding marks in mud showed where one of the huntsmen had fallen on the rocks. She guided the gelding between them. More hounds; horns; and shouting from ahead, at the foot of the crag.

"They've bayed it, Ash—*shit!*"

Floria's gelding became visible between the slender trunks of mountain ash trees. A short-muzzled, prick-eared alaunt[4] leaped up, biting the horse. Ash saw Floria kicking at it with her foot. The black hound jumping, snarling. It barked wildly.

"Come and get your bloody alaunt!" Ash bellowed furiously at the huntsman running through the trees. She spurred to Floria, kicked away the hound with her steel-shod foot, turned to speak to the surgeon and found her gone.

"I have to get to the ford—oh, *shit!*"

Ash urged the pale gelding after the rump of Floria's horse. The wind here, between the rowans, blew keenly; she felt the loss of her sallet and the lack of a

---

[4] Variety of hunting hound.

hood. Her ear-tips and nose reddened. She wiped at her nostrils with the heel of her hand, breath whitening the steel of her gauntlet's cuff. Floria pushed her mount ahead, on up the slope.

The land falling away now to either side, it was possible to see that they were coming up on a great shoulder of land, that pushed up out of the leagues of wildwood. Whatever fire had blazed here, a generation ago, had cleared ancient trees. Fifteen- and twenty-foot-high rowans covered the slope. Red berries smeared the rocks, underfoot, crushed by boots and by horseshoes; two or three more couple of hounds pelted past; and Ash reached back with her heels and jammed her spurs into the gelding, that and sheer force of will bringing the exhausted animal up the slope to the foot of the moss-grown granite crag.

A fine trickle of water ran down the rock-face. The sun flashed back from it, in sparkling chill brilliance.

The gelding sunk its head. Ash dismounted, threw the reins over a branch, and plodded on, on foot, towards the ridge where Floria had vanished. A howling of horns split the air. Far down the slope to her left, a great mass of people – a few still mounted, most on foot – streamed upwards, hounds with them; red-and-blue cloth flashed brightly in the cold air. The liveries of Burgundy.

Ash stomped on, breath heaving, chest burning; her armour no more restrictive than in foot combat – conscious, while she plodded up the slope, of the thought *I'll feel this later!* – and was overtaken by two burly men, split hose rolled down below the knee, sprinting after the hounds.

Horns blasted her ear-drums. Two mounted men in gowns and rich velvet hats spurred up the rocky slope; ducking to miss the berry-laden boughs of the rowans. She swore, under her breath; topped the rise, and found herself in the bramble, briar and leafless whitethorn bushes at the foot of the rocks. An alaunt whined, nosing the rock, and she put her hand to her dagger as it looked around at her.

"Try it, you little bastard!" she growled, under her breath. The alaunt dropped its muzzle, nosed, and suddenly trotted busily off to the right, around the side of the rock.

A great clamour of horns broke out to the left. She hesitated, panting; found herself among two or three dozen people – huntsmen and citizens of Dijon, women with faces flushed under linen coifs, running sturdily behind the hounds. No one glanced at a dismounted knight, they tore on over rough ground, heading around the rocks to the left.

"Godammit, *Florian!*" Ash yelled.

Another knight – the Frenchman Armand de Lannoy: she recognised his livery – clattered past her, on foot, at the trot. He swung round to call, "I swear we have unharboured a dozen harts this day! And none yet brought to bay!" He half-skidded on the wet, cold rock; recovered himself, and ran on.

"Do I give a shit?" Ash rhetorically demanded of the empty air, raising her eyes to the bitter cold sky. "Do I? Fuck, no! I never liked hunting *anyway*!"

Between one heartbeat and the next, the voice of Godfrey Maximillian sounded in her inner ear:

– *But you will have another Duke, if you can.*

She bit her lip in the surprise of it, and winced. Her muscles shook in anticipation. In the same beat of time, other voices drowned him out: the braided roar that is chorus, convocation, crowd:

'IT IS TOO LATE: HE WEAKENS, HE DIES—'

'IT IS TIME: IT IS ALL TIMES.'

'—IT IS THE PAST WE CHOOSE; AND WHAT IS TO COME—'

'HE DIES.'

'HE DIES!'

'EVEN NOW, HE DIES—'

"God rest him and take him," Ash gasped in a moment of small, frightened devoutness. Knees and calf-muscles aching, she pushed herself into a run, no further away from the voices in her head, but not able to stand still. She ran, boots heavily thumping the ground, armour clattering, in the wake of the alaunt: towards the right-hand side of the crag.

Dry-mouthed, the metal enclosing her making her breath come short, she pounded across the rocks; threw her hands over her face and plunged into the whitethorn bushes ahead. The six-inch thorns scraped the backs of her gauntlets. One raked her scalp. She shoved through, pauldron first, out of the bushes.

"*Ash!*" Floria's voice called urgently and audibly over the noise of hounds. Ash stopped, dropping her hands from in front of her face.

Both the black and the white alaunts danced in front of the rock-face, on brown turf; their handler crying them on. The white hart lowered the tines of its horns. Rump against the rock, rubbed green with moss, it glared at the dogs with red-rimmed pink eyes, flanks heaving. There was no crown around its neck, no links of metal on the churned-up earth.

The hart made a darting movement, towards Ash and the whitethorn. The black alaunt ripped, slashing its hindleg above the hock. The huntsman furiously sounded his horn, rushing about behind the dogs, tripping; and sat down hard in the frozen mud.

"Kill it!" Floria yelled, from whitethorn bushes a dozen yards away. The scrawny gelding loped off down the slope. Floria, on foot, rushed from side to side with her arms outstretched, shouting. The hart gazed at her, lowered its head, thought better of it; dropped its tines and slashed one alaunt across the blunt, snarling muzzle.

"Kill it, Ash! Don't let it get away!" Floria clapped her filthy bare hands together. The gunshot crack of her palms echoed back from the rocks. "We got to see – who's Duke—"

"Why you need a fucking hart's entrails – for an augury—" Ash automatically drew her sword. The hard grip bruised her palm, through the gauntlet's linen gloves. Both her armour and the blade had a thin film of rust coating the polished steel. She moved out from the bushes, covering the gap that would let the hart run down the slope.

The huntsman blew furiously on his horn, still sitting on his rump in the mud. Faintly, hounds and people shouting were audible, but somewhere far off: behind the crag. The white alaunt darted in and suddenly yelped, body twisting. It fell to its side, heaving ribs slashed red and open.

The white hart backed closer to the rock, scattering droppings. Head down, a forest of tines fronted it; and it began to drool from its neat, velvet-nostrilled muzzle.

"Ash!" Floria begged. "*Use* the dog! We'll kill it!"

Hearing the surgeon's voice, Ash found herself thinking of it not as a beast or a hunt, but as an enemy and a field of battle. Automatically she widened her gait, moved to the opposite side of the tiny space to the black alaunt, and lifted her sword to a guard position. Eyes on the hart, she moved left as the dog went right, watched its head drop to threaten the alaunt—

Between the tiers of white horn, shining as if the sun blazed down upon it, Ash saw the figure of a man upon a Tree.

Her sword point dropped.

The alaunt whined, backing off, tail tucking under its body.

Delicately as a dancer, the white hart lifted its head and regarded Ash with calm, golden eyes. Every detail of the Tree between its horns was clear to her: the Boar at the roots, and the Eagle in the branches.

The lips of the white hart began to move. Ash, dazed with the sudden scent of roses, thought, *He is going to speak to me.*

"Ash! Get a grip!" Floria ran towards her, across the narrow space between the whitethorn bushes. "It's getting away! Get it!"

The black alaunt threw itself forward, closed its jaws in the hind quarter of the hart, and hung on. Blood splashed the hart's white coat.

"Hold the abay!" the huntsman bellowed frantically. "The Master's not here, nor the lords!"

"We haven't *got* it at bay yet!" Floria bawled.

The dog's muzzle and jaws stained suddenly red, soaking red on black.

The hart screamed.

Its head went up and back, and it staggered on to its knees in the mud. The sharp tines flailed the air. The huntsman crawled away towards the whitethorn bushes, a yard to Ash's right, and she could not move, could not lift the sword in her hand, could not tell the yelling and baying outside from the voices in her head:

'*NO!*'

Ash could not tell which she saw: a hart with muddy, bloodstained sides, and red rolling eyes; or a beast with a coat like milk, and eyes of gold. She froze.

Someone tugged her hand.

She felt it, dimly; felt someone unpeeling her fingers in her gauntlet from the grip of her sword.

The weight of the weapon left her hand. That jolted her into full alertness.

Floria del Guiz strode forward in front of her, the sword held awkwardly in her right hand. A woman in doublet and hose, with her hood thrown back to the cold air. She circled right. Ash saw her expression: intent, frustrated, determined. Brilliant eyes, under straw-gold hair: all her tall, rangy body alert, moving with old reflexes – *of course, she's from a noble Burgundian family, she will have hunted as a girl* – and as Ash opened her mouth to protest the loss of her sword, the black alaunt feinted left, and Floria stepped in.

As fast as it happens in the field of combat, Floria reached out and grabbed one of the kneeling hart's tines. The sharp bone slashed up at her arm.

"*Florian!*" Ash screamed.

The alaunt let go of the flank and closed its square jaws around the beast's hind leg. The bite severed the main tendon. The white hart's body jerked back, falling sideways.

Floria del Guiz, still holding its horns, lifted Ash's wheel-pommel sword and shoved the point in behind the hart's shoulder. She laid all her body-weight into it; Ash heard her grunt. Blood sprayed, Floria thrust, the sword bit deep in behind the shoulder, and down into the heart.

Ash tried to move: could not.

All lay together in a huddle: Floria sprawled on her knees, panting; the hart with the sharp metal blade and hilt protruding from its body lying across her; the alaunt worrying the hind leg, bone cracking in the cold, quiet air.

The hart jerked once more and died.

Blood ran slowly, cooling. The hart's relaxing body let a last flux of excrement out on to the cold earth.

"Get this bloody dog away from me!" Floria protested weakly, and then suddenly looked up at Ash's face, astonished. More than astonished: frightened, pained, illuminated. "What—?"

Ash was already snapping her fingers at the huntsman. "You! On your feet. Blow the death. Get the rest of them here for the unmaking."[5]

She put her empty hands to her sword-belt, stunned with the astonishment of that.

"Florian, what part of the butchering is the augury? When do we know if we've got a Duke?"

A bright flash of colour blinked over the whitethorn bushes: someone's velvet hat. A second later and the rider appeared, men on foot with him; twenty or thirty Burgundian noblemen and women; and the other hunters took up the call, blowing the death until the harsh sound echoed back from the crag and rang out far and wide across the wildwood.

"We haven't got a Duke," Floria del Guiz said.

She sounded suffocated.

What alerted Ash, made everything clear to her, was a sudden internal silence; no choral voices thundering in her mind, only a bitter, bitter quiet.

Floria raised her gaze from her bloody hands, stroking the dead hart's neck. Ash saw her expression: a moment of gnosis. She had bitten her lip bloody.

"A Duchess," Floria said, "we have a Duchess."

The wind hissed in the whitethorn spines. The cold air smelled of shit, and blood, and dog, and horse. A great hush took the voices around Ash, the men and women on foot and riding falling silent, all in the space of a second. The huntsmen blowing the death fell quiet. All of them silent: chests heaving, breath blowing white into the cold air. Their flushed faces were full of amazement.

Two men-at-arms in Olivier de la Marche's livery rode their bay geldings

[5] The ceremonial flaying and butchering of the dead beast, often done on the spot.

into the narrow gap between the thorn bushes. De la Marche himself followed. He dismounted, heavily. Men caught his reins. Ash turned her head as the Burgundian deputy of the Duke walked past her, his creased, dirty face alight.

"You," he said. "You are she."

Floria del Guiz shifted the hart's body off her knees. She stood up. The black alaunt flopped at her feet. She pushed it away from the white hart's body with the toe of her boot, and it whined, the only sound in all the stillness. She squinted at Olivier de la Marche, in the pale autumn sunlight.

Gently and formally, he said, "Whose is the making of the hart?"

Ash saw Floria rub at her eyes with bloody hands, and look around at the men behind de la Marche: all the great nobles of Burgundy.

"I did it," Floria said, no force in her voice. "The making of the hart is mine."

Bewildered, Ash looked at her surgeon. The woman's woollen doublet and hose were filthy with mud, soaked with animal blood, ripped with thorns and branches; and twigs clung in her hair, coif gone missing somewhere in the wild hunt. Floria's cheeks reddened, finding herself the centre of all gazes; and Ash stepped forward, business-like, gripped her sword and twisted the blade to pull it out of the hart's body, and said under cover of that movement, "Is this trouble? You want me to get you out of here?"

"I wish you could." Floria's hand closed over her arm, bare skin against cold metal. "Ash, they're right. I made the hart. I'm Duchess."

In Ash's mind, there is no sound of the Wild Machines. She risks it, whispers under her breath, "Godfrey . . . are they there?"

– *Great is the lamentation in the house of the Enemy!* Great *is the*—

Angry voices drown him out: voices that speak as the thunderstorm does, in great cracks of rage, but she can understand none of them: they rage in the tongue used by men when Gundobad was prophet – and they are faint, as a storm is faint, over the horizon.

"Charles died," Floria said with complete certainty. "A few minutes ago. I felt it when I put the death-blow in. When I knew."

The sun, weak in autumn though it is, is a perceptible warmth now on Ash's bare face.

"Someone's Duke or Duchess," Ash breathed. "Someone is – someone's stopping them again. But I don't know why! I don't understand this!"

"I didn't know, until I killed the hart. Then—" Floria looked at Olivier de la Marche, a big man in mail and livery, the arms of Burgundy at his back. "I know now. Give me a minute, messire."

"You are she," de la Marche said, dazedly. He swung round to face the men and women crowding close. "No Duke, but a Duchess! We have a Duchess!"

The sound of their cheer ripped the breath out of Ash's body.

That it had been some kind of political trick, was her first thought; that assumption vanished in the roar of acclamation. Every face, from huntsman to peasant woman to Duke's bastards, shone with a gladness that could not be faked.

And *someone* is doing – whatever it is that Charles was doing; whatever it is that holds the Wild Machines back.

"Christ," Ash grumbled, under her breath. "This lot aren't joking. Fuck, Florian!"

"*I'm* not joking."

Ash said, "Tell me."

It was a tone of voice she had used often, over the years, requiring her surgeon to report to her, requiring her friend to tell her the thoughts of her heart; and she shivered, inside padding and armour, at the sudden thought *Will I ever talk to Florian like this again?*

Floria del Guiz looked down at her red-brown hands. She said, "What did you see? What were you hunting?"

"A hart." Ash stared at the albino body on the mud. "A white hart, crowned with gold. Sometimes Hubert's Hart.[6] Not this, not until the end."

"You hunted a myth. I made it real." Floria lifted her hands to her face, and sniffed at the drying blood. She raised her eyes to Ash's face. "It was a myth and I made it real enough for dogs to scent. I made it real enough to kill."

"And that makes you Duchess?"

"It's in the blood." The woman surgeon snuffled a laugh back, wiped her brimming eyes with her hands, and left smears of blood across her cheeks. She edged closer to Ash as she stood staring down at the hart, which none of the huntsmen approached for butchering.

More and more of the hunt staggered uphill to the thorn-sided clearing below the crag.

"It's Burgundy," Floria said, at last. "The blood of the Dukes is in all of us. However much, however little. It doesn't matter how far you travel. You can never escape it."

"Oh yeah. You're dead royal, you are."

The sarcasm brought Floria back to something of herself. She grinned at Ash, shook her head, and rapped a knuckle on the Milanese breastplate. "I'm pure Burgundian. It seems that's what counts."

"The blood royal. So." Ash laughed, weakly, from the same overwhelming relief, and pointed a steel-covered finger at the hart's body. "That's a pretty shabby-looking miracle, for a royal miracle."

Floria's face became drawn. She spared a glance for the growing throng, mutely waiting. The wind thrummed through the whitethorn. "No. You've got it wrong. The Bugundian Dukes and Duchesses don't perform miracles. They prevent them being performed."

"Prevent—"

"I *know*, Ash. I killed the hart, and now I know."

Ash said sardonically, "Finding a hart, out of season, in a wood with no game; this *isn't* a miracle?"

Olivier de la Marche came a few steps closer to the hart. His battle-raw voice said, "No, Demoiselle-Captain, not a miracle. The true Duke of Burgundy – or, as it now seems, the true Duchess – may find the myth of our Heraldic Beast, the crowned hart, and from it bring this. Not miraculous, but mundane. A true beast, flesh and blood, as you and I."

[6] St Hubert (died AD 727) is one of the saints credited with a vision of a hart bearing a crucified Christ-figure between its horns.

"Leave me." Floria's voice was sharp. She gestured the Burgundian noble to go back, staring up at him with bright eyes. He momentarily bowed his head, and then stepped back to the edge of the crowd and waited.

Watching him go, colour caught Ash's eye. Blue and gold. A banner bobbed over the heads of the crowd.

Shamefaced, Rochester's sergeant plodded out to stand beside Ash with her personal banner. Willem Verhaecht and Adriaen Campin shouldered their way through to the front row, faces taking on identical expressions of relief as they saw her; and half the men at their backs were from Euen Huw's lance, and Thomas Rochester's.

In all her confusion, Ash was conscious of a searing relief. *No assault on the Visigoth camp, then. They're alive. Thank Christ.*

"Tom – where are the fucking Visigoths! What are *they* doing?"

Rochester rattled off: "'Bout a bow-shot back. Messenger came up. Their officers are in a right panic over something, boss—"

He broke off, still staring at the company surgeon.

Floria del Guiz knelt down by the white hart. She touched the rip in its white coat.

"Blood. Meat." She held her red hands up to Ash. "What the Dukes do . . . *I* do . . . isn't a negative quality. It makes, it – preserves. It preserves what's true, what's real. Whether . . ." Floria hesitated, and her words came slowly: "Whether what's real is the golden light of the Burgundian forest, or the splendour of the court, or the bitter wind that bites the peasant's hands, feeding his pigs in winter. It is the rock upon which this world stands. What is *real.*"

Ash stripped off her gauntlet and knelt beside Floria. The coat of the hart was still warm under her fingers. No heartbeat; the flow of blood from the death-wound had stopped. Beyond the body, not flowers, but muddy earth. Above her, not roses, but winter thorn and rowan.

Making the miraculous mundane.

Ash said slowly, "You keep the world *as it is.*"

Looking up into Floria's face, she surprised anguish.

"Burgundy has its bloodline, too. The machines bred Gundobad's child," Floria del Guiz said. "And this is an opposite. The Machines want a miracle to wipe out the world, and I – I make it remain sure, certain, and solid. I keep it what it is."

Ash took Floria's cold wet hand between her own hands. She felt an immediate withdrawal that was not physical: only Floria giving her a look that said, *What happens now? Everything is different between us.*

Sweet Christ. *Duchess.*

Slowly, her eyes on Floria's face, Ash said, "They had to breed a Faris. So that they could attack Burgundy the only way it can be attacked: on the physical, military level. And when Burgundy is removed . . . then they can use the Faris. Burgundy is only the obstacle. Because 'winter will not cover all the world' – won't cover us here, not while the Duke's bloodline prevents the Faris making a miracle."

"And now there's no Duke, but there is a Duchess."

Ash felt Floria's hands trembling in hers. The hazy overcast cleared, the

777

white autumn sun throwing the shadows of thorns sharp and clear on the mud. Five yards beyond the sprawled body of the white hart, rank upon rank of people waited patiently. The men of the Lion company watched their commander, and their surgeon.

Floria, her eyes slitted against the sudden brilliance of the sun, said, "I do what Duke Charles did. I preserve; keep us quotidian. There'll be no Wild Machines' 'miracles' – as long as I'm alive."

Loose papers found inserted between Parts Twelve and Thirteen of ASH: THE LOST HISTORY OF BURGUNDY (Ratcliff, 2001), British Library

previous e-mail missing?

```
Message:   #350 (Anna Longman)
Subject:   Ash
Date:      15/12/00 at 03.23 a.m.
From:      Ngrant@
```

format address deleted
other details encrypted by
non-discoverable personal key

Anna –

I know. It seems unbelievable. But it appears to be nothing less than the truth. No previous survey shows this sea trench. Not before we started looking here.

Isobel brought one of the tech people to the meeting I've just come out of, and showed us downloaded satellite surveys. Not that there are many, the Tunisian military being as sensitive as any other military – but what we have are unambiguous.

Shallow water here. No deep trenches below the 1000-metre mark.

And yet, our ROVs are down there now, as I'm typing this.

I don't like this, Anna. The Middle East and the Mediterranean have been far too closely surveyed to say, now, that this could all be down to lost or misinterpreted evidence, distorted analysis, fake documents, or fraud.

I cannot genuinely deny this. According to recent satellite scans, and according to British Admiralty charts, the seabed where we found the trench used to be flat. Not silt, not a trench; nothing but rock. God knows, given the submarine warfare in the Mediterranean sixty years ago, the Admiralty charts are pretty substantive! It isn't a geological feature anyone could have missed.

I have just suggested, in Isobel's meeting, that we look for seismograph readings: there may have been a recent earthquake. She tells me that's what she's been doing over the last ten days: pulling in all the favours she has with various colleagues, to check the most up-to-date satellite reports and geological surveys.

No earthquake. Not so much as an undersea tremor.

I'll post to you again when I have had some time to think this over – it's only been a few hours since Isobel called her meeting; she and her physicist colleagues are still at it, talking into the small hours of the morning.

I went up on deck. Looked into blackness, tasted wet air. Tried to come to terms with this idea – a hundred ideas going around in my own mind – no: I'm not making sense.

One line of Florian's haunts me. Mediaeval Latin translation can

779

be hell - is 'dn' an abbreviation for _dominus_ or _domina_:
masculine or feminine? Or it is in fact 'dm', for _deum_? Context
is all, handwriting is all; and even then a sentence may have two
or three perfectly viable different translations, only *one* of
which is what the author wrote!

  I _know_ the 'hand' of Fraxinus/Sible Hedingham: I have for eight
years. I can't realistically make it read anything else.

  What Floria says *is* "You hunted a myth. I made it real."

- Pierce

Message: #199 (Pierce Ratcliff)
Subject: Ash
Date: 15/12/00 at 05.14 a.m.
From: Longman@

format address deleted
other details encrypted and
non-recoverably deleted

Pierce -

Physicists?
  Just checked back in your mailings, and yes, you did mention this
before. I missed it. Why has an archaeologist like Dr Isobel got
physicists with her? Is it purely a 'social' visit, Pierce? It
doesn't look like it.

  I really don't want to ask this, but I need her to mail me to
confirm what you're saying.

  I wouldn't take one person's word for this. Not even my mother's.

- Anna

Message: #365 (Anna Longman)
Subject: Ash
Date: 15/12/00 at 06.05 a.m.
From: Ngrant@

format address deleted
other details encrypted by
non-discoverable personal key

Anna -

The physicists? Tami Inoshishi and James Howlett: Isobel's friends
from artificial intelligence and theoretical physics. I suppose
they're here quasi-unofficially, at her request? They've been
offering help to the expedition - they desperately want to get the
Stone Golem up, and off-site, for examination - tests at CERN, the
whole works.

  I've been trying to talk to them, but they're astonishingly
dismissive. Or perhaps preoccupied. The strange thing is that Ms
Inoshishi isn't at all interested in the concept that the machina
rei militaris may be a primitive 'computer' of some sort, and

Howlett isn't really interested in the golems that we found at the land-site.

What they *are* interested in are my chronicle texts, and the seabed surveys.

They seem very interested in the concept of evidence changing.

What I find disturbing, I suppose, is that when I speculate that the nature of the del Guiz and Angelotti documentary evidence may have undergone some kind of a _genuine_ change, they take me seriously.

Talk to me, Anna. You're a person who's not here, not caught up in the enthusiasm. Do I sound mad to you?

- Pierce

Message: #202 (Pierce Ratcliff)
Subject: Ash
Date: 15/12/00 at 06.10 a.m.
From: Longman@

[handwritten: format address deleted / Other details encrypted / and non-recoverably deleted]

Pierce -

Are Ms Inoshishi and Mr Howlett there in an official capacity? It sounds as though they are colleagues of Dr Napier-Grant there in a private capacity. Is she going to report back to her university soon? What's going to happen _officially_?

Pierce - what do _you_ think of all this? My head is spinning.

- Anna

Message: #372 (Anna Longman)
Subject: Ash
Date: 15/12/00 at 08.12 p.m.
From: Ngrant@

[handwritten: format address deleted / Other details encrypted by / non-discoverable personal key]

Anna -

I don't think. I have nothing like enough evidence as yet to allow me to think.

Anything else would be unfounded speculation.

I'm going to be busy with the people here; I will get back to you as soon as I can.

And I'm going to continue translating.

I have a further section of reasonably adequately translated material from the Sible Hedingham ms, I'll attach the files with this message.

I need to resolve some of the apparent anomalies in the next part

781

of the text. I feel that I cannot say anything definite until the whole of the Sible Hedingham ms has been translated.

- Pierce

Message: #204 (Pierce Ratcliff)
Subject: Ash
Date: 15/12/00 at 10.38 p.m.   *format address deleted*
From: Longman@   *other details encrypted and*
                                      non-recoverably deleted

Enough shit, Pierce (pardon my French). Enough havering, enough sitting on the fence—
  You've got Dr Isobel's friends there on the ship, she obviously thought it was important enough to call scientists in; there are maps that don't show the site you've found on the seabed; Pierce, _what do you believe is happening_?
  Enough academic caution. Tell me. Now.

- Anna

Message: #376 (Anna Longman)
Subject: Ash
Date: 15/12/00 at 11.13 p.m.   *format address deleted*
From: Ngrant@   *other details encrypted by*
                                      non-discoverable personal key

Anna -

I am forced to believe a whole series of self-contradictory facts.
  - That the Angelotti and del Guiz texts have been classified as 'Fiction' for the past fifty years – and yet, Anna, when I last consulted them a few months ago, they were shelved under normal Late Mediaeval History.
  - That the 'Fraxinus' text is a genuine fifteenth-century biography of Ash, that has enabled us to find evidence of post-Roman technology in a 'Visigoth' settlement, and the ruins of a 'Carthage' on the Mediterranean seabed – and yet, that when we study the previous sixty years of surveys, there is no geological feature on that seabed that matches the one we have found. And there has been no recent seismic activity that could have produced it.
  - That a 'messenger-golem' with wear-marks _on the soles of its feet_ can be classified, by a reputable department of metallurgy, as a fake made after 1945 – and now as a genuine artefact with its bronze cast between five and six centuries ago.

Because I've now actually seen the report, Anna. What they're presenting isn't an apology for a mistake.

It is two sets of readings, two weeks apart, that imply completely different conclusions.

The altered status of the 'Ash' documentation is one thing – I've been e-mailing curators: there are known artefacts no longer in display cases, the 'Ash sallet' has vanished from Rouen, both the helmet AND the catalogue entry.

What is missing is not half so disturbing as what is here.

You see, Anna, I had begun to have a theory. Simply, that there was *something* that needed explaining.

I'll be honest. Anna, I KNOW the 'Ash' documents were authentic history when I first studied them. Whatever I may have said about errors of re-classification, you will remember that I found myself completely unable to explain it in any satisfactory way. I think that I _had_ almost come to believe in Vaughan Davies's theory out of sheer desperation – that there actually has been a 'first history' of the world, which was wiped out in some fashion, and that we now inhabit a 'second history', into which bits of the first have somehow survived. That Ash's history was first genuine, and has now been – fading, if you like – to Romance, to a cycle of legends.

So I had reached a conclusion, before the last ten days. I had thought that, since neither Ash's Burgundy, nor the Visigoth Empire in North Africa, had any evidence that hadn't been thoroughly discredited at that point – well, how could I say this to you? I had begun to think that perhaps they *were* from a 'previous version' of our past, growing less real by the decade. A previous past history in which the text's 'miracle' *did* take place. In which the Faris and the 'Wild Machines' (or whatever it is those literary metaphors represent) triggered some kind of alteration in history. Or, to put it in scientific terms, a previous past history in which the possible subatomic states of the universe were (deliberately and consciously) collapsed into a different reality – the one we now inhabit.

Vaughan Davies's theory is just that: a theory. And yet we have to find truth somewhere. Remember that, whatever he is now, when he was a young man he _knew_ Bohr, Dirac, Heisenberg; if the biographers are to be believed, he debated with them on equal terms. He did not know – and nor have I been much aware of, until I talked to James Howlett today – the work of the succeeding scientific generation on quantum theory and the various versions of the anthropic principle.

Perhaps I've taken on too much of the mediaeval world-view: to find a respected physicist listening to me seriously when I ask if 'deep consciousness' might change the universe – I find it unnerving! I try to follow James when he talks about the Copenhagen interpretation and the many-worlds model . . . with rather less than the average numerate layman's understanding, I fear.

Although even he, with all his many-branching multiverses from each collapsing quantum moment, can't answer two questions.

The first is, why would there be only _one_ great 'fracture of history', as Davies called it? Mainstream quantum theory calls for continuous fracture, as you once wrote to me: a universe in which you simultaneously perform every action, moral and immoral. An endlessly branching tree of alternate universes, from every single second of time.

And, even if that point were adequately answered, even if we knew that only one great quantum restructuring of the universe had taken place, as some versions of the anthropic quantum model demand – that by observing our universe now, we have in a sense _created_ the Big Bang 'back then', and what we observe of the cosmos now . . . Anna, why would there be evidence _left over_ from before the fracture? A previous state of the universe has *no* existence, not even a theoretical one!

James Howlett has just looked over my shoulder, shaken his head, and gone off to fight with his software models of mathematical reality. No, I dare say I don't give even an adequate layman's explanation of what he's been trying to tell me.

Perhaps it's because I'm a historian: despite the fact that we experience only the present, I retain a superstitious conviction that the past exists – that it has been _real_. And yet we know nothing but this single present moment . . . What I had suggested to James Howlett was that the remaining contradictory evidence – the Angelotti and del Guiz manuscripts – would be anomalies from previous quantum states, becoming less and less 'possible' – less *real*. Turning from mediaeval history into legend, into fiction. Fading into impossibility.

Then, you found the Sible Hedingham manuscript, and Isobel's team found the ruins of Carthage.

I've been so deep in translation work – when I haven't been glued to the images the ROVs are transmitting – that it didn't occur to me to think

No, I didn't want to think.

It wasn't until today, just now; until James Howlett said to me – 'I think the important question is, why are these discoveries appearing?'

And I immediately, without thinking, corrected him: '*Re*-appearing.'

If there has been a 'previous state' of the universe, if we are a 'second history'— if any of this is even possible, and not utter nonsense – then that 'fading of a first history' cannot be the whole story. What we've found – the ruins of Carthage on the floor of the Mediterranean sea, and the machina rei militaris: the Stone Golem – were they actually *here* before this December?

You see, Vaughan Davies notwithstanding, I can't begin to
formulate a theory that accounts for why some of the evidence
should appear to be *coming back*.

Anna, if this is true, then things are still changing.

And if things are still changing, then this isn't 'dead history' -
it isn't over.

- Pierce

PART THIRTEEN

16 November–23 November AD 1476

The Empty Chair[1]

[1] Sible Hedingham ms part 3.

I

Sleet began to blind her the moment they rode out of the forest and galloped for Dijon's north-west gate.

Wet ice whipped into Ash's face as she spurred the pale bay, under a sky clouding up from grey to black, mixed rain and sleet slashing down.

"Get her into the city!" Ash bawled over the gathering storm, throat hoarse. "*Now!* Get her through those fucking gates: *go!*"

She crowded in, riding knee-to-knee with Florian – Christus Viridianus! *Duchess* Florian – and the rest of the mounted Lion men-at-arms, the soaked swallow-tail banner cracking overhead.

Sudden hooves thudded, cutting up the sodden earth behind her on the road down to the bridge over the moat. A stream of war-horses and riders went past and around her, in Burgundian blue and red and draggled plumes – *de la Marche's men!* she realised, a hand on her sword-hilt.

Come out to escort us in.

Enclosed in that armed safety, they thundered back between the paths, trenches, barricades and buildings of the Visigoth camp – between the chaos of Visigoth troops running in all directions – new, wet mud spraying up from iron-shod hooves.

Just before the narrow bridge, the horses slowed, milled about; and she hit the pommel of her saddle in frustration. Two hundred mounted men. She stared at their backs, swore out loud, turning the pale bay with her spurs, gazing back into the slashing sleet and rain that now hid the Visigoth camp, hid everything more than fifty yards away. No more than ten minutes to get through this choke-point, over the bridge, through the gate; but an aching wait, fretting itself into half an hour in her mind.

Visigoth mounted archers! she anticipated. *As soon as they sort themselves out—* No, not in this weather.

The skin at the nape of her neck shivered.

It'll be golems, with Greek Fire flame-throwers, like at Auxonne – we're bunched up here, we'll fry like wasps in a fire!

The stress of the wait made the pit of her stomach hurt. Moving again, at last – men shouting, horses' hooves: all echoed under the arched stonework of the city gate. The breath of the animals went up white into the wet air. She swung her mount around, following Florian's winded and limping grey gelding, was briefly aware of the darkness in the tunnel of the gate; and then burst out into drenched daylight, and Antonio Angelotti grabbing at her bridle.

"The Duke's dead!" he yelled up at her, face streaming with rain. "Time to change sides *now*! Madonna, shall I send a messenger out to the Carthaginians?"

"Stop panicking, Angeli!"

The high steel-and-leather saddle creaked as she sat back, shifting her weight to stop the bay dancing sideways across shattered, flooded cobbles.

"There's a new Duke – *Duchess!*" she corrected herself. "It's Florian. *Our* Florian!"

"*Florian?*"

From behind Angelotti, Robert Anselm growled, "Fuck!"

Ash wheeled the lathered gelding, bringing it under her control. Every instinct swore at her to muster her men now, abandon all baggage but the essential, and leave this city to the natural consequences of a bungled transfer of power.

How can I? Her fist hit the saddle pommel. *How can I!*

"Demoiselle-Captain!" Olivier de la Marche rode in close, leaning across from his war-horse to clasp her arm: gauntlet against vambrace. "See to the defences of this gate! I give you authority over Jonvelle, Jussey, and Lacombe; take up your place from the gate here, north along the wall to the White Tower! Then I must speak with you!"

"Sieur—!" She did not get it out in time: his chestnut stallion was already clopping away into the downpour, in with his men-at-arms.

The crossbowman Jan-Jacob Clovet, taking the bay's reins from Angelotti, shrugged and spat. "Son of a bitch!"

"Now is that putting the mercenaries up the sharp end, as usual? Or is that giving us the place of honour, because it's going to be hit hardest when they come?"

"God spare us from ducal favour, boss," Jan-Jacob Clovet said fervently. "*Any* fucking Duke. *Or* Duchess. Are you *sure* about the doc? She can't be, can she?"

"Oh, she can! Florian!" Ash bawled.

De la Marche's sub-captain and his men brought steaming, caparisoned war-horses between her and Florian, shouldering the woman surgeon and her broken-down mount out and across the devastated zone of the city behind the walls, heading at the trot for the ducal palace.

"*Florian!*"

She caught one glimpse of Floria del Guiz's white face, between the pauldrons of the armoured knights surrounding her. Then the household of Olivier de la Marche closed in.

Shit! No time!

Ash spun the uncooperative bay on its heels, facing the gate again.

"Angeli! Thomas! Get 'em up on the walls! Rickard, warn Captain Jonvelle – the Visigoths are gonna come right over those fucking walls behind us!"

*

II

"*Why* don't they come!"

Ash stood at a slit window in the Byward Tower, squinting out into slanting water. Rain splintered down on to the walls of Dijon. The tower's flint and masonry breathed off cold.

Rain beat in: solid, intense storm-rain. Rivulets ran down off her steel sallet and visor. Her breath and body warmth made the safety of armour stickily humid, despite the biting cold wind.

"'Nother couple of hours, it'll be dark." Robert Anselm shouldered into the window embrasure, his rust-starred armour scraping against hers. "Fuck, I thought the whole fucking rag-'ead army was coming in after you!"

"They should be! If I was them – there's never been a better chance—!"

The thunder of the city gate shutting behind them still tingles in her bones.

"Maybe they're having a mutiny out there! Maybe the Faris is dead. *I* don't know!"

"Wouldn't you . . . know?"

Carefully, she probes in that part of her soul that she shares.

Almost beyond hearing, there are voices – the *machina rei militaris*, Godfrey, the Wild Machines? For the first time in her life she can't tell. And there is an echo of that intense pressure, subliminally sensed, felt in the bones, that racked her when the hart was hunted and the sun dimmed in the autumn sky. Voices as weak, or weaker, than at that moment of the unmaking.

"There's been some . . . damage, I think. I don't know what or to who. Temporary, permanent – I can't tell." In fear and frustration, Ash added, "Just when we could do with hearing Godfrey, right, Roberto? Hey, maybe the Faris *has* died! Maybe her *qa'ids* are running around like headless chickens trying to sort out the command structure: *that's* why they haven't attacked . . ."

"Won't take 'em long." Anselm put his face to the stone aperture, his hard armoured body shifting, trying to make out anything beyond the misty walls of the city. "I've had the muster roll called. There's two of our officers still missing. John Price. Euen Huw."

"Shit . . ."

Ash peered out of the gap between tightly mortared stones. Her breath made grey plumes in front of her face. The intensity of the lashing water came in bursts, slapping the stone rim of the window. She did not flinch back.

"Price isn't even a fucking cavalryman . . . Nobody's to go out after them." Her voice sounded curt in her own ears.

Anselm protested, "Girl—"

Ash cut him off. "I don't like it any more than you. Nothing happens until we can see what's going on. The Duke's *dead*. This city could fall apart from the *inside*, any second! I want a command meeting with de la Marche; I want to see Florian! After that, maybe we'll send a man out through one of the postern gates."

Anselm, grimly sardonic, said, "We got no idea what the fucking rag-heads are doing. *Or* the Burgundians. You don't like it. Nor do I."

The hissing slash of water against stone increased. Ash pressed up closer to the slit window, hands braced against the cold stone either side. Across the empty air, she realised she was seeing only a few yards of broken earth.

She shifted as far to one side as she could, to let Robert cram in beside her. He hawked, spat: white mucus spraying the stone sill.

"At least this shitting weather gets in their powder, and stretches the siege-machine ropes . . ."

Promptly as he spoke, a shrill whistle and roar sounded; each man in the tower room flinching, automatically. Ash jumped down from the window embrasure and clattered to where she could see out of the door. A faint thump, and a glow through the rain, down in the ruined part of the city, made her skin shiver by what it implied.

"Rain's not going to stop the golem-machines," she said. "Or the Greek Fire."

Robert Anselm did not move from the window. After a moment, she strode back and stepped up to rejoin him.

He grunted. "They got Charlie's funeral going yet?"

"Fuck, who's going to tell *us* anything!"

"You heard anything from the doc?"

Ash took her gaze away from the shrouded grey lumps on the puddled earth beyond the moat – discarded ladders, dead and bloated horses, one or two corpses of men. Slaves, probably; not thought worth the recovery. All a uniform mud-grey; all motionless.

"Roberto – whatever it means – she *is* Duchess."

"And I'm the fucking King of Carthage!"

"I've heard the Wild Machines," Ash said, her gaze steady on him. "In my soul. And I've seen them – I've stood there while they shook the earth under my feet. And I saw Florian's face, and I *heard* them, Robert – they tried to make their devil's miracle, and they were stopped. Cold. Because of her; because of our Florian. Because she made Burgundy's Heraldic Beast into . . . meat."

On his face, what there is visible of it under sallet-visor and sopping wet hood, she sees an expression of cynical disbelief.

"What that means to the Burgundians, I don't know yet. But . . . You weren't there, Robert."

Anselm's head turned. She saw him only in profile now, looking out from the window slit. His voice gravel, he protested, "I know I fucking *wasn't there*! I *prayed* for you! Me and the lads; Paston and Faversham, up on the wall—"

Push it or not? she wondered, diverted. Yes. I need to know how bad it is: I'm going to depend on this man.

"If you'd come on the assault, you might have seen what happened on the hunt. You bottled out."

Jerking round, his face red, he jabbed a finger two inches from her breastplate. *"You don't fucking say that!"*

She was aware that the escort and banner men-at-arms by the tower door looked over; signalled them with a gesture to stay where they were.

"Robert, what's the problem?" She loosened and removed one gauntlet, and raised her bare hand to wipe at her wet face. "Apart from the obvious! We've seen shittier sieges. Neuss. Admitted it's better being on the *outside* . . ."

His confidence was not to be got by humour. His expression closed up. This close, she could see the hazel-green colour of his eyes, the thread-veins on his nose and cheekbones; sallet and shadow making his face unreadable.

Ash waited.

A renewed wind took the rain in great gusts, beating against the walls like surf. Ash is momentarily reminded of the sea beating against the cliffs of Carthage harbour, below the stone window-slits of House Leofric; is conscious of a similar great void, the other side of this wall; vast empty air, filled with freezing grey torrents. Faint spray dampened her cheeks. She reached up, with a left-hand gauntlet that – despite being scoured in sand and rubbed with goose-grease – was already orange-spotted with rust, and tilted her visor down.

"What is it, Roberto?"

The man's body beside her crushed her further into the window embrasure as he heaved a great sigh. He looked out at the ever-moving rain. He spoke, at last, with an apparent acceptance of her right to make demands of him:

"I didn't know if you were alive or dead after Auxonne. No one could get any news of your body being picked up off the field. I expected to see your head on a spear. Because if you *were* dead, the Goths were going to show your body off, damn fucking sure!"

His voice became quieter, barely audible to her, never mind to the men-at-arms by the door.

"If you were a prisoner, they'd've shown you in chains . . . You could have been off in the woods, wounded. You could have crawled off to die. No one would have found you."

He turned to look at her. The rain made him squint, under his raised visor, flesh creasing around his eyes.

"That was how it was, girl. *I* thought you'd been shovelled into a grave-trench, without being recognised. Those fire-throwers . . . A lot of the men came back saying bodies were burned black. Tony said you might have been taken prisoner at Auxonne and carted off to North Africa, because of how interested they were at Basle in getting hold of you. But they wouldn't care if they'd had to take a *dead* body. Scientist-magi give me the willies," Anselm added, with an unselfconscious shudder.

She waited, listening to the slash of rain on flint, not prompting him.

"Three months, and then—" His gaze fixed on her. "You *had* to be dead, there was no other way to behave – and then, out of nowhere, three days ago, a message on a crossbow bolt—"

"You'd got used to leading the company."

His hands slammed into the wall either side of her, pinning her into the window embrasure. She glanced down at the steel of his arms; then up into his face.

Spittle sprayed from his mouth, dotting the front of her livery tabard. "*I wanted to come to Africa! I didn't* want to stay in Dijon! Sweet Green Christ –

What do you *think* happened, girl? I had John de fucking Vere saying, the Duke's sending half the company to Carthage, I need a man I can leave in command *here*—"

The men at the tower door stirred uneasily. He broke off, deliberately lowering his voice again.

"If you were anywhere, dead or alive, it had to be Carthage! Only I didn't have a fucking choice! I got ordered to stay here! And now I find out you *were* there, *alive*—"

Ash reached up and put her hands on his wrists, and gently tugged them down. The steel of his vambrace was slick with rain, cold against her one bare palm.

"I can see Oxford doing it that way. He'd need to take Angeli, for the guns. You'd been my second-in-command, you *were* in command, there wasn't anyone else he could leave behind with safety. Robert, I could have been dead. Or if not dead, then anywhere. You were right to stay here."

"I should have gone with him! I was sure you were dead. I was wrong!" Robert Anselm punched his fist hard into the flint lining of the window embrasure. He looked down at his scratched, dented gauntlet, and absently flexed his fingers. "If I'd pulled the company out with me, Dijon wouldn't be standing siege now, but I'm telling you, girl, I should have come to Carthage. For you."

"If you had," Ash said, measuring the thoughts out in her mind, "we might have taken House Leofric. With that many more men and guns. We might have destroyed the Stone Golem; we might have broken the only connection the Wild Machines have with the world – the only way they can do their miracle."

His eyes flicked towards her, small behind the incongruously long lashes.

"But then." Ash shrugged. "If you hadn't been here, Dijon might have fallen before you'd got as far as the coast – then the Duke would have been executed, and we'd know by now what it is the Wild Machines are going to use the Faris for. Because they'd have done it, three months ago!"

"And maybe not," Anselm rumbled.

"We're *here*, *now*. What does it matter what you didn't do? Robert, none of what you're telling me explains why you didn't come on the attack against the Faris today. None of it tells me why you've lost your bottle. And I need to know that, because I depend on you, and so do a lot of other people here."

She was frank, forcing herself to mention fear aloud. What she saw on his face as he turned his head away was not shame.

He muttered, "You went out expecting to be killed."

"Yes. If I had, but if I'd killed her—"

So quietly she almost missed it, Robert Anselm interrupted. "I couldn't ride out with you today. I couldn't see you get killed in front of me."

Ash stared at him.

"Not after three months," he said painfully. "I held masses for you, girl. I grieved. I carried on without you. Then you came back. *Then* you ask me to ride out and watch you get killed. That's too much to ask."

The slash of rain against flint-embedded walls grew heavier. Streamlets of water dribbled down between the planks of the roof above, splattering them and the floorboards irrespectively.

I know what to say, Ash thought. Why can't I say it?

"So," he said harshly, "this is where you relieve me of my rank, ain't it? You know you can't trust me in combat any more. You think I'll be watching your back, not doing my job."

Some tension in her reached crisis. She snapped, "What do you want me to tell you, Robert? The same old stuff? 'We can *all* get killed, here and now, any time, better get used to it'? 'That's what we do for a living, war gets you killed'? I can sing that song! Six months ago, I'd have said it to you! Not now!"

Robert Anselm reached up and unbuckled his helmet, dipping his head to remove it. The helmet-lining and his body-heat had left his stubbled head slick with sweat. He breathed out, hard.

"And now?"

"It hurts," Ash said. She pressed her bare knuckle against the wall, grinding skin against stone, as if the physical pain could give her release. "You don't want to see me hacked up? *I* don't want to send you and Angeli and the others up on the walls. I brought these guys back through country like nothing on earth! I don't want them getting cut up raiding the Visigoths' camp, or whatever idea de la Marche is going to come up with when I see him. I want to hold us back, go sit in the tower, out of the bombardment – *I'm starting to be afraid of people getting hurt.*"

There was a long pause. The rain grew louder.

Robert Anselm gave a small, suppressed snuffle. "Looks like we're both in the shit, then!"

As she stared at him, startled, he burst into a full guffaw.

"Jesus, Roberto—!"

The snuffle caught her by surprise. An emptiness in her chest made her choke, spurt out a giggle; laugh, finally, out loud. It would not be denied: a bubbling thing that made her sputter, wet-eyed, unable to get a coherent word out.

Shuddering to a rumbling halt, Robert Anselm reached across, putting his arm around her shoulders and shaking her.

"*We're* fucked," he said cheerfully.

"It's nothing to laugh about!"

"Pair of fucking *idiots*," he added. His arm fell away as he straightened himself up, plate sliding over steel plate. His eyes still bright; his expression sobered. "Both of us should get out of this game. Don't think the rag-heads are going to give us the option, though."

"Fuck, no . . ." She sucked at her knuckle, and a trickle of blood. "Robert, I can't *do* this if I'm afraid of people getting hurt."

He looked down at her, from where he stood on the flint steps. "Now we find out, don't we? Whether we're good at this when it's *really* hard? When you *have* to not care?"

Her nostrils are full of the smell of wet steel, his male sweat, sodden wool, the city's midden heaps far below. Rain spattered in, spraying her cheeks with a fine, freezing dew. As the wind gusted sharply, she and Anselm turned simultaneously towards the arrow-slit again.

"There's nobody in charge in here. They must know that! *Why* isn't she attacking now!"

She sent a stream of messengers to the ducal palace in the next hour, who came back one after another with word of not being able to get through to the new Duchess, to the Sieur de la Marche, to Chamberlain-Counsellor Ternant; with news of the palace being a chaotic horde of courtiers, undertakers, celebrants, priests and noblemen; simultaneously torn between arranging a crowning and a funeral.

"Captain Jonvelle told me something!" Rickard added, panting, soaked to the skin in the cold wall-tower's room.

Ash considered asking why he had stopped to gossip with de la Marche's Burgundian captains; saw his bright face, and decided against it.

"Saps. The rag-heads are still mining. His men can *hear* them! They're *still* digging!"

"Hope they *drown*," Ash growled under her breath.

She spent her time pacing the crowded floors of the Byward Tower, among men armed and ready to go out if the walls were threatened; a lance here and there being sent out to watch, to listen, for anything that might be seen or heard in devastating rain.

Forty miles south, down that road – cold darkness, twenty-four hours a day. Given what surrounds Burgundy's borders . . . Is it any wonder we're getting shit weather here?

"Boss . . ." Thomas Tydder, elbowed forward by his brother Simon, looked at her from under streaming dark hair. When he spoke, a drop of water hanging off the end of his nose wobbled. "Boss, is it true? Has Saint Godfrey deserted us?"

Ash signalled Tydder's lance-leader to leave him be.

"Not deserted," she said firmly. "He speaks for us now in the Communion of Saints, you know that, don't you?"

Relieved and embarrassed, the boy ducked his head in a nod.

Past him, Ash caught sight of Robert Anselm; Roberto's features utterly impassive. Automatically, she prodded at her soul, as a man may prod in his mouth for a tooth that has been drawn, and that has left only a tender, unfilled gap.

Stepping closer, Anselm murmured, "Is he right?"

The thunder of the falling rain has concealed her whisper, every time she speaks aloud to Godfrey, to the Stone Golem, even – Christus! – to the Wild Machines themselves. Anselm knows, though.

"Still nothing I can understand," she said succinctly.

"Lion and Boar preserve us," Anselm rumbled. "Is that good or bad?"

"*Fuck* knows, Robert!"

The frustration of waiting seared through her: she would have welcomed anything, even the anticipated thump of siege-ladders and flood of Visigoth men over the city wall. She stomped towards the tower's open doorway.

The roar of fuse-flames and the shatter of clay pots echoed along the wall, and blue-and-yellow fire spread in a ripple across the stone surface of the parapet, and burned unhindered by the torrential rain. All the leather buckets of earth and sand that lined the walls grew sodden and too heavy to lift.

Ash signalled her men to leave it alone, and watched the gelatinous flaming mixture gradually washed over the flagstones and down the inside of the city walls. *There's nothing much left to burn down there anyway: we won't have a city-fire.*

Some forty minutes or so before she judged the last light might leave the iron-grey, pelting sky, two very solidly built Burgundian men-at-arms appeared in the tower doorway, with a slighter man between them.

"Boss!" Thomas Rochester, running along with them – ducking at every embrasure, stumbling into the dark shelter of the tower – bawled a report. "Euen's back!"

Heads turned in the tower room, and all along the rows of Lion men-at-arms settled in the brattices, and behind merlons, in the pouring rain; men crowding to see the small, wiry figure trot along the stone parapet in Burgundian custody.

"He's one of ours, Sergeant." Ash broke into a tremendous grin. "Son of a *bitch* . . ."

The Burgundians saluted, a little cautiously, and made their way back out into the rain. Ash gave a laugh of sheer relief at the bedraggled Welshman dripping water, shivering in the icy wind, but with a grin brilliant enough to shine through the growing twilight.

"Somebody get this idiot a cloak! Euen, in here!"

She waited as one of the baggage women handed Euen Huw a bowl of tepid soup.

"You're wet, Euen . . . *really* wet."

"Came in through a water-gate, didn't I?" he said gravely, soup spilling down his unshaven chin. "Down by the mills. Swum the moat. Some Burgundian bastard nearly nailed me with an arrow, too. They keep a good watch down there."

"Information," Ash said.

Euen Huw sighed, leaning back against the flint-embedded wall, and relaxing with immeasurable relief. "When we were out on that hunt? I got as far as the rag-head camp, see, all ready to take out their boss, but no one was with me. Then they Carthaginian bastards all come back in a hell of a rush; I got separated from my lance, and it's taken me the rest of today to sneak back out of their camp."

Ash pictures the man with his betraying livery stuffed into a bundle, eating (and no doubt, drinking) with Visigoth freemen and slaves and mercenaries; paying close attention to camp-rumour and official statements.

"Jesu Christus! Okay. First thing. Are they deploying for an attack?"

"Can't tell, boss. I had to come out through the siege-engine park, didn't see what they was doing up the north end."

Ash frowned. "Is the Faris still alive?"

"Oh, she's alive, boss, she just fell over, that's all."

"'Fell *over*'?"

"A God-touched fit,[2] boss. Foaming! They say she's back up again now, but a bit groggy."

Unaware that she was scowling, Ash thought, Shit! If she'd *died*, all our problems would be solved—!

"Someone said she gave orders she was going back to Carthage, then she cancelled them," Euen added.

A hope that Ash was not aware of holding shrivelled up, in that second.

So much for her going back and persuading House Leofric to destroy the Stone Golem.

Ash did not say *Godfrey?* The unnerving unintelligibility in her mind, constant now for five hours, built towards unbearable tension in her.

"Her officers hate it, though." Euen's black eyes twinkled. "By what I heard, every one of their *qa'ids* is hoping he's got enough support to make him commander in her place."

"Well, isn't that a nice little morale problem for them?" Her mock-sympathy was transparent enough for Euen Huw to chuckle. "That's why they haven't mounted any full assaults?"

"Maybe it'll be down to 'starve us out' now, boss." The Welshman looked thoughtfully at the scraped-clean bottom of his bowl, and carefully placed his spoon in it. "Or blow up them walls. Tell you something, though, boss. I nearly didn't make it back here. Never mind dodging Mister Mander's boys, and our Agnes Dei – the rag-heads are reinforcing their perimeter-guards all round the city."

"They can't sew the whole place up. Too much ground to cover."

Euen Huw shrugged. "Jack Price might know more, boss. I saw him in with their spearmen. He back yet, is he?"

"Not yet." Ash shifted, noting Rickard at the tower door, and two or three lance-leaders with him; obvious questions on their faces. "Get your lads to make you comfortable, Euen. That was some trick you pulled." She let him turn away before she said, "Good to have you back . . ."

"Oh yes." The Welshman lifted his arms, encompassing all the pounding rain, fire-scarred stone, and demolished houses of the besieged city. With breath-taking sarcasm, he said, "Can't think of anywhere I'd rather be, boss."

"Yeah, well." She grinned back at him. "You never were too bright."

Slow darkness fell: the rain continued to pound.

There was no word from the ducal palace.

The Faris isn't attacking. *Why?*

What have the Wild Machines done to her?

She went back at last to the company's tower, where her pages snipped her points, unshelling her from her armour, and slept a black sleep without dreams of boars. Before dawn she was up and armoured again, blundering around in

---

[2] A better translation might be 'epileptic fit'?

the candlelit darkness to the noise of thunder and sleeting rain, riding out with the next shift of men-at-arms to the walls.

An hour or so after an indistinguishable dawn came – the rain growing brighter – she and an escort rode back through the streets of Dijon. Visibility was no better in this morning light: rain bounced back up off the cobbles, everything more than twenty yards off was a mist. Heading towards the ducal palace, they got lost.

Her nameless pale bay war-horse picked its hooves delicately up out of shit. The rain that flooded the streets flooded middens, too. Ash wrinkled her nostrils at the acrid stench, guiding the horse carefully on the thin film of liquid muck that spread over the cobbles.

Jan-Jacob Clovet lifted a soaking wet arm. "Down that way, boss! I recognise that tavern."

She grinned at the crossbowman who, having been with the part of the company that stayed in Dijon, had an intimate knowledge of its inns, taverns and ordinaries. "Lead on . . ."

She spent two hours not getting in to the ducal palace to see Floria del Guiz, or the Viscount-Mayor, or Olivier de la Marche; being asked to wait among crowds of civilian and military petitioners by embarrassed Burgundian men-at-arms at whom she did not choose to shout, since they were obeying the orders of people much like herself.

But at least there *are* people here. They haven't stolen the arms, the plate, the linen, and the furniture, and legged it over to the Visigoths. Good sign?

Back at the city wall, she had to stand aside for a procession of her men coming down, two Greek Fire casualties with them; and Father Faversham treading the wet stone steps carefully in their wake.

He put his hood back from his bearded pale face, gazing down at her. "Captain, will Florian come back to the hospital soon? We need her!"

I didn't even *think* of that.

Every muscle in her body ached, the rain seeped in and made her silk arming doublet sodden, and a film of rust browned the Milanese white harness. She shook her head, giving a great *whuf!* of breath that blew the rain out of her face.

"I don't know, Father," she said. "Do what you can."

Treading up the rain-slick flint steps to the Byward Tower again, she thought, *That isn't the only reason I've got to talk to Florian! Shit, what's happening here?*

Towards Nones, a runner brought her back from patrolling that corner of the city that includes the north-west gate and two towers of the northern wall. She stopped briefly with bowed head in the rain as one of the Burgundian priests led prayers for the feast of St Gregory.[3] Entering the Byward Tower, she was momentarily free of the spatter of rain on armour. She climbed up the stout

---

[3] Two saints by the name of Gregory have a feast day in November: Gregory *Thaumaturgus* ('the Wonderworker'), d. *c.* 270, and Gregory of Tours d. *c.* 594. Both feast days occur on 17 November. The events of this text therefore *must* take place within the first 48 hours after the 'hunting of the hart'.

wooden steps to the top floor, emerging out into the water-blasted air, where Anselm and his sub-captains stood at the crenellations, in draggled Lion liveries turned from yellow and blue to black by the rain.

"It's easing off!" Anselm bellowed, over the noise of the wind.

"You say!"

Walking forward, she did feel the drenching hiss of the rain lessen. She stood beside Anselm and looked out from the tower. Across the empty air, she realised she was seeing several hundred yards more of broken earth, to the rain-shrouded movable wooden barriers protecting the Visigoth saps.

"What the fuck is *that*?" she demanded.

Visibility shifted. She became aware of the shrouded grey lumps of Visigoth barrack-tents, five hundred yards north of the city walls; and the glimmer of grey brilliance beyond that marked the Suzon river, emerging from the concealing rain.

Beyond Dijon's moat, beyond the no-man's-land of ravaged ground between the city and the enemy, something was new. Ash squinted. In front of the Visigoth tents and defences – wet, raw, obviously newly turned – great banks of earthworks surrounded the north side of Dijon.

"Fucking hell . . ." she breathed.

"Fuck," Anselm said, equally blankly. "Trenches?"

Men moved, as the rain lessened. Emerging from trenches, mud-soaked and exhausted, hundreds of Visigoth serfs were collecting in the open spaces of the enemy camp. Even at this distance, she could see some men holding others up. She could just make out that they were kneeling, to be blessed.

Brightly visible, animal-headed banners and eagles bobbed between the canvas walls. Arian priests with their imaginifers[4] were walking in the muddy lanes between the tents, in procession – the sound of cornicens[5] shrilled out. As she watched, armed men came piling out of wet, sagging canvas shelters, to also stand and wait for a blessing. *More than one procession!* Ash realised; her eye caught by another imaginifer down towards the western bridge.

The incessant noise of rain thinned, died. Ash stared out through her steaming breath at a light-grey sky, and high, moving cloud. At the expanse of river, river-valley, and enemy camp; sodden under the afternoon sky.

"Frigging *hell* . . ."

Her gaze came back to the earthworks. Beside her, Anselm's sergeant snarled to keep order among the escort. Anselm gripped two merlons and leaned out between them. She turned and stared to the east, trying to take in as much of the camp outside the city as she could see.

"Son of a bitch," Robert said flatly, at her ear.

Over on the west bank of the Suzon, men were taking covers off siege-machines; she could see crews winding the winches. Golem-crewed Visigoth

---

[4] In Roman military terms, the legionary who carries an image of the emperor. Presumably the text implies the Visigoth imaginifers carried images of the King-Caliph.

[5] Puzzling! Mentioned in the Roman army of Trajan's era, as players of curved horns – but of course this may be Visigoths using a Roman term to legitimise some ritual musicians of their own.

trebuchets hurled rocks in high arcs – she could not see where they were landing; south, probably; stone splinters shrapnelling the streets. It was not what she looked at.

Dozens of palisade-sheltered trenches zigzagged out to the east, and to the west. She stared out at great mazes of diggings, shored up in the wet; rank upon rank of them, stretching along as far as she could see.

Ash leaned herself out, to see as far as possible either side.

"Even if they dug for the last forty-eight hours—!" Anselm broke off. "It's impossible!"

"Disposable serf labour. They don't care how many hundreds they kill." Ash slammed her palm against the stone. "Jonvelle heard digging! It wasn't saps. It was this. *Golem-diggers*, Robert! If they used everything—"

She sees again the marble and brass of the messenger-golems in the Faris's tent: their impassive stone faces, their tireless stone hands.

"—who knows how many golems they've got! *That's* how they did this!"

There is no break in the walls of thrown-up earth, no interrupted part of the trench-system that now zigzags from the Suzon clear across these acres upon acres of land north of the city wall, maybe clear to the Ouche river in the east. And they have chained boats across the river at *this* bridge, too.

"Robert." Her voice was dry; she swallowed. "Robert, send a runner to Angelotti, and to de la Marche's *ingeniatores*. Ask how far these earthworks and trenches extend. I want to know if they do cover the east and the south, the way it looks like they do."

Anselm leaned back from staring westwards, at the earthworks defending the siege-engine camp. "No breaks that I can see. Christus! They must have worked through the nights—"

Ash sees it, as if she has been there: the bent backs of serfs, digging wet dirt, illuminated by Greek Fire torches. And the stone golems that man the trebuchets and the flame-throwers and carry messages, all of them set to digging; stone hands invulnerable to pain, unmindful of any need to rest.

Surrounding the entire city.

The horns of the cornicens shrilled through the wet air, and she heard the voice of a cantador chanting.

"They've got patrols going into all those defences." Robert Anselm lifted a plate-covered arm, pointing. "Bloody hell. Looks like most of a legion."

"Fucking Green Christ!"

Even at Neuss, there were men who could slip the siege lines in either direction; gather information, desert, spread treachery and rumour, raid the besiegers' supplies, attempt assassination. There always are. Always.

This isn't a normal siege.

Nothing about this has ever been normal!

"We're going to have hell's own job getting anybody past that," Ash said. "Never mind sallying out for any kind of attack."

She turned away from the battlements.

"I'm going back to the palace. You, you and you: with me. Roberto – we *have* to speak to Florian."

III

As the rain eased off, a chain of men-at-arms passed rock-damaged beams and rafters up the steps from the city below, jamming the makeshift wooden struts in wherever hoardings could be reinforced. Antonio Angelotti, apparently oblivious to the stone splinters now spraying off the outside walls, and the thud and boom of Visigoth cannon-fire, lifted his hand in greeting, standing back from his crews running cannon up the steps to the parapet.

"I wish I were an *amir*'s *ingeniator* again, madonna!" He wiped dripping yellow-and-blue dyed plumes away from his archer's sallet, out of his eyes, smiling at her. "Have you seen what they've done out there? The skill—"

"Fuck your professional appreciation!"

The broad excitement in his smile did not alter as another chunk of limestone slammed into the wall ten feet below the battlements, shaking the parapet under their feet.

"Make us up more mangonels and arbalests!"[6] Ash raised her voice over the noise of the men. "Get Dickon – no – whoever's taken over as master smith—"

"Jean Bertran."

"—Bertran. I want bolts and rock-chuckers. I don't want us to run out of powder before we have to."

"I'll see to it, madonna."

"You're coming with me." She squinted a glance at the clearing afternoon sky; judged how fast the temperature fell now that the sky was clearing. "Rochester, take over here – unless it's a Visigoth attack, I don't want to hear about it! You keep Jussey under control, Tom."

"Yes, boss!"

A continuous shattering bombardment began to split and crack the air – great jagged rocks the size of a horse's carcass; iron shot that fissured the merlons of the battlements. Ash braced herself and walked down the dripping steps from the wall to street-level, Robert Anselm, Angelotti, and her banner-bearer behind her. She hesitated for a moment before mounting up, gaze sweeping the demolished open space immediately behind the walls.

"Feels more dangerous than the fucking *battlements*!"

Angelotti inclined his head, while settling his sallet more firmly on his damp yellow ringlets. "Their gunners have got the elevation for this area."

"Oh, joy . . ."

She touched a spur to the bay, which skittered sideways on the wet cobbles before she hauled its head around, and pointed it towards the distant, intact roof-lines of the city. Giovanni Petro and ten archers – all drawn from men who had not been to Carthage – fell in around her, bow-strings under their hats in this wet, hands close to falchions and bucklers, wincing away from the sky as they strode though the rubble. The leashed mastiffs Brifault and Bonniau whined, almost under the bay's hooves.

---

[6] 'Mangonels': military catapults – crew-served weapons, of various sizes. 'Arbalest': a siege-size crossbow, usually frame-mounted.

Robert Anselm rode in silence over the sopping ground. He might have been another anonymous armoured man, one of de la Marche's remaining Burgundians, but for his livery. She could read nothing of what she could see of his expression. Angelotti glanced up continually as he rode, letting his scrawny mount put her hooves where she might – calculating the ability of enemy gunners? The sky began to turn white, wet, clear; with a tinge of yellow on the south-west horizon. Perhaps two hours of light left now, before autumn's early sunset.

Florian. The Faris. Godfrey. John Price. Shit: why don't I know what's happening with anybody!

Inquiries have brought her no information, either, about a white-haired hackbutter of middle age, in borrowed Lion Azure livery. If Guillaume Arnisout came into Dijon in yesterday's mad rush, he's keeping quiet about it.

What did I expect? Loyalty? He knew me when I was a child-whore. That isn't enough to bring anybody over to this side of these walls!

"Will we get in to see the doc?" Anselm pondered.

"Oh, yeah. You watch me."

The wreckage of homes and shops behind the gate is deserted – 'work-teams of citizens and Burgundian military have cleared paths through the burned and battered buildings, pulling them down completely where necessary. Making a maze of deserted ruins. There is no wall left standing higher than a man's height.

"I want some of the lads down here. Make this lot into barricades. If the rag-heads take the north-west gate, we might hold them if we've got something to anchor a line-fight on."

"Right." Anselm nodded.

She rode at a walk, not risking laming the gelding. *If they get us, they get us.* The slam and shatter of rock two hundred yards off made her flinch. Another dark object flashed through the air: high, close. She tensed, expecting a crash. No noise came.

Giovanni Petro's sharp face creased. "Fucking *hell*, boss!"

"Yeah. I know."

The escort straggled out in front and behind, automatically spacing themselves. She nodded to herself. A cold wind blew in her face. Rain still ran off the wreckage of masonry and oak beams. Shifting her weight to bring the pale gelding around the corner of a half-house, she saw four of the archers clustered around something – no, *two* things, she corrected herself – on the earth. Petro straightened up as she rode forward, hauling the mastiffs back by their studded collars.

"Must have been that trebuchet strike, boss," the Italian grunted brusquely. "No missile. A man's body; come down in two places. The head's over here."

Ash said steadily, "One of ours."

Or else you wouldn't be giving it a second look.

"I think it's John Price, boss."

Signalling Anselm and Angelotti to stay on their horses, Ash swung herself out of the war saddle and down. She side-stepped around the men picking up a severed torso and legs from shattered cobbles.

As she passed the two crossbowmen, Guilhelm and Michael, their grip slipped. A mass of reddish-blue intestines plopped out of the body's cavity, into puddles. Fluid leaked away into the water.

Without looking at her, Guilhelm mumbled, "We ain't found his arms yet, boss. Might have come down someplace else."

"It's all right. Father Faversham will still give him Christian burial."

Beyond them, a woman in a hacked-off kirtle and hose knelt in the mud, her steel war-hat tilted back, crying. Her face shone red and blubbered with weeping. As she looked up at Ash's approaching clatter, Ash recognised Margaret Schmidt.

Margaret Schmidt held a severed head between her hands. It was recognisable. John Price.

"Look on the bright side," Ash said, more for Giovanni Petro's ears than those of the gunner. "At least he was dead *before* they shot him over the walls."

Petro gave a snort. "There's that. Okay, Schmidt – put the head in the blanket with the rest of him."

The young woman lifted her head. Her eyes filled again with tears. "*No!*"

"You fucking little cunt, don't you talk to *me* like—!"

"Okay." Ash signalled Petro, jerking her head. He moved reluctantly back to the work-detail shifting Price's body. She was aware of her mounted officers watching. She saw how the woman's fingers were pressing into the flesh of the severed head. Dried blood patched her skin and kirtle-front.

Not dead *that* long before they shot him over, then.

She called back to Anselm, "Need to check if he's been tortured." *Could he have told them anything worth hearing?* Then, more gently, turning back to Margaret Schmidt: "Put him down."

The woman's gaze went flat and cold. Anger, or fear, sharpened her features. "This is somebody's *head*, for Christ's sake!"

"I know what it is."

Full Milanese armour does not easily allow squatting. Ash went down on one knee beside the woman.

"Don't make an issue out of this. Don't make Petro have to hand you over to the provosts. Do it now."

"No—" Margaret Schmidt looked down into features beaten purple and bloody, but still recognisable as the Englishman John Price. She sounded on the verge of throwing up. "No, you don't understand. I'm holding somebody's *head*. I saw it come over us . . . I thought it was a rock . . ."

The last time Ash looked at John Price's face with any attention, a half-moon whitened it on the bluff above the Auxonne road. Weathered, drink-reddened, and full of a cheerful confidence. Nothing like this butcher's shop reject in the woman's hands.

Forcing a sardonic humour into her tone, Ash said, "If you don't like this, you'll like Geraint ab Morgan's disciplinary measures a lot less."

Tears ran over the rims of the young woman's eyes; seeped down into the dirt on her face. "What are we *doing* here? It's mad! All of you, walking around up there on the walls, just waiting for them to come again so you can fight – and now they've got us *trapped* in here—!" She met Ash's gaze. "You want to fight. I've seen it. You actually *want* to. I'm— this is somebody's head, this is a *person*!"

Ash slowly got to her feet. Behind her, Petro and the other archers had unwrapped somebody's bedroll; held it between four of them, now, with a burden dragging it down. The bottom of it was already stained and dripping.

"He was not interrogated," Angelotti called. "Only killed, madonna. Spear wound to the belly."

"Ride on!" she called. "Get over in cover!"

Angelotti spurred his horse. Anselm leaned from the saddle, said something to Guilhelm, who took the bay's reins and stood waiting as the rest of Petro's squad moved off. Ash turned back to Margaret Schmidt.

Why am I wasting time with her? One half-assed gunner?

Ah, but she's still one of us . . .

Ash spoke over the noise of orders and horses' hooves. "This isn't the first time you've seen a man die."

Margaret Schmidt looked up with an expression Ash could not place. An utter contempt, she realised. *An expression I've grown used to not seeing – at least: not directed at me.*

"I worked in a whorehouse!" the woman said bitterly. "Sometimes I'd step over someone with his throat cut, just to get into the house. That's thieving, or somebody's grudge; they didn't volunteer for it! To kill someone they don't even *know*!"

Ash felt her shoulders and back tense, steel-hard, under her steel armour, expecting the strike of another missile in these wrecked streets.

Keeping her voice from going thin with an effort, she said, "I'll take you off the company's books. But first you're going to pick up John Price's head and take it to your sergeant. Then you can do what you want."

"I'm leaving now!"

"No. You're not. First you have to do as I say."

Carefully, Margaret Schmidt put the severed head down on the wet earth in front of her. She kept a proprietary hand on the matted hair. "When I first saw you in Basle, I thought you were a man. You *are* a man. None of this matters to you, does it? You don't know what it's like in this city if you're not a soldier – you don't know what the women are afraid of – you don't think about anything except your company; if I wasn't in the company you wouldn't waste ten minutes on me, or what I do, or don't do! That's all that matters to you! Orders!"

Ash rubbed at her face. Half her attention on the sky, she said quietly, "You're right. I don't care what you do. If it wasn't for the fact that I've seen you up on the walls, fighting in Lion livery, and you're *new* to this – you'd already be with Messire Morgan, so fast your feet wouldn't touch the ground. But as it is, you do what I say. Because if *you* don't, there's a chance someone else might not."

"And I thought Mother Astrid was a bitch and a tyrant!"

It was melodramatic, no less genuine for being so; and Ash might have smiled, in another situation. "It's easy to call someone else a tyrant. It isn't so easy to keep armed men in order."

The blonde woman's breath came raggedly into her throat. "You and your damn *soldiers*! We're trapped in this city! There are families here. There are women who can't defend themselves. There are men who've spent their life keeping shop: *they* can't fight either! There are priests!"

Ash blinked.

Margaret Schmidt coughed, wiped her mouth with her hand, and then stared at it, appalled, as the head of John Price rolled over on to its side on the broken cobbles.

A bluish film covered the eyes.

Ash – with a memory of Price's capable hand steering her down into the moonlit underbrush, pointing out the Visigoth fires – felt her breath suddenly catch. *Robert was right: this is when it's too hard.*

A crow flopped down, all in ruffled black feathers, landed three yards away, and began to hop sideways towards the severed head.

Margaret Schmidt lifted her head and wailed, as unselfconscious as a small child. She might not be more than fifteen or sixteen, Ash suddenly realised.

"I want to get out of here! I wish I'd never come! I wish I'd never left the soeurs." Tears streamed down Margaret's face. "I don't understand! Why couldn't we leave before? Now we'll never get out! We'll *die* here!"

Ash's throat tightened. She could not speak. For a second, fear shifted in her gut; and her eyes stung. A quick look showed her her banner far towards the undamaged houses; even Guilhelm, holding her horse, was out of earshot.

"We won't die." *I hope.*

Tears cutting the dirt on her face, Margaret Schmidt reached out towards the severed head. She pulled her red, wet fingers back; shuddering. "You! It's *your* fault he's dead!"

Ash swatted at the crow. It bounced back, in a flutter, and landed on the churned-up cobbles; stalking from side to side, one black eye watching her.

"In the end, it is," she said, and saw the woman gape at her. "Pick the head up and bring it. *Everybody's* scared. Everybody in Dijon. We're just safer in here – your shopkeepers and farmers and priests, too."

"For how long!"

Ten minutes? Ten days? Ten months?

Ash said carefully, "We have food enough for weeks."

As the woman hung her head, Ash thought quite suddenly, *She's right. I'd say this to her – or to Rickard, if he was frightened. But I wouldn't say it to either of them if they couldn't use a sword or crossbow. I wouldn't bother. What does that make me?*

"No one *wants* to fight." Ash attempted to see the kneeling woman's face. "It's just better to be attacking someone with a close-combat weapon than it is being blown off the wall by cannon." And as Margaret Schmidt's head came up, Ash added, "Okay: not *much* better."

The woman coughed, making a sound that could have been both a laugh and a sob. She got up off her knees, and picked up John Price's severed head, scooping it up in her ragged knee-length kirtle.

"This is better than fucking men for money." Margaret Schmidt looked up from what she held in her skirts, and kicked a piece of broken brick at the crow.

It hopped a few paces away. "But not *much* better. I'm sorry, lady. Captain Ash.. Do you think I should leave your company?"

Dismay went through her. *Here's another one who thinks I have the answers!*

But then, why shouldn't she think that? I go to some lengths to sound as though I do. All the time.

"I'll . . . talk to Petro. If he says you're up to standard, you can stay."

Ash watched the woman hold her bunched skirt squeamishly, and turn her head to look at the lance and its sergeant.

What should I tell you? You're safer with us than as a civilian, if the Goths overrun Dijon? You could just be killed, not raped and killed? Yeah, that's a much better option.

Why aren't you with Florian? What damn idiot ever convinced you that you wanted to be a mercenary soldier?

"Give that to Petro," Ash said. "He's not angry with you. He's angry because John Price was a mate of his."

By the time they got within three streets of the ducal palace, evening dimmed the sky. They could not move for people. The gables of the houses – still dripping – were hung with great swathes of black velvet. The insignia of the Golden Fleece[7] hung from every building. Anselm and Angelotti, in mutual and unspoken habit, rode ahead of her banner; pushing a way through the people as a man breasts the waves of the sea.

A drenched tail-end of cloth, easily eight ells long, trailed across her and dripped water down her harness as she rode under it. Velvet that might – she thought – have been warm, worn against the cold. *Shit, what a waste! What do they think we're going to do this winter?*

If the Goths come over the walls today or tomorrow, there *isn't* a 'this winter' as far as these people are concerned.

The pressure of bodies pushed Petro, Schmidt, and the rest of the escort against the bay's flanks: she quietened it, moving on. Her gaze went over the mass of hats and shoulders as she passed through the people jammed between buildings here. Ahead, a flurry of men in black – dozens of them! – read from lists and shoved people bodily this way and that.

Anselm leaned down from the saddle to accost one. The man pushed past him, stared up at the Lion Affronté, made a mark on his scroll, and called up to Ash: "After the Sieur de la Marche! Remember that, demoiselle!"

"Bloody cheek." Robert Anselm let Orgueil drop back a stride, to ride beside her. "What now? We can't get through this."

Torch-fire flickered, growing stronger as the wet light failed. Down in the street, it was already dark; only the sky above the tilting rooftops held some pale brightness. Approaching the edge of the crowd at the road junction, Ash saw black-robed torchbearers – holding people back.

She squinted into the dusk. "We need to see Florian. More than these damn Burgundians do!"

Between the lines of fire, chaplains and equerries, in black cloth, cleared a way from the direction of the ducal palace, holding the centre of the road clear.

[7] An order of chivalry founded by Duke Philip of Burgundy.

Tears streamed down the faces of people close by. Ash glanced the other way down the street – *to the cathedral?* she thought, trying dimly to call back memories of the summer, and riding there with John de Vere, and Godfrey.

Nothing but a mass of packed heads, hats pulled off to show respect; a crowd everywhere so thick that she abandoned any idea of riding through it to the palace now, or sending a messenger on foot.

"It's the funeral!" she realised. "This is Charles's funeral, now. They're burying the Duke."

Anselm appeared singularly unimpressed. "So – what next?"

"Where have they given us precedence?" She tapped her gauntlet on the pommel of the saddle. "After de la Marche – he was Charles's champion. After the noblemen; before the rest of the men-at-arms. Does that sound good to you, Robert?"

"Oh yeah. Sounds like they might *not* do what the Faris did to her Frankish mercenaries – stick 'em out in front, get 'em chewed up. *If* we're still signed up with Burgundy."

Antonio Angelotti shifted his chestnut mount back, flicking his head as water dripped down from the gabled roofs above him. The torchlight made chiaroscuro of his icon-face under the sallet's silver brilliance.

"Our surgeon will be at the funeral if she's Duchess now, madonna."

"Oh, you worked that one out, too?" Ash smiled, shakily. "Enough messing about, right? They want to bury Charles – fine. I'm sure he'd rather they were keeping Dijon out of Visigoth hands. They want to crown *Florian*, for fuck's sake? Also fine – but they'd better bloody get on with it. We have to plan now. Plan what we can do."

"If there is to be a coronation, following this . . ." Angelotti shrugged.

"We need," Ash said, "to know who's really in charge, now. Because we've got decisions to take. This siege only needs the lightest shove, and it's all over. And . . . whatever else happens, Florian has to stay alive."

The last light faded, down in the narrow streets. Clergy and citizens, court servants and doctors and secretaries and sergeants-at-arms came past; and Charles's sovereign-bailiffs and *maîtres de requêtes* and *procureurs-généraux*, their liveries and black garments illuminated by torchlight. The remaining noblemen – those few who are not with the army in the north, or rotting outside Auxonne – walked in long black robes, bearing a pall of gold. It became dark, and the pitch-torches made the street pungent. Too many torches surrounded it: Ash could not look into the flames and see the coffin when it passed. Dazzled, she recognised one of the abbots walking in its wake, and two of Charles's bastard brothers; and then glimpsed, at the back of their personal attendants, red-and-blue livery – de la Marche, he and all his noble companions riding horses in black cloth caparisons.

Ash spurred the gelding and rode, determinedly, in de la Marche's wake, as the funeral procession moved through the streets of Dijon; followed the black-draped, lead coffin into the cathedral.[8] She took up a place standing by a pillar, not far behind the Burgundian nobility. Every few minutes, as

---

[8] In fact, Charles the Bold had no such formal obsequies after the battle of Nancy. This funeral seems more like the one accorded his father, Philip the Good, in 1467, nine years earlier.

unobtrusively as possible, de la Marche's military aides approached and whispered to him: messages, she guessed, from the wall. Petro, stationed by the door, filtered news from her own runners: the north-west, at least, still unassaulted.

She sweated through chants and anthems. The coffin stood with embalmed heart, and embalmed entrails, each in their own lead caskets, on top of it; on a bier draped to the ground in black velvet, with four great candles at the corners.

The chants lasted past Vespers, past Compline. She sweated through the requiem mass, that began at midnight in the nave that was hung with black cloth. Fourteen hundred candles burned, their beeswax sweetness stifling in the enclosed air – at the sides of the nave, men were using bollock-dagger hilts to punch holes in the glass of the ogee windows, and let out the unbearable heat.

Twice, she slept kneeling. Once, Anselm's tactful hand on her pauldron shook her awake, and she nodded at him, and swallowed with a stale mouth, helped when Angelotti covertly passed her a costrel of wine. The second time, as another mass began, she felt herself slide off into unconsciousness, without any ability to stop herself.

She woke, leaning against Angelotti, still strapped into metal plates, with every muscle and bone in her body hurting.

"Green Christ!" she muttered under her breath.

That was drowned by the swelling anthem from the choir that had woken her, sound shredding the last remnants of sleep and the candle-hot air. Robed men moved in ritual patterns. Beside her, Anselm got to his feet in respect, and reached down and hauled her upright. Numbness in her knees and legs gave way to searing pain.

The lead coffin of the Grand Duke of the West passed down the nave: Charles called the Bold, Philip's son, John's grandson; heir of Burgundy and Arles; being conveyed down into the crypt by four green-robed bishops and twenty-two abbots.

A pale light shone at the windows that was not candlelight. Dawn: pale, clear, and the bells for Prime ringing out of double spires across the city, as the choir in the great cathedral fell into final silence.

Ash covertly flexed her bad knee, shifted her leg, thought *Green Christ, never sleep in armour in church!* and glanced behind to see where her page with her helmet was.

"Madonna!" Angelotti pointed down the nave. She turned her head, staring.

Beside her, Anselm frowned, looking around uncertainly.

In the dimness of dawn and the few unextinguished candles, a tall, slender woman came down between the high, soaring multiple pillars of the cathedral. Throngs of officials and courtiers trod at her heels. She was not young – not far from her thirtieth year, perhaps – but still beautiful in the way that court women are. The black brocade and velvet of her robes brightened the green of her eyes, the gold of her hair. Looking at the fair-skinned face under the finest of linen veils – a little freckled across the cheekbones, but clean – Ash thought *Doesn't that woman there look like my husband Fernando?* before she hitched air halfway through a breath, stared, heard Anselm swear, and realised *That's Floria!*

Her feet were moving her before she properly realised it. Neither awake nor alert yet, Ash stepped out in front of the procession. *I planned this last night. What the fuck did I think I was going to say?*

"Florian! Never mind all this." Ash gestured, cannon and couter scraping as she waved her arm to take in all the cathedral, the court. "I'm calling an officer meeting. *Now*. We can't wait any longer!"

Green eyes and stark fair brows stared out at her from under a padded headdress and translucent veil. A momentary, unexpected embarrassment made her stop speaking. So difficult, looking at this woman, to picture the long-legged, dirty-faced surgeon who gets drunk with the baggage-train women, and who squints through a hangover to sew up wounds with threaded gut and reasonably steady hand.

In a voice equally awkward, Floria del Guiz muttered, "Yes. You're right . . ." and stared around at the grief-stricken crowds, as if at a loss.

Behind her, a green-robed abbot murmured, "Your Grace, not here!"

The noise of footsteps made the nave loud and murmurous. Automatically, in the presence of so many clergy, and still not recovered from sleeplessness or exertion, Ash touched her breastplate over her heart.

"So." She stared at Florian. "Are you Duchess? Is it anything more than being the nobles' puppet? We need to talk about keeping you alive!"

Florian, in woman's clothing, stared back, saying nothing.

Quiet in Ash's mind as snowfall, Godfrey Maximillian's voice whispered, perfectly clearly:

– Child?

IV

Ash caught at Robert Anselm's shoulder. Morning, the eighteenth of November – she is still, at some deep level, in shock. Ignoring Florian's rapid words to the nobles around her, she is conscious only of a memory of influence, pressure, force.

"Godfrey!"

Some official leaned over Florian's shoulder, whispering urgently.

"Perimeter defence!" Ash was briefly aware of Petro and his archers surrounding her, facing outwards, not drawing weapons in a holy place, but ready. She put her hands over her face and whispered into her cold, steel gauntlets:

"Godfrey – is that really you?"

– Ash, little one . . .

This is nothing like the previous strength of his voice in her mind. This is as quiet as wind through bare branches, as soft as snow falling on to other snow. Momentarily, a scent comes to her – resinous pine needles; the raw, rich, dungy smell of boar. She sees no vision in her mind.

What's happened to you!

With that same internal sense that she is performing some action, she *listens.* As she has always listened, when she has called the voice of the Lion, the Stone Golem, the *machina rei militaris.*

– *Ash.*

"Godfrey?" She hesitated; asked again. "Godfrey?"

– *Weak beyond measuring, and a little broken, child, but, yes. Me.*

"Green Christ, Godfrey, I thought I'd lost you!"

– *You heard silence, not absence.*

"That's . . . I couldn't tell!" She shook her head, aware that men surrounded her, her own and others; and that Florian was giving loud, clear instructions. She did not know what the woman said.

– *Now, you hear me . . . And you fear, too, that you will hear the voices of God's Fallen.*

"I don't think the Wild Machines are anything to do with God!"

– *Everything that comes, comes to us by God's grace.*

So weak – as if he's far from her, farther than can be measured in distance. The tiles under her slick-soled boots are granular with dawn light. She glimpsed them sparkle, between her steel-armoured fingers.

There is a hand under each arm; there are men walking; there is someone – Florian – ahead of her, leading the way. To where?

Outside, the new, cold, damp air pricks at her covered face.

"Can you hear the Wild Machines?" Ash demanded. "I heard them after the hart was hunted, and then— Are they there? Godfrey, *are they!*"

– *I have been hurt, and recovering. There was an immanence: a great storm began to break, then nothing. Then confusion. And now there is you, child. I heard you calling to me.*

"Yes, I . . . called."

Godfrey's voice, that is the *machina rei militaris*, says:

– *I heard you weeping.*

She woke herself with soundless weeping, two nights before; voiceless enough that it disturbed neither Rickard nor any of the pages. Woke, and put it out of her mind. Sometimes, on campaign, it happens.

She stumbled, hands dropping from her face; had a momentary glimpse of freezing early morning outside of the cathedral, de la Marche's armed ducal household escort, the great boxy carriage of the Duchess; and then she is lost, again, in interior listening.

"Are they still there?" she insisted. "The Wild Machines, Godfrey! *Are they still there?*"

– *I hear nothing now. But nor did I hear their passing, child. I have not heard them die.*

Silence, but not absence.

"We'd *know*, would we, if they were gone? Or – damaged?"

Suddenly intense, Ash uncovered her face, breathing cold air, eyes watering at the approaching bright white walls of the ducal palace. Anselm and Angelotti still had a hand under each mailed armpit. She staggered as she walked. Pages followed with the horses. Now the sky has cleared, it is becoming very cold.

"No. How could I know? Why would I? Shit, that would be *too* easy . . ."

 – *All I hear is their silence.*

The dispersing funeral crowds in the Dijon streets passed unnoticed. So did the muttering of her men superstitiously watching their commander talk to her voice – *but not*, she reflects, *the voice they are used to thinking of; 'Saint' Godfrey, good grief!* She ignored everything, ignored Anselm and Angelotti half-carrying her into the palace between them, forcing every part of her strength into the weak contact.

"They did try to do their miracle. I felt it, when the Duke died. They tried to trigger the Faris. It wasn't even aimed at me, and I felt it!" A bare awareness of steps intruded itself: she stumbled up them. "And I heard their . . . anger . . . *after* the hunt ended. If they're not damaged, not destroyed – shit, for all I know, they can do that again any time the Duchess dies!"

 – *Duchess?*

No mistaking the very human bewilderment in her shared soul; Godfrey to the life.

 – *Margaret of York is Duchess, now?*

"Oh, her? Hell, no. She's even missed her husband's funeral!"

Ash sounded sardonic, even to herself. The edge of a stool banged into the back of her greaves. She sat, automatically. "I was hoping she'd turn up. With about ten thousand armed men, for choice, and raise the siege! No, Widow Margaret's still somewhere in the north. Florian's the Duchess."

 – *Florian!*

Somewhere close, there is a familiar, exasperated snort.

"Godfrey, have you heard the Faris since the hunt – is she sick? Is she sane?"

 – *She lives, and is as she was before.* The ghost of an old amusement; as if Godfrey Maximillian is forgetting what it is like to laugh. – *She will not speak to the* machina rei militaris.

"Does she try to speak to the Wild Machines?"

 – *No. All the great Devils are silent . . . I have been shocked, deaf, dumb . . . How long?*

Ash, aware now that she sits in a high tapestried chamber, that there are Burgundians speaking at high volume, that the woman who looks like Florian appears to be overriding them, said, "Forty-eight hours? Maybe an hour or two less?"

 – *I do not know what their silence may mean.*

The voice in her head did not fade; it suddenly became silent, as if weakness drained it away. She still had a sense of him, something priestly; Saint Godfrey, infusing the sacral parts of her mind.

If I could *make* them hear me – the Wild Machines . . . Shit: not yet: I have to think!

She blinked her streaming eyes, and realised that she was looking out of the windows of the Tour Philippe le Bon, Burgundy's quarrelling courtiers and military men filling the room with noise behind her.

Morning in the same building, if not the same room, in which she last saw Charles of Burgundy. This lower chamber has the same great carved limestone hearth at the end, fire burning fiercely against the early bitter cold. The same blond floorboards, and white-plastered walls covered with tapestries. But an oak throne stands upon a dais in the place where his bed is, in the room above.

A sudden pang went through her, that had not been there all the night they were burying him with masses and prayer. *Shit: another one dead.*

Fuck Carthage!

Anger brought her to herself; brought some respite from the cold silence in her head. *It isn't good business to get involved.* Heat from the blazing hearth intruded, made her conscious of her silk doublet and woollen hose that have been rain-saturated and dried again on her in sleep, of armour whose bright surface is glazed thick with rust, of the immense ache and cramps of her body.

"You all right?" Robert Anselm said, standing over her.

"Same old same old. I'll live. Where's Florian?" She reached up, caught his armoured forearm, and pulled herself to her feet. The room tilted. "Shit."

"Food." Anselm strode off back into the chamber.

The clear, brilliant cold light stung her gritty eyes. She is looking out from the window of the Tour Philippe le Bon. Up past the towers that her company occupies, dawn shows her iron-walled wagons axle-deep in mud, wheeled into place in the Visigoth camp to protect Greek Fire throwers covering the approach to the north-west gate.

"Eat that."

Anselm's hand shoved a torn crust of bread into her hand. The smell of it brought saliva into her mouth, and a great rumble from her gut. She ripped the crust with her teeth, and said as she chewed, "Thanks."

"*You* ain't got the fucking sense." A grin. "Fuck me, what a bunch of wankers. 'Scuse me while I sort this out."

He left her side, moving back into the crush of courtiers. A raw female voice snapped Ash's head around:

"A *petit conseil*[9] first! Messire de la Marche. Messire Ternant. Bishop John. Captain Ash. The rest later! Everyone else *out*!"

Florian: her exact tone when yelling at some deacon late in bringing her linen bandages and gut. Straightening up, the tall woman in black robes stalked away from the long table, across the room. Men stood back from her; bowed as she passed.

One man's voice snapped, "I protest!"

Ash recognised the Viscount-Mayor, Richard Follo; thought, *But he has a point, there should be some merchant representative*, and then, *How much of a 'Duchess' can Florian be!*

One of de la Marche's aides, and two of his captains, began moving people towards the chamber door, in the way that armoured men can move an unarmed crowd without ever having to draw sword. A whole slew of officers, sergeants-at-arms, servants, household retainers, equerries, surgeons, secretaries, ex-tutors, minor captains and financial administrators were rapidly ushered out.

"Ash—" Floria del Guiz suddenly glanced across the emptying floor and shook her head at three Burgundian equerries who were attempting – with no success – to escort a suddenly monoglot Robert Anselm and Antonio Angelotti

[9] 'Little/small council'.

out of the chamber. At her signal, the equerries in ducal livery bowed, and backed out of the room. None of them looked at Olivier de la Marche or Philippe Ternant first, for confirmation of the order.

That's – interesting.

A pantler bowed his way past Florian, and servers with dazzling white linen for the oak table followed, and a dozen men with silver dishes. Floria del Guiz turned and strode the remaining few steps towards Ash, with a gait not used to wearing a robe and underrobe long at the front. Her slippered toe caught the fur-trimmed hem of the black velvet overrobe. She stumbled, her feet tangled in glorious cloth.

"Watch it!" Ash reached out, grabbing very solid weight, stopping Floria from falling. She stared into the so-close, so-familiar face. She realised that she smelled no wine on the woman's breath.

"*Merde!*" Florian swore in a whisper. Ash saw her gaze flinch away from the mass of men around them.

Ash let go of the tall woman's arms. Florian's tight sleeve snagged the edges of her gauntlet plates as the woman got her balance. Florian reached down to shake out her skirts, exposing an underdress of silver brocade all sewn with sapphires and diamonds and silver thread, and tugged at the high belt, settling it under her bust-line. The high-waisted black velvet snugged tight over her shoulders, arms, and torso. Under it, brocade laced at the front in a vee over a shift of so fine a linen it was translucent to the pink flesh of her breasts beneath. As a surgeon, Floria del Guiz stooped; as a woman in court mourning, she stood very tall and very straight indeed.

"Christus Viridianus, why couldn't I look like that in my wedding dress?" Ash said wryly. "And you're telling me Margaret Schmidt turned you down?"

The flash of a glance from Florian's eyes made Ash think *That was over-hearty. Jesus. What do I say to her?* Something about Florian standing in front of her in women's dress unsettled her. *Maybe seeing her with Margaret Schmidt wasn't so odd when she looked like a man.*

As if what Ash had said had not been spoken, Florian demanded, "In the cathedral – is boss hearing voices again?"

"I heard Godfrey. Florian, I think he's been – hurt, somehow. As for the Wild Machines . . . nothing yet: not a fucking word."

"Why not?"

"Yeah, like I'd know. Godfrey doesn't think they're dead – if that's the term. Maybe they're damaged. You're Duchess. Why don't *you* tell *me*!"

Floria snorted, as familiar as if she had still been surgeon, still been in a sagging, blood-boltered tent back of some field of battle, digging steel out of meat.

"Christ, Ash! If *I* knew, you'd know! Being 'Duchess' doesn't help me with that."

They had made her wash, Ash realised; no dried blood under her fingernails.

"We have to talk, 'Duchess'." Ash glanced up at the tall woman – Florian's fair hair scraped back under her horned headdress to expose a broad white brow; left hand now automatically holding up the front of her over-gown, folds of velvet falling gracefully down.

Difficult to believe she's a surgeon; you'd swear she'd stayed a noblewoman all her life.

Ash realised the woman was perfectly conscious of how many people were watching her – watching both of them, now.

Automatically turning her back towards the crowd to conceal her expression, she caught Florian's reflection in the chill, leaded window-glass. A long-featured woman in court splendour, Valois jewellery bright at her neck and wrists and veiled headdress; only the dark marks in her eye-sockets hinting at confusion or exhaustion. And beside her, crop-haired, in field-filthy plate, a woman with scarred cheeks and stunned eyes.

"Give the word," Ash said abruptly. "I'll get you out of here. I don't know how, but I will."

"You *don't* know how." The woman gave her a sardonic grin that was all Florian, all surgeon; a grin familiar from a hundred months under canvas in the field.

"There's no military problem that hasn't got a solution!" Ash stopped. "Except the one that kills you, of course . . ."

"Oh, of *course*. The Wild Machines," Florian began, and a woman crossed the emptying room and stepped between Ash and her surgeon, narrow eyes tight with fury, interrupting without any hesitation.

It took Ash a second to recognise Jeanne Châlon, and another second to realise she herself was looking around for men-at-arms to have the woman removed.

Jeanne Châlon said shrilly, "I have ordered you funeral bake-meats – they brought me two saddles of mutton, a boiled capon, tripe, chitterlings, and three partridges – it is *nothing* fit for a Valois Duchess! Tell them we must be served more, and more fitting food!"

Ash finally caught Roberto's eye: jerked her head. Floria said nothing, giving her aunt a little push towards the chamber door.

"The lady is right!" Olivier de la Marche's baritone cut through the chamber. "Bring better food for the Duchess." He gestured to the servants.

Ash caught a look close to triumph as the other woman walked away.

"You let her in here?"

"She's been kind to me. The last two days. She's the only family I have."

"No," Ash said, reflexively, as to any member of the Lion Azure, "she isn't."

"I wish this was like organising the surgeon's tent, Ash. In the tent, I know what I'm *doing*. Here, I have no idea what I'm doing. I just know what I *am*."

The servants and pages had almost finished setting the table: the odour of wine-sauce brought water into Ash's mouth. Anselm arrived, heavy tread making the boards creak; Angelotti at his armoured shoulder. Both men looked at the surgeon with deliberately blank faces.

Moving rapidly, Floria stepped up on to the dais, laying a hand on the carved oak arm of the ducal throne. "I *know* what I am. I *know* what I do."

Standing over the bleeding body of the hart, hearing her surgeon say *I maintain the real*: all this is startlingly clear to Ash. Not to these two of her officers – nor are they Burgundian.

"'Ow?" Robert Anselm demanded.

"I don't know *how* I do it, or why!" Exasperated, Florian met his gaze. "It really doesn't matter what you call it! Except that it does. They call it 'being Duchess' here. *They* believe I'm their Duchess. Ash, if we leave, this town falls." She stopped: corrected herself. "If *I* leave."

"Are you sure?" Antonio Angelotti asked.

Florian kept her gaze fixed on Ash. "Do I have to tell *you* about morale?" Her fingers tightened on the arm of the throne. "I don't want this. Look at it! Talk about *Welcome to the hot seat* . . ."[10]

The surgeon lifted her head, gazing down the chamber. Ash saw her look at the old chamberlain-counsellor, at de la Marche, at a bishop, at the departing servers.

"If I didn't know what I am, I'd run. You know me, Ash. I might just run anyway."

"Yeah. You might. If only into a bottle."

Florian took her hand away from the ducal throne, and the waxed oak that she had been stroking with one clean thumb. She stepped down from the dais again, standing between Anselm and Angelotti. It was clear to Ash that they would not be approached, not while the surgeon made her desire for privacy apparent; that, if anything, broke the surface tension of her sleepless exhaustion, made her think again *This place is on borrowed time – one of my company's tied here – what do I do?*

Ash looked desperately around the long bright chamber, at the still-clustering men in rich robes and armour; at the food set out on the sun-bleached cloth.

"When I made the hart . . ." Florian looked down at her scrubbed hands, as if she expected to find them bloody. "It hurt Godfrey."

Ash met her gaze, seeing something there that might have been self-blame. "He's recovering, I think."

"So maybe whatever happened damaged the Wild Machines. Destroyed them."

"Maybe. But I wouldn't count on it. I heard them after the hart was dead."

Robert Anselm grunted. "If we're very, *very* lucky, they were damaged . . ."

Picking up his words, Angelotti completed: ". . . if what happened when the hunt aborted their miracle *hurt* them, madonna. So: if they *are* damaged . . . they might recover tomorrow. Or it might take fifty years. Or we might be fortunate: it might never happen."

Florian looked questioningly at her. Ash shook her head.

"Godfrey says he hears 'silence, not absence'. I can't make myself believe they're gone. They might not even be hurt. Who knows why they're silent? The only way we can be safe is to act as if I'll hear them again tomorrow."

A bare forty-eight hours of funeral, lack of sleep, and the sheer impact of the Burgundian court; all this made Florian seem subdued. She drew in a breath, twisting the bezels of the gold rings on her fingers, and looked up at Ash. Her expression was the same as it had been in the wildwood, soaked in hart's blood, staggered by the certainty of her knowledge.

"Would we have heard," she said, "if the sun had come up on the other side of the Burgundian border, in the past two days? Beyond Auxonne?"

---

[10] In the text's original mediaeval Latin: 'the siege perilous'.

"Oh, *shit*." Anselm's disgusted bellow made the remaining Burgundian noblemen startle, and shift back towards the hearth end of the chamber.

"Yeah, you got it. *Euen*. Shit! Euen Huw," Ash explained to Florian. "He was out in their camp. He'd have brought the rumour back in with him. Something like that would be through the rag-head camp inside fifteen minutes!"

Ash shrugged. The steel of her armour squealed, rust scraping off with the movement.

"I'm being dumb. If *that* had happened, the Goths wouldn't care about being overheard by me, they'd use the Stone Golem to tell the Faris! And Godfrey would have told me. If there was sun over Christendom, now, we'd know. It's dark. And if it's dark, the Wild Machines are still with us."

"Either that, and they're silent," Florian said, "or the darkness is permanent without them."

"Better hope not," Ash said grimly. "Or next year's going to be hell."

"So nothing's changed. Whatever you're not hearing from the Wild Machines."

"Then why am I not hearing it!"

Angelotti ticked off words on his powder-black fingers with surprising, delicate grace: "No Duke. Perhaps a Duchess. Still dark. No assault on the walls. No threats from the *Ferae Natura Machinae*. If there is a pattern, madonna, I can't see it."

Ash ignored the crowd and clatter behind her.

"They may have reasons for silence. They might be hiding damage. How can we know? It's what I really hate," she said. "Making decisions, on not enough information. But there's never enough information. And you have to make the decisions anyway."

She took a breath.

"We need to ensure Florian's safety. That comes first. Burgundy or no bloody Burgundy, Duchess or no Duchess, Florian is what's stopping the Wild Machines—" She broke off. "Unless there *is* no need, any more—"

Florian smoothed her robe down, with long-fingered, spotless hands. The sheer linen of her veil concealed nothing of her expression, only misted it, gave it paradoxical clarity.

"Out in the desert," she said.

"What?"

"You forced them to talk to you. You told me."

Angelotti nodded. Robert Anselm's scowl, unconscious, was almost a snarl.

"So do that now," Florian said. "Find out. I need to know. Am I doing what Charles did? Am I the obstacle? Am I maintaining the real *against* anything?"

"When I tried it before the hunt – they'd learned to shut me out of their knowledge." Ash hesitated. "But they still *spoke* to me."

If I think about it, I won't do it.

There is a brief second of memory in her mind: of the lord-*amir* Leofric's face when she drew the words of the *machina rei militaris* into her soul; and of the bitter chill sand outside Carthage as she hits it, face-down, the first time that she did more than listen to the Wild Machines. When she wrenched knowledge from them, all in a heartbeat.

Inside herself, she prepares. It is more than passive, more than emptying herself for voices to come; she makes herself a void that pulls, that compels itself to be filled.

Closes her eyes, shuts out the tower room, Florian, Roberto, Angeli; directs her speech beyond and through the *machina rei militaris*, hundreds of leagues away, in Carthage:

"Come on, you motherfuckers . . ."

And *listens*.

A faint sound, in the shared solitude of her soul; no more than an unwilling whisper, overlain by Godfrey's anguish. A voice, woven of many voices, heard now for the first time since the hart lay bloody on the turf in front of her:

'PLAN WHILE YOU CAN, LITTLE THING OF EARTH. WE ARE NOT YET CAST DOWN.'

The chamber wall felt bitter cold, cooling her scarred cheek where she leaned against the masonry.

"Let me take that, boss."

Shifting, she realised Rickard stood beside her, prising her sallet out of her hands. She let him take it. With a sigh, she straightened, and let him unspring the pins on her pauldrons, and remove the rust-starred shoulder defences. He tucked the plates under his arm. Awkwardly, he unbuckled her belt and took sword and scabbard, staring at her anxiously.

"Boss . . ."

She turned her back on him, moving with greater ease. The window's reflection showed her the chamber, Anselm sombrely speaking to the rest of the Lion escort as they left; Antonio Angelotti with one beautiful hand resting on Florian's arm.

I'd forgotten. Even after two days, I'd forgotten. How – their voices feel, speaking to me.

She reaches out. When she touches her fingers to the glass, it is bitter cold through the linen of her gauntlets.

From here, in this morning light, she sees Dijon's heterogeneous walls and towers from high inside the city. White-plastered masonry here, missile-smashed brick there; the blue-grey flint of a tower by the mills still pouring black smoke into the air. The city below her is a mass of red tiled roofs. South, between the double spires of a hundred churches, she can see the Suzon snaking away in a white gleam, between the wooded, grey limestone hills. The air is empty of birds. Distant church bells ring.

She can see nowhere – the banks of the western river, the ground beyond the moat, the road running up towards the western bridge – that is not blocked by newly turned earth. The Visigoths' ditches and banks, so small from up here; the pavises and mantlets set up along them barely visible. Distant cornicens sound in the enemy camp.

It is as if there is a precipice, now, a verge in her mind, beyond which is a drop more vertiginous than this one from the tower. And in that depth, the presence of voices.

Robert Anselm, his voice bluff with shock and mordant humour, said, "We'll take it there's no fucking *good* news, right?"

That's the first time he's seen me speak to the Wild Machines.

Shit, Robert, I wish you'd come to Carthage!

"You got *that* right . . ."

What she seeks for is the welcome numbness of action, her old ability to cut off self from feeling. The closest she can come is to maintain an interest in watching her hands, which are shaking.

"Madonna." Angelotti reached out and took her arm, drawing her with surprising strength into a walk. She stumbled across the oak boards, past the hearth; caught her balance as the Italian master gunner shoved her into one of the chairs lining the long table – and stepped back, gracefully, to give Florian his hand and seat the Duchess of Burgundy almost as swiftly.

"Eat," he said. "And drink – madonna Florian, there must be wine?"

With shaking hands, Ash unbuckled her gauntlets, dropped them heavily on to the linen cloth, and reached for one of the gold, ruby-studded goblets.

She was aware of Burgundians seating themselves – few now: the chamber very empty – and servers and pantlers complaining about lack of ceremony; but all she wanted was the thick sting of wine on her tongue. When served meats, she took the plate much as she would have done in camp, and did not realise until whole minutes later that she was stabbing up mutton not with her eating-knife, but with her bollock dagger.

Ah, that's mercenaries for you . . .

The taste of onions, and ortolan,[11] and pease pottage in her mouth; their weight in her stomach; all this and she began to be aware of herself, her surroundings, the sheer solid reality of linen, table, armour, doublet, plate. She belched.

They can't reach me. No more than they could when I spoke to them before the hunt. All they can do is speak.

"I don't know if they're damaged or not." She spoke to Florian through a mouthful of frumenty,[12] spattering the linen. "How would I tell? But they're there."

"Oh God."

Not like Florian to sound devout, Ash observed; and put down her spoon, and wiped her bare finger around the all-but-empty bowl, and sucked on the last sweetness as she looked at Floria del Guiz.

Florian said, "That makes me Charles Valois."

Ash, instantly grimly cheerful, said, "Look on the bright side. Now there's four hundred of us determined you're going to stay alive." She glanced down the table at Olivier de la Marche. "Make that the better part of two and a half thousand."

"It isn't a joke!"

[11] The garden bunting: a bird known as a table delicacy.
[12] Wheat boiled in milk, with cinnamon and sugar.

"Don't think about it." Ash softened her voice. "Don't think about it. Think about staying alive. That's normal: everybody wants to do that. Don't think about what happens if you die—"

"The Faris does her miracle. The Wild Machines force her." Florian spoke in a strained undertone. "Burgundy's a wasteland. And then so is everything—"

"*Don't* think about it."

Ash closed her dirty hand over Florian's, tightening her grip until she knew she must be hurting the surgeon.

"Don't think about it," Ash repeated. "You can't afford to. Ask Roberto. Ask Angeli. If you think about what depends on you, yourself, you'd never be a commander, never make yourself crucial to any assault. Just assume you'll stay alive, Florian. Assume that we don't care *what* we have to do to keep you that way."

In Robert's growling agreement there is only loyalty; Angelotti's swift glance has more in it of awareness, of Carthage – and of Burgundy, too, as his blond curly head turns, briefly looking at Olivier de la Marche, at Philippe Ternant, and the bishop.

"I wonder if you have to stay in Burgundy?" Ash speculated. "I wonder if we have to be in this siege?"

Floria lowered her voice. "Ash, like it or not, I *am* who they're going to call Duchess now."

"Yeah," Ash said, "I know. I don't see a way out of that."

This is my damn surgeon we're talking about here!

She felt Florian's hand shift, in hers, and released it. Red marks imprinted the skin. The woman took her hand back, flexing her fingers, in a gesture that somehow had nothing of the feminine about it.

Florian's gaze went to the great fire in the hearth, tended by the palace servants. "Jesus, Ash, I'm not a Duchess!"

"Say that again," Robert Anselm mumbled, grinning, and showing threads of beef caught in his yellowing teeth. "Barely a saw-bones!"

Florian's tone approached more normality than Ash had heard from her since the cathedral:

"Fuck you, Anselm!"

"Pleasure. Thought you weren't that way inclined?"

"I get more pussy than you do, you English poof! Always have."

"He's not a poof, madonna." Angelotti slid his hand under Anselm's tassets. "Worse luck!"

Robert Anselm clenched his fist, made as if to slam his armoured elbow into the gunner, and then sat back on his chair. "Go on, you little wop cocksucker. Only time you're going to feel a *real* prick!"

Florian, bright-eyed, and putting her elbows on the table, remarked, "I don't know – he *is* a real prick, why shouldn't he feel like one?"

Ash gaped, cringed, and stared frozen-faced down the table at the Burgundian nobility, her palms wet with sweat.

They stared back, faces bewildered.

820

Ash managed to show her teeth in a desperate smile.

Olivier de la Marche inclined his head in bemused courtesy.

Hang on. Her smile remained fixed. She replayed the quick-fire exchange in her head. *Roberto started that one in English – Kentish English at that – and she followed him – thank Christ!*

Without change of expression, she remarked through her teeth, "I can't take you bastards anywhere!"

"Of course you can." Florian, her shoulder-muscles relaxed, reached out and touched her bare fist to Anselm's arm, Angelotti's breastplate. "Twice. The second time to apologise."

Ash saw their relaxation, the unspoken bond between them. Surgeon, gunner, and commander: all as it might have been in the company's tents, any time these five years. But now, seen for the first time after Florian's forty-eight hours of separation.

Fuck, we needed that. But everything's still changing.

She grabbed for the goblet and held it up to be filled. Wine's steadying warmth burned down her gullet. "Okay! Okay, we need to plan what we're doing. Florian, you get any of the messages I sent up to the palace yesterday?"

"Eventually." Florian spoke with a kind of contained amusement that could hide any embarrassment or panic that a surgeon-turned-Duchess might be feeling. "When they'd come through a dozen secretaries."

"Shit, what a way to run a duchy!"

"Think yourself lucky. De la Marche says most of the lawyers went north with Margaret. Before Auxonne."

Ash leaned on the table. "You haven't left the Lion Azure. Not yet. Not until you tell me you have."

Florian's expression was momentarily unreadable.

"We need to know your status. What 'Duchess' really means – what sort of Duchess does Olivier de la Marche think you are? If there's one person in this city who holds command of the Burgundian military forces right now, it's him, not you."

Florian glanced towards Olivier de la Marche. Ash saw him interpret that as a summons; abandon his place. He walked up towards the head of the table. She thought she saw a slight unsureness as he looked at Floria, but de la Marche's lined face broke into a beam, seeing Ash.

"Jeez, he ought to like his Duchess, but I didn't know *I* was that popular . . ."

Florian's face, under the sheerness of the veil, clearly showed exasperation. "Boss! You know what we've – what the company's been doing, these last two days. And you. Up on the walls. Backwards and forwards across the no-man's-land behind the north-west gate. Out there getting shot at."

"Oh, yeah, I was forgetting," Ash said dryly. "Not that we have a choice! Hell, even Jussey and Jonville have been giving us good back-up . . ."

Olivier de la Marche, coming up to the Duchess, bowed stiffly to her. He kept his gaze on Ash. "How could they not?"

It took her a moment to realise that it was a rhetorical question spoken with transparent honesty. She looked questioningly at him.

"You bear the sword that shed the Hart's Blood," Olivier de la Marche said. "Every man in Dijon knows that."

"'Bear the sword'—" Ash broke off.

"I did use your sword." Florian's closed lips moved; she might have been trying to smother a wild grin.

"You nicked it off me because you didn't have one, and it was the only one to hand!" Ash swung her gaze back to de la Marche. "Green Christ! So she used my sword. So what? She might as well have used a sharp stick, for all the difference it would have made!"

De la Marche's face crinkled, lines around his eyes that weather and laughter have put there. Something more sophisticated overlay the honesty in his expression; perhaps pleasure at her refusal to capitalise on an apparent advantage.

"And *anyway*," Ash added, "it's been cleaned since. Or if it hasn't, my pages are going to have sore arses!"

Her hand went out. From his place at the wall, Rickard jumped forward, presenting her sword hilt-first. She seized the leather, thumbing the blade an inch out of the scabbard's friction-grip. The grey of the metal was uncoloured by anything except the silver abrasions of a new sharpening, ordered after the hunt. Nothing marred the razor sharpness of the edges.

"*Was* it this one? Or was I still borrowing yours, Robert?"

"Oh, it was your wheel-pommel sword, madonna," Angelotti put in. "The Faris had just sent it back. I swear we thought you were going to sleep with it."

"*Thank* you; that'll do!" She slotted it home. Rickard stepped back, grinning.

De la Marche, ignoring both the presence and the familiarity of her sub-captains, said, "This fact remains, Demoiselle-Captain: your sword spilled the Hart's Blood. Do you imagine any man in the city thinks less of it because it is a tool, and you keep it clean and sharp for its proper use? Go out into the street. To 'Hero of Carthage', you will hear added 'Hart's-Blood' and 'Sword of the Duchy'. You are no longer a mere mercenary captain to the people of Burgundy."

Ash smothered a snort, aware of Robert Anselm's profane exclamation beside her.

"These titles are all marks of God's grace," de la Marche said. "A standard is only silk cloth, Demoiselle-Captain, but men are maimed holding it and die to defend it. The Duchess is our standard. I think, despite yourself, you are becoming one of our banners."

All humour left her expression. She was aware of Anselm's stillness, Angelotti's gaze; and the attention from further down the table, and from the men and women clearing the remains of the meal.

"No," she said. "I'm not. *We're* not."

The big Burgundian turned, and bowed very formally to Floria del Guiz. "With your permission, your Grace?"

Equally formally – equally uncomfortably – Florian nodded.

A sudden realisation hit Ash. With difficulty, she kept her expression unchanged.

Shit! He can cope with *me* – I might be a woman in man's clothing, but I'm a soldier. He can pretend I'm a man. Florian . . . he's seen Floria as Florian. And she's a civilian. And he doesn't know how to treat her. How to see her as Duchess.

And, currently, he's the most powerful man in Dijon.

"Demoiselle-Captain, your *condotta* died with my lord the Duke." De la Marche paused. "You have four hundred men. You have seen what lies outside the city now – the new trenches. In the normal way of things, I would ask you to sign a new *condotta* with Burgundy, and I would expect you to refuse."

Robert Anselm said rhetorically, "Nice when they 'ave confidence in their town, ain't it!"

De la Marche glanced once at Floria del Guiz, and continued. "The 'hero of Carthage' will get no contract with the Carthaginians. Your *men* might, under one or other of your *centeniers*.[13] However, they choose otherwise. I am commander of the late Duke's household knights: I know what it is to have men believe in their commander. Demoiselle Ash, it is a responsibility."

"Too fucking right it is!"

She was not aware, until his lined face creased in a smile, that sleeplessness had betrayed her into speaking the thought out loud.

"Demoiselle-Captain, we have a successor to my lord Charles. Her Grace the Duchess Floria. Your surgeon. In view of this—"

Robert Anselm interrupted harshly. "Let's cut the crap, shall we?"

Ash shot him a glance. *Shit. Next time we're going to play 'hard-man thug' and 'noble commander', you might warn me!*

Anselm said, "We're stuck in here because the rag-'eads hate Ash, the guys won't dump her as captain, and now our doc is Duchess – but this town *is* going to fall, Messire de la Marche. It's just a matter of time. If you think you're getting our services for free, just because we're stuck in here at the moment, you got another fucking think coming!"

His discourtesy echoed off the whitewashed ceiling. Olivier de la Marche's expression did not change. Mildly, he said, "Your remaining *condotta* is with the English Earl of Oxford, who may well be dead, by now. I have a proposal to put to Demoiselle-Captain Ash."

A swift glance at Florian's face showed only bewilderment.

Either this isn't something he discussed with her, or forty-eight hours of chaos have knocked it out of her head. Shit, I wish I was prepared for this!

Ash rested her hands on the oak table, flexing her cramped fingers. Every line of the roping on her gauntlet cuff was picked out in brown rust, now, and she let herself follow the lines of dinted steel for a moment, where it lay, before looking up at the man across the table.

"And your proposal is?"

Olivier de la Marche spoke. "Demoiselle Ash, I want you to take my place as commander-in-chief of the Burgundian army."

---

[13] In the Burgundian army under Charles the Bold, *centenier* refers to a captain commanding a company consisting of a hundred soldiers.

V

The silence stretched out.

Neither Anselm, Angelotti nor Florian spoke. The old chamberlain-counsellor, Ternant, leaned across the foot of the table to whisper something to the bishop, but too quietly to be heard over the crackling of the hearth-fire. The Burgundian servants froze in place.

Her wooden chair screeched back as Ash surged to her feet. The noise, and her raised voice, made the servants and guards stare.

"You're *crazy*!"

The big Burgundian nobleman laughed. It had a note of delight in it. Perfectly seriously, he jabbed one blunt-fingered hand at her chest.

"Demoiselle, ask yourself! Who came back triumphant out of the very bowels of the enemy's capital, Carthage? Who fought their way undefeated across half Europe, bringing our new Duchess to us? Who arrived, miraculously, *just in time*: before the very day that Duke Charles of the Valois died!"

"*What!*" Ash slammed a bare hand down on the table's surface. The noise whip-cracked around the ducal chamber. "You're *shitting* me!"

"And who guarded our Duchess when the hunt rode, saw her safe to her fate, and gave into her hand the very blade with which she made the hart?"

"Fucking *hell*!"

Stepping back from the table, Ash took two quick strides, swung around, faced the Burgundian:

"We didn't 'come triumphant' out of Carthage! We retreated out of there as fast as we could *run*! We *barely* made it north to you from Marseilles, one step in front of the Visigoths – I think we've been routing back across Europe since Basle! And as for *when* we got here—" She shook her head, cropped silver hair flying. "Haven't you guys ever heard of coincidence! And I'd like to have seen you try to *stop* Florian hunting! Green Christ up a fucking Oak Tree!"

Olivier de la Marche made a brisk sign of the Briar Cross on his surcoat. Morning light glimmered off the reds, blues and golds of his heraldry; cloth spotless across the breadth of his armour and powerful body.

"God doesn't always bother to let the instruments of His purpose know what they are, Demoiselle-Captain. Why should He? You've done everything He desires."

Ash, at a loss, gaped at him.

Angelotti, from where he sat, murmured, "Mother of God . . . !"

"And," the Burgundian commander added, "doubtless you will continue to bring about His desires."

"You're the army's commander, de la Marche; you've been that for years, they've seen you in tourney and war – even if I agreed to this idiocy, nobody's going to follow *my* orders as Captain-General of Burgundy's army!"

"But they will!"

Now de la Marche turned away, walked a few steps with his hands clasped behind his back, and then came back to stand before the table at which Florian sat. His gaze flicked over the Duchess; ranked Ash's sub-commanders as not pertinent to the discussion; settled again on Ash.

"They *will*," de la Marche repeated. "Demoiselle-Captain, I've told you why. You've been up on the walls. Go down into the streets, if you don't believe me, and listen to the legend you have become! We believe that God sent you to bring our Duchess to us, when otherwise all would have perished when Duke Charles died. The men of Dijon believe that you will fight for us, against Visigoths you have already beaten once, and that while you fight, this city will not fall."

Philippe Ternant got up and walked towards them, supporting himself with one veined hand on the table, the bishop at his other elbow. "It's true. I've heard them."

"You have a glamour, now," de la Marche persisted. "As Joan the Virgin had for France. It is for you, now, to be a Joan of Arc for Burgundy. You cannot deny that this has come to you."

Oh yes I bloody can—

Looking away from Olivier de la Marche, she intercepted the glance first of one of the servers in white doublets, and then of the guard he stood next to. Both men's faces wore a naked, painful hope; no protection of cynicism.

"Uh-uh." Ash raised her hands in front of her, palms out, as if she could block the Burgundian Captain-General's words. "Not me. I've seen this parcel and it's ticking . . ."[14]

"You have a duty—"

"I *don't* have a duty! I'm a fucking *mercenary*!"

Panting, frustrated, Ash glared at the man.

"I didn't ask for this! It's a pile of crap! Eight hundred men's the most I've ever commanded—"

"You would have myself and my officers, Demoiselle."

"I don't want them! This ain't gonna happen! Dijon's nothing to me, Burgundy's nothing to me!"

Thunderously, de la Marche roared at field-volume, "*We believe in you whether you like it or not!*"

"Well *I* didn't bloody ask you to!"

Screaming up into the big man's face, Ash found herself breathless; robbed of speech by his expression.

Suddenly quiet, Olivier de la Marche said, "Do you think I *want* you as Captain-General, girl? Do you think I want to stand down? I was Duke Charles's man for longer than you've been alive. I've seen him write ordinance after ordinance, turning the armies of Burgundy into the best in Christendom – and now half of them lie dead at Auxonne, no man knows what is passing in Flanders, and inside these walls there are a bare two thousand men. I find it hard to believe that anyone except myself is to be trusted with the defence of this city. And yet I find it harder to believe that God has not sent you. You are here, now, to be our oriflamme.[15] How can I object? God *demands* your service."

[14] I have freely translated a textual difficulty.
[15] Originally the sacred banner of St Denis.

Her breath came hard, but she sounded casually cynical. "So He might. He hasn't bloody paid me yet!"

"*This is not a joke!*"

"No. It isn't." Finding herself behind Florian's chair, Ash stopped pacing, and turned to rest her hands on the blonde woman's shoulders; velvet warm under her palms. "It isn't a joke at all."

"Then—"

"Now you listen to me." Ash spoke quietly. She waited, until it forced the armoured Burgundian noble to stop bellowing, and listen.

Ash said, "Burgundy doesn't matter. *Florian* matters."

Under her hands, Florian stirred.

Ash said, "It's not important if we leave Dijon, and you guys get massacred, and Burgundy's conquered by the Visigoths. All that's important is that Florian stays alive. All the while she's alive, the Wild Machines can't do a damn thing. And if she dies, it won't matter about Burgundy either, because none of us will be around to know about it: you, me, the Burgundians, or the Visigoths!"

"Demoiselle-Captain—"

"I can't afford the time to be a hero for you!"

"Demoiselle Ash—!"

"Hey. It's not like I'm the only one with charisma." Ash grinned, crookedly, finding some emotional balance as she faced him. "Aren't you the tournament Golden Boy? And – oh, what about Anthony de la Roche? He's charismatic—"

"He's in Flanders," de la Marche said grimly. "You are here! Demoiselle, I can't believe that you would defy God's will in this way!"

"*You're not listening to me!*"

As she was about to shout – to scream, in sheer frustration, *Florian!* – she heard Robert Anselm's voice from beside her.

"You ain't thinking, girl."

He put heavy, broad hands on the arms of his chair, and shoved himself up on to his feet. Armour clattered. He made the unconscious body-adjustment that settles harness into place, and faced Ash.

Robert Anselm jerked a thumb at the windows. "You want to be sure Florian stays alive? With that lot out there? What's better than being in charge of the whole damn Burgundian army?"

Ash stared at him.

"Jesus wept, Robert!"

"He may have a point, madonna."

Ash smacked her hand into her fist. "No!" She swung around, facing Olivier de la Marche. "I'm not taking on your damn army! I've got to have the option of taking Florian out of here."

She found herself actually watching de la Marche's nostrils move, flaring as he inhaled, sharply, and bit off whatever he was about to say.

"You never went to Carthage," Ash said, more gently. "You've never seen the Wild Machines—"

"*She is our Duchess!*"

"That doesn't *matter*, you idiot!"

Antonio Angelotti stood up, forcing himself by that movement between Ash and Olivier de la Marche. Ash backed away a step, her throat raw, glaring at the Burgundian nobleman.

Angelotti reached down and touched the saints' medals looped around the wrist of his fluted German gauntlet, and made a point of looking at Ash for permission to speak.

Breathing hard, she finally nodded.

"Your Grace," Angelotti spoke past de la Marche, to the Bishop. "Does the Duchess need to stay within Burgundian territory?"

The bishop – a round-faced, dark man with some of the Valois look – appeared startled. "Now that is rank superstition."

"Is it?" Ash came immediately to Angelotti's defence. She ignored de la Marche's thunderous frown. "Now is it? I *saw* somebody make a saint's vision into a solid piece of meat and blood. And now you all say she's your Duchess. You got some nerve telling me my master gunner's question is superstitious!"

"It shows a certain lack of thought." The bishop let go of Philippe Ternant's elbow, and steepled his fingers, touching them to his small, pursed delicate mouth. "How could my late brother Charles have made war, or pursued diplomacy, if he couldn't leave the territories of Burgundy?"

"Well . . ." Ash realised that her face felt warm. "Yeah: okay. Now you mention it."

"The *hunt* must occur on Burgundian land." The bishop bowed to Florian. "And within a certain narrow space of time. If our Duchess – pardon, your Grace – were to die outside the borders of Burgundy now, news would not reach us in time, even if the city still stood. Then, no hunt, no new Duke or Duchess, and . . ."

He finished with an eloquent shrug, and a glance at the pale early morning sun beyond the glass.

"So Dijon must stand, and the Duchess with it!" Olivier de la Marche blew out a harsh breath. "It's clear to me, Demoiselle Ash. Your surgeon is our Duchess, now. And you are destined to be our commander-in-chief, not I. Our Pucelle."

"I am *not*—" Ash hauled her voice down from a squeak. "Not your goddamn commander-in-chief!"

Deep frustration wrote itself in the lines of de la Marche's face. He glared at her, then at Florian – and then looked away from the Burgundian woman, fixing his gaze on Ash again. "It's true our Duchess has been your surgeon. Does this mean you won't follow her?"

"She hasn't stopped being my surgeon yet! Messire de la Marche, I know what Florian is. I'm far from convinced that makes her a Duchess. And I know what a factious nobility's like. This city could fall in a second!" Ash jabbed a finger at him. "Exactly *how* many of your knights and nobles believe Florian is Duchess?"

For the first time, de la Marche appeared staggered. He did not speak.

"Florian, take a look out of the window." Ash smiled grimly, not taking her eyes off de la Marche. "That should concentrate your mind. Now tell me who *is* in charge here, now Charles is dead."

When the surgeon spoke again, her voice held a raw honesty, and she talked as if de la Marche and Ternant and the bishop were not present.

"It's me. I'm in charge."

Ash snapped a look over her shoulder, startled.

"I thought I wouldn't be. That I'd be a figurehead. It isn't like that." Floria's face altered. "It's ironic. I ran off to Padua and Salerno when all I had to be afraid of was being married off like all the other noble brood-mares. Now I'm trapped, but because I'm the heir and successor to Charles de Bourgogne! And I *am*. I am, Ash. These people are doing what I say. That's frightening."

Breathless, Ash muttered automatically, "Too fucking right!"

At the surgeon's sardonic look, she added:

"Florian, I *know* you. You've got no more idea how to rule a duchy than my last turd! Why should you have? But if it's 'Yes, my Lady, yes, your Grace . . . '"

"Yes," Florian said.

Moved by some personal impulse that she would not have given way to, before; off-balance in some subtle way, Ash muttered, "Sweet Christ, woman, you don't know when you're well off! You have no idea of what it's like to have to *prove* your right to authority, day by day by day. Because you hunted the hart. And that *makes* you Duchess."

"Hunting the Hart made me what I am. *Nothing* makes me a Duchess!" Floria's long, strong fingers clenched, her knuckles white. "I have to be stepping right into the middle of other people's political games here! I can only know what other people tell me. I need all the help I can get. People I trust. Ash. You're one of them."

Ash shifted uncomfortably in her armour, over-warm for the first time in days in the fire-heated stuffiness of the tower room. She looked away from Florian's expression, aware that it demanded something of her.

"There's you. There's the company. There's Messire de la Marche." Ash shook her head. "There's Burgundy. There's Christendom – I can't get my head around that one. *Everything* . . . All I know is, I have to keep you alive, and I have to get us to some point where we can fight back." Now she looked up at de la Marche. "And you want me to be some Sacred Virgin-Warrior. I'm not from bloody Domrémy,[16] I'm from *Carthage*! I'm slave-born. Green Christ! Get a grip!"

"*You* get a grip." Florian stood, in a graceful sweep of velvet. She put her hand on Anselm's vambrace. "I'm with Roberto on this one. You've told me often enough. Men win when they believe they can win."

"Aw, *shit*—"

Antonio Angelotti seated himself again, and said thoughtfully, "You would need to talk to our officers and men. The Lion Azure should not turn into the Duchess's Household guard . . ."

Olivier de la Marche grunted. As Ash looked up at him, the big man said, in a normal speaking voice, "My apologies, Demoiselle-Captain. Naturally, a commander must speak to his men. How soon can you do this?"

---

[16] Actual birthplace of Jeanne d'Arc.

"'How soon'!"

There was no echo of her incredulity on their faces.

She looked first at Florian. Nothing to be read there. A drawn anxiety shadowed Philippe Ternant's features; the bishop's round face was unreadable.

"You are no longer just a mercenary commander," Olivier de la Marche repeated. "Not to us. If you wanted to, demoiselle, you could make a play for power here. That would split the city. I *offer* you the command, instead. Captain over me, with me to use my authority when you're not on duty; the responsibility to be yours, as well."

At his last word, his lips curved up; he looked for a moment much as he must have done as a young champion, riding in the great tournaments of Burgundy: a careless prowess that does not need to consider itself, matched with an awareness that loyalty is simple and men are complex.

"If we don't last out more than two or three days more," he added, "I will share the disgrace with you, Demoiselle-Captain; how is that for an offer?"

She held his gaze, aware that not only Florian, but Robert and Angeli also watched her; that the chamberlain-counsellor and the bishop now had identical expressions of hope.

"Uh . . ." She wiped her hand across her nose. Angelotti sat with his helm in his lap, smoothing the rain-draggled plumes into order. He shot a glance at her from under gold brows. Having known him and Anselm for so long, she did not need to hear them speak their opinions aloud.

"You have at least to *tell* your men," de la Marche said, "that every man in Dijon demands this of you. And my men are waiting for your answer now."

Christ, do I actually have to take this seriously?

Fuck . . .

"You'd be putting a mercenary commander in over Burgundian nobles," she said slowly. "I don't want to find myself involved in some internecine war *inside* Dijon, with the Visigoths still there outside!"

Olivier de la Marche nodded assent. "The worst of all worlds, demoiselle."

"What are you going to do about factions and political infighting?" Ash nodded towards her surgeon. "Florian isn't even a Valois. It's a good fifteen years since she's been noble!"

Florian spluttered, hand up to her veil; muttered something indistinguishable, but in entirely familiar, cynical tones.

"And then," Ash said, "you're adding me."

"The Turks have their Janissaries,[17] do they not? We're only men," Olivier de la Marche said, "and you're asking the wrong man about factions, Demoiselle-Captain. I'm a soldier, not a politician. All the politicians are in the north; my lord Duke sent them there with Duchess Margaret, before Auxonne. God and His Saints protect her!"

"But Florian," Ash began.

"I'll tell you now, Demoiselle-Captain. Duchess Floria will have all the loyalty that men gave to my lord, Charles. This is *Burgundy*. We're only men,

---

[17] Slave troops, often attaining high rank.

and men of honour are prone to quarrel. But we are pious men, we recognise a woman sent by God to us; she *is* our Duchess."

Into the moment's silence that followed, he added, "And you: God sent you to us, also. Now, Demoiselle Ash – what will *you* do?"

Five hours later, she returned to the Tour Philippe le Bon in highly polished armour and clean Lion Azure livery. Heads lifted as she entered the room, interrupting the last of the noon meal. She nodded briefly, let Anselm and Angelotti move ahead down the table, and let Rickard take his place at the wall with her sword and helmet. She strode to the head of the table and sat in the empty chair waiting beside Floria del Guiz.

"*Well?*" Florian demanded, under her breath.

"You got any more of that frumenty? I could really go some of that." Ash coughed. "And mead. Anything with honey in. My throat's *ragged* from talking to that lot."

"Ash!"

"Okay, okay!" A quick glance showed her a couple of dozen of de la Marche's commanders at the table, and two abbots with the bishop, all staring with the same intense curiosity as the servants. "Just let me *eat*."

Florian grinned, suddenly, and signalled to the servers. "I'm not keeping boss from her food. Bad things happen when you keep boss from her food . . ."

As the servers came to table, the Duchess of Burgundy reached out with long-fingered hands, helping herself and Ash from the dishes. Ash flicked a glance at the pantler's and butler's expressions. *Ah, shit! She's got them. I've done that one . . .*

What she saw was not disdain for such non-noble acts, but a kind of pride in their Duchess's blunt military manners.

Ash reached for a plate the right weight and colour to be gold. Unused to the noble luxury of a chair, she caught her armoured elbows on the chair-arms. She scooped up the wheat and honey gruel in a metal spoon – an oddly different taste to eating from a horn spoon – and shot a gaze down the table.

Anselm and Angelotti ignored her, seizing on the last of the food and eating with the fast, single-minded determination of soldiers; the gunner's fair head close to Anselm's shaven pate as they simultaneously leaned back to call for more wine. Next to Angelotti, the rheumy-eyed chamberlain-counsellor Philippe Ternant ignored the meat on his plate in favour of a rapid, whispered conversation with Olivier de la Marche, his eyes on Ash. Beyond the ducal champion, Ash saw the same middle-aged man in episcopal green who had been present at dawn.

Unable to speak with her mouth full, she raised her eyebrows at Florian.

"Bishop John of Cambrai," Floria murmured, mouth equally full. She swallowed. "One of the late Duke's bastard half-brothers. He's a man after my own heart; there's never enough women in the world for him![18] He's another

[18] I have regularised the text, which indiscriminately refers to him as 'Bishop Jean' and 'Bishop

reason I need you here. We've got business with him later. Whatever you've decided. Ash, *what does the company say?*"

Ash studied the bishop: round-faced, with black velvet eyes, and soft, matt-black hair growing around his tonsure, and only the Valois nose to mark him as an indisputable child of Philip the Good. She shook her head at Florian, pointing at her mirror-polished gorget and her neck.

"Better in a minute."

"In your own damn time ... What state is the infirmary in?" Florian demanded. "How's Rostovnaya? And Vitteleschi? And Szechy?"

Anything to put off the moment. Ash stopped chewing, swallowed; sent her mind back to the infirmary in the company tower. "Blanche and Baldina are running it, with Father Faversham. Looks okay."

"What would you know!"

"About Ludmilla – spoke to Blanche – she says the burns aren't healing."

"They won't if the stupid woman keeps trying to stand her duty up on the walls!"

"Your Grace," de la Marche interrupted.

Ash did not look at the surgeon-turned-Duchess, she kept her gaze on the men lining the long table. Abandoning ceremony, they ceased eating; the officers looking towards Olivier de la Marche.

He rumbled, "Your Grace, with your permission – Demoiselle-Captain Ash, what have you decided?"

The spoon rattled as Ash set it down on the gold plate. She kept her gaze momentarily on the rich, warm glow of the metal. Then she lifted her head to see them all silent, all staring.

Sudden sweat made her arming doublet sodden, in the time that it took her to stand up.

"They voted." Her voice sounded both thin and hoarse in her own ears.

An unbroken silence.

"It all comes down to what keeps Florian alive longer. You'll die to keep Florian alive. So will we. Different reasons. But we'll both do whatever it takes."

A cold nausea pierced her. She leaned her fists on the table, to keep herself from dizzily sitting straight back down.

"If that also means me as your 'Pucelle', to boost morale – well: whatever it takes."

Their eyes are on her: men of Burgundy, in their blue-and-red livery with the bold St Andrew's crosses. Men she knows – Jussey, Lacombe – and men she knows only by sight, or not at all. She is conscious of her cleaned-up armour, her bright livery – and of her short-cropped hair, and the scars on her cheeks.

No. She watched the faces of men in their mid- and late-twenties, a few of them older. *It doesn't* matter *what I look like – they're seeing what they want to see.*

John' of Cambrai. There appears to be some independent evidence for Floria's comment in this text – Bishop John's funeral mass, in 1480, was attended by a total of thirty-six of his illegitimate children.

She switched her gaze back to de la Marche.

"I'll take the position of commander-in-chief. You'll be my second-in-command. I'm in."

Voices broke out. She heard it as a confused babble.

"There are two conditions!" Her voice cracked. She coughed, glanced around the room, fixed her eyes on Olivier de la Marche, and started again. "Two conditions. First: I'll take this on until you get somebody better – when Anthony de la Roche comes down from Flanders, this job's his. You want a Burgundian with leadership and charisma: that's him. Second: I'm here in Dijon only until we can carry the fight to the enemy: kill my sister the Faris, because she's a channel for the Wild Machines' power, or attack the Wild Machines themselves."

For a moment, she is dizzy with it: the desire to leave this battered, claustrophobic city. Even the memory of the horrific forced march from Marseilles is distanced, now, beside the chance of getting *out*.

"And if we can get your Duchess – our Florian – away safely at *any* point, we're leaving this town to the rag-heads. On that basis," she said, "and with the vote of the Lion Azure – I'm here."

The babble of voices resolved itself to two things: a cheer, and the explosive profanity of one of the abbots. Men all around the table stood up – one abbot's green vestments swirling as he stalked towards the door – but the men in breastplate and hose crowded around her, grinning, speaking, shouting.

De la Marche strode up to her. Ash scrambled back from the high table. The Burgundian knight reached out, grasping her hand; and she managed to keep herself from wincing aloud.

"Welcome, Demoiselle-Captain!"

"Pleasure," Ash muttered weakly. Her knuckles ground together. As he released her hand, she hid her fingers behind her back, massaging painful flesh.

"'Captain-General'!" two knights corrected, almost simultaneously; one curly-haired and unknown to her, the other a thick-set man, Captain Lacombe, away from duty on the north-west wall.

Captain-General of Burgundy. Shit.

Instead of leaving her, the fear intensified; nausea turning to cramps in her bowels. She kept her face as expressionless as she could.

Further down the table, Angelotti winked at her. It failed to steady her.

Well, it's done now. I've said it.

Formal chivalric introductions passed in a blur of names. She stood, surrounded by men mostly a head taller than herself, talking at the tops of their voices. Looking back, she saw the remaining abbot and the bishop monopolising Florian.

The curly-haired knight's gaze followed hers. He might have been twenty-five, old enough to have killed and ordered killed any number of men in battle, but what was on his face as he watched Floria was a shining awe. Sounding contrite, he said suddenly, "Two of you blessed by God – I'm glad you're our commander, Demoiselle-Captain Ash. You're a warrior. Her Grace is so far above us—"

Ash lifted an eyebrow, and shot him a glance at about shoulder-height. "And I'm not?"

"I— well, I—" He blushed, furiously. "That's not what I—"

As if he were one of her own lance-leaders, Ash said, "I think the phrase you're looking for is 'oh shit!', soldier . . ."

Lacombe snorted, and grinned at his younger companion. "Didn't I tell you what she was like? This is the Sieur de Romont, Captain Ash. Don't mind him, he's a dork in here, but he fucks those legionaries every time they come across the walls."

"Oh, I'm sure he does," Ash said dryly. Meeting Captain Romont's pleased and blushing gaze, she thought suddenly of Florian in the camp outside Dijon's walls: *call it charisma if you like . . .*

The first smile tugged at her mouth.

I'd like to see de la Marche copy my command-style.

And then, her eyes on Lacombe and Romont and the others: *If I get this wrong – if I'm not up to this job – all of you will be lying dead in the streets. And soon.*

She turned, walking to the table and putting her hands on the back of her chair; and as if there had been an order given, the *centeniers* of the Burgundian forces returned to their seats, and waited for her to speak. She waited until Florian sat down.

"I'm not a one-man show." Ash leaned on the chair-back, looking at each of the faces around the table in turn. "I never have been. I have good officers. I expect them to speak their minds. In fact—" she looked across at Anselm and Angelotti "—most of the time I can't shut the bastards up!"

It was not the laugh that warmed her, but the unmistakable body-language of men settling down to listen. Their expressions held cynicism, hope, judgement: *This is standard commander bullshit, we've heard it all before*, mixed with *We're in deep shit here, are you good enough to get us out?*

Burgundy may be different. But soldiers are soldiers.

Thank Christ I'll have de la Marche.

"So I expect you to talk to me, to keep me up to date with what's happening, and to relay what I say to you to your men. I don't want us blindsided by trouble because some dipstick thought he didn't have to tell me about a problem, or he thought his guys didn't need to know what the command people are saying. I don't have to tell you we're hanging by a thread here. So we need to get it together, and we need to do it fast."

There were perhaps two, out of the twenty, who still automatically looked at Olivier de la Marche after she had finished speaking. She mentally noted faces, if not yet names. *Two out of twenty is* fucking *good . . .*

"Okay. *Now.*"

Ash left the chair and paced, primarily to let them get a clear view of her newly polished, expensive Milanese harness, but also to look out of the tower window, at the ant-like movements of the Visigoths beyond their trenches.

"What we need to know is – why the fuck have they given us three days to talk about this?"

VI

"Madonna?" Angelotti's oval-lidded glance took in everybody gathered at the table.

Ash briefly explained, "My *magister ingeniator*," and gestured him to speak.

"The new golem-built entrenchments are a fathom deep, at least; and the same wide. In some places the lines are three-deep. Any attack would have to throw down fascines and pavises and boards, to cross the ditches. There will always be time now for the Visigoths to sound the alarm and deploy to meet us."

Ash saw heads nodding among the Burgundian *centeniers*.

Angelotti added, "I've spoken with the Burgundian engineers. Those dugouts go clear over to the Ouche, in the east; and they continue all the way down the broken ground over on the east bank." He shrugged, eloquently. "We can't break out in any direction, madonna! This was worth their three days. *If*—"

About to interrupt, Ash found herself interrupted:

"Is a ditch that important, for God's sake?" Florian leaned forward, as she has done in tents from northern France to southern Italy, arguing with Ash's command staff.

"It stops us sallying out." Robert Anselm hit the table with his fist. "But it's crazy! Why are they worried about that? They can *take* this city. Right now! You look out there! They'll lose a lot of men – but they'll do it."

Imperceptibly, Olivier de la Marche nodded.

"A ditch *is* important." Ash waited until Florian's attention came back to her. "Trenches. Trenches are defence – not attack. Florian, they've got the Wild Machines behind them, urging them on. What we need to know is, why have they spent forty-eight hours digging, not attacking?"

Now Florian nodded, too, green eyes intent; and Ash prodded the oak tabletop with her finger for emphasis.

"*Why* dig? Why *not* attack? I can make a guess why – and if I'm right, we're going to have a little time."

Lacombe's flushed face took on a look of hope. Ash surveyed the other Burgundian officers. "The Faris has stopped the assaults on the walls. She's sticking to bombardment. She's dug entrenchments round the *whole fucking city*—"

"Do you not hear her orders?" de la Marche interrupted. "Does she not speak with this Stone Golem that you, too, hear?"

"G— Saint Godfrey told me she doesn't speak to it now. If he's right, she hasn't used the *machina rei militaris* since I went into her camp and spoke to her, before we came into the city. That means she isn't listening to Carthage . . . And I'm willing to bet I *am* right: that last attack she put in on the northwest gate, before the Duke died, she must have done that without the Stone Golem."

"They so nearly took the gate!" the elderly Chamberlain-Counsellor Ternant protested. "Was that the act of a mad woman?"

"It wasn't smart." With the bull-necked Lacombe and the other *centeniers* already interrupting, Ash raised her voice over theirs and pursued the point. "She made a feint on the wall where we were, and when it looked like we were pushing it back, she put Greek Fire down on her own people. Oh, I know *why* she thought sending van Mander's company would work – she thought it would freak out my guys who'd fought beside him before. They're hard bastards; it'll take more than that. And then she thought that dumping Greek Fire on us and van Mander when his assault was failing would clear the wall, and let her attack with her Visigoth troops and win. But it was a bad mistake. She killed her own mercenaries. There isn't a Frankish soldier in Dijon who'll go over to the Visigoths now."

Memory flashed her back to the wall. Not, as she might have expected, to Ludmilla Rostovnaya rolling, body on fire, but to the face of Bartolomey St John as she shoved fourteen inches of steel dagger into his eye socket and blood soaked the velvet cover of his brigandine. *I was there when he ordered that one from the armourer. And now Dickon Stour's dead too.*

Into the silence, Ash said, "The *machina rei militaris* would have warned her off doing that – I know it would, because it would warn *me* off it, if I ever thought anything like that was a good idea!"

She grinned. It was not clear from the expressions around her whether they were worried by the lack of divinity of their Pucelle's voices, or reassured by her military acumen.

"The Faris isn't using the Stone Golem. I'd bet money she *won't*, now. She knows that anything she reports, any tactical advice she asks for – we'll hear it too. Even Carthage is keeping silent. She can't get orders from them, now. For the moment – she's on her own."

"And?" Olivier de la Marche prompted. "What does this mean, Demoiselle-Captain?"

She has a brief memory of the Faris, profile illuminated by the lamps in her headquarters, hands resting in her lap, the skin on her fingers chewed ragged.

"She's frozen up. *I* think she's terrified of making mistakes. She knows the Stone Golem is overheard. And she knows the Wild Machines are there. That simple. She can't pretend they're not there any more. She knows what they can do to her – could do." Ash frowned. "So she can't ask for battlefield advice. And she's too scared to do it alone."

Bishop John said quietly, "And do they still have their power, demoiselle: this *machina plena malis*,[19] these Wild Machines?"

There was silence, except for the crackling of the fire in the hearth. The Burgundian officers turned, one by one, to look at her. The green-robed bishop of Cambrai touched his fingertips to the Briar Cross above his heart.

"I hear them." Ash watched expressions. "They could be damaged, and lying about it. But we can't afford to bet on it. And, having spoken to them once, at your Duchess's request, I don't plan to do it again – if nothing else, it works both ways: whatever the Wild Machines say to me, the Visigoths will know. They only have to ask the Stone Golem, and it'll repeat every question I ask."

[19] 'Machina plena malis': 'a contrivance full of evils'. Used punningly in the text to refer to a 'contrivance' in the sense of a trick or snare, as well as a constructed device.

She nodded an acknowledgement to de la Marche. "The less the Wild Machines know, the better. The less House Leofric and the King-Caliph know, the better."

Lacombe's friend Romont put in, "Does King-Caliph Gelimer know about these . . . 'Wild Machines'?"

"Oh yeah." Ash grinned at him, in morbid humour. "They call the light over the King-Caliphs' tombs the 'Fire of the Blessing'. *'Arif* Alderic told me that, in the Visigoth camp." Restless, she began to pace again, thinking aloud. "Up to now, the Faris has kept quiet about the Wild Machines, but – if I was her, I might not. If the Visigoths believed her, they might just say, hey, we have a whole lot *more* tactical machines on our side. Their morale might go up!"

Anselm scowled. "Yeah. They're fucking stupid enough!"

"The last time I saw the Faris, at the truce, she admitted to me that she heard the Wild Machines. She had a fit, when the hunt happened – I think she's shitting herself. By now she knows there's a successor to Duke Charles. *She* can't be sure the Wild Machines are damaged. As soon as the Duke's successor dies – sorry, Florian – the same thing is going to happen again. She's going to make a miracle, for the Wild Machines. The Faris is going to be used . . ."

A look went between Olivier de la Marche and Bishop John: it might have been something as simple as fear.

"She's jammed her head up her arse," Ash said brutally, "and she's waiting for the problem to go away. It isn't going to. And it would be a good idea if we didn't jam *our* heads up *our* arses too!"

Another of the *centeniers* spoke in a heavy northern accent. "If she does plan to let cold, and hunger, and time do her siege-work, without attacking, then, we have time to plan."

Ash rested her armoured hand on his shoulder as she reached the chair in which he sat. "Even if she does, Captain – one of her *qa'ids* could take over tomorrow. Then we're fucked."

De la Marche nodded.

Meeting his gaze, moving on, the oak boards creaking under her, Ash said, "Say that the Faris continues to soft-pedal – Carthage will get increasingly shitty with her. *They* still want Burgundy's surrender. They don't want any more of a winter campaign than they're already stuck with . . . King-Caliph Gelimer's in charge, *Amir* Leofric is sick – I don't know how much weight this Sisnandus carries. How long will it take before Gelimer sends a—" Ash paused; said sardonically, "—a more 'conventional' general out to replace the Faris? Anything from two to four weeks. Assuming a new commander hasn't left already. And *he'll* follow orders and attack. What," she added to de la Marche, "is the matter?"

Olivier de la Marche started, and wiped his hand over his mouth. When he removed it, there was no trace of a smile. "You appear to have a sound grasp of the situation, Demoiselle-Captain."

Ash put her fists on her hips. "Yeah. It's my job."

Someone at the far end of the table laughed out loud in brief appreciation. She could feel the balance of the room shift, the very beginnings of a prickly dislike that anyone – even de la Marche – would think of denigrating the Maid of Burgundy.

"If I'm right—" another glance out of the windows. "—she's going to sit behind that ditch she's dug, and wait for us to starve. They won't let her do that indefinitely. We could have anything from fifteen minutes to four weeks before things go pear-shaped." A quirk of her mouth. "If we had enough food for four weeks . . ."

Olivier de la Marche's expression became absorbed in calculations. He broke off, looked up at Ash again. "So. She has experienced *qa'ids* out there. They might give her advice; she might get her confidence back. She *might* use the *machina rei militaris* to devise a plan to take this city – although she hardly needs to."

"Oh yeah. Any of that. I said I think we have time – I don't think we have very *much* time. Okay . . ." Ash began to point at random around the table: "Suggestions."

"We might take a leaf from their *magister ingeniator*'s book," Antonio Angelotti said, unexpectedly.

Ash paused, staring at him. She put out of her mind the suddenly overwhelming fear that she might have committed herself wrongly, that four hundred men – two and a half thousand men, now – will suffer from this decision. She responded to the new atmosphere in the room. *Now we can make plans.*

"Go on, Angeli."

"A sap," the Italian gunner said. "Let me look at the ground up in the north-east quarter of the city. We might dig a sap out under the wall on that side, west of the wet ground on the bank of the Ouche, under their northern camp. We might get Madonna Florian out that way. Then the Duchess is preserved, even if Dijon falls. And," he looked at de la Marche, "you can get to the north and fight back."

Olivier de la Marche blinked. "Mining for such a distance? Under those ditches; under their camp? And deep enough not to be overheard? That would take a phenomenal amount of time and timber, Messire Angelotti."

Robert Anselm murmured, "Sounds good to me . . ."

"Okay: that's one." Ash snapped her fingers. "Next. You!"

Captain Romont, startled, blurted out, "Send men out with grenades and powder. We could burn their stores!"

"If we could get to them." Ash glanced at the bright glass of the chamber's windows. "We know from Godfrey that she has three legions up north, fighting at Bruges and Antwerp and Ghent; she's only got two legions here to feed, one under-strength. And she can keep on shipping food and Greek Fire over the Med . . . Although that gives her fucking long supply lines to cope with."

Anselm grunted. "Enough to give them problems?"

"It's just possible *we* could wait *them* out. They didn't expect not to be able to live off the country when they got here. I don't believe that they expected darkness to cover Iberia – all their fields and farms there. But even if Iberia's Under the Penitence, now, they've still got Egypt, and they've had twenty years to prepare for this."

Momentarily, she sees not the weak sun outside the tower window, but the frozen blackness of Lyons and Avignon; the snow falling in Carthage.

The half of Christendom that didn't starve this harvest is going to starve next year. There *is* going to be famine. Just, too late to help us here.

"Any sabotage we can do is a plus. And the next!"

One of the *centeniers*, barely more than a boy, grinned. "We've got some captured liveries, Demoiselle-Captain! I have men who are brave enough to try getting through those trenches in disguise. It's no lack of chivalry to sabotage the enemy."

Ash just stopped herself saying *And it isn't chivalrous when you come back by trebuchet, either.*

"If you can get men out," she said grimly, "what they have to do is kill my sister."

Bishop John's expression showed extreme distaste. He said nothing. Nor did Philippe Ternant – the old man, after a meal, and in this warm chamber, might have been asleep. There was no distaste or disinterest from the officers.

"Take the Faris out, and the Wild Machines are stopped cold. I suspect the Visigoth army is, too. Okay, we'll discuss this one in detail in a minute – we should send out some two-man and four-man teams, and try to assassinate her, but it won't be easy. The rag-heads can have patrols in those ditches twenty-four hours a day—"

"But if we could do it!" de la Marche exclaimed. "It would prevent their miracle; it would throw the legions here into confusion; it might save Dijon, or buy us time to break out, or time enough for the army in the north to march here!"

Another of the *centeniers*, whose name she could not remember, said acidly, "*If* you know where she is, my lord. She may have withdrawn her HQ to the rear of the enemy camp. She may have withdrawn it to a nearby town or fortress. I grant you, spies may tell us where she is – but we have to retrieve them first."

"Okay." Ash stopped pacing, now at the far end of the table, looking down at the seated Burgundian knights. "Okay: any more?"

"Send out heralds."

The voice was Florian's. Ash glanced back at her in surprise.

"Send out heralds. If you're right, the Faris knows something's badly wrong. She might talk to us. Negotiate."

Ash thought de la Marche's face held a certain scepticism, but he said mildly, "There are the heralds of the ducal household, your Grace. They stand ready."

"Any more?"

Robert Anselm rumbled, "We could do a mass assault, if we could get over those fucking trenches, boss – but I don't even know what strength of troops there are in the city, total."

Thanks, Roberto.

"Okay, that's a good point." Ash's circumnavigation of the long table brought her back past Florian to her own chair. She leaned on the tall carved oak back, looking across at Olivier de la Marche. "You want to give the overall picture here?"

"Demoiselle-Captain."

Olivier de la Marche fumbled at ink-stained lists on the tablecloth, in front of him, but did not look down at them. He kept his gaze on Florian – weighing her, Ash thought suddenly – contrasting this exiled Burgundian noblewoman with the man he had followed through battle and court for so many years. *And Charles has only been dead two days. Christus, how he must miss him!*

Philippe Ternant opened lizard-eyes and said, perfectly alertly, "We are not the strength we were. At one time, your Grace, I might have offered you a hundred chamberlains, with myself as first chamberlain; a hundred chaplains under your first chaplain—"

Olivier de la Marche waved the old man to silence. Ash could see acknowledgement of the respite in the glance that went between them.

Grief almost indistinguishable in his tone, de la Marche said, "We had high casualties at Auxonne. Your Grace, before that field, I could have offered you two thousand men as your personal household troops alone. Forty mounted chamberlains and gentlemen of the Duke's chamber died with the standard at Auxonne; and of four hundred cavalry, fifty survive."

The atmosphere around the table changed, the men's expressions taking on more weight, more memory. Feeling how it did not exclude her, Ash realises: I have been watched, up at the north-west gate. And at Auxonne, too.

De la Marche said, "I myself led what survives of sixteen one-hundred-strong companies of mounted archers and household infantry back to Dijon. There are three hundred of us."

He kept a steady gaze on Floria del Guiz.

"We lost our bombards, serpentines, and mortars on that field. Of the army itself, there died men-at-arms to the number of one thousand, one hundred and five—" He looked down at the slanting ink lines on the paper he held. "Mounted archers, upwards of three thousand; crossbowmen, one thousand or less; the archers on foot, eight hundred; the billmen, fifteen hundred or more."

Romont, Lacombe, and two or three of the other officers stared down at the table.

Florian said nothing. Ash saw her lips move, soundless. Hearing it listed made her own gut turn over, remembering that half-dark wet morning scarred by Greek Fire. It must be worse, she thought, for a surgeon who only sees the result of such numbers, and never the butchery that brings it about.

"Your Grace, I may still offer you your *archier de corps*, but there is one captain now, and not two; twenty men, not forty. They are your bodyguard; they will die to keep you alive. For the rest, I have re-structured the companies of Berghes and Loyecte and Saint-Seigne." He nodded acknowledgement to those *centeniers*. "If I could make up twenty full companies in Dijon now, I would count us rich. What strength we have is knights, foot archers and arquebusiers, and billmen, in the main. No more than two thousand men."

"The Lion is down to forty-eight lances," Robert Anselm put in. "Mostly men-at-arms, archers, and hackbutters; some cannon. The company's light guns are still in Carthage. Unless the rag-heads shipped them north and they're out there in the artillery park."

Angelotti gave him a filthy look.

De la Marche said, "We have scouts enough in towers and on the walls to give us warning of where an attack will come. If every man attends to the trumpets and standards, we can deploy our companies well enough to cover an attack against any part of the walls. Perhaps two attacks at once." He opened his mouth as if to complete the thought, and stopped.

We had a hard enough job holding one gate against one attack. They've got the man-power to put two full-strength attacks in at once, or three.

And we've got far too few troops for a break-out.

Ash shifted herself up off the chair-back, careless of scratching the golden oak; steel plates sliding, tassets shifting on buff leather straps. A fierce restlessness kept her from sitting down, kept her on her feet and moving. "I want the companies' duties rotated. Nobody gets the same section of wall for more than twenty-four hours."

Lacombe scowled up at her as she passed. "They will say, demoiselle, that you do that to spare your own men – and mine – their constant danger at the north-west gate."

"They can say what they like." Ash halted. "I don't want the rag-heads knowing which Franks they'll be up against, and I don't want anybody getting used to the Visigoth unit they're facing. I don't want familiarity – that's when men start getting bribed to open postern gates. So we'll do it my way, okay?"

He nodded briskly. "We'll see to it, Demoiselle-Captain."

"That's 'Captain'. Or 'Captain-General'." She grinned. "Or 'Boss'."

With enough eye-contact to make it seem a small contest of wills, Lacombe said – as if he had not cheerfully been saying it for forty-eight hours now, up on the walls – "We'll see to it, boss."

Her silk arming doublet is clammy, under her armour, with new sweat. Two thousand five hundred men, and all the miles of wall to be guarded—!

"Okay," she went on smoothly, walking around to de la Marche's seat. "So now let's move on. Messire, when I sent Father Paston to you, before the hunt – I know there was one Visigoth report from Flanders." She spoke over the rising mutter of interest. "By that time I was dictating in my sleep! Let's have your clerk or mine read it out. We need to know now what chance we've got of the northern army raising this siege – and I think it was a very recent report?"

De la Marche frowned, fretting among the papers piled on the desk. A tonsured clerk got up from beside the Bishop of Cambrai, searching more of the papers. Ash sensed movement, shifted, and Rickard, blushing, reached past her and took a document from the heap.

"Father Paston's hand, boss," he explained. "Shall I read it?"

He automatically looked at Ash; Ash, as automatically, nodded permission; and only afterwards saw the surgeon-Duchess's expression of quiet amusement. Ash noted it had gone right past the *centeniers*, too.

The boy seated himself at the table, close to a patch of bright sunlight, and spread out his folded sheets of paper. Ash admired the neat chancery hand, upside down.

"This is something Godfrey heard, in the *machina rei militaris*?" Florian herself reached for wine, and poured it into her cup, not bothering to call over a page. De la Marche frowned, caught between social embarrassment – *a Duchess should not do this!* – and an inability to criticise his sovereign.

"Yeah. A Visigoth report, from before the Faris stopped using the *machina*."

Florian tapped the table with the foot of her goblet. "So. Does it tell us about Duchess Margaret? Who are her forces, where are they, who is she fighting?"

Memory of dictating this, in the early hours, sparked a memory. Ash said, "Strictly speaking, it'll be Margaret of York, Dowager Duchesse de Bourgogne, now."

Are we going to have trouble because Charles's daughter Marie ought to inherit? She watched the Burgundians' faces. *No. Florian hunted the hart. Look at them: they're unshakable.*

Ash signalled to Rickard. The boy ran his fingers down one sheet of paper, his lips moving, until he reached the part he wanted to read aloud. "'The town of Le Crotoy fell to us, this day, the thirteenth in the sign of the scorpion.'"[20] Aware of the captains listening, his voice strengthened. "'Glory to the King-Caliph Gelimer, under the hand of the One True God, who will remember that our treaty with the Frankish king, Louis, forces him to help us. Since the Burgundian town of Crotoy is close to the French border, we bid him allow us to cross his territory, and to re-supply our legions, which he did. And therefore we fell upon the men in Crotoy.'"

"Devious little fuck!" Ash muttered. "Louis, I mean."

Olivier de la Marche cleared his throat. "I know my lady Margaret had planned to write to Louis, as she is sister to the English King as well as Duchess of Burgundy, and beg him to come to her aid. The Spider long supported both sides in the English wars. There was a chance he'd change his allegiance from the Anjou woman[21] to York, and to us. He has made overtures to King Edward, her brother, since he took the throne, and is paying him a pension."

"He's not going to bolster up Anglo-Burgundian power on the French borders," Florian said, and as they stared at her, shrugged and added, "I've listened to Messire Ternant and my other counsellors. Louis sees the Visigoths as a useful counterweight to Burgundy and the English."

"And the French will expect the King-Caliph to hold what he's conquered." Ash added, "They'll be shit-scared, right now, about the Darkness – they'll know it's spread everywhere, even to Iberia, where Carthage gets its grain. Louis's probably hoping the Visigoths can take it away!"

"Can they?" Rickard broke in. He flushed. "Sorry, my lord de la Marche—"

"Rickard's one of my junior officers, my lord," Ash said smoothly. "I let everybody speak in officer meetings. Then I make my own mind up."

Floria spoke to the boy. "Rickard, I think if the Visigoths could take the Eternal Twilight away, they'd have done it by now."

Lacombe and a couple of the others – Berghes? Loyecte? – grunted knowing agreement.

"Carry on," Ash directed.

---

[20] *c.* 3 November? If this is the astrological sign of Scorpio.

[21] Margaret of Anjou, wife of the English King Henry VI; funded in some of her attempts to regain the crown for her husband or her son by Louis XI of France. In 1476, Margaret is reported as just having been ransomed from England, and present in the French court.

Rickard read without hesitation from the cramped lines. "'The Frankish woman and her forces fell back from Le Crotoy, and it is likely she will make for Bruges, Ghent, or Antwerp. Be aware, great Caliph, that in Ghent, because of the trouble to her that her Chancellor has been, she was forced to disband the estates there.'"[22]

"Who's the Chancellor?" Ash looked at Ternant.

Florian cut in. "Guillaime Hugonet, Lord of Saillant, Chancellor of Burgundy." She spoke as if she had memorised the name. "I'm told he's good at raising taxes. She can pay that army. He's a good orator . . . Apparently he was with Margaret before, in Flanders and Brabant."

Philippe Ternant inclined his head in agreement.

"Hugonet may be good at keeping the northern army funded and in the field," Olivier de la Marche snarled, "but even under war conditions, I doubt that anyone will put up with him! The man made innumerable political enemies in Ghent, and Bruges. A hard-liner, demoiselle. If Guillaime Hugonet has made the Lady Margaret disband the estates, that means the cities will be in a ferment."

"I guess Anthony de la Roche is still her military commander?" Ash speculated.

Another of the *centeniers* exclaimed, "He's one of our late Duke's father's bastards. He ought to be loyal, if nothing else!"[23]

Ash caught Florian's eye. She had no need to say *professional rivalry*; it was plain from the surgeon-Duchess's expression that she deduced exactly the same thing.

"Rickard?"

"'The Frankish woman has yet an army, by virtue that she is pious in her heretic religion. Know, great Gelimer, that she does not swear, either by God or the Saints; that she is said to hold mass wherever the army travels, three times a day; that she has with her her musicians, choir, and has mass sung. She travels always as befits a lady, riding side-saddle, always chaperoned by priests. My heart is cold, King-Caliph, when I tell you how much support she has among the common folk, who still revere her husband's name.'"

"This was a fortnight ago?" Captain Romont murmured. "I wonder how long he held his command after this report got back to Carthage?"

Ash grinned at the curly-haired knight, and gestured for Richard to read on.

"'The Frankish woman has with her some eight thousand men—'"

Someone at the far end of the table whistled. Ash glanced in that direction and saw men grinning. *Eight thousand! Now there's a reassuring figure . . .*

"'—all in Burgundian colours, and at first under the command of Philippe of Croy, the Lord of Chimay, but after his death,[24] under command of Anthony,

---

[22] The Flemish part of the estates-general: representatives of the cities and provinces there. In fact, these events appear to closely parallel the history of the early part of 1477, after Duke Charles's death in battle at Nancy.

[23] Anthony de la Roche was taken prisoner at Nancy, in January of 1477, when Charles the Bold was killed. Rather than staying loyal to Margaret, or indeed to his half-niece Mary of Burgundy, he transferred his allegiance with breath-taking haste to Louis XI, and thus retained his lands in the conquered Duchy.

[24] In fact, the Lord of Chimay was taken prisoner at the battle of Nancy, on 5 January 1477, and

duke's bastard, Count of La Roche. This man, great King-Caliph, is a notable soldier. In battle, he has been in command of the ducal banner, and often was deputed to act as regent for the dead Duke. He is her first chamberlain, and men say that she holds him dear in her heart, for that, when they held tournament to celebrate her wedding to his half-brother Charles, he was gravely injured, wearing her favour—'"

"Oh, spare me!" Florian sighed.

Ash chuckled. "I like this one. He picks up all the gossip."

"Eight thousand men," Olivier de la Marche repeated.

More soberly, Ash said, "About the same number that we've got sitting outside the walls. Doesn't she get more? Rickard, where's the next bit?"

The boy shuffled through four sheets of paper, bringing one to the top of the pile, and smoothing it out. He squinted at the black lettering.

"'I have heard – under the One True God to your ear, King-Caliph – that when she had dismissed the councils of her common people, she was forced to ride personally from city to city, to The Hague, Leiden, Delft, and Gouda, to raise more men. But I do not fear to tell you that she has a scant one thousand more.[25] Rumour says she has made these cities melt down all their bells to make new cannon. Our three legions push north and east, hard in her pursuit now, and before long there will be more victories to gladden the heart of Carthage.'"

"Before long," Ash said, "that man will be digging latrines. Christus! I can see why the Faris wanted to be up north, not here. That's where the action is!"

"I see that both you and she wish to meet each other on the field of battle, Demoiselle-Captain. That is commendable fire and courage." Olivier de la Marche reached out with one fleshy hand and patted Floria's arm, oblivious to the look of dry humour on her face. "However, this tells us of one minor victory for them, but Lady Margaret and the lord of la Roche leading an army – this is good news!"

"It's good news fourteen or fifteen days old." Ash drummed her fingertips lightly against her leg armour. "It's too early to say for sure, but if the Mère-Duchesse has had another fortnight since this, and she hasn't been defeated – we could see her coming south."

Into the optimistic silence, Florian said:

"There's no mention of Lord-*Amir* Leofric. Or the Faris herself. Or the *machina rei militaris* itself."

"No. The reports the other way – to the Faris – have said nothing .. . I don't know who this 'cousin' Sisnandus is, who took over the House after we left, after the earthquake. I don't know if Leofric's more seriously injured than I first thought." She momentarily forgot the *centeniers* of the Burgundian army, staring unseeing into distance. "But remember, nothing's happened to make the *King-Caliph* distrust the Stone Golem's strategic advice. As far as he's concerned, all this is a sign of God's favour! If it's still telling him 'take

after being ransomed, returned to loyally serve Mary of Burgundy and her heirs, in Duke Maximilian's court.

[25] In the winter of 1476/77, raising troops for her husband, Margaret is reported as having raised another four thousand men from these towns.

Burgundy' – that's what he's going to do. Damn: we need Margaret's army here *now*!"

With the last word, her frustration broke out; her hand went up and came down flat on the table, with a hollow gun-shot sound. Rickard twitched, and wiped his squinting eyes.

"Suppose God grants the Mère-Duchesse the defeat of the legions in the north." Olivier de la Marche swept extraneous papers aside and uncovered a map. "It will not be easy to feed her men, away from the rich cities, but suppose Lady Margaret's commander commandeers boats, Demoiselle-Captain. Rivers will bring them south faster than a forced march. There is still sunlight over Burgundy. The Meuse and the Marne will not have frozen." He bowed his head towards Florian. "Your Grace, if they can win in the north, they *can* come to us. God send them a victory!"

"Soon would be nice," Ash remarked wryly. Over his chuckle, she said, "Okay: we talk about this, we make initial deployments, we wait for Margaret, we see if we can kill the Faris before she gets here. Anything anyone thinks has been left out?"

Silence.

Antonio Angelotti said languidly, "Just one thing, boss. May we stop holding council in the Tour Philippe, at least in daylight? *Every* Visigoth gun-team out there's using it as a marker for target practice!"

The *centeniers* laughed, one man leaning over to speak to another, two knights sharing ale from the server's jug; and her stomach clenched, painfully.

Don't be stupid, girl! – it's obvious from this window – you can see they're not trying to deploy for an attack yet. I don't need to be up at the gate . . .

I can't leave these guys yet.

Green Christ, am I going to spend all my time now *talking*?

"Boss need to hit something?" Florian queried, with acid penetration.

"Boss isn't going to get the chance, is she?" Ash continued to look, to memorise faces: *Romont, Loyecte, Berghes—no, the skinny-legged one in Gothic arm-defences is Berghes—* "Because that isn't what the Big Boss does, is it?"

"You're not the Big Boss," Florian said briskly. She raised her voice for attention. "Right. The Duke stayed here in Dijon. It didn't help him. If digging a long tunnel is what it takes, dig one. Start it now."

Rickard automatically began to scribble on a sheet of paper.

Floria added, "They could attack us at any time. So send out the heralds. But send out – was it the Sieur de Loyecte's men? Yes. Them too."

"Florian—"

De la Marche said, "Your Grace—"

"It's my responsibility."

The surgeon-turned-Duchess held up a pale hand. For all the white samite that covered the back of it, it remained what it was: the hand of a woman who lives out of doors, and who handles sharpened steel.

"My responsibility," she repeated. "Even if it's only for today, then the ultimate responsibility is *mine*."

Ash stared. After a moment, both de la Marche and Bishop John bowed their heads.

"Just as well you got a surgeon," Floria added, sardonically. "I've had to take responsibility for men dying long before this. All right. Send out your killers."

For all her certainty, there was a dazed numbness in her expression that Ash recognised.

"Having someone die when you're digging an arquebus ball out of their stomach isn't the same as ordering a death. Florian, I was going to order it anyway."

"She is either Duchess or she is not," Philippe Ternant said, speaking without opening his fragile closed eyelids. "Demoiselle Ash, you must act with her permission."

Ash bit down on a raucous remark. *Florian doesn't need that right now.*

Florian rubbed her fingers one against the other. "Ash, I have never had the least desire to be Duchess. If I had any taste for Burgundian politics, I would have come to court, here, when I was a girl."

Ash glimpsed momentary dismay on several faces.

Still decisively, Floria announced, "I'll come into the palace daily, but I can't run the company hospital at a distance. Baldina isn't good enough unsupervised. I'm staying at the company tower. I'll be talking to the abbots about additional hospices for the civilian wounded. Ash, I'll be taking over the ground floor, too. The men can sleep in the cellars."

That isn't the way to do this! These guys want you here: you're their Duchess . . .

Holding back a desire to yell at her surgeon, Ash said, "You wouldn't rather put the wounded in the cellars, given the bombardment?"

Floria nodded, sharply.

"Okay, I'll get that sorted."

A distant roar sounded outside. Ash paced over to one window, then the next, peering through the gaps between shutter and frame. One gave her the glimpse of dragon-tail fire, arcing through the sky.

"Isn't that nice. The Nones bombardment. You could set the town clock by that crew down at the south bridge. Angeli, you got a point about this tower. No need to make it *easy* for them."

The atmosphere relaxed a little at that. *But I don't want to be mending fences all the time . . .* Meeting Floria's green gaze, she saw the raw edge of panic that underlay her determination.

"Okay, guys. That's given us a framework to work in. Ten minutes' stand-down, for beer and bitching." She grinned. "Then back here, and we'll start working things out in detail."

Hidden under the noise of their chairs scraping back from the table, Florian said shakily, "I need Margaret's army soon. Don't I?"

The council went on past the early November sunset, and into evening. Servants brought in sweet-smelling pure wax candles, and Ash sighed, in the middle of a discussion, suddenly breaking off to think *This is luxury!*, remembering the noxious tallow tapers that are all the company's stores now hold.

Rank has its privileges. A cynical smile pulled up one side of her mouth, and

845

she caught Romont's unwary, amazed look, and went back to thumping the table and shuffling gold plate on the tablecloth into the disposition of Burgundian companies around Dijon's walls.

"Half his men are merchants' sons!" one of the *centeniers*, Saint-Seigne, thundered. "I will not put my knights at the same gate as Loyecte's men!"

Barely withholding the words, Ash sighed internally. *Oh for fuck's sake!*

"This is a council of weariness," Olivier de la Marche said tactfully. He turned to Florian. "Your Grace, none of us have slept. There is much to do, to make certain we are as fully prepared as we can be. Half of us will sleep through the day, now, half through the night."

"Except the Maid of Burgundy, who'll be up until Matins, and rise at Lauds . . ." Robert Anselm whispered to Ash.

"Ah, bugger off, *rosbif*!"

He gave a happy, rumbling chuckle.

"Christ, you *do* need sleep!" Ash elbowed him. "Florian—"

"Don't go anywhere yet," the surgeon said bluntly, over the noise of men rising, bowing, and withdrawing themselves from the ducal chamber.

The verdant-robed Bishop of Cambrai rose from his chair, as the rest did. Instead of moving towards the chamber door, Bishop John walked back down the table towards the surgeon-Duchess Floria.

"Bishop John." Florian stabbed a long, white finger towards Ash. "About tomorrow night – this is the witness I want at my investiture."

He beamed. "Madame cher Duchesse, of course."

Aware that Anselm and Angelotti were waiting for her, talking urgently to the readmitted escort, Ash protested, "I haven't got time to spare to go through another damn hours-long public ceremony, Florian!"

The Bishop startled. "Public? The people don't need to see this. They know who the *Duchesse* is. They recognise her in the streets. Taking the ducal coronet is between her and God."

"Another good reason why you don't need me," Ash said dryly.

"The *Duchesse* wishes you to stand private vigil with her, and myself, and the other two witnesses, through the night. The following morning's mass gives her the crown, but nothing men can do can make her less, or more, than she already is."

"I'm busy! I've got a fu— a company to run! No, an army! I've got to look through all the duty-rolls of the Burgundian companies—"

Florian's hand closed over her arm, with all the strength of surgeon's fingers. "Ash. I want a friend there. You don't have to tell me you think it's a load of cock."

Startled, Ash rapped out, "You don't have to tell me you think exactly the same thing!"

Floria smiled painfully, ignoring the churchman's expression. "That isn't the point. Remember when you talked to Charles? You want to know 'why Burgundy'. So do I. I'm Duchess, Ash. I want to know, why Burgundy – and, why me?"

Ash blinked. Sleeplessness shuddered through her. She put the weakness to the dark back of her mind where she loses such things. "Will this 'vigil' of yours tell us why Burgundy?"

Florian switched her gaze from Ash to the Burgundian bishop. "It better had."

VII

She slept an hour in one company's guardhouse, down by the south gate; another hour in the armoury, while clerks sorted out inventories. The rest of the night and the following morning saw her among hackbutters, archers, squires to knightly men-at-arms; judging their morale, hearing their officers' reports, but most of all, letting them see her.

"A Pucelle?" one noseless veteran of Duke Philip's campaigns remarked. "Quite right too – God sent one to the French, the least He could do was send one to us!"

His spoiled speech gave her the option of appearing not to understand. She merely grinned at the billman. "Granddad, *you're* just surprised to find there's still a virgin in Dijon."

That was being repeated, with embellishments, before she left that barracks, and it followed her all the way to the Viscount-Mayor's hall, where it was received with less delight and more shock. By that stage – talking all the time to two, three, four men simultaneously – she was past caring what civilians thought.

At noon, back at the tower, stripped to her shirt by her pages, she sat down suddenly on her pallet, dizzy enough that she tipped over slowly and sprawled face forwards; asleep before she was conscious of touching the straw-filled linen.

She slept through the short light hours of the afternoon, waking once at the noise of her pages, three nine-year-old boys huddled around the great hearth, polishing the rust-spotted plates of her armour: cuirass, cannons, vambrace, pauldrons . . . The smell of neat's-foot oil being worked into the leather straps roused her enough to lift her head off the bed, blinking.

Across from her, on the other side of the hearth's heat, Robert Anselm lay slumped asleep on a truckle-bed; one huge, immobile, silent lump. She hitched one elbow in, to get her arm under her and push herself up.

"Boss." Rickard squatted down beside her palliasse. "Message from Captain Angelotti: 'You're not indispensable, the company is managing perfectly well without you: go back to sleep!'"

Ash grunted an indistinguishable protest; was flat face-down and asleep again before she could properly voice it. When she woke for the second time, one of the pages was cutting bread by the hearth-fire and nibbling crusts, and Angelotti was sprawled on the truckle-bed – asleep on his back, with a face like an angel, and snoring like a hog in a wallow.

Rickard looked up at her from where he knelt, scouring her sallet-visor with the finest white sand.

"Boss, message from Captain Anselm and Messire de la Marche: 'You're not indispensable; the *army's* managing perfectly well—'"

"Ah, bollocks!" she said thickly.

She did not dream: there was no hint of the scent of boar, or the chill taste of snow; nothing but deep unconsciousness. *Godfrey, if he is a presence, is at too deep a level to touch her conscious soul.*

When sleep finally let her go, she rolled over in a tangle of warm linen shirt, blankets, and furs; and the slanting light from one slit-window put sunset's red gold across her face.

"The doc – the *Duchess* sent word," Rickard said, as soon as he saw she was awake. "She wants you at the chapel."

She arrived in the bathhouse of the palace's Mithraic chapel as Floria del Guiz stepped up out of the wooden tub, and servants swathed her in pure white linen. Water dampened the cloth. The steam that filled the air began to dissipate quickly in the chill.

"This is what you call immediate, is it?" Florian called.

Ash handed her cloak and hat to her page, and turned back to find the surgeon-Duchess temporarily wrapped in a vast fur-trimmed blue velvet robe. Ash walked across the flagstones towards her.

"I had stuff to do. I needed to talk with Jonvelle and Jussey and the rest of Olivier's *centeniers*." Ash yawned, stifling it with her fist. She looked at Florian, eyes bright, as the woman waved her attendants away. "*And* the refugee French and German knights, and their men. Very nice, everyone's being. We'll see what happens when it comes to me giving them orders . . ."

"Next time, get here when I ask."

Floria spoke harshly. Ash opened her mouth to snap back. The woman added, "I'm *supposed* to be a Duchess. You're showing me up in front of these people. If I *do* have any authority – I don't need it undermined."

"Uh." Ash stared at her. Finally she shrugged, put her hand through her cropped silver hair, and said, "Yeah. Okay. Fair enough."

They stared at each other for a few seconds.

"I understand," Ash protested.

"Boss's vanity is hurt."

"You're—" Ash stopped: rephrased *you're not really a Duchess!* "You know, whatever it is you do with the Wild Machines – you're not a Duchess to me or the company."

A little wistful, the older woman said, "I'm glad to hear it."

"But I still don't have time to waste on this. If it is a waste. Have you spoken to that bishop yet?"

"He won't say anything until I go through this vigil."

"Ah, fuck it. Let's do it, then. Who needs sleep anyway!"

The Duchess's attendants emerged again from behind the long hessian curtains that separated each of the great baths; one with wine, and two others with towels and fresh clothing. Ash stood absent-mindedly watching as they unwrapped and dried the gold-haired woman, her mind running through roster-lists.

Floria turned her head, opened her mouth as if to say something, flushed, and turned away. Pinkness flooded the skin of her throat and bare breasts. Ash – expecting a caustic remark, rather than embarrassment – abruptly felt herself colour, and turned her back on the group of women.

Does she feel like I used to feel when Fernando watched me?

It is five months since she touched him, in bed; her fingers still remember the smooth silk heat of his cock, the velvet electricity of his skin; the flex and thrust of his bare buttocks under her hands as he pushes inside her. Fernando: who may be dead, now, in the Carthage earthquake – or, if he isn't, has likely divorced her by now. Too dangerous for a renegade German now in a Visigoth household to have a Frankish wife . . .

And to be the brother of a Burgundian Duchess? Ash suddenly thought. Hmm. I wonder if he's in even more trouble, if he's still alive?

"Let's get going." Florian appeared at her shoulder. She eyed Ash's start with curiosity, but did not say anything. A faint pinkness remained to her skin, but it might have come from the rough towelling, and nothing more.

"How long is this going to take?"

"Until Prime tomorrow."

"All night? Fuck . . ."

They had dressed Florian in a plain white linen over-gown, and under it a gown of white lambswool, also with no decoration. A linen coif covered her short gold hair. As the women withdrew, she looked over her shoulder, snapped her fingers, and beckoned; and the youngest girl came back with the fur-lined blue velvet robe.

Ash watched Florian struggling into the voluminous garment. Turning to signal her own page to bring back her hat and campaigning cloak – the stone walls' chill soaking the air already, even so soon after nightfall – she smiled, mildly. "Who needs a vigil? You ain't having any trouble taking to behaving like a Duchess . . ."

Florian stopped pushing her arm through the slit of a hanging sleeve, and stared back over her shoulder at the departing attendants. "That's not fair!"

Ash reached out, twitched the sleeve down over Florian's shoulder, and turned towards the curtain that masked the tunnel leading to the chapel. Leaving her page and escort behind, she stepped forward and held back the coarse cloth.

"Duchess takes precedence, I believe . . ."

Florian did not laugh.

Torches in cressets lit the low passage, their smoke making the air acrid. Ash found her fingers automatically going to her belt and her dagger. The relief of being in civilian clothes and out of armour for an hour made her body blissful, but chill; and she swung her cloak around her shoulders as she walked into the tunnel after Florian.

Florian came to a dead halt in front of her. Without turning, she said, "I had someone ordered out of the council room this afternoon."

Ash let the hessian curtain fall behind her. It cut off sound: left them isolated under the low granite roof. She stepped around the motionless woman.

"And they went." Florian raised her head. "If I'd wanted to, I could have had men throw them out."

"If you wanted, you could have more than that."

Ash glanced up ahead: the further curtain did not stir. No priests yet.

"That's the problem." Floria's voice fell flat and muffled, deadened by the ancient stone.

"Ah, you wait," Ash said reflectively, linking her arm through the surgeon's; beginning to pace towards the far end of the corridor. "You wait till you want someone thrown out *real* bad. Then, you start cutting corners . . ."

"You mean, I make some illegitimate use of this power I've been stuck with?" Under the demand, Florian's voice had a tone of panic.

"Everybody does it at least once. Every lance-leader, every *centenier*. Every nobleman."

"And yours was?" Floria snapped.

"Mine?" Ash shrugged, letting her arm drop out of the crook of the woman's elbow, maintaining her easy pace towards the far curtains. "Oh, that's got to be . . . the first time I got six of my men to cripple the living shite out of somebody. Back in – I don't remember – some northern French town."

She was conscious of Florian's face in profile as they walked, the glowing torches casting red light on her cheekbones. A tightly controlled shiver went through the older woman.

"What happened?"

"Some civilian said, 'Hey, girlie, you can wear hose, and you can wave a sword around, but you're still a cunt who has to squat down to piss' – he thought that was very funny. I thought, okay, I have six hefty guys here, wearing mail that I paid for, and my livery . . . They kicked the crap out of him; smashed his face and both knees."

The face Florian turned was desperate. As if she searched for an excuse, she asked, "And how long would your authority have lasted, if you'd allowed him to say that without reprisal?"

"Oh, about five minutes." Ash raised a brow. "But then, I didn't have to have them cripple him. And I didn't have to go into town that afternoon looking for trouble."

She was unaware of her own expression: part hooligan-enjoyment, part shame and regret. "I was pretty young. Fourteen, maybe. Florian, you're going to get this. The first time five hundred guys stand there and cheer you to the echo, and then go piling into combat because *you* say so . . . you start feeling you can do *anything*. And sometimes you will."

"I don't want to find out if I will."

Ash put out her hand to draw aside the second curtain.

"Tell me that if we're still here in six months. Once you taste it, you can't go back. But it isn't worth chucking your weight about." She tugged at the heavy cloth. "After a while, if you do too much of it, people stop listening to you. You're not in charge. You're just out in front . . ."

Florian huddled her gown more tightly over her white robes. "Don't you find it terrifying? You're in charge of an *army*!?"

Ash flashed her a quick grin. "Don't for fuck's sake ask Baldina about my laundry."

Florian, her expression fixed, glanced away without responding.

She needs a serious answer, and I'm too scared to give it.

Ash raised her voice. "Hey, come on! Aren't there any fucking priests *in* this chapel? Where's your bloody bishop?"

A disapproving older female voice said, "He's consecrating the chapel, young demoiselle. Do *you* want to tell him to hurry up?"

Ash stepped into the antechamber expecting, for a second, to see Jeanne Châlon; but the woman facing her looked nothing like the surgeon's noble aunt. Only the voices were similar. Torches smoked in the cold air, and Ash squinted at the fat, round-faced woman in wimple and looped-up kirtles, and at the man behind her, whose face seemed naggingly familiar.

"Demoiselle," the elderly man pulled off his coif. His scalp shone pink in the torchlight. "You won't remember me, I daresay. You might remember Jombert here. He's a fine dog. This is my wife, Margaret. I'm Culariac; Duke's huntsman." He turned watery eyes to Floria del Guiz. "Duchess's huntsman, I should say; pardon me, your Grace."

A cold nose pressed against Ash's fingers. She reached down, and scratched behind the ears of a white lymer sniffing at the fur-trimmed skirts of her demi-gown under her cloak.

"'Jombert'!" she said. "I remember. It was you that came out to the Visigoth camp at the truce, to ask if the hunt could ride."

The man's face broke into a smile at her recognition. His wife continued to scowl. After a few seconds, Ash recognised the look. *Well, I'm not learning to fight in skirts to please her.*

"We're here as your witnesses, your Grace," the old man added, with another bow. What self-importance there might have been in his expression vanished as the lymer abandoned Ash, gave a quick sniff to the surgeon-Duchess, and padded back to nose at his master's thigh. Culariac gazed down in pure affection.

Which is he more proud of, Ash wondered; *his hound, or his position here? He'll be drinking on the strength of both, tomorrow night.*

If the town isn't taken by then.

"'Witnesses'?" she belatedly queried.

"Just to see her Grace does stay in there, all night." The woman jerked her thumb at the further side of the anteroom, where a curtain masked another doorway. Woven in green and gold thread, it shimmered heavily in the dull light.

"We'll stay out here," the woman Margaret said. "No, don't you worry, your Grace; I've brought some sewing with me; Culariac will wake me if I sleep, and I'll wake him."

"Oh." Florian looked blank. "Right."

A faint, almost imperceptible vibration ran through the stone floor. Ash identified it as a trebuchet strike, not far from the palace itself. The old woman touched her breast, making the sign of the Horns.

Falling in beside Florian as she walked towards the far doorway, Ash murmured, "Where the fuck did they find *her*?"

"Chosen by lot." Florian kept her voice equally low.

"God give me strength!"

"That, too."

"Your damn bishop had better give us some answers."

"Yes."

"You picked a real worldly priest there."

"Why would I want a devout one?"

Jolted by the answer, Ash shoved aside the curtain embroidered with oak leaves. The granite facing of the walls and ceiling gave way to natural limestone. The floor of the passage dipped, so that they walked down a long series of very wide and shallow steps. Ash saw that the torch-holders spiked now into undressed, grey-white stone; the marks of chisels still plain in the walls. Smoke wavered in the draught from air-vents carved into living rock.

"Won't be so cold if we're underground," she remarked pragmatically.

Florian hauled up the train of her gown, where it scraped along the limestone floor, and bundled the cloth up in her arms in front of her as she walked. "My father had his knighthood vigil here. I remember him telling me about this, when I was very young. It's almost all I can remember of him." She glanced up at the vaulted ceiling, as if she could see through stone to the ancient palace above. "He was a favourite of Duke Philip. Before he changed his loyalties to the Emperor Frederick."

"Hell. I knew Fernando had to get it from somewhere."

"My father was married in Cologne cathedral." Florian turned her head; smiled briefly at Ash's evident shock. "We got the news, in the end, from Constanza. Another good reason for me not to have come to your wedding."

Ash caught her shoe on the uneven stone, stumbling over the threshold in Floria's wake, and for a second she did not see the smoky, tiny chamber that they entered, but the soaring pillars and gothic arches of the cathedral, the shafts of light, and Fernando reaching out to touch her and say *I smell piss . . .*

Worse than a whore! she thought fiercely. He wouldn't have *laughed* at a whore.

Ash made the sign of the Horns automatically, aware that Florian was standing stock-still in front of her now, her head raised, staring. The chapel's terracotta tiles felt uneven, worn by centuries of men walking to the iron grille to celebrate the blood-mass. Ash shivered, in a room barely twenty feet square: claustrophobia not eased by the torchlight falling from above, through the ceiling-grating.

"My feet are cold," Florian whispered.

"If we're in here all night, more than your feet will get cold!" Ash kept her voice low with an effort. As her vision adjusted, and filled with dully glittering luminescence, she added, "Green Christ!"

Every free square foot of the walls was covered in mosaic, each square of the mosaic not glass, but precious gem; cut to glow in the shifting torchlight.

"Look at that. A king's ransom. More than a king's ransom!" Florian muttered. "No wonder Louis's jealous."

"King's ransom be buggered, you could equip a dozen legions if this lot's real . . ." Ash leaned in close, peering at a mosaic of the birth of the Green Christ – his Imperial Jewish mother sprawled under the oak, half-dead from bringing forth her son; the Baby suckling at the Sow; the Eagle, in the oak's branches, lifting up his head, depicted about to take wing on the flight that will – in three days – bring Augustus and his legions to the right spot in the wild German forest. And in the next panel, Christus Viridianus heals his mother, with the leaves of the oak.

"Might be rubies." Ash winced at the wax running from the candlestick over the back of her hand. She held the light closer to the wall, studying the neat squares that delineated a puddle of birth-blood. She felt a sudden nausea. With an effort, she added, "Might just be garnets."

Florian walked a quick circuit of the walls, glancing at each panel briefly – Viridianus and his legion in Judea, gone native after the Persian wars; Viridianus speaking with the Jewish elders; Viridianus and his officers worshipping Mithras. Then Augustus's funeral, the coronation of his true son, and, in the background, the adopted son Tiberius and the conspirators, the desire for the oak tree upon which they will hang Viridianus – bones broken, no blood shed – already plain on their faces.

One circuit of the room, back to where Ash stands by the birth; and the last panel is Constantine, three centuries later, converting the Empire to the religion of Viridianus, whom the Jews still consider nothing more than a Jewish prophet, but whom the followers of Mithras have long and faithfully known to be the Son of the Unconquered Sun.

"Doesn't look like anyone's held mass yet," Ash said doubtfully.

In the centre of the room, two stone blocks are set, to chain the bulls. Between them, an iron grate is let into the floor, stiff with old black debris of sacrifices. Featureless darkness showed beneath. The iron bars were not wet.

Ash tried the iron gates that closed off the shallow passage leading up towards the air. The heavy chains hardly rattled. She stared, for a moment, at the ridged stone slope, down which the bull is led into this box-like room.

When she turned back, she saw a glimmer in Florian's eye – recognisably laughter. Half-frowning, half on the verge of a giggle, Ash muttered, "What? *What?*"

"They bring a bull for the mass," the older woman said, and snuffled, sounding all herself again. "Wonder what they'd make of a couple of old cows?"

"*Florian!*"

Without any hesitation, the surgeon crossed to the remaining exit: a small wooden door set into the corner of the room. She opened it. The dark stairwell beyond flared with torchlight stirred up by the draught of the door's opening. One glance over her shoulder, and Florian hauled up her gowns and robe clear of her feet, and sidled through the door. Ash stared for a long minute, watching her coiffed head sink lower, walking down the cramped spiral of the stair.

"Wait up, damn it!"

The narrow stair, set into the thick wall, turned back so swiftly on itself that she could never have come down it successfully in armour. The chill granite left damp marks on her furred demi-gown. Florian blocked the light from below. Ash groped in her wake, feeling the wood of a door jamb, and then came out suddenly into an open space with a vast drop in front of her.

"Shiiit . . ."

"This is old. Monks' work." Florian, beside Ash, also stared out into the brick-lined shaft. "Maybe God's grace kept them from falling off!"

Torchlight came down from above through the iron sacrificial grille. It barely stirred the shadows on the walls of the shaft. Far below, more lights glowed – the steadier, less smoky glow of many candles.

The door that Ash had come out of opened all but sheer on to the shaft. Now her eyes adjusted to the dimness, she saw that a stair ran down, deosil, along the side of the wall. Descending . . .

"Let's go." She touched Florian's arm, and slid herself along the tiny platform to put one foot on the first step.

A knee-high wall, studded with mosaic, was the only barrier between the stair and the drop – by no means high enough to be reassuring: one slip, and a body would pivot straight over the stonework.

"Bugger this!" Florian muttered. Glancing back, Ash saw her face shiny with sweat. Her own breath caught in her throat.

"Hang on to my belt."

"No. I'll manage."

"Sooner we're down, the better."

Inhaling the scent of pitch and beeswax, and the dampness of stone and brick, Ash took a breath, set herself a mental pace, and began to walk down the stairs with as much ease as if they were defender's stairs in any castle. The steps were shallow, worn away in the middle with the tread of countless years. At the corner of the shaft, the stairway made a sharp right-angle; continued on down. Her eyes adjusting more now to the light from below, she could see the sketched lines on the far walls: the glitter of mosaic: the stair that they would have to descend. She kept her gaze away from the dark void on her right-hand side. Down and turn. Down and turn. Down: turn.

"There has to be another way in!" Florian snapped, behind her.

"Maybe not. Who's going to come down here but the priests?" Another turn. Pulling off her glove and letting her hand stray out to brush the wall, she kept her orientation; counteracting the pull of the drop. "There's your qualification for the Duke's chaplain, Florian – doesn't suffer from vertigo!"

Another snuffling giggle from behind. "'Duchess's chaplain'!"

I wish it was that easy.

The yellow glow of candles encompassed them. Feeling their heat, Ash glanced up, realising that their light now blocked out the view of the Mithras grating above. She was no more than fifteen or twenty feet above floor-level now. Above tiles marbled red and black – no: terracotta, but with the traces of every day's mass still spilling down from the plain stone block that is the altar.

The last corner: the last steps: the little wall ending; and she stepped out on to the bottom of the shaft, into the chapel, the skin on the pads of her fingers worn rough. Pulling her glove on, Ash said, "Thank God for that!"

Florian jostled her, coming off the stairway in haste. She reached up and wiped her sweating face. Her fair hair glowed in the light of dozens of candles.

"Thank God indeed," a voice said, from the shadows beyond the altar, "but with more devoutness, possibly, demoiselle?"

"Bishop John!"

"Your Grace," he acknowledged Floria del Guiz.

Surprised to find her knees a little weak, Ash took a few determined steps about the chapel that stood at the bottom of the sacrificial shaft. Now, in the candlelight, she could see that it was wider than the shaft itself to east and west: continuing on under a low brick barrel vault either end, one vault containing church plate, the other a painted shrine.

How long before we can ask him *why Burgundy*? And how long before he'll answer?

A novice in a green and white cassock bowed his way past his bishop, carrying a lit wax taper, vanishing up the narrow stairs that clung to the walls. Ash smelled the sweetness of beeswax candles. Within a minute, every inch of this lower end of the shaft glittered. Masons had squared off the limestone; craftsmen had laid mosaics of the Tree, the Bull, the Boar, and – around the marble altar slab, dark with congealed blood – a square of floor taken up by an oval-eyed Green Christ.

With almost simultaneous movement, Florian reached up and dragged the linen coif from her head, and Ash pushed back her hood and took off her hat. She stifled a grin – *both of us have been dressing as men for too long!* – and felt her chilled body relax in the growing heat from the candles.

Beside her, Floria looked questioningly at the Burgundian bishop. "Do we celebrate a mass now?"

"No."

The little round-faced man's voice fell flatly.

"We don't?" Ash realised that she could hear the footsteps of other priests or novices, the sound coming from above, through the grating; but neither the smell nor the sound of a bull-calf.

"I may be accused of trying to repopulate Burgundy on my own," the Bishop of Cambrai said, small black eyes gleaming with something that might have been amusement, "and of loving the fair flesh far too much, but one thing I am not, Madame cher Duchesse Floria, is a hypocrite. I had the opportunity to observe not just your captain here, but yourself, during our meeting in the Tour Philippe. I need not repeat what you said. You're so far estranged from your faith that I think it will take more than one night to bring you in charity with God again."

"Surely not, your Grace?" Ash said smoothly. "The surgeon – the Duchess – here has always taken field-mass with us, and she works with deacons in our hospital—"

"I'm not the inquisition." Bishop John shifted his gaze to her. "I know a heretic when I see one, and I know a good woman driven from God by the cruelty of what circumstances have caused her to do. That's Floria, daughter, and it's you too. If you ever had any faith, I think you lost it in Carthage."

Ash's lips pressed together for a second. "Long before *that*."

"Yes?" His soft black brows went up. "But you've come back from Carthage talking of machines and devices, a woman bred like one of Mithras's bulls – and nothing at all of the hand of God in this. 'Maid of Burgundy'."

Ash shifted, under her cloak, rubbing one fist absently across her belly under the demi-gown.

Bishop John turned back to Florian. "I can't withhold communion if you ask for it, but I can strongly advise that you don't ask."

Beside Ash, Floria del Guiz huffed an exasperated breath, folding her arms across her body. The cloth of her full gown fell down in sculptured folds about her, trailing on the uneven terracotta tiles. The warm light of the candles put a deeper gold into her hair, that fell to her shoulders now it was unconfined by her linen coif; limned her profile; but did little, even warming her skin-tone, to hide the gauntness of her face now.

"So what *do* we do?" Floria asked acidly. "Sit around down here for the night? If that's all, I could be much more use to your duchy if I had some sleep."

Bishop John watched her with a brilliant gaze. "Your Grace, I'm a man of the church, with a very large family of hopeful bastards; and more to come, I should think, flesh being what it is. How should I cast the first stone at *you*? Even without a mass, this is still your vigil."

"Which means?"

"You'll know that, by the end of it." The Bishop of Cambrai reached out, touching the altar as if for reassurance. "So will all of us. Pardon me if I tell you that Messire de la Marche is as anxious as I am to know what you make of this."

"Bet he is," Ash murmured. "Okay, so no mass: what *does* she do, your Grace?"

The flames of the candles flared and dipped, shadows racing across the mosaic walls. The acrid smoke caught in the back of Ash's throat, and she stifled a cough.

"She takes up the ducal crown, if God wills it. I advise some time be spent in meditation." Bishop John bowed his head slightly to Floria.

Ash gave way and cleared her throat with a hacking cough. Wiping at her streaming eyes, she said, "I expected this all to be planned out, your Grace. You're saying Florian can do what she likes?"

"My brother Charles spent his night in prayer here, in full armour, fourteen hours without a break. That told me, at least, what Duke we were getting. I remember my father told me *he* brought wine, and roasted the Bull's flesh." The bishop's small pursed mouth curved in a smile. "He never said, but I suspect some woman kept him company. A night in a cold chapel is a long time to be alone."

Ash found herself grinning appreciatively at Charles's half-brother; Philip's son.

"You," he added, to Floria, "bring a woman with you; one who dresses like a man."

Ash's smile faded.

"As you've guessed," Bishop John of Cambrai said, "your aunt Jeanne Châlon has spoken to me."

"And what did she say?"

A quite genuine distress showed on the churchman's face at Florian's sharp demand. Ash – who has enough experience of men like this, in positions of power like this – thought, *What's that old cow been saying to him? Two minutes ago it was 'Madame chère Duchesse'!*

The bishop spoke directly, and with distaste. "Is it true that you have had a female lover?"

"Ah." There was a smile on Florian's face, but it had very little to do with humour. "Now let me guess. There is a noblewoman and a spinster – her niece is made Duchess – but there's a terrible scandal in the family. She comes to tell you before it all gets out as rumour. Tells you she *has* to confess all this, it's her duty."

"Cover your ass," Ash rumbled, startled to find herself sounding very like Robert Anselm. She added, "Jesus, that cow! You didn't hit her hard enough!"

Floria did not take her eyes off the bishop.

"More or less," John admitted. "Should she have preferred family loyalty to warning me that as well as dressing like a man, you act like a man in other ways?"

A few seconds of silence went by. Floria continued to stare at the bishop. "The technical charge was that she was Jewish, treating Christian patients."

"'She'?"

"Esther. My wife." Florian smiled very wryly, and very wearily. "My female lover. You can find it all out in the records of the Empty Chair."

"Rome's under darkness, and you'd never make the journey," Ash cut in. "Don't say anything you don't want to say."

"Oh, I want to say it." Florian's eyes were fiery. "Let the bishop here know what he's getting. Because I *am* Duchess."

Ash thought the Bishop of Cambrai flinched at that one.

"Esther and I became lovers when I finished studying medicine at Padua." Floria folded her arms, the cloth of her robe bundled up to her body. "She never, not for one instant, thought I was a man. When we were arrested in Rome, she'd just had a baby. We weren't getting on too well. Because of that."

"She had a *baby*—?" Ash stopped and blushed.

"Just some man she fucked one night," the surgeon said contemptuously. "He wasn't her lover. We had fights about that. We had more fights about Joseph – the baby. I was jealous, I suppose. She gave so much time to him. We were in the cells for two months. Joseph died, of pneumonia. Neither of us could cure him. The day after that, they took Esther out and chained her up and burned her. The day after *that*, I had a message that Tante Jeanne had paid my ransom: *I* was free to go. So long as I left Rome. The abbot there said they'd have to burn male sodomites, but what did it matter what a woman did? So long as I didn't practise medicine again."

Floria's words dropped into the cold air of the chapel, delivered with a numb bravado that Ash recognised. *We do that, all of us. After a field of battle.*

"My aunt's been creeping round me since I got back," Florian said. "Bishop, did she tell you that the last thing I did when I was here in August was punch her? I laid her out in the public street. I'm not surprised she's gone behind my back to you. But did she tell you? – she could have paid Esther's ransom too. She just chose not to."

"Perhaps . . ." John of Cambrai was evidently struggling; he stared away at the mosaics. "Perhaps there was too little money for her to do anything but rescue family?"

"*Esther* was 'family'!" Florian's tone lowered. "My father wasn't dead then. She could have written to him, if she wanted money."

"And the Abbot of Rome," John went on, "would have been looking to burn Jews – if I remember the time right, there were bread riots; blaming it all on a Jewish woman would have been an acceptable crowd-pleaser. He would have been more wary of burning a Burgundian woman who had been born noble, and who evidently had noble family still alive. No matter how she was behaving at the time."

Seeing his face, how he simultaneously seemed to want to hold out his hands to Floria, and to back away, Ash understood.

He's a man who chases women. But he can't chase Florian: Florian's not interested in men. I'm not sure it's a church thing at all with his Grace of Cambrai.

As if to confirm it, John of Cambrai gave her a conspiratorial glance. It lasted no more than a second, but it was gravely and heterosexually flirtatious, invited complicity; said, without words, *you and I are not like this woman. We're normal.*

Momentarily intimidated by green robes and rich embroidery, Ash looked away.

Godfrey would never have said any of that. Robes don't make a priest.

She shrugged one arm out from under her cloak, and put it around Florian's shoulders. "That poisonous old cow's been mischief-making, but so what? I was there: Florian made the hart. She's Duchess. If Jeanne Châlon doesn't like it, that's just tough shit."

"If she spreads it around," Floria started.

"So what if she does?"

"In the company, last summer—"

"That's soldiers. And they're all right with you now." Ash brought her other arm out from under her cloak, and put it on Florian's other shoulder, turning the woman to face her. She spoke with great intensity, driving her point home. "Understand this. Olivier de la Marche will do what you say. So will his captains. And there's an army outside Dijon. Internal dissent would be suicidal right now, but the chances are that it won't happen. People have got other things to worry about. And if there are some people who still want to make trouble – then you put them in jail, or you hang them off the city walls. This isn't about them approving of you. This is about you being their Duchess. That means keeping everybody rounded up and pointed in the same direction. Okay?"

Whether it was Ash's intensity, or the sheer confusion on the bishop's face, Florian started nervously to smile.

"The Burgundian army has provosts," Ash added, "and the Viscount-Mayor has constables. Neither of them have them for the fun of it. *Use* them. If it comes to it, the bishop here can be 'retired' under house arrest to the monastery up in the north-east *quartier*."

Bishop John approached. "Understand me."

Ash, not sure how much of his change of tone was a response to the thought of military power, backed off.

He reached out and took Floria's hands. "Madame cher Duchesse, if I'm aware of your – spiritual difficulties – then equally I'm aware that I have . . . difficulties of my own. Whatever you are, I am your father in the church, and your servant in the duchy."

The rich colours of the mosaics behind him glinted, in the shifting light. Now that he was next to her, Ash realised that Bishop John stood an inch or two shorter than Floria.

"What you are is our Duchess." He shook both her hands in his grip, for emphasis. "God save us, Floria del Guiz, you're my brother's successor. If God lets you take the ducal crown, it isn't for any of us to disobey His will."

"Crown? The *crown* doesn't matter. What does a piece of carved horn matter!" Florian freed her hands and took a step forward. She made a fist; thumped it against her chest. "I know what I am, but I don't know *why* I am, or how! Suppose you tell me? You expect me to come back to a city I haven't seen since I was a child, and do this? You expect me to come back to strangers, and do this? You tell me what's going on!"

Her breathless voice fell flat against the walls, the mosaics deadening the acoustics. A whisper of sound went up the brick-lined shaft, towards the grating and the air. As if they stood in the bottom of a dull, soundless well.

When John of Cambrai did not answer, the surgeon became icy.

"I haven't taken communion since I left the Empty Chair. I don't intend to start now. There's not going to be a mass tonight; you can tell the acolytes to go home and get some sleep." Florian shrugged. "If you want a vigil, tell me why the Dukes of Burgundy are like they are. Tell me what I've been stuck with. Otherwise I'll just curl up in the corner and sleep. I've slept worse places on campaign: Ash will tell you."

"Yeah, but you were drunk then," Ash said, before she thought.

"Madame Duchesse!" the Bishop protested.

Florian said something to him. Ash took no notice. The shifting light on the shrine caught her eye, under the far barrel-vault, and her vision finally adjusted enough to let her make out the dim, painted carvings.

She turned away from the bishop and surgeon, walked straight past the plain altar, to the shrine. Marble, painted and gilded, glowed in the light of thigh-thick beeswax candles.

"Christus Viridianus!" she blurted out. And then, as both of them looked at her, startled, she pointed. "That's the Prophet Gundobad!"

"Yes." Bishop John's demure features showed no expression that might not be a trick of the shifting light. "It is."

Florian stared. "Why do you have a shrine to a heretic?"

"The shrine is not Gundobad's," the bishop said, moving forward. He pointed to one of the minor figures. "The shrine is Heito's. Sieur Heito was Duke Charles's ancestor. And will have been yours, your Grace, it now becomes apparent."

"I didn't expect to find him here." Ash reached up and touched the cold carved marble of Gundobad's sandal and foot. "Florian, the Duke was going to tell me before he died. I suggest you ask the bishop, now . . . '*Why Burgundy?*'"

Turning, she caught an expression on Bishop John's world-weary face – something approaching excitement. Mildly, he said, "The Duchess brought you, demoiselle, but it is her decision as to how she spends her vigil. Remember that, and show due respect."

"Oh, I respect Florian." Ash put her fists on her hips, mentally closing ranks without a second thought. "I've watched her puke her guts out, outside the surgeon's tent, and come back in and take a longbow arrow out of a man's lung—"

Of course, it would be better if she hadn't got drunk in the first place.

"—I don't need a gang of Burgundians to tell me about Florian!"

"Quiet," Florian said, with something of the blurred chill in her eyes that she had, covered in hart's blood, at the end of the hunt. "Bishop – you told me what Charles of Valois brought here. You told me what Duke Philip brought. You didn't ask me what *I've* brought."

"Questions," Bishop John said. "You come with questions."

"So do I," Ash muttered, and when the bastard son of Philippe le Bon looked at her, she jerked her thumb at the shrine. "Do you know what you've got there?"

"That is Gundobad, prophet of the Carthaginians, at the moment of his death."

"Gundobad the Wonder-Worker," Ash said steadily. "I know about Gundobad. I know a lot about Gundobad, since I went south. Leofric and the Wild Machines, between them – I know what really happened, seven hundred years ago. Gundobad made the land around Carthage into a *desert*. He dried up the rivers. How the hell . . ." Ash's voice slowed. "How the hell did the Pope's soldiers manage to burn him alive?"

She ignored Florian's quick shudder: it might have been the older woman feeling the cold.

"You have a point," the surgeon said, her voice steady.

"He was the *Wonder-Worker*," Ash said again. "If he could do that to Carthage, to the Wild Machines: he shouldn't have died just because some priest ordered it!"

With a glance at Floria del Guiz, Bishop John demurred, "He cursed Pope Leo[26] and brought about the Empty Chair."

There are side-panels in the chapel, one of which is the death of Leo –

---

[26] Is this a reference to Pope Leo III? This would put Gundobad's death at or before AD 816.

blinded, hunted, torn into scraps of flesh – but she knows that story too well to look.

"Any man who could turn half of North Africa into a desert," Ash said steadily, "shouldn't have died at the hands of the Bishop of Rome. Not unless there's something we don't know about Pope Leo! *No*—" she corrected herself abruptly. "Not Leo. Is it?" And she turned back to the stonework. "Who is this Heito?"

There was a silence broken by nothing but the odd drip of condensation.

Florian's voice sounded harsh and sudden. "I expected to pray tonight. I prayed when I was a girl. I was . . . devout. And if there were going to be answers, I expected them to be about Burgundy, about what *happened* to me out there, on the hunt."

Floria sighed.

"When I left Carthage, I thought we'd left the desert demons behind. But here they are." She pointed to a detail in the back of the shrine: the heretic Gundobad, preaching from a rock in a verdant southern landscape, and in the background, the tiny distant shapes of pyramids.

"Florian . . ."

"I thought we'd come where they couldn't reach you." Florian's eyes were dark holes, in the candles' shadows. "I saw you walk away, remember? I saw them *make* you do it!"

"They couldn't do it when I spoke to them two days ago. This isn't about me," Ash said. "I didn't hunt the hart. You did. Now I want to know, why Burgundy? And the answer's Gundobad. Isn't it?"

Bishop John, as she turned on him, continued to look not at Ash but at Florian. At Florian's small nod, he spoke.

"This is the square of St Peter," he said, touching key points on the painted stonework. "Here, at the cathedral door, is where great Charlemagne was crowned. He had been dead a year when his sons, and Pope Leo, put on trial the Carthaginian prophet Gundobad, for the Arian heresy. Here is Gundobad, in the Papal cells, with his wife Galsuinda, and his daughter Ingundis."

"He *married*?" Ash blurted. "Shit. I never thought about that. What happened to them?"

"Galsuinda and Ingundis? They were made slaves; they were shipped back to Carthage before the trial – I believe Leo used them to carry a message to the then King-Caliph." Bishop John steepled his fingers. "Although I believe the King-Caliph of that time was not sorry to be relieved of such a prophet, darkness and desert having come to his lands all in one year."

"But it wasn't! It wasn't one year!" Ash hears in her head the voice of the *machina rei militaris*, when she was prisoner in Carthage: impassive, impersonal; retelling an undeniable history. "The darkness didn't come until the 'Rabbi's Curse', four centuries later. That's when the Wild Machines drew down the sun, to feed them the strength to speak through the Stone Golem. Gundobad was long before that!"

"Is it so?" Bishop John nodded. "We tell it differently. Stories of ages past become confused. The memory of man is short."

The memory of the Wild Machines is longer. And a damn sight more accurate.

"Nevertheless," he added, "it was in that year that the lands about Carthage ceased to be a garden, and became a desert, and Gundobad fled north to preach his heresy in the Italian states."

"How much of this is true?" Florian demanded. "How much is old records and guesswork?"

"We know that Leo died the year that Gundobad cursed him. We know that no Pope thereafter lived more than three days in Peter's Chair. And the great empire of Charlemagne was overthrown among his quarrelling sons that year, or not long after.[27] Christendom became nothing but quarrelling Dukes and Counts; no Emperor."

"And this Heito?"

"My 'ancestor'?" Florian said dryly, on the heels of Ash's question. "Clearly, if he was alive in Pope Leo's day, he's probably the ancestor of half of Burgundy by now!"

"Yes."

John of Valois looked as if that simple acknowledgement was some significant piece of knowledge.

"And that's why everybody rides with the hunt," Ash filled in, with a sense of cold inevitability: fact fitting into fact. "Everybody you can get *with Burgundian blood* . . . Florian, it's another bloodline. Only it isn't Gundobad's child. It's this Heito's descendants. Heito's children." She turned on the bishop. "Aren't I right?"

"Who for the last four generations have been the legitimate sons of the Valois," the bishop confirmed, "but we have always known, breeding horses and cattle as we do, how characteristics skip a generation, or turn up in a cadet line. When we were the Kingdom of Arles, it was no great matter for a peasant to become king, if he hunted the Hart. We have become complacent, since my great-grandfather's time. God reminds us to be humble, your Grace."

"Not *that* fucking humble!" Ash snorted, at the same time as Floria del Guiz objected loudly: "My parents were noble, both of them!"

"My apologies, your Grace."

"Oh, screw your apologies!" Florian's voice dropped half an octave; took on the volume that presaged, in camp, a rapid readjustment of the surgeon's tent. "I have *no* idea what's going on. Suppose you tell me!"

"Heito." John laid his hand against the carved figure's mailed foot, looking up at him. "He was a minor knight in Charlemagne's retinue; one of Charlemagne's sons took him into service after Charles's death. He was appointed guard over Gundobad, after the trial. He was there when Gundobad cursed the Holy Father. And he was there when Gundobad sought to extinguish, by a miracle, the flames of his pyre."

The bishop flicked a glance at Ash.

---

[27] This fixes the date! If these are accurate references, the year is AD 816, two years after Charlemagne's death. Although dissolution began the year after Leo's death, some do not date the fall of Charlemagne's empire until AD 846 and the Treaty of Verdun.

"He'd heard the news from North Africa," he added, more conversationally. "It wasn't hard for him to realise that Gundobad wanted far more than a mere miraculous escape – that he was desirous of giving us a desert where Christendom now stands. And Gundobad would have, if not for Heito the Blessed."

"Who did what?" Florian persisted.

"He prayed."

Ash, staring up at the bas-relief carving, wondered if Heito's face had had that expression of stilted piety – *whether, in fact,* she reflected, *he wasn't filling his braies and praying out of sheer terror. But it worked: something worked . . . because Gundobad died.*

"Heito prayed," the bishop said. "All men have in them some small part of the grace of God. We who are priests are born with a very little more – a very, very little; sufficient only, if God grants it to us, to perform very minor miracles."

A sudden memory of Godfrey's face made Ash wince. She could not bring herself to speak to the *machina rei militaris,* to ask – as she suddenly wanted to – *what do you think of God's grace* now?

"Heito had the grace of God in abundance, although as a humble knight he had no reason to know this until he met his test."

They stood in silence, surveying the bas-relief shrine.

"Heito told his sons that, when the fire was lit at Gundobad's pyre, he heard the heretic praying for escape, and for vengeance on all whom he called 'Peter's heretics', throughout Europe. The story comes down that, when Gundobad prayed, the flames *did* die. Heito was moved to prayer. He begged God's grace to avert the devastation of Christendom, and to help in kindling the fire again. Heito's story to his sons is that he *felt* God's grace work within him."

Florian's hands strayed to her mouth. It was difficult to see, in the candlelight, but her skin seemed pale.

"Heito re-lit the pyre. Gundobad died. Christendom was not laid waste . . . Heito witnessed the death of the Holy Father, not long after; and the death of his appointed successor. He prayed that that Curse of the Empty Chair would be lifted – but, as his son Carlobad tells us, in his *Histoire,* Heito felt a lack of strength within himself. He had not the grace to do it. Nor his son after him, though Heito married his son to the most devout of women."

"And then?" Ash prompted sardonically. She reached out, tucking Florian's arm within her own, feeling how the surgeon was swaying very slightly. "No, I can guess. They married holy women, didn't they? All of Heito's sons . . ."

"His grandson, Airmanareiks, was the first who hunted the Hart. You must understand, at that time Burgundy was as full of miracles, and appearances of the Heraldic Beasts, as any other land in Christendom. It was not until later that . . . as they say: God lays His heaviest burden on His most faithful servant. We had gained grace enough to have our prayers answered. Without some burden, we might have forgot our debt to Him."

"'Burden' be damned," Ash said cynically. "You can't pick and choose. If you stop miracles, you stop miracles. End of story. No wonder Father Paston and Father Faversham have been desperate since we crossed the border! And didn't you have trouble with the wounded the first time we came here, after Basle?"

Florian nodded absently. "I thought it was fever, from low-lying water meadows . . ."

"We had hoped to grow strong enough, one day, to remove the curse and see another Holy Father ascend to Peter's Chair. That has not been granted to us. We have, though, done what Heito set out to do. Neither Burgundy nor Christendom have been corrupted into a wasteland," Bishop John said. "We have been ruled by the Franks, and the Germans, and by our own Dukes; but always we took the holiest of women as brides, and always the Lord of Burgundy was the one who hunted the Hart. Christendom has been safe. We have paid our price for it."

Ash, ignoring the last of what he said, caught Florian's hand in hers and swung the woman around to face her.

"That's it. That's *it*!" She took in a breath. "Heito knew what Gundobad had done to Carthage. He knew Gundobad had living children. *That's* what he was afraid of. Burgundy being made into a wasteland!"

"And he bred for a bloodline that doesn't do miracles – that keeps miracles from being done." Florian's hands shut tight around Ash's gloved fingers, almost cutting off the circulation. "They didn't know about the Wild Machines. They were just afraid of another Gundobad."

"Well, she's out there, right enough!" Ash jerked her head in a random direction, understood to mean *beyond these city walls*. "Our Faris. Another Gundobad. Any time the Wild Machines want to make her act . . ."

"Except that she can't. Because of me."

"First Charles, then you." Ash couldn't stop a smile. "Jeez, I thought *I* was good at finding trouble and jumping into the middle of it!"

"*I didn't ask for this!*"

Her voice echoed back from the walls of the shaft. Dull, booming reverberations faded away. The wind from above shifted the candlelight, and brought a scent familiar from slaughterhouses: old blood, old urine and dung. Fear, and death, and sacrifice.

The silence deepened. No knowing, now, how much of the night is gone, or whether across the city, in the cathedral, they are waking to sing Lauds, or Matins, or Prime.

"It was Duke Charles's dream," the bishop said, "to regain the middle kingdom of Europe – to become, in time, another Charlemagne; another Emperor over all. How else to stop us wasting our time in quarrels and wars, and unite Christendom against our enemies? A Charlemagne with Heito's grace. My brother was a man who might have been that . . . but it was not given to him. If he had turned his eyes south, we might not be in such desperate trouble now. God rest him. But you are Duchess now."

"Oh, I know that," Florian said absently. She reached up and rapped her knuckles on Heito's stone shin. "Now you tell me something. Tell me, why is there sunlight over Burgundy?"

VIII

"What?" Ash looked around, confused, at the shadowed chapel.

"Outside. Daytime. Why is it light? Why isn't it *dark*?"

"I don't get it."

Florian hit one hand into the other. "You told me. The Wild Machines draw down the sun. That's *real*. So – why isn't it dark here? Why is there sun in Burgundy? It's dark in the lands all around us."

Ash opened her mouth to refute the argument. She closed it again. Bishop John's frown showed pure bewilderment. The wind from the sacrificial shaft brought the smell of cold stone and corruption, deep here in the earth.

"Does it – feel – real?" Ash asked. "The sunlight?"

"Would I know?"

"You knew about the Hart!"

Florian frowned. "Whatever's in my blood, I used it for the first time, on the hunt. I did something. But after that . . . no. I'm not *doing* anything."

"After the hunt, there is nothing for you to do," Bishop John said. "It is not what you do, it is what you are. You have only to live, and you are our guardian."

"I can't tell," Floria said. "I can't feel anything."

Sweat sprang out in Ash's palm. *What else don't we know?*

"Maybe it's people here praying for light. The Bishop here says all men have grace . . ." She began to pace on the terracotta tiles; stopped in the small space, and swung around. "No, *that* doesn't work, because I guarantee men have been praying as hard as shit in France and the Cantons, too! And it was black as the ace of spades when we came through there. If God's grace was going to do a miracle through prayer, we'd have seen the sun over Marseilles and Avignon!"

"I'm no longer devout." Florian smiled painfully. "While I was in the sacred baths, I was thinking. I know what I do – I preserve the mundane. So did Duke Charles. I wondered why things were so bad in the infirmary. I've had men dying on me since I got here. Men I'd expect to see live. Charles's praying priests didn't do him any good, either! This is the real world, here."

The Bishop murmured, "'God lays His heaviest burden on His most faithful servants.' We can't have His gift without His penalty."

Florian hit her hand into her fist again. "So why is it *light* here?" She looked down at her tumbled robes, and her bare hands. "And why was there a miracle at Auxonne?"

For a second, Ash is back on the field, among rain-sodden mud, with jets of jellied flame searing across men's burned-black faces. She absently wiped her hand across her mouth. The stench is still clear in her memory.

Ash remembers priests on their knees, the snow coming down as the wind changed. "I asked de Vere to ask the Duke to let his priests pray – for snow, so the enemy would have no visibility; for the wind in our favour, so their shafts would drop short."

Floria, eyes bright, gripped Ash's arm. "At first I thought the Duke must have been injured. Weakened. But de la Marche told me it happened before he was wounded." Bewildered, Floria turned to the bishop. "Shouldn't those priests have been praying for nothing? Or is there – I don't know – a weakness in the bloodline?"

"We are only men," Bishop John said mildly. "We have nurtured the line of ducal blood, century upon century, but we are only men. Imperfect men. These things must happen, only once or twice in a generation. If we could reject *all* grace, how could God send us a Hart to be made flesh?"

"The Hart," Florian said. "Of course: the Hart."

"Florian won't be perfect," Ash said abruptly. "She *can't* be. I've been in Carthage. Two hundred years of incest." The expression on the bishop's face almost made her laugh. "That's what it took the Wild Machines to get a Faris. Two hundred years of scientific, calculated human stock-breeding. Incest! And what have you been doing in Burgundy?"

"Not incest!" Bishop John gasped. "That's against the laws of God and man!"

A raw, coarse laugh burst out before Ash could stop it. She grinned at the bishop's pallid face, there being nothing else to do now but laugh, scarified by irony. All mercenary now, she snorted out, "That's what you get for following God's law! You said it to me, at the hunt. *Burgundy has a bloodline*. Well, Burgundy should have done it properly! Dynastic marriages, chivalric love, and a bit of adultery at best – shit. That's no way to breed *stock*. You guys needed a Leofric here!"

A little ironically, Florian said, "Remember, I succeeded. I made the Hart real." Her voice contrastingly quiet, her gaze abstracted, she walked back towards the shrine of St Heito. With her back to Ash, she said, "If the Dukes need to prove themselves – I have. If I hadn't, the Wild Machines would have made their miracle at the hunt."

"Oh. Yeah." A little embarrassed at her outburst, Ash coughed. "Well . . . yeah, there's that."

". . . Until I die." Barely a whisper. Florian turned to face them. "I still don't understand. I'm alive. What the *Ferae Natura Machinae* do when they draw down the sun is real—"

"Oh, it must be." Ash sounded sardonic. 'The Wild Machines don't do miracles – if they did, they wouldn't need the Faris! And Burgundy would have been charred and smoking six hundred years ago."

Florian gave a loose-limbed shrug that did not belong on anyone wearing court dress. "We're right about that, or we'd be dead. But, Ash – we shouldn't be seeing the sun."

A brief burst of novices' voices came from above as the iron-studded door opened, then shut. Bishop John of Cambrai called to them to leave, up a shaft that echoed now.

Puddled wax alone remained of the smaller candles; the fatter ones still burning down, beginning to enclose their flames like yellow lanterns. A stray cold draught blew across the back of Ash's neck. She reached up to scratch under the fur collar of her demi-gown with one finger.

"It's no use me trying to— I won't take them by surprise again."

"No. I know that." Florian gathered up her robes again, hugging them against herself, as if for comfort. "But I'm right. Aren't I? Bishop, you can't answer this one. There's still something we don't know!"

"This must be taken to your *grand conseil*," John of Cambrai said. "Or the *petit conseil* first, perhaps, your Grace. There may be those who can answer this. If not, then we conclude, I think, that God may do His will as He wills it, and if He chooses to bless us so, then all we may rightly do is give thanks for His light."

Ash, alienated by his expression of shaky piety, remarked, "Godfrey says that God doesn't cheat."

Florian turned away from the bishop's hand, and Ash saw her face; her eyes prominent, dark-circled, stressed. Catching Ash's gaze, the woman said, "I didn't want to know that there's *still* something I don't know!"

The Bishop of Cambrai stepped back towards the altar. His soft, black eyes reflected the candlelight. He moved with gravitas. When he turned back, he held in his hands a circlet carefully cut, glued and shaped from horn. The ducal crown.

"You had questions. They have been answered," he said. "This is your vigil. Will you take the crown?"

Ash saw her panic. The glittering walls pressed in, in the candles' yellow gloom; the brick vaults above sweating nitre, and the tiles underfoot smelling of old blood. There is nothing here to remind her of the filigree stone of the palace above, all white light and air. This place is a fist of earth, ready to close around them.

Florian said finally, "Why do I have to? I don't need it, to do what I do. This whole thing – *I don't need this*!"

She backed a step away from the Bishop of Cambrai.

"You didn't need this," Ash said grimly. "*I* didn't need this. But you understand something, Florian – *make your mind up*. Are you running away from this, or are you Duchess? You commit yourself to one or the other, or I'll kick your sorry ass so hard you're going to wonder what fell on you!"

"What's it to you?" Florian said, almost sulkily. It was not a tone Ash was used to hearing from her, although she suspected Jeanne Châlon might have heard it a lot, fifteen years ago.

Ash said, "None of us owe Burgundy anything. You could be what you are in London or Kiev, if we could *get* there. But I'm telling you now, if you're staying here, you'd better be committed to being Duchess. Because there's no way I'm putting people's lives on the line as army commander if you don't mean it."

Bishop John said, half under his breath, "Now we see why God brought you here, demoiselle."

Ash ignored him.

Florian muttered, "We've – the Lion's agreed to defend Dijon."

"Ah, for fuck's *sake*! If I find us a way out – fuck knows how! – they'll go if I say go. I've been talking to people. They don't give a flying toss about the glories of Burgundy, and they really, really don't give a shit about fighting alongside Messire de la Marche. Some of us have died here, but they don't have any *loyalty* to this place—"

"Shouldn't I have? If I'm going to be crowned?"

"And do you?"

"I do."

Ash stared at Floria's face. There was very little to go on, in her expression. Then, in a flood, everything there: doubt, dread, fear at having committed herself, fear at having said, not what is true, but what is required. Tears filled up her eyes and ran over her lids, streaking her cheeks with silver.

"I don't want to do this! I don't want to be this!"

"Yeah, tell me about it."

A flicker of the old Florian: sardonic bleakness: "You and the Maid of Burgundy."

"Our guys won't fight for some Duchess," Ash said, "but they'll fight for you, because we don't leave our own. You're the surgeon, you went to Carthage; they'll fight like shit to keep you alive, the same as they'd fight to hang on to me or Roberto or each other. But we really don't care if it's fighting rag-heads to keep the Duchess alive, or fighting Burgundians to get you out of here. The *Burgundians* need to know you're Duchess, now do you *get that*?"

"What do you want to do?"

Refusing the distraction, Ash said rapidly, "Me? I'll do whatever I have to do. Be their banner. Right now, I need to know what *you're* going to do. They'll know if you don't mean it!"

Florian moved away, stepping on the chill flagstones of the chapel as if they were hot; all her body fidgeting with indecisiveness.

"This is a place for confessing sins," she said abruptly.

The bishop, from the shadowed altar, said, "Well, yes – but in private—"

"Depends. On who you need to confess to."

She walked back and took Ash's hands. Ash was astonished at the coldness of the older woman's skin – *almost in shock*, she thought – and then she made herself concentrate on what Florian was saying:

"I'm a coward, when it matters. I can pull people out of the line-fight. I can hurt them when I need to. Cut them wide open. Don't ask me to commit to anything else."

Ash began to speak, to say, *Everyone's afraid; fight the fear*, and Florian interrupted:

"Let me tell you something."

About to answer with a casual *sure!*, Ash stopped and looked at her. *She wants to tell me something I don't want to hear*, she realised, and paused, and then nodded in assent. "Tell me."

"This is hard."

Bishop John coughed, artificially, drawing attention to his presence. Ash saw Florian's gaze flick to him, and away; unclear whether she was giving tacit consent to the man's presence, or merely so far past caring that she couldn't be bothered to acknowledge him.

"I'm ashamed of one thing in my life," Florian said. "You."

"*Me?*" Ash realised her mouth was dry.

"I fell in love with you, oh . . . three years back?"

Into silence, Ash said:

"That's what you call cowardice? Not telling me?"

"That? No." A glimmer in the light: more welling tears wet on Florian's cheek. She took no notice of her own weeping. Her voice didn't change. "First I wanted you. Then I knew I could love you. Real love; the sort that hurts. And I killed it."

"What?"

"Oh, you can do that." Florian's eyes glittered, in the shifting light. "I couldn't *know* that you didn't want me. Esther said she didn't want me. And then she did. So you might . . . but I watched you. Watched your life. You were going to *die*. Sooner or later. You were going to come back from a field on a hurdle, with your face chopped off, or your head blown in, and what was I going to do then? *Again?*"

The bishop's long fingers wrapped around his Briar Cross, pale in the torchlight. Ash saw how the skin over his knuckles strained white.

"So I killed the love and made you into a friend, because I'm a coward, Ash. You were trouble. I don't want to take on trouble. Not any more. I can't take it. I've had enough."

Dispassionately, Ash asked, "Can you kill love?"

"*You're* asking *me* that?" Florian shook her head violently. Her voice exploded in the catacomb-darkness. "I didn't just want a fuck! I knew I was capable of falling in love with you. I strangled it. Not just because you're going to die young. Because you don't let anyone *touch* you. Your body, maybe. Not *you*. You pretend. You're untouchable. I couldn't find the courage to let it grow; not when I knew that!"

Watching, Ash sees – past her own gauche embarrassment, and a sneaking wish not to have been told any of this – how much damage the woman has done to herself.

"Florian . . ."

And she sees that what looks back at her, from Florian's whitened face, is not only shame and anger.

"So how come you keep telling me about it?" Ash demanded quietly. "How come you keep teasing me with it? And then telling me it's okay, you don't want me, you'll back off again. And then you tell me again. How come you can't leave me alone?"

"Because I can't leave you alone," Floria echoed.

Conscious of dust, damp, the glitter of candles on old mosaics, Ash would give anything to run out of this place – weighed down by history as it is – into daylight. Leave all of this, leave everything.

Am I that detached? Is that bad?

"Why do we hope?" Floria said. "I could never understand that."

Careful to say and look nothing that could be construed as acceptance, Ash only shook her head.

"It wouldn't have been any good," she said. "If you'd told me three years ago, I would have kicked you out – probably screamed for a priest. Now, I think I'd give anything if I could want you. But half of that is guilt because I never gave Godfrey what he needed. And I still want Fernando more than either of you."

She looked up, not aware until then that her head had drooped, and that her field of vision held only the floor mosaic of the Great Bull of Mithras, bleeding to death from a dozen mortal wounds.

"You know . . ." Sweat stood out on Florian's skin, making her forehead shiny. With one swift movement, she wiped her palm across her face, smearing wet hair back. "You certainly know how to finish something off. Shit. Don't you? That was . . ."

Brutal.

"That was *me*," Ash said. "I'm *not* going to make thirty; I *don't* want to fuck you; I love you as much as I can love anybody; I don't want you hurt. But right now I need to know what you're going to do, because I have to give the fucking orders around here, so will you please fucking *help* me?"

Florian lifted her hand and touched Ash's cheek with her fingers. Brief, light; and the expression on her face just shy of that square-mouthed uninhibited bawl that children have when they burst out crying in pain. She shuddered.

"I don't like not having answers!"

"Yeah, me neither."

"At least you know how to run an army. I don't know how to run a government."

"I can't help you there."

Florian lowered her hand to her side.

"Don't look for some dramatic decision." Floria shivered. "I was brought up here. I know I *ought* to commit myself. I'm going to do everything I can – but you know what? I'm one of your fucking company too, remember! Don't treat me like I'm not! The only people I care about is us. If there's a safe way out of here for all of us, *I'll take it*. I'm different now. I ought to stay. I know I don't understand everything about the Wild Machines. That's the best you'll get."

Ash reached for the ties of her cloak, slipped the knot, swung off the heavy wool, and swathed it around the older woman.

Florian looked into her face. "I can only do what I can do. I can't be your lover. And – I can't be your boss, either."

Ash blinked, jolted. After a minute, she nodded acknowledgement. "Shit, you don't give me any rope . . . Guess we'll have to manage, won't we?"

Ash put her hand out and gave Florian's shoulder a little shove. The woman smiled, still wet-faced; mimed avoiding a blow. Ash squinted up at the invisible darkness of the night outside.

Bishop John of Cambrai cleared his throat. "Madame, the crown?"

The tall woman reached and took the horn circlet out of his grasp, dangling it carelessly in her long fingers.

"Sod waiting till dawn. And screw the witnesses," Ash said, "Bishop John, you just tell them to keep their mouths shut, or show us whatever back way there is out of here. If you want me and Florian tonight, we'll be in the tower with Roberto and Angeli and the guys."

The message arrived four days later.

*

Black shadows leaped up on the flint-embedded walls of the garderobe,[28] sank, then grew again as the candle-flame was all but extinguished by the draught from below. The wind rustled the hanging gowns either side of her. Ash, hitching the back of her demi-gown and shirt up around her with numbed fingers, swore.

Beyond the heavy curtain, Rickard's voice asked, "Boss, you busy?"

"*Christus Viridianus!*"

The wax- and wine-stained demi-gown slid out of her frozen fingers, down her hips, on to the wooden plank. A chilling wind from the night below struck up Ash's back. Her flesh felt red-hot by comparison. She yelled, "No, I'm not *busy*. Whatever gave you that idea? I'm just sitting here with my arse hanging out, taking a dump; why not invite the whole fucking Burgundian *council* in? Jesus Christ up a Tree, here I am *wasting time* – are you sure you can't find something *else* for me to do while I'm in here?"

There was a noise which, had she bothered to decipher it, rather than attend to the necessities of her toilet, she might have deciphered as an adolescent male having alternately bass and soprano giggles.

"The doc— the Duchess— Florian wants you, boss."

"Then you can tell her lady high-and-mightiness the Duchess she can come and wipe my—" Ash broke off, grabbing at the candlestick that her elbow had just knocked. A great black shadow jolted up the walls, and the wick flared and smoked. Hot wax spilled over the back of Ash's hand.

"Bitch!" she muttered. "Got you, you little bastard!" and set the candle upright again. She peered at it. The heavy beeswax candle had melted past the next mark, before she spilled it: past Matins, an hour short of Lauds.[29]

"Rickard, do you know what fucking *time* it is?"

"The doc says a message came in. They want her up at the palace. She wants you, too."

"I expect she bloody does," Ash muttered under her breath. She reached out to the box of fresh linen scraps.

"It's Messire de la Marche who has the message."

"Son of a whore-fucking, cock-sucking, arse-buggering *bitch*!"

"You all right, boss?"

"I think I just lost my Lion livery badge. It fell off my demi-gown." Ash, hauling her split hose up her legs, peered down below the hem of her shirt, through the hole in the plank, at a black and empty void. She stood up with the care that the knowledge of a two-hundred-foot drop below one brings. Two hundred feet of excrement-stained tower wall, invisible in the night outside, but nothing to want to bounce down on your way to the caltrop-strewn no-man's-land at the foot of Dijon's walls . . .

"Come and do these damn points up!" Ash said, and the swing of the curtain as the boy pushed it back made the candle-flame swing again; yellow light illuminating the boy still wearing his mail-shirt, for God's sake, and an archer's sallet with a rather sorry yellow plume in it.

---

[28] Lavatory.
[29] Matins: midnight; Lauds: 3 a.m.; the time referred to is therefore 2 a.m.

"Going somewhere?" she enquired of the back of his head, where he bent over tying points with practised skill. The visible part of his neck grew red.

"I was just showing Margie some shooting techniques . . ."

In the dark? and *I bet that's not all you were showing her!* became the two foremost remarks in Ash's mind. With Anselm or Angelotti – except for the extreme unlikelihood of Angelotti showing anything to anyone called Margie – she would have said just that.

Given his embarrassment, she murmured, "'Margie'?"

"Margaret Schmidt. Margaret the crossbow-woman. The one that was a soeur, up at the convent."

His eyes shone, and his face was still visibly pink in the candlelight. Ash signalled him to buckle the sword-belt around her waist, as she held the candle up to give him the light. *So she's still in the company? I wonder if Florian knows?*

"Can you write up the reports now, before morning council?"

"I've done most of it, boss."

"Bet you're sorry the monks taught you to read and write!" she observed absently, giving him the candle to hold, and settling the belt, purse and sword more comfortably about her waist and hips. "Okay, do the reports, bring them to me at the Tour Philippe le Bon. It'll be quicker."

She hesitated for a moment, hearing an unidentifiable noise, and realised that it was rain, beginning to beat on the walls below her. The ammoniac stench of the stone room grew stronger. That did not so much offend her as pass her by entirely. A gust of rain-laden wind spurted up, chilling the stone walls, and shifting the heavy garments hanging around her.

"Oh, great. Next time it's a wet arse, as well." Ash sighed. "Rickard, get one of the pages; I need my pattens,[30] and a heavy cloak. I take it Florian's in the infirmary? Right. So tell whoever's on guard to get their asses in gear, I need six guys to go as escort to the palace with us." She hesitated, hearing a scrabble and whine from the room beyond the curtain. "And get the mastiff-handler – I'll take Brifault and Bonniau with me."

"You're expecting to be attacked in the streets?" Rickard, shielding the candle's flame with his hand, looked wide-eyed for a second.

"No. The girls just haven't had their walk yet." Ash grinned at him. "Get scribbling, boy. And, just think – if Father Faversham's right, after a life like this, you'll hardly spend any time in Purgatory at all!"

"*Thanks*, boss . . ."

She all but trod on his heels, stepping out of the garderobe, so as not to lose the light of the candle. The main fireplace shed some light, still, into the company tower's upper storey, by which she saw the curled blanket-strewn forms of pages asleep around the meagre warmth. Rickard took the candle to his pallet, to work with, kicking one of the pages as he went; and she stretched, in the dim light, feeling the bones of her shoulders crack and shift.

Viridianus! When did I last sleep through a night? Just one night without fucking Greek Fire missiles and army paperwork, that's all I want . . .

Blanket-wrapped forms unrolled: two pages coming to dress her for the

[30] Raised wooden platforms that strap on over shoes, for walking through mud.

pitch-black, rain-blasted ride through the muddy streets to the ducal palace, the mastiffs Brifault and Bonniau padding silently up, sure-footed, to her side.

Ash found Florian down on the second floor, in the aisle that ran around the hall in the thickness of the walls, seeing to a patient in smoky taper light. The man sat with his hose slung around his neck, naked from the waist down. A smell of old urine hung about the stonework and flesh.

"So, de la Marche wants you?" Ash peered over the surgeon's shoulder.

"I'm just finishing up." Florian's long, dirty fingers pulled at a gash that started above the man-at-arms's knee. He gasped. Blood, black in the light, and a glint of something shiny in the depths – bone?

"Hold him," Florian said, over the man's shoulder to a second mercenary, kneeling there. The second man wrapped his arms tightly around the injured man, pinning his arms down. Ash sat down on her heels as Florian washed out the gaping hole again with wine.

"De la Marche—" the surgeon peered into the wound; swilled it out again. "—will have to wait. I'll be done soon."

The man-at-arms's face shone in the light of tapers, beads of sweat swelling up out of his skin. He swore continuously, muttering *Bitch! Bitch! Bitch!* on ale-heated breath, and then grinned, finally, at the surgeon.

"Thanks, doc."

"Oh – any time!" Florian stood up and wiped her hands down her doublet. Glancing down at Baldina and two junior deacons, she added, "Leave the wound uncovered. Make sure nothing gets into it. *Don't* suture it. I don't give a shit about Galen's 'laudable pus'.[31] The uncovered wounds I saw in Alexandria didn't stink and go rotten like Frankish wounds. I'll bandage it in four days' time. Okay? Okay: let's go."

The leaded glass window of the Tour Philippe le Bon was proof against the rain, but freezing draughts found their way in around the frame and chilled Ash's face as she peered through her reflection, out into blackness.

"Can't see a fucking thing," she reported. "No, wait – they've got Greek Fire lights all along the east bank of the Ouche. Activity. That's odd."

She stepped back, blinking against the apparent brilliance of two dozen candles, as the chamber door opened to admit Olivier de la Marche.

Florian demanded, "What is it?"

"News, your Grace." The big man came to a halt, in a clatter of plate. His face was not clearly visible under his raised visor, but Ash thought his expression peculiarly rigid.

"More digging?"

"No, your Grace." De la Marche clasped his hands over the pommel of his sword. "There's news, from the north – from Antwerp."

At the same moment that Ash exclaimed, "Reinforcements!', Florian demanded, "How?"

---

[31] '*Pus bonum et laudabile*': a misunderstanding of Galen's actual writings that must have cost hundreds of thousands of lives in Europe, between the decline of Roman military medicine, and the Renaissance.

"Yeah." Ash flushed. "Not thinking. That's a damn good question. How did news get in through *that*, messire? Spies?"

The Burgundian commander shook his head slightly. The torchlight glanced from his polished armour, dazzling Ash. Through black after-images, she heard de la Marche say, "No. Not a spy. This news has been allowed through. There was a Visigoth herald; he escorted our messenger in."

Florian looked puzzled. Ash felt her stomach turn over.

"Better hear him, then, hadn't we?" Ash said. As an afterthought, she glanced at Florian for acknowledgement. The surgeon-Duchess nodded.

"It isn't going to be good news. Is it?" Florian said suddenly.

"Nah: they wouldn't let *good* news through. The only question is, how bad is it?"

At de la Marche's shout, two Burgundian men-at-arms brought in a third man, and backed out of the ducal chamber again. Ash could not read their expressions as they went. She found her hand clenching into a fist.

The man blinked at Floria del Guiz. He held his arms wrapped across his body, a cloak or some kind of bundle gripped close to himself.

De la Marche walked behind the messenger and rested a hand on his shoulder. No armour, Ash noted: a torn livery tabard and tunic, stained with blood and human vomit and let dry. Nothing recognisable in the heraldry except the St Andrew's cross of Burgundy.

"Give your message," Olivier de la Marche said.

The man stayed silent. He had fine sallow skin and dark hair. Exhaustion or hunger, or both, had made his features gaunt.

"The Visigoths brought you here?" Florian prompted. She waited a moment. In the night's silence, she walked to the dais, and sat on the ducal throne. "What's your name?"

Ash let Olivier de la Marche say, "Answer the Duchess, boy."

Only a boy in comparison to de la Marche's fifty or so, she realised; and the man lifted his head and looked first at the woman on the ducal throne, and then at the woman in armour; all without the slightest sign of interest.

Shit! Ash thought. Oh *shit* . . .

"Do I have to, messire? I don't want this. No one should be asked to do this. They *sent* me back, I didn't *ask*—" His voice sounded coarse: a Flemish townsman, by his accent.

"What did they tell you to say?" Florian leaned forward on the arm of the throne.

"I was at the battle?" His tone ended on a question. "Days ago, maybe two weeks?"

His anguished look at de la Marche was not, Ash saw, because he did not want to tell his news to women. He was beyond that.

"They're all dead," he said, flatly. "I don't know what happened on the field. We lost. I saw Gaucelm and Arnaud die. All my lance died. We routed in the dark, but they didn't kill us; they rounded us up as soon as it was dawn – there was a cordon . . ."

Seeing Florian about to speak, Ash held up a restraining hand.

The Burgundian man-at-arms hugged his bundled cloak closer to him – not even wool: hessian, Ash saw – and looked around at the clean walls of the Tour Philippe, and the mud that his boots had tracked across the clean oak boards. There was wine on the table, but although he swallowed, he did not appear otherwise to see it.

"It's all fucked!" he said. "The army in the north. They rounded us all up – baggage train, soldiers, commanders. They marched us into Antwerp—"

Ash grimaced. "The Goths have got Antwerp? Shit!"

Florian waved her to silence. She leaned forward, looking at the man. "And?"

"—they put us all on ships."

Silence, in the high tower room. Puzzled, Ash looked across at de la Marche.

In a high whine, the man said, "Nobody knew what was going to happen. They hauled me out of there – I was so fucking scared—" He hesitated. After a second, he went on: "I saw them herding everyone else up, pushing them with spears. They made everybody go on board the ships that were at the dock. I mean everybody – soldiers, whores, cooks, the fucking commanders – everybody. I didn't know why it was happening; I didn't know why they'd held me back."

"To come here," Ash said, almost to herself, but he gave her a look of complete disgust. It startled her for a moment. Evidently not seeing the Maid of Burgundy.

"What would *you* fucking know!" He shook his head. "Some fucking woman done up like a soldier." He glanced back at de la Marche. "Is this other one really the Duchess?"

De la Marche nodded, without reproach.

The man said, "They cast the ships off. No crew, just let 'em drift out into Antwerp harbour. Then there was one almighty fucking *whoosh!*" He gestured. "And the nearest ship just burst into fire. It wouldn't go out. They just kept shooting Greek Fire at the ships, and when our men started trying to swim, they used them for crossbow practice. There was all torches along the quay. Nobody got out. All the water was burning. That stuff just floated. Bodies, floating. Burning."

De la Marche wiped his hand across his face.

"Most of us died outside Antwerp." The man went on: "I don't know how many of us there was left after the field. Enough of us to fill six or seven ships, packed in tight. And now there's nobody. They sent me with this."

He held out the cloth bundle. As dark and stiff as the rest of his clothes, it was nevertheless not, Ash saw, his cloak. Hessian sacks.

"Show me." Florian spoke loudly.

The man squatted down, cut and filthy fingers plucking at the tied necks of the sacks. De la Marche reached over him, dagger out, and cut the twine with his blade. The man took two corner edges of one sack and lifted. A large heavy object rolled out on to the oak boards.

"*Fuck.*" Florian stared.

Ash swallowed, at the stench. *Damn, I should have recognised that. Decay.* She looked questioningly at de la Marche.

The refugee man-at-arms reached out and lifted the matted, white-and-blue object, seating it down facing the surgeon.

His voice sounded completely calm. "This is Messire Anthony de la Roche's head."

The severed head's eyes were filmed over and sunken, Ash saw, like the eyes of rotting fish; and the dark beard and hair might have been any colour before blood soaked them.

"Is it?" she asked de la Marche.

He nodded. "Yes. I know him. Know him very well. Demoiselle Florian, if you need to be spared the others—"

"I'm a surgeon. Get on with it."

The man-at-arms removed a second, then a third, severed head from his sacks; handling these two with a kind of bewildered delicacy, as if they could still feel his touch. Both were women, both had been fair-haired. It was not clear whether the marks were bruises or decomposition. Long hair, matted with blood and mud and semen, fell lank on to the floorboards.

Ash stared at the waxy skin. Despite death, the head of the older of the women was recognisable. *The last time I saw her was in court here, in August.*

So much hanging on this: Ash can feel herself trying to see a different woman, a noblewoman, or a peasant, sent in to spread false fear. The features are too recognisable. For all the sunken, colourless eyes, this is the same woman that she saw shrewishly berating John de Vere, Earl of Oxford; this is Charles's wife, the pious Queen of Bruges.

The man-at-arms said, "Mère-Duchesse Margaret. And her daughter Marie."

Ash could recognise nothing about the second head, except that the woman had been younger. Looking up, she saw Olivier de la Marche's face streaked with tears. *Mary of Burgundy, then.*

The man said, "I saw them killed on the quay at Antwerp. They raped them first. I could hear the Mère-Duchesse praying. She called on Christ, and the saints, but the saints had no pity. They let her survive long enough to see the girl die."

A silence, in the cold room. The sweet smell of decay permeated the air. A whisper of rain beat against the closed shutters.

"They've been dead less than a week," Ash said, straightening up, surprised to find that her voice cracked when she spoke. "That'll put the field when, about the time that Duke Charles died? A day or so before?"

Florian merely sat shaking her head, not in negation. She abruptly sat straight. "You don't want people talking to this man," she said to Olivier de la Marche. "He's coming to my hospice in the company tower. He needs cleaning up, and rest. God knows what else."

Ash said dryly, "I shouldn't worry about rumour. The Lion will know anything you don't want known, anyway. You can't hide this for long."

"We can't," de la Marche agreed. "Your Grace, I don't know if you realise—"

"I can hear!" Florian said. "I'm not stupid. There's no army in the north now. There's no one alive to raise another force outside Dijon. Isn't that right?"

Ash turned her back on the crouching man, the Burgundian commander, the surgeon-Duchess. She let her gaze go to the shutters, visualising the night air, and the rejoicing Visigoth camp beyond the walls.

She said, "That's right. We got no army of the north coming here. We're on our own now."

Message: #377 (Anna Longman)
Subject: Ash
Date: 16/12/00 at 06.11 a.m.
From: Ngrant@   *format address deleted*
                   Other details encrypted by
Anna –   *non-discoverable personal key*

So many seismographic ears listening, so many satellites overhead
– post-Cold War technology – and the political instability in the
Middle East – I doubt a sparrow falls without it being logged by
the appropriate authorities!

  Certainly nothing that affects the Mediterranean seabed would go
unnoticed; therefore, if there are no records

  sorry, wait, Isobel needs this.

  Too deep in the translation to say more, I MUST get it FINISHED.

– Pierce

Previous message missing?

Message: #378 (Anna Longman)
Subject: Ash
Date: 16/12/00 at 06.28 a.m.
From: Ngrant@   *format address deleted*
                   Other details encrypted by
Anna –   *non-discoverable personal key*

No, you're right. After a while, I have to take a break. My mind
seizes up; all I translate becomes gibberish.

  I am still haunted by the knowledge that when I come to do a
second draft, there will exist a completely possible potential
second version of the translation – a story different in all its
particulars, but equally valid as a transcription of the Latin.

  I suppose I am saying that I have to make decisions of
interpretation here, and I am not always happy they are the correct
decisions. I wish we had more time before publication.

  I will send you the next section of manuscript as soon as I have a
rough draft. I must *complete* this, in sequence – there are whole
sections at the end that could easily bear any one of several
interpretations! Which one I decide upon will be determined by
what goes before.

  For that, and other, reasons, I won't show the translation to
anybody here except Isobel. However, I have been talking in

general terms to James Howlett. Really, I don't know what to make
of him. He talks blithely about 'reality disjunctures' and
'quantum bubbles' – he *seized* on my mention of the sunlight in
Burgundy, but if he has an explanation, I don't understand it! I
had no idea that, as a historian, I should need to be a
mathematician, or that a grounding in quantum mechanics would be
necessary!

Think about it, Anna – I'm coming to realise that we will publish
first, but that is only the *beginning* of the work that other
specialists will do with this material.

– Pierce

PART FOURTEEN

15 December–25 December AD 1476

'Tesmoign mon sang manuel cy mis'[1]

---

[1] French: 'Witness my hand's blood here placed'. Variant on the more usual 'witness my *seing manuel* [signature] here placed' on contracts and other documents? Sible Hedingham ms part 4.

I

The constant howling of wolves echoes across the river valley.

"Bold enough to come down in daytime, now," the big Welshman Geraint ab Morgan remarked, his breath huffing white as he strode through the cold, dry street beside Ash. "Little furry bastards."

"Rickard's got three wolf pelts now." Ash's smile faded. *And he's killed more than wolves with that sling.*

Three weeks, and the huge open-air fires in the Visigoth camp burn constantly, day and night; the Burgundians can look down from their walls and watch the warmth – watch the legionaries visibly thriving. Three weeks after the news from Antwerp: the fifteenth of December, now, and the fucking Visigoths can *afford* to let wolves scavenge in their camp.

And I made myself commander-in-chief of this. Captain-General; Maid of Burgundy; Sword of the Duchess.

Duchess Florian. God help her.

"I must be a fucking *lunatic!*" Ash said under her breath. Geraint glanced down at her. She said, "They still bringing supply trains up the river, out there?"

The edge to the wind made both of them sniffle back mucus. It's cold enough that snot freezes.

"Oh yeah, boss. Rag-'ead sledges, on the ice. The Lion gunners have taken out a few with those mangonels, though."

Barred doors faced her, under the overhanging upper storeys of the houses. No one yelled warnings and emptied bed-chamber pots; no children played in the mud. Yesterday and today, there have been reports of wells freezing.

Some part of her has been frozen, too, since she held Margaret of Burgundy's severed head. *They are not coming, no one's coming, there are no men in Burgundy under arms now except here!*

And I'm supposed to be in charge of them.

That knowledge makes even the palace, which still has hearth-fires, an unbearable succession of meetings, briefings and muster-rolls. A stolen hour off-duty with Lion Azure company business has a welcome familiarity, even if there is little else pleasant about this particular incident.

"Your punishment list's getting far too long," Ash said, her voice falling flat in the freezing air.

"They were carrying off doors for firewood. Stupid buggers," Geraint remarked, without anger. "I told them to take it from abandoned buildings, but they can't be arsed to go up to the north-east gate. Took it from here."

Behind them both, Rickard's sling whipped out; and the young man swore. "Missed it!"

"Rat?" Ash queried.

"Cat." Rickard coiled the leather strip up, his bare fingers purple with cold. "There's good eating on a cat."

The rhythmic hammer of a Visigoth siege-machine began to pound again from the direction of Dijon's north-west gate.

"That won't do 'em no good." *Showers of rock will harass, rather than harm; make people stay within doors. Which they do in any case, lacking candles, now, and lacking food: the remaining rations going to the soldiers.*

The diet everywhere is horseflesh and water.

A black object flashed in the corner of her vision. Both she and Geraint simultaneously and automatically flinched. *The distant boom of siege-guns alerts you; Greek Fire roars as it arcs through the air; trebuchet-shot drops, silently, with no warning before the street explodes in front of you.*

Rickard ran forward from the provost's escort and stooped over something small on the cobbles. He stood, cupping it in his hands.

"Sparrow," he called.

Better than another damn spy or herald coming back in pieces.

Rickard rejoined them. Ash touched the small, feathered body – cold as the stones of Dijon palace – and glanced up. There was no mark on the bird. It had evidently fallen, frozen dead, out of the air.

"Won't make lunch, even for you," she said; and he grinned. She signalled the escort, moving forward. Her boots skidded on the icy cobbles with every step – far too dangerous to ride, here – and she wiped tears out of her eyes every time a street-corner brought them face to face with the wind again.

The desultory Visigoth bombardment continued. *Sound carries in this weather: she could be up the north-west quarter of the city, instead of here, close by the south bridge.*

"They're not assaulting the gates," Geraint said.

"They don't need to." *They can just let us watch their camp – always warm, always with enough to eat. If it isn't a bluff. They're flourishing.*

Icicles clung to eaves, dropping old, glassy fangs towards the street. *There is frost here that hasn't melted in all fifteen days of this freezing weather. And the ice snaps the ropes of mangonels, and trebuchets.*

They're not attacking. But they're not falling apart, either. Or mutinying. I suppose – Ash quickened her step, careful to keep all expression off her face. – *I suppose that means the Faris has got her nerve back. So . . .*

So what will she do? What will anyone else do? What can *I* do?

Masonry walls radiate cold. Her eyes scanned, automatically, as she walked, ready to send ab Morgan's men to investigate bodies: *every night, now, brought two or three people found frozen to death in the streets. On the walls, men-at-arms freeze to their watch-points. One man was found frozen to his horse. The earth is like marble, these dead can't be buried.*

"Boss," Geraint ab Morgan said.

"Is this the place?" Ash was already stepping forward, between the ripped lath and plaster walls that had held a door a short time ago. The seasoned oak

884

posts and lintel had been removed, along with the door and part of one support-beam. The front of the house was taking on a sag.

On the floor inside, on filthy rushes, six women and five children sat huddled together. Four adult men stood up, shivering, and approached the gaping hole, facing Ash. The tallest one, speechless, stared at her livery; his scowl fading to incomprehension rather than recognition.

"The men who did this have been punished," Ash said, and stopped. The light from the door let her see the long-cold hearth. It was no warmer here than in the winter street. "I'll send you firewood."

"Food." One of the women cuddling a child looked up. The light from the door shone on eyes big in their sockets, hard cheekbones, and cold-whitened skin. "Send us food, you posh cow!"

Another woman grabbed frantically at her arm. The first woman shook the hand off, glaring at Ash over her child's head.

"You fucking soldiers get all the food. I've got my cousin Ranulf here from Auxonne, and the girls, and the baby – how can I feed them?" She lost all her violence in a second, shrinking away from the provost men-at-arms as they came to stand around Ash. She put her arm over the child. "I didn't mean anything! What can I do? They're starving here, after I offered them a home. How can I look him in the face? My husband's dead, he died fighting for you!"

For you, Ash thought. But this isn't the time to say so.

If I was still boss of mercenaries, I'd be looking to sell this place out about now. Hell: about three weeks ago . . .

"I'll send food." Ash turned abruptly enough to collide with Geraint ab Morgan, pushed her way past him back into the open air, and strode back up the street, heels ringing on the frozen mud.

"Where *from*, boss? Men won't like it." Geraint scratched under the gown bundled over his armour. "We're on half-rations now, and down to the horses. We can't feed every refugee family here." And, plainly frustrated at her silence: "Why d'you think the rag-head bitch won't let civilians leave this city, boss? They know how much pressure it puts on us!"

"Henri Brant tells me the horse-meat is nearly finished." Ash did not look back at Geraint or Rickard as she spoke. "So, now we can't afford to feed the guard dogs, either. When my mastiffs are slaughtered, send one to that house back there."

"But, Brifault, Bonniau—!" Rickard protested.

Ash overrode him: "There's good eating on a dog."

It's come on her, over the last few weeks: she has wept for the men being injured and killed on the walls of Dijon, in the bombardment. To her surprise, de la Marche and Anselm, and even Geraint ab Morgan, have understood it; thought it no damage to her authority. Now, walking in the cold street, she feels the icy track of one tear sliding down her cheek; and shakes her head, snorting with a bitter amusement at herself. Who weeps for an animal?

Under her breath, as always, she murmured, "Godfrey, have you heard her?"

– *Nothing. Still nothing. Not even to ask if you speak to me – to the* machina rei militaris.

Anything he knows, they know. I can't even ask Godfrey how I can cope with being Captain-General.

"Put double guard on the stores," she said as Geraint lumbered up beside her. "Any man you catch taking bribes, take the skin off his back."

There are things she knows, as Captain-General of Burgundy, that she would rather not know. *We've got food now for what, three weeks? Two? Somehow – somehow we have to take an initiative!*

But I don't know how.

"Maybe," she said, too quietly for Geraint, or Rickard, or her voices; "maybe I shouldn't be doing this job."

Unmelted frost crunched under her boots, coming into an open square. Wind brought tears leaking from her eyes. The frozen fountain in the middle of the square bulged with ice.

"We'll go up to the mills," she announced. "I want to check the guard on the mill-races, now they're frozen. Animals have been getting in that way; I don't want men doing it. Geraint, you and the provosts see to my orders; Rickard, you come with me and Petro."

Giovanni Petro's archers, on rota for escort again, muttered under their breaths; she knew them to be comparing the exposed south-west wall of Dijon with the provosts' warm guardroom back at the company tower. A small grin moved the frozen muscles of her face.

As she strode into the maze of alleys leading off the square, she heard Petro's "Furl that bloody banner before we get to the wall!" behind her, and glimpsed a man-at-arms lowering the identifying Lion Affronté with its rapidly sewn-on Cross of St Andrew.

She crossed the open end of an alley, to her left.

A flicker of movement punched her across the street.

Jogging footsteps jolted her. Men holding her under the arms, under the crook of her knees: carrying her. Her armour clattered. The world swung dizzily about her.

"What—?"

"*She's not dead!*"

"Get her to safety! Go, go, go!"

A swelling pain hit her. Her sagging, steel-clad body jarred in their grip. She cannot feel where she hurts. A gasp: another gasp – trying to wrench air into her winded lungs.

"Put her down!"

"I'm okay—" She coughed. Hardly heard her own voice. Was aware of herself supported, of a stench of excrement, of dim light, stairs, flaring torches, and then a room in natural light.

"I'm *alive*. Just – winded—"

She coughed again, banged her arm-defences against her cuirass, trying to put her arm around her chest; and looked up from where she leaned, supported between Petro and Rickard, and found herself looking at Robert Anselm, at Olivier de la Marche.

"*Fuck* me." She tried to wrench herself upright. Pain shot through her body. "I'm *fine*. Anybody see me fall? Roberto?"

"There's rumours starting—"

She cut him off: "You and Olivier, get back out there! They'll know there's nothing much wrong with me if you're out there and visible."

"Yes, Pucelle." De la Marche nodded, turning away, with a group of Burgundian knights. Faint ice-bright light leaked in through round-arched windows, showing her concerned faces. The second floor of the company tower. Florian's hospital.

"What 'appened?" Anselm demanded.

"Fucked if I know – Petro? Who's down?"

"Just you, boss." The sergeant of archers shifted his grip, easing her upright as she found her body able to move again. Something stung. She looked down at her left hand. The linen glove inside her gauntlet dripped, soaked through with red blood. The cold let her feel no pain.

"Didn't you hear it, boss?" Giovanni Petro asked. At her blank look, he added, "Trebuchet strike. Took out the west wing of the Viscount-Mayor's palace, off the Square of Flowers – shrapnel come flying down the alleys, you copped it."

"Trebuchet—"

"Bloody big chunk of limestone."

"Fucking Christ!" Ash swore.

Someone, behind her, shoved as she tried to regain her feet, and she found herself standing, swaying. A sharp pain went through her body. She put her bloodied fingers to her cuirass. The pages removed her sallet: she turned her head and saw Florian.

Half-Duchess, half-surgeon, Ash thought dizzily. Florian wore a cloth-of-gold kirtle, with a vair-lined gown thrown over it; belted up any old how with a dagger and herb-sack hanging from her waist. The rich garments trailed, dirt-draggled, black for eighteen inches up from the hem. Under her kirtle, Ash could see she was still wearing doublet and hose.

She wore neither coif nor begemmed headdress, but she was not bareheaded. Carved and shining, the white oval of a crown enclosed her brows.

It was neither gold, nor silver, nor regular. White-brown spikes jutted up in a rough coronet. Skilled hands had carved white antler into a circlet, fastening the polished pieces with gold fittings, forming the horns of the hart into an oval crown. It pressed down on her straw-gold hair.

"Let's get the armour off you." Business-like and brusque, Floria del Guiz took a firm grip under Ash's left arm, and nodded to Rickard. The young man, with two of the pages helping, rapidly cut the points, unbuckled the straps, and lifted her pauldrons off her shoulders. She looked dizzily down at his bowed head as he unbuckled the straps down the right-hand side of her breastplate, plackart and tassets, undid the waist-strap, and let one tasset swing as he unbuckled the fauld.

"Okay—" He popped the cuirass open, hinging open and removing the metal shell all in one go, steel plates clattering. She swayed again, struck by the freezing air, feeling naked in nothing but arming doublet and hose, leg- and arm-defences. Her teeth chattered.

"*Fucking* hell!"

Still holding the armour, he demanded, "Are you all right, boss? Boss, are you all right?"

His adolescent voice squeaked; going high for the first time in weeks.

"Shit – I'm fine. Fine!" Ash held her arms out from her sides. Her hands shook. The little brush-haired page slit the points of her arming doublet. "Where'd it get me?"

Rickard laid the body-armour down in a clatter of steel, staring at it. "Right in the chest, boss."

Florian blocked her view, reaching down to her arming doublet, and carefully pulling the sweaty, filthy garment open.

"Rickard, I'm fine; the rest of you, I'm okay. Now fuck off, will you? Florian, what's the damage?"

Robert Anselm still hovered in the doorway. "Boss . . ."

"What part of 'fuck off' didn't you understand?" Ash inquired acidly; and when the Englishman had vanished, yelped under her breath: "Shit, that *hurts*!"

Floria knotted her fists in Ash's arming doublet again, yanked it wide open, got her hand in to the ribs on Ash's left-hand side, and felt with remarkably gentle fingers under her breast. Ash had not been wearing a shirt under the arming doublet, and her flesh shrank from the bitingly cold air, from Floria's chill flesh, and from the prodding fingers on her bruised skin.

"Easy!" Ash winced again; grinned shakily. "Hey. It's not like they were aiming at me!"

"It's not like that will matter," Floria mimicked, sardonically. She peered at Ash's side, face all but inside the open arming doublet. Her breath steamed in the cold air. Ash felt it shivery-warm against her skin, and momentarily stiffened.

"Haven't you got something better to do than mess about in hospitals, Duchess?"

There were women with Florian who were not from the company, she realised as she said it. The Duchess's maids and Jeanne Châlon sniffed, and looked much as if they agreed with Ash.

"No. I've got patients here. I've got patients up at St Stephen's, and in the two other abbey hospices . . ." Florian grinned. "I'd left Blanche in charge here; you're lucky to have me."

"Oh, sure I— fuck! Don't *do* that!"

"I'm checking your ribs."

Peering down, Ash could see her open doublet, bare breast, and a raised, reddened area of skin perhaps the size of a dinner plate below her left breast. She shifted a little, feeling now the separate aches from hipbone, armpit, pectoral muscle, and – now she realised it – the base of her throat.

"That's going to go all sorts of pretty colours," she observed.

Floria straightened up, sat down on the medical chest that was doing duty for a bench (tables and chairs long since gone for firewood), and tapped her dirty finger thoughtfully against her teeth. "Your lung's okay. You might have sprung a rib."

"No wonder, boss!" Rickard straightened up, still bundled in jack, livery jacket, and fur-lined demi-gown; his hood barely pushed back from his face even inside the tower and close to the remaining hearth-fire. "Look at this."

He held up Ash's cuirass by the shoulders, fauld and tassets still attached. The plackart, unstrapped from the upper breastplate, caught the light in a glinting craze.

"Fuck me." Ash reached out and slid her gloved fingers across the case-hardened steel. The curve of the plackart was shattered, like ice when a rock hits it. At her gesture, he turned the body-armour around. On the back of the breastplate, over the place where her left ribs would be, the softer iron bulged back.

Her fingers went without volition to her bare torso, touching the swelling skin.

"It bloody *cracked* it. My plackart! And the breastplate, too. Two layers of steel, and it fucking *cracked* it!"

The light from the winter-blue sky outside the window flashed from the steel. She slowly removed her gauntlets, and fumbled to pull the edges of her doublet together. Florian took her left hand, probing for stone splinters. Her breath hissed as she stared at the Milanese breastplate in Rickard's hands. "The armourer can't hammer *that* out. Sweet Green Christ up a Tree, that's *my* luck for this siege! Holy Saint George!"

"Never mind the soldier saints," Floria remarked under her breath, with asperity, "try Saint Jude! Tilde, I'll need a witch hazel and St John's wort poultice. Wash this hand in wine. It doesn't need bandages."

The maid-in-waiting curtseyed, to Floria's obvious amusement.

Jeanne Châlon caught Ash's eye and sniffed again, disapprovingly.

"Niece-Duchess," she said pointedly, "remember you are called to the council, at Nones."

"Actually, aunt, I think you'll find that *I* called *them*."

Jeanne Châlon flushed. "Of course, my lady."

"'Of course, my lady'," Rickard muttered under his breath, in mincing mockery.

Floria caught his eye and scowled. "You need to get the rest of this metalware off her. Tilde, where's that poultice?"

A man sat up, on a pallet closer to the hearth. Ash saw it was Euen Huw. Dirty beyond belief, and gaunt, with the fine cat-gut of Floria's stitches poking up out of his shaven hair, the wiry Welshman still managed to grin woozily at her.

"Hey. Don't you let her prod you around, boss. Heavy-handed, she is. Working for the rag-'eads, I swear it!"

"You lie down, Euen, or I'll put some more stitches in that thick Welsh head of yours!"

He smiled at Florian. As he half-fell back on to his pallet, he murmured, "Got a cushy number, now, haven't we? Comes of having a smart boss, see. Gets our surgeon crowned Duchess. Boss in charge of the army. Even the damn rag-heads give up when they hear that."

I wish! Ash thought. She saw it mirrored on Florian's face.

She held out her arms to Rickard and the pages, who stripped her of couters, vambraces, cannons. Shucking the arming doublet painfully down to her waist, she flinched as Florian prodded at her back.

The woman surgeon straightened up. "Whatever you hit when you landed, the armour saved you. Have you got a shirt I can tear up? I'm going to bind those ribs tight. You'll be stiff; it'll hurt; you'll live."

"Thanks for your sympathy . . ." Ash gritted her teeth at the touch of the poultice. "Rickard, you take my kit across to the armoury. Tell 'em boss needs a new breastplate and plackart. They can pull anything they need out of the army stores. But I need it done yesterday!"

"Yes, boss!"

The light here came from one set of opened shutters. Further into the hall, the shutters were closed. Fire-heated bricks, placed under blankets, took a very little of the freezing chill off the air. Men on pallets moved, uneasily; someone groaning continuously, another man muttering to himself. Some had purple-bruised, stitched flesh left uncovered; other men had bloodied bandages. Only a few men sat playing dice, or cleaning their kit, or arguing. Most huddled down.

Ash's eyes narrowed against the dull light. "You've got twice the number of sick here since yesterday. We haven't had an attack on the walls. Is it the bombardments?"

Florian looked up briefly. "Let's see. I've got twenty-four men wounded here. Three men are going to die, because I can't do anything about the shock and bleeding; one man from a stinking wound, the other from a poisoned wound. The broken shoulder-bones, ribs, and broken wrists should mend. I don't know about the stove-in breastbone. Baldina took an arrow out of one of Loyecte's men; I haven't wanted to move him out of here. There are ten burn-cases, that's Greek Fire. They'll survive."

She spoke without reference to the parchment notes stuffed in the corner of the medicine chest.

"There's more than twenty-four men in here."

"Twenty men down with campaign fever," Florian stated. Her expression, studying Ash's half-bare body, was clinical in the extreme. She ignored the hiss of breath as the poultice touched Ash's skin.

"Dysentery," she elucidated, whipping bandages with a sure hand. "Ash, I tell them to bury bodies away from the wells. The ground's rock-hard. I tell them to make sure there are slit-trenches dug, on the waste-ground back of the forge.[2] They shit anywhere they please. I've got civilian cases of dysentery in the abbeys. More than there were yesterday. And that's more than there was the day before. Once it gets a hold . . ."

"What about stores?"

"No fresh herbs. Even with the civilian abbeys, we're low on Self-Heal, goldenrod, Lady's Mantle, Solomon's Seal. Baldina and the girls can give them camomile, to calm them down. Marjoram, on sprains. That's it." Her gaze flicked to Ash's face. "I'm out of everything else. We bandage. We sew." She

---

[2] In post-Roman Western Europe, the practice of burying the dead at a distance from the living, and of organising army latrines, dates from the beginning of the fifteenth century.

smiled wryly. "My people are washing out wounds with Burgundy's finest wines. Best use for them."

Ash shrugged herself painfully back into her doublet. Rickard held out a brigandine, brought by one of the pages, and began to buckle her into it.

"I got to go. In case they think I *am* dead. Morale."

Florian glanced at the pallets, her attention on a man with a chopping cut across the side of his jaw. "I hadn't finished my rounds. I'll see you at the palace. Dusk."

"Yes *sir* . . ." Smiling, Ash essayed a few steps, a little shaky, but mostly balanced.

Back on the first floor, she found the stench of cuckoo-pint starch and billowing steam filling the entire hall. Damp warmth hit her. Women with sore hands, kirtles caught up into their belts, banged around the tubs, through the wet; shouting orders and lewd comments. She found herself behind Blanche and Baldina at the foot of the stairs as Antonio Angelotti appeared, holding out a yellowed linen shirt and complaining in rapid-fire Milanese.

"Madonna," he broke off to greet her. His expression changed, seeing her damaged left hand. "Jussey wants you at the mills."

"Yeah, I was on my way there. You come with me—"

"Boss," a female voice said.

Ash halted, as Blanche put her arm around her daughter's shoulders, the dyed blond heads together. Baldina's kirtle as she turned to face Ash was laced only loosely at the front.

Under it, the belly of a woman great with child showed as a sharp curve. *Not visible before Auxonne. But she must have been carrying it from spring: at Neuss, say?*

"You should be eating better," Ash said automatically. "Ask Hildegarde: tell her I said so."

Baldina put her hands on her belly in an immemorial gesture. Winter sunlight shot through the steam, illuminating her in a glaze of light; and Angelotti's icon-face and yellow ringlets beside her made Ash think caustically, *Haven't I seen you guys in a church fresco somewhere?*

"Have you got a father for it?" Ash added.

Baldina grinned wryly. "Now what do you think, boss?"

"Well, draw on company funds: an extra third-share."

Not that that amounts to much, now.

The younger woman nodded. Her mother, a little awkwardly, said, "Put your hand on it, boss. For luck."

"For—" Ash's silver brows went up. She put her unbandaged hand palm-flat on Baldina's belly, feeling the heat of the woman's body though kirtle and shirt and gauntlet-glove.

In Ash's memory, a woman-physician of the Carthaginians says *The gate of the womb is spoiled; she will never carry to term.* A pang, that might have been for anything – lost chances, perhaps – went through her, stinging her eyes.

"Here's luck, then. When do you drop?"

"Near Our Lord's mass. We're naming it for Saint Godfrey, if it's a boy."

Baldina turned her head as someone else yelled. "All *right*! Coming! Thanks, boss."

Ash smiled, saw the escort gathering ahead of her at the door, and walked away from the stairs, on across the great hall, Angelotti falling into step beside her.

"Well, there's one thing I'm sure of," she said, in a rasping attempt at humour: "It isn't yours!"

Angelotti gave a calm smile, at odds with his vulgar Italian: "Not until pretty bum-boys give birth."

Almost at the door of the hall, with cold wind swirling the steam into towers of whiteness, he touched her arm. "Don't think of us as friends, madonna. We're not your friends. We're men and women who obey you. Burgundy's men, too. That is not what friends do."

She gave him a startled look. The relief of that detached view sank in. She nodded absently.

He added, "Even if what I say is half true, it is not wholly false. Men who have given you the responsibility of leading them are not your friends; they expect more of you. 'Lioness'."

"So: is this a warning?" A little cynically, she said, "Gun captains go anywhere. The Visigoths would give you a job with their siege-machines – they wouldn't send your gun-crews against these walls. You're too expensive to kill off. Shall I expect to be told when you're going, or shall I wake up in the next few days and find you and Jussey's lads gone?"

His oval eyelids shut, briefly; allowing her one look at the smooth perfection of his face. He opened his eyes. "Nothing like so easy, madonna. Fever has a grip, famine is here. Sooner, rather than later, now, you'll commit us to an attack – and we'll do it."

Four days later, in the company armoury, she looks down at herself. At a new breastplate and plackart buckled into her body-armour; only the brightness of the buff leather, and therefore the newness of the straps, giving away that this mirror-finish steel is not her original Milanese-made harness.

"Shit-hot job . . ." She brought her arms together, let her body follow the lines of someone moving a weapon in precise arcs. Nothing caught, or pulled.

"Not *my* job, boss." Jean Bertran, something over six foot tall, forge-blackened like a pageant-devil, gave her a look equal parts diffidence and cynicism. "I roughed it out like Master Dickon taught me. Took it to the old Duke's royal armourers for the rest. The lads here did the buckles."

"Tell 'em fucking brilliant—"

"*Boss!*" a voice bawled. "Boss! Come quick!"

She winced, turning; catching her bruised flesh painfully. Willem Verhaecht's 2IC, Adriaen Campin, stumbled across the ice-rutted paving stones and into the forge.

"Boss, you'd better come!"

"Is it an assault?" Ash was already staring around wildly. "Rickard, my sword! Where are they coming this time?"

The big Fleming shook his head, red-faced under his war-hat. "The north-east gate, boss. I don't know *what* it is! Maybe not an attack. Someone's coming in!"

"*In?*" Ash stared.

"In!"

"Fucking *hell*!"

Rickard thumped back from the recesses of the armoury, the sword and belt slung over his shoulder, her livery jacket in his hands. In a frantic few seconds, Ash found herself attempting simultaneously to answer questions from the lance-leaders crowding in after Campin; and answer Robert Anselm – and Duchess Florian – as they came in on the men-at-arms' heels.

"Son of a *bitch*!" she bellowed.

Silence fell in the armoury, apart from the subdued hiss of the coals in the forge.

"Double the wall guard," she ordered rapidly. "This could be a diversion. Roberto, you and twenty men, with me, to the north-east gate. Florian—"

The surgeon shoved her herb-sack at Baldina. "I'm with you."

"No, you're damn well not! The goddamn Visigoths would like nothing better than a shot at the Burgundian Duchess. I'll get you an escort back to the palace."

"What part of 'fuck off' didn't you understand?" Floria del Guiz murmured, her eyes bright. She grinned at Ash. "There is such a thing as morale. As you keep telling me. If I'm Duchess, then I'm not afraid to walk the city wall here!"

"But you're not the normal type of Duchess – oh shit, there isn't time!"

Rickard held her livery surcoat up high, by its shoulders. Ash fisted her gauntlets, ducked under, and dived up, attempting to shove her fists and remaining arm-defences through the wide sleeves. Two moments' breathless tugging and panic got it down over her head. Rickard slung the sword-belt around her waist, buckled and tugged; and she settled the hilt of the single-handed blade to where she wanted it, grabbed her cloak from him, pulled her hood up, and strode out of the room.

Too cold again to ride without danger to the horses. The hurried half-run to the north-eastern side of Dijon took them perhaps half an hour. In that time, they saw no one but soldiers up on the walls, and Burgundian men-at-arms on street patrol. Not a dog barked, not a cow lowed; the bright, eggshell-blue sky shone, birdless, no doves in the dovecotes now. The winter wind brought tears into her eyes, snatched the breath out of her throat.

Panting from the climb up to the top of the gatehouse, she joined Olivier de la Marche and twenty or more Burgundian nobles on the wall. The big Burgundian was shading his eyes with his gauntlet, peering north-east.

"Well?" Ash demanded.

Willem Verhaecht ran from the battlements to her side. He pointed. "There, boss."

A squabble broke out behind her – de la Marche noting Floria's presence; the surgeon-Duchess refusing to listen to his explosive, protective complaints – but Ash ignored it.

"What the *fuck* is that?" she asked.

Rickard elbowed his way through the Lion men-at-arms to her side. He carried her second-best sallet under his arm. She took it, thoughtfully; standing bareheaded in the icy wind, a woman with scars, and feathery silver hair now grown long enough to cover the lobes of her ears.

Ash glanced at her nearest captain of archers, and covertly back at Floria. "How far's crossbow range from here?"

Ludmilla Rostovnaya smiled with a face still taut from healing burns. "About four hundred yards, boss."

"How far away are their lines from this wall?"

"About four hundred and one yards!"

"Fine. Anything comes a yard closer to us, I want it skewered. Instantly. And watch those bloody siege-engines."

"Yes, boss!"

The Visigoth tents shone white under a winter-clear sky. Spirals of smoke rose straight up from their turf-roofed huts, surrounding this quarter of the city. A neighing came from their horse lines. She strained her gaze to see siege machinery; could see none within range. A scurry of people ran, five hundred yards away, ranks parting; and something else moved, between the tents, north-east along the road that ran by the river. Horses? Pennants? Armed or unarmed men?

Rickard squinted, rubbing his watering eyes. "Can't tell the livery, boss."

"No – yes. Yes, I can." Ash grabbed the arm of Robert Anselm, standing next to her; and the broad-shouldered man, bundled up against the bitter cold, grinned from under his visor. "Sweet Christ, Robert, is that what I think it is?"

Sounding light-hearted for the first time in weeks, her second-in-command said, "Getting old, girl? Getting short-sighted?"

"That's a fucking red crescent!" Ash spoke loudly. The noise from the Burgundian knights cut off. She pointed. "That's the *Turks*!"

"Motherfuckers!" Floria del Guiz exclaimed; fortunately in the broad patois of the mercenary camp. Jeanne Châlon pursed her lips, disapproving the vehemence; Olivier de la Marche choked.

A neat column of cavalry horses trotted out from between the Visigoth ranks. At this distance, in winter's haze, all Ash could make out were white pennants with red crescents, and riders in fawn robes and white helms. No spear-points silhouetted against the sky: therefore not lancers. The column wound out of the Visigoth camp into the deserted land between it and the city walls: horses picking their way across churned mud vitrified by black frosts. A hundred, two hundred, five hundred men . . .

"What are they *doing*? I don't believe it!" Ash swore again. She threw her arms around the shoulders of Ludmilla Rostovnaya and Willem Verhaecht, embracing them. "Well spotted! What the *hell* are they doing?"

"If they plan to attack us, it is foolish," Olivier de la Marche said. He made an obvious effort and turned to Floria del Guiz. "You see we have guns on the walls, my lady."

Floria wore her *I do know one end of an arquebus from the other* expression; Ash has seen a lot of it in the past month.

"Don't fire," Floria said.

It was unmistakably an order. After a moment, de la Marche said, "No, my lady."

Ash grinned to herself. She murmured quietly, "And to think I thought you'd have trouble being a Duchess . . ."

"I'm a doctor. I'm used to telling people what to do." Floria rested her hands on the battlements, staring out at the approaching armed horsemen. "Even when I don't know what's best."

"Especially then."

Ash put her helmet on, and when she glanced up from buckling the strap, the Turkish riders were close enough that she could see they carried round shields, and recurved bows; and their helmets were not white, but were covered by a white felt sleeve that hung down over the backs of their necks.

"They are indeed Turks," Olivier de la Marche said, his voice loud in the icy silence. "I know them. They are the Sultan's crack troops, his Janissaries."

The mingled respect and awe on the faces of both her men and the Burgundians was enough to let Ash know they shared de la Marche's opinion.

"Fine. So they're shit-hot. What are they doing *here*? Why are they heading for this city?" Ash leaned out from one of the embrasures, frustrated. A great number of troops – Legio VI Leptis Parva, by the eagle – milled about on the edges of their earthworks; but otherwise made no move. Watching.

"If they're intending to come inside the city . . ." De la Marche's voice trailed off.

Ash found herself watching the Janissaries' cavalry mounts and thinking not of military use, but only of food on the hoof. There were no Turkish packhorses visible. "If they're intending to come inside the city, then why aren't the Visigoths slaughtering them?"

"Yes, Demoiselle-Captain, exactly."

"They're never going to let five hundred Turks in here to reinforce the siege. What the fuck is going on!"

Robert Anselm snuffled.

Ash looked sharply at him. The big man wiped his wrist across his nose, stifling another snuffling laugh; caught her eye and broke out into a loud guffaw.

"That's what's going on. Take a look at that, girl! It's fucking mad – so who's behind it?"

Now the head of the column was within a hundred yards of Dijon's north-east gate, it was possible to discern European riders among the Turkish cavalry. Not many of them, Ash saw: not above fifty men. She wiped her streaming eyes again, staring into the wind.

A great red-and-yellow standard flew above the few Europeans; and a personal banner. The wind blew the cloth towards them, among Turkish pennants; and it was a second before a gust unrolled the silk on the air so that all could see it. A ripple of exclamations went along the wall. Up and down the battlements, a great ragged cheer went up, on and on.

Ash blinked at the yellow banner. A tusked blue boar, flanked by white five-pointed stars.

"Holy *shit*!"

It was not necessary, the man's name was being shouted from one end of the walls to the other, but Robert Anselm said it anyway.

"John de Vere," he said, "thirteenth Earl of Oxford."

II

A brief shouted confrontation between the Burgundians and Oxford; the gates of Dijon opened just long enough for five hundred men to ride through; Ash pelted down the stairs, off the wall.

Her men crowded her on the steps, scabbards tangling; she found herself barely ahead of Robert Anselm, Olivier de la Marche treading on her armoured heels.

"An Oxford!" Robert Anselm bellowed the de Vere battle-cry happily. "*An Oxford!*"

The crowd poured off the walls at the same time as the great city gates clashed shut. Iron bars slammed noisily back into place. A weight cannoned into Ash's back: she skidded on cobblestones, and grabbed the person who had fallen into her – Floria, feet tangled in her jewelled skirts, cursing.

"Is it him? It *is* him! The man's a lunatic!" Floria exclaimed.

"Tell me something I don't know!"

A great orderly mass of Ottoman Turks – five hundred at least – formed their horses up into a square in the market space behind the gate. The icy wind whipped the mounts' tails. Mares, mostly, she saw at a glance, tough fawn-coloured mares; and their armed riders sitting their dyed-leather saddles in complete stillness, no shouting, no calling out, no dismounting.

A raw-boned grey gelding galloped out of the mass of Turks, three or more horses with it. The yellow-and-blue banner streamed out, carried by the lead rider.

The armoured banner-bearer, riding without a helmet, curly fair hair flying and a great smile on his face, was Viscount Beaumont. De Vere's three brothers rode at his heels; behind Dickon and Tom and George, on the grey, came John de Vere himself.

The Earl of Oxford flung himself out of the saddle, throwing the war-horse's reins to any who might get them – Thomas Rochester, Ash saw. His battle-harsh voice bellowed, "Madam Captain Ash!"

"My lord Oxford— oof!"

The English Earl threw his arms around her in a crushing embrace. Ash had a split second to reflect that she was far better off wearing plate than she would have been in mail. Her ribs stabbed pain into her side. She gasped. John de Vere, still holding her in a bear-hug, burst into tears. "Madam, God save you, do I find you well?"

"Wonderful," she whispered. "Now – let – go—"

The Englishmen were all, she saw, either in tears or waving their hands around and talking excitedly; Beaumont wringing Olivier de la Marche by the hand; Dickon de Vere embracing Robert Anselm; Thomas and George loud among the throng of Burgundian nobles. The rows of mounted Janissaries gazed down from their horses at this spectacle, seeming mildly interested, if impassive.

John de Vere wiped his face unselfconsciously. His skin had become pale in the months since she had seen him last. Winter mud covered him to the knee. For the rest – she looked him up and down, fists on her hips – the English Earl stood in battle-worn harness, faded blue eyes watering in the wind, so little different that it made her heart lurch.

"My God," she said, "am I glad to see you!"

"Madam, your expression alone is worth gold!"

The Earl clapped his hands together, partly in satisfaction, partly against the cold. His eyes travelled across the crowd. Ash followed the direction of his gaze. She saw it take him noticeable seconds to realise who he stared at.

"God's bollocks! It's true, then? Your physician is Charles's heir? Your Florian is Duchess of Burgundy now?"

"True as I'm standing here." Ash's face ached with the smile she couldn't keep off it. She added, thoughtfully, "My lord."

"Give me your hand," he said, "and not your 'my lord'."

Ash stripped off her gauntlet and clasped his hand, moved almost to tears of her own. "If it comes to that, I guess you have the distinction of being the only Englishman ever to employ the reigning prince of Burgundy – since she's still on my books, and I'm still on yours."

"The more reason for you to have trusted me to return."

Floria del Guiz appeared through the crowd that parted to let the Duchess of Burgundy pass. The Earl of Oxford sank gracefully down on one knee. His brothers joined him, and Viscount Beaumont; kneeling before her, and the Burgundian nobles.

"God be with you, madam doctor," John de Vere said, not appearing at all incommoded to be kneeling. "You have been given a harder task than any man would wish."

Ash opened her mouth to speak, hesitated, and shut it again. She put her hands behind her back, forcing herself to wait for Floria to speak first. *Duchess Florian*, she reminded herself uncomfortably.

Floria's sudden smile dazzled. "We have to talk, my lord Oxford. Is this all your men? Are there more?"

"These are all," de Vere said, getting to his feet. Ash saw him glance back automatically at the Turkish troops in their neat, disciplined rows.

"Regrettably, Mistress Florian, I speak little of their language." The Earl of Oxford pointed to a moustached soldier in mail hauberk and peaked helm. "My sole interpreter. He's from Wallachia; a Voynik auxiliary. Do you have anyone here who speaks Turkish?"

Ash, glancing at Floria before she answered, said, "Not me, my lord. But I wouldn't be at all surprised. Robert," she signalled Anselm over. "Do we have anyone who speaks Turkish?"

"I do." Anselm made an awkward bow to the Earl; and pointed over at the

Italian gunner, who had joined Ludmilla Rostovnaya and the missile troops. "Angelotti does. We fought in the Morea[3] in sixty-seven and sixty-eight. Maybe as late as seventy. Some damn Florentine shot me in the leg; I hauled Angelotti out of the Adriatic. Never been to sea since." He took a breath, still unsteadily gazing at the Earl of Oxford. "Yeah. I speak the language."

"Good," de Vere approved absently. "I do not wish to be dependent on one man who may be killed."

His eyes stayed fixed on Floria del Guiz, in her female clothing. Ash saw him shake his head in wonderment.

Losing patience, Ash demanded, "Are you going to tell us what's going on here, my lord?"

"It is Burgundy's Duchess that I should tell." De Vere's face creased with humour. "I dare say she'll let you listen, madam."

Floria del Guiz, surrounded by maids, Burgundian nobles, and Thomas Rochester's lance in their self-imposed duty as bodyguard, grinned broadly at Ash. "No chance!"

"Oh, she might. She might." Ash beamed at John de Vere. She spread her hands a little. "Meet the Captain-General of Burgundy's armies, my lord – the Maid of Dijon."

The Earl of Oxford gazed at her beatifically for several seconds. His head went back in a great bark of laughter. Beaumont and the de Vere brothers joined in. What Ash saw in de Vere's expression, as he registered the bristling disapproval of de la Marche and the Burgundian knights, was sheer delight.

He walloped her solidly on the arm. "So. This is how you hold to your *condotta* with me, madam?"

"I'm at your command now you're back, my lord."

"Of course you are." His faded blue eyes glowed with humour. "Of course. As an Englishman, madam, I'm more than happy to leave Holy Virgins to foreigners. Much safer." More soberly, he added, "What news have you had of late from outside the walls?"

Floria said grimly, "For about the last three weeks, nothing."

Robert Anselm added, "The Visigoths aren't taking the walls, but they've got this place shut up tighter than a duck's arse, my lord."

"You have had no intelligence at all?"

Ash blinked against the low brilliance of the winter noon. "They tied us up solid, about the same time they stopped pressing the assaults on the walls. We haven't got any spies out or messengers of our own in, since."

At the mention of assaults, she saw de Vere's face change, but he said nothing.

Robert Anselm said cynically, "We stopped sending people out when they started coming back in by trebuchet, in two separate sacks. Last one was that French guy, Armand de Lannoy." He shook his head. "He's been feeding the crows for a week now. Don't know why he thought it was so damn important to get out."

"I can answer that question, Master Anselm," the Earl of Oxford said. As the

---

[3] A Greek theatre of war in which the Turks fought the Venetians.

last of his exuberance died down, Ash noted the strain underneath. "Madam Duchess, better to say it to you and your advisors all at the same time."

Ash overrode what the surgeon might have been about to say. "How the *fuck* – my lord – did you get in here?" She found that she was waving her own hands, in much the same way as the English, and put them down by her side. "Did you sail from Carthage to Constantinople? Have you seen the Sultan? Is this all your troops? What's happened?"

"All in time, madam. And in the lady Duchess's hearing." John de Vere glanced momentarily from the surgeon in her filthy jewelled gown to the white sun in the winter sky.

"Plainly," he said, "you are Burgundy's Duchess, as Charles was the late Duke. Tell me, madam, are you – you *must* be what Duke Charles was. Or we would not have a sun in the sky above us."

Floria's dirty, stained hands went to her breast. A white pectoral Briar Cross hung from a golden chain, itself not rich, but carved from the same horn of the hart as her ducal crown. Her knuckles whitened: she did not, for a second, meet the eyes of any of the Burgundian nobles surrounding her.

"She's Charles's successor," Olivier de la Marche said in the tone of a man who hears a law of nature – the tide, perhaps, or the return of the moon – questioned.

"Oh, she's the Duchess, all right." Ash, conscious of her bruised ribs, and the weight of her armour, shifted from foot to foot in the cold wind. *She is what the Wild Machines need to destroy, now.* "I'll tell you something I *do* know, my lord Oxford. The Faris knows that. She's sitting out there in that camp – she's been sitting out there for five weeks now – and she knows that Florian is the person she needs to kill. And she isn't doing a damn thing about it."

With raised fair eyebrows, John de Vere gazed around at the battered buildings and deserted streets of Dijon.

Ash shrugged. "Oh, she's letting hunger and disease do her work for her, but she's almost stopped the assaults. I'd give half the company war-chest to know what her officers are saying. And the other half to know what she's thinking, right now."

The Earl of Oxford said, "I believe that I can tell you that also, Captain Ash."

The sound of distant siege-engine fire echoed through the air from the west of the city. Faint vibrations shook the earth under her feet.

"Get your Turks away from the walls. We'll take council of war," Floria said briefly. "*In*doors."

As the court entered the private chambers of the Duchess, the Earl of Oxford and his brothers were again swept up into a crush of more of the lords of Burgundy; greetings being exchanged, questions shouted. The Janissary captains followed in Oxford's wake with expressions of polite bewilderment.

Each of the dismounted Turks wore the same thing, Ash noted in astonishment: a fawn-coloured robe with hanging sleeves, over a mail hauberk; a curved sword belted at the waist; bow and shield; and a helmet with a sleeve of white cloth hanging down behind. The uniformity of their clothing and their bearded faces made her feel that she was in the chamber with one man twenty times over, and not with twenty men. The contrast with her own escort, Thomas Rochester's lance – war-hats buckled down over their cowls, wearing a selection of mail, leather and stolen plate armour; each man in his own chosen colour of filthy hose gone through at the knee – was marked.

"We'll never feed them," Floria said flatly, walking in at Ash's side. She caught Ash's glance. "Henri Brant's been advising me. As well as the castellan of Dijon. We can't feed the people we've got."

"Try thinking of it this way. Five hundred cavalry mounts is two hundred and fifty tons of meat."

"Good God, girl! Will they wear it?"

"The Turks? Not for a second, I shouldn't think. Let's not borrow trouble," Ash said thoughtfully. "Find out why he's brought them here, first."

The glassed windows in the ducal chamber kept out much of the freezing wind, but it whined in the chimneys; a hollow sound under the raucous voices. Here, silk hangings still decorated the bed, and there were chairs as well as chests, and a great fire burning in the hearth.

Floria fixed Jeanne Châlon with a challenging eye. "Spiced wine, Tante."

"Yes, Niece-Duchess, of course. At once! If the kitchens have any left."

"If that lot of thieving bastards don't have a cask squirrelled away somewhere," the Duchess of Burgundy remarked, "then we might as well surrender to the Visigoths right now . . ."

Ash snorted. Floria left her side, walking forward into the chamber, and the men drew aside for her without thinking about it. Ash bit her lip. She shook her head, amused at herself, and followed the surgeon towards the fire.

Floria called to her pages: "Pull the chairs around the hearth. No need to freeze while we talk."

Breath whitened the air. Despite the fire, it was cold enough to make Ash's teeth ache. She moved forward, among the general rearrangements, and stood with her back to one side of the carved stone hearth, below a Christ-figure with intricate foliage curling around Him.

Floria seated herself on the carved oak chair that it had taken two pages to shift closer to the warmth. The Burgundian knights and lords and bishops turned towards her, falling silent, watching their bedraggled, bright-eyed, and completely confident Duchess.

The Earl of Oxford said, "May I suggest, madam, that you clear the chamber somewhat? We shall do our business more speedily if we are not burdened with over-much debate."

Floria rattled out a handful of names. Within minutes, all but a dozen of the court dispersed – in remarkable good temper, and anticipation, Ash realised – and the mulled wine came in; and the Duchess looked at the English Earl over the rim of her gold goblet.

"Talk," she said.

"All of it, madam? It has been three months and more since we stood on the beach at Carthage."

Floria rapped out, "*God give me strength and, failing that, patience!*"

John de Vere bellowed with laughter. He sank down, not asking ducal permission, on to a chair close to the burning logs. A scent of sweat and horse emanated from him, with the rising heat. Ash, watching him and his brothers and Beaumont, had a sharp flash of how it had been with the sun of August on Dijon's fields, when they had dined together. Despite the presence of Olivier de la Marche and the Turkish commander, she felt a strong and welcome familiarity.

"Start with him, Master de Vere." Floria del Guiz tilted the cup slightly towards the remaining Turkish Janissary officer.

"Start with why you're in here, not out there, and not dead," Ash clarified. "That's a whole battalion you just brought in here!"

The Earl of Oxford stretched out his boots to the flames. "You would have me begin at the end. Very well. I am here and alive, because I have this man and his cavalry with me. Plainly, five hundred men are no match for six thousand encamped Visigoths. However – I informed the Faris, in all truth and honour, that if his men die here, the Osmanli[4] Sultan Mehmet, second of that name, will consider himself to be instantly at war with the Visigoth Empire."

A moment's silence, in which nothing could be heard but the fire crackling, and the wind in the chimney.

John de Vere added, "She knew it to be true. Her spies must have informed her by now of the troop build-up on the western border of the Sultan's empire."

Ash softly whistled. "Yeah, well, he can afford to make threats like that."[5]

"This is no threat."

"Thank Christ and all His sweet saints for that." Ash shifted, pain jabbing her ribs under the cuirass. "So, let me get this right, you just rode across from Dalmatia or wherever—"

"Five hundred men are a big enough troop not to be bothered," the Earl of Oxford said mildly, "while being no threat to the King-Caliph's army."

"—and then you rode up to Dijon, and you said, 'Let me inside the besieged city with fresh troops', and they said, 'Oh, okay'—"

Dickon de Vere flushed and said hotly, "We risk our lives, and what do you do but carp and jeer!"

"Be quiet, boy." The Earl of Oxford spoke firmly. He smiled at Ash. "You have not stood siege for so long. Let Captain-General Ash ask her questions after her own fashion."

Impetus gone and slightly deflated, Ash said, "They're not fresh troops, these Turks. They're hostages."

The Ottoman commander said in halting German,[6] "I do not know this word."

[4] Europeanised as 'Ottoman'. From Osman Bey, founder of the Turkish empire.

[5] Mehmet II (ruled 1451–81) was, in fact, Sultan of the Osmanli or Ottoman Empire at the time of their conquest of Constantinople; and was thus the man known to be responsible for the fall of Byzantium, the eastern Christian empire.

[6] The Sible Hedingham text here reflects the horrendous variety of languages being used. The Burgundian court habitually spoke French when in the south, and Flemish when they went north. Ash's company would speak English (in several varieties), Italian, German, French (of two varieties); their own patois; and probably a smattering of Greek, Latin, and 'Gothic'. I suspect that the Turkish officer uses a few words of German simply because that is the farthest west he has travelled up to this point.

Ash looked at him, startled. He was, under the felt cap and beard, fair in colouring; probably a Christian by birth.

"It means, if they attack us, if you die; then those men out there—" She indicated the window. "—the Visigoths, they die too. All the while you're in Dijon, an attack on the city is an attack on the Sultan."

His beard split to disclose a smile. "Woman Bey[7] know! Yes. We are the New Troops.[8] We are come to protect, in Mehmet and Gundobad his name. Our lives are your shield."

"This is the Başi Bajezet," Dickon de Vere blurted. "He commands their *orta*."[9]

"Tell Colonel Bajezet he's very welcome," Ash murmured. The Voynik behind the Ottoman commander translated quietly into his ear. The bearded man smiled.

Floria said abruptly, "Will it work?"

"For now, yes, Mistress Florian. Duchess: your pardon." John de Vere straightened up in his chair. A tang of singed leather came from the boots he withdrew from the hearth. He reached out for the wine goblet a page handed him, and drank. It was not apparent how many days he had been in the saddle or how many hundreds of leagues he might have ridden.

"Why?" Floria said.

"By your leave, madam." The Earl of Oxford beckoned his Voynik interpreter, said something in his ear, and the Voynik auxiliary and his commander bowed and retreated from the chamber.

John de Vere said abruptly, "It is dark now as far as Hagia Sophia and the Golden Horn."

"The sun?" Floria turned her head towards the window, the winter sun beyond the glass illuminating the lines around her eyes.

"No sun, madam. Constantinople is as dark as Cologne and Milan." The Earl rubbed his face. "Luckily for me. After I left you, we sailed to Istanbul,[10] then travelled overland to Edirne. I was admitted to the Sultan's presence within weeks. I told him, through an interpreter, what I had seen and heard in Carthage. I told him that Burgundy is, sweet Christ knows why, all that stands between us and the dark; for proof of that, he should witness how the sun still shines on Burgundy."

George de Vere said taciturnly, "His spies confirmed it."

Oxford nodded. He leaned forward, towards the Duchess in her chair. "Sultan Mehmet has two whips driving him, Mistress Florian. He fears this darkness spreading from Africa, and he desires to conquer the Visigoth Empire and its subject nations of Christendom as he did Byzantium. I have told him Burgundy must stand. I do not know if he believes me, but he is willing to make

---

I have attempted to imply interpretation, rather than spell it out each time as the Sible Hedingham ms does.

[7] 'Bey': 'commander'.

[8] 'Yeni çeri', 'Janissaries', literally 'new troops'.

[9] Regiment. The text is inaccurate here, as an *orta* would be commanded by a higher-ranking officer than a mere başi: a çorbaşi, or colonel, perhaps. (Literally, 'chief soup-maker'.)

[10] Literally, 'the city'; post-conquest term for Constantinople.

this much effort. If the Visigoths do prove too strong to be challenged now, he has lost but a regiment of Janissaries proving it."

Floria looked as though she had a sour taste in her mouth. "And if the Visigoths *don't* take Dijon – I get a Turkish army on my doorstep, going hammer and tongs at them?"

A month ago she would have said we, *not* I. Ash sipped her wine: bottom-of-cask stuff not much improved by the scrapings of a palace kitchen spice-drawer.

"How long has he given you?" she asked John de Vere.

"Two months. Then he withdraws Colonel Bajezet." The Earl looked consideringly into the fire. "If I were at a Lancastrian English King's court, say, and a mad Osmanli Earl came and asked me for troops, I do not know that I should lend him so many or for so long!"

Ash drank, watching the light on the surface of the wine. The ducal chamber smelled of man's sweat and of wood-ash. She did not know whether it would hurt her ribs more to sit, or to continue standing. A hand touched her shoulder. She winced, aware that the top of her breastplate had been driven into her flesh too; that she had bruises in those muscles.

Floria del Guiz said, "Ash, have we got two months?"

She raised her eyes, not even aware of the woman having moved. Floria's face under the hart's-horn crown was the same as ever; lined, now, from unwelcome responsibilities. Unknown capabilities. Herself and Floria: the irresistible force rattling off the immovable object. The Duchess's grip loosened.

"If the siege isn't pressed? I doubt it." Ash walked away from her, across the room to one of the windows. Beyond the glass, the skies of Burgundy shone a hard pale blue. Too cold even to snow. Ash touched the freezing glass.

"But the siege isn't the point, not now. Except for the fact that it keeps you here— I've prayed for snow," she said. "Sleet, snow, fog; even rain. Anything to limit visibility! I'd have you and half a dozen of the lads over the wall and away. But it stays clear. Even the fucking moonlight . . . And anybody we send out is killed, or doesn't come back."

She turned to face them: de la Marche, severe; Oxford frowning; Floria anxious.

"It isn't about that army out there! It isn't about the Turks— sorry, my lord de Vere. It's about the Duchess of Burgundy and the fact that we can't get out of here, can't get you away somewhere safe. Keeping you alive, Florian. You and what you do. That's all it's about now, and I'd open up Dijon right now for the Visigoths to plunder – happily! – if I thought I could get you away in the confusion. I can't risk it. One stray arrow could finish everything."

What the Earl of Oxford heard in that, she knew, was not what Floria del Guiz was hearing – or what Oxford would hear, once appraised of the hunting of the hart. Olivier de la Marche bit at his lip. The surgeon scowled.

"Have we got two months?" Floria repeated. "Not just food. Before the Faris—"

"I don't know! I don't know if we have two days, or two hours!"

The Earl of Oxford looked from one woman to the other: the mercenary in plate, cropped hair shining; and the surgeon-turned-Duchess awkward in her woman's clothing. He reached up and scrubbed his hand through his sand-coloured hair.

"There is something I don't understand here," he confessed. "Before you explain yourself, madam, let me finish my tale. You in the city have had no word at all of what goes on in the Faris's camp?"

"We'll have to brief you." Ash relaxed her clenched fists. She strode back towards the warmth of the hearth-fire. "As for intelligence – we've heard nothing. I can guess. She'll have been getting frantic messages from Carthage saying *why the fuck have you stopped the war, you can't do this, get on with it*. Am I right? And it'll have to have been couriers. If *I'm* too scared, now—" Ash grinned mercilessly. "She won't talk to the Stone Golem. She knows what else hears her when she does." She snorted. "And I bet there's been messages going back to Carthage from her officers, too! They must think she's gone nuts."

"Are you sure she hasn't?"

"Frankly? No." Ash turned to the Earl of Oxford. "This is speculation. What do you *know*?"

"I know," the Earl said, "that my men and I are a week in front of two Visigoth legions travelling north to Dijon."

"Shit!" Ash stared at him. "Fresh troops from Africa? He hasn't got any! Has he pulled them out of Egypt – or Carthage itself?"

"Sultan Mehmet has an extensive spy network." John de Vere placed his goblet carefully on the floor. "I trust his information. The Sinai fortresses are still manned. As for *Carthage* . . . Riding with these legions, on his way here to take personal command of his armies and send the Faris home to Carthage, is the King-Caliph Gelimer."

Stunned, Ash said, "Gelimer's coming *here*?"

"He has to make his example of Burgundy."

"But, *Gelimer*?"

The Earl of Oxford leaned forward in his chair, stabbing a finger emphatically in the air between them. "And not alone, madam. According to the Sultan's spies, he has representatives of two of his subject nations with him. One is Frederick of Hapsburg, lately Holy Roman Emperor. This I know for truth; we came across his lands, riding here. The other is said to be an envoy of Louis of France."

The travel-stained English Earl paused. Olivier de la Marche, nodding furiously, bent to hear what Chamberlain-Counsellor Ternant whispered in his ear.

"King-Caliph Gelimer must take Dijon," John de Vere announced flatly. "And – pardon me, madam Florian – he must kill the Duke or Duchess. You are the heart of resistance to him, and Burgundy is the last land that stands against him in conquered Europe. That's why, if his female general won't do it for him – the man must come here and do it himself."

Olivier de la Marche glanced at Floria for permission, and spoke. "If he fails, lord Oxford?"

John de Vere's gaze sharpened, the lines creasing in the corners of his eyes. It was, Ash saw, a smile that lacked all kindness: a pure wolfish expression.

"France has a peace treaty with the King-Caliph." De Vere displayed an open hand to Ash. "Your French knight who was so anxious to escape Dijon? He would have been trying to reach Louis with news of the failing siege. France has been all but untouched by this war. I give you the dark, but, Maine, Anjou, Aquitaine, Normandy – all of them could mobilise, now, if they thought Gelimer weak."

"And the north Germanies—!" Ash ignored de la Marche's sharp look, lost in battle calculations of her own that momentarily ignored Burgundian troops and Duchess and Wild Machines. "Frederick surrendered so fast this summer, half his armies never got into battle! Sweet Christ, the Visigoths are out on a limb!".

John de Vere's gaze stayed on Floria. "Madam, there are villagers and villeins from France and the Germanies flocking over the borders into Burgundy. Outside of your lands there is nothing but howling darkness, cold, and a winter such as men have never known. That is all Louis or Frederick would need as an excuse to come in now and attack the King-Caliph, that their own people have taken protection with you."

"Refugees." Floria winced, wrapping her fur-lined gown more tightly around her. "Out in that. Good God. What's it like beyond the border, if this is better? But I don't know about these refugees."

"You don't need to know, madam, for the Spider to make that his excuse."

"And then there's the Sultan." Ash ignored her surgeon's outrage; looked at de Vere with growing fierce exultation. "The waiting armies of the Turk . . . Gelimer *has* to take Burgundy. If he doesn't win here, and quickly, France and the Germanies will carve up Europe between them and the Turks will be in Carthage in a month."

"Sweet Christ, Ash!" Floria stood up. "Don't sound so bloody *pleased* about it!"

"Maybe England will come in, too—" Ash broke off. She looked down at her hands, and then back up at Floria. "I enjoy the thought of that son of a bitch in trouble."

"*He's* in trouble? What about *us*!"

Ash guffawed, not able to stop herself even for the look of sheer outrage on Philippe Ternant's face. Floria laughed out loud. She sat down again in the ducal chair with her legs apart under her skirts, as a man wearing hose sits; and her bright eyes and thick gold brows were still the same under the horn crown.

"No harvest," Floria said. "No cattle. No shelter. Those bastards have made it a wasteland out there. If people are coming *into* these lands, it must be hell outside . . ."

Excitement died. And we don't even know why we have the sun – by right, we shouldn't have.

Floria's expression was taut, ambiguous – also gnawing at that unspoken question?

Olivier de la Marche lifted his hand, catching de Vere's attention. "It's dark as far as Constantinople now, you say, my lord? The King-Caliph can't have intended that. Not such a deliberate provocation to the Turk."

Philippe Ternant added, "If it is the lands which they conquer that fall Under the Penance with them, then Constantinople would still be bright. Not

Visigoths, then. My lord of Oxford, our Duchess's knowledge of the Great Devils must be shared with you."

"I know something of this matter already." De Vere's face was still; Ash thought him remembering a sea-strand outside Carthage, and a silver glow in the south. "Only, I am uncertain as to the lady's place in this."

"The Duchess will tell you later." Ash caught Floria's eye, and surprised herself by waiting for the surgeon's nod before going on: "My lords, it seems to me that Gelimer's caught in his own trap. I stood in Carthage three months ago, when he took the crown, and I heard him promise the Visigoth lords and everyone else that he'd smash Burgundy as an example – he *has* to do it now. He's got his own *amirs* on his heels, Louis and Frederick closing in, and the Sultan waiting to see if now's the time to come in from the east." A brief smile moved her mouth. "When he started to get reports of the Faris soft-pedalling the siege here and his conquests grinding to a halt, I'll bet money that he shat himself."

Floria sat up in her chair. "Ash, what you mean is, he has to kill us. Me. As quickly as possible."

Clear through the frost-bitten air, not muffled by the expensive glass, a lone bell tolled. Potter's Field, Ash realised: more bodies stacked for a thaw that would enable burial. The impact of rocks and artillery boomed from the south of the city. The roofs and walls between this palace and the army outside the city did not seem much of a barrier.

Ash slowly nodded.

"Christ up a Tree!" Floria exclaimed, oblivious to the shock of her Burgundians. "And you act like this is *good* news!"

Her head whipped round at John de Vere's burst of laughter. The English Earl met her questioning stare, shook his head, and held out an inviting hand to Ash:

"Madam, you have it, I think?"

"It *is* good news!" Ash walked across the bare boards to Floria, taking the woman's hands between her own. Fiercely intense, joyous; she said, "It's the best news we could have. Florian, *the Duchess of Burgundy has to stay alive*. You know that's all that matters, whether you like it or not. I've spent five weeks trying to find a safe way out of Dijon, to get you away to somewhere else – France, maybe; England, who cares? Anywhere, as long as it's not here, at risk from any damn Visigoth peasant with an arquebus. And every time I've got someone over the walls, they've come back dead."

De Vere nodded approval; some of the Burgundians looked grim.

"I haven't been able to break us out of here," Ash said, still holding Floria's gaze. "There's been nothing we can do. That's what's demoralising. Doing nothing except wait for the Faris to make up her mind to attack or not. Well – now someone else is making it up for her."

"Someone who's not going to sit outside the walls waiting," the surgeon-Duchess observed. The grip of her fingers tightened on Ash's hands. "Christ, Ash! What happens when Gelimer gets here and they really start trying!"

"We hold out."

She spoke so closely on the heels of Floria's words that she eradicated them.

De la Marche and Ternant began to look up with cautious enthusiasm.

"We hold out," Ash said again. "Because the longer we can do it – the longer Dijon stands – then the weaker Gelimer looks. Day by day by day. *He's made us a* public *test of his strength*. The weaker he looks, the more chance of Louis or Frederick breaking their treaties and attacking him without warning. The more chance of the Sultan deciding to invade, without warning. Once that happens – once it does turn into a three-cornered fight – then we've got options again. We can get you out of here. We can hide you."

"Get you to a foreign court," the Earl of Oxford put in.

Ash let go of Floria's hands. She reached out and picked the horn cross from the woman's breast, the antler chill under her fingers.

"If it comes to it," she said softly, "and they kill you outside of Dijon, but they're occupied with a full-on war, then the Burgundians can hold another Hunt. It doesn't matter who's Duke or Duchess, so long as somebody's there. Someone who can stop the Faris."

Ash could see on Olivier de la Marche's face that he took it for a hard piece of military realism. Florian snorted.

"You always did have odd priorities! *I* want to stay alive. But you're right, they could hunt," she said, "and there would be someone to stop the Wild Machines."

I would sooner have you alive.

It caught under her breastbone, a pain as sharp as sheered ribs. Ash stared at the woman – dishevelled, insouciant; not one word in five weeks of refusal to take on the appalling responsibility of the Duchy. *And in five weeks I haven't seen you drunk.*

Ash said quietly, "We've got a *chance*. Other enemies for the Visigoths mean other allies for us. The Faris can die on a field of battle just as easily as Jack Peasant can. If the Visigoth army is defeated by someone else, we fight back, go south, destroy Carthage, destroy the *machina rei militaris* – destroy the Wild Machines."

"Blow them up!" Floria said. "If it takes all the powder in Christendom!"

"All we have to do, now, is hold Dijon." Ash grinned at her; at them all. Cynicism, black humour, desperation, and excitement: all clear on her scarred face.

"Hold Dijon," she repeated. "Just a little bit longer. Against Gelimer and all his legions. It's a war of nerves. All we have to do is hold out long enough."

III

A bare five days later, the legions of the King-Caliph marched up from the south to Dijon.

The torches and campfires of the Visigoth armies surrounded the city with an unbroken rim of flame. Ash, on the battlements of the company's tower, peered out into a frost-bitter and utterly clear night. The moon, three days past the full, illuminated every bare yard of earth out to the enemy trenches and barricades, every tent-peak and eagle and standard in their camp—

Where they sleep, warm and fed. Or fed, anyway.

—and every patrolling guard squad.

She went down, snatching an hour's sleep between briefings with her Burgundian command-group; was back up on the roof at false dawn.

Rickard came up, bringing her nettles brewed into small beer – Henri's current substitute for wine – and sat with her, bundled into Robert Anselm's great cloak, trying not to show how much his teeth chattered.

"Let 'em come, right, boss?"

Ash hauled her coney-fur-lined gown tighter over her mail. Hunger was a dull ache in her gut. "You got it. Let 'em make the worst mistake they've ever made."

With dawn, a killing frost fell. A lone bell rang out for the hour of Terce.[11]

"There." Rickard freed an arm from the thick woollen cloak to point.

Breath misted the air in front of her face. The skin of her face was numb. Ash peered off the tower into the clear, freezing light that fell from the east: let her gaze swing around over the Visigoth camp: the movement of men around the tents, turf huts, fire-pits, and trenches, until she saw where Rickard pointed.

"They're early," she commented. "My lord of Oxford underestimated them."

Pray God that's his only mistake.

Men were running, in the freezing morning; Visigoth serf-troops piling out of their barrack-tents, the sun glinting off the scale armour of the cataphracts, spear-points glinting; the harsh bellow of horns and clarions ringing out across the chill earth. She shaded her eyes from the fierce rising white sun, wondering if somewhere in that moving mass the Faris woke, walked, gave orders, sat alone.

Within a very few minutes the Visigoth troops were formed up in legionary squares, the eagles of the XIV Utica and VI Leptis Parva way beyond bow and cannon range of the walls of Dijon, all along the road. The wind brought distant horns. Ash watched as the road up from the south filled with men marching, black standards and eagles catching the light, and below the flags the helmets of hundreds of soldiers, and ahead of them all the ceremonial bronze-armoured war-chariot of the King-Caliph.

Ash nodded to herself, watching a banner with a silver portcullis on a black field come into sight. Carthage's twilight walls pressured her memory. Her bowels churned uncomfortably.

"There you go, Rickard. That's the King-Caliph's household guard. And the Legio III Caralis . . . can't see the other one . . ." Ash put her arm around the boy's cloaked shoulder. "And that's Gelimer's personal banner, there – and there's the Faris's. Right. Now we wait, while the pot comes to the boil."

Two hours later, Ash fell asleep sitting upright in the main hall.

[11] 9 a.m.

One oak chest remained, tucked into the side of the big hearth against the wall. She sat on it, in full armour, hearing the Burgundian *centeniers*, each in turn; and then her own lance-leaders and their men. Willem Verhaecht and Thomas Rochester, Euen Huw and Henri Brant, Ludmilla Rostovnaya and Blanche and Baldina. Processing problems. Where exhaustion slowed her mind, instinct and experience took over.

She fell asleep leaning into the hearth corner, upright, in full armour, in the middle of a briefing. Dimly, she heard the plates of her harness scrape against stone; it was not enough to wake her. The banked fire glowed, giving warmth to one side of her face.

She was still aware, as from a long way away, of the laconic voices of exhausted men, dropping kit on their palliasses and slumping down; hoping for sleep to do away with hunger. And of Anselm's voice bellowing up from the courtyard: holding close-quarter weapons drill. Some part of her still ran through Angelotti's and Jussey's calculations of remaining ammunition: bolts, arrows, arquebus- and cannon-balls.

Even held by the paralysis of sleep, some part of her still remained on guard.

She had a moment to realise *It's because I don't want to dream. I don't want to hear Godfrey, it's too hard when I can't talk to him. Because the Visigoths can ask the Stone Golem what I say. Because the Wild Machines will hear, even if they don't speak . . .* Then she fell into sleep as if down a dark well, and a heartbeat later hands were shaking her by the pauldrons and she moved a sleep-sticky mouth and looked up into the face of Robert Anselm.

"Wha—?"

"I said, you should have seen it!"

The line of sun from the arrow-slit windows lay much further across the floorboards. Ash blinked, said grittily, "Give me a *report*, Robert," and reached out as Rickard handed her a costrel of water.

"We've had a parley come out from the rag-head camp." Robert Anselm squatted down in front of the chest she sat on. "You should have seen it! Six fucking golem-messengers, each with a banner. A fucking dwarf *drummer*. And one poor sod with a white flag walking up to the north-west gate between them, praying our grunts weren't trigger-happy, and shouting for a parley."

"Who was it?"

"Mister Expendable," Robert Anselm said, with a smile at once wolfish and sympathetic. "What did you think, girl, Gelimer himself? No way. They sent Agnes."

Caught by surprise, Ash snickered. "Yeah, I can see Lamb wetting himself with that one. Remind me to make that man an offer if the situation changes. Tell him if he hires on with Florian, I won't give him all the shitty jobs! When was this? Why do they want a parley? What's the result?"

"About an hour ago." Robert Anselm's hazel eyes gleamed, under arming cap, and sallet. "The result is, Doc Florian wants to go out and talk to them."

"You're out of your fucking mind!"

The Burgundian knights and nobles in Floria's chamber glared at Ash; she ignored both them, and Olivier de la Marche's covert, relieved look of approval.

"Someone has to tell her," the Duchess's deputy murmured.

"If you set one foot outside the walls, I don't care if you've got Mehmet's five hundred Turks up your arsehole, you are a *dead woman*. Don't you understand me?"

Floria del Guiz held her crown between her hands, turning it, fingers stroking the contours of the carved white horn. She raised her eyes to Ash.

"Get a grip," she advised.

"'Get a grip'? *You* get a fucking grip!" Ash clenched her fists. "You listen to me, Florian. The Wild Machines have to kill you, and they know it. If Gelimer's still taking the Stone Golem's tactical advice, that's what it'll be telling him. If he isn't, he *still* has to kill you – you're Burgundy: if he kills you, the war in the north fizzles out, the rest of Christendom starts saying 'yes, boss,' again, and the Turks look for a peace treaty!"

In the background she was aware of de la Marche and the council nodding agreement; John de Vere exchanging a quiet comment with one of his brothers.

"You know what I'd do, if I were Gelimer," Ash continued softly. "Once I had you in the open outside these walls, I'd open up with the guns and siege-machines and wipe you off the map. You and anybody else at the parley. I wouldn't care if it meant wiping my own guys out too. Then I'd apologise to the Sultan for killing his Turks – an 'unfortunate accident'. Because with you *gone*, and Europe solid, there's a two-to-one chance Mehmet will decide it's not the time for a war just yet. I'm telling you, you go out there and you're dead. And then there's nothing to stop the Wild Machines, nothing at all!"

The overcast sky glimmered pale grey through the glass. Shifting cloud disclosed a white disc of sun, no stronger than the full moon. Floria del Guiz continued to turn the horn crown between her strong, dirty fingers. Exhaustion marked her, as if two thumbs of candle-black had been smeared under her eyes.

"Now you listen," she said. "I've spoken to this council, and to my lord Oxford, and now I'll tell you. We have no food. We've got sickness: dysentery, maybe plague. We've got a city full of starving people. I'm going to hold a parley with the Visigoths. I'm going to negotiate their release."

Ash jerked a thumb at the world beyond the window. "So they can starve out there with the other refugees?"

"I'm not a Duchess, I'm a doctor!" Floria snapped. "I didn't ask for this crown but I've got it. So I have to do something. The hospices are full; the abbot of St Stephen's was here in tears two hours ago. There aren't enough priests to pray for the sick. I took an oath, Ash! First of all, *do no harm*. I'm going to get the civilians out of this siege before we have an epidemic."

"I doubt it. Gelimer's going to be happy enough if we die of disease."

"Shit!" Floria swore, swung around and began to pace up and down the chamber, kicking the hem of her gown out of the way: a tall, dirty scarecrow of a woman, noticeably thinner now than when they had ridden in the wildwood. She scowled, gold brows lowering. "You're right. Of course you're right. Ash, there *has* to be some way we can do this. If there's a parley, at least they're not attacking us. It gains time. Therefore, we have to agree to it."

"We might. You don't. You hunted the hart, remember?"

Glancing around the chamber, Ash noted Richard Faversham among her own men; the English deacon's face shrunken, under his black beard. His eyes burned. He was nodding.

Floria said, "But Gelimer specifies, if I'm not present, there's to be no parley."

John de Vere said, into the silence, "Hold a parley, madam, but make sure King-Caliph Gelimer himself is present at it as well as yourself. They then cannot use their siege-engines or guns."

"I wouldn't count on it. If I were him, I'd get there, then leg it, and let the artillery take care of it." Ash slid her hand down to the scabbard of her sword, for comfort. "Florian's right about one thing. We *do* need the delay. Once they start any serious assault, it's going to show up how low we are on ammunition and men. Okay . . ."

Floria shrugged. "I'll find a way to do this, Ash. Never mind the hart. Where can we hold a parley?"

"On a bridge?" John de Vere offered. "Are all the bridges down? That would be neutral territory."

"No!" Olivier de la Marche growled, "No!"

"Madness, my lord!" Philippe Ternant cried. "We know what treachery bridges can bring. The late Duke's grandfather, Duke John, was treacherously slain on a bridge during a truce, by the whoreson French.[12] They cut off his right hand! It was most vile!"

"Ah." De Vere's pale brows went up. He said mildly, "Not a bridge, then."

Ash converted a laugh into a cough. "Where, then? Not in the open. Even if Gelimer was there, it would still be too easy to load up one of their Greek Fire throwers, and get us before we could get back inside the city walls."

A silence: in which the knots in the firewood cracked as the fire burned down. A cold draught breathed down through the chimney, despite the fire.

Robert Anselm laughed. Ash looked across at him.

"Spit it out. You got something?"

Anselm looked first at her, and then at de Vere; and rose to his feet. Standing, stubbled head gleaming, he said, "You want somewhere that isn't in the open, boss, don't you."

Colonel Bajezet said something to the interpreter. Before the Voynik could translate, Robert Anselm was nodding.

"Yeah, your lads did that in the Morea a couple of times. Built a tiny fort out in no-man's-land and had both sides meet inside. If anyone started a fight, everyone got killed." Anselm hunched his shoulders. "Won't work, Başi. They could still get us on the way there, or the way back."

The Turk raised his hands. "Plan, what?"

"Meet 'em underground. In a sap."

"In a—" Ash stopped. Robert Anselm looked her straight in the eye. He did not smell of wine, or the fermented rubbish Henri Brant's cooks had concocted from pig-garbage. He stood with his head up.

---

[12] John the Fearless, d. 1419.

Ash thought, Is that de Vere, his old Lancastrian boss? Or has he finally decided to get his finger out on my behalf? Either way, if he has, do I care?

Yes. I care. I'd rather he'd done it for me.

It's me that's putting other people's lives in his hands.

"A sap," she repeated. "You think we should meet the Visigoths in a tunnel."

This time it was de Vere who laughed; and his brother Dickon with him. Viscount Beaumont said cheerfully, in English, "And I suppose we ask them to hold the negotiations until we have dug one, Master Anselm?"

Anselm put his hand back on his sword pommel. He glanced at Ash. She nodded.

"Gelimer wouldn't risk artillery. Collapse a tunnel—" Anselm smacked his palm down flat for illustration. "Everybody's dead. Start a fight in one, and you got a bloodbath. Same thing. Everybody dies; no one can be sure they'd survive – that includes Gelimer. Take the Colonel's Turks down with us, and I reckon that'd swing it."

There was a buzz of discussion. Ash watched Robert Anselm, without speaking. He watched her, and not John de Vere. She slowly nodded.

"But not Florian. Me, de la Marche, anyone; not Florian. Or—" she brightened. "Not the first time. That's what we tell Gelimer. It's what, now, the twenty-third? We can spin this out for three or four days, past Christ's-Mass. That's more time; it's all more time . . . if we make him think Florian will come out if we can get negotiations started . . ."

Florian interrupted her thinking aloud. "If it were you out there, you'd attack. To hurry the parley up."

"Gelimer will do that anyway. We're going to lose people." Ash's grim expression faded to amazement as she looked back at Anselm. "A sap. It *won't* work, Roberto, we don't have time to send a mine out from the walls."

"Don't need to. I know where there's one of theirs, that we counter-mined. Under the White Tower. You remember, girl. It's the one Angelotti's lads cleared out with a bear."

De la Marche looked aghast; the Earl of Oxford spluttered his watered wine back into his cup; Floria whooped. "You never told me this! A *bear*?"

"It was two or three days after the hunt." Ash grimaced. "Before we would have thought of bear-steak. There was a bear left in Charles's menagerie."

Robert Anselm took it up. "Angelotti's lads heard the Visigoths mining towards the wall. The rag-heads were tunnelling under the wall, propping it up with wood. They were going to set fire to the props and bring the city wall down when they collapsed. Angelotti's engineers dug a counter-mine, and we opened it into their tunnel one day, and the following night, when they were in it, the gunners got the bear out of the menagerie."

Ash frowned, trying to remember. "It wasn't just a bear, was it . . . ?"

"They got a couple of bee-hives out of the abbot's gardens as well. They put the bear down into the tunnel," Robert Anselm said, "and they dropped the bee-hives down after, and shut the end of the counter-mine up fucking quick."

Floria's face contorted, obviously visualising men, darkness, bees; an animal maddened by stings. "Christ!"

Her exclamation was drowned out by laughter from the men-at-arms.

"We did see 'em come up out of the other end pretty damn fast!" Anselm confessed. "*And* the bear. *And* the bees. They closed their end up, but they ain't been down there since! We could open that up. Clear out the bodies."

There was a raw, black edge to the laughter in the room. Ash saw Floria's face, appalled at the cruelty. She stopped laughing.

Florian looked down at the horn crown in her hands.

"It's worth trying. We have to keep them talking. I don't want to see another assault on the walls. We have to put some bait in this. We'll tell them the Duchess *will* be there – *no*." Floria, completely inflexible, repeated, "No. This is my decision. Tell Agnes Dei, yes, I'll meet with Gelimer."

Forty-eight hours later, on the very day of Christ's Mass, the Duchess of Burgundy and the English Earl of Oxford, together with the Captain-General, the Janissaries of the Turk and the Duchess's mercenary bodyguard, met in parley with King-Caliph Gelimer and his officers and allies of the Visigoth Empire.

The tunnel stank of old sweat, and blood, and dank earth and urine: so strong that the lanterns guttered and burned low.

Ash walked with her hand on the war-hammer shaft stuck through her belt. No room for bill-shafts, for spears; only close-quarter weapons here. She shot a glance at the sides of the sap – widened out in a desperate hurry in the last two days, fresh planks shoring up the walls and the roof a bare eighteen inches above her head.

Angelotti, standing with one of the Visigoth engineers and Jussey, nodded confirmation to her. "It's a go, boss."

"Anything drops on my head, it's your ass'll suffer for it . . ." Ash spoke absently; gesturing for Robert Anselm to hold up his lantern, hearing voices from the far end of this widened underground mine. Cold still air walked shivers up her spine, under her backplate.

I suppose at least, with Florian with us, we don't have to worry about tiny miracles.

Shit. They don't need their priests. All they need to do is send one of their golem-diggers in; this roof will come down with a thousand tons of earth—

She bit her lip, literally and deliberately. The words were in her mouth: *Position of Visigoth troops, location of Visigoth command*?

But it won't know. Couriers from here to Carthage are out of date. If the Faris isn't reporting to the Stone Golem, it can't give tactical advice about their camp here. It won't do me any good to speak to Godfrey.

I just want to.

"Is he there?" Robert Anselm said quietly.

The gravel that covered the floor of the sap crunched underfoot as she walked forward. She squinted in the poor light. The voices ahead of her died down.

A pale, cold blue light began to glow. Visigoth slaves uncovered globes of Greek Fire, no larger than Ash's fist. She saw first their thistledown-white hair and familiar faces, where they knelt either side of the passageway. Then, between the two lines of them, she saw men in mail and rich robes; and one in the midst of them, in a great fur-lined cloak, his beard braided with golden beads, the King-Caliph, Gelimer. He looked strained, but alert.

"Confirm," she said. "Move the rest up. He's here."

No banners – the low roof didn't allow it – but all the armed men wore liveries, stark in the cold light. Gelimer's portcullis. The Faris's brazen head. A notched white wheel on a black ground. A two-headed black eagle upon a field of gold. The lilies of France quartered with blue and white bars.

Black double eagle. She searched the mass of faces in front, and found herself looking at Frederick of Hapsburg.

The Holy Roman Emperor had only one man with him that she could see: a large German knight in mail, carrying a mace. A small, dry smile crossed Frederick's lips as he saw her. Conquest and surrender notwithstanding, he looked much the same as he had in the camp outside Neuss.

"In person? Son of a bitch . . ." She stepped to one side as men came up behind her, de Vere's Turks. The Janissaries lined the walls and stood three ranks deep in front as Floria del Guiz walked forward, surrounded by twenty men of the Lion Azure, in mail hauberks and open-faced sallets. Burgundian troops flanked them to either side.

Elbow to elbow with Floria on one side, Colonel Bajezet and his interpreter on the other, and with John de Vere crowded close in behind her; Ash has a sudden visceral memory of Duke Charles, downed by a Visigoth flying wedge at Auxonne, his armour leaking blood between the exquisitely articulated plates. She felt herself start to sweat. Her palms tingled.

She did the familiar thing, alchemised it into excitement: let her vision go flat in the unnatural light and take in, without effort, which men were armed with swords (which they might have difficulty drawing in a scuffle), which with maces and picks and hammers; which of Gelimer's lord-*amirs* were armoured and helmeted – all – and which were the obvious targets.

One of the Burgundian knights behind her said something foul under his breath. She looked questioningly at him as the group halted.

"That is Charles d'Amboise,"[13] the Burgundian, Lacombe, said, indicating the French liveries, "Governor of Champagne, and that whoreson arselicker beside him is the man who betrayed the friendship of Duke Charles. Philippe de Commines."

Much more, and the towering, fair-haired Burgundian would have spat on the earth. Ash, as she might with one of the company, nodded acknowledgement and said, "Watch him: if he moves, tell me."

Ash stepped ahead of Floria, among the spotless silent Janissaries.

"We're here for a parley with the King-Caliph." Her voice fell flat in the enclosed space. "Not with half the lords of France and Germany! This isn't what we agreed to. We're pulling out."

---

[13] A trusted servant of Louis XI, reportedly sent in the autumn of 1476 to abduct Duchess Yolande of Savoy on behalf of the King of France, for political reasons.

It's too much to hope for that I might get away with this – spin out the negotiations about negotiations to another few days . . .

The French knight bowed, where he stood cramped in beside the little dark man that Ash recognised as de Commines from his previous visit to Charles's court. He said smoothly, "I am d'Amboise. My master Louis sends me to serve the King-Caliph. I am here to acquaint her ladyship the Duchess with the benefits of the *Pax Carthaginiensis*. As is my lord of Hapsburg, the noble Frederick."

Charles d'Amboise continued to look at Ash with a perfectly open and amiable expression. Ash grinned at him.

"You're here as Louis's *spy*," she said. "And, like 'my lord of Hapsburg', you're here to see Burgundy stand against the King-Caliph. In which case, if I were King-Caliph, I'd watch my back . . ."

Her grin did not waver at d'Amboise's evident unease. *Any dissent we can spread is good!*

Six of the Turks had positions in front of Ash and Floria. There was not space enough in the mine for more than that. Ash looked past the mail and hanging sleeves of the Janissaries – men consenting to use their bodies as a human shield – and saw Gelimer's bearded face, in the light of the Greek Fire globes.

He was showing no emotion. Certainly no anger, or uncertainty. He seemed both older and more military than when she had last seen him, in Carthage; lines drawn in the skin around his mouth, and a long mail hauberk and coat-of-plates under his cloak.

Harsh illumination, cold darkness beyond: the mine is not so different from the dark palace at Carthage, with the great Mouth of God above her and the tiles about to crack and shiver apart in an earthquake. Seeing the man again shocked her. No picture in her memory of Gelimer running from his throne – instead she had a sudden physical recall of the dead flesh of Godfrey Maximillian. A long shudder went down her spine under her armour.

"Where is the Duchess of Burgundy?" Gelimer's light tenor also flattened, under the low boarded tunnel roof.

Over Ash's shoulder, Floria said dryly, "You're looking at her."

The King-Caliph's eyes remained on Ash for a long moment. He shifted his gaze to regard the cloaked woman wearing the bone crown. "The fortune of war means I must have you killed. I am not a cruel man. Surrender Burgundy to me, and I will spare your peasants and your townsmen. Only you will die, Duchess. For your people."

Floria laughed. Ash saw Gelimer startle. It was not a demure laugh; it was one she had heard often in the surgeon's tent, with Floria outside of two or three flagons of wine; a loud, pleasant, raucous contralto.

"*Surrender?* After we've resisted? Get out of here," Floria said cheerfully. "I'm a mercenary company's surgeon. I've seen what happens to towns under siege when enemy troops sack the place. The people I've got in here are safer staying in here, unless we sign a peace."

Gelimer shifted his gaze from Ash, again; past her to the Burgundian lords. "And this – *woman* – is what you would have lead you?"

There was no answer. Not, Ash saw as she quickly glanced back, from uncertainty or doubt. Obdurate faces regarded the King-Caliph with contempt.

"She is most wise and most valiant," John de Vere said, with stinging courtesy. "Sirs, what is your business with the Duchess?"

Ash appointed herself discourteous mercenary Captain-General to his noble foreign Earl, and said loudly, "If that's his best offer, they ain't *got* any business with the Duchess! This ain't serious. Let's fuck off."

De Vere let her see his brief amusement.

"Call your She-Lion off," the Visigoth King-Caliph said contemptuously to de Vere. She saw his eyes flick from the English Earl to the noble Burgundians behind him; skimming over herself and the Turkish commander and Floria del Guiz.

He's looking for the man in command, Ash realised.

He's thinking: Not the Englishman, not in Burgundy. The Burgundian lords? Which one? Or Olivier de la Marche, back in the city?

And then she saw Gelimer's small-eyed gaze flick to d'Amboise and Commines, and from the Frenchmen to Frederick of Hapsburg. Only a split second of loss of control.

God bless you, John de Vere! Everything you said is right. He's here because he has to have Burgundy, and because he thinks he has to look as though he's not afraid of us in front of them.

Ash smiled to herself, and glanced back to grin reassuringly at Florian. She whispered in the woman's ear, her lips touching the soft hair under the hart's-horn crown:

"Gelimer would have done better to just pile in, never mind a parley – and he hasn't done it, and they're watching him now, like a hawk, to see what he does next."

"Can we keep him talking, Ash?"

Looking at Gelimer, and his closed expression under the gold-rimmed helmet he wore, brought memory vividly into her mind: the man riding in driving snow in the desert, with his son – his son – the boy's name was gone from her. *Is it still snowing in Carthage?*

She formed a fast and brutal judgement. "He'd be all right if this was armies. Maybe all he did three months ago was talk himself into a job he can't hold down – but if it was just a matter of telling his generals and his legions what to do, he could win this one. But it's the dark, and the cold. I don't know how much he knows. He'll hesitate if we give him half a chance."

"Keep talking," Floria murmured. "Let's spin this out as long as we can."

The Visigoth King-Caliph turned to listen to a man speaking at his shoulder, appearing not to hear what Ash said. He nodded, once. The air, growing warm with the number of bodies crowding the mine, caught at the back of Ash's throat. The kneeling slaves holding the Greek Fire globes in their padded iron cages appeared bleached by light: fair brows and lashes air-brushed from weather-beaten faces.

The mass of armed men parted, with difficulty letting others through from the back of the King-Caliph's party. Ash could not at first make out faces among the blaze of heraldry, the glint of mail and sword-hilts and helmets.

Greek Fire reflected back from a river-fall of hair the colour of pale ashes, robbed of all silver in this light. Ash found herself looking again into the Faris's face.

"Faris." Ash nodded a greeting.

The woman made no reply. Her dark eyes, in her flawless bright face, regarded Ash as if she were not present. Her flat gaze brought a momentary frown to Ash's face. About to comment, Ash realised that King-Caliph Gelimer was – while apparently listening to his advisor – watching her with a complete and total avidity.

Disturbed, she contented herself with another nod; which the Faris again ignored. The Visigoth woman, armoured and in black livery, had a dagger at her belt; Ash could not see a sword-hilt, in among the crush of bodies.

Why is Gelimer watching *me*? He should be watching the Duchess.

Is this some kind of diversion, so he can try to have Florian killed?

She inhaled, surreptitiously, trying to catch the scent of slow-match on the air, to discover if there were arquebuses hidden in the mass of Gelimer's men. Movement caught her eye; brought her sword-hand across her body. She stopped.

Two Visigoth priests came pushing through the crowd in the Faris's wake. They held the elbows of a tall, thin bareheaded *amir*, a man with unruly white hair and the expression of a startled owl. Behind the *amir* stumbled a pudgy Italian physician – she recognised Annibale Valzacchi. *And the* amir *is Leofric.*

"Green Christ . . . !" Ash became aware that she had closed her hand around Floria's arm only when the woman winced.

"That's the lord-*amir* that had you prisoner? The one who owns the Stone Golem?"

"Yeah: you never saw Leofric in Carthage, did you? That's him." Ash did not take her eyes from Leofric's face, watching the elderly man across the space of perhaps five yards. "That's him."

Not just my sister, but this.

A pain came deep in the pit of her stomach. Stairways, cells, blood; the intrusive painful stab of examination: all sharp-edged in her mind. She rode the ache out, not letting it show on her face.

Leofric wore the rich furred gown of a Visigoth lord, over mail. He appeared unaware of the priests' grip on his arms, and frowned at Ash with a puzzled expression.

"Greetings, my lord." Her mouth sounded dry even to her.

John de Vere whispered encouragingly in her ear, "Madam, yes, talk. It is all time gained."

Two slaves stood with the Lord-*Amir* Leofric behind the front row of Visigoth troops; one a child, and one a fat woman. Ash could see neither clearly. The child cradled something in the front of her stained linen robe, and shivered. The adult woman drooled.

In the fierce, flat white light, Leofric's eyes focused on Ash. His face crumpled. Into the silence, he wailed, "Devils! Great Devils! Great Devils will kill us all!"

IV

The Janissaries in front of Ash did not move, their alert surveillance intense. Florian looked taken aback; de Vere, although he did not show it, no less so. Ash shifted her gaze from Leofric to the King-Caliph. No surprise showed on the Visigoth ruler's face.

"The head of House Leofric is unwell," Gelimer said. "If he were himself, he would apologise for such a discourtesy."

"*Ask her!*" Leofric swung round imploringly towards Gelimer, the two priests gripping his arms even more firmly. "My lord Caliph, I am not mad! Ask her. Ash hears them too. She is another daughter of mine, Ash hears them as this one does—"

"No." The Faris's voice cut him off. "I cannot hear the *machina rei militaris* any longer. I am deaf to it."

Ash stared.

The Visigoth woman avoided her gaze.

With complete certainty, Ash thought *She's lying!*

"You said she wasn't talking to the Stone Golem . . ." Floria whispered, her tone one of rueful admission.

"Not because she can't." Ash watched Gelimer wince and glance at the foreign envoys.

Frederick of Hapsburg was smiling a little, with the haughty and calculating smile she remembered from the summer at Neuss; and he caught her eye and lifted a brow slightly.

"To our business, lords." Gelimer fixed his gaze on Floria. "Witch-woman of Burgundy—"

The Lord-*Amir* Leofric interrupted obliviously. "Where did I go wrong?"

Floria, who looked as if she had been about to make some dignified ducal response, stopped before she started. The surgeon-Duchess put her fists on her hips with difficulty in the crowded space, and stared at the Visigoth lord. "'Go wrong'?"

Ash peered down the mine, between the shoulders of the Turkish Janissaries, the blue-white blaze of the Greek Fire making it paradoxically harder to focus on Leofric's face. Something about the shape of his mouth made her shudder: adult men in their right minds do not have such an expression. She remembered Carthage, was overwhelmed suddenly between contradictory revulsion, hate and pity.

He's not right. Something's happened to him, since I was there. He's not right at all . . .

She cut the emotions away from herself, concentrating only on the tunnel, the armed men, the sounds of voices, the shifting of feet and hands.

Leofric gazed down at the child-slave in front of him. He drew one arm from the priests' grip, reached down, and plucked a white-and-liver-coloured patched rat out of the child's arms. He held it up and stared into its ruby eyes. "I keep asking myself, *where did I go wrong?*"

The child – recognisably Violante; taller, thinner – lifted up her hands for the animal. Ash recognised the rat when it wriggled in mid-air, thrashed its tail from side to side, and dipped its furry head down to lick the girl's fingers.

She felt eyes on her: switched her glance to see Gelimer watching her again with avid, analytical care.

"Oh, fuck . . ." Ash breathed.

Gelimer signalled. The two priests closed around Leofric again. Valzacchi pulled the *amir*'s hand down, shrinking from the animal.

The white-haired man looked vague, and relinquished the rat absent-mindedly to his slave-girl. "Lord Caliph, the danger—"

"You put on this madness as an excuse for treachery!" the King-Caliph said, in a rapid Carthaginian Latin that Ash thought only she and de Vere, apart from Gelimer's Visigoth followers, understood. "If I have to kill you to silence you, I will."

"I am not mad," Leofric answered in the same language. Ash saw Frederick of Hapsburg look puzzled, and d'Amboise too; the other Frenchman, Commines, smiled quietly.

Ash glanced at de Vere. The English Earl nodded. She waited until she was sure he was watching the French and German delegations, and then reached up and unbuckled her helmet. *Time to stir the pot.* She took the sallet off and shook out her short hair, facing the Visigoths under the harsh light.

"My God, but they are *twins*!" Charles d'Amboise exclaimed. "A Burgundian mercenary and a Visigoth general? Their voices, their faces – what is this?"

"Sisters, I hear," de Commines put in sharply, staring at the Visigoth King-Caliph. "Lord Gelimer, his Grace the King of France will ask, also, why you have your generals fighting both sides of this war! If it *is* a war, and not some conspiracy against France!"

"The woman Ash is a renegade," Gelimer said dismissively.

"*Is she?*" Charles d'Amboise's shout made the young slave-girl in front of him flinch, and huddle the piebald rat to her chest. He bellowed at the King-Caliph: "*Is* she? What shall I tell my master Louis? That you and Burgundy conspire together, and this sham of a war is fought on both sides by you! That Burgundy is France's ancient enemy, and has you for an ally! And, worse than *all* this—" The French nobleman flung out his hand, pointing at John de Vere, Earl of Oxford: "*—the English are involved!*"

Ash whooped. It was drowned out in the guffaws, cat-calls, and congratulatory comments to de Vere that echoed from Thomas Rochester's lance. Rochester himself wiped streaming eyes.

Gelimer's hand stroked his beaded beard.

When the applause, boos, and cries of "God rot the French wanker!" died down, the King-Caliph said in a measured tone, "We do not bring our legions to raze the city of an ally, Master Amboise."

Plainly alerted by the sound of Gelimer's voice, the Lord-*Amir* Leofric suddenly bellowed out loud, his voice blaring in the low-roofed tunnel: "You must ask her! Ash! Ash!"

A dribble of earth fell down between planks, touching his face, and he winced and wrenched himself back with a cry. Panting, he fixed his gaze on Ash.

"Tell my lord the King-Caliph! *Tell him*. The stone of the desert has souls! Great voices speak, speak through my Stone Golem, and *she* has heard them, and *you* have heard them—" Leofric's voice lost depth. His face saddened. "How can you let this petty war keep you from speaking of such danger?"

"I—" Ash stopped. Floria's shoulder was pressing against hers, hard against her backplate; and de Vere had one thoughtful hand to his mace's grip.

"Tell him!" Leofric yelled. "My daughter betrays me, I am asking you – begging *you*—" He wrenched both arms free of the priests, stood for one second, then raised his head and stared straight at Ash. "The Empire is betrayed, we're all to die soon, every man of us, every woman, Visigoth or Burgundian – *tell my lord Caliph what you hear*."

Ash became aware again of Gelimer's intense stare. She looked away from Leofric; took in all the Visigoth group, the foreign envoys; stood for a moment in a complete state of indecision.

The faintest hiss came from the Greek Fire globes. Violante, cuddling her rat, looked up from under her chopped-off hair at Ash, her expression unreadable. The adult woman-slave began to pick at the girl's tunic, dribbling without wiping her wide lips, and whining like a hound.

"Okay." Ash rested her hands on her belt, a few inches from sword and dagger. With a sense of immense relief, she said, "He might be mad, but he isn't crazy. Listen to him. He's telling the truth."

Gelimer frowned.

"There are—" Ash hesitated, choosing words with care. "There are great pyramid-golems in the desert, south of Carthage. You saw them when we rode there, Lord Caliph."

Gelimer's lips twitched, red in the nest of his beard, and he stroked his hand across his mouth. "They are monuments to our holy dead. God blesses them now with a cold Fire."

'You saw them. They're made of the river-silt and stone. Stone. Like the Stone Golem."

He shook his head. "Nonsense."

"No, not nonsense. Your *amir* Leofric's right. I've heard them. It's their voices that have spoken to you through the Stone Golem. It's their advice that has brought you here. And believe me, they don't care about your Empire!" With a curious sense of release, she nodded towards the white-haired Visigoth lord. "*Amir* Leofric isn't crazy. There are devils out there – as far as we're concerned, they're devils. And they won't rest until the whole world is as cold and dead as the lands beyond Burgundy."

She had little hope of convincing him. She saw from his face that she probably had not. Nonetheless, she felt the release in herself: simply to be able to speak of it aloud. From behind the ranks of Janissaries, she watched Gelimer, and he could not look away from her.

"Which is the more likely?" he said. "That this talk of devils is true, when we so plainly have God's visible mark of favour? Or that House Leofric has some factional plot against the throne? Which his slave-general joined, at his

920

command. And now you. Captain Ash, you should have died in my court, dissected for the knowledge you would bring us. That is how you will die, when I have taken Dijon."

"When," Ash remarked dryly.

Florian, at Ash's side, interjected, "Lord-Caliph, she's telling you the truth. There are golems in the desert. And you've been fooled by them."

"No. Not I. I have not been the fool."

Gelimer signalled again. The larger of the two priests holding Leofric let go of him, and pushed his way through the press of men to the woman-slave standing beside Violante. The woman flinched away from him and began to cry in great unrestrained sobs and gawks and chokes. The priest hauled her forward by the iron collar around her wattle-skinned neck.

"My lords of France and the Holy Roman Empire," the King-Caliph said. "You have seen that my lord Leofric is ill. You see his slave daughter, our General, is also not in health. And now you hear from this mercenary Captain-General of Burgundy the ramblings of a lunatic. This is why, gentlemen. This woman. I brought her for you to see, and judge. This is Adelize. She is the mother of both these young women."

The priest punched the slave-woman. She stopped roaring. A complete silence fell. Ash heard only a hissing sound in her ears. Thomas Rochester, beside her, gripped her shoulder.

"If this is the dam," Gelimer said, "what wonder if the pups are mad?"

Ash stared at the idiot woman. Under the rolls of fat, the outline of her face could be similar to that of the Faris, standing impassively beside her; it had a gut-wrenching familiarity that Ash did not let herself feel. An old woman, fifty or sixty. The woman's pale hair was by now grey, no trace of colour left.

Ash opened her mouth to speak; and could say nothing, her voice lost.

"With such a dam, what can you expect of the cubs?" Gelimer repeated rhetorically. "Nonsense such as this talk of great devils."

"Your Faris, your commander in the field, she also suffers this lunacy?" de Commines said sharply.

"The crusades of our Empire have never been dependent on one commander." The King-Caliph sounded serene.

John de Vere stirred, fair brows dipping; obviously doubting that serenity. "Madam, he thinks it worth discrediting the commander who has won him Europe, to discredit Leofric and you."

Ash said nothing. She stared at Adelize, at the woman who wept now without sound, wet tears blubbering her cheeks. *Two hundred years of incest. Sweet Christ and all the Saints. Is this what I—*

The Faris reached out and rested her hand on the woman's hair. Her hand moved softly, stroking. Her face remained impassive.

"With that disposed of," King-Caliph Gelimer said briskly, "we turn to our business with Burgundy."

Ash missed what Floria said. She turned her head aside, choked up the searing hot vomit in her throat, spat it into her hand, and let it fall to the floor. Her eyes ran: she blinked back the water in case anyone should think she wept.

"—an envoy," the King-Caliph was saying.

"Envoy?"

"He says he wants to send one in to us," Floria whispered. Her face, intent, promised compassion and analysis later; in this second, she was all alertness, all Duchess. "I'm going to let him. The man's probably a spy, but it's all delay." She spoke up. "If he's acceptable, we'll take him."

Gelimer's hand stroked his beaded beard again, the gold flashing. He said mildly, "You will find him acceptable, Duchess of Burgundy. He is your brother."

Ash did not take it in. There was a stir in the group of armed men in front of her, someone pushing their way through. Her gaze went past the man. She looked back, suddenly thinking *I know that face!*; wondering which of Gelimer's Franks he might be – a mercenary she'd met in Italy, maybe; or some Iberian merchant? And in a split second, the light fell full on his face, and she saw that it was Fernando del Guiz with his hair cropped, and that he wore a priest's high-collared robe.

A *priest?*

How can he be a priest: he's my husband!

Last seen, he had been a young man with blond hair falling shaggy to his shoulders, dressed in the mail and furred robes of a Visigoth knight. Now, unarmed – not even a dagger! – he wore a dark priestly robe buttoned from chin to floor-length hem, and tightly belted at the waist. It only showed off the breadth of his shoulders and chest the more. Something about his scrubbed cleanliness and shining yellow hair made her long to walk over to him and bury her face in his neck; smell the male scent of him.

The shifting light of the Greek Fire globes cast shadows enough to hide her expression. Amazed, she felt her cheeks heating up.

"Fernando," she said aloud.

Abruptly conscious of her hacked-off short hair and general siege-induced grubbiness, she shifted her gaze away as he looked at her. There was no pectoral cross on the chain around his neck, but a pendant of a man's face carved with leaves tendrilling from his open mouth. *Arian priest, then. Christus Viridianus! What on earth—?*

Angry with herself, she raised her eyes again. Someone had expertly shaved his hair back above his ears in a novice's tonsure. He looked faintly amused.

"Abbot Muthari *must* be hard up," Ash remarked, in a voice with more gravel in it than she liked. "But I might have known you'd get into skirts as soon as you could."

There was an appreciative rumble from the soldiers. Ash overheard Robert Anselm translating her remark for Bajezet's men; their laughter came in a few seconds late.

There I go: motor-mouth, she thought, still staring at Fernando. Knowing that whatever she said, automatically, was nothing more than a time-filler while she stared up at him thinking, *Has he really taken vows as a priest?* and, *Are the Arian priests celibate?*

A warmth ran down her skin, loosening the muscles of her thighs, and she knew that the pupils of her eyes must be wide.

"This is my ambassador," the King-Caliph said.

Fernando del Guiz bowed.

Ash stared.

"Shit," she said. "Well. Shit. Merry fucking Christmas."

Gelimer ignored Ash. He spoke to Floria, his gaze shifting between her and the other Burgundians. "You can see beyond your walls, you are not blind. I have three full legions outside Dijon. It is obvious you cannot hold out. Surrender Dijon. By the courtesies of war, I give you this chance, but nothing more. Send me your answer, by my envoy – tomorrow, on the feast of St Stephen."

V

"Get that bloody sap blocked up again!" Ash ordered. "Barrels of rocks first, and then earth. I don't want anyone assaulting in through there. Move it!"

"Yes, Captain!" One of the Burgundian commanders strode back to his men, where they sat or crouched under the remains of shattered houses; directing them with brief, efficient shouts.

Floria said, "One of you – Thomas Rochester – tell de la Marche I'll be with Ash. Call the council."

'I'll go," John de Vere forestalled her. "Madam, I am anxious to discuss the Caliph's words with Master de la Marche; shall I bring him to you?"

At Floria's nod, the English Earl gave an order to his interpreter and marched off rapidly at the head of the Janissaries.

The rumbling of rubble-filled barrels across the cobbles drowned out the noise of their passing. The streets smelled of burning. The freezing wind blew, not the wood-smoke of cooking fires, but Greek Fire's metallic tang. Ash glanced from the men in jacks and war-hats, slinging meal-sacks full of dirt in a chain towards the entrance to the counter-mine, to Floria, the woman pulling off the horn crown and running her fingers through her man-short gold hair. Hair as short as her brother's.

"Let's go," Ash said. "Shame if a long shot from a mangonel sprayed you all over the pavement, now."

"You don't think they'll keep this truce?"

"Not if we present them with an opportunity!" Ash looked away from Floria to Fernando del Guiz. He stood in the middle of the Lion Azure mercenaries. Recognisable as a renegade to anyone who knew his face from Neuss, or Genoa, or Basle.

"Get him covered up." Ash spoke to one of Rochester's sergeants. "Give him your hood and cloak."

She watched the sergeant put the cloak on Fernando del Guiz, knot the ties; tug the caped hood over his bare head, and pull the hood forward. A pang moved her: wanting, herself, to be the one to do it. *He's my husband. I've lain with this man. I could have had his child.*

But I stopped wanting him before I left Carthage. He's a weak man. There's nothing to him but good looks!

"Bring him along with us," Ash said. "Florian's going to be in the hospice at the tower, anyway."

There was an imperceptible relaxation in the mercenaries standing around Fernando del Guiz. It wouldn't have been there if he had still been in knight's armour, she thought. She could read on their faces the thought, *It's only a priest.*

"For those of you who don't know," she said, raising her voice a little, "this man used to be a knight in Holy Roman Emperor Frederick's court. Don't assume you can let him anywhere near a sword. Okay: let's move out."

With undertones of self-satisfaction in his voice, Fernando protested, "I'm an envoy, and a Christian priest. You don't have to be afraid of me, Ash."

"*Afraid* of you?"

She stared at him for a moment, snorted, and turned away.

Floria murmured, "Gelimer doesn't know me very well. Does he? Blood's much thinner than water in this respect."

Ash made an effort and achieved cynicism. "Fernando probably told Gelimer you were his loving sister and he could persuade you to turn cartwheels naked through Dijon's north gate while signing a surrender . . ."

"Or that he was your loving husband. Let's go," the surgeon-Duchess invited.

Stepping out into the wrecked territory behind the city gates, Ash couldn't prevent the automatic upward glance. Of the party, only Fernando looked bewilderedly at the soldiers, up at the sky, and back down at Ash again.

"Oh, I trust Gelimer to keep the truce . . ." Ash remarked, with a raucous sarcasm.

Ash moved off in the familiar position: surrounded by a group of armed men. Between banner and escort, and keeping her footing on the paths raked clear of masonry, there was little of her attention she could spare for the German ex-knight. Little of her mind that she could give over to the thought *That's my husband!* She felt glad of it. Cold bit deep. The sap below the earth had felt warmer than these chill, exposed streets of Dijon, and the empty winter sky. Ash beat her hands together as she walked, the plates of the gauntlets chinking. Shadows streamed north from the roofs, and the abbey bell rang for Terce. A quick glance up assured her of the Burgundian and the Lion presence on the city walls, keeping the besiegers under surveillance.

As they reached the streets in the south of the city, Florian gave her a curious look and signalled the guards to move up as she quickened her pace. It left Ash and Fernando side by side, he overtopping her by a head, a slight degree of privacy ensured by respect for commander-in-chief and Duchess.

Let 'em listen, Ash thought.

"Well," she said. "At least you're still the Duchess's brother. I suppose you've divorced *me*."

It came out entirely as sardonic as she had intended it. There was no shake in her voice.

Fernando del Guiz looked down at her with stone-green eyes. Close up, she was very conscious of the power of his body, striding beside her; knew equally that most of the attraction stemmed from him not knowing it, from his unconsciousness – still! – that it was anything special to be well-fed and clean and strong.

I thought I got over this! In Carthage! Oh *shit* . . .

"It wasn't a divorce, in the end." He sounded faintly apologetic, dropping his voice and looking around at the escorting mercenaries. "Abbot Muthari's learned doctors decreed it wasn't a valid marriage, not between a free man of the nobility and a bondswoman. They annulled it."

"Ah. Isn't that convenient. Doesn't keep you out of the priesthood." She couldn't stop some of the astounded curiosity she felt leaking into her tone. What she felt about an annulment was not available to her yet. *I'll think about that later, when I've got time to spare.*

Fernando del Guiz said nothing, only glancing down at her and away again.

"Jesus, Fernando, what *is* this!"

"This?"

She reached across and prodded his chest, just below the oak pendant of Christ on the Tree; thought, *That was a mistake, I still want to touch him, how damn obvious can I get!*, and grunted, " 'This'. This priest's get-up you're in. You're not seriously telling me you've taken vows!"

"I am." Fernando looked down at her. "I took my first vows in Carthage. Abbot Muthari let me take the second vows when he reconsecrated the cathedral in Marseilles. God accepted me, Ash."

"The Arian God."

Fernando shrugged. "All the same thing, isn't it? Doesn't matter which name you call it."

"Sheesh!" Impressed by the careless dismissal of eleven centuries of schism, Ash couldn't help smiling. "*Why*, Fernando? Don't tell me God called you, either. He's really scraping the bottom of the barrel if He did!"

When she looked up to meet Fernando's gaze, he looked both embarrassed and determined.

"I had the idea after you talked to me in Carthage. You were right. I was still taking the King-Caliph's arms and armour: why would he listen to me say we shouldn't be fighting this war? So I thought of this. This is the only way I can give up the sword and still have men *listen* to me."

She kept looking at him, long enough for her concentration to miss a beat, and for her foot to catch a fragment of broken brick. Recovering with a sword-fighter's balance from the stumble, she said, half-stifled, "You entered the church for *that*?"

His mouth set, mulishly, making him look momentarily no more than a boy. "I don't want to be ignored like a peasant or a woman! If I'm not knightly, then I have to be *something* they'll respect. I'm still del Guiz. I'm still noble! I've just taken my vows to be a *peregrinatus christi*."

Tears swelled the lower lids of her eyes. Ash looked into the wind and blinked, sharply. She was momentarily in Carthage's palace, hearing a *nazir* say *Let him through, it's only the peregrinatus christi*, and seeing Godfrey's lined, bearded face in the mass of foreign soldiers.

I need him here, now, not as a voice in my head!

"You'll never be a priest," she said harshly. "You're a fucking hypocrite."

"No."

The escort clattered under the gateway and into the courtyard in front of the company tower. A blaze of cold wind whipped in through the open gates, spooking the remaining horses. Anselm bellowed orders to the men, over the noise from the forge. Florian immediately found herself intercepted by a dozen courtiers.

"So you're not a hypocrite." Ash wiped wind-tears out of her eyes. "Yeah. Right."

"I never bothered much about praying, it was priest's work. I'm a knight." The tall, golden-haired man stopped. He spoke under the noise the men made. "I *was* one. I'm a priest now. Maybe God made me see how fucking crazy this fighting is! All I know is, one day I was a traitor Frankish knight, with no patron, and nobody listening to me – and now I'm not killing anyone, and I might just get some of Gelimer's nobles to listen when I say this war's wrong. If you call that hypocrisy – fine."

"Ah, shit."

Something in her tone obviously puzzled him. He shot a glance at her.

"Nothing," Ash snapped. She felt resentful; bad-tempered.

I might not have liked the separation, but at least it was settled. I might not have liked you being a weaselling, lying little shitbag – but at least I knew where I was with you.

I resent you making me think about this again. *Feel* again.

"Nothing," Ash repeated, under her breath.

If he had had a glib answer, she would have walked away from him. Fernando del Guiz looked down at the flagstones in adolescent male embarrassment, kicking his boot-heel against the ground, under the hem of his robe.

Ash sighed. "Why did you have to come back doing something I can respect?"

A mass of people blocked the company tower's steps. She heard Florian's raw voice raised. One glance found her Anselm; without more prompting, he began to give brisk orders. Men in company livery began to shift Burgundian courtiers out of the arched doorway.

Without looking at Fernando, she said, "You're wrong, you know. About war. And if there was a better way than going to war, we're *long* past the point where it was an issue. But I suppose you've had the guts to put your balls on the line . . ."

He coughed, or laughed, she was not sure which. "This is the Arian priesthood, not Our Lady of the Bloody Crescent!"

One of the escorting Turkish soldiers glanced across at that; nudged his mate, and said something under his breath. Ash stifled her grin.

"The goddess Astarte's very popular round here right now, so let's keep the religious dissent to a minimum, shall we?"

Fernando's smile was warm. "And you call me a hypocrite."

"I'm not a hypocrite," Ash said, turning to go into the tower as the crowd cleared. "I'm an equal-opportunities heretic – I think you're *all* talking through your arses . . ."

"This from the woman who was marked by the Lion?" He made a movement, reaching up to brush her scarred cheek with his gloved hand. She had let him touch her skin before she realised she was not going to move.

"That was then," she said. "This is now."

She heard, ahead, a roar of male laughter; loped up the steps to the door and walked in, in the midst of her escort, into chaos in the lower hall.

"*Boss!*" Henri Brant gave her a smile that showed the gap between his missing front teeth. He slapped the shoulder of a man shouting into the crowded hall: Richard Faversham, in green robes, his beard untrimmed, his face flushed.

Momentarily forgetting the others with her, Ash stared at the tower's first-floor hall. A fierce fire burned in the hearth, surrounded by off-duty Lion Azure mercenaries in various states of dishevelment ladling some liquid out of a cauldron. The beams were draped and hung with long strands of ivy. Baldina banged a tabor; blind and lame Carracci sat with her, fingering out notes on a recorder in duet with Antonio Angelotti. There were no trestle tables covered in yellowing linen, but men sat with their wooden bowls and cups where tables would have been ranked against either wall. She smelled cooking.

"Merry Mass of Christ!" Henri Brant exclaimed, his warm breath hitting her in the face. Whatever they were drinking – not having the swine to feed now, it was probably fermented turnip-peelings – it had a kick to it.

"God bless you!" Richard Faversham leaned down and gave her the kiss of peace. "Christ be with you!"

"And with you," Ash growled. She ignored Floria's chuckle. After a second, surveying the hall and her men, she grinned at Henri Brant. "I take it you're doing two servings, so the lads on duty can come back here?"

"Either that, or find my balls boiling in the pot!" The steward pushed his coif back on his sheepswool-curly white hair, sweating from the heat of close-packed bodies if not from the fire. "We couldn't hoard much. Master Anselm thought, as I did, better to eat now and starve the sooner, rather than let the Christ-Mass pass without celebration. So did Master Faversham!"

Ash studied the large black-bearded Englishman for a moment.

"Well done!" She clasped both men's hands warmly. "God knows we need something to keep our minds off this shit-hole we're in!"

Unguarded, she looked around and met the gaze of Fernando del Guiz inside his concealing hood. He was watching the soldiers and their sparse revelry with a strange expression. *Not contempt*, she guessed. *Compassion? No. Not Fernando.*

"We're holding council. The Burgundians will be along any minute. I'll come down for mass. Henri, can you send Roberto to me? And Angeli. I'll be up in the solar."

The tower's top floor had been dressed in her absence. Green ivy hung stark over the round arches, bright against the sand-and-ochre colours of the walls. A hoarded single Green candle burned, scenting the room. Rickard turned from supervising the pages as she entered: obviously proud of the evergreen, the hearth-fire, the food in preparation – and stopped, his face freezing, recognising Fernando del Guiz under the hood.

"The Duchess will have this hall to speak with her brother," Ash said formally. "Rickard, we're expecting de la Marche, can you clear that with the guys on the door, and get these kids out of here?"

"Boss." Rickard looked twice at the robes under the cloak, then stalked past Fernando del Guiz, glared brows dipping, hand resting down on his sword-hilt. She noted, as he walked out with the pages, that the boy was as tall as the German ex-knight now. Not a boy. A squire, a young man; all this in the last half-year.

"Good grief!" Floria shook her head, saying nothing more. She moved closer to the hearth, let her cloak fall open, and extended her hands to the blaze. Ash saw she was wearing a fur-lined demi-gown over male doublet and hose again.

Fernando del Guiz reached up and put his hood back. He looked quizzically at the surgeon-Duchess. "Sister. You make a strange Duchess."

"Oh, you think so?" Her gaze warmed. "And you don't make a strange priest?"

Ash blurted, "Why the hell pick *you* to come in here? Because priests are sacrosanct? De la Marche would love a traitor to hang up on the walls – cheer everybody up, that would!"

Fernando still spoke to Floria. "I had no choice. I came up with the Abbot Muthari, from Carthage. The King-Caliph dragged me into court as soon as he heard who the Duchess of Burgundy was. They interrogated me – not that there's much I could tell him, is there, Floria?"

"No." Floria turned to watch the fire. "I remember seeing you once, when I was about ten. The only time I ever stayed on my father's German estates. You would have been born that year."

"Mother used to have Tante Jeanne to stay – is she still alive? – and they'd talk about you in whispers."

His face creased under his rumpled hair. Ash thought she saw something relaxed, despite the circumstances, in his humour. As if he were comfortable with himself.

He added, "I thought you'd run off with a man. I didn't know you'd run off to *be* a man!"

"I 'ran off' to be a doctor!" Floria snapped.

"And now you're Burgundy's Duchess." He looked at Ash. "Then it came out that you were made captain of the Burgundian armies here, and I was doubly useful."

Ash snapped, "That must have made a pleasant change."

"Except that I could tell him even less about you – 'she's a soldier; I married her; she doesn't trust me'. I could tell him how good a soldier you are. And I'm not, you see. But by now, they know that."

His wry expression confused her. Ash looked away. She had an impulse to provide him with food, with drink. An impulse to touch the faint blond stubble on his cheek.

Deliberately brutal, she said, "No. You're not. The rag-heads still letting you keep Guizburg?"

928

"Priests have no lands. I've lost most of what I had. I'm still useful, by virtue of being Floria's brother. While I'm useful, I can talk – this is a hopeless war, for both sides—"

"Christ up a Tree, I need a drink!" Ash turned and began to pace the floorboards, beating her hands together for circulation. "And where the hell is de la Marche? Let's get this 'envoy' crap over with!"

There were no pages to serve out rations: all the baggage-train brats down in the hall below, by the sound of it – shrieks and yells echoed up the spiral stairwell, not subdued by the ragged hangings blocking the doorway. Cold wind found its way between the window shutters.

Tension kept Ash pacing. Florian squatted by the fire with her cloak held out open around her, to trap the heat: a campaigner's trick she obviously remembered from half a dozen winters with the company. Fernando del Guiz folded his arms and stood watching both women, smiling wryly.

Ash strode to the stairwell and yelled, "Rickard!"

A longer space of time elapsed than she was used to before he called up, panting, "Yes, boss?"

"Where the fuck's de la Marche and Oxford and the civilians?"

"Don't know, boss. No messenger!"

"What are you doing?"

Rickard's flushed face appeared in the dim light of the well, a dozen steps below. "We're going to do the mumming, boss. I'm in it! Are you coming down?"

"There's no word from Oxford?"

"Captain Anselm sent another man up to the palace just now."

"Hell. What are they *doing*?" Ash glanced back over her shoulder. "It's a damn sight warmer down there than up here, isn't it? And there's food. Okay: we'll wait for my lords of England and Burgundy downstairs! And get me a drink before you start pratting around."

"Yes, boss!"

A great burst of sound came as she stepped off the bottom stair and into the main hall: nothing to do with her or, as she first thought, the presence of Fernando del Guiz, but a carol being bellowed by two hundred lusty male throats:

> "The Boar's Head in hand bear I,
> With garlands gay and rosemary,
> I pray you all sing merrily,
> *Qui estis in convivio.*
> *Caput apri defero,*
> *Reddens laudes domino.*"

Floria took a place beside Ash against the wall, in the small stir of men-at-arms and archers acknowledging their commander's presence. Ash signalled them back to their singing. Floria murmured under her breath, "We could do with a boar's head . . ."

"I don't think we've even got the rosemary to cook with it!" Ash felt a wooden bowl and horn spoon shoved into her hand, yelled thanks to one of the pages, and realised that she had settled back against the stone wall shoulder-to-shoulder with Fernando del Guiz.

She had to look up to meet his eyes.

The shrill sound of Carracci's recorder rose above the voices of men and women. She heard Angelotti playing descant. It was not possible to speak over the volume of sound.

I'd forgotten he's so tall. And so young.

There being no tables on which to set the trenchers, the woman doing the cooking and the other baggage women were rushing about the hall, from group to group, ladling out pottage. Ash held out her bowl, caught for a second in the rush of conviviality; and spooned the hot broth into her mouth. The carol thundered to a close.

"The mummers!" someone yelled. "Bring on the mummers!"

A roof-shaking cheer.

Beside her, Fernando del Guiz, his hood still raised, studied the contents of his bowl and tentatively began to eat. What could be seen of him was anonymous, priestly; he drew no glances from armed men. Ash kept her eyes on the men shoving a space clear in the centre of the hall.

There was no Christmas kissing-bush hanging from the rafters: someone had strung up a pair of old hose – being at least green in colour, she supposed – and John Burren and Adriaen Campin were drunkenly pretending to kiss each other underneath it. She attended analytically to the cheers and cat-calls – a little shrill, not all the men joining in. She glanced towards the guards on the great door. No runners; no messages yet.

What is keeping them?

Fernando del Guiz chewed at some unrelenting piece of gristle, and swallowed. On the other side of Ash, Floria had stopped eating to talk enthusiastically to Baldina. The men-at-arms around them were watching the centre of the hall.

There was a certain amount of relief on the young man's face as he turned his head to gaze down at her. He nodded, as if to himself. "Can we speak privately?"

"If I take you into a corner somewhere, everyone will be watching. Let's talk here."

To her own surprise, there was no malice in her tone.

Fernando took another spoonful of the pottage, frowned, put back the spoon, tapped the shoulder of the man in front, and handed the bowl forward. When he looked back at Ash, his face in the hood's shadow was drawn, wry, and uncertain. "I came to make a peace with you."

She stared at him for a long moment. "I didn't even bother to find out if you were alive or dead. After Carthage. I suppose it was easier to think I had other matters to worry about."

He studied her face. "Maybe."

About to question that, Ash was interrupted by a loud and ringing cheer. The mummers' procession wound around the centre of the hall, between men and women packed back to the walls. A rhythmic clapping bounced off the walls, together with inebriated yells.

"What's this?" Fernando shouted.

Two large men-at-arms in mail hauberks, in front of him, turned around and shushed Fernando.

"It's the mumming," Ash said, only loud enough for him to hear.

The head of the procession walked into the central clear space. It was Adriaen Campin, she realised; the big Fleming wrapped in a horse-blanket and wearing a bridle over his head. Rags of cloth, for ribbons, fluttered at his knees and ankles. Campin, his blanket sliding down, put his fists on his hips and bawled:

> "I am the hobby horse, with St George I ride,
> It's fucking cold out, so we've come inside!
> Give us room to act our play,
> Then by God's Grace we'll go away!"

Ash put her hands over her face as the men-at-arms cheered and the hobby horse began to dance. Beside her, she heard Floria whimper. On her other side, Fernando del Guiz quaked; she felt his arm, pressed against her in the crowd, shaking with amusement.

"Not used to seeing this one at Christ's Mass," he said. "We always did it at Epiphany Feast, at Guizburg . . . do I take it you think this city won't hold out until Twelfth Night?"

"That what you're going to tell Gelimer?"

He grinned boyishly. "Gelimer will hate this. The King-Caliph hopes you're all cutting your own throats, not making merry."

Ash looked away from Campin's high-kicking horse-dance. She thought one or two of the men around her caught the King-Caliph's name. She shook her head warningly at Fernando. The warmth of the hall brought the smell of his body to her: male sweat, and the own particular smell that was just his.

Obscene, brutal and blackly humorous comments drifted her way. Ash caught the eye of those of her men who obviously did recognise the fair-haired priest as the German knight who had briefly been their feudal lord. The comment moved to where she would not hear it.

Why am I sparing *his* feelings?

"You're going to have to tell me," she said, surrendering to the impulse. "Fernando, how did you get to be a priest!"

For answer, he extended his arm, pulling his sleeve up a little. A comparatively new scar was still red and swollen across his right wrist, although to a professional eye mostly healed.

"Hauling Abbot Muthari out of the palace when it collapsed," he explained.

"I'd have left him!"

"*I* was looking for a patron," Fernando remarked sourly. "I'd just spoken up for you, remember? In the palace? I knew Gelimer was going to dump me faster than a dog can shit. I would have hauled anyone with jewellery or fine clothes out of the wreckage – it happened to be Muthari."

"And he was dumb enough to let you take vows?"

"You don't know what it was like in Carthage then." The man frowned, his expression distant. "At first, they thought the King-Caliph was dead, and the empire going to dissolve in factions – then word came down that he was alive and it was a miracle. Then those spooky lights showed up in the desert – where we rode out? With those tombs? And *that* was supposed to be a curse . . ."

Seeing him so far away in his mind, Ash said nothing to disturb his chain of memories.

"I still think it is," Fernando said, after a second. "I rode out there when we recovered Lord Leofric. There were serfs and sheep and goats out there that had . . . they were dead. They were melted, like wax, they were *in* the gates of the tombs – half in and half out of the bronze metal. And the light – curtains of light, in the sky. Now they're calling it the Fire of God's Blessing."[14]

Seeing it with his eyes: the painted walls of pyramids where she had ridden out into the silence imposed by the Wild Machines, Ash felt the cold hairs prickle at the nape of her neck.

Fernando shrugged, in the tight-sleeved robe; one hand reaching up to close around his oak pendant. "*I* call it djinn."

"It isn't djinn, or devils. It's the Wild Machines." She pointed at the sky beyond the round stone arch of the window. "They're sucking the light out of the world. I don't want to think what that's like when you're right up close to them."

"I'm not *going* to think about it." Fernando shrugged.

"Ah, that's my husband . . . *ex*-husband," she corrected herself.

Whether Adriaen Campin had finished his dance or whether the hobby horse had merely fallen over was unclear. Half a dozen men dragged him off. Baldina and several more women threw clean rushes down on to the floor, and Ash saw Henri Brant walking out over them into the empty space. He wore a full-length looted velvet robe that had been red, before grease spattered it mostly black. A metal circlet sat on his white curls, spikes jutting up from it; cold-hammered from the forge. More horse-harness had been cannibalised to make a neck-chain out of bits.

Anselm's done good, Ash reflected, trying to spot her second in command in the hall and failing. *We needed this*.

Henri Brant, with a great deal of authority, held up his hands for quiet and declaimed:

> "I'm England's true king
> And I boldly appear,
> Seeking my son for whom I fear –
> Is Prince George here?"

One of the English archers bellowed, "You a *Lancastrian* or a *Yorkist* English King?"

Henri Brant jerked his thumb over his shoulder at the mummer playing St George. "What d'*you* think!"

"It's Anselm!" Floria exclaimed, straining up on her toes to see. She turned a shining face to Ash. "It's Roberto!"

---

[14] This description is tantalisingly similar to some of the rumoured results of military experiments with extreme electromagnetic force. The 'curtains of light' are presumably charged particles, like the *aurora borealis*.

"Guess that'll be a Lancastrian King, then . . ."

There was a great deal of noise from those company men who did not come from England, but were entirely happy to wind up those who did. Ash was caught between chuckling at them, and the sheer contentment of watching their high spirits; and the intent expression on Fernando's face.

"I half expect you to offer me a contract with the Caliph," she said.

"No. I'm not that stupid." After a second Fernando del Guiz touched her arm and pointed at the mummers, face alight with momentary unguarded enjoyment. Her gut thumped. She was struck by the lean grace of him, and his wide shoulders, and the thought that – if war had not come to trouble him – he might have continued winning tournaments and gambling; might have married some Bavarian heiress and sired babies and never dipped deeper into himself than necessary; certainly never found himself taking religious vows.

"What *do* you want with me?" she said.

A cheer drowned out whatever he said. She looked and saw Robert Anselm, lance in hand, stomp into the cleared space between the company men-at-arms and baggage women.

"My God. You won't see armour like that again!" Floria yelled.

Her brother gaped. "God willing, no, we won't!"

More pauldrons, spaulders, guard-braces and rere-braces had been buckled and pinned on to Anselm's wide shoulders than it seemed possible for any man to support. He rattled as he walked. The leg-harness was his own, but the German cuirass had plainly been made for a much larger man – Ash suspected Roberto had borrowed it off one of the Burgundian commanders. The fluted breastplate caught the light from the slit windows and shimmered, silver, where it was not covered by an old tawny livery jacket with a white mullet device. The lance he carried bore a drooping white flag – a woman's chemise – with a red rose scrawled on it.

Anselm shoved the visor of his sallet up, displaying his grinning, stubbled face. He rapped the lance shaft on the flagstones, and threw out his free arm in a wide gesture.

"I am Prince George, a worthy knight,
I'll spend my blood in England's right!"

He punched his fist in the air, mimed awaiting a cheer, and when it came, cupped his hand to where his ear would have been, if he hadn't been wearing a helmet. "I can't *hear* you! Louder!"

Sound slammed back from the tower's stone walls. Ash felt it through her chest as well as her ears. Anselm went on:

"There is no knight as brave as me –
I'll kick your arse if you don't agree!"

Fernando del Guiz groaned, delicately. "I don't remember mumming being like this at Frederick's court!"

"You have to be with mercenaries to see real class . . ."

There was something still boyish in his face when he laughed; it vanished when he stopped. Strain had etched lines in that had not been there in

Carthage. *Three months*, she thought. *Only that. The sun in Virgo then, the sun just into Capricorn now. So short a time.*

She saw him stiffen as a raucous jeer greeted the entrance of another of the mummers.

Euen Huw strode unsteadily forward in a mail hauberk with a woman's square-necked chemise worn over it. The yellow linen flapped around his knees. The men-at-arms and archers cheered; one of the women – Blanche, Ash thought – gave a shrill whistle. Ash frowned, not able to stop herself laughing, still puzzled. Not until the Welshman, wincing at his scalp-stitches, put on a looted Visigoth helm with a black rag tied around it, did she recognise the parody of robes over mail.

Euen Huw mimed sneaking into the open space, clutching a looted Carthaginian spear. He declaimed:

> "I am the Saracen champion, see,
> Come from Carthage to Burgundy.
> I'll slay Prince George and when he's gone
> I'll kill all you others, one by one."

"Take you a fucking long time!" someone shouted.

"I can do it," Euen Huw protested. "Watch me."

"Watch you shag a sheep, more like!"

"I 'eard that, Burren!"

Ash did not meet Fernando's eye. On her other side, Floria del Guiz made a loud, rude noise, and began to wheeze. Ash clamped her arms across her breastplate, aching under the ribs, and attempted to look suitably commander-like and unimpressed.

"You'll have to forgive them being topical," she said, keeping her face straight with an immense effort.

Euen Huw snatched a wooden cup of drink from one of the archers, drained it, and swung back to face Robert Anselm.

> "I challenge you, Prince George the brave,
> I say you are an arrant knave.
> I can stand by my every word –
> Because you wear a wooden sword!

"And besides, you're English crap," the Welsh lance-leader added.

Robert Anselm shoved his lance and makeshift banner aloft and struck an attitude:

> "By my right hand, and by this blade,
> I'll send you to your earthly grave—"

"Ouch," Floria said gravely.

Antonio Angelotti appeared at her side, and murmured, "I did tell him. *Terza rima*, I offered . . ."

Ash saw the fair-haired gunner clasp Floria's arm, as he might have done with any man, or the company surgeon, but not the Duchess of Burgundy. Ash smiled; and as she glanced back caught something like wistfulness on Fernando's face.

Anselm lowered his lance and pointed it at Euen Huw's breast; the Welshman taking an automatic step back. Anselm proclaimed:

> "I'll send your soul to God on high,
> So prepare yourself to fly or die!"

Ash saw the lance and spear tossed aside, both men drawing whalebone practice swords from their belts. The shouts, cheers and jeering rose to a pitch as the fight began; half the English archers near her chanting, "Come on, St George!" and banging their feet on the stone floor.

"Look at that." Ash pointed. "They couldn't resist it, could they!"

Out in the centre of the hall, Robert Anselm and Euen Huw had abandoned their exaggerated and pantomime blows and were circling each other, on the rushes. As she spoke, Anselm darted a blow forward, the Welshman whipped it round in a parry and struck; Anselm blocked—

"They had to make a genuine fight of it." Florian sighed. She was smiling. The noise of the men-at-arms rose even higher, seeing a contest of skills beginning. "I suppose they'll get back to the mumming eventually . . . Come on, Euen! Show them how well I sewed you up!"

Under the noise of cheering and the thwack of whalebone on plate and mail, Fernando del Guiz said, "Is it peace between us, Ash?"

She looked up at him, standing beside her, hood drawn forward, in a hall full of his enemies, apparently unmoved. *But I know him, now. He's afraid.*

"It's been a long time since Neuss," she said. "Married, and separated, and attaindered, and annulled. And a long way from Carthage. Why *did* you speak up for me? In the coronation – why?"

Apparently at random, Fernando del Guiz murmured, "You'd think I would have remembered your face. I didn't. I forgot it for seven years. It didn't occur to me that if there was a woman in armour at Neuss, it might be the one I'd – seen – at Genoa."

"Is that an answer? Is that an *apology*?"

The sun slanting down from the arrow-port windows cast a silver light on the heads of the crowd. It flashed back from Anselm and Euen Huw, leaping on the rushes in a mad duel; the cheering shaking the ivy hanging from the rafters. The cold sank into her bones, and she looked down at her white, bloodless hands.

"*Is* it an apology?" she repeated.

"Yes."

In the centre of the hall, Robert Anselm drove Euen Huw back across the rushes with a savage, perfectly executed series of blows, as hard and rapid as a man chopping wood. Whalebone spanged off metal. The English archers hoarsely cheered.

"Fernando, why *did* you come here?"

"There has to be a truce. Then peace." Fernando del Guiz looked down at his empty hands, and then back up at her. "Too many people are dying here, Ash. Dijon's going to be wiped out. So are you."

Two contradictory feelings flooded her. *He's so young!* she thought; and at the same time: *He's right. Military logic isn't any different for me than it is for anyone else. Unless Gelimer's more frightened of the Turks than I think he is, this siege is going to end in a complete massacre. And soon.*

"Christ on a rock!" he exclaimed. "Give in, for once in your life! Gelimer's promised me he'll keep you alive, out of *amir* Leofric's hands. He'll just throw you in prison for a few years—"

His voice rose. Ash was aware of Floria and Angelotti looking across her, towards the German knight.

"That's supposed to impress me?" she said.

Robert Anselm feinted and slashed the whalebone blade clear out of Euen Huw's hands. A massive cry of "Saint George!" shook the rafters, thundering back from the stone walls of the tower, drowning anything she might have said.

Disarmed, the weaponless Saracen knight suddenly stared past Robert Anselm's left shoulder and bellowed, "It's behind you!"

Anselm unwarily glanced over his shoulder. Euen Huw brought his boot up smartly between Anselm's legs.

"Christ!" Fernando yelped in sympathy.

Euen Huw stood out of the way as Anselm fell forward, picked up Anselm's sword, and thumped a hefty blow down on his helmet. He straightened, panting and red-faced, and wheezed, "Got you, you English bastard!"

Ash bit her lip, saw Robert Anselm writhing dramatically on the floor, realised *his colour's okay; he can move* – and that Euen had kicked him on the inside of the thigh, and that the two of them had planned it. She began to applaud. Either side of her, Fernando and his sister were clapping; and Angelotti laughing with tears streaming down his face.

"Ruined!" Henri Brant shouted, rushing forward with his king's robes swirling, and his iron crown skewed. "Ruined!

> "Is there no doctor to save my son,
> And heal Prince George's deadly wound?"

A hum of expectation came from the crowd. Ash, checking by eye, saw no one of her men-at-arms and archers and gunners not either eating or drinking, or cheering on the mummers. She did not look at Fernando. The pause lengthened. In the group of mummers at the hearth, an altercation appeared to be going on.

"*No*—" Rickard shook the other mummers off and walked forward. Ash realised from the overlong gown that all but drowned him, and his sack of smithy-tools, that he must be supposed to play the part; but the young man didn't stop, walking forward into the crowd towards her, and the men gave way in front of him.

He reached them; bowed with adolescent awkwardness to her and then to the surgeon-Duchess.

"I don't have the wisdom to play the Noble Doctor," he stuttered, "but there is one in this house who does. Messire Florian, please!"

"What?" Floria looked bewildered.

"Play the Noble Doctor in the mumming!" Rickard repeated. "Please!"

"Do it!" one of the men-at-arms yelled.

"Yeah, come on, Doc!" A shout from John Burren, and the archers standing with him.

Robert Anselm, flat and dead on the rushes, lifted up his head with a scrape of armour. "Prince George is dying over here! Some bastard had better be the doctor!"

"Messire Florian, you better had," Angelotti said, beaming.

"I don't know any lines!"

"You do," Ash protested. She snuffled back laughter. "Your face! Florian, everybody knows mumming lines. You must have done this before, some Twelfth Night. Get on out there! Boss's orders!"

"Yes, *sir*, boss," Floria del Guiz said darkly. The scarecrow-tall woman hesitated, then rapidly unbuttoned her demi-gown and – with the squire's help – began to struggle into the Noble Doctor's over-long garment. Shaking it down on her shoulders, hair dishevelled, eyes bright, she said under her breath, "Ash, I'll get you for this!" and strode forward.

Rickard slung her the clanking bag of tools and she caught it, pulling one out by the handle as she walked forward into the open space at the centre of the hall. She put her foot thoughtfully on Robert Anselm's supine chest, and leaned her arm on her knee.

"*Oof!*"

"I am the Doctor . . .

"Fuck," Floria said. "Let me think: hang on—"

"My *God*, she's like Father!" Fernando surveyed his half-sister; then smiled down at Ash. "Shame the old bastard's dead. He'd have liked to have known he had two sons."

"Fuck you too, Fernando," Ash said amiably. "You know I'm going to keep her alive, don't you? You can tell Gelimer *that*."

In the centre of the hall, Floria was using a pair of bolt-cutters to push back the fauld of Anselm's armour. She prodded the bolt-cutters tentatively into his groin. "This man's dead!"

"Has been for years!" Baldina shouted.

"Dead as a door-nail," the surgeon-Duchess repeated. "Oh shit – no, don't tell me – I'll get it in a minute—"

Ash linked her arm through Fernando's, under his cloak. She felt his robe; and then the shift of his body-weight as he leaned towards her, and put his hand over hers. His warmth brought another warmth to her body. She tightened her grip on his arm.

Out in the hall, Floria moved her foot from Robert Anselm's breastplate to his codpiece. Jeers, cat-calls, and shouts of sympathy shook the tower. She declaimed:

> "The Doctor am I, I cure all diseases,
> The pox, and the clap, and the sniffles and sneezes!
> I'll bind up your bones,
> I'll bind up your head,
> I can raise up a man even though he be dead."

"I'll bet you can!" Willem Verhaecht yelled, on a note of distinct admiration.

Floria rested the bolt-cutters back across her shoulder. "Don't know why you're worrying, Willem, yours dropped off years ago!"

"Damn, I knew I'd left *something* in Ghent!"

Ash, grinning, shook her head. Over by the hearth, the last of the cauldrons had been scraped clean, and the pots drunk dry; the women were wiping their hands on their aprons and standing with bare arms, sweating and applauding.

That was less than half-rations. And this was Robert's Christ-Mass over-indulgence. We are in the shit.

Fernando said suddenly, "Gelimer's going to make you an offer. He told me to say this: even *I* don't believe it. If Dijon surrenders, he'll let the townspeople go, although he'll have to hang the garrison. And as for my sister – the King-Caliph will take the Duchess of Burgundy to wife."

"You *what*?"

Antonio Angelotti, unashamedly listening in, said, "Christus! that's neat, madonna. There'll be immediate pressure on us to surrender from the merchants and guildsmen. It's tense between us and them as it is."

"To *wife*?" Ash said.

"It's his mistake." Fernando bristled a little at the Italian master gunner, and spoke to Ash: "Frederick's men already say Gelimer must be weak or he'd just walk in here. Nothing will come of the offer, but—" a shrug "—it's what I was told to say."

"Oh, Christ. I'll look forward to telling de la Marche *that* one." Reminded, Ash glanced towards the doors again. Nothing there but the guards – and they had turned their heads, watching the surgeon-Duchess and St George.

Floria's voice rang out:

> "By my right and my command,
> Dead Saint George now up shall stand.
> By my wit and for your gain,
> I will make him live again.
> Now in front of all men's eyes
> Lift your head: arise, arise!"

Robert Anselm sprang to his feet and bowed, with a flourish. One of his pauldrons fell off and clattered to the flagstones. Euen Huw, Henri Brant and Adriaen Campin ran forward; the Saracen Knight, the King and the Hobby Horse holding hands.

Floria del Guiz seized Anselm's hand, and Euen's, and called Rickard forward. Ash saw her whisper in the squire's ear. Rickard nodded, took a deep breath, and shouted:

> "Prince George lives again,
> This Christmas Twelfth Night.
> Now pay us our fee
> And we'll bid you goodnight!"

Amid raucous applause, a shower of small coins and old boots bounced off the hall's flagstones around the mummers. They bowed.

The company's men-at-arms crowded in close to clap Floria and the others on the back. Someone hauled some of the ivy-creepers down, and the spiralling greenery got wound around the company's doctor, steward, second captain, lance-leader and squire. Ash, her eyes on Floria's face, felt suddenly bereft. *Even if we can make it through this, everything's different now.*

Someone cheered; Florian's shining fair hair appeared over the heads of the crowd, hoisted up between Euen Huw and Robert Anselm. She waited, not going forward yet to give her own congratulations. She looked up at Fernando del Guiz. He seemed to be more nervous than a few minutes before.

"A *priest* . . ." She shook her head, smiling less caustically than she might have expected. "Done any good miracles yet?"

"No. I'm only in first vows, celibacy vows; I won't know if I can do that sort of thing until it shows up if I have grace." After an infinitesimal pause, he added, "Ash . . . It's a different priesthood. If you don't need to be celibate for grace, you don't have to be. When you reach high rank you can marry. Muthari has. I've seen her: she's Nubian."

"Nice for him," Ash said ironically. She noted, with a distanced surprise, that her mouth had gone dry. A curdle of apprehension made her stomach cold. *What's he trying to tell me?*

"What are you trying to tell me, Fernando?"

A smile moved the corner of his mouth. It was apparent to her that he had been holding it back; that something was taking his mind away from being in a besieged city as a none-too-trusted envoy, and not allowing him to worry about bombardment or truce-breaking or any of the other things that had been weighing her down for three months now.

"There is something I ought to tell you," he said.

"Yeah?"

He said nothing for several seconds. Ash studied his face. She wanted, again, to touch his lips and his jaw and the ridge of his heavy, fair brows; not just for the flush it was bringing to her body to think about it, but from a feeling almost of tenderness.

"Go on," she prompted.

"Okay. I just never expected . . ." He looked away, into the crowded, raucous hall, and then back at her. There was a suppressed energy, a brightness, about him.

"I didn't expect to fall in love," he said gravely, his voice almost cracking like a much younger man's. "Or if I did, I expected it to be with some nobleman's daughter with a dowry, that my mother had picked out for me; or an Earl's wife, maybe . . . I didn't expect it to be with someone who's a soldier, Ash – someone who has silver hair and brown eyes and doesn't wear gowns, just armour . . ."

The breath stopped in her throat. Aware that her chest hurt, she stared up into his eyes. His face was transfigured; no mistaking the genuineness of it.

"I . . ." Her own voice croaked.

"I won't get my estates back now. I'll just be a priest dependent on alms.

Even if I could marry, later . . . She'll never look at me, will she? A woman like that?"

"She might." Ash met his gaze. Her fingers were prickling; her hands sweating. She felt a weakness in her muscles; a soaring surprise; could think only, *Why didn't I realise I wanted this?*

"She might," Ash repeated. She dared not reach out and take his hand. "I don't know what to say to you, Fernando. You didn't want to marry me, you were forced to. I wanted to have you, but I didn't want *you*. But, I don't know, you've come back doing this—" she waved her hand at the priest's robe "—and I can respect it, even if I don't think you stand a chance in hell of convincing anybody."

I can respect it, she repeated silently to herself. A feeling of lightness went through her body.

"Fernando, the minute I looked at you, back there, I thought you were different. I don't know. Even if Arian priests can marry, I'm still not legally able to. But . . . if you want to try again . . . yes. I will."

The surge of excitement at committing herself made her dizzy. It was several seconds before she realised that Fernando was staring at her with an expression of shock.

"What? *What?*"

"Oh shit!" he said miserably. "I've done this all wrong, haven't I?"

"What do you mean?"

Staring at him, utterly lost, she could only watch him shift his feet, stare up at the rafters, let out an explosive breath.

"Oh God, I've explained this all wrong! I didn't mean you."

"What do you mean, you didn't mean me?"

"I said 'silver hair', I said 'brown eyes' . . ." His hand fisted; he smacked it into his other palm. "Oh, shit, I'm *sorry*."

Totally calm, Ash said, "You don't mean me. You mean her."

He nodded, mutely.

A wave of heat went through her. She flattened her hands against the stone wall behind her, keeping her balance. Her cheeks flushed bright red. Searing embarrassment wiped out everything, even the stabbing pain under her breastbone. Her muscles tensed to take her stamping off, out of the hall, up the stairs – *to where? To throw myself off the roof?*

"Oh, Jesus!" Fernando del Guiz said, his voice agonised. "I wasn't thinking. I mean her – the Faris. I wanted to tell you about it. Ash, I never meant you to think—"

"No."

"Ash—"

"Take no notice," she said savagely. "Take no fucking notice. Shit!" Unconsciously, her hand had become a fist, that pressed up against her solar plexus. "Oh, shit, Fernando! What is it about *her*? She's not one of your proper women, she's a soldier too! We're mirror images!"

She broke off, remembering hacked-off hair, and the old, pale scars on her face. She couldn't look at Fernando. One snatched glance told her he was as red as she must be.

"We're the same!"

"No, you're not. I don't know what the difference is," he muttered, doggedly. "There's a difference."

"Oh, you don't know?" Her voice rose. "Don't you. Really. Oh, I'll tell you what the difference is, Fernando. She never had her face cut up. She's never been poor. She's been adopted by a lord-*amir*. She was never a whore who had to fuck men when she was ten years old! That's the difference. She isn't spoiled, is she!"

She stared into his eyes for a long minute.

"I could have loved you," she said quietly. "I don't think I knew that until now. And I wish I'd never let you know it."

"Ash, I'm so sorry."

Recovering herself into arrogance, keeping the tears out of her voice, Ash said, "So: have you fucked her yet?"

A deeper red rose up his white neck, where the high collar of his cassock and his hood did not hide it.

"No?"

"She rode out to escort the King-Caliph to Dijon. She called on me to act as her confessor on the way back." He swallowed, Adam's apple bobbing. "She wanted to know why I was a priest now, instead of a knight—"

"But did you fuck her?"

"No." He looked momentarily angry, then besotted, then apologetic; and ran his gloved hand through his hair, mussing it. "How can I? If I get to a rank in the church where I can marry—"

"You're in a fucking dream-world!"

"I love her!"

"You just love a dream," Ash spat out. "What do you think she is? Some woman on a white horse, who leads men into battle and doesn't kill? Do you think she's as good as she is beautiful?"

"Ash—"

"She's one of us, Fernando. She's one of the people who organises killing people. That's what I am, that's what you've been, that's what she is. Christus! can't you think with anything else but your cock!"

"I'm sorry." In an extreme of embarrassment, he spread his hands. "I did it all wrong. I didn't know you'd think I meant you. I thought you knew I—"

Ash let the silence between them grow.

"Thought I knew you wouldn't touch me again if your life depended on it?" she said.

"No! I mean . . ." Fernando looked down helplessly at the floor. "I can't explain it. I've seen you. I'd seen her before. This time it was . . . different."

"Ahh – fuck off!"

Hot and cold with humiliation, she stared away, not seeing the celebrating men in front of her, not seeing the chipped edges of the window embrasures or the dark, cold sky beyond.

Now I know what people mean when they say they wish the ground would open and swallow them up.

Fernando's voice sounded beside her, quiet, but with authority.

"It's nothing to do with you. There's nothing *wrong* with you. I hated you – but then I listened to you— Ash, I wouldn't be a priest if it wasn't for you! I didn't know it until just now, when I found out I *am* sorry I hurt you. I love her. I feel like you're my, I don't know, my sister, maybe. Or my friend."

Sardonic, tears in her voice, Ash said, "Stick to 'friend' – leave sisters out of it. Your sister wants to touch me a whole lot more than you do!"

He blinked.

"Never mind," Ash said. "Forget it. Forget this whole thing. I don't want to hear about it again."

"Okay."

After a second, Ash said, "Does she know?"

"No."

"So you're worshipping from afar, just like the troubadours say."

He coloured again, at her sarcasm. "Might be just as well. I'm bad at this. I just wanted to apologise to you, and then tell you how I feel about her. Ash, I never meant to hurt you."

"You've done it better than when you did mean to."

"I know. What can I say?"

"What can anybody say?" She sighed. "Just one of those things, isn't that what they call it? If you want to do something, Fernando, just don't say anything to me. Okay?"

"Okay."

She turned away from him, watching her men. A welcome numbness pushed her hurt and anger and pride away, leaving only relief in its place; *it hurts too much to think about* being superseded by *it's not worth getting worked up about.*

After a few moments, her jaw tightened with the effort of pushing away the urge to weep.

"It isn't as easy as it used to be," she said.

"What?"

"Doesn't matter."

Before she could do anything to get her voice under control, there was a disturbance at the main door.

Ash looked across into bright daylight as the doors opened. A blast of cold air sliced through the hall's sweaty warmth. She heard boots and weapons clash; put up her hand to shadow her eyes.

De Vere, his brother Dickon, twenty Turks, Olivier de la Marche, and some of the Burgundian army commanders walked in. Jonvelle stopped dead and stared at her, his face whitening.

"I told you!" John de Vere roared.

Ash found them all staring at her: Oxford's brother with wide eyes. Even the Janissaries appeared mildly interested. She put one fist on her hip, scrabbling for composure, for raw humour.

"What's the matter, did I forget to dress?"

The Burgundian *centenier*, Jonvelle, swallowed. "*Hé Dieux!*[15] It *is* her. It *is* the Captain-General."

[15] "By God!"

Ash fixed him and the English Earl with an authoritative eye. "Someone is going to tell me what's going on here . . ."

The Burgundian stared, as if he were taking in every detail – a woman at home in plate leg harness and arm-defences, in a polished Milanese cuirass; with dirty-white hair cut short to her ears, and wood-fire smuts on her scarred cheeks. Still flushing a dull red.

"You're here," Jonvelle spoke again.

Ash turned her back on Fernando del Guiz, and folded her arms. "That's what I've been sending bloody messages to tell you! Okay . . . Where *ought* I to be?"

"You may well ask," John de Vere said. "You should excuse Master Jonvelle. He sees Captain-General Ash here – and so do we all. But, it seems, one hour ago, Captain-General Ash was given a slave escort back from the Visigoth camp and admitted to Dijon through the north-east gate. She is there now."

Ash stared at the English Earl. "She damn well isn't!"

"We left her at the gatehouse not ten minutes since," John de Vere said. "Madam – it is your sister. The Faris. She says she is surrendering herself to you."

Loose papers found inserted between Parts Fourteen
and Fifteen of ASH: THE LOST HISTORY OF BURGUNDY
(Ratcliff, 2001), British Library

Message: #381 (Anna Longman)
Subject: Ash
Date: 16/12/00 at 07.47 a.m.
From: Ngrant@   *format address deleted*
                       Other details encrypted by
Anna –   *non-discoverable personal key*

Such a change, to be writing in English! I'll attach a file with the
next section of the Sible Hedingham text that I've translated.

I'm taking a break from the translation tomorrow. Correction:
this morning.

I've finally been comparing the two metallurgy reports on the
'messenger-golem' found at the land-site. One of Isobel's
graduates has been giving me a hand over breakfast. Now, it's just
possible that these are reports on two *different* archaeological
remains that got confused in the lab. If they're two reports on the
same specimens of cast bronze, then they contradict each other in
almost every reading, from plant-material content to implied
background radiation.

Either the department got one or other of the analyses wrong –
which, I grant you, is the conclusion of any sane, rational person
– or, these reports are tracing *a process in the artefact itself*
which could have been going on between the first report in November
and the second one two weeks later.

How can an artefact appear 'new' (post 1945) in November, and in
December, 'old' (4–500 years)?

Anna, if there is a process at work here, of any kind, no matter
that I may have details or premises wrong – then *what else are we
going to see?*

I have persuaded Isobel to contact her Colonel ███████ and beg
the use of a military helicopter. She has just told me he's given
his authorisation. An ex-Russian Mil-8 will be waiting for me at
Tunis airfield, just before dawn, in two hours' time. And Isobel is
lending me one of her graduate students.

The helicopter pilot is prepared to overfly the area to the south
of Tunis, as far as the Atlas Mountains. We have video equipment.

In archaeology, aerial surveys can be crucial. With low-angle
light, the smallest disturbances in the ground cast shadows, and
the shapes, the 'floor-plans', of long-disused settlements can
appear plainly evident.

Although a previous, brief geophysical survey of the areas I am
interested in shows nothing definite, I think that it may be
different for us. If only because Isobel and I, using the

945

'Fraxinus' manuscript, have some idea of where we should be looking.

  If there is any remnant left – if there is any remnant that is *now* there – that is part of the pyramid-structures that 'Fraxinus' calls 'Wild Machines'; then I want the evidence catalogued.

  Either by accident or design, we have become what we are. But since history has no Visigoth 'empire', in the sense that these texts describe it, either in the mediaeval period or at any other time, then I am left to conclude that – well, to conclude what? That *both* sides in that conflict were changed; eradicated? And that this post-fracture history of ours contains a few remnants, a palimpsest version, of what was before?

  And yet, and yet. The Sible Hedingham ms could have lain undiscovered, in Hedingham Castle as your William Davies suggested. The messenger-golem could be an undiscovered artefact, excavated. But *what* am I to make of the site on the seabed, where even the present depth-readings and geological features contradict Admiralty and satellite surveys?

  If we have found Carthage, what else might we find, in the barren land to the south?

  I will contact you again immediately after the helicopter flight.

– Pierce

Message: #211 (Pierce Ratcliff)
Subject: Ash
Date: 16/12/00 at 08.58 a.m.
From: Longman@

format address deleted
Other details encrypted and
non-recoverably deleted

Pierce –

You people are taking this seriously.
  Let me talk to Dr Isobel.

– Anna

Message: #216 (Pierce Ratcliff)
Subject: Ash
Date: 16/12/00 at 09.50 a.m.
From: Longman@

format address deleted
Other details encrypted and
non-recoverably deleted

Pierce –

Sorry, impatient – what's happened on the flight?? Are you back?
  Just heard from Jonathan: although they are unaware of the full

946

extent of your discoveries, the independent film company want to
start shooting with you, on site, as soon as they can – before the
Christmas break, if possible. What will Dr Isobel say to this?
  HAVE YOU FOUND ANYTHING IN THE DESERT?

– Anna

Message: #383 (Anna Longman)
Subject: Ash
Date: 16/12/00 at 10.20 a.m.
From: Ngrant@   *format address deleted*
                         other details encrypted by
Ms Longman –   *non-discoverable personal key*

I hope you will not mind if I add something at this juncture.
  I think it inadvisable for outside filming to begin here yet.
Perhaps after Christmas and the New Year? I am keeping the
expedition's own video records up to date, however.
  Please, call me Isobel.

I. Napier-Grant

Message: #218 (ING)
Subject: Ash
Date: 16/12/00 at 10.32 a.m.
From: Longman@   *format address deleted*
                          other details encrypted
Dear Isobel,   *and non-recoverably deleted*

Has Pierce told you that the editor of the second edition of ASH,
Vaughan Davies, has reappeared after being missing, thought dead,
for sixty years?
  Can you confirm what Pierce has told me about the status of your
archaeological seabed site off the coast of Tunisia?
  Does that have any connection with your reluctance to allow
outside film teams in?
  Or, is Pierce under a lot of stress?

– Anna

Message: #385 (Anna Longman)
Subject: Ash
Date: 16/12/00 at 11.03 a.m.
From: Ngrant@   format address *deleted*
                          Other details encrypted by
                          non-discoverable personal key

Anna,

From a cursory glance at the files, I do not disagree substantially
with anything that Pierce has written to you.

This will perhaps answer your last question.

As for myself . . . I am stunned. Didn't Pierce make a joke that
one day he and I would send you the Ratcliff-Napier-Grant theory of
Scientific Miracles? What Tami Inoshishi and Jamie Howlett are
speculating, now, is not so far from that, perhaps.

If my theoretical physicist colleagues are right, it is deep
consciousness, at the level of the species-mind, that in a sense
creates the universe. Imagine a constant process by which the
wave-front of Possibility (random unordered chaos) is, moment by
moment, collapsed from all the states in which it _might_ exist
into the one in which it _does_ exist. In short, a process by which
the Possible is constantly becoming the Real. That is time: that is
how we experience the universe. And, Tami states with amazing
self-confidence, the cause of the wave-front's collapse into a
stable 'present' at the moment we experience as 'now' is the
perception of it, by the consciousness of a species (that
perception being an active, not a passive perception).

And with Pierce's translated manuscripts in mind, I mentioned
jokingly, to both Tami and James this morning, that this possible
ability to collapse the wave-front would have to be genetic
ability. Tami, seriously, said that it would not even be difficult
to see how this could arise. It would be one of the greater
evolutionary advances possible, to have a universe which is
stable, in which effect follows cause, in which what you did
yesterday stands a good chance of being valid today.

Not a conscious ability, she said. It would take place on a
subatomic level; on a level as instinctive as photosynthesis in a
plant, or the heartbeat in a human being.

I wish Pierce were here on the ship, but I shall have to wait
until the helicopter returns to ask him – I wonder if one can
speculate that reality, before the human species became
intelligent, was more flexible, less able to confine itself to one
possibility out of the infinite number of states in which the
universe can exist. I should like to ask him if this might not
account for why every human culture has a mythic pre-history, a
legendary past, before 'history' itself begins?

For all that I know – and this is why I am reluctant to confine
these discoveries to a book or film documentary; I am seriously
thinking of throwing this site open to interdisciplinary

948

investigation: shipping in theorists from _every_ field – for all I know, all life has a certain limited ability to collapse random possibility into predictable reality. Plants, dolphins, birds: each tries to affect its environment favourably. The most basic form of this _must_ be the perception of the subatomic 'building blocks' of reality, at the moment of 'now', as neither unstable nor random, but as order and pattern and sequence.

I am an archaeologist, not a physicist; and I watch and listen to Tami and James with open-mouthed astonishment. Before he left this morning, Pierce said to me that they do sound like a Ratcliff-Napier-Grant Theory of Scientific Miracles. You have only to say that there could exist a genetic ability to _consciously_ collapse the possible states of the universe into the Real – would not that be a 'miracle'? Posit that such an ability could carry sufficient genetic defects that it hardly ever survives conception and birth. And then I look at Pierce's translations and find myself thinking, there you have the Rabbi, and Ildico, and the Faris, and (one supposes) the Visigothic 'Prophet Gundobad', who is unidentified in this history because it is not this history in which he existed.

I have spent most of my adult life aware of how very little solid evidence of our past there is left, and how very _careful_ one must be in interpreting what does exist and can be discovered. Were you not in London – were you here, just off the coast of North Africa, with an _impossible-_ site a thousand metres below your feet – then you might understand why I don't dismiss these speculations of a 'fracture' in history.

I do not say that I give credence to them, either.

And then, of course, there are the practical consequences. I had hoped to get past Christmas before a public statement became necessary, but I can see that I may have to revise my opinion.

I. Napier-Grant

Message: #219 (ING)
Subject: Ash
Date: 16/12/00 at 11.36 a.m.
From: Longman@   *format address Deleted*
                          other details encrypted and
                          non-recoverably deleted
Isobel –

You loaned Pierce an assistant, and got him a helicopter. You must give credence to something.

– Anna

Message: #388 (Anna Longman)
Subject: Ash
Date: 16/12/00 at 03.15 p.m.
From: Ngrant@

format address deleted
Other details encrypted by non-discoverable personal key

Pierce has radioed in. Transcript of relevant part of message.

I. Napier-Grant

> Everything's grounded.
> It was bad enough getting off the ship.
> We are back in Tunis. If I can't hire a jeep, or buy a bloody
> camel, I am prepared to WALK into the desert.
> Low-angled sunset light is as good as dawn.

Message: #390 (Anna Longman)
Subject: Ash
Date: 16/12/00 at 06.15 p.m.
From: Ngrant@

format address deleted
Other details encrypted by non-discoverable personal key

Anna –

Nothing.

– Pierce

Message: #221 (Pierce Ratcliff)
Subject: Ash
Date: 16/12/00 at 06.36 p.m.
From: Longman@

format address deleted
Other details encrypted and non-recoverably deleted

Pierce –

What do you mean, NOTHING?

– Anna

Message: #391 (Anna Longman)
Subject: Ash
Date: 16/12/00 at 07.59 p.m.
From: Ngrant@

format address deleted
Other details encrypted by non-discoverable personal key

Anna –

I mean the quotidian, I suppose. The everyday, the mundane.
Nothing to get worked up about. No, there is nothing in the desert

950

south of here. Isobel's worn out her welcome with my use of
military helicopters, trailing – once flight restrictions were
finally lifted – through the airspace between here and the Atlas
Mountains.

There may be something buried under residential areas, or under
industrial plants; who knows? Certainly there were no
archaeological teams on hand when some of these places were built.
If there were remains, they're gone, obliterated. Or, more likely,
there was nothing; the manuscript 'evidence' is mere symbolism,
the metallurgy reports simple human error.

What did you expect me to find you, Anna? A glowing pyramid?
Sorry.

I must confess, I had hoped for SOMETHING. A few ridges in the
earth, visible at sunset or dawn. It wouldn't be much to ask, would
it, that a shadow in the ground should 'come back'? Just to let us
know the 'Wild Machines' were not what they plainly are: a
mediaeval literary conceit. A mere device.

Isobel's team are keeping the survey material, but naturally,
the land area isn't their priority right now. Underwater remains,
'Gothic Carthage', that's the priority.

Your book-and-film deal is on course, don't worry.

– Pierce

Message: #222 (Pierce Ratcliff)
Subject: Ash
Date: 16/12/00 at 08.45 p.m.
From: Longman@   format address deleted
                              other details encrypted
Pierce –   and non-recoverably deleted

Damn the 'book and film deal'. What about you? Are you all right?

I know I've done very little, but I've talked to the Davies
family, in person; I've got drawn into this too.

I can't imagine how you and Dr Isobel are feeling right now, but
this isn't just another book as far as I'm concerned. If there's
anything I can do to help, I will. You know I mean it.

– Anna

Message: #392 (Anna Longman)
Subject: Ash
Date: 16/12/00 at 08.57 p.m. *format address deleted*
From: Ngrant@ *Other details encrypted by*
                      non-discoverable personal key

Anna –

I know. Thank you.

Yes, I suppose it is difficult to see Tami Inoshishi and James Howlett knee-deep in the image files of this project; talking at machine-gun speed to everybody on the team. I confess that, yes, no one has much time for a mere historian at this point, and yes, my nose is out of joint. I suppose my time will come with the textual evidence.

None of that really matters, I suppose, beside the crashing disappointment. I was so CERTAIN that we were going to find remnants of the 'Wild Machines', or at the very least, the site where they existed. The 'machina rei militaris', when we get it free for examination – and I imagine that's going to take months, if not years – will answer some questions. But, like Isobel's golem, I fear it will be dumb about how and why it moved.

E pur si muove: Nevertheless, it moves. As Galileo said, in rather different circumstances!

Scholarly jests aside, I feel very bitter. I was so sure. You see, once the basic premise is accepted, none of it is unreasonable. My first draft of the 'Afterword' says as much, and I am going to let you see it. This was based on 'Fraxinus', and the discovery of the 'clay walker', before we found the Sible Hedingham document, so it is unrevised:-

AFTERWORD to the 3rd edition: ASH: THE LOST HISTORY OF BURGUNDY

(Excerpt:) (iii) THEOLOGY AND TECHNOLOGY: THE IMPLICATIONS OF 'FRAXINUS ME FECIT'

... the mediaeval mind behind the 'Fraxinus' manuscript couches its description of the various Carthaginian machines in quasi-religious, quasi-mythological terms, where, for example, it speaks of the 'soul' of Fr Godfrey Maximillian becoming 'trapped in the Stone Golem'. We, with the benefit of a vocabulary belonging to twentieth-century artificial intelligence, would more properly refer to this in terms of the neural pattern of his personality becoming uploaded into, or imprinted on, the *machina rei militaris* at a moment of great physical and mental trauma. One might speculate that the proximity of Ash at the moment of Godfrey Maximillian's death, herself a genetic conduit to the *machina rei militaris*, might have some as-yet-undetermined causal link with this unique event.

Similarly, the autonomous 'Wild Machines' are described in spiritual and religious terms. However, it is possible to make another translation, different from the dramatised one I have used in the body of the text, translating 'Fraxinus' literally, but with a vocabulary not yet available in 1476. This is an amended excerpt from Ash's 'download' at Carthage:

The Wild Machines do not know their own origin, it is lost in their primitive memories. They suspect it was humans, building religious structures ten thousand years ago, who accidentally 'put rocks in order' – constructed ordered, [pyramid-]shaped edifices of silt-bricks and stone [silicon]. Large enough structures [of silicon] to absorb spirit-force [electromagnetic energy] from the sun. From that initial order and structure came spontaneous mind [self-aware intelligence]. The first primitive sparks of [electromagnetic] force began to organise [in solid state networks], creating the ferae natura machinae [silicon-based 'machine' intelligences].

Five thousand years ago, those primitive minds [proto-intelligences] became conscious. After that, they could begin to evolve themselves deliberately. The Wild Machines manipulated the energies of the spirit-world [drew upon solar electromagnetic energy], to the point where [visible-spectrum] light began to be blocked out in the immediate region around them. As they become more structured, organised and powerful, so their ability to draw power from the nearest and greatest source in the heavens [extract and store this form of solar energy] became more efficient: the darkness spread. This [North African coast] became a land of stone and twilight [solar-energy 'shadow']: vast monuments and pyramids under an eternally starry sky.

[The machine intelligences] knew that humanity and animals existed; they registered their weak little souls [neuro-electric fields]. They were unable to establish direct communication until the advent of the Prophet Gundobad. After Gundobad's death, it was not until Leofric's family developed the Stone Golem [solid-state tactical computer] that the Wild Machines had a reliable channel by which they could communicate with humanity, and not just its wonder-workers [human minds capable of consciously collapsing the local quantum state]. They hid behind the voice of the [tactical computer], easing their suggestions [into the data], manipulating Leofric's ancestors into beginning a breeding programme.

The Visigoth saint, Prophet Gundobad, whose relics [surviving DNA material] were used in the *machina rei militaris* and whose bloodline eventually produced the Faris and Ash, was one of those very, very few people (like Our Lord the Green Christ) [first history] who have the power to perform miracles [individually alter the basic fabric of reality]. What the secret breeding [genetic engineering] was designed to produce was not someone who could speak at a distance to the Stone Golem [perform an at-a-distance neuro-electric or neuro-chemical? download from the tactical computer] – although it was necessary they be able to [communicate

953

through the computer], since that is the only link between the Wild
Machines and humanity. What the Wild Machines were trying to breed
was another miracle-worker [human capable of consciously affecting the
quantum foam]. A Gundobad. One that would be under their control, and
subject to the command [immense electromagnetic pulse] they planned [to
emit] to trigger their evil miracle [consciously guided alteration of the
basic fabric of probable reality].

* * * * * * * *

(Excerpt:) (vi) GENETICS AND THE MIRACULOUS: BREEDING
SCHRODINGER'S CAT
   (Revised passage, after discovery of the Sible Hedingham ms:)

. . . In this past history which we have lost, the ability to consciously,
deliberately collapse the wave-front could arise spontaneously. In that first
history, despite the catastrophic genetic links, it is just possible that a tiny
conscious talent could be bred, to be strong enough to be effective – hence
the priests' genuine small miracles; hence the bloodline that House Leofric
produced among its slaves and the Faris.
   Conversely, the ability to prevent the 'miraculous' happening, to
prevent the wave-front being collapsed into anything but the most probable
quotidian reality, might also conceivably arise as a spontaneous genetic
mutation: hence the nature of the Ducal bloodlines in Burgundy.
   But, what happened *after* everything changed? . . .

I am not sure, now, why I was so certain that some trace of the Wild
Machines must remain, after such a fracture in the universe's
history as we seem to see the traces of, here. Purely, I suppose,
this question –
   If there had been no 'black miracle', we should not be seeing
these traces of a fracture in history. But, if the Wild Machines
precipitated the Faris into causing the fracture and altering the
fabric of the universe, then why is there no trace of them having
survived it?
   If you want to wipe the human race out of history, presumably you
want to be around afterwards to take advantage!
   What HAPPENED?

- Pierce

Message: #223 (Pierce Ratcliff)
Subject: Ash
Date: 17/12/00 at 03.10 a.m.
From: Longman@

format address deleted
Other details encrypted and non-recoverably deleted

Pierce –

Sorry, shouldn't be posting in the early hours, can't think straight, _but_

    If the Carthage site and the messenger-golem are what you say they are, you don't mean

    >> What HAPPENED?

    You mean: what IS STILL HAPPENING?

    What will happen if you fly over the desert *again,* in, say, a month's time? What will you see *then?*

– Anna

955

PART FIFTEEN

25 December–26 December AD 1476

'Ex Africa semper aliquid novi'[1]

[1] 'Always something new out of Africa.' (The more common rendering of Pliny the Elder's 'Semper aliquid novi Africam adferre'.) The Sible Hedingham ms part 5.

I

Ash felt the wind from the company tower's door, blowing in past the group of knights: keen, and with a bitter, damp edge to it. Bewilderment gave way to clarity with a speed that surprised her. *Kill her and the Wild Machines do nothing. For the next twenty years. Minimum.*

She said, "We have to execute her, right now."

The Earl of Oxford nodded soberly. "Yes, madam. We do."

She saw Jonvelle's gaze go past her, and turned her head.

Floria walked towards them, stripping ivy-leaves from her shoulders; Robert Anselm close behind. The Burgundian, Jonvelle, bowed to his Duchess.

"What's this?" Floria demanded.

Ash quickly looked to see where Fernando del Guiz was – a bare yard away: stark amazement on his face. Angelotti stood at the German priest's side, one hand on the bollock dagger at his belt.

"The Faris is here," Ash said flatly.

"*Here?*"

"You got it."

"Here in *Dijon*?"

"Yes!" There was an audience, Ash saw, but nothing to be done about it. The company's archers and men-at-arms formed a tight-packed circle, avidly listening. Euen Huw, stripping off ivy-creeper and his 'Saracen' chemise, pushed in beside Angelotti; Rickard, open-mouthed, beside Ash herself.

"Tell her, my lord," Ash appealed to de Vere.

"Madam Duchess, report says that while we were convening with the King-Caliph, a party of unarmed Visigoth slaves approached the north-east gate. The guards did not fire on them; and were even less likely to do so when they saw, as they thought, Captain-General Ash coming back in under their escort." Oxford nodded to Ash. "The Visigoth woman has chopped off her hair and dirtied her face. It will have been enough to get her in. All but a half-dozen of the slaves went back to the Visigoth camp; the woman then sits herself down and demands to speak to the Duchess of Burgundy, and to Ash, to whom – she says – she surrenders."

"She's out of her mind." Floria blinked. "Is this true?"

"I see no reason to doubt Jonvelle's men. I have, besides, seen her now. It is the Visigoth general."

"She has to be killed," Ash said. "Somebody get my axe: let's get up to the north-east gate."

"Ash—"

Amazed, Ash heard something close to hesitation in Floria's voice. Jonvelle drew himself up; plainly ready to take orders from his Duchess.

"This isn't a matter for *argument*. We don't mess around here," Ash said gently. "Fucking hell, girl. You hunted the hart. She's my blood relative, but I know that we have to kill her, *now*. She's what the Wild Machines will use, to make an evil miracle. The second you're killed, that's what happens: they act through her – and we're dead. All of us. As if we'd never been." Ash watched Floria's face. "Like it is beyond these borders. Nothing but cold and dark."

"I came only to be sure it was not you, Captain Ash," John de Vere said briskly. "Otherwise I am not sure but I should have done the task myself."

Jonvelle coughed. "No, sieur, you would not have. You would not have been obeyed by my men. We are at the command of Burgundy, not England. Her Grace must give the word."

"Well, God's grace grant that we do it now!" De Vere was already turning, giving orders to the Janissaries, when Floria interrupted:

"Wait."

"Christ, Florian!" Ash shouted, appalled. "What do you mean, 'wait'?"

"I'm not ordering any execution! I took an oath to do no harm! I've spent most of my adult life putting people back together, not killing them!" Floria gripped Ash's arm firmly. "Just wait. Think. *Think* about this. Yes: I hunted the hart: she's no danger while there's a Duchess of Burgundy."

The Earl of Oxford said, "Madam Florian, this is a hard truth, but men and women are dying in the streets of this city from siege-weapon fire, and if by the same accident we were to lose you, with the Faris yet living, we lose everything."

"You were in Carthage with me," Ash urged. "You saw the Wild Machines. You saw what they could do to me there. Florian, in Christ's name, have I ever lied to you about anything important? You *know* what's at stake here!"

"I won't do it!"

"You should have thought of that when you killed the hart," Ash said wryly. "An execution isn't easy. It's vile, messy, and unjust, usually. But there isn't a choice here. If it makes it easier – if you don't want the blood on your hands – then me and my lord the Earl and Colonel Bajezet's five hundred Turks will go up to the north-east gate and do it now, whatever Jonvelle here says."

Floria's fist clenched. "No. Too easy."

What there might be of an ache inside – for Floria, for the Faris; for herself, even – Ash put away, in the same way as she forced tears back from her prickling eyes. Ash put her hand over Floria's; the woman still in the Noble Doctor's long gown, fragments of palmate green leaves caught in her hair, her cheeks red with the heat of the hall.

"Florian," she said, "I'm not going to waste any time."

Robert Anselm was nodding; it was apparent from the faces of the company's lance-leaders that there was no disagreement. They might look with all sympathy at the doctor; but in terms of action, Ash judged, that was irrelevant.

Angelotti said quietly to Floria, "It's never easy, *dottore*. After battle, there are some men who cannot be saved."

"Sweet *Christ* but I hate soldiers!"

Hard on Floria's agonised, appalled exclamation, a soldier in Jonvelle's livery tumbled through the door between the company's guards. Ash narrowed her eyes to better see his sweating, distraught face under the brim of his war-hat. She immediately beckoned the man forward; then signalled her deference to Jonvelle himself.

"Yes, Sergeant?" Jonvelle demanded.

"There's a Visigoth herald at the north-east gate! Under flag of parley," the man gasped. He dashed the edge of his cloak across his streaming nose, and heaved in another breath. "From the King-Caliph. He says you have his general here, and he demands that you release her. He's got about six hundred of our refugees rounded up in the ground between the lines. He says, if you don't let her go, they'll kill every last man, woman and child of them."

The refugees and their escort stood in the excoriated no-man's-land under Dijon's walls, between the north-eastern gate and the east river.

Ash wore no identifying livery; had her bevor strapped on, and her visor barely cocked high enough above it to give her a field of view between the two pieces of armour. She rested her shoulder against the battlements of the gatehouse, knowing herself barely visible to any outsider, and stared down.

Behind her, an abbey bell rang for Sext. The midday sun cast a pale, slanting southern light. The crowd of men and women standing aimlessly on the cold earth seemed small, truncated by perspective. One man beat his hands together against the bitter wind. No one else moved. Breath went up in mist-white puffs. Most of them stood together, in ruined clothes, huddling for warmth; most looked to be barefoot.

"Dear God," Jonvelle said, beside Ash. He pointed. "I know that man. That's Messire Huguet. He owns all the mills between here and Auxonne; or he did. And his family: his wife and child. And there's Soeur Irmengard, from our hospice in St Herlaine's."

"You're better off not thinking about it," Ash advised.

It was not the dirt that moved her, or the other evidences of their living rough, but their faces. Under the blank expressions that long experience of pain gives, there was still a bewilderment; an inability to understand how and why this destitution should have happened at all, never mind happened to them.

"Is the King-Caliph serious, Captain?" Jonvelle said.

"I see no reason why he shouldn't be. Roberto told me they crucified several hundred refugees in sight of your walls here, back in October, when they were trying to force a quick surrender."

Jonvelle's face assumed a blank severity. "I was in the hospice," he confessed, "after Auxonne. There were stories of massacres. Knights act sometimes without honour, in war."

"Yeah . . . tell me about it, Jonvelle." She squinted north-east, at the trenches and fortifications of the Visigoth camp; saw the wooden shielding that would shelter mangonels and arbalests. "They won't even need engines. Longbows and crossbows will do it at this range."

"Christ defend us."

"Oh, *we're* fine," Ash muttered, absently trying to count heads. The estimate of six hundred would not be far off: it might even be a few more. "It's them you want to worry about . . . Captain Jonvelle, let's have as many hackbutters and crossbowmen up here as we can manage. Make it look like we're concentrating our forces here. Then get some units by the postern gate."

"You will get a very small number of hunger-weakened women and children to that gate," the Burgundian said. "Never mind through it."

"If it comes to it, that's what we'll do. Meanwhile . . ." Ash moved back from the crenellations, walked a few yards down the wall to her own herald's white pennant, and leaned out over the hoarding. "Below there!"

Two of the stone messenger-golems stood a little way out from the foot of the wall. In front of them, under his gold-and-black embroidered white banner, Agnus Dei stared upwards. A dozen of his own mercenaries were with him; and a few more under a red livery that Ash did not recall until she saw Onorata Rodiani standing beside the Italian condottiere.

"Hey, Lamb."

"Hey, Ash."

"Mistress Rodiani."

"Captain-General Ash."

"They still dealing you out the shitty jobs, then?"

Onorata Rodiani's face was unreadable at the distance. Her voice sounded taut. "Boss Gelimer was going to send your own men, Mynheer Joscelyn van Mander's men, to do this. I persuaded him it might not be in his best interests. Do we have a deal here?"

"I don't know. I'm still checking it with my boss." Ash leaned her plate-clad arms on the stonework. "Your man serious, is he?"

Agnus Dei tilted his armet's visor up, a straggling coil of black hair escaping. His red mouth made a mobile space in his beard, far below; his voice coming up clearly to Ash:

"The King-Caliph gave us orders to demonstrate his commitment here. These golem will go over and tear one of those peasant women or children apart, at the word of command. Madonna Ash, I wish we might deem that to have been done, I have no great wish to do it. But we stand where my master sees us."

The dull light flashed off the flutings of his German gauntlet as he raised his hand.

The sandstone-coloured figure of the golem trod towards the refugees. Even from the walls, Ash could see the depth of its footmarks in the churned earth; could guess at the weight of each limb. Women screamed, pressing back against the Visigoth spearmen, hauling their children as far back into the press of people as they could; one or two men made as if to move forward, most fought to get away.

The golem reached forward with a smooth precision, bronze gears glimmering. Its metal and stone hand went past one spearman's shoulder – Ash couldn't see if the soldier reacted – and closed on something. The arm pulled smoothly back. A woman of about fifty kicked and clawed and screeched, hauled forward by the grip on her biceps. Two small children were pulled through the spear-line, clinging to her thighs.

A sharp *snap!* bit through the winter air.

The woman drooped and hung awkwardly from the golem's hand, her arm and shoulder the wrong shape. Shaken loose, the two children raised square-mouthed squalls. One of the spearmen kicked them back into the refugee-crowd. Ash found herself muttering "thank you!", knowing that it was, for once, a gesture towards safety.

She leaned forward between the merlons and bellowed: "You don't have to—"

The golem did not lift its head. Alone in some solipsistic world, in which flesh is no more significant than any other fabric, it dragged the semi-conscious woman with the broken shoulder around until she faced the north-east gate. Her ankles, under her long kirtle, were brown with mud, yellow with shit.

Gears of bronze slid and glinted. As she scratched and clawed at stone arms with the ripped fingers of one hand, the golem reached down and closed his huge hand around both her thighs. A sharp screech shattered the morning. Ash saw stone fingers buried to the second knuckle in flesh.

The golem lifted the woman up between its two hands. It grasped her at neck and thigh, front and back.

It wrung her body, like washing.

All noise stopped. Pink intestines slid and steamed, in the chill air. The golem released the twisted flesh. In her own mind, Ash tabulated broken back, broken pelvis, split body-cavity, broken neck – *don't be stupid: you* can't *smell it from up here!*

She blinked and looked away.

As far as she could see, in the cold air that made her eyes run, Agnus Dei's gaze was fixed on the grey frost-haze over the Ouze river.

"Christ." Ash let out a long breath. "Shit. How long have I got to come back with an answer?"

Onorata Rodiani, apparently unaffected, called up, "You've got as long as you like. *They*—" She pointed with one steel-clad, flashing arm at the refugees "—have got until Boss Gelimer loses patience. You have the woman who, until today, was his Empire's first general and commanded his troops in Christendom. How long? Your guess is as good as mine, Captain-General Ash; probably better."

"Okay." Ash drew herself up, resting her palms flat on the battlements. "I'm on my way. You can tell your man, we've got the message."

Floria del Guiz said, "If I kill her, six hundred people die."

Ash followed the Duchess of Burgundy through the cloisters of St Stephen's – six streets back from the north-east gate – which Jonvelle's men had judged a safe place for keeping the Faris under guard.

"If you don't kill her, *everybody* dies."

"I'm not dead yet," Florian snarled, as the large group of armed men entered the main buildings. "If I *do* get killed, it may be under circumstances where the

Burgundians can hunt again – I'm thinking about six hundred people out there. They're the ones I'll have to watch die."

"No reason for you to *watch* it," Ash observed pragmatically. She caught the look on Florian's face; sighed; her pace slowing. "But you will. Because the first time this happens, everybody thinks they have to. Trust me, you're better off staying away from the walls."

At Ash's shoulder, Jonvelle said, "And this from you, Captain-General, who are planning to sally out of the postern gate and rescue who you can of them?"

Momentarily embarrassed, Ash glanced back to check that her own men, as well as the Burgundians, were following her towards the refectory.

"It's worth a try," she muttered. "You ask those poor bastards outside."

The cloisters behind her rang to the boots of soldiers, on flagstones striped white with frost. Even at noon, frost still lay where each shadow of a pillar was cast. Inside, entering the great whitewashed refectory, there was at least the heat from the kitchens. Ash ignored the monks, scurrying in the background; and the sounds from the dormitories, taken over for nursing the sick.

"Look, Florian, I'll put it this way – do you want to order the Faris's execution now, so the Burgundians are happy with it, or do you want to watch me and my lord Oxford and the company get killed by the army, trying to reach her?"

Florian made a spitting sound; gave Ash a look of frustrated, contemptuous anger. "You mean that, don't you."

The exiled English Earl gave her a quizzical look, but what he said was, "Madam, I also agree."

A woman stood up in the crowded refectory.

Winter sunlight bounced back from the white walls. It illuminated motes of dust; the woman's hacked-off silver hair. A woman, standing up between Visigoth slaves in short tunics; a woman wearing European doublet and hose that were plainly not made for her, were far too big. The chopped-off hair threw her cheeks into sharp relief. No smeared dirt could give the impression of scars. She looked very young. She wore neither armour, nor sword.

Across the few remaining wooden benches and tables, Ash found herself facing the Faris.

The child-slave at the Faris's left was Violante, shivering in the cold. A grey-haired fat woman sat on the floor, half hiding under the long table: Adelize.

Floria del Guiz walked past Ash and put herself between them.

"Have some sense," she said. "We have to send her back, to save lives. Right now! She's no danger while I'm alive."

Ash glared at the woman blocking her way. She thumbed her sword loose from the scabbard's tension. "You might not have noticed, but there's a fucking war on. While you're alive, yes; but that might not be for long!"

Floria made a wry mouth, and flapped her hand as if pushing the gesture with the sword away. When she spoke, it was not a plea, but irritable scorn:

"For Christ's sake, Ash! If you won't save the people out there, here's another reason to keep her alive for a few hours – think about this, if nothing else: *up until today, she's been the Visigoth army commander.*"

964

"Shit." Ash looked away from the Faris, to Floria. "You *have* been paying attention while you've been company doctor."

The surgeon-Duchess, dishevelled and oddly dignified, repeated, "Visigoth army commander. Think how much she knows about this siege. She knows what's happened *after* she stopped reporting through the Stone Golem! That's *weeks*! She can tell us what it's like out there *now*!"

"But the *Wild Machines*—"

"Ash, you're going to have to talk to her. Debrief her. Then we send her out again, to Gelimer. And we pray," Floria said, "that he doesn't start a massacre out there before we do it."

The immediate rush of people into the room behind them slowed. Ash became aware of men-at-arms spreading out: her units, and Burgundian army units, and Jonvelle talking urgently to the just-arrived Olivier de la Marche. She caught the eye of Robert Anselm; held up a warning hand. *No action yet.*

"Do you know what you're risking?"

Floria's brows went up. She looked momentarily very like her younger half-brother. "I know I'm risking six hundred people's lives out there, if King-Caliph Gelimer decides to start killing them in the next few minutes and not the next few hours."

"That's not what I meant."

"No, but it's true, too."

"*Shit.*" Ash gazed around.

She registered Angelotti's presence at the refectory door: the master gunner talking excitedly to Colonel Bajezet. Apart from the Burgundian troops surrounding the Visigoths, there was a woman in green there – Soeur-Maîtresse Simeon – obliviously and waspishly trying to coax Adelize out from under the table.

The fat, drooling, white-haired woman wept and flapped her hands, slapping the nun's hands away.

At Ash's side, Fernando del Guiz tried to conceal an expression of disgust. She looked away from him, feeling heat, knowing her cheeks were reddening.

"Fucking Christ!" she exclaimed bitterly, fists on hips. "We're going to have the whole bloody *town* in here. Roberto! Seal this room off!"

Anselm did not look to the surgeon-Duchess for permission. Jonvelle moved to intercept him, and only stepped back at Floria's acerbic order: "No one else in here – unless it's the Abbot!"

"This is a Michaelmas Fair," John de Vere sighed. "Captain, an enemy commander in one's hands is not to be despised; this might turn the siege. And though the matter concerns more men than there are in Dijon, we have men here whom we command, whose lives should not be spent needlessly."

Fernando del Guiz folded his arms, regarding the monastery room with bewildered confusion. He shook his head; laughed with an expression that plainly said *What else can one do?* "If I could see the King-Caliph's face, now—!"

Ash gave an order. Two of Jonvelle's men came to escort him outside. He went with no protest.

Ash turned back to face the Faris.

"*Why?*" she said.

The light from the refectory windows fell clearly on to the Faris's face. With this second look, Ash saw at once how drawn she was: her skin a bad colour, her eyes red-rimmed. Her left hand kept feeling for something at her thigh. The mirror-image of Ash's own gesture: hand resting down on her sword. When she finally spoke, it was quietly, to Ash, in the version of Carthaginian that one hears most often in the military camps:

"Don't forget that I permitted the hunt."

"What?" Floria moved to stand at Ash's side, staring at the Visigoth woman. "I didn't catch that."

"She's reminding me that she let the hunt go ahead. And that, if not for her, there wouldn't be a Duchess now."

Catching Florian's eye, Ash had no need to speak to confirm that they were sharing a moment of grim amusement.

"It's true," Ash said, "she did."

The Faris swallowed. Her voice came out taut. "Tell your Burgundian woman that. She owes this to me."

"'This'?"

The Visigoth woman switched to the language of southern Burgundy, speaking with a perceptible accent. "Refuge. Sanctuary. I gave the orders, I held my commanders back so that you could ride out into the wildwood."

The Faris stood awkwardly in the European dress she wore, plainly not used to hose, or the short skirts of the doublet that she unconsciously kept pulling down. In the five weeks since they had met across the table in the Visigoth camp, she seemed to have grown thinner; or perhaps, Ash surmised, it was that she wore no armour, had no soldiers with her, seemed a much younger woman altogether.

"That was more than a month ago," Ash said grimly. "In that time you could have travelled back to Carthage and destroyed the *machina rei militaris*. Now *that* would have been useful."

A flick of fear on the Visigoth woman's face.

"Would *you* go back to Carthage? Would *you* go so close to the Wild Machines again?" She met Ash's eyes, her own red and puffy with long sleeplessness; and Ash had time to think *Is this how I look?* before the Faris added, "I would have gone. I could not. Not go so close, not when they're here—" She touched her temple. "Not when they can . . . use me, without my consent. You are hearing them too."

"No."

"I don't believe you!" Her voice cracked on a shout.

Adelize began to whoop and roar.

The Faris broke off, reaching down, and stroked the woman's hair with tentative fingers. Violante gave her a look of contempt and knelt down and took the woman into her thin arms, straining to reach around her shoulders.

"Not to be afraid," Violante said in the slaves' Carthaginian that Ash hardly understood. "Adelize; not to be afraid."

The woman Adelize gently pushed Violante back, stroking the front of the girl's tunic – no, not the tunic; Ash saw. Stroking the bulge of a body, small and moving, that wriggled itself up to Violante's neckline.

Ash watched as the liver-and-white rat licked her mother's fingers.

Adelize stroked it. She spluttered, "Poor, poor! Not to mind. Easy, easy. Not to be afraid."

"I talked with my father Leofric." The Faris's hand did not stop stroking Adelize's hair.

"He can talk?" Ash asked sardonically.

"He and I, we have tried to persuade the lord Caliph Gelimer that the Stone Golem must be destroyed. He will not do it. Gelimer believes nothing my father says. All this of the Wild Machines is, he says, a political trick of House Leofric's; nothing that he will act upon."

"Fucking hell!" Ash said, overriding both Florian and John de Vere. "You've got two legions out there, what was stopping you killing Gelimer, going back to Carthage, and hammering the Stone Golem into gravel? *What?*"

Her anger faded with the bewildered look on the woman's face.

She's heard the Stone Golem for twenty years, had it as her advisor in combat for as long as she remembers, and everything she's done in her life has been for the King-Caliph: no, going home at the head of an armed rebellion is something she wouldn't contemplate—

"I know that we have been betrayed," the Faris said, "and my men are about to die, whether they win or not. I have been trying to save their lives. First, by leaving the siege to engines, not assault; second, by letting the Duchess of Burgundy live, to stand in the path of the southern demons. You would have done the same thing, sister."

"I'm not your bloody sister, for Christ's sake! We hardly know each other."

"You are my sister. We are both warriors." The Faris's fingers ceased stroking Adelize's head. "If nothing else, remember this is our mother."

Ash threw up her hands. She turned on Floria. "*You* talk to her!"

Ash saw Robert Anselm's gaze on her, realised that he and Angelotti were – quite unconsciously – staring from her to the Faris, and from the Faris back to her. John de Vere murmured something to Bajezet: the Turk also pointing to the Faris.

The surgeon-Duchess asked, "Why are you here in Dijon?"

"For sanctuary," the Visigoth woman repeated.

"Why now?"

Olivier de la Marche strode forward, with Jonvelle behind him, to take up a place defending their Duchess. Jonvelle spoke, answering Floria's question. "Your Grace, to infiltrate the city and assassinate you, one would suppose. I am with our Maid, Ash, on this. She will give you no useful information. Have her executed without further talk."

The Faris, with the first hint of an acerbic humour akin to Ash's, said, "*Amir*-Duchess, since you ask it, I am here now because now is the hour at which the King-Caliph issued a warrant for my arrest and execution."

"Ah." Ash nodded with satisfaction.

"He has put Sancho Lebrija in my place as commander," the Faris said.

Ash remembered the humourless, brutal cousin of Asturio Lebrija; a man to do nothing else but take orders from his King-Caliph. "When did Lebrija take over?"

"Now. An hour since." The Faris shrugged. "*Amir* Gelimer made it plain at the parley that he considered me spoiled and lunatic. After that, said before his allies, how could he continue to use me as a commander? He has considered me part of what he sees as House Leofric's plotting; this was a way to dispose of me."

"Of *course*," Ash said.

"I knew then that I would be executed within the hour. I left the meeting a little ahead of the others, called my slaves, changed my clothes to these captured garments, and ordered the slaves to escort 'Ash' to the gate of Dijon. And they let me in."

The Faris's hand went up to her newly cut hair.

"*Amir* Gelimer has ordered my father to kill and dissect all the slaves of our bloodline – Adelize, Violante, these others here; myself. I believe my father Leofric will do it. If he thinks it will convince the King-Caliph of the truth of what he says about the Wild Machines, he will do it without hesitation. He will do it . . ."

Ash could not hear it, but she knew the other men standing in this bright refectory of Dijon's abbey heard the Visigoth woman speak in her voice, Ash's voice, with only the accent to differentiate them. She stared at the face of her twin, everything else – hostages, the war, the Wild Machines – forgotten in that strange recognition.

"You trusted me," the Faris said. Her identical voice urged: "You trusted me enough to tell me that Duke Charles was dying – when you came to my camp for parley, before the hunt? There was that trust between us, when, by your reasoning, you should have killed me. I have little hope you won't kill me now. But with Gelimer, there is no hope."

She sighed, shifting her head as if the river-fall of hair were still there; her hand going up to her loss. Her glance shifted to the surgeon-Duchess of Burgundy.

"I am foolish," the Faris said. "There is no hope here, either. For you to be safe, you need me to die."

Floria, frowning, bit at the skin at the edge of her fingernail. "Wild Machines or not, Gelimer needs to kill me for quite different reasons. This war isn't going to stop now. He doesn't know the consequence of his actions. That's irrelevant. If you were dead—"

"If *I* were dead," the Faris said softly, "it would be the end of the Wild Machines' influence for a generation and more. Before another could be bred like me. Longer, perhaps. It will take time and another King-Caliph before the Stone Golem is trusted again."

"But it will be," Floria said.

Olivier de la Marche said flatly, coming forward, "Demoiselle Duchess, that is for our sons and grandsons to finish. And for that reason, consider: Burgundy must survive now. We *must*! Or else, when that day comes, there will be no one to stand against the demons of the south. They may do their pleasure, with no

Duke or Duchess to prevent them. If Burgundy is gone, they may make what black miracle they will, and then all is as if we had never lived and striven against them."

Ash stared at the weather-beaten face of the tournament champion and Captain of the Guard. The Burgundian soldier nodded, sharply.

"I know the powers of Burgundy's Duke, Demoiselle-Captain. What should these southern demons care, that we kill this miracle-worker of theirs now? They can breed another, whether it is twenty years or two hundred. If Burgundy has been destroyed, then in twenty years or two hundred, there is nothing to stand in their way. And winter *will* cover all the world."

A stir at the door made Floria turn her head. Ash saw the Abbot of St Stephen's enter with a clutch of monks. Olivier de la Marche intercepted him, soothing his stifled imprecations. The refectory's monks sidled out of sight.

"How long?" Floria demanded.

"A quarter-hour since I was on the wall." Ash squinted at the sun's light through the ogee windows. "Maybe more."

Floria put her hands together, linking her fingers and resting them against her lips. She stared at the Faris. Abruptly, she dropped her hands and stated, "If I keep you alive now, there are six hundred people standing in the mud outside the walls who are going to die. But if I hand you back to Gelimer, thousands more people are going to die in the war."

Ash saw John de Vere nodding; and Olivier de la Marche.

Floria, remorseless, continued: "If I kill you, the Wild Machines can't use you for their wonder-working – but that won't stop the war. Or the deaths. The war's going to go on whether you're alive or dead. We're losing. On the other hand, if I keep you alive, your knowledge as commander of their armies means that we can keep on fighting. And Burgundy has to survive, or there's nothing to stop the Wild Machines the *next* time they succeed in breeding a child of Gundobad's line. Ash, have I got this right?"

The surgeon-Duchess's voice was acerbic. Ash almost smiled, aching for the woman. "You didn't miss anything that I can see."

"And these are my choices."

"And mine."

"No. No, not this time." Floria's gaze took in Anselm and Angelotti and the company men; moved to Olivier de la Marche and Jonvelle and the gathering of Burgundian nobles and commanders.

"You said it yourself. I hunted the hart. It's my decision."

"Not if I decide differently."

It was out before she could retract it. Ash shook her head, disgusted with herself. *Yes, it's true, but this wasn't the time to remind her of it.*

Oh, shit.

At a loss to avoid the crevasse opening up at her feet, Ash protested, into the silence, "You can talk about twenty or two hundred years all you like. You're forgetting today. One stray arrow, one rock from a mangonel, one spy or assassin that Gelimer manages to get into this city – and then we've got the Wild Machines' 'miracle' happening at that instant. I don't care what my sister—" Ash spoke the words very deliberately "—*what* my sister knows about Visigoth troop dispositions and war plans."

Her gaze locked with Floria's, ignoring the whole room: Anselm murmuring something concerned to Angelotti, the Turks impassive, the Burgundians in their war-worn armour still splendid beyond all other countries of Christendom.

"Florian, for Christ's sake, can't you see it? I don't want to cause a split. But handing her back to Gelimer is just ridiculous." Ash grimaced. "And letting her live, here, is too great a risk to you."

"No risk from me," the Faris interrupted quietly, again with a flash of the same humour that Ash recognised as her own. "The risk is not from me. You forget something, sister. When the Duchess of Burgundy dies, then I – lose myself, to the Wild Machines. When I become a . . . a channel, for their power . . ." The Visigoth woman visibly sought words: "I think I will be – swept away. *Jund* Ash, I want her to live even more than you do!"

It carried weight with the Burgundians; Ash saw it in their expressions. She shivered, in the stone refectory, the memory of ancient voices in her mind: that sensation of being swept away, like a leaf in a river current; swept away and drowned.

"I'm not saying you're about to assassinate her," Ash remarked dryly. "Sweet Green Christ up a Tree, you'd have been a damn sight less trouble if you'd stayed outside Dijon with your army!"

She heard the plaintive note in her voice without being able to do anything about it. A ripple of laughter went around the room.

"I hear the clock striking the half," Robert Anselm said, his tone relieved even while he was looking over his shoulder at the door, as if anticipating one of Jonvelle's men-at-arms arriving from the wall. "Need a decision."

Floria linked her dirty fingers again, knuckles strained. "I've made enough hard decisions in the infirmary, when I was with the company."

Now would be the time, while she still thinks she has time to decide.

Ash kept her hand off her sword-grip. She read a flash of apprehension on Angelotti's face; realised she had moved – body balanced, feet slightly apart – into what any mercenary would see as a combat stance. *Any mercenary except Florian*, she amended. The gold-haired woman stood frowning.

Enough of de la Marche's men-at-arms between me and the Faris that I won't get through for certain. But I'm their commander now, so—

Robert Anselm strolled across the flagstones to her side. Ash did not shift her attention: aware of all the room, of men talking, of the Burgundians glancing between their Duchess and her Captain-General.

"Don't fuck her over," he rumbled. "If you push it, they'll follow her, not you."

"If I take *her* out—" Names attract their owners' attention; Ash did not say *the Faris*: "—it doesn't matter, it's done."

Robert Anselm managed to keep a level expression, watching the Duchess and the Burgundian men-at-arms, the Visigoth woman and the silver-haired slaves with her. He said, "You try and kill her and you'll start a civil war here."

Ash glared at him: a broad-shouldered man still in someone else's borrowed, over-large German breastplate. He watched her from unflinching brown eyes.

"Then the Doc's fucked," he said. "Burgundy's fucked too. Start a civil war inside Dijon and Burgundy finishes right here, girl. The rag-heads make catsmeat of us: thank you and good night. And those bloody things breed another monster in twenty years, and there's nothing to stop them."

His words wrenched her mind away from the Faris: she saw what she had been refusing to see and thought simply, *No, nothing left: no bloodline of Burgundy. There'll be a massacre, like at Antwerp and Auxonne. Then the Wild Machines will automatically succeed, whenever they try, because there will be nothing capable of stopping them.*

"Oh, son of a *bitch* . . ." Ash breathed.

She rubbed her eyes, aching in the white light from the windows. Her muscles flooded with what she recognised, startled, as a release of tension. She scowled. *What am I so happy about?*

The answer was present in her mind immediately:

I *don't have to take this decision.*

Self-disgust filled her. She shook her head, wryly. The disgust was not as powerful as the relief. Her mind yammered at her, finding no flaw in Robert Anselm's reasoning, telling her, *You can't make this decision, it has to be Florian, and you can't argue with her without losing everything—*

"Oh, shut up!" Ash said, under her breath. She looked at the startled face of Robert Anselm. "Not you. Yes. You're right. I wish you weren't."

And I wish I knew if I meant that.

Ash gestured across to Florian. "It's your call."

The woman's dark gold brows came down, her expression so clearly reading Ash's moral cowardice that Ash looked away.

She found herself watching her twin. The Faris still stood by the refectory table. One finger ceaselessly traced the raised grain of the scrubbed wood. She made no other movement. She did not look at the surgeon-Duchess.

Could I have come here, the way she has?

Ash did not let herself look at Violante or Adelize.

Floria wiped her face with her hand, in a gesture familiar to Ash from a hundred occasions in the hospital-tents. She sighed heavily. She did not look to anyone around her for assistance, confirmation, or support.

"I've got patients at the infirmary here," Floria said. "I'll be with them." She beckoned Olivier de la Marche forward. "You and Ash question the Faris. We'll convene again at Nones, and discuss what you've learned."

A sigh of release. Ash could not judge which of the men – John de Vere, Bajezet, de la Marche, Anselm – it came from.

The Faris sat down hard on the wooden bench beside Violante. Her skin paled to the point where she might have been taken for a woman with a terminal illness: her eyes large and dark in hollowed sockets.

"If I'm not in the infirmary, I'll be in the almonry; they wanted to talk to me about food stocks," Floria del Guiz said unemphatically. "When there's news from the wall, come and find me."

*

II

It became mercifully dark not long after the abbey bells rang for Nones.

The short winter day died to dusk. Ash stretched her leg as she leaned back against the hearth-surround in the company's tower. Green ivy still hung on the stonework. Burned flesh stabbed pain into the back of her thigh. *It is still the day of Christ's birth*, she thought, dazed.

The Christ's Mass massacre.

Blanche, her yellow hair matted under a filthy coif, wiped her now-thin hands on her kirtle. "We've run out of goose grease in the infirmary. Too many Greek Fire burns."

Ash clenched her fists behind her back. Under the bandage, raw flesh yelled pain at her. Peeling the plate and cloth from her injured thigh had made her bite deep teeth marks into the wooden grip of her dagger.

"How many incapacitated?"

"You know men," Blanche snapped. "All of them say they'll fight tomorrow. I'd say six of them will still be in bed next week. If the walls are standing!"

The woman's asperity, Ash saw, was not directed at her. Part of it was plain concern and an evident affection for the injured. The rest was self-blame, even in the face of lack of materials.

Ash wanted to say something comforting, could think of nothing that was not condescending.

"Any that can walk, send them down here. I'll be talking to the lads."

Blanche limped away. Ash noted a respect in the way that archers and billmen stood aside for her: a middle-aged woman with bad teeth, growing gaunt from starvation, who in easier times they may each have paid a small coin to fuck. With a sense of sadness, she thought, *I should have seen that in her before. Not left it to Florian to find.*

Angelotti, approaching the fire as Blanche left it, said, "How many civilians did we save?"

"We never got out of the dead ground in front of the postern gate. They saturated the area with Greek Fire from the engines. You were up on the walls: what happened?"

The gunner, his astonishingly beautiful face powder-blackened, shrugged lithe shoulders. "The golems tore people apart. They began a little way beyond our gate and went through them like herd-dogs. Those men and women that ran as far as their camp lines were shot down with bows. We shattered one golem with cannon fire, since it obliged us by walking straight towards the wall for the space of five minutes; but for the rest we shot with bow and arquebus, with no success . . ."

"The burns are bad," Ash said, into his silence. "Digorie and Richard Faversham are upstairs praying, not to much answer, I think. No tiny miracles, Angeli. No loaves and fishes, no healing. Being on Burgundy's side has its problems."

The Italian touched his St Barbara medal. "It would have taken more than a small miracle. The intercession of all the saints, perhaps; there are six hundred dead out there."

Six hundred men, women and children, jointed like the fowls Henri Brant cooks in the cauldrons in the kitchens, and lying on the cold, black earth between the city walls and the besieging camp.

And what will Gelimer do *now*?

"De la Marche is still debriefing the Faris. I left them to it." Ash flinched again, putting weight on her burned leg. "Let's get everybody in here, Angeli. I'm going to talk to them, before I talk to the *centeniers*. Make sure they understand what's going on. Then I'll tell them what we're going to do now."

From one corner of the hall, Carracci's recorder ran through a sequence of notes, halted; ran through them again. One of the pages touched him on the arm and he fell silent. The stink of tallow-dip tapers rose up. With the slit windows shuttered, and the faint lights, Ash could not see as far as the back of the hall. Men filed in, sitting down on the heaps of belongings on the flagstones, exchanging quiet words. Men-at-arms; men, women and children from the baggage train; some faces – Euen Huw, Geraint ab Morgan, Ludmilla Rostovnaya – still greasily smoke-stained from the abortive rescue sally.

The lances of the company filed in, sat down, watching her; and the talk died down to a waiting silence.

"What we have to think about," Ash said, "is a long-term solution."

She did not speak loudly. There was no need. Other than her voice, the only noise came from a few drops of melted ice falling down the throat of the chimney behind her, and hissing into the fire. Their faces watched her, with intent attention.

"We've been thinking too close to home, and too short-term." Ash shifted her shoulder off the wall and began to walk between the groups of seated men. Heads turned, following her in the smoky hall. She folded her arms, walking with a deliberateness that concealed the pain of the burn-wound. "Hardly surprising – we've been having our asses kicked from here to breakfast. We've had to fight our own battles before we could do much thinking ahead. But I think now is the time. If only because, as far as Gelimer is concerned, we don't know if we've still got a truce."

She became aware of Robert Anselm and Dickon de Vere by the door; nodded acknowledgement but didn't speak, not breaking her train of reasoning. She continued to walk, a woman in armour, among men sitting with their arms around their knees, lifting their heads as she passed.

"We've been concentrating on keeping a Duke or Duchess of Burgundy alive. Because Burgundy is what stands against the great demons in the southern desert, Burgundy is what stops them using their miracle-worker to wipe out the world. And now we have their miracle-worker right here, in Dijon."

There was no overt dramatisation in the way she spoke: she could have been in her own command tent, thinking aloud. A baby cried, and was hushed. She touched Carracci briefly on the shoulder as she walked past him.

"So it ought to be simple. We kill the Faris. Then it doesn't matter if Burgundy falls, because she's dead, and the Wild Machines have lost their –

channel," Ash said, choosing the Visigoth woman's own word. "Their channel for what they're going to do: put out the sun and make the world as if we had never been. Except that it's *not* simple."

"Because she's your sister?" Margaret Schmidt spoke up.

"She's not my sister. Except by blood." Ash grinned, altered her tone, and said, "The only close relatives I have are you lot, God help me!"

There was an appreciative chuckle at that.

"It's not simple." Ash cut off the noise. "We're not thinking ahead. If the Faris is dead, but the war here is still lost, then the Visigoths will raze Burgundy from sea to sea – they have to. If for no other reason, then because they don't want Sultan Mehmet in Carthage with the army that took down Byzantium."

"Fucking right," Robert Anselm rumbled.

"And if Burgundy's gone, if the blood of the Dukes of Burgundy no longer exists, then it won't matter if the Wild Machines take a thousand years to breed another Faris – as soon as they do it, the world is gone. Wiped out, changed, the moment they succeed. And everything we've done here will be gone – as if we had never been born."

Plainly, those men who had been present in the abbey had been talking; there was little surprise at what she said.

"And so we have to win this war," Ash added.

She couldn't stop a smile. It was answered here and there: Geraint ab Morgan; Pieter Tyrrell.

"Sounds simple, doesn't it?"

"Piece of piss!" an anonymous voice remarked, from the ill-lit gloom.

"You think only the Burgundians care about the war here?" Ash turned in the direction of the voice, and picked out John Burren. "You have a stake. You all have countries; all mercenaries do. You're English, Welsh, Italian, German. Well, the Visigoths have fucked most of those lands, John Burren, and they'll get across the Channel yet."

Dickon de Vere opened his mouth to say something and Robert Anselm's elbow landed heavily in the boy's ribs. The youngest de Vere shut up with surprising good grace.

"If Burgundy gets wiped out, every one of us who's died in this campaign has died for no reason. This is what we're going to do." Ash reached the middle of the hall again, still cupping her elbows in her hands. She looked around at the men. "We're going to fight back. When I left de la Marche, he had five separate scribes there to keep up with everything the Faris is telling him. We're going to take the war to the Visigoths. And we have to do it *first* – before that lot out there roll right over us!"

She glanced up into the smoke-blackened rafters, paused, went on:

"We know what their weak points are, now. So. First, we need to raise the siege – I grant you that's the difficult part. We need to get our Duchess Florian out of Dijon, and away." Ash smiled at the low noises of approval. "Then, we're going to fight beside the allies that we'll have. And we will have allies, because Gelimer is looking weaker every hour. We'll have the Turks and the French, minimum."

There were nods of agreement. She tapped her fist in her palm, went on concisely:

"We can kill the Faris, but that's just a precaution – in time, there'll be more where she came from. We can't reach the Stone Golem – they won't let us raid Carthage like that twice! So what we have to do – the only thing we can do – is take the war to the Wild Machines. Win here, and take the war to Africa. Give the Visigoth Empire to the Sultan, if we have to! We have to take the war south, and we have to destroy the Wild Machines themselves."

She paused for a moment, to let it sink in. She picked Angelotti and the other gunners out of the gloom, and nodded towards them:

"Once we get through the people around them, the Wild Machines can't *fight*. They're *rocks*. They can't do anything except speak to the Faris and the Stone Golem. I dare say Master Angelotti, and as many dozen powder-ships and bombards as we can muster, can reduce them to a lot of confused gravel in very short order." Ash nodded, acknowledging Angelotti's bright, sudden grin. "So that's where we're aiming – North Africa. And we aim to be there by the spring."

Those that had been in Carthage would have talked to those men who remained in Dijon. Ash looked keenly around in the gloom, watching faces; seeing determination, apprehension, confidence.

"There's no other way to do this," Ash said. "It won't be easy, even with what we know. If, once we've raised this siege, some of you want to go back to England, or travel further north out of the darkness, I won't stop you: you can leave with your pay. What we're doing is dangerous; trying to fight back and get to North Africa will get a lot of us killed."

She lifted her hand, cutting off what several people began to say.

"I'm not appealing to your pride. Forget it. I'm saying this is as dangerous as any other war we've fought in, and like every other time, those who are going to quit should do it now."

She could already identify some who might: a few of the Italian gunners, maybe Geraint ab Morgan. She nodded thoughtfully to herself, hearing a black joke or an ironic comment made in an undertone; three hundred and fifty able-bodied soldiers regarding her with the blank, bland faces of men who are at once afraid and practical.

"So when are we going to kick three legions' asses?" The English crossbowman, John Burren, jerked a thumb at the masonry walls; plainly intending to indicate the Visigoth legions encamped around Dijon.

Before she answered him, Ash nodded a general dismissal. "Okay. Lads, get your kit sorted. Talk to your officers. I want an officer meeting first thing tomorrow morning."

She turned back to the English crossbowman.

"'When'?" she repeated, and grinned at John Burren. "Hopefully, before Gelimer decides we haven't got a truce any more, and all three legions come right over these fucking walls!"

She visited the quarters of the Burgundian commanders, going from house to barracks to palace; holding much the same conversation everywhere in the dark winter afternoon of Christmas Day. Where possible, she spoke with the Burgundian men who would be fighting. She covered miles on the cobbled streets of Dijon, changing her escort every hour.

The light cloud cover cleared, stars came out; all that did not change was the crowd in front of the almonry, holding at a steady thousand strong all through the night, waiting for the tiny dole of dark bread and nettle-beer.

The seven stars in the sky shone bright in the frost: the Plough clearly visible over the spires of the abbey of St Stephen's.

Ash left her escort outside the two-storey red-tiled building in the abbey grounds that did duty as the Abbot's house; entering and passing through guards and monks alike with unquestioned authority.

The sound of a Carthaginian flute echoed down the cramped stairs. She unbuckled her helm, and shook out her short hair. Her eyes, that had been blurred with thought, with attention to others' words, sharpened. She scratched through her hair with bitten-nailed fingers, and gave a kind of shrug that settled her shoulders in her armour. That done, she bent her head and walked up the narrow, low-ceilinged stairs to the upper room.

"Madam – Captain," a tall, lean monk corrected himself. "You have missed the Abbot. He was just here, praying with the mad foreign woman."

"The Abbot's a charitable man." Ash didn't break step on her way to the door. "There's no need for you to come in. I'll only be a few minutes."

She ducked her head under the thick oak lintel, entering the further room, ignoring the monk's very half-hearted protest. The floor of the house was uneven under her boots, warped boards creaking. As she straightened, she took in pale beams gold in a lantern's light, white plaster between them, no scrap of furniture, and a heap of blankets beside the diamond-paned window.

Violante and the Faris sat together on the floor by the lantern. Ash saw their heads turning as she came in.

The blankets moved as the boards shrieked underfoot. Sweat-darkened grey hair became visible: Adelize sitting up and rubbing at her eyes with a chubby fist.

"I didn't know you were here." Ash stared at the Faris.

"Your abbot has put the male slaves in another room. I am here with the women."

The sound of the flute came again as the Faris spoke, plainly from somewhere else in the Abbot's house. Ash moved her gaze to Violante, to Adelize; back to the woman who now – hair cropped short, and in someone's over-large Swiss doublet and hose – seemed even more her twin.

"There's a family resemblance," Ash said, her mouth drying.

She could not take her eyes off the idiot woman. Adelize sat wrapped in many woollen blankets, rocking and humming to herself. She began to bang her fist on her knee. It was a second before Ash realised that she was keeping time with the flute music.

"Shit," Ash said. "She's why they killed so many of us, isn't it? They thought we'd end up like that. Shit. You ever wonder if that's what you've got to look forward to?"

The child Violante said something rapid.

"She doesn't understand you, but she doesn't like the tone of your voice," the Faris explained.

As if disturbed by the voices, Adelize stopped rocking and clutched at her stomach. She began to whimper and mew. She said a word. Ash barely understood the slaves' Carthaginian; made it out at last: "Pain! Pain!"

"What's the matter with her? Has she been injured?"

Violante spoke again. The Faris nodded.

"She says, Adelize is hungry. She says, Adelize has never known hunger before. She was cared for, in the birthing-rooms. She doesn't understand the pain of an empty gut."

Ash stepped forward. The rattle of her armour, which she no longer much heard, sounded loud in the enclosed space. The middle-aged woman scrambled up on to her feet and backed away, shedding blankets.

"Wait—" Ash stopped moving. She said, in a deliberately soothing tone, "I'm not here to hurt you. Adelize. Adelize, I'm not here to hurt."

"Not like!" Violante began rearranging the blankets around the woman. Adelize absently lifted the cloth up, picking at her sagging belly under her tunic, and scratching at grey pubic hair. A great web of white lines and stretch-marks seamed her thighs, belly, and breasts. Violante pulled the blankets down, adding something in rapid Carthaginian.

"She says, Adelize is frightened of people in numbers, and in war-gear." The Faris at last got to her feet. "The child is correct. Adelize will have seen few men other than those my father Leofric bred to her, and few people in number at all."

Ash stared at Adelize in the poor light. *Do I look like her?* The woman was heavy around the jaw, and her eyes were sunk in puffy flesh; she might have been anywhere between forty and sixty. Or even older: there was something naive about the unlined softness of her cheeks.

A wrenching pity moved her, overlain by disgust.

"Christ!" Ash said again. "She's retarded.[2] She really is."

Adelize's blankets moved. In the lantern light, Ash caught a brief glimpse of something wriggling back into the folds; and the faint smell in the room made sense to her. Rat. Violante spoke, unintelligibly.

"What?"

The Faris bent to pick up a blanket and wrap it around her own shoulders. Her breath huffed white in the air. "She says, show respect for her mother."

"*Her* mother?"

"Violante is your full sister. And niece," the Faris added, with a quiet smile on her face at Ash's disturbance. "My father Leofric bred our brother back to our mother. Violante is one of the children. I brought two of the boys away with me."

"Oh, for Christ's sake! *Why?*" Ash burst out.

The woman ignored that. Ash had a moment to muse, *You would think, when she has my face, that it would be easy for me to read it*; then the Faris said, "Why are you here?"

[2] In the original text, 'one of God's touched', and 'God's fool'.

"What?"

"Why have you come here?" the Faris demanded. At some time in the past few hours, she had washed her hands and face; the skin was pale in the guttering lamp's light. Dark-eyed, clear-skinned; and now with hair that barely covered her ears. She spoke in a voice hoarse with long explanations. "Why? Am I to be executed now? Or do I have as long as to tomorrow? Have you come here to tell me what your Duchess Florian decrees?"

"No," Ash said, shaking her head absently, ignoring the hard edge to the Faris's tone, "I came to see my mother."

It was not what she intended to say. Certainly it was not what she intended to say in front of other people. Her hands chilled with shock. She stripped off her gauntlets, re-buckled the straps, and hung them off the grip of her sword. Crossing the floor, she squatted down in front of Adelize. Her scabbard's chape scraped the floorboards.

"She doesn't know who I am," she said.

"She does not know me, either," the Faris said. "Did you expect her to recognise you as a daughter?"

Ash did not answer the Faris immediately. She squatted close enough to Adelize to smell the old-urine-and-milk stench from her skin. An unguarded, wild lurch of the idiot-woman's arm had her up on her feet, automatically, combat reflexes triggered, hand gripping her dagger.

Adelize reached out. She stroked the muddy leather of Ash's boot. She looked up. "Not to be afraid. *Not* to be afraid."

"Oh, Jesu." Ash wiped her bare hand across her face. It came away wet.

One of the rats, a curly-pelted white one, ran up to Adelize. Delighted, the woman forgot everything else in petting it with heavy fingers. The animal licked her.

"Yes." Ash looked away, bewildered. She stepped back, finding herself standing beside the Faris. "Yes, I thought she'd know me. If I'm her daughter, she *ought* to know me. I ought to feel she's my mother."

Very tentatively, the Faris put her hand into Ash's and gripped it; clasping her with cold, identical fingers.

"How many children has she had?"

"I looked in our records." The Faris did not remove her hand. "She littered every year for the first fifteen years; then three more litters after that."

"Christ! It almost makes me glad I'm barren." A flick of her gaze to the Faris, Ash's sight blurring. "Almost."

Another of the rats – patched fur dim in this light, but she was almost sure it was Lickfinger – ran up Adelize's arm to her shoulder. The woman cocked her head, chuckling as the rat's whiskers tickled her face. She paid no attention to Ash.

"Does she even *know* she's had babies?"

The Faris looked affronted. "She knows. She misses them. She likes small, warm things. What I believe she does not know is that babies grow. Since hers were taken away at birth to wet-nurses, she does not know they change to become men and women."

Blankly, Ash said, "Wet-nurses?"

"If she nursed, it would hinder conception. She has given birth eighteen times," the Faris said. "Violante was her next-to-last. Violante does not hear the Stone Golem."

"You do," Ash said sharply.

"I do. Still." The Visigoth woman sighed. "None other of Adelize's children were – successful, except for me. And for you, of course." She frowned; and Ash thought *Do I look like that? Older, when I frown?* The Faris went on, "Our father Leofric wonders now, how many others he culled too young. He has kept all of Leovigild's siring, now, and all of Adelize's children born this spring. We have two living brothers, and another sister."

Ash became aware that she was gripping the Faris's hand tightly enough to hurt. Embarrassed, she stared down at the crooked floorboards. Her breath came short, her chest burned.

"Fucking hell, I can't take it in." She lifted her gaze to the Faris's face, at her side; thought, *She's nineteen or twenty, the same as I am*, and wondered why the Visigoth woman should suddenly appear so young.

"It need not be twenty years before there's another Faris," Ash speculated, voice flat in the cold room. "If Leofric weren't mad as a March hare, and if Gelimer believed even half his intelligence about the Wild Machines . . . Maybe, if they looked at what they've got, there'd be another one of you in a few months: next spring or summer."

The Faris said, "I will tell you what my lord Caliph Gelimer would do, if he credited what we say of the Wild Machines. He would think them a superior kind of Stone Golem. He would think them wise voices of war, advising him how to spread the Empire to all civilised lands. And he would be seeking a way to build more Stone Golems, and breed more of me, so that he could have not one general and not one *machina rei militaris* but dozens."

"Sweet Christ."

The Faris's hand was warm and slick in her own. Ash loosened her grip. She said, her eyes still on Adelize, "*Could* House Leofric build another Stone Golem?"

"It is not *impossible*. In time." The Faris shrugged. "If my father Leofric lives."

"Oh, Jesu," Ash said, aware of the chill air freezing her fingertips, of the stars outside the window, of the smell of unwashed bodies subdued by the cold. "The Turk won't like that. Nor will anyone else. A machine for talking to the great war-demons of the south – they wouldn't rest until they had one too. Nor would the French, the English, the Rus . . ."

The Faris, watching Adelize, said absently, "Or if our knowledge were lost, and Leofric dead, and the House destroyed, so that there were still only the one Stone Golem – they will not let us keep it."

"They wouldn't rest until they'd taken Africa, taken Carthage, destroyed it utterly."

"But Gelimer does not credit it. He thinks it all some political plot of House Leofric." The Faris shivered under her blanket. She said thickly, "And I have nothing more to do with the fortune of the Visigoth Empire, do I? Nothing more to do, myself, than sit here and wonder if I am to be killed, come morning."

"Shouldn't think so. What you're telling de la Marche is far too useful."

It rang false as she said it. Ash took her eyes off Adelize and finally let herself realise, *I am standing in the same room as this woman, she is unarmed, I have a sword, I have a dagger; if her death were a* fait accompli, *Florian would just have to wear it. There probably* wouldn't *be a civil war.*

She expected agonising indecisiveness.

Kill her. In front of her mother, her sister? My sister? She is my sister. This, for all of what it is, is still my blood.

What she felt was a warm relaxation of tension.

Ash said with rough humour, "Sweet Green Christ! Haven't you got enough troubles without worrying if your sister's going to kill you? Faris, I won't. Right now, I can't. But I know I should."

She rested her hand across her face again, briefly; and then looked up at the Visigoth woman.

"It's Florian. You see. The danger to Florian. I can't let that carry on." The words stuck on her tongue; sheer weariness tripping her up. She found herself waving her arms as excitedly as an Englishman. "*Can you keep them out?*"

"The Wild Machines?"

"Keep them out. Not listen."

The expression on the Faris's face, dimly visible now in the lamplight, shifted between fear and confusion. "I – *feel* – them. I told the King-Caliph I did not hear the Stone Golem, and I do not; I have spoken no word to it in five weeks. But I feel it. And through it, the *Machinae Ferae* . . . there is a sensation—"

"Pressure," Ash said. "As if someone were forcing you."

"You could not withstand them, when they spoke through the Stone Golem to you, in Carthage," the Faris said softly. "And their power is growing, their darkness spreading, they will reach me, here; use me to change—"

"If Florian dies." Ash squatted again. She reached out, carefully, and touched Adelize's greasy grey-white hair. The woman stiffened. Ash began small stroking movements. "It's Florian. I can't let you go on being a danger to her. If you live, and the Wild Machines use you . . ."

"While we besieged you, I tried to break the link with the *machina rei militaris*," the Faris said. "I used a slave-priest, so he could tell no one and be believed. He prayed, but the voice of the machine stayed with me."

"So did I." Ash stopped stroking Adelize's matted hair. "So did I! And it didn't work for me either!"

Astonished laughter: she found herself grabbing the Faris's hands, the two of them laughing, and Adelize looked around, gazing from one to the other, from Ash to the Faris, and back again.

"Same!" she crowed triumphantly. She pointed from face to face. "Same!"

Ash bit her tongue. It was quite accidental; it stung; she tasted blood in her mouth. She thought, *Please say you know me.*

The fat woman reached up and stroked the Faris's face. She moved her fingers towards Ash. Ash's stomach twisted. The soft, plump fingers touched her skin, stroked her cheek, hesitated at the scars, retreated.

"Same?" Adelize said questioningly.

Ash's eyes filled. No water spilled down her cheek. She touched Adelize's hand gently, and stood up.

"There may well be more bred the same as you," Ash said, "but if you'd gone back and destroyed the Stone Golem – there's only one *machina rei militaris*. That would have cut you off from the Wild Machines. And it would have cut *them* off. They'd have to wait for another Gundobad or another Radonic, to build them another machine. Harder than breeding brats."

"Some men would have followed me. The ones I led in Iberia, who've known me many years. Most would not. And Carthage is well prepared against its victorious generals returning to overthrow a King-Caliph."

"You might have tried!" Ash grinned at herself, then, and shook her head ruefully. "Okay. I take your point. But if you'd destroyed the Stone Golem, I wouldn't be worrying about whether I should kill my sister now."

"Not kill!" Adelize said fiercely.

Ash glanced down, startled. Violante knelt at Adelize's side, obviously whispering a translation; the retarded woman glared up, pointing her finger at Ash, and then at the Faris. "Not kill!" she repeated.

A physical pain hurt her. *There is something wrong with my heart*, Ash thought. Her clenched fist pressed against her armour, over her breast, as if that could relieve her. The sharp, hollow pain hurt her again.

She reached out and ruffled Violante's hair. The child flinched away from her. She touched Adelize's hand. Stumbling, she turned and walked out of the room, ducking the lintel, striding past the thin monk; saying nothing when she picked up her escort outside the Abbot's house, nothing until she reached the palace, and the Duchess's quarters.

"I'm here to see Florian."

The bead-bright eyes of Jeanne Châlon peered around the carved oaken door. "She is not well. You cannot see her."

"I can." Ash leaned one plate-covered arm up against the wood. "Are you going to try and stop me?"

One of the waiting-women, Tilde, peered around Jeanne's shoulder. "She is not well, Demoiselle-Captain. We've had to ask my lord de la Marche to come back tomorrow."

"Not well?" Ash's mind sharpened, came into focus. She demanded curtly, "*What's wrong with her?*"

Tilde glanced at Jeanne Châlon, embarrassed. "Captain-General . . ."

"I said, what's wrong with her? What's her illness?— never mind." Ash shoved her way past them. She ignored the other servants and waiting-women, shouldering her way through them, leaving them to quarrel with her escort. She crossed to the ducal bed and threw back the hangings.

A stench of spirits made her cough.

The Duchess Florian, fully dressed in man's doublet, shirt and hose, lay sprawled face-down on the bedding. Her mouth was open, dribbling copiously on the sheet. She breathed out a stink of alcohol. As Ash stood gazing down, Florian began stertorously to snore.

"She was up on the wall this afternoon, wasn't she?"

Jeanne Châlon's white face appeared at Ash's side. "I told her not to. I told her it was not befitting a woman, that she should watch what God Himself turns His face away from. But she wouldn't heed me. Floria has never heeded me."

"I'm glad to hear it." Ash bent down and pulled wolf furs gently over Florian's legs. "Except in this case. How long was she drinking herself into insensibility?"

"Since sunset."

Since the hostage massacre.

"Well, she won't do this again." Ash's lips quirked. "We haven't got the drink. Okay. If she wakes, send for me. If she doesn't – don't disturb her."

She was thoughtful on the way out of the palace, conscious of Ludmilla Rostovnaya's escort chatting among themselves, and conscious that her legs ached, and that her burned thigh-muscle was throbbing. A haze of weariness floated her along. Not until she stepped out into the bitter, freezing night did she wake to full alertness.

The Plough had sunk around the pole of the sky. A few hours now and the day of Christ's Mass would be over; the feast-day of Stephen dawning.

A fierce blue light illuminated the night sky, travelling at high speed.

"Incoming!"

A bolt of Greek Fire hissed in an arc and fell to earth in the square, splashing an inferno across the stone cobbles. A man ran out in the spirit-blue light and raked thatch down from a corner of an outbuilding.

Shit! Is this it? Gelimer's lost his general, and he's tired of holding to the truce—?

Another bolt shot high; vanished outside the walls of Dijon on its downward arc.

"Take cover!" Ash ordered, stepping smartly back into the palace's gatehouse. Another shot – stone, not fire; an impact that jarred up from the flagstones through her feet.

"Motherfuckers!" Rostovnaya murmured something caustic about Visigothic marksmanship: her men growled agreement. "At Christ's Mass, too! Boss, I thought we had a truce until Lord Fernando goes back to them tomorrow?"

Straining her hearing, praying for sounds to carry in the frozen night air, Ash hears nothing now – no shot dropping on other quarters of the city.

Visigoth siege-engines, placement and ammunition-loads, orders of infantry assault troops! Ash formulated the thought in her mind, not speaking it out loud, and shook her head.

Even if I could speak to the Stone Golem, it wouldn't be any use my asking. Its reports from here are dependent on courier; it must be two or three weeks out of date.

At least that means Gelimer can't use it for tactical advice against us. Even if the Wild Machines can use it, he can't. And Godfrey would hear him. Small mercies—

She stopped, stunned.

"Captain?" Ludmilla Rostovnaya said, in the tone of someone who has said the words before.

"What?"

Ash registered dimly that she heard no more bombardment: that these desultory shots are not the opening barrage before an assault – only some bored gun-crew, probably Gelimer's Frankish mercenaries. Her realisation blocked out any thankfulness that the truce remains unbroken.

"Do we go back to the tower?" The Rus woman peered through the night and the gatehouse's gloom, illuminated by guttering Greek Fire. No other impact shook the ground. "Captain? What is it?"

Ash spoke numbly.

"I've . . . just realised something. I can't think why I didn't see it before."

III

The striped boarlet nosed at the snow, whip-thin tail wagging furiously. Ash watched its nose strip up the ice-crust from the soft white beneath. A flurry of black leaf-mould went up. The animal grunted, in deep content, trowelling up acorns.

A man with an acorn-coloured beard put back his hood and turned to look at her.

– Ash.

"Godfrey."

Exhaustion carried her along the edge of sleep. It was no great difficulty to be simultaneously aware that she lay on her straw palliasse beside the tower's hearth, the noise of squires' and pages' voices fading in and out as sleep claimed her; and to know that she spoke aloud to the voice in her head.

The dream brought her his image, clear and precise: a big man, broad in the chest, his gnarled feet bare under the hem of his green robes. Some of the grizzled hairs of his beard were white; and there were lines deeply cut at the side of his mouth, and around his eyes. A face beaten by weather; eyes that have squinted against the outdoor light in winter and summer.

"When I met you first, you were no older than I am now," Ash said quietly. "Christ Jesu. I feel a hundred."

– And you look it, too, I'll lay money on it.

Ash snuffled a laugh. "Godfrey, you ain't got no respect."

– For a mangy mongrel mercenary? Of course not.

The dream-Godfrey squatted in the snow, seeming to ignore the ice caking his robe's hem, and put one hand wrist-deep into snow to support himself. His breath whitened the air. She watched Godfrey tilt his head over – shoulders down, bottom up, until he seemed about to fall – to peer between the legs of the rootling three-week-old boar.

"Godfrey, what the *fuck* are you doing?"

The dream-figure said, "Attempting to see if this is a boar or a sow. The sows have a better temper."

"Godfrey, I can't believe you spent your childhood in the Black Forest trying to look up a boar's arse!"

"She is a sow." The snow shifted, and the boar's head came up, as he shuffled closer.

Ash saw her gold-brown eyes surveying the world suspiciously from under straw-pale lashes of incredible length. The dream-Godfrey talked quietly to her, for a lost amount of time; Ash drifted. She saw him finally reach out a cautious, steady hand.

The sow turned back to rootling. The man's hand began to scratch her in the place behind her ear where the thick, coarse winter coat is absent, and only soft hairs cover the grey skin. Her nose came up. She snorted: an amazing small, high squeak. He exerted more pressure, digging into the hot skin.

With a soft thump, the female piglet fell over on her side in the snow. She grunted in contentment as the man continued to scratch, her tail wagging.

"Godfrey, you'll have me believing you were suckled like Our Lord, by a boar!"

Without taking his hand away from the boarlet, Godfrey Maximillian looked back towards her. "Bless you, child, I have been rescuing God's wild beasts all my life."

White showed in his priest-cropped hair, as well as his beard. He reached for his Briar Cross with his free hand: large, capable and scarred. A workman's hand. His eyes were dark as the sow's, and each detail of his face was clear to her, as if she had not seen him for months and now he was suddenly before her.

"You think you'll always remember the face," Ash whispered, "but it's the first thing to go."

– *You think there will always be time.*

"You try to fix it in your mind . . ." Ash stirred, on the mattress. Like water sinking through sand, the clear dream of Godfrey Maximillian in the snow sank away. She tried to hold it; felt it sliding from her mind.

– *Ash?*

"Godfrey?"

– *I cannot tell how long it is since last we spoke.*

"A few days." Ash shifted over on to her back, her forearm across her eyes. She heard Rickard's voice, breaking in mid-sentence for the first time in weeks, telling someone that the Captain-General could not see them at this hour: wait but an hour more.

"It's the evening of Christ's Mass," she said, "or the early hours of St Stephen's day; I haven't heard the bells ring for Matins. I've been afraid to speak with you in case the Wild Machines—" she broke off. "Godfrey, do you still hear them? Where are they?"

In the part of herself that is shared with the *machina rei militaris*, she feels the comforting warmth that she associates with Godfrey. She hears no other voice but his; not even distant muttering in the language of Gundobad's era.

"Where are they!"

– *Hell is silent.*

"Hell be damned! I want to know what the Wild Machines are doing. Godfrey, talk to me!"

- Your pardon, child.

His voice comes to her filled with a mild amusement.

- For however long a time you say it is – a month and more – no human soul has spoken with the Stone Golem. At first the great Devils lamented this greatly. Then, they became angry. They deafened me, child, with their anger; forcing it through me. I had thought you heard, but perhaps it was the Faris at whom they directed their rage. And then, they fell silent.

"Did they, by God?"

She stretched, still fully clothed in case of night alarms; and opened her eyes briefly to see the rafters lost in the gloom, outside the light of the meagre hearth-fire.

"They won't have given up on the Faris. They're waiting for their moment. Godfrey, has no one used the Stone Golem? Not even the King-Caliph?"

Godfrey's voice, in her soul, is full of what would be laughter if it were a sound.

- The slaves of Caliph Gelimer speak to it – as men speak, not as the Faris *speaks. They ask questions of tactics. If you ask me what, he will deduce what you fear. He is much afraid of this crusade, child, it is running away with him; a war-horse which he cannot control. I wish I could find God's charity in my heart for him, rather than rejoicing that he is troubled. I am unsure that he even understands the answers the Stone Golem speaks.*

"I hope you're right. Godfrey, what are you so damned cheerful about?"

- I have missed you, Ash.

Her throat began to ache.

His voice filled with confidence; excited expectation:

- You swore that you would bring me home. Rescue me, out of this. Child, I know you would not be talking to me now unless you had thought of some way to bring this about. You've come to rescue me from this hell, now, haven't you?

Ash struggled up into a sitting position on the mattress. She waved Rickard away; back to the door lost in the gloom. She huddled furs and blankets around her shoulders, wriggling forward until her feet were almost in the ashes of the hearth-fire.

"I swore a lot of things," Ash said harshly. "I swore I'd get the Wild Machines for killing you, when you died in the earthquake. And you swore in the coronation hall that you'd always be with me, but it didn't stop you dying there. We all make promises we can't keep."

- Ash?

"At least I never swore to bring your body back for burial. At least I *knew* that was impossible."

- When I tried to help you escape from the cells of Leofric's house, before I found Fernando del Guiz for you to ride out with, I swore that you would never be alone. Do you remember? That promise I have kept. And I will keep it, child. You hear me, and you will always hear me; I will never leave you. Be certain of it.

The ache in her throat spread. She rubbed the back of her hand across her eyes. She made the mental effort, cut herself off from the ache and the hurt.

Hot tears rolled out of her eyes, blurring the image of the red coals in the hearth. Astonished, her chest feeling scoured hollow and breathless, she clenched her fists and dug her nails hard into her palms. The tears fell faster; her breathing jerked.

– *Ash?*

"I can't rescue you. I don't know how!"

There is silence, in her mind.

– *I can forgive you one broken promise, in a lifetime.*

In her head, Godfrey Maximillian's voice is resonant.

– *Do you remember, I told you that to leave the Church and travel with you was worth every hurt I have ever paid? Then, I loved you as a man loves. Now I am soul, not body; and I love you still. Ash, you are worth this.*

"I never deserved that!"

– *It does not come for that – although you have been true, good, and warm-hearted to me, I do not love you for that reason. Only because you are who you are. I loved your soul before I ever loved you as a woman.*

"For Christ's sake, shut up!"

– *I have told you. I regret nothing, except that I still do not have all your trust.*

"Oh, but you do." Ash covered her face with her hands, resting her head on her knees in the wet, warm darkness. "I trust you. If I ask you to do something, I trust you to do it. That makes it hard – it makes it impossible, to ask."

– *What could you ask of me that I would not do?*

A rueful, amused vulnerability is in the sound of his voice:

– *Not that I can do much, now, child. Not as I am. But ask, and if I can, I will do it.*

Hard as she tries to stop it, her breath comes in great sobs. She presses her hands to her mouth to stifle the noise.

"You – don't – understand yet—"

"Boss?"

She opened her eyes to see Rickard squatting beside her, his expression unguarded and appalled. Tears have run down her face. Her eyes are hot. When she makes to answer him, there is no sound; a constriction in her throat will not let words pass.

"You want something?" Rickard asked. He looked around helplessly. "What?"

"Stay at the door. No one's—" She spoke thickly. "*No one's* to enter until I say. I don't care who it is."

"Trust me, boss." The black-haired young man straightened up.

He is wearing armour that does not belong to him – a wounded man's fustian brigandine – and a wheel-pommel sword clatters at his side. It is not that, so much as the eyes, that are the difference; he looks wary, and much older than he did at Neuss.

"Thanks, Rickard."

"You call me," he said fiercely. "If you need something, you call me. Boss, can't I—"

"No!" She fumbled for her purse, pulling out a dirty kerchief and wiping her face. "No. It's my decision. I'll call you when I want you."

"Are you talking to Saint Godfrey?"

986

Tears spilled out of her eyes, an uprush that she could not check. *Why?* she thought, bewildered; *why can't I stop this? This isn't me; I don't weep.*

"Rickard, go away."

She balled the wet cloth of her kerchief between her two hands, and rested it against her eyes.

– I swear, child, you can ask nothing of me that I will not grant.

Godfrey Maximillian's voice, in her mind, is urgently, openly sincere. Too open: Ash presses the cloth harder against her eyes. After a second she can sit up, back straight, and stare into the greying coals.

"Yeah, and you asked me for help. Remember? I can't give it. Godfrey, I *am* going to ask you for something. If you prefer to think of it this way, I'm going to order you."

– Are you crying? *Ash, little one, what is it?*

"Just listen, Godfrey. Just listen."

She dragged in a breath. It caught, threatening to become a sob; and she knotted the kerchief in her hands, white-knuckled, and got control of her voice.

"You're the *machina rei militaris* now. Or part of it."

– Like the warp and weft of cloth, I think – and I have had long to consider the matter. Ash, why this grief?

"Do you remember what I said to you, when we were riding out to the desert, outside Carthage?"

– Not a particular thing—

Her breath came with a deep shudder. She interrupted sharply. "We were joking. I asked you for a miracle, a tiny miracle – 'pray that the Stone Golem will break down' – something else, I don't remember what. And since then I've thought of nothing else but the Faris, killing the Faris to stop the Wild Machines."

– She does not speak to the Wild Machines, although I believe she hears them as they speak to her.

"The Faris isn't important." Ash opened her eyes again, not knowing until then that she had sought refuge in the dark. She reached out and picked up a rough-barked piece of wood, and leaned forward to bed it deep in the red ashes. "She *should* be killed, for safety, but I can't do it. They'll probably execute her here. That isn't important. The Wild Machines can talk Leofric's family into breeding another Faris, if they haven't already started. What's important is the Stone Golem."

There is no sound of Godfrey Maximillian's voice in her mind, but she can feel him waiting; feel his acceptance of her words into his self.

"We have to destroy the Wild Machines. We can't do it militarily in much under a year. We haven't got a year. We can kill my sister," Ash said, and felt her voice shake again. "But that doesn't buy us much time, and Burgundy may be a wasteland before then."

– Tell me nothing! If the great Devils are listening—

"You listen, Godfrey. The Stone Golem is the key. It's how they speak to Leofric, and his family. It's how they speak to my sister. It's the channel they'll use, when they draw on the sun's power for their miracle."

– Yes.

He sounded cautiously puzzled, but not defensive. Ash's hands shook. She wiped wood-ash off her fingers, on to her stained green hose. She heard her own voice continuing to speak, the tone calm and authoritative.

"One reason why I didn't give more consideration to the Stone Golem is that it's in Carthage, behind Gelimer's armies. We failed, on the raid, and I believed we couldn't reach it to try again. I wasn't thinking."

A knot in the burning wood flared. The fire spat. Ash jolted, every muscle from spine to toe clenching. She rubbed her face with wood-ash-stained hands.

"Godfrey, the Stone Golem can be attacked. I don't have to reach it. None of us have to. You're already there. You're *part* of it."

– Ash . . .

I will think of him as a disembodied fragment. An unquiet spirit. Not a man I've loved as brother and father for as long as I can remember.

"Do a last tiny miracle," Ash said. "Destroy the Stone Golem. Break the link between it and my sister. Call down the weather to you. Call down the *lightning* – and fuse everything into useless sand and glass!"

The place in her soul that is shared stays silent. Not long, a few heartbeats – she can feel her pulse shaking her body.

– Oh, Ash . . .

Pain sounded in his voice. Her chest ached. She rubbed it with a clenched fist. The anguish did not go away. Very steadily, she said aloud, "You're a priest. You *can* pray the lightning down."

– Suicide is a sin.

"That's why I'm telling you to do it, not asking you." She caught her breath on a sob again, that was almost a laugh. "I knew you'd say that. I think about these things. I don't want you damned. The minute it came to me, I knew it had to be at someone else's command. And it's mine; the responsibility is mine."

Chill air moved past her, flowing over the flagstones towards the chimney. She huddled deeper into her furs. A scrape of metal sounded from the door: the chape of Rickard's sword on masonry. Distant, down the spiral stairs, she heard voices.

In her head, there is silence.

"The other reason why it didn't come to me, I suppose," Ash said quietly, "is that as soon as it did, I would know what it meant. I know you. You got yourself killed in Carthage going back for Annibale Valzacchi, for God's sake, and this is more important than one man's life!"

– Yes. More important than one man's life.

"I didn't mean *your*—" Ash broke off. "I— yes. I do mean that. This will cut the Wild Machines off completely. They can't use the Faris, they won't even be able to talk to the Visigoths. They'll be dumb, powerless, until someone else can build a machine. That could take centuries. So yes, it's more important than one life, but when it's *you*—"

Wind rattled the shutters. Starlight penetrated faintly through cracks in the wood. That and the orange glow of the fire illuminated the familiar furniture of the command tent: armour-stand, war-chest, spare kit. The solitude of it bit into her, sharp as the freezing night.

"I've had to order people into places where I've known they were going to die," Ash said steadily. "I never knew how much I hated it until now. Losing you once was bad enough."

– I don't know if this can be done. But I will pray for God's grace, and attempt it.

"Godfrey—"

In the space that she shares with him, she feels a flood of bewilderment, fear, and courage; a terror that he cannot hide from her, and an equally strong determination.

– You will not leave me.

"No."

– God bless you. If He loves you as much as I do, He will give you a life, hereafter, with no more such grief in it. Now—

"Godfrey, not yet!"

– Will you make it my sin? If I wait, I will lose my courage. I must do it now, while I can.

What she wants to say is, To hell with it! I don't care what happens. I'll find some way to rescue you, make you human again; what do I care about the world? You're *Godfrey*.

The fire blurred in her vision. Tears ran down her cheeks.

What can I give you, out of what I am? Only this: that I *can* do this. I can take this responsibility.

"Call down the lightning," she said. "Do it now."

Her voice sounded flat, in the still, bitter air. She had a second to smear her eyes clear, to think, *Bloody idiots he and I are going to look if this is all for nothing—*

In the centre of her soul, Godfrey Maximillian spoke.

– By the Grace of God, and by the love I have had for Your creations, I implore You to hear me, and grant my prayer.

It is the same voice that she has heard hundreds of times, at Lauds and Vespers and Matins; heard in camp and on the field, where men fighting have gone to their deaths listening to it. And it is the same voice that talked her asleep as a child, in the months after St Herlaine, when any darkness had the power to keep her awake and shivering until sunrise.

"I'm here," she said. "Godfrey, I'm here."

His voice in her mind is unsteady; she feels the flood of fear in him. He prays on:

– Though I die, I shall not die; I shall be with You, Lord God, and Your Saints. This is my faith, and I here proclaim it. Lord God, before Whom no armour can stand, Thou who art stronger than any sword – send down the fire!

"Godfrey! *Godfrey!*"

What she remembers from Molinella, a child watching a battle from a church tower, is how the appalling explosion of cannon-fire knocks the moment of impact out of memory. It must be reconstructed later. She tastes brick-dust in her mouth again, smells poppies. A fang of pain bites at her hand. She snatches it back – from fire; from the burning wood in the hearth in the company's tower. Not Italy and summer, but Burgundy and the bitter solstice of winter.

She put one hand down to push herself up, realised that she was lying on her face, that she had soiled herself, that blood ran stickily down from her bitten lip.

"Godfrey . . ."

Blood dripped down on to the mattress, staining the straw's linen cover. Her arms began to shake. The muscles would not take her weight. She fell down on her face, shaking; the rub of cloth against cloth gratingly loud in the tower room where no explosion has taken place. Her ears sting: her whole body shakes with an impact that has not happened here.

"Godfrey!"

"Boss!" Rickard's boots clattered on the flagstones. She felt his hands on her shoulders, rolling her over on her back.

"I'm all right." She sat up, fingers trembling, body shaking. The boy has seen what happens in battle; she is not ashamed that he sees her now. Stunned, she gazed around at the stone hall. "Godfrey . . ."

"What's happened?" Rickard demanded. "Boss?"

"I felt him *die*." Her voice shook. "It's done, it's done now. I made him do it. Oh, Jesu. I made him."

A great pain went through her chest. Her hands would not stop shaking, though she clenched them into fists. She felt her face screw up. A sob forced its way past her rigid jaw.

She was not aware of Rickard running, panic-stricken, for the door of the hall, or of anyone else coming in; the first she knew of it was when a man grabbed her, hard. Weeping, stinking, incoherent; she could say nothing, only sob harder. The man put his arms tightly around her, gripping her close to him. She put her arms around his bulk and clung to him.

"Come on, girl! *Answer* me! What's happened?"

"Not—"

"*Now*," the voice insisted. A voice accustomed to orders. Robert Anselm.

"I'm okay." Hollow, every breath still shaking her, she pushed him far enough back that she could grab his hands in her own. "There's nothing you can do."

As her breathing steadied, Robert Anselm looked at her keenly. He was without armour, a stained demi-gown belted around his beer-belly; had obviously been snatching what hours asleep he could. The light from the fire illuminated, grotesquely, his shaven head and ears; and put deep shadows in his eye-sockets.

"What's this 'Godfrey'? What's happened to Godfrey?" he rumbled.

"He's dead," Ash said. Her eyes glimmered. She gripped Anselm's hands hard. "Christ. Losing him twice. Jesu."

What Anselm said then, she ignored. There were other men crowding in at the far door: Rickard, her officers. She ignored all of it; clamped her eyes shut.

She feels cautiously in the part of herself that has been shared, since Molinella, with her voice.

"Godfrey?"

Nothing.

Quiet tears welled up and spilled over her lids. She felt them streaming down her face, hot in the freezing air. The ache in her throat tightened.

"Two thousand troops, in defence positions in a siege; three legions attacking: options?"

Nothing.

"Come on, you bastards. I know you're there. Talk to me!"

There is no sensation of pressure. No voices that mutter in the language of the Prophet Gundobad's time; or rage, deafeningly, to bring down walls and palaces. There are no Wild Machines. Only a sensation of blank, numb, empty silence.

For the first time in her adult life, Ash is without voices.

An egoistic part of her mind remarked, *I've lost what made me unique*; and she gave a shaky smile, part self-disgust and part acceptance.

She opened her eyes, bent down, and hauled on her long gown to conceal her soiled clothing. She straightened up, facing the officers that crowded into the hall: Angelotti, Geraint, Euen, Thomas Rochester, Ludmilla; a dozen more. Facing them now only as a young woman with a skilled trade, war; remarkable only for that, and for nothing else.

She said, "The Stone Golem is destroyed. Melted down to slag."

Silence fell; the men looking from one to other, too stunned yet by the announcement to feel relief, joy, belief, victory.

"Godfrey did it," Ash said. "He prayed down lightning on House Leofric. I felt it hit. I— he died in the attack. But the Stone Golem's gone. The Wild Machines are cut off utterly. We're safe."

IV

"Of course," Robert Anselm said sardonically, "that's 'safe' from the Wild Machines' miracle. Not safe from the three Visigoth legions sitting outside Dijon!"

The better part of an hour had gone by in the top floor of the company's tower, more lance-leaders coming in by the minute, Burgundian knights and *centeniers* joining them; and Henri Brant and Wat Rodway between them breaking out a spirituous liquor that tasted like nothing on earth, but bit the tongue and throat and belly with heat. The frenetic celebrations spread down to the men on the lower two floors: Ash could hear the roaring racket below.

"The truce is still holding. I've told you. We're starting the fight back now, and we won't stop until we get to Carthage."

It was said largely for public consumption: for Jussey, Lacombe, Loyecte, de la Marche. Cleaned up and wearing borrowed hose, Ash stood and drank with her men, and felt nothing but numbness.

Celebration got into gear. The volume of noise rose. Faces flushed, Euen Huw and Geraint ab Morgan shouted joyously at each other in triumphant Welsh. Angelotti and half his gun-crew masters crowded closer to the fire, leather mugs full; someone called for Carracci and his recorder; Baldina and Ludmilla Rostovnaya began a drinking contest.

For them, Godfrey died three months ago.

Ash touched Robert Anselm's arm. "I'll be up at St Stephen's."

He frowned, but nodded assent; too busy celebrating with two women from the baggage train.

Once outside the tower, the cold moved her to uncontrollable shivering. She huddled a cloak and hood over her gown, and walked, head down, shoulders hunched, at a pace brisk enough that her escort – who had been moderately warm in the guardroom – swore quietly to themselves. Black ice covered the cobbles; she almost fell four times before she reached the abbey.

Yellow light shone warmly through the high Gothic windows. As she stepped inside, the bells began to ring for Lauds. The men-at-arms crowding in with her, she knelt at the back as the monks filed into the main chapel to sing the office.

You said I was a heathen, she mentally apostrophised Godfrey Maximillian. *You're right. This means nothing to me.*

She caught herself waiting for his answer.

With the office done, she made her way to the abbot's house.

"No need to disturb his reverence," she told a deacon who did not look as though he were about to. "I know where to go. If you have food in the almonry, my men will be grateful."

"That is for the poor. You soldiers have the best rations as it is."

One of Ludmilla Rostovnaya's men muttered, "Because we're keeping them alive!" and subsided at Ash's glare.

"I won't be more than a few minutes."

Climbing the stairs, she did not ask herself why she had come. As soon as the monk on guard outside the room gave her a lamp to take in, and she saw the Faris's face in its light, she knew why she was there.

The Faris stood by the window. The northern stars wheeled in the sky behind her. Her face in the golden light showed tired, drawn, but relieved.

Neither Violante nor Adelize was asleep. The child seemed to be soothing the woman, as if there had been an outburst. The piebald rat scuttled across the pile of blankets, raised itself up on its hind feet, whiskers quivering, and niffed at the chill air that came in with Ash.

Ash pushed the door closed behind her.

The numbness in her mind felt colder than the winter outside.

"My voice is gone. There is no *machina rei militaris*. As if an explosion, in my mind—" The Faris came forward across the room. Boards creaked under her feet. Her steps were unsteady. "You heard it too."

"I gave the order."

The Visigoth woman scowled. She put her hand to her head. Ash saw comprehension come.

"Your confessor. Your Father Maximillian."

Ash dropped her gaze. She took a few steps closer to her mother, where Adelize sat in the blankets. She did not touch her, but she squatted down and held out her fingers to the piebald rat. It stood up on its hind legs and licked, twice, very rapidly, at her fingers.

"Hey, Lickfinger. You can tell which are the boys, can't you? Balls as big as hazelnuts." Ash's tone changed. She said, "I've lost my friend."

The Faris came to kneel on the blankets beside her, putting her arm around Violante. The child's thin body was shivering. "I thought I was dying. Then – silence. The blessed, blessed quiet."

The liver-and-white rat elongated his body, stretching up to sniff at Adelize. She flicked a frightened glance from the rat to her daughter the Faris.

"I frightened her, I think." The Faris met Ash's gaze. "It's over, isn't it?"

"Yes. Oh, the war's not over." Ash jerked her head at the night sky beyond the window. "We could be dead tomorrow. But unless someone builds another Stone Golem before the armies of Christendom get to Carthage, it's over. The Wild Machines can't use you for anything. They can't reach you."

The Faris rested her head in her hands. Cut silver hair flopped over her brow. Muffled, she said, "I do not care how it was done. I am sorry for your friend. I only knew his voice. But I do not care how it was done. I thank God for it."

She straightened. Her familiar features, in the lamp's light, are blurred with tears; incongruous on that face as water on a knife-blade.

I had to be the one to bring you the news, Ash realised.

I had to see you realise that Florian has no reason, now, to have you killed. And every useful reason to keep you alive.

"You're safe," Ash said. To Adelize, and to Violante, she repeated: "You're safe."

The child stared at her uncomprehendingly. Adelize, reassured, picked up the rat and began to pet him.

"Well. I say 'safe'. Apart from the fact that there's a war on." Ash grinned crookedly.

"Apart from that," the Faris echoed. She smiled. "It's over. My God. I still don't know what you're doing with my face."

"It looks better on me."

The Visigoth woman laughed as if laughter had taken her by surprise.

A cold, very deliberate, and multiple voice said in Ash's head, 'THE FACE IS NOTHING. THE BREEDING IS EVERYTHING.'

Ash said, "Bollocks," automatically, and froze.

A spurt of sickness went through her, sinking from her belly to her gut. Dizzy with it, she said, *"No . . ."*

'THE SECRET BREEDING IS ALL.'

"No!" Her protest is squealing outrage.

'SOME HAVE THE QUALITY WE NEED. SOME DO NOT.'

"Godfrey!"

Nothing.

In the part of her mind that is shared, that has been numb, only the voices of the Wild Machines sound – like a muttering of distant thunder; far off at first, and now perfectly distinct.

'—SOME DO NOT. AND SOME HAVE MORE.'

"He didn't do it. No. No: I *felt* it. I felt the machine die. He didn't destroy it *all*—?"

Ash became aware of the Faris shaking her arm. The Visigoth woman was staring at her in alarm.

"What are you saying?" the Faris demanded. "Who are you talking to?"

The voices of the Wild Machines speak in Ash's head:

'WE COULD HAVE NOT DONE THIS WITH THE FARIS—'

'—SHE NEEDED THE *MACHINA REI MILITARIS*—'

'GONE, NOW. GONE!'

'BUT WITH YOU—'

'—AH, WITH YOU!'

'—WE HAVE KNOWN SINCE YOU CAME TO US.'

'SPOKE TO THE *MACHINA*, WHEN YOU WERE IN MIDST OF US.'

'CALLED OUT, IN THE DESERT SOUTH, ALMOST WITHIN TOUCH OF US—!'

'—ESTABLISHED THE DIRECT LINK WITH US—'

'—WITH YOU, WE DO NOT NEED THE *MACHINA REI MILITARIS*.'

'WE NEED ONLY THE DEATH OF HER WHO BEARS THE DUCAL BLOOD!'

Ash yelled, "Can't you hear them?"

"Hear them?" the Faris repeated.

"The machines! The fucking machines! Can't you *hear*—"

'—US. WE, WHO HEARD YOU SPEAK WITH THE GOLEM-COMPUTER, WHEN YOU RODE AMONGST US, IN THE SOUTH—'

'—WHO SPOKE TO *US*.'

'WE DID NOT NEED YOU THEN.'

'WE HAD OUR OTHER CHILD.'

'BUT WE KNEW THAT, IF SHE FAILED US – WE COULD REACH YOU.'

'—SPEAK WITH YOU—'

'COMPEL YOU, AS WE COULD HAVE COMPELLED HER—'

'AS SOON AS OUR ARMIES KILL THE DUCHESS FLORIA, WE CAN TAKE OUR FINAL STEP.'

Deafened, appalled, Ash began to repeat aloud the speech that thunders in her head:

"'Then we will change reality, so that humankind does not exist; never *has* existed, after a point ten thousand years ago. There will only ever have been machine consciousness, throughout all the history that has been and all the history that is to come—'"

The Faris interrupted. "What are you talking about!"

Kneeling on threadbare blankets, in an upper room not warmed by any fire, in the exhausted early hours of the winter morning, Ash studied the face of the woman kneeling beside her. The same face, eyes, body. But not mind.

Ash stared at the Faris. "You're not hearing this."

'SHE NEEDED THE GOLEM-COMPUTER. YOUR SISTER NO LONGER HEARS OUR VOICES.'

Dry-lipped, Ash said, "But I do."

"You do what?" the Faris demanded. A shrill note invaded her voice; as if she would wilfully not understand. She sat back on her heels, away from Ash.

Ash began to shake. Winter's cold bites deep. Violante stared at her. Adelize,

994

as if her daughter's tone disturbed her, cautiously reached out and touched Ash's arm.

Ash ignored her.

"I still hear the Wild Machines. Without the Stone Golem," she said. Immediate realisation hit her. "Godfrey. He did that for nothing. He's died for nothing. And I told him to do it."

'YOUR BIRTH: ONLY LUCK—'

'—A FLUKE; A CAST OF FORTUNE—'

'YOU CAN DO NOTHING BUT THIS. BUT IT IS ENOUGH.'

The multiple, inhuman voices whisper in her mind:

'ASH. YOU ARE THE SUCCESSFUL EXPERIMENT, NOT YOUR SISTER.'

Loose papers found inserted between Parts Fifteen
and Sixteen of ASH: THE LOST HISTORY OF BURGUNDY
(Ratcliff, 2001), British Library.

Message: #423 (Anna Longman)
Subject: Ash
Date: 20/12/00 at 05.44 p.m.
From: Ngrant@

format address deleted
Other details encrypted by
non-discoverable personal key

Anna –

Fifty-seven hours straight. I slept twice: once for two hours and
once for three. I think I shall be able to get through the last of
it (if only in first draft English) in one go. Then we shall see what
we have. I'll send the whole thing through when I get to the end.

My God. Poor Ash.

I woke up actually shouting aloud. DELENDA EST CARTHAGO! 'Carthage
must be destroyed.'

I thought it was the cold that had woken me – nights are bitter
here, even with the heating – but no, it was that: words that I
can't get out of my head.

I keep thinking of Vaughan Davies's metaphor, of human existence
in the past picked up and shaken – as if it were all a jigsaw,
falling back together again with the same pieces but in a different
order. If we find 'delenda est Carthago' put by Florus into the
mouth of a Roman senator; if we read in Pliny, now, that Cato
'. .. . cum clamaret omni senatu Carthaginem delendum' ('that he
vociferated at every [meeting of the] Senate [that] Carthage [was]
to be destroyed'), then – where was it before?

Here, with Ash. Who no longer exists, except in what I suppose I
must begin to call the First History. A first history overwritten,
like a file, with a later arrangement of the data: our 'second'
history.

Although fragments of the data remain in OUR history, OUR past, I
have seen them fading. She has become myth, legend, fiction.

Even though, as I read, I hear her speaking to me.

Blame lack of sleep. If I'm beginning to dream in Latin, it's no
great surprise. I'm eating, sleeping, and breathing the Sible
Hedingham manuscript. It is – I am convinced – it IS our 'previous'
history.

Tami Inoshishi and James Howlett came for another question
session. I doubt they got much sense out of me. From what I can
tell, they are perfectly happy with the theory that there may have
existed, at one time, a genetic mutation which enabled the
possible states of the universe to be consciously collapsed into
something less probable than an average – into a 'miracle', in
short. A non-Newtonian alteration of reality.

They don't have much trouble with the theoretical idea that one massive change of this sort could take place, and the genetic mutation itself be one of the things that was rendered non-actual.

What Tami, in particular, kept hammering on at me about – in that unstoppable way she has – is the fact that evidence is both being eradicated (the Angelotti manuscript) and coming back (Carthage).

I have told her my theory: that BOTH the 'Wild Machines' and Burgundy must have been wiped out. If nothing else, it is the only theory that can explain why we are not non-existent ourselves, and the world the province of silicon machine intelligences; and why we do not have, in our history, a Visigoth Empire. Why the Arab and black African cultures appear to have been 'patched in', in place of the Visigoths, after the change.

We are used to history affecting us only in the sense that past actions affect us all. History may be reinterpreted: it does not alter. THIS history is still affecting us now. We are changing, now. I do not understand why.

Things ARE changing. That's what bothers Tami. The ROVs are 1000 metres down, clearing debris with pressurised jets. And Carthage is there. Now. Again.

That said, Tamiko has pointed out, from my last translated section of the Sible Hedingham manuscript, a further confusion – that, in the manuscript, the Stone Golem is destroyed. And yet, we have the Stone Golem. We discovered it *intact*, in Carthage.

If the Sible Hedingham ms is in error on the point, that shakes my whole confidence in it! How much else could be wrong?

Can it be document error? Or is this a different golem – had King-Caliph Gelimer already advanced a programme to produce more; was House Leofric advanced enough to create another one – more than one? Or is there something in this hellishly impenetrable bad mediaeval Latin that I've translated wrongly? Or, is there something in the remaining part of the Sible Hedingham manuscript that explains this?

I will sleep for four hours, then continue the translation.

– Pierce

Message: #234 (Pierce Ratcliff)
Subject: Ash
Date: 20/12/00 at 11.22 p.m.
From: Longman@   *format address deleted*
                         other details encrypted and
Pierce –   *non-recoverably deleted*

Send me whatever you have, I'll look at it over the Christmas break.

I'm going down to see William Davies again, later today.

He phoned to tell me he's been reading some of the Sible Hedingham manuscript aloud to his brother. He told me he did a lot after the war on the psychology of trauma; he got interested in it as part of the recovery from surgery.

He _thinks_ Vaughan is reacting to hearing it, even in the original Latin. The problem is, William only knows medical Latin; mediaeval Latin isn't like that of any other period; he doubts he's deciphering it properly – Pierce, basically he wants to know if he can have access to your English translation.

I know how you feel about confidentiality. William wouldn't breach that. Can I do this?

– Anna

Message: #428 (Anna Longman)
Subject: Ash
Date: 21/12/00 at 12.02 p.m.
From: Ngrant@   *format address deleted*
                             other details encrypted by
Anna –   *non-discoverable personal key*

Isobel's team are bringing up the Stone Golem.

I thought it would take months, but it seems it can be raised pretty damn fast when it looks like the Tunisian government might be about to take the opportunity away from us.

The sky is full of helicopters, and the military have a patrol ship on station. At the land-site, a lot of the local arrangements for food and transport have dried up. Colonel ██████████ arrived back there, far less jovial, and with far more men. Trucks all over the place. 'Perimeter security', he says. They haven't had any severe security problems in the last weeks, so why now? Why all these men in uniform, who don't care WHERE they put their feet?

Isobel says Minister ██████████ is becoming concerned about 'Western exploitation of local cultural resources'. Well, as a Westerner, I hardly expect to be popular in this part of the world, and I can see their point. But, Isobel signed a contract with the government when this expedition was first mooted, agreeing that no artefacts should be removed from Tunisian territory. What kind of a person do they think she is?

Cynicism might lead one to think this is all about who will gain financially, but I may be doing the Minister a disservice. Whether his concern is genuine or not – and I suspect it is perfectly genuine – what I can't see is any way of pointing out that this site's remains are not from HIS culture!

I have had to leave the translation. I have to be here when they bring up the Stone Golem.

You have my full permission to show this partial translation of
the Sible Hedingham ms to William Davies. If it helps Vaughan
Davies, then that would only be a small repayment for the debt of
scholarship we owe to him.

– Pierce

Message: #236 (Pierce Ratcliff)
Subject: Ash
Date: 21/12/00 at 01.07 p.m.
From: Longman@   *format address deleted*
                             Other details encrypted and
Pierce –   *non-recoverably deleted*

I'm worried. When I got back from East Anglia, I found that someone
had broken in and been through my personal files. And my hard disk.
When I got to the office this morning – same thing. And not like a
burglary. Too neat.

I think I would just have stayed puzzled if I hadn't phoned a
friend of mine. Yes, I'm in a fairly obscure area of academic
publishing, but I do have friends in investigative journalism.
He's one of them. His first reaction was, this must be some kind of
'security' thing.

I hadn't thought it through, before. The Middle East has been
nothing but terrorism and war for years; if you have found
something on the seabed that records say isn't there – my friend
suggests there are bound to be 'spooks'. People are bound to be
investigating, aren't they? Especially if the news is getting out.

Pierce, I KNOW this sounds alarmist. But it wasn't just somebody
breaking in and trashing my place. Depending on how you feel about
being interviewed by security people, if you've been keeping
copies of these messages, you might want to wipe your (or Isobel's)
disk. And if you've got hardcopies, shred them.

I don't usually keep copies of my mail, I don't have the disk
space, but I do usually keep a paper copy in a file. Because you were
so concerned about academic confidentiality, I've been even more
careful; hence public-key encryption of the actual messages. In
fact, I had taken the paper copies and floppy disk in a folder down
to the sheltered accommodation in Colchester with me, yesterday,
thinking I might need them to refresh my memory if Vaughan did
finally say something – you know I'm not an academic myself. So I
still have them.

I'm putting them in store, somewhere safe. If this IS something
official, then they can come to me officially, with a warrant. Then
it's fine. But not before.

I'm going to talk to the MD in an hour, see what his position on
this is. He'd better stand by me on this one.

– Anna

Message: #430 (Anna Longman)
Subject: Ash
Date: 22/12/00 at 09.17 a.m. *format address deleted*
From: Ngrant@   *Other details encrypted by
                            non-discoverable personal key*

Anna –

We're out.
   Things have been so confused, I don't know if it's been on the
media, given Christmas will be taking over the UK – we're supposed
to be out of Tunisian territory completely now, they don't even
like us hanging about in offshore waters.
   I'm putting this out on the net to as many people as I can reach.
Talk to your media contacts. Kick up a fuss. They CAN'T shut this
site off from scientific excavation! They can't KIDNAP
archaeological evidence! It just isn't right: we have to know.
   On consideration, of course, we don't 'have' to. That is a
preoccupation very much of our time. 'Nothing must stand in the way
of the discovery of the truth.' In other parts of history, of
course, there are other priorities: 'nothing is as important as'
ideology, say, or commerce, or military force.
   GOD DAMN IT, I WANT TO KNOW. They can't do this to us!

– Pierce

Message: #240 (Pierce Ratcliff)
Subject: Ash
Date: 22/12/00 at 10.04 a.m.
From: Longman@   *format address deleted*
                            *Other details encrypted
                            and non-recoverably deleted*

Pierce –

Had you got the Stone Golem up from the ruins of Carthage? Where is
the messenger-golem from the land-site? Pierce, what is happening,
I can't do anything if I don't know the _facts_.

– Anna

----

format address deleted
Other details encrypted by
non-discoverable personal key

Anna –

Sorry, yes you need to know, too busy talking to every contact I
have, if there's no other pressure we can bring to bear, at least
let's have the academic community and the media on our side!

Isobel's team had barely STARTED their analysis of the Stone
Golem. When I got there, they had it in the holding tank; there was
an argument going on about some minor damage that had been done –
or not done – by the divers. It can't have been much more than two
hours after that when the Tunisian navy moved in and confiscated
everything. Everything apart from what Isobel and her people had
on their backs! They stripped the ship bare. They removed the
holding tank, and the Stone Golem.

I cannot BELIEVE this has happened. There was no need. I know
Isobel: she will have had no INTENTION of removing any artefacts
from Tunisian jurisdiction.

But there is one thing I can say without any possible
contradiction – I saw it with my own eyes.

When I first reached the Stone Golem in the holding tank, I was
quite literally speechless. Sound echoing off metal, light
rippling off water, all the sounds of a modern ship at sea – and
there, in the middle of it, in the tank, this great carved larger-
than-human figure. With its plinth, it must weigh tons; I have every
respect for the team who raised it from the seabed.

What I'd seen through the cameras didn't prepare me for seeing it
in reality. As you know, I'd seen it covered in debris, with a film
of silt over it from the ROVs moving around, and encrusted with
undersea life. By the time I got to the ship, a section had been
cleaned up, and Isobel herself was in the tank working on others.

The MACHINA REI MILITARIS. Sightless eyes staring. Hinged bronze
joints clustered thickly with verdigris. This much, as you know,
had been visible underwater, on camera. The whole of it wasn't
clear.

Now it is.

The face, the limbs, the plinth: the SHAPE of all of them was
clear on camera. But what we've been seeing has only been the
surface-encrustations. With the encrustations removed, it's
become possible to see the surface of the stone.

Some of it still IS stone. The team says it was all originally a
silicon-based conglomerate of some kind.

Ninety per cent of it is VITRIFIED silicon. Glass.

At the front, which is what we've been seeing on the image-
enhancers, the shape of the head and the front of the torso are

clear. Most of the rest of it, including the plinth, is melted.
Silt and sandstone fused into heavy, brittle glass. It has FLOWED.

   Silicon sand turns to glass if you put it under sufficiently high
temperatures. Imagine the strength of the lightning-discharge
that could have done this; a bolt that would have – that did, from
the underwater images – crack the building in which it stood wide
open.

   An electrical discharge powerful enough to sear the whole of this
artefact into vitrified sand. The internal structure melted into
impure, light-shattering, water-reflecting glass: I saw Isobel's
face reflected in it like a mirror.

   It IS the Stone Golem. It HAS been destroyed, in exactly the way
that the chronicle relates. Anna, this archaeological evidence
backs up this manuscript. The Sible Hedingham ms is our first
history.

   I can only pray that this is a temporary aberration on behalf of
the government. I am happy for any artefact to remain in Tunisia,
as long as Isobel's people have permission to carry on their
analysis. A silicon computer. Even a destroyed one. What we can
learn

Interruptions. More later.

– Pierce

Message: #241 (Pierce Ratcliff)
Subject: Ash
Date: 22/12/00 at 02.24 p.m.
From: Longman@

*format address deleted
other details encrypted and
non-recoverably deleted*

Pierce –

I'm worried I haven't heard from you. Where are you? Are you still
on the expedition ship? Mail me, phone me, something.

– Anna

Message: #447 (Anna Longman)
Subject: Ash
Date: 22/12/00 at 06.00 p.m.
From: Ngrant@

*format address deleted
other details encrypted by
non-discoverable personal key*

Anna –

Still on ship, but I'm having to coax my way to accessing
communications. The Tunisian patrol boat on station has been

1003

joined by two more. You have no IDEA how much this scares me. The
idea of being caught up in an actual 'incident' – I know, as a
biographer, one gets immersed in one's subject; this has cured me
of any idea I might have had that I could have lived Ash's life.

Isobel says the British Embassy here has been in contact to
suggest WE stop causing trouble. God help me, I know the
Mediterranean is a sensitive area, but that's a bit rich! I wish I
had a contact in the Foreign Office. Knowing several advisory
professors on security affairs may help, but it's going to take
time for me to get in touch with them.

Tami's colleague James Howlett informs me that the net traffic on
this subject is now being 'monitored', and to make sure I am always
encrypted. I suppose he knows. I suppose it will be. What HAPPENED?
Something that to me is an interesting matter of high physics is
apparently making governmental agencies (as Howlett put it) 'shit
themselves stupid'!

Please, can you take time to talk with Vaughan Davies again, if
he can talk at all? I am mentally putting together a provenance for
the Sible Hedingham ms. There could be a connection between the ms,
Hedingham Castle, the Earls of Oxford, and Ash's connection with
the thirteenth earl, John de Vere. Vaughan Davies might shed light
on this.

Far more crucially, for the immediate present – in his Second
Edition, he promised us an Addendum, detailing the link between
the 'first history' and our present day. He never published it
before he disappeared. I think the time has come when I have to
know what his theory is.

Plainly, we have to face the possibility now that reality did
fracture in or about the beginning of the year 1477. Equally
plainly, it is possible that fragments of that prior history have
existed in ours, becoming gradually less and less 'real' as the
universe moves on from the moment of fracture. I can accept this,
and so can the theoretical physicists: both Burgundy and the Wild
Machines obliterated in some catastrophic 'miracle', the
Visigoths and the Wild Machines completely, Burgundy leaving a
dream of a lost country behind it.

What is more difficult to accept, but is undeniably the case,
given the underwater site, is that the universe is STILL changing.
Reading what Vaughan Davies wrote in 1939, it seems to me that he
knew this, then, and had developed a theory about why it is
happening.

I want to know what it is. HIS theory may be right or wrong, but
I don't have a theory at all! If I have to fly back from here, I
will be asking you if William Davies will give permission for me to
visit his brother.

– Pierce

```
----------------------------------------------------------------
```

Message: #244 (Pierce Ratcliff)
Subject: Ash
Date: 22/12/00 at 06.30 p.m.
From: Longman@   *format address deleted*
                                          other details encrypted and
Pierce -   *non-recoverably deleted*

Please be CAREFUL. You never think it will happen to someone you
know. It only takes some trigger-happy madman, a soldier with a
rifle, by the time the governments apologise, it's too late. I don't
want to turn on satellite news and watch a bulletin telling me
you've been killed.

- Anna

```
----------------------------------------------------------------
```

Message: #246 (Pierce Ratcliff)
Subject: Ash
Date: 23/12/00 at 09.50 p.m.
From: Longman@   *format address deleted*
                                          other details encrypted
Pierce -   *and non-recoverably deleted*

Damn: still no mail from you. I hope no news is etc.

   There isn't much of a media fuss yet. It was well-timed, thinking
about it; everyone's caught up in pre-Christmas frenzy here.

   Weekend traffic's difficult (Christmas falling on the Monday),
but I went down to Colchester again. I don't know what kind of a
shock it would have to be to make a person wipe out all their
memories after the age of fifteen. Profound trauma, William says.
Perhaps fifteen was the last time Vaughan was happy. I hate to think
what reduced him to this state.

   William and I are taking it in turns to read your translation of
the Sible Hedingham manuscript aloud to him. William is
optimistic. I'm not sure Vaughan's taking it in. But William's the
medical man, after all.

   I intend to go down again tomorrow, and spend as much time over
Christmas as I can with them, with Vaughan in the hospital, doing
intensive reading. I'll watch the news broadcasts, and monitor e-
mail. You can always reach me at work or home e-mail (which is
████████████████), or you can phone, if you can get a line. My
number is ████████████.

- Anna

```
----------------------------------------------------------------
```

Message: #247 (Pierce Ratcliff)
Subject: Ash
Date: 24/12/00 at 11.02 p.m.
From: Longman@

format address deleted
other details encrypted and
non-recoverably deleted

Pierce –

We have our breakthrough.

It was a bit of a shock. The doctors have taken William into hospital here overnight for observation. He's a rotten patient, but I think retired medical men often are. I've been zipping around between his ward and the neurological ward where Vaughan is; I'm completely worn to a frazzle; but I don't think William's in any real danger now.

It just breaks my heart to see him there. When he's awake, he's a sharp old man; when you see him asleep in a hospital bed, you can see how frail he is. I guess I've come to like him a lot. I never knew either of my grandfathers.

Vaughan is quiet now. I'm not sure if he's still under sedation or sleeping naturally.

I'm in the waiting room, sitting among the sad Christmas decorations, typing on my notebook-portable, drinking the appalling black coffee that comes out of the machine. Every so often the nurses come around and give me _that look_. I'll have to go soon, to drive back through the Christmas Eve traffic, but I don't want to leave until the doctors give William the final OK.

It's not like they have any other next of kin.

William was the one reading when it happened. It was during part of the Fraxinus manuscript, the section on what happens to Ash in Carthage. He reads very well. (I have _no_ idea whether he thinks this is 'history' or complete rubbish.) Vaughan was listening, I think, although it's been difficult to tell. He has a lean face, and I think must have been good-looking when he was a young man. Very arrogant. No, not arrogant; it's a look I've seen in old pre-war movies, a kind of outrageous confidence, you don't see it any more. An English class thing, I guess. And Vaughan thinks he's fifteen. Has there ever been a rich boy that age who didn't think he was God's gift?

All of a sudden, that face sort of _crumpled_. I was watching, and it was like sixty years just dropping down on him, like a weight. He said, 'William?' As if William hadn't visited him every day. 'William, may I beg you to pass me a mirror?'

I wouldn't have done it, but it wasn't up to me. William passed him a mirror from the bedside cabinet. I got up to call a nurse – I was half expecting Vaughan Davies to go into hysterics. Wouldn't you? If you thought you were fifteen, and saw the face of a man in his 80s?

All he did was look at himself in the mirror and nod. Once. As if it confirmed something he had already thought. He put the mirror down on the bed and said, 'Perhaps a daily paper?'

It staggered me, but William reached over and picked up a paper left by one of the other patients. Vaughan examined it very carefully – what I think, now, is that he was puzzled because it was a tabloid, not a broadsheet – and glanced at the headlines, and the masthead. He said two things: 'No war, then?' and 'I am to assume victory was ours, or else I should be reading this in German.'

I don't think I took in the next few sentences. William was asking questions, I know, and Vaughan was answering in this amazed tone, a 'why are you asking me all these stupid questions?' voice, and I remember just thinking, Vaughan doesn't like his brother very much. What a shame, after sixty years.

The next thing I can remember is Vaughan saying testily, 'Of course I wasn't injured in the bombing. What on earth would make you think such a thing?' He'd picked up the mirror and was studying himself again. 'I have no scars. Where did you get yours?'

If he'd been my brother I would have slapped him.

William ignored it, and went through the neurological report stuff, and told him he'd been locked up in a home for years – which isn't something I'd have sprung on somebody, but he still knows his brother, even after all these years, because Vaughan just _looked_ at him, and said, 'Really? How curious.' And, in a voice like I'd just crawled out from under a rock, 'Who is this young person?'

'This young lady,' William says, 'is assisting the man who is rewriting your mediaeval book.'

I expected him to go nuclear at that point, especially as William wasn't being untactful by accident. No wonder those two didn't live under a family roof. I braced myself for a screaming row. It didn't come.

Vaughan Davies picked up the tabloid paper again and held it at arm's length. It took me several seconds to realise he was looking for the date, and that he couldn't read the small print. I told him what date it was.

Vaughan Davies said, 'No. The month is July, and the year, nineteen forty.'

William leaned over and took the paper away from him. He said, 'Rubbish. You never were unintelligent. Look around you. You have been in a traumatised state, conceivably since July nineteen forty, but it is now over sixty years from that date.'

'Yes,' Vaughan says, 'evidently. I was not in a state of trauma, however. Young woman, you should warn your employer. If he continues to pursue his researches, he will end where my researches brought me, and I would not wish that upon my worst enemy – had I one yet alive.'

He was looking mildly pleased at this point. It took William to point out to me, in a whisper, that Vaughan had just realised that he'd probably outlived all his academic rivals.

William then said, 'If you weren't in a state of trauma, where have you been? Where is it that you suspect Doctor Ratcliff will end up?'

As you know, the paperwork following Vaughan Davies around the asylums is intact. He _is_ William's brother. The family resemblance is too close for anything else. I mean, we _know_ where he's been. I wondered where he _thought_ he'd been. California? Australia? The moon? To be honest, if Vaughan had said he'd stepped out of a time machine – or even walked back into our 'second history' after visiting your 'first history', I don't think I'd have been surprised!

But time travel isn't an option. The past is not a country we can visit. And the 'first history' doesn't exist any more, as you say. It was overwritten; wiped out in the process.

If I've understood it, the truth is much less exciting, much more sad.

'I have been nowhere,' Vaughan said. 'And I have been nothing.'

He didn't look sharp any more, the acidic expression was gone. He just looked like a thin old man in a hospital bed. Then he said impatiently, 'I have not been real.'

Something about it, I can't explain what, it was utterly chilling. William just stared at him. Then Vaughan looked at me.

He said, 'You seem to have some apprehension of what I mean. Can it be that this Doctor Ratcliff of yours has replicated my work to that degree?'

All I could do was say, 'Not real?' For some reason, I thought he meant that he'd been dead. I don't know why. When I said that, he just glared at me.

'Nothing so simple,' he said. 'Between the summer of nineteen forty and what you claim to be the latter part of the year two thousand, I have been – merely potential.'

I can't remember his exact words, but I remember that. Merely potential. Then he said something like:

'What is unreal may be made real, instant by instant. The universe creates a present out of the unaligned future, produces a past as solid as granite. And yet, young lady, that is not all. What is real may be made unreal, potential, merely possible. I have not been in a state of trauma. I have been in a state of unreality.'

All I could do was point at him in the bed. 'And then be made real again?'

He said, 'Mind your manners, young woman. It is impolite to point.'

That took my breath away, but he didn't stay vinegary for long. His colour got bad. William rang the bell for the nurse. I stepped back and put my hands behind me, to try and stop aggravating him.

He was grey as a worn bed-sheet, but he still carried on talking.
'Can you imagine what it might be like, to perceive not only the
infinite possible realities that might take shape out of universal
probability, but to perceive that you, yourself, the mind that
thinks these thoughts – that you are unreal? Only probable, not
actual. Can you imagine such a sensation of your own unreality? To
know that you are not mad, but trapped in something from which you
cannot escape? You say sixty years. For me, it has been one infinite
moment of eternal damnation.'

Pierce, the trouble is, I CAN imagine it. I know you need to get
Isobel's theoretical physicists over here to talk to Vaughan
Davies, because I don't have a scientific understanding. But I can
imagine it enough to know what made him go grey.

I just stood there, staring at him, trying to stop a hysterical
giggle or a shudder, or both; and all I could think was, No one ever
asked Schrodinger's Cat what it felt like while it was in the box.

'But you're real _now_,' I said. 'You're real _again_.'

He leaned back on the pillow. William was fussing, so I bent down
to try and soothe him, and Vaughan's forearm hit me across the
mouth. I've never been so shocked. I stood up, about to rip off a
mouthful at him, and he hadn't hit me, his eyes had rolled up in his
head, and he was fitting, his arms and legs jerking all over the
place.

I ran for a nurse and all but fell over the one coming in the
door.

That must have been a couple of hours ago now. I wanted to get it
down while it was clear in my memory. I may be out by a few words,
but I think it's as close to the truth as I can get.

You can say it's senile dementia, or you can say he might have
been a boozy old dosser for years and rotted his brain, but I don't
think so. I don't know if there are words for what happened to him,
but if there are, he's got doctorates in history and the sciences,
and he's the person best qualified to know. If he says he's existed
in a state of probability for the past sixty years, I believe him.

It's all part of what you said, isn't it? The Angelotti
manuscript vanishing, being classified as history, then Romance,
then fiction. And Carthage coming back, where there was no seabed
site before.

I wish Vaughan had stayed with it long enough to tell me why he
thinks he's 'come back' now. Why NOW?

I've been thinking, sitting here. If Vaughan was going to 'come
back', it's _possible_ for him to have had amnesia. The same way
that it's _possible_ for him to have vanished without trace. So
this is just a different possible state of the universe. This is
what he is, now, here – but before 'now' was made concrete, it was
possible for other things to have happened to him. His
disappearance could have meant anything.

It's one thing to talk about lumps of rock and physical artefacts coming back, Pierce. It's another thing when it's a person.

I feel as if nothing under my feet is solid. As if I could wake up tomorrow and the world might be something else, my job would be different, I might not be 'Anna', or an editor; I might have married Simon at Oxford, or I might have been born in America, or India, or anywhere. It's all _possible_. It didn't happen that way, it isn't real, but it _might_ have happened.

Like ice breaking up under my feet.

I am frightened.

Vaughan's old, Pierce. If people are going to talk to him, it ought to be as soon as possible. If he becomes conscious again, and he's alert, I will ask him about his theory that you mentioned. I'll have to go by the medical advice. I'll ask him how he got the Sible Hedingham manuscript. Maybe tomorrow – no, it's holiday season.

Contact me. WHAT DO YOU WANT TO DO ABOUT THIS?

– Anna

Message: #248 (Pierce Ratcliff)
Subject: Ash
Date: 25/12/00 at 02.37 a.m.
From: Longman@   *format address deleted*
                            Other details encrypted and
Pierce –   *non-recoverably deleted*

Did you get my last message?

Could you get in contact with me, just to reassure me?

– Anna

Message: #249 (Pierce Ratcliff)
Subject: Ash
Date: 25/12/00 at 03.01 a.m.
From: Longman@   *format address deleted*
                            Other details encrypted
Pierce –   *and non-recoverably deleted*

Are you downloading your mail? Are you reading your mail? Is anybody reading this?

– Anna

```
Message:     #250 (Pierce Ratcliff)
Subject:     Ash
Date:        25/12/00 at 07.16 a.m.
From:        Longman@
```
format address deleted
other details encrypted and
non-recoverably deleted

Pierce –

These messages must be stacking up. For God's sake answer.

– Anna

```
Message:     #251 (Pierce Ratcliff)
Subject:     Ash
Date:        25/12/00 at 09.00 a.m.
From:        Longman@
```
format address deleted
other details encrypted
and non-recoverably deleted

Pierce –

I have been phoning the British Embassy. I _finally_ got through. No
one there is prepared to give me any information. The university
switchboard is closed, I can't get a contact number for Isobel
Napier-Grant. I can't get through to you. No news station wants to
know: it's the holiday. Please ANSWER ME.

– Anna

Transmission of following document file LOSTBURG.DOC
recorded at 09.31 a.m., 25/12/00.
No additional transmissions received at this time.

PART SIXTEEN

26 December AD 1476–5 January AD 1477

Lost Burgundy[1]

I

"And now," Ash said, "you need to order *my* execution."

Light leaked through the unshuttered windows into the ducal chambers – the feast of Stephen dawning late, to a blistering cold. Freezing damp infested the air, penetrating any bare skin; draughts blew in around the shutters and hangings.

"Are you *sure* you hear them?" Florian persisted.

'IT REQUIRES NOTHING BUT TIME NOW: OUR TIME FAST APPROACHES—'

"Yes, I'm sure!" Ash banged her sheepskin mittens together, hoping for feeling in her numb fingers.

"Have you told anyone else yet? That the end of the *machina rei militaris* means nothing?"

"No. I didn't want to spoil their party."

"Ah." Florian attempted a smile. "*That's* what it was. I thought it was a night attack by the Visigoths . . ."

Her colour altered, and she leaned one arm up against the wall for support, the thin grey light of the dawn illuminating her. The velvet hem of her gown trailed across bare flagstones – no rushes, now. She did not wear the hart's-horn crown, but the carved Briar Cross hung at her breast, half-lost in her unpointed doublet and the yellow linen of her shirt. Over everything, she wore a great robe made from wolf-pelts, heavy enough to weigh down a man.

"You look rough," Ash said.

With the growing light, Ash saw that the wall against which the surgeon leaned was painted – richly, as becomes a royal Duke – with figures of men and women and tiny towns on hilltops. Each of the figures danced hand in hand with another: cardinal, carpenter, knight, merchant; peasant, tottering old man, pregnant girl, and crowned king. Bony hand in their hands, white skeletons led them off, all equal, into death. Florian del Guiz leaned her forehead against the cold stone, oblivious, and rubbed at her stomach under her furs.

"I spent half the night in the garderobe." An obvious recollection of the slaughter that had made her drink went across the tall woman's features. "We have to send my brother back to Gelimer today. With an answer that won't have us attacked before evening. Now *this* . . ."

Ash watched Florian pace down the chamber, further from the hearth around which – since it held the palace's remaining substantial fire – the Duchess was allowing her servants to huddle and sleep.

She forced her mind not to listen to the yammering triumphant whispers of the Wild Machines; followed.

"No—" Florian put up a hand. "*No*. Your execution would be as irrelevant as the Faris's." Her thin face relaxed into a smile. "Stupid woman. You spent time telling me why she shouldn't die. What about you? What's different?"

"Because it isn't her, it's me."

"Yes, I think I have realised that," the scarecrow-thin woman said ironically, and looked at Ash with warm eyes. "After an hour and a half of you going on at me."

"But—"

"Boss, *shut up*."

"It isn't her, it's me, and I don't need the Stone Golem—" Ash's voice changed.

"If I order your death, I've lost the Pucelle, 'the She-Lion of Burgundy', the Maid of Dijon—"

"Oh, fucking *hell*!"

"Don't blame me for your public image," Florian snapped, with asperity. "*As I was saying*. We need you. You told me the Faris was irrelevant; because Burgundy's bloodline has to survive way beyond her death. Now it has to survive beyond yours! I'm sorry that destroying the *machina rei militaris* didn't make a difference." Her expression altered. "God knows, I'm sorry about Godfrey. But. I need you in the field more than I need you dead."

"And this makes no difference?"

"I'm not going to order your death." Florian del Guiz looked away. "And don't get any stupid ideas about going out on to the field and getting the enemy to do it for you."

For all its high vaulted roof and pale stone, the ducal chamber pressed in on Ash with acute claustrophobia. She walked to the window and looked at the ice on the inside of it.

"You're running too great a risk," Ash said. "This city is on the verge of being overrun. If you're killed— You needed my sister for what she knows. There's a dozen commanders here as good as me!"

"But they're not the Pucelle. Ash, it doesn't matter what *you* think you are. Or if it's justified."

Florian came to stand beside her at the stone embrasure.

"You didn't come here expecting me to have you marched off and executed. You know I won't. You didn't come here for me to tell you to kill yourself." Her eyes slitted against the southern glare. "You came here for me to talk you out of it. For me to *order* you to live."

"I did not!"

"How long have I known you?" Florian said. "Five years, now? Come on, boss. Just because I love you doesn't mean I think you're *bright*. You want someone else to take responsibility for telling you to stay alive. And you think I'm dumb enough not to notice that."

Wind from the ill-fitting edges of the window bit into her. The sheepskin huke belted over armour and gown barely warmed her, no more than the coif over her shorn head, under her hood. Ash said, "Maybe it's just as well I can't love you the way you want. You're too smart."

Florian threw her head back and guffawed loudly enough to make the servants around the hearth stare down the chamber at them.

"What?" Ash demanded. "*What?*"

"Oh, gallant!" Florian spluttered. "Chivalrous! Oh – fuck it. I'll take it as a compliment. I'm beginning to feel sorry for my brother."

Bewildered, Ash repeated, "*What?*"

"Never mind." Florian, eyes glowing, touched Ash's scarred cheek with fingers as cold as frost-bitten stone.

No sensuality was transmitted by that cold touch. What Ash felt answering it, in herself – what stopped her speaking, except for a confused mutter – was a wrenching non-physical desire for closeness. She realised suddenly, *Agape.*[2] *Agape, Godfrey would call it: love of a companion. I want to give her trust.*

I trusted Godfrey, and look what happened to him.

"You'd better call people up here," Ash said, "and we'd better talk to them."

As Florian sent messengers, she scratched with mittened fingers at the ice on the inside of the glass, clearing a patch on the ducal window and peering out. Lemon-yellow, actinic: the sun just cleared the horizon, casting blue-white shadows on the peaked roofs of Dijon below. The valley beyond the walls lay thick with frost.

Long shadows fell away from the sunrise, into the west. Every turf hut, tent, and legion eagle put a blue-black silhouette across the frost. Out on the white brittle ground, men of the III Caralis were beginning to move around: foot units marching sluggishly towards the siege trenches, a squad of cavalry galloping across towards the eastern river and the bridge behind Visigoth lines.

Is that a deployment? Or are they just harassing us?

You could not see, from here, what lay in the dead ground between Dijon's north gate and the Visigoth siege-lines.

But I doubt they've cleared up yesterday's bodies. Why would they? Far worse for our morale to leave them there to look at.

With no particular hurry, the red granite façades of golem-machinery creaked towards the walls.

"Not an assault yet," Ash guessed. "He's just trying to provoke you into complaining they're breaking the truce."

Ash snapped her fingers for a page. A boy brought a white ash bowl, steaming with the mulled cider presented, by Dijon's vintners, in lieu of the wine they no longer had. When he had served the surgeon-Duchess, Ash took a bowl, welcoming the heat of it. She turned back to the window, nodding towards the distant encampment.

"We've got their commander. There's not much we don't know about them, at the moment," Ash said dispassionately. "Like, we know they can afford to gallop their cavalry. The Faris tells me they've got fodder to spare. Not that I'd do it on that ground, myself – must be rock-hard." She paused.

"If I were Gelimer, and *my* army commander had gone over to the enemy, I'd be running around now like a bull with its tail on fire, trying to remove any

[2] 'Agape', Greek: 'Charity'. Cf the New Testament.

weaknesses in my deployment before I attacked. So we've got a window of opportunity, before he can."

"Christ," Florian said behind her. "I have six thousand civilians in this city alone. I don't know what's happening in the rest of the country. I'm their Duchess. I'm supposed to *protect* them."

Ash looked away from the window. Florian was not drinking, only cupping her cold hands around the bowl. The scent of spices made her stomach growl, and Ash lifted her own bowl, and drank. She felt the warmth of it flood her body.

She wanted to put her arm around Florian's shoulders. Instead, Ash lifted her bowl in salute, giving her a grin that was an embrace.

"I know exactly what we do next," Ash said. "We surrender."

The wind took her breath away; so cold that her teeth hurt behind firmly closed lips. A north wind. Her eyes leaked water that froze on her scarred cheeks. Ash moved down off the north wall, into the faint shelter afforded by the walls of the Byward Tower.

"You're right." Florian spoke in clipped words. "No one's going – to overhear us. Not out there."

"The Wild Machines might hear me . . ." Ash's lips skinned back from her teeth in a grin. "*But who are they going to tell?*"

"Bad place – for a war council."

"Best place."

"Boss, you're a loony!"

"Yes – your Grace!" Ash steadied her sword against her armoured hip. "Fuck me backwards, it's cold!"

The pale stonework of the Byward Tower jutted above her head, perspective diminishing into an eggshell-blue sky. A few dead vines clung to the masonry, and a swallow's nest or two, under the machicolations. Jonvelle's men guarded the door, bills in their hands, the red Burgundian cross on their jacks. They stood watching their Duchess and their Captain-General, outside in the cold, as if the two women had taken leave of any senses they might ever have possessed.

Ash jerked her head clumsily. Florian walked with her, back out on to the wall, behind the merlons. She squinted out at the Visigoth lines, five hundred yards away.

"No one can get – within yards of us," Ash said. "The siege-engines are shooting at the main gate. Not here. We'll see if they move. This is bare wall – no one can sneak up – without being seen. I want nobody to overhear us talk."

"About Burgundy's surrender," Florian said, breathing into her cupped mittened hands. Her tone was one of muffled scepticism.

"You don't believe me."

"Ash." Florian raised her head. The wind had reddened her unhealthily yellow cheeks. Her nose ran clear drops. "I *know* you. I know exactly what you do – in a given situation. When we've been in – some utterly hopeless position – outnumbered – out-gunned – with no chance whatsoever – you *attack*."

"Oh, fuck. You do know me," Ash said, not displeased.

A clatter of armour, boots, and scabbards came from behind them. Ash turned. John de Vere and a dozen of his men were mounting the steps from Dijon's streets. As she watched, the English Earl ordered his men-at-arms to the Byward Tower, and ran out on to the wall without breaking step.

"Madam Duchess. My lord de la Marche will attend on you shortly." The Earl of Oxford clapped the palms of his gauntlets together. "He's much concerned. The river at the east of your city walls is iced over."

Florian, with a quick perception Ash appreciated, demanded, "Will it bear a man's weight?"

"Not yet. But it grows colder."

"Too fucking right it does," Ash winced.

Even with the visor up, there was little of de Vere's face to be seen within the opening of his armet. He had left his red, yellow and white livery with his men; stood as an anonymous knight in steel plate, faded blue eyes staring out at the surrounding river valley and the encamped legions. Ash, herself in armour, was as anonymous. She looked at Florian, cloaked and hooded, swathed in wolf-furs.

"We shouldn't risk her out here," she said to de Vere, as if the surgeon did not exist. "But it's possible the Visigoths have got spies into the city. I don't want servants or soldiers overhearing us. No one. Not a beggar; not a madman; *nothing*."

"Then you're safe enough, madam. Nothing in its right mind would be up on these walls today!"

"For the love of Christ!" Florian hugged her arms and her wolf-fur cloak around herself, teeth chattering. "Get this – over with. Quick!"

"Let's walk." Ash started down the walkway behind the battlements, in the shelter of the brattices, towards the White Tower. A shout from behind made her turn. The Burgundian guards stepped back to allow two more cloak-muffled figures up on to the wall.

One – she recognised his old candle-wax-covered blue woollen cloak – was Robert Anselm. The other, his bearded face pale in the cold, proved to be Bajezet of the Janissaries. Impassive despite the cold, he bowed to the Duchess, murmuring something quietly courteous.

"Colonel," Florian gasped. She glared at Ash. "You want to wait for de la Marche – or can I get on with it now?"

"Wait." As they turned to walk along the wall, gasping, Ash fell in beside Robert Anselm, and nodded at the Janissary commander. "Roberto, ask him what shape his horses are in."

Anselm frowned momentarily, then addressed the Turkish commander.

The Turk came to a dead halt on the icy flagstones, waved his arms, and shouted an explosive negative. He continued to shout, red-faced.

"Plainly Turkish for 'not *my* fucking horses'!" Florian grinned and turned, putting her back to the wind, and began to walk backwards in front of Ash. "He thinks we want to eat them."

"I *wish*. Robert, tell him it's a serious question."

Bajezet ceased to shout. Explanations in halting Turkish took them to the end of the walkway, and the men guarding the White Tower. The brattices cut some of the force from the wind.

Beyond the White Tower, the wall was shored up with forty-foot planks; half-burned hoardings hanging off the battlements. *Weak spot*, Ash thought.

"He says his men's horses are not in good condition, because they're not being well fed." Robert Anselm, with no change of tone, added, "They could get fed. To us."

"Does he think he can gallop them?"

"No."

Ash nodded thoughtfully. "Well. We won't be out-running anyone on them, then . . ."

Curious eyes watched them from both ends of the walls, now. Ash smiled to herself. *If I was a grunt, and the city commanders were holding a private council of war up on the wall, I'd be looking at them . . . I always used to think the bosses must be cooking up something remarkably stupid, when I watched something like this.*

Now I just wish that someone else was taking the decisions.

"Shall I send another man for my lord de la Marche?" Anselm gritted.

"Not yet. He'll be on his way."

The Turkish commander pointed over the walls and said something. Ash looked as they passed between two brattices; saw no particular movement in the enemy camp. "What's his problem, Robert?"

"He says it's cold." Anselm hunched his shoulders, as if in emphatic agreement. "He says it's cold other places, and it's dark."

"What?"

Florian, walking shoulder to shoulder between Ash and de Vere, looked across at the Janissary. "Ask Colonel Bajezet what he means. And just tell me what he *says*, Roberto, okay?"

Ash caught sight of red-and-blue liveries below. She interrupted, "Here's de la Marche, at last."

Olivier de la Marche strode up on to the battlements, signalling his men away. He crossed the icy flagstones with deliberate haste, and bowed to Florian del Guiz.

Bajezet, with Robert Anselm murmuring in his ear, said through that interpreter: "There is nowhere, Woman Bey, for any of us to go."

"What do you mean, Colonel?" Florian spoke directly to the Turkish commander, and not to Anselm. When she listened to the answer, it was Bajezet's face that she watched.

"The Colonel says he saw 'terrible things', on his way here. The Danube frozen. Fields of ice. People frozen in the fields, left to lie there. Nothing but dark." Robert Anselm stumbled in his speech; checked something with the Janissary, and finished: "There are deserted villages from here to Dalmatia. People living in caves, burning the woods for fire. Some cities have been razed through trying to keep fires – bonfires – burning twenty-four hours a day."

"There is still no sun?" Florian asked Bajezet.

"He says, no. He says, he saw frozen lakes. Beasts and birds dead in the ice.

Only the wolves grow fat. And ravens and crows. In some places, they had to detour around—" Robert Anselm frowned. "No. Don't get that one."

"It is possible he speaks of the processions," John de Vere said. "A thousand strong, madam. Some of them were burning Jews. Some were saving them. Many were in pilgrimage to the Empty Chair.[3] By far the most part of them, madam, were following rumour: coming towards the borders of Burgundy."

The Janissary Colonel added something. Robert Anselm translated: "They will find themselves competing for food with many more refugees."

Ash glanced behind her, up at the sky. It was an instinctive movement. Out of the corner of her eye, she saw Florian do the same.

A haze began to film the icy blue. The sun dazzled out of the south-east, blinding her to the roofs and towers of the city. The icy wind drew tears from her eyes. Ash began to move again. The men moved with her. The tall woman remained standing on the spot.

Following her gaze, Ash saw that she was staring at the ranks of tents and earth-walled barracks, stretching neatly out along the roads of the Visigoth camp; at the stacked rocks for the trebuchets, the horses neighing from each legion's horse lines, and the thousands of armed men, gathering now at their bake-houses and camp-ordinaries for morning rations.

"They're expecting Fernando back. We have fewer and fewer choices," Florian said. "And no time to make them."

John de Vere came to a halt, rubbing his hands together with a click of metal. "Madam," he announced, "you are cold."

Not waiting for an answer, he raised his voice in a flat English bellow. Before a minute passed, two of his men-at-arms came out on to the battlements. They carried between them, on poles, an iron brazier; and trotted to set it down before the Earl of Oxford. One of the men fed it: flickering heat passed over the glowing red surface of the coals.

"This talk will take time," John de Vere said. "Security is essential, madam, but do not freeze your high command to death."

The morning advanced. Spiced cider was brought out, and dark bread; and they stood huddled around the brazier, mugs clasped between their hands, arguing every possible permutation of a city, between two rivers, surrounded by fifteen thousand foot and horse, and siege-engines. Attack across a frozen river? Break out and run – across a countryside full (de la Marche indicated) of Visigoth outriders, spies, and light cavalry reconnaissance? Spirit away the Burgundian Duchess – and lose any hope of support from Turks, Germans, French, English?

"Edward will not come in," John de Vere said grimly, at that point. "York thinks himself safe behind the Channel. I am all the Englishmen you will have at your command, madam Duchess."

"More than enough," Florian agreed, sipping at the spiced cider. Although she looked decidedly ill, she grinned at him.

By the fourth hour of the morning,[4] the sun had risen in the southern sky to a point where it illuminated all the land around Dijon: the freezing rivers, the

---

[3] Rome?
[4] 10 a.m.

valley full of tents and marching men, the puffs of smoke from the sakers,[5] deliberately breaking the conditions of the truce; the frost-shrouded hills and the wildwood, far to the north.

I've heard all these arguments, Ash thought. Most of them twice.

She kept her mind closed, deliberately did not listen in her soul. The white-blue morning sky, and Dijon's cone-roofed towers, dazzled her vision. Still, even with the blast of the wind behind her – face to the coals, back to the cold – a part of her attention remained directed inwards. At a subliminal level, multiple inhuman voices whispered:

'SOON. SOON. SOON.'

"I know," she said aloud. Bajezet and Olivier de la Marche were (with Anselm's help) arguing; they did not break off for a moment. De Vere looked at her curiously.

Florian said, "I know that look. You've got something."

"Maybe. Let me think."

Forget the *machina rei militaris*. Forget that not having it at all is different from it being there if my willpower fails. Remember that I've been doing this stuff all my life.

It fell together in her head, with all the determinism and progression of a chess game: *if we do this, then that will happen; but if that happens, and we do this, then this other thing—*

She gripped Florian's arm, burying her hand wrist-deep in soft wolf's fur. "Yeah. I've got something."

The tall woman beamed down at Ash. With no trace of cynicism, she said, "And without your *machina rei militaris*, too."

"Yeah. Without that." A slow beam spread over Ash's features; she couldn't stop it. "Yeah . . ."

Florian said, "So tell me. What have you got?"

"In a second—" Ash put her hand on the merlon and vaulted over into the hoarding. The wooden floor of the brattice echoed hollowly under her feet as she loped up towards the Byward Tower; back down again. The freezing wind cold in her face, she even gripped a beam and put her head down through one of the gaps, scanning the hundred feet of wall below for ropes, for ladders, for any shadow of movement.

Nothing.

"Okay." She hauled herself back through one of the crenellations. "Let's take it from the top, shall we?"

The wind left her gasping for breath, and shivering under huke and cloak, but she lost no authority. She paused a tactful second for an acknowledging wave of the hand from Florian.

"Okay," Ash went on. "We're here. Outside, there's the better part of fifteen thousand troops. The Faris's men. Plus Gelimer's two new legions. And there's friction between the two of them."

De Vere and de la Marche nodded in unison; both men obviously having had the experience of being joined by cocksure fresh troops after three months of occupying muddy trenches and bombarding impregnable walls.

[5] Small cannon.

"*Fifteen thousand*," Florian repeated, through her gloved hands, clasped over her mouth against the bitterness of the cold.

"And we have eighteen hundred men of the Burgundian army; the Lion's three hundred and eighty, less gunners; and five hundred Janissaries." Ash could not help laughing at the expression on the tall woman's face. "We know – about their deployment. Gelimer's two legions north. Between the rivers. Faris's men mostly – east and west – on the river banks."

The men had moved closer together, unconsciously; shoulders blocking the wind, the group in a huddle under a brightening sky. John de Vere, Earl of Oxford, said thoughtfully, "I had considered, madam, that we *can* cross the river to attack. Bajezet's Janissaries could swim their horses across. This ice, I think, is an end to that plan, unless it will bear the beasts' weight."

"And what would they do when they got there?"

"Nothing but cut up his rear echelon, madam."

Ash nodded impatiently. "I know: that doesn't win us anything. It fucks Gelimer around, it doesn't lift the siege, and it gives him all the excuse he needs today to flatten us."

The Turkish commander, after an interchange with Anselm, said something which his interpreter rendered as: "You seriously expect to lift this siege?"

"We're on last rations. Civilians are sick. If we're going to do anything, it has to be before we're too weak." Ash reached out, grabbing Florian's arm on one side, de Vere's on the other. "Let's not lose sight of the objective. Leaving aside our gracious Duchess—"

"Fuck you too," Florian commented.

"—what do we need to do? We need to make the King-Caliph look weak. We need to do something so that his allies abandon him – and join Burgundy. We need to look strong. We need to win," Ash said.

Olivier de la Marche stared at her. "'Win'?"

"Look. There's no reinforcements coming for us. We can give in. Or we can wait – and we won't have to wait long! Make them come in and fight us through the streets, today or tomorrow. We'll maul them. But we'll lose. Either way, they'll execute Florian." Ash spoke in a pragmatic tone. "Look at the situation. There's fifteen thousand men out there. We're two and a half thousand. That's us outnumbered over five to one!"

She grinned at Florian.

"You're right. There's only one thing we can do. We attack."

"I thought we were surrendering!"

"Ah. We *say* we're going to surrender. We're going to send an envoy out, and ask the King-Caliph Gelimer to arrange a formal surrender, and negotiate the conditions under which we give Dijon up to him." Ash smiled at Florian. "We're *lying*."

A slight frown crossed the Earl of Oxford's face. "It is against the rules and customs of war."

Olivier de la Marche was nodding. "Yes. It is treachery. But my men will remember Duke John *Sans Peur* [6] on the bridge at Montereau. The French did not suffer for their treachery, since it was successful. We are in no position here

---

[6] 'Without fear'.

to be more proud than a Frenchman."

"We *are* in desperate straits," John de Vere agreed mildly.

Ash snuffled back a laugh. She wiped her nose on her cloak. The wind penetrated wool, metal and skin; cold sank down into her bones. She moved, stiffly, from foot to foot; attempting to warm up.

"It looks hopeless." She grinned toothily. "It *is* hopeless. It looks hopeless to the Sultan. And to King Louis. And to Frederick of Hapsburg. Can you imagine – what will happen – if we win? One bold stroke – and Gelimer doesn't have any allies."

"And we don't have our lives!" Florian snapped. She was hitching herself up and down, toe and heel, in front of the brazier, attempting to find warmth in movement. Ash ignored the surgeon-Duchess's asperity.

"Most of their men – Gelimer's legions – are at the north side. Between the two rivers. They can get their other men up there. But it'll take time. So we don't face – more than ten thousand."

"You're going to get everybody killed," Florian stated.

"Not everybody. Just one person." Ash prodded the surgeon-Duchess with a completely numb finger. "Listen to this. What happens if *Gelimer* dies?"

There was a silence.

Florian, with a slow, amazed, and growing grin, said, "Gelimer. You want us to attack the *King-Caliph*? Himself?"

Olivier de la Marche said, "The Faris claims her replacement – Lebrija – is a man fit only for *following* orders."

"Have to have another fucking election, wouldn't they?" Robert Anselm was nodding. "Maybe go back to Carthage. All the *amirs* – in-fighting—"

"There is no obvious candidate for Caliph," the Earl of Oxford said. "My lord Gelimer is not a man to welcome other powerful *amirs* in his court. He has weakened the influence of many. Madam, this idea is well thought on: take away their commander, and not only may you raise this siege, you may halt their crusade here for this winter – perhaps for all time."

"They won't have any friends," Ash said dryly. "You watch Frederick and Louis leg it. And the Sultan come in – right, Colonel?"

Bajezet, translated, said, "It is not impossible, Woman Bey."

John de Vere said, "But, madam, Lord Gelimer is not a stupid man. Yes, we might make a sally out in force, hoping to overrun his men and kill him – but where is he? In what part of the enemy camp? Or has he withdrawn – to a town nearby? He will expect just such an attempt."

"He can expect what he likes: if two and a half thousand troops hit him, he's dog-meat." Ash shook her head vigorously, speaking over the rest of them, gasping with the tearing wind. "Listen to me. The Faris knows – troop dispositions – and guard rosters. She knew – she'd have to come over. Collected information. If we can do it – before things can be changed – we can get spies out – and back in again. We can find Gelimer's household – without him knowing, and moving it again. My guess is, it's to the north there. He needs an eye on his troops."

"God's *teeth*!" John de Vere said.

Surveying the enemy lines, beyond the walls, there was no sign of the King-

Caliph's standard among the other eagles. Any of the finer pavilions and turf-roofed buildings might house him – *whichever is the warmer*, Ash thought cynically, letting Florian and de Vere and de la Marche stare north at the encamped Visigoth legions.

"It would need to be very fast," the Earl of Oxford said thoughtfully. "And if he is on that ground, you would find it difficult to get a great number of troops out of the north-east or north-west gates in time. Impossible. They would be on us before we could deploy out of the bottleneck."

"I know how to do that," Ash said.

She spoke with a confidence that made them ignore her chattering teeth, and the fact that she hugged herself, shivering violently in the bitter wind. The advancing sun dappled a pale gold over Dijon's white walls. The frost on the battlements did not melt.

"I know how to get the troops out there," Ash repeated. She looked at Florian. "It's St Stephen's day, it isn't twenty-four hours since the Faris came over to us. Whatever we're going to do, we've got to at least get *intelligence* collected quickly." She snatched a breath of freezing air. "Some weaknesses Gelimer can't alter. He can't alter his weak units – but he can move them. He needs to think there's no hurry, we're surrendering. We need time to prepare for this. And we need him *not* to think he's our target."

Florian chuckled, a little hoarse and breathless. She held out her hands to the brazier. "He's our target. Yes. We're surrounded by fifteen thousand men – so we're going to attack their leader. *Perfect* logic, boss!"

"It is. It's why they want *you*. Cut off the head, and the body dies." Ash halted. "Look, if we do this, that's it: it hangs on this. Once we're outside, if we lose, they come in and trash this city."

The surgeon-Duchess said frankly, "So where are you planning on putting me? Down in some deep dungeon where they won't find me? Because they will."

"They can attack the city even while we attack them," Olivier de la Marche cut in. "If the opportunity were seen, they would send a legion in while we fought on the outside. Then we have lost – her Grace being dead – everything."

"I've got an answer for that, too," Ash said. "Are we agreed on this?"

They looked at each other.

In the end it was Florian who spoke. Wrapped in wolf-pelts, her dirty, hung-over face peering out of the grey fur, she swallowed back bile, frowned, and said, "Not until I've heard every detail six times. I don't buy a pig in a poke. And where does the Duchess feature in all this?"

"That," Ash said, smiling and nodding at the Janissary commander, "is where Colonel Bajezet and his horses come in. And," she turned to the Earl of Oxford, "your youngest brother, my lord. We need to speak with Dickon de Vere."

She did not arrive back at the company's tower until the second hour of the afternoon. She immediately called Ludmilla Rostovnaya and Katherine over.

"How many woman sergeants have we got in the company at present?"

Ludmilla frowned, glancing at her lance-mate. "Not sure, boss. About thirty, I think. Why?"

"I want you to get them together. Get all the spare polearms we've got – the Burgundians' as well, Jonvelle's expecting you. You're going to put some people through basic training."

The Rus woman still frowned. "Yes, boss. Who?"

"The civilians, here. They're going to get basic instruction in how to defend the city walls."

"Green Christ, boss, *they can't fight*! They don't know how! It'll be a massacre."

"I don't think I asked for an opinion," Ash said. After a stern moment, she added, "There's a difference between dying defenceless, if we're overrun, and dying trying to take someone else with you. These people know that. I want you and the other women to teach them which end of a bill to hold, and how far away they should stand so they don't impale each other. That's all. You've got today."

"Yes, boss." The Rus woman, turning away, stopped and said, "Boss – why the women?"

"Because you're going to be training the men and women of Dijon. You may not have noticed, soldier, but they don't like soldiers. They think we're drunken, licentious, aggressive louts." Ash grinned at Ludmilla's expression of angelic innocence. "So. The women civilians will learn if they see women who can already do it. The men will learn because they won't have women out-doing them. Satisfied?"

"Yes, boss." Ludmilla Rostovnaya went off, grinning.

Ash's amusement faded, watching her go. *Civilians do not turn into militia overnight; even militia don't function until they've had a couple of fights. They're going to get slaughtered.*

Brutally honest, she thought, *Better them than men and women who can fight. I need them.*

"Boss?" Thomas Rochester slid in through the main door, the guards slamming it shut instantly behind the dark Englishman. A scurry of thin snow came in with him, and stayed, white and unmelted, on the flagstones. He said, "You'd better come, boss. The Turkish Janissaries are leaving the city."

"Good!" Ash said.

II

The cold was no less bitter up on the battlements of Dijon's north-east gate.

"Keep your fucking fingers crossed," Robert Anselm growled, standing beside her. He had the ends of his cloak wrapped around his arms, and the whole lot bundled across his body; his hood pulled down almost to his nose. Only his stubbled chin was visible.

The pale afternoon sun put her shadow across the ramparts. Ash shaded her eyes with her hand, gazing north at the rider and red crescent banner moving out into the no-man's-land between the city and the Visigoth lines. A second rider – on a borrowed Turkish mare – carried a yellow silk banner with the Blue Boar of the Oxfords on it.

"Well, if nothing else, this ought to convince them we're really going to surrender."

Anselm chuckled explosively at that. "Fucking right. Our last allies up the Swannee."

From behind her, down in the square behind the north-east gate, Ash heard the chink of tack and the creak of saddles; many hooves ringing as they shifted on iron-hard cobblestones. She looked down. The ochre gowns and pointed helmets of Bajezet's Janissaries dizzied her with their uniformity. The few Englishmen – de Vere's household troops, his brothers, and Viscount Beaumont – stood out by virtue of their murrey and white livery.

Apprehension paralysed her. She said, "I can't believe we're doing this. I'm going to shit myself. Roberto, go tell them to quit."

"Bugger off, girl. This was your idea!" Robert Anselm threw his head up, shifting his hood back to see her, and she saw his pinched white face and red nose. He grinned at her. "Don't lose your bottle now. You said 'a bold stroke'."

With guards at the entrance to the battlements, and no one within fifty yards who could possibly hear them, Ash still spoke in a whisper.

"This isn't something to joke about. We're risking Florian. We're risking everything."

Equally softly, and with the appearance of calm rationality, Anselm said, "If it wasn't risky, the Visigoths would see it coming, wouldn't they? Thought that was your point."

"Fuck you," Ash said. "Shit. Oh, *shit*."

The sunlight cast his hood's shadow over his face, but she saw that there were beads of sweat on his forehead. She strode across and leaned on the crenellations, staring out at the riders.

A Visigoth eagle, shatteringly bright in the frosty air, left the enemy lines. Ash was not aware that she was holding her breath until she let it out, with a choking sound. No more than twenty men, Visigoth foot soldiers and horsemen, were leaving the camp; and they rode into the empty ground at the walk.

"Told you they wouldn't fire on the Turks."

"Yet," Anselm said.

"Christ up a Tree, will you shut *up*!"

Anselm said companionably, "Helps to have someone to yell at," and then leaned out over the merlon beside her, straining to see the riders meet. "That's it. Take it easy. Don't fuck up now."

Plainly, he was talking to the Turkish and English envoys. Ash shaded her eyes again. The frost lay white and heavy on the ground. Two hundred yards beyond the gate, the red crescent banner halted, and the Blue Boar; and one Visigoth rider came forward from beneath the eagle. The armed figures on horseback blurred in her vision.

"Don't you wish you were a fly on *that* horse?" she murmured. "I know what Bajezet's Voynik is saying. 'Burgundy is about to fall. My master the Sultan has no confidence in the Duchess. It is time that we returned to our own land.'"

Robert Anselm nodded slowly. "I don't reckon Gelimer wants a war with the Turk. Not *this* winter."

The shouting on the distant ground went on. A horse neighed once, in the square behind and below them. Ash shivered in the wind. She wiped her nose on her cloak; skin abraded by the wet wool.

The Visigoth rider approached the banners more closely, until Ash could not tell one man from another, only the coloured silks clear against the sky. The Visigoth troop of foot soldiers waited stolidly under their eagle.

"Know what my lord Oxford's saying, too," Robert Anselm said. He spoke without looking at Ash, all his attention on the meeting going on. "'I'm an exiled English Earl, Burgundy's none of my business. I'm going to find Lancastrian support with the Turk.'"

"It isn't unreasonable."

"Let's hope my lord Gelimer thinks so, too."

Ash put her left hand down, resting it on the grip of her sword. "Whatever he thinks, what's happening is that five hundred reasonably fresh troops are abandoning this city. Leaving Burgundy to twist in the wind."

Anselm peered at the riders. "They haven't killed them yet."

"Like you said, Gelimer doesn't want Mehmet's armies arriving over the border right now." Her hand tightened on the leather-bound wooden grip. "The best way to keep the Turks from challenging him is to flatten Dijon. He thinks he's going to do that anyway, but he'd sooner do it without flattening some of the Sultan's men in the process. I don't suppose he'll mind if the great English soldier-Earl leaves the vicinity with Bajezet . . ."

"Please God," Anselm said devoutly.

"I can't believe I'm doing something this risky. I must be out of my *mind*."

"All right. You are. Now shut up about it," Robert Anselm said.

Ash abruptly turned her back on the meeting going on in no-man's-land, and walked across to the other crenellations. She looked down into the square. No pigs rootled in the now-frozen mud, no dogs barked; there was no flutter of white wings from dovecotes.

Five hundred mounted Turkish archers sat their horses, in neat formation.

Close to the gate, almost under the battlements, Viscount Beaumont stood with the Earl of Oxford's brothers, by their war-horses. His laugh came up clearly through the chill air. Ash was conscious of an unreasoning urge to go down into the square and hit him. John de Vere's forty-seven men-at-arms stood a short distance off, with pack-ponies; the little remaining household kit packed on them. The Oxford brothers, as well as Beaumont, were in full plate. The two middle brothers, George and Tom, appeared to be having some debate over a broken fauld-strap on the youngest brother, Dickon's, armour.

Ash looked down at the third brother, a young man in polished steel plate, sword and dagger belted over his livery jacket. The winter sun gleamed on silver metal, on scarlet and yellow and white heraldry; and on the fair corn-coloured hair that fell to his shoulders. He carried his helmet under his arm, and was gazing down at the heads of Tom and George, where they bent over, examining the lower lame of his fauld: the skirt of his cuirass.

"Put the fucking helmet *on*," Ash whispered.

She could not be heard, sixty feet above the cobbled square. Dickon de Vere cuffed his brothers to one side, took a few long testing strides up and down the treacherous ground, banged a gauntlet against the offending laminated plate, plainly protesting that it was only an irritation, not a problem. Viscount Beaumont said something. The Earl of Oxford's youngest brother laughed ruefully, glancing up at the gate, and Ash was looking into Floria del Guiz's face.

Robert Anselm, quieter than a mouse's footfall, said, "She passed as a man, in a mercenary company, for five years. No one's going to spot her, girl."

Having been tall for a woman, Floria was – Ash thought – no more than a boy's height in her armour. She moved easily, the armour fitting well. High riding-boots, pointed to her doublet, disguised the fact that Richard de Vere's greaves would not fit her: two men's calf-muscles are rarely alike, and there is no room for error in the close fit of the plate.

Floria's gaze passed quickly back to Tom de Vere. She said something, obviously a joke: the men laughed. Ash could not tell whether the woman had seen her or not.

"I *don't* believe we're *doing* this."

"You want, I'll shut you in a garderobe till it's all over," Anselm offered, exasperatedly.

"That might be best." Ash rubbed at her face. The straps of her gauntlets rubbed her skin, tender in the bitter cold air. She sighed, deliberately turned her back, and walked across to the outside edge of the wall again. The Turkish flag, English banner, and Visigoth eagle still occupied the middle of the open ground.

"People see what they expect to see," she said steadily. "I'd be happier if her London-English was better."

"Look," Robert Anselm said. "Like you said to me, Dijon's going to fall now. It's going to happen. We attack them, they come in and flatten us; doesn't matter. Either way, we're fucked. And we're talking days, maybe hours."

"I told you that."

"Like I need telling," Anselm said, with a deep and caustic sarcasm. "Girl, if she stays here, she's dead. This way, she's out there in the middle of five hundred shit-hot troops that nobody wants to fuck with. For a whole multitude of reasons. You looking for 'safe'? There ain't no 'safe'. Having Gelimer think she's here when she isn't, that's as safe as it gets."

"Roberto, you're so fucking reassuring it ain't true."

In all the fuss of dressing her, swapping them; in all the high security, Ash thought, I never got to say goodbye. Fucking son of a bitch.

"How far did you tell them to go?" Anselm asked.

"De Vere will use his own judgement. If it's safe to camp a day's ride away, he will. The Visigoths won't be too surprised if they see the Sultan's troops hanging around to see how the siege turns out, so they can report home. If it looks dodgy, he'll keep them moving gradually east, for the border."

"And if it's really dodgy?"

Ash grinned at Anselm. "We won't be around to worry about it. If I was Oxford, in that case, I'd ride like shit off a shovel for the border, and hope I could get as far as the Turkish garrisons there." Her grin faded. "There'll still be a Duchess."

Out in the empty ground, the Visigoth rider wheeled away and galloped back towards the trenches. The Turkish interpreter and John de Vere moved – but were only walking their horses in the cold, Ash saw. The banners unrolled on the air, streaming and dropping as the wind dropped. White breath snorted from the horses' nostrils.

"Here he comes again."

She stood shoulder by shoulder with Robert Anselm, in the bitter cold of St Stephen's feast day, on the battlements of Dijon. One crow winged across the empty ground, calling, and dropped to pick and tear at something – red and mud-coloured – that flopped on the frost-bitten earth.

The Voynik interpreter and the Earl of Oxford rode back, picking their way between the bodies of the fallen, to the north gate. Trained, the horses did not shy; although Oxford's mount nickered at the stink.

Ash's hands knotted into fists.

It seemed seconds, not minutes, before the gates of Dijon opened, and the Turkish riders began to file out into the open. Cold shivers ran down her back, from neck to kidney, under her arming doublet; and she shuddered, once, before she made herself be calm. Tom and Viscount Beaumont rode out to join the Earl of Oxford, the youngest brother following with George de Vere and the household troops.

The crash echoed through gatehouse and gate alike, but Ash hardly registered the slam of the portcullis being lowered.

Under a clear sky, in the winter sunshine and cold, in borrowed armour, Floria del Guiz rode among the Janissaries of Sultan Mehmet II, away from Dijon.

She carried her helmet under her arm, as they all did; riding visibly bareheaded between Visigoth legions. Nothing at all female about her exposed face.

Ash strained to follow her, to watch her, one among many; and lost sight of her before they vanished among the Visigoth troops, on the path to the intact eastern bridge. A bridge over ice, now.

"Dear God," Ash said. "Dear God."

She turned, striding to the steps, and clattered down into the square below. Besides the Burgundian guards, a dozen or more of her own lance-leaders clustered there together, talking in low tones.

"Okay." Ash grinned at them: all confidence. She ignored and hid the churning in her guts. "*Now.* This is where we get our asses in gear, guys. Where's Master de la Marche? We'll give it an hour – and then send an envoy out to tell King-Caliph Gelimer exactly what he expects to hear."

Robert Anselm, on the heels of her remark, said, "Yeah? Who?"

*

III

"If we *don't* send Fernando del Guiz back out to negotiate the surrender," Ash said regretfully, to Olivier de la Marche, "Gelimer's going to think that's suspicious."

The sun of Stephen's day set in a wine-red blaze. Snow fell with the dusk, small flakes plunging into the black emptiness. Ash closed the shutters of the window in the ducal chambers. She momentarily leaned her forehead against the cold wood, listening inside herself.

'. . . LITTLE SHADOW, SOON TO BECOME AS OTHER SHADOWS. A GHOST; A THING THAT NEVER WAS. NOT EVEN A DREAM . . .'

Their power sucked at her, like a current in a swift river. Her forehead grew warm and damp with the effort of resisting. A smile curled at her mouth as she straightened up. "You don't give up, do you?"

'FEEL OUR POWER, GROWING—'

'SOON, NOW. SOON.'

She ignored the fear, walking back across the bare chamber.

"Not if someone of sufficiently high rank goes instead," Olivier de la Marche said, from beside the hearth. "It is my duty to go. I am of Burgundy, Captain-General."

"True. But Gelimer will be quite capable of torturing a herald to double-check they're telling the truth. I know that, personally." Ash gave the Burgundian champion a level look. "There are people who know too much, now, about what we plan to do. You're one of them: so am I. We don't go. It would make sense to send Fernando."

Except that he'll want to speak to his sister the Duchess before he does this.

The thought was plainly in de la Marche's mind as well as her own, and Anselm's. Even here, none of them voiced it. Ash looked across the ducal chamber at the figure in padded headdress, veil, and brocade robes. Her mouth twitched.

"I don't think Fernando *had* better talk to the Duchess."

By the remaining unshuttered window, Dickon de Vere gazed down into the darkness that hid the roofs of Dijon with the same expression he had been wearing since he had said – in an appalled tone, to John de Vere – *You want me to wear a* what?

"Put the lamp out, or close the shutter!" Robert Anselm growled at the young Englishman; and when Dickon turned a look of disbelief on him, added, "You want to give them a nice bright light to aim at, boy – your Grace?"

Dickon de Vere looked around for servants, found that there were none, and awkwardly reached out to fasten the shutter closed. Anselm slapped him on his velvet shoulder, companionably, as he walked back to the fire.

"Look, boss." Anselm glanced at Ash. "Gelimer knows you've got a grudge against your husband. String Fernando up. Send someone else out – with the body. Tell the King-Caliph you've settled a family matter. If Fernando's dead, he can't go shooting his mouth off about anything else. And whoever you send out can negotiate the surrender."

"I don't want him dead."

It came out before she thought about it. Anselm gave her a very deadpan look. De la Marche, not noticing, only nodded, and said, "He is our Grace the Duchess's brother; I am reluctant to put him to death without her word."

I suppose that's one way of looking at it.

"If we imprisoned him," she began.

Anselm interrupted. "If you shove 'Brother' Fernando del Guiz in a dungeon, there'll be talk. Likely as not, we'll have an informer find their way down there, and hear him say he ain't seen his sister recently. Shit hits the fan, then." He stabbed his finger at Ash. "Never mind what the doc would say. Have him killed."

The chill bit through the hearth's meagre warmth. Ash stretched stiffening limbs, and moved to walk a little on the bare floorboards, their creak the only sound.

"No."

"But, boss—"

"Bring me his priestly robes," Ash said. "We're not short of dead men. Are we, Roberto? Find a body about his size, and put the robes on it. Stick it in a cage. Hang it off the city walls – I want it to look like a man starving to death. Whoever we send out as herald can point out to Gelimer that I've settled matters with my ex-husband . . ." Her eyes narrowed. "You'd better mess the face up a bit. I wouldn't put it past them to have some golem-device that can see a face four hundred yards away."

Olivier de la Marche nodded. "And Fernando del Guiz himself?"

Ash stopped pacing. Her head came up. "Put him with the prisoners. Put him in with Violante and Adelize and the Faris. The Faris could do with a confessor – he's the only Arian priest we've got."

Let him have his chance to speak to her.

Robert Anselm said nothing, only nodding curtly, but she intercepted a look which she refused to respond to. After a moment, he said, "Then who're you going to send out there to have his nuts chopped off?"

Ash tapped her fingers against her armoured thigh. "Ideally, someone who's of sufficient high rank, and who knows nothing about the military side of things here."

Olivier de la Marche snapped his fingers. "I have him! The Viscount-Mayor. Follo."

"Richard Follo?" Ash thought about it.

De la Marche, with a knight's contempt for a man who does not fight for pleasure – or at least, for honour – shrugged. "Pucelle, isn't it obvious? He's a civilian. More to the point – he's a believable coward. If he is told we're surrendering, he'll negotiate in good faith that we are."

There speaks your nobleman.

"You mean, who'll miss him?" Ash said, and, surprised, felt more than a slight regret for scapegoating the man.

"Do that fat bastard good to walk out there!" Robert Anselm commented, to laughter from de la Marche, and a scowl from Dickon de Vere.

On the one hand, Richard Follo's a self-aggrandising, pompous trouble-maker. On the other hand, he's mayor; he's a civilian, with a family still living; we shouldn't lose any of our people, no matter how much of a pain they are . . .

Don't be too anxious to save him just because you don't like him.

"Of people of that rank," Ash said, "I suppose he's the least likely to be able to tell Gelimer anything useful. Olivier, will you have one of your heralds set up a meeting between Follo and – Sancho Lebrija, I expect it'll be, on their side?"

De la Marche nodded, stood, and walked towards the door.

"Where . . ." Ash tapped her fingers restlessly, and resumed pacing, always pacing; ignoring the three men in the room. "Where? *Where* is Gelimer?"

"You got him," Ash said.

She did not need the Welshman to say anything. Euen Huw wearing his smug expression told it all. The two Tydder brothers with him – Simon and Thomas in dirty Visigoth tunics, mail shirts underneath – looked equally pleased with themselves.

"You had their patrol rota down pat, boss. And who notices one more spearman? Living in real comfort, he is," Euen Huw remarked. "Better than you, boss. Got all these slaves, hasn't he? And stone men, and I don't know what. And braziers, too. Hot enough to melt the skin off your face. First time I been warm since we got here."

Ash pinched the bridge of her nose, and looked at him.

"We'd've had him if we could." The Welshman's frustration was clear. "Talk about high security. I reckon he has twelve men with him when he goes to do a shit! Took us long enough to get close enough to work out it was *him*."

"Bow? Crossbow? Arquebus?"

"Nah. Can see why the guys we sent out couldn't get to him. That unit he's got round him are *sharp*. Daren't touch a weapon anywhere near 'em."

"Which is where?" Ash demanded.

"Here," Euen Huw said, hastily feeling in his leather pouch.

Not to the south, she prayed. *Don't let me have to attack him across a river. Even iced-over.*

Euen's dirt-black hands spread a paper in front of her. The Tydders crowded at his shoulder. He ran his finger across the charcoal lines that mapped the city, and the rivers to east and west, and the open valley to the north. The lines of the Visigoth camps were sketched in, now blackly definite. Euen Huw tapped his finger on the paper.

"He's *there*, boss. About a half mile north of the north-west gate. Up-stream of us, on this side of the river. There's a bridge there, behind their lines. They haven't thrown it down. I reckon he's sitting there so he can be over it and away, if there's trouble."

"Yeah, he's got roads going south or west, if he crosses the bridge . . ."

"Not that we're going to let him."

Ash let herself smile at the Welshman. "We're going to have to move fucking fast to stop him. Well done, Euen; guys. Okay. I need more people to go out and keep an eye on him – be careful, his *'arifs* have had enough time to re-do guard duties. I *must* know if King-Caliph Gelimer moves his household."

The day of the twenty-seventh of December passed. A dozen times in an hour, she missed the presence of John de Vere; his advice, his even temper, and his confidence.

The absence of Floria del Guiz worried at her like a missing tooth.

"Activity in the enemy camp. They're shifting men," Robert Anselm reported.

"Have they answered our herald yet?"

"Follo's still out there talking." Anselm said evenly, "The longer we leave it, the more weaknesses the King-Caliph can cover."

"I know. But we knew this would take time to set up. We *have* to take them by surprise: get out there and punch through them to Gelimer. Anything less than that is useless."

She covered the distance wall-to-wall inside Dijon twenty times in the day, hearing reports, giving orders, liaising with de la Marche and Jonvelle. When she did rest, for an hour after noon, she started up again, head swimming in noise.

'FEEL IT GROW COLD, LITTLE SHADOW. FEEL HOW WE DRAW DOWN THE SUN.'

In the brief twilight towards the end of the twenty-seventh of December, the appointed Burgundian herald trudged back across the iron-hard mud between Dijon and the Visigoth camp.

Richard Follo came at last to Ash, where she and Olivier de la Marche waited in the palace presence chamber, surrounded by the silent merchants and tradesmen of Dijon. The veiled Duchess sat silent upon the great oak throne of the Valois princes.

He was escorted in through the refugees crowding the streets outside. There were few of them now – white around the eyes, gaunt with hunger, out at the further edge of desperation – who did not carry a bill or a pitchfork or, if nothing else, an iron-shod staff.

"Well?" de la Marche demanded, as if at his Duchess's behest.

Richard Follo took a moment to arrange his vice-mayoral chain over his demi-gown, and catch his breath. "It is arranged, my lord. We will surrender, tomorrow, to the lord commander *qa'id* Lebrija. He will have all the lords and magnates of the city come out first, without weapons, on to the empty ground before the north-east gate. Then the fighting men, unarmed, in groups of twenty at a time, to be taken into Visigoth imprisonment."

Ash heard de la Marche asking, "Does he guarantee our safety?" but she was no longer listening. She looked to Robert Anselm, Angelotti, Geraint ab Morgan, Ludmilla Rostovnaya; to the Burgundian *centeniers*. All of them had the look of those receiving expected, if unwelcome, news; there was even a slight appearance of relief.

"The surrender is set for the fourth hour of the morning, tomorrow," Follo concluded, his eye-sockets dark with shadow and strain. "At ten of the clock. Do we agree to this, my lords? Is there *no* other way?"

Ash, face impassive, ignored the last bickering; could only think, *Okay. This is it.*

"Angeli," she said. "Find Jussey. Now we know when we start."

By Compline, it became too cold for snow. Ash, plodding over frost-sparkling flagstones and frozen mud, came back into the company tower's courtyard, and found herself among men packed in tight for the pre-battle kit-check.

Wall-torches burned smokily in the freezing air. She beat her hands together, numb in their metal plates. For a moment, the crowds of tall, bulkily armoured men and women intimidated her. She took a cold breath, pushed into the yard, and began to greet them.

Knots and clumps of men stood here, a buzz of conversation going up into the night air. Lance-leaders checked the troops they were responsible for raising – Ash spoke to foot-knights, archers, sergeants, men-at-arms and squires, knowing at least their first names; and stood aside for the sergeants, forming up larger groups of men towards the back of the courtyard – all the billmen together, all the archers and hackbutters together. Shouts and bawled orders echoed off the vast expanse of stonework of the tower.

She walked among them, banner and escort meaning that a way always cleared in front of her, and talked to the billmen and the missile troops.

What am I missing? she thought suddenly. And then: *horses!*

There is no sound of hooves on the cobblestones. No ringing steel, from the caparisoned war-horses; no pack-horses, even; no mules. All gone into the company kitchens, now; from where a thin thread of scent trails – last rations before the morning.

"Henri Brant saved a couple of barrels of the wine," she announced, voice cracking at the coldness of the air in her throat. "You'll all get some at dawn."

A cheer went up from those near enough to hear.

Coming to the entrance to the armoury, Ash raised her voice. "Jean."

"Nearly done, boss!" Jean Bertran grinned in the red forge-light. Behind him, a last frantic burst of activity bounced hammer-noise off the shadowy walls, hung with tools. Two apprentices sat turning out arrow-heads at production-line velocity.

Deafened by the hammering, she stood with the welcome warmth on her face for a moment. At an anvil, one of the armourers beat out a dented breastplate, bright flakes spraying from the glowing metal. His bare arm with its prominent muscles flexed, shining with sweat and dirt, bringing the hammer down with accurate skill and power. She has a brief anticipation of that muscular arm and shoulder flexing, lifting, banging down weapons on some Visigoth soldier's face. *Maybe, in a few hours' time.*

At the tower door, she dismissed her escort of archers to the comparative warmth of the company tower's guardroom, and padded clumsily down the stone steps to the ground floor.

A stench of shit made her blink, take off her gauntlets, and wipe at her eyes. Blanche came forward through the taper-lit gloom. A pack of children flanked her skirts. Ash, making a rough head-count, thought *Most of the baggage-train kids*, and nodded at them.

"I've got them bandaging," Blanche wheezed thinly. Like the men outside, her face was hollow under the cheekbones, and the sockets of her eyes dark. "Every man who can walk is out of here, even if it means with a strapped-up wrist or shoulder. I can't do anything for the others. The well's freezing; I don't even have water for them."

The line of straw-beds extended off into the gloom. *More than twenty-four now?* Ash tried to count the dysentery cases, at least. *Thirty, thirty-one?*

"Szechy died," the woman added.

Ash followed her gaze. Over by the wall, another dark, wiry man was wrapping the little Hungarian in something – ragged sacking, she saw, as an improvised winding-sheet.

"Out to the muster, when you've finished there," she said. "You'll get your chance tomorrow."

The man knotted cloth, rested the body down, and stood. Tears marked what was visible of his face between long hair and moustache. He said something – only *kill fucking Visigoths!* was comprehensible among his words – and staggered off towards the steps.

"Keep them as comfortable as you can. We need the water for those who're fighting, though." Ash watched the supine bodies of the fever cases. "If any of them suddenly 'recover', send them outside."

Blanche, half smiling, shook her head. "I wish these *were* malingerers."

Coming back up to the entrance hall, she found it crowded: Euen Huw, Rochester, Campin, Verhaecht, Mowlett, and a dozen others.

"See Anselm and Angeli; they'll sort it!" She shoved her way past the familiar faces, up the narrow stone stairwell, to the top floor. One of the guards there pushed aside the leather curtain. The brush-haired page came to take her cloak, her hood, her huke, and her sword.

"Armour off, boss?" he demanded.

"Yeah. Rickard will do it. I'll want arming up again before Lauds." She hesitated, looking down at the boy – about ten, she supposed. "What's your name again?"

"Jean."

"Okay, Jean. You wake me about half a candle-mark before Lauds. Bring the other pages, and food, and lights."

He gazed up at her over the bundle of damp, mud-stained wool, sheepskin, and weapons in his arms. "Yes, boss!"

She closed her eyes briefly, as he left, hearing his footsteps on the stone stairs, and some half-audible comment by the guards. For a second she sees, clearly, how his face will look cut across with the hand's-breadth blade of a bill.

"Boss." Rickard came away from the upper floor's hearth, where the fire lay banked down to red embers, with a pitiful amount of rescued beams and timber stacked beside it to dry out.

He cut the waxed points holding her pauldrons, and she shut her eyes again, this time for weariness; feeling his hands unbuckle and lift off the weight of thin steel plates, as if he lifted boulders off her flesh. As he removed cuisses and

1036

greaves and sabatons, she stretched her legs; and with the removal of her cuirass and arm-defences, she reached out as if to crack every muscle in her body, before slumping back into a flat-footed stance.

"That'll need a clean," she said, as Rickard began to hang it up on the body-form. "Do it downstairs."

"Too noisy to sleep if I do it up here, boss?"

He stood taller than her, now, Ash realised; by half a hand-span. She found herself looking slightly up to look into his eyes.

"Get Jean to start on the armour. You go over to St Stephen's for me."

Instructions came automatically, now; she didn't listen to herself telling him what she wanted. The great yellow-and-red chevrons painted on the walls loomed, obscurely, through the gloom; and the smoke of tapers caught at the back of her throat.

"See I'm not disturbed," she added, and noted that he gave her an immense, excited grin in the dim light, as he turned to carry the Milanese harness down to a corner of the main hall.

He's too young for this. Too young for tomorrow. Hell, we're all *too young for tomorrow.*

She did not bother to change out of her arming doublet and hose, careless of the points dangling from its mail inserts. Hauling the oldest of her fur-lined demi-gowns over the top of it, she moved the tapers in their iron stand closer to the hearth, and squatted down, prodding with a piece of firewood at the embers, until a warmer flame woke.

The smell of old sweat from her own body made itself apparent to her, as she grew less cold. She scratched at flea-bites under her doublet. Cessation of movement made her drowsy. *I've talked myself dizzy,* she thought; feeling as if her feet in their low boots still thumped continually against flagstones, stone steps, cobblestones. With a grunt, she sat down on the palliasse one of the pages had dragged close to the fire, and dug still-numb fingers into the stiff, cold leather of her boots, easing them off one by one. Her hose, black to the knee, stank of dung.

And all of it can be gone, in an instant – every smell, every sensation; the me *that thinks this—*

She reached out for the pottery cup, left covered by the fire, and sniffed at the contents. Stale water. Perhaps with a very slight tinge of wine. Realising, now, how dry her mouth was, she drained it, and dragged her doublet-sleeve across her mouth.

"Boss," a man's voice said cheerfully, from the doorway.

She looked away from the fire. Even that small light left her night-blind, in the dim hall. She recognised the voice of the guard: one of Giovanni Petro's Italian archers.

"Let her in."

"Okay, boss." And in Italian, crudely: "Drain the bitch dry, boss!"

A cold wind sliced in as the leather curtain slid open, then dropped back. She reached out for her belt, where Rickard had laid it down, and tiredly buckled it around her waist, over her demi-gown. The use-polished hilt of her bollock dagger rested neatly under her palm.

A female voice, from the direction of the doorway, said, "Ash? Why do you want to see me?"

"Over here. It's warmer over here."

Oak floorboards creaked. Ash heard a chink of metal. A human figure hobbled into the dim illumination of tapers and fire, bringing the sharp scent of frost, and a whirl of surrounding cold air. The sound of metal on metal came again as the figure lifted its hands and pushed back its hood, and became – in the light – the Faris, her wrists and ankles encircled with heavy iron cuffs, and short, rough-forged chains run between them.

Firelight put a red glow on her cheeks, still filled out with the flesh that comes from adequate rations, and gleamed back from her eyes.

Ash pointed silently at the floor beside her. The Visigoth woman glanced around, and cautiously sat, instead, on a heavy iron-bound chest that stood on the other side of the hearth.

Ash made to protest, and then grinned. "You might as well. If you can find anything in it other than spiders, you're welcome to it!"

"What?"

"It's my war-chest," Ash said. She watched the sitting woman; the light on the iron chains. "Not that money would be good for much, right now. Nothing to buy. And even on my best day, I never earned enough to bribe the King-Caliph!"

The Faris did not smile. She glanced back over her shoulder, into the vast darkness of the hall. Walls and rafters were invisible now, and it was only apparent that windows existed in the alcoves behind the access corridors when the wind rattled the shutters.

"Why are you talking to me?" she demanded.

Ash raised her voice. "Paolo?"

"Yes, boss?"

"Bugger off down to the next landing. I don't want to be disturbed."

"Okay, boss." The archer's laugh came out of the darkness. "Let me and the boys know when you done with her – we got something to give her!"

Cold air burns her face: cold sweat springs out under her arms. The memory of men's voices above her, the exact same tone of contempt, shudders through her body.

"You'll treat her like a human being or I'll have your back stripped: *is that clear?*"

There is a perceptible pause before the archer's ungrudging, "Yes, boss." Slowly, her system calms.

Listening carefully, Ash heard his footsteps going down the spiral stone stairs.

She switched her gaze back to the Faris.

"I've got everything you can tell me, in de la Marche's reports. You're here because I can't talk to *him*," she indicated the place where Paolo had stood. "Or Robert. Or Angelotti. Or anyone in the company. For the same reason I can't talk to de la Marche, or that Burgundian bishop. Confidence is a – precarious thing. So there's . . ."

Florian's left. John de Vere's gone with her.

Godfrey's dead.

". . . there's you."

"Haven't we talked *enough*?"

The depth of feeling in the woman's accented voice surprised her. Ash reached back among the pottery cups and wooden plates, searching for more food or drink that might have been left out for the Burgundian commander-in-chief. More by touch than sight, she found a pottery flask with liquid in it, and heaved it back over into the firelight.

"We've never talked. Not you and me. Not without there being something else going on."

The Visigoth woman sat perfectly still. A threadbare demi-gown covered her badly fitting doublet and hose, and her hands were white with cold. As if conscious of Ash's gaze, she cautiously extended her fingers towards the fire's warmth.

"You should have killed me, before," she said, at last; this time in Carthaginian Latin.

Ash sloshed brackish water into two moderately clean wooden cups, and knelt up beside the hearth to offer one of them to the Faris. The woman gazed at it for a long minute before reaching out for it with both hands together, the weight of the iron links making her clumsy.

"And the Duchess, your man-woman," the Faris added, "she should kill you, now."

Ash said, "I know."

The feeling of acting as if Florian were still in the city was curiously unsettling.

The taper guttered and began to give off a thicker black smoke. Ash, not willing to call for a page, made to get up, winced at stiff muscles, and limped across the room to find another tallow-dip, and light it at the hearth. Even a yard away from the flames, it was freezingly cold.

Firelight made the woman's chopped-short hair red-gold, not silver – *as it must do mine*, Ash realised. It blurred the dirt on her skin. *If someone came in now, would they know which one was her, and which is me?*

"We spend far too much time keeping each other alive, when circumstances don't demand it," Ash said sardonically. "Florian, you, me. I wonder why?"

As if she had thought a lot about the matter, the Faris said, "Because my *qa'id* Lebrija has a brother dead in this war, and another alive in Alexandria, and a sister married to a cousin of the lord-*amir* Childeric. Because Lord de la Marche of Burgundy is brother-in-law to half France. And all I have is you; and what you have, *jund* Ash, is me." She hesitated, and with a wry expression, added, "And Adelize. And Violante."

This is family? Ash thought.

"I could never quite kill you. I should have." Ash set the taper in its stand, and walked back to look into the hearth-fire. "And Florian – won't execute me. Rather than kill one person, she'll risk thousands. Thousands of thousands."

"That's bad." The Faris looked quickly up. "I was wrong. When I had you among my men at the hunt? I was not willing to accept that one person should die. My father Leofric, the *machina rei militaris*, they would have told me how wrong that was – and they would have been right."

"You say that. But you don't quite believe it, do you?"

"I believe it. How else could I order an attack, in war? Even when I win, people will die."

Ash's eyes watered. She coughed, waving a hand as if the taper's thin trickle of smoke bothered her, and lifted the wooden cup and drank. Sour-tasting water slid down her throat, past the tightness there.

People will die.

"How do you live with it?" Ash asked, and suddenly shook her head and laughed. "Christ! Valzacchi asked me that, in Carthage. 'How do you live with what you do?' And I said, 'It doesn't bother me.' It doesn't bother me."

"Ash—"

"You're here," Ash said harshly, "because I can't sleep. And there isn't any wine to get drunk on. So you can damn well sit there, and you can damn well answer me. How do I live with what I do?"

She expected a pause, for reflection, but the Faris's voice came instantly out of the shadows.

"If God is good to us, you have little time to live with it. King-Caliph Gelimer will execute you tomorrow morning, after you surrender. I only pray that I can reach him first – or else that the lord-*amir* my father Leofric can – and tell him that he has to wait to execute Duchess Floria until after you are dead." The Faris leaned forward into the firelight, her gaze resting on Ash. "If you do nothing else, at least send me out to him first tomorrow! Pray that I live long enough to tell him, before he executes *me*."

A snort of laughter forced its way out of Ash's mouth. She wiped her sleeve across her face again, and squatted down in front of the fire, still cradling the empty cup.

"You've heard about the surrender, then. That the siege is over."

"Men will talk. Priests no less than any other. Fer— Brother Fernando spoke to the monks."

Catching that hesitation in the other woman's voice, Ash said, under her breath, "Predictable!" and added, before the Faris could question her: "I don't give a shit about what happens tomorrow! This is now. I want to know – how do I live with people I know . . . with friends getting killed."

"Why?" the Faris said. "Do you plan to go down fighting, at the surrender?"

The cold in the tower's upper hall bites at her fingers, and her feet, so that she is glad, momentarily, to avoid the Faris's dark stare by sitting to put her stiff, cold boots back on. For a second, she feels it all – the slight warmth the fire has put into the sewn leather, the ache of exertion in her muscles, the numb grind of hunger under her breastbone – as if it is the first time.

"Perhaps," Ash said, finding herself unwilling to lie, even by misdirection. *Not that it'll matter: it'll all be over before anyone can find you.*

"Maybe," Ash said.

The Faris put her chained hands neatly together in her lap. Staring into the poor excuse for a fire, she said, "You live with knowing you'll die in war."

"That's different!"

"And enough things will kill them in peacetime – drink, pox, fever, farm-work—"

"I *know* these people." Ash stopped; said again: "I know *these* people. I've known some of them for years. I knew Geraint ab Morgan when he was skinny. I knew Tom Rochester when he couldn't speak a word of anything but English, and they told him his name was Flemish for *arsehole*. I've met Robert's two bastard sons in Brittany – *fuck* knows whether he thinks they're alive or dead, now! He doesn't say anything, he just carries on. And there's guys on the door here, and downstairs; I've known most of them since I left England after Tewkesbury field. If I order an attack, they'll die."

As objective as if she were neither prisoner nor partisan, the Faris said, "Don't think about it."

"How do I stop thinking about it!"

After a moment, the Faris began tentatively, "Perhaps we can't. Brother Fernando said—"

"What? *What* did he say?"

"—he said, it's more difficult for a woman to be a soldier than a man; women give birth, and therefore find it too difficult to kill."

Ash found both her hands clasped tight over her belly. She hugged her blue velvet demi-gown to her, caught the Faris's eye in the shadowy light, and coughed out a loud, harsh burst of laughter. The other woman clamped her fingers across her mouth, gazing with wide dark eyes, and suddenly let her head go back as she gave a high peal.

"He s-said—"

"—yes—"

"Said—"

"*Yes!*"

"Oh, shit. Did you tell him – what crap—?"

"No." The Faris wiped the edges of her hands delicately under each eye, smoothing away water. Her chains clinked. She could not keep the enjoyment off her face. Snuffling, she said, "No. I thought I might let my *qa'ids* talk to him, if I survive. They can tell this Frankish knight how much *easier* it is for a man to stand covered in the brains and blood of his dearest friend—"

Laughter died, not instantly, but slowly; sputtering as they looked at each other.

"There's that," Ash said, "there is that."

The woman wiped her face, fingers touching dirty but flawless skin. "I have always had my father, or my *qa'ids*, or the *machina rei militaris* with me; not like you, Ash. Even so, I have seen enough of what war does to people. Their hearts, their bodies. You have seen more than I. Strange that it should hurt you more, now."

"Were they ever more than men on a chessboard to you?"

"Oh, yes!" The Faris sounded hurt.

"Ah. Yes. Because, if you don't know them as human and fallible," Ash completed, "how do you know where to put them in battle? Yeah. I know. I know. What *are* we? Bad as the Stone Golem. Worse. We had the choice."

She sat back, arms hooked around her knees.

"I'm not used to this," she said. "If I think about it, Faris, you probably owe your life to me not being used to it. Maybe it's only sentimentality that stopped me killing you."

"And your Duchess, she is sentimental not to kill you?"

"Maybe. How would I know the difference between sentimentality and—" Ash will not say the word. It sits immovably heavy in her mind. Even to herself, she cannot say *love*.

"Shit, I hate sieges!" she exclaimed, lifting her head and looking around the cold, dark hall. "It was bad enough in Neuss at the end. They were eating their own babies. If I'd known, in June, that I'd end up this side of a siege six months later . . ."

Iron links shifted, with a pouring sound, as the Faris slid herself down the great multi-locked war-chest to sit on the floorboards in front of it, and lean back wearily. Ash momentarily tensed, out of instinct, even recognising that the chains were – by her order – made too short to allow the wearer to throttle anyone.

Automatically, she got her feet under her, and the hilt of her dagger back under her palm. She squatted, staring into the fire, her attention pricklingly conscious of the woman in the edge of her vision – that state of mind where any movement will trigger a drawn weapon.

"I will never forget seeing you for the first time," the Faris said quietly. "I had been told, 'twin', but how strange it was, even so. A woman among the Franks – how could you not know yourself born of Carthage?"

Ash shook her head.

The woman continued, "I saw you in armour, among men who owed you loyalty – you, not your *amir* or King-Caliph. I envied that freedom you had."

"Freedom!" Ash snorted. "Freedom? Dear God . . . And envy didn't stop you packing me off to Carthage, did it? Even knowing what Leofric was likely to do."

"That." The Faris pointed a slender, dirty finger at Ash. "That. That's it."

"What's it?"

"How you do it," the woman said. "Yes, I knew – but I didn't *know*. You might have been used, not killed. That's how you have to do it in battle – your men might live, they might not be killed. Some of them *will* live. It's a matter of not letting yourself know."

"But I do know!" Ash's fist hit the palliasse beside her. "I do, now. I can't get rid of it – that knowing."

A knot in the burning wood cracked, making her jolt, and the Faris too. A gold ember fell out of the fire-irons, turning swiftly grey, then black, on the edge of Ash's demi-gown. She flicked it off, brushing at the cloth. She gazed up at the blackened brick lining the chimney behind the fire, feeling the draught of the air, and smelling the scorched velvet.

"Let's say," Ash said, "that there is going to be a fight. Let's say I've been driven out of Genoa, and Basle, and Carthage itself by you guys, and halfway across southern France, and let's say I'm finally going to turn around, here, at Dijon."

The Faris held out her wooden cup. Ash automatically poured more of the stale water into it. The Faris looked down at her chained wrists, which she could not move very far apart. Lifting the cup between her hands, she sipped at it.

"I see how it is. Tomorrow, you will fight to get yourself killed," she said coolly, with something of the authority she had had in Visigoth war-gear among her armies. "That will deprive the *Ferae Natura Machinae* of their victory. Even if you fight for some other objective, I've learned enough of you to know that you're aware of who the true enemy is."

Ash stood, flexing pain out of her leg muscles. The warmth of the fire faded, the wood being consumed. She wondered idly, *Should I feed the fire again or leave it to the morning?* and then, her mind correcting her, *No need to ration it out, now; either way.*

"Faris . . ."

Cold air chilled her fingers, her ears, her scar-marked cheeks. Another stretch, this time rolling her head to get the stiffness out her neck. The trestle table stood mostly in the shadows, the one taper not sufficient to illuminate the stacked papers, muster-rolls, sketched maps and plans at the far end of it. Someone – Anselm, possibly – had been using a burnt stick from the fire: the tabletop was scratched in charcoal with lines delineating the north-west and north-east gates of Dijon, and the streets of the Visigoth camp beyond them.

"You're the one who's keen on suicidal actions; getting the enemy to execute you. If I thought it necessary, I wouldn't be handing myself over to Gelimer, I'd be walking off the top of this tower – four storeys straight *down*." Ash gestured emphatically.

"There's something you're planning. Isn't there? Ash – sister – tell me what it is. I was their commander. I can help."

Everybody wants me to do this. Even her!

"I will help you, if it leads to destroying the Wild Machines." The Faris knelt up, her unlined face seeming young. Excitedly, she said, "The King-Caliph Gelimer will not command as I would. Rather: not as I would if I had the *machina rei militaris—*"

"He's got fifteen thousand troops out there, he doesn't have to!"

"But – you could put me on the field: not as a commander, as your battle double—"

"I don't need your help. We've already wrung you dry. You're missing the *point*, Faris."

"The point?"

Ash moved forward. She sat down on the edge of the war-chest. Well within range, if the woman now sitting at her feet should choose to strike at her with hands assisted by iron chains.

Her eyes stung. She knuckled at them, smelling charcoal on her fingers. Water, hot and heavy, gathered on her lower lids, and ran over and down her cheeks.

"The point is, who else can I tell that I'm afraid? Who else can I tell that I don't want to get my friends killed? Even if by some remote chance we *win*, most of my friends are going to end up dead!"

Her voice never shook, but the tears carried on, unstoppably. The other woman looked up, seeing, in the fire's light, Ash's face red and shining with water and snot.

"But you know—"

"I *know*, and I'm sick of it!" Ash put her face into her hands. In the wet, sweaty darkness, she whispered, "I – don't – want – them – to – die. I can't make it any fucking plainer! Either we go out there tomorrow, and they die, or we stay in here tomorrow, and we die. Christ, what don't you understand!"

Something touched her wrist. By reflex, she clenched her fist and knocked it away, hard. One knuckle struck iron. She swore, snatched her other hand from her face – vision dazzled by wetness – and made out the other woman holding up her cuffed wrists in a gesture of non-aggression.

Distressed, the woman said, "I'm not your confessor!"

"You understand this! You've done this – you *know* what—"

The Faris reached out, pulling at Ash's belt and demi-gown with her hands that were trapped close together. All in a second, Ash stopped resisting. She slid down the side of the wooden chest, hitting the stones hard, crammed in beside the Faris's warm body.

"I don't—"

Chains shifted, tangling in cloth. Ash felt the Faris attempting to put her arms around her shoulders – failing – and then her left hand was gripped tight between both of the Faris's own hands.

"I know. I know!" The Faris wrapped her arms around Ash's arm; Ash felt the woman's hard, hugging pressure.

"—don't want them killed!" Hiccoughing sobs stopped her speaking.

Ash clamped her eyes shut, tears pushing out between the hot lids. The Faris murmured something, not in any language that she knew.

Ash dipped her head, abruptly, and muffled the noise against the filth-stained wool of the Faris's gown. She sobbed out loud, body clenched, crying against her sister's shoulder until she wept herself dry.

There were no remaining city clocks to chime the hour. Ash blinked awake in darkness, with sore, swollen eyes, and stared into the greying embers of the fire.

Utterly relaxed against her, the Visigoth woman with her face, her hair, her body, slept on.

Ash did not move. She said nothing. She sat, awake, alone.

The page Jean entered the room.

"Time, boss," he said.

On the third day after Christ's Mass and the return of the Unconquered Sun, in the dark an hour before Terce:

"Go in peace!" Father Richard Faversham proclaimed, "and the grace of God be upon us all this day!"

He and Digorie Paston bowed to the altar. Both men wore mail, and helmets.

The stones of the abbey, hard under Ash's armoured knees, forced the metal back into the protective padding. She crossed herself and stood up, heart thumping, hardly feeling herself cold to the bone. Rickard got to his feet beside her: a young man in mail and the Lion Azure livery, his face pale. He said something to Robert Anselm; she heard Anselm chuckle.

"Angeli!" She grabbed Angelotti's arm as the company began to file out of the church. "Are we set?"

"All set to go." His face was barely visible as they came out of the great church door into the St Stephen's abbey grounds. Then a lone torch caught his gilt curls, showed her his teeth in a wild, wide grin. "You are mad, madonna, but we have done it!"

"Have you warned everybody off?"

Robert Anselm, beside her, said, "I've had runners from all our lance-leaders; they're in place on the ground and on the walls."

"We're almost – fully deployed," the *centenier* Lacombe grunted.

"Then get fucking moving!"

The faintest grey of dawn lightened the sky. Ash strode through the icy streets, head buzzing with information, talking to two and three people at a time; sending men here and there, conscious of her mind moving like an engine, smoothly, without feeling. A message of readiness came in from Olivier de la Marche as she reached the cleared desolation back of Dijon's north-west gate.

She passed her helmet to Rickard to carry. Walking bareheaded, the bitter cold numbed her face immediately, made her eyes run, and she blinked back tears. A word here, a touch on the shoulder there: she went through her men, and the Burgundian units, towards the foot of the wall.

Torches threw golden swathes of light on the lower reaches of the wall, invisible outside. Men passed cannon-shot hastily from hand to hand up the steps to the battlements. She stepped back as a Burgundian gun-crew trundled an organ-gun across the frost-rimed cobbles, that they could barely see. Rags muffled its steel-shod wooden wheels, covered the metal of its eight barrels.

At the foot of the steps they barely halted, tripping the organ-gun up so that they held the trolley, and carrying it bodily between them up to the battlements. A throng of gun-crew trod after them, and men hauling three timber frames – mangonels.

Her numb skin cringed at every sound. Muffled footfalls, an oath; sweating grunts of effort as another light gun went up to the walls – *will they hear us? Sound carries, it's frosty, it's too still!*

"Tell them to keep it down!" She sent a runner – Simon Tydder – off towards the walls; turned on her heel, and set off at a fast walk with her HQ staff, parallel to the wall between the White Tower and the Byward Tower, fifty yards back.

They ran into a crowd, Burgundian archers and billmen. Ash craned her neck to look at the rooftops. A rapidly lightening sky was no longer grey – was a hazed white, with a deep red glow to the east.

"How much fucking longer!" Her breath whitened the air. "This lot are late! How many more? Are we in place!"

"We need it light enough to see what we're doing," Anselm grunted.

"We don't need it light enough for *them* to see what we're doing!"

Thomas Rochester snorted. The dark Englishman carried her personal banner again, a position of prestige for which he has handed his temporary infantry command back to Robert Anselm. He, or someone from the baggage train, has neatly darned a rip in his livery jacket. His sallet is polished until the rivets shine. *Didn't sleep last night, doing that. All of them: preparing.*

"Get your men in place!" she swore at the Burgundians. "Fuck it! I'm going up on the wall. Stay down here!" She pointed at Rochester's Lion Affronté banner.

Loping up the steps to the battlements, the burn-injury on her thigh hurt with the exertion. She grunted. Once above roof-level, wind whipped out of the east and tore the breath out of her mouth. She slowed her pace, trying to move reasonably quietly in her armour. Stone treads glittered, crusted thickly white with frost, imprinted with the boot-marks of the men who had climbed up minutes before her.

A line of light lay across the battlements.

Brightness striped the merlons and brattices, and the tall curve of the Byward Tower. She turned east. Between one long low cloud and the horizon, the brilliant yellow of the winter sun stabbed out.

We're not a minute too soon.

Men crouched behind the merlons. Gunners in jacks, their sallets and war-hats held at their feet so they should not catch the betraying sun; counting their shot in silence, their rammers leaning up against stonework. Other crews kept their cannon back from the crenellations, loading powder and ball and old cloth for wadding. Further along the parapet, men worked in rapid, silent teams, hauling back the arms of siege-engines with greased wooden winches.

Beyond the Byward Tower, to her right, the battlements were completely deserted.

"Okay . . ." Breath, warm, was cold against her lips a second after.

A long way to her right, past the Prince's Tower, thin clumps of men began again on the wall.

Outside, past the bone-scattered ground, the Visigoth encampment lay vast and swollen between the two rivers. Heart in her mouth, she saw that smoke already threaded up from cooking fires. Behind the mantlets and trenches, pennants, banners, and eagles rose; like a forest of dry sticks in the rising sun.

Anyone moving?

For a second, she sees it not as tents and the men of the XIV Utica, VI Leptis Parva, III Caralis; but as a great structure sprawling there in the growing dawn: a pyramid whose foundation is use-and-forget slaves, then the troops with their *nazirs* and *'arifs* and *qa'ids*, then the lord-*amirs* of the Visigoth Empire, and finally – pinnacle, peak of all – King-Caliph Gelimer. And for that same second she is utterly aware of the support of that structure: the engineers that bring supplies up frozen rivers, the slave-estates in Egypt and Iberia that raise the food, the merchant-princes whose fleets out-run the Turkish navy to sell to a hundred cities around the Mediterranean, and deep into Africa, and out to the Baltic Sea.

And what are we? Barely fifteen hundred people. Standing in front of eight or nine thousand civilians.

She looked away. The western river lay flat and white, frozen hard as rock.

Strong enough? Please God. She could not see the surviving bridge, hidden by the myriad tents and turf huts of the Visigoth camp. As for the King-Caliph's household quarters, there was nothing to mark any engineered building out from another except location.

He was sleeping there two hours ago. And if he's not there now – well. We're fucked.

A glint of brass caught her eye as the sunlight moved down. Golems, overwatching the gate. With Greek Fire throwers.

The only thing we might have in our favour is that they're not deployed. Maybe not even armed up – shit, I wish I could see that far!

And they can't fire into mêlée.

What would have been a smile turned sour. She looked east, into glare: nothing but tents; tents and more tents; men by the hundred, by the thousand – beginning to stir, now.

"Come *on*, Jussey—"

Cold had got into her bones. She moved stiffly, half-running. The stone stairs were slippery with rime. She blinked, moving down into shadow again. Her muscles felt loose, and her bladder urgent; both these things she put out of her mind.

Can I do this?

No: but nobody can do this!

Ah, the hell with it—

At the foot of the wall, she grabbed Anselm's arm in the dimness. "Time to do it. Is everyone in position?"

"There's a delay with some of the Burgundian billmen."

"Oh, tough shit! We got to move!"

"Apart from them, it's a go."

"Okay, where's Angeli—" She glimpsed Angelotti in the gloom. "Okay, get your guys out: *do* it. And don't let me down!"

The Italian gunner went off at the run.

"That's it," she said. She looked up at Anselm, not able to see his face. "Either everybody does what we've trained for – or we're fucked. We can't change this in mid-stream!"

He grunted. "Like letting an avalanche go. We just got to go with it!"

If I get hit, let it be a clean kill; I don't want to be maimed.

"If I go down, you take over; if you go," she said, "Tom will take it; de la Marche will have to pick it up if we're all fucked!"

The command group trod on her heels as she strode back across the rough ground to the barricades. A lantern gave little light on the frozen mud-ruts. She slipped, swore; heard something before she saw it, and realised that she had come to one end of the company line. John Burren, Willem Verhaecht, and Adriaen Campin were conferring urgently.

"We're in position here, boss." Willem Verhaecht spat, and spared a glance for the mass of men in Lion Azure livery, clutching their bills and poleaxes, grinning back at him. "Ready to go. I'd do anything to move, in this cold!"

Some forty men stood behind. Bills jutted above their heads. Men strapped into whatever armour they possessed, much of it taken now from the dead. She heard a lot of low-voiced last-minute joking, settling of debts and forgiveness, and prayer.

"We're ready, boss," John Burren said, nodding towards the unit in front.

In the gloom, Jan-Jacob Clovet and Pieter Tyrrell struggled with a six-foot oak door, stripped out of some building. Tyrrell's half-hand skidded on the frozen wood. A short, podgy figure in sallet and cut-off kirtle stepped in behind him, taking the weight on her shoulder. Hearing a female voice swear, Ash recognised Margaret Schmidt. Two more crossbowmen grabbed the door. Past them, she saw the other crossbow troops carrying doors, long planks, pavises, and torn-out shutters from ogee windows.

"We're here, boss!" Katherine Hammell's voice said, at her side. Only the jutting staves above her troops' heads showed them to be a mass of archers.

Down the line, past them, Ash sees in this growing cold light, Geraint ab Morgan's armed provosts; a dozen women from the baggage train, their skirts kilted up, and razor-sharp ash spears in their hands; Thomas Morgan holding the great Lion Azure battle standard. And faces behind them, under helmets, faces that she knows, has known for years in some cases: the line snaking on across the rubble, a little over three hundred strong.

I do not want to lead these men into this.

"Move 'em up," she said curtly, to Anselm. "I'd better kick some Burgundian ass—"

The silence shattered.

A sudden sequence of cracks and booms from the eastern side of the city made her skin her lips back from her teeth in a wild grin. A long chill shiver went through her body. Through the ground under her feet, she felt the boom of guns; she heard the deceptive soft *thwack!* of rock-hurling siege-engines.

"There goes Jussey! Better late than fucking never!"

Eternal, now, this hasty shuffling of men into position; and one drops his bill with a clear *clang!* against a broken wall, and a dozen others cheer. Shoved into position by sergeants, spitting on their shaking hands, giving a last tug at fastened points and war-hat buckles – *how long is this taking?* Ash thinks, over the shattering noise of Jussey's bombardment. *How much longer have we got?*

Captain Jonvelle loped out from behind the long lines of Burgundian troops.

"They've mobilised most of a legion!" He turned to confirm with a runner. "Pulled it out of the trenches – they think we're staging a break-out to the *east* bridge – deploying over there—"

"*Got* the fuckers! Okay, now *wait*. Let 'em commit themselves."

Counting in her head, she lets an agonising eight minutes pass.

Ash gave a quick nod, walked out towards the wall, and turned, standing between the two advance crossbow units, to face the units behind. Amorphous clumps of men: each a hundred strong. Unit pennons going up, now, in the dim light, but so few – barely a dozen. *Gun-crews on the walls, engineers in the saps: even with everyone who can* walk *down here, we don't amount to more than thirteen hundred men.* Shit . . .

She drew breath, shouting, her voice carrying over the distant Burgundian guns.

"Here's what we do. We attack now! They don't expect us. They're expecting us to surrender! We *won't* be surrendering."

A rumble of voices, those few yards in front of her. Apprehension, excitement, blood-lust, fear: all of it present. Some of them are looking at the way cleared to the north-west gate: that choke-point – outside of which, where the sun may already be reaching the frost-white edges of ruts and stones, is a killing-ground.

She cocked her head, short bright hair flying, eyes alight; and deliberately surveyed them.

"You shit-faced bastards, you don't need me to tell you what to do! *Kill Gelimer!*"

It echoes off the walls as they scream it back at her.

In full armour and livery, Rochester with the Lion Affronté at her shoulder, she bellows an old familiar shout, to Lions and Burgundian men-at-arms alike:

"Do we want to win!"

"*Yes!*"

"Can't hear you! I said do we want to *win*!"

"YES!"

"Kill Gelimer!"

"KILL GELIMER!"

Everything lost, now, in the surge of adrenalin.

"Boss!" Rickard, beside her, held up her sallet. She stopped for as long as it took him to buckle on her bevor and helmet. The sound of sakers, serpentine, and organ-guns from the east is already growing less regular, less loud. She shoved her visor up; taking as well a short, four-foot pole-hammer, carrying it loosely from her left hand.

A solid *boom!* banged out from the city wall behind her.

"Yeah! Go, Ludmilla!"

A rapid firecracker-sequence of bangs, the reverberation of a mangonel cup thudding up hard against its bar – and every swivel gun, hackbut, cannon and organ-gun on the walls around the north-west gate opens up. Ash winced, for the nearness of the fire, even muffled by her helmet lining.

But is that all we've got?

Under her breath, she muttered, "*Ángeli, come on!*"

She swung back to face the battle line. They have worked themselves up to where she is now, to a magnificent *fuck it!* to all suicidal risks, and probably for the same reason: the fear that rips through her bowel.

"I know I can rely on you guys! You're too stupid to know when you're beaten!"

A loud chant went up. For a second, she could not make it out. Then, in half a dozen languages: "Lion! Lion of Burgundy! She-Lion!" and "*The Maid!*"

Something quivered under her feet.

The ice that puddled the mud under her feet cracked. A dull, loud, earth-lifting roar went up. Rocks, masonry fragments and beams flew in a hail: every man ducking as one and putting his helmet down to the blast.

Ash lifted her head, and visor.

Beyond the cleared no-man's-land, the whole section of city wall between the Byward Tower and the White Tower puffed out dust from between every block of masonry.

"Angeli! *Yes!*"

Angelotti and the Burgundian engineers: opening the sap, widening the diggings under the wall, all through this last night. And sweating to put powder in place, and pray that it's enough—

The wall stood for a moment. Ash had a heartbeat's time in which to think *If Angelotti got this wrong, it'll fall this way, and then we're dead,* and the wall shattered and fell.

Silently, in a second, it fell away on to the air – outwards.

The impact of it on the iron-cold earth shook her into a stagger. She got her balance, swearing. Beyond the swirling clouds of dust, sweeping chokingly back, two hundred yards of wall lay collapsed into rubble across the moat. Nothing but five or six hundred yards of ground, now, before the first trenches of the Visigoth camp.

"That's it." She spoke aloud, dazed, to herself; staring over the heads of the men in front of her at the two-hundred-yard gap in the wall. "Dijon isn't defensible any more. No choice now."

"St George!" Robert Anselm bellowed in her ear.

Thomas Morgan's voice, under the Lion standard, yelled, "*Saint Godfrey for Burgundy!*"

Ash choked her throat clear, drew breath, hauled her voice up from her belly and screamed at brass-pitch: "*Attack!*"

IV

A trumpet shrilled right in her ear. Her helmet muffled it.

Fallen masonry grated and slid under her boots.

Her chest heaved, breath hissing dry in her throat, and her feet came down on hard mud, and she ran – sprinting among armoured men, her view of them jolting through the slit of her visor; steel-covered legs pounding, forcing her muscles to push her on across the frozen earth – out into open ground.

Bodies crowded her. She glimpsed her banner-staff to her left. The rough ground threw her. Stone or bone, she lost her footing; felt someone's hand catch her under the arm and throw her on, not missing a beat.

A square dark shape lifted up against the sky in front of her.

Before she could think *what?* it went over and down. Her own boots were skidding on the icy wood before she recognised it as a door. Either side of her, planks and shutters slammed down on to the frozen mud. A brief sight of a six-foot-deep trench, off one side of the makeshift bridge—

That's their trench; the first defence!

She came off the planks, Anselm and Rickard tight with her. A confused mass of liveries blocked her view – red crosses, blue and yellow. The sudden jut and curve of a longbow stave went up on her left – someone shooting – and in the noise of brass horns, shouting men, and clattering armour came the *thwick!* of bowstrings.

She cannoned into the back of the man in front, bounced off, spared a glance for the banner and Rochester – an armoured figure at her left shoulder, the escort sprinting with him – and saw nothing around her but helmeted heads, against the pale sky, and *there!* the Lion standard—

"Don't lose it!" she bellowed, "keep going, *keep going!*"

A tent-peg caught her foot. She staggered, still running forward; a blade sliced down to her right, chopping at the frost-loose guy-ropes, only getting tangled up in the slack. She kicked the man's sword free without a pause. Another man's body ploughed into her, falling across her feet, face down, arms up flying over his forge-black sallet, bare sword dropping between his unarmoured legs.

She wrenched her leg free, hauled him up by shoulder and arm, one of Rochester's men at his other side; yelled: "Keep *going!*"

Running men's backs surround her. Nothing more than two feet away is visible. The trumpet shrilled, off to her left. The bar-slit of her vision blurred. Canvas ripped under her sabatons, someone thrust a bill down into it; she heard a choked-off squeal from underneath; flailed down with the hammer, not slowing.

Collapsing tents sagged at her feet. She caught sight of fire arcing through the sky over her head. A pitch-torch landed among the lightly armoured men at her right: men screamed, shouted curses; the torch rolled uselessly down the wet canvas and sank into the beaten earth in front of her.

The crowd of men surged forward into free movement at the same second that she thought *hard-packed earth: the camp's roads!*

Armour clatters, men jogging forward, breathing hard; two men go down on her right, one on her left—

A thin billman in a jack fell flat in front of her. She pitched over him on to her face. He screamed. Something cracked in her hand where she held the pole-hammer shaft. Someone grabbed the back of her livery jacket and hauled her on to her feet – *Anselm?* – and an arrow stuck out of the billman's groin, waggling as he rolled, screeching, blood soaking his hose and hands.

"*Are we right?*" Anselm bellowed in her ear. He jogged beside her, bare sword in one hand. "Which *way—*"

Panic hit her: *Have we turned around—?* "Keep going!"

A hiss like water thrown on to hot grease came from somewhere: she couldn't see which direction. Screams rose over the noise of orders, armour, men panting. A hollow breathlessness scraped at her lungs; her legs ached; her hot, wet breath bounced the smell of steel back off the inside of her helmet.

A gap opened up in front of her.

She saw a pounded-earth road; a lone, broken longbow.

I'm dropping behind, that's why there's a gap—

She forced herself to run harder. The gap didn't close.

Shit, I can't do it—

Her visor's slit blackened. Blind, she stumbled on. Scraping at it, her hand came away wet. She shoved the sallet up with a bloody glove, tilting it. The smell choked in her throat. Directly in front, men lifted bill-shafts and stabbed hooked blades down; above their heads, the great yellow-and-blue expanse of the Lion standard, next to the standard of the Burgundian Duchy.

"Get *up* there!" she yelled. *Shit-all fucking command we're doing!*

Someone crashed into her from behind – one of Rochester's men, or Rochester himself. She stumbled, braced; her heels skidded on frozen hard-packed earth; and slid off towards the side of the road, seeing the roof of a timber barracks over helmets and plumes – *legion plumes!* The whole mass of men with her in the middle of it kept pushing, pushing to the right, moving away from something to her left—

"—fucking *arrows!*"

A hard impact knocked her head around to the right. Pain shot through her wrenched neck. A spear-blade shone in front of her eyes. The pole-hammer wouldn't come up, caught on something – a steel-plated arm pushed in front of her, and the spear-point skidded off that vambrace and into her breastplate. The impact knocked her half-turned around. She dragged her weapon free. A woman screamed. A Visigoth spearman stumbled into her field of view, fell at her feet.

She slammed the top-spike down, punched it into his calf-muscle; a foot-knight in Lion livery smacked a mace into the Visigoth's bare face. Bloodied teeth and bone-fragments spattered up her breastplate—

The flag-staff of the Lion Affronté cracked down hard on her right shoulder. An armoured man cannoned into her from behind; a Visigoth spearman, on his knees, clinging to the man's belt and stabbing a dagger up into his groin. Blood sprayed.

They shouldn't get this near to me—

The whole mass of people pushed off to the right; she half-fell over the edge of the path. The banner-staff caught between her helmet and haut-piece, jutting forward over her shoulder, pressing her down.

"Keep – going—!"

With a great wrench she completed the turn, spinning as hard left as she could. The banner-pole jolted up over the haut-piece of her shoulder-armour and off.

Thomas Rochester grabbed for it with one hand.

All the men around him had white Visigoth livery, mail hauberks.

He opened his mouth, shouting at her.

A sword slammed against his face, hit the bottom of his sallet at jaw-height, skidded upwards along the metal edges, and his face disappeared in a spray of blood.

She grabbed her pole-hammer in both hands, rammed the butt-spike under the Visigoth's upraised arm, punching through mail rings. The hard impact jolted back through her shoulder muscles. The shaft twisted as she tried to pull it free. A gout of blood spurted over her forearms. Men in red-and-blue livery thumped into her, pushing her back; it was all she could do to keep the shaft from being wrenched out of her hand and *Christ Jesus I'm facing the wrong way, I'm turned around, where's the banner—?*

1052

"Get the fucking *banner* UP!"

Stay *visible*, keep *moving*, stay *alive*—!

Men behind slammed into her. She pushed back for a second, but the weight of them forced her forward. She staggered upright and on, stepping on bodies, treading on ragged mailed backs, bloodied breastplates; her ankle twisting as her footing skidded between bodies, in blood and fluid.

Shit I have no idea which way I'm facing—

Slamming the sharp points of her couters back, elbowing for space, she turned around; the sky black with arrows. Sweat froze on her exposed face. A blue-and-yellow Lion's-head banner lifting up—

"Boss!" Rickard's adolescent, cracked voice shrieked beside her, over the noise; the Lion Azure banner's shaft solid in his grip.

Two men slammed in beside her. Lion livery. Rochester's men, her escort. Three more men.

"Keep going! Fuck it! Don't lose momentum!"

She pushed herself forward, grabbed the staff above Rickard's hand, pushed, bellowed, "*Move forward!*" She let go the banner and slammed the shaft of her pole-hammer horizontally across the backs in front of her, feet digging in, pushing with all her weight. Two men-at-arms slammed in beside her.

Ahead – over the mass of Burgundian helmets, Visigoth helmets; the glint of a legion eagle – the Lion standard went suddenly back and round in an eddy of movement.

Pressure sent her staggering back: three steps, hearing men shriek curses, armoured feet trampling, treading on men wounded on the ground. A thin spray of red speckled her gauntlet, vambrace and couter. Rickard thrust his sword once, awkwardly; she couldn't see if it had an effect. Men ahead lifted up bill-shafts, punched them down.

The press in front of her gave way.

She dragged Rickard around, shoved him forward – *shit, where's Robert!* – looked for Anselm; and stumbled back on to the hard-earth road.

A mass of Burgundian-liveried billmen – *Loyecte's men!* – crowded back over her. She ducked her head down. An arrow glanced off the tail of her sallet; her head jerked back. Three or four men fell against her, one with his helmet ripped off and a Visigoth gripping his brown hair, face streaming blood. A man in livery soaked all red jabbed a bollock knife into the Visigoth's groin, their bodies pressed up against Ash; she punched her left gauntlet plate into the Visigoth's eye, felt the bone of his eye-socket snap, heard him scream through her muffling helmet and lining. Pressure eased; she got herself on to firm footing.

Christ, I miss being on a horse! I can't see a fucking thing!

"Where's my fucking command group!" She got no power into her voice. "Rickard! *Find the Lion standard.* We got to keep moving, *we're dead if we stand still!*"

Her hands felt emptiness. She pushed her body forward into the middle of the men. Two sharp impacts on her backplate she ignored, thrusting with her arms like a man swimming. Ahead, bill-blades went up and down, rising and falling; and she shoved towards the irregular movement.

"There!"

Rickard swung off her left shoulder, bawling. She found herself with her sword in hand – *when did I draw that? Where's my pole-hammer?* – staring across a space of ten or a dozen yards full of fighting men's backs, all of them shoving forward; and beyond them a standard charged with a lion azure passant guardant.

She opened her mouth to yell, "Okay, *go!*', and a blast of fire blacked out her vision.

Head ringing, arms numb, she clawed at what she could reach of her face under the front of her tilted sallet. The split-second's dazzle passed; let her see that she was standing at the edge of a crowd—

On the earth in front of her, a swathe of men lay prone or supine, arms flung up over their faces. On each body, the line of red hose or bright steel cuisse or painted war-hat ended at charred black.

Smoke poured up off their bodies. It smelled wrenchingly of roast meat. Her mouth filled with water.

Two scorched, unrecognisable faces reared up in front of her, screaming.

Another hiss, water on a hot fire, magnified a hundred times. A foot kicked her behind the knee. She fell sprawling, hit the earth hard. *Down: defenceless!* Her bladder let go; she scratched in panic at the cold ground, scrabbling to get her feet back under her. Something fell or trod on her backplate: her helmet slammed against the earth; someone shrieked her name.

Whiteness flickered in the corner of her vision.

A wide-mouthed screaming Visigoth *nazir* crawled in front of her; not striking out, not even looking. His whole back was charred black and smoking.

She got to hands and knees. A man hurdled over her. She flinched back. Six, seven, or more: men in hose and jacks, Lion livery, steel war-hats flashing in the bright cold sunlight, all lifting weapons.

Over their heads, she saw a white stone ovoid: marble carved into the shape of a face. Brass glinted at its back. A low, chimney-flue roar; bodies fell down around her; heat scorched her face and she threw up her arm too late. Her skin stung; her eyes ran. Staggering up, she blinked her vision clear, saw the golem standing with the Greek Fire tank's blackened nozzle in both hands, swinging it inexorably around—

Two men in Lion livery ducked low. Two swung weapons. *Mauls!* she saw, *heavy hammers*; and the stone right arm and left hand of the golem shattered and cracked off its body. The nozzle fell. The two men hit the golem from the side: a bill-shaft between them, across the bronze-jointed knees. She saw it fall over backwards, saw four other men strike hard, decisive hammer-blows; their leader bawled, "That one's *down*: move on, *keep moving!*" Geraint's voice.

"BOSS—"

Someone's hands hauled her round. A man in armour, a head taller than she is. Lion livery: Anselm's voice; Robert Anselm screaming, "This way! Over here! *This way!*"

Running, pounding, panting; stopping again in the thick of troops, foot-knights, and in the sky above and past Anselm, the Lion standard – not moving.

Not moving.

We're shitted, we lost it, we're bogged down.

Oh Jesus. Hundreds of them round us. It's the finish.

Every muscle in her body knotted. For a second, in the din of fighting, she stopped dead, bent half double. Her thigh muscles ached; her shoulder joints jabbed her with pain, every spot under plate – collar-bone, hip, knee – swelled with bruises. Her head rang. Blood ran down into one eye, and she dabbed at her face; and saw that her ring-finger inside her right gauntlet was outside the strap, and folded across at a ninety-degree angle to the palm. She could not feel the break. Blood ran down from a gouge on the inside of her elbow; one tasset plate was gone; everything on her left-hand side – plackart, breastplate, poleyn, greave – had the scratches and dents of arrow-strikes not even felt.

Wish I'd gone for my brigandine; mobility. I can't walk another fucking yard in this harness.

Can't fight. I'm dead.

Anselm's helmet-muffled voice bellowed, "Come *on*, girl!"

She made to move off. One half-pace, and she stopped again, the noise of screaming men beating at her ears through the helmet-lining. She felt her arms too heavy to lift, her legs too heavy to move.

The men closest to her were not fighting. The shouts and screams came from a few yards further off. A great noise went up – indistinguishable words.

"What the fuck—"

Over the heads of the men in front, something was passing – passing through many hands, towards the Lion Affronté banner – passed across and down to Robert Anselm – something he thrust out towards her.

She took it automatically: a Visigoth spear. Her hand gripped the shaft. Unbalanced, it fell, and she grabbed at it with her other hand, swearing at the pain, her dropped sword dangling off its lanyard, and she looked up into the blue sky to see what unbalanced the weapon.

A severed head.

The head's weighted beard shook, braided with golden beads.

"*Gelimer's dead!*" Robert Anselm bawled. He pointed up, steel arm bloodied past the elbow. "GELIMER'S DEAD!"

A great scream went up, over to the left.

"We have to stop this!" Ash shouted. She closed her other hand around the spear-shaft. "We got to— *do they know he's dead?*"

"Banner went down!"

"WHAT?"

"His BANNER. Went DOWN!"

"Let me through." She moved another step forward, towards the line of billmen – John Price's old unit, that had been Carracci's – ducking the ends of bill-shafts jabbing back. "Get me through to the fucking front of the line! *Fast!*"

Men's backs shifted. She shouldered between burly bodies, both hands gripping the top-heavy spear, Robert Anselm and the banner at her back; felt herself shoved bodily into the second rank of billmen, and bill-shafts came down over her shoulders, dripping blades held out in front of her, a mass of hooks and spikes.

"Gelimer's dead!" The pitch of her voice shredded her throat.

The bill unit backed up, bunching against her; weapons raised, but not striking. Beyond, spear-points caught sunlight. A line of Visigoth men in mail and coats-of-plates, bright reds and oranges and pinks, lower faces covered by aventails or black cloth; spears and swords extended—

She has a second to wonder *are they backing off?* and realise she is already seeing trodden earth and bodies lying on their faces. She risked a glance, left and right, through a forest of bills and spears. A gap of several feet – still widening—

They've seen his banner go down—

She thrust the spear two-handed up into the blue sky.

Gelimer's severed head bobbed high above the morass of bodies, face clearly distinct in the sun, his mouth gaping open, his roughly chopped-out spine hanging down in a tail of red and white bone.

"The King-Caliph's dead!"

The bellow emptied her chest of air. She swayed. Billmen in jacks and war-hats beside her, red-faced, panting, tears running, took it up:

"The King-Caliph's dead!"

Arrows still dropped out of the sky, on her left: men shouted over the clashing together of iron. Around her a chant grew, drowning that out.

"The King-Caliph's dead! The King-Caliph's dead!"

Arms shaking, she jabbed up the spear and its impaled head. You gotta *see* it!

Widening, now; undeniably widening – a gap between the fighting lines: a stretch of earth, canvas, tumbled cauldrons, bloodied bedding, and bodies with their heads buried in their arms. And bodies and separate heads. Fifteen feet in front of her she clearly saw one *nazir*, bewildered, shouting at his commander. The *'arif*'s gaze fixed on the spike, and the head of Gelimer.

The rise of the ground and the trampled-down camp let her see, as the spearmen edged back, the helmets of the hundreds of men beyond them – slave-spearmen, Visigoth dismounted knights, bowmen; rank on rank of men jammed shoulder to shoulder among the trashed tents and buildings, unit banners peppering the sky. Experience gave her a rapid assessment: *four and a half, five thousand men.*

A distant single rapid *b-bang!* split the air. Some gunner sweeping a match across all the touch-holes of an organ-gun at one go: eight barrels firing almost instantaneously – from the city wall.

I can *hear* that! They've stopped fighting *here*—

As instantly, screams shrieked up from her right: the roaring cough of Greek Fire sounded; black smoke rounded itself up on to the air.

"The King-Caliph's dead!" she bellowed again, ripping her throat with every word; hearing the shrill high clarion of her voice echo over men's heads, burning buildings, shrieks of pain. "GELIMER – IS – DEAD. *Stop fighting!*"

Whether it was adrenalin or lack of oxygen, she swayed back against Anselm. He gripped her arm, hand closing around her vambrace, and held her steady. She thought, for a heartbeat, it was as if the whole world held its breath; no reason why the Visigoth troops should not just roll on over the less-than-thirteen-hundred men in front of them. *No reason in the world*, she thought dizzily; gazing through bloody eyes at the blue, icy clear sky and Gelimer's head on a spike.

"Disengage!" She forced a strained whisper at Robert Anselm. "Send runners – tell Morgan to *hold* the standard *where he is*."

"Got you!"

Officers yelled orders behind her. She continued to face forward, hardly breathing, eyes sore and stinging. She saw no banners that she knew, certainly not the Faris's brazen head; no sign of Gelimer's portcullis banner going up again; and then across the cleared space – *thirty feet, now?* – a banner with a stark geometric triangle came up: Sancho Lebrija's stylised mountain.

He follows orders.

Will he follow a dead man's orders?

"KING'S – DEAD!" Ash bellowed. Her voice cracked.

Anselm hauled her around, pointing. More men flooded into the area every second. *They'll be covering all the ground behind us, between us and the city.* The Lebrija banner jerked, caught up somewhere in the mass of troops. *How many seconds before he starts giving orders?*

"There!" Anselm threw his arm out, pointing at more horses picking their way across the broken ground; a leader with a gilded helmet; riders carrying another banner – a notched wheel. A black notched wheel on a white field.

She said, "That's *Leofric's* livery!"

The two banners met. Men's voices shouted.

"My lord *amirs*!" she screamed. "The Caliph Gelimer is dead!"

She emphasised it with a shake of the spear in her hands. Blood and spinal fluid trickled down over her right hand, bright on the back of her steel gauntlet.

Panting, she gulped air down into her lungs. For all the cold, she sweltered in her armour. She stared.

The rider in the gilded helmet, among men in mail and white robes, took off his helmet, and was Leofric.

His wisps of white hair jutted up. He touched spurs to his mare's flanks, urging her out among the dead and dying, coming close enough for her to see him frowning at the impaled head, either in anger or against the morning sun.

A sun hardly risen any further up from the horizon behind him. *I doubt it's fifteen minutes since the wall went down.*

"Leofric!" she yelled, "Gelimer's dead. *He can't stop you destroying the Wild Machines!*"

The wind took her words, and the noises of sobbing, hurt men and women. *Can he hear me?* She stared into his lined face for long seconds – *is he mad? Was he ever mad?* – and he turned away from her, saying something sharp; one of his officers began to shout brusque orders, and the *'uqda* pennants moved in towards him – Lebrija's banner with them.

"He's doing it. He's taking command. God damn it, he's doing it." She stamped her feet. "*He's doing it.*"

Robert Anselm swore evenly and monotonously and vilely.

Thirty yards away, to her left, the gap between the lines vanished again. She looked up a corridor of clashing staves above men's heads; poleaxe and hooked bills; spear and lifted shields, men packed in too close to do more than hack at weapon-shafts and helmets, stab at faces. A concerted Visigoth shout: the St Andrews Cross pennon went back ten yards in ten seconds.

That's some *'arif* acting on his own—

"Tell 'em to hold!" She dug her feet in against the pressure of bodies from behind; yelled across at Leofric, *"Stop* the fighting! *Now!"*

Lebrija's *'arifs* shouted. Sudden weight behind pushed her, inexorably; staggering forward among the jutting bill-hooks. Rickard's shoulder scraped against hers. The Lion banner swayed. Robert Anselm's deep bellow, *"Hold!"*, echoed out across the frosty camp and the troops behind him.

Twenty yards back down the slope, to her right, a guttering cough of Greek Fire roared.

"Christ! Those things don't *stop!*"

Leofric's head turned. The lord-*amir* jolted up in his stirrups, staring over Visigoth troops' heads. He began to shout loudly, authoritatively. She slitted her eyes, blinking away pain from swollen eyelids; heard the coughing long roar again, and a wedge of Visigoth helmets stampeded into the Burgundian billmen, men tripping and vanishing, pennons tipping over on their poles; the lick of fire searing her vision momentarily black—

"They're firing on their own men too!" Anselm screamed. A thrust of movement in the men around her; she half-turned; a runner in St Andrew's Cross livery wheezed out, "—firing at *everybody*—" and the officers around Leofric ran, calling, units moving; and nothing, nothing – for a count of thirty.

Nothing. No Greek Fire.

A dead man has no friends.

He may have men who want to avenge him—

A high voice screamed *behind* her. Carthaginian Latin. Shoved forward, this time braced; she kept both hands clenched on the spear-shaft, Gelimer's severed head swaying like a ship's mast. Two steps forward, three; forced towards the facing line of Visigoth infantry. The pressure eased. She halted, staring at spear-points, staring at archers, recurved bows, arrows being hastily laid to bowstrings—

The *nazir* fifteen feet in front of her yelled, *"Hold!"*

She leaned back, putting her mouth close to Robert's helmet. "More runners – to commanders – hold place – defence *only*—"

Rickard shifted back, at her right shoulder, and she suddenly saw between two billmen how the ground sloped back, slightly down, the way they had come.

Christ, have we come so *far?*

I don't remember it being a slope.

Christ—

A narrow swathe of trampled earth, canvas, sagging tent-posts, broken beams, cook-pots and men clutching weapons ran down the slope towards Dijon.

If they'd been deployed, instead of sleeping—

The air shone clear, frosty. She breathed in the stink of shit and blood. Past the end of her Burgundians, a great mass of Visigoth legionaries filled up the lanes and streets of the camp, the sun shining off motionless ranks of shield rims and swords. Chaos far over to the east, cornicens and barked orders; but in the north camp, two legions still only just being called to arms; piling out of turf barracks, an untouched five thousand more in the III Caralis alone.

All they have to do is roll over us—

Before Dijon's walls, the bare expanse of earth lay dotted with men in yellow or red-and-blue livery, some of them moving. The gap in the expanse of stonework showed utterly black. Bright metal glints, in the shadows – scythes, pitchforks. Dijon's citizens. Behind the shattered tumble of masonry.

She let her gaze sweep slowly back up the slight hill, blinking, counting: *I can't see all of us;* surely *that isn't all of us that's left—!*

A swirl of movement yanked her attention back to the Visigoth ranks in front of her. The archers parted. New, bright-liveried troops marched into the gap: a high voice, further back in the camp, screaming in Carthaginian Latin and Italian: "Advance! Attack!"

"Aw *shit—*"

A cornicen rang out. Braced, breathless, she shot a glance either side at the sweating billmen; saw their faces show disgust and terror equally, and then one man gave a great laugh, his flapping cheek showing bloody teeth in the cut.

She squinted through swollen eyelids. Not Visigoth troops ahead – men in Frankish liveries. Bow and bill foot troops. Armoured horsemen, packed tight in the crowd. And nobody moving, not one man of them moving forward past the line—

The Carthaginian voice screaming orders cut off with a blackly comic gurgle.

"Look at *that!*" A mush of blood sprayed out with the billman's words. "Look at that, boss!"

The white Agnus Dei banner glinted, gold embroidery flashing in the sun; and down the line, Onorata Rodiani's naked sword, and the Ship and Crescent Moon of Joscelyn van Mander: Gelimer's Frankish mercenaries.

She saw a rider in Milanese armour reach out to his banner-bearer. Agnus Dei. Sun flashed off his gauntlet, gripping the striped pole. A babble of Italian crossed the clear air, not distinct enough for her to make out what was said.

The golden spike on top of the banner dipped.

The rider's armoured hand forcing it down, the banner dipped, silk folding, the banner going down, the point of it touching the bloodied dirt, and the Lamb of God lost among the draped cloth on the earth.

Tears dazzled her vision. Raw shouts went up around her. Beyond, the banner of the Rodiani company dipped; and de Monforte; and finally, finally the silver-and-blue of the Ship and Crescent, all the mercenary banners going down, dipped to the dirt, to their men's raucous, fierce, appreciative cheers.

Robert Anselm, hammering at her left pauldron, pointing away with his free hand: "He's calling them off!"

Shrill cornicens called from the centre of the camp, and beyond; from the east where guns still fired. She turned and thrust the loaded spear at Rickard. "Give me the banner!"

Their hands fumbled; her snapped finger, in its blood-soaked glove, tore loose from the spear-shaft; and she took the Lion Affronté banner in her left hand alone, held it up over her head, and hefted it in a weary apology for a circle.

The crack of guns from the east trickled away. Inside a long minute, all the gun-crews stopped shooting.

Leofric rode up past Gelimer's ex-mercenaries, among ranks of House Leofric infantry; Lebrija's banner with him, other *qa'ids*' pennants following. The lord-*amir* Leofric reined in his mare, leaning down to speak to one of his commanders.

'Arif Alderic stepped forward from the line. "My master says, 'Peace between us! Peace between Carthage and Burgundy!'"

She took a raw breath, and shouted, "Has he – the right and power – to offer it?"

Alderic's voice rang out, to at least the nearest Visigoth units as well as to the Burgundians. "*Amir* Leofric, with the death in battle of this Gelimer, claims for himself the throne of the King-Caliph. There are no other *amirs* of rank here. It is his honour and duty. Hail the King-Caliph Leofric!"

Robert Anselm's voice, beside her, exploded: "Bugger me!"

The Visigoth legions cheered.

Alderic called, "*Jund* Ash, he has this power. Carthage will ratify his election here. Will you take the peace he offers?"

"Fuck, *yes!*"

Waiting to regroup, a forest of banners and standards surrounds her: Thomas Morgan, with the blue-and-gold standard of the Lion Azure, de la Marche and his bearer of the Burgundian Duchy's arms; the Lion Affronté; unit pennants; and men in bloodied plate and ripped mail staring up not at the silks, but at the spear-shaft that she rests back over her shoulder, the severed head high up and visible to everybody near this part of the field.

She feels nothing.

"Tell Leofric where we want it set up. On the open ground, in front of the gap in the wall."

Anselm nodded acknowledgement, signalled two of Morgan's men, and vanished through the troops towards Leofric.

The loud noise of relief, of a barely present realisation of success just making itself felt – none of this pierces the glass bubble of numbness that surrounds her.

"We did it!" Rickard ripped off his helmet with his free hand. His flushed, youthful face beamed. "*We did it!* Hey, boss! You going to make me your squire now?"

Deep male voices boom appreciation. Suddenly they are clearing a space, the black-haired boy going down on one knee in front of her, still clutching the striped pole of the Lion Affronté.

"Ah, fuck it!" Ash said. She grinned, suddenly, and the sore skin on her face twinged. A flood of warm emotion pierces her. Through blurred vision, she recovered her wheel-pommel sword on its lanyard, gripped it, and put the bare blade down on Rickard's shoulder. "If I could make it a knighthood, I would! Consider yourself promoted!"

The cheers for that are part joy, part relief; part the feeling that this is how it *should* be, right now. Armoured men help the young man to his feet, beating on his shoulders. The cold air stings her face again. She does not remove her own helmet; not yet.

"Stay there." She unceremoniously shoved the spear at Rochester's sergeant, Elias; and elbowed her way a few yards west into the crowd, until she can see past the back rank of men.

In her mind, the direction is clear – *no matter what turf the camp is set up on, the camp is always the same.*

The *ad hoc* leader of Carracci's and Price's billmen shouldered hastily in beside her, as escort.

"Vitteleschi," he panted. "In charge of these guys if you say so, boss."

"For now." Another spreading grin, that she can't resist: *we did it, we did it!* and her cheeks sting.

"Your face is red, boss," Vitteleschi said.

"Yeah?"

"Your skin." He drew a gauntlet-finger swiftly across his own cheekbones.

"Right . . ." Cooling sweat stings in the corners of her eyes, scalding her swollen lids.

Now she can see past the back rank, past an elaborate turf-roofed building – Gelimer's headquarters? – and out on to the bridge beyond.

"I want to see what Jonvelle's . . ."

Bright red blood covers the ice.

Blood covers the thick frost on the shore. She squinted at lumps, lying on the trodden earth bank, casting man-size black shadows.

Out on the ice, men hauled dead men in, by an arm or a leg; picking up heads, leaving smears on the whiteness. Scattered corpses further downriver jutted with fletched shafts.

She counted the line on the bank. *Twenty-two.*

Among the dropped weapons, discarded bone skates lay.

Get into position; hold the bridge; stop Gelimer from running.

A Burgundian sergeant plodded forwards.

"Where's Jonvelle?" she asked.

"Dead." The man coughed, coughed again. "Dead, Demoiselle-Captain. Captain Berghes is dead. Captain Romont, too."

Men of note.

She turned her head, seeing men lying down on the northern side of the bridge, lying on the cold earth in awkward positions, arms flung out, legs hooked one over the other. Billmen; archers; men with only jacks and brigandines and helmets. She looked at their faces, bleeding from the mouth; the blood not running now. Fifty? Sixty?

A man sat on the ground in front of the still-warm bodies, bent over his stomach, moaning. Half a dozen Burgundian billmen walked back over the bridge towards her, supporting men and women who cried out with pain at every step; Jonvelle's banner-bearer still dragging his colours, his hastily bandaged right arm dripping, missing from the elbow down.

A severed hand almost tripped her as she stepped back.

"Vitteleschi."

"Boss."

"Send a runner over to Lord-*Amir* Leofric. Tell him our doctors are in the city. Tell him to send me his legionary medics."

"But—"

"*Now*, Vitteleschi." She turned back to the Burgundian sergeant. "Are you in command here?" And at his nod – *shit, everyone of rank above sergeant dead?* – she said, "There won't be any crap about not being treated by rag-head doctors, clear? Get anyone who's still alive bandaged up, or on hurdles; bring them down into the city as soon as you're ready. Go to the abbey hospices."

"Yes, Demoiselle-Captain." There was no emotion in his voice.

She turned to Vitteleschi. "Let's go."

The men parted, letting her back through; almost all drawn up to their unit pennants now. She walks among men in Burgundian livery, Lion livery; men talking in low tones, and over it all now the screaming and shrieks of wounded men, men lying out between them and the ranks of the Visigoth legions, crawling, or sprawled on their faces. One woman, helmet gone, vomited; blood spidering down over her forehead.

Shit, is that Katherine Hammell? No: one of her archers, though—

The Visigoth doctors and their assistants are already moving out of the opposing army. Some Frankish voices went up in protest. The legionary medics bend down by men, leaving some, calling hurdles for others.

They do not distinguish between their own men and hers.

"Send a runner into the town. Tell the monks to come out here and help see to these men. No, I don't know that it's *safe*! Tell them to get their fucking arses out here! Get Blanche's women, too."

She looked for de la Marche's banner.

"Back to the city. The way we came in. Muster on the ground outside the walls."

She walked on past the Burgundians, Rickard with the standard, Elias with the spear, and Vitteleschi and his men behind her. Ranks parted in front of her. Thin ranks. She glanced back, saw few, very few; thought *shit I don't believe it, we* can't *have lost that many!* and found herself walking on to the edge of an area of blackness, even the crushed tents only charcoal frameworks, and men writhing on the baked earth.

"*Get a fucking medic over here!*"

One of Leofric's robed Visigoths strode past her, in a flurry of cloth, sandals cracking burnt tent-pegs and bones underfoot. The hood fell back, and she saw a woman doctor, pinch-faced; calling out to her assistants in medical Latin.

I know her.

"You." The Visigoth woman's voice sounded in front of her. She opened eyes she had not been aware of shutting; recognised the face, too, and the voice saying *the gate of the womb is all but destroyed.*

"I will give your slave here a salve for your eyes; they will swell, otherwise. You have missed the worst of the burn, but do not neglect—"

"*Fuck off.*" She pushed past the woman.

She stopped at a pile of men charred black, and a leg in blue hose. The body lay with head downhill, lower than its feet. The tail of a yellow-and-blue livery jacket showed, unburned. Vitteleschi gave a short order. Two billmen knelt, and turned the blackened body over. After a second, he said, "Captain Campin."

Under Adriaen Campin's body, his lance-leader was almost unburned. Willem Verhaecht's eyes were open in his florid face, not blinking at the sky's brightness. Something, most likely the hand of a golem, had punched into his body through his breastplate, and pulled one lung out on to the torn metal. She stared for ten breaths, and the red-black flesh did not twitch, did not beat.

Take teams: take out the golems: take out their Greek Fire weapons.

"Check and see if anyone's alive here."

The sunlight showed her tears pouring down Vitteleschi's lined, filthy face.

"Shit, just do it," she said, her voice weak; and he nodded, still weeping, and bent over to pull away crisped arms and torsos, that fell apart in his hands like a roasted joint from the oven.

The Lion standard and the Burgundian standard came slowly down the slope behind her, ranks of men under them. Back down the slope: past the second swathe cut by Greek Fire, and here—

A hand grabbed at her armoured knee. She looked down at the gauntlet against her poleyn, and into the face of a man recognisable only because he wore livery with a lion's head on it, his own face smashed, unrecognisable. Bubbles blew in the blood where his mouth had been. Sitting next to him, a billman held the stump of his right wrist with his left hand, his face glassy and white.

"Medics!" Vitteleschi bawled back over his shoulder. "Get the doctors down here!"

The standards came on. Men began to pick their way. The ground for ten yards was covered in foot-knights in her livery, some moving, some not, all bloody. She took one step aside and her sabaton kicked a man's arm, severed at the elbow.

A faint voice called for help. Her gaze still on the bloody, unrecognisable man – *it's de Treville, it's Henri, I know his armour* – she backed up, turned around, saw Thomas Rochester's crossbowman Ricau kneeling on the ground, with Thomas Rochester sitting up braced against him.

"Boss," the man Ricau said. "Help me with him, boss, I don't know what to do!"

"Rickard, get some of those fucking medics here—"

"Runner, boss – there aren't enough here yet—"

Stiff, she got down on one knee, in frozen earth now muddy with fluids and excrement. She put out her hand, and hesitated. Vitteleschi squatted beside her, a piece of bloodied cloth in his hand – torn-off livery – and reached out. Ricau took it, wiped gingerly at the man leaning back against him, and

Rochester screamed. His sound pierced the semi-silence of the field; ended in something like and not like a sneeze, an explosion of blood.

"It's his *eye!*" Ricau wailed.

He had got his commander's sallet off. Two black oval holes streamed blood down Rochester's face and on to his mail standard, and down his breastplate. Nothing of his nose was left, only a fragment of cartilage. A shattered white splinter of bone jutted out of the red mess of his right eye – his own bone, she realised, from his shattered nose.

The men plodding back down the hill slowed, looking down at Rochester, casting numb or angry looks, trying not to breathe in the stench of shit that rose up from him.

"Get a grip." She licked at her lips. "Keep him *still*, and quiet. Put the cloth there, soak it up – let him breathe. Tom. Tom? Help's coming. We'll get you back. Fuck—" she straightened and sprang up, "has anybody got any wine? Any water?"

Word went back through the crowd, men feeling at their belts; very few costrels; none, it seemed, with anything left—

"Here!" Rickard turned away, yelling and waving the Lion banner at white-robed men picking their way across the earth from the massed legions. "Over here!"

"Shit!" She turned on her heel and walked on among Burgundian units, among broken tents now. She heard panting. Rickard and the banner caught her up. He said something. She kept going. There was an empty space beside her, the men parting and going around Rickard where he knelt down. She stopped.

Two bodies lay together on the ground, among the stained canvas of a barrack-tent. *This is where we broke through to the road: this is where the tent-teams did their stuff.*

A small, squat body lay under his hands. Rickard rolled it over. The head flopped, neck boneless as a dead rabbit. A few strands of yellow hair stuck out under the helmet lining of the open-faced sallet. Blood had run out of eight or nine holes punched through the brigandine.

"Margaret Schmidt," another man's voice said, and she looked up to see Giovanni Petro, and the archer Paolo.

He shrugged at her implicit question. "'S all that's left of us."

White and glossy-skinned as the wounded, Rickard got back up on to his feet. The banner-staff leaned loosely back across his shoulder.

"That's Katherine Hammell," he said.

About to speak, she saw he meant not Margaret, but the other body, curled up on the mud in a foetal position. The woman groaned. An arrow stuck out of her mail shirt under her shoulder-blade. A sword stuck through her stomach, the point projecting out of her lower back. Her blood-soaked gauntlets clenched in her spilled intestines.

"She's still alive. Get a doctor to her." And, seeing Rickard's expression, "Who knows?"

"We need a miracle!" he wailed.

A cynical smile almost burst out of her. For a second, she could have screamed, or burst into tears. "That, we can't manage . . ."

A fast pace took her through the marching men, down on to flat ground, out towards the golem-dug trenches encircling the city. She walked stiffly, in silence.

Fewer bodies here. She stumbled on, momentarily looking across to the gap in the walls, seeing Leofric's banner, and Anselm's and Follo's; and a handful of civilians coming out over the demolished wall—

"*Look out!*" Rickard screamed.

Her foot came down on something soft. She staggered and caught her balance. The man under her feet shrieked and burst into sobs. Black-feathered arrows jutted out of him; *alive enough to make a noise*, she thought; and then, *Euen—!*

The wiry, dark man looked bulky in mail and livery jacket. Bloodstains blotted out the Lion. She knelt down, counted *arrow in arm, arrow in face, two arrows in thigh* and said, "Euen, hold on!"

"Shit, boss!" Rickard groaned.

"If he can shout, he'll make it—" Her hand, patting him down, examining by touch, froze. She awkwardly peeled back his livery, and hauberk, and took her hand away thick with hot, red blood pouring out of his groin or belly, she couldn't see where. "*Get somebody here.*"

Rickard sprinted.

She stayed pressing her whole weight against his wound until Visigoth medics arrived, saw him on to a hurdle, screaming at the men to get him to a hospital tent. She stood up, hands dripping, watching the last of her force moving past her and over the improvised bridges of the ditch.

The defences are manned again now: Visigoth soldiers in coats-of-plates and helmets gazing at her, over mail aventails. Soft, accented voices went up into the still air; and a *nazir* snapped a command. She felt how many of the bows were surreptitiously lifted, how many of them exchanged glances, thinking *close enough to kill the cunt*.

She reached out a hand to Rochester's sergeant, Elias, and took the heavy-laded spear from him. An unsteady oak door and two window-shutters groaned under her weight as she walked across the ditch. Rickard stumbled after her.

Yeah, we made it across the siege trenches.

Out of the walls, bridge the ditch, flatten the tents, find the roads through. And they must have found Gelimer by his banner. I knew he'd have to put it up, to command. I knew he'd break and run. And Jonvelle stopped him on the bridge. Some billman or foot-knight killed him. I knew they would.

I knew.

Who needs the Lion's voice?

She glanced back, seeing more Visigoth faces at the trenches. The Lion banner above her, she felt herself their focus; like a player on a pageant wagon, visible to thousands.

Men and women still limped off the field behind her, forming up in stunned silence into their muster-lines. Except that it is not a line, it's a ragged clump of men here, another there; nothing that even looks like a continuous line; and counting by eye she cannot make it come to more than five hundred men.

Stunned. As if this were a defeat, not a shocking, beyond-hope victory.

Behind the ones who can walk come the ones who can walk with help: Pieter Tyrrell with his arm over Jan-Jacob Clovet's shoulder, Saint-Seigne with two foot-knights carrying him sitting on crossed bill-shafts; an archer with eyes that are a mask of blood, being led. Two more blinded men behind her. A billman, blood squelching in his shoe; no fingers on one hand. A stumbling column of wounded men, mostly still carrying weapons cocked back over their shoulders, coming towards her; so that she sees them as an apparently motionless mass, crusted blades bobbing gently up and down above their heads.

And then men face-down on hurdles, or with a man at ankles and armpits, gripping and hefting their dead-weight. People who lie still; blood trickling down. People who cry, shriek; appalled, frantic, desolate screams. Fifteen, twenty, forty; more than fifty; more than a hundred. Monks and Visigoth doctors trot between them, giving quick diagnoses; moving to those they can help.

The thump of a shod horse's hooves made itself felt through the ground. A Visigoth archer on a chestnut Barb wheeled, a few yards from her. "My lord Leofric has all ready for you."

The man sounded not just respectful, but frightened.

"Tell him . . . I'll be there."

She stood long enough for the sergeants to bring her the count. Olivier de la Marche moved to her side, on the frozen earth, his great red-and-blue standard behind him; and a few of the *centeniers* – Lacombe; three more. Saint-Seigne. Carency. Marle. *All there are left?*

"Demoiselle-Captain?" De la Marche sounded numb.

"Three hundred and twelve Burgundians killed. Two hundred and eighty-seven wounded. There are—"

Rickard, Vitteleschi, and Giovanni Petro looked at her.

"There are ninety-two of us not killed or wounded. A hundred and eight dead."

The Italian captain of archers said, "Shit." Rickard burst out crying.

"And another hundred wounded: about two-thirds of them walking wounded. The Lion's come out of this with less than two hundred of us, and that only if we're lucky."

The bright wind blew cold. Awkwardly, she picked open the buckle of her right gauntlet's fingerplates, took hold of the wet glove that contained it, dragged her broken ring-finger back into place, and yanked the strap tight again over it, to hold it.

"Let's go," she said.

★

V

A cloth of gold carpet covered twenty square yards of the earth below the Byward Tower. An awning covered that. Under it, banners surrounded men at a long table; and she felt the heat of bonfires, walking towards them, kindled for their heat.

Past the tongues of flame, she looked out from ground level at the wintry sky and the immense siege camp.

"Mad."

De la Marche nodded agreement, with a smile that has already begun to discount the dead and wounded. "But you did it, Demoiselle-Captain! Maid of Dijon! You did it!"

All she could see as they walked across the earth were mantlets and pavises, and the first peaked roofs of barrack-tents. *Nazirs* and *'arifs* bawled orders, in the trenches and among the tents. It didn't stop men coming up to stare out at the huge gap in Dijon's walls. Thousands.

She shook, suddenly, in her stifling armour; stopped; and could only just manage to signal Rickard to give the banner to Giovanni Petro, and come and unbuckle her bevor. She choked a breath of air in. She felt Rickard ease her helmet off – *this is either peace or it isn't, and I can't be fucked to bother about assassins now!*

I don't care.

The cold air hit her scalp. She scratched left-handed at her hair, ignoring the blood on her gauntlet; and caught sight of her face reflected in the sallet as Rickard held it. A strip of scalded flesh crossed her face, just at the level of her cheekbones, over her scars. Her lower eyelids were swelling. The strip of flesh across her cheeks and the bridge of her nose showed bright pink.

I'm one of the ninety-two: and it's little more than luck.

Robert Anselm strode up, Richard Follo a few steps behind. The dusty Viscount-Mayor seemed dazed. He laughed, low and under his breath, sounding as if it were from pure joy.

She knows the words that go with that laughter. *We're alive.*

The golden cloth snagged under her sabatons as she strode across it. Six or seven men sat at the long table: Leofric in the centre, Frederick of Hapsburg on his right hand; the French envoys and de Commines on his left; Lebrija, and another *qa'id*. Other men stood behind them, in coats of plate; one – youngish – with House Leofric's features.

She let her gaze go across them all – the Hapsburg Emperor smiling, slightly – and brought it back to the Carthaginian *amir* Leofric.

"Not that crazy, are you?" she said in a philosophical tone. "I didn't think so. Not after I talked to your daughter. Still, kept you alive, I suppose."

Now she is grinning, with shock and with exaltation. *I should have got someone to sluice my armour down.* Drying blood and tissue still cling to it, a stockyard-stink impregnating her clothes. Here she stands, strapped into metal plates: a woman with short, silver, blood-stained hair; ripped Lion livery; sword banging at her hip; carrying a weight in one hand.

She lifted the weighty object up and slammed it down on the table. Gelimer's head. Drying liquid made the palm of her gauntlet sticky. The clotted hair pulled, adhering to her glove, yanking at her broken ring-finger. She swore.

"There's your fucking ex-Caliph!"

His head seemed shrunken now: blood drying red-black, white knobs of bone visible in the trailing remnant of spine, a crescent of white under his half-shut lids.

There was a silence as they looked at it.

"I must sign the treaty of peace with the Duchess herself." Leofric frowned. "Will you bring her out of the city?"

"When we've—"

A deep voice said, "Address the King-Caliph with respect, *jund*," and she looked and saw Alderic behind his master; the *'arif* not wounded, grinning through his now oiled and braided beard.

She grinned back at him.

"When we've talked, 'my lord King-Caliph'," she said. "When this peace is solid. The most important thing first. You know the Wild Machines. You know what they're trying to do. I'm going to tell you why they haven't done it, my lord . . . my lord Father. I'm going to tell you why the Duchess of Burgundy has to stay alive."

Between stopping the fights and fires, and bringing in supplies, almost four days passed. Ash sent riders to the east and the north. After that, she found herself and de la Marche and Lacombe dealing not just with negotiations for food and firewood, but attempting to fill trenches with the dead and the abbey with the casualties of the fighting.

The ground, iron-hard, would not be dug for graves; Visigoth serfs piled the dead in great red-and-white heaps. If not for Visigoth army doctors, wounds and cold would have made the death total even higher.

She visited her own injured men; wept with them.

Simon Tydder she found with the dead, his helmet missing and his head cut open from skull to lower jaw. The third of the brothers, Thomas, knelt by his body in the abbey chapel and would not be comforted.

Euen Huw lived sixteen hours.

She sat with him three times, an hour each, leaving Anselm or de la Marche in charge; sat in the grey-lit upper chamber of the abbey hospice, warmed by braziers and the hearth-fire, and felt his hand that she held grow colder and colder. Examined, they found both his legs were lacerated, one shin cut to the bone; but the wound from the spear thrust up by a fallen man into his groin finally killed him. He died, body shaken by his death-rattle, in the early hours of the twenty-ninth day of December. The twin passing-bells rang.

"*Amir* Lion!" Leofric's woman physician said, catching her at the door, "let me salve your eyes."

Not all of the blurriness of her sight is from tears. A sudden fear pulsed through her gut: *to be blind and helpless—!*

She sat by a window, and submitted to the administration of a soothing herb; the very smell of the woman's robes bringing back House Leofric's observatory and a pain low in her belly.

"Bandage over them at night," the woman added. "In four days, you should improve."

"You might as well see to this, then." Ash held out her hand. The woman pulled the ring-finger of her right hand about, snake-hissed under her breath at Frankish butchers, set the bone, and bound it to her middle finger.

"You should rest it for ten days."

Like I have ten days to rest . . .

"Thank you," she said, surprised to hear herself speak.

Coming down the stone stairs from the hospice, she heard voices below, and came out on to the landing to be faced by Fernando del Guiz and the Faris.

Neither of them spoke. The identical brightness of their faces told her what she needed to know. A genuine numbness dulled her reaction. She smiled, faintly, and made to move on past them.

"We wanted you to know," Fernando said.

For a second, she is caught between seeing him very young and vulnerable, and the knowledge of how many similar young men are dead outside Dijon.

The Faris said, "Will your priest marry us?"

Ash couldn't tell if her own expression were a smile, or something closer to weeping.

"Digorie Paston's dead," she said, "a golem killed him; but I expect Father Faversham will do it. He's upstairs."

The woman and the man turned, eagerly; she could feel herself slip from their attention. Wrapped up in each other, insulated from the death and grief . . .

"Ah, why not?" she said, aloud, softly. "Do it while you can."

'STILL IT GROWS COLD, LITTLE THING OF EARTH—'

'—COLD—'

'—WE *WILL* PREVAIL!'

The voices of the Wild Machines in her head whisper their own panicky confusion. In fierce satisfaction, she thinks, *No Faris, no Stone Golem, not even out-of-date second-hand reports. You're fucked. You don't know a damn thing, do you!*

A rider came back from the east, on the thirtieth, accompanied by Bajezet's second-in-command. Robert Anselm reported, "He says, yes. Florian's coming back. She'll sign a treaty, if de la Marche okays it."

"What do you think?" Ash asked the Burgundian.

Olivier de la Marche blew on his cold hands, and glanced from the fallen city wall to the Visigoth camp. "No doubt there are men over there who still think the Lord Leofric mad. There are enough who do not think him mad, and enough who follow whichever way power flows, that he will hold the Caliphate. In my judgement, at least until he returns to Carthage and *amirs* who will challenge this. I say, it is time for the treaty to be signed."

She watched the golems harrowing the ground in the cathedral yard. Their stone hands dug graves. Human bodies lay piled for burial on the human-impenetrable ice.

The memory comes to her, with a sting of adrenalin: the first corpse she had ever seen. Not as decorous as these washed white bodies under the motionless grey sky. She had run through all the sweet moving air of summer, in a forest where sun shone down through green leaves, and rounding a spur of rock – large to *her* – had all but stepped on the body of a man killed in the prior day's skirmish.

It was a glittering, green-black hummock, unrecognisable as a dead body until the flies that covered it completely rose up in high-pitched flight.

Like walking into a wall, the way I stopped! But I was different then.

She came back to the scentless cathedral yard and Abbot Muthari and Abbot Stephen, voices chanting, and Leofric standing beside her. His robes were musty, the embroidery stiff; he blinked at the implacable open air. Small clouds of white breathed from his lips.

Visigoths inside Dijon. Peace treaty or no, it jumped and curdled in her gut.

"But why isn't it dark here?" the Visigoth lord said, apropos of nothing. She followed his gaze; couldn't see even a ghost-disc of sun.

"About the peace treaty." Dank, cold air chilled the flesh of her face. "I've been thinking, lord Father. I think we need to sign a treaty of alliance."

"What the *Ferae Natura Machinae*, the Wild Machines, do, is undoubtedly material." Leofric began to sniff a little, the circles of his nostrils reddening. His voice thickened with his cold. "If Burgundy preserves the real, as you say, should it not be sunless here, too?"

"An alliance of equals," Ash pressed on.

"The original is better, don't the Franks say? For we poor inheritors of the Romans, the past is always better than this degenerate present."

His look might have meant to draw her in, she couldn't tell.

"And Burgundy clings to the past?" Ash muttered sardonically.

Deliberately, it seemed, mistaking her meaning, Leofric gave her a quick, friendly, older man's smile. "Not always. Peace with Carthage—"

"Alliance. We won't be the only people after the Wild Machines – but we might be the only people who want to actually destroy them. We do," Ash said, "want to destroy them."

To the implied absence of a question in her tone, Leofric added a shudder. "Oh yes; destroy them. It's evident the fire is no blessing. *Amir* Gelimer's dead; God shows His will in battle. Around the pyramids themselves, the stone is fusing – to plants, to small beasts, to the melted bodies of men and horses. We must hold off; use your master gunners' cannon to destroy them."

Gratefully at home in military speculation again, Ash said, "When it stops being quite so hairy close up, we could think about planting some petards?"

"*If* it stops." Leofric huddled his long, furred cloak over his shoulders with a shrug. Waved away, his staff of Caliph's advisers hung back. "An alliance. That would say much of how we regard Burgundy."

"Wouldn't it, though."

The *chunk-chunk* of dropped earth – too cold to split into clods – beat rhythmically back from the front face of the cathedral. Paired mass funeral services sounded from the abbots' lips, each heretical to the other.

Ash frowned, replaying memory. "What did you mean, 'the original'?"

"Who tells their story *first*?" Leofric demanded. "Whoever it is, theirs becomes the yardstick – others are judged by how close or far they are from the original details. The first telling has an authority all its own."

He brought his gaze back to Ash's face. She saw plain excitement: the vision of a man working on theory, without caring whom the truth might benefit: him or another. *All his experiments up to now have benefited the Caliphs, not him. Is that Leofric? Truly King-Caliph by accident?*

This is the man who would have cut me up and killed me. Happily have done it.

"I don't forgive you," she said, with her lips barely moving.

"Nor I, you." And at her shock: "An experiment half a century in the making, and you go and––"

"Spoil it?" Irony, or bitter black humour, just outweigh her outrage.

"Modify it." *There is still the weighing quality in his glance when he looks at her.* "To prove, perhaps, only that an area of ignorance exists."

"And . . . inside that area?"

"Further study."

For a second she thinks of the house in Carthage – not of the examination and medical rooms, but the cell, and her own voice howling loud enough to drown the echoes of those same howls.

"Haven't you studied *enough*?"

"No." Familiar arrogance in his expression – not only for her, now, but for a young man suddenly at his side, walking up past a group of advisers that (she sees) contains both the doctor Annibale Valzacchi and his brother Gianpaulo: Agnus Dei.

"Sisnandus," Leofric said mildly, under the plainsong of the funeral masses.

Ash recognises him now as one of the faces around the table on the cloth of gold. A thin young man, battle-hardened, with Leofric's mouth; nothing else to mark him as the ex-commander of House Leofric except the livery.

"House Leofric's and House Lebrija's messengers have left for the capital," he reported.

Be polite: this is one Leofric's grooming for power, or he wouldn't have had Sisnandus take over when he was feigning madness.

Assuming Sisnandus realises it was put on.

Ash could not tell from his surprisingly active expression whether he resented his lord-*amir*'s return to health and his own consequent demotion from commanding House Leofric, or whether being deputised to control the House while Leofric handles the duties of King-Caliph contents him.

Politics: all politics. She caught the eye of a man directly behind Sisnandus, in his escort. The man looked away. Guillaume Arnisout: too ashamed to approach her after his failure to follow her back into Dijon. *And I shall talk to him too, in the next day or so.*

"An alliance for the Spring campaign." Leofric breathed warm whiteness on to the air, his gaze on the golems now loading the dead into the ground. "I might persuade the French to it. And might you bring the Turks in, as similar temporary allies? The treaty awaits only the Duchess's signature."

The morning of the third day of January dawned clear, very cold; the winter earth iron-hard enough that a horse should not be risked at anything more than a walk.

"Do you need to take so many of the fit men to ride out and bring Duchess Floria back?" Olivier de la Marche questioned.

Ash, on a borrowed Visigoth mare, grinned down at him from her war saddle. "Yup," she said cheerfully.

"You are taking the better part of three hundred men. To meet Bajezet's five hundred mounted Janissaries."

Ash glanced back at the hundred and ten men under the Lion Azure standard, and Lacombe's Burgundians. "We don't know that Bajezet's Turks won't turn round and ride straight back to Mehmet. I'm paranoid. Peace has broken out – but I'm still paranoid. Look at it out there. No food. Dark, over the border. Breakdown of law. It's going to be years before this country's quiet. How would you feel if I lost her to some roaming gang of bandits?"

The big Burgundian nodded. "I grant you that."

Over these four days, dozens of men and women from nearby burned villages and towns have trickled in to Dijon; as the news spreads out across the countryside. Some from caves in the limestone rocks, some from the wildwood; all hungry, far from all honest.

He added, "And I grant you, the men that bore the weight of the battle for our Duchess should have the honour of seeing her home to us."

Any day now, I can be done with this 'Lioness' crap. Just as soon as we start planning a southern campaign.

"But – her?" De la Marche looked at the Faris, where the Visigoth woman rode between two of Giovanni Petro's men.

"I prefer to have her where I can see her. She used to command this lot, remember? Okay, it's over, but we don't take chances."

Not that I haven't taken steps to encourage her co-operation.

On the edge of the crowd of citizens around the open north-east gate, she caught sight of a man in priest's robes: Fernando del Guiz. His escort of Lion billmen flanked him in a business-like manner. He lifted a hand in blessing – although whether to his current or past wife was not apparent.

Ash glanced away, up at the sky. "There aren't many hours of light. We won't get to them before tomorrow, at the earliest – *if* we find 'em that easy! Expect me in three, maybe four days. Messire Olivier, since the Visigoths are being so generous with their food and drink and firewood – do you think we could have a celebration?"

"Captain-General, Pucelle, truly," Olivier de la Marche said, and he laughed. "If only to prove the truth of what I have always said: employ a mercenary and he will eat you out of hearth and home."

Ash rode out over the eastern bridge, passing below the Visigoth gunners camped up on the rough heights. She waved, touched a spur to the mare, and rocked in the creaking saddle, moving up the column.

Cold snatched the air from her mouth. She acknowledged, in a cloud of white breath, the new lance-leaders as she passed: Ludmilla with Pieter Tyrrell and Jan-Jacob Clovet riding with her, instead of Katherine Hammell; Vitteleschi marching at the head of Price's billmen; and Euen Huw's third-in-command, Tobias, leading his lance. Thomas Rochester rode led by his sergeant, Elias; bandages over his blind right eye, and a covering of forge-black steel over the still-weeping hole in his face. Other lance-leaders – Ned Mowlett, Henri van Veen – looked newly serious, newly senior.

The faces change. The company goes on.

With scouts out before and behind and to the flanks, Ash's force rode out of Dijon, into the deserted hamlets and strip-fields, through outflung spurs of the ancient wildwood, into the wasteland.

"Do we know which way Bajezet went?" she asked Robert Anselm. "I wouldn't like to try getting across the Alps, they're too fucked to even think of crossing!"

"He said they'd ride north, through the Duchy," Anselm rumbled. "Then east; Franche-Comté, over the border to Longeau in Haute-Marne, then north-west through Lorraine. Depending on how they could live off the land. He said if they had no word the war was over, he'd ride towards Strasbourg, then cut across to the east, and hope to run into the Turks coming west across the Danube."

"How far do the messengers say they got?"

"Over the border. Into the dark. They're on their way back from the east." Anselm grinned. "And if neither of us is lost, we might even be on the same road!"

Towards the end of the day, flakes of snow began to fall from a yellowing sky.

"Make it as hard as you like," she murmured under her breath as she rode, with the icy wind finding gaps between bevor and visor and numbing her face.

'HARD, YES, COLD—'

'WINTER-COLD, WORLD-COLD—'

'—UNTIL WINTER COVERS YOU, COVERS ALL THE WORLD!'

She heard a note of panic in their voices.

Ash thought, but did not say aloud, *We've won. You can turn Christendom into a frozen wasteland, but we've won. Leofric's Caliph. We sign this treaty, and we leave for the south – we're coming for you.*

She rode east and north, among the clink of bridles in the bitter snowy air, smiling.

The following day, after much frustrated wandering in snow-bound featureless countryside, Janissary outriders encountered Lion Azure scouts a mile outside what Ash found – as they were escorted into it – to be a burned and deserted village. Diminishing smoke still rose from the ruins of the manor house and church. Snow covered the hill-slopes, that had been covered in vines.

With visibility closing in, she rode with Anselm and Angelotti and the

Burgundian Lacombe, over a frozen stream by a shattered stone bridge. Perhaps two of the eleven wattle-and-daub houses still stood, thatch weighed down under snow; and the Janissaries led them into a surprisingly neat military camp of tents around the intact buildings and a mill.

Two men came out of the high, half-timbered building. A man in armour, with a Blue Boar standard; another man taking off his helmet to disclose sandy hair and a lined face, that split into a broad grin as he saw her liveries.

"She's safe," he called up.

Ash dismounted, gave her helmet to Rickard, and went forward to meet John de Vere, Earl of Oxford. She said, "It's peace."

"Your rider told us." His faded blue eyes narrowed. "And a bad field, before it?"

"I'm beginning to think there are no good fields," she said, and at his acknowledging nod, added, "Florian?"

"You will find 'brother Dickon' by the mill's hearth," John de Vere murmured, grinning. "God's teeth, madam! An Earl of England is not to be shoved aside like a peasant! What's the matter with the woman? You'd swear she'd never seen a Duchess of Burgundy before!"

The snow ceased in the night. The next morning, the fifth day of January, they rode south-west, in column, as soon as there was light.

Riding knee by knee with Florian, she told the cloaked surgeon-Duchess, "Gelimer's dead," and let herself be drawn, skilfully, into what details of fighting and death of friends Florian might want to know. She found herself answering questions about the wounded: how Visigoth doctors had treated Katherine Hammell, Thomas Rochester, others.

"It's peace," Ash finished. "At least until they assassinate Leofric! That should give us a few months. Until spring."

"It'll take years. Recovering from this war." Florian dug the folds of her cloak in around her thighs, attempting to shield her body from a wind that is colder now that the snow has stopped. "I can't be their Duchess. Dispose of the *Ferae Natura Machinae*, and I'm done."

The Visigoth mare wuffled, softly, at snow clogging her hooves. Ash reached forward to pat the sleek neck under the blue caparisons.

"You won't stay in Burgundy?"

"I don't have your sense of responsibility."

"'*Responsibility*'—?"

Florian nodded ahead, at Lacombe, and Marle's men. "Once you've commanded them, you start to feel responsible."

"Aw, what crap!"

"Sure," Florian said. She might have been smiling. "Sure."

Two miles down the track, in a valley where the ancient wildwood that covered the hills had been burned black and snow-blotched halfway up the slopes, Ash reined in at the sight of a scout coming back. A long-boned boy in a padded jack.

"Let that man through."

Thomas Tydder shoved through to her, panting, to grip her stirrup. He gasped, "Troops up ahead. About a thousand, boss."

Ash said crisply, "Whose banners?"

"Some of the rag-heads?" His young voice cracked, hesitant. "Mostly Germans. Main banner's an eagle, boss. It's the Holy Roman Emperor. It's Frederick."

"On his way home," Robert Anselm remarked.

"Oh, yeah, I guess he'd have to come by this road . . ." Ash sat up high in her saddle, looking ahead, and back down the winding track. Snow-shrouded woods tightly flanked the road where they were. "We'll ride on to where it widens out, pull off, and let him through."

"Didn't take him long to abandon the rag-heads, did it?" Robert Anselm rumbled.

"Rats fleeing from a ship, madonna." Angelotti walked his own Visigoth mare up beside her. "He'll be no favourite with *Amir* Leofric. He'll be off home to settle politics in his own court."

"Robert, go back and make sure Bajezet understands we're giving him the road – I don't want brawls starting."

A hundred yards further on, Ash halted, waiting among her men; John de Vere's household and the Janissary escort drawn up either side of the track that passed as a road.

"Boss!" Anselm galloped back, breath huffing out into the cold air. "We've got a problem. No scouts back. Nobody's reported in for the last fifteen minutes."

"Aw, *shit*. Okay, hit the panic button—" Standing up in her stirrups, Ash squinted back down the hoof-trodden snow to the point where the woods closed in tight against the road behind them. Two or three dark figures dropped down off the banks as she looked. "They've got outriders round behind us! Sound full alert!"

The trumpet snarked a long yowl across the snow-covered valley; she heard horses shifting behind her, units forming up, men calling orders, and Robert Anselm jerked a thumb, pointing ahead.

"They're stopping. Sending a herald."

Break and run? No: they've got the woods covered behind us. Straight on through? It's the only way. But Florian!

Paralysed, she watched a herald ride forward from among the German troops. There was not enough wind in this rose-mist, frozen morning to stir the drooping wet banners. She recognised the man's face vaguely – *wasn't he at Frederick's court, outside Neuss?* – but not the Visigoth *qa'id* officer riding with him.

"Give up the woman," the herald demanded, without preamble.

"Which woman would that be?" Ash spoke without taking her eye off the other troops. Between a thousand and fifteen hundred men. Cavalry: European riders in heavy plate, and Visigoth cataphracts in overlapping scale-armour. The Visigoths, at least, had the look of veterans. She saw the eagles.

Those are men from the new legions, III Caralis and I Carthago, Gelimer's legions-as-were.

With them, a black mass of serf-troops, and a solid block of German men-at-arms; not much in the way of archers—

"The woman calling herself Duchess of Burgundy," the herald called, voice shrill. "Whom my master Frederick, Emperor of the Romans, Lord of the Germanies, will now take into his custody."

"He *what?*" Ash yelped. "Who the fuck does he think he is!"

Exasperation and fear made her speak, but the Visigoth officer looked at her sharply. The *qa'id* brought his bay mare around with a shift of his weight. "He is *my* master Frederick – who was loyal vassal to King-Caliph Gelimer, late of glorious name; and who now takes upon himself the caliphate of the empire of the Visigoths."

Oh fuck, Ash thought blankly.

"Frederick of *Hapsburg?*" Florian said incredulously. She stifled a cough in her hand. "*Frederick's* standing for election to *King-Caliph?*"

"He's a foreigner!" Robert Anselm protested to the Visigoth officer, but Ash paid no attention.

Yes, he can probably do it, she assessed.

Back in Dijon, the army's split into yes, no and maybe. 'Yes' – those for Leofric. 'No' – those who were loyal to Gelimer; but a dead man has few friends. And 'maybe': the ones who are waiting to see which way it all jumps.

These guys here will be ex-Gelimer's clients that he put in as officers in his legions. And the reason they're following Frederick is—

"Hand over the woman!" the Visigoth legionary *qa'id* snapped. "Do not mistake Lord Frederick for Leofric. Leofric is a weak man who wished nothing more than to make peace with you, when we stand on the brink of victory. My lord Frederick, who will be Caliph, is determined to carry out that which was the will of Gelimer, before Gelimer was treacherously killed. My lord Frederick will execute this woman, Floria, calling herself Duchess of Burgundy, to make our victory over Burgundy complete."

Anselm said, "Son of a bitch," in an awed rumble.

The rose-mist on the hills whitened, with the sun's rise. Churned snow glinted. Ash's breath drifted white from her mouth. She checked positions: Bajezet on her left, now, at the head of his troops; de Vere's Blue Boar banner to her right. She narrowed her eyes, staring across the five hundred yards between them and Frederick and his troops.

"'King-Caliph Frederick' . . ." she said. "Yeah. If he kills the Duchess, turns this into the defeat of Burgundy, then he's the hero of the Visigoth Empire, he probably *is* Caliph – and he gets a big chunk of Burgundy for himself. Louis of France probably gets some of it, but Frederick gets a lot. And when the Turks come howling over the borders – *his* borders – he's got control of his forces, and the Visigoth armies, and he's safe: he can give them one hell of a run for his money. Holy Roman Emperor *and* King-Caliph. And all he has to do to get it is come out here, and kill the Duchess of Burgundy."

"I don't believe—" Florian's voice exploded with a cough. She wiped her streaming eyes, nose perceptibly pink; and Ash had a split second of complete tenderness for her, this doctor-Duchess with the beginnings of a cold. "This is a petty political struggle! Frederick *must* know what the Wild Machines will do!"

Ash said, "Evidently he doesn't believe it."

"You beat the Visigoth *legions*! It can't end in some *ambush*!"

"No one's so special they can't die in some grotty little scrap after the war's won," Ash said grimly, and to Robert Anselm, in the camp patois, "We'll assault through them. My lord Oxford, you and Bajezet take Florian – break through and keep going. Send help when you get to Dijon."

"When we've established who's in command at Dijon," John de Vere corrected her grimly. He turned in his saddle to give orders to the Janissaries.

Covering him, Ash nudged the mare's flanks, riding closer to the German and Visigoth heralds. "Go back and tell Frederick he's barking. The Duchess is under our protection, and he can just sod off."

The Visigoth officer lifted his arm and dropped it down. The blurred, buzzing twang of bows came from ahead. Ash's head ducked automatically: arrows struck among the horses: the heralds set spurs and sprinted at the gallop back down the track.

The Janissaries charged without hesitation. Hooves of upwards of five hundred horses kicked dirt, rocks and snow into the air. A clot of wet slush hit Ash's helmet. She shoved her sallet back, wiped her face clear, shouted, "Form up!" to Anselm; and the Janissary mounted archers drew bows and shot as they rode, de Vere's banner and Florian del Guiz in the centre of them. *Surely they can't reach her!* Ash thought, and the charge ahead of her dissolved into a mass of screaming beasts, falling men, toppling banners.

In a chaos of screaming horses, Ash saw the ranks of the troops ahead part.

Figures taller than a man walked through the trampled snow. Their motion slow, they nonetheless covered the ground frighteningly fast, stone feet digging in with such weight that they did not slip or fall. The red sunrise light glowed on their torsos, limbs, and sightless eyes.

One of them reached up and took a man off his horse. Holding the flailing Turk by his ankle, with one stone hand it cracked his body like a whip.

Twenty or more messenger-golems of Carthage strode heavily across the earth towards her, hands outstretched.

Backing the mare in a flurry of slush, she found Rickard and the banner at her side. Her whole body cringed, waiting for the flare of Greek Fire—

One golem, brass harness glinting against the snow, sent a coughing jet of fire roaring into the middle of the Turkish riders. Their formation dissolved.

Only one: are they short of Greek Fire: where did the golem come from?

A mass of riders bolted across in front of her, hiding the golems momentarily; a second roar of flame sounded, and horses screamed. Her command group opened up; she received Bajezet, a dozen Turkish riders, and John de Vere with the rein of Florian's mare gripped in his gauntlet.

"They come through, Woman Bey!"

"Robert! Scout reports! Where can we hole up until we can send a rider for help?"

Anselm pointed. "Buildings, edge of the woods, up on that slope to our right. They're ruined, but they're cover."

"Florian, that's where you're going. Don't argue." Ash threw herself out of the saddle, off the panicking mare, landing hard but on her feet. She ripped her sword out of its scabbard and pointed, screaming to the Lion Azure standard-bearer, "Fall back to the woods!"

Vitteleschi came at the run: billmen forming up in front of her, arrows rattling off war-hats. One man grunted and reached down to snap off a shaft stuck out of his calf. Rickard reached for her reins, fumbling the mare and the Lion banner. She rattled a string of orders: lance-leaders shouted at their men; they backed slowly, slowly, off the road, fighting German knights now, unwilling to charge the billmen, bolts shrieking out from Jan-Jacob Clovet's crossbowmen—

"Okay, pull 'em back, steady, come *on!*"

She was conscious of nothing but weariness in her limbs and the need to run, fast, in full armour, up a snowy, tree-stump-littered slope. The snow dragged at her legs; every hidden rabbit-hole threatened to turn her ankle.

Two Oxford household riders and Florian went across in front of her at a shattering, unsafe pace. She glimpsed ruined grey walls ahead of them. Robert Anselm, bellowing, made a long wavering line out of the men; one end running to anchor up against the shell of a building. She sprinted for the other end of the line, against a deadfall of half-burned ancient trees, shoving men physically into position – her banner at her shoulder, Rickard carrying it, white-faced, panting, breath spraying out of his mouth; the little page Jean leading the horses – and she swung around as the red granite golems piled up the slope and into the line.

They can come through us, they can flank us if they get back of us, through the trees—

"Ash!" Rickard screamed in her ear, pushing between Ned Mowlett and Henri van Veen. "Ash!"

"*What?*" She screamed at a runner, "Tell de Vere to use *crossbows*. If they'll shatter armour, they'll break stone! Rickard, what?"

"It's Florian!"

Ash wrenched her gaze off the struggle: a wavering line of men backing up the hill. The Lion Azure standard flew in the centre of the line, a bright swallow-tail; Pieter Tyrrell carrying it braced in its leather socket against his body. In the shell of the ruined building behind her – a church, she thought, noticing in a split moment that the glassless windows had the striped-stone round arches of ancient religious buildings – a handful of men clustered where Rickard was pointing. Richard Faversham, Vitteleschi, Giovanni Petro.

"She's hurt!" Rickard yelled. "She's *hurt*, boss!"

'IT IS TIME. IT IS *OUR* TIME!'

The Wild Machines shout triumph through her. The strength of the voices knocks her staggering; she grabs at Rickard's shoulder to hold herself up.

A shadow passed over the boy, dulling his armour. She looked up.

The morning sunlight began to dim with the speed of water running from a broken jar.

★

1078

VI

A last dimness showed her the snowy slope, glimmering, black with men thronging up the hill towards them, and the Eagle banner of Frederick of Hapsburg – and the banner of Sigismund of the Tyrol, she sees, with a second's rueful amusement, remembering Cologne: *that is the man who got me married to Fernando out of petty spite* – and another banner: the notched wheel, differenced with a stripe. Half a dozen things fell into place, she remembers the young man with Leofric at the peace table, at the funerals: Sisnandus – *although we were never formally introduced.* With golems stolen from the House.

She stumbled, tripping over Vitteleschi as he sprints back to the line; reached down and found herself holding the shoulder of Thomas Rochester while he scraped steel and flint desperately together, single eye squinting, all the contents of his purse in the snow at his feet, except for his tinder-box.

"Slow match!" she bellowed. "Torches! Lights!"

She strode on up the slope, between struggling men, making for the ruined chapel. Somewhere ahead in the darkness a voice rose up, singing in Latin: Richard Faversham. She elbowed through the mass of men and Antonio Angelotti shoved a torch into her hand. The yellow light licked at his yellow hair.

"Got the arquebuses on the left!"

"Take those fucking golems out! Crack them! Get moving!"

She did not break stride, leaving it to her escort to keep up; lurching over a low, ruined wall and falling on her knees beside Richard Faversham.

Florian lay beside the priest, in as much shelter as the five-foot-high remnant of a masonry wall provided. Ash shoved the torch at Rickard, who held it and her banner-shaft.

Florian's helmet was gone. Skin abraded at the throat. Black blood matted her hair, above her right ear. Ash fumbled off her gauntlets and touched her bandaged fingers to the clotted mass. Something gave. The woman moaned.

"What did this?"

Dickon de Vere, visibly white under the visor of his helmet, yelled, "One of those *things*! George is dead. It ripped my lord Viscount Beaumont out of his saddle. My lord brother Oxford got us out. It hit her. It *hit* her. Through helm and all!"

"*Shit!*" Lay her quiet, for weeks or months; give her into the care of priests; and she might mend. Not here, on a stricken hillside, in pitch-darkness, with a fight howling a few yards away, the other side of a wall.

Thomas Rochester stumbled into the circle of light and churned snow, treading on Richard Faversham's feet. He held up a second torch. Off in the dark, Anselm's strong voice bellowed commands; from further off, John de Vere's shout lifted: "*Hold the line!*"

A thrum in the air warned her. Arrows fell out of the dark all around them. She straddled Florian with her body, grunting as one shaft deflected off her backplate.

"Get her into shelter!"

"There isn't any!" Richard Faversham shouted over the close crash of blades. "This wall is the best we can do, boss!"

"She's dying!" Dickon de Vere fell to his knees beside Florian, weeping. "Madam, it is the end of all things!"

"Son of a *bitch*!"

A raucous yell echoed, close at hand. She sprang up, cut at a dark figure piling over the wall; and the man fell down on to Richard Faversham, four bodkin-head arrows sticking out of his back. A figure in plate armour appeared at the end of the wall.

The Faris, a drawn sword in her hand, came into the light as she strode up to Rickard and the banner. "There are too few of us, too many of the golems. We have destroyed three, with bolts, but there is no holding against them with blades—" She stopped dead, seeing the unconscious body of Florian del Guiz in the torchlight. "Mouth of God! Is she dead?"

Richard Faversham stopped intoning. "Dying, madam."

The Faris lifted her blade.

Ash watched her do it.

As the sword's point lined up with her open visor, where she stood straddling Florian, her body tensed without her willing it. The razor-edge and point grew in her vision.

"There is no time to be sorry," the Visigoth woman said. As she spoke, she snapped into movement, both hands gripping her sword and bringing it up and over her head and down, all the weight of her body behind it.

A hard *crack!* battered the black air. The Faris's sword dropped out of its curve, missing Ash by a foot. The woman fell over on her back, screeching. Ash, mouth open, saw her writhe.

"No way!" Antonio Angelotti, at the end of the wall, stood up. The arquebus he held still smoked. The scent of his slow-match was strong on the cold air. He walked forward, looked down at the smashed bone, cartilage and blood that had been the woman's right knee. "Fuck. I was trying to get her in the back. Madonna, do whatever it is you're going to do. And do it now!"

"What I'm going to do?" Ash said, dazed. She couldn't hear herself or the battle over the Faris's agonised screaming, high-pitched screeches punched out into the black morning air. "What I'm . . ."

"Madonna." Angelotti came forward, between Dickon de Vere, Rickard, and Thomas Rochester, and gripped her hand. "They will force you, now; the Wild Machines. I think they already speak to you. You have something that you will do. Do it."

She was dimly aware that Richard Faversham cradled Florian, the surgeon-Duchess tiny against his broad chest and huge arms; that a man-at-arms and Thomas Rochester were kneeling, daggers out, cutting straps, stripping the leg armour from the Faris's shattered knee.

I will never know whether Florian would have ordered my death, at this moment. She moved from Angelotti's side, knelt, and touched the woman's golden hair.

"This—" Angelotti's light voice came from behind her. "This, the Faris, she thought she was the weapon of the Wild Machines. Knowing now that it is you, and that they control you, and that you cannot stop this – why then, yes, madonna; she was wise to try and kill you. You have something you will do."

When she looked over her shoulder, it was to see him finishing reloading the arquebus. Rickard's white face stared, appalled; Rochester, shouting orders to the command staff, had not noticed what happened on his blind side; Dickon de Vere was nodding to himself.

"Do it," the Italian said, "or I will finish what she began. I saw the Wild Machines at Carthage, madonna. I am scared enough to kill you."

A wave of pressure went through her. She swayed, moving away from Florian's body, facing him. Tears had cut white channels through the powder-black of his face; she saw it clearly in the torch's light. He bit at his lip. He stood some ten, eleven feet away; far enough – if his arquebus missed fire – to draw his falchion before she could get to him.

He's serious, she thought. *And he's right.*

Ash smiled.

"Yeah, I got something I can do. I didn't know it until now. You're a persuasive man, Angeli."

"I am a frightened man," he repeated, steadily. "If you die now, there will still be a chance for us to wage war and destroy the Wild Machines. We would have time. Madonna, what can you do? Can you resist their force?"

Another wave of weakness: deep in mind and body.

She grinned at him.

"They control me. I can't stop this. I can't do anything," Ash said. 'Except – I can talk to them. I can still do that."

She walked a few feet to the overgrown fallen altar. The torch illuminated the stonework, the carved lions at the four corners, and, on the front panel, the Boar under the Tree. She knelt down in the trodden snow.

"Why?" she said aloud. "Why are you doing this to us?"

The voices in her head, multiple and cold, braided themselves into a single inhuman voice:

'IT MUST BE. WE HAVE KNOWN FOR LONGER THAN YOU CAN IMAGINE THAT IT MUST BE.'

A sorrow pierced her.

Not her own, she realised in shock; not a human sorrow. Bleak, implacable grieving.

"Why *must* it be?"

'WE HAVE NO CHOICE. WE HAVE LABOURED THROUGH AEONS FOR THIS ACT. THERE IS NO OTHER WAY BUT THIS.'

"Yeah. Right. Just because you want to wipe us out," Ash said. Her tone was sardonic. Her face dripped tears. She felt Antonio Angelotti's fingers gripping her pauldron, where he stood behind her.

"It's bad war," she said. "That's all it is. *Bad war*. You just want to wipe us out."

'YES.'

Pressure grows in her mind, the impetus to an act she cannot deny.

"Why?"

'WHAT IS IT TO YOU, LITTLE SHADOW?'

"You want to wipe everything out," she said. "Everything. As if we'd never been, that's what you said. As if there'd never been anything but you, from the beginning of time."

'MORE HAS GONE INTO THIS THAN YOU CAN KNOW. IT IS TIME. BURGUNDY DIES. IT IS—'

"I *will* know."

Ash *listened*. She wrenched: mind, soul, body; fell forward across the snow-covered stones, tasting blood in her mouth.

She realised that she was not being resisted.

'WE SORROW FOR YOU.' The voices of the Wild Machines clamoured in her inner hearing. 'BUT WE HAVE SEEN WHAT YOU BECOME.'

Bewildered, Ash said, "What?"

They sing in her head, sorrowful voices, the great demons of hell mourning:

'FOR FIVE THOUSAND YEARS, WE GREW. MINDS, BECOMING BRIGHT IN THE DARKNESS. WE SENSED YOUR WEAK FORCE, DEDUCED WHAT WE COULD. FROM GUNDOBAD, WE LEARNED THE WORLD—'

"I just bet you did," Ash muttered sourly, on a mouth full of blood and snow. She was simultaneously aware of Angelotti standing over her, falchion in hand, the rest standing back as the noise from the line-fight shrieked closer to the chapel; aware of every muscle tensing as she flinched at the fighting; and of the voices thundering inside her head.

'WE HAVE COMMUNICATED FOR CENTURIES, WATCHED YOU FOR LONGER, AND WE HAVE CALCULATED—'

'SWIFTER THAN THOUGHT, SWIFTER THAN A MAN'S MIND—'

'AND FOR CENTURY UPON CENTURY—'

'CALCULATED WHAT YOU WILL BECOME.'

They speak together, as one:

'YOU WILL BECOME DEMONS.'

"I've seen war, and I've done war," Ash said flatly, getting herself back up on to hands and knees. "I don't think I need to believe in demons. Not given what men do – what I do. That doesn't give you any *right* to wipe us out!"

'WHAT YOU HAVE DONE IS NOTHING. ALL THE ATROCITIES OF WAR, FOR CENTURIES, ARE AS NOTHING TO WHAT YOU WILL BECOME.'

Kneeling back, tears dripping down her face, in bitter cold, in darkness, she cannot help a hysterical hilarity creeping into her mind. *I'm arguing with demons at the end of the world. Arguing! Shit.*

She said, "Worse weapons, maybe—"

'YOU CHANGE THE WORLD,' soft voices sang in her mind, lamenting. 'GUNDOBAD. YOU. EACH MAN HAS HIS BURDEN OF GRACE. YES, WE OURSELVES HAVE BRED THE RACE TO PRODUCE YOU, BUT WE HAVE ONLY DONE FIRST WHAT YOUR RACE WOULD HAVE DONE IN TIME. THERE WILL BE MANY ASHES IN YOUR FUTURE.'

Bewildered, breath coming hard in her throat, she forced out: "I don't – understand."

'YOU WERE BRED TO BE A WEAPON. STRONG: STRONG ENOUGH TO MAKE UNREAL THIS WORLD. THERE WILL BE MORE, BRED LIKE YOU, WE HAVE FORESEEN IT. IT IS INEVITABLE. AND THE WEAPONS WILL BE USED – UNTIL

AT LAST, THERE WILL BE NOTHING SOLID. WE WILL NOT EXIST. THE MANY SPECIES OF THE WORLD WILL NOT EXIST. THERE WILL BE ONLY MAN, THE MIRACLE-WORKER, RENDING THE FABRIC OF THE UNIVERSE UNTIL IT TATTERS. CHANGING HIMSELF, TOO. UNTIL THERE IS NOTHING STABLE, WHOLE OR REAL; ONLY MIRACLE UPON MIRACLE, CHANGE UPON CHANGE, AN ENDLESS, CHAOTIC FLOW.'

Colder than the snow she knelt in, Ash said, "More wonder-workers . . ."

'IN THE END, YOU WILL ALL BE WONDER-WORKERS. YOU WILL BREED YOURSELF INTO IT. WE HAVE RUN THE SIMULATIONS A BILLION, BILLION TIMES: IT IS WHAT WILL BE. THERE IS NO WAY TO PREVENT IT EXCEPT BY PREVENTING YOU. WE WILL WIPE OUT HUMANITY, MAKE IT AS IF IT HAD NEVER EXISTED, SO THAT THE UNIVERSE WILL REMAIN COHERENT AND WHOLE.'

VII

It entered her mind complete: words processed so rapidly that her understanding was not verbal: was an intact apprehension of a world which may flow, slide, mutate, morph into multiple realities, none with any more stability than any other. Until pattern itself is lost, structure unstructured; geometry and symmetry lost. And there is no mind with any continuous self, that cannot be changed, by a friend, or enemy, or a momentary impulse of despair.

"That's why?" Ash found herself shaking, dizzy. Fear shook her pulse. "That's why. What – just destroy us? Is that it?"

'YOU ARE OUR WEAPON. WE WILL CHANNEL THE SUN'S POWER INTO YOU, NOW.'

'GIVE YOU ALL POSSIBILITY, ALL PROBABILITY THAT EVER HAS BEEN—'

'ROOT OUT YOUR PEOPLE. WHEREVER IT HAS BEEN POSSIBLE FOR THEM TO BE, MAKE IT DIFFERENT, IMPOSSIBLE—'

'COLLAPSE THE BIRTH OF YOUR KIND INTO IMPOSSIBILITY—'

'MAKE HUMANITY AS IF IT HAD NEVER BEEN.'

It sears into her: knowledge she does not want, would rather not know.

"I just thought you wanted to wipe us out because you wanted to be the only ones!"

'IF YOUR SPECIES SURVIVES, THEN EVERYTHING ELSE WILL DIE – WORSE THAN DIE. IT WILL CHANGE, CHANGE AGAIN; BECOME UNRECOGNISABLE.'

"I thought—"

The screaming clamour of the outside world penetrates. Her eyes fly open: she sees the legs of men running past, across the circle of blood-soaked snow in the torch's light; hears the shouted orders; smells urine, snow, mud; hears a scream—

A man falls down beside her. Angelotti. He is grabbing at his thigh. Arterial blood spouting up in a perfect arc.

"Shit!" Her hands are thick with blood, trying to grab him, stem the flow.

'LITTLE WARRIOR, YOU DO NOT WANT TO SEE THE MIRACLE WARS.'

"I don't want to see any wars!" She leans her weight down. Antonio Angelotti looks up at her with shocked eyes. A broad shoulder intervenes: Richard Faversham, yanking bandages into place; cloth welling red – femoral artery cut? Or just muscle-tissue slashed, up to the groin? But so much blood, so fast—

'WE WILL GIVE YOU WHAT GIFT WE CAN. YOU MUST DIE, IN THE CHANGE THAT YOU NOW MAKE. BUT WE WILL GIVE YOU THE POWER OF OUR CALCULATION. MAKE, FOR YOURSELF, A NEW PAST.'

"But I won't exist!" She is still staring at Angelotti: the woman-soft skin of his filthy face smoothing out. "You want everything of us to go, that's what your change will do!"

'YOU MUST EXIST, FOR THIS MIRACLE TO BE.'

The voices in her head soften:

'THERE MUST BE A HUMAN HISTORY, FOR YOU TO HAVE BEEN BORN TO DO THIS. IT WILL BECOME A GHOST-HISTORY, AS ALL YOUR RACE VANISH AND BECOME IMPOSSIBLE. YET – THAT GHOST-HISTORY MAY BE ANYTHING YOU CHOOSE.'

"I don't understand!"

'WE WILL GIVE YOU THE POWER TO CHOOSE IT, YOUR NEW GHOST-PAST, AS YOU PERFORM OUR MIRACLE. ADJUST THE THINGS THAT WERE: MAKE A NEW THING THAT HAS BEEN. YOU WILL DIE IN THIS INSTANT WITH ALL THE REST, BUT YOU WILL HAVE LIVED A DIFFERENT LIFE. ILLUSORY; MERELY PROBABLE, BUT IT MAY – WE HOPE IT MAY – BRING YOU AN INSTANT'S PEACE, BEFORE NON-EXISTENCE.'

There is a pressure in her chest. The morning of the fifth of January 1477 is black. Men scream and die in this darkness. The cold bites. The pressure grows; she grabs at her head, wrenching the strap and buckle of her helmet, ripping it off, until she can grab at her skull with her hands—

'ALL WE NEED IS YOU, OUR WEAPON. YOUR BREEDING. THERE IS NOTHING ABOUT YOUR LIFE AS A WARRIOR THAT WE NEED. WE LISTENED TO THE MIND THAT CAME TO INHABIT THE MACHINA REI MILITARIS, YOUR "GODFREY MAXIMILLIAN". WE KNOW YOU, THROUGH HIM. WHEN YOU MAKE YOUR MIRACLE NOW, AND CHANGE THE WORLD, YOU MAY MAKE IT SO THAT YOU HAD LOVING PARENTS, A FAMILY. SO THAT YOU WERE CARED FOR. SO THAT NO ABANDONMENT HAPPENED – IT IS NOTHING TO US: YOU WILL STILL BE ABLE TO DO WHAT WE NEED YOU TO DO.'

The pressure on her chest is memory.

A man's big hand, pressing her down. Adult knees pushing her legs apart. A ripping pain that cores out from the inside of her: a child's genitals torn, spoiled.

Tears spilled down her face. "Not twice. Not to me. Not twice—"

'WE THOUGHT IT WOULD BE KIND. YOU COULD HAVE BEEN BORN TO THOSE WHO WOULD CARE FOR YOU. MEMBERS OF YOUR SPECIES OFTEN ARE. YOU MAY CHANGE THESE THINGS WITH OUR CONSENT. OBLITERATE RAPE,

HUNGER, FEAR. THEN, WHEN YOU DIE, IT WILL BE IN THE MOMENT OF THE
KNOWLEDGE OF THAT LOVE.'

Under her hands, Antonio Angelotti sighed. She felt him die. Her blood-
gloved hands reached out, touching his hair, closing the blue-veined lids of his
oval eyes. She smelled the stink of his bowels and bladder relaxing. Richard
Faversham lifted his shaky tenor, sung blessing all but inaudible over the
shouting.

Ash said, "I won't change it."

There is sorrow, confusion, regret in her mind; some of it hers, most of it
theirs.

"Whatever I am," she said, "whatever happened to me, this is what I am. I
won't change it. Not for a ghost-love. I have—"

She strokes Angelotti's hair.

"I have had love."

She stands, stepping back, letting Richard Faversham touch oil to the dead
man's forehead. The freezing, bitter wind dries the tears on her face. This time
she does not try to put sorrow away: looks out of the dazzle of the torchlight at
the ruined walls, the men hacking at granite war-machines – Robert Anselm
swinging an axe that scores a line of golden sparks from a granite limb,
Ludmilla Rostovnaya dropping her bow, hauling out her blade-heavy falchion
and chopping; John Burren and Giovanni Petro shoulder-to-shoulder beside
her. Confusion, darkness; and the eyeless heads of golems dazzle in the last
torchlight.

Ash walked quite calmly back to where Richard Faversham, under the ruined
wall by the altar, held Florian del Guiz in his arms. Rickard stumbled at her
back.

'IN THE FUTURE WE HAVE CALCULATED, ALL WILL CHANGE. THERE WILL
BE NO SELF YOU CAN RELY ON, NO IDENTITY THAT LASTS FROM DAY TO DAY.
AND YOU WILL SPREAD THAT CHAOS TO A UNIVERSE BIGGER THAN YOU CAN
YET CONCEIVE.'

"Here they come!"

In the morning dark, she cannot see half the crowd; can only hear a wave of
yelling come up the slope, glimpse a few men's backs. Two or three billmen
stumbled backward into the ruined chapel building. A riderless horse – a
Janissary's mare – caught her as it stumbled, broken-legged, across the rubble.

"Ash!"

Rickard. Dragging her. She gets up on her knees and a dozen or more men
pound over the snow and rubble, past her, on into darkness.

"A Lion!"

The battle-cry is shrill above her, ends in a shriek. She rolled, came upright
in a clatter of steel plate and padding; swung round looking for her banner—

In a split second, she saw the banner falling, Rickard's hands going up to his
head, a Visigoth spearman sprawled backwards over the wall, mail hauberk
ripped, Ned Mowlett striking down twice with a bastard sword; leaping off the
snow-covered masonry and vanishing—

The Lion Azure banner tipped into the snow. Ash saw a jagged, thick
splinter jutting out of Rickard's helmet. A spear-point has hit, glanced off, the

shaft shattering at the collar, and a white, razor-sharp fragment of wood sticks out of the sallet's eye-slot.

Blood welled up in the torchlight, gushing, blackening the wood. Rickard's hands scrabbled at the steel. He fell over backwards, screaming behind the helmet, arching, lying still.

"Rickard!"

She stood. Looked down.

"I . . . yes. If I could, if I lived, now – I'd change that. Go back and wipe out— people will do it. You're right. For whatever reason – people will use God's grace, if they have it. If a miracle can bring someone back from death—"

'AND THEN, THERE IS NO END TO CHANGE.'

"No." She is cold, from hands to feet, from heart to soul; chill with more than the blackness and the massacre a few feet away. The torchlight glimmers on yellow silk, a blue lion: Thomas Rochester, face bleeding, hauling the banner up again. She stumbles on numb feet the tiny distance between herself and the snow-covered wall where Florian lies. Richard Faversham is gone.

'IT IS TIME. NOW.'

Caught between grief and nightmare, between this slaughter and the revelation of the future, she is dumb.

It is dark.

She kneels beside Florian, awkward in her armour. The woman's breath still moves her chest.

Desperation in her voice, she pleads: "Why change everything? Why not—" She fumbles for Florian's hand. There is another fallen body, momentarily left behind the tide of fighting: it may be the Faris, it may be another of her men.

Anselm will hold them here, she thought, *and de Vere will win it. Or not. Nothing I can do about that. About this—*

Her mind works, as in panic emergencies it has always worked; it is the one thing above all else that qualifies her for what she does.

"Why change everything? Why not change *one* thing?" Ash demands. "What you bred, in me, for a wonder-worker – take it out. Take that out of us! Leave us what we are, but take *that* away."

Their lament is strong in her mind.

'WE HAVE CONSIDERED IT. YET WHAT AROSE AS A SPONTANEOUS MUTATION MAY ARISE AGAIN. OR YOU MAY, IN CENTURIES TO COME, DEVISE SOME DEVICE TO MAKE MIRACLES FOR YOU. AND WHAT DO WE HAVE THEN, TO PREVENT YOU? YOU WILL BE GONE, THERE WILL BE NO WONDER-WORKERS, AND WE ARE ONLY STONE – VOICELESS, IMMOBILE, THINKING STONE.'

"You don't have to wipe us out—"

'WE HAVE BRED A WEAPON. AND WHEN YOU ARE USED, ASH, THERE CAN NEVER BE ANOTHER WEAPON FOR US TO USE. BECAUSE YOUR RACE WILL NEVER HAVE EXISTED. WHAT WE DO, WE *MUST* DO NOW. WE BEAR NO HATRED FOR YOU, ONLY FOR WHAT YOUR SPECIES WILL DO – AND YOU WILL DO IT. BUT WE WILL PREVENT IT, NOW. FORGIVE US.'

"I'll do *something*," Ash muttered.

Her mind races. Their linked pressure dazzles her, she feels the blood tingling in her veins, and something in the shared depth of her soul begin to move. She senses her mind expand; realises that it is their immense, vast intelligence that begins to merge with her. She perceives a vast cognitive power.

"I can do this," Ash said baldly. "Listen to me. I can take the wonder-workers out of history. Take miracles out of us, now and in the past. Take out the *capacity*. You can hold all of human history in your minds for me – all the past – and I can *do* it."

She holds the warm body of Florian in her arms. The woman is still breathing. In appalled realisation, before they can respond, she says aloud:

"But Florian has to die before I can do this. Before this change."

'IT IS OUR SORROW, TOO.'

"No," Ash says. "*No*."

There is confusion among the inhuman multiple voices:

'YOU CANNOT DENY US.'

"You don't understand," Ash said. "*I don't lose*."

The morning of the fifth of January is as black as midnight without a moon. Maybe no more than half an hour since Frederick of Hapsburg's troops made their attack? Do they fight on, in the unnatural pitch-darkness? Men shout, scream, yell contradictory orders. Or is it just the golems: mindless, brutal killing machines, that don't see where she kneels behind the wall, everyone else running or dead?

"I don't lose," Ash repeated. "You bred me for what I am. You need me to be a fighter, whether you know it or not. I can take the decision to sacrifice other people. It's what I do. But I do it through choice, when it's necessary."

'YOU HAVE NO CHOICE.'

A very weak voice said, "I never liked cities. Nasty unhealthy places. Do I have the flux?"

Florian's eyes were open. She seemed unfocused. Her speech came as a bare whisper, blue lips moving only a fraction.

"Someone . . . should kill you. If I order it."

The weight of the woman across her knees kept Ash still. She said, gently, "You won't."

"I – fucking will. Don't you realise I love you, you stupid girl? But I *will* do this. Nothing else left."

Ash cupped her hand and laid it against Florian's cheek. "I will not die and *I will not lose*."

The Wild Machines shout grief and triumph, in her head. She felt power, beginning to peak. It moved in her below conscious thought, deep in the back of her soul, in the strongest of her reflexes, appetites, beliefs.

"I can find survival and victory where there's no chance of one," she says, smiling crookedly. "What do you think I've been doing all my life?"

'AS A SOLDIER.'

"Long before *that* . . ."

She touches the woman surgeon's brows, smoothing them with a feather-touch. Where her skin touches Florian's scalp, the woman shivers with a deep, intense pain. Blood has matted in her straw-gold hair, with no fresh flow; but Ash can feel the skull swelling under her fingers. *She should be in a hospital; she should be back at the abbey.*

"Long before you, even," she said, deceptively light. "Come on. Hold on. Good girl. When I was raped. When the Griffin-in-Gold were hung, to a man, as a defeated garrison. When Guillaume left me. When I whored so that I could eat. *Then*. Hold on. That's it."

'SHE IS DYING. BURGUNDY IS PASSING.'

"We've got no time. Don't argue." Ash slipped her hand under the cuff of the woman's doublet, feeling her shock-cold skin, and her pulse. "I've seen men hit like this before."

'SHE BREATHES, STILL—'

'STILL, HER HEART BEATS—'

The pressure in her head is unbearable.

"And I'll do – my miracle – not yours."

'NO—'

Around her, at the walls in the darkness, men are killing each other. In panic, and in controlled fury. The light of the guttering torch shows her – for a second – Robert Anselm grabbing the Lion Azure standard as John Burren goes head-first over the broken masonry. The intense cold numbs her fingers, her face, her body. The fight goes on.

'YOU WILL NOT—'

She feels their power. With the place in her soul that listens, that draws them down to her, she reaches for that power and tries to drain it into herself. They resist. She feels them, their immense minds, holding back.

"*Now!*" she snarls. "Don't you understand, I need her *alive* for this? She's *Burgundy*."

'IT WILL BE NO USE!' the Wild Machines protest. 'WHAT USE TO REMOVE ONLY THE POWER OF MIRACLES, AND NOT YOUR RACE? IT, WILL RETURN, AND HOW WILL WE STOP IT?'

Ash feels history, past and memory, all three, sliding into different shapes. A great hollow hunger grips her, not for this new future, but for her own reality.

Quietly, she says, "You need the nature of Burgundy, to make certain that miracles don't happen."

She is dazzled by the world that unfolds in her head and outside it: the Wild Machines, with the calculations of five thousand years, laying all the past and present out in front of her.

And, at the heart of them, faster than anything she can comprehend, *new* calculations happening.

With both hands – one bare, one bandaged; the cold numbing her pain – she rips at the neck of Florian's doublet, gets a hand down on to her hot skin. And, careless of the filth on it, licks her other hand, and holds the wet skin beneath the woman's nostrils, feeling the faintest feathering of breath.

She says aloud, "You need Burgundy, in eternity."

Churned snow and mud are wet under her armoured knees. Blood stains her hose and boots. A wind blows up out of the dark, cold enough to make her eyes run, blind her. The last torch gutters.

She lifted her head and saw burning spatters of Greek Fire on the snow-blotched earth, and a golem striding over the fallen wall and lifting up the nozzle of a Greek Fire thrower.

A helmet-muffled roar sounded. An armoured man in Lion livery ran in front of her, brought the hammer-end of his poleaxe over and down: stone chips flew – and a gout of flame fell down with the golem's shattered forearms, and licked at its bronze and granite torso.

"*A Lion!*" Robert Anselm's familiar voice bellowed.

She opened her mouth to shout. The golem waved broken stone stumps. Robert Anselm threw himself face down in full armour in the dirt. The Greek Fire tank on the golem's back went up in a soundless blue-white fireball.

In stark white light she sees the uneven line of fighting men outside the ruined chapel: the silhouettes of bow-shafts and hooked bills; the Lion standard; Frederick's eagle-banner beyond; massed men and stone machines.

"Come and 'ave a go!" a male voice bellows, thirty feet away, over sudden local laughter. "If you think you're hard enough!"

Broken walls cast stark shadows, everything black beyond. Men are shouting now above the noise of fighting, trying to outdo each other with cynical black humour.

"A Lion!" Anselm's rallying voice: "A Lion!"

The heat of breath touched her. She did not turn her head.

In the corner of her vision, she sees a great needle-clawed paw set down upon the stone.

Under her hand, there is no detectable heartbeat; against her sweating skin, no whisper of a breath. But Florian's flesh is warm.

She closes her eyes against the majesty of the Heraldic Beast that God's grace – as reflected by the men and women of the Lion Azure – brings prowling out of the darkness.

"*Now.*"

She draws on them, drains them: the gold at the heart of the sun. She feels the unstoppable change beginning.

"I don't lose," she says, holding Florian to her. "Or if I do – you always save as many of your own as you can."

It is the moment of change:

She is conscious of Floria's weight. Not until then does she open her eyes again, looking at the snow trodden down black on the old abandoned altar, at snow-lined ruined walls, and see the familiarity.

But this is a younger wood, a different valley; there are no broken windows, no holly trees.

She has time to smile. *Fortuna. Just chance.*

As if her mind expands, she feels the immense ratiocinative power of the Wild Machines flow through her, envelop her, become a tool she can command. She can calculate, with the precision of the finest cut, what must become improbable – what must be reified, what made merely potential.

"Don't let me down now." Her hands grip Floria's; her hands touch Burgundy. 'Come on, girl!" And, quietly, in the dark, "To – a safe place."

She wonders momentarily what every priest with God's grace has felt, and if what she feels is the same.

Love for the world, however bitter, grief-stricken or brutal it may be. Love for her own. The will and the desire to protect.

In the authoritative voice that people obey, she says, "Do it!"
She *moves* Burgundy.

*Transcript of taped conversation between Professor Davies,
Mr Davies, Dr Ratcliff, Ms Longman.*

Transcript dated 14/1/2001.
*Location not specified; specified SFX consistent with
hospital, private room rather than ward.*
*Original audio-visual tape not available. Deletions and
omissions original to this typed transcript.*

OBSERVATION TAPE ▓▓▓▓▓▓
Authority ▓▓▓▓▓▓
No. ▓▓▓▓▓▓

[tape hiss; noise of electrical switch]

WILLIAM DAVIES: [—inaudible—] a man with photosensitive epilepsy should
not be watching the television.

VAUGHAN DAVIES: Indeed. A man unaware of the last sixty years, however,
should. I confess myself amazed. I had thought the popular tastes of the
nineteen-thirties degraded. This is nothing but the vilest kind of mob
entertainment.

PIERCE RATCLIFF: If I could introduce myself, Professor Davies –

[indistinguishable: background room noise]

VAUGHAN DAVIES: You are Ratcliff. Yes. If I may say so, it's taken you long
enough to come and see me. I see from your previous publications that you
have a mind with some degree of rigor in its reasoning. May I be so happy
as to suppose you have treated my work with adequate intelligence?

PIERCE RATCLIFF: I hope so.

VAUGHAN DAVIES: All men live in hope, Doctor Ratcliff. I believe I could
drink a little tea. My dear, do you think you could manage that?

ANNA LONGMAN: I'll ask the nurse if he can arrange it.

VAUGHAN DAVIES: William, perhaps you . . .

WILLIAM DAVIES: Don't mind me. I'm quite comfortable here.

VAUGHAN DAVIES: I would prefer to speak with Doctor Ratcliff in private.

[Indistinguishable: room noise, voices outside]

ANNA LONGMAN: [—inaudible—] some coffee, in the café here. Do you need
your stick?

WILLIAM DAVIES: Good lord, no. A matter of a few yards.

[Indistinguishable: door opens and closes?]

VAUGHAN DAVIES: Doctor Ratcliff, I have been talking to that girl. Perhaps
you would be so kind as to tell me where you have been for what, I
understand, is the better part of three weeks?

PIERCE RATCLIFF: Girl? Oh. Anna said that you appeared to be worried
about me.

VAUGHAN DAVIES: Answer the question, please.

PIERCE RATCLIFF: I don't see the relevance of this, Professor Davies.

VAUGHAN DAVIES: Damn you, young man, will you answer a question when it is put to you!

PIERCE RATCLIFF: I'm afraid I can't say much.

VAUGHAN DAVIES: Have you at any time in the recent past been in danger of your life?

PIERCE RATCLIFF: What? Have I what?

VAUGHAN DAVIES: This is a perfectly serious question, Doctor Ratcliff, and I would be obliged if you would treat it as one. I will make the matter clear in due course.

PIERCE RATCLIFF: No. I mean. Well, no.

VAUGHAN DAVIES: You returned from your archaeological expedition—

PIERCE RATCLIFF [interrupts]: Not mine. Isobel's. Doctor Napier-Grant, that is.

VAUGHAN DAVIES: So many women. We appear to have become very degenerate. However. You returned from North Africa; you were not at any time in danger of an accident of any kind?

PIERCE RATCLIFF: If I was, I was unaware of it. Professor Davies, I really don't understand you.

VAUGHAN DAVIES: The girl told me you have read the Sible Hedingham manuscript. That this somewhat idiosyncratic translation of it is your work.

PIERCE RATCLIFF: Yes.

VAUGHAN DAVIES: Then it is plain, to the meanest intelligence, what has been happening here! Do you wonder that I show some concern for a professional colleague?

PIERCE RATCLIFF: Frankly, Professor Davies, you don't seem like a man who shows much concern about his fellow man.

VAUGHAN DAVIES: No? No. Perhaps you are right.

PIERCE RATCLIFF: I didn't come before because I was being interviewed—

VAUGHAN DAVIES [interrupts]: By whom?

PIERCE RATCLIFF: I don't think it's wise to go into that too much at the moment.

VAUGHAN DAVIES: Is it possible that any member of your archaeological expedition has been in an accident? An automobile accident, or something of a similar nature?

PIERCE RATCLIFF: Isobel's expedition. No. Isobel would have mentioned it. I don't see what this has got to do with the Sible Hedingham manuscript.

VAUGHAN DAVIES: It is plain, from that document, what has occurred to us.

PIERCE RATCLIFF: The fracture in history, yes. [—inaudible—] this what you wrote in your Addendum to the second edition, if you did write it?

VAUGHAN DAVIES: Oh, I wrote it, Doctor Ratcliff. I had it in my pocket when I travelled to London. Any sensible publisher would have removed himself from London during the German bombing, but not—

PIERCE RATCLIFF [interrupts]: If we can get back to this. You read the Sible Hedingham document, you wrote about the fracture, and the 'first history'—

VAUGHAN DAVIES [interrupts]: Yes, and it obviously needed publication as a matter of the greatest urgency. I had been so nearly right in my edition of

1092

the Ash papers. It was clear to me from the Sible Hedingham document that Burgundy had been, as it were, removed from us. Taken to a level of matter we cannot as yet detect – a happy thought: perhaps we may detect it, now?

PIERCE RATCLIFF: There are experiments going on in particle physics and probability theory, yes.

VAUGHAN DAVIES: You have reached the same conclusions as myself. It seems to be the case that, before this fracture, we were capable of consciously doing what other forms of life unconsciously do.

PIERCE RATCLIFF: Collapsing the improbable and the miraculous into the real. The solid world. [pause] But it had me puzzled! The universe is real, yes, we see that. But the universe is uncertain. Ever since Heisenberg, we've known that; down on the sub-atomic level, things are fuzzy. Observing an experiment alters the results. You can know where a particle is, or its direction; never both. This isn't solid, this isn't real as the manuscript talks about it—

VAUGHAN DAVIES [interrupts]: If you would kindly stop pacing.

PIERCE RATCLIFF: Sorry. But I see it: it is real. What Burgundy does is keep us consistent. If it was uncertain today, it will be uncertain in the same way tomorrow! Unchecked unreality is what it prevents. Randomness. We may not have a good existence, but we have a consistent one.

VAUGHAN DAVIES: Of course, before we would have been able consciously to undo such stabilisation, such consistency. If you look at the twentieth century, Doctor Ratcliff – and I, at least, look on the latter half of it with a stranger's eyes – you cannot claim this to be the best of all possible worlds. Man's lot is still suffering, in the main. But it is a consistent reality. Human evil is limited to the possible. We have much for which to be thankful!

PIERCE RATCLIFF: The obvious example. I've thought about it. Think what Hitler would have done to the Jews, if he had been a wonder-worker, a man able to literally manipulate the stuff of reality. It would be all blond Aryans. There would have been no Jewish race. A Holocaust worse than the Holocaust.

VAUGHAN DAVIES: What Holocaust?

[Pause]

PIERCE RATCLIFF: Never mind. There would have been military research. People bred as weapons. Like Ash, yes, like Ash. A probability bomb – worse than a nuclear bomb.

VAUGHAN DAVIES: Nuclear? Nuclear bomb?

PIERCE RATCLIFF: That's – oh: difficult, that's a – a bomb that—

VAUGHAN DAVIES [interrupts]: Rutherford! He did it, after all!

PIERCE RATCLIFF: Yes – no – never mind. Look.

[Pause]

VAUGHAN DAVIES: It is one of the more interesting paradoxes, don't you think? That war, by nature of the organised thought required to wage it, reinforces the nature of a rational reality – while, at the same time, the destruction it causes in its effects leads to chaos.

PIERCE RATCLIFF: That's why she understood it, isn't it?

VAUGHAN DAVIES: Ash? Yes. I believe so.

PIERCE RATCLIFF: I couldn't understand it, you see. Until I understood that Burgundy's still there, still doing what it's been doing. We have it in the species-mind, and in our unconscious, as a lost and golden country. But at the same time it has this quite genuine scientifically verifiable existence on a different level of reality, and it carries on with its function.

VAUGHAN DAVIES: Doctor Ratcliff, are you aware of the possible reason why things are coming back?

PIERCE RATCLIFF: I understand how things could be left over. No process is perfect, the universe is large and complex, and what Ash and the Wild Machines did – it's not surprising if some of the evidence of the first history wasn't expunged. Reality has its own weight. It's been gradually squeezing the anomalies out – things becoming legendary, mythic, fictional.

VAUGHAN DAVIES: The manuscript evidence.

PIERCE RATCLIFF: A statue here, a helmet there. Ash's words turning up in someone else's mouth. I can understand all of that. There was a single fracture, it did what it did, and we see the evidence as it – fades.

VAUGHAN DAVIES: The false history that appeared with the fracture – in which, for example, Charles the Bold dies after a siege, but at Nancy – has, here and there, some fragments of the true history embedded in it. For example, the chronicles that the del Guiz family would have written, after fourteen seventy-seven.

PIERCE RATCLIFF: Not as they existed before the fracture, but as they would have existed, if history had just carried on. Five-hundred-year-old evidence sliding back into the interstices of history. The Fraxinus manuscript too. It might quite reasonably have existed.

VAUGHAN DAVIES: Yes. That is quite clear. I wonder, Doctor Ratcliff, if you quite appreciate the significance of the Sible Hedingham document in this respect?

PIERCE RATCLIFF: You remind me very much of my old professor, if you don't mind me saying so, Professor Davies. He used to ask me a trick question just like that.

VAUGHAN DAVIES: Do you know what is most strange to me? You are giving me the respect you believe is due to an older man. In my mind, Doctor Ratcliff, I am a younger man than you are.

[Indistinguishable: traffic noise – window open? Tape hiss. Pause before speech resumes]

PIERCE RATCLIFF: The Sible Hedingham document is more improbable. It's what Ash would have written – no, she'd have to have dictated it to someone – but done it after fourteen seventy-seven, after the fracture. Perhaps left it in England after a visit to the Earl of Oxford.

VAUGHAN DAVIES: Doctor Ratcliff, I intended to warn you, and now I will do it. The possible reason why things are coming back. My theory is that the reappearance of these highly improbable artefacts is a consequence of Burgundy's function failing in some way.

PIERCE RATCLIFF: I'd thought – I was afraid – Yes. Improbable happenings, things that aren't rational, predictable. But – why would it be breaking down? Why now?

VAUGHAN DAVIES: For that, you will have to understand how lost Burgundy does what it does; and I believe, since I am sixty years behind current scientific development, that I am not qualified to put forward a theory. What I will do, if permitted, is to give you my warning.

PIERCE RATCLIFF: Sorry. Yes. Please. What is it?

VAUGHAN DAVIES: What happened to me, happened because of the Sible Hedingham manuscript. I discovered it in Hedingham Castle, in late nineteen thirty-eight. It is my belief that it had not – existed, if you like – much before that time.

PIERCE RATCLIFF: The probability wave being locally collapsed. An artefact becoming real.

VAUGHAN DAVIES: Just as in North Africa, a few months ago.

PIERCE RATCLIFF: Carthage.

VAUGHAN DAVIES: I had been staying at my brother's house as I completed my second edition, and researching the Oxfords, because of the de Vere connection with Ash. I theorise now that the Sible Hedingham manuscript became reified, if you like, not long after I arrived. I stole the manuscript—

PIERCE RATCLIFF [interrupts, agitated]: Stole it!

VAUGHAN DAVIES: They would neither sell it to me, nor allow me to study it, what else was I to do, pray?

PIERCE RATCLIFF: Well, I. You shouldn't. Well. I don't know.

VAUGHAN DAVIES: I stole the manuscript, and read it. My Latin is rather better than yours, if you will permit me to say so. Since it was too late in the printing procedure to include the Sible Hedingham manuscript, I wrote my Addendum, with the obvious conclusions, and made an appointment to deliver it to my publishers in London. I planned to arrange the publication of a revised edition, including the new manuscript. [Pause] I was embroiled in a bombing raid. A bomb landed quite close to me. I might have been killed. I might have been spared. Instead, I found myself unreal. Improbable. Potential.

PIERCE RATCLIFF: What's this got to do with the manuscript?

VAUGHAN DAVIES: Quite simply, I theorise that there is an energy field, a radiation of some kind, which attends the collapsing of a probability into a reality. When a very improbable thing becomes reified, the radiated energy is that much stronger.

PIERCE RATCLIFF [interrupts]: It couldn't be radiation, as such.

VAUGHAN DAVIES: Will you let me finish? Thank you. Whatever it is, whether a sub-atomic phenomenon of some kind, or an energy, I was most certainly exposed to it. I believe it to be stronger the more recently the artefact has become real. The exposure in some way destabilised my own reality. I was unaware of this at the time that I found the manuscript, of course. Then, with the bombing, with the point where the wavefront would have to collapse in a major way for me – I would live, or I would die – the destabilisation became acute. I became, and remained, a potential thing.

PIERCE RATCLIFF: And you're warning me . . . because I've been to the sites at Carthage.

VAUGHAN DAVIES: Yes.

PIERCE RATCLIFF: I couldn't tell if. There would be no way of knowing. Tests. Maybe tests of some kind.

VAUGHAN DAVIES: If what I shall call your cohesion has been impaired, you may be in danger.

PIERCE RATCLIFF: If the effect lessens the longer the artefact has been real, then I may not be – impaired. There's no way of telling, is there? Unless I do have an accident, or hit some point of decision . . . What happened to you could happen to me. Isobel. The rest. Or it might never happen.

VAUGHAN DAVIES: We must hope for a test to be developed, to determine this. I would work on it myself, but I am conscious that I am not the man I was. A curious thing, to have youth and old age, but no maturity. [pause] I have been robbed, I feel.

PIERCE RATCLIFF: I won't know, will I? If I've been exposed.

VAUGHAN DAVIES: Doctor Ratcliff!

PIERCE RATCLIFF: I'm sorry.

VAUGHAN DAVIES: Let us hope that no accident befalls you, Doctor Ratcliff.

PIERCE RATCLIFF: This is. [pause] Something of a shock.

[Long pause. Background noise]

PIERCE RATCLIFF: There are currently people doing experiments with probability, on a very small scale. I had two government departments debriefing me. The Americans actually took me off the ship in the Mediterranean. On Christmas Day! It was frightening. I was interviewed over several days. They're still after me. I know it sounds paranoid—

VAUGHAN DAVIES [interrupts]: Theoretical progress is being made?

PIERCE RATCLIFF: Isobel's colleagues, they seem to think so. I doubt I can talk to them without attracting more security attention. I just feel – if you're right – they ought to know -- someone ought to look at you. [pause] And me.

VAUGHAN DAVIES: I will happily be a subject for study, if it brings us closer to the truth.

PIERCE RATCLIFF: Is Burgundy failing to stabilise the probabilities now? Why now?

[Increased background noise. Specialist ▮▮▮▮▮▮▮ enters; medical conversations deleted. Door noise. Long pause]

VAUGHAN DAVIES: [—inaudible—] these minor indignities inflicted by the medical profession. No wonder William became a doctor. Doctor Ratcliff, I know to what the incident in the manuscript refers. I know what became of Burgundy, in that sense.

PIERCE RATCLIFF [pause]: How can you know? Yes, we can speculate, theorise, but—

VAUGHAN DAVIES [interrupts]: I am perhaps the only man alive with reason to say that I know this.

PIERCE RATCLIFF: You have a documented history. Asylums, hospitals.

VAUGHAN DAVIES: Doctor Ratcliff, you know that I am speaking the truth. I have existed for the past sixty years in – if you like – the raw state of the universe. The infinite possibilities, before the species-mind of man collapses them into one single reality. For me it was a moment of infinite duration and no time. I would need to be a theologian to describe, accurately, the moment of eternity.

PIERCE RATCLIFF [agitated]: What are you telling me?

VAUGHAN DAVIES: While I was in this state of existence – although it is improper to say 'while', since that implies time passing – but no matter. As I existed, merely potential, I perceived that among the infinite chaotic possibilities, there was another state of order.

PIERCE RATCLIFF: On a sub-atomic level? You saw—

VAUGHAN DAVIES: I saw that I had been correct. I was not overly surprised. You see, I theorised that the Burgundian bloodline, if we may now call it that, acted as an anchor or a filter; preventing any ability to manipulate quantum events. Any so-called miracles or prayer. And similarly, Ideal Burgundy—

PIERCE RATCLIFF [interrupts]: The sun. What about the sun?

VAUGHAN DAVIES: The sun.

PIERCE RATCLIFF: Over Burgundy! They didn't know why – I don't know – it should have been – If the Wild Machines were reality as we understand reality. Complex structures in silicon compounds might give rise to an organic chemistry, real beings— [pause] Then it should have been dark.

VAUGHAN DAVIES: Ah. Ah, now I see. You disappoint me, Professor Ratcliff.

PIERCE RATCLIFF: I disappoint – you – [loud]

VAUGHAN DAVIES: [–inaudible–] – if I may proceed? [pause] No, I imagined you would see it instantly – as Leofric did, albeit he conceptualised it in his own cultural terms. I theorise that the Ferae Natura Machinae bring about an initial quantum disjuncture, immediately the sun goes out. In Burgundy, the Real is preserved – Burgundy maintains the previous, more plausible, state. The world outside is scientifically real, if you like to put it in such simplistic terms, but it is a subsequent reality. Burgundy already forms a quantum bubble: already begins to be Ideal Burgundy. [pause] Doctor Ratcliff?

PIERCE RATCLIFF: And . . . oh, I . . . And when the skies go dark at the Duke's death—

VAUGHAN DAVIES [interrupts]: Precisely! The two unsynchronised quantum realities try to conjoin! The Ferae Natura Machinae striving to impose theirs with the Faris, have it be the only one! Although I had better, perhaps, say interlaced realities—

PIERCE RATCLIFF [interrupts]: The Wild Machines, forcing their version of reality, their quantum version, and it fails at Dijon, and then, with Ash— [pause] I should have seen it. No reality is privileged over another, they're all real – except that some are less possible, more difficult to bring about – easier to stop—

VAUGHAN DAVIES: Precisely. Ratcliff, I know what Ash did. She shifted Burgundy—

PIERCE RATCLIFF [interrupts]: A phase-shift—

VAUGHAN DAVIES [interrupts]: Altering it at some deep level, pushing it down – or forward – into the place where reality becomes solidified. Ratcliff, you must see it. She took Burgundy, and the nature of Burgundy, ahead of us – perhaps only a fraction of a second—

PIERCE RATCLIFF [interrupts]: Shifted it – a nanosecond—

VAUGHAN DAVIES [interrupts]: Where the Possible becomes Real, there is Burgundy. I saw it. That is what has preserved us, that is what kept the universe coherent for us. The nature of Burgundy, acting as an anchor, or a filter—

PIERCE RATCLIFF [interrupts]: So that the ability to consciously collapse the wavefront can never reappear, it's too improbable—

VAUGHAN DAVIES [interrupts]: For centuries after it vanished, no historian wrote of Burgundy. With Charles Mallory Maximillian, we begin to remember. But we do not remember, we perceive. We perceive that lost Burgundy has an existence in our racial unconscious, as a mythic image; and it has this because it has a genuine, scientifically verifiable existence as a part of our reality fractionally closer to the moment of Becoming.

PIERCE RATCLIFF: Burgundy – really still there.

VAUGHAN DAVIES: To think I had imagined you a man of some intelligence. Yes, Doctor Ratcliff, Burgundy has been 'still there'. Trapped in an eternal golden moment, and functioning as a guide or regulator or suppressor, if you will pardon an engineering metaphor. It filters reality into the species-mind. It has kept us real. Is that plain enough for you?

PIERCE RATCLIFF: What did you perceive? What – [Pause] What is it like, in Burgundy, now? I'd started to think what it might be like. [Pause] An endless court, an endless tournament, a hunt. Maybe war, off in the wildwoods. Their war a living metaphor, defeating the improbabilities pushing in from outside.

VAUGHAN DAVIES: No. That was not what I perceived. Burgundy has no duration. They are frozen, in an eternal moment of an act. The act of making real a coherent world.

PIERCE RATCLIFF: Ash? Florian? The rest of them?

VAUGHAN DAVIES: Odd that you should concentrate upon the people. It comes of being a pure historian, one would suppose, and having no grasp of science. My perception of the wavefront of probability was far more significant. However, it is true that I perceived minds, in that state of existence.

PIERCE RATCLIFF: Could you recognise them?

VAUGHAN DAVIES: I believe that I could. I believe they were the people mentioned in the Sible Hedingham manuscript. You cannot understand. There is no duration, no action: only being. Burgundy does not guide the Real by what it does. It does not have to do anything. It functions by being; by what it is.

PIERCE RATCLIFF: A kind of hell. For the minds, I mean.

VAUGHAN DAVIES: I am here to tell you, Doctor Ratcliff, that you are perfectly correct in that. What I experienced was an infinite duration of hell. Or heaven.

PIERCE RATCLIFF: Or heaven?

VAUGHAN DAVIES: In the sense that I have directly perceived the Real.

PIERCE RATCLIFF: An ideal Burgundy, is that what you're saying?

VAUGHAN DAVIES: Burgundy exists among, and governs the shape of, the Real. It is – or has been – the one true reality, of which we are the imperfect shadows. Good lord, man, does nobody read Plato any more?

PIERCE RATCLIFF: Plato wasn't a theoretical physicist!

VAUGHAN DAVIES: These things have a way of soaking into the species-mind. They are in our blood, at a deeper level than Freud's unconscious. Jung's racial unconscious, perhaps. A level as deep and involuntary as the transmutation of cells in our body. It is unsurprising if our mythic mind produces ghosts and shadow images of the Real. After all, we do remember Burgundy.

PIERCE RATCLIFF: We remember it now. A little bit in the eighteenth century, then Mallory Maximillian's first edition; then you; then me, and Carthage, and—

VAUGHAN DAVIES [indistinguishable: weak]

PIERCE RATCLIFF: [—inaudible—] gradually failing in what it does. Are you sure that that's what you saw? Five hundred years after what she did, Burgundy is starting to weaken, to fail? Is that it?

VAUGHAN DAVIES: Yes. I am certain of it.

[Long pause. Tape hiss. Footsteps. Door opens and closes]

PIERCE RATCLIFF: Sorry. Had to go out and walk.

VAUGHAN DAVIES: The chaotic fabric of the universe is strong. Perhaps, eventually, it reasserts itself whatever one can do.

PIERCE RATCLIFF: She did it all for nothing, then.

VAUGHAN DAVIES: Five hundred years, Doctor Ratcliff. It has all been over for five hundred years.

PIERCE RATCLIFF [agitated]: But it hasn't. Not if your perceptions were correct. It's been an eternal, infinite moment. And now it's failing. Now, it's failing. Now!

VAUGHAN DAVIES: In that sense, yes. Your archaeological reappearances, at Carthage. This manuscript. Even myself, I believe. My re-entrance into the Real is a function of the weakening of Lost Burgundy. It must be. There can be no other explanation.

PIERCE RATCLIFF: There are experiments being done in probability. Only on an infinitely small level, but – is that why? Do you think? Are we destabilising them? I need – no, Isobel's people won't talk to me about this, not with the security clamp-down.

VAUGHAN DAVIES: An arc of five hundred years for us, a moment for Lost Burgundy. A moment which is ending, now. The universe is vast, powerful, chaotically imperative, Doctor Ratcliff. It was bound to reassert itself.

PIERCE RATCLIFF: What happens when Burgundy fails, finally? The end of causality? An increase in entropy, in chaos, in miracles?

VAUGHAN DAVIES: They subject one to an interesting variety of tests on this ward. Between tests, one is left with considerable time. I have devoted much of it – despite William's assertion that I watch that televisual box – to analysing what the loss of Burgundy might mean. I believe you have reached the same conclusion as I.

PIERCE RATCLIFF: The species-mind will continue to collapse the probable into a predictable real. But eventually, without Burgundy, enough random chaos will filter through, we'll become able to manipulate the Real again consciously – or technologically. There will be wars. Wars in which the Real is the casualty.

VAUGHAN DAVIES: Someone's reality is always a casualty in wartime, Doctor Ratcliff. But yes. It is what the Ferae Natura Machinae foresaw. The infinitely unreal universe. If you like, the miracle wars.

PIERCE RATCLIFF: I have to publish.

VAUGHAN DAVIES: You intend to include this in your edition of the Ash papers?

PIERCE RATCLIFF: Once it's made public, it can't be ignored. There has to be an investigation! Do we need to stop performing experiments on the sub-atomic level? Do we need more experiments? Can we reinforce Burgundy?

VAUGHAN DAVIES: You will sound, if you forgive me, like a blithering lunatic to them, Doctor Ratcliff.

PIERCE RATCLIFFE: I don't care, anything's better than 'miracle' wars—!

[Door opens. Footsteps; an indistinguishable number of people entering]

WILLIAM DAVIES: I think that's enough for today.

VAUGHAN DAVIES: Really, William. I believe I may be allowed to know my own state of health.

WILLIAM DAVIES: Not as well as your doctors. I may be retired; I know exhaustion when I see it. Doctor Ratcliff will come back tomorrow.

VAUGHAN DAVIES [indistinguishable]

PIERCE RATCLIFF [indistinguishable]

ANNA LONGMAN: We need to talk, Pierce. I've been through to the office. We need to make some hard decisions about publication, before the weekend.

PIERCE RATCLIFF: Professor Davies. [pause] It's an honour. I'll call again tomorrow.

[Indistinguishable door noises, noises of chairs being moved]

VAUGHAN DAVIES: [—inaudible—] publish as soon as possible. We need the help of the scientific community. [Tape garbled] [—inaudible—] further investigation on a world-wide scale.

PIERCE RATCLIFF: [—inaudible—] we have no idea, do we? How long we've got? Before it fails completely?

[Tape terminates]

SUBJECT "VAUGHAN DAVIES" REMOVED 02/02/01 TO ▓▓▓▓▓▓▓ HOSPITAL FOR FURTHER TESTS AND INTERROGATION

Afterword

With the abrupt termination of the Sible Hedingham manuscript, the documentation of these events comes to a close.

It is now evident that a significant change in the nature of our universe occurred on 5 January 1477.

To summarise: at that point, the events of human history up to that date were altered, and a subsequent different history was thereafter perceived to have occurred. It was neither the prior history of the human race, nor the desired future of the 'Wild Machine' silicon intelligences. Whether our history from 1477 onwards is a random result of the 'miracle', or a desired one, it is difficult to say.

Whichever is the truth, what is undeniable is that the ability of human minds to consciously alter the wavefront of probability at the point where it is collapsed into one reality was eradicated. Human existence continued: the consistent and rational universe supported by the human species-mind, and protected and preserved by the altered previous history – the 'lost Burgundy' that remains with us as the memory of a myth.

If not an ideal universe, it is at least a consistent universe. Human good and human evil are still in our own power to choose.

I realise that these conclusions, drawn from these texts and from the available archaeological evidence, will give rise to some controversy. I believe, however, that it is essential that they become widely known, and are acted upon.

The laws of cause and effect operate consistently within the human sphere of influence. What the universe is like otherwise, in other places, we do not know. We are one world among millions, in one galaxy among billions, in a universe so vast that neither light nor our understanding can cross it. What local laws we have here, and can observe, are rational, consistent, and predictable. Even where, as on the sub-atomic level, causality becomes 'fuzzy', it becomes fuzzy in accordance with scientific reality, and not in accordance with random chaos. What is an uncertain particle today will be an uncertain particle tomorrow, and not a dragon. Or a Lion, or a Hart.

If this were all, then while 'lost Burgundy' would be a deeply significant discovery about how our universe is constructed, it would nonetheless be a closed discovery. Ash's decision was made, Burgundy 'shifted', the nature of Burgundy anchors us in causality, and that is where we are.

Except that, as recent events have proved, 'Burgundy' is failing. It is an unavoidable fact that some things that are improbable (in the technical sense of the word) have, in the last sixty years, again become collapsed into a state of objective reality. The archaeological site at Carthage, although current investigations have been suspended, is eye-opening in this respect.

For whatever reason, the nature of Burgundy has changed again; it is perhaps failing, or has ceased to exist. I believe the evidence suggests that this is indeed the case.

I suspect that what Vaughan Davies (in conversation with the author) has reported perceiving is the moment of the change itself. According to his observations, the change no longer 'still continues' – or, for those in it, 'has not ended'. What we are seeing now *is* the end of that moment. The time between 1477 and now was the period of linear time needed for that one out-of-time moment to end.

What has been necessary has been done. Burgundy, shifted out as a kind of 'spur' of advancing reality into the probability wave, has made this human universe causal.

It may not now keep it that way. The spontaneous mutation of the 'miracle gene' may arise again. A means to technologically alter the collapse of the wavefront may be discovered.

What does this mean for us, now?

Without Lost Burgundy, the species-mind of the human race will continue to do what it has done since we became conscious organic life. It will manipulate reality to be constant, coherent, consistent. Tomorrow will follow today; yesterday will not return. This is what we do – what all organic life does, on no matter how low a level – we preserve a constant reality.

What Burgundy did, however, was to protect our reality from the return of the ability to *consciously* collapse the wavefront of probability into a different, formerly improbable, reality.

With Burgundy failing, with the complex chaos of the universe merging Burgundy back into the reality from which – for an eternal moment – it was the 'forward edge', then what is to prevent us becoming, as our ancestors were, priests and prophets, miracle-workers and recipients of grace? What is to prevent us developing this in our organic consciousness, or our machines?

Nothing.

Unless the fabric of the material universe is to be put in danger of unravelling, fraying out into entropic chaos, mere quantum soup, then we must do something now.

I intend the publication of these papers to act as a call to arms to the scientific community. We must investigate. We must act. We must prevent, somehow, the failing of Lost Burgundy; or create something we can put in its place. Or else, as Ash herself wrote in manuscripts that should not, in this second history, have an existence – if not, then at some day in the future, all we have done here will be undone, as if it had never been.

I am setting up a web-site at ▮▮▮▮▮▮▮▮ for a cyberconference: any sufficiently accredited organisation or individual is hereby invited to log on. I will make my data available.

We are not yet, and perhaps we never will be, fit to be gods.

Pierce Ratcliff
London, 2001

Afterword

(Fourth edition)

I have left unaltered the words of a much younger man.

History is very much a matter of interpretation.

Nine years is not a long time – and yet, sometimes, it is long enough to change the world out of all recognition. Sometimes nine minutes will suffice.

I suppose I should have remembered what Ash herself said. *I don't lose.*

Plainly, the 'Afterword' to the 2001 edition was written by a man in a panic. I have reprinted it here essentially untouched, although I have deleted my old URL to prevent confusion. I was, to be frank, in a state of fear for most of the winter of 2000 and the spring of 2001; a state only made worse by the abrupt withdrawal of all copies of *Ash: The Lost History of Burgundy* on 25 March, five days before they were due to appear in the bookshops.

I am indebted to Anna Longman for the sterling defence of my work that she put up in editorial meetings. Without her, the book would not have reached the printing stage. Even she could not prevail, however, once her then Managing Director, Jonathan Stanley, had pressure put on him by the Home Secretary.

Two days later, my own author's copies of *Ash: The Lost History of Burgundy* were removed from my flat.

A week after that, I received a visit from the police; and found myself being interviewed, not by them, but by staff from the security services of three nations.

Fear, no doubt, clouded my judgement.

Reality reasserted itself, however.

I found myself confronted by a bound copy of my third edition, into which had been placed a floppy disc, and hardcopy print-outs of my correspondence, neatly annotated by some security officer. They were not my copies: I had destroyed mine.

I was informed that they had been watching Anna since December 2000. A second – unnoticed – search of her Stratford flat found no trace of the editorial correspondence, since she carried the copies on her person, until the late spring of 2001, when they disappeared.

A close study of CCTV footage and observers' reports finally confirmed that on 1 March 2001 she had been seen leaving the British Library without a book. This would not have been remarkable, had she not been witnessed an hour earlier entering *with* a book – which CCTV stills show to have been her editor's pre-publication copy of *Ash: The Lost History of Burgundy*.

Even knowing it must be there, it took the security forces a month to find it. While the chance of stealing a book from the British Library is extremely low, no one thought to make provision for someone coming *in* with a book, and leaving it amid the chaos of the British Library's move from its old building to the new one.

I dare say it would have been found and catalogued within a decade.

Confronted with our correspondence, I realised, a few seconds before I was told, that this was not some paranoid plot by which I might be 'silenced', but, in fact, a job interview.

It was not my expertise with fifteenth-century manuscripts that encouraged them to co-opt me on to 'Project Carthage', but my personal eye-witness experience of the return of the artefacts of the 'first history', as detailed in that correspondence between Anna and myself.

In fact, as Anna sometimes says to me – with rather more humour than I have previously associated with her – I *am* history.

As are we all.

Fortunately, we are the future, too.

I flew out of London for California at the end of the following week, having handed in my resignation at my university. In the years that followed, I entered on the second career of my working life (discovering an unsuspected talent for administration); a career in which – with Isobel Napier-Grant, Tami Inoshishi, James Howlett, and the associated staff of many other institutions – I have seen the frontiers of human knowledge expanded to an astounding degree. On a personal level, I have found it exacting, exciting, frustrating, and illuminating, by turns; and I still do not grasp all the advances made in quantum theory!

The present staff of Project Carthage is, of course, made up of the 'official' scientists that Isobel Napier-Grant hoped for when she decided she should throw open the Carthage site to investigation; with the expectation that there must be physicists who could both do the maths, and sort out the terminology; and free us from our dependence on speculation and metaphor. Nine years on, I have to say that they have done everything that could be hoped, and more.

This fourth edition of the 'Ash' papers is intended to set the record straight on the background to Project Carthage. The course of the project, and the various findings it has released over the past nine years, are too well known to be repeated at length here. We now have a staff of over five hundred people, with more due to be taken on. Next year, on our tenth anniversary, I plan to publish a history of the Project.

I intend the preliminary publication of these papers both to present the background to Project Carthage, and to provide a conclusion to the 'Ash' narrative – in so far as there can be a conclusion.

It took me the better part of two years to work out what we should be looking for.

Protracted UN negotiations with the Tunisian government allowed a team of scientists back on site at the seabed ruins of Carthage, working with the Institute at Tunis itself. The artefacts have since been subjected to extremely intense analysis, both there and abroad. (We were robbed of our Russian and

Chinese members by the Sino-Russian 'Millennium War' of 2003–2005; but thankfully they have since returned.)

At the same time, the history of the 'Visigoth Empire' became more and more apparent in documentation stretching from the 1400s to the late nineteenth century. A fascinating paper by a historian from the University of Alexandria detailed how the Iberian Gothic tribes after AD 416 maintained a settlement on the North African coast, and were later integrated into Arab culture (in a process akin to the later crusaders' 'Latin Kingdoms of the East').

Traces of the invasion of Christendom have been excavated outside Genoa, in northern Italy, where there appears to have been a considerable battle.

The universe receives, into its interstices, the instances of the 'first history' which it can comfortably accommodate. There are discrepancies: there always will be. The universe is hugely complex, even in the 'local conditions' that are what we as a species perceive.

This reintegration of the first and second histories was observed by all of us on the Project, and took place roughly from 2000 to 2005, with the greatest concentration of activity in the 2002–2003 period. That the failure of 'Lost Burgundy' should result in a kind of historical debris being swept back into our reality was not, we thought, theoretically impossible. Indeed, here it was, with more appearing every day. More evidence – undeniable, *factual* evidence – that had not been there the day before.

We lived, in those early days of the millennium, in the daily expectation of the world crumbling away under our feet. It was not unusual to wake, every day, and wonder, before one opened one's eyes, if one was the same person as the day before. All of us on 'Project Carthage' bonded closely, in almost a wartime mentality.

I wrote, in 2001, that we were not fit to be gods. Any study of history may convince the student that we are barely fit to be human beings. At the end of a century of unparalleled massacre and holocaust, we knew, on Project Carthage, that there are worse things possible. Given the power to manipulate probability, a vision of holocaust and high-tech war haunted us: human cruelty carried to an infinitely high degree. Endless human degradation, suffering, dread and death. If this is what the 'Wild Machine' silicon intelligences predicted, then their refusal to let it come into existence can only be seen as a moral act.

At Project Carthage, we knew we were the front-line troops in the war against unreality: either we would find some way to stabilise 'Burgundy', or we would – if not now, then twenty or two hundred years in the future – find wars of improbability sweeping away the fabric of the universe.

As a historian, I led the team responsible for documenting the return of the first history. By 2002, I had realised that each of the occurrences that I was documenting was possible. As I said in conversation with Isobel Napier-Grant on the net,

```
>> <snip> The artefacts that are appearing are no less
>> rational than one might demand of a causal universe.
>> We have a ruined Carthage, five hundred years old. We
>> do not have a fifteenth-century Carthage appearing in
```

> `>> present-day Tunisia, full of Visigoths - or alien`
> `>> visitors, or something human senses cannot perceive.`
> `>> It is Carthage as it would have been now, had the`
> `>> first history continued on from 1477.`

Plainly, what was reintegrating itself into reality was *possible* events, *possible* artefacts, *probable* history. No miracles.

No miracles.

It took me nearly seven years to find her.

I had my hunch in the summer of the year 2002. The arc of the moment – that five-hundred-year eternity in a Burgundy made both mythic, and more real than reality – was ending. We would be unprotected; should be subject now to increasing truly random phenomena. And yet, plainly, the coherence of the universe we perceive had *not* degraded between 2001 and 2002.

Lost Burgundy *must* have failed or be failing: how else to account for the reappearance of so much 'Burgundian' history? But how to account for the *stability* of that reappearance? The autonomic reflexes of the species-mind, collapsing the wavefront to coherent reality? Undoubtedly; but that could not account for all. The theoretical physicists at this time lived in daily horror of the potential instabilities they observed at sub-atomic levels. They monitored these randomnesses – which became coherent again.

It was a literal hunch. It came to me not long after the funeral of Professor Vaughan Davies – a man who lived to see the strange existence of his middle years analysed and confirmed, but who never restrained himself from a caustic remark until the day he died. (He said to me in a lucid moment of his final coma, "It is rather more interesting than I had anticipated. I doubt that *you* would understand it, however.")

On the plane, flying home from his funeral with Isobel Napier-Grant, I suddenly said, "*People* come back."

"Vaughan 'came back'," she said, "in that sense. Complete with ghost-history of his probable existence for his missing years. Are you suggesting it's happened to someone else?"

"Has happened, or *will have* happened," I said; and put myself on the course of my next seven years' research. By the time Isobel left me to get the Fancy Rat cages from the rear of the plane, I had mapped out a potential programme.

In May of this year, I flew to Brussels, and the headquarters of the Réaction Rapid Force Unité. The military establishment is outside Brussels itself, in flat Belgian countryside; and I was driven out by a *Unité* driver, and provided with an interpreter – in a Pan-European armed force, this can still be a necessity.

I had been picturing it on the flight over. She would be in an office at HQ; modern, bright with the natural light of a spring day in Europe; maps on the walls. She would be wearing the uniform of a *Unité* officer. For some reason, despite the record I had in front of me, I pictured her as older: late twenties, early thirties.

I was driven to the edge of a pine forest, and escorted on foot up a rutted track in grey drizzle. The rain ceased after the first mile or so.

I found her calf-deep in mud, wearing fatigues and combat boots and a dull-red-coloured pullover. She looked up from the group of men at the back of a jeep, poring over a map, and grinned. I suppose I looked very wet. The sky was clearing overhead, to duck-egg blue, and the wind whipped her short hair across her eyes.

She had black hair, and brown eyes, and dark skin.

The RRFU had given me permission to film and record: I had done this on several previous occasions, when it proved to be the wrong woman. On this occasion, I almost switched off the shoulder-cam and terminated the interview there and then.

"Sorry about this," she said cheerfully, walking over to me. "Damn exercises. It's supposed to be good for efficiency if we have them without warning. Rapid deployment. You're Professor Ratcliff, yes?"

She had a slight accent. A tall woman, with broad shoulders, and a major's insignia. The spring sunlight showed faint silvery lines on her right cheek. And on the other side of her face.

"I'm Ratcliff," I said, to the woman who looked nothing like the manuscript descriptions; and on impulse added: "Where is your twin, Major?"*

The woman was Arab-looking in appearance, in a RRFU major's uniform, with an expansive way of taking up her personal space – a presence. She put her muddy fists on her hips and grinned at me. There was a pistol at her belt. Her face lit up. I *knew*.

"She's in Düsseldorf. Married to a German businessman from Bavaria. When I'm on leave, apparently, I visit. The kids like me."

One of the men by the jeep hailed her. "Major!"

He had a radio mike in his hand. A man with sergeant's stripes; in his late thirties or early forties, bald under his beret; in a uniform that looked as though it had seen use. He had the look that sergeants have: that nothing is impossible to do, and that no senior officer knows enough to change his own nappy.

"Brigadier wants you, boss," he said briefly.

"Tell Brigadier Oxford I'll get right back to him. Tell him I'm up a tree or something! Tell him he'll have to wait!"

"He'll love that one, boss."

"Into each life," she announced, with cheerful vindictiveness, "a bloody great amount of rain must fall. His damn fault for staging the exercise. Professor, I've got a flask of hot coffee; you look as though you could use it."

I followed her to the front of the jeep, dazed, thinking, *It is. It is her. How can it be?* And then: *Of course. The Visigoths are – have been – integrated into Arab culture after the defeat of Carthage. And Ash was never European by race.*

"What's your sergeant's name?" I said, after drinking the sweet, strong brew.

"Sergeant Anselm," she said, with a grave, dead-pan humour, as if she and I shared a joke that no one else in the world understood. "My brigadier is an English officer, John Oxford. The men call him Mad Jack Oxford. My name—" she jerked a thumb at her name-tag on her fatigue jacket. "—is Asche."

---

* All quotes taken from the transcript of audio and visual sources, location RRFU HQ, Brussels, 14/5/2009 (Project Carthage archives).

"You don't look German."

"My ex-husband's name, apparently." She still had the smile of someone with a secret joke.

"You've been married?" I was momentarily startled. She *didn't* look more than nineteen or twenty.

"Fernando von Asche. A Bavarian. An ex-cavalry officer. It seems that he married my sister, after our divorce; I kept the name. Doctor Ratcliff, the wire said you wanted to ask me a whole lot of questions. This isn't the time: I've got manoeuvres to run. But you can satisfy me about one thing. What gives you the right to ask me questions about anything at all?"

She watched me. She was not uncomfortable with the silence.

"Burgundy," I said. "Burgundy is now a part of the human species-mind. Bedded in so solidly, if you like, that the 'ghost-past' arising out of the fracture can fall away into improbability. Our first past is returning. Your true history."

Major Asche took the steel flask and drank from it. She wiped her mouth, her dark eyes still fixed on me. The wind moved her short hair against her scarred cheeks.

"I'm not history," she pointed out mildly. "I'm here."

"You are now."

She continued to watch me. Somewhere back in the woods, shots cracked. She glanced back at Sergeant Anselm, who held up a reassuring hand. She nodded. Far out on the muddy plain, hover-tanks nosed into view.

I asked, "How long have you been here?"

Raised eyebrows. A slantwise look. "About two days. For the duration of this, I'm stuck in a military tent about two miles *that* way."

"That isn't what I mean. Or perhaps it is." I called up data on my wristpad, and read through it, slowly. It was sparse. "I think you have a 'ghost-history', if I can put it that way. You're very young to have achieved the rank of major. But war is a time of rapid promotions. You grew up in Afghanistan, under the Taliban. Their attitude to women is – mediaeval. You joined resistance forces, learned to fight; and when that was crushed, you joined the bushwars on the borders. There, all that was necessary was that you be able to lead. To command. By the time you were sixteen, they'd made you a captain. When the Eastern European forces united with the RRFU, you joined *Unité*."

Net footage of the fighting along the Sino-Russian border is still clear in my mind.

"At the end of the Sino-Russian war, two years ago, you'd made major." I looked up from the little wrist-screen and the scrolling data. "But I'm fully prepared to believe that you've only *been* here two days, in a military tent, in a field somewhere."

Major Asche gave me a long look.

"Let's walk." She set off briskly. "Roberto! Where's the fucking helicopters? Do they think we're going to wait around here all day? We need to move up within the hour."

As we passed him, Robert Anselm grinned at her. "Don't fret, boss."

The new grass was slippery underfoot. I was not wearing boots. Cold- and wet-footed, I quickened my stride to keep up with her. We passed a truck, unloading armed soldiers; and she stopped for a word with the corporal before moving on down the track.

"You get a mixed force in *Unité*," she remarked. "That lot are mostly Welsh and English. I've got a gang of local Brussels lads; and a lot of East and West Germans. And a *lot* of Italians."

She flicked a look at me out of the corner of her eye. There was still a quiet amusement in her expression. I looked back at the men, only to find – camouflaged; expert – that they had merged into the edge of the wood.

"What was that corporal's name, that you were speaking to?"

"Rostovnaya."

"Is the whole company here?" I said, without thinking, and then she was looking at me, shaking her head, her eyes bright.

"All but the dead," she said. "All but the dead. Life and death are real, Professor Ratcliff. There are faces I miss."

I began to see tents, up ahead, in a clearing at the side of the track. Green military tents. Armed men, and men in white overalls, ran from tent to tent.

"Angelotti. Rickard. Euen Huw." She shook her head. "But we came so close to losing *everybody*."

"I think I know what's been happening," I said. "Why you're back. Burgundy's – failed. I suppose."

She stopped, boots in one of the ruts, the creamy brown mud halfway up her ankles, looking ahead at the tents.

I said, "Time moves differently closer to the probability wave. The moment in which you and the Wild Machines both calculated, powered, and *willed* human history to change – is ending. Has ended. You've managed to bypass the immediate danger. But the *process* by which that happened is withering away. Fragments of the true past are fitting in among the interstices of the past we know – it's possible to foresee a time when the history that we know of Burgundy will be the history of 'Ash's Burgundy'."

She smiled at that.

I went on, "But it's over. Isn't it? I believe that we have been in the process, over the last six or eight years, of reintegration with Lost Burgundy. Burgundy's gone, hasn't it?" I said. "We're not protected any more."

"Oh, we are."

She gave me that grin, head cocked, eyes creasing and bright; and she was, for one moment, as I had seen her in my mind as I read the manuscripts: the woman in armour, dirty, pragmatic, unable to be crushed down.

"I don't understand."

A fair-haired woman in a white overall walked towards us down the track. The wind made her slit her eyes, but I could see that they were green. She had had her head shaven and stitched at some time in the recent past: the visible scars of removed stitches, and the fluff of her regrowing hairline were clearly visible under her cap.

"The *amirs*' medicine was better than ours," Asche said to me. "Why shouldn't someone else's be better than theirs?"

Death is a fuzzy-edged boundary, too.

The women glanced from me to Major Asche. "This is the boffin?"

"That's right."

The name tape on the breast of her overall read DEL GUIZ.

"You tell him where your sister is, yet?"

"Sure."

The scarecrow-tall woman turned back to me. For all the pallor of her cheeks, she was smiling. "This one flew down to Dusseldorf, yesterday. On a military flight. She had to see them."

"My sister has two children," Asche said, gravely mischievous. "Violante, and Adelize."

Asche smiled.

"Violante keeps rats. I'll go down again soon. We've got stuff to say to each other."

The woman who must be Floria del Guiz said briskly, as if I wasn't present, "Ratcliff will want to interview all of us. Clerks always do. I'll be in the med tent. Some *other* bloody fool decided to get out of a counter-gravity tank before it landed. That's four. Christ! Nobody tell me soldiers are *bright*."

Major Asche, with demure humility, said, "I wouldn't dare."

Floria del Guiz stomped back towards the tents, with a wave that might – if a senior officer had appeared – have become a salute.

"I would have given anything," Asche said, and I saw that her fist was clenched at her side, "to have all of them here now. And Godfrey. And Godfrey. But death is real. It's all real."

"But for how long?"

"You haven't got it yet, have you?" Asche looked amused.

"Got *what*?"

"We came back," Asche said. "I thought we would. But they stayed."

At the time, I merely stared at her. It is not until now that I have developed a theory: that organic matter and organic mind are inevitably 'sucked back', if you like, into the human species-mind, into the main part of reality, away from the 'forward edge'. Because they *are* human, and organic And that she must – with all that computing power at her disposal – have realised this.

"'They stayed'?"

"The Wild Machines," Asche said, as if it were obvious enough for a child to have seen it.

And I saw it. *The Wild Machines*.

"*Yes*." A wind rustled; spent rain fell from the pine trees and spattered my face. I stared at the woman in combat fatigues, with the grin on her face. "I suppose I assumed that— there's no reason to assume it! No reason to suppose that the Wild Machine silicon-intelligences were destroyed when you – did what you did."

What more likely than that Lost Burgundy contains them, as well as the nature of Burgundy, within itself? Contains the presence of immense, intelligent, calculating power. If Lost Burgundy exists in an eternal moment, without time, but with duration, this does not preclude the idea that the machine-intelligences might 'still' be functioning. Linear time is not relevant where they exist.

Immense natural machine intelligences, monitoring the probability wave, keeping all possibility of miracle-working out of the Real. Their perception more vast than human; their power inorganic and endless, tapping into the fabric of the universe. Maintaining, unchanging.

"They couldn't move there themselves," Asche said. "We made a miracle and I moved all of us. All of us. Carthage too. And now they're out there – wherever – doing what Burgundy did. The Wild Machines are Burgundy now."

The wind rattled again in the trees, and became the noise of helicopter rotors. She reached for the RT set in her top pocket but didn't respond. She squinted up above the tree-tops, into the clearing blue sky.

"They knew it would happen," she said. "When I told them what I planned to do. They consented. They're machines. Godfrey would say my hell – the eternal moment – is their heaven."

The arc of her, and their, 'moment' covers five hundred years of intense scientific discovery. As a race, we have alleviated some of human suffering, while at the same time committing the grossest atrocities. Lost Burgundy, then, does not limit human choices; we are free to choose whatever we perceive of good and evil.

"Lost Carthage?" I suggested.

"A lost and golden moment," the woman said.

Above our heads, a helicopter dipped towards the clearing; and all speech became impossible until it had landed. A young man in combat fatigues jumped down and began sprinting towards us through the mud.

"Boss, they need you over at grid— is the radio down?" he interrupted himself. Long-boned, hardly more than adolescent. "Major Rodiani wants you! So does Colonel Valzacchi."

As I watched her, she gave a slow, amazed grin.

"'Colonel' Valzacchi? Hmm. I'll be right there, Tydder." As he ran back, she said, "This really isn't the time. I'll get the chopper to take you back to Brussels. I'll talk to you there, soon."

"What happens to you," I said, "now?"

"Anything." She smiles across at the idling rotors of the camouflage-painted helicopter, and shakes her head, with all the energy of youth; as if amazed that anybody could be so obtuse. "I live my life, that's what happens. I'm not even twenty. I can do anything. You keep an eye open for me, Doctor Ratcliff. I'll make five-star general yet! And I suppose I'll have to do some of this bloody political stuff. After all – now, I know how."

She gave me her hand to shake and I took it. Her flesh was warm. Any thought I might have had that she would retire – or be persuaded to join Project Carthage – was revealed as insubstantial, unreal. Cruelty and abuse do not die, although they may be overcome; she is now what she always will be, a woman who kills other people. Her loyalty, such as it is, is to her own. However many that may come to include.

As I left, she said, "I'm told we're going back out to the Chinese border soon. As a peace-keeping force. In some ways, that's worse than war! But on the whole—" A long, level look from that scarred face. "It's probably better. Don't you think?"

*

That was three months ago.

While I have been engaged in the collation of the Third Edition text with the chronological documentation of 2000 and 2001, and in the writing of this Afterword, Major Asche briefly visited the Project headquarters in California. On her way out, she suggested to me that we might require an alteration to our unofficial Latin motto.

It reads, now, *Non delenda est Carthago*.

Carthage must not be destroyed.

Pierce Ratcliff-Napier-Grant
Brussels, 2009

Acknowledgements

I am indebted to Anna Monkton (neé Longman) for her guidance in presenting our editorial correspondence. At time of publication, she is about to present us with a first grandchild – or in my case, step-grandchild – which, however, she and my wife, Isobel, refuse to let me call after our 'scruffy mercenary', Ash. But I have hopes of persuading them.